Praise for Chris Wooding:

'Will surprise, delight and horrify' *SFRevu*

'Chris Wooding takes care to undercut fantasy clichés with skilful characterisation, an oriental location and complex sexual politics' *Guardian*

'A triumph' *Dreamwatch*

'On every level, *Retribution Falls* is a triumph' *Guardian*

'*Retribution Falls* is the kind of old-fashioned adventure I didn't think we were allowed to write anymore, of freebooting privateers making their haphazard way in a wondrous retro-future world. A fast exhilarating read' Peter F. Hamilton

'*Retribution Falls* picks you up, whisks you swiftly and entertainingly along, and sets you down with a big smile on your face' Joe Abercrombie

Also by Chris Wooding from Gollancz:

The Fade

Tales of the Ketty Jay
Retribution Falls
The Black Lung Captain
The Iron Jackal

THE BRAIDED PATH

CHRIS WOODING

GOLLANCZ
LONDON

First published in Great Britain in 2006 by
Gollancz
An imprint of the Orion Publishing Group
Orion House, 5 Upper St Martin's Lane,
London WC2H 9EA
An Hachette UK Company

This edition published in Great Britain in 2011 by Gollancz

1 3 5 7 9 10 8 6 4 2

A CIP catalogue record for this book is available from the British Library

ISBN 978 0 575 07881 9

Typeset at The Spartan Press Ltd,
Lymington, Hants

Printed in Great Britain by CPI Mackays,
Chatham, ME5 8TD

www.chriswooding.com
www.orionbooks.co.uk

CONTENTS

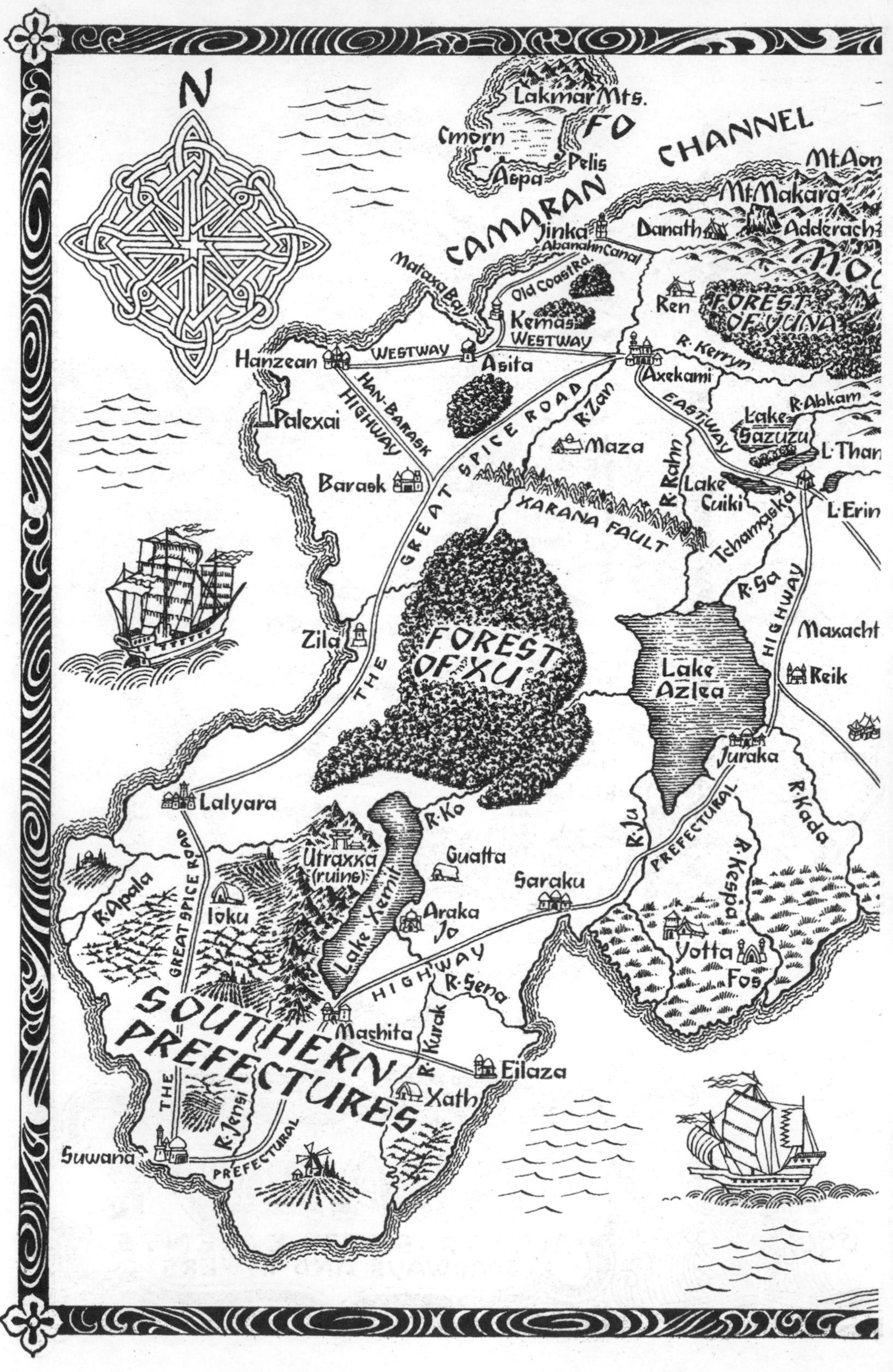
N
Lakmar Mts.
FO
Cmorn
Pelis
Aspa
CAMARAN CHANNEL
Mt. Makara
Jinka
Danath
Adderach
Abanahn Canal
Mataka Bay
Old Coast Rd.
Ren
FOREST OF YUNA
Kemas
WESTWAY
Hanzean
WESTWAY
Asita
R. Kerryn
Axekami
HAN-BARASK HIGHWAY
THE GREAT SPICE ROAD
R. Zan
EASTWAY
R. Abkam
Lake Sazuzu
L. Than
Palexai
Maza
R. Rahn
Lake Cuiki
Barask
L. Erin
XARANA FAULT
Tchamaska
R. Sa
HIGHWAY
Maxacht
Zila
FOREST OF XU
Lake Azlea
Reik
Juraka
Lalyara
R. Ko
R. Ju
PREFECTURAL
R. Kada
Utraxxa (ruins)
Guatta
R. Kespa
R. Apala
GREAT SPICE ROAD
Saraku
Ioku
Lake Xemii
Araka Jo
Yotta
Fos
HIGHWAY
R. Sena
SOUTHERN PREFECTURES
Machita
R. Kurak
Eilaza
Xath
THE
R. Jensi
Suwana
PREFECTURAL

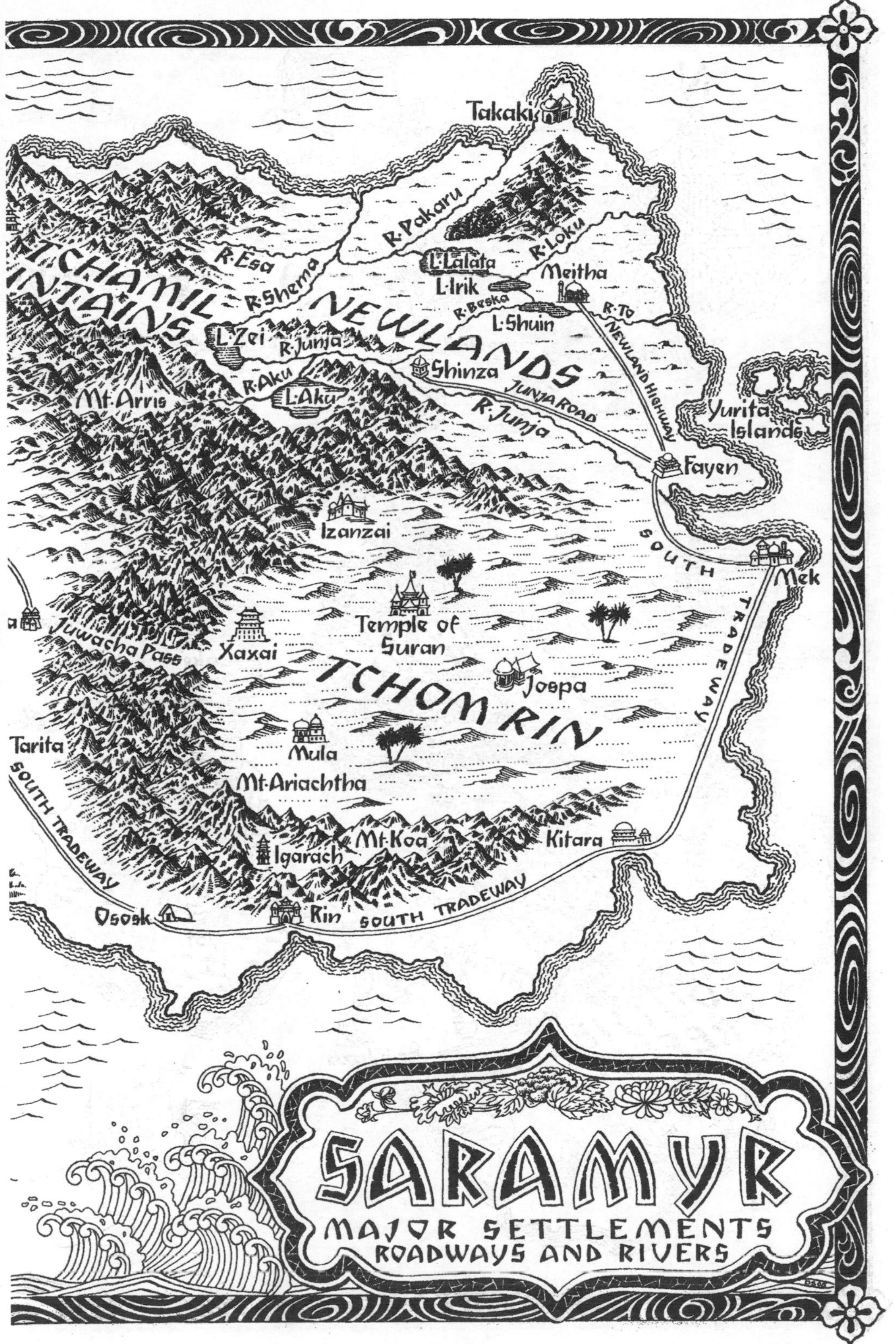

Takaki
R·Pakaru
R·Loku
R·Esa
L·Lalata
Meitha
L·Irik
R·Shema
NEWLANDS
R·Beska
R·To
L·Shuin
NEWLAND HIGHWAY
L·Zei
R·Junja
Shinza
JUNJA ROAD
R·Aku
L·Aku
Mt·Arris
R·Junja
Yurita Islands
Fayen
Izanzai
SOUTH TRADEWAY
Mek
Temple of Suran
Juwacha Pass
Xaxai
TCHOM RIN
Jospa
Tarita
Mula
Mt·Ariachtha
SOUTH TRADEWAY
Mt·Koa
Kitara
Igarach
Ososk
Rin
SOUTH TRADEWAY
SARAMYR
MAJOR SETTLEMENTS
ROADWAYS AND RIVERS

WESTERN
SARAMYR
MAJOR SETTLEMENTS
ROADWAYS
and
RIVERS
FO
TMORN
DUST ROAD
PELIS
ASPA
CAMARAN CHANNEL
ABANAHN CANAL
JINKA
OLD COAST ROAD
KEMAS
WEST WAY
ASITA
HANZEAN
HAN-BARASK HIGHWAY
SPICE ROAD
R. ZAN
MAZA
PALEXAI
BARASK
XARANA
THE GREAT
AZILA
FOREST OF XU
LALYARA
R. KO
GUATTA
SOUTHERN PREFECTURES

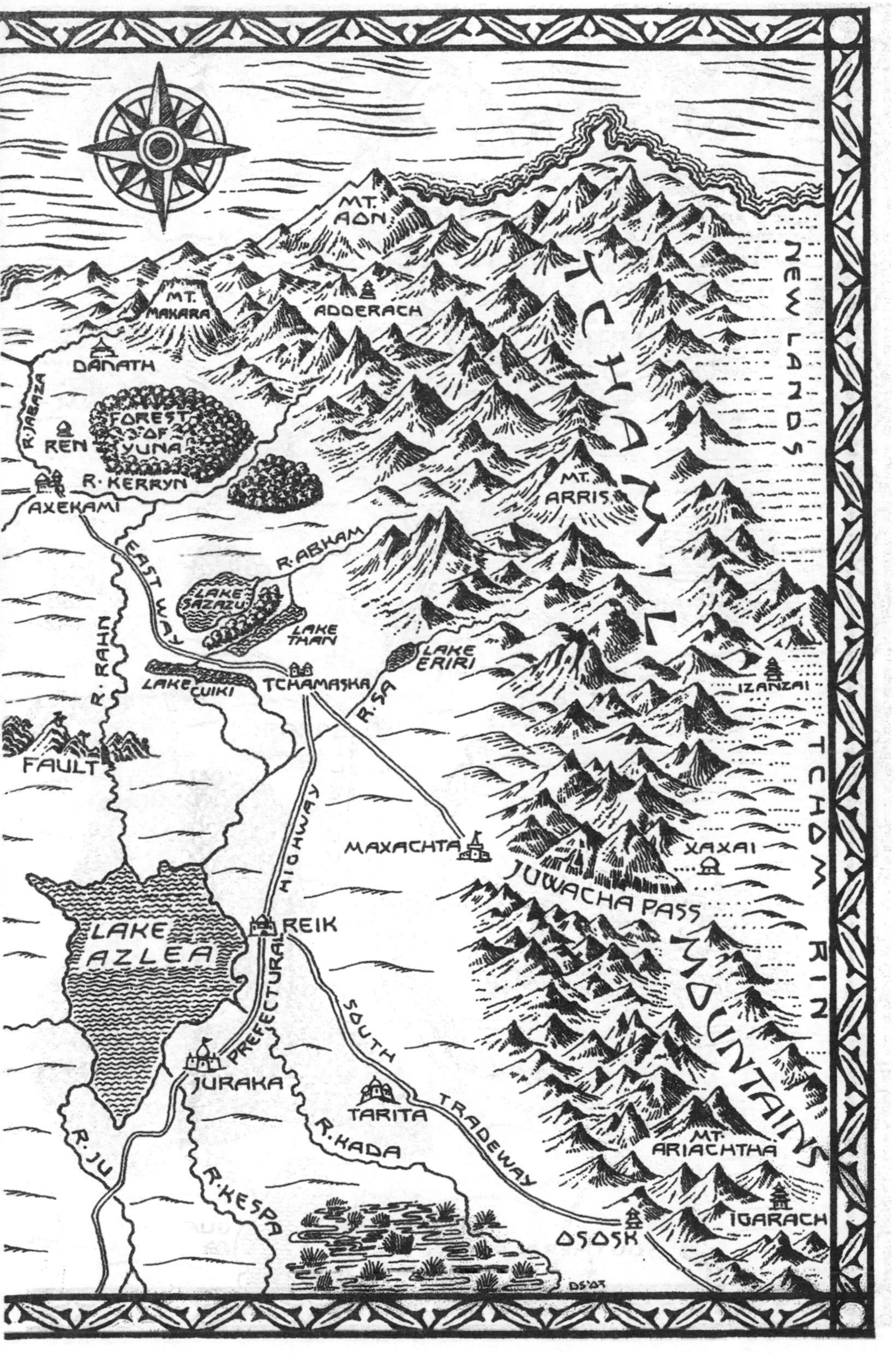
MT. AON
MT. MAKARA
ADDERACH
DANATH
R. JABAZA
FOREST OF YUNA
REN
R. KERRYN
AXEKAMI
EAST WAY
R. ABKAM
LAKE SAZAZU
LAKE THAN
LAKE ERIRI
MT. ARRIS
TCHAMASKA
LAKE CUIKI
R. RAHN
R. SA
FAULT
HIGHWAY
MAXACHTA
XAXAI
IZANZAI
JUWACHA PASS
REIK
LAKE AZLEA
PREFECTURAL
SOUTH
TRADEWAY
JURAKA
TARITA
R. KADA
R. JU
R. KESPA
MT. ARIACHTHA
OSOSK
IGARACH
NEW LANDS
TCHOM RIN
TCHAMIL MOUNTAINS
DS'03

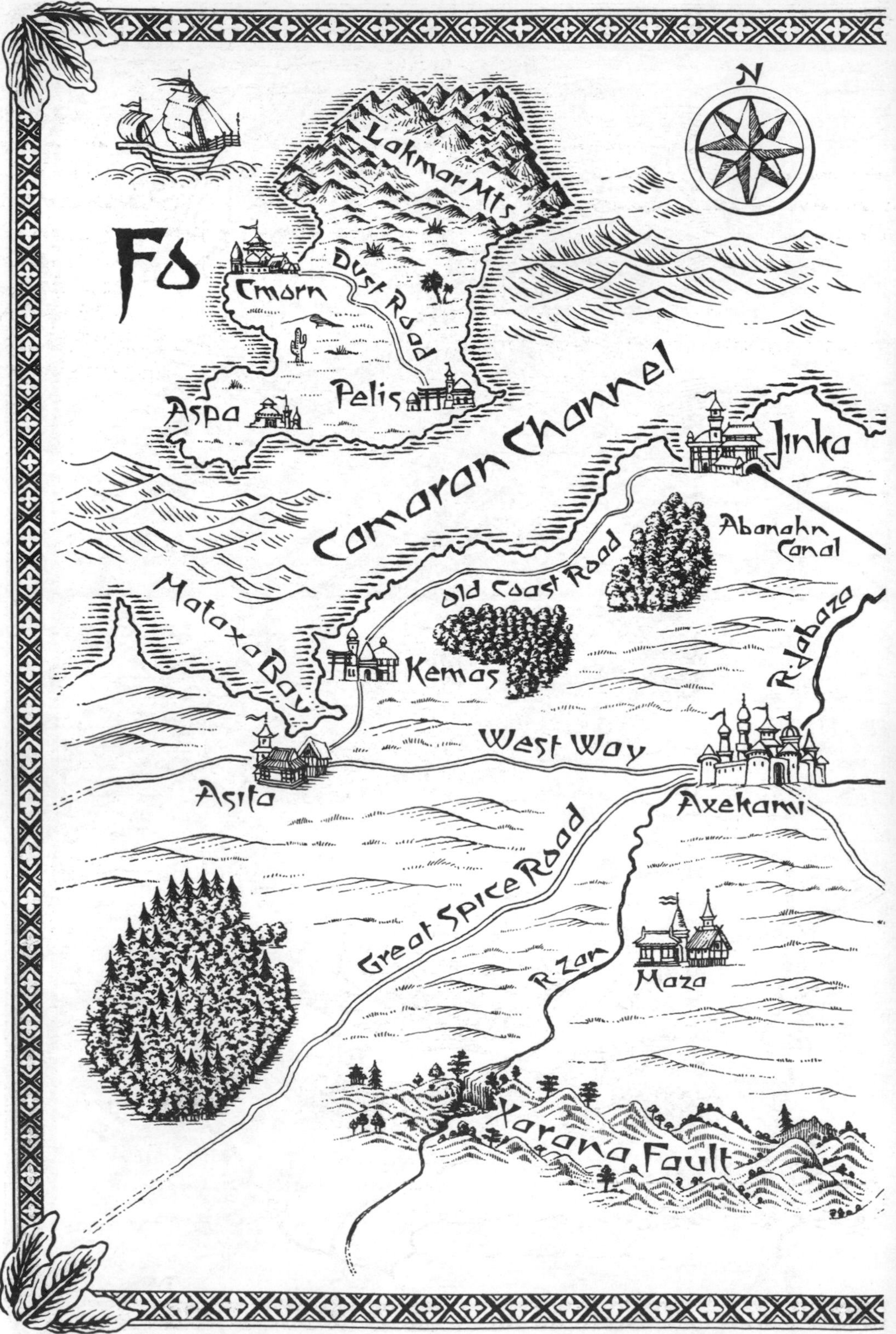

N
Lakmar Mts
Fo
Cmorn
Dust Road
Pelis
Aspa
Camaran Channel
Jinka
Abanahn Canal
Old Coast Road
R. Jabaza
Mataxa Bay
Kemas
West Way
Asita
Axekami
Great Spice Road
R. Zan
Maza
Xarana Fault

NORTHWESTERN
SARAMYR
MAJOR SETTLEMENTS
ROADWAYS
and
RIVERS
Mt. Makara
Mt. Aon
Adderach
Donath
Tchomil Mountains
Forest of Yuna
Ren
R. Kerryn
R. Abkam
L. Sazazu
East Way
L. Than
R. Rahn
Tchamaska
L. Cuiki
L. Eriri
R. So
DS'02

THE WEAVERS OF SARAMYR

ONE

Kaiku was twenty harvests of age the first time she died.

There was no memory of how she had come to this place. Recollection evaded her, made slippery by ecstasy, the sensation of tranquillity that soaked every fibre of her body. And the sights, oh, such sights as would have made her weep if she could. The world to her was a golden shimmer, millions upon millions of tiny threads crowding her gaze, shifting, waving. They tugged and teased her gently, wafting her onward towards some unseen destination. Once they parted to delineate a shape that slid through them, a distant glimpse of something vast and wondrous, like the whales she used to watch off the coast at Mishani's summer house. She tried to catch it with her eye, but it was gone in a moment, and the tapestry had sewn shut behind it.

These are the Fields of Omecha, she thought. Yet how could that be so? She had not passed through the Gate yet, not met the guardian Yoru, the laughing, pot-bellied dwarf with his red skin and piggy tusks and ears, carrying the endless jug of wine given to him by Isisya to ease his long vigil. No, not the Fields, then; merely the approach to the Gate, the soft path to the entrance of the realm of the blessed dead.

She felt no remorse or sorrow. She was full of such harmony that she had space in her heart for nothing else. She thought she might burst from the wonder of the golden, glittering world she drifted through. This was what the monks strived for when they crossed their legs and sat for years upon a pillar in contemplation; this was what the old addicts in their smokehouses sought when they sucked on their pipes of burnt amaxa root. This was completeness.

But suddenly there was a wrench, a terrible burning in her breast. She felt a shudder through the shimmering fibres that caressed her, felt them draw back . . . and then, appallingly, she was being pulled away, down, back to where she had come from. She thought she saw the outline of the Gate in the distance, and Yoru laughing and raising his jug in farewell to her. She wanted to scream, but she had no voice. The beauty was deserting her, fleeing her heart, draining like water through a holed bucket. She fought to resist, but the force pulled harder now, the burning stronger, and she was sucked away . . .

*

Her eyes flew open, unfocused. Lips were on hers, soft lips pressing hard, and her lungs seared as agonising breath was forced into them. A face, too close to determine; black hair lying against her cheek.

She twitched, a single brief spasm, and the lips left hers. The owner drew back, and Kaiku's vision finally found its focus. They were on her sleeping-mat, in her room, and straddling her hips was her handmaiden Asara. She brushed the long, sleek fall of her hair back over her shoulder and regarded her mistress with eyes of liquid darkness.

'You live, then,' she said, strangely.

Kaiku looked about, her movements frightened and bewildered. The air felt wrong somehow. Flashes of purple flickered in the night outside, and the thrashing of rain underpinned the terrible screeching roars from the sky. It was no ordinary thunder. The moonstorm her father had been predicting for days had finally arrived.

Her surroundings slotted themselves into place, assembling an order from her fractured consciousness. The once-familiar sights seemed alien now, disjointed by a slowly settling unreality. The intricately carved whorls and loops of the shutters looked strange, subtly off-kilter, and when they rattled in the wind the clacking was like some desert snake. The deep night-shadows that gathered among the polished ceiling beams seemed to glower. Even the small shrine to Ocha that rested in one corner of the minimally furnished bedroom had changed. The elegantly laid guya blossoms nodded in sinister conspiracy with the storm, and the beautifully inlaid pictographs that spelt the name of the Emperor of the gods swarmed and shifted.

Behind Asara, she could see a sandalled foot poking from the hem of a simple white robe. The owner lay inert on the hard wooden floor.

Karia.

She sat up, pushing Asara off her. Karia, her other handmaiden, was sprawled as if in sleep; but Kaiku knew by some dread instinct that it was a sleep she would never wake from.

'What is this?' she breathed, reaching out to touch her erstwhile companion.

'There is no time,' Asara said, in a tone of impatience that Kaiku had never heard before. 'We must go.'

'Tell me what has happened!' Kaiku snapped, unaccustomed to being talked to in such a way by an inferior.

Asara grabbed her hard by the shoulders, hurting her. For a moment, Kaiku was seized by the wild notion that she might be struck by her handmaiden. 'Listen,' she hissed.

Kaiku obeyed, mostly out of shock at the way she was being treated by the usually meek and servile Asara. There *was* another sound over the awful screeching of the moonstorm and the pummelling tattoo of the rain. A slow, insectile tapping, coming from above; the sound of something moving across the roof. She looked up, then back down at Asara, and her eyes were full of terror.

'*Shin-shin*,' her handmaiden whispered.

'Where's Mother?' Kaiku cried, springing up and lunging for the curtained doorway. Asara grabbed her wrist and pulled her roughly back. Her expression was grim. It told Kaiku that all the things she feared were true. She could not help her family now.

She felt her strength desert her, and she fell to her knees and almost fainted.

When she raised her head, tears streaked her face. Asara was holding a rifle in one hand, and in her other she held a mask, an ugly thing of red and black lacquer, the leering face of a mischievous spirit. She stuffed it unceremoniously inside her robe and then looked down at her mistress. Kaiku's feathered brown hair was in disarray, forming a messy frame around her face, and she wore only a thin white sleeping-robe and the jewelled bracelet at her wrist that she never took off.

A scream sounded from somewhere in the house; thin, cracked. Kaiku's grandmother. Asara seized Kaiku and pulled her towards the doorway. A moment later came the sound of a shin-shin, rattling across the roof slates. Something darted past the shutters, crawling down the outside wall of the building. Kaiku saw it and shuddered.

Asara took her hand and looked into her eyes. They were wild and panicked.

'Listen to me, Kaiku,' she said, her voice firm but calm. 'We must run. Do you understand? I will take you to safety.'

Trembling, she nodded. Asara was satisfied.

'Stay with me,' she said, and she slid aside the thin curtain in the doorway and stepped out on to the balcony beyond.

The country retreat of Ruito tu Makaima – Kaiku's father and a scholar of some renown – was built in a clearing in the midst of lush woodland, a hollow square enclosing a central garden. It was built with an eye for aesthetics, in the fashion of the Saramyr folk, ensuring ostentation was kept to a minimum while the spare beauty of its form was picked out and assembled in harmony with its surroundings. The austere simplicity of its pale walls was contrasted by ornate wooden shutters and curved stone lintels shaped into graceful horns at either end. It sat in eerie serenity even amid the howling storm. A ruthlessly tamed lawn surrounded it, with a simple bridge vaulting a stream and a path leading from the front door that was so immaculate it might have been laid only yesterday. Within the boundaries of the clearing, the more untidy edges of nature had been excised for the sake of perfection; it was only where the clearing ended that the forest regained dominance again, crowding around the territory jealously.

The upper floor had a long balcony running around its inside wall, looking out over rockeries and miniature waterfalls, tiny bridges and sculpted trees. All the rooms, Kaiku's included, faced on to this balcony; and it was on to that balcony they emerged, Asara with her rifle held ready.

The night was hot, for it was early summer, and the rain that lashed the house ran off carven gutters to pour down in torrents to the garden below. Thin pillars stretched from the waist-high wooden barrier to the sloping roof. The air was full of drumming and rattling, the voice of a thousand drips and splatters; and yet to Kaiku it seemed eerily silent, and she could hear the pounding of her heart loud in her ears.

Asara looked one way, then another, distrusting the empty balcony. Her hands gripped hard on the rifle. It was a long, slender piece of metal, its barrel decorated with sigils and a sight cleverly fashioned in the form of a breaking wave. Far too expensive and elegant for a handmaiden like Asara to own; she had stolen it from elsewhere in the house.

Kaiku jumped as Asara moved suddenly, levelling the barrel down at the garden. Something dark moved across the rockeries, inhumanly fast, racing on four spindly legs; it was too quick for Asara, and she withdrew without firing.

They edged along the balcony towards the stairs. Kaiku was almost paralysed with fright, but she forced herself to move. She felt overwhelmed and helpless; but Asara, at least, seemed to be in control. She followed her servant. There was nothing else she could do.

They reached the top of the stairs without incident. Below it was dark. No lanterns had been lit tonight, and there was no sign of movement. The sky howled again. Kaiku looked up instinctively. The clouds were being torn ragged up there, tossed about by the changing winds, swirling and curling, occasionally reaching out to each other as a bolt of purple lightning bridged a gap or lanced down to earth.

She was about to say something to Asara when she saw the shin-shin.

It was creeping out of the darkness at one end of the balcony, a demon of shadow that made Kaiku quail in terror. She could barely see it, only its outline, for it seemed part of the blackness that concealed it; but what she could see was enough. Its torso was like that of a human, but its forelegs and forearms were terribly elongated and tapered to a thin spike, so that it seemed like a man walking on four stilts. It was tall, much taller than she was, and it had to crush itself down to fit under the roof of the balcony. She could see no other detail except the eyes; they glittered in the darkness like lamps, twin points of burning brightness in the gloom.

Asara swore an impolite oath and pulled Kaiku after her, down the stairs. Kaiku needed no second prompting; all else had fled her mind at that moment, and the only remaining urge was to get away from the demon that stalked towards them. They heard the clatter as it gave chase, and then they were thundering down the stairs into the room below.

The entrance hall was wide and spacious, with elaborately carved wooden archways to the other ground-floor rooms. This house was built for the stifling heat of summer, so there were no interior doors, and attractively dyed screens stood about which could be moved to better allow the warm evening breezes through. The unnatural lightning of the moonstorm flickered through the ornamental shutters, stunning the room in brightness.

Kaiku almost fell down the final few steps, but Asara pushed her aside and aimed her rifle up the stairs at the archway leading on to the balcony. A moment later, the spindly silhouette of the shin-shin darted into view, eyes blazing in the dark oval of its face. Asara fired, and the report of the rifle cracked deafeningly through the house. The doorway was suddenly empty; the demon had been deterred, at least for a short time. Asara reprimed the bolt on her weapon and hurried Kaiku towards the door to the outside.

'Asara! More of them!' Kaiku cried, and there they were, two of the creatures, hiding in the archways of the entrance hall. Asara clutched her mistress's wrist and they both froze. Kaiku's hand was on the door, but she dared not tear it open and run, for the creatures would cut her down before she had gone ten metres. Raw, choking fear began to claw its way up her throat. She was blank with panic, disorientated, caught in a waking nightmare.

Slowly the shin-shin came into the hall, ducking their torsos beneath the archways as they angled their long, tapered limbs with insectile grace. They were the more terrible because Kaiku's gaze refused to fix on them properly, allowing only hints of their form; only the glitter of their eyes was solid and visible. She was conscious of Asara reaching for something: a lantern, dormant and unlit on a window-ledge. The demons crept closer, keeping to the deepest darknesses.

'Be ready,' Asara whispered; and a moment later, she threw the lantern into the centre of the room. The shin-shin whirled at the sound, and in that instant Asara brought up her rifle and fired it into the slick of lantern oil on the floor.

The room was suddenly bright, a roaring sheet of flame, and the demons shrieked in their unearthly tongue and scattered away from the brilliance. But Kaiku was already through the door and out into the storm, racing barefoot across the grass towards the trees that surrounded the house. Asara came close behind, leaving the fire to lick at the wooden walls and paper screens. They rushed through the rain, cringing at the great screeches coming from the sky. Not daring to look back, not knowing if Asara was following or not, Kaiku plunged into the forest.

The three moons were out tonight, clustered close above the slowly writhing clouds. Vast Aurus, the largest and eldest of the sisters; Iridima, smaller but brighter, her skin gullied with blue cracks; and the tiny green moon Neryn, the shyest of them all, who rarely showed her face. Legends told that when the three sisters were together, they fought and tore the sky, and that the screeching was Neryn's cries as her siblings teased her for her green skin. Kaiku's father taught a different tale, that the moonstorms were simply a result of the combined gravity of the moons playing havoc with the atmosphere. Whatever the reason, it was accepted wisdom that when the three moons were close moonstorms would follow. And on those nights, the Children of the Moons walked the earth.

Kaiku panted and whimpered as she ran through the trees. Thin branches whipped at her from all sides, covering her arms and face with wet lashes. Her sleeping-robe was soaked through, her chin-length hair plastered to her cheeks, her feet muddied and slimed. She fled blindly, as if she could outrun reality. Her mind still refused to grip the enormity of what had occurred in the previous few minutes. She felt like a child, helpless, alone and terrified.

Finally, the inevitable happened. Her bare foot found a rock that was more slippery than it looked, and she fell headlong, landing against a root that was steadily emerging from washed-away layers of mud. Fresh tears came at the pain, and she lay in the dirt, filthy and sodden, and sobbed.

But there was no rest for her. She felt herself gripped from behind, and there was Asara, dragging her upright. She shrieked incoherently, but Asara was merciless.

'I know a safe place,' she said. 'Come with me. They are not far behind.'

Then they were running again, plunging headlong through the trees, stumbling and slipping as they went. The air plucked at them, trying to lift them up, charged with a strange energy by the storm. It played tricks on their senses, making everything seem a little more or less than real. Grandmother Chomi used to warn her granddaughter that if she jumped too high in a moonstorm she might never come back down, but drift into the sky. Kaiku pushed the thought away, remembering instead the scream she had heard earlier. Her grandmother was gone. All of them were gone.

They came out of the trees at the edge of a rocky stream, which was swollen and angry with the rains. Asara looked quickly left and right, her long hair soaked to deepest black and sluggish with moisture. She made her decision in moments, heading downstream, tugging Kaiku after her. The latter was almost at the limit of exhaustion, and it told in her staggering steps and lolling head.

The stream emptied into a wide clearing, a shallow bowl of water from which humped several grassy islands and banks, scattered with the bald faces of half-buried rocks and taut clusters of bushes. The largest island by far was the pedestal for a vast, ancient tree, overwhelmingly dominating the scene by its sheer size. Its trunk was twice as thick as a man was tall, knotted and twisted with age, and its branches spread in a great fan, leaves of gold and brown and green weeping a delicate curtain of droplets across the water below. Even in the rain, the clearing seemed sacred, a place of untouched beauty. The air here was different, possessed of a crystalline fragility and stillness, as of a held breath. Kaiku felt the change, the sensation of a presence in this place, some cold and slow and gentle awareness that marked their arrival with a languid interest.

The sound of a breaking twig alerted Asara, and she spun to see one of the shin-shin high up in the trees to their right, moving with impossible dexterity between the boughs while its lantern eyes stayed fixed on them. She pulled Kaiku into the water, which came up to their knees and soaked through their robes. They splashed across to the largest island, and there they clambered out. Kaiku collapsed on the grass. Asara left her there and raced to the tree.

She put her palms and forehead against it and murmured softly, her lips rapid as she spoke.

'Great ipi, venerated spirit of the forest, we beg you to grant us your protection. Do not let these demons of shadow defile your glade with their corruption.'

A shiver ran through the tree, shaking loose a cascade of droplets from the leaves.

Asara stepped back from the trunk and returned to Kaiku's side. She squatted down, wiping the lank strands of hair from her face, and scanned the edge of the glade. She could sense them out there, prowling. Three of them, and maybe more, stalking around the perimeter, hiding in the trees, their shining eyes never leaving their prey.

Asara watched, her hand near her rifle. She was no priest, but she knew the spirits of the forest well enough. The ipi would protect them, if only because it would not let the demons near it. Ipis were the guardians of the forest, and nowhere was their influence stronger than in their own glades. The creatures circled, their stiltlike legs carrying them to and fro. She could sense their frustration. Their prey was within sight, yet the shin-shin dared not enter the domain of an ipi.

After a time, Asara was satisfied that they were safe. She hooked her hands under Kaiku's shoulders and dragged her into the protection of the tree's vast roots, where the rain was less. Kaiku never woke. Asara regarded her for a moment, soaked as she was and freezing, and felt a kind of sympathy for her. She crouched down next to her mistress and stroked her cheek gently with the back of her knuckles.

'Life can be cruel, Kaiku,' she said. 'I fear you are only just beginning to learn that.'

With the moonstorm raging high overhead, she sat in the shelter of the great tree and waited for the dawn to come.

TWO

Kaiku awoke to a loud snap from the fire, and her eyes flickered open. Asara was there, stirring a small, blackened pot that hung from an iron tripod over the flames. A pair of coilfish were spitted on a branch and crisping next to it. The sun was high in the sky and the air was muggy and hot. A fresh, earthy smell was all about as damp loam dried from last night's downpour.

'Daygreet, Kaiku,' Asara said, without looking at her. 'I went back to the house this morning and salvaged what I could.' She tossed a bundle of clothes over. 'There was not a great deal left, but the rain put out the blaze before it could devour everything. We have food, clothes and a good amount of money.'

Kaiku raised herself, looking around. They were no longer in the water-logged clearing. Now they sat in a dip in the land where the soil was sandy and clogged with pebbles, and little grew except a few shrubs. Trees guarded the lip of the depression, casting sharply contrasting shadows against the dazzling light, and the daytime sounds of the forest peeped and chittered all about. Had Asara carried her?

The first thing she noticed was that her bracelet was missing.

'Asara! Grandmother's bracelet! It must have fallen . . . it . . .'

'I took it. I left it as an offering to the ipi, in thanks for protecting us.'

'She gave me that bracelet on my eighth harvest!' Kaiku cried. 'I have never taken it off!'

'The point of an offering is that you sacrifice something precious to you,' Asara said levelly. 'The ipi saved our lives. I had nothing I could give, but you did.'

Kaiku stared at her in disbelief, but Asara appeared not to notice. She made a vague gesture to indicate their surroundings. 'I thought it best not to start a fire in the ipi's glade, so I moved you here.'

Kaiku hung her head. She was too drained to protest any further. Asara watched her in silence for a time.

'I must know,' Kaiku said quietly. 'My family . . .'

Asara put down the spoon she had been using to stir the pot and knelt before Kaiku, taking her hands. 'They are dead.'

Kaiku's throat tightened, but she nodded to indicate she understood. 'What happened?'

'Would you not rather eat first, and compose yourself?'

Kaiku raised her head and looked at Asara. 'I must know,' she repeated.

Asara released her hands. 'Most of you were poisoned,' she said. 'You died as you slept. I suspect it was one of the kitchen servants, but I cannot be sure. Whoever it was, they were inefficient. Your grandmother did not eat at the evening meal last night, so she was still alive when the shin-shin came. I believe that somebody sent the demons to kill the servants and remove the evidence. With no witnesses, the crime would go unsolved.' She settled further on her haunches.

'Who?' Kaiku asked. 'And why?'

'To those questions I have no answers,' she said. 'Yet.'

Asara got up and returned to the pot, occasionally turning the fish. It was some time before Kaiku spoke again.

'Did I die, Asara? From the poison?'

'Yes,' replied the handmaiden. 'I brought you back.'

'How?'

'I stole the breath from another, and put it into you.'

Kaiku thought of Karia, her other handmaiden, who she had seen lying dead on the floor of her room.

'How is that possible?' she whispered, afraid of the answer.

'There are many things you do not understand, Kaiku,' Asara replied. 'I am one of them.'

Kaiku was beginning to realise that. Asara had always been the perfect handmaiden: quiet, obedient and reliable, skilled at combing out hair and laying out clothes. Kaiku had liked her better than the more wilful Karia, and often talked with her, shared secrets or played games. But there had always been the boundary there, a division that prevented them from becoming truly close. The unspoken understanding that the two of them were of a different caste. Kaiku was high-born and Asara was not, and so one had a duty to serve and obey the other. It was the way in Saramyr, the way it had always been.

And yet now Kaiku saw that the last two years had been a deception. This was not the person she thought she knew. This Asara had a steely calm, a core of cold metal. This Asara had saved her life by stealing another's, had burned down her house, had taken her most valuable token of her grandmother's love and given it away with impunity. This Asara had rescued her from demons.

Who was she, truly?

'The stream is nearby, Kaiku,' Asara said, pointing with her spoon. 'You should wash and change. You will catch a chill in that.' It had not escaped notice that since last night she had ceased to call Kaiku 'mistress', as was proper.

Kaiku obeyed. She felt she should be ashamed of the state of herself, half undressed with her thin white sleeping-robe mussed and filthy. Yet it seemed insignificant in the wake of what had gone before. Weary despite her sleep, she went to the stream, and there she threw away the soiled robe and washed herself clean, naked in the hot sunlight. The feel of the water and warmth on her bare skin brought her no pleasure. Her body felt like only a vessel for her grief.

She dressed in the clothes Asara had brought her, finding that they were sturdy attire for travelling in. Leather boots, shapeless beige trousers, an open-throated shirt of the same colour that would belong better on a man. She had no complaints. She had always been a tomboy, and she fitted as easily into the trappings of a peasant as those of a noble lady. Her elder brother had been her closest companion, and she had competed with him at everything. They had fought to outride, outshoot and outwrestle each other constantly. Kaiku was no stranger to the gun or the forest.

When she returned to the campfire, the air was alive with sparkling flakes, drifting gently from the sky like snow. They glittered as the sun caught them, sharp flashes of light all about. It was called starfall: a phenomenon seen only in the aftermath of a moonstorm. Tiny, flat crystals of fused ice were created in the maelstrom of the three sisters' conflict, thin enough to float on their way down. Beauty after chaos. Much prose had been written of starfall, and it was a recurring theme in some of the finest love poetry. Today, it held no power to move her.

Asara handed her a bowl of coilfish, vegetables and saltrice. 'You should eat,' she said. Kaiku did so, using her fingers in the way she had as a child, barely tasting it. Asara arranged herself behind, and gently untangled Kaiku's hair with a wooden comb. It was an act of surprising kindness, in the face of everything; a gesture of familiarity from a girl who now seemed a stranger.

'Thank you,' Kaiku said, when Asara was done. The words meant more than simple gratitude. There was no need to thank a servant for a duty that was expected to be rendered. What seemed a mere pleasantry was a tacit acceptance that Asara was no longer subservient to her. The fact that Asara did not correct her proved it.

Kaiku was unsurprised. Asara had altered her mode of address towards Kaiku, and was now talking to her as if she was social equal, albeit one who was not close enough to be called a friend. It spoke volumes about the new state of their relationship.

The Saramyrrhic language was impenetrably complex to an outsider, a mass of tonal inflections, honorifics, accents and qualifiers that conveyed dense layers of meaning far beyond the simple words in a sentence. There were dozens of different modes of address for different situations, each one conveyed by minute alterations in pronunciation and structure. There were different modes used to speak to children, one each for boys, girls, and a separate one for infants of either sex; there were multiple modes for social superiors, depending on how much more important the addressee was than the speaker, and a special one used only for addressing the Emperor or Empress. There were modes for lovers, again in varying degrees with the most intimate being virtually sacrilegious to speak aloud in the presence of anyone but the object of passion. There were modes for mother, father, husband, wife, shopkeepers and tradesmen, priests, animals, modes for praying and for scolding, vulgar modes and scatological ones. There were even several neutral modes, used when the speaker was uncertain as to the relative importance of the person they were addressing.

Additionally, the language was split into High Saramyrrhic – employed by nobles and those who could afford to be educated in it – and Low Saramyrrhic, used by the peasantry and servants. Though the two were interchangeable as a spoken language – with Low Saramyrrhic being merely a slightly coarser version of its higher form – as written languages they were completely different. High Saramyrrhic was the province of the nobles, and the peasantry were excluded from it. It was the language of learning, in which all philosophy, history and literature were written; but its pictographs meant nothing to the common folk. The higher strata of society was violently divided from the lower by a carefully maintained boundary of ignorance; and that boundary was the written form of High Saramyrrhic.

'The shin-shin fear the light,' Asara said in a conversational tone, as she scuffed dirt over the fire to put it out. 'They will not come in the daytime. By the time they return we will be gone.'

'Where are we going?'

'Somewhere safer than this,' Asara replied. She caught the look on Kaiku's face, saw her frustration at the answer, and offered one a little less vague. 'A secret place. Where there are friends, where we can understand what happened here.'

'You know more that you say you do, Asara,' the other accused. 'Why won't you tell me?'

'You are disorientated,' came the reply. 'You have been to the Gates of Omecha not one sunrise past, you have lost your family and endured more than anyone should bear. Trust me; you will learn more later.'

Kaiku crossed the hollow and faced her former servant. 'I will learn it now.'

Asara regarded her in return. She was a pretty one, despite the temporary ravages of grief on her face. Eyes of brown that seemed to laugh when she was happy; a small nose, slightly sloped; teeth white and even. Her tawny hair she wore in a feathered style, teased forward over her cheeks and face in the fashionable cut that young ladies wore in the capital. Asara had known her long enough to realise her stubborn streak, her mulish persistence when she decided she wanted something. She saw it now, and at that moment she felt a slight admiration for the woman she had deceived all this time. She had half expected the grief of the previous night to break her, but she was finding herself proven wrong. Kaiku had spirit, then. Good. She would need it.

Asara picked up a cured-leather pack and held it out. 'Walk with me.' Kaiku took it and slid it on to her back. Asara took the other, and the rifle, from where it had been drying by the fire. The previous night's rain had soaked the powder chamber, and it was not ready to use yet.

They headed into the forest. The branches twinkled with starfall as it gently drifted around them, gathering on the ground in a soft dusting before melting away. Kaiku felt a fresh upswell of tears in her breast, but she fought to keep them down. She needed to understand, to make some small sense of what had happened. Her family were gone, and yet it did not seem real yet. She had to hold together for now. Resolutely, she forced her pain into a tight, bitter corner of her mind and kept it there. It was the only way she could continue to function. The alternative was to go mad with sorrow.

'We've watched you for a long time,' Asara said eventually. 'Your house and family, too. Partly it was because we knew your father was one who was sympathetic to our cause, one who might be persuaded to join us eventually. He had connections through his patronage in the Imperial Court. But mostly it was because of you, Kaiku. Your condition.'

'Condition? I have no *condition*,' Kaiku said.

'I admit I had my doubts when I was sent here,' replied her former handmaiden. 'But even I have noticed the signs.'

Kaiku tried to think, but her head was muddled and Asara's explanation seemed to be throwing up more questions than answers. Instead, she asked directly: 'What happened last night?'

'Your father,' Asara said. 'You must have remembered how he was when he returned from his last trip away.'

'He said he was ill . . .' Kaiku began, then stopped. She sounded foolish. The illness he had feigned had been an excuse. She *did* remember the way he had seemed. Pale, quiet and lethargic. There had been a haunted look about him, a certain absence in his manner. Grandmother had been that way when Grandfather died, seven years ago. A kind of stunned disbelief, such as soldiers got when they had been too long exposed to the roar of cannons.

'Yes,' she agreed. 'Something happened, something he would not speak of. Do you know what it was?'

'Do you?'

She shook her head. They trudged a few more steps in silence. The forest had enshrouded them now, and they walked a zigzagging way through the sparsely clustered trees, stepping over roots and boulders that cluttered the uneven ground. A dirt ridge had risen to waist-height on their right, fringed with gently swaying shadowglove serviced by fat red bees. The sun beat down from overhead, baking the wet soil in a lazy heat that made the world content and sluggish. On any other day Kaiku would have been lost in tranquillity, for she had always had a childlike awe of nature; but the beauty of their surroundings had no power to touch her now.

'I watched him these last few weeks,' Asara said. 'I learned nothing more. Perhaps he wronged someone, a powerful enemy. I can only guess. But I am in no doubt that it was he who brought ruin on you last night.'

'Why? He was just a scholar! He read *books*. Why would someone want to kill him . . . all of us?'

'For this,' Asara said, and with that she drew from her robe the mask

Kaiku had seen her take from the house. She brandished it in front of Kaiku. Its red and black lacquer face leered idiotically at her. 'He brought it with him when he returned last.'

'That? It's only a mask.'

Asara brushed her hair back from her face and looked gravely at the other. 'Kaiku, masks are the most dangerous weapons in the world. More than rifles, more than cannon, more than the spirits that haunt the wild places. They are—'

Asara trailed off suddenly as Kaiku's step faltered and she stumbled dizzily.

'Are you unwell?' she asked.

Kaiku blinked, frowning. Something had turned in her gut, a burning worm of pain that shifted and writhed. A moment later it happened again, stronger this time, not in her gut but lower, coming from her womb like the kick of a baby.

'Asara,' she gasped, dropping to one knee, her hand splayed on the ground in front of her. 'There's . . . something . . .'

And now it blossomed, a raw bloom of agony in her stomach and groin, wrenching a cry from her throat. But this one did not recede. Instead it built upon itself, becoming hotter, a terrifying pressure rising inside her. She clutched at her belly, but it did not abate. She squeezed her eyes shut, tears of shock and incomprehension dripping from the corners.

'Asara . . . help . . .'

She looked up in supplication, but the world as she knew it was no longer there. Her eyes saw not tree and stone and leaf but a thousand million streams of light, a great three-dimensional diorama of glowing threads, stirring and flexing to ebb and flow around the objects that moved through it. She could see the bright knot of Asara's heart within the stitchwork frame of her body; she could see the ripple in the threads of the air as a nearby bird tore through it; she could see the lines of the sunlight spraying the forest as it slanted through the canopy, and the sparkle of starfall all about.

I'm dying again, she thought, *just like the last time.*

But this was not like the last time, for there was no bliss, no serenity or inner peace. Only something within, something huge, building and building in size until she knew her skin must split and she would be torn apart. Her irises darkened and turned red as blood. The air stirred around her, ruffling her clothes and lifting her hair. She saw Asara's expression turn to fear, the threads of her face twisting. Saw her turn and run, fleeing headlong into the trees.

Kaiku screamed, and with that venting, the burning force found its release.

The nearest trees exploded into flaming matchwood. Those a little further away ignited, becoming smoking torches in an instant. Grass crisped, stone scorched, the air warped with heat. The power tore from her body, ripping through her lungs and heart and searing them from the inside.

She never stopped screaming until she blacked out.

*

She did not know how long unconsciousness held her before releasing her back into reality, but when it did, calm had returned. The air was thick with smoke, and there came the harsh crackle and heat of burning trees.

She levered herself up, her muscles knotting and twitching, her insides scoured. She found her feet and her balance. She was alive; the pain told her so. Slowly she looked around the charred circle of destruction that surrounded her, and the sullenly smouldering trees beyond. Already the dampness from yesterday's rains was overcoming the hungry tongues of flame, and the fire was subsiding gradually.

She fought to reconcile the scene with the one she had been walking through when the pain struck her, and could not. Blackened rock faces hunkered out of soil gone hard and crisp. Scorched leaves curled into skeletal fists. Trees had been split in half, roughly decapitated or smashed aside. The very suddenness of the obliteration was almost impossible to understand; she could scarcely believe she was still in the same place as she had been when she had fainted.

The mask, unharmed, lay on the ground nearby, its empty gaze mocking. She stumbled over to it and picked it up. There was a terrible weariness in her body, a hazy blanket over her senses that smothered her towards sleep or unconsciousness or death – she was not sure which, and welcomed all equally.

Her eyes fell upon the crumpled white shape lying nearby. Numb, she staggered over to it, absently stuffing the mask into her belt as she went.

It was Asara. She lay strewn in a hollow where she had been thrown by the blast. One side of her had caught the brunt. Her robe was seared, her hair burned and smoking. Her hand and cheek were scarred terribly. She lay limp and still.

Kaiku began to tremble. She backed away, tears blurring her eyes, her fingers dragging at her face as if she might pull the flesh off and find the old Kaiku underneath, the one that had existed only yesterday, before chaos and madness took her in a stranglehold. Before she had lost her family. Before she had killed her handmaiden.

A choking sob escaped her, a sound not sane. She shook her head as she retreated, trying to deny what she saw; but the weight of truth crushed down on her, the evidence of her eyes accused. Panic swam in and seized her, and with a cry, she ran into the forest and was swallowed.

Asara lay where she was left, amid the smoke and the ruin, the gently drifting starfall settling on her to twinkle briefly and then die.

THREE

The roof gardens of the Imperial Keep might have seemed endless to a child at first: a vast, multi-levelled labyrinth of stony paths and shady arbours, of secret places and magical hidey-holes. The Heir-Empress Lucia tu Erinima, next in line to the throne of Saramyr, knew better. She had visited all of its many walls, and found that the place was as much a prison as a paradise, and it grew smaller every day.

She idled down a rough-paved trail, her fingers dragging over a vine-laden trellis. Somewhere nearby she could hear the rustle of a cat as it chased the dark squirrels that wound around the thin, elegant boles of the trees. The garden was an assembly of the most delicate foliage and flowers from all over the known world, arranged around a multitude of sheltered ornamental benches, statues and artful sculpture. Sprays of exotic foreign blooms stirred in the minute breeze. Birds hop-swooped back and forth, their gullets vibrating as they chattered staccato songs to each other. Distantly, the four spires of the Keep's towers lanced upward, rendered pale by haze. Closer by, the dome of the great temple at the centre of the Keep's roof was visible over the carefully placed rows of kamaka and chapapa trees. Today it was hot and balmy with the promise of a summer soon to come. The sun rode high in the sky, the single eye of Nuki, the bright god, whose gaze lit the world. She basked in his radiance as she watched the squirrels jumping through the treetops and spiralling along the boughs.

The Saramyr people tended towards tanned skin and a smooth beauty. Lucia's paleness was striking by contrast. More so was her hair, for true blonde was rare among the Saramyr, and her round face was framed by a flaxen cascade that fell down her back. She wore a dress of light green and simple jewellery. Her tutors demanded that she learned to present herself elegantly, even when there was nobody to see her. She listened with a dreamy vacancy of expression, and they retreated in exasperation.

She envied her tutors sometimes. They had a marvellous ability to focus their concentration on one thing to the exclusion of all others. It was inconvenient that they could not understand her situation in the way that she understood theirs; but Zaelis, at least, knew why she rarely seemed to be more than partially interested in any one thing. She had a lot more to think about than those with only five senses.

By the time she had learned to speak – at six months old – she already knew this to be a bad thing. She sensed it in the instinctive way of infants, in the sadness her mother's eyes held when she looked down at her baby. Even before Lucia had begun outwardly to manifest her talent, her mother the Empress knew. She was hidden from the world and put inside this gilded cage deep in the dark, sprawling heart of the Imperial Keep. She had been a prisoner ever since.

The cat emerged from a cluster of trees nearby on to the path. It looked her over with an insulting lack of respect and then turned its attention to the squirrels that raced about above it, watching those who were heading dangerously near to ground level. A moment later, it sprang off after them. She felt the alarm of the squirrels as it blundered in, their fast animal thoughts blaring.

Her animals were her friends, for she had no others. Well, that was not quite true. She supposed Zaelis was her friend, and her mother in a strange way. But them aside, she was alone. The solitude was all she knew. She was quite content with her own company; but when she dreamed, she dreamed of freedom.

Her mother Anais, Blood Empress of Saramyr and ruler of the land, visited her at least once a day, when she was not constrained by official business. As the author of her confinement, Lucia sometimes considered hating her; but she hated nobody. She was too forgiving for that, too ready to empathise. There was not a person she had met yet who was so black-hearted that she could find no redeeming quality to them.

When she told Zaelis this, he reminded her that she hadn't met many.

It was her mother who taught her to keep her talents secret, her mother who had seen to it that her tutors were kept silent about the true nature of the child they taught. It was her mother also who had confirmed what she already knew: that people would hate her, fear her, if they knew what she was. That was why she was hidden.

The Empress had begged her daughter's forgiveness a hundred times for keeping her locked away from the world. She wanted nothing more than to let Lucia run free, but it was simply too dangerous. Anais's sorrow was, she said, as great as Lucia's own. Lucia loved her mother because she believed her.

But there were dark clouds massing beyond the horizon; this she knew. Her dreams of late had been plagued by an unseen menace.

Often, as she slept, she walked the corridors of the Imperial Keep, beyond the confines of her rooms. Sometimes she visited her mother, but her mother never saw her. Lucia would watch the Empress sew, or bathe, or gaze out of the windows of the Keep. Sometimes Lucia would listen to her consult with advisors about the affairs of the realm. Other times she would walk through the rooms of the servants as they gossiped and cooked and coupled. Occasionally someone would see her, and panic ensued; but most just looked straight through her.

Once she asked her mother about some things she had seen in her dreams. Then her mother's face grew a little sad, and she kissed her daughter on the forehead and said nothing. From this, Lucia knew not to mention them again; but she also knew that these were no ordinary dreams, and that what she was witnessing was real.

Through her dreams she learned a little about the world outside, but still she was confounded by the perimeter of the Keep, unable to roam beyond it. The city of Axekami, that surrounded the Imperial Keep, was simply too far outside her experience. She could not dream it. She had only widened the walls of her pen.

It had been a little over a year since she had first begun dream-walking. Not long after that the dream lady had appeared. A fortnight ago, another stranger had come. Now she woke sweating and shaking, her body taut with fear at the nameless presence that stalked her through the corridors of nightmare, prowling inexorably behind.

She did not know what it was, but she knew what it meant. Something bad had found her; perhaps the very thing her mother had tried to hide her from. Change was coming. She did not know whether to feel joyous or afraid.

On the far side of the roof garden, something stirred. The gardeners had been working here of late, digging up the dying winter blooms to replace them with summer flowers. A wheelbarrow sat idle by the path, forks and spades laid askew within it. Beneath the thick screen of trees, newly turned earth lay moist and black and fertile in the sun, waiting for the seeds it could impart its life to.

The turf shuddered. First a small movement, and then a great disturbance as the man buried beneath it rose up, sloughing off dirt. A tall, thin man, nearing his fortieth harvest, with short, greying hair and stubbled cheeks. He pulled himself free and spat out the short, thick bamboo tube that had been his breathing apparatus. He dusted himself off as best he could and straightened.

Purloch tu Irisi had always been lucky, but luck could only last for so long. Already he had evaded enough dangers to put off even the most determined intruder. He had slipped past sentries, rappelled down sheer walls, crept past observation posts. He had made a blind jump across a fifty-foot drop to a lightless wall, trusting only his instincts to find and grip the edge. Frankly, he believed he should have been caught or dead by now. He prided himself on being the most adept cat-burglar in the city, capable of getting into anywhere; but even he had been a whisker's breadth from discovery three times since last night, and twice had edged by death with barely an inch to spare. The Heir-Empress was guarded more closely than the most precious jewel.

The person who had come to him with the offer was an obvious middleman, a hireling sent to protect the identity of the real brain behind the plan. Purloch had met enough to know. He only became interested when he learned what they wanted him to do. To get to the Heir-Empress's chambers . . . such a thing was close to impossible!

But the middleman was remarkably well informed, with detailed plans of the Keep to hand and information about sentry movements and blind spots. The price he offered was enough for Purloch to retire on and live wealthy for the rest of his life. It would be an illustrious end to his career. He would be left a legend among the underworld, and his days of risk-taking would be done.

Still, the mission was too dangerous to be taken on faith. So he shadowed the middleman back to his home, and observed as he met another man later that day, and that man met another the next night, and through him Purloch finally traced the offer to its source. It had taken all his skill just to keep up with them, even though they had been unaware he was following. They were undoubtedly good. He was assuredly better.

The source, then: Barak Sonmaga, head of Blood Amacha. They were powerful among the high families, and old antagonists to Blood Erinima, to which the Empress and her daughter belonged. Purloch could divine nothing of Blood Amacha's plans, but he could surmise that he was being made part of something huge, a pawn in the game between two of the empire's greatest families.

It was a terrible risk, now that he knew the stakes. But though he had to admit he was puzzled by the nature of his task, he could not turn it down. He had taken every precaution he could – including what retribution he could muster against his employer if he should be double-crossed in some way – but in the end, the money and glory were too great to resist.

Now he was wishing he had listened to sense, and turned down the offer.

He had spent days posing as a servant, observing the forms and rhythms of the Keep before he moved. Getting in had been the easy part; there were forgotten ways, paths that history had lost but which he had unearthed again. But it was the slow process of planning a way to penetrate the defences at its core that was the true art. Even with the detailed information his employer had given him, it was abominably hard to conceive of how he might get to the Heir-Empress. Only a select few had ever seen her at all – the most trusted guards, the most honoured tutors – and the circle of people surrounding her was so small that infiltration by disguise or deception was not even remotely viable.

But Purloch was patient, and clever. He talked with the right people, asked the right questions, without ever drawing suspicion to himself. And soon his opportunity came.

He had made a special point of befriending some of the gardeners, a guileless, honest group whose loyalty to their liege was beyond question, inspired by the almost religious awe that the peasantry felt towards their masters and mistresses. They were forbidden on pain of death to talk about the Heir-Empress, even though they had never seen her, for the gardening was done only in those hours of the day when Lucia was not outside. But they were still informative enough, in their way. It was clear they were honoured to be gardeners to the future ruler of Saramyr, and they talked about the minutiae of their jobs endlessly. Purloch had learned they were digging new beds to plant a fresh batch of summer flowers that would not wilt in the heat. It had given him the idea he needed. And so the plan had formed.

He had infiltrated the garden at night, for it would certainly have been impossible during the day. There were too many guards, too many rifles. But with the cover of darkness, and the moons all but hidden beneath the horizon, he had made it. Barely.

Once inside, he had searched for his place to hide. A light poison in the drinks of the gardeners had seen to it that they were forced to spend the next day in bed – he wouldn't like to find his guts pierced by a fork as he lay under the turf. He buried himself expertly before the dawn came, and then waited in his earthen cocoon for daybreak.

His contact had informed him that guards searched the garden in the morning, before the Heir-Empress was allowed up. They were just as aware as Purloch that the concealing shadows of night might afford an intruder a slim chance of getting past the sentries, and even that slim chance was too much. The information was good. Purloch heard the clatter of pikes as they passed him by. The newly turned soil of the flower bed showed no sign of the disturbance Purloch had created while digging himself into it.

Now the guards were gone, and the child was here alone. Time to do what had to be done. Slipping silently along, he undid the clasp of the dagger at his belt.

He found the girl in a small paved oval hemmed in by trees. A cat was chasing its tail, while the Heir-Empress watched it with a strangely detached look on her face. The cat was absorbed in its own capering, so much so that it did not notice his approach. Lucia did, however, though he had made not a sound. She slowly looked into the foliage, right at him, and said: 'Who are you?'

The man slid out from behind a tumisi tree, and the cat bolted. Lucia regarded the newcomer with an unfathomable gaze.

'My name is of no consequence,' Purloch replied. He was nervous, glancing about, eager to be gone.

Lucia watched him placidly.

'My lady, I must take something from you,' he said, drawing his dagger from its sheath.

The air around them exploded in a frenzy of movement, a thrashing of black wings that beat at the senses and caused Purloch to cry out and fall to his knees, his arm across his face to shield it from the tumult.

As quickly as it had begun, it was over. Purloch lowered his arm, and his breath caught in his throat.

The child was cloaked in ravens. They buried her, perching on her shoulders and arms: a mantle of dark feathers. They surrounded her, too, a thick carpet of the creatures. Dozens more perched in the branches nearby. Now and then one of them stirred, preening under a wing or shuffling position; but all of them watched him with their dreadful black, beady eyes.

Purloch was dumbstruck with terror.

'What did you want to take?' Lucia asked softly. Her expression and tone reflected none of the malevolence the ravens projected.

Purloch swallowed. He was aware of nothing more than the ravens. The birds were *protecting* her. And he knew, with a fearful certainty, that they would tear him to bloody rags at a thought from the child.

He tried to speak, but nothing came out. He swallowed and tried again. 'A . . . a lock of your hair, my lady. Nothing more.' He looked down at the dagger still in his hand, and realised that his haste to get his prize and escape had made him foolish. He should not have drawn the blade.

Lucia walked slowly towards him, the ravens shuffling aside to let her pass. Purloch stared at her in naked fear, this monster of a child. What *was* she?

And yet what he saw in her pale blue gaze was anything but monstrous. She knew he was not a killer. She did not think him evil; she felt sympathy for him, not hate. And beneath it all was a kind of sadness, an acceptance of something inevitable that he did not understand.

Gently, she took the dagger from his hand, and with it cut away a curl of her blonde, tumbling hair. She pressed it into his palm.

'Go back to your masters,' she said quietly, the ravens stirring at her shoulder. 'Begin what must be begun.'

Purloch drew a shuddering breath and bowed his head, still kneeling. 'Thank you,' he whispered, humbled. And then he was gone, disappearing into the trees, with Lucia watching after and wondering what would come of what she had done.

FOUR

It was four days after the murder of her family that Kaiku was found. The one who discovered her was a young acolyte of the earth goddess Enyu, returning to the temple from a frustrating day of failed meditation. His name was Tane tu Jeribos.

He had almost missed her as he passed by, buried as she was under a drift of leaves at the base of a thick-boled kiji tree. His mind was on other things. That, he supposed, was the whole problem. The priests had taught him the theory behind attuning himself to nature, letting himself become blank and empty so he could hear the slow heart of the forest. Yes, he understood the theory well. It was just that putting it into practice was proving next to impossible.

You cannot feel the presence of Enyu and her daughters until you are calm inside. It was the infuriating mantra that Master Olec droned at him every time he became agitated. But how calm could he be? He had relaxed to the best of his ability, evacuated his mind of all the clutter, but it was never enough. Doubly frustrating, for he excelled at his other studies, and his masters were pleased with his progress. This lesson seemed to elude him, and he could not understand why.

He was turning over sullen thoughts in his mind when he saw the shape buried beneath the leaves. The sight made him jump. His first reaction was to reach for the rifle slung across his back. Then he saw what it was: a young woman, lying still. Cautiously he approached. Though he saw no threat from her, he had lived his whole life in the forests of Saramyr, and he knew enough to assume everything was dangerous until proven otherwise. Spirits took many forms, and not all of them were friendly. In fact, it seemed they were getting more and more hostile as the seasons glided by, and the animals grew wilder by the day.

He reached out and poked the girl in the shoulder, ready to jump back if she moved suddenly. When she did not respond, he shoved her again. This time she stirred, making a soft moan.

'Do you hear me?' he asked, but the girl did not reply. He shook her again, and her eyes flickered open: fevered, roving. She looked at him, but did not seem to see. Instead she sighed something incoherent, and murmured her way back to sleep again.

Tane looked around for some clue about her, but he could see nothing in the balmy evening light except the thick forest. She seemed starved, exhausted and sick. He brushed back her tangled brown hair and laid a hand on her forehead. Her skin burned. Her eyes moved restlessly beneath their lids.

As he was examining her, his hand brushed across the leaves that were covering her, and he paused to pick one up. It was fresh-fallen. In fact, all of them were. The tree had shed them on the girl as she lay, not more than half a day past. He smiled to himself. No tree-spirit would harbour an evil thing in such a way. He straightened and bowed.

'Thank you, spirit of the tree, for sheltering this girl,' he said. 'Please convey my gratitude to your mistress Aspinis, daughter of Enyu.'

The tree made no response; but then, they never did. These were young trees, not like the ancient ipi. Barely aware, all but senseless. Like newborn children.

Tane gathered up the girl in his arms. She was a little heavier than he had expected, but by her lithe figure it was apparent that it was muscle and not fat. Though Tane was no great size himself, forest life had toughened him and tautened his own muscles, and he had no trouble carrying her. It was a short walk to the temple, and she did not wake.

The temple was buried deep in the forest, situated on the banks of the River Kerryn. The river flowed from the mountains to the north-east, winding through the heart of the Forest of Yuna before curving westward and heading to the capital. The building itself was a low, elegant affair, with little ostentation to overshadow the scenery all around. Temples to Enyu and her daughters were intentionally kept simple out of humility, except in the cities where gaudiness was a virtual prerequisite for a place of worship. It was decorated in simple shades of cream and white, supported by beams of black ash, artfully describing lines and perimeters across the structure. It was two storeys high, the second one built further back than the first to take advantage of the slant of the hill. Gentle invocations were inscribed in the henge-shaped frame of the main doors, picked out in unvarnished wood, a mantra to the goddess of nature that was as simple and peaceful as the temple itself. A prayer-bell hung above a small shrine just to one side of the doors, a cairn of stones with bowls of smouldering incense inside. Long-stemmed lilies and fruit were laid out on a ledge before an icon of Enyu: a carved wooden bear statuette, with one mighty paw circling a cub.

A curving bridge arced from one side of the Kerryn to the other. Carven pillars etched with all manner of bird, beast and fish sunk deep into the river bed. The river was a deep, melancholy blue, its natural transparency made doleful by the salts and minerals it carried down from the Tchamil Mountains. It threw back the sun in fins of purple-edged brightness, dappling the smooth underside of the bridge with an endless play of shifting water-light. The effect, intentionally, was that of calm and beauty and idyll.

Tane consulted with his masters, and an aged priest examined her. He concluded that she was starving and fevered, much as Tane had said, but there were no more serious afflictions. She would recover with care.

'She is your responsibility,' Master Olec told him. 'See if you can keep your mind on something for a change.'

Tane knew Olec's withered old tongue too well to be offended. He put her in a guest room on the upper storey. The room was spare and white, with a sleeping-mat in a corner beneath the wide, square windows. The shutters were locked open against the heat of oncoming summer. Like most windows in Saramyr, there was no need for glass – much of the year it was too hot, and shutters worked just as well against adverse weather.

As evening wore on to a dark red sunset, Tane brewed a tea of boneset, yarrow and echinacea for her fever. He made her sip and swallow it as hot as he dared, half a cup every two hours. She muttered and flinched, and she did not wake, but she did drink it down. He brought a bucket of cool water and mopped her brow, cleaned her face and cheeks. He examined her tongue, gently holding her mouth open. He checked the flutter of her pulse at her throat and wrist. When he had done all he could, he settled himself on a wicker mat and watched her sleep.

The priests had undressed her – it was necessary to determine if she had suffered from poison thorns, insect bites, anything that might influence her recovery – and given her a sleeping-robe of light green. Now she lay with a thin sheet twined through her legs and resting on her ribs, pushed out of place by her stirrings. It was too hot to lie under anyway, especially with her fever, but Tane had been obliged to provide it out of respect for her modesty. He had cared for the sick before, young and old, male and female, and the priests knew it and trusted him. But this one interested him more than most. Where had she come from, and how had she got into the state she was in? Her very helplessness provoked in him the need to help her. She was incapacitated and utterly alone. The spirits knew what kind of ordeals she had gone through wandering in the forest; she was lucky even to be alive.

'Who are you, then?' he asked softly, fascinated.

His eyes ranged over the lines of her cheekbones, a little too pronounced now but they would soften with the return of her health. He watched her lips press together as she spoke half-formed dream-words. The light from outside began to fade, and still he stayed, and wondered about her.

The fever broke two days later, yet there was no immediate recovery. She had beaten the illness, but she had not overcome whatever it was that plagued her waking hours and haunted her dreams. For a week she was nearly catatonic with misery, unable to lift herself from the bed, crying almost constantly. Very little of what she said made sense, and the priests began to doubt her sanity. Tane believed otherwise. He had sat by her while she sobbed and raved, and the few fragments of what he could understand led him to the conclusion that she had suffered some terrible tragedy, endured loss such as no human should have to undergo.

He was excused from some of his less pressing duties while he cared for his patient, though there was little he could do for her now that she was physically well again. He made her eat, though she had no appetite. He prepared a mild sedative – a tincture of blue cohosh and motherwort – and gave it to her to gentle down some of her worse fits of grief. He made an infusion of hops, skullcap and valerian to put her to sleep at night. And he sat with her.

Then one morning, as he came into her room with a breakfast of duck eggs and wheatcakes, he found her at the window, looking out over the Kerryn to the trees beyond. Insects hummed in the morning air. He paused in the doorway.

'Daygreet,' he said automatically. She turned with a start. 'Are you feeling better?'

'You are the one who has been looking after me,' she said. 'Tane?'

He smiled slightly and bowed. 'Would you like to eat?'

Kaiku nodded and sat down cross-legged on her mat, arranging her sleeping-robe about her. She had little recollection of the past two weeks. She could remember impressions, unpleasant moments of fright or hunger or sadness, but not the circumstances that attended them. She remembered this face, though: this bald, shaven head, those even, tanned features, the pale green eyes and the light beige robes he always wore. She had never imagined a young priest – to her, they had always been old and snappy, hiding their wisdom inside a shell of cantankerousness. This one had some of the air of gravity she usually associated with the holy orders, but she remembered moments of light-heartedness too, when he had made jokes and laughed at them himself when she did not. By his speech, she guessed he had come from a moderately affluent family, somewhere above the peasantry though probably still local. While he was educated, he was certainly not high-born. The complexities of the Saramyrrhic language meant it was possible to guess at a person's origins simply by the way they used it. Tane's speech was looser and less ruthlessly elocuted than hers.

'How long has it been?' she asked, as she slowly ate.

'Ten days since we found you. You were wandering for some time before that,' Tane replied.

'Ten days? Spirits, it seems like it was forever. I thought it would never pass. I thought . . .' She looked up at him. 'I thought I could never stop crying.'

'The heart heals, given time,' Tane said. 'Tears dry.'

'My family are gone,' she said suddenly. She had needed to say it aloud, to test herself, to see if she could. The words provoked no new pain in her. She had mastered her grief, sickened of it; though it had taken a long time, her natural wilfulness would not let her be kept down. Her sorrow had spent itself, and while she doubted it would ever leave her entirely, it would not swallow her again. 'They were murdered,' she added.

'Ah,' said Tane. He could not think of anything else to say.

'The mask,' she said. 'I had a mask with me . . . I think.'

'It was in your pack,' said Tane. 'It is safe.'

She handed her plate back to him, having eaten only a little. 'Thank you,' she said. 'For taking care of me. I would like to rest.'

'It was my honour,' he replied, getting up. 'Would you like a tea to help you sleep?'

'I do not think I will need it, now,' she said.

He retreated to the door, but before he reached it he stopped.

'I don't know your name . . .'

'Kaiku tu Makaima,' came the reply.

'Kaiku, there was someone you mentioned several times in your delirium,' he said, turning his shoulder to look at her. 'Someone you said was with you in the woods. Asara. Perhaps she is still—'

'A demon killed her,' Kaiku replied, her eyes on the floor. 'She is gone.'

'I see,' Tane replied. 'I'll come back soon.' And with that he left.

A demon killed her, Kaiku thought. *And I am that demon.*

She did rest for a time, for she was weakened by her ordeal. She felt more drained than she had ever thought it was possible to feel, more exhausted than she could ever remember. The feeling spurred a memory that she had not come across for months, a random jag of pain that emerged to worry at the fresh wound of her loss. She steeled herself against it. She would not forget. Some things were worth remembering.

It had been at Mishani's summer house by the coast, where she and her brother Machim often stayed. They had always been competitive, and growing up with a brother had left her with some hopelessly unfeminine tendencies – one of which was a stubbornness that verged on mule-headed. One morning, she and Machim had become embroiled in their usual game of boasting who was better at what. The stakes were raised and raised until between them they had devised an endurance course involving archery, swimming, cliff-climbing, running and shooting that was far beyond the capacity of most athletes, let alone two youths who had rarely tasted hardship. Out of sheer unwillingness to concede, they both agreed to attempt it.

The archery they handled easily – they had to shoot ten arrows, and a bullseye meant that they could run down to the beach and swim across the bay to the cliffs. Machim succeeded before she did. The swimming was hard work, for she was trying to catch up with her brother and narrow his head start. She gained ground on the cliffs, but by now the ache in their bodies was evident, and their muscles were trembling. Machim was flagging badly, and he barely made it over the top before collapsing in a panting heap. Kaiku could have given up then and claimed the victory; but it was not enough for her. She began to run back along the cliff top to Mishani's house, where they had set up a makeshift rifle range. Her body burned, her vision blurred, she wanted to be sick, but she would not let herself stop. She reached the house, but the effort of picking up the rifle was too much for her, and she fainted.

She was put to bed then, and until now she had never felt anything like the exhaustion she had experienced on that day. The challenge had taken everything out of her, and it seemed like there was barely enough left to go on surviving. Mishani chided her for her stubbornness. Her brother sneaked in and congratulated her on her victory when nobody else was around.

But however bad that had been, this was worse. Her very soul felt exhausted, used up in the effort to expel the grief of her family's death. She found that thinking of her brother now brought no tears, only a dull ache. Well, she could endure that, if she must.

It was not only the loss of her family that troubled her, however. It was the power . . . the terrible force that had claimed Asara's life in the forest. Something had come from within her, something agonising and evil, a thing of raw destruction and flame. *Was* she a demon? Or had she one inside her? Could she even let herself be around other people, after what she had done to—

'No,' she said aloud, to add authority to her denial. It was useless to think that way. She had fled from the horror once already; now she had to face it. Whatever was the cause of Asara's death, it would not be exorcised by hiding herself away from the world. Besides, it had shown no sign of reoccurring in the time since that first cataclysmic event. She felt a hard coil of determination growing inside her. Suddenly she resented the presence of this side of herself that she had never known before. She would understand it, learn about it, and destroy it if necessary. She would not carry around this unnamed evil for the rest of her life. She refused to.

Asara. She had been the key. She had spoke of a cause. They had been watching her father, hoping to persuade him to join them. And they had been watching her, for two whole years.

Mostly it was because of you, Kaiku. Your condition.

Condition? Could she have meant the cruel flame that took her life? How long had it slumbered inside her, then, since Asara had come to her two years before this *condition* ever manifested itself? She thought back to the circumstances that might have attended her arrival. One of her previous handmaidens had disappeared without word or warning, that was true. Was there anything suspicious in that? Not at the time – after all, she was only a servant – but in retrospect it made her uneasy. No, she had to think before that.

She had heard the tales of the spirits of the forest turning bad. She knew the stories of the achicita, the demon vapours that came in the swelter of summer and stole in through the nostrils of sleeping men and women, making them sick on the inside. She knew about the baum-ki, who bit ankles like snakes and left their poison dormant in the body, to be passed on through saliva or other, more personal fluids. The poison hopped from person to person, becoming lethal only when it came across a baby in a womb, killing mother and child in one terrible haemorrhage.

It was the only sense she could make. There was something within, something unknown, something that had lashed out and killed. Had the shin-shin been after her, to claim whatever was inside her? What was she carrying? What was the *condition* Asara had spoken of?

But Asara was gone, and all she had left behind were questions. What manner of thing was she, who could suck the breath from one person and give it to another? Another demon, sent to look after her own? Who were her masters, the ones who had sent her? And what had her father been involved in, that such a tragedy should be visited on their house?

She slept, and her dreams were full of a face of black and red, a cackling spirit that haunted her in the darkness with the voice of her father.

The priests allowed her to use their sacred glade to make an offering to Omecha, the silent harvester, god of death and the afterlife. It lay along a narrow, winding trail that wove up the hill to the rear of the temple. Tane led the way, taking her hand when she stumbled. Having spent so long in convalescence, her muscles were shockingly weak, and the incline was almost too much for her to take. But Tane was there, keeping a respectful silence, and with his help she made it.

The glade was a spot of preternatural beauty, scattered with low, smooth white stones that peeped from the undergrowth, upon which complex pictograms were carved and painted red. There appeared to be no man-made boundary or border to separate it from the surrounding forest – in fact, were it not for the stones and the shrine, Kaiku would have not recognised it as a sacred place at all. There was a thin stream running through the glade, with the far bank rising higher than the near side, and a great old kamaka tree surmounting it, its thick roots knotted through the soil and its pendulous leaf-tendrils hanging mournfully over the water in flowery ropes. On the near side of the stream was the shrine, little bigger than the one that sat in front of the temple. It had been carved from the bole of a young tree, and the interior was hung with wind-chimes and tiny prayer scrolls. Fresh flowers had been laid inside it, and incense sticks smouldered in little clay pots to either side.

She gave Tane a nod and a wan smile, and he bowed, murmured a swift prayer to Enyu to excuse himself from the glade, and retreated down the trail.

Alone, Kaiku took a breath and assembled her thoughts. There was no emotion involved in this; she had spent that entirely by now. This was ritual. Her sorrow had eaten her from the inside and then turned and devoured itself into emptiness. All that was left was what was inevitable, what honour and tradition demanded she do. She acceded without complaint. Everything had fallen apart around her, but this at least was inviolable, and there was some comfort in that.

She knelt among the incense in the grey votive robe the priests had given her, for she had no formal wear and it was necessary to be respectful here. She prayed to her ancestors to guide her family through the Gate, past laughing Yoru into the golden Fields. She named each of them aloud to

Omecha, so that his wife Noctu might write them in her great book, and record their deeds in life. And finally she prayed to Ocha, Emperor of the gods and also god of war, revenge, exploration and endeavour. She begged for strength to aid her purpose, asking for his blessing in finding the one that struck down her family. If he would aid her, she swore to avenge them, no matter the cost.

And with that oath, her course was set.

When she left the glade, she felt exorcised somehow. She had left a part of herself behind there, the part that was confused and frightened and heavy with grief. She had a new path now. It was what her family's honour demanded. She would not let them die forgotten; she would right the injustice. There was no other course open to her.

After she had walked back to the temple with Tane, she reclaimed the mask from the priests and looked at it often, turning it about in her hands. Asara said her father had been killed for this mask. What was it, and what did it mean? Sometimes she toyed with the idea of putting it on, but she knew better. Even if Asara had not warned her, she had heard enough tales of the Weavers to learn caution.

Masks are the most dangerous weapons in the world.

The next morning, Tane brought her clothes with her breakfast.

'You've been lying about too long,' he said. 'Come outside. You should see this.'

Kaiku nodded muzzily. She had no particularly strong inclination to do anything, but it seemed easier to go along with his suggestion than to refuse it. When he had gone, she stood up and stretched her limbs, then clambered into her travel clothes that the priests had washed and mended. Someone – presumably Tane – had added a purple silk sash to the bundle, a splash of colour amid the beige and brown. She tied it loosely round her waist, letting it hang down her thigh. It made her attire a little more feminine, at least. She laced up the open-throated shirt and gave herself a perfunctory examination. A smile touched her lips, more wry than humorous. The sash made her look like some flamboyant bandit.

She joined Tane outside in the bright glare of the sun. It was a good time to be out, before the ascending heat became uncomfortable. She appreciated the warmth of Nuki's gaze on some dim and distant level, but it did not seem to penetrate as it had done in the days when her family were still alive. Rinji birds were drifting down the Kerryn, their long, white necks twisting down to snap at fish and beetles that strayed too close. Tane was watching them distractedly.

'They're early this year,' he observed. 'It's going to be a long, hot summer.'

Kaiku shaded her eyes and followed the languid procession with her gaze. Several of the priests had paused in their work and were studying the birds with contemplative expressions. As children, she and Machim used to head out to the riverbank every morning in early summer, to wait for the rinji to come down from their nesting sites in the mountains, down to the plains where the better feeding was. With their long, gangly legs tucked beneath them and their massive wings folded, they glided with effortless grace, riding the currents of the Kerryn towards the lowlands.

When the first rinji had drifted out of sight – there were only a dozen or so, the vanguard of the impending exodus – Tane led Kaiku down to the bank. At her request, they crossed over the bridge and sat on the south side, looking over the shimmering deep blue expanse towards the unassuming temple.

'This is the way we always watched them,' she said by way of explanation. 'Machim and I.' Watching the birds going from left to right instead of the opposite had jarred with her memories and made her unaccountably uncomfortable.

Tane nodded. Whether it was simple preference, or if she was consciously trying to recapture the fond moments she shared with her dead sibling, he was prepared to indulge her.

'It seems there are fewer and fewer each year,' Tane said. 'Word comes down from the mountains that their nesting grounds aren't so safe any more.'

Kaiku raised an eyebrow. 'Why not?'

'Fewer of the eggs hatch, that's one thing,' he replied, rubbing his bald scalp, rasping his palm against the stubble. 'But they say there are things in the mountains now that can climb up to where they lay. And those things are multiplying. It wasn't like that ten years ago.'

Kaiku found herself wondering suddenly why Tane had troubled to bring her out here at all, why they were sitting together and talking about birds.

'I have watched them every year since I can remember,' she said. 'And I used to stay up in the autumn and look out for them flying back.'

It was an aimless comment, a lazy observation thrown out into the conversation, but Tane took it as a cue to continue his train of thought.

'The beautiful things are dying,' he said gravely, looking upstream to where the Kerryn bent into the trees and was lost to sight. 'More and more, faster and faster. The priests can sense it; *I* can sense it. It's in the forest, in the soil. The trees know.'

Kaiku was not quite sure how to respond to that, so she kept her silence.

'Why can't we *do* anything about it?' he said, but the question was rhetorical, an expression of impotent frustration.

They watched the birds come down the river all that day, and it did seem that there were fewer than Kaiku remembered.

She stayed another week at the temple while she regained her strength. The waiting was chafing her, but the priests insisted, and she believed they were right. She was too weak to leave, and she needed time to formulate a plan, to decide where to travel to and how to get there.

There was never really any doubt as to her destination, however. There was only one person who might be able to help her learn the circumstances that surrounded her father's death, and only one person who she felt she could trust utterly. Mishani, her friend since childhood and daughter of Barak Avun tu Koli. She was part of the Imperial Court at Axekami, and she was privy to the machinations that went on there. Kaiku had not seen her much since they both passed their eighteenth harvest, for Mishani had been enmeshed in the politics of Blood Koli; yet despite everything, she found herself growing excited at the thought of seeing her friend again.

She walked with Tane often during that week, traipsing through the forest or along the river. Tane was interested in her past, in who she was and how she had come to be under that tree where he had found her. She talked freely about her family; it made her feel good to recall their triumphs, their habits, their petty foibles. But she never spoke of what happened at her house that night, and she made no mention of Asara's fate again. He was light-hearted company, and she liked him, though he tended to swing into unfathomably dark moods from time to time. Then she found him unpleasant and left him alone.

'You're leaving soon,' Tane said as they walked side by side in the trees behind the temple. It was the hour between morning oblations and study, and the young acolyte had asked her to join him. Birds chirruped all around and the forest rustled with hidden animals.

Kaiku fiddled with a strand of her hair. It was a childhood habit that her mother used to chide her for. She had thought she had grown out of it, but it seemed to have returned of late. 'Soon,' she agreed.

'I wish you would tell me what you are hurrying for. Are you fleeing your family's murderers, or trying to find them?'

She glanced at him, faintly startled. He had never been quite so blunt with her. 'To find them,' she said.

'Revenge is an unhealthy motive, Kaiku.'

'I have no other motives left, my friend,' she said. But he was a friend in name only. She would not let him close to her, would not divulge anything of true worth to him. There was no sense inviting more grief. She knew she was leaving him; it was necessary, for she still did not know the nature of the demon inside her, and she feared she might harm him as she had Asara. By the same token, she was terribly afraid of endangering Mishani by her presence; but she knew if Mishani were asked, she would willingly take that chance, and so would Kaiku for her. There was some comfort in that, at least. Their bonds of loyalty went beyond question. And there was scarcely any other choice, anyway; it was the only course she could see.

'I'd like it if you stayed,' he said solemnly. She stopped and gave him a curious look. 'For a while longer,' he amended, colouring a little.

She smiled, and it made her radiant. For a moment, she felt something like temptation. He was physically attractive to her, there was no doubt of that. His shaven head, his taut and muscular body honed by outdoor chores and an ascetic diet, his deep-buried intensity; these were qualities she had never encountered in the high-borns she had met in the cities. But though they had spent much time together in the past week, she felt she had not learned anything about him. Why had he become a priest? Why was he driven to heal and help others, as he professed? He was as closed to her as she was to him. The two of them had fenced around each other, never letting their guards down. This was the nearest he had got to real honesty. She exploited the opening.

'What is it I mean to you, Tane?' she asked. 'You found me, you saved my life and sat with me through it all. You have my endless gratitude for that. But why?'

'I'm a priest. It's my . . . my calling,' he said, frowning.

'Not good enough,' she said, folding her arms beneath her breasts.

He gave her a dark look, wounded that she would pressure him this way. 'I lost a sister,' he said. 'She would not be much younger than you are. I could not help her, but I could help you.' He looked angrily at the ground and scuffed it with his sandals. 'I lost my family too. We have that much in common.'

She wanted to ask how, but she had no right. She would not share her secrets with him, nor he with her. And therein lay the barrier between them, and it was unassailable.

'One of the priests is going downriver to the village of Ban tomorrow,' she said, unfolding her arms. 'I can get a skiff from there to the capital.'

'And you think your friend Mishani will be able to help you?' Tane asked, somewhat bitterly.

'She is the only hope I have,' Kaiku replied.

'Then I wish you good journey,' said Tane, though his tone suggested otherwise. 'And may Panazu, god of the rain and rivers, guard your way. I must return to my studies.'

With that, he stalked away and back to the temple. Kaiku watched him until he was obscured by the trees. In another time, in another place . . . maybe there could have been something between them. Well, there were greater concerns for now. She thought of the mask that lay in her room, hidden behind a beam on the ceiling. She thought of how she would get to Axekami, and what she might find there.

She thought of the future, and she feared it.

FIVE

It had to come to this, Anais thought. *I was only putting off the inevitable. But by the spirits, how did they find out?*

The Blood Empress of Saramyr stood in her chambers, her slender profile limned in the bright midday sunlight, the hot breath of the streets reaching even here, so far above. Below her lay the great city of Axekami, heart of the Saramyr empire. It sprawled down the hill and away from her, a riot of colours. Long red temples shunted up against gaudy markets; smooth white bathhouses huddled close to green-domed museums. There were theatres and tanneries, forges and workhouses. Distantly, the sparkling blue loop of the River Kerryn cut through the profusion on its way to meet its sister, the Jalaza, and combine to form the Zan. Axekami was built on the confluence of the three rivers, and their sweeping flow served to carve the city neatly up into districts, joined by proud bridges.

She let her eyes range over the capital, over *her* city, the centrepiece of a civilisation that stretched thousands of miles across an entire continent and encompassed millions of people. The life here never ceased, an endless, beautiful swelter of thronging industry, thought and art. Orators held forth in Speaker's Square while crowds gathered to jeer or clap; manxthwa and horses jostled in their pens while traders harangued passers-by and jabbered at each other; philosophers sat in meditation while across the street new lovers coupled in fervour. Scholars debated in the parks, blood spewed on to tiles as a bull banathi's throat was slashed by a butcher's blade, entertainers leered as they pulled impossible contortions, deals were made and broken and reforged. Axekami was the hub of an empire spread so wide that it was only possible to maintain it via the medium of instantaneous communication through Weavers. It was the administrative, political and social fulcrum on which the entire vastness of Saramyr balanced. Anais loved it, loved its constant ability to regenerate, the turbulence of innovation and activity; but she knew well enough to fear it a little too, and she felt a ghost of that fear brush her now.

The Imperial Keep stood high and magnificent on the crest of a hill, looking out over all. It was a vast edifice of gold and bronze, shaped like a truncated pyramid, with its top flattened and surmounted by a wondrous temple to Ocha, Emperor of the gods. It swarmed with pillars and arches, broken up by enormous statues that grew out of the walls, or which snaked along the grandiose façade to wind around shining columns. At the four points of the compass stood a tall, slender tower, reaching high above the main body of the Keep, each one dedicated to one of the Guardians of the Four Winds. Narrow bridges ran between the towers and the Keep, spanning the chasms between. The whole was surrounded by a great wall, decorated with carvings and scrollwork all along its length, and broken only by a mighty gate, with its soaring arc of gold inscribed with blessings.

Anais turned away from the vista. The room was wide and airy, its walls and floor made from a smooth, semi-reflective stone known as *lach.* Three tall arches gave her the view of her city; several smaller ones provided access to other rooms. A trickling fountain was the centrepiece, fashioned in the shape of two manta rays, their wings touching as they danced.

Messages had been arriving all day, both by hand and across the Weave, calling for a council. Her allies felt betrayed, her enemies incensed, and nothing she could do would assuage them. The only heir to the throne of Saramyr was an Aberrant. She should have been killed at birth.

Weave-lord Vyrrch was in the room with her; the very last person she wanted to see right now. The Weavers were the ones who did the killing, and she could feel glowering disapprobation in every syllable he spoke. He was at least wise enough not to berate her for hiding her child away from them, even though she knew that was what he was thinking. Did that foul ghoul seriously expect her to give up her only child to their tender mercies?

'You must be very cautious, Mistress,' he gurgled. 'Very cautious indeed. You have few options if you wish to avert a disaster.'

The Weave-lord was wearing his Mask, and for that, at least, she was thankful. His horribly deformed features were hidden behind a bronze visage, and though the Mask itself was distressing to look upon, it was far preferable to what lay beneath. It depicted a demented face, its features distorted in what could be pain, insanity or leering pleasure. The very sight of it made her skin crawl. It was old, very old; and where the True Masks were concerned, age meant power. She dreaded to think how many minds had been lost to that Mask, and how much of Vyrrch's remained . . .

'What do you advise then, Weave-lord?' she replied, concealing her distaste with a skill born through many years of practice. Silently, she dared him to suggest having her daughter executed.

'You must appear conciliatory, at least. You have deceived them, and they will expect you to acknowledge that. Do not underestimate the hatred that we of Saramyr bear for Aberrants.'

'Don't be ridiculous, Vyrrch,' she snapped. Though slender and willowy, with petite features and an innocent appearance, she could be iron when she wanted to be. 'She's not an Aberrant. She's just a child with a talent. *My* child.'

'I know well the semantics of the word, Mistress,' he wheezed, shifting his hunched body. He was clothed in ragged robes, a patchwork of fibres, beads, bits of matting and animal hide cannibalised together in an insane fashion. All the Weavers wore similar attire. Anais had never had the desire to delve deep enough into their world to ask why.

The Weavers had been responsible for the practice of killing Aberrant children for more than a hundred years. They were gifted at tracking down the signs, searching with their unearthly senses across the Weave to root out corruption in the purity of the human form. Though they were reclusive as a rule, preferring to remain in the comfort of noble houses or in their monasteries in the mountains, they made exception where Aberrants were concerned. Weavers travelled from town to village to city, appearing at festivals or gatherings, teaching the common folk to recognise the Aberrant in their midst, urging them to give up the creatures that hid among them. The visit of a Weaver to a town was an almost religious event, and the people gathered in fear and awe, both repulsed and drawn by the strange men in their Masks. While there, they listened to the Weaver's teachings, and passed on that wisdom to their children. Though the content of the teachings never varied, the Weavers were tireless, and their word had become so ingrained in the psyche of the people of Saramyr that it was as familiar as the rhymes of childhood or the sound of a mother's voice.

Vyrrch waited for Anais's gaze to cool before continuing. 'What I think of the matter is not relevant. You must be prepared for the wrath of the families. The child you have borne is an Aberrant to them. They will make little distinction between Lucia and the twisted, blind, limbless children that we of the Weavers must deal with every day. Both are . . . *deviant.* Until today, they believed the line of Erinima had an heir. Sickly, perhaps – I believe that was your excuse for hiding her away from us? – but an heir nonetheless. Now they find it does not, and many possibilities will—'

'It *does*, Vyrrch,' Anais smouldered. 'My child *will* take the throne.'

'As an Aberrant?' Vyrrch chuckled. 'I doubt that.'

Anais turned to the fountain to cover the tightening of her jaw. She knew Vyrrch spoke the truth. The people would never suffer an Aberrant as ruler. And yet, what other choice was there?

Apart from her phenomenal speed at picking up speech, Lucia had displayed few outward signs of her abilities until she reached two harvests of age; but Anais knew. If she was honest with herself, she had known instinctively, early in the pregnancy, that the child in her womb was abnormal. At first she did not dare believe; but later, when she faced the reality of the situation, she did not care. She would not consider telling her doctor; he would have counselled poisoning the child in the womb. No, she would not have given Lucia up for anything.

Perhaps that would be her downfall. Perhaps, if she *had* given up Lucia, she would have borne many healthy babies afterward. But she made her choice, and through complications she was rendered barren in giving birth. She could have no more children. Lucia was the only one there would ever be. The sole heir to the realm of Saramyr.

And so she had hidden her child away from the world, knowing that the world would despise her. They would ignore her gentle nature and dreamy eyes, and see only a creature *not human*, something to be rooted out and destroyed before its seed could pollute the purity of the Saramyr folk. She had thought that the child might learn to hide her abnormalities, to control and suppress them; but that hope was dashed now. Heart's blood, how did they learn of it? She had been so careful to keep Lucia from the eyes of those that might harm her.

This land was sick, she thought bitterly. Sick and cursed. Every year, more children were born Aberrant, more were snatched by the Weavers. Animals, too, and plants. Farmers griped that the very soil was evil, as whole crops grew twisted. The sickness was spreading, had been spreading for decades and nobody even knew what it was, much less where it came from.

The door was thrown open with a force that made her judder, and her husband thundered in, a black tower of rage.

'What is this?' he cried, seizing her by the arm and dragging her roughly to him. '*What is this?*'

She tore free from his grip, and he let her. He knew where the power lay in this relationship. She was the Blood Empress, ruler by bloodline. He was Emperor only by marriage; a marriage that could be annulled if Anais wished it.

'Welcome back, Durun,' she replied sarcastically, glowering at him. 'How was your hunt?'

'What has happened while I've been gone?' he cried. 'The things I hear . . . our child . . . what have you done?'

'Lucia is *special*, Durun. As you might know, if you had seen her more than once a year. Do not claim that she is *our* child: you have taken no hand in her parenting.'

'So it's true? She's an Aberrant?' Durun roared.

'No!' Anais snapped, at the same time that Vyrrch said 'Yes.'

Durun gazed in astonishment at his wife, and she, unflinching, gazed back. A taut silence fell.

She knew how he would react. The Emperor was nothing if not predictable. Most days she despised him, with his tight black attire and his long, lustrous black hair that fell straight to either side of his face. She hated his proud bearing and his hawk nose, his knife-thin face and his dark eyes. The marriage had been purely political, arranged by her parents before their passing; but while it had gained her Blood Batik as staunch and useful allies, she had paid for it by suffering this indolent braggart as a husband. Though he did have his moments, this was not one of them.

'You gave birth to an Aberrant?' he whispered.

'You fathered one,' she countered.

A momentary spasm of pain crossed his face.

'Do you know what this means? Do you know what you've done?'

'Do you know what the alternative was?' she replied. 'To kill my only child, and let Blood Erinima die out? Never!'

'Better that you had,' he hissed.

There was a chime outside the door then, forestalling her retort.

'Another messenger awaits you,' Vyrrch said in his throaty gurgle.

Flashing a final hot look at her husband, Anais pulled open the door and strode past the servant before he had time to tell her what she already knew. Durun stormed away to his chambers. For that, Anais was thankful. She still had no idea how she would handle the anger of the high families, but she knew she would do it better without Durun at her side.

The chambers of Weave-lord Vyrrch were a monument to degradation. They were dingy and dark, hot and wet as a swamp in the heat of early summer. The high shutters – sealed closed when they should have been open to admit the breeze – were draped in layers of coloured materials and tapestries. The vast, plush bed had collapsed and settled at an angle, its sheets soiled and stained. In the centre of the room was an octagonal bathing pool. Its waters were murky, scattered with floating bits of debris and faeces. At the bottom, staring sightlessly upward, was a naked boy.

Everywhere there was evidence of the Weave-lord's terrible appetites when in his post-Weaving rages. All manner of food was strewn about in varying states of decay. Fine silks were ripped and torn. Blood stained the tiled floor here and there. A scourge lay beneath the broken bed. A corpse lay *in* the bed, several weeks old, its sex and age mercifully unidentifiable now. A vast hookah smoked unattended amid a marsh of spilled wine and wet clothes.

And in the centre, his white, withered body cloaked in rags, the Weave-lord sat cross-legged, wearing his Mask.

The True Mask of the Weave-lord Vyrrch was an old, old thing. Its lineage went all the way back to Frusric, one of the greatest Edgefathers that had ever lived. Frusric had formed it from bronze, beaten thin so it would be light enough to wear. It was a masterpiece: the face of some long-forgotten god, his expression at once demented and horribly, malevolently sane, his brows heavy over eyes like dark pits. The face appeared to be crying out in despair, or shrieking in hate, or calling in anger, depending on what angle the light struck it.

Frusric had given the new Mask to Tamala tu Jekkyn, who had worn it till his untimely death; it was then handed on to Urric tu Hyrst, a master Weaver himself. From Urric, it could be traced through seven subsequent owners over one hundred years, until it had come into the possession of Vyrrch, given to him by his master, who recognised in the boy a talent greater than any he had seen.

The True Masks took all their owners had, draining them, rotting them from the inside out. They kept a portion of what they took, and passed it on to the next wearer. It *changed* them, imbuing shreds of its previous owner's mind and memories and personality. With each owner, it took more and passed more on, until the clash of influences, dreams and experiences became too much for the mind to bear. The older the Mask, the greater the power it gained, and the swifter it drove the wearer to insanity. Lesser apprentices would have died of shock at just putting this Mask on. Vyrrch was laid low three seasons, but he mastered it. And the power it had granted him was nothing short of magnificent.

What it had taken from him, though, was less glorious. He was nearly forty harvests of age, but he creaked and wheezed like a man of thrice that. His face had been made hideous. A thousand more minor corruptions and cancers boiled in his broken body, and the pain was constant. And though he did not realise it, the Mask had subtly been eroding his sanity like all the others, until he teetered daily on the brink of madness.

But he felt none of the pains in his body now, for he was Weaving, and the ecstasy of it took him away on a sea of bliss.

Like all Weavers, he had been taught to visualise the sensation in his own way. The raw stuff of the Weave was overwhelming, and many novices had found its beauty more than they could bear, and lost their will to leave. They wandered forever somewhere between its threads, lost in their own private paradise, bright ghosts mindlessly slaved to the Weave.

For Vyrrch, the Weave was an abyss, a vast, endless blackness in which he was an infinitesimal mote of light. And yet it was far from empty. Great curling tunnels snaked through the dark, grey and dim and faintly iridescent, like immense worms that thrashed and swayed, their heads and tails lost in eternity. The worms were the threads of the Weave, and he floated in the darkness in between, where there was nothingness, only the utter and complete joy of disembodiment. A creature of sensation alone, he felt the sympathetic vibration of the threads, a slow wind that swept through him, charging his nerves. On the edge of vision, huge whale-like shapes slid through the darkness. He had never understood what they were: a product of his own imagining, or something else altogether? Nor had he ever found out, for they eluded him effortlessly, remaining always out of his reach. Eventually he had given up trying, and for their part they ignored him as being beneath their notice.

Swiftly he glided between the immense threads, a gnat against their heaving flanks. By reading their vibrations he found the thread he sought and, steeling himself, he plunged into it, tearing through its skin into the roaring tumult inside, where chaos swallowed him.

Now he was a spark, a tiny thing that raced along the synapses of the thread with dizzying speed, selecting junctions here and jumping track there, flitting along faster than the mind could comprehend. From this thread to that he flickered, racing down one lane after another, a million changes executed in less than a second, until finally he reached the terminator of a single thread, and burst free.

His vision cleared as his senses reassembled themselves, and he was in a small, dimly lit chamber. It was unremarkable in any way, except for the crumbling yellow-red stone of its walls, and the pictograms daubed haphazardly across it, spelling out nonsense phrases and primal mutterings, dark perversions and promises. The ravings of a madman. A pair of lanterns flickered fitfully in their brackets, making the shadow-edges of the bricks shift and dance. A peeling wooden door was closed before him. Though he was far from any mark by which to recognise his surroundings, the walls exuded a familiar resonance to his heightened perception. This was Adderach, the monastery of the Weavers.

The room was empty, but he sensed the approach of three of his brethren. While he waited, he thought over the news he had to report.

He could not imagine how she had stayed hidden for so long. That the Heir-Empress could be an Aberrant . . . how could he have not seen it before? It was only when he began to hear reports from frightened servants of a spectral girl walking the corridors of the Keep at night that he began to suspect something was amiss. And so he had begun to investigate, searching the Keep for evidence of resonances, tremors in the Weave that would indicate that someone was manipulating it, in the way a spider feels the thrashings of the fly through her web.

He found nothing. And yet something was there. Whatever was causing these manifestations was either too subtle to be detectable even by him, or was of a different order altogether.

Eventually his searching bore fruit, and he found the trail of the wandering spectre as she prowled the corridors of the Keep, a tiny tremor in the air at her passing that was so fine it was almost imperceptible. Yet though he sensed himself drawing close time after time, he never caught up with her; he was always evaded. Frustration gnawed at him, and his efforts became more frantic; yet this only seemed to make her escapes all the easier. Until one day one of his spies overheard Anais consulting a physician about her daughter's odd dreams, and the connection was made.

Like many, he had never laid eyes on the Heir-Empress, but he had spied on her from time to time. The Heir-Empress was far too important for him to abide by her mother's wish for her to be kept sheltered and secret. He knew at once that she was not so sickly as Anais made out, but he also knew there were many good reasons why a child as important as this one should be kept safe from harm. He had simply attributed it to Anais's paranoia about her only daughter – the only child she could ever have – and forgotten about it. It had not seemed urgent at the time, and as the seasons came and went he forgot about it, the thoughts slipping through the gauze of his increasingly addled mind and fading away.

It was his assurance of his own abilities that had led him to discount the little Heir-Empress from his initial investigations concerning the spectre. Surely, he would have sensed something if she had been unusual in any way. He had not looked closer at first, because he should have detected it when he first spied on her.

The night he heard about the Heir-Empress's dreams, he had used his

Mask to search for her, to divine what she truly was. It was something he should have done a long time ago. Yet when he tried, she was impossible to find. He knew who and where she was, but she was still invisible to him. His consciousness seemed to slip over her; she was unassailable. The rage at his failure was immense, and cost the lives of three children. All this time, there had been an Aberrant under his very nose but it had taken him eight years to see it.

He knew now that he was dealing with something unlike anything he had encountered before. He considered what she was and what it might mean, and he feared her.

And yet still he needed proof, and it must be a proof that could not be connected to him in any way. So he had sent a message to Sonmaga tu Amacha's Weaver, who had advised the Barak, who had employed a series of middlemen to obtain a lock of the Heir-Empress's hair. Anyone who followed the trail would find it led to Sonmaga tu Amacha's door; the only one who knew of Vyrrch's involvement was Sonmaga's Weaver, Bracch.

The conclusive proof of Aberration could only be carried out by a Weaver if he were physically within sight of the person, or if he had a piece of the person's body to study. With the lock of hair Bracch was able to convince Sonmaga of the truth.

The girl was a threat that had to be eliminated. Though the situation was yet far from desperate, she had the potential to become a great danger to the Weavers. With good fortune, the Baraks and high families would deal with her for him, but if not . . . well, maybe then more direct methods would have to be employed.

The door to the chamber opened then, and the shambling, ragged figures of the three Weavers came inside. To them, he appeared as a floating apparition, barely visible in the dim, flickering light.

'Daygreet, Weave-lord Vyrrch,' croaked one, whose mask was a tangle of bark and leaves shaped into a rough semblance of a bearded face. 'I trust you have news?'

'Grave news, my brothers,' Vyrrch replied softly. 'Grave news . . .'

SIX

The townhouse of Blood Koli was situated on the western flank of the Imperial Quarter of Axekami. The original building had been improved over the years, adding a wing here, a library there, until the low, wide mass sprawled across the expanse of the compound that protected it. Its roof was of black slate, curved and peaked into ridges; the walls were the colour of ivory, simple and plain, their uniformity broken up by a few choice angles or an ornamental cross-hatching of narrow wooden beams. Behind the townhouse was a cluster of similarly austere buildings: quarters for guards, stables, and storage rooms. The remainder of the compound was taken up by a garden, trimmed and neat and severe in its beauty. Curving pebble paths arced around a pond full of colourful fish, past a sculpted fountain and a shaded bench. The whole was surrounded by a high wall with a single gate, that separated the compound from the wide streets of the Imperial Quarter. The morning sun beat down on the city, and the air was humid and muggy. Not too distantly, the golden ziggurat of the Imperial Keep loomed at the crest of a hill, highest of all the buildings in the city.

Within the townhouse, Mishani tu Koli sat cross-legged at her writing desk and laboured through the last season's fishing tallies. Blood Koli owned a large fishing fleet that operated out of Mataxa Bay, and much of their revenue and political power was generated there. It was common knowledge that crabs and lobsters stamped with the mark of Blood Koli were the most tender and delicious (and hence the most expensive) in Saramyr. It was a benefit of the unique mineral content of the bay's waters, so Mishani's father said. For two years now she had been rigorously educated in every aspect of the family's holdings and businesses. As heir to the lands of Blood Koli and the title of Barakess upon her father's death, she was expected to be able to handle the responsibility of heading them. And so she tallied, her brush flicking this way and that as she made a mark here, crossed a line there, with a single-minded focus that was alarming in its intensity.

Mishani was a lady of no great height, slender and fine-boned to the point of fragility. Her thin, pale face, while not beautiful, was striking in its serenity. No involuntary movement ever crossed her face; her poise was total. No flicker of her pencil-line eyebrows would betray her surprise unless she willed it so; no twitch of her narrow lips would show a smirk unless she wished to express it. Her small body was near-engulfed by the silken mass of black hair that fell to her ankles when she stood. It was tamed by strips of dark blue leather, separating it into two great plaits to either side of her head, and one long, free-falling cascade at her back.

A chime sounded outside the curtained doorway to her room. She finished the tally line she was working on and then rang a small silver bell in response, to indicate permission to enter. A handmaiden slipped gracefully in, bowing slightly with the fingertips of one hand to her lips and the other arm folded across her waist, the female form of greeting to a social superior. 'You have a visitor, Mistress Mishani. It is Mistress Kaiku tu Makaima.'

Mishani looked blandly at her handmaiden for a moment; then a slow smile spread across her lips, becoming a grin of joy. The handmaiden smiled in response, pleased that her mistress was pleased. 'Shall I show her in, Mistress?'

'Do so,' she replied. 'And bring fruit and iced water for us.'

The handmaiden left, and Mishani tidied up her writing equipment and arranged herself. In the two years since her eighteenth harvest, she had been kept busy and with little time for the society of friends; but Kaiku had been her companion through childhood and adolescence, and the long separation had pained her. They had written to each other often, in the florid, poetic style of High Saramyrrhic, explaining their dreams and hopes and fears. It did not seem enough. How like Kaiku, then, to turn up unannounced like this. She never was one to follow protocol; she always seemed to think herself somehow above it, that it did not apply to her.

'Mistress Kaiku tu Makaima,' the handmaiden declared from without, and Kaiku entered then. Mishani flung her arms around her friend and they embraced. Finally, she stepped back, holding Kaiku's hands, their arms a bridge between them.

'You've lost weight,' she said. 'And you seem pale. Have you been ill?'

Kaiku laughed. They had known each other too long to be anything less than brutally honest. 'Something like that,' she said. 'But you look more the noble lady than ever. City life must agree with you.'

'I miss the bay,' Mishani admitted, kneeling on one of the elegant mats that were laid out on the floor. 'I will admit, it is galling that I have to spend my days counting fish and pricing boats, and being reminded of it every day. But I am developing something of a taste for tallying.'

'Really?' Kaiku asked in disbelief, settling herself opposite her friend. 'Ah, Mishani. Dull, repetitive work always was your strong suit.'

'I shall take that as a compliment, since it was you who was always too flighty and fanciful to attend to her lessons as a child.'

Kaiku smiled. Just the sight of her friend made the terrors that she had endured seem more distant, fainter somehow. She was a living reminder of the days before the tragedy had struck. She had changed a little: shed the last of her girlhood, her small features become womanly. And she spoke with a more formal mode than Kaiku remembered, presumably picked up at court.

But for all that, she was still that same Mishani, and it was like a balm to Kaiku's sore heart.

The handmaiden gave a peremptory chime and entered; she needed no answering bell when she had already been invited by her mistress. She laid a low wooden table to one side of Kaiku and Mishani, placed a bowl of sliced fruit there, and poured iced water into two glasses. Finally, she adjusted the screens to maximise the tiny breaths of the wind that stirred the hot morning, and unobtrusively slipped away. Kaiku watched her go, reminded of another handmaiden from a time before death had ever brushed her.

'Now, Kaiku, to what do I owe this visit?' Mishani said. 'It is not a short way from the Forest of Yuna to Axekami. Are you staying long? I will have a room prepared. And you will need some proper clothes; what are you *wearing*?'

Kaiku's smile seemed fragile, and the sadness within showed through. Mishani's eyes turned to sorrow and sympathy in response. 'What has happened?' she asked.

'My family are dead,' Kaiku replied simply.

Mishani automatically suppressed her surprise, showing no reaction at all. Then, remembering who it was that she was talking to, she relaxed her guard and allowed the horror to show, her hand covering her mouth in shock. 'No,' she breathed. 'How?'

'I will tell you,' Kaiku said. 'But there is more. I may not be as you remember me, Mishani. Something is within me, something . . . *foreign*. I do not know what it is, but it is dangerous. I ask for your help, Mishani. I *need* your help.'

'Of course,' Mishani replied, taking her friend's hands again. 'Anything.'

'Do not be hasty,' Kaiku said. 'Listen to my story first. You are in danger just by being near me.'

Mishani sat back, gazing at her friend. Such gravity was not Kaiku's way. She had always been the wilful one, stubborn, the one who would take whatever path suited her. Now her tone was as one convicted. 'Tell me, then,' she said. 'And spare nothing.'

So Kaiku told her everything, a tale that began with her own death and ended in her arrival at Axekami, having bought passage on a skiff downriver from Ban with money she found in her pack. She talked of Asara, how her trusted handmaiden had revealed herself to be something other than what she seemed; and she told of how Asara died. She spoke of her rescue by the priests of Enyu, and the mask Asara had taken from her house, that her father had brought back from his last trip away. And she told of her oath to Ocha: that she would avenge the murder of her family.

When she was finished, Mishani was quite still. Kaiku watched her, as if she could divine what was going on beneath her immobile exterior. This new poise was unfamiliar to Kaiku; it was something Mishani had acquired accompanying her father in the courts of the Empress these past two years. There, every movement and every nuance could give away a secret or cost a life.

'You have the mask?' she asked at length.

Kaiku produced it from her pack and handed it to her friend. Mishani looked it over, turning it beneath her gaze. The mischievous red and black face leered back at her. Beautiful and ugly at the same time, it still looked no more remarkable than many other masks she had seen, worn by actors in the theatre. It seemed entirely normal.

'You have not tried to wear it?'

'No,' Kaiku said. 'What if it were a True Mask? I would go insane, or die, or worse.'

'Very wise,' Mishani mused.

'Tell me you believe my story, Mishani. I have to know you do not doubt me.'

Mishani nodded, her great cascade of black hair trembling with the movement. 'I believe you,' she said. 'Of course I believe you. And I will do all I can to help you, dear friend.' Kaiku was smiling in relief, tears gathering in her eyes. Mishani handed the mask back. 'As to that, I have a friend who has studied the ways of the Edgefathers. He may be able to tell us about it.'

'When can we see him?' Kaiku asked, excited.

Mishani gave her an unreadable look. 'It will not be quite as simple as that.'

The chambers of Lucia tu Erinima were buried deep in the heart of the Imperial Keep, heavily guarded and all but impregnable. The rooms were many, but there were always Guards there, or tutors pacing back and forth, or nannies or cooks hustling about. Lucia's world was constantly busy, and yet she was alone. She was trapped tighter than ever now, and the faces that surrounded her looked on her with worry, thinking how the poor child's life must be miserable, for she was hated by the world.

But Lucia was not sad. She had met many new people over the last few weeks, a veritable whirl compared to her life before the thief had taken a lock of her hair. Her mother visited often, and brought with her important people, Baraks and ur-Baraks and officials and merchants. Lucia was always on her best behaviour. Sometimes they looked on her with barely concealed disgust, sometimes with apprehension, and sometimes with kindness. Some of those who came prepared to despise her departed in bewilderment, wondering how such an intelligent and pretty child could harbour the evil the Weavers warned of. Some left their prejudices behind when they walked out of the door; others clutched them jealously to their breast.

'Your mother is being very brave,' said Zaelis, her favourite of all the tutors. 'She is showing her allies and her enemies what a good and clever girl you are. Sometimes a person's fear of the unknown is far, far worse than the reality.'

Lucia accepted this, in her dreamy-eyed, preoccupied kind of way. She knew there was more, deeper down; but those answers would come in time.

It was while she was with Zaelis one balmy afternoon that the Blood Empress Anais brought the Emperor.

She was sitting on a mat by the long, triangular windows in her study room, with the sunlight cut into great dazzling teeth and cast on to the sandy tiles of the floor before her. Zaelis was teaching her the catechisms of the birth of the stars, recounting the questions and answers in his throaty, molten bass tones. She knew the story well enough: how Abinaxis, the One Star, burst and scattered the universe, and from that chaos came the first generation of the gods. Sitting neatly and with her usual appearance of inattentiveness, Lucia was listening and remembering, while in the back of her head she heard the whispers of the spirits of the west wind, hissing nonsense to each other as they flowed across the city.

Zaelis paused as a gust ruffled through the room, and Lucia looked quickly upwards, as if someone had spoken by her shoulder.

'What are they saying, Lucia?' he asked.

Lucia looked back at Zaelis. He alone treated her abilities as if they were something precious, and not something to be hidden. All the tutors, nannies and staff were sworn to secrecy on pain of death with regards to her talents; they looked away if they caught her playing with ravens, and shushed her if she spoke of what the old tree in the garden was saying that day. But Zaelis encouraged her, believed her. In fact, his fervour worried her a little at times.

'I don't know,' she said. 'I can't understand them.'

'One day maybe you will,' said Zaelis.

'Probably,' Lucia replied offhandedly.

She sensed Durun's arrival a moment before she heard him. He frightened her with his intensity of passion. He was a knot of fire, always burning in anger or pride or hate or lust. In the absence of anything that heated his blood, he lapsed into boredom. He had no finer emotions, no intellectual interests or stirrings of mild introspection. His flame roared blindingly or not at all.

The Emperor strode into the room and halted before them, his black cloak settling reluctantly around his broad shoulders. Anais was with him. Zaelis stood and made proper obeisance; Lucia did so as well.

'So this is she,' Durun said, ignoring Zaelis completely.

'It is the same *she* as you saw previously, on every occasion you bothered yourself to visit her,' Anais replied. It was clear by their manner that they had just argued. Anais's face was flushed.

'Then I had no idea that I was harbouring a viper,' Durun answered coldly. He looked Lucia over. She returned his gaze with a placid calm. 'If it weren't for the distance in those eyes,' he mused, 'I would think her a normal child.'

'She *is* a normal child,' Anais snapped. 'You are as bad as Vyrrch. He breathes down my neck, eager for the chance to—' She stopped herself, glanced at Lucia. 'Must you do this in front of her?'

'You've told her, I suppose? About how the city is rising against her?'

Zaelis opened his mouth and shut it again. He knew better than to interfere on behalf of the child. If the Emperor would not listen to his wife, he certainly would not listen to a scholar.

'You'll bring this land to ruin with your ambition, Anais,' Durun accused. 'Your arrogance in making this abomination the heir to the throne will tear Saramyr apart. Every life lost will be on your head!'

'So be it,' she hissed. 'Wars have been fought for less important causes. Look at her, Durun! She is a beautiful child . . . *your* child! She is all you could hope for in a daughter, in an heir! Don't be blinded by a hatred wrapped up in *tradition* and *lore*. You listen too much to the Weavers, and think too little for yourself.'

'So did you,' he replied. 'Before you spawned *that*.' He flung out a finger at Lucia, who had been watching the exchange impassively. 'Now you use arguments that you would have scorned in days gone by. She's an Aberrant, and she's no child of mine!'

With that, he turned with a melodramatic sweep of his cloak and stalked away. Anais's face was tight with rage, but one look at her daughter and it softened. She knelt down next to Lucia, so that their faces were level, and hugged her.

'Don't listen, my child,' she murmured. 'Your father doesn't understand. He's angry, but he'll learn. They all will.'

Lucia didn't reply; but then, she seldom did.

SEVEN

Six sun-washed days had passed in the temple of Enyu on the banks of the Kerryn, and Tane felt further from inner peace with every dawn.

He had wandered far today, after his morning duties were performed. As an acolyte, the priests gave him leisure to do so. The way to Enyu was not made up of rituals and chores, but of community with nature. Everyone had their own way to calm their spirit. Tane was still looking for his.

The world was tipping over the heady brink between spring and summer, and the days were hot and busy with midges. Tane laboured through the pathways of the forest with his shirt tied around his waist and his torso bare, but for the strap of the rifle that was slung across his back. His lean, tanned body trickled with sweat in the humid confines of the trees. The sun was westering; soon he would have to head back, or risk being caught in the forest after dark. Ill things came with the night, more so now than ever.

All around was discontent. The forest seemed melancholy, even in the sunlight. The priests muttered about the corruption in the land, how the very soil was turning sour. The goddess Enyu was becoming weak, ailing under the influence of some unknown, sourceless evil. Tane felt his frustration grow at the thought. What good were they as priests of nature, if they could only sit by and lament the sickness in the earth as it overtook them? What use were their invocations and sacrifices and blessings if they could not stand up to defend the goddess they professed to love? They talked and talked, and nobody was doing anything. A war was being fought beyond the veil of human sight, and Tane's side was plainly losing.

But such questions were not the only things that preyed on his mind and ruined his attempts at attaining tranquillity. Though he worked hard to distract himself, he found he was unable to forget the young woman he had found buried in leaves at the base of a kindly tree. Pictures, sounds and scents, frozen in memory, refused to fade as others did. He remembered the expression of surprise, the whip of her hair, as she whirled to find him standing unexpectedly behind her; the sound of her laugh from another room, her joy at something unseen; the smell of her tears as he watched over her during her grief. He knew the shape of her face, peaceful in sleep, better than his own. He cursed himself for mooning over her like a child; and yet still he thought on her, and the memories renewed themselves with each visit.

He found his feet taking him to a spring, where cold water cascaded down a jagged rock wall into a basin before draining back into the stone. He had been here a few times before, on the hotter days of summer; now it seemed a wonderful idea to cool himself off before returning home. A short clamber up a muddy trail brought him to the basin, hidden among the crowding trees. He stripped and plunged into the icy pool, relishing the delicious shock of the impact. Sluicing the salty sweat off his body with his palm, he dived and surfaced several times before the temperature of the pool began to become uncomfortable, and he swam to the edge to climb out.

There was a woman in the trees, leaning on a rifle and watching him.

He stopped still, his eyes flickering to his own rifle, laid across the bundle of clothes near the edge of the pool. He might be able to grab it before she could raise her own weapon, but he would have no chance of priming and firing before she shot him. If indeed that was her intention. She appeared, in fact, to be faintly amused.

She was exceedingly beautiful, even dressed in dour brown travelling clothes. Her hair was long, with streaks of red amid the natural onyx black, and was left to fall naturally about her face. She wore no makeup, no hair ornaments; the dyed strands of her hair were the only concession to artificiality. Her beauty was entirely her own, not lent to her by craft.

'You swim well,' she commented dryly.

Tane hesitated for a moment, and then climbed out to retrieve his clothes. Nudity did not bother him, and he refused to be talked down to while he trod water in the pool. She watched him – equally unfazed – as he pulled on his trousers over the wet, muscular curves of his legs and buttocks. He stopped short of picking up his rifle. She did not seem hostile, at least.

'I am looking for someone,' the stranger said after a time. 'A woman named Kaiku tu Makaima.' He was not quick enough to keep the reaction off his face. 'I see you know that name,' she added.

Tane ran his hands over his head, brushing water from his shaven scalp. 'I know that she suffered a great misfortune at someone's hands,' he said. 'Are you that someone?'

'Assuredly not,' she replied. 'My name is Jin. I am an Imperial Messenger.' She slung her rifle over her back and walked over to him, pulling back her sleeve to expose her forearm. Stretching from her wrist to her inner elbow was a long, intricate tattoo – the sigil of the Messengers' Guild. Tane nodded.

'Tane tu Jeribos. Acolyte of Enyu.'

'Ah. Then the temple is not far.'

'Not far,' he agreed.

'Perhaps you could show me? It will be dark soon, and the forest is not safe.'

Tane looked her over with a hint of suspicion, but he never really considered refusing her. Her accent and mode spoke of an education, and possibly high birth, and besides, it was every man and woman's duty to offer shelter and assistance to an Imperial Messenger, and the fact that her message was for Kaiku intrigued him greatly. 'Come with me, then,' he said.

'Will you tell me of this . . . misfortune on the way?' Jin asked.

'Will you tell me the message you have for her?'

Jin laughed. 'You know I cannot,' she replied. 'I am sworn by my life to deliver it only to her.'

Tane grinned suddenly, indicating that he had been joking. His frustrated mood had evaporated suddenly and left him in high spirits. His humours were ever mercurial; it was something about himself that he had learned to accept long ago. He supposed there was a reason for it, somewhere in his past; but his past was a place he had little love of revisiting. His childhood was darkened by the terror of the shadow that stood in his doorway at night, breathing heavily, with hands that held only pain.

They talked on the way back to the temple, as night drew in. Jin asked him about Kaiku, and he told her what he knew of her visit. He made no mention yet of her destination, however. He had no wish to reveal everything to a stranger, Imperial Messenger or not. He felt protective towards Kaiku, for it was he who had saved her life, he who nursed her to health again, and he treasured that link. He would make sure of Jin before he sent her on the trail to Axekami.

As they walked, Tane realised to his chagrin that he had misjudged the time it would take to travel back from the spring. Perhaps he had unconsciously been slowing his pace to match Jin's, and he had been so preoccupied in conversation that he had not noticed. Whatever the reason, the last light bled from the sky with still a mile to go. The looming bulk of Aurus glowed white through the trees, low on the horizon. Iridima, the brightest moon, was not yet risen, and Neryn would most likely stay hidden tonight.

'Is it far yet?' Jin asked. She had politely restrained from asking him if he was lost for some time now.

'Very close,' he said. His embarrassment at the miscalculation had not diminished his good humour one bit. The single moon was enough to see by. 'Don't concern yourself about losing the light. I grew up in the forest; I have excellent night vision.'

'So do I,' Jin replied. Tane looked back at her, about to offer further words of encouragement, but he was shocked to see her eyes shining in a slant of moonlight, two saucers of bright reflected white, like those of a cat. Then they passed into shadow, and it was gone. Tane's voice went dry in his throat, and he turned away, muttering a quiet protective blessing. He reaffirmed his resolve to tell her nothing of Kaiku's friend Mishani until he was certain she meant no harm.

They were almost at the temple when Tane suddenly slowed. Jin was at his shoulder in a moment.

'Is something wrong?' she whispered.

Tane cast a fleeting glance at her. He was still a little unnerved by what he had seen in her eyes. But this was nothing to do with her, he surmised. The forest felt *bad* here. The instinct was too strong to ignore.

'The trees are afraid,' he muttered.

'They tell you so?'

'In a way.' He did not have the time or inclination to elaborate.

'I trust you, then,' Jin said, brushing her hair back over her shoulder. 'Are we close to your home?'

'Just through these trees,' muttered Tane. 'That's what worries me.'

They went carefully onward, quietly now. Tane noted with approval how Jin moved without sound through the forest. His mood was souring rapidly into a dark foreboding. He unslung his rifle, and his hands clasped tightly around it as they stepped through the blue shadows towards the clearing where the temple lay.

At the edge of the trees, they crouched and looked out over the sloping expanse of grassy hillside that lay between the river on their left and the temple. Lights burned softly in some of the temple windows. The wind stirred the trees gently. The great disc of Aurus dominated the horizon before them, lifting her bulk slowly clear of the treeline. Not an insect chittered, and no animal called. Tane felt his scalp crawl.

'Is it always so quiet?' Jin whispered.

Tane ignored her question, scanning the scene. The priests were usually indoors by nightfall. He watched the temple for some time more, hoping for a light to be lit or extinguished, a face to appear at one of the windows, anything that would indicate signs of life within. But there was nothing.

'Perhaps I'm being foolish,' he said, about to stand up and come out of hiding.

Jin grabbed his arm with a surprisingly strong grip. 'No,' she said. 'You are not.'

He looked back at her, and saw something in her expression that gave her away. 'You know what it is,' he said. 'You know what's wrong here.'

'I suspect,' she replied. 'Wait.'

Tane settled himself back into his hiding place and returned his attention to the temple. He knew each of its cream-coloured planes, each beam of black ash that supported each wall, each simple square window. He knew the way the upper storey was set back from the lower one, to fit snugly with the slope of the hill. This temple had been his home for a long time now, and yet it never felt as if he belonged here, no matter how much he tried. No place had ever truly been home for him, however much he tried to adapt himself.

'There,' Jin said, but Tane had already seen it. Coming over the roof from the blind side of the temple, like some huge four-legged spider: *shin-shin.* It moved stealthily, picking its way along, its dark torso hanging between the cradle of its stiltlike legs, shining eyes like lanterns. As Tane watched with increasing dread, he saw another one come scuttling from the trees, crossing the clearing in moments to press itself against one of the outer walls, all but invisible. And a third now, following the first one over the roof, its gaze sweeping the treeline where they crouched.

'Enyu's grace . . .' he breathed.

'We must go,' said Jin urgently, laying a hand on his shoulder. 'We cannot help them.'

But Tane seemed not to hear, for he saw at that moment one of the priests appear at an upper window, listening with a frown to the silence from the forest, unaware of the dark, spindly shapes that crouched on the roof just above him.

'You cannot fight!' Jin hissed. 'You have no weapon to use against them!'

'I won't let my priests die in their beds!' he spat. Shaking her off, he stood up and fired his rifle into the air. The report was deafening in the silence. The glowing eyes of the shin-shin fixed on him in unison.

'Demons in the temple!' he cried. 'Demons in the temple!' And with that he primed and fired again. This time the priest disappeared from the window, and he heard the man's shouts as he ran into the heart of the building.

'Idiot!' Jin snarled. 'You will kill us both. Run!' She pulled him away, and he stumbled to his feet and followed her, for the sensation of the shin-shin's eyes boring into him had drained his courage.

One of the demons hurled itself from the roof of the temple and came racing towards them. Another broke from the treeline and angled itself in their direction. Two more shadows darted across the clearing, slipping into the open windows of the temple with insidious ease, and from within the first of the screams began.

Tane and Jin ran through the trees, dodging flailing branches and vaulting roots that lunged into their path. Things whipped at them in the night, too fast to see. Behind they could hear the screeches of the shin-shin sawing through the hot darkness as they called to each other. Tane's head was awhirl, half his mind on what was happening back at the temple, half on escape. To run was flying in the face of his instincts – he wanted to help the priests, that was his way, that was his *atonement* for the crimes of his past. But he knew enough of the shin-shin to recognise the truth in Jin's words. He had no effective measure against them. Like most demons, they despised the touch of iron; but even the iron in a rifle ball would not stop them for long. To attack them would be suicide.

'The river!' Jin cried suddenly, her red and black hair lashing about her face. 'Make for the river. The shin-shin cannot swim.'

'The river's too strong!' Tane replied automatically. Then the answer came to him: 'But there is a boat!'

'Take us there!' Jin said.

Tane sprang past her, leading them on a scrabbling diagonal slant down the hillside. The decline sharpened as they ran, and suddenly he heard a cry and felt something slam into him from behind. Jin had tripped, unable to control her momentum, and the two of them rolled and bounced down the slope. Tane smacked into the bole of a tree with enough force to nearly break a bone, but somehow Jin was entangled with him, and as she slithered past he was dragged down with her. They came to rest at the bottom of a wide, natural ditch; a stream in times gone by. Jin hardly paused to recover herself; she was up on her feet in an instant, dragging Tane with her. She scooped up her rifle as it clattered down to rest nearby. The screeches of the shin-shin were terrifyingly close, almost upon them.

'In here!' Tane hissed, pulling against her. There was a large hollow where the roots of a tree had encroached on the banks of the ditch, forming an overhang. Tane unstrapped his rifle – which had miraculously stayed snagged on his shoulder during the fall – and scrambled underneath, wedging his body in tight. There was just enough space for Jin to do so as well, pressing herself close to him. Mere moments later, they heard a soft thud as a shin-shin dropped out of the trees and landed foursquare in the ditch.

Both of them held their breath. Tane could feel Jin's pulse against his chest, smell the scent of her hair. Ordinarily, it might have aroused him – priests of Enyu had no stricture of celibacy, as some orders did – but the situation they were in robbed him of any ardour. From where they hid at ground level, they could see only the tapered points of the shin-shin's stilt-legs, shifting as it cast about for its prey. It had lost sight of them as they tumbled, and now it sought them anew. A slight fall of dirt was the only herald of the second demon's arrival in the ditch; that one had followed their trail down the slope, and was equally puzzled by their disappearance.

Tane began a silent mantra in his head. It was one he had not used since he was a child, a made-up nonsense rhyme that he pretended could make him invisible if he concentrated hard enough. Then he had been hiding from something entirely different. After a few moments, he adapted it to include a short prayer to Enyu. *Shelter us, Earth Goddess, hide us from their sight.*

The pointed ends of the shin-shins' legs moved this way and that in the moonlight, expressing their uncertainty. They knew their prey should be here; yet they could not see it. Tane felt the cold dread of their presence seeping into his skin. The narrow slot of vision between Jin's body and the overhang of thick roots and soil might be filled at any moment with the glowing eyes of the shin-shin; and if discovered, they were defenceless. He fancied he could sense their gaze sweeping over him, penetrating the earth to spot them huddled there.

Time seemed to draw out. Tane could feel his muscles tautening in response to the tension. One of the shin-shin moved suddenly, making Jin start; but whatever it had seen, it was not them. It returned to its companion, and they resumed their strange waiting. Tane gritted his teeth and concentrated on his mantra to calm himself. It did little good.

Then, a new sound: this one heavy and clumsy. The shin-shin stanced in response. Tane knew that sound, but he could not place it in his memory. The footsteps of some animal, but which?

The yawning roar of the bear decided the issue for him.

The shin-shin were uncertain again, their reaction betrayed by the shifting of their feet. The bear roared once more, thumping on to its forepaws, and began to advance slowly. The demons screeched, making a rattling noise and darting this way and that, trying to scare it away; but it was implacable, launching itself upright and then stamping down again with a snarl. There was the loping gallop as the bear ran towards them, not in the least cowed by their display. The shin-shin scattered as it thundered along the ditch, squealing and hissing their displeasure; but they gave the ground, and in moments they were gone, back into the trees in search of their lost prey.

Tane released the pent-up breath he had been storing, but they were not out of danger yet. They could hear the bear coming down the wide ditch, its loud snuffling as it searched for them.

'My rifle . . .' Jin whispered. 'If it finds us . . .'

'No,' he hissed. 'Wait.'

Then suddenly the bear poked down into the hollow, its brown, bristly snout filling up their sight as it sniffed at them. Jin clutched for the trigger of her rifle to scare it away; but Tane grabbed her wrist.

'The shin-shin will hear,' he whispered. 'We don't fear the bears in Enyu's forest.' He was less confident in his heart than his words suggested. Where once the forest beasts had been friends to the priests of Enyu, the corruption in the land had made them increasingly unpredictable of late.

The bear's wet nose twitched as it smelt them over. Jin was rigid with apprehension. Then, with a final snort, the snout receded. The bear lay heavily down in front of their hiding place, and there it stayed.

Jin shifted. 'Why did it not attack us?' she muttered.

Tane was wearing a strange grin. 'The bears are Enyu's creatures, just as Panazu's are the catfish, Aspinis's the monkeys, Misamcha's the ray or the fox or the hawk. Give thanks, Jin. I think we've been saved.'

Jin appeared to consider that for a time. 'We should stay here,' she said at length. 'The shin-shin will be waiting for us if we emerge before dawn.'

'I think she has the same idea,' Tane said, motioning with his eyes towards the great furred bulk that blocked them in.

The bear lay in front of their hollow throughout the night, and in spite of their discomfort the two of them slept. Jin's dreams were of fire and a horrible scorching heat; Tane's, as always, were of the sound of footsteps approaching his bedroom doorway, and the mounting terror that came with them.

EIGHT

Weave-lord Vyrrch shuffled along the corridors of the Imperial Keep, his hunched and withered body buried in his patchwork robes, his ruined face hidden behind the bronze visage of an insane and ancient god. Once he had walked tall through these corridors, his stride long and his spine straight. But that was before the Mask had twisted him, warped him from the inside. Like all the True Masks, its material was suffused with the essence of witchstone, and the witchstones gave nothing without taking something away. His body was thronged with cancers, both benign and malignant. His bones were brittle, his knees crooked, his skin blemished all over. But such was the price of power, and power he had in abundance. He was the Weave-lord, the Empress's own Weaver, and he wanted for nothing.

The Weavers were a necessity of life in the higher echelons of Saramyr society. Through them, nobles could communicate with each other instantly over long distances, without having to resort to messengers. They could spy on their enemies, or watch over their allies and loved ones. The more effective Weavers could kill invisibly and undetectably, a convenient way to remove troublesome folk; the crime could only be traced by another Weaver, and even then there were no guarantees.

But the most important role of a Weaver was as a deterrent; for the only defence against a Weaver was another Weaver. They were there to stop their fellows spying on their employers, or even attempting to kill them. If one noble had a Weaver in their employ, then his enemies must have one to keep themselves safe. And so on with their enemies, and theirs. The first Weavers had begun to appear around two and a half centuries ago, and in the intervening time they had become a fixture of noble life. Not one of the high families lacked a Weaver; to be without one was a huge handicap. And while they were widely reviled and despised even by their employers, they were here to stay.

The price paid to acquire a Weaver was steep indeed, and the employer never stopped paying till the Weaver died. Money was an issue, of course; but that money was not paid to the Weavers themselves, but to the Edgefathers in the temples, for they made the Masks that the Weavers wore, and such was the purchase price of the Mask. For the Weaver, there was only this: that whatever comfort he sought would be attended to, every need fulfilled, every whim satisfied. And that he would be cared for, when he could not care for himself.

Weaving was a dangerous business. The Weavers brushed close to madness each time they used their powers, and it took years of training to deal with the energies inherent in their Masks. The Masks were essentially narcotic in effect. The sublime delights of the Weave took the mind and body to a dizzying high; but when the Weaver returned to himself, there was a corresponding backlash. Sometimes it manifested itself as a terrible, suicidal depression; sometimes as hysteria; sometimes as insane rage or unquenchable lust. Each Weaver's needs were different, and each had different desires that had to be satisfied lest the Weaver turn on himself. No employer wanted that. A dead Weaver was merely a very expensive corpse.

The Weavers were mercenaries, selling their services to the highest bidder. To their credit, once bought they were loyal; there had never been a case of one Weaver defecting to another family for a higher price. But all owed a higher loyalty, and that was to Adderach, the great mountain monastery that was the heart of their organisation. The Weavers would do anything and everything for their employers, even kill other Weavers – it was hard to maintain a conscience in the face of the atrocities they committed in their post-Weaving periods – but they would not compromise Adderach or its plans. For Adderach was the greatest of the monasteries, and the monasteries kept the witchstones, and without the witchstones the Weavers were nothing.

Vyrrch reached the door to his chambers, which were high up at the south end of the Keep. He encountered few people here. Though there were servants within calling distance whose job it was to satisfy whatever desire took him, they had learned that it was safer to stay out of his way unless needed. Vyrrch's preferences were unusual, but then it was common for a Weaver's requests to become more random and bizarre as the insanity took hold.

He had become increasingly paranoid about theft of his belongings one summer, convinced that whispering figures were conspiring to strip his chambers of their finery. He gnawed on his thoughts until he had reached the point of mania, and several servants were executed for stealing things which had never existed in the first place. After that, he declared that no servant would be allowed to enter his chambers; they were accessible by only one door, which was kept locked, and he was the sole owner of a key. Beyond that door was a network of rooms in which no servant had trodden for several years now.

He drew out the heavy brass key from where it hung around his scrawny white neck, and unlocked the massive door at the end of the corridor. With a heave, he pushed it open. A moment later, something darted out and shot past his feet. He whirled in time to see a cat, its fur in burned patches, racing away down the corridor. A momentary frown passed beneath the still surface of his Mask. He did not even remember asking for a cat. He wondered what he had done to it.

He stepped into the dim chambers, closed and locked the door behind him. The stench coming from within was imperceptible to him; it was the smell of his own corrupted flesh, mixed with a dozen other odours, equally foul. The light from outside was muted by layers of hung silks, now besmirched by dust and hookah smoke, making the rooms gloomy even at midday. He shuffled into the main chamber, where the octagonal bathing pool was. Vyrrch had rid it of its centrepiece of a drowned, naked boy by ordering a tank full of scissorfish and dumping them in the pool. They made short work of the boy, and later of each other, but now the water was dark red and chunks of flesh floated in it. The decayed lump that shared his broken bed was still there, he noted with distaste. It was beginning to offend him. He would do something about it soon. For now, though, he had a more important task of his own.

The Empress was facing the council on the morrow. It was a dangerous time for her, and potentially ruinous to Blood Erinima. The nobles and high families had assessed the Lucia situation by now; they had formed into alliances, struck deals. They were ready with threats which they were fully prepared to deliver, ready to declare their intentions regarding Lucia's claim to the throne: support, or opposition.

Vyrrch had spent the last few days relaying communiqués between Blood Erinima's allies, of which there were more than he expected. The news that Lucia's Aberration was not overtly dangerous, nor outwardly visible, had gentled the storm somewhat, and many of Blood Erinima's staunchest friends had opted to stand by them. Even Blood Batik, the line to which Anais's husband belonged, had given their support, despite Durun's obvious abhorrence to the child. They believed the tradition of inheritance by blood should be adhered to. Other, smaller families, seeking the opportunity of raising themselves, had also shown their colours in Lucia's defence. They hoped that allying themselves to the Empress in her time of need would win them reward and recognition.

Vyrrch was a little dismayed, but not put off. The opposition – who believed in the good of the country over tradition – were easily as strong, and there were still many families drifting undecided. The debate could swing either way.

It was Vyrrch's intention to lend his own weight to the swing, and not in his employer's favour. For the accession of Lucia was dangerous to the Weavers and to Adderach, and so he worked quietly to betray the Empress and her daughter.

He settled himself in his usual spot near the pool, cross-legged and hunched over, curled up small. Once he had become still, he waited while the ache in his joints slowly faded, allowing his phlegmy breathing to deepen. He relaxed as much as was possible, for his body constantly pained him. Gradually, he meditated, allowing even the pain to numb and retreat, feeling the eager heat of the witchstone dust embedded in his Mask. It seemed to warm his face, though its temperature did not rise; and its surface began to shimmer with an ochre-green cast.

The sensation of entering the Weave was like swimming upward through dark water to bright skies above. The pressure of the held breath expanding in the lungs, the feeling of being near bursting, the anticipation of the moment of relief; and then, breaking water with a great expulsion of air, and he was floating once again in the euphoric abyss between the gargantuan threads of the Weave.

The bliss that swamped him was unearthly, making all sensation pale by comparison. For a time, he shuddered in the throes of a feeling far past any joy that physical pleasure could provide. Then, with a great effort of will, he reined himself in, keeping the ecstasy down to a level he could tolerate and function in. The Weaver's craft was born of terrible discipline; for the Weave was death to the untrained.

He took himself to a territory often visited by him at his mistress's behest. It was the domain of Tabaxa, a young and talented Weaver who worked in the service of the Barak Zahn tu Ikati. This time, though, he was coming not to convey a message or to parley. This time he was entering unnoticed.

Blood Ikati were a sometime ally of Blood Erinima. The two families had too many conflicting interests ever to become loyal friends, but they were rarely at odds; more often, they remained respectfully neutral with each other. Blood Ikati, while not being especially rich or owning much land, had an impressive array of vassal families who had sworn allegiance to them. In their heyday, they had been the ruling family, and many treaties forged then still held today through careful management. Blood Ikati by themselves were not the most powerful family in the land by a long shot, but when one counted in the forces they brought to the table they became a factor to be reckoned with.

Barak Zahn had struck a deal with the Empress – in secret – meaning that he would declare his support for her during tomorrow's council. Anais knew better than to send a message through Vyrrch if she did not have to, and she had wisely decided not to rely on his loyalty in this affair. It pleased Vyrrch to see her distaste at being forced to use him to communicate over distance, for she was well aware of the Weaver's standpoint on the matter of Lucia. Instead she had invited the Barak to meet with her in person in the Keep. But this was Vyrrch's domain, and there was little that went on within these walls that he did not know about; so he listened in from afar anyway, unbeknownst to the plotters.

Anais was relying heavily on Blood Ikati's support to help her win over the council; or at least to stop them becoming openly hostile. Vyrrch had other ideas. He planned to change the Barak's mind.

It was a dangerous undertaking, but these were dangerous times. If he was discovered, it would mean scandal for the Empress – which was no bad thing – but it would also give Anais the excuse she needed to get rid of him. There were rules to prevent employers throwing Weavers out once they became an annoyance, as they inevitably did; but committing sabotage without her order was breaking those rules.

The Weavers' position depended on their trustworthiness. The nobles resented them for their necessity, and despised the fact that they had to take care of the Weaver's ugly and primal needs; yet without them the vast empire would be hopelessly crippled. It was a curious balance, a symbiotic relationship of mutual distaste; and yet, for all the strength of the Weavers, they were still only involved in Saramyr society as mere tools of the nobles who employed them, and like tools they could be discarded. No one could feel safe with creatures which could read their innermost secrets, and yet it would be worse to have those secrets read by a rival.

The Weavers balanced on a knife edge, and if one as prominent as Vyrrch was shown to be undermining his employer the repercussions would set Adderach's plans back decades. If they were suspected of being less than absolutely loyal, the retribution would be terrible, and their security relied on the nobles not acting in concert to remove them. Anais would love to have a new Weaver, and Vyrrch was too infirm to survive without a patron now.

Tread carefully, he thought to himself, but the words seemed as mist in the bliss of the Weave.

Tabaxa was no easy opponent, and so the strategy relied entirely upon stealth. The Barak or his watchdog must not realise that Vyrrch had been there, subtly tinkering with his thoughts, turning them against the Empress.

Tabaxa had woven his domain as a network of webs, their gossamer threads reaching into infinity. It was the most common visualisation of the Weave, taught by the masters to their pupils, but Vyrrch could not help a small stir of awe at the sight.

The vastness of the web defied perspective. It hung in perfect blackness, layer over layer stretching away at angles that baffled logic, anchored by threads chained somewhere so distant that perspective had thinned them to oblivion. It was far more complex than the simple geometry of a spider's construction; here, unconstrained by laws of physics, webs bent at impossible angles that the eye refused to fix on, joining in abstractions that could not have existed in the world outside the Weave. Between the thick strands, gauzy curtains of filmy gossamer seemed to sway in a cold wind, the tomblike breath of the abyss. A faint chiming sounded as the massive construction murmured and shifted.

Vyrrch was forced to adapt, shifting his perception to match that of his opponent. He knew it was not really there, only a method of allowing his frail human brain to see the complexities of the Weave without being driven mad. He hovered in nothingness, a disembodied mind, probing gently with his senses, seeking gaps in the defence. Net upon net of webwork spread before him, each one representing a different alarm that would bring Tabaxa. Vyrrch was impressed. It was subtly and carefully laid; but not so carefully that a Weave-lord could not penetrate it.

He shifted his vision to another frequency of resonance, and saw to his delight that much of the webbing was gone. Clearly Tabaxa had not been careful enough to armour his domain across the entire spectrum. There were very few Weavers who could alter their own resonance to a different level – in a sense, enter a new dimension within the Weave. Vyrrch could. Gratified, he gentled his way forward, invisible antennae of thought reaching out all around him, brushing near the threads but never touching them. He could feel the thrum of Tabaxa's presence, a fat black spider many hundreds of times his size, brooding somewhere near.

A tremor caught the edge of his senses, and in his mind he saw something descending from above, a ghostly veil, flat and transparent, drifting through the gaps between the webbing. Almost immediately, he sensed others nearby. None seemed to be heading for him, so he remained still until they passed by, like ethereal wisps of smoke.

He's clever, Vyrrch thought. *I've never seen that before.*

The things were sentinels, roaming alarms that existed on a plane high up in the resonance of the Weave. They were invisible at normal resonance. If Vyrrch had tried to penetrate the web as he had originally found it, he would have been unable to see them until they bumped into him and alerted their creator.

The Weave-lord was enjoying this. Slowly, patiently, he penetrated deeper into the gossamer shell of Tabaxa's domain. The illusory wind sighed through the framework of alarms, shifting them from side to side. In reality, Tabaxa had set the alarm network to vary slightly across the Weave, the better to catch unsuspecting intruders, but the effect manifested itself to Vyrrch's senses as a stirring of the web. Vyrrch had to dodge aside as a huge thread of silver lunged past him. He kept himself small, a tight focus of consciousness, and crept through, deeper, inward.

That was when the alarm was tripped.

Vyrrch panicked as the web around him erupted in a deafening din, a stunning cacophony of resonances. For an instant, he flailed; then he regained himself, and cast about for the cause. Nothing! There was nothing! He had been careful! He could feel the sudden, urgent movement of Tabaxa as he hefted his bulk up and came racing down the web, searching for the intruder. Vyrrch tried to move, to get out before he was identified, but he was trapped, his consciousness snared. Frantically, he shifted back down to normal resonance, and there, to his horror, he found himself engulfed in some grotesque, slippery thing, half mist and half solid, a vile amoeba that was clutching his mind tightly.

Vyrrch cursed. Tabaxa had not only employed alarms that were visible exclusively in the higher spectrum – the filmy ghosts he had seen before – but he had used ones that could only be seen in the normal spectrum too. Vyrrch had been caught out; he should have been switching between the two resonances.

Enraged suddenly, he annihilated the amoeba with a thought, disassembling its threads in fury. But Tabaxa was almost upon him now, a dark, massive shape, eight legs ratcheting as he raced along the threads of his weave to see what was amiss. It was too late to avoid a conflict, too late to escape and remain anonymous. Tabaxa would know he, Vyrrch, had been here.

Heart's blood! he thought furiously. *There's nothing else for it now.*

He tore out through the webbing of alarms, tattering it behind him, and crashed into the spider-body of his opponent. His world dissolved into an impossible multitude of threads, a rushing, darting tapestry of tiny knots and tangles, and he was *in* the threads, controlling them. Tabaxa was here too; Vyrrch sensed his angry defiance. He was puzzled as to why Vyrrch had come into his domain, but eager to demolish the older Weaver. There would be no quarter given, and none asked.

The conflict was conducted faster than consciousness could follow. Each sought a channel into the other, so they dodged and feinted down threads, finding one suddenly knotted against them, untangling this one or that, reaching dead-ends and loops that had been laid as traps or decoys. Each wanted to confuse the other long enough to break through the defences, while simultaneously shoring up their own. By manipulating the threads of the Weave, they jabbed and parried, darting back and forth, creating labyrinths for their opponent to get lost in or frantically unwinding a complex knot to create a channel into their enemy.

But in the end experience won out, and Tabaxa slipped up. Vyrrch had left him a tempting channel as a lure, and he impetuously took it; but it came up against a dead-end, and Vyrrch was waiting. With a speed and skill unmatched among the Weavers, he fashioned an insoluble knot behind Tabaxa, trapping him. Tabaxa tried to skip threads, to get out of the trap, but he only came up against another trap, and another, and by that time it was too late. Vyrrch was already away, burrowing through his defences, and Tabaxa could not get out in time. Vyrrch had identified a knot in Tabaxa's wall that was fraying, and he tore it open and raced through, into Tabaxa's mind like a meathook into a carcass, lodging in there and *rending* . . .

He could feel the force of his enemy's haemorrhage as he withdrew, feel the flailing embers of Tabaxa's consciousness as they were pulled back to his dying body. Tabaxa was even now spasming on the floor of his chamber, his brain ripped from the inside by the force of Vyrrch's will. The Weave-lord himself was retreating, the agony receding behind him rapidly as he raced out of the Weave, following the threads back to his own body, cursing and raging.

Vyrrch's eyes snapped open in the dim, filthy room where he sat. He shrieked in frustration, consumed by an anger that could not be borne. He had been careless! He, Vyrrch, the Weave-lord, had been caught by a trap he should have avoided with ease, *would* have avoided a year ago. What was wrong with him? Why could his mind not assemble his thoughts, lessons, instincts as it used to? He was perhaps the most formidable Weaver in the land, and yet he had blundered into Tabaxa's trickery, and been forced to kill him to protect his own identity. And all without getting close to Barak Zahn. A failure; an unmitigated failure.

Vyrrch rose suddenly, another shriek coming from beneath his Mask. He picked up the unidentifiable corpse on his bed and tossed it into the bloodied pool. He swatted aside a crystal ornament that stood in the corner of the room, one he did not recall seeing before. It dashed into shards on the tiles, a fortune destroyed in an instant. Like a whirlwind he swept through his chambers, breaking and throwing anything he could pick up, screaming like a child in a tantrum before flinging himself to the floor and scratching at it until his fingernails snapped.

The pain of his broken nails brought him to a momentary calm, a lull in the storm. He lay panting for a moment, before getting to his feet and stumbling to where a mouthpiece was set into the wall, connected by an echoing pipe to the quarters of his personal servants.

'Get me a child!' he rasped. 'A child, I don't care what sort. Get me a child, and . . . and bring me my bag of tools. And food! I want meat! Meat!'

He did not wait for a response. He threw himself to the floor again and lay there, his emaciated ribs heaving, waiting, drooling in anticipation. He did not know what would happen when the child got here. He never knew what would happen. But he thought he was going to enjoy it.

NINE

The compound of Blood Tamak was on the other side of the Imperial Quarter from Blood Koli's, but Mishani chose to walk anyway. For one thing, it was a beautiful day, with cool breezes from the north offering relief from the usual stifling heat of the city. For another, she preferred that her business this afternoon remained a secret.

The streets of the Imperial Quarter were wider than the usual thoroughfares of the city, and less trafficked. Tall, ancient trees lined the roadside, and the rectangular flagstones were swept for leaves every morning. Fountains or ornamental gutters plashed and trickled, collecting in basins where passers-by could drink to quench their thirst. Carts rattled by with deliveries piled high upon them. Mishani passed many gates, each one belonging to an important family, each one with their ancestral emblem wrought upon them somewhere. The Imperial Quarter was made up mainly of the town-houses of the various families – not only the high families who sat on the councils, but a multitude of minor nobles as well.

She glanced up at the Imperial Keep, its angled planes sheening in the sunlight. One such council was going on now, and it was one that she should well be attending. The Heir-Empress was an Aberrant, and the Empress in her hubris still seemed intent on putting her on the throne. Mishani would never have believed it possible – not only that Lucia had been allowed to reach eight harvests of age in the first place, but also that the Empress was foolish enough to think the high families would allow an Aberrant to rule Saramyr. Her father would be angry that she had not been there to lend her support to his condemnation of the Empress; but she had something else to attend to, and it had to be done while all eyes were on the Keep.

The divisions brought about by the revelations in the Imperial Family had come swift and savage. Longtime allies had separated in disgust, driven apart by their inability to condone the other's viewpoint. Arguments had erupted and turned to feuds. Most of it was down to men and their posturing, Mishani thought with a wrinkle of contempt. Her father was an example. He and Barak Chel of Blood Tamak had been political allies and good friends a month ago. Mishani had often accompanied him on visits to the townhouse of Blood Tamak. Then Chel's support of the Empress in the matter of the succession sparked a debate in which both said regretful things to each other, and now they were bitter enemies and would not speak.

That, unfortunately, was contrary to Mishani's interests, for within the house of Blood Tamak lived a wise old scholar by the name of Copanis, whose particular field of expertise was antique masks. And whatever the state of play between their two families, she intended to see him. The risk to herself was not inconsiderable. Her reputation would suffer greatly if she was caught in defiance of her father's wishes, not to mention the embarrassment that would be caused by her presence in her enemy's house. But there were greater matters at play here. Kaiku's only clue to her father's murder was the mask, tucked now beneath Mishani's blue robes; and if anyone could tell them about it, it was Copanis.

She just had to get to him.

She worried about her friend as she walked a winding route through the Imperial Quarter: across sunlit, mosaic-strewn plazas with restaurants in the shady cloisters, down narrow and immaculate alleyways where thin, short-furred cats prowled and slunk, through a small park in which couples strolled and artists sat cross-legged on the grass, their brushes hovering above their canvases. She had a great affinity for the Imperial Quarter, and on most days she found it tantalising, a place of beauty and intrigue, where the peripheral machinations of the court were played out in the gardens and under the arches. She was aware that it was heavily sanitised and rigidly policed in comparison to the sweaty bustle of the rest of the city, but she was content to avoid the crush and press when she could, and she preferred the calm and beauty of these streets to those of the Market District or the Poor Quarter.

But today her mind was not on the sights and sounds surrounding her. Her concern for Kaiku consumed her thoughts entirely. If what Kaiku had told her was true – and she had no doubt that Kaiku, at least, believed it – then her situation was grave. She was convinced she was possessed by something, which was bad enough; the alternative – that she was mad, and had merely created the story of the shin-shin and the burning of Asara as a hysterical reaction to the death of her family – was scarcely better. And yet she seemed lucid, which tended to discount either of those possibilities; unless the madness or possession was of a more insidious kind, that did not show itself as raving lunacy but in a subtle mania instead.

A chill ran through her, a cool bloom that counteracted the bright afternoon sun on her skin. Heart's blood, what if she *was* possessed? Mishani knew the stories of the dark spirits that haunted the forests and mountains, the deep and high and secret places of the world; but they had always seemed distant, powerless to affect her. She had heard about the gathering hostility of the beasts; it had been a small but persistent concern in court circles for a long time now. Enyu's priests and their sympathisers never stopped talking about it. Was it so much of a stretch, then, to believe the possibility that her friend had become . . . *infested* by the emboldened spirits?

She shook her head. What did she know about spirits? She was frightening herself with conjecture and guesswork. There would be answers, there *had* to be answers, and she and Kaiku would hunt them out; but first, she had another task to perform.

Blood Tamak's compound was set on a hillside, the main body of the townhouse supported by a man-made cliff of stone to make it sit level. It was a squat, flat-roofed building, its beige walls sparsely panelled in dark, polished wood, without any of the ornamentations, votive statues or icons that were usually present somewhere around the exterior of Saramyr households. Beneath it were the gardens, an unprepossessing lawn with curving flagstone paths and sprays of blooms, spartan even by the minimalist norms of Saramyr.

Mishani knew the layout well, for she had been shown around it often during her father's visits. At the side of the compound, a narrow set of sandstone steps ran from the street in front to the one behind, which was set higher in the hill. There was a servants' gate there, used for unobtrusive errand-running. It was here that Mishani took herself and waited.

She had timed her arrival excellently. Less than five minutes later, a short, sallow servant girl appeared, half opening the gate. Recognition widened her eyes as she saw who was outside.

'Mistress Mishani,' she gaped, blanching. She looked up and down the steps. 'You should not be here.'

'I know, Xami,' she replied. 'Heading to the market for flour?' Xami nodded. 'I thought so. Ever punctual. Your master would approve.'

'My master . . . your father . . . we must not be seen talking!' Xami stammered.

Mishani was the picture of elegant calm. Her tone was unhurried but firm. 'Xami, I have a favour to ask.'

'Mistress . . .' she began reluctantly, still standing in the gateway with the gate obscuring her partway, like a shield between them.

Mishani reached in and took the servant girl's hands in hers, and within was the crinkle of money. *Paper* money, which meant Imperial shirets. 'Remember the services I performed for you, in days when the heads of our houses were friends.'

Xami put the money inside her robe without looking at it. Her wide, watery eyes wavered in indecision. Mishani had passed love letters between her and a servant boy in the Koli house many times. It had seemed an interesting diversion then – and, additionally, Xami's clumsy attempts at poetry in the vulgar script of Low Saramyrrhic always made her smirk – but now it seemed it might serve a useful political purpose as well.

'Let me in, Xami,' Mishani said. 'You did not see me; you will not be blamed if I am caught. I promise you.'

Xami deliberated a few moments longer. Then, more because she feared somebody seeing them together than because she wanted to, she opened the gate fully. Mishani went in, and Xami slipped out and shut the gate behind her.

Mishani found herself in a narrow, vine-laden passageway that led around to the back of the main house, where the servants' quarters were. Most of the servants – indeed, much of the household – would be at the Keep now, for in matters of state the nobles liked to arrive in full pomp and splendour whenever they could. Copanis would not. He was a scholar, not a servant; the Barak Chel was his patron.

The thought brought uncomfortable resonances of Kaiku's father, Ruito tu Makaima. If he had had a patron, maybe there would have been somewhere to start, somebody that suspicion might devolve upon who might have a reason to kill him and his family; but it was a dead-end. Ruito had been in the rare position of being independently wealthy enough to survive without patronage, having had several works of philosophy in circulation among the literati of the empire that had generated enough income for him to buy himself free a long time ago.

Mishani made her way around to the back. She refused to sneak; she walked instead as if she owned the place, her long, dark hair swaying around her ankles as she went. Those servants that were still about would be engaged in menial duties now, but thankfully none seemed to have taken them outside, and she was able to slip into the house through the rear entrance undetected.

The interior of the house was very spare and minimal, with polished wooden floorboards and only the occasional wall hanging or mat to draw the eye. Chel liked his house as he liked his pleasures – respectable and sparse. Upstairs lay the family rooms and the ancestral chambers, where the house's treasures were kept. She would have no chance of getting up there; they were always guarded. But Copanis's study was on the ground floor, near the back of the house. Trusting to luck and Shintu, god of fortune, she made her way down a wide corridor, hoping that no one would come to challenge her.

Shintu smiled upon her, it seemed; for she reached the study without seeing another soul. Unusually, it had a door instead of a curtain or screen, but then the old scholar valued his privacy. She tapped on it. An instant later it was opened irritably, as if he had been lurking on the other side for just such an opportunity to surprise those who dared to interrupt him.

His face turned from annoyance to puzzlement as he saw who it was. Before he could protest, she laid a finger on her lips and slid inside, shutting the door behind her.

Copanis's study was uncomfortably hot, even with the shutters open to admit the breeze from outside. A low table was scattered with scrolls and manuscripts, but everywhere were concessions to ornamentation that were not present in the rest of the house. A sculpted hand; a skull with glass jewels for teeth; an effigy of Naris, god of scholars and son of Isisya, goddess of peace, beauty and wisdom. All was a clutter, but it conveyed the intensity of its author.

'My, my,' he said. 'Mistress Mishani, daughter of my master's newly embittered enemy. I take it you have something very important you need, to come see me like this. And miss the council with the Empress, too.'

Mishani looked over the old man with an inner smile that did not show on her face. He always was quick, this leathery, scrawny walnut of a scholar. His clothes seemed to sag off his lean frame, as his flesh did; but his eyes were still feverishly bright, and he was capable of running rings round intellectuals half his age.

Mishani decided to dispense with the preamble. She drew out the mask. 'This belongs to a dear friend of mine,' she said. 'Our need is most pressing to discover all we can about it. I can tell you no more than that.'

Copanis scrutinised her for a short while. He was making a show of deliberation, but it was not hard to see how his eyes were drawn to the mask. He was too cantankerous to fear to balk the authority of his master, and he was never one to hoard his knowledge when he could share it. With a mischievous quirk of one eyebrow, he took the mask and turned it around in his hands.

'You take a great risk, coming here,' he murmured.

'I seek to right a grave wrong, and aid a friend in desperate straits,' she replied. 'The risk is little, weighed against that.'

'Indeed?' he said. 'Well, I won't inquire, Mistress Mishani. But I dare to say I can help you in my small way.'

He placed the mask in a small wooden cradle, so that it faced the sunlight from the windows. After that, he found himself a small ceramic pot of what looked like dust. This he sprinkled over the face of the mask. Mishani watched with fascination – disguised, as ever, behind a wall of impassivity – as the dust seemed to glitter in the sun.

'Draw the shutters,' he said. 'Not this one; the others.'

Mishani obeyed, darkening the room until only a single shutter remained, shining light on to the mask's dusty face. After a time, Copanis shut that one himself, plunging the room into darkness. He turned the mask so they could both see it. The dust glowed dimly, phosphorescent in the darkness – but its life was momentary, and it faded.

Copanis harumphed. He told Mishani to open the shutters again. She did so, enduring his peremptory tone because she needed his help. After that, he sat cross-legged at his desk and brushed the dust off the mask, then turned it over in his hands and studied it. He held it near to his face without letting it touch. He closed his eyes and spent a short time chanting softly, as if in meditation. Mishani waited patiently, kneeling opposite him with her hair pooled around her.

Eventually he opened his eyes. 'This is indeed a True Mask,' he said. 'It has been infused with witchstone dust, and there is power here. However, it is very young. Less than a year old; I would estimate no more than two previous wearers, neither of them possessing any remarkable mental strength. It is valuable, of course; but as far as the True Masks go, it is weak, like a newborn.'

'You can tell all that? I am impressed,' Mishani said.

He shrugged. 'I can only tell you in the vaguest of terms. A True Mask picks up strength from its wearers . . . or, rather, it saps it from them. There are ways to tell a True Mask from an ordinary one, and guess at its age; but little else can be done. There is a simple way to learn more, of course, but I cannot counsel it.'

'And that is . . . ?'

'To put it on, Mistress,' said Copanis with a sour smile.

'Surely anyone who did that would die, unless they were a Weaver and trained in the arts.'

'Ah, not so. A common misconception,' Copanis replied, stretching. His vertebrae cracked like fireworks. 'The older the Mask, the greater the peril; but one as young and weak as this . . . why, you or I might put it on and suffer no ill effects. Nightmares, maybe. Disorientation. That said, I repeat I cannot counsel it. There is still an element of risk. Should the mind prove to be susceptible, insanity and death would surely follow. The chance is small, but it exists.'

Mishani considered this. 'Can you tell me where it comes from?'

'Ah, that is easy. The hallmarks are obvious. See this wave pattern in the wood on the inside? And the indentation here, to accommodate the wearer's philtrum? This comes from one of the Edgefathers at Fo; although from which part of the isle, I cannot say. I would guess at the north, simply because of the marked lack of mainland influences on the carving. The one who carved this either had little contact with the ports in the south of Fo and the people there, or he spurned the craft of the mainland Edgefathers.' He passed it back to her, the red and black face seeming to grin mockingly. 'That is all I can tell you.'

'It was more than enough,' she replied, bowing. 'You have my gratitude. Now I must go; I've put you in peril already.'

He stood up, knee joints popping, and cackled. 'Hardly peril, Mistress. Here, I'll help you get out,' he said. 'Let me spy out the lie of the land for you, then you can make it to the servants' gate. You know where it is?'

'I know,' replied Mishani, standing also, her hair cascading around her.

'I thought you might,' he replied.

Kaiku was unused to spending the summer months in the city; her father had always sent his family to their cooler property in the Forest of Yuna while he worked. Though it was only just climbing the slope towards the truly miserable heat of midsummer, Kaiku had become drowsy and felt the need for a siesta, and she had slept while she waited for Mishani to return.

In her dreams, the shin-shin came.

This time they were even more dark and nebulous than she remembered. They stalked unseen in the corridors of her mind, fearful presences that emanated dread, which she could not see but sense. She fled through a labyrinth that resembled her father's house in the forest, but seemed infinitely bigger and endless. She found doors, hatches, corners that brought her shuddering to a stop, for she knew with dream-certainty that death was lurking there, *felt* them waiting just beyond with a terrifying, hungry patience. And each time she came up against one of these invisible barriers of fear, she turned and ran the other way, her skin clammy with the proximity of the end. But no matter how far she went, they were everywhere, and inescapable.

Flailing helplessly, trapped forever, she knew there was no escape for her, and still she tried. At some point, she became aware of another presence, one even more malevolent than the shin-shin. This one lived inside her, in her belly and womb and groin, and it grew whenever she thought about it, feeding on her attention. She desperately tried to distract herself, but it was impossible not to feel the thing inside her skin, and she sensed its mad glee as it suckled on her terror. Desperate, driven by some illogical prescience that she had to get out of the house before this new entity consumed her, she raced onward, trying new routes with increasing panic, finding all blocked against her by the lurking, unseen shin-shin. Her chest ached, and her heart pounded harder and harder, but she could not stop even though her body burned with fatigue, and suddenly it was all too much and—

Her eyes flew open to agony, and the room ignited.

She threw herself off her sleeping-mat with a shriek, warned by some instinct that caused her to react before her conscious mind could arrange itself. She was fortunate: so quick was she that the ripples of flame that sprang from the weave of the mat only licked her, and it was too brief to do more than singe her sleeping-robe. She scrambled to her feet, gazing wildly around the room. The curtain that hung in the doorway was ablaze; the window shutters smoked and charred, blue flames invisible in the bright sunlight. The timbers of the room had blackened but not caught light; an arrangement of guya blossoms in a vase had crisped to cinders. A wall-hanging, that had once depicted the final victory of the first Emperor, Jaan tu Vinaxis, over the primitive Ugati people that had occupied this land in the past, ran with fire. Thin, deadly smoke was rising all around her.

She dashed immediately for the doorway, an automatic response, and then retreated as she saw it was impassable while the curtain still burned. The windows were no option either. More terrifying than her animal fear of fire was the knowledge that she was trapped by it. She tried to cry for help, but the intake of breath made her chest blaze in pain. Her every muscle was in agony, and the blood seemed to boil and scorch as it pumped through her veins. The demon inside her had returned in her sleep and tormented her with fires inside and out.

Steeling herself against the torture, she found her voice and shouted, hoping to alert the servants to her plight. But no sooner had she done so than the flaming curtain began to thrash, and she saw Mishani beyond it, slashing at it with a long, bladed pike that had been part of an ornamental set in the corridor outside. She hacked at the disintegrating cloth and it came to pieces, falling to the floor where a servant girl threw a bucket of suds across it and reduced it to a black mush. Shielding her face with one blue-robed arm, Mishani called to her friend; Kaiku ran to her in desperate relief. Mishani pulled her clear of the room, out into the corridor. Voices were raised all about the household as servants ran for water.

Kaiku would have embraced her friend then, if it were not for the gasp of horror that the servant girl gave. Kaiku looked to her, confused, and the girl quailed and made a sign against evil. Mishani's face was stony. She grabbed the servant girl's wrist, pulling her roughly to face her mistress.

'On your life, you will speak of this to no one,' she said, her voice heavy with threat. 'On your *life*, Yokada.'

The servant girl nodded, frightened.

'Go,' Mishani commanded. 'Find more water.' As Yokada gratefully fled, she turned to Kaiku. 'Close your eyes, Kaiku. Let me lead you. Feign that you are smoke-blinded.'

'I—'

'As I am your friend, trust me,' Mishani said. Kaiku, shaken and scared still, did what she was told. Mishani was several inches shorter than Kaiku, but she seemed many years older then, and her tone brooked no argument. She took her friend by the hand and led her away, hurrying so that Kaiku feared to trip. She opened her eyes to see where her feet were, and Mishani caught her and hissed at her to keep them shut. Servants rushed past them in a clatter of feet, and she heard the swill of water in buckets. After a time, Mishani drew back a curtain and led her into a room.

'Now you can open them,' Mishani said, sounding weary.

It was Mishani's study. The low, simple table was still occupied by neat rows of tally charts, an inkpot and a brush. Several shelves held other scrolls, not one of them out of place. Sketch paintings of serene glades and rivers hung on the walls, next to a large elliptical mirror, for Mishani often entertained guests in here and she understood the importance of appearance.

'Mishani, I . . . it happened again . . .' Kaiku stammered. 'What if you had been with me? Spirits, what if—'

'Go to the mirror,' Mishani said. Kaiku quieted, looked at her friend, then at the mirror. Suddenly, she feared what she might see. She shuddered as a spasm of pain racked her body.

'I need to rest, Mishani . . . I'm so tired,' she sighed.

'The mirror,' Mishani repeated. Kaiku turned, bowing her head as she stood before it. She did not dare see whatever it was that Mishani wanted her to.

'*Look at yourself!*' Mishani hissed, and there was an edge to her voice that Kaiku had never heard before, one that made her afraid of her friend. She looked up.

'Oh,' she murmured, her fingers coming up to rest on her cheek.

Her eyes, gazing back at her, were no longer brown. The irises were a deep and arterial red, the eyes of a demon.

'Then it's true,' she said, slowly, brokenly. 'I am possessed.'

Mishani was standing at her shoulder in the mirror, her head tilted down so that her hair fell across her face, her gaze averted.

'No, Kaiku,' she said. 'You are not possessed. You are Aberrant.'

TEN

The council chamber of the Imperial Keep was not vast, but what it lacked in size it made up for in opulence. The walls and tiers of the semi-circular room were drenched in grandeur, from the enormous gold and crystal chandelier overhead to the ornate scrollwork on the eaves and balconies. The majority of the room was lacquered in crimson and edged in dark gold; the ceiling was sculpted into a relief of an ancient battle, while the floor was of reflective black stone. The flat wall at the back – where the speaker stood to talk to those on the semi-circular tiers above – bore a gigantic mural of two scaled creatures warring in the air, their bodies aflame as they locked in mortal combat above a terrified city below.

The assembly was silent as Anais tu Erinima, Blood Empress of Saramyr, walked to stand in front of the mural, her dress a dark red like that of the room. She wore her flaxen hair in her customary long plait, with a silver tiara across her brow. Next to her walked an old man in robes of grey, his hood masking his face so that only his hooked nose and long, salt and pepper beard could be seen. High, arched windows lit the scene, brighter on the west side where the sun was heading toward afternoon.

Anais hated this room. The colours made her feel angry and aggressive; it was a poor choice for a place of debate. But this had been the council chamber for generations past, through war and peace, famine and plenty, woe and joy; tradition had kept it virtually unaltered for centuries.

Maybe I will be the one to change it, Anais thought to herself, masking her nervousness with bravado. *Maybe I will change many things, before my days are done.*

She took her place on the central dais, a petite and deceptively naïve-looking figure in the face of the assembly. The Speaker in his grey robes stood next to her. Facing her, on three tiers that rose up and away, were representatives of the thirty high families of Saramyr. They sat behind expertly carven stalls, looking down on their ruler. She scanned the room, searching out her supporters, seeking her enemies . . . and finally finding Barak Zahn tu Ikati, whom until a few minutes ago had been the former. Now she had no idea where she stood in his regard.

She had in her pocket a letter from the Barak, informing her of the sudden and extremely suspicious death of his Weaver, Tabaxa. It said nothing more than that. The letter had been delivered to her by a servant just before she entered the chamber. If the move had been calculated to unnerve her, it had succeeded admirably. Now she studied him in the stalls, a tall man with a short white beard and pox-pitted cheeks, trying to divine what he meant by it; but his face was blank, and gave no indication of his thoughts.

By the spirits, does he think I did it? she asked herself, and then wondered what she would do if the Barak withdrew his support, when her position was precarious enough already.

'The Blood Empress of Saramyr, Anais tu Erinima,' the Speaker announced, and then it was her time to speak. She took a breath, showing nothing of the fear she felt.

'Honourable families of Saramyr,' she began, her usually soft and gentle voice suddenly strong and clear. 'I bring this council to session. Thank you for coming; I know some of you have travelled far to be here today.' She paused, allowing the echoes of her pleasantries to fade before she launched into the fray.

'I am certain you are aware of the matter before us. The issue of my daughter is of great importance to all of you, and to Saramyr as a whole. I know of the division over this situation, both among the high families and those not of noble birth. If compromise can be reached to heal this division, then I am willing to compromise. There are many aspects to this matter that will bear negotiation. But know this as a fact: my daughter is of Blood Erinima, and the daughter of the Blood Empress. Some may call her Aberrant, some may not: it is a matter of opinion. But the point is moot in the laws of succession. She is the sole heir to my throne, and she will be Blood Empress after me.'

The council, predictably, broke out in uproar. Anais faced them without flinching or lowering her gaze. Many of them had been hoping that she had seen sense and decided to abdicate, if only to spare her daughter's life. But Anais had never been more sure of anything. Her child would be as good a ruler as any, better than most. Whatever the dangers to herself, she would bring her child to throne.

Unless, of course, she was deposed by the council.

The thirty high familes were nominally vassals to the ruling family, but it rarely worked exactly that way. Blood Erinima ruled Saramyr, meaning that they – in theory – spoke for all the families. The Baraks each owned vast tracts of land, effectively dividing up Saramyr into manageable chunks. The Baraks further subdivided their land to ur-Baraks, who dealt with smaller portions, and the ur-Baraks left the management of villages within their territory to the Marks. With as many powerful families as there were in Saramyr, the question of loyalty was never clear-cut.

The council of the high families represented only the Baraks, and some of the more influential ur-Baraks who were related by blood. Though there was a strong tendency to support the ruling family, fuelled by tradition and concepts of honour, it was by no means a guarantee. The council had turned against their lieges before, and for much less. A vote of no confidence from the council was damning, and left only two real options: abdication, or civil war. Saramyr's history was spotted with bloody coups. Though the ruling family always had the greatest army by far – for their post entitled them to the protection of the Imperial Guards, who owed allegiance only to the throne and not Blood – an alliance of several strong Baraks could still challenge them and win.

The Speaker raised his arm, and in his hand was a small wooden tube on a thin red rope. He spun it quickly, and a high keening wail cut through the room. When it died, silence had returned. Anais's eyes flickered over the assembly. She could see other members of Blood Erinima in the stalls, approving of her declaration. Her old enemies in Blood Amacha looked furious; though she noted that Barak Sonmaga's expression was almost smug. He relished the fight.

'To those who oppose me, I say this!' she cried. 'You are blinded by your prejudices. Too long have you listened to the Weavers, too long have you been told what to think on this matter. Many of you have never even seen an Aberrant. Many of you are ill educated in what makes an Aberrant at all. Those of you who have met my daughter know her to be gentle and kind. She bears no deformities. She may possess perceptions greater than ours, senses that we do not understand: but don't the Weavers have the same? She has harmed no one and nothing; she is as well-adjusted as a child can be expected to be. And if exceptional intelligence is an undesirable trait for a ruler of Saramyr, then let us be ruled by half-wits instead, and see how long our proud country lasts!'

There was silence again for a short moment. She was coming dangerously close to defying the Weavers outright, and who knew the ruin that would bring? Anais was only glad that no Weavers were present; they played no part in the country's politics. Still, she was sure that they were listening somewhere . . .

Barak Sonmaga tu Amacha stood. She might have known he would be the first. The Speaker announced his name.

'Empress, nobody doubts the love you have for Lucia,' Sonmaga said. He was a broad-chested, black-bearded man with heavy eyebrows. 'Which of us could say that we would not do the same, were it our own son or daughter? Who among us could bear to deliver our own child to the Weavers, even if they were . . . unnatural?'

Anais did not react to his choice of words. They were intended to provoke.

'But this is a matter greater than your feelings, Empress,' he continued, his voice lowering in tone. 'Greater even than ours, here in this council. The *people* are the issue here. The people of Saramyr. And I tell you they *will not bear* an Aberrant to sit on the throne. She might have the potential to be a great ruler – I'm sure no mother would think any less of her child – but how long will she rule, how effectively, when she is reviled by the people beneath her?'

Anais kept her face calm. 'Barak Sonmaga, the people have a long time to get used to her. By the time she sits the throne, they will have learned to accept. They, like many of the honourable Baraks and Barakesses in this chamber, will find their opinions changed upon seeing my daughter, and witnessing her nature.'

Sonmaga opened his mouth to speak again, but Anais suddenly remembered another point she had meant to make, and got in first. 'And never forget, Barak Sonmaga, the lessons of the past. Our people have suffered tyranny under the madness of Emperor Cadis tu Othoro. They have been brought to famine and ruin by the ineptitude of Emperor Emen tu Gor; and then suffered terrible and entirely preventable plagues under his successor, because he refused to clean up the cities. None of these brought the people to revolution. I offer a child with extraordinary intelligence, impeccable sanity and a kind nature, and the only count against her is that she is unusual. I hardly think the people will take up arms at that. I say you exaggerate, Barak Sonmaga tu Amacha. It is no secret that you have your own preferences as to who should sit on the throne.'

Sonmaga's eyes blazed. Such a direct accusation was a hair's breadth from insult, but it was also inarguably true. Blood Amacha had never been a ruling family, and they had always coveted the throne. He knew it well enough, so he could not take umbrage without weakening his own position. Anais, for her part, gazed coolly around the chamber. She did not glance at the representatives of Blood Gor, whom she had regrettably reminded of their past failures. Blood Othoro had thankfully dwindled long ago, and taken its madness with it. Her gaze passed across Barak Zahn and lingered there for a moment, but he was as impassive as before. His letter had unnerved her considerably; she had no idea if she could count on his support or not. The deal they had made could be in tatters if he suspected that Anais had tried to kill him or his Weaver . . . but why should he think such a thing? They were allies, weren't they?

An elderly Barak stood up then, his lean body draped in heavy robes.

'Barak Mamasi tu Nira,' the Speaker announced.

'I beg that you consider this matter well,' said Mamasi. He was a neutral, as far as Anais knew. He disliked getting his family involved in disputes of any kind if he could help it. 'To force a council vote on this matter can only bring ruin. Opinion among the Baraks is deeply divided: you know this. Abdicate, Empress, for the good of the land and for your daughter. If you stay, civil war must follow, and Lucia's life would be in great danger were you to lose.'

'Barakess Juun tu Lilira,' said the Speaker, as she stood and made a sign that she wished to speak in support of Mamasi.

'Now, of all times, we must remain united,' declared the ancient Barakess. 'The very land turns against us. Evil things haunt the hills and forests, and grow bolder by the day. My villages are besieged by ill spirits; the earth sickens and crops fail. A civil war now would only add to our misery. Please, Empress, for the good of your people.'

'I say no!' Anais cried. 'I say my abdication would weaken the country more than Lucia ever could. There are at least three houses who hold power enough to challenge for the throne. I will name no names, and I do not presume to know their intentions, but a war of succession would follow should Blood Erinima relinquish their claim on the throne, and all of you know it!'

Silence again. She spoke the truth. Blood Batik claimed rights by marriage, but there was no way Anais would pass the responsibility for Saramyr into the hands of her wastrel, womanising husband. Blood Amacha claimed rights by sheer power; they owned the most land, and a large private army. And Blood Kerestyn were most powerful of all; they had been the ruling family before Erinima, and they had never lost the desire to reclaim the throne.

'I know the horror that the word "Aberrant" awakens in all of us,' she continued. 'But I know also that there are many interpretations of that word. Not all Aberration is bad; not all Aberrants are evil. It took the birth of my child to make me see that, but I see it now. And I would have all of you see it, too.'

She raised her hand to forestall another of her antagonists. 'I ask for the vote of the council in support of my daughter's claim to the throne.'

'The council will vote!' the Speaker called.

Anais stood where she was, her hands laid across each other, clammy with sweat. She could feel herself trembling inside. If the council approved by a majority, she could consider herself safe for a time. As the Barakess had said, nobody wanted a civil war now. But if her support was lacking, then she was in terrible danger. Would she truly abdicate, even for the sake of her child? At least, that way, Lucia might live . . .

'Blood Erinima, family of my heart. How do you say?' she asked.

'We support you as always, Empress,' said her great-aunt Milla. As eldest, she was the head of the family, even though her niece was Empress.

Anais looked about the chamber, scanning the grandiose tiers. She would have to ask each of the thirty families in turn, and the order that she chose them was crucial. Some families who were wavering might be swayed if a more powerful ally took the lead. Blood Erinima was easy. She asked then three other families, all certainties, who assured her of their support. A fourth one, whom she had thought she could rely on, decided to remain neutral.

Then, reasoning that it was best not to use up all her support this early in the vote, she chose an obvious enemy: Blood Amacha.

'We oppose you, Empress, with all our strength and vigour,' Barak Sonmaga replied, somewhat unnecessarily.

She asked several other families, receiving mixed reponses. The powerful Barak Koli voted against her; his daughter Mishani was noticeably absent. Blood Nabichi threw unexpected support behind the Empress. But there was one to whom many of the lesser families were looking: Blood Ikati. Anais took a breath; their support was vital for snaring in some of those who sat on the fence.

'Blood Ikati,' she said, her voice echoing across the chamber. 'How do you say?'

Barak Zahn tu Ikati unfolded his lean, rangy body from behind his stall. He regarded Anais carefully. Anais met his gaze with her own, unfaltering.

I have done him no wrong, she told herself. *I have nothing to fear.*

'Blood Ikati supports your daughter's claim, Anais tu Erinima,' the Barak said, and as he sat down Anais felt herself weaken at the knees.

The ritual of asking each family was a nerve-racking affair, and by the time it had concluded there was no clear majority. Her supporters and opponents were evenly matched, and there were few who abstained. The council was divided, split down the middle.

Anais felt a thrill of mixed relief and trepidation. If the council had voted heavily against her, she would have been tempted to consider abdication, whatever the cost to Blood Erinima. Her daughter's life would surely be forfeit if Anais tried to put her on the throne with no support. But now her course was set. Though it was risky, she had enough strength behind her to dare this, even if she was sorely tempting the prospect of civil war. When they left the chamber, Blood Amacha would be gathering their allies and Blood Kerestyn theirs. The only comfort she took was that the opposition was divided, whereas her support was as solid as she could hope for.

'My daughter sits the throne,' she said. 'I bid you all a safe journey.' And with that, she left, her composure threatening to break as she stepped from the dais; but she did not allow herself to cry until she was alone in her chambers.

It was perhaps an hour later when Barak Zahn tu Ikati came to her chambers.

Ordinarily, Anais would not have received visitors after council; but for him she made an exception. They had known each other long enough that formality was unnecessary, so she had Zahn shown into a room with plush chairs and gently smoking scented braziers, and she appeared wearing a simple dress and her hair, freshly brushed, worn loose. The décor was relaxed and homely, calculated to put him at his ease. Here some concession had been made to luxury over aesthetic beauty, and the room had a cosy air about it, with rugs on the *lach* floor and curtains of coloured beads hanging over the tall, narrow window arches.

'Zahn,' she said with a bright smile. 'I'm glad to see you.'

'You too, Anais,' he said. 'Though I wish the circumstances were somewhat different.'

She gestured him to a chair and sat opposite him. 'Troubled times indeed,' she said.

'I cannot stay, Anais,' said Zahn, scratching his neck with his thumb absently. 'The afternoon is drawing on, and I have to journey back to my estate. I came to bring you a warning.'

Anais adopted an attentive posture.

'A servant found my Weaver, Tabaxa, as he lay dying,' Zahn said, frowning slightly. 'He was struck down very suddenly, it seems, and was bleeding from the ears and eyes; yet there was not a mark on him.'

'It sounds like another Weaver did it,' Anais said. 'Or perhaps poison.'

Zahn made a negative grunt. 'Not poison. The servant removed Tabaxa's mask, and he said a word before he died. Very clearly.'

Anais suddenly pieced together the puzzle: why Zahn had sent that letter; why he had seemed so cold in the council chamber. 'Vyrrch,' she said.

Zahn did not reply, but his eyes told her she was right.

'Then why . . . ?'

'Did you know of it, Anais?' Zahn demanded, suddenly lurching forward towards her.

'No!' she replied instantly.

Zahn paused, half out of his chair, and then sank back with a sigh. 'As I thought,' he said. 'A single word is a slim rope to hang so much weight on, Anais. But you must watch him, your Weave-lord. Perhaps he seeks to undermine you. Have you thought what it might mean for the Weavers if Lucia sits the throne and there *isn't* a revolution?'

Anais nodded grimly. 'She is a mockery of all their teachings about Aberrants. They have killed Aberrant children for so long, and so young . . . Lucia is living proof that they do not always turn out evil, if at all. If she becomes Empress, they fear what she will do.'

'Perhaps,' said Zahn, 'it is something that needs to be done.'

Anais nodded slightly, her gaze turning to the windows, where Nuki's eye watched benevolently over Axekami from behind the bead curtains.

'Why did you vote for me, Zahn, if you thought I had sent Vyrrch to spy on you?'

'Because I trust you,' he said. 'We have been allies and opponents by turns for a long time now, but you have never broken a deal with me. Also, I confess, I wanted to see how you reacted when you saw me; I would have been able to tell, I think, if you had been guilty.'

'Maybe you would,' said Anais with a faint smile. 'Still, I am grateful for your trust.'

'I must go now,' said Zahn, standing up. 'I shall see myself out. Please, Anais, take warning. Do not turn your back on Vyrrch. He is evil, and he will kill your child if he can.'

'And I can do nothing to him without proof,' she replied sadly. 'And perhaps not even then. Goodbye, Zahn. I hope we meet again soon.'

'Indeed,' said the Barak, and he left Anais alone in the muggy warmth of the afternoon, thinking.

ELEVEN

The morning sun dawned red as blood behind the barge as it lumbered westward into Axekami. They called it the Surananyi – the fury of Suran. Somewhere in the eastern deserts of Tchom Rin, great hurricanes were tearing across the desolate land, flinging the red dust into the sky to mar the light of Nuki's single eye.

Legend told how Panazu, god of rivers and rain, had been so besotted with Narisa, daughter of Naris, that he had asked a wise old apothecary to make him a potion that would cause her to fall in love with him. But the old apothecary was none other than Shintu the trickster in disguise, and Shintu put a feit on Panazu so that he would think the first woman he saw was his beloved Narisa. So it came to pass that he returned to his home, and the first to greet him was his sister Aspinis, goddess of trees and flowers. Panazu, thinking his sister was Narisa, chose the moment to slip his potion into Aspinis's drink, and she fell under its influence. And so they coupled, and when the morning came and their eyes were cleared they were horrified at what they had done.

But worse was to come; for they were the son and daughter of Enyu, goddess of nature and fertility, and from their coupling grew a child. They dared not tell their mother, for the child was not natural, conceived as it was of incest; and they knew well how their mother could not condone anything that was not complicit with her laws. Aspinis fled, hiding her shame. But she was beloved of the gods, and sorely missed; and so Ocha and Isisya ordered that all should search for her until she was found.

So began the Year of the Empty Temples, when the people of Saramyr suffered greatly, for the gods turned their faces away from the land and hunted through the Golden Realm for their lost kin. Crops failed, cruel winds blew, famine struck the land. Even Nuki turned away from them, and the sun was dim that year. And though the people thronged to the temples to pray for deliverance, their gods were not present.

Then, joy. Aspinis returned from the wilderness, and all the Golden Realm celebrated. In Saramyr the crops flourished, the fish were plentiful and the livestock grew fat once again. Aspinis would not speak of where she had been; but Shintu, who had guessed what had happened, threatened to tell her mother Enyu unless she revealed to him where the baby was. Aspinis – who had no inkling of Shintu's hand in the affair – told him that the baby was in a cave deep in the desert, where she would have long died.

Shintu, eager to see the results of his meddling, travelled to the cave, and there he found the baby not dead, but very much alive. She was being fed by snakes and lizards who brought her morsels, and she was a wrinkled and ugly thing with long, tangled hair and odd eyes – one green and one blue. But Shintu was struck with pity then, and he took the baby to his own home and nurtured her in secret, and named her Suran. She became a bitter girl, for in the way of the gods she remembered what had been done to her as an infant, and when she was grown she left Shintu and went back to the desert to dwell among the lizards and the snakes, to become the antithesis of everything her hated parents stood for. Suran was the outcast, the goddess of deserts and drought and pestilence; and when she raged, the whole of Saramyr saw red.

Tane's heart felt heavy in his breast as he sat on the forecastle of the barge, feeling the slow surge of the ship beneath him as it bore him onward. It was a low, clumsy craft, laden heavy with ores and minerals from the mines in the Tchamil Mountains. The rough cries of the bargemen sounded in his ears, hollering in their jagged dialect; peeping birds banked and swirled high above, mistaking the barge for a fishing vessel and hoping for breakfast; hawsers creaked and timbers groaned. All around him, life; and yet he felt lifeless.

He looked down at the planks between his knees, their colour stained red by the bloody sun, and traced the grain of the wood with his gaze. How like himself those lines were, he thought. They travelled their solitary way, sometimes brushing near to another line but rarely touching. Sometimes they were swallowed by a whorl or knot, sucked into a tangle; but always they emerged on the other side, always returning to an aimless and lonely path. He felt himself flailing inwardly, scrabbling for a greased rope of purpose that eluded his grip. Of what worth was he, one among thousands, millions; what right had he to expect the forbidden happiness of belonging? The gods meted out their gifts and blessings as they chose, and there were certainly many more worthy than him. Though he was a priest, he was still lower than these simple bargemen; for he had taken the order to atone for his past, not out of nobility or generosity. To pay off his guilt and regain his innocence. How many lives, how many sacrifices would it take before the gods were satisfied?

He felt sorrow for the priests of the temple that he had left behind, but no real grief. He and Jin had returned to Tane's erstwhile home at daybreak, and found it in terrible disarray. The priests were scattered haphazardly about like discarded dolls. They scarcely seemed real to Tane as he identified each of them: effigies only, as if the faces he had known these past few years had been replaced by waxy sculptures with glazed, glassy eyes and dry mouths gaping and lolling purple tongues.

'They were looking for something,' Jin said.

'Or someone,' Tane added.

He took Jin's silence to mean she had guessed who he referred to.

Later, he brought the priests out of the temple and laid them on the grass. There, he named them silently in prayer to Noctu, that she might record their deaths and inform her husband Omecha. He said another prayer to Enyu while Jin waited patiently, and he was just finishing when Jin's sharp intake of breath warned him that something was amiss.

When he opened his eyes, he saw the bears. They waited at the edge of the clearing, massive black and brown shapes hidden in the foliage, watching and waiting. Tane bowed to them, and then led Jin away to the boat which the priests used to travel to the nearby settlement of Ban and back.

'Is there to be no burial?' she asked.

'That is not our way,' he replied. 'The forest beasts will have them. Their flesh will return to the cycle of nature; their souls to the Fields of Omecha.'

They had bought passage on a barge from Ban. During the six-day journey, Tane had been given plenty of time for introspection. He sought inside himself for the well of loss, but found nothing. He was confused by the absence. His home, all the faces he had known, his tutors and friends and even old Master Olec were gone in a single night. Yet he could not bring himself to grieve; and in fact, he felt a guilty excitement at the prospect of moving on. Maybe he had never belonged there at all, and he had simply not admitted it to himself until now. Maybe that was why he could never find the inner peace he sought.

Enyu has another path for me, he thought. *She has spared me the slaughter and set me on my way. I, the least worthy of her followers.*

The thought made him strangely happy.

The sun had risen high in the eastern sky by the time they reached Axekami, but it had still not cleared the veil of desert dust that hung before it, and the capital of Saramyr glowered angrily in brooding red. The approach to the city proper was through the sprawling shanties of the river nomads, whose stilt huts and rickety jetties crowded the river banks. Withered, wiry old men poled back and forth, seeming to take their lives in their hands as they cut into the path of the barge. The barge master did not slow or pay any attention. The nomads sat outside their wooden homes and shops, scraping leather or weaving, and their eyes were suspicious or indifferent as they passed over the hulking barge that plied past them down the Kerryn. Nomads only trusted their own kind, and likewise were mistrusted by all.

Jin came and sat by him as the shanties gave way to buildings, mostly warehouses and shipyards initially. She brushed her hair back over her shoulder and watched the wine-coloured water.

'I think you want to find this Kaiku tu Makaima for more reasons than simply helping me deliver my message,' she stated.

Tane looked at her sidelong. She was still gazing out over the gunwale. He studied her profile; it was flawless. She truly was beautiful; and the curious thing was she seemed to grow more beautiful by the day. If anything, she seemed *too* perfect in aspect. Even the great beauties had imperfections: a freckle, or a slight unevenness about the lip, or the colours of their irises mottled slightly. The imperfection heightened their beauty by contrast. But Jin had not even that.

She puzzled him. She had proved herself during their conversations these past six days to be luminously intelligent and well-travelled. Coupled with her appearance, she had the world in her lap. He found it hard to imagine anything she could not do, any position she could not attain with ease if she had the will. Why, then, an Imperial Messenger? Why choose a dangerous and dusty road, always on the move, never settling? Who *was* she, in truth?

She turned to him expectantly then, and he realised she wanted an answer. He gave her none. Let her speculate as she liked. Even he could not fathom why he was following Kaiku's trail; only that she was the last destination left to him after his home was gone.

'Do you think we can find her?' he said at length.

'I can find this Mishani you spoke of with ease. She is Mishani tu Koli, daughter of Barak Avun. If Kaiku is with her, our task is that much easier.'

Tane nodded. He hoped he had not made a mistake in revealing what he knew to Jin; but he could scarcely have done otherwise. They were companions, at least for a short while, and he had no idea how to find someone in a city the size of Axekami without her. Still, his suspicions about her had hardly been eased by the apparent knowledge she displayed of the shin-shin, and led him to wonder once again about that strange light he had seen in her eyes back in the forest.

'We are safe from them, at least for the moment,' she had told him. 'Whatever brought them to your temple, they cannot track us on the water. They may guess where we are heading, and possibly follow us downstream on the north bank, but once near Axekami they will not come any closer. The city is the place of men, where spirits do not belong.'

'And they'll stop tracking us then?' Tane had asked.

'Shin-shin are persistent, and they do not let their prey go easily. But if they are tracking us at all, they may give up when we reach the city. Or they may wait outside and hope to pick up our trail again when we leave.'

Tane had wanted to ask her how an Imperial Messenger had learned so much about spirits and demons, but in the end he decided that he would rather not know.

The vast capital swelled around them, domes and spires and temples crowding together, hugging in close to the Kerryn. To the north, the land sloped upwards and the buildings rose with it, until it became too steep to build on and rose almost sheer in a great bluff, upon which stood the mighty Imperial Keep, its skin burnishing red-gold in the dust-hazed sunlight. The city streets were a canvas of tinted whites, weathered greens, columns and fountains and parks. Here a clutter of warehouses in the worst state of dereliction; there a gallery, a bell tower, a library, all elegant sweeps of stone and wood and inscribed in fine metals across their entranceways. An enormous prayer gate lunged across the border of the Imperial Quarter, a tall ellipse of stone and gold, its edges dazzling even in the muted rays of Nuki's eye.

To the south was the famous River District, where there were no roads but only canals, a place both exquisitely fashionable and extremely dangerous. It was as chaotic and beautiful as the rest of the city, only concentrated in a smaller area, with buildings of extraordinary design crowding over each other on tiny, irregular islands. The people that walked to and fro or were poled along the canals by puntmen were swathed in extravagant and impractical fashions, such as would make respectable society blush; but in the River District, nothing was too extreme.

Tane took it all in with wonder. He had been to Axekami before on odd occasions, but it still held the power to awe him. His world had been the quiet of the forests, where the only loud noise was the sharp crack of a hunting rifle or snap of a fire. Already he could hear the pummelling blanket of sound that came from the city; many thousand voices jabbering, the rattle of carts, the lowing of manxthwa as they plodded through the streets. The city seemed to seethe on the shores of the river, waiting to consume him as soon as he stepped away from the sanctuary of the barge, an inescapable din that might drive a man mad. Tane was afraid of it and desired it all at once.

The same, he thought, could be said of his future.

Kaiku knelt before the mirror in the sparsely furnished guest bedroom, and looked at herself. The face that returned the gaze seemed unfamiliar now, though the red of her irises had long faded back to their natural brown. The world had turned but once since she had learned of her condition, and yet it seemed she had forever been this way, a stranger to her own perceptions.

Outside she could hear the sounds of the servants returning from the burial. Mishani would be with them. Kaiku had not thought it appropriate to go.

She had not cried. She would not. *Keep the tears to quench the flame*, she had thought in a fanciful moment; but the truth was, she felt no sadness. Sorrow had belaboured her past the point of tolerance, and still it had not broken her back. It held no power over her now. Instead, she felt a hard point of bitterness in her breast, a small stone forming in the chambers of her heart like a polluted pearl inside an oyster. She was sick of sorrow, sick of pain. How could she trust anything now, even the evidence of her eyes and ears, when twenty harvests of safety and happiness had come and gone in her life only to be smashed aside in a single day of tragedy? How could she rely on anything again? Weighed against that, grief and remorse were useless. All that was left was giving up, or going on.

She chose the latter.

Mishani had closed herself up like a fan since the fire of yesterday afternoon. The blaze was mercifully checked quickly and caused little damage to the house, but the damage it had done to their relationship was immeasurable. Her once-friend was cold to her now, an impassive veneer rigidly locked in place. And though she did speak, her words were robbed of feeling, and it seemed that it took great effort to converse.

'You died, Kaiku,' she had said the previous day, in the wake of her accusation. 'It is not uncommon for Aberration to lay dormant for years, until something . . . wakes it up. All this time, you have carried it inside you and not known it.'

'How can you tell?' she had demanded, desperate to refute her host. 'You are not a priest; how can you tell? How can you tell what is inside me is not a demon, a malevolent spirit?'

Mishani turned away. 'We learned little of Aberrants from our tutors, you and I. They taught us manners, calligraphy, elocution; but not about Aberrants. They were not fit for polite young noblewomen like ourselves. But I have learned much since I have come to court, Kaiku, and I know how they preoccupy even the greatest of the high families.' She spoke quietly, as if fearing someone would overhear; though the lack of doors in most Saramyr houses meant that eavesdropping was severely frowned upon, and repeating what one heard was tantamount to obscenity. 'Our catches in Mataxa Bay grow more befouled by the year. Each haul brings in more three-clawed crabs, more fish with extra fins, more eyeless lobsters. Aberrations.'

Her voice was taut, suppressing disgust. The fact that Kaiku could tell at all meant that Mishani wanted her to know how she felt about it. In the background, Kaiku could hear the sounds of the servants racing to put out the fire she had started; the creaking of bucket handles, the slosh of water, shouts of alarm. They seemed impossibly distant.

'I have seen a girl in a village on my family's land,' she continued, her back to her visitor. 'She was hideous to look at, a freak of melted skin and hair, blind and lame. Where her hands touched, flowers grew. Even on skin, Kaiku. Even on metal. We found her being kept in a pen. She had killed her mother as an infant, after the poor woman allowed her daughter to feel her face. The mother's eyes were bored through by flower roots, and she choked on blossoms that grew in her mouth.' She paused, reluctant to go on; but she did so anyway. 'I have never seen a person possessed by a spirit, but I have seen and heard of many Aberrants, and I have heard of several who brought flame simply by being in a room. Most burned themselves to death; the rest were executed by the Weavers. They had two things in common, though, the fire-bringers. All were female. All of them had your eyes when the flames came. Your red eyes.' She faced Kaiku at last, and her gaze was hard and grave. 'Aberrants are dangerous, Kaiku. *You* are dangerous. What if I had been in that room with you?'

That had been yesterday. Since then, she had been left alone, given the bare minimum of attention by her host, given time to think on her condition. She had done a lot of thinking.

She could hear the weeping of the servants as they neared the house. Yokada, the servant girl who had been the only witness to Kaiku's condition as she escaped the fiery room, had died. It had been said she left a brazier burning in Kaiku's room, sparking the blaze. She had drunk poison last night, a suicide to atone for her crime. Kaiku doubted that the suicide was voluntary. She wondered if Yokada had even known she was drinking poison at all.

Mishani had grown ruthless in her time at court.

Kaiku had no illusions. Being at her lowest ebb afforded her a wonderfully clear perspective on things. Mishani had not been protecting her; she had been protecting herself. Blood Koli's standing would suffer terribly if it was found that they were harbouring an Aberrant. Worse, that the heir to the family had been fast friends with that unclean creature all through childhood and adolescence. The taint would be on Mishani's family then; they would be shunned. Their goods would fall in price, and stories about the strange fish in Mataxa Bay might start circulating. Kaiku's presence in their home was enough to ruin Blood Koli. Mishani could not risk the loose tongue of a servant girl undoing generations of empire-building.

Mishani came into the room without ringing the chime. She found Kaiku still sitting before the mirror. Kaiku turned her gaze to Mishani's reflection.

'My servants tell me you did not eat this morning,' she said.

'I feared to find something deadly in my food,' Kaiku replied, her manner chilly and excessively formal, her mode of address altered so that she spoke as if to an adversary.

Mishani betrayed no reaction. She met Kaiku's eyes in the mirror levelly, her small, thin face in amid the mass of black hair.

'I am not so monstrous that I would order your death, Kaiku, no matter what you have become.'

'Perhaps,' Kaiku replied. 'Or perhaps you have changed much these past years. Perhaps I never really knew you.'

Mishani was perturbed by this shift in character. Kaiku was not properly and rightfully ashamed of what she was; instead, her tone condemned Mishani for her lack of friendship, her lack of faith. Kaiku had always been stubborn and wilful, but to be an Aberrant was surely indefensible?

Kaiku stood and faced Mishani. She was a few inches taller than the other, and looked down on her now.

'I will go,' she said. 'That is what you came to ask, is it not?'

'I was not intending to *ask*, Kaiku,' Mishani replied. 'I have told you what I know about the Mask. It is better if you go to Fo and seek answers for yourself. You understand, I am sure.'

'I understand many things,' said Kaiku. 'Some less palatable than others.'

There was a long silence between them.

'It is a measure of our friendship that I have not had you killed, Kaiku. You know how dangerous to my family you are. You know that, by revealing yourself as an Aberrant, you could hurt us badly.'

'And be executed by the Weavers,' Kaiku retorted. 'I would not throw my life away like that. It is precious. You thought so too, once.'

'Once,' Mishani agreed. 'But things have changed.'

'*I* have not changed, Mishani,' came the reply. 'If I was ill with bone fever, you would have sat by me and nursed me even though you might have caught it yourself. If I was hunted by assassins, you would have protected me and used all your family's powers to keep me safe, though you yourself would have been endangered. But this . . . this you cannot condone. I am afflicted, Mishani. I did not choose to be Aberrant; how, then, can I be blamed for it by you?'

'Because I see what you are now,' she replied. 'And you disgust me.'

Kaiku felt the blow of her words as an almost physical pain. There was nothing else that needed to be said.

'There are clothes in that chest,' Mishani said. 'Food in the kitchens. Take what you will. In return, I ask this courtesy. Leave after sunset, that you may not be seen.'

Kaiku tilted her chin proudly. 'I ask no favours of you, nor will I grant any. I want only what is mine: my father's Mask, and the clothes and pack I came with. I will leave as soon as I have them.'

'As you wish,' Mishani replied. She paused then, as if she wanted to say something else; but the moment passed, and she left.

Kaiku walked boldly out of the front gate once the servants had brought her belongings. Barak Avun – Mishani's father – was away, so she was spared the dilemma of whether to thank him for his hospitality and bid him goodbye. She could feel the servants watching her leave. The sight of their noble lady's friend departing in trousers and boots – travelling clothes – was odd enough. Perhaps some of them also blamed Yokada's suicide on her. She cared little. They knew nothing of her affairs. They were only servants.

I have a purpose, she thought. *A destination. I will go to the Isle of Fo. There I will learn of the ones who killed my family.*

The afternoon was sweltering and muggy now that the sun had climbed clear of the obscuring red dust of the Surananyi, and so bright that her eyes narrowed unconsciously. The Imperial District's streets were as clean and wide and beautiful as ever. She had money in her pack. Her first destination would be the docks. She would not think about Mishani, nor about what had been done to her, until she was far away from this place. She would not look back.

She left the compound of Blood Koli, turned a corner into a narrow side-street sheltered by overhanging trees, and almost walked into Tane, coming the other way with a woman at his side.

Surprise paralysed them both for a moment, before Kaiku found her voice. 'Tane,' she said at last. 'Daygreet. Shintu's Luck, no?' The latter was a phrase expressing amazement at an unlikely coincidence – in this case, their meeting here.

'Not luck,' he replied. 'We have been searching for you. This is Jin, an Imperial Messenger.'

Kaiku turned to the woman who walked with him, and the colour drained out of her. The sound of the city birds chirruping in the trees lining the lane seemed to fade. She became aware that, in this narrow passageway, she was all but invisible to anyone on the main thoroughfare.

'Is something wrong?' Tane asked, putting a hand on her shoulder in concern. 'Are you ill?'

Kaiku's mind whirled in denial even as her senses bludgeoned her with their evidence. A subtle difference in the bone structure, in the hairline, the lips, the skin . . . but none of those mattered. She saw the eyes, and she recognised her. Impossible as it was, she recognised her.

'She is not ill,' said Jin, grabbing Kaiku by the front of the shirt and pulling her roughly so they were face to face, their noses almost touching. Tane was too startled to intervene. 'You know me, don't you, Kaiku?'

Kaiku nodded, suddenly terrified. 'Asara,' she breathed.

'Asara,' said the woman in agreement, and Kaiku felt the sharp prick of a blade at her belly.

TWELVE

The temple of Panazu towered over the River District of Axekami, its garish blue colliding with the greens and purples and whites and yellows of the surrounding buildings and overwhelming them with sheer grandeur. It rose tall, narrow in width but extending far back into the cluster of expensive and outrageously ostentatious dwellings that huddled on the small island of land. Steep, rounded shoulders of blue stone were swirled and crested like whirlpools and waves, and curved windows of sea-green and mottled silver glided elegantly across its façade. Panazu was the god of rain, storms and rivers, and so it made sense that here, where there were no roads but only canals, he should reign supreme.

The River District was an archipelago of buildings, sheared into irregular shapes by the passage of the canals that ran asymmetrically through the streets like cracks in a broken flagstone. It sat just south of the Kerryn, a florid clump of houses, gambling dens, theatres, shops and bars. Long ago it had been a simple heap of old warehouses and yards, convenient for storage of small items; but as Axekami grew and larger cargo barges began to arrive, the narrow canals and the small amount of space to build in the River District necessitated a move to larger, more accessible warehouses on the north side of the Kerryn. The River District became a haven for criminals and the lower-class element for many years, until a group of society nobles decided that the eccentricity of living in a place with no roads was too much to resist. The cheap land prices there triggered a sudden rush to buy, and within a decade large portions of the District had been swallowed by insane architectural projects, each newcomer trying to outdo his neighbours. The criminal element already present boomed with the new influx of wealthy customers; soon the drug hovels and seedy prostitution bars were replaced by exquisite dens and cathouses. The River District was for the young, rich and bored, the debauched and the purveyors of debauchery. It was a dangerous, cut-throat place; but the danger was the attraction, and so it flourished.

'I thought she was dead,' Kaiku said.

Tane looked over at her. Slats of light shining through the boards above drew bright stripes across her upturned face. The room was dark and swelteringly hot. It was the first thing she had said since Asara – the one he had called Jin – had left them here.

'Who is she?' Tane asked. He was sitting on a rough bench of stone, one of the square tiers that descended into a shallow pit at the centre of the room. This place had been a steam room, once. Now it was empty and the air tasted of disuse.

'I do not know,' Kaiku replied. She was standing on the tier below, on the other side of the pit. 'She was my handmaiden for two years, but I suppose I never knew who she was. She is something other than you see.'

'I had my suspicions,' Tane confessed. 'But she had the mark of the Imperial Messenger. It's death to wear that tattoo without Imperial sanction.'

'She was burned,' Kaiku said, hardly hearing him. 'I saw her face, burned and scarred. It is her and yet not her. She is . . . she is more beautiful than before. Different. I would say she was Asara's sister, or a cousin . . . if not for the eyes. But she was *burned*, Tane. How could she heal like that?'

Asara had been angry. Kaiku could still feel the press of her dagger against her skin, that first moment when they met outside Blood Koli's compound. For a fleeting instant, she had expected Asara to drive it home, thrust steel into muscle in revenge for what Kaiku had done to her.

But what *had* Kaiku done to her? Up until that moment, she had thought her uncontrollable curse had killed her saviour and handmaiden; now she found she had been mistaken. It was not an easy thing to accept.

'You left me to die there, Kaiku,' Asara said. 'I saved your life, and you left me to die.'

Tane had been too surprised to react until then, but at that moment he made a move to protest at Asara's handling of the one they had come to find.

'Stay there, Tane,' Asara hissed at him. 'I have given a lot to ensure this one stayed alive, and I will not kill her now. But I have no such compunctions about you, if you try and stop me. You would be dead before your hand reached your sword.'

Tane had believed her. He thought of the flash of light he had seen in her eyes back in the forest, and considered that he did not know who or what he was dealing with.

'I thought I had killed you,' Kaiku said, her voice calmer than she felt. 'I was scared. I ran.' She had considered adding an apology, then thought better of it. To apologise would be to admit culpability. She would not beg forgiveness for her actions, especially in the face of Asara's deceit.

'Yes, you ran,' Asara said. 'And were things otherwise I would hurt you for what you did to me. But I have a task, and you are part of it. Come with me.' She turned to Tane, her face still beautiful, even set hard as it was. 'You may accompany us, or go as you wish.'

'Where?' Tane replied, but he had already made up his mind. He would not abandon Kaiku like this.

'To the River District,' said Asara.

She had put her dagger away as they walked, warning both of them not to attempt escape. Neither had any intention of doing so. Though there was violence in her manner, they both sensed that Asara did not mean them actual harm. When Kaiku added up all she knew about Asara, she came to one conclusion: Asara had been trying to take her somewhere ever since the night her family died. If it had been kidnap she intended, she could have done it long ago. This was different. Kaiku was part of Asara's task, and she guessed that the task involved getting her to the River District of her own will. She could not deny more than a little curiosity as to *why*.

They had crossed the Kerryn at the great Gilza Bridge into the gaudy paveways that fronted the houses of the District. The sudden profusion of extravagance was overwhelming, as if the bridge formed a barrier between the city proper and this nether-city populated by brightly plumed eccentrics and painted creatures. Manxthwa loped past, laden with bejewelled bridles and ridden by men and women who seemed to have escaped from some theatrical asylum. There were no wheeled vehicles allowed here, even if they had been practical on the narrow paveways that ran between the stores and the canals, but the punts and tiny rowboats more than made up for them, explosions of colour against the near-purple water.

Asara had taken them to an abandoned lot behind a strikingly painted shop that proclaimed itself as a purveyor of narcotics. The lot was almost bare but for a low wooden building that had apparently been a steam room in days gone by, and an empty pool. All else was dusty slabs and the remnants of other, grander buildings.

'Wait here,' said Asara, ushering them into the old steam room. 'Do not make me come and find you. You will regret it.'

With that, she was gone. They heard the rasp of a lock-chain on the door, to further ensure that they stayed. She had answered none of their questions as they walked, shed no light on their destination. She merely left them in ignorance, for hours, until the sun was sinking into the west.

They talked in that time, Tane and Kaiku. Tane recounted the fate of the priests at the temple; Kaiku told him what they had learned of the origin of her father's Mask. But though conversation between them was as easy as it had been when they first knew each other, their guard was undiminished, and each held back things they did not say. Kaiku made no mention of her affliction, nor why Mishani had sent her away, nor what had passed between her and Asara back in the forest. Tane did not reveal how he felt about the death of the priests, the strange, growing excitement he was experiencing at being cast adrift and sent on some new destiny.

So they waited, and speculated, both curiously unafraid. Once Kaiku had surmounted the initial shock, she was happy to let these events unfold as they would. The worst that could happen was that she would be killed. Considering her condition, she wondered idly if that would not be for the best.

The beams of light coming through the overhead boards – once sealed with tar that had been stripped or decayed long ago – were slanted sharply, climbing the eastern wall, when the door opened and a stranger stepped into the hot shadows.

She was tall, a tower of darkness. Her dress was all in black, with a thick ruff of raven feathers across the shoulders. Twin crescents of dusk-red curved from her forehead, over her eyelids and down her cheeks; her lips were painted in red and black triangles, alternating like pointed teeth. Her hair, as dark as her clothes, flashed night-blue highlights in the shafts of sun, and was fashioned into two thick ponytails, side by side to spill down her back. A silver circlet adorned her brow, with a small red gem set into it.

She glided into the room, Asara following and closing the door behind them.

'Welcome,' she purred, her voice like cats' claws sheathed in velvet. 'I apologise for the venue, but secrecy is necessary here.'

'Who are you?' Tane demanded, studying her outlandish attire. 'A sorceress?'

'Sorcery is a superstition, Tane tu Jeribos,' she said. 'I am far more unpleasant. I am an Aberrant.'

Tane's eyes blazed, and he switched his wrath to Asara. 'Why have you brought her here?'

'Calm yourself, Tane,' Kaiku interceded, though she herself had felt a thrill of disgust at the mention of Aberrants, an ingrained reaction deeply at odds with her current position. 'Let us listen.'

Tane flashed a searing glare at the three women in the room, then snorted. 'I will not listen to the talk of one such as her.'

'Go, then,' Asara said simply. 'Nobody will stop you.'

Tane looked to the door, then back to Kaiku. 'Will you come?'

'She must stay,' said Asara. 'At least until she has heard what we have to say.'

'I will wait for you outside, then,' he said, and with that he stalked to the door and was gone.

'A friend of yours?' the tall lady asked Kaiku, with a faintly wry edge to her tone.

'It would seem so,' said Kaiku. 'Though who can say?'

The stranger smiled faintly in understanding. 'It is good that he has gone. I would have the things I am to discuss with you kept private, for your sake. He may come round, later.'

'Kaiku tu Makaima,' Kaiku said, introducing herself as a roundabout method of learning the name of the one she was addressing.

'I am Cailin tu Moritat, Sister of the Red Order,' came the reply. 'We have been watching you for quite some time.'

'So Asara told me,' Kaiku said, glancing at her former handmaiden. She had hinted as much in the forest, the morning after the shin-shin had come to their house, but Kaiku had not known who she meant until now. 'What do you want with me?'

Cailin did not answer directly. 'You are changing, Kaiku,' she said. 'I am sure you know that by now. Fires burn within you.'

Kaiku could not meet Asara's gaze, so she kept her eyes on Cailin. 'You know what they are?'

'I do,' she replied.

Kaiku ran a hand through her hair, suddenly nervous, fearing to ask her next question. Both stood on the lowest of the stone tiers, on opposite sides. She faced Cailin across the gulf of the stifling steam pit, the two of them striped by dusklight from outside. Motes danced in the air between them.

'Am I an Aberrant, then?'

'You are,' Cailin replied. 'Like myself, and like Asara. But do not attach so much weight to a word, Kaiku. I have known Aberrants who have taken their own lives in shame, unable to bear the burden of their title.' She looked down on Kaiku from within the red crescents painted on her face. 'You, I believe, are stronger than that. And I can teach you not to be ashamed.'

Kaiku regarded her with a calculating eye. 'What else can you teach me?'

Asara noted with approval the difference in manner between this Kaiku and the one she had dragged out of the burning house. She had suffered much, and learned many unpleasant truths; yet she was unbowed. Perhaps Cailin's faith in this one had been well founded.

'You do not know how to control what you have,' Cailin said. 'At the moment, it manifests itself as fire, as destruction; childish tantrums. I can teach you to tame it. I can help you do things you would never have dreamed.'

'And what would you ask in return?'

'Nothing,' came the reply.

'I find that hard to believe.'

Cailin stood very still as she spoke, a thin statue wrapped in shadow. 'The Red Order are few. The Weavers get to most of our potential candidates before we do; that, or they unwittingly burn themselves to death, or kill themselves in horror at what they are or what they have done. We teach them how to cope with what they have before it consumes them. They then choose their own path. Each of us is free to leave and pursue what lives we may. Some become like me, and teach others. I would teach you, Kaiku, before your power kills you or those around you; whether you then decide to join us is up to you. I would take that risk.'

Kaiku was unconvinced. She could not marry the appearance and manner of this lady with such apparent altruism. What *did* lie behind this offer of assistance, then? Was it simple narcissism? A desire to mould another in her image? Or was it something more than that?

'Is *she* one of you, this Red Order you speak of?' Kaiku asked, inclining her head towards Asara.

'No,' said Asara, and elaborated no further.

Kaiku sighed and sat down on the stone tier. 'Explain yourself,' she said to Cailin.

Cailin obliged. 'The Red Order is made up of those who have a specific Aberration. You have the power within you that we call *kana*. It manifests itself in different ways, but only to women. It is a privilege of our gender. Aberrations are not always random, Kaiku. Some crop up again and again, recurring over and over. This is one such. It is not a handicap or a curse, Kaiku; it is a gift beyond measure. But it is dangerous to the untrained.

'In recent years we have become skilled at finding those who carry the power, even when it has not manifested itself. Some display the power early, in infancy; they are usually caught by the Weavers and executed. But some, like yourself, only find your talent when it is triggered, by trauma or extreme passion. You have great potential, Kaiku; we knew that some time ago.'

'You sent Asara to watch me,' Kaiku said, piecing the puzzle together. 'To wait until I manifested this . . . *kana*. And then she was to bring me to you.'

'Exactly. But events conspired against us, as you know.'

Kaiku let her head fall, her forearms crossed over her knees. A moment later, the short wings of brown hair began shaking as she laughed softly.

'Something is amusing you?' Cailin asked, her voice edged with a brittle frost.

'Forgive me,' she said around her mirth, raising her head. 'All this tragedy . . . all that has happened to me, and now you are offering me an *apprenticeship*?'

'I am offering to save your *life*,' Cailin snapped. She did not appear to appreciate the humour.

Kaiku's laughter trailed away. She cocked her head elfishly and regarded Cailin. 'Your offer intrigues me, have no doubt. There seems to be a great deal I do not know, and I am eager to learn. But I cannot accept.'

'Ah. Your father,' Cailin said, the chill in her voice deepening.

'I swore vengeance to Ocha himself. I cannot put aside my task for you. I will travel to Fo, and find the maker of my father's Mask.'

'You still have it?' Asara asked in surprise. Kaiku nodded.

'May I see it?' Cailin asked.

Kaiku was momentarily reluctant, but she drew it from her pack anyway. She walked around the tier and handed it to Cailin.

A breath of hot wind stirred the still air inside the abandoned steam room, shivering the feathers of Cailin's ruff as she studied it.

'Your power is dangerous,' she said, 'and it will either kill you or get you killed before long. I offer you the chance to save yourself. Turn away now, and you may not live to get a second chance.'

Kaiku gazed at her for a long time. 'Tell me about the Mask,' she said.

Cailin looked up. 'Did you not hear what I said?'

'I heard you,' Kaiku said. 'My life is my own to risk as I choose.'

Cailin sighed. 'I fear your intransigence will be the end of it, then,' she said. 'Allow me to offer you a proposal. I see you are set on this foolishness. I will tell you about this Mask, if you will promise to return to me afterwards and hear me out.'

Kaiku inclined her head in tacit agreement. 'That depends on what you can tell me.'

Cailin gave her a slow look, appraising her, taking the measure of her character, searching for deceit or trickery therein. If she found anything there, she did not show it; instead, she handed the Mask back to Kaiku.

'This Mask is like a map. A guide. Where it came from is a place that you cannot find, a place hidden from the sight of ordinary men and women. This will show you the way. Wear it when you are close to your destination, and it will take you to its home.'

'I see no profit in being cryptic, Cailin,' Kaiku said.

'It is the simple truth,' she replied. 'This Mask will breach an invisible barrier. The place you are seeking will be hidden. You will need this to find it. That is all I can tell you.'

'It is not enough.'

'Then perhaps this will help. There is a Weaver monastery somewhere in the northern mountains of Fo. The paths to it were lost long ago. It would have been considered to have disappeared, but for the supply carts that come regularly to the outpost village of Chaim. They deliver masks from the Edgefathers at the monastery, untreated masks for theatre, decoration and such. They trade them for food and other, more unusual items.' She gave a dismissive wave of her hand. 'Go to Chaim. You may find there what you are looking for.'

Kaiku considered for a moment. That jibed with Copanis's guess, at least. 'Very well,' she said. 'If what you say proves to be true, then I will return to you, and we can talk further.'

'I doubt you will live that long,' Cailin replied, and with that she stalked out, leaving Kaiku and Asara alone.

Asara was smiling faintly in the hot darkness. 'You know she could have made you stay.'

'I suspect she wants me willing,' Kaiku said.

'You have quite a stubborn streak, Kaiku.'

Kaiku did not bother to reply to that. 'Are we finished here?' she said instead.

'Not yet. I have a request,' Asara said. She brushed the long, red-streaked fall of her hair back behind her shoulder and set her chin in an arrogant tilt. 'Take me with you to Fo.'

Kaiku's brow furrowed. 'Tell me why I should, Asara.'

'Because you owe me that much, and you are a woman of honour.'

Kaiku was unconvinced, and it showed.

'I have deceived you, Kaiku, but never betrayed you,' she said. 'You need not be afraid of me. You and I have a common objective. The circumstances behind your family's death interest me as much as you. I would have died along with you if the shin-shin had been quicker, and I owe somebody a measure of revenge for that. And need I remind you that you would not even have that Mask if not for me, nor your life? The breath in your lungs is there because *I* put it there.'

Kaiku nodded peremptorily. 'I wonder that you are not telling me your true reasons. I do not trust you, Asara, but I do owe you,' she said. 'You may come with me. But you will not have my trust until you have earned it anew.'

'Good enough,' Asara replied. 'I care little for your trust.'

'And Tane?' Kaiku asked. 'You brought him here. What about him?'

'Tane?' Asara replied. 'I needed his boat. He is a little backward, but not unpleasant. He will come, if you let him, Kaiku. He seeks the same answers we do; for whoever sent the shin-shin to kill your family were also responsible for the slaughter at his temple.'

Kaiku looked at Asara. For a moment she felt overwhelmed, swept along by the pace of events as if on a wave, unable to stop herself from hurtling headlong into the unknown. She surrendered herself to it.

'Three of us, then,' she said. 'We will leave in the morning.'

The estates of Blood Amacha stood between the great tines of a fork in the River Kerryn, many miles east of Axekami. There the flow from the Tchamil Mountains divided, sawn in half by the inerodable rock formations that lanced from the earth in jagged rows. Passing to the north of them, as almost all traffic did, the Kerryn became smoother, fish more plentiful, and there was only a trouble-free glide downstream to the mighty capital of Axekami. To the south, however, the new tributary was rough and treacherous: the River Rahn, shallow and fast and little-travelled.

The Rahn flowed east of Blood Amacha's estates before curving into the broken lands of the Xarana Fault, and there shattering into a massive waterfall. Only the most adventurous travellers, in craft no bigger than a canoe, might be able to negotiate the falls by carrying their boat down the stony flanks to the less dangerous waters beneath; but the Xarana Fault had its own perils, and not many dared to enter that haunted place. The Fault effectively shut off all river travel between Axekami and the fertile lands to the south, forcing a lengthy coastal journey instead.

From the fork in the rivers, the rocky spines gentled into hills, tiered with earthen dams and flooded. Paddy fields of saltrice lapped down the hillside in dazzling scales. Cart trails ran between them, and enormous irrigation screws raised water from the river to supply the fields. Atop the highest hill sprawled the home of Blood Amacha, an imposing litter of buildings surrounding an irregularly shaped central keep. The keep had high walls built of grey stone, and was tipped with towers and sloping roofs of red slate. It was constructed to take advantage of the geography of the hilltop, with one wing dominating a rocky crag while another lay low against the decline of the land, where the wall that circumscribed the building did not need to be quite so high. The buildings clustered around it were almost uniformly roofed in red, and many were constructed using dark brown wood to follow the colours of the Amacha standard.

West of the keep, the hills flattened out somewhat, and here there were no paddy fields but great orchards, dark green swathes pocked with bright fruit: oranges, likiri, shadeberry, fat purple globes of kokomach. And beyond that . . . beyond that, the troops of Blood Amacha drilled on the plains, an immensity of brown and red armour and shining steel, five thousand strong.

They trained in formations, vast geometric assemblies of pikemen, riflemen, swordsmen, cavalry. In the sweltering heat of the Saramyr midday, they grunted and sweated through mock combats, false charges, retreats and regroups. Even in their light armour of cured, toughened leather, they performed admirably under the punishing glare of Nuki's eye, their formations fluid and swift. Metal armour was impractical for combat in Saramyr: the sun was too fierce for most of the year, and the heat inside a full suit of the stuff would kill a man on the battlefield. Saramyr soldiers fought without headgear; if they wore anything at all, it was a headband or bandanna to protect themselves from sunstroke. Their combat disciplines were based on speed and freedom of movement.

Elsewhere, swordsmasters led their divisions in going through the motions of swordplay, demonstrating sweeps, parries, strokes and maneouvres, and then chaining them all together into sequences of deadly grace, their bodies dancing sinuously around the flickering points of their blades. Fire-cannons were targeted at distant boulders, and their bellowing report rolled across the estates. Ballistae were tested and their capacities gauged.

Blood Amacha was gearing up for war.

Barak Sonmaga tu Amacha rode solemnly through the heat and dust of the drilling ground, his ears ringing to the rousing cries of battle all around him, the barked commands and the tumultuous responses of the training groups. The air smelt of sweat and damp leather, of horses and the sulphurous reek of fire-cannons and rifle discharges. He felt his chest swell, his pride a balloon that expanded inside him. Whatever his misgivings, whatever his fears for the land he loved, he could not help but feel overwhelmed by the knowledge that five thousand troops stood ready to give their lives at his command. Not that he appreciated their loyalty – after all, it was their duty, and duty along with tradition were the pillars on which their society was built – but the feeling of sheer *power* that it brought on made him feel close to the gods.

He had spent the morning making inspections, conferring with his ur-Baraks and generals, giving speeches to the troops. His decision to make them train without a break all through the hottest part of the day was heartily approved of by his subordinates, for the soldiers needed to be able to fight under any conditions. Not that the Barak had expected any dissent even if they had disagreed; the discipline of the Saramyr armies was legend, and Sonmaga was not accustomed to having his orders questioned.

Seized by a suddenly poetic mood, he spurred his horse and angled through the rows of soldiers towards the keep that sat distantly to the east, made pale and half real by graduated veils of sunlight. But it was not the keep that was his destination; instead, after a short ride, he reined in some way up the hillside that looked out over the dusty plains, and there he dismounted.

He was standing on a low bluff, where a short flap of rock had broken through the even swell of the hillside to provide level ground. Behind him and a little way upward were the first dry-stone walls that marked the edge of his orchards, and beyond that the grassy soil was subsumed in a mass of leaves and trunks and roots and fruit. He left his horse to crop the grass and walked out on to the bluff, and there he surveyed the arrayed masses of his troops.

The size of the spectacle took his breath away, but more humbling was the vastness of the plains that made even his army seem insignificant. The massive formations of men seemed antlike in comparison, their magnificence outshone by the world around them. The sky was a perfect jewel-blue, untroubled by cloud. The flow of the Kerryn was a blinding streak of maddening brightness, twinkling and winking in the fierce light of Nuki's eye, tracing its unstoppable path towards Axekami, which was hidden beneath the horizon. The plains were dotted with clusters of trees, dirt roads, the occasional settlement here and there; Sonmaga fancied he could see a herd of banathi making its slow way across the panorama, but heat haze made his vision uncertain.

Sonmaga offered a silent prayer of thanks to the gods. He was not a tender man, but what softness he had he reserved for moments like these. Nature awed him. This land awed him, and he loved it. His gaze swept over the tiny formations of his troops below, and he felt his doubts dissipate. Whatever came of this, he would know that he had done what his heart dictated. There were greater matters at play than thrones here.

He did not deny to himself that he wanted power. To elevate Blood Amacha to the ruling family would enshrine his name forever in history, and the honour would be immense. But a coup would be enacted on *his* terms, *his* way. He did not want a civil war, not now. The time was not right; it was too precipitate. Events had conspired to force his hand.

But there was a higher motive for victory than simple power. Sonmaga's deep, abiding love for the land made him sensitive to it, and the blight he saw creeping into the bones of the earth scarred him deeply. He saw the evidence even in his own orchards, the decline that was too gradual to spot until he compared tallies over the years and saw that more and more fruit was spoiling on the branch, more trees withering or coming up twisted. Though the blight had barely brushed his lands when compared to some other, less fortunate areas, he felt an unholy abhorrence of it, as if the corruption crept slowly into him as well as the soil. And then there were the Aberrants, children of the blight, born to peasants on his land; and he feared that if the time should come that he would marry and father a child, it might turn out like them, mewling and deformed and terrible. He would snap its neck himself if he saw a child of his born Aberrant.

And now, Lucia. The Heir-Empress, an Aberrant? There could be no greater affront to the gods, to nature, to simple *sense*. Now was not the time for *tolerance* of these creatures – a tolerance that would surely increase if Lucia reached the throne. They were symptoms of an evil that was killing Saramyr, and to encourage them to thrive was lunacy.

No, the desire for power would not have been enough to make Sonmaga war against his Empress, not at this juncture. But to arrest the progress of the poison in the land? For that, he would dare almost anything.

He brought out the letter in his pocket and read over it again, the letter that had been sealed with the stamp of Barak Avun tu Koli, and wondered if he might not be able to turn things around yet.

THIRTEEN

The isle of Fo lay off the sloping north-western coast of Saramyr, a day's travel across the red-tinged waves of the Camaran Channel. The wind had freshened as the afternoon wore on, and it cooed and whistled through the ratlines of the enormous junk, rippling the sails that sprouted from its back like the spined fins of some magnificent sea creature. The *Summer Tide* was a merchant vessel belonging to the wealthiest trading consortium in Jinka, and it showed. Her gunwale was moulded into the likeness of stormy waves, chasing each other from bow to stern, and in amongst them frolicked seals and whales, sea-spirits and imaginary beasts of the deep. The sails were a magnificent array, with polished wooden ribs holding great fans of beige canvas between them, and painted with the red sigil of the consortium. It was a thing of beauty, carrying a cargo of beautiful things: silks, perfumes, spices; and several passengers, two of whom were watching the desolate isle draw ever closer.

Kaiku was lounging against the thick oaken rail on the foremost deck, her feathered hair whipping restlessly against her tanned cheeks. It was not especially ladylike; but then, neither were her clothes, and she had ever been a tomboy. She wore trousers of heavy, baggy fabric and soft boots wound around with leather to keep them tight. In addition, she had on a light shirt of blue, wrapped right over left – men wore their shirts the opposite way – and belted around her waist with a sash of red. She felt the sun on her skin and flexed like a cat, luxuriating in the warmth. Tane, standing nearby, watched her with a hungry eye.

A week had passed since they had left Axekami and taken a barge upriver to Jinka. Upriver travel was necessarily slower on craft that had no sails, but the Jabaza's current was not strong at this time of year, and the barge had plenty of wheelmen hired. These swarthy folk rarely came up on deck; their journey was spent in the treadmills at the hot heart of the barge, turning the massive paddle-wheels that powered the craft against the flow. For three days they had watched the flattened peak of Mount Makara rise slowly from the horizon, until it bulked vast among the surrounding mountains, a pale blue-green, and they could see the wisps of smoke that issued from its volcanic maw.

That leg of the journey, from Axekami up the Jabaza, had been easy and pleasant, and the weather was good; yet Tane's recollection of it was polluted with disgust. For it had not been an entirely uneventful trip. Among the passengers on the *Summer Tide* had been a Weaver on his way to Jinka.

The Weaver had a separate cabin at the back of the boat, where he spent almost all his time. There was a cabin boy who saw to his needs, a fresh-faced lad of twelve years or so that brought in his food and took out his chamber-pot. His name was Runfey, and he was an ever-smiling presence aboard the barge, his high laugh often heard across the deck.

One day, as dusk approached, Kaiku was stricken with a sudden faintness. Tane was with her at the time; Asara was elsewhere, alone, as she usually preferred.

Kaiku had moaned aloud as her head went light; then she seemed to notice Tane, and fell quiet. Tane could not help feeling galled at the way she clammed up, hoarding whatever secret she kept. He did not pretend to understand her, but he sat with her until the faintness passed. Twenty minutes later, the noises began.

Kaiku had gone to lie down, and Tane was out alone, watching the moons rise as the darkness deepened. The river was a peacefully undulating abyss picked out in Iridima's light. The only sound was the sighing lap of the water against the hull of the barge, and the creak of her timbers. Tane had felt strangely peaceful then, calmer than he had been for a long time, even back in the forest when he had been trying to master his meditations.

The shrieking and raging started all of a sudden, coming from the Weaver's cabin. Tane moved closer, curious. The Weaver seemed to be in a fit of terrible anger, smashing things and throwing himself around inside. Two guards posted at his door made no attempt to disperse the small crowd of sailors that gathered at the noise, but they would let no one in. No one except Runfey.

He was brought by another guard, led by the arm to the Weaver's door. He was not struggling, but the naked fear in his eyes as they met Tane's would haunt him for a long time afterward. The guards opened the door, and all went quiet inside, a predatory kind of silence that made Tane cold. Then they put Runfey in there, and closed the door behind him.

Tane and six of the sailors stood there that night, and heard the screams of Runfey as the Weaver vented his anger on the boy. They heard him beg and plead as he was battered, heard him shriek and wail as other tortures were visited on him that Tane could only guess at, heard him cry out as he was raped repeatedly. Two hours they stood there as witnesses to the horrors that were carried out in that cabin, while their vile guest's post-Weaving rage exhausted itself. None would move, for it would be an unpardonable shame to turn their backs; and yet none dared intervene, either.

Only when silence fell did Tane leave to pray. He was still praying in the dead of night, when he heard the splash of something heavy tipped overboard. They saw no more of Runfey. Nobody spoke of it again. The next day it was business as usual, and Kaiku was still not even aware anything had happened. Tane had elected not to tell her; it would do no good to anyone.

After that, they had turned west into the Abanahn Canal. Tane felt an unfamiliar sweep of patriotic pride at the sight. He had heard of it only in tales: a vast man-made waterway that connected the Jabaza with the coast, one of the mightiest feats of engineering in Saramyr. Enormous walls of white stone rose on either side, dotted with towers and gates and locks. Immense mechanisms with cogs that were half the size of their barge lay dormant, but Tane had heard how they could be used to raise impenetrable gates to prevent enemies sailing up the canal from the sea and reaching the interior of Saramyr. They passed beneath a curved prayer gate of monolithic size, arcing from one side of the canal to the other, its inscription offering the blessing of Zanya, goddess of travellers. In both directions sailed such a profusion of gaudy boats and barges that Tane spent all his daylight hours on the deck, watching them in amazement as a child watches a procession. Moments like this reminded him how painfully limited his life had been until now, spent almost exclusively in the Forest of Yuna.

What he saw of Jinka was even more hectic than the streets of Axekami. They disembarked at the docks amid the babble of hundreds of labourers, the creak and groan of pulleys and thick ropes as they unloaded crates and bales, the raucous laughter of sailors in the taverns. The Weaver had gone about his business elsewhere, while Asara took them to a boat master she professed to know. The boat master did not appear to remember her, but after a few words in private, he beamed and said he would be delighted to arrange them transport. Asara kept her silence.

And so they had stayed the night in a clean and respectable temple inn. Temple inns were resting places owned by the priesthood of one god or another, and the only place they were unlikely to be bothered by prostitutes or drunks or cut-throats while staying in the docks. Tane had fretted to himself about the shin-shin, unable to dispel their memory and remembering Asara's comment about how the demons might track them when they left the safety of the capital. But they had entered Axekami by water and left by water, and it seemed that their trail had gone cold. Nothing disturbed them that night.

When dawn came they were taken to the *Summer Wind*, and set sail for Fo.

Tane leaned against the railing now, next to Kaiku. She was radiant in the westering light. Not so beautiful as Jin – *Asara*, he corrected himself – but possessed of some different kind of attraction, and one that was stronger. Perhaps it was something to do with the way he had met her, her total vulnerability. She had appealed to his need to heal, and he had nursed her strength back. Perhaps it was their similarities: both had lost their families, both had their secrets. Or perhaps it was something altogether different.

Lucia dreamed.

Her dreams had always been strange, informed as they were by subconscious nonsense-whispers emanating from the life that surrounded her. When she dreamed, she heard the slow, childlike thoughts of the trees in the roof garden, the rapid and unintelligible gibber of the wind, the obsessively focused ravens and the impossibly ancient ruminations of the hill upon which the Keep stood, for whom the completion of a single thought would take longer than a human lifetime. It was never silent for Lucia, and the sounds all around her translated into strange images when she slept.

She had stopped dream-walking entirely of late. The unseen presence that had suddenly begun to stalk her was too frightening, and too dangerous. She felt its monstrous attention gnawing at the edges of her consciousness even now, however. It was ravenous, hungry, frustrated by her elusiveness. She would not let it catch her.

Over the year since she had begun exploring the Keep in her dreams, she had learned to control her abilities somewhat. Whereas at first she had no say over where she would find herself when she closed her eyes, and was only a spectator to her own wanderings, she had soon divined how to guide herself, and how to choose which places to visit. More importantly, she learned how *not* to dream-walk, so that she could suppress it if she wanted and sleep untroubled. She rarely felt rested after a night wandering the Keep's corridors in her mind; but in those early days, her curiosity about the world outside her prison kept her going back again and again. By day, she was a rumour among the folk of the Keep; by night, she was a ghost.

But other things had changed, too. Whatever it was that she had set in motion when she had given a lock of her hair to the man in the garden, it was gathering pace, and she felt it daily.

She dreamed that she stood on the edge of a high, rocky crag, a great promontory that dropped away hundreds of feet to jagged rocks below. The landscape spread out and away beneath her, an impossible chaos of ridges and shattered stone, tree-choked valleys and plateaux. It was thick with spirits down there, invisible in their hollows, and they cooed and whispered to each other in the night.

The night. The three moons hung before her in a velvet sky, so close that they were overlapping. Aurus seemed near enough to touch, looming immense in the star-pocked darkness. She was not in the least perturbed by the impossibility of the three moons being in such close proximity without the howling maelstrom of a moonstorm lashing the land. With the easy logic of sleep, she knew that it was simply not the right time yet.

She sensed the dream lady watching her before she turned to look. The sloping table of rock she stood on jutted out from a thick wood, and in the shadows of the treeline she could see the blurred, unclear shape of the mysterious stranger. She was a smear of black and white, a child's charcoal drawing, stretched thin and tall with a cloak folded close around her like a bat's wings. Always too far away to see clearly, always evading Lucia's sight. This one had found her when the unseen monster could not; but Lucia was not afraid of the dream lady. There was no malice there, only an unsettling intensity. Often she was simply present on the sidelines of Lucia's dreams, watching silently from some distant point, a rooftop or a cavern, her gaze unwavering as she followed the Heir-Empress. Sometimes she spoke, and though Lucia did not like her voice, her words were very clear and she told Lucia things about the world outside. Lucia, desperately curious, would converse whenever she could with the dream lady; but often the newcomer would not reply, would simply watch her disconcertingly, always from far away. Lucia did not know what to make of it all, but she had the impression that the dream lady told Lucia exactly as much as she wanted the young Heir-Empress to know, and nothing more.

Still, as time went on, she learned who and what the dream lady was, and she began to think of her as a strange kind of friend.

Tonight she was not talking, it seemed. She hung in the shadows, a half-seen haze, and stared. Lucia ignored her. She had learned by now that it was pointless doing anything else. Distractedly, she sensed the unseen malevolence, hunting for her again. It was far away, and no threat to her here.

There was no sound but the sigh of the cool wind and the calling of the spirits in the cracked landscape below. Lucia wandered to the edge and looked down, her blonde hair tumbling over her shoulder. When she turned back, the dream lady was gone.

It gave her a fright. She was quite accustomed to the dream lady's visits, but her sudden disappearances were always a surprise. Before, she had only ever vanished when the dark presence that stalked her had become too strong, got too close. She had told Lucia she must stay away from the presence, must not let herself be detected. Lucia had accepted that, but when she asked what the presence was, the dream lady would not say.

Now, however, the air seemed to become light, taking on a coppery taste, and the fine hairs on Lucia's skin stood up. She felt as if she was being lifted, dragged upward towards the sky, though her feet remained firmly on the ground. The atmosphere had become charged, and the spirits hidden in the panorama beneath her had gone silent.

She felt a hand touch her on her shoulder, far bigger than any human hand, thin white fingers tipped with hooked nails. Her heart seemed to slow to a stop. She did not dare turn around. She could feel them, their presence making her consciousness crawl. Ageless, endless, mad things, the three sisters that stalked the earth when the three satellites shared space in the night sky. The Children of the Moons.

The touch was both dreadful and divine, filling her with terror and awe in equal measure. She squeezed her eyes shut, knowing that behind her there was no ground to stand on, that the spirits hung in the air over the precipice, massive and cold and fearful. She could not bear to look at them, could not face the depthless void of their eyes, where motivations boiled that were as alien to humanity as the gods were. And though some part of her knew this to be a dream, it brought her no comfort; for dreams were no refuge from beings such as these.

Words were spoken, but they came as an awful, thin, sawing noise, making Lucia shudder. She could not hope to comprehend them. She trembled, bowing her head, her lower lip shaking and her eyes screwed firmly closed.

Then they were before her instead of behind, the three of them looming, and though she could not see them she could *feel* their outlines through her eyelids. She felt something brush the side of her hair, and she shivered. A fingernail. It brushed her again, infusing her anew with panic and wonder, the strange current that passed into her from the contact. It took her a breathless moment to realise what the spirit was doing. It was stroking her, using only a single finger, as a person might do to a delicate animal, or a mother to a newborn baby. Gentling her. The voice came again, and once more it was horrible to the ear; but this time softer somehow, a tonal quality that transcended language and meaning.

Lucia did not know what they wanted. She did not even know if *wanting* was a concept that applied to them. But she said a tiny prayer to the moon sisters, and then opened her eyes, and looked upon their children.

The Imperial bedchamber was shadowy and quiet. Warm night breezes blew in through elegantly curved window arches, stirring the thin veils that hung before them. Against one wall, the enormous bed was a rolling landscape of opalescent sheets, gold and white and crimson. At each corner stood one of the Guardians of the Four Winds, carved in precious metals and reaching up to hold aloft the canopy that roofed the whole of the grand structure.

Anais tu Erinima, Blood Empress of Saramyr, stood by a dresser of finest wood, leaning gently against the wall with a silver cup of amber wine in her hand. Her light hair was loose, falling about her deceptively innocent face and over the shoulders of the black silk nightdress she wore. The jet-coloured *lach* of the floor was cold against her bare soles – apart from its reflective properties, *lach* was a stone valued for its reluctance to take up heat, and hence keep a room cool.

She sipped her wine and waited, nursing her fury.

How she hated him. As if the Emperor Durun had not been enough of a trial before, this business with Lucia had made him a hundred times worse. He seemed to be going out of his way to anger and humiliate her. His drunkenness, always apt to get a little out of hand, was appalling now. He caroused at feasts, bawling and vomiting until even his hunting companions seemed uneasy. The hunts themselves were a mercy, because they got him out of the Keep for a few days at a time; but he used them as an excuse to stand up important guests and often reeled home in a worse state than he had left.

She seethed as she thought on it. At least she had the small revenge that his family, Blood Batik, had thrown their support behind her at the council. But this in itself was a double-edged sword. If Blood Batik had declared against her, she would at least have had the comfort of annulling her marriage to Durun; now she was forced to suffer him, for she could not do without the support of his family. Durun was too stubborn and bullheaded to toe the family line in this matter, and his frustration was evident. He and his father Barak Mos – a firebrand to equal his son – had bellowed at each other often in the past weeks, but each confrontation only sent Durun away with a renewed desire to embarrass himself. After that, the Barak had come as near as he ever came to apologising to Anais, asking her to forgive his son's transgressions and promising to make up for them in the future. Anais knew how much it had taken for him to overcome his not inconsiderable pride to do this, and she was touched; but it did not abate her anger one bit.

Durun's indiscretions with the ladies of the Keep had been an open secret for years now. Usually he preferred the younger ones; impressionable daughters of minor nobles who were visiting court, too flattered by the Emperor's attentions to think of the consequences. Other times he laid with servants who dared not say no to him. Sometimes he brought whores from the cathouses into the Keep. At first it had only been on rare occasions, and Anais had tolerated it. This was not a marriage of passion, but of politics; she was happy to do anything to make it more endurable. But gradually he had become less discreet, and the rumours began.

Anais initially felt humiliated by the whole affair, bound by the notion that she should be good enough at bedplay to keep him on her pillow; but then, as always, she had not been in a position where she could do Blood Batik the grievous insult of divorcing their favourite son. The strength her marriage provided was what had got Blood Erinima to where it was, and she could not throw it away, not even when their vows were being so flagrantly abused.

Eventually, she ceased to care. Let him do as he would. In the main, she was indifferent to him as a husband anyway. Sometimes, just sometimes, when he turned the bright flame of his passions on to something worthwhile – or more rarely, on to her – she saw a glimpse of the man he might have been, the marriage as it could be. But those moments were too brief and far between; only enough to frustrate her with possibilities. He wasted himself on idiot passions, fighting and drinking and whoring.

But now Durun had gone too far.

Tonight he had come back from a hunt, roaring drunk, and ordered a feast for himself and his companions. There in the hall they had made pigs of themselves and swilled wine. Durun, flushed with triumph at killing a boar single-handed, had been even more out of control than he usually was. When one of the servants had come to pour him another drink – a simple, slender and plain-faced girl whose lack of wit or beauty was made up for by a disproportionately large chest – he pulled her around him and on to the table, scattering greasy food and cups of wine, and had her there. Anais's handmaiden, whom she had charged with delivering a message to the Emperor when he returned from the hunt, walked in then. She found him between the legs of the servant girl, her breasts exposed between the torn halves of her shirt, gasping with each thrust while Durun's hunting companions gathered round and cheered. She had reported a slightly less graphic version of events to the Empress.

Anais was livid. Rumours were one thing; people could pretend to ignore them. But this was intolerable. The Emperor of Saramyr, rutting like an animal in a hall full of servants and the sons of nobles, flouting his infidelity for all to see. It was more than she could bear.

The heavy, unsteady footsteps that approached the bedroom door heralded the arrival of her wayward husband. He pushed the door open and lumbered through unsteadily. With his sharp, knifelike features, his bearing was proud and haughty even in such a state as he was. He saw Anais standing by the dresser, and shut the door behind him. Brushing back the long fall of fine black hair – spotted with grease and matted with wine now – he raised an eyebrow at her.

'Wife,' he said. 'You seem angry.'

She crossed the room in three strides and threw the cup of wine in his face.

'You disgusting excuse for a man!' she hissed.

He sputtered, instinctively backhanding the silver cup out of her grip. It clashed and clattered across the *lach* floor and rolled to a stop. She slapped him, hard. He recoiled, more surprised than hurt. She hit him again, more violently this time. A small part of her was telling her that an empress should not act this way, but the wine and her pent-up fury overrode it. She was seized by the need to hurt him, encouraged by her first assaults; and she hit him again, and again, pounding against him with her fists.

He shook off his initial bewilderment as the pain seeped through his drink-fogged brain. Anais's next blow was arrested by a black-gloved hand, seizing her wrist. Instinctively, she struck with the other one, but he caught that too, holding her arms apart. She struggled desperately against him, suddenly wanting to escape. She saw the blaze in his eyes and feared she had gone too far. He was much larger and stronger than her, and he held her with effortless ease.

'Let go of me!' she hissed. 'Bastard!'

His dark eyes threatened her with pain, and she twisted to be out of his grip; then suddenly he was lifting her up by her arms, slamming her against the wall hard enough to knock the breath from her.

'Heart's blood, Anais,' he husked. 'It's been too long since you've had this kind of fight in you.'

And then he was kissing her, hard and savagely, biting her lips and her tongue. She struggled against him, making sounds of protest through her nose; he slammed her against the wall again.

'Now will you behave?' he demanded.

She sagged. 'Bastard,' she said again, but there was no strength in it. He stepped back and let her go. She regarded him for a time in the shadows, her eyes baleful and wary all at once. Spirits, she truly hated him; but she wanted him as well. It was only his heart and mind that were weak and stupid; when he towered over her like this, when she was at bay before him, she could imagine that he was the powerful, dangerous man she had wished for a husband, instead of the indolent sluggard that she got.

Well, why shouldn't she take what pleasure she could from him? She got so little else. And she only needed his body . . .

Surging forward, she grabbed his head, her fingers like claws at the back of his skull, drawing him into a kiss as brutal as the one he had given her. She tasted wine on his breath, mingled with other things less pleasant, but it did nothing to dampen her suddenly awakened ardour. He shoved her against the wall again, and this time she saw the animal lust on his face. He did not want *her*, not specifically; he wanted woman, any woman. Well, that would suit her. She wanted a man, and he would do for now.

Grabbing the front of her nightdress, he tore it half away in one great swipe. She had braced herself against it, but she was still overwhelmed by his strength, pulled into him by the force. He pushed her back again, and with a second effort he rent it from her completely. She stood before him, her pale and slender form naked in the shadows, her small, hard breasts rising and falling with her breath. Then they fell to each other.

Their congress was rough and forceful, each using the other's body without thought of tenderness. Anais tore her husband's clothes away as eagerly as he had hers, running her hands over the taut muscles of his body and the thin covering of fat overlaying them, the legacy of too much drink and rich food. He thrust into her over and again as they rolled across the bed, each seeking the dominant position. Finally she pinned him down and he relented. She drove herself against him faster and faster. For all that he was drunk, and all his many failings, he still possessed a certain endowment beyond that of most men. In the morning they would be as they always were, argumentative and spiteful; but for now, with the weight of the realm on her shoulders and more worries than she could count, she took the passion she craved so desperately, and found her release therein.

She wanted to tell him that she hated him but the words, when they came in the throes of orgasm, were quite the opposite.

FOURTEEN

When the night came, Asara hunted.

They had arrived in the port of Pelis before sunset, the crossing made swift by favourable winds. The folded sails and rigging of the other junks that swayed in the harbour were silhouettes against the red-orange flamescape on the western horizon. Shadows were long, and the air was full of the bawdy sound of chikkikii as they cracked and rattled their wing-cases from invisible hiding places. Though the ubiquitous dockhands and sailors were present here as at every trading port, the work proceeded at a quieter, more leisurely pace, as if in reverence to the coming dusk. Lantern-lit bars and provincial-style shops idled lazily in the warmth of the dying day. It was a time for lovers to walk arm in arm, for seduction behind closed shutters.

Kaiku was plainly taken by the atmosphere of the place, even before the *Summer Tide* had creaked into its bay and the mooring lines were thrown to the men on the dockside. Such a short divide from the mainland, and yet even a stranger could tell at a glance that things were done a different way here on Fo. Asara had been here many times before, and always disliked it for the very reasons that appealed to Kaiku. It was peaceful in Pelis, and peace meant boredom to Asara. She looked forward to moving on, into the wilder parts of Fo, where life was not so easy.

Once disembarked, Asara declared that she would find them passage north tonight, and they would leave in the morning if they could. She advised Kaiku to buy herself a rifle; she would need protection where they were going. Kaiku was excited at the thought. She had always been an excellent markswoman, and recent events had meant that she had slipped out of practice. She and Tane went off to buy supplies and weaponry.

Asara was left alone, as she liked it.

It was an easy matter to get them a ride on a trade caravan going to Chaim. Her previous visits had taught her who to go to, though she looked radically different now than she did then, and nobody recognised her. Only one caravan was departing in the morning, but it was well-guarded enough and suitable to their needs. She approached the caravan master as he was overseeing the loading of the cargo. He gave them a very good price for passage. It was so easy to manipulate men, looking as she did. She was coldly aware of the effect her beauty had on the male mind. She went through the motions of flirtatiousness, bored inside, executing a sequence of smiles, laughs, tilts of her body, small touches. Her victim's arousal was plain on his face. Sometimes the sequence took a little tailoring to suit the individual, but usually not. She sighed to herself as she walked away, the agreement done. What brainless animals men were: like dogs, simple to train, begging for treats, eager in heat and appetite. She had little enough respect for anyone – with a few notable exceptions – but at least most women had some modicum of dignity. Men were just embarrassing.

Her transaction done, she met up again with Tane and Kaiku, who informed her of the inn they had found where they would all be staying. Asara knew it well, and it was a safe choice. She told them to go back and rest; she had some business to conclude before retiring. They accepted her explanation, knowing better than to pry. There had been questions on their journey: where were the burns she had suffered; why did she look different? More gratifying was Tane's shock when she appeared on the deck of the barge with short sleeves, and he saw that the tattoo of the Messengers' Guild that had run the length of her inner arm was now only a dark smear like a bruise. The next day it was gone entirely. She gave them no answers. She was not a freak for their curiosity.

She walked the town while the inky shadows of night seeped through the narrow, picturesque streets. Aurus and Neryn shared the sky, the vast pearl moon and her tiny green sister. Iridima, the brightest, was not to be seen; her orbit took her elsewhere, it seemed. In the pale, green-hued glow, Asara wandered down lantern-lit lanes, killing time. She passed a street of bars and restaurants, silhouettes moving in the windows as conversation and laughter drifted out; but it all seemed alien to her, and made her feel unaccountably lonely. This place was possessed of a wonderfully historic charm, with its balconies and coiled-metal railings and uneven alleyways, but it did not have the power to touch Asara.

Gradually, the town of Pelis gentled itself to sleep. She waited, patient as a spider. She had already chosen her prey for the night, spotted him waddling home, puffing at the exertion of hauling his fat frame up the sloping cobble streets. Usually she preferred women – the sensuous curves of their bodies, their fragrance appealed to her – but her encounter with the caravan master had given her a perverse desire for someone bloated and disgusting. He was a fishmonger, by the smell of him, and he lived in an unremarkable corner house of a quiet street. Usually she would have spent more time studying him before she struck – ensuring that he lived alone, observing his habits – but tonight she would have to allow herself a little recklessness. There was no telling when she might next get a chance, and the need was pressing at her.

Her rifle she had stashed underneath a row of bushes; it would only get in her way here. She haunted the street until she was sure that nobody was observing her, and then crossed to the wall of the house and pressed herself flat against it. The ground floor was secure, but on the second storey the shutters were open to let the summer night breezes blow through the house.

Asara tested the texture of the wall. It was of local stone, rough and weathered, and it provided more than enough handholds for her.

She took a final look about and then climbed. In four swift movements she had scaled up to the window-ledge, where she looked inside. The room beyond was bright with green-edged moonlight, and cluttered with the fishmonger's voluminous clothes, heaped untidily about the tiled floor. It was simple and sparse, built to be cool and airy to combat the heat. The fishmonger himself was a mountain of flesh on a mat in one corner, rolled on his side with his back to her, half covered by a thin sheet. His shoulders, dusted with curls of hair, rose and fell as he slept. She slipped inside, over the ledge and on to the floor without a sound.

She padded silently towards him, glancing warily at the dark, uncurtained doorway leading into the rest of the house. When she reached the edge of his sleeping-mat, she straightened and brushed her hair back behind her ear, looking down on him. She could smell the acrid night-sweat rising from his skin, pungent with the scent of the fish he had eaten and handled. And something else too, another faint smell: perfume, and coitus. Her eyes fell to the shallow depression in the mat next to his bulk, too small and light to have been made by him.

She whirled just as the woman appeared at the doorway, returning from whatever nocturnal desires had made her get up. She was dressed in a simple grey nightgown, her black hair tangled and her eyes muzzy with sleep. For the briefest of instants, she froze as she saw Asara standing over her lover; then she screamed.

Asara was on her in an eyeblink. She lashed a kick across the woman's face, sending her spinning in a whirl of hair and arms to crash into the wall and collapse. Whether dead, unconscious or only stunned, Asara had no more time to deal with her. The fishmonger was scrambling off the bed, crabbing away from her frantically on his heels and elbows, a small cry of bewilderment and alarm coming from his lips. She pinned him down with a hand to his flabby throat and trapped his arms with her knees; he was too slow to resist, and by the time he realised what she had done, it was too late. She sat on the rise of his hairy belly, feeling his legs kick uselessly behind her, trying to get a knee up into her ribs but foiled by the gut in between. She took a glance over at the woman, still slumped against the wall, her face covered by her hair. Then she returned her attention to the fishmonger, who was flailing ineffectually beneath her even though he was easily double her weight. His faint cries were strangled by her grip. His eyes bulged in fear.

'Shh,' she said softly. 'I only want a kiss.'

She moved her lips to his as fast as a snake taking a mouse, and sucked.

The fishmonger went rigid as something seemed to tear inside him, something not physical, and gush out through his mouth and into hers. It glittered, this thing, and sparkled; a rushing, bright stream that flickered between their lips as she robbed it from him. For a few long seconds, he felt as a ghost must, fading in the rays of the dawn; and then the horror in his eyes waned, and his pupils grew dark and dim, and his body relaxed in death. Asara let him go with a gasp, wiping her mouth with the back of her hand. His head smacked hard against the tiled floor with a nauseating sound. She took a few heavy breaths in and out, relishing the swelling warmth inside her, and then she got off him.

She had no understanding of what it was in her body that made her this way. There was no anatomical comparison for her to draw against. Arbitrarily, she thought of it as a coil, a tight whorl of fleshy tubing nestled just behind her stomach and before her spine. When glutted, it was thick, and she could feel its warm presence there; when starved, it was flaccid and thin, and the space where it had shrunken from ached with an emptiness a hundred times worse than hunger. Using her talents drained it, like exercise promotes appetite. When she had no need of them, the hunger came on her only rarely; just enough for her body to keep at bay the onset of age. But recently, since her first encounter with the shin-shin, she had been forced to excessive use.

Healing herself after Kaiku had left her near death had almost been too much for her. She had been helped by two foresters who had come to investigate the blaze and found instead a scorched and disfigured handmaiden. The sustenance they provided restored her health more than any care they could offer. Sloughing off the burned skin of her face and hands, regrowing her hair: these took time and effort and strength, and that strength had to come from somewhere. Altering her features was more of a whim, executed after she had restored herself to her satisfaction. She had been careful not to seem outstandingly beautiful while posing as Kaiku's handmaiden, and settled for being merely pretty for two years. But she had a vain streak, and she decided that the time had come to indulge it once again. The slightest shift in aspect rendered her from pleasant-faced and demure to an object of lust. How awful it must be, she thought, for those who are condemned with the face they are born with.

But then, she reflected ruefully, she never knew hers.

Seized by a suddenly maudlin air, she walked over to the woman and pushed her head back. A black bruise was already forming on her cheek. She was unconscious, still breathing. Asara tilted her head first to one side, then to the other. She was not pretty, but possessed of a certain voluptuousness that Asara found faintly intoxicating. If she had not come in, had not seen Asara's face, then Asara would have let her live. But now, she could not.

Asara enfolded the woman in her arms and flicked her hair back over her head, then put her lips to the partly open mouth of her victim.

The Empress Anais tu Erinima stalked along the corridors of the Imperial Keep, in a foul mood. She had barely had time to get into her bath after a day of meetings, arguments and reports before she had received the news that Barak Mos, her husband's father and the power behind Blood Batik, had arrived with an important message for her. Anyone else she would have let wait – with the possible exception of Barak Zahn – but Mos was too important to take even the slightest risk of offending. Batik was the single strongest ally she had, and she needed all she could get right now.

Her route took her around the edges of the Keep, where sculpted arches looked out over the soft night beyond. Neryn was peeking out from behind her mighty sister Aurus, a pale green bubble on the edge of the mottled, pearl-skinned disc that loomed huge in the star-littered sky. Thin streamers of moon-limned cloud drifted in the lazy warmth of the summer darkness. Below, the city was a net of lantern lights, deceptively peaceful and quiet. She had wanted nothing more on this night than to relax on a balcony and sip wine, and let the cares of the past weeks ease out of her; but it was not to be, it seemed.

Every day was like this now. She had barely a moment to herself in daylight, and her nights were no longer sacrosanct either. Each morning brought a new crisis: a protest demonstration somewhere, news of the famed agitator Unger tu Torrhyc stirring trouble among the people, another noble who wanted to beg favour or make veiled threats, an allegiance changed, a suspicion of deceit, an appointment, a dismissal, an oath . . . everything was important now, everything had to be attended to. She had stirred up Saramyr, for better or worse. Now she was surrounded by enemies, and few of them wore their colours overtly.

The one positive aspect of all this chaos was a surprising one. Her relationship with her husband had smoothed somewhat; in truth, a part of her tiredness was due to the fact that she took out her frustrations on him in the bedchamber, vigorously and every night. With all the cares of the realm clamouring for attention, and each day more hectic than the last, her need for release manifested itself with increasing intensity. Durun matched her, which was more than she could say of most men. And though they still could not be said to *like* each other, Durun had at least ceased to be quite so antagonistic to her, and she noticed he had stopped finding excuses to be absent from the Keep so he could be in the bedchamber when she got there.

She should have realised it before. The best way to keep him on a leash was to keep him in her bed. It was a mutually beneficial arrangement, but no more than that. Not to her, anyway.

She was sweeping along the corridor, her shoes tapping on the veined *lach* of the floor, when she saw the Weave-lord Vyrrch emerge from a door ahead of her. A familiar worm of disgust twitched in her gut at the sight of the shambling, bent figure, buried under a robe of patchwork rags, mismatched material stitched haphazardly layer over layer. The hideous, immobile bronze face turned to her within the frame of his tattered hood.

'Ah, Empress Anais,' he croaked, with feigned surprise. She knew by his tone that this meeting was no accident, but she had no patience for it.

'Vyrrch,' she acknowledged, curt enough to be rude.

'We must talk, you and I,' he said.

She passed him by without slowing. 'I have little to say to one who desires the death of my child.'

Vyrrch wasted a moment on surprise, then followed her with his peculiar, broken gait. Twisted and corrupted his bones might have been, but he was not as slow as his appearance suggested.

'Wait!' he cried, outraged. 'You dare not walk away from me!'

She laughed at his bluster. 'The evidence points to the contrary,' she replied, relishing his discomfort as he hobbled along, falling behind her.

'You dare *not*!' he hissed, and Anais felt herself suddenly wrenched as if by some great force, an invisible hand that seized her and whirled her around to face him. She tottered, stunned for a moment; and then the hand was gone.

Vyrrch regarded her icily from behind his Mask.

'I should have you executed for that,' Anais said, her cheeks flushed with fury.

Vyrrch was not cowed. 'We are displeased with you, Anais. Very displeased. If you get rid of me, no Weaver will take my place. We are bound to Adderach above all other loyalties, and you are working against the interests of our kind. None of us will claim the title of Weave-lord if I am removed. Do you think you will survive the civil war you are bringing upon us all, without a Weaver to defend you?'

'My Weaver works to *betray* me,' she hissed. 'Do you think I am not aware of that? Perhaps I would be better with none.'

'Perhaps,' he replied. 'Though without any way to contact your far-flung interests – unless, of course, you care to revert to horse messengers or carrier birds – I cannot imagine you will make an effective empress any more.' She thought she could hear a smile in his withered and broken voice, and it angered her more; but she reined herself in, made her anger go cold and hard like new-forged metal plunged into ice water.

'Do not threaten me, Vyrrch. You know well that if the hand of the Weavers was suspected of meddling in the politics of the land, then my enemies and allies alike would destroy you. Your insane kind are an accessory to government, not a part of it; and you know as well as I that the high families would sooner see an Aberrant on the throne than a Weaver. You may have ingratiated yourself so much that we think we cannot do without you; but you are here on our sufferance, and you would do well to remember that. Like rebellious dogs, you will be put down if you try and bite your masters. And the Weavers grow altogether too bold.'

'Do you think so?' Vyrrch mocked. 'Perhaps, after you have persuaded the people to accept an Aberrant freak as their ruler, then you will persuade the high families to get rid of us? I don't think it likely, do you?'

'Do not speak of *freaks* to me, you vile thing. I have no interest in the Weavers' displeasure. You are not part of the government of this land, and you have no say in it. Now I am late for a meeting.'

She turned and stalked away, and Vyrrch did not call her again; but she felt his gaze burning into her back all the way along the corridor.

Barak Mos was a man of great presence, though physically he was not as tall as his son. He was broad-boned, with a wide chest and shoulders and thick arms, and there was a squatness about him – with his strong, bearded jaw, flat head and short limbs – that lent him an impression of impressive solidity. At just under six feet in height, he towered over Anais; but she had never faced him in anger, and she knew him to be gentle towards her. She had dealt with enough of the son's tempers to be able to field his father's, anyway.

She met him in a room of her chambers that she particularly liked, dominated by a massive ivory bas-relief of two rinji birds passing each other in flight, their long necks and white wings outstretched, their ungainly, sticklike legs curled up beneath them. The three-dimensional effect of one bird occupying the foreground as it flew between the viewer and the other bird had always appealed to Anais. It appealed to Mos too, apparently, for he was admiring it as she entered.

'Barak Mos,' she said. 'I apologise for keeping you waiting.'

'No trouble,' he replied, turning towards her. 'Rather, let me apologise for the inconvenient hour. I would not have come, but I have grave information.'

Anais gave him a curious look and then invited him to sit. For such a gruff man, he was being excessively polite. The apology was a pleasantry; to get Barak Mos genuinely to say sorry was like getting blood from a stone, which is why she had been so impressed when he had asked her forgiveness for his son's debauched ways.

Two elegant couches were arranged around a low table of black wood, looking out across the room through a partition to the open balcony beyond. On the table was a bowl of kama nuts, giving off a fragrance that was bitter and fruity and smoky all at once. It was the recent fashion among young ladies of the court to keep some kama seeds in their pockets to lend them this enticing fragrance, and Anais had grown to like the scent.

They settled themselves, Anais reclining and Mos sitting on the edge of his couch, leaning forward with his hands clasped before him. She noticed suddenly and with embarrassment the lack of refreshments in the room. Mos caught her gaze and waved absently.

'Your servants came,' he said. 'I sent them away. I won't be here long. Order something for yourself, if you like.'

That was more like the Mos she knew; tactless. As if she needed his permission to call for refreshments in her own home. She decided against it, more concerned with hearing the Barak's news.

'I don't have to tell you that this goes no further than us,' he said, giving her a serious gaze.

'Of course not,' she replied.

'I am only telling you this out of concern. For you, for my son, for my granddaughter.'

A small smile of surprised gratitude flicked over the Empress's face at the term. She had not expected to hear him acknowledge Lucia so.

'I understand,' she replied.

He seemed satisfied. 'Your Weaver, Vyrrch. Weave-lord, sorry. Why is that?'

'Why is what?'

'Why is he a Weave-lord?'

Anais was bewildered. She thought a man in Mos's position should know *that*, at least. 'It is the title bestowed upon the Emperor or Empress's Weaver. Usually it is also because they are the best at their craft.'

Mos harumphed, seeming to digest this. 'Do you trust him?'

'Vyrrch? Heart's blood, no. He would murder my daughter if he thought he could get away with it. But he knows what would happen if the high families thought a Weaver had slain the Heir-Empress. Aberrant or not.' She hesitated to use the word, but there was no other that fitted her purposes.

'That's true enough,' he said, shifting his broad bulk. 'Let me be blunt, then. I suspect that Weave-lord Vyrrch and Barak Sonmaga tu Amacha are working together against you.'

Anais raised an eyebrow. 'Indeed? It would not be a surprise to me.'

'This is bad business, Anais. I have spies, you know that. I don't much approve of them, but they're as necessary as Weavers are in the game we play. I sent them to find out what they could after this whole business began, and I suppose one of them struck lucky. We heard about a man named Purloch tu Irisi. He's a cat-burglar of some renown and great skill. I can vouch for that: he got into this Keep, and into the roof gardens, and he got to Lucia.'

Anais felt a jolt of terror. 'He got to Lucia?'

'Back when all this started. Weeks ago. He could have put a knife in her, Anais.'

The Empress was rigid on her couch. Why had Lucia said nothing? Of course, she should not have been surprised. A life of being hidden had made her secretive, and she was so unfathomably introverted at times. At those times, Anais did not understand her child at all. It made her sad to think of the gulf between them, that her daughter would not mention something so important. But that was just her way.

'Murder wasn't his mission, though,' Mos was continuing. 'He got a lock of hair instead. He wasn't after her; he didn't know anything more than what he was sent for.'

'Why? Why the hair?' Anais asked, her eyes darkening.

'His employer needed proof she was an Aberrant, so he could spread the news and stir up the nobles. The Weavers have some test, some way of telling. The gods only know the ins and outs of their science. But they need a part of the body: skin, hair, something like that.' He shrugged. 'Anyway, this Purloch was clever. He wouldn't take on a task like that without insurance. Too smart to be someone's pawn. He wanted to know who it was that hired him; so he traced the middlemen back to their source. Sonmaga.'

Anais nodded to herself. She had never solved the mystery of how this furore suddenly started, how the high families all seemed to know at once about her child being different. Sonmaga! It *would* be him.

'Do you have proof of any of it?'

Mos looked momentarily embarrassed. 'Purloch disappeared directly after he had completed his task. There is no testimony against Sonmaga, and if there were, it would be useless. A thief's word against a Barak's?'

'Did this . . . Purloch know about Vyrrch's involvement?'

'He knew nothing, or he said nothing,' said Mos. 'There is no link, or at least none that anyone but a Weaver could follow. But there was one thing that sat uneasily with me about the whole affair. Purloch's fee was huge. All that effort and expense on Sonmaga's part, just to hire a man to steal a lock of hair. Points to one conclusion.'

'Sonmaga must have suspected,' she said.

'He already knew she was Aberrant,' Mos agreed with a nod. He seemed to have no problem with the word, used in conjunction with the one he had called 'granddaughter' moments ago. She took heart in that.

'Because somebody told him so,' she concluded. 'Vyrrch.'

'He found out somehow,' Mos said. 'It's the only answer.'

'Not the only answer,' Anais replied cautiously. 'Others knew. Tutors, a few servants . . .'

'But none more likely than Vyrrch,' Mos countered. 'None with so much to lose by an Aberrant taking the throne. What if she *does* become Empress? She'll know the Weavers would have killed her at birth, given the chance. What if she stops the Weavers killing Aberrant children? What if she tries to undermine them, drive them out? The Weavers know they could not thrive in a realm where an Aberrant ruled. They would suddenly find they have to fear retaliation for over two hundred years of rooting out deviancy.'

'Maybe it's what we need,' Anais said, thinking over her conversation with Vyrrch. 'Gods-cursed parasites. We'd be better off without them. We should never have let it get this far, never have allowed them to become indispensable.'

'You'll find no stronger agreement than mine,' Mos said. 'I despise their slippery ways. But beware of setting yourself squarely against them, Anais. You walk a precarious edge.'

'Indeed,' said Anais, musing. 'Indeed.'

FIFTEEN

The compound of Blood Amacha was enormous, the largest in the Imperial Quarter of Axekami, larger even than that of the ruling family, Blood Erinima. It rested on a flat tabletop of land, a man-made dais of earth that raised it up above the surrounding compounds by a storey. Within its walls, a virtual paradise was wrought: lush tropical trees imported from distant continents, sculpted brooks and pools, wondrous glades and waterfalls. In contrast to the usual minimalism of Saramyr gardens, this place was abundant to the point of gaudiness; but even here, the tendency towards neatness was still in effect, and there were no fallen leaves on the paths, no chewed branches left on the trunks, no blighted leaf uncut. Unfamiliar fruits hung in the branches, and sprays of strange flowers nestled amid the bushes. There were even foreign animals here, chosen for their beauty and wonder – and their inability to harm those who wandered the gardens of the compound. It was like stepping into another land, a storybook realm of magic.

Mishani tu Koli sat on a wooden bench that was carved into the living root of an enormous chapapa tree, a slim book of war sonnets by the swordsman-poet Xalis in her hand. A kidney-shaped pool lay before her, fed by a trickling fall of water over red rocks, with exotic fish lazing within. The afternoon air hummed with the benevolent drone of insects.

She counted the ostentation of Blood Amacha's compound as faintly vulgar, considering it the highest arrogance to raise themselves above the other nobles in such a way; yet she could not deny the thrill of walking their gardens, nor the pleasure of knowing that she was sitting on a tree that was seeded on another continent entirely. Amacha's gardens had been growing for over three hundred years, and this tree had been here for most of that time, imported as a sapling from the jungles of Okhamba.

For all its breathtaking splendour, though, she could not find her ease here. Her mind would not stay on the verses on the page, and the tranquillity of the gardens did little to soothe her. She ached inside with a feeling of such loss and sadness that she wanted to weep, and worse was the knowledge that she had created her own misery.

She played the moment over and over in her memory, hearing her own voice come back to her, watching the reaction on the face of her friend.

Because I see what you are. And you disgust me.

With those words she had sawn through ties twenty harvests in the making. With those words, she had overcome the weakness of indecision, committed herself to the course she knew was right. By banishing Kaiku, she protected her family, protected her *father* from dishonour. It was a daughter's duty to do so, to hold her family above all else, sometimes even the Empress herself.

With those words, she had turned her back on her lifelong friend, and now she wanted to scream with the pain of it.

But she didn't scream. That was not her way. She showed outwardly no sign at all of her grief, nor of the warring forces of recrimination and justification that battled behind her calm, dark eyes.

Her father had had questions for her when he returned. News of the death of Kaiku's family had been slow in escaping the Forest of Yuna, but when it did it was all over the court. Barak Avun had been canny enough not to reveal to anyone that Kaiku was staying with his daughter until he had been given the opportunity to talk to her. He never got the chance. She was gone by the time he came back, and had effectively disappeared.

Mishani feigned shock, pretending that Kaiku had said nothing about the slaughter of her family. Barak Avun did not believe her, but he did not challenge her either. He knew his daughter well, knew how loyal she was. If he demanded, she would tell him; but the fact that she was not telling him meant it was something he would be better off not knowing. That, on top of the strange fire on the day of the council meeting and the curious deaths of Kaiku's family, had him mightily suspicious; but he trusted her, and let the falsehoods settle.

She was protecting his honour by risking her own. He allowed it, but the message between them was unspoken. Even though her intentions were good, even though it were better that she did not tell him, she was still neglecting a daughter's duty by lying to her father. She owed him greatly.

Mishani had tried to distract herself from her thoughts of Kaiku by burying herself in the family business and the intrigues of court. The Barak indulged her by confiding closely in her. The court was a hotbed of power-plays in the wake of the council meeting and the Empress's announcement that the Aberrant child would sit the throne. New alliances were being forged, uniting against the ruling family. Agitators had taken to the streets.

In particular, one man, Unger tu Torrhyc, was stirring up a storm with his fiery orations against the Heir-Empress. Mishani had attended one of his demonstrations in Speaker's Square, and been impressed. The anger in the city was rising to fever pitch. Violent protests had already been quelled by the Imperial Guards in the poorer districts. The Empress might have enough support among the nobles to keep a precarious hold on her throne, but she had made no overtures to the common folk, and they were solidly opposed to the idea of an Aberrant ruler. Whether oversight or arrogance, it could prove to be her downfall.

Yet all the rhetoric that flew about the streets and the court rang hollow to

Mishani now. The cries that Aberrants were freaks, a blight, that they were *evil* by birth . . . what had previously made so much sense now seemed like the hysteria of foaming zealots. How could it apply to Kaiku? She was no more 'born evil' than Mishani was. She was no more evil *now* than Mishani was. And if it did not apply to her, then how many others did it also exclude? What evidence was there that Aberrants were evil at all?

And yet there was still the fear and disgust. That she could not deny. She had been repulsed by Kaiku, though her friend had not changed physically one bit beyond the colour of her eyes. It was the *knowledge* that repulsed her, the thought that Kaiku was Aberrant. But the more she thought on that, the more she found there was no weight to the reasoning. She was repulsed because Kaiku was Aberrant. But she could not come up with any other reason than that. The danger of being near her did not bother Mishani; as Kaiku had said, she would have stood by her if she had been suffering from an infectious disease. But Aberrancy was different.

Wherever she turned in the corridors of her mind, she came up against the same phrase: *because she is Aberrant.* It was phantom logic, a dead-end in the pathways of thought. So deeply ingrained in her was it that it required no more reason than it *was*, no evidence to back it up. If she was asked why the sun was in the sky, she could tell the story of how Ocha put his own son's eye out because two were too bright, and then set him to watch over the world; and how Nuki was chased round the planet by the three amorous moon-sisters, giving us night and day. She could explain why the birds sang, why the wind blew, why the sea rippled; but ask her why Aberrants were revolting and terrible, and she had only this answer: *because they are.*

Suddenly, it did not seem good enough.

A benefit of her father's strong opposition to the Empress was that Blood Koli found themselves in the favour of Blood Amacha. Blood Amacha and Blood Kerestyn were the only two families with the power to lay claim to the throne except for Blood Batik, the Emperor's family – but they had chosen to side with the Empress, despite the Emperor's obvious detestation of his daughter. Those who had voted against the Empress at the council were being feted or bullied by the two claimants as they gathered their forces in anticipation of conflict; but Blood Koli and Blood Kerestyn had a history of antagonism, so the increased friendship between Barak Sonmaga tu Amacha and Barak Avun tu Koli seemed natural under the circumstances.

Her father and Barak Sonmaga had been in conference most of the day. She and Avun had joined their host for breakfast, enjoying a delicious meal on the porch of the sprawling wooden townhouse that hid among the exotic fauna. There they had watched strange deer as they ate, and heard the chirruping of hidden animals in the foliage. Afterward, the men had gone to talk. Usually Mishani would have been allowed to join them; but this meeting was of the gravest secrecy, and she was excluded. She did not mind. She was not in the mood for parley anyway.

Now she heard the soft tread of feet on the path behind her, and she put down her book, stood up and bowed to her father and the Barak Sonmaga, fingertips of one hand to her lips and the other arm folded across her waist. Sonmaga bowed slightly in return, put a hand on her father's shoulder with a meaningful glance, and then walked on, leaving them alone. Mishani noticed that her father was carrying something, securely tied in a canvas bag.

'Father,' she said, 'are we leaving now? Did all go well?'

'Soon,' he said. 'May I sit with you for a while?'

'Of course,' she said, moving her book and sitting back down, her ankle-length hair thrown over one slender shoulder.

Barak Avun sat, the bag put aside. He seemed nervous to be holding it. Like his daughter, he was fine-boned and lean. Sharp cheekbones stood out on a tanned and weathered face, and his hair had receded from his pate and now held out in a horseshoe shape from ear to ear. He gave the impression of being permanently tired and weary, though it was a misleading assumption to make. Mishani loved her father, but she respected him more. He was a ruthless and eminently successful player in the games of the court, and she could not have asked for a better tutor.

'Daughter, there are things we must speak of,' he said. 'You know that the discovery of the Heir-Empress's secret has come at a bad time for Saramyr. The harvest promises to be lean this year, despite the weather, as the blight in the earth takes hold. The wild places are more dangerous than ever. We cannot afford a civil war now.'

'Agreed,' Mishani said. 'But since the Empress is determined to see her child on the throne, it seems unlikely that any other option is available. Even if we conceded to her, I doubt that the people would. Axekami is tipping towards revolt.'

'There is another way,' he said. 'The Empress is sterile. Birthing that spawn of hers has made her barren. If the Heir-Empress were removed, then Blood Erinima would have no choice but to forfeit their position as ruling family once Anais died. And probably before.'

'If Lucia were . . . removed,' Mishani said carefully. She did not like the way this conversation was going. 'Then the Empress would stop at nothing to hunt down whoever was responsible, and civil war would likely ensue anyway.'

'Not if she had nobody to blame. No target on which to vent her wrath.' Barak Avun grew sly. 'Not if it was the work of the gods.'

'Speak plainly, Father,' she said, her thin face set. 'What have you in mind?'

'The Empress is wooing the nobles as well as she can, by introducing them to the Aberrant child so that they may see she is not deformed or freakish. Reports say she is, on the contrary, quite pretty if a little . . . odd. But pretty or not, she must be removed if the stability of the country is to be maintained.'

'Am I to take it from this,' Mishani suggested daringly, 'that Blood Amacha is not quite prepared for civil war yet, and finds the thought of revolution unappealing at the moment? I would think they would prefer to bide their time and strike when they are assured of their ability to beat Blood Kerestyn to the throne.'

Barak Avun regarded his daughter with eyes gone dull as a lizard's. 'You are clever, daughter, and you fill me with pride. But be obedient now. You have a task.'

Mishani bowed her head a little in submission, letting her black hair fall across her face.

The Barak settled back, satisfied. 'You will go to see the Heir-Empress, and give her a gift.' He motioned to the canvas bag next to him, but Mishani noted that he was still chary of being near it. 'You were absent at council; Anais does not know whether you are opposed to her or not. She will welcome the chance to change your mind. Go see the child, and offer her a present.'

'What is in the bag, Father?' Mishani asked, feeling her blood begin to run cold. She knew what the Barak was asking her, and knew equally that she could not refuse him. He had not mentioned her absence at council by accident; he was making another point of her recent disobedience.

'A nightdress,' he said. 'Beautifully embroidered; a work of art. It is infected with bone fever.'

Mishani had expected as much, and made no reaction.

'The Heir-Empress will sicken within a week, die a few weeks later. Perhaps a few others in her chambers will catch it too. Bone fever strikes at random; nobody will suspect the gift. And even if they do, it cannot be detected, and thus cannot be traced to you or me,' he said.

Or Sonmaga, Mishani thought sourly, knowing him to be the author of this plot. She wondered what he had promised Avun for using his daughter this way. The use of poison was still counted an acceptable, if not honourable, method of assassination. But use of disease was abhorrent, and rarely even considered. Only barbarians would do such. What depths her father and Sonmaga had stooped to; and what depths they would condemn her to, if they made her their accomplice.

No, she thought. *Not accomplice. Scapegoat.*

She looked hard into her father's eyes. She believed he thought it would work, and he thought he was doing what was good for the country. But she knew also that if she were somehow caught, he would cut her loose like an anchor from a ship to save his family. She had seen moves like this a hundred times in court, but she had never been the subject of them before. Never had she felt so cheapened, never so much a pawn as now; and the one who wounded her this way was the one she trusted most in the world. She felt fundamentally betrayed, and in that she felt the love she bore for her father curl up and die. She was shocked at how fragile a thing it must have been.

Mishani gazed at the stranger on the bench next to her a moment longer, then dropped her eyes to the pool before them. Sun glittered in the edges of the ripples.

'I will do as you say,' she said. She could scarcely do otherwise.

At the foot of Mount Aon, the great monastery of Adderach crouched and glowered, a testament to the insanity of its architects. Its form was bewildering to the eye, the sand-coloured stone of its skin moulded so that it seemed to melt from one form to another: here a narrow walkway, terminating over a drop; here a sculpture of howling demons; there a redundant minaret, a half-constructed window, a corkscrewing spire. One wall of an entirely disused wing was crafted in the shape of a screaming face, thirty feet high, teeth bared and eyes wild. Statues stalked the desolate surroundings, the delirious babblings of mad minds scoured by cold winds from the upper altitudes. Lonely walls stood, guarding nothing. Inside, staircases went nowhere, whole wings were inaccessible because nobody had thought to build a door, cavernous halls vied with tiny rooms too small to stand up in.

It was a masterpiece or an atrocity, born of a thousand projects of whim and caprice that somehow fused together seamlessly into one; and it was such a place that the Weavers had made their cradle of power, from which they watched over the land of Saramyr and made their plans.

The Weavers had no recognisable hierarchy. Their structure was anarchic, random and operating under uncertain values; but there was one overarching principle that united them all, and that was the good of the whole. Though individually their motives were saturated in dementia, they each worked together towards the same goal at any given time. None questioned this strange group consciousness; nobody asked who set the goals, who directed their efforts, whether it was a majority decision or the determination of a select few. It simply *was*. The force that kept them coherent was a web that bound them all together, like the sublime threads of the Weave.

The monastery was built over a vast, labyrinthine mine. It had lain disused for over two hundred years now, but still it stood, and creatures of a foulness beyond imagining roamed its tunnels in the blackness. The mine had been the site where the first of the witchstones had been found, two and a half centuries ago, buried deep beneath the earth, and from there the Weavers had sprung.

At first the miners had no idea what they had found. They were simple, tough and honest folk, working a seam of iron deep in the Tchamil Mountains, far from civilisation; at that time, the mine was new, and nothing Aberrant stalked the dark passageways as they did today. Living as remotely as they did, the miners had built settlements, and among them were stoneworkers and carpenters and the like: artisans. They came to view the thing that the miners had found, and it was they that gave the substance its name.

It was plain from the first that this was no ordinary stone. For one thing, a man could sense it just by being close. The hairs on his arm would stand on end, his skin would crawl, his teeth tingle. Not in fear, but because he stood in the presence of energy. The air felt charged around the stone, like it was before a moonstorm, and even the most pragmatic of those hardy folk were forced to admit that.

The second odd thing was the state in which it was found. It was a vast, uneven hulk of black, grainy stone, like an outcrop of volcanic rock; except that it was discovered deep underground, whole and unattached, inside a small cave. The surrounding stone had been melted to glass by unimaginable heat, and no matter how they mined, there was no evidence of a seam anywhere. It was impossible that it could have formed naturally. Which begged the question: how did it get there? Could it have been a relic of the Ugati, the native folk who had lived in Saramyr for uncountable years before the first Emperor drove them out?

The history of the Weavers was not clear on exactly what happened next. All that was certain was that the artisans began rubbing dust from the surface of the witchstone and infusing it into their crafts. Perhaps it was the strange properties of the stone that attracted them, or the novelty of an entirely unheard-of substance integrated into their work. Carpenters rubbed the dust into the grain of benches, stonemasons mixed it in with mortar. It was an odd craze, but no odder than a hundred thousand others across the land. The empire in general knew this much about the origin of the Weavers only because some of the folk from the settlement made the trek across the mountains to try and sell their wares, confident that their new edge would appeal to the markets in the west. Their samples were well received; the raw sense of energy they gave out amazed buyers. During that time, the folk of the settlement told people about their strange discovery. When they had sold their samples, they returned home to fulfil the orders that eager customers had made. They never came back.

The settlement was silent for years. Remote as it was, buried in the trackless mountains, it faded into memory. The initial flurry of excitement in the markets diminished and the witchstone artefacts were forgotten.

What happened during that time is a matter of speculation.

At some point, the decision was made to introduce witchstone dust to the craft of mask-making, and during that period some experimenter must have discovered the other powers of witchstone dust. There is no telling how the process began, or how it went on. Perhaps, at first, they used it as a narcotic, for long-term exposure to witchstone caused disorientation and euphoria. Later they discovered that having it close to the face – and hence the brain – was the most effective method of attaining that feeling. From there, small and rudimentary effects in the physical world were noticed. While under the delirium of the witchstone, a cup would be moved without anyone touching it; a flame would flare or gutter; a man might know the thoughts of his friend and be suddenly aware of his innermost secrets. It can only be guessed how arduous the path was from simple addiction to an unknown substance to gaining control of it. How many of them stumbled unwittingly into the full light of the Weave, and lost their minds and souls to its glory? How many atrocities of rape and murder and mutilation were committed in the agonies of post-Weaving withdrawal? History does not recall. But when they emerged again from that settlement after their long silence, no women and children were left.

Two centuries ago, the first Weavers appeared in the towns and cities of Saramyr. Their powers were weaker then, and cruder; but they already moved with one purpose, operating to a master plan. Subtly, they infiltrated the homes of the noble classes, making themselves invaluable. In those days, the people of Saramyr were naïve to the Weavers, and those that proved an obstacle to them were simply *influenced*, their minds and opinions changed to suit the plan. In a matter of a decade, they were integrated; and from there they began to grow, and build, and scheme.

In a firelit chamber somewhere in the depths of Adderach's convoluted arteries, an apparition of Weave-lord Vyrrch hung in the air. It was a dim and blurred ghost, a mottled smear of brown and grey and orange, approximating the colours of his patchwork robe. Curiously, the form seemed to gain definition the closer it came to his Mask, as if the Mask was the focus of the phantom. It was the only thing sharply defined, a translucent bronze face amid the ether of Vyrrch's body.

The three Weavers that Vyrrch faced were different to the last three, and they had been different to the three before. Lacking a hierarchy, the Weave-lord had no superiors to report to; instead the three Weavers present would disseminate the information throughout the network using the Weave. They, in turn, spoke for the others.

'The Empress is being less than cooperative,' observed one, whose name was Kakre. His Mask was of cured skin stretched over a wooden frame, and made him look like a corpse.

'I expected no less,' said Vyrrch, his croaking voice seeming to come from the walls around them. 'But the situation turns to our advantage. It would be . . . inconvenient if she abdicated now.'

'Explain yourself,' demanded Kakre. 'Is not the Heir-Empress's claim to the throne a great threat to the Weavers?'

'Indeed,' Vyrrch replied. 'And as things stand, the forces on either side are evenly matched. But I have not been idle in the Imperial Keep. The Baraks dance to my tune.'

'And what advantage for us?' whispered a fat Weaver, his face a blank oval of wood with a long, braided beard of animal hair depending from it.

Vyrrch turned his gaze to that one. 'Brother, I have plans in hand to rid us of the Empress and her troublesome brood. I have struck a pact with the most powerful player in this game; and when he becomes Blood Emperor, we will be raised up with him. We will no longer be merely an accessory to government; we will be the power behind the throne!'

'Be careful, Vyrrch,' warned Kakre. 'They do not trust us, do not want us here. They will turn on us if they can. Even your Barak.'

'They suspect,' added the third weaver, whose black wooden Mask wore a snarl. 'They suspect what we are about.'

'Then let them suspect,' Vyrrch replied. 'By the time they realise the truth, it will be too late.'

'Perhaps,' said Kakre, 'you had better explain to us your intentions.'

Vyrrch returned to himself shortly afterward, his consciousness flitting down the synapses of the Weave to arrive back at his physical body. His breathing fluttered, and his eyes, which had been open and glazed, focused sharply. He was sitting in his usual place, amid the stench and rank squalor of his chambers. For a time he composed himself, awaiting the backlash of withdrawing himself from the sheer bliss of the Weave. Recollection slotted into place around the usual patches of amnesia, and he looked around quizzically. He vaguely remembered having a girl brought to him yesterday, a particularly spirited little thing as it turned out. He'd had her trussed up, like a spider with a fly, intending to keep her and feed her and use her as necessary. The motive behind it eluded him; perhaps he had wanted instant relief for his next post-Weaving psychosis rather than having to wait for the servants to bring him what he needed on request. The clever bitch had slipped her bonds somehow and was loose in his chambers, hiding. She was trapped in here with him, for he wore the only key to the heavy door that would give her freedom, and he never took it off. He liked that. A little game.

He felt no desire for her now, though. Instead, he felt a sudden and overwhelming compulsion to rearrange his surroundings. An alien and quite dazzling logic had settled on him, a way things should be done, and he saw as if in a vision from the gods how he should alter his living space. He got up to do so, knowing it to be just another form of mania, but powerless to prevent it anyway. The girl could wait. Everyone could wait.

Then when he was ready, he'd have them all.

SIXTEEN

They travelled north along the great Dust Road that curved from the south-east to the north-west of Fo, terminating in the mining town of Cmorn on the far coast. The sun was barely up in the east as they set off, and Neryn was still doggedly high in the sky and would have remained visible until the afternoon, clouds permitting. They did not. By midday, what had begun as a few wisps of cirrus had marshalled into a humped blanket that muted the sun, slowly cruising overhead. The heat did not diminish in proportion to the light, but Tane found himself glad of the shade anyway. Life under a forest canopy had not prepared him for the exposure of recent days, and he still found himself becoming woozy if he stood in the glare of Nuki's eye for too long.

Their caravan was pulled by a pair of manxthwa, whose enormous strength powered a train of seven carts. The hindmost five were covered with tarpaulin and lashed down, packed with a wide variety of supplies for the isolated village of Chaim. The foremost two were for passengers, fitted with a narrow bench on the inner lip of each side so that six people could sit in each cart. A further seat was provided at the front for the driver, a withered, crotchety-looking old man who wore a thin shirt over his ropy frame, and the fat caravan master. Kaiku, Asara and Tane sat in the front passenger cart; the one behind them was full of guards, muttering between themselves and leaning on their rifles.

Tane studied the manxthwa idly as they travelled the Dust Road. They were seven feet high at the shoulder, with short back legs and long front ones in the manner of apes. Their knees crooked backwards, and ended in spatulate black hooves to take the weight of their immense frame. Their bodies were covered in a thick and shaggy fur of a dull red-orange, a legacy of their arctic origins; and yet the heat of Saramyr seemed not to bother them one bit. Their wide faces were drooping and sad and wrinkled, lending them a misleading impression of aged wisdom, and two stubby tusks protruded from beneath their lower lips, jutting out from squared chins.

What odd creatures they were, Tane thought; and yet perfect. Enyu's creations were each a wonder, even those things that preyed on man. A shadow seemed to settle on his heart as he thought of the Aberrant lady they had met in Axekami. She may have been outwardly unblemished, but inside she was a corruption of Enyu's mould, a horror. The goddess of nature created her children each for a reason, and Aberrants were a mockery of that.

Towards the end of the day, they turned off the thoroughfare, leaving behind the traffic of rickety carts and painted carriages to head northward. The Dust Road had been aptly named, for each step of the manxthwa stirred up the stuff, powdered stone blown off the surrounding land. Most of Fo was a vast, flat waste of rock and scree, with little vegetation but the hardiest, thorny scrubs. It was high above sea level, higher than the mainland, and its soil was unforgiving. Its bones had been bared by millennia of wind and rain, and made it stark and bleak.

Once the Dust Road was behind them, they travelled on rougher paths, barely more than shallow ruts worn into the ground by the passage of caravans like theirs. They had not gone more than a mile along that way when the driver turned them off the track and circled the caravan.

The caravan master bustled round to help Asara down from the passenger cart. He was bald and rubber-lipped, with tiny eyes and a nose buried in a mass of corpulent, blubbery features. There was a slightly fish-like aspect to his face. His name was Ottin.

'Why are we stopping?' she asked, as she accepted his hand. His skin was clammy and cold.

'It's best not to travel too near the mountains at night,' he replied. 'Dangerous. We will reach Chaim tomorrow, you'll see.'

A fire was made, and Kaiku was surprised to feel the temperature begin to drop hard as the sun fled the sky. The guards took shifts in walking the perimeter of the circle of caravans, while the others sat in the restless light of the blaze. The unfamiliarity of this land, the strangers surrounding her and the promise of danger had combined to make Kaiku feel quite intrepid. She relaxed and listened to the talk at the fireside, and a strange contentment took her.

'There's a blight on the isle, no doubt of that,' the driver was saying. It was a common complaint in Saramyr, but they had never heard it applied to Fo. 'Cancer in the bones of the earth.'

'It's the same on the mainland,' Tane said. 'A malaise for which we can't find a source. Once the forests were safe to walk; now we know better than to be caught out at night. The wild beasts are becoming more aggressive; and the spirits that haunt the trees are cold and unfamiliar.'

'I don't know from forests, but I can tell you the source all right. Up in the mountains. That's where it's coming from.'

'Such superstitious nonsense!' declared Ottin, glancing at Asara to see if she approved of his outburst.

'Is it?' the driver replied sharply, fixing him with a wrinkly squint. 'You tell me if we don't start to see it in the land, the further north we go. North is the mountains. Makes sense to me.'

About that, at least, the driver was right. By midday it was difficult not to notice. Bare trees thrust out of the soil, their limbs crooked and misshapen, oozing sap from some places where the bark was thin as human skin, and in others bowed down by a tumescent surplus of it. They saw one whose branches grew in loops, straggling out of the trunk at one point only to curve back and bury themselves into it elsewhere. Thin, hooked leaves stood out like spines along the tangle of boughs.

The guards were more alert now. Kaiku noted how they faced outwards from their cart with their rifles ready, and never stopped scanning. She began to pick up on their wariness, and fiddled with her hair nervously. Ottin, apparently oblivious to it all, continued his inane attempts at banter with Asara. She bore it with remarkable patience. It seemed that the discounted fare the caravan master had offered came with a hidden price: taken with Asara's beauty, he tried ceaselessly to insinuate himself into her affections. Kaiku and Tane exchanged glances and smiled in amusement.

But Tane's amusement was only fleeting. Nowhere in the Forest of Yuna had he ever seen the signs of the corruption in the earth as obviously as here. His tanned brow furrowed as he looked out over the empty landscape towards the ghostly peaks of the Lakmar Mountains in the distance. A sudden flurry of movement among the guards drew his attention to their right, where something darted among an outcrop of rocks, making a throaty cackling sound that echoed in the still air. They kept their rifles ready, but it made no further appearances.

'See?' said the driver suddenly, pointing up. 'Those things are so common, they even have their own name. Gristle-crows, we call them.'

The passengers looked, and saw above them a trio of black birds, swooping and turning. Indeed, they did seem like crows at first glance, but it was only when Tane asserted his perspective that he realised they were much higher than he thought, and therefore larger.

'How big are they?' he asked, unable to credit the evidence of his senses.

'Six feet wing-tip to wing-tip,' the driver croaked back.

Kaiku swore under her breath, an old habit borrowed from her brother and one she had often been reprimanded for as unladylike. It scarcely seemed to matter out here.

Tane peered up into the clouded sky at them. It was difficult to make out details, but the more he looked the more he reconsidered their likeness to their namesakes. Their beaks were thick and malformed, more like keratinous muzzles with a hooked lip at the front. Their wings were sharply kinked in the middle, in the manner of bats' wings, though they were thickly shagged with untidy black feathers. He grimaced and looked away, hoping never to be any closer to them than he was now.

'Interesting,' said Asara. When she said nothing else, Kaiku took the bait.

'What is interesting?'

'This is not the first type of Aberrant that has become so common as to constitute a species,' she said, gazing pointedly at Tane, who ignored her. 'In amongst all the freaks of nature produced by this . . . *corruption* in the land, there are many that have flourished. For every hundred useless aberrations there may be one that is useful, that provides its bearer an advantage over its kin. And if that one survives to breed, and pass on its—'

'There's nothing new in what you're saying, Asara,' Tane snapped. 'Those ideas have been part of Jujanchi's teachings for decades.'

'Yes,' said Asara. 'He was one of Enyu's priests, wasn't he? A great thinker, by all accounts. He used his theories to explain diversity in animals. Strange how his teachings apply to Aberrants, then, when your creed dictates that they are not children of Enyu.'

'Aberrants follow the *laws* of nature,' Tane replied, 'because they are corruptions of the same basic root. It doesn't make them natural, or any less foul.'

What about me, Tane? Kaiku thought. *What would you think of me, if you knew what I was?* In truth, she wondered that Tane did not suspect Asara of being an Aberrant, but it seemed that he would rather not know.

'But perhaps this corruption is not corruption at all,' Asara posited. 'Maybe it is only accelerated change. Those things up there may be foul to your eyes, but as big as they are they will rule the skies. Does that not make them a superior breed? Consider, Tane: more new species have probably arisen in the last fifty years than in the last five hundred.'

'Change in nature is slow,' Tane countered angrily. 'It is that way for a reason: so that everything around it can adapt. And besides, this is not just a matter of animal speciation. Crops are dying, *people* are dying. Not only that, but the spirits are changing, Asara. They grow hostile. The guardians of natural places are fading, being overrun by things like . . . like the *shin-shin*.'

'The shin-shin were summoned,' Asara replied. 'To get back that Mask. Or to get Kaiku. That was not the random anger of the spirits that killed your priests. They followed the trail to your temple. If they could get across the Camaran Channel, they would follow it here too; but I suspect we lost them in the city, and the trail is cold now.'

'Then whoever summoned the shin-shin knows how to treat with the dark spirits,' Tane said, suddenly calming and becoming contemplative. 'Could it be that they're also responsible for the sickness in the land?'

The reply that Asara was about to give was swallowed in a sudden riot of movement and noise. Kaiku yelped in surprise as she saw a blur of black lunging out from the stony soil of the roadside, and then their cart was tipped violently and they were flung to one side of it. Tane and Asara were thrown into Kaiku, and the three of them pitched over on to the road as the cart toppled with a loud splintering of wood. Tane rolled away out of instinct as the cart was dragged towards them, but mercifully it did not tip again, or it might have crushed the passengers beneath it. They scrambled clear amongst the shouts and chaos of the guards, who had been similarly surprised, and there they saw what had befallen them.

The Aberrant thing was huge, an ungodly fusion of teeth and limbs that had lain in a burrow by the roadside, disguised by a thin covering of shale, until it had sensed their approach. It was still half in the burrow, with only the foremost part of its body visible. Kaiku caught a horrified impression of a blind, eyeless face that was all jaw and teeth, a mouth stuffed with yellowed, crooked fangs amid a multitude of spiderlike legs that had crammed out of the burrow and enwrapped one of the manxthwa at the lead of the caravan. Both the manxthwa were lowing and bellowing in fear. Ottin had pulled himself clear, but the driver was screaming, trapped and entangled in the tethering ropes that served as bridles for the great beasts.

'Heart's blood, *shoot it*!' Ottin shrieked at the guards, but they already had their rifles up and ready. A volley of gunfire tore into the Aberrant creature and it squawked in fury, but it would not let go of its prize. It was dragging the manxthwa closer to its burrow, with the driver and the rest of the caravan pulled in by the force. Those spider limbs that were not engaged with the manxthwa waved tremulously in the air, seeming poised to strike at anything that came near.

The driver screamed again, begging incoherently as the Aberrant made another effort and dragged its prey another foot closer.

Kaiku reacted suddenly and without thinking. She ran back to the passenger cart, which was still on its side, and clambered on to it. Tane shouted at her to come back, but she barely heard him. The Aberrant thing gave another great pull, and the whole caravan shifted. Kaiku grabbed on and rode the lurch, praying that the cart would not tip further. It didn't. Heart thumping, she edged along it to where the manxthwa were bridled.

Ottin was yelling orders at the guards as they reloaded, though nobody was listening to him. He had backed away to the other side of the road, keeping the caravan between him and the horror that attacked them. As he saw Kaiku climbing towards where the driver was trapped, he shrieked something at her too. Whether he was encouraging her or otherwise, she never knew; for as she looked up at him, the second Aberrant creature burst out of its burrow behind Ottin and enfolded him in its vile arachnid legs. The scream that tore from his throat then was like nothing Kaiku had ever heard or wanted to again, but it was quickly silenced as he was stuffed into the creature's toothy maw with a cracking of bones and a flood of gore.

She scrambled onward, breathing hard in horror. Tane and Asara were firing on the first Aberrant creature, trying to dissuade it from the panicking manxthwa, but it held fast. Kaiku reached the front of the caravan, wedging herself into a corner formed by the overturned driver's seat. The terrified driver was gibbering at her, spittle bubbles flecking his lips. She saw that he was lashed tight to the flank of the manxthwa by the tautened tethering ropes. The spider legs of the Aberrant flexed within a few feet of her, each as thick as her arm, encircling the heaving flanks of the thrashing beast.

And then suddenly the fire was there, leaping into life inside her. She felt it stir with a flood of panic, which only seemed to double its intensity. It wanted out of her, wanted escape from the confines of her body, awakened by the spark of fear and excitement. She grabbed on to the tethering ropes and shut her eyes.

No, she willed it. *No, you will stay where you are.*

For the first time, she realised what she had done when she turned down Cailin tu Moritat's offer to help her control her power. In one moment she saw clearly what her recklessness had achieved, the price of her impatience, her eagerness to avenge her family. If she let it go here, they would all die.

'Kaiku!' It was Tane, calling her name. He could see that something was wrong with her, but the air was awash with rifle fire, and she could not hear him.

She tried to forget the cries of the driver; deafened herself to the report of the rifles. Peripherally, she realised that some of the guards had noticed the second Aberrant beast and were rushing around to the other side of the caravan to deal with it. She turned her thoughts inward, forcing the heat back into her abdomen as if trying to keep down vomit or bile. The driver howled at her to help him, unable to understand why she had suddenly frozen. She ignored him.

And now it faded, reluctantly receding, defeated by the barrier of her will. Her eyes flicked open, bloodshot and tear-reddened, and she gasped and panted hard. The physical effort had been immense. But she had won out, for now.

The Aberrant beast hauled on the manxthwa again, bringing her roughly back to reality as the caravan was wrenched another few feet closer to the burrow. The manxthwa in its grip was apoplectic with fear, almost within biting distance of the thing. Kaiku cringed as the thing's chitinous limbs stroked the air above her.

She pulled a knife from her belt. It had been with her ever since the Forest of Yuna, when Asara had given her travel clothes to change into; she had scarcely noticed it until now. It was a good forest knife, adapted to skin animals or cut wood with equal ease. Swiftly, she began to saw at the tethering ropes that held the driver. He squirmed, attempting to break free before she had even got through the first one.

'Stay still!' she hissed, and he did so.

Tane and Asara fired, and fired again. The creature that had hold of the manxthwa was by no means immune to the bullets, for they could see the dark splashes of blood that spattered its black body; but it seemed possessed of a suicidal persistence, and would not release the bucking manxthwa from its grip. Tane's weapon fired dry, and he broke it open to put new ignition powder in the chamber, glancing at Kaiku as he did so. She was frantically working on the ropes, her arm pumping as she cut, her face red and sweaty.

The creature braced and hauled with a greater effort than before, desperate to get its meal and get away from the stinging rifle balls. It could not understand why the manxthwa was so heavy, for it had not the brain to realise it was tethered. The puzzle frustrated it mightily. It applied brute strength.

Kaiku cried out as the entire caravan shifted a metre across the road. Asara and Tane had to scatter as the passenger cart finally toppled upside down.

Kaiku was pitched over with it, landing heavily on the stony dirt of the road and rolling to a stop a short way distant. The driver gave a strangled shriek, and then the tethering ropes, weakened by Kaiku's efforts, finally gave way. With a triumphant squawk, the Aberrant monstrosity bundled the manxthwa into its burrow and dragged it underground.

Tane scrambled to Kaiku's side, but she was already levering herself up on her elbows. Asara stood over the two of them, framed against the clouded sky, her rifle trained towards the Aberrant burrow.

'Are you hurt?' Tane asked, almost touching her and then thinking better of it.

Kaiku shook her head. 'I do not think so.' She stood up. 'Bruised,' she elaborated. 'Why have the guns stopped?'

Tane and Asara noticed it at the same time. The guards on their side of the caravan pricked up their ears. The train of carts that was snarled and corkscrewed along the centre of the road formed a barrier that prevented them seeing to the other side.

'Ho! Is all well over there?' one of the guards called.

'All's well,' came the reply.

They hurried around the end of the caravan, and there they saw the remainder of the guards clustered around the grotesque corpse of the second Aberrant creature. Its massive jaw lay on the road, its legs limp around it, half out of its burrow.

'It must have been a lucky shot,' said one, prodding it with the barrel of his rifle. 'We got the brain.'

'We should move out of here,' said a short, grizzled guard, evidently the leader. 'Take the remaining manxthwa, and two carts for passengers. Leave the rest.'

'Leave the goods?' another protested.

'There's no caravan master to sell them. We're not paid to deliver goods.' The leader jerked a hand at the approximate location of the other burrow. 'And that thing is still alive, and it will be out again as soon as it's finished its meal.'

All of them began to untangle the carts and right those that could be righted. Three guards stood near the burrow entrance, from which the sounds of crunching bone could be heard as the unfortunate manxthwa was devoured. The driver was disentangled from the ropes, but it was too late for him. His neck had been broken, and he stared glassy-eyed towards the earth.

'What was his name? The driver?' Tane asked as he lent his back to the effort of tipping a cart back on to its wheels.

'Why?' one of the guards replied.

'He should be named,' Tane grunted. 'To Noctu, recorder of lives.'

But nobody knew his name.

They managed to get two carts tethered to the remaining manxthwa, who could smell the blood of its departed companion and was snorting skittishly. The Aberrant beast did not emerge again, even after the sounds of feeding had ceased. Leaving the train of goods on the road, they took the body of the driver, wrapped in a tarpaulin, and bundled it in with them. In that manner, they drove on towards Chaim.

'Those monsters are your Aberrants, Asara,' Tane said as they set off, dejected and shocked and tired. 'Those are your *superior breed.*'

Overhead, the gristle-crows circled and swooped.

SEVENTEEN

Chaim had little to offer the traveller. It was a skeletal, sparse mountain village, with low houses of wood or stone scattered around a few rocky trails that wound haphazardly through the village. Everywhere the eye roamed it struck a hard plane; there was no softness of foliage, no sprinkle of mountain flowers or grass. Even the people seemed hard, squat and compact with narrow, dull eyes and brown, wind-chapped skin. It could not have been more different from the quaint, provincial charm of Pelis; this place seemed to have been scratched from the mountainside and built out of grudging necessity, and it loured in a stew of its own bleak misery.

It was not a place that welcomed strangers, but neither was it hostile to them. Kaiku, Asara and Tane found themselves simply ignored, their questions responded to with unhelpful grunts. Kaiku tried asking about for anyone who might remember her father passing through, but what began as a slim hope petered to nothing in the face of the villagers' stoic rudeness. In this place, a person either lived here or they didn't, and outsiders got short shrift from the natives.

They arrived in Chaim in the late afternoon. The caravan guards bade them a peremptory farewell, and they were left to themselves. Wandering through the simple streets of the village, buffeted by occasional gusts of cold wind and frowned upon by the rising peaks all around them, they felt curiously alone.

Asara's talents for procuring aid failed them in this desolate place. Their inquiries after a guide were met with ignorance and surliness, and her striking beauty appeared to have no effect on the men here. It piqued her mightily, Kaiku was amused to note.

'Probably they find their relief with their pack animals,' she muttered.

Eventually it was a guide who found them, as night gathered and lanterns were lit.

They were sitting in what passed for a bar here, merely the downstairs portion of someone's house that sold a raw local liquor. It was devoid of joy or atmosphere, a simple scattering of low, round tables cut from rough wood and a few threadbare mats for patrons to sit on. A stone-faced woman meted out measures of the liquor from behind a counter in the corner. Lanterns half-heartedly held back the gloom, while simultaneously contributing to it by the fumes from the cheap, smoky oil they were filled with. Despite being so small, and half-full with villagers who muttered to each other over their tumblers, the place still managed to feel cold and hollow. Kaiku could scarcely believe that a place like this existed. She had no illusions about the state of many bars in the Poor Quarter of Axekami, but she had always imagined them to be at least raucous, if not exactly brimming with celebration. This place seemed like a gathering of the condemned.

The three companions were contemplating their next move when a short, scrawny figure sat down with them. He was buried in a mound of furs that dwarfed his bald head, making him seem like a vulture. By the condition and tone of his skin, he was a mountain man like the rest of them, but when he talked it was in a rapid chatter that seemed quite at odds with his kinsfolk.

'I'm told you're looking for the mask-makers, that right?' he said, before any of them could wonder who he was. 'Well I'm here to tell you that it can't be done, but if you still want to try I'm your guide. Mamak!'

'Mamak,' Kaiku repeated, unsure if that was his name or some local exclamation that they did not understand. 'You will take us, then?'

'What do you mean, it can't be done?' Tane interrupted.

'As I said. The paths have been lost, and not even the greatest of mountain men have ever found them.'

'We knew that,' Kaiku said to Tane, laying a hand on his arm. 'Do not be discouraged.' She knew him well enough by now to see the signs of an impending mood swing, and Tane had been overdue for a plunge into miserable despair for hours, beleaguered as they had been by the events of the day. Apart from the frustration they had experienced since their arrival in Chaim, Tane had been dwelling on the fate of the driver of their caravan. The lessons of his apprenticeship to the priesthood were gnawing at his conscience. Nobody should die without being named to Noctu, he said; and yet it was only the caravan master who hired him who must have known the driver's name, and he was gone.

'If you cannot take us there,' said Asara coolly, resting her elbows on the table, 'then why do we need you?'

'Because you'd be lost within an hour,' he said with a quick grin, showing long teeth narrowed into crooked, browned columns by decay and neglect. 'And up in the mountains there's creatures so warped that you'd never be able to guess what kind of animal they originally came from. Like the thing that nearly had your lives on the way here.'

Asara did not trouble to ask how he knew about that. The guards had been talking, it seemed.

'Listen,' he said. 'It's not my way to pry into your business. You say you knew you were looking for a place that couldn't be found, and you still want to look. I'd guess you know something I don't. Or you think you do.' He sat back, splayed his fingers on the coarse wood of the table before him. 'I can take you to where the monastery *ought* to be. It still shows up on old maps, and nobody knows the mountains better than me. But when we get near, you'll see what I mean when I say it can't be found. You'll be walking down a trail, heading north, and all of a sudden you realise you've ended up a mile south, though you could've sworn you were checking your bearings every step of the way. There's something there, clouds a man's mind, turns you around, and no amount of care can get through it. Believe me, people have tried.' He tipped them a conspiratorial wink. 'Still want to go?'

'How much?'

'Five hundred poc. No, round it up to ten shirets.'

'You can have it in coins. I do not have paper money,' Kaiku lied. Her grandmother had always warned her about showing money in public, especially in places like this. Presumably Mamak thought he was overcharging, but it was still cheap by city standards.

Mamak shrugged. 'Five-seventy poc, then,' he said. 'In advance.'

'Three hundred now,' Asara said. 'The rest when we are up in the mountains.'

'As you'll have it,' he said.

'Good. When do we leave?'

'Have you booked into the inn yet?'

Asara made a sound to the negative.

'Then we can leave right now.'

'It's dark,' Tane pointed out.

Mamak rolled his eyes. 'The first stretch is a trail as big as a road. It'll take a few hours. We camp at the end of that, and in the morning we tackle the rough stuff. I suppose you have some kind of warm clothing?'

Asara showed him what they had brought. He tutted. 'You'll need more. This isn't the mainland. The nights up there aren't so warm, and the weather's a beast even in summer.' He stood. 'I have a man we can see. Best to get going.'

The next few days were hard.

Both Tane and Kaiku were quite used to the physical exertions of long journeys. Both had hunted in the forests, chased down deer and travelled far to lay traps or find a picturesque spot to fish or bathe. Tane, for his part, had often made forays for rare herbs into the lesser teeth of the Tchamil Mountains, which blended into the Forest of Yuna on its eastern edge until the soil gave way to rock and the trees disappeared. But neither of them was quite prepared for the sense of wilderness that overtook them as they ascended into the Lakmar Mountains that dominated the northern half of Fo.

The mountains seemed to exude a sense of something that was like death but yet not: the absence of life. The unforgiving rock shouldered all around them in great, flattened slopes, yet there was rarely more than a fringe of tough grass or hardy weeds to be seen. What trees there were served only to remind them of the caravan driver's warnings of blight in the mountains; they were gnarled and crooked, sometimes with several scrawny trunks sharing the same withered branches, joined seamlessly together. Jagged peaks reared across the horizon, made bluish by distance; but the world around them was grey and hard. The silence was oppressive, and seemed to stunt conversation. The only one who seemed unaffected was Mamak, who chatted away as he walked, telling them old legends and stories of the mountains, many of which were variations of ones they knew from the mainland.

Kaiku, at least, was glad of his talk, for it distracted her from fatigue. The paths had become progressively steeper and harder as they travelled onward, and they were forced to climb often. This was the first serious exercise she had undertaken since her convalescence in the temple of Enyu, and her muscles ached. Tane seemed to be doing better, though his pride would not let him show fatigue; Asara was tireless.

Given time to contemplate, Kaiku found herself wondering more and more about Asara. During her time as Kaiku's handmaiden, they had been good friends, and shared many secrets. They had talked about boys, made fun of her father's foibles, teased the cook and picked on Karia, Kaiku's other handmaiden. And even though she knew it now to be a charade, and that Karia had ended unwillingly giving her life to resurrect her dead mistress, she missed that person Asara had been. This new Asara – presumably the real one, though how could she be sure? – was colder and harder, fiercely asserting her independence from everybody. She did not need reassurance or company, it seemed; she had no interest in talking about herself, nor did she appear to care about Kaiku or Tane. Tane accepted this as the way she was, but Kaiku was not so certain. Sometimes she caught glimpses of a stubborn child in Asara, balling its fists and scrunching its brow and protesting that it *didn't* want to talk to anyone. She was an Aberrant, that much Kaiku knew; but beyond that, her beautiful companion was still a mystery.

She thought about Tane, too. Before she had left the temple, he had made some small overtures to her in his awkward way about staying with him. She had been forced to deny him then, because she had to move on. He had followed her and joined her instead. He had told her of how the shin-shin had destroyed his temple, and how he was seeking the ones who had summoned them to exact his revenge; but Kaiku knew there was more to it than that, and she felt something . . . unfamiliar in response. Yet whenever she allowed herself to dwell on it, whenever her eyes roamed across his back and imagined the taut play of lean muscles beneath, her thoughts became soured. For Tane was a priest of nature, and she was an Aberrant. It was in his blood to hate her. And sooner or later, inevitably, he would find her out. Like Mishani.

She clamped down on her sorrow as soon as it bunched to spring. Mishani. That was a name forever in her past now. If she must live on, she must prepare herself to be shunned and despised, even by the ones she held most dear. Perhaps she was merely being obtuse, unwilling to accept what seemed the obvious truth: that Cailin tu Moritat and her Red Order were the only ones who would accept her now, the only ones who *wanted* her. Though she suspected their motives, she could not deny that. To everyone else, she was simply an Aberrant, and no different from the foul things which attacked their caravan.

Mamak seemed a capable guide, and they felt as safe in his hands as it was possible to feel in such an alien place. Many times he made them backtrack to avoid a bluff, or to take advantage of an overhang. Rarely did he explain why – one of the few things he was not overly vocal about – but whenever they wondered about the absence of the dangerous creatures they had been warned of, they thought of these detours and suspected it was thanks to him they had not met any. They did see smaller breeds, however: some whole and strange, and some malformed. These latter flopped inefficiently about, searching for food. They were usually cubs or chicks, for they would not survive to adulthood before becoming a meal for some superior predator. The evidence of these predators came at night, when the whistling wind was joined by eerie baying and yelping from unnatural throats. On the second night they had stayed awake, listening to the cries come closer and finally encircle them. But Mamak had not allowed a fire that night, and though they shivered, the creatures passed them by.

On the third day, the weather worsened.

They were caught out on a long, slanted table of bare rock when the storm hit, seemingly out of nowhere. Kaiku was shocked at the speed that the cloud cover darkened to glowering black, and the ferocity with which it unloaded on them. She was used to the slow, ponderous buildup of humidity on the mainland, when it was possible to sense precisely when a storm was about to break; here, there were no such indications. Mamak cursed and increased the pace, leading them up the exposed tilt of the rock towards shelter; but it would take several hours to traverse the open ground, and they feared the storm would overwhelm them by then.

Kaiku had never felt anything like it. The rain, icily cold, battered and smashed at her with such force that it stung the skin of her face. Lightning flashed and tore the air, and thunder blasted them and rolled through the creases of the mountains. It seemed that by being this high they were disproportionately closer to the cloud, and the violence of the storm's roar was enough to make them cringe. The wind picked up steadily until it pushed at them with rough shoulders, snapping from different directions in an attempt to tip them and send them tumbling away. As Mamak had advised, they had bought heavy coats for the journey, and they were never more glad than now; but even with their hoods pulled over their heads, the wind and rain slashed them with brutal force.

They bowed to the fury of the elements, forging on with their packs tugging at their backs. Their teeth chattered and their lips and cheeks were numb, but they wearily forced one foot in front of the other and hurried up the rocky slope, slick with rain. And each time Kaiku thought she could take no more, that she must somehow stop this assault immediately or just curl up and collapse, she looked up at the steep cliff they were heading towards and moaned in misery at how little ground they seemed to have made.

Eventually, the unendurable ended, and they stumbled into a cave, frozen and soaking and shivering. It was a good size for the four of them, its walls a ragged mess of black stone, shot through with scrappy veins of quartz which glistened as if moist. The floor was tilted slightly upward from the mouth, so it had mercifully stayed dry, even though they would still have taken shelter there if it had been inches deep. Mamak stalked to the back of the cave and angrily pronounced it unoccupied. Then he shouted and swore and stamped, profanities echoing off the uneven walls, cursing the gods in general and Panazu specifically for the storm.

'He seems annoyed,' Asara deadpanned, and Kaiku was so surprised that she started laughing, despite it all.

'I'm glad you two are in such good spirits,' Tane said morosely, and by his tone Kaiku guessed that the black mood which had been hovering over him of late had finally descended.

Mamak was leaning against the cave wall, his head rested on his forearm, breathing hard to relax himself. 'Warm yourselves as best you can,' he said. 'I'll make a fire.'

'With what?' Tane snapped, depression making him thorny. 'There's no wood on this damned mountain!'

It was not strictly true, but Mamak did not bother to correct him. 'There are other ways of making fire in the mountains,' he said. 'I have done this before, you know.'

Tane flashed him a sullen glare and marched to the entrance of the cave, where he sat alone, looking out at the lashing rain, with the fur lining of his hood rippling as stray gusts found their way in. Kaiku sat dripping against one of the walls, hugging her coat close around her, her jaw juddering from the cold. Asara sat down next to her. Kaiku gave her a look of vague puzzlement, for she had expected the other to sit alone; then Asara opened her coat, and put one arm around Kaiku, gathering her into the voluminous furred folds. Kaiku hesitated a moment, then relented, curling up into Asara with her hooded head on her companion's breast. Asara's damp coat enfolded her completely, like a wing, and Kaiku burrowed into the warmth of her body. In the hot, dark place that Asara had provided for her, she felt the shivering recede to the rhythm of Asara's heartbeat in her ear, and before she drowsed and slept she felt safer and more content than she had for a long time.

When she awoke, it was to a new heat. A fire was burning in the cave. Asara sensed her stirring and unfolded her wing; Kaiku blinked muzzily and relinquished Asara's body with some reluctance. She sat upright, meeting Asara's gaze, and gave her an awkward smile of thanks. Asara inclined her head in acceptance. Tane was watching them from the other side of the blaze, with undisguised disapproval in his eyes and something that he was loathe to admit as jealousy. Outside, the sky boomed and the storm raged unabated, but here in the cave there was a pocket of warmth and light that robbed its thunderous threats of potency.

'Awake then?' Mamak said cheerily. 'Good. We're going to have to sit this out. No telling how long it will be.'

Kaiku squinted at the flames. The fire burned with an amber hue, and at its base was not wood but a black, crinkly skeleton of thin fibres like spun sugar.

'Fire-moss,' Mamak said, anticipating her question. He held up a handful of the stuff; it was a black, soggy puffball. 'Weighs almost nothing, burns for hours. It secretes an inflammable residue, but its structure is extremely tough and takes a lot of heat to burn through. Useful tip if you don't have any wood to hand, and extremely portable.'

Inevitably, they talked. The storm showed no sign of abating, and so Mamak produced a jar of a sharp, murky liquor and passed it around to them. They had brought provisions for two weeks' travel, and so there were plenty of ingredients for a pot of vegetables and cured meat. Once their stomachs were full and their tongues loosened, they discussed and laughed and argued over a range of subjects. But it was Asara who introduced the one that occupied them most of the night: the affair of the Heir-Empress and the rising unrest in Axekami. The argument that ensued was not new to them, pitched between Asara, who was intent on challenging Tane's religious prejudice, and Tane, who was intent on defending it. Kaiku stayed out of it, unsure of her own feelings on the subject, and Mamak didn't care one way or another about Aberrants as long as they didn't try and eat him. Tane was in the midst of an assertion that the Heir-Empress could not possibly be good for the country because the country would never have an Aberrant as leader when Asara stopped him dead with a single question.

'Do any of you know what the Heir-Empress can actually *do*?'

There was silence. Tane fought for an answer, and found none. The fire was eerily silent, for there was no snapping of wood. Outside, the storm raged on, and if there were any Aberrants brave enough to venture out in it, they heard none.

'I thought not. Let me educate you, then, for you may find this very interesting. You especially, Tane. Have you heard of the Libera Dramach?' Before any of them could answer, she went on, 'No, you won't have. Their name is known among the people of Axekami, but they are only a rumour at present. That will soon change, I think.'

'What are they, then?' Kaiku asked, the shadows of her face wavering in the light of the burning fire-moss.

'In the simplest terms, they are an organisation dedicated to seeing the Heir-Empress take the throne.'

Tane snorted, making a dismissive motion with one hand. 'It's been scarcely a month since anyone even knew the Heir-Empress was an Aberrant at all.'

'We have known for years,' Asara replied levelly.

'We?' Mamak inquired, passing her the jar of liquor.

Asara sipped. 'I belong to no master or mistress,' she said. 'But as much as I can be said to be part of something, I am part of the Libera Dramach. Their aims and mine coincide, and have from the start.'

'And what are their aims?' Tane demanded.

'To see the Heir-Empress on the throne,' she repeated. 'To see the power of the Weavers destroyed. To stop the slaughter of Aberrant children. And to stop the blight that encroaches on the land.'

'How will the Heir-Empress's succession have any bearing on the malaise in our soil?' Tane asked. This had caught his interest.

Asara leaned forward so that her face was underlit in orange flame. 'She can talk to spirits, Tane. That is her gift. Spirits, animals . . . she is an element of nature, closer to Enyu than any human could be.'

'That's blasphemy,' Tane said, but not angrily. 'An Aberrant can't be *anything* to Enyu. And besides, her priests can talk to spirits. *I* can, to some degree.'

'No,' Asara corrected. 'You can listen. You can feel the spirits of nature, sense their mood; even the greatest among you has little more that a rudimentary understanding of them. They are to humans like the gods are: distant, unfathomable, and impossible to influence. But she can *talk* to them. She is eight harvests of age, yet already she can converse with a skill far beyond the best of Enyu's priests. And she gets better ever day. This is not something she has learned, it is something she was born with that she is learning to *use*. It is her Aberrant ability, Tane.'

Tane was silent for a time, head bowed. Mamak and Kaiku, sensing that this was between Asara and the acolyte, stayed out of it and waited to see what his reaction would be. Presently he stirred. 'You're suggesting that she could be a bridge to the spirits? Between us and them?'

'Exactly,' Asara said. 'For now, she is kept at the Imperial Keep, in the city, where men and women rule. But you know and I know that there are places in our land where the great spirits dwell, places where people such as us dare not go. But *she* could go. She is an ambassador, don't you see? A link between our world and theirs. If there is any hope of turning back the tide that is slowly swallowing us, then she is it.'

'How do you know?' Tane asked. He sounded . . . *overwhelmed*. Rather than the stoic denial Kaiku had expected from him, he seemed to be listening. Truly, he was an unpredictable soul. 'How did you know of it, before the rest of us?'

'That, I cannot tell you,' said Asara, with a soft sigh. 'I wish I could do so, to make you believe me. But lives are at risk, and loose talk can still undo what has been done.'

Tane nodded slightly. 'I think I understand,' he replied. He said nothing further for the rest of the night, merely stared into the fire, meditating on what he had been told.

*

The storm did not abate by the morning, nor the morning after that. They did not speak again of the Heir-Empress or the Libera Dramach; in fact, they spoke little of anything at all. Kaiku was becoming worried; she had never seen a storm that lasted so long, never imagined the sky could sustain such fury. And despite Mamak's assurance that such storms were not unheard of, the atmosphere in the cave became strained. When Tane suggested that Mamak might have been unwise to curse Panazu, god of storms, the two men nearly came to blows. Asara cleaned her rifle for the twentieth time and watched them owlishly.

As the day waned on the third night in the cave, Mamak announced that they had to turn back.

'This storm can't hold much longer,' he said, throwing another wad of fire-moss from their diminishing supply on to the small blaze they had going. 'But it's a good two days' journey yet to the site of the monastery, and that makes five to return to Chaim. If everything went perfectly to plan, if we left tomorrow and we found the monastery immediately and came right back, we would still only have a day's margin of food. You don't take risks like that in the mountains. I don't, anyway.'

'We cannot turn back!' Kaiku protested. 'I swore an oath to Ocha. We have to go on.'

'The gods are patient, Kaiku,' said Asara. 'You will not forget your oath, and nor will Ocha; but you cannot rush blindly at this. We retreat, and try again.'

'You'll die if you don't, besides,' Mamak put in.

Kaiku's brow was scored with a line of frustration. 'I cannot turn back!' she reiterated. Asara was puzzled at the desperation in her voice.

'But we must,' she said. 'We have no choice.'

Tane awoke several hours later. The storm howled and boomed outside, its tumult now a background noise. Kaiku was sitting at the fire, staring into its heart. She had been banking it up with fire-moss. Tane, still lying on his side, blinked at her and frowned. He had been withdrawn since his conversation with Asara, fiercely preoccupied with his own thoughts; now he noticed that Kaiku had lapsed into a similar attitude.

She jumped slightly when he spoke.

'Kaiku?' he observed. 'Why aren't you asleep?'

'When I sleep, I dream of boars,' she replied.

'Boars?'

'You turn back so easily, Tane,' she said, her voice soft and contemplative. 'I swore to the Emperor of the gods, yet you turn back so easily.'

He was still barely awake, and his eyes drowsed heavy. 'We will try again,' he mumbled. 'Not giving up.'

'Perhaps this was not your path to take after all,' she murmured to herself. 'Perhaps it is mine alone.'

If she said anything else Tane did not hear it, for he was drawn back into oblivion once more.

The next morning, Kaiku was gone. She had walked into the storm with only her pack and her rifle. And with her went the Mask.

EIGHTEEN

Mishani wore a robe of dark green for her audience with Lucia, and a wide sash of blue around her slender waist. The sash was more than decorative, for pressed against her lower back was the gift she had been charged to deliver. The slight bulge it made was hidden by her thick, ankle-length hair, which she had bound with blue strips of leather. A flat square of elegant wrapping paper, and within it the nightdress that would be the Heir-Empress's death.

It took every ounce of her carefully cultivated self-control to keep herself calm as she was escorted into the presence of the Empress. Quite aside from anything else, the prospect of having a garment riddled with bone fever pressed close to her skin was terrifying. Her father had assured her that the package was sealed tight, and its wrapping treated with odourless antiseptics to keep the disease inside; and besides, it was a very low-grade infection, and it would only take effect if breathed in over a period of time, such as in sleep. Mishani sneered inside at his words; it was bitterly obvious that he knew nothing about bone fever, that he was merely parroting the blithe assurances of Sonmaga. What had the Barak of Blood Amacha promised, that had turned her father into his lapdog, and *her* into his cat's-paw?

She was taken aback by her own vehemence. Before all this, she would never have allowed herself to think so uncharitably about her father. But as she was shown into the room where Anais was waiting, she was still certain that everything she felt was justified. He knew she could not refuse him, and he betrayed her by using that assurance for his own ends. She did not want to be party to murder; and to make her an assassin of the lowest kind, the sort of filth who would use *disease* as a weapon . . . The raw shame if she was caught would drive her to suicide.

And what of the shame if I succeed?

Her father was full of meaningless words: she would be averting a civil war, saving many lives, doing a great service for Saramyr. She heard none of them, knew them for the empty platitudes they were. She wanted to weep, to hug him and then shout in his face: *Do not do this, Father! Can you not see what will happen to us? It is not too late; if you change your mind now, I can still be your daughter.*

But he had not changed his mind. And she felt the bonds between them sawn apart so brutally that she could barely look at him. Suddenly she saw every annoying tic, every blemish on his face, every unpleasant quirk of his character. She did not respect him any longer, and that was a terrible thing for a daughter to admit.

She would murder for him, because she must. But after that, she was no longer his. She suspected he knew that, but he sent her anyway.

Sonmaga. Her hatred for him knew no bounds.

Mishani talked with Anais for some time, though afterward she hardly remembered what was said. The Empress was trying to divine Mishani's standpoint on Lucia's accession to the throne, but Mishani revealed nothing in her pleasant responses. Anais inquired after her father also, obviously hoping to learn why Mishani had come when the Barak was such a staunch opponent to her. Mishani said enough to assure Anais that she was approaching the situation with an open mind, and she did not believe in judging somebody she had never met.

But a cold dread was settling slowly on to Mishani as she spoke to the Empress. Was her mask slipping, and her own fear and trepidation showing through? Certainly it seemed as if the Empress was procrastinating, unwilling to show Mishani through to Lucia's chambers. She seemed frankly nervous. The package pressed against Mishani's lower back burned with the heat of the shame it bore. Could the mother sense she meant harm to the child? She felt perspiration prickle her scalp.

Then Anais was inviting her through, up to the gardens that nestled among the confusing maze of the Imperial Keep's top level. The temple to Ocha that was the centre point of the roof rose magnificently against the midday sky, and the four thin needles at each corner of the Keep reached higher still. The uppermost level of the sloping edifice was a labyrinth of gardens, small buildings, waterways and stony trenches which served as thoroughfares between them, like sunken streets. From below it was impossible to see there was anything up here, and Mishani had always borne the assumption that the roof was flat and featureless apart from the temple which was easily visible from anywhere in Axekami. Now she realised she was wrong; it was like a miniature district of the city. Mishani noticed also several squat guard towers around the gardens, and soldiers with rifles watching within.

'I apologise for all the guards,' Anais said as they came out into the blinding sunlight. She had noticed Mishani's furtive glance. 'The security of Lucia is paramount, especially now.'

'I understand,' Mishani said, feeling her throat tighten. She had hidden her package because she had little knowledge of how closely Lucia was guarded, and did not want to risk it being opened and checked. Though it would be a grave insult to imply that she meant the Heir-Empress harm, she did not dare take the chance. She wanted to give her gift to Lucia in secret if possible; but she doubted now that the opportunity would arise.

Anais seemed about to speak, thought better of it, then changed her mind again. 'I learned that someone had . . . got close to Lucia recently,' she intimated. 'Someone who could have done her harm.'

'How awful,' Mishani said, but inside she felt the tension slacken like an exhaled breath. So that was why she was nervous. She did not suspect Mishani.

They came across Lucia in the company of a tall, robed man with a close-cropped white beard. They were standing in a small square that formed a junction between several paths, and were playing some kind of learning game that involved arranging black and white bead-bags in different formations on the flagstones. Trees rustled around them with the activity of squirrels and the stirring of the hot, sluggish air. As the Empress and Mishani arrived, they looked up and bowed in greeting.

'This is Mishani tu Koli,' she said to the group at large. 'And here is Lucia, and Zaelis tu Unterlyn, one of her tutors.'

Zaelis bowed. 'It's an honour to meet you, Mistress,' he said in a throaty bass.

Mishani acknowledged him with a nod, but she had barely taken her eyes off the Heir-Empress since she arrived. Lucia, in turn, was regarding her steadily with her pale blue, dreamy gaze, an almost fey expression on her face. Her blonde hair stirred in a soft gust of warm wind.

'Come and walk with me, Mishani,' Lucia said suddenly, holding her hand up.

'Lucia!' Anais exclaimed. She had never behaved in such a way before with guests; usually she was the model of politeness. Such an imperative request from a child to an adult was nothing short of impertinent.

'Lucia, remember your manners,' Zaelis cautioned.

'No, it's quite all right,' Mishani said. She looked to Anais. 'May I?'

Anais hesitated a moment, caught between her desire to have the child where she could see her and winning over Mishani. In the end, she did the only thing she really could. 'Of course,' she smiled.

Mishani took Lucia's hand, and it was as if some spark passed between them, a minute current that trembled up Mishani's arm. Her face creased slightly in puzzlement, but Lucia beamed innocently and led her away from the others down a paved path, across an immaculate lawn bordered by a dense row of tumisi trees, hemmed in from the rest of the gardens.

They walked in silence a short way. Mishani felt a creeping nausea in her stomach. The child next to her seemed only that: a child. Like Kaiku, she was physically unmarred by her Aberrance.

I am to murder a child, she thought. *And by the foulest means imaginable.* It was what she had been thinking ever since her father asked her to do this, but now the reality of the situation crowded in on her and she began to suffocate.

'You must get tired of seeing people like me,' she said, feeling the sudden need to talk to distract herself. 'I expect you have met a lot of nobles over these past weeks.' It was an inanity, but she felt disarmed and it was all she could find to say.

'They think I'm a monster,' Lucia said, her eyes placid. 'Most of them, anyway.'

Mishani was taken aback to hear such words from an eight-harvest child's mouth.

'You don't, though,' she said, turning her face up to Mishani's.

She was right. It was different with her than it had been with Kaiku. She could not even consider this child as being Aberrant; not in the sense that she knew it, anyway. She felt the nausea in her gut become painful.

Spirits, I cannot do this.

They turned from the lawn into a shaded nook, where there was a simple wooden bench. Lucia turned them into it and sat down. Mishani sat next to her, smoothing her robe into her lap. They were away from the sight of anyone, but for a single raven perched on a distant wall of the garden, watching them with disconcerting interest.

I cannot . . . cannot . . .

Mishani felt her control teetering. She had almost hoped the Empress would stay with them, that the opportunity to give Lucia the parcel would not present itself; but the child was unwittingly making it easy for her.

'I have a gift for you,' she heard herself say, and her voice sounded distant over the blood in her ears. She felt the package slide free from her sash as she tugged it out, and then it was in her hands. Flat and square, gold-embroidered paper and a deep blue bow.

Lucia looked at it, and then at her. A sudden surge of emotion welled inside Mishani, too fast for her to suppress; she felt her lip quiver as she took a shuddering breath, as if she were about to weep. She forced it down, but it had been an unforgivable breach in her façade. Two years she had been practising the stillness and poise of court, two years of building her mask; but now she felt as a young girl again, and her confidence and poise had fled. She was not as strong as she had thought she was. She flinched and railed at her responsibility.

'Why are you sad?' Lucia asked.

'I am sad . . .' Mishani said. 'I am sad because of the games we play.'

'Some games are more fun than others,' Lucia said.

'And some are more serious than you imagine,' Mishani answered. She gave the child a strange smile. 'Do you like your father, the Emperor?'

'No,' Lucia replied. 'He scares me.'

'So does mine,' Mishani said quietly.

Lucia was silent for a time. 'Will you give me my gift?' she asked.

Mishani's blood froze. The moment that followed seemed to stretch out agonisingly. A sudden realisation had hit her: that she was no more prepared now to kill the child than she ever had been. She thought of her father, how proud she had always made him, how he had taught her and how she had loved him.

She shook her head, the tiniest movement. 'Forgive me,' she said. 'I made a mistake. This gift is not for you.' She slid it back into her belt.

Lucia gazed at her blankly with her strange, ethereal gaze. Then she slid along the bench and laid her head on Mishani's shoulder. Mishani, surprised, put her arm around the child.

Do not trust me so, she thought, burning with shame, *for you do not know what kind of creature I am.*

'Thank you,' Lucia whispered, and that destroyed the last of her composure. She felt the swell of tears expand behind her eyes, and then she wept, as she had not wept for years. She cried for Kaiku, and for her father, and for herself and what she had become. She had been so sure, so certain of everything, and yet all the certainties had been shattered. And here was the daughter of the Empress thanking Mishani for choosing not to murder her, and—

She looked up and into Lucia's eyes, her weeping suddenly arrested. It hit her then. She knew. The child *knew*. And yet Mishani wondered if she would not have taken the gift anyway, and worn it, and died if it were offered. She had the sudden prescience of being at the fulcrum of some terrible balance, that uncounted futures had depended on that single instant of decision.

Lucia gave her a shy smile. 'You should go and see the dream lady,' she said. 'I think you would like her.'

The crowd in Speaker's Square that evening was immense.

The square was a great flagged quad, bordered by tall rows of grand buildings. Its western side was almost entirely taken up by the enormous Temple of Isisya, the façade a mass of swooping balconies, mosaics and carvings, its lowest storey shaded by an ornamental stone awning that encroached on to the square, supported by vast pillars. The other buildings were similarly impressive: the city library – ostensibly public, but whose volumes were illegible to the peasantry, written as they were in High Saramyrrhic; the central administrative complex, where much of the day-to-day running of Axekami took place; and a huge bathhouse, with a bronze statue of a catfish resting on a plinth set into its broad steps, the earthly aspect of Panazu.

In the very centre of the square was a raised platform over which a carven henge was raised, its two upright pillars elegantly curving up to support the bowed crossbeam, on which was written in languid pictograms a legendary – and historically dubious – quote from the Blood Emperor Torus tu Vinaxis: *As painting or sculpture is art, so too the spoken word.*

The crowd crammed around the speaker's podium and spread all the way to the edges of the square, clogging the doorways of the surrounding buildings and spilling out into the tributary streets. Its mood was ugly, and it told in the scowls on people's faces and the frequent scuffles that erupted as patience ran out and fuses burned down. Its cheers in support of the speaker – and these were often and heartfelt – had a savage edge to them. Most of the crowd knew what they felt about the matter of the Heir-Empress already; they had come to hear someone who could articulate the rage and frustration and revulsion they nursed in their breasts, and agree with him. That someone was Unger tu Torrhyc.

Zaelis watched from beside one of the marble pillars of the city library, scanning the throng. They milled in the slowly declining heat of the evening, when the sun's light had reddened and the shadows of the buildings to the west stretched across the convocation, a sharp border dividing them into light and darkness. As Unger delivered a particularly barbed comment about the Heir-Empress, the crowd erupted in a roar, and Zaelis saw the glimmer of primal fury in the city folk's eyes, age-old hatred rooted so deep that they did not even remember its origins. Barely any of them knew that it was the Weavers who had planted that seed, the Weavers who had instigated and encouraged humankind's natural fear of Aberrants, and had been doing so for two centuries or more.

On the central platform of the square, Unger stalked between the red wooden pillars of the henge, prowling here and there while he orated, his voice carrying to all corners of the gathering as his hands waved and his wild hair flapped. He was not a handsome man, a little too short for his frame and his features large and blocky; but he had charisma, nobody could deny that. The passion was plainly evident in his voice as he harangued the multitude of the dangers that would beset Saramyr with an Aberrant on the throne. He used the stage like a master theatre player, and his tone and manner rode the swell of the crowd, becoming louder and louder until he was almost screaming, whipping his audience to fever pitch. What he was saying was nothing new, but the way in which he said it was so persuasive, the arguments he posited so unassailable, that he was impossible to ignore. And as his fame had grown over these past weeks, so his listeners had multiplied.

Zaelis felt a cold foreboding as he looked out over the crowd. The tension in the air was palpable. Axekami teetered on a knife-edge, and its Empress appeared to be doing nothing about it. Zaelis wondered in despair if Anais had even listened to her advisors as they explained the growing discontent in the streets of the capital, or if she had still been thinking of ways to win the high families round to her side. She was so preoccupied by the reports of Blood Amacha and Blood Kerestyn massing their forces that she had no time to consider anything else; and as much as he respected and admired her, he had to admit that she was guilty of the arrogance of nobility. Deep down, she did not believe that the underclasses were capable of organising themselves enough to hurt her. She saw Axekami as a creche, swarming with unaccountably wilful children who had to be kept in line to prevent them from harming themselves. The idea that they might throw off their loyalty to her over this matter had occurred to her on a superficial level, but no more. She suffered from a lack of empathy; she could not understand the level of hatred they bore for her beloved child. She underestimated the dread the word *Aberrant* still evoked in the common man.

But Zaelis's real concern was for Lucia. With two factions already building their forces against her, Anais could not afford to fight on a third front, this one *inside* the walls of her city. If any of the forces opposed to her won the victory, then Lucia's life would be forfeit. No matter that she was not the monster they imagined her to be – though he had to admit she frightened even him at times, and the gods only knew what kind of power she would wield in adulthood if she continued developing at the rate she was going. She would have to be killed because of what she represented.

Zaelis thought about that for a time, ignoring the rhetoric that Unger tu Torrhyc threw out to the crowd like bloody bones to baying hounds. Then he left, his thoughts dark, pushing his way through the throng and back towards the Imperial Quarter.

He did not notice the man in grubby baker's clothes as he passed by on the outskirts of the gathering. Nor would he have troubled himself about it if he *had* noticed; he had more important things on his mind than that. Perhaps he would have puzzled over the man's odd expression – a combination of furtiveness, defiance and feverishness. He might have noticed the heavy pack the baker carried, triple-strapped shut. And if he had waited long enough, he might have seen the second man arrive, also carrying a heavy pack, and the grim mutual recognition passing between them, as of two soldiers meeting on a battlefield over the carnage of their dead companions.

None of that would have meant anything to Zaelis, had he not simply walked on by. And besides, it was only one of many similar meetings across the city that had been going on ever since the news of the Heir-Empress broke. Only a seed, another small part of one of Axekami's endless intrigues.

The baker and his new companion – neither of whom had met before – slipped away from the crowd without a word, towards a place that both of them knew but neither had ever been to. A place where others of their kind were gathering, each carrying another deadly load in their packs.

NINETEEN

In the mountains, the snow fell thick, carried on a wind that blew down from the peaks and whipped the air into a whirling chaos of white, a blizzard that wailed and blustered along the troughs and passes.

A solitary woman walked in the maelstrom wearing a red and black Mask, using her rifle as a staff to support her exhausted body. She staggered through the knee-deep crust, beneath a skeletal cluster of trees that rattled their snow-laden branches violently at her. She slipped and fell often, partly from the treacherous, uneven floor of stone under the crust, but more because her legs were failing, her strength eroded with every gust of wind that buffeted her. Yet each time she fell, she rose again and forged onward. There was little else she could do. It was that, or lie down and die there.

The mountains had become one endless, featureless ascent; a blanket of white delineated only by the lines, ridges and slopes where the black rock of the mountains poked through. Some distant part of her told her it was unwise to be trudging up this shallow trench, a wide furrow in the mountainside with stone banks rising to shoulder-height on either side. Something about snowdrifts. But the voice was fractured, and she could not piece it together enough to make sense of it.

Kaiku barely knew where she was any more. The cold had numbed her so much that she had lost sensation in her extremities. Exhaustion and incipient hypothermia had reduced her to a zombie-like state, slack-jawed and clumsy, pushing herself mechanically onwards with no clear idea of where she was going. She was a being entirely of instinct now, and that instinct told her to *survive.*

She had lost count of the days since she had left the cave where she had sheltered with Tane, Asara and Mamak. Five? Six? Surely not a week! A miserable week spent in this forsaken wilderness, starving, frightened and alone. Each night huddled and shivering in some hole, each day a torture of frustration and terror, searching for paths while cringing at every sound, and hoping that whatever made it might be something she could catch and eat rather than something that would catch and eat *her*.

How much longer would Ocha test her so?

Back in the cave, she had been visited by the same dream every time she closed her eyes. In it she saw a boar, and nothing more. It was huge, its skin warty and ancient, its tusks chipped and yellowed and massive. The boar said nothing, merely sat before her and looked at her, but in those animal eyes was an eternity, and she knew she was looking at no mere beast but an envoy of Ocha. She was struck by awe, filled with an ache and a wonder more potent than any meditation she had ever been able to achieve, a vast sorrow mingled with a beauty so enormous, so overwhelming and fragile that she could not help but weep. But there was something else in the boar's eyes, in its doleful face. It *expected* something of her, and it mourned because she was not doing it, and its grief tore her heart apart.

She woke each time with tears running down her cheeks, and the sadness lingered long into the morning. She did not speak of it to the others. They would not have understood. Nor did she understand, then. It was only in that moment of perfect clarity, when she had stared into the fire after all were asleep, that she knew. Ocha had heard her oath made in the Forest of Yuna. She was to avenge her family. He would not brook delay or retreat; he demanded action and strength of heart.

And so she did the only thing she could do: she took the Mask, and walked into the storm. Though the wind tore at her and the rain lashed her with freezing darts, she knew at that moment what she was doing was the will of the Emperor of the gods.

After that, things deteriorated.

For a day she stumbled through the furious wind and rain and lightning. The pain of endurance seemed nothing to her at first, for she knew it was not without purpose. But soon it began to wear at her resolve, as her teeth chattered and her skin prickled with freezing droplets. She pulled her hood tighter to her head and staggered on, not knowing where she was going, trusting to Ocha to guide her.

How she survived that first day, she did not know; her existence had degenerated into a nightmare in which the very air was against her, trying to push her over with great gusts and whipping her exposed skin mercilessly. Her lips were cracked and her eyes bloodshot, her cheeks tender and raw.

She found herself an overhang for shelter, little more than a scoop of rock in a sheer, broken face. It kept off the rain from above, but water still ran along the ground from upslope and the wind howled through her niche. At some point during the day, unnoticed by Kaiku, the thunder had passed on, and this was her first glimmer of hope; for though she believed she could not make another day in this storm, she knew she would be moving on whatever the weather at dawn. She prayed to Panazu for an end to the downpour.

Somehow, she slept, exhaustion overcoming the excruciating discomfort of her meagre shelter. That night, she dreamt nothing.

She awoke to the splash and patter of water, and the dazzling light of a cold, clear sky turning the flat planes of wet stone to sparkling brightness. The storm had passed.

Painfully, she pulled herself from her shelter and tried to stand up in the glare of Nuki's single eye. A crippling cramp put her back down on to her knees, the legacy of sleeping on freezing rock. One of her arms and one thigh were numb, and she could not curl her fingers more than a feeble twitching. But soon the blood returned to her body, and she flexed her hand into a fist; and though she ached, she felt an inner rejoicing, and sent thanks to Panazu for answering her prayer.

She stood up then, and looked about. The mountains seemed so different when she was standing on them than they did from a distance. From afar, their immensity rendered them simple, vast ridges of rock that tapered towards a peak. But once among the folds and crevices and slopes and bluffs that formed their skin, it was suddenly more complex, for stone reared high all around and it was difficult to imagine a world outside, where the land was flat and not circumscribed by frowning buttresses of grey and black. Perspective became skewed, and navigation ceased to be as easy as it seemed from a vantage outside the mountains.

She took the Mask from her pack and looked at it. It leered back at her, an insouciant, disrespectful smirk frozen on its red and black face. For this, her family had died. For this a temple of Enyu had been destroyed, its priests slaughtered. She turned it over and examined it. She held in her hands a True Mask, and if she believed what she had been told, it would show her the path to the place where it was made. The hidden monastery where the Weavers lived.

She had been putting the moment off as long as she could, fearful of that small margin Mishani had warned her about, the slim chance that she might slide through the seams in the wood into insanity and death. But really, she had made her choice when she decided to walk out of the cave, and procrastination felt false now.

The time had come. She put it to her face.

The effect, if anything, was something of an anticlimax. She did not die, nor go insane. She felt a certain strangeness, a sensation of being detached from the world she saw through the carven eyepieces; and the wood of the Mask seemed to warm and soften against her face, feeling more like a new layer of thick skin than something rigid. Then there was an overwhelming contentment, like sinking into the plush folds of a soft bed. After a time this faded as well, and she felt only faintly foolish for having been so worried.

She set off again. She had not known what kind of guidance she might expect from the Mask, and for a time she doubted it was guiding her at all. Then she remembered what Cailin had told her, that the Mask would only work once they neared the monastery. But how far was that, and in what direction? It could be on the other side of the mountains!

She shook herself mentally. Such thoughts brought her no profit. She had taken this journey as an act of faith, and faith was needed to sustain her. She believed that Ocha would not abandon her so, when it was he who had set her on this path. But then, who knew the ways of the gods, and what mortal pieces they might discard or forget in whimsy or caprice?

The next few days were progressively worse. Her meagre rations dwindled to nothing; most of the food had been in Mamak's pack. She wandered higher and higher into the mountains, taking no direction, choosing instead that the gods should determine her way.

She came across small Aberrant creatures time and again, often so malformed that they were slow enough to catch with her hands, or pick off with her rifle. But she would not eat Aberrant flesh; she mistrusted it abominably. Out of desperation, she tried a fleshy root that poked from cracks in the stone at the base of rivulets and small waterfalls, feeding tough, thorny weeds. It made her gag and retch, but it was subsistence. She dared not try others she saw, for the trees and plants they supported seemed warped by blight, and she feared poisoning herself. She broke away bundles of brittle twigs from the crooked trees for firewood, but they were near-impossible to burn, and she could only ever manage a small blaze after an hour of effort, by which time it seemed scarcely worth it.

By the next day the fleshy root disappeared entirely, and she was forced to spend most of her day foraging for food, which slowed her further. The temperature dropped sharply. Her route was taking her higher into the peaks, and frost dusted the ground, even in the sunlight. She wrapped her coat tight around her, but the cold seemed to seep in anyway, and her teeth chattered whenever she stood still for more than a few minutes. She stuffed the coat with grass and whatever bitter foliage she could find and used it as insulation.

The terrain became hard, and she found herself climbing. Twice she escaped death by pure chance, when some instinct warned her a handhold was about to crumble or a ledge was unstable. Other times she hid in fear as great, shaggy man-things lumbered past her, or stood in grey silhouette, haunting the horizon. The Aberrants bayed at night, when she froze in hollows or crevices she had squeezed herself into for shelter; but miraculously, though it seemed they were all around, she did not come across a single one at close quarters. They were distant things, suggested shapes that moved in valleys far below or lurked in shadows. Gristle-crows glided overhead now and again, but they did not seem interested in the stumbling figure beneath them. Perhaps they recognised her purpose, and kept away.

This is my test, she repeated to herself, a mantra that kept her walking and putting one foot in front of the other. *This is my test.* But at some point her mind wandered, and when it came back to her the mantra had changed. *This is what I deserve. This is what I deserve.*

And she knew then the real reason why she had walked out into the storm that night. Starvation and exhaustion had chased the clutter from her mind. Here, though she sweated and reeked and felt like an animal rather than a woman, though she had scrabbled in the dirt for foul roots to abate the ache in her stomach, she had found self-knowledge and clarity.

She hated herself.

I am Aberrant, she thought. *And I will pay for it, and pay again, until my debt is met.*

And then the blizzard came, howling out of nowhere and catching her unawares. There was no shelter for her, no respite from the maelstrom. She felt the cold of death settle into her marrow. Her lips were tinged blue, her tanned skin pale, her muscles cramped and aching. Tiny crystals of ice hid in her eyelashes, having found their way through the eyepieces of the Mask. She shivered uncontrollably as if palsied. Such weather would have tested the hardiest of mountaineers, but Kaiku was starving, tired, and under-equipped. Soon the cold seemed to seep away, and she began to feel the heaviness of sleep upon her, dragging her down, dulling her mind.

When I sleep, I die, she said to herself, and some force inside her kept her walking, powered by will alone. She had something she had to do, something she was meant to . . . something . . . something . . .

Then, a light. She blinked away snow, disbelieving. There was fire, burning within a cave, bright with warmth. Heedless of danger and bereft of thought, she staggered towards it, knowing only that warmth meant life. Her rifle, which she had been using as a walking staff, still trailed in her numb hand, cutting trenches in the snow behind her. Now she could smell cooking meat, and her hunger quickened her pace. She tripped and stumbled the last few feet, almost falling into the cave, a small avalanche of snow around her boots.

There was something sitting at the fire, a shape confusing enough that her bewildered and deadened brain could not at first pick it out. Then it shifted, and a long sickle gleamed in a hand. None of this really registered with Kaiku, until she heard a shriek and saw a flurry of movement come racing towards her; then instinct took over, and she brought up her rifle to protect herself. There was a chime of metal, and her rifle was jarred in her hand by the sickle; then the report of the weapon, deafening at such close range, as something warm and heavy crashed into her. They went down together in silence, landing in the snow, Kaiku still too confused and stunned by the noise of the rifle to understand what was happening. She did not even realise it had been primed.

They lay there, still, the musty smell of the thing atop her slowly pervading Kaiku's senses.

This was strange, she thought.

Then she felt the liquid warmth spreading across her collarbone and throat and down her chest. Blessed warmth! The feeling brought back the memory of the fire, suddenly like a beacon to her. Slowly and by degrees, she shifted the bulk of the thing that had attacked her, not even caring what it was or why it had stopped moving. She crawled to the fire, and the heat of the blaze made her skin sear and itch; but she endured it long enough to pull the roasting creature from the spit before she retreated to a less painful warmth. The gods knew what it was, but it was the size of a small rabbit. She tore off her Mask. Aberrant or not, she no longer cared. Greedily, she ate the meat half-cooked, blood running down her chin to meet the blood that soaked her neck and breast, but before she got past halfway she had fallen asleep, sitting cross-legged with her head hanging inside its furred hood.

*

She awoke several times throughout the next few days, though she remembered virtually nothing of them afterwards. There was a small hoard of firewood stacked at the back of the cave, and a pack with delights such as bread, rice and a jar of sweet fried locusts, hunks of dried meat and even a smoked fish. Like a dream-walker, Kaiku rose periodically, motivated by bodily needs too primal to bother her conscious mind. Somehow the fire kept going, even though it almost burned out twice; Kaiku automatically dumped firewood on it when her precious source of warmth seemed ailing. She ate, too, mechanically dipping into the pack and eating the food therein with no preparation; she did not cut the meat, nor the bread, but bit mouthfuls of both off and then fell asleep again.

Finally, she returned to true wakefulness and realised that she was still alive. It was night, but the fire was burning low, and the blizzard had stopped. Shadows shifted disconcertingly across the rock walls with the capricious sway of the flames. The whimpering cry of an Aberrant beast sounded distantly, echoing across the peaks. For a time she lay where she was, trying to remember. She could not think how long she had slept, or even recall how she came to be here. The last thing she remembered was the blizzard.

She put fresh firewood on the blaze, thanking providence for this haven but still utterly confused, and it was then that she saw the thing at the mouth of the cave. Puzzled, she walked over to it. At first it seemed like a heap of discarded cloth in a tailor's store. Looking closer, she saw that it was a robe, a heavy garment patched together from a multitude of different hides and materials with no sense of order or symmetry. With her boot she pushed the corpse over on to its back.

The robe was indeed heavy, with a cowl that was far too big, threatening to swallow the face it sheltered. But it was not a face; it was a Mask. A strange, blank thing, white, its brow quirked as if curious, with a carven nose but no mouth. The right side, from cheek to chin, was bored with small holes such as might be found on a musical pipe or a horn, set in no particular pattern. The left side was cracked and shattered by a rifle ball, and its ivory colour stained and bloody. The furs around the stranger's neck were flaky red with dried gore.

She looked down at the figure for a long while before gingerly removing the Mask. The face beneath was pale and hairless, with bulbous eyes frozen wide in death and narrow, white lips. A little freakish in appearance, perhaps, but definitely a man. A Weaver. She had killed a Weaver.

The stranger's coat looked warm. Kaiku set about stripping it off the corpse. Suddenly energised, as if in reaction to the days of inactivity in the cave, she took snow in her hands and scrubbed out as much of the blood as she could, then set it to dry by the fire.

When she was done, she stripped the corpse's underclothes – even the soiled and wet leggings that felt like sealskin – and washed them too. Her fear of the cold was greater than her disgust at the voiding of the man's bladder and bowels in death. With those set to dry, she rested by the fire.

Later she dressed herself anew, stuffing her own clothes into her pack. The leggings and hide vest fit snugly, and the heavy robe of patchwork fur was extremely warm. She began to sweat in the heat of the fire, and relished the discomfort for its novelty.

Whoever this Weaver was, he had been on a journey when he was caught in the blizzard. He had provisions for several days' travel, and he had gathered firewood before the snows became too bad. He was digging in to wait for the snowstorm to pass. It was this stranger's foresight – and the fact that he had conveniently managed to die – that had saved Kaiku's life.

This man came from somewhere, Kaiku thought. She wondered how far away that somewhere was.

She ate, slept, and woke with the sun. It was a new dawn, fresh snow was on the ground, and the sky was a clear blue. Today was the day she would leave.

She picked up her father's Mask and looked at it, as she had done many times before. Its vacant gaze held no answers. She put it on, and once again it gave her nothing.

'I am not done yet, Father,' she mumbled to herself, and set forth into the snow again.

TWENTY

The Barak Avun's rage knew no limit.

'You had her alone, you offered her the gift, and then you *took it back*?' he cried.

Mishani looked at her father, all glacial calm and studied poise. Her hands were tucked into the sleeves of her robe and held before her; her hair fell in black curtains to either side of her thin face. They were in his study, a small, neat room with dark brown furniture and a matching wooden floor. Fingers of evening light reached through the leaves of the trees outside and in through the shutters, tickling bright motes and making them bob and dance.

'I did, Father,' she replied.

'Ungrateful child!' he spat. 'Do you know what we were promised for your service? Do you know what your family would have gained?'

'Since you saw fit to exclude me from your dealings with Sonmaga,' she said icily, 'I do not.'

Mishani was really quite surprised by the vehemence of her father's reaction to her news that the Heir-Empress had not received the infected nightdress. He seemed to have abandoned all dignity, red-faced and shaking with anger in a way that she had not seen him before. The remnants of the old Mishani wanted to comfort her father, or at least fear his wrath; but in her heart, she was scorning him. How easily she had torn away his façade of unflappability. She had told him the honest truth about what had happened in the roof gardens of the Imperial Keep. She could have lied, told him that Lucia was too well guarded or that they had intercepted the gift she brought; but she would not degrade herself so. She held herself with pride in the face of her father's fury. If not for years of conditioning, she would not even have troubled to maintain the formal mode of Saramyrrhic used to address a parent.

'Where did I fail with you, Mishani? Where is your loyalty to your family?' He paced around the room, unable to stand still. 'Do you know how many lives would have been saved if you had done what I asked?'

'If I had murdered an eight-harvest child?' Mishani replied. Her father glared at her. 'Say it, then, Father. Do not hide behind euphemisms and evasive language. You are quite willing to have me bear the burden of your actions; at least have the courage to admit them to yourself.'

'You have never spoken to me this way, Mishani!'

'I have never had cause to until now,' she said. Her voice was perfectly level, chilling in its rigidity. 'You dishonour yourself, Father, and you dishonour me. I do not care to know what Sonmaga promised you. Even if it were the keys to the Golden Realm itself, it would not have been worth what you asked me to do. You made yourself his pawn for a reward; that I could understand. But you made me your pawn because you knew I could not refuse. You took advantage of me, Father. I would have done anything you asked if I could have done it with honour, no matter how hard it was. I have killed to protect you before!' His eyes widened at this; though he had suspected the death of Yokada to be no accident, the admission was still a surprise. 'But *this*? To give an infected nightdress to a child, and have her die a lingering death? I will not stoop so low, Father. Not even for you.'

Avun was almost choking with rage. 'How dare you suggest that your honour is greater than mine in this matter?'

'I suggest nothing,' said Mishani. 'You went through with this deed. I, at the last, did not.'

'She is an Aberrant!' Avun cried. 'An Aberrant, you understand? She is no *child*. She should have been killed at birth.'

Mishani thought of Kaiku, and the words came from her mouth before she could stop them. 'Perhaps that is not the way things should be, then.'

Her vision exploded in a blaze of white, and she was on the floor, her hair like a black wing over her fallen body. It took a few seconds to realise that she had been struck, hard, across the face. Surprise and pain threatened tears, but she swallowed them back and quelled any reaction on her face. She looked up at her father with infuriating calm. His bald pate was sweating, his eyes bulged. He looked ridiculous.

'Viperous girl!' he said. 'To turn on your own family this way! You will go back to Mataxa Bay tomorrow, and there you will stay for the season, and when winter comes we may see if you are my daughter again.'

He glared at her a moment longer, waiting to see if she dared to offer a rejoinder that he could punish her for. She would not give him the satisfaction. With a snort, he stalked out of the study.

She went to the servants' yard almost immediately, detouring past her room on the way to apply a face powder that would hide the bruise on her jaw. It did an adequate job, though it made her look a little sickly. Well, it would have to do. If she was leaving for Mataxa Bay tomorrow – and she could scarcely stay with things as they were – then she had business to attend to this evening.

She found Gomi currying the horses in the stables. He was a short, stocky man with a shaven head and flat features, managing to combine an impression of wisdom, earthiness and reliability in their assemblage. He bowed low when he saw her silhouetted in the light at the stable door, but Mishani fancied she saw something unpleasant in his eyes as he did so. Yokada, the servant girl Mishani had poisoned to protect her family's reputation, had been his niece.

'Bring the horses and prepare the carriage,' she said. 'I wish to go out.'

A short time later they were travelling through the streets of the Imperial Quarter, heading down the hill towards where the burnished ribbon of the River Kerryn slid through the city. Gomi was driving, sitting at the front with the reins of the two black mares in his hands. The carriage was as black as the horses, chased with elegant reliefs of blue lacquer and edged in gold around its spokes, a testament to the wealth of Blood Koli.

Mishani sat inside, looking out of the window. The clean, well-maintained thoroughfares of the Imperial Quarter seemed bland now, where before she had always enjoyed the sight of the ancient trees, fountains and carvings that beautified the richest district in the city. Vibrant mosaics had lost their colour; the play of shadow and reddening sunlight across the plazas was no longer attractive. Where once the wide streets and narrow alleys that sprawled up the contours of the hill had seemed to harbour intrigue and whisper of secrets, now they were just streets, robbed of mystery. She felt washed-out somehow, a lifetime of assumptions and conditioned responses turning to driftwood in the current of events. Her mind strayed to Kaiku again and again, and a single question weighed on her heart like a tombstone.

Was I wrong to do what I did?

The streets of the Imperial Quarter gave way to the Market District, and traffic thickened around them. Though Nuki was fleeing westward and the ravenous moons would soon come chasing into the night, the markets did not sleep until long after dark. They clustered together in an interlinked series of squares, set at uneven angles to each other and connected by winding sandstone alleys. The city here had a rougher edge, less well maintained than the Imperial District, but it was possessed of a comforting vibrancy. The squares were thick with noisy stalls, multicoloured awnings of all shapes and sizes piling on top of each other for space. The air smelled of a dozen kinds of food: fried squid, potato cakes, sweetnuts, saltrice, all mingling amongst the jostle of cityfolk that milled to and fro.

But even the steadily growing babble and ruckus ahead did little to lift her spirits; where once it had seemed a thriving hive of life, now she heard only a senseless cacophony of meaningless cries, like the voices of madmen.

She thought of her destination, and wondered if she herself was entirely rational. *You should go and see the dream lady*, the Heir-Empress had said; and when she left the Imperial Keep, Mishani had realised that she knew where the dream lady was, without a word on the subject being spoken between them. She knew, as if something had touched her heart and shown her.

The child both terrified and fascinated her. There was no questioning that she was special; but was she evil? *Could* an eight-harvest child be evil? She thought of the malformed infant who made flowers grow wherever her fingers touched. Had *she* been evil, or just dangerous? The difference was important, but it had never seemed to matter until now.

And here she was, on her way to see Lucia's dream lady. What she might expect, she had no idea; but she knew that she had to find out before she was sent away from the city. For Kaiku, for Yokada, for her father, she wanted to be shown a truth.

Gomi, perhaps out of spite, had chosen a route that skirted the edge of the busiest market square in the district, and they were soon slowing as they forced their way through roads crowded with lowing animals and jabbering cityfolk who darted between the carriages and carts that choked the roadway, carrying with them baskets of fruit and bread or hurrying furtively away to their homes.

Mishani frowned. Even preoccupied, she noticed the atmosphere that prevailed here. The sounds of the Market District *were* different, and not only to her ears. She saw other passengers and drivers looking about in confusion. Stalls were packing up and being deserted. Customers were fleeing the square. It was not happening all at once, but rather an unevenly spread phenomenon. Everywhere Mishani looked, she saw people locked in intense discussion before hurrying to their friends to pass on what they had heard. The traffic had choked almost to a halt now, and Gomi scratched the thin rolls of fat at the back of his neck and shrugged to himself.

Mishani leaned out of her carriage door a little way and called to a boy coming up to his twelfth harvest. It was undignified to do so, but she had a creeping concern that there was something happening she should know about. The boy hesitated, then came over to her, subservient to her obvious status as a noble.

'What is going on here?' she asked.

'The Empress has arrested Unger tu Torrhyc,' the boy said. 'Over at the Speaker's Square. Imperial Guards took him away.'

Mishani felt a shadow of dread climb into the carriage with her. She did not need to, but she gave the boy a few coins anyway. He took them gratefully and ran. She sensed the air of impending panic, and feared it. The people knew as well as her what would come of arresting the most popular and outspoken opponent to the Empress among the common people. Mishani cursed silently. She had thought the Empress arrogant before in the way she ignored the cityfolk and concentrated only on the nobles; now she was staggered by her foolishness. To inflame an already enraged populace by publicly arresting their figurehead was nothing short of an incitement to riot.

'Gomi!' she called, leaning out of the window again. 'Can you get us away from here?'

She saw him turn around to reply, his mouth opening in an O, and then the world exploded around her.

The carriage was lifted from the road in an ear-shattering tumult and a flash of light. She felt herself thrown heavily back inside the carriage as it was swatted aside by the force, and a split-second later the door where her head had been punched inward, smashing into splinters. The whole side of the carriage crumpled in on her, splitting into wooden daggers, but she had neither the time nor the purchase to react, and instead she could only watch in shock as the confining wooden box she rode gathered in to crush her life away.

Suddenly, overwhelmingly, there came a single picture in her mind, strong enough to be a vision. Time seemed to freeze outside, and Mishani was once again on the beach at Mataxa Bay, with the summer sun sparkling on the rippling waves. She was perhaps ten harvests old, and laughing, running breathlessly through the surf. Behind her came Kaiku, holding a sand-crab the size of a dinner plate before her, laughing also as she pursued her friend. And there was nothing in Mishani's heart at that moment but joy, and carelessness, and freedom.

Then: reality. She blinked.

The side of the carriage had crumpled and splintered, and the broken blades of wood had stopped mere inches from her.

She began to breathe again. Sounds from outside filtered in. Screams arose; first a single one, then many. She heard the hungry growl of flame, running feet, cries for help. Stunned, she could not piece together the evidence of her senses to determine what had happened. Instead, she concentrated on freeing herself from the coffin that her carriage had become. She had been thrown up against one door when the other one caved in, but it had been buckled by the impact and would not open when she tried it. Twisting herself within the dark confines of the carriage, she elbowed the shutters open – which had been closed by the force of the explosion – and mercifully they gave easily. She clambered out, her hair snagging on loose bits of wood as she emerged into the evening light.

It took only moments to see what had happened. The epicentre of the blast was clearly visible by soot marks. Something – perhaps a cart, for it was now impossible to tell – had exploded by the side of the road, destroying the fascia of a money-house. Shattered wreckage of carriages and horses reduced to smoking meat surrounded the epicentre; they had absorbed the blast that would have otherwise killed Mishani. Instead, her carriage had been thrown against the side of another carriage to her right; the two of them had merged into a mess of wreckage.

All around, the carnage was horrific. Men, women and children lay still on the road, or hung impaled where they had been flung against a heap of jagged debris. The wounded moaned and writhed or staggered among them, some newly bereft of a limb. The air tasted of blood and sulphur and acrid smoke. Plaintive wails issued from a noble lady who was kneeling by the scorched corpse of her husband. Gomi lay next to the dead horses that had drawn her carriage, his brains dashed out on the road. A fire was burning somewhere, and outside the blast area people were shrieking and fleeing in headlong panic. Mishani flinched as another explosion tore through the air nearby, and a hail of pebbles and splinters pattered across her head. The screams were silenced, only to begin anew.

She gazed at the mayhem with the dull, slack face of a sleepwalker. Then, slowly, she began to walk, not hearing the cries for help or seeing the bloodied hands that reached out in supplication. There was no sense in returning home, back to the protection of a father who had betrayed her. She was heading for the River District, and the dream lady.

The Guard Commander was thrown to his knees before his Empress in a clatter of armour.

'You gave the order,' she accused.

The throne room of the Imperial Keep was less ostentatious than some of the state rooms, but its décor was heavy and grave, befitting the business that was conducted there. Arched windows were set high in the walls, slanting light down on to thick hangings of purple and white, the colours of the Blood Erinima standard. Braziers smoked gently with incense, set on high, thin poles, corkscrews of silver that stood on either side of the dais where the thrones rested. The thrones themselves were an elaborate fusion of supple, varnished wood and precious metals, coils of bronze and gold interweaving across its surface in seamless unity.

Anais rarely came in here except during times of crisis or meetings of extreme importance; the air of intimidation that the throne lent her was an edge she did not usually need. She had been receiving report after hurried report for an hour now, but it all came down to one thing: Unger tu Torrhyc had been arrested by Imperial Guards. But she had not told them to do any such thing.

'Empress, I did give the order,' the man replied, his head bowed.

'Why?' Anais demanded. Her tone was cold. This man's admission had already signed his own death warrant.

The Guard Commander was silent.

'*Why?*' she repeated.

'I cannot say, Empress.'

'Cannot? Or will not? Be aware that you are already dead, Guard Commander, but the lives of your wife and children depend on your answer.'

He raised his head then, and she saw the terror and confusion on his face. 'I gave the order . . . but I do not know why. I know full well the consequences of my action, and yet, at that moment . . . I thought of nothing, Empress. I cannot explain it. Never before has . . .' He faltered. 'It was an act of madness,' he concluded.

Anais's anger was only fuelled by his unsatisfactory answer, but she kept her passions well reined. She flicked her gaze to the Guards that stood at the kneeling man's shoulder.

'Take him away. Execute him.'

He was pulled to his feet.

'Empress, I beg of you the lives of my family!' he cried.

'Concern yourself with the last moments of your own life,' she replied cruelly, dismissing him. He wept in fear and shame as he was led away. She had no intention of punishing his family, but he would go to his death not knowing that. For a man who had jeopardised her position with such gross stupidity, she was in no mood for mercy.

She motioned to a robed advisor who stood near her throne, an old academic named Hule with a long white beard and bald head.

'Go to the donjon and bring Unger tu Torrhyc to me. See he is not mistreated.'

Hule nodded and departed.

The Empress settled back on her throne. Her brow ached. She felt besieged, conspired against by events. The chain of explosions that had ripped across the city in the last hour had happened too fast and were too well coordinated. They had already been in place, awaiting the spark to ignite them. Torrhyc's arrest threw that spark. There seemed to be no specific targets in mind; they occurred in crowded streets, on ships at the docks, even outside temples. Whoever was behind them, she suspected that their intention was to sow mayhem. Their method was effective. She had already been forced to send over half her Imperial Guards to quell riots in different districts of the city, but the sight of their white and blue armour only seemed to agitate the crowds.

The Guard Commander's idiocy had put her in a dire position, but it was not irretrievable yet. Unger tu Torrhyc's influence was evidently greater than she had first imagined. She knew he was an agitator and an orator of great skill; now it seemed apparent that he had a subversive army working for him. It was not hard to see how a man of his charisma could inspire that kind of loyalty in his followers.

Someone had planted those bombs. She suspected that Unger tu Torrhyc could tell her who.

At that very moment, the subject of the Empress's thoughts brooded in a cell, deep in the bowels of the Keep.

The prisons of the Imperial Keep were clean, if a little dark and bare. His cell was unremarkable, the same as every other cell he had been put in. And he would be released with his head held high, just like every other time. Noble lords, landowners, even local councils had incarcerated him before. His calling made him many enemies. The rich and powerful did not like to be brought to account for the injustices and evils they brought upon the common folk.

He had begun to view being arrested as part of the process of negotiation now. He had become too dangerous, a threat to the safety of the city. Stirring up trouble, inciting revolution. He had expected arrest; it was a mere flexing of muscle, to show that they were still the ones in power. Afterwards, they would talk to him. He would bring them the people's demands. They would agree to some, but not all. He would be released, hailed as a hero by the people, and use that status to resume haranguing the Imperial Family until the people's remaining demands were met.

This time the people's demands were simple, and not open to negotiation. The Aberrant child must not sit the throne.

Anais had been a good ruler, as far as the frankly despotic system of Imperial rule went. Even Unger would admit that. But she was blind, and arrogant. She was so high up on her hill, in this mighty Keep, that she did not see what was happening in the streets below. Furthermore, she did not appear even to be interested. She dallied with politicians and nobles, winning the support of armies here and signing treaties there, and all the time forgetting that the people she ruled were crying out in an almost unanimous voice: *We will not have her!*

Did she think her Imperial Guards could keep the people of Axekami in line? Did she plan to rule them by force? Unacceptable! Unacceptable!

The people would be heard, and Unger tu Torrhyc was their mouthpiece.

He had been placed far away from other prisoners, so that he could not spread his sedition among them. A high, oval window beamed a grille of dusk light on the centre of the stone floor. There was a heavy wooden door, banded with iron, with a slat for guards to look in that was now closed. Otherwise, the cell was absolutely bare, hot and gloomy. Unger sat in a corner, his legs crossed, his eyes closed, and thought. He was a plain man, plain of dress and plain of speech, but he questioned all and everything. That made him a threat to those who relied on tradition for their advantage. And whatever his feelings on Aberrants were, the Empress could not be allowed to foist upon the people a ruler that they so vehemently did not want.

His eyes flickered open, and his heart lurched in his chest. There was someone in the cell with him.

He scrambled to his feet. The cell had darkened suddenly, as though a bank of cloud had swallowed the last of the day's light. Yet, by the dim rays coming through the window, he saw the faintest shape in the far corner of the room. It filled him with an unwholesome dread, emanating malevolence. There had been nothing in here before, and the door had not opened. Only a spectre or a spirit could have come to him this way.

It did not move, and yet he never for a moment doubted the shrieking report of his senses. The air seemed to whine in his ear.

'What are you?' he breathed.

The shape moved then, shifting slightly, an indistinct form that brightness seemed to shy from.

'Are you a spirit? A demon? Why have you come?' Unger demanded.

It walked slowly towards him. He took a breath to cry for help, to rouse the guard outside; but a gnarled and withered hand flashed into the shaft of dusk from the window, one long finger pointing at him, and his throat locked into silence. His body locked also, every muscle tensing at once and staying there, rendering him painfully immobile. Panic sparkled in his brain.

The intruder moved into the dim light. He stood hunched there, his small body buried in a mountain of ragged robes and hung with all manner of beads and ornaments. He wore a Mask of bronze, contorted into an expression of insanity; and as Unger watched, he slowly unfastened the latch strap and removed it.

He was like a man, but small and withered and grotesque, his skin white and parchment-dry. And his face . . . oh, there was ugliness such as Unger had never seen. His aspect was twisted so far out of true that the prisoner would have shut his eyes if he could. One side of the sallow face seemed to have melted, the skin becoming like wax and sliding off the skull to gather in folds of jowl and chop, a flabby dewlap depending from his scrawny neck. His eye on that side laboured to see from beneath the overhanging brow; his upper lip flopped over his lower one. But his right side was no less repulsive: there, his lips had skinned back as if they had simply rotted away, exposing teeth and gum in a skeletal rictus; and his right eye was huge and blind, an orb that bulged from the socket, milky with cataract.

'Unger tu Torrhyc,' croaked the intruder, his malformed lip flapping. 'I am the Weave-lord Vyrrch. How pleasant to meet face to face.'

Unger could not reply. He would not have had the words anyway. He felt a scream rise inside him, but there was nowhere for it to go.

'You've served me well these past weeks, Unger, though you didn't know it,' the foul thing continued. 'Your efforts have accelerated my plans tenfold. I had expected it would take so much more than this to set Axekami on its way to ruin. I had to tread carefully, to keep my hand hidden, but you . . .' Vyrrch wagged a finger in admiration. 'You stir the people. Your arrest has angered them mightily. I never would have thought it so simple.'

Unger was too terrified to think where Vyrrch was leading this; the sensation of having bodily control robbed from him was overwhelming his reason.

'It was quite a risk, even the little push it took to make the Guard Commander do what I needed. I had thought there would be outrage, *counted* on it . . . but even I had underestimated the effectiveness of your secret army of bombers, Unger. I would hate to see them stop the good work they are doing.'

'Not . . . not . . .' Unger managed, forcing the words in a squeak past his throat.

'Oh, of course they're not yours. They're *mine.* But the people and the Empress alike assume you are responsible, so let us not disabuse them of that notion.'

The creature was close enough to touch him now, and Unger could see that it was not wholly real, but faintly transparent. A spectre, after all. It ran a finger down his cheek, and the sensation was like freezing water.

'Your cause needs a martyr, Unger.'

The spectre seized him savagely by the back of the head, and despite its apparent intangibility, Unger felt its massive strength. His muscles loosened, and he screamed as it propelled him against the wall of the cell, smashing his skull like a jakma nut on a rock, leaving a dark wodge of blood and hair above his corpse.

The gates to the temple of Panazu in the River District of Axekami stood open as dusk set in. Mishani stood beneath them, looking up at the tall, narrow façade that towered over her, its shoulders pulled in tight and sculpted into the form of rolling whirlpools. She was bedraggled, exhausted and suffering from shock, and yet she was here, at the abode of the dream lady. The sounds of Axekami beginning to tear itself apart were audible across the Kerryn. New explosions could be heard, and bright flames rose against the gathering dark. Voices were raised in clamour, mob roars made weak and thin by distance. This night would be an evil one for all concerned.

She walked up the steps to the temple, through the great gates and into the cool sanctuary of the congregation chamber. The interior of the temple was breathtaking. Pillars vaulted up to domed ceilings, painted with frescoes of Panazu's exploits and teachings. The walls were chased with reliefs of river creatures. The vast curved windows of blue, green and silver in the face of the building dappled the temple in shades of the sea floor, and seemed to stir the light restfully to heighten the illusion. The sound of water was all around: splashing, trickling, tinkling, for the altar was a fountain from which many gutters ran, directing the crystal liquid into artful designs carved into the blue-green *lach* on the floor. The congregation area, where the oblates came to kneel and pray, was surrounded by a thick trench of water in which swam catfish, the earthly aspect of Panazu, and bridged by short arcs of *lach*.

There was nobody here. The place was peaceful and deserted. Mishani shuffled in, and did not even turn around when the gates closed behind her of their own accord. She walked listlessly down the central aisle, her mind and body still numb from the tragedy she had witnessed in the Market District.

'Mishani tu Koli,' a soft voice purred, echoing around the temple. Mishani looked to the source of the sound, and found her standing to one side of the chamber. The dream lady. She looked more like something in a nightmare, a tall, slender tower of elegant black, her face painted with crescents of red that ran over her eyelids from forehead to cheek. Her lips were marked with alternating triangles of red and black, like teeth. A ruff of raven feathers grew from her shoulders, and a silver circlet with a red gem was set on her forehead.

She crossed the chamber to the central aisle, emerging between the pillars to stand before Mishani. She took in Mishani's unkempt appearance without a flicker of an expression.

'My name is Cailin tu Moritat. Lucia calls me the dream lady. She told me you would be coming.' Cailin took her by the elbow. 'Come. Rest, and bathe. Your journey has not been easy, I see.'

Mishani allowed herself to be led. She had nowhere else to go.

TWENTY-ONE

Time did not pass in Chaim. Rather, it elongated, stretching itself flat and thin, sacrificing substance for length. Tane had ceased counting the days; they had merged into one great nothing, a relentless, frowning wall of boredom and increasing despair.

The disappearance of Kaiku had hit them hard. At first there was something akin to mild panic. Had something been into the cave and taken her while they slept? Mamak searched and found no sign. It took a short while before Tane remembered the strange things Kaiku had been saying to him while he drowsed:

Perhaps this was not your path to take after all. Perhaps it is mine alone.

The storm kept them in the cave another day. Mamak flatly refused to let them search.

'If she's out there, the fool is dead already. When this storm breaks, I go home. You can come with me, or stay in this cave if you wish.'

Tane begged him, offered him triple his fee if he would find her. He told her that Kaiku had money, and lots of it. Mamak's eyes lit at the prospect, and for a moment Tane saw greed war with sense on his face; but in the end, his experience of mountain travel tipped the balance, and he refused. Asara shook her head and tutted at Tane for his loss of dignity in desperation.

'I want her back!' he snapped in his defence.

Asara shrugged insouciantly. 'But she is gone, Tane. Time for a new plan.'

When the storm gave up the next morning, they accepted the inevitable and returned to Chaim. Tane talked of raising an expedition to search the mountains for Kaiku – or her body – so that they might at least retrieve the Mask. Tane had not forgotten that without that Mask he had no hope of discovering who had sent the shin-shin that had massacred the priests of his temple. But the plan was unsound, and everyone knew it. Even Tane knew it. There was not a prayer of finding her in all the vastness of northern Fo, with her tracks erased by rain and wind. By the time they came down out of the mountains and were back on the path to Chaim, he had stopped talking about it.

Tane and Asara found themselves rooms in Chaim's single lodging house, a bare and draughty construction that catered for the few outside visitors the town received. Neither intended to leave, or even spoke of such.

'She decided to go on alone,' Tane said. 'If she makes it, she'll come back here.'

'You are chasing false hope,' Asara told him, but she did not argue further, nor make any move to depart herself.

There was nothing to do in Chaim. The unfaltering rudeness of the locals began to wear on them after a time, and they talked to nobody but each other. At first, there was little for them to speak of. Too many barriers existed between them, too many deceptions. It was just like it had been with Kaiku.

Gods, do we ever take our masks off, even for a moment? Tane thought in exasperation.

But gradually their enforced solitude bred conversation, as the slow trickle of water through a holed dam will erode the surrounding stone till it cracks. After what might have been a week of waiting and wondering, they found themselves back in the makeshift bar where they had first met Mamak.

'You know what I am, Tane,' Asara said.

The statement, put casually in the midst of the conversation, brought the young acolyte up short. 'What do you mean?' he asked.

'No games,' she said. 'The time has come for honesty. If you are to walk the same paths as I, as seems increasingly to be the case, then you should face up to what you already know.'

Tane glanced around the bar to ensure they were not being overheard, but it was almost empty. A bleak, wooden, chilly room with a few locals in a corner minding their own business. A scatter of low, rough-cut tables and worn mats to sit on. A grouch-faced barmaid serving shots of rank liquor. Spirits, he hated this town.

'You are Aberrant,' he said quietly.

'Well done,' she replied, with a hint of mockery in her voice. 'At last you admit it to yourself. But you are a strange one, Tane. You listen. You are ready to learn. That is why I will tell you this, for you may one day come to my way of seeing. So swallow your disgust for a moment, and hear what I have to say.'

Tane leaned forward over the table, his cheeks flushed. With the lack of anything to do in the town, Chaim's inhabitants had a lot to drink about, and the potency of the liquor attested to that. Asara was dead sober, as always; her Aberrant metabolism neutralised alcohol before it could affect her, and she did not know how it felt to be drunk.

'I am old, Tane,' she said. 'You cannot guess how old by looking at me. I have seen much, and I have done much. Some memories bring pride, others disgust.' She turned the wooden tumbler of liquor inside the cradle of her fingers, looking down into it. 'Do you know what experience is? Experience is when you have handled something so much that the shine wears off it. Experience is when you begin to see how relentlessly predictable people are, how generation after generation they follow the same simple, ugly pattern. They dream of living forever, but they do not know what they ask. I have passed my eightieth harvest, though it does not show on me. Since I reached adulthood, I have not aged. My body repairs itself faster than time can ravage it. That is my curse. I have already lived the span of a normal lifetime, and I am bored.'

It seemed such bathos that Tane almost laughed, a bitter hysteria welling within him; but the tone of Asara's voice warned him against it. '*Bored?*' he repeated.

'You do not understand,' Asara said patiently. 'Nor, I think, will you ever. But when so much has become jaded, all that is left is the search for something new, something that will fire the blood again, if only for a short while. I was purposeless for a long time before I met Cailin tu Moritat, seeking only new thrills and finding each less satisfying than the last. When I found her, I saw something I had never seen before. I had thought I was a freak, a random thing; but in her I saw a mirror to me, and I saw a purpose again.'

'What did you see?' asked Tane.

'A superior being,' Asara replied. 'A creature that was human and yet *better* than human. An Aberrant whose Aberration made her better than those who despised her.'

Tane blinked, wanting to shake his head and refute her. He restrained himself. Her words were preposterous, but he would listen. He had learned her opinions on the subject of Aberrancy over the weeks they had spent together, and while he did not agree with much of what she said, it had enough validity to make him think.

'I saw then the new order of things,' Asara continued. 'A world where Aberrants were not hated and hunted but respected. I saw that Aberrancy was not a fouling of the body, but merely a changing. An evolution. And as with all evolution, many must fall by the way for one to emerge triumphant. If I am to live in this world for a long time to come, I will do all I can to make it a more pleasant experience for myself. And that means I must work towards that new order.'

'I think I see,' he said, recalling other snatches of conversation they had shared over the period of their self-induced confinement in Chaim. 'You help the Red Order because they represent Aberrants whose abilities make them greater than human. And the Libera Dramach . . . they work for the same thing you want; so you help them too.'

'But the Red Order and the Libera Dramach are working together for the time being, with one common goal in mind,' Asara said, enmeshing her fingers before her.

'To see the Heir-Empress take the throne,' Tane concluded.

'Exactly. She is the key. She is the only one that can reverse the blight on our land. She is the bridge between us and the spirits, between the common folk and the Aberrants.' Asara grabbed Tane's wrists and fixed him with an iron gaze. 'It *must* be this way. And we must do what we can to make it so.'

Tane held the gaze for a moment, then countered with a question. 'Why did you watch over Kaiku for so many years?'

He regretted it almost immediately. It had come out without thought, seeming to trip from his subconscious to his tongue without routing through his brain; and yet he knew by some terrible prescience what would be Asara's reply.

Asara smiled faintly and released him. She sat back and took a sip of liquor. 'I became her handmaiden at the behest of the Red Order. Her previous one met with an accident.'

Tane let this one pass. When he did not react, Asara continued.

'They found her through whatever method they have; their ways are a mystery to me. They knew she would manifest . . . powers sooner or later, and they asked me to watch her until she did. There was no way she would be coerced to join until she had her first burning. Who in their right mind would believe they were an Aberrant without any evidence?'

Asara's words dropped into Tane's consciousness like a stone into thick honey. The world seemed to slow around him, the whispering of the other denizens of the bar becoming a meaningless susurrus in the background. Across the coarse wooden table he could see Asara's beautiful eyes watching his face, evaluating the effect of what she had just told him.

'But you knew that, didn't you?' she asked.

Tane nodded mutely, his gaze falling. She relished it, he realised. He had asked her a question he already had the answer to, and she was amused that he still felt her response like a pikestaff in the ribs.

'Small things,' he murmured, when he could bear her wry silence no longer. 'When first I met her, she was raving about a woman named Asara. She told me you had been killed by a demon in the forest. Later you reappeared. No explanation was given, and I didn't ask for one.'

'You thought it was not your place to enquire,' said Asara scornfully. 'How like a man.'

'No,' he said. 'No, I suppose I didn't want to know. I was cowardly. Then there was you. I suspected you from the start. Add to that the lengths you went to to bring her to the Aberrant woman Cailin, the secrets you held between you that I was not privy to, the way you seemed to change . . .' He sighed, a strange noise of resignation. 'I'm not feeble-minded, Asara. I've been walking with Aberrants since my journey began.'

'Yet you believe your journey was ordained by your goddess, that you were spared for a purpose; but there is no greater foulness to Enyu than an Aberrant. Reconcile these things, if you can.'

Tane bowed his head, his shaved skull limned in dim lantern light. 'I can't. That's why I've been avoiding them.'

'Here it is in the open, then,' said Asara, brushing back the red-streaked fall of her hair behind one sculpted ear and leaning forward. 'She is Aberrant, gifted with the ability to mould the Weave as the Weavers do. But she is dangerous to herself and others; she needs schooling. I came to Fo for several reasons, but one was to stop her committing suicide. Every day she spends here increases the risk that her powers will break their boundaries again.

Eventually, she will either burn herself or be killed by those that fear her.' She relaxed back, her gaze never leaving Tane, never ceasing to calculate him. 'I told Cailin I would bring her into the fold, and I will. Assuming she still lives, of course. I will wait in this spirit-blasted wasteland until hope is gone. That may be weeks, it may be months; but age has a way of foreshortening time, Tane, and I am a patient woman.'

Tane was silent. The sensation of drunkenness felt suddenly unpleasant, having soured within him.

'Join us, Tane,' said Asara. 'You and I share the same goals. You may hate Aberrants, but you would see the blight on this land stopped. And the Heir-Empress is the only chance we have.'

'I do not . . .' Tane began, feeling the words stall and clutter in his mouth. 'I do not *hate* Aberrants,' he said.

'Indeed not,' Asara said, raising one eyebrow slightly. 'For you love one of them, I suspect.'

Tane flashed her a hot glare, forming a retort that died before it could be born. Instead, he became sullen, and did not reply.

'Poor Tane,' Asara said. 'Caught between your faith and your heart. I'd pity you, if I had not seen it endless times before. Humankind really is a pathetically predictable animal.'

Tane slammed his hands on the table, spilling their liquor. He arrested himself just as he was about to lunge at her. She had not moved a muscle, staying relaxed on her mat, watching him with that infuriating amusement on her face. The others in the bar had their eyes on him now. He wanted to strangle her, to hit her, to slap her hard and show her that she could *not* speak to him that way.

Like father, like son, he thought, and suddenly he went cold, the rage in him flickering and dying out. He slammed his hands on the table again in one last, impotent display of frustration, got up and stalked out of the bar and into the night.

The chill air and knife-edge wind sawed through him eagerly. He welcomed the discomfort, hurrying away from the bar, away from the lights in the windows, seeking only to distance himself from Asara and all she had said. But he could no longer avoid it now. There was no question, no element of doubt any more. He had been treasuring that margin of uncertainty, for in that small space he could still stay with Kaiku and not offend his goddess, could still protest that he was never certain she was Aberrant. Now it was gone, and he was forced into a quandary.

There were few people on the rough trails that passed for streets in Chaim. No lanterns burned except through grimy windows. The moons were absent tonight, and the darkness was louring and hungry. He let himself be swallowed by it.

After a time, he came to a sloping, craggy rock atop a slope that looked out over the faint lights of the grim village, and there he sat. It was bitterly cold, but he had his coat on and his hood pulled tight. He meditated for a time, but it was hopeless. No enlightenment could come to a heart in such turmoil. Instead he prayed, asking Enyu for guidance. How could she have sent him on this way to ally himself with Aberrants, if Aberrants were corruptions of her plan? What was he supposed to do? So many uncertainties, so many unanswered questions, and he was left scrabbling for purpose once again. How could something as simple as faith be so contradictory?

It is my punishment, he thought. *I must endure.*

And there it was: his answer. This agony of indecision was only part of his penance. He must accept it gladly, and act as he thought best, and bear the consequences of that.

I owe the gods a life, he told himself. It was a phrase he had been using to account for his suffering ever since he was sixteen harvests of age, and he had murdered his own father.

He had no clear recollection of anything before the age of eight or nine, except of the fearful dark shape that lumbered through his embryonic memories, and the crushing inevitability of the pain that was to follow. Pain was a part of the jigsaw of Tane's childhood as much as joy, hunger, triumph, disappointment. In some form or another it visited him daily, whether it were a sharp cuff on the ear while he ate his oats or a thrashing in the corner for some real or imagined mischief. Pain was a part of the cycle of things: random and illogical and unfair, but only in the way that illness was or any other misfortune.

His father, Eris tu Jeribos, was a member of the town council of Amada, deep in the Forest of Yuna. Politics had always been his ambition, but while he was shrewd and clever enough to make headway time and again, he was forever dragged back by those facets of his personality that alienated him from his fellows.

He was pious, and nobody could fault him for that; but his extreme and puritanical views met with little favour among the other councillors. He made them uneasy, and they feared to let him gain any more power than he had in the council; yet though he knew this, he was a man of such conviction that he could do nothing but continue to expound his beliefs. And so he was always frustrated, and each time a little more of the humanity inside him shrivelled to a bitter char.

But there was something other than his obvious piety: an almost indefinable quality that he projected to only the most subtle of senses, so that his peers shrank from him without knowing why. He was cruel. And though he took pains never to show a hint of it in public, somehow it seemed to emanate from him and put people on edge. Perhaps it was the flat bleakness of his hooded eyes, or the curl on the edge of his voice, or his thin, gaunt, stooped body; but whatever it was, the things he did in private carried themselves to his public life whether he wanted them to or not.

Tane had been taught to hunt by his father when he was ten harvests old. He was a remarkably adept pupil, and he applied himself vigorously, having finally found something that pleased the strict patriarch. And if he noticed the gleam in Eris's eyes was a little too bright as he watched a rabbit thrashing in a snare, or that he took a fraction too much pleasure in snapping a wounded bird's neck, then he counted himself lucky that his father was happy, and less likely to turn on him without warning as he usually was.

When he was twelve, he was out walking in the woods and he came across his father skinning a jeadh – a long-muzzled, hairless variety of the wild dogs that haunted the northern end of the Forest of Yuna. The jeadh was still very much alive, staked to the ground with its legs forced apart. The spirits knew how Eris had subdued it like that. Tane had been attracted by the muffled whimpers and yelps that it forced through the crude muzzle Eris had formed when he tied his belt around its mouth.

He stood and watched, unnoticed by Eris, who was too engrossed in what he was doing to pay attention to anything else. He watched the slow, careful way his father parted the layers of skin and subcutaneous fat with his knife, drawing back a bloody flap to expose the glistening striations of pink muscle beneath. For half an hour he was motionless, standing in full view in the clearing, but his father never saw him as he meticulously took the beast apart, piece by piece, unpeeling it like an orange until he could see its heart beating in terror between its ribs. Tane looked from the animal to his father's face and back, and for the first time he truly understood that he was the son of a monster.

Tane's mother Kenda was a pale, mousy woman, small and shy and grey and quiet. It had occurred to him in later life that her marriage to Eris might have made her this way, but strangely Eris's cruelty never extended to his wife, and he never beat her as he did Tane. At most, he snapped at her, and she would scuttle away like a startled shrew; but then, since she seemed to possess no will of her own and dared not accomplish the smallest task without being told to do so by Eris, she never gave him a reason to be displeased with her. Tane remembered his mother as something of a non-entity, a pallid extension of his father's wishes, a menial thing that swept and scampered and was wholly ineffectual on her own.

Kenda had bore Eris two children. Each had brought her close to death, for her weak body could barely stand the trials of pregnancy; but Tane doubted that she had even considered herself or her health in the equation. Tane's sister Isya was six harvests younger than him, and he loved her dearly. She was the one anchor of humanity in their household. Somehow she grew up unsullied by the parents who raised her, taking on none of their traits as most children are wont to do. Instead, it was as if her personality were formed in the womb, crystalline, rejecting any possibility of absorbing outside influences.

She was a happy child where Tane was serious, a dreamer, a creature of imagination and boundless energy, who would cry when she found a broken chick that had fallen from its nest, or laugh and dance when it rained. Tane envied her passion for life, her carefree joy; and he treasured it also, for just to be near her was to feel the warmth she gave off, and the world seemed better for her being in it. She endured the bumps and scrapes of childhood like any other, but he was always there for her, to bandage a skinned knee or soothe her tears. It was through learning to care for her that he first realised the healing properties of herbs, and began to apply them to his own bruises too. For her part, Isya adored her older brother; but then she adored everyone, and not even the stern manner of their father – who was careful never to beat Tane within her earshot – or the nervous shyness of their mother were enough to deflect her affection.

It was Isya and Isya only that made life bearable for Tane as he grew into adolescence. It was as if his father had somehow sensed the disgust his son now felt for him, after seeing him torture the jeadh in the forest. This, coupled with his increasing frustration at the town council, led to the regular beatings that Tane suffered suddenly intensifying. He would be set impossible tasks of learning, told to go to the library in Amada and memorise entire chapters of Saramyr history to recite word for word. If he failed, as he inevitably did, he was thrashed until his body was bruised black and his lungs rattled for breath.

He took to retreating into the deeper forest for days at a time. His father's lessons in hunting and survival served him well during these periods when he was away, and he began to yearn more and more to stay on his own, surrounded by the animals and trees, none of whom could possibly be as cruel to him as the lean ogre who waited at home. But there was one thing that always drew him back: Isya. Though his father's casual violence had been hitherto directed only at Tane, he did not dare leave his sister to Eris's mercies, in case one day he might seek a new target to vent himself on.

When he was sixteen harvests and Isya was ten, that day came.

He had been away for a week, searching the stream sides and rocky nooks for a particular shrub called iritisima, whose roots were a powerful febrifuge, used to bring down fevers. By now most of the time he was not away he was at the library, learning the intricacies of herblore alongside the futile task of keeping up with his father's lessons. Isya missed him, but he was faintly dismayed to see that she got along fine in her own company, and did not need her older brother half as much as he liked to think. She had cultivated friends in the village, too; real friends, not the acquaintances Tane had. He could never begin a true friendship while he still had to hide the bruises and mysterious convalescences that were part of his routine.

When he returned home to the cabin, sitting beneath the shade of the overhanging oaks that leaned over the low cliff at its back, he found it silent. The day was warm and humid, and his shirt was damp with sweat. Using his bolt rifle as a walking staff – the way his father had warned him never to do – he made his tired way to the door and peered inside. A quiet house usually meant Eris was away, but this time there was a certain malevolence about the peace, something that prickled at his intuition.

'Mother?' he called as he propped his rifle inside the porch. Her face appeared in the doorway to the kitchen, a flash of fright, and then she disappeared. He felt something cold trickle into his chest. Striding quickly, he went to Isya's door and opened it without waiting to knock.

She was huddled in a corner by her simple pallet bed, curled up like a foetus, her hair a straggle and her face puffy with tears. In that moment, in one terrible second, he knew what had happened – hadn't he always feared it, secretly? His breath stopped, as if to plug whatever it was that was rising from his belly to his throat. Seemingly in a dream, he crossed the room and crouched next to her, and she threw herself into his arms and hugged him tight, desperately, as if she could crush him into her and he could take away the pain as he had always done before. The veins on his neck throbbed as she screamed into his shoulder; his eyes fell to the spatters of dark, dark blood on her pallet, the bruises on her thin arms where Eris's hands had gripped. Her saffron-yellow dress was a dull rust-brown where she had gathered it between her knees.

He remembered holding her. He remembered brewing her a strong infusion of skullcap and valerian that put her to sleep. And then he went out, into the forest, and did not return till the next morning.

His father was back by then, sitting at the round table in the kitchen. Tane went in to check on Isya, who was still asleep, and then sat down opposite Eris. He swung a half-full bottle of liquor on to the table. His father watched him stonily, as if this were a day like any ordinary day, as if he hadn't ruined and dirtied the one precious thing he had ever created, forever destroyed the fragile innocence of a creature more beautiful that the rest of her family combined.

'Where did you get that?' he asked, his voice low, as it always was before he struck.

'It's yours,' Tane said. 'I took it.'

His mother, who had been hovering by the stove, began to scuttle out quickly, sensing the rising conflict.

'Get us two cups, Mother,' Tane said. She stopped. He had never *ordered* her to do anything before. She looked to his father. He nodded, and she did as she was bade before retreating.

'You're drunk.'

'That's right,' said Tane, filling the two cups. Eris rarely drank, but when he did it was always this: abaxia, a smooth spirit from the mountains.

Eris looked steadily at Tane. Ordinarily, Tane would be rolling and pleading beneath his fists or the buckle of his belt by this point. But Eris had sensed he had gone too far this time, crossed some invisible line, and Tane was strong enough now to stand up to his father. There was a belligerence about his manner, and beneath that a look in Tane's eyes that he had never seen before. A kind of emptiness, like something had died inside him and left only a void. For the first time in his life, he secretly feared his son.

'What do you think you're doing?' he asked slowly, warily.

'You and I are going to take a drink,' Tane replied, pushing his cup towards him. 'And then we're going to talk.'

'I'll not be told what to do by you,' Eris said, rising.

'You'll sit *down*!' Tane roared, slamming his fist on the table. Eris froze. His son glared at him with raw hatred in his eyes. 'You'll sit down, and you'll take a drink, or the gods help me I'll do worse to you than you did to Isya.'

Eris sat, and with that the last of his authority was gone. For so many years he was used to his word being unchallenged in his own home that he simply did not know how to react when it was. His hands were trembling as Tane composed himself again, brushing a flick of dark hair back from his forehead. His skull was unshaven then.

'A toast,' Tane said, raising his cup. Shakily, Eris did the same. 'To family.'

With that, he drained his cup in a single swallow, and his father followed him.

'She was all I had, Father,' Tane said. 'She was the only good thing you ever did, and you've ruined her.'

Eris's eyes would not meet Tane's.

'*Why?*' he whispered.

His father did not reply for a long time, but Tane waited.

'Because you weren't here,' Eris said quietly.

Tane let out a bitter laugh.

Eris looked at him then. 'What are you going to do?'

Tane tapped the bottle of abaxia with a fingernail. 'I've already done it.'

His father opened his mouth to speak, but no words came out. The expression of horror on his face was something Tane had never seen before.

'Tasslewood root,' he said. 'First it paralyses your vocal cords, then robs the strength from your limbs. After that it gets to work on your insides. It takes up to fifteen minutes to die, so the books say. And best of all, it's practically undetectable and the cadaver is unmarked, so it seems like a simple heart failure.'

'You . . . but you drank . . .' Eris gasped. He could already feel the numbness at the base of his throat, his larynx swelling.

'It's quite a plant, really, the tasslewood,' Tane said conversationally. 'The leaves and aerial parts provide the antidote to the poison in the roots.' He opened his mouth, displaying a wad of bitter green mush that he had kept concealed under his tongue. He swallowed it.

His father tried to reply, to plead or beg; but instead he slumped off his chair and fell to the floor. Tane got down and crouched next to him, watching him twitch as he lost control of his limbs. His father's eyes rolled and teared, and Tane listened dispassionately to the soft bleats of agony that were all Eris could force from his body.

'Look what you made me, Father,' Tane whispered. 'I'm a murderer now.'

He took the cups and the bottle when he left. They were the only evidence that could be used in accusation against him for his father's death. Not that he believed he would be accused. His mother did not have the initiative. He walked into the woods with the sound of her rising scream coming from the cabin behind him, as she discovered the body of her husband.

That day he roamed the woods, half mad with grief and self-loathing. He had no idea what would come afterwards, how they would keep going, what would become of them. He knew only that he would look after Isya, protect her, and never let a man such as Eris harm her again. He only hoped she would emerge from her ordeal as the same girl he had known before.

He returned to the cabin at night, and it was once again silent. He found his father still lying in the kitchen. Of his mother and Isya, there was no sign. At first he felt a flood of panic; but then reason calmed him. They had gone to a friend's house, or to have Isya seen to by the physician in Amada. Whatever else, his mother did not have the strength of character to leave her home permanently. He took the corpse away and buried it in the darkness, and settled to wait for their return.

After a week it became apparent that they were not coming back. He had underestimated his mother. Perhaps her need to run had overcome her fear of facing the outside world without her husband. Perhaps she truly loathed her son for what he had done. Perhaps she was terrified that he would come back and kill them, too. He would never know. She had gone, and taken his sister with her. He had lost the one he meant to protect, and now there was no one and nothing. Only him.

Towards dawn, he returned to the lodging house briefly to collect his possessions. He avoided Asara's room, not wishing to face her. There was much he had to think on, insoluble questions he had to find answers to. He could not do it here in Chaim, and he could not do it in company. He would leave Asara to watch out for Kaiku's return for the time being. He trusted her that far, at least.

He had gathered everything from his draughty, rickety wooden room and was about to leave when he saw a note on his bed, signed in Asara's flowing hand. Hesitantly, he picked it up.

Should you change your mind, he read, *take this note to the priests at the Temple of Panazu in Axekami. Tell them you wish to come to the fold. They will understand.*

A ghost of a frown crossed his tanned brow, and then he pocketed the note and left. There would be trader carts going south with the sunrise. He intended to be on one of them.

TWENTY-TWO

The snow crunched beneath her heavy boots as Kaiku forged her way westward through the high peaks of the mountains. From a distance, she looked like a shambling mound of fur, buried as she was in the patchwork coat she had taken from the dead man in the cave three days ago. Her voluminous cowl flapped over the smooth red and black Mask that she wore on her face, and she walked with the aid of a tall staff, her rifle slung across her back.

Heart's blood, she thought to herself. *When does it end?*

The last of her stolen rations had been consumed yesterday, and she was once again faint from hunger. Some inner voice had told her to push on with all her strength, to travel through the night and make good time while she still had something more than snow in her belly. That voice had told her that the peaks must give up their secrets soon, that she could not be more than an overnight trek from the monastery. Now, at mid-afternoon of the next day, the voice was conspicuously silent.

She rested for a moment, leaning on her staff like a crutch. There was no chance of catching anything to eat out here, and the snow had buried any plants or roots beneath three-foot drifts. The wilderness was a bleak, empty maze of white, and the only signs of life were the distant cawing of gristle-crows and the occasional howl of the Aberrants at night. Once again, she was facing starvation, and all she could do was keep going.

The Mask felt natural on her now, as if it had moulded itself subtly to the contours of her face. She remembered the fear and trepidation she had felt at the thought of putting it on, her worries of insanity or addiction. How ridiculous that seemed now. The Mask was not her enemy. In fact, it was perhaps her only hope of survival out here. She trusted the Mask, took comfort in it; and though it had proved remarkably ineffective thus far, her faith had seemed to grow still. And it was here, after many days, that her faith was finally rewarded.

She raised her head and saw a gorge she recognised.

Crossing to it, she stood at its snowy lip and puzzled over it for a time. She was certain she had been here before, and yet she would have remembered coming across such a vast rent in the landscape, and she could not recall seeing it on her journey. At its southern end was a path that led in between two of the more foreboding peaks; she knew that, too, with a certainty that seemed strangely groundless, as she was equally certain that she had not passed it since she began her trek into the mountains.

When she investigated, she did indeed find a path, and she took it.

As the day wore on, she found more and more landmarks she knew: an enormous, twisted tree that raked out of the snow and held crooked fingers to the sky; a flat, glassy plain of ice that was passable by following a rocky spine of black stone through its midst; a forked mountain peak, split asunder by some great and ancient disaster. Each sight triggered a memory that was not hers, but which belonged to one of the previous wearers of the Mask, and which had been absorbed into its wooden fibres by some incomprehensible osmosis.

Father, she thought. She could feel tears threatening. It seemed as if the wood smelled of Ruito, a cosy, musky smell of old books and fatherly affection, the scent she got when she sat in his lap as a child and burrowed into his chest to sleep there. She sensed him as a ghost in her mind, frustratingly elusive but present nonetheless, and she felt as that child again.

The next day, hungrier and weaker, she came across a strange phenomenon. Walking along an unremarkable curve of rock, an insect in the snowy waste, she felt the Mask grow suddenly warm. Her head began to feel light. The sensation was not unpleasant, but a little worrying. As she moved onward, the heat grew greater; experimentally, she tried backtracking, and to her surprise the heat faded.

There is something there, she thought.

There was nothing to do but go on. She walked slowly, feeling the presence of something vast and invisible before her. Instinctively, she put out a hand, fearing to walk into something, though there was nothing that any of her five primary senses could tell her.

Her hand brushed the barrier, and the glittering Weave opened up to her.

It was breathtaking: a vast, sweeping band of golden threads, stretching from horizon to horizon. It lacked the definition a wall would have; rather, it was a thickly clustered mass of whorls and loops, slowly revolving, turning inside out, swallowing each other and regenerating once again. The shining threads of the Weave were thrown into turmoil here, as if the stitching of the world had caught and snarled into a seething mess. And yet the barrier followed the contours of the land, always staying at approximately six metres high and six deep. Chaos within an ordered framework. This was no accident, nor some freak of nature. This was placed here on purpose, and by beings who knew how to manipulate the world beyond human sight with great skill.

With a gasp, she drew her hand back, and the barrier faded from sight. The Mask was radiating in response, making her dizzy. This was how the monastery had stayed hidden all this time. The barrier turned an unprotected mind around, misdirecting it, disorientating. Only with the Mask could someone hope to break through.

More firmly now, Kaiku put her hand out to the barrier. A slight pressure, and the stirring fibres slid apart to admit her. She closed her eyes, took a breath and said a short prayer to the gods, then stepped into it.

She was engulfed in light, swallowed by the womb of the Weave. The fibres surrounded her, a gently swirling sea of wonder, and she felt she could simply let herself be swept away by it and never have another care again. But she was not so unguarded against the dangers of the Masks that she would surrender herself to her desire. This was how it felt when she had died, this beauty, this perfection of ecstasy; and so she knew there would be no coming back if she yielded. She remembered that this was how the world appeared to her when the burning came upon her, when her irises turned to red and she saw the Weave that sewed its way beneath the skin of human sight. She feared that, and held on to that fear, for it kept her anchored to reality. She pushed onward, through the sublime paradise, and broke through to the ugly and harsh light of the world on the other side.

It felt as if she had been robbed of something beautiful, like a lover's betrayal. She looked over her shoulder, but the barrier had receded into invisibility again. For a moment, she wanted nothing more than to be back there, enfolded in the light instead of this cruelty of cold and hunger. Then she turned her head, and walked on, the Mask cooling on her face.

Over time, she had developed a tendency to mutter to herself, an unconscious reaction to the oppressive loneliness of her journey. Most of her monologue was random and meaningless, but a lot of it involved her condition, a rambling and repetitive confession that she was an Aberrant and a danger to others, that she should stay out here in the wilderness where there was nobody to harm and nobody to shun her. Sometimes she talked to her father and brother as if they were beside her. Sometimes she imagined a huge boar was walking with her, just out of sight on the edge of her vision, and its presence comforted her.

Delirium and hunger had lent these fantasies strength, and they had taken hold of her weakened mind and fastened there. They were what kept her going when her endurance flagged, and they would have kept her walking till she dropped and died, had she not come across the monastery when she did.

She saw it first through a gap between two mountain slopes to the south. It was a clear day, or she might have missed it entirely; but the air was cold and sharp as crystal, and her eyes were still keen. It was buried in the mountainside a mile or two away, a great façade hewn out of the surrounding rock, massive and stolid. She found it hard to make out any detail at this distance, but she could see the narrow stone bridge that arced from the entrance to the other side of a deep gorge, and presumed that it was there she should be heading if she wanted access.

It took her most of the day to find the way up to the monastery, which was a set of wide, steep steps carved out of the mountain's stony skin. The sheer scale of it provoked a vague awe through the haze of exhaustion. The steps had been carved centuries ago, their edges weathered to curves and crumbling; if the Weavers truly lived at the top, then they must have occupied the monastery rather than built it, for the stairway was older than the Weavers were. Snow-buried statues guarded it from pedestals set to either side, but when Kaiku cleared away the snow she found them moss-covered and worn smooth by the elements, so she could not tell what they were. The seemingly endless stairway sapped what little stamina she had remaining, and she was asleep on her feet by the time it ended.

The change in the rhythm of her steps woke her out of her shallow drowse, and she found herself on a narrow path, part of a small outpost that clung precariously to the flanks of the mountain. There were several buildings of brick and stone, linked by curving paths that went where the shape of the mountain would allow. The dwellings were old and looked abandoned, waiting silently with their shutters creaking in the freezing breeze. They were ugly and simplistic, like the houses in Chaim but more sturdy. A little further up, she saw where the bridge began, a stout and unornamented span of stone that leaped across the massive divide, where only a snowy murk drifted below. There was no sign of life.

By now exhaustion had claimed her, and she knew she would soon be unable to go no further. Stumbling towards the nearest building, she pushed open the wooden gate and found that it was a chicken barn, long empty but still retaining some mouldy hay in the pens. She clambered into one, gathered the hay about her, and was instantly asleep.

Cramps in her stomach woke her rudely from slumber, and she was dragged unwillingly into awareness again. She lay with her eyes closed for what seemed a long while, until the scuffing of someone's feet in the hay next to her made her jerk in alarm.

Someone was leaning over her. For one terrifying moment, she thought it was the ghost of the man she had slain in the cave; but though the clothes were similar, they were not identical. This one's ragged robes were of different kinds of fur, and the Mask that peered at her was pale blue, and made of wood rather than bone. It was a portrait of idiot curiosity, a fat moon-face with a pooching lower lip and wide, dark eyes set in an expression of surprise. Kaiku scrambled back, but her progress was impeded by the stone wall behind her. Her rifle lay nearby, though not near enough so she could easily lunge for it.

The moon-face tipped its head to one side, then bobbed closer, peering intently. It was like being sniffed by some wild animal who was trying to decide whether she was food or not. Kaiku did not move.

Silently, the blue moon-face withdrew and lost interest. The Weaver turned and climbed out of the chicken pen, pausing to examine a few other things on the way. Then he left, closing the gate behind him.

Kaiku's heart was pounding. What did this mean? In the days since she had left the cave in the mountains, she had never once considered that the death of the man whose robes she wore might have repercussions. Now she knew it had been a foolish oversight. What if they recognised each other by their robes as much as their Masks? What if the Weaver who had worn this red and black Mask was known to them? Kaiku's father might have killed him as Kaiku had killed the Weaver in the cave. If they found that the one wearing these blood-spotted robes, this leering Mask was not the man they knew . . .

. . . the man . . .

It hit her then, something so obvious that she had overlooked it in her delirium. The Weavers were exclusively male. No women were allowed in their order. It was only by grace of their heavy, disfiguring garments that her body shape was not recognisable; yet even then the slope of her breasts could be faintly determined, unless she hunched her shoulders forward. If she so much as spoke, she would be discovered.

Feeling sudden panic welling within her, she grabbed her rifle and hurried to the door of the building. Opening the gate a little, she feared to see Moonface running towards the monastery to raise the alarm; but instead she saw the shambling figure wandering about a little way down the path, idly poking and pushing things or picking up stones for closer scrutiny.

She stepped out warily. It was morning, bitterly cold and damp. The snow-dusted flanks of the gorge were hidden by white mists, churning far below. The bridge hung in the air nearby, spanning the chasm. It seemed impossibly fragile, the worse because its lack of ornamentation made it feel temporary, incongruous with the carven façade on the other side. Kaiku looked at it, and at the mouth of the monastery beyond. She was suddenly afraid. What had she been hoping for when she climbed up here? Why had she not considered the danger? Why had she not held back and observed?

A pang in her stomach reminded her. She could not afford the time to wait and spy out the land, for she was starving. To return to the wilderness far below meant certain death.

There was no choice.

A quick search of the outpost – carefully avoiding the attentions of Moonface – revealed nothing but deserted buildings, and yielded no morsel to eat. So it was that Kaiku found herself crossing the narrow stone bridge to the monastery, leaning on her staff like an old man, and hoping only that whatever was within would not question her disguise.

The monastery façade was stern and simple. Great pillars held up a roof that sloped back to merge with the rock of the mountainside, and beneath it there crouched four mighty statues, four creatures all haunch and scale and fang. As Kaiku approached, she saw that the pillars were decorated with thousands of tiny, intricate glyphs and pictograms, and that the statues were not weathered like their inferior counterparts on the stairway she had climbed yesterday. These were so carefully carven that it was almost possible to believe they breathed. The portal to the monastery had heavy stone gates, but they were open and inside it was dark.

Kaiku hesitated. The statues made her skin crawl. She had a notion that their eyes were on her, a sensation too strong to be put down to nerves. She looked back across the bridge and saw Moon-face watching her from the other side of the gorge. The fear of discovery assailed her anew; but she could not turn back. Steeling herself, she walked onward and into the stone throat of the monastery.

The corridor she came into bore torch brackets but no torches. By the morning light that shone in through the square portal, she could see hints of statues to either side, deformed beasts that pawed at her or gathered themselves to leap. Beyond that, all was black. She went forward, her shadow preceding her, gradually merging with the darkness until she was swallowed by it.

Her eyes adjusted slowly as she went, tapping her staff before her. This place seemed as deserted as the outpost, and yet Moon-face had come from *somewhere.* Though she was weak and fragile, her hunger drove her onward, even after the light from the entrance had disappeared with the turn of a corner.

And then she saw new light, and became aware of someone coming towards her from below. She stopped still at the top of a staircase she had been about to tumble down. The flickering torch came nearer, until she could see that it was held by another creature of motley and rags, this one with a face like a grinning skull, made of blackened bone. The newcomer came up the stairs and halted a few steps below Kaiku. She was stooped so that her robes buried her, the better to conceal her femininity; but she felt her heart begin to accelerate as the Weaver regarded her. Was he waiting for her to speak? She could not: to open her mouth would be to give herself away. After a short pause that seemed to stretch agonisingly, he grunted and handed Kaiku his torch, then walked past her, without fear of the darkness. Kaiku let out a pent-up breath.

The steps took her down to a new corridor, and as she progressed along this one she found that the torch brackets were occupied more often than not, and smoky flames cast warm reddish light about the pathways of the monastery. The walls, ceiling and floor were built of massive bricks of a sandy-coloured stone, and decorations were strewn haphazardly about: here a little votive alcove, there a hanging, chiming talisman. Sometimes there were tiny carven idols standing on shelves, and sometimes Kaiku had to duck beneath hanging streamers. She could discern no pattern to the imagery; it was as if someone had hoarded the detritus of a dozen religions together. There were icons from far-off lands, heathen dolls from the jungle continent of Okhamba, ancient Ugati carvings, depictions of the Saramyr pantheon including some of those gods who had been all but forgotten. She even saw a graven fountain, now dry, that had the three aspects of Misamcha set into its pedestal in the classical Vinaxan style, from the very beginning of the Saramyr Empire.

The corridor split off into two, and that into four, and soon Kaiku was hopelessly lost within the subterranean maze of the monastery. She wandered through chamber after chamber, finding them arranged utterly without order or direction, as if planned by some madman. She passed other masked Weavers several times, but all of them ignored her, and she began to relax a little, content that her disguise hid her gender well enough.

Presently, after walking for some time down deserted ways, she came across an area which she took for some kind of prison. There was no light burning and nobody present, but the sound of shuffling and scraping from the dark recesses of the cells told her that at least some of them were occupied.

Curiosity overcame hunger, and she crept inwards. What kind of prisoners did the Weavers keep? The chamber was little more than a short, wide corridor between two rows of barred cell doors. The silence as she stepped inside became total; even the shuffling stopped. Her torch showed her only the bars, and did nothing to illuminate what was behind them.

She stood indecisive for a time. Then, slowly, she stepped over to one of the cells, holding her torch up. There was something pressed back there in the shadows, something . . .

It sprang at her without warning, crashing into the bars and lunging with one clawed arm. She yelled and pulled herself away, the claws missing her by centimetres. The torch fell from her hand to the floor, rolling back a little way, out of the creature's reach.

An Aberrant. She had seen its kin many times in the mountains, but never one like this. This one was a true grotesquerie, a malformed abomination of muscle and tooth. It had four arms, but all were different sizes, ranging from withered to massively swollen. A single eye blinked balefully from a face that was black and wizened, and its lower portions were a terrible tangle of half-grown limbs and tentacles, wrapped around each other, some crooked and broken. Its back was a shiver of spines and fins. It looked like the collision of several different types of creature, all fighting to represent themselves by a limb or a feature and resulting only in a horrible clutter of nauseating aspect.

'. . . *kkilll yoooou* . . .' the thing gurgled in Saramyrrhic, and Kaiku's heart froze.

Suddenly, all around her, the cells were alive, things rattling the bars of their cages or reaching out of the darkness for her. Roars and bleatings became mangled words from deformed mouths, pleadings, curses, even some awful noise that sounded like weeping. Kaiku recoiled in terror, snatching up the torch, but she dared not take her eyes off the thing that had spoken first. It retreated slowly out of the light, letting the darkness take it once more, and as it did so it spoke again.

'. . . *lookkk wwwhatt yoou've ddooone ttto ussss* . . .'

She fled the prison, horror making her blood cold as she ran, and she did not stop until she was beyond the reach of the clamour. There she leaned against a wall, panting, listening to her heart slow. The shock of having that thing attack her had been bad enough, but to hear it speak . . . it was almost more than she could bear, in her weakened state. They were *full-grown*

Aberrants in the midst of a Weaver monastery. Intelligent, aware, and imprisoned. What could it mean?

Seeking to distract herself from the memories, she stumbled onward, thoroughly lost. The possibility had occurred to her several times that she might be unable to escape this maze before she starved, but for the moment her hunger was forgotten. Instead, she pressed onward, knowing no direction but away from that prison.

After a time, she became aware of a dull hum coming from somewhere ahead of her. By now she had passed into unlit corridors that were little more than crude tunnels, and there were no torch brackets here. She had seen nobody for some while, and had resigned herself to the fact that she had strayed far from the beaten path. She had been about to turn back to where there was a greater likelihood of finding food, but the hum intrigued her enough to keep her going.

A light further up the tunnel drew her to it, and she found a wide rent in the side of the corridor which let out on to a broad ledge in a vast chamber. The hum was coming from the chamber, and the light from within shone on her, a strangely uneasy glow of an indefinable hue.

The ledge blocked her view of the chamber below, so she wriggled through the rent and crawled to the lip, and there she looked over and saw what was beneath.

The chamber was more ornate than anything she had seen so far in this place. It was possessed of a powerful, stony grandeur, its sandy walls curved into pillars or gliding into mighty stone lintels above the gold-etched gates at floor level. Kaiku was very high up, her ledge only a little below the flat ceiling. On either side of her, a cluster of enormous gargoyle-like creatures leered over the proceedings below, smaller cousins to the vast statue that dominated the far end of the chamber. That one was fully fifty feet high, its shoulders scraping the ceiling as it squatted in the unnatural light. The creatures were foul beyond imagining, eyeless things with gaping maws whose proportions seemed to defy sense. They were monstrously malformed, just humanoid enough to be recognisable as such but twisted so far out of true that Kaiku could not help but doubt the sanity of the mind behind them. They were lit from below, their hideous features made more menacing by shadow.

But it was what was happening in the centre of the chamber that drew Kaiku's attention. There was the source of the light: a massive rock, perhaps forty feet in length and half that in height. It was not like any rock Kaiku had ever seen.

The shape of the thing was utterly irregular, and doubly so for a mineral. It seemed to have *sprouted*, like a plant or a coral reef, so that great roots and lumpen antlers of stone reached out from its core and buried themselves in the floor, walls and ceiling of the chamber. It seethed with an unnatural glow. Kaiku narrowed her eyes behind her Mask and felt a sickness creep into her belly. It made her feel ill just to look upon it.

I know of these, she thought to herself, the memory of the Mask coming to her. *This is a witchstone.*

She was gazing on the source of the Weavers' power, and their most jealously guarded treasure.

There were twelve Weavers surrounding the rock, attired as Kaiku was in patchwork robes and odd Masks. There was a thirteenth person as well, but this one was naked: a thin, emaciated man struggling weakly in the clutches of two of the robed figues. Kaiku watched as they dragged him up a set of steps and pulled him on to the jagged back of the witchstone. She guessed what was going to happen even before one of them drew his sickle and cut the unfortunate man's throat.

The man slumped forward on his face. One of the robed figures retreated while the other turned him over and cut him from chin to manhood, opening him up to expose his insides. These he roughly began to hack at, pulling them out one by one without finesse, laying them aside on the rock when they were free. Heart, kidneys, liver, intestines . . . in moments, he was surrounded by the man's organs.

Kaiku had been watching this with no particular horror. The fate of that man did not concern her, nor the method in which he was despatched. But there was something wrong with what she was seeing, and it took her a little time to understand what it was.

There was no blood. Oh, certainly, the man *bled*, and the Weaver's garments were sprayed with gore; but the rock, where almost all the blood had eventually fallen, was spotless. Where the heart had been taken out and laid aside, it lay as clean and dry as an apple. Where the intestines should have rested in a pool of red, they were rubbery and blue and immaculate. The blood was coming out, all right, but where was it going? It was as if the rock absorbed it somehow.

Or *drank* it.

Kaiku frowned at the thought, but she could see now that the witchstone was beginning to darken, the foul glow fading and being drawn inwards, until the cavern was almost pitch black. The only source of light was within the rock, and the rock was full of veins, a network of glowing lines hanging in the pure darkness, as if its skin had become transparent and its own innards were exposed. And at its core, a pulsing chamber like a human heart, pushing the bright white blood around it.

By the spirits, Kaiku thought. *The witchstone. It is alive.*

The memories hit her then, a sudden rush of understanding that flooded into her brain, triggered by the realisation. Connections that she had never considered before became suddenly obvious, each one sparking another and another until the circuit was complete and she saw the whole of the grand design, as her father had seen it. Kaiku knew, in a flash, what Ruito tu Makaima had found out, why he had run, and why they had killed him for that knowledge.

The witchstones were alive. And just as the dust of the witchstones in the

Weaver's Masks corrupted and warped their bodies, so the witchstones were corrupting and warping the earth in which they lay.

It opened up to her then as a vision. Ruito in his study, in a hired apartment in Axekami, poring over a map and a heap of charts and scrolls. A project he had been working on in secret for years, a passion, a suspicion. In her vision, Kaiku stood with him at the moment of realisation – though she had not been present in real life – when all the facts and figures and distances fell into place. There was a correlation between the reports of Aberrant births and their proximity to Weavers. He saw that the epicentre of Aberrancy always lay at the site of a Weaver monastery, and the monasteries were always built around the witchstones. How could nobody have seen this before? How many people had been killed or dissuaded, to keep their silence? But Ruito saw, and determined to investigate, to gain the proof he needed to confront the nobles with. So he had come here, and seen this, and then he had run.

But they had known. Somehow, they had known, by some carelessness that even Ruito was not aware of. An invisible trigger, a misplaced word . . . who could say? By the time he returned to the mainland, it was hopeless. Only in secrecy could a man such as he hope to overcome the Weavers. Once they were forewarned, he would never be able to so much as get a message to the nobles. They would not even let him leave his house, watching his every move like vultures. Perhaps if he had gone straight to Axekami, tried to spread the knowledge to others, they would have killed only him. But he had come home, shattered by what he had seen, to think and recuperate; and they had been following him all the way. It was only then they had let themselves be seen, let him know they were on him like a shadow. They allowed him to come all the way home, back to his family, and then they showed themselves.

And Ruito knew that his life was at an end; he had discovered too much.

Kaiku felt she would choke on sorrow as she felt him make his choice. There was no escape, and no way to unknow what he knew. He would be killed, and so would his family. But they could at least leave the player's table with honour, instead of at the foul hands of whatever creatures the Weavers would employ. He would not let his family be subject to tortures or interrogation, to have their minds laid bare and flayed by the monsters he had stirred up.

It was no assassin who poisoned the evening meal that day, no agent of the Weavers who killed Kaiku that first time. It was her father.

When they were assured of his impotency, once they had scoured his apartment in Axekami and removed all his work, the Weavers sent the shin-shin. But the shin-shin were too late to do anything but clean up the evidence, and it was only through the strength of Asara that anyone was left to tell of it at all.

Kaiku's eyes flooded with tears. She felt all the despair, all the loss, the terrible realisation that her father had borne. No wonder he had seemed haunted when last he returned to their home; he had been broken by the scale of the conspiracy he had uncovered, shattered by the knowledge that neither he nor his family would be allowed to live. Destroyed by the choice he had to make, to poison his loved ones or leave them to a far worse fate.

The Weavers had killed Aberrants for two hundred years, preached hatred towards them, used their positions of power to ingrain it into the consciousness of the people of Saramyr. But they were not doing it out of the desire to keep the human race pure, nor for any religious reason. They were cleaning up their own mess, covering their tracks, destroying the evidence.

The source of the Weavers' power was also the source of the blight that was wasting the land.

This final realisation was too much for her. Starving, exhausted and frightened, she slid back through the crack in the wall and away from the ledge. She did not know how long she stumbled until she fainted, but she welcomed oblivion with open arms.

TWENTY-THREE

Anais tu Erinima, Blood Empress of Saramyr, stood at the top of the Imperial Keep and looked over the city below. A pall of smoke was drifting up from the north bank of the Kerryn, joined by several thinner cousins nearby, polluting the evening sky. The air was as dry and hot as the inside of a clay oven. Behind her and to her left, Nuki's eye was a westering ball of sullen orange, setting the horizon afire behind the grand bulk of the temple to Ocha that lay in the centre of the Keep's roof. Beneath the walkway that supported her lay the Keep's sculpture garden, a frozen forest of artistic shapes and constructions, open to the sky. The strange forms that inhabited the garden cast long, warped shadows across their neighbours. Narrow white paths wound through carefully tended lawns, gliding between the pedestals that the sculptures rested on.

She laid her pale, elegant fingers on the low wall that protected her from a dizzying drop, and let her head bow. An Imperial Guard in white and blue armour stood at his post further along the walkway, pretending not to notice.

She wanted to scream, to throw herself from this height and tumble to her death below. Wouldn't that make an ending? Wouldn't that be worth a song, or a poem? If the war poet Xalis was still alive today, he would make a good fist of it, describing her sharp and sudden finale in his equally sharp and sudden verse, the words like the cut and thrust of a sword.

The city was tearing itself apart. Most of the nobles had fled by now, back to their estates where they gathered what armies they had and waited to see which way the wind was blowing. The court had scattered, and that made the Weavers more important than ever; civil war was in the offing, and every house was scrambling to ensure they would keep their heads above water when the conflict came. In her heart, Anais knew that the author of her misery was within her own Keep: Vyrrch. And yet the alternative to him was to blind and cripple herself, to leave herself without a Weaver in the face of her enemies. Vyrrch may have dared to act in secret, but he could not overtly refuse to defend her or keep messages from her, or he would reveal his hand and the power of the Weavers would be jeopardised. If it was once proved that Vyrrch had meddled, then the nobles would retaliate. But not, she suspected, until after they had done their level best to kill her child.

The frustration was abominable. Even her supposed allies within her camp were against her. Why could none of them see? Did her years of sound rule count for nothing? By the spirits, it was her *child*! Her only child, and the only one she could ever have. Lucia was supposed to rule. She was bloodline!

But what price for a mother's love? How many would die for her pride in her daughter? How many would lose their lives before the people saw that Lucia was no freak, not a thing to be loathed, but a thing of beauty?

The unfairness of it rankled. She had been coping with the disorder until that idiot Guard Commander had ruined everything by arresting Unger tu Torrhyc. And then, when she was prepared to release him and show the people the generosity of their ruler, Unger was found dead, having smashed his own brains out against the wall of his cell. The stories circulated in the streets already, of how he bravely sacrificed himself before the Empress's torturers could make him retract his words.

And at the centre of the web, Vyrrch. She knew it was him. But she had no way to prove it.

'Anais!' came the cry from below. She stirred from her maudlin reverie and looked down into the sculpture garden, where Barak Zahn tu Ikati was hailing her. She raised a hand in greeting and made her way down to him. He met her at the bottom of the steps. For a moment they regarded each other awkwardly; then Zahn put his arms around the Empress and hugged her, and she, surprised, returned the embrace.

'To what do I owe this undue affection?' she murmured.

'You look like you need it, Anais,' he replied.

He released her, and she smiled wearily. 'Does it show so much?'

'Only to one who knows you such as I,' Zahn replied.

Anais inclined her head in gratitude. 'Walk with me,' she said, and she took his arm as they strolled through the sculpture garden.

The sculptures of the Imperial Keep dated back to pre-Empire days, monuments to the acquisitive instincts of the second Blood Emperor, Torus tu Vinaxis. Only good fortune had made him decide to choose Axekami as the place to keep his treasures, for the first capital of Gobinda was swallowed by cataclysm shortly after his reign ended, and much would have been lost. He was responsible for starting most of the art collections in the current capital; a man too sensitive and creative to be a good ruler, as history told when he was usurped by the now-dead bloodline of Cho. Anais found some of them restful, others interesting, but few inspiring. She had not the heart of an artist, which was why – she told herself – she had been such an effective Blood Empress.

'Things are turning for the worse, Zahn,' Anais said, as they ambled past a curving mock-organic whirl of ivory. 'The people are becoming uncontrollable. My Imperial Guards are already stretched to the limit, and their presence only seems to incite the people more. Every riot put down breeds two smaller ones. The Poor Quarter is burning. Unger tu Torrhyc's cursed band of followers are causing untold damage in the streets of my city.' Her eyes dimmed. 'Things are turning for the worse,' she said again.

'Then what I have to tell you will not improve your mood, Anais,' said Zahn, rubbing his bearded cheek with a knuckle.

'I already know,' she replied. 'Blood Kerestyn have marshalled their forces to the west. They are marching on the capital.'

'Did you also know that Barak Sonmaga and the forces of Blood Amacha are marching from the south to meet them?'

Anais looked up at him, and for a moment there was the aspect of something hunted in her eyes. 'To join with Kerestyn?'

'Doubtful,' said Zahn. 'At least, there has been no intelligence to that effect. No, I believe Sonmaga intends to block Kerestyn from entering the city.'

'At least until he can march in himself,' Anais scowled.

'Indeed,' Zahn said ruefully. There was a silence between them, as they walked through the looming aisles of sculpture, their shoes crunching on the gravel path.

'Say it, Zahn,' Anais prompted at length. 'You came here for more important reasons than to deliver a message.'

Zahn did not look at her as he spoke, but fixed his eyes on an imaginary point in the middle distance. 'I came here to beg you to reconsider your decision to keep the throne.'

'You are saying I should abdicate?' Anais's voice hardened to stone.

'Take Lucia with you,' Zahn said, his tone flat and devoid of emotion. 'Leave the throne to those who desire it so much. Choose your child's life over your family's power. You can live in peace and prosperity the rest of your days, and Lucia will be safe. But your position is worsening, Empress, and you know what will happen if Blood Amacha or Blood Kerestyn have to take this city by force.'

Anais was furiously silent.

'Then I will say it, if you won't,' Zahn continued. 'You, they may well allow to live. But they will execute Lucia. They cannot risk her being a threat to their power, and the people will want their blood.'

'And if I abdicate?' Anais spat. 'They will get to her, Zahn. She is still a threat even if I give up all claim to the throne. As many people who hate Aberrants, there are some who don't and she will become a focus for their discontent, an icon for them to rally behind. Whether Kerestyn or Amacha become the ruling family, whether I abdicate or not, they will kill Lucia. They will send assassins. She is *too dangerous to live*, don't you see that? The only way I can keep my child alive is to stay Empress and *beat* them!'

She was aware suddenly that she was shouting. Zahn put his hands on her shoulders to calm her, but she swatted him away.

'Don't touch me, Zahn. You have no right any more.'

'Ah,' the Barak said bitterly. 'Yes, I have heard that you have taken to sharing your bed again with your wastrel husband. I remember when you—'

'That is *not* your business!' Anais snapped, her pale skin flushing.

Zahn held up his palms placatingly. 'Forgive me,' he said. 'I forget myself. Do not let us argue; there are more important things at stake here.'

Anais searched his eyes for hints of mockery, but she found him honest. She relaxed. When Zahn saw she was ready to listen, he spoke again.

'If you are adamant on staying, Anais, at least let your allies help you,' he said. 'There could be a thousand troops here in two days, ten times that in a week. You could put down the uprising, keep the people safe, and once within the city we would be unassailable. Amacha or Kerestyn would not dare enter.'

'Zahn,' Anais said wearily. 'I trust you. But you know I cannot allow a force like that into Axekami. There are too many families involved, too many political uncertainties.'

'Word has reached me that Barak Mos of Blood Batik has offered his troops, and that you accepted.'

'Your spies are inept, my Barak,' Anais said without rancour. 'Mos has offered me troops, but I have not accepted yet. He is a different matter, anyway. My defence is in his interest: he has his son and granddaughter to protect. Durun would just as likely be killed as I if either Blood Amacha or Blood Kerestyn took Axekami.'

'Mos is also the head of the only other family strong enough to take the throne,' Zahn reminded her.

'His son already *has* the throne,' Anais replied. 'I have not annulled our marriage through these years despite the obvious unsuitability of my husband. He has no reason to think I might now.'

'Do you believe you can hold Axekami against your enemies, with the very people of the city against you?' Zahn asked.

'The people will learn to accept Lucia,' said Anais. 'Or I will *make* them learn. As to now, they are like children in a tantrum, and must be punished. I will keep them in order.'

They turned a corner, into the long shadow of a rearing thing that might have been a stone cobra, or perhaps a man and woman entwined. The evening sun shone through the gaps in the sculpture, reddening imperceptibly as dusk came on. Zahn gave it barely a glance. They walked on for a time in the sultry heat of the Saramyr summer before Anais spoke again.

'I owe you an apology,' she said.

Zahn was surprised. 'For what?'

'I have been presumptuous. I have been so busy trying to win my opponents over that I have not considered one of my greatest allies. For weeks I have been introducing Lucia to the high families in an attempt to dispel the myths that have arisen about her; but you have supported me from the start in this, and I have never once invited you to see the cause you fight for.'

Zahn inclined his head. She knew as well as him why he was on her side. 'You are right, of course. I never have met her. I would be honoured if I might do so now.'

*

The Heir-Empress Lucia had finished her lessons for the day, so she went up to the roof gardens to enjoy the last of the evening light. Zaelis had stayed with her. She liked the tall, white-bearded tutor. He indulged her relentlessly, and his deep, molten voice was comforting. She knew – in the unique way that she knew things – that he had her best interests at heart. She also enjoyed the freedom she felt when she was alone with him. He was the only one around whom she could use her talents overtly.

They were sitting together on a bench, a picturesque arbour within a shaggy fringe of exotic trees. Berries hung in colourful chains amid the deep, tropical green of the leaves. Insects droned and clicked from a hundred different hiding places, occasionally swooping past them in languid curves or hurried, darting rushes. Ravens perched all around them. The ravens of the Keep had learned to accept Zaelis, and he had learned to relax in their presence. They were fiercely protective of the young Heir-Empress. Saramyr ravens had a strong territorial instinct, and it bred in them a desire to guard and protect. They watched over Lucia as if she was an errant chick, motivated by parental drives they were not intelligent enough to understand.

'Are you worried, Lucia?' Zaelis asked.

She nodded. He had become adept at reading her moods, even though they rarely showed in the dreamlike expression she always wore.

'About what is happening in the city?'

She nodded again. Nobody had told her anything – the tutors and guards had been instructed to keep outside matters secret after Durun's outburst in front of the child – but Lucia knew anyway. How could you keep something like that from a girl who could speak to birds? Zaelis had ignored the edict and elaborated on the situation for her. Lucia had not told him that the dream lady had informed her of most of it anyway.

'This was my fault,' she said quietly. 'I started this.'

'I know you did,' Zaelis replied, in the casual mode of address used for – and by – children, even the Heir-Empress. 'But we've been waiting for you to start it for a very long time.'

Lucia looked up at him. 'You'll look after me, won't you?'

'Of course.'

'And my mother?'

Zaelis hesitated. There was no point lying to her; she saw right through him. 'We'll try,' he said. 'But she won't see things the way we do.'

'Who is "we"?' Lucia asked.

'You know who *we* are.'

'I've never heard you say it.'

'You don't need to.'

Lucia thought about that. 'Do you think I'm wicked?' she said after a time.

'I think you were inevitable,' Zaelis replied.

She seemed to understand; but then, with Lucia, who could say?

'Mother's coming,' she murmured, and almost simultaneously the ravens took wing, disappearing in a raucous flutter of black feathers, rising into the red sky.

A moment later, the Blood Empress came into view, walking with Zahn along a tiled path between a stand of narrow trees. She glanced once at the departing ravens, but no other reaction crossed her face. Zaelis got to his feet, ushering Lucia up with him.

'Barak Zahn tu Ikati, allow me to present my daughter Lucia,' the Empress said.

But her words seemed scarcely heeded by either the Barak or the child. The two of them were staring at each other with something like amazement on their faces. Anais and Zaelis exchanged a puzzled glance as the moment became awkward; and then Lucia's eyes filled with tears, and she flung herself at the Barak and hugged him around the waist, burying her head in his stomach.

'Lucia!' the Empress exclaimed.

Zahn folded his hands over the little Heir-Empress's blonde tresses, a strange look in his eyes, a mix of bewilderment and shock. Lucia pulled herself away suddenly, glaring at him through her tears; then with a sob she turned and fled, disappearing into the leafy folds of the garden.

All three were dumbstruck for a moment before Anais found her voice.

'Zahn, I cannot apologise enough. She never—'

'It's quite all right, Anais,' Zahn said, his voice sounding distant and distracted. 'Quite all right. I think I should go now; I seem to have upset her.'

Without waiting for her leave, Zahn turned and began to walk slowly to the entrance of the garden. Anais went with him, leaving Zaelis alone on the path. He sat back down on the bench.

'Well, well, well,' he murmured to himself, and an odd smile creased his face.

TWENTY-FOUR

Asara killed again in Chaim. It was an unwise risk, for she had no need to feed; but she sought diversion, and there was no other in the bleak, empty trading village to interest her. She chose a man this time, because she had less respect for them than for women, and she was less likely to suffer something like guilt for robbing their life as a source of amusement. This one was drunk, a leathery, tough brawler who had no fear of the short, dark route from the bar to his house, where no lights burned. Asara taught him otherwise.

Afterward, when she had hidden the body far away where it would not be discovered for days, she returned to her room. She was not worried about being caught. There was not a mark on him, nothing to link them. He had simply got lost on his way home in the dark, and fallen victim to exposure. Or perhaps his heart just stopped. He was a drinker, after all, and well-known for it.

She sat in her room, alone. As she preferred it. As it always was.

Her room at the lodging house was as spartan as everything else in Chaim. There was a double bed in the centre, its woollen covers dark with age and moth-ragged. There was a lantern on the wall, and bare, ill-fitting floorboards. Beyond that, there was nothing. The mountain winds cooed outside, sending chilly fingers in through the cracks in the wall to brush across her skin. The lantern was unlit, which made little difference to Asara – her night vision was near-perfect, like a cat's. It was freezing, as always, for the winds cut to the bone here even in summer. She listened to the night, and the sudden, sharp gusts that whipped around the rickety lodging house.

The bliss of feeding was short-lived, and when it left her she was maudlin. She sat cross-legged on the tatty bed and looked at the empty room. Alone, ever alone. She did not know any other way. For there were none like her, not even the other Aberrants. She was a reflection, a cypher, without identity or cause. She was nothing, not even herself.

There was no memory of her childhood. There had been a time when she had wished she could gaze upon herself at the moment of her birth, thinking that if she could see her first face, even if it was the scrunched-up red ball of a newborn, then she might have a fix on her identity, a base line from which all her other selves grew. But it was fancy. She suspected anyway that she would not like what she saw there.

Her mother died in the pregnancy. During her early years, in her lonely quest for herself, she had tracked down the place where she had been born. She learned of a woman there who had become pregnant, and within three months had wasted away to the point of death. Yet the woman's belly was so swollen that the physicians of the village cut her open, and they found a fully grown babe within. Asara had no doubt that it was her. She had sucked her mother dry from inside the womb.

What happened to the baby, nobody knew. Perhaps it was given away, perhaps lost and found. It was remarkably hard to trace her own trail, when with each new location she was a different person.

She remembered several mothers and fathers, foster parents who took her in. She was irresistible to them. With a child's eagerness to please, she unconsciously changed herself, day by day, to accommodate her new parents' vision of the perfect offspring. She bewitched them by fulfilling their heart's desire. But always, sooner or later, the time came to leave. When a relative marked the drastic alterations since they had visited last year, too gradual for her parents to see but obvious to one who had been away for a while; when her cravings and appetites had claimed too many lives; when people began to question where she had come from: that was her time to move on, leaving only the memory of a curious ailment known as the Sleeping Death behind her, a disease that struck at random and left not a mark on the victim's body. As if their life had simply left them.

She grew fast. When she was six harvests old, the craving began, and instinct taught her how to sate it in the same way it taught babes to suckle or adolescents to kiss. She was clever even then, and careful never to be caught, though there were times when she had come close. In the early days, the hunger was worse, for she was growing as well as changing. By the time she was thirteen harvests of age she had the form and understanding of an eighteen-harvest girl. In those days, she seemed to absorb something of her victims, shreds of understanding and knowledge that kept her mind apace with her body; that talent she had lost with the passing of childhood, and never regained. To her, it was simply a part of growing up.

Her uncanny growth meant that she was forced to move on frequently, and learn hard lessons in life; but she was a good pupil, and an attentive one, and she survived the fate that most Aberrants suffered. She avoided the Weavers and the hatred of those around her, until she had mastered herself enough to disguise her condition.

As time went on, she grew bitter and resentful. She searched for her past and found fragments, each as unsatisfying as the last. In the end, she gave up. And yet the feeling remained, even now, eighty harvests after her birth. She had no core. She was a mirrored shell, reflecting other people's ideas of beauty, but under it all there was nothing. A void that sucked in life, and was never quite filled. It demanded that she prey on the things she imitated, desperately drawn to their light like a moth to a candle. She was an effigy, a parasite . . . anything but a person.

Time had given her ample opportunity to change, both in conviction and form. She had spent a few years as a man before deciding that it did not suit her. She had briefly tried to struggle against her need to feed and liberate herself from it, but in the end she could not convince herself of the worth of human beings, and she still saw most of them as a brand of cattle only slightly more unpredictable than oxen or cows. The rest were dangerous to her: the Weavers and the nobles, those who would hunt her down and slay her because she was a threat to them. No, she owed humanity no favours, and though she still hung on to a vestigial semblance of guilt and regret at sacrificing a particularly pretty life to her hungers, it was more in the manner of having been forced to break a beautiful vase.

But all changes led back to the same void, the same boredom and emptiness. And so she sat, alone, in her room in Chaim, and wondered when it might ever end.

Asara awoke at mid-morning, a moment before there came a knock at her door. She dressed hurriedly, already alert, and opened it.

The owner of the lodging house was there, a thin, grizzled, wiry man with few teeth. She dismissed him from her gaze, shifting it immediately to the one who stood next to him. Their eyes met, and the other managed a smile so weak that it told all the story it needed to tell.

Kaiku.

'This one wanted you,' the owner said. 'Was asking around.'

Kaiku stepped into the room. She looked half the weight she had been when they set off into the mountains, three weeks ago. Asara embraced her gently; she felt frail and thin, all bone.

'Bring us food,' she said to the owner. 'Meat, fish.'

'She'll be staying in this room, then?' the owner queried, a note of disapproval in his voice.

'Yes,' Asara replied bluntly. 'She will.'

By the time she had turned back, Kaiku was lying on the bed, asleep.

They did not leave the room for three days. Kaiku slept most of that time, and Asara watched over her. She seemed withdrawn, hollowed-out, and by the look in her eyes Asara knew it was something more than a physical trial she had suffered. She barely talked the first day, and only a little more on the second. Asara did not press her, not even to ask whether she had found the monastery or not. She knew Kaiku had, anyway. Her father had borne that same look about him when he returned to their house in the Forest of Yuna, shortly before the shin-shin came. Instead Asara simply waited, and guarded her while she recovered.

At Asara's behest, the owner knocked and brought them food at intervals. He was well paid for his trouble. The wealth that Asara and Kaiku carried between them, while not impressive by city standards, was a small fortune in Chaim. Kaiku ate, at first a little and then a lot as her shrunken stomach stretched to the prospect of life-giving energy. She was ravenous. At night, they slept huddled together. Asara had the owner bring extra blankets, but Kaiku shivered anyway.

By the third day, Kaiku's strength had returned somewhat. Without prompting, she suddenly began to talk.

'I imagine you are curious to know where I have been,' she said to Asara, who was sitting on the edge of the bed combing her hair.

'The thought had crossed my mind, yes,' she replied dryly.

'Forgive me my silence,' Kaiku said. 'I have had much to think about.'

Asara finished her combing and twisted to face Kaiku, who was wrapped in a blanket, hugging her knees. 'You have suffered,' she observed as a way of excusing her.

'No more than I deserve,' she replied. Then she told Asara about what she had seen and done, of her journey across the mountains and the slaying of the Weaver whose robes she stole, of the Mask and the crossing of the barrier that hid the Weavers from the world. She talked of the monastery and the strange things within, of the foul prison full of Aberrants and the creature's accusation: *Look what you've done to us . . .*

Asara's eyes widened as Kaiku recounted what she had seen in the chamber of the witchstone, and the vision the Mask had given her. She did not weep as she spoke of her father and his fate; but tears stood in her eyes, marshalling behind her lashes. Finally, she told Asara of the true nature of the witchstones. The jealously guarded source of the Weaver's power was also the despoiler of the land. Kaiku, Asara, Cailin, the Heir-Empress Lucia . . . all the Aberrants were merely a side-effect of the witchstones' energy that the Weavers harnessed in their Masks.

As she spoke, Asara found herself breathless with wonder. Each word seemed to increase the sensation of incredulity. The witchstones were the *source* of the blight? The Weavers were responsible for the very Aberrants they murdered? For the first time in longer than she cared to remember, she felt she was on the cusp of something truly worthwhile. All she had been working for these last years, with the Red Order and the Libera Dramach, in her time as Kaiku's handmaiden . . . all of it flexed into focus at this moment, and she felt the pounding of blood through her body and was *alive*.

'Do you know what you have discovered?' Asara managed. 'Do you know what you have *found*?' She grabbed Kaiku's arm. 'Are you sure? Are you sure it was no delirium you saw, but your father's memories?'

'As sure as I can be,' Kaiku said wearily. 'But Father's notes burned with the house, and if there were any left in his apartment in Axekami, I doubt there is any trace now.'

'But this could topple the Weavers!' Asara enthused. 'If the nobles knew, if we could *prove* it . . . the rage at being deceived would be . . . spirits, even if we *cannot*, we can plant the seed, help them ask the right questions! Why has nobody thought of it before?'

'They have,' Kaiku said. 'But most scholars are patronised by a noble, who in turn has a Weaver. They usually met with accidents before they could get far into their research, I imagine. My father was independent, and he kept his research secret, and even then he was discovered.'

Asara was barely listening. 'How did you get away, Kaiku? From the monastery?'

Kaiku shrugged minutely. 'It was easy.'

She told the rest of her story then. When she had woken from the faint induced by stress and hunger, she had forced herself to her feet and attempted to find her way back to the more central areas of the monastery, where food would be. Whether the Mask was helping her or not she could not divine, but she found a kitchen not long after, populated by short, scurrying servants whom she had not encountered until now. They were almost dwarfish in stature, wiry and swarthy, and their bunched-up faces revealed nothing about their thoughts, if indeed they thought at all. They seemed a simple, servile breed.

By pointing to a bone plate and to the stove, Kaiku procured herself a meal of root vegetables, a curious kind of rice-potato hybrid, and chunks of dark red meat swimming in an oily sauce. She retreated to solitude to eat, tipping her Mask up and spooning the food beneath, afraid in case anyone should see her face. It was surprisingly delicious, but the relief of putting food in her belly again made it seem all the more wonderful. She returned for more and the servants filled her plate unquestioningly. From then on, Kaiku navigated by that kitchen, using it as her base point so she always knew where to return to after she had done wandering.

It took her several tries to find her way out of the monastery, by which time she had become confident enough that her disguise would not be seen through. The Weavers kept themselves to themselves, and they were an eccentric breed. She came across some of them squatting in corners, rocking themselves gently and muttering gibberish; others sprang shrieking out of hiding at her and then fled. Most just passed her by. She soon realised that a Weaver who did not speak was a minor oddity among the insanity of the monastery, and she took comfort in that.

She had not known what plan she had in mind for when she found her way to the open air once again. Perhaps she had thought to walk back into the wilderness and trust to Shintu's luck to get her through. But Shintu smiled on her in other ways.

When she did emerge into the harsh, snow-crisp light, there was some kind of activity going on in the tiny settlement that clung to the mountain-side opposite the monastery. She crossed the bridge that spanned the chasm and investigated. Several dozen of the dwarfish servants were hauling sacks and boxes down the immense stone stairway that led to the foot of the mountain. She watched them for a while before guessing what they were about. They were loading up carts! Suddenly excited, she made her way past them and began her descent of the stairway. It was no short trip, but she had a sense that if she missed this opportunity she may never get another.

At the bottom, she saw her efforts had not been in vain. Three large carts with great wheels wrapped in chains sat there, and manxthwa were being tethered to them. Several Weavers were bustling around. A moment's consideration led her to discard the idea of hiding in the carts, so she did the only thing she could think to do. The driver's bench was wide enough for three, and there only appeared to be one driver for each cart. She clambered on to one of the carts and waited.

It seemed like hours before the servants had finished loading, during which time Kaiku sat still, praying that nobody would question her. She was trusting to the shield of the Weaver's insanity to let her get away with this; she had seen many far more random acts in the short time she had spent wandering the monastery. After a time, one of the dwarf servants clambered into the seat next to her. He looked at her incuriously for a moment, and then snapped the reins, and the manxthwa hauled away. Kaiku let out a breath; the Weavers were staying behind.

It took them several days by cart-trails to get back to Chaim. The servants spoke between themselves in an incomprehensible dialect, but never to Kaiku. They did not remark on how she always took her food away to eat, or how she disappeared to make toilet. At some point, they passed through the Weave-sewn barrier that surrounded the monastery again, but the servants seemed unaffected by its disorientating effects and drove right through. Kaiku was exposed to the momentary surge of bliss that accompanied that golden world of waving threads, and then it was snatched from her again with enough force to make her heart ache afresh. She settled into quiet misery, and endured. Over the entire length of the journey, she did not speak a word, and when they arrived at Chaim she could have wept with relief at the sight of the grim, squalid little town.

'When we reached here,' she concluded. 'I found a place to hide and changed back into my clothes. The Mask and robes are in my pack.' She motioned with her head towards the bulging bag in the corner of the room. 'I hoped you would have waited for me. One of you, at least.'

Asara let the unspoken question about Tane go unanswered, and that was all the answer Kaiku needed. She did not ask again.

'Kaiku, what you have done . . . it is a wondrous thing,' she said, as some sort of consolation.

'Wondrous?' Kaiku queried, and her eyes fell to her blanketed knees. 'No. I am condemned over again. Don't you see? I swore to the Emperor of the gods to avenge my father's death. The Weavers are responsible for that. Not just one, acting alone. *All* of them. How can I . . . how can one person face the Weavers? How can I destroy creatures that can kill with a thought, that can read a person's mind? My task is impossible, but my oath still stands.'

'Then you should come back to the mainland with me. To the Red Order. You have done enough here, Kaiku . . . more than enough. One person cannot destroy the Weavers; but you have done more with your strength of heart than dozens who have gone before you. And you have allies.'

Kaiku nodded, though there was no conviction in her. 'You are right. I promised Cailin I would be back. There is nothing more to be done here. We will leave tomorrow.'

Night fell, the cold, bleak night of the mountains. They ate again, then slipped into their nightclothes and into the bed with a practised rapidity. The thought of leaving this place was on both of their minds, but there was still that question lingering unsaid, and so it was no surprise to Asara when Kaiku began to weep softly. She did not need to ask what it was that troubled her; she knew well enough.

'He is gone,' she whispered, and there was a shift of blankets as she moved closer and buried her head in Asara's shoulder.

Asara made a noise of confirmation. 'I told him. About you, about me. It was right that he should know.'

'Father, Mother, Grandmother Chomi, Machim . . . even Mishani. And now Tane,' Kaiku whispered. 'They all leave me, one way or another. How much more of this am I to endure, Asara?'

'Everyone you become close to will leave you, Kaiku,' Asara said softly, feeling an uncomfortable welling of emotion herself, 'until you accept what you are. Would you rather Tane left us now . . . or when he saw your eyes after a burning? He has many contradictions he needs to resolve, Kaiku. Do not lose heart. He may find you again.'

The words gave new strength to Kaiku's tears. 'Do you think he will?'

'Maybe,' Asara said, her breath stirring Kaiku's fine hair as her lips lay close. 'Maybe not. He was learning, and accepting. Perhaps there was more to him than I guessed.' She placed a hand on Kaiku's head, stroking it gently. 'You are not alone. But you must choose to be Aberrant, Kaiku. Stop thinking of yourself as one of *them. They* hate you now. *They* are like Mishani: even the most trusted will turn their back on you. You have nobody but your own kind. For now at least, you have me.'

Kaiku drew away from Asara's shoulder, and wiped her eyes with the back of her wrist. She could sense Asara's gaze in the darkness, through she could see only the faintest glitter of light from her unnatural, night-seeing eyes.

No, she caught herself. *Not unnatural. Beautiful. She need never fear the darkness, as I must.*

'You are beyond them,' Asara said quietly. 'Forget the restrictions, all the rules you have learned. They do not apply to you; use them only when necessary to disguise yourself among them. Why should you submit to what you have been taught, when your teachers would have you executed if they could? Listen no longer. Disobey. Fight back.'

'Fight back,' Kaiku breathed, her fingertips touching Asara's cheek. She was overwhelmed, her heart seeming to swell to bursting at Asara's words, and she tasted a cocktail of fear and terror and excitement and freedom such as she had never known before. There was a moment in which something seemed to shift between them, when the sharing of their body heat became suddenly magnetic, a moment in which all things seemed possible and thus became so. And in that moment, Kaiku put her lips to Asara's, who was already meeting her halfway, caught in the same tide.

They melted into one, soft skin pressing together. Their lips were dry from the wind, but they moistened swiftly in the fervour, tongues touching and sliding as they tasted each other. Kaiku's hand slid along the curve of Asara's waist and the swell of her hip, feeling the taut muscle beneath. Asara gripped the back of her neck, rolling her weight so that Kaiku was underneath her, the sound of her breath quickening in the darkness. She sat astride Kaiku's hips, and Kaiku felt Asara's hot palms on her face, running down across her shoulders, over the swell of her breasts and the apex of her nipples, across her flat stomach.

Asara's breathing was rapid now, almost panting; Kaiku experienced a moment of doubt, that something was wrong, that she had become too excited too quickly.

'You shouldn't . . .' Asara sighed. 'Don't make me . . .'

But Kaiku, swept up in the rush, ignored her. She raised herself up to kneel on the bed and brought her lips to Asara's again, kissing her hard, all warmth and sensation and darkness. Asara's hair fell across Kaiku's uptilted face; she was straddling Kaiku's knees now, and she pulled herself closer, their bellies and breasts pressed together with only the twin layers of silken nightrobes separating skin from skin. Kaiku's nails raked down her back, as if they could slice through the barrier to what was beneath.

'You don't . . . you don't know what you do . . .' Asara murmured in protest, but Kaiku had slid one strap from her shoulder, pulling it down to her elbow, and her mouth had found Asara's nipple and was sucking it gently. She shuddered in involuntary pleasure, sweeping her hair back from her face, her hips rocking against Kaiku, her breath shallow gasps.

She seized Kaiku then, roughly, and pushed her down to the bed. Her fingers gripped clawlike on either side of the younger woman's skull, and she brought her lips to Kaiku's with a predatory lunge that she had practised a thousand times before. Something inside her was warning her to stop, to stop, but her hunger and desire had been maddened by Kaiku's passion, and the voice was weak and unheeded. Suddenly, she desperately wanted what was inside Kaiku, wanted to take back the life *she* had given, to suck out the part of herself that had gone into Kaiku when she stole the handmaiden Karia's breath and blew it into her dead mistress's lungs. A piece of Asara had gone with that breath, a sliver of her life had lodged in Kaiku's heart, and Asara knew in a flash that that was the true reason why she had returned to Kaiku after Kaiku had almost killed her in the Forest of Yuna.

Kaiku sensed something in Asara's urgency, but in her heat she did not know whether it was passion or anger or something altogether different, and her senses were too overloaded to rely on. Asara kissed her hard, harder, and Kaiku felt a pain inside her, as if some organ in her breast were about to rip free, her heart about to tear from its aortal mooring. Asara sucked, powerless to stop herself, wanting only to sate herself in the most complete way she knew how.

The door to the room burst inwards.

Asara tore herself away, and Kaiku flung herself across to the other side of the bed, gasping like one who had been an inch from drowning. Her body had sensed the proximity of death although her mind had not, and she felt the terror and panic crash in on her even as Mamak and three other heavyset men rushed into the room, wielding picks and shovels. They stopped at the sight that met them: the two women, one with her nightrobe hanging from her shoulder and her right breast exposed, breathing hard and caught in surprise. A leer began to spread across Mamak's face, and then Kaiku screamed, and he exploded.

The surge of *kana* ripped through her like a stampede. The world switched from reality to the infinity of golden threads, warp and weft, a diorama of beautiful light that burned her from within like molten metal in her veins. Her irises darkened to a deep red, and she lashed out in reaction to the fear, the passion, the surprise. She saw the bright pulse of Mamak's heart as a rushing junction of threads, the stream of his blood as it passed beneath his transparent skin, and she rent it apart with a thought. He burst in a shower of flaming gore, spattering his stunned companions and spraying the bed with shards of charred bone and brain. Asara shrieked and threw herself backwards, her instincts reminding her of what had happened the last time she had seen Kaiku like this.

But this time it was tighter, more focused. This time there was no surprise in its coming, and Kaiku managed to steer the rush, to force it away and direct it. With a sweep of her hand, she blasted the other men in the room, shredding through their fibres; and where the threads snapped, flame followed, an explosive release of energy. Mamak's companions became blazing pillars of fire, their howls silenced in seconds as their lungs and throats charred, their eyes bubbled, cooking from inside and out. One of them lunged at Kaiku in a last, idiot attempt for revenge or supplication, but he only slumped on to the bed and ignited it.

Kaiku felt the *kana* blow itself out like a candle in a gale, and her vision seemed to fade back to normality, the golden threads disappearing beneath solid forms and the light from the blaze that lit the shadowy room.

The blaze.

The room was afire.

It took her a moment to assimilate her surroundings again. Asara was already up, her nightrobe pulled back into place to preserve her modesty, eyeing Kaiku warily. She seemed unable to decide which was more dangerous – the flames, or the one who had brought them. The air was filling with a choking, sickly reek of burning flesh, and black smoke gathered on the ceiling.

Kaiku swayed, feeling her head grow light. The effort of corralling the *kana* so as not to incinerate the entire room had brought her to the brink of fainting. Asara saw her weaken, and was on the bed with her in a moment, grabbing her arm.

'Come on,' she hissed. 'We have to go.'

Kaiku allowed herself to be pulled, her head lolling on her neck like a marionette's, her red eyes drowsing. Asara gathered up their clothes in a single scoop and threw them over the burning corpses, through the open doorway and out into the corridor. Then she slung both packs and rifles on her back and propelled Kaiku off the burning bed. The flames were licking up the walls now. Mamak's charred remains lay across the doorway, still ablaze, blocking their exit.

'We have to jump him.'

'I cannot jump,' Kaiku murmured.

Asara slapped her, hard. She recoiled, her eyes focusing.

'Jump,' she hissed.

Kaiku took a two-step run and sprang over Mamak's corpse, too fast for the flames to find purchase on her gown. The corridor outside seemed freezing in comparison to the room she had escaped from. She could hear voices and footsteps downstairs, but she was already grabbing her trousers and tugging them on over her nightrobe. Asara burst through the doorway then, following Kaiku's lead. She pulled on her travel clothes just as the owner of the lodging house and several tenants with water pails came up the stairs and into the corridor, and a moment later they found themselves staring at the barrel of a rifle.

'I assure you, I am a very good shot,' Asara said, her eye to the sight.

'What happened?' the owner demanded.

'Our erstwhile guide decided he was tired of waiting for us to rehire him and intended to liberate us of our money,' Asara replied. She had surmised as much by their entrance, and by the unwise way Tane had flaunted their money on the trip down from the mountains.

'Get out of the way!' one of the men behind him cried. 'The place is burning, by the spirits.'

'Pick up the packs,' she said quietly over her shoulder. Kaiku obeyed wearily. The burning of the *kana* was already causing her to spasm in pain, jolts of agony pulsing through her body.

'What do you want?' the owner cried. 'Let me put out the fire! This is my livelihood!'

'Two horses, from your stables,' Asara said. 'We can buy them from you, or we can take them by force. Choose.'

'Heart's blood,' breathed another man suddenly. 'Look at her eyes!'

It was Kaiku he was referring to.

'Aberrant!' somebody hissed.

'Yes, Aberrant,' Asara replied. 'And she will do to you what she has done to that room if you get in our way. The horses, *now*, or we stay here until this whole place burns down.'

'I'll take you,' the owner snapped. 'You men, put out that fire!'

With Kaiku in tow, Asara edged down the corridor. The men rushed past her, shying back from Kaiku with mingled disgust and fear, carrying their buckets to the blaze.

'Good horses,' said Asara, 'and we'll pay you the worth of this place.'

The owner looked at her hatefully, but he knew what it might mean. A new start, in a new place, where life was not so hard and grim. 'You have the money now?'

Asara nodded.

'Then let the place burn. Come with me,' he said.

They rode that night, driving their horses, heading south through the biting wind across Fo, putting as much distance as they could between themselves and Chaim. Kaiku slept lashed to the saddle, for her *kana* had burned her out from within, and Asara kept by her side to guide her mount.

How strange the ways that the gods take us, Asara thought, and rode on as dawn lightened the east.

TWENTY-FIVE

The Xarana Fault lay far to the south of Axekami, bracketed at its east and west end by the rivers Rahn and Zan. It was a place of dark legend, a vast swathe of shattered land haunted by the ghosts of ill memory and stalked by restless spirits, who had been shaken awake in the tumult of its formation and never quite settled again.

The histories told of how Jaan tu Vinaxis, venerated founder of the Saramyr Empire, had built the first Saramyr city of Gobinda in that place as a commemoration of the defeat of the aboriginal Ugati folk. At that time the land was flat and green, and Gobinda prospered and became a great city on the banks of the Zan. But Torus, Jaan's son, was usurped by the third Blood Emperor, Bizak tu Cho. Stories speak of the debauchery that Bizak entertained, orgies of godlessness and excess. Then came Winterfall, the day on which all men must give praise to Ocha for the beginning of a new cycle of the year. Bizak, after a three-day celebration, was too exhausted to attend. He sent his daughter in his stead.

At that, Ocha was angered. The histories tell that wise men dreamed of a great boar that night, with breath of fire and smoke and jagged tusks, who stamped the earth and split it asunder. They warned the Emperor to make amends to Ocha, reminding him that he was only Emperor of men, and Ocha was Emperor of the gods. But Bizak in his hubris would not listen, and so they fled.

There were few survivors of Ocha's mighty retribution, but those who escaped painted a terrifying picture. The ground roared and bucked and split, breaking into sections like stone hit with a hammer and pitching the people of Gobinda howling into the yawning chasms. Magma spewed from the earth, belching ash into the sky and blackening the sun, turning the world to a seething cauldron of fiery red light. Huge sections of the land plummeted suddenly hundreds of feet; rock shattered; lightning flashed; and over it all was a bellowing and screeching, as of a vast, enraged boar. Gobinda fell into the earth and was swallowed, and Bizak tu Cho, his daughter and all his bloodline went with it.

When the destruction was over, the land was buckled and ruined. The Rahn and the Zan, which had previously flowed true, were now kinked with immense waterfalls as they dropped to the newly sunken landscape. The

Xarana Fault – as it came to be known, when more was understood of tectonics and the ways of the inner earth – was a maze of folds, juts, plateaux, valleys, moraines and promontories: a landscape of utter chaos. In the many hundred years since the cataclysm, it had grown new grass and trees that smoothed over its edges somewhat; but its lessons had never been forgotten. It was still a place of bad luck and ill fortune, and was seldom visited by the honest folk of the city. Spirits were abundant there; some benevolent, most of them not.

But some dared to make their home in the hard lands of the Xarana Fault. Those who sought solitude, or needed to hide; those who would risk the dangers for the rewards of precious metals and gems unearthed by the ancient upheaval; those who had found nothing for them in the cities and the fields, and wanted a new start. There were as many reasons as there were people living in the lands of the Fault, and amid the turbulent landscape dozens of small communities lived side by side, some in harmony and some in hostility. But all had the single understanding: the business of the Fault stayed in the Fault, and was not the outside world's to know.

Cailin tu Moritat sat high in the saddle of a black mare, framed against the hot mid-morning sky. Beneath her, the ground fell in massive semicircular steps, irregular plateaux that piled haphazardly on top of each other. On the backs of these plates of earth was built a small town: dense clusters of houses, supply stores, an occasional bar and a smattering of tiny shrines nestling off the dirt tracks that passed as streets. Bridges and stairways linked the disparate levels together. It was a jumble, an accretion of a hundred different styles of architecture; this place had not been planned, but built as necessity dictated, and by many different hands. The angular, three-storey houses of the Southern Prefectures rose out of a clutter of low, broad Tchom Rin dwellings; balconied and ornamented houses that would not have looked out of place in Axekami's River District were shamed by the crafty austerity of their neighbours. Some of the dwellings had been here twenty years or more – a long time in the turbulent environment of the Fault – whereas others were still being built, wooden ribs and angle joists bristling from the wounds in their exteriors. Most of the building had been done around six years ago, when the Libera Dramach had engulfed the existing dwellings and begun to draw in people from all over Axekami, some of whom were construction engineers of no mean skill.

At the top, where the steps ran up against a mighty flank of stone, there were caves that went far into the hillside, their entrances decorated with whimsical etchings, blessings for those who entered and supplications to the gods. There, hidden within, a labyrinth of chambers lay, a secret network enshrouded in impenetrable rock.

From her vantage point on a nearby ridge, overlooking all, Cailin could see the scale of the industry that went on here. Everywhere there was movement. Workers scuttled back and forth with orders for this and that. Foremen hollered at their men. Towers were being erected, their skeletons aswarm. On one plateau, a score of men and women were being trained in the sword, jabbing and thrusting in unison to their master's barked commands. The steps were littered with wooden cranes, lifts and bamboo scaffolding. Stacks of crates and bundled supplies were being hauled to and fro by carts that ran on curving tracks. Outposts were perched on the lips of the plateau, and sentries watched within, their eyes ranging out beyond the broken slopes to the short expanse of flat earth that surrounded them and the frowning walls of grim rock beyond. The rise of the neighbouring land sheltered this place from view so efficiently that it was only possible to see it from the edge of the valley that cradled it. There was no kind of organised army here, but the Xarana Fault was a brutal place, and any settlement that did not think and act as a fortress would soon find itself overrun.

Cailin allowed herself a tiny smile, the red and black triangles painted on her lips curving slightly. This was the Fold, the home of the Libera Dramach and, for the time being, also home to a small sisterhood of the Red Order. She could not help but admire the realisation of their leader's vision. Few even knew of the existence of the Fold. For years now the Libera Dramach had been recruiting and gathering in secret, drawing from all sources equally. Bandit gangs had been offered the chance to end their hand-to-mouth existence and join; scholars had been persuaded of the rightness of their cause; common folk who had a grudge against the Weavers – and these were legion – came in search of a way of striking back at those who had hurt them. With them came physicians, apothecaries, disenchanted soldiers, wives who had been turned out of home, vagrants, debtors. All found a place here. All were brought into the Fold. At the core were the Libera Dramach themselves, those sworn to the organisation, picked from among the hundreds who came. As to the rest, some believed in the cause, and some did not; but all found themselves a part of a community, self-governed and free of the laws of nobility or the Weavers; and that was a precious thing to many.

She still found it faintly surprising that such a disparate group of individuals might have kept a secret so large for so long, especially as most of the Libera Dramach spent their time away from the Fold, in the cities, going about their daily business. These were the spies, the suppliers, the network. But, though it was a potent rumour among common folk, word of the Fold had yet to reach the nobility – or, which was more likely, they had ignored it. The Xarana Fault was a place of secrets; there were vast illegal farms of amaxa root that supplied the cities without paying their taxes, whole enclaves of people who worshipped forbidden gods, monasteries where contact with the outside world was utterly shunned. Mention of the Fold would scarcely merit the attention of a noble. At least, not one who was not already part of the organisation. For the Libera Dramach had eyes even in the courts of the Empress, and there were many who believed as they did. Aberrants were not evil. The Heir-Empress should sit the throne.

A tribute to the skill and learning of their leader, then, that they had got this far, and were ready when the long-expected crisis came. The

Heir-Empress had been discovered by the world at large. Now was the time for the Libera Dramach to take action.

Cailin turned her mount and headed down the grassy ridge towards the Fold. There had been several new arrivals of late, and the moment had come to bring them all together.

'I can scarcely believe it all,' Kaiku said. She stood fearlessly at the lip of one of the uppermost plateaux of the Fold, above the main mass of the buildings, and gazed in wonder at the landscape tumbling away from her below, the maze of different-shaped rooftops an overlapping and multi-layered jigsaw. The packed-dirt streets were seething with people from all over Axekami, a collision of makeshift fashions such as Kaiku had never seen. The afternoon sun beat down on her skin, warming her with its rays; birds winged and jagged through the sky overhead. She tilted her face up, closed her eyes, and felt Nuki's eye looking down on her, a red glow behind her lids. 'It is perfect.'

Asara sat on a large, smooth rock that towered aslant out of the grassy plateau. She did not know what Kaiku was referring to as perfect: the Fold, the sunlight, or a more general expression of contentment? She dismissed it, anyway. Kaiku's spirits had been restored with a vengeance since leaving Fo and taking the River Jabaza back towards Axekami. They had disembarked some way north, warned by sailors coming upriver that Axekami was in turmoil and no boats were getting in. Taking the horses they had gained in Chaim, they rode south, crossed the Kerryn by ferry east of Axekami, and then made good time to the Xarana Fault. There, Asara had taken them by one of the few relatively safe routes through the maze of broken land, and thence to the Fold.

The journey had been a strange one. Kaiku appeared to have surmounted her loathing of herself, perhaps because there was nobody left that she cared much about who could leave her or hurt her. Her family were dead; Mishani and Tane had betrayed her by their reactions to the news that she was Aberrant. Rock bottom was a wonderful place in which to re-examine oneself, and she seemed finally to have accepted what she was and made the decision to live with it. Her initial despair at the impossibility of the oath she had sworn to Ocha had warmed and turned to determination, a rigid focus, an unswerving direction she could cling to. By the end of their journey, Kaiku had been urging Asara on, desperate to get to the Fold as quickly as possible and begin to assess what chances she had of avenging her family against the unassailable might of the Weavers.

And yet, though there was this general lightening of heart about her, she had closed up to Asara again, just when she was beginning to feel something like trust in her former handmaiden. Asara told herself that the release of passion in that cold, draughty room in Chaim was a demonstration of Kaiku's decision to discard the old rules that no longer applied to her as an Aberrant, proof to herself that she had no boundaries left; only that, and nothing more. But she had stirred something between them that refused to go away, and it hid in glances and loaded comments and darted out unexpectedly to sting the other. Kaiku was wary of Asara for another reason as well. She had never asked what had happened in that room, when Asara's kiss turned to something more than lips and tongues, and she sought to suck the breath from Kaiku's body; but she had sensed the danger on an instinctive level, and now she would not allow her guard down again.

Still, she was here, in the Fold. Asara had discharged her duty, an agreement taken on more than two years ago now. She felt something of a satisfaction in herself. She lounged on the warm rock, observing Kaiku's back as she admired the vista before her and soaked in the simple glory of a summer day.

'You have my deepest thanks, Asara,' Cailin purred next to her. Asara was quick enough to prevent herself starting and giving away her surprise at the dark lady's appearance. 'You have kept her safe. She is quite a precious asset to me.'

'I am afraid I did not do quite the job of keeping her safe that I could have done,' Asara replied, not looking up. 'But we have such things to tell you, Cailin.'

Cailin arched an eyebrow at her tone. 'Really? These I must hear.'

'Later. In private,' Asara said. She would pick the time and place. 'She has already started to get her *kana* under control,' Asara added. 'It is still wild, but not untameable. That is a rare thing, I understand.'

'Rare indeed,' Cailin replied, never taking her eyes off Kaiku. 'But then, we knew she would be strong. And you have put yourself in great danger for my sake. Once again, I thank you.'

'Not for your sake,' Asara corrected. 'For mine. She interests me. I have watched her lose everything, and become the thing she most despised; and I have watched her fight back and regain herself again. In my time in this world, I have seen the same loves, hates and struggles played over and again in endless monotony; but hers is a rarer story than most, and she still surprises me even now. I almost feel guilty for bringing her into your sphere of influence. You may fool her with your altruism, but not me. What are you planning, Cailin?'

'I believe you are fond of her, Asara,' said Cailin, a smile in her voice as she avoided the question. 'And I thought you too cynical for such fancies.'

'My heart and soul are not dead yet,' Asara replied, 'only dusty and jaded from lack of interest.'

Cailin laughed, and the sound made Kaiku turn and notice them for the first time. She walked over to them, away from the precipice.

'I am glad to see you are a woman of your word,' Cailin said, inclining her head in greeting. 'Did you find what it what it was you were looking for?'

'In a manner of speaking,' Kaiku said, and did not elaborate.

'The time approaches for action,' Cailin said, studying Kaiku from within the painted red crescents over her eyes. 'That is partly why I asked to meet you here.'

'What kind of action?' Kaiku demanded.

'Soon,' Cailin promised. 'But first, I have some people you might like to meet.' She waved a hand at where two newcomers were approaching along the plateau.

Mishani and Tane.

For a moment, Kaiku could not find the words to say, nor dare to think what this might mean. But then Mishani approached her, seeming strangely smaller now than before, her immense length of hair tied in a loose knot at her back. She hesitated for an instant, and then put her arms around Kaiku; and Kaiku embraced her in return. She sobbed a laugh, clutching Mishani tight to her. 'I'm so happy you're here,' she said; but the last of the sentence was incomprehensible with the tightening of her throat, and the tears that fell freely from her. Cailin flashed a triumphant look at Asara, who quirked her mouth in a smile.

The two of them held each other for a long time, there in the sun. Kaiku had no idea why she had come, or what had turned her around, but she knew Mishani well enough to realise what it meant. Eventually they released each other, and Kaiku looked to Tane, who smiled awkwardly.

'I had a little time to think,' he said, and that was all, for Kaiku embraced him too. He looked faintly abashed by the contact, but he held her also, and was a little disappointed when she withdrew much sooner than she had with Mishani.

Kaiku wiped her eyes and smiled at Cailin, who was watching her benevolently with her deep green gaze.

'People have a way of turning up when you least expect them to, Kaiku,' the tall lady told her. 'The four of you walk a braided path; your routes are intertwined, and they will cross again and again until they are done.'

'How can you know that?' Kaiku asked.

'You will learn how I know,' said Cailin. 'If you choose to take the way of the Red Order.'

'Is there a choice for me?'

'Not if you want to live to see the next harvest,' Cailin answered simply.

Kaiku demurred with a shrug. 'So, then.'

Cailin laughed once again, throwing her head back, her white teeth flashing between the red and black of her lips. 'I have never had an offer accepted with such poor grace. Do not be afraid, Kaiku; this is not a lifetime commitment you are making. A Sister of the Red Order is nothing if she is unwilling. All I ask is that you let me teach you; after that, you may choose your own way. Is that acceptable?'

Kaiku bowed slightly. 'I would be honoured.'

'Then we shall begin as soon as you are ready,' she said.

There were three Sisters in the room apart from Cailin. All of them wore the accoutrements of their order: the black dress, the red crescents painted over their eyes, the red and black triangles on their lips like teeth. Asara found their poise uncanny, but not unnerving.

In the conference chamber of the house of the Red Order, lanterns glowed against the night, placed in free-standing brackets in the corners. The red and black motif was mirrored in the surroundings: the room was dark, its walls painted black but hung with crimson pennants and assorted other arcana. Its centrepiece was a low, round table of the same colour on which a brazier breathed scented smoke into the room. The Sisters all stood, but Asara lounged in a chair. She had digested the importance of the news she brought long ago; it amused her to watch the reactions of the Sisters now.

'Do you trust her?' one of the Sisters asked, a slender creature with blonde hair.

'Implicitly,' Asara replied. 'I have known her for years. She would not lie; certainly not about this.'

'And yet there is no proof,' another pointed out.

'Not unless any remains in her father's apartment in Axekami,' Asara said. 'But I doubt that.'

Cailin bowed her head thoughtfully. 'This bears research of our own, dear Sisters. If a single scholar can assemble enough evidence to convince himself to travel all the way to Fo for proof, to risk himself and his family . . .' She trailed away.

'We must contact our Sisters further afield,' suggested another.

Asara raised an eyebrow. The Red Order had their ladles in more pots than anyone knew, she suspected. Though she had no clear idea of their membership, they were careful never to gather in one place in any great number. Indeed, four was the most she had ever seen together. She had gathered hints from Cailin that the Sisters were scattered all over Saramyr and beyond, engaged in hunting for new recruits like Kaiku or inveigling themselves into other organisations; but she believed there was another reason why they never congregated. They were paranoid. They knew well how fragile they were, how small their Sisterhood, and they feared extinction. While they were all connected by the Weave, there was no need to gather together, and hence no way the whole could be destroyed. Oh, she did not doubt that each of them was using their powers to further the Sisterhood, but she suspected fear was at the root. They were selfish, and sought power to stabilise themselves. The Red Order and the Weavers were not as different as Cailin would like to think.

'There is another matter,' Cailin pointed out. 'The caged Aberrants Kaiku came across. What do they mean?'

'Perhaps they are studying the effects of the witchstones on living beings. Perhaps they are searching for a cure to Aberrancy.'

'Perhaps,' Cailin replied. 'Perhaps it was merely a product of their insanity. Or maybe it is a clue to something much greater.'

'We should think on this,' agreed one of the other Sisters.

'But this changes nothing,' Cailin said, her voice rising decisively. 'Kaiku's discovery is only a first step, a breakthrough that demands our attention. But we have other, more pressing concerns now. This can wait. We must disseminate the information and ensure it becomes spread so wide that it cannot be suppressed, we must plan and research and investigate . . . but all that is for the future.' She made a sweeping gesture as if to clear it from their minds. 'For now, we have another task. Axekami is falling apart; the city is in the midst of revolution. The Imperial Guards cannot contain it. The armies of Blood Amacha and Blood Kerestyn squabble just outside the city. The Weave-lord Vyrrch works from within to undermine the Empress and kill her child.' She paused, and her eyes flicked to each of them in turn. 'This must not be allowed to happen. She is the only hope we have of turning the people of Saramyr away from the Weavers' teachings, making them understand that Aberrants are not the evil they imagine us to be. I do not care who takes the reins of the Empire if Blood Erinima is overthrown, but I will not lose the Heir-Empress. I have met her in her dreams, and I know something of what she can do. She is too rare and powerful a creature to die on the end of some ignorant foot soldier's blade. Perhaps Blood Erinima will emerge triumphant, but I count the chances as slim. The Empress has set herself squarely against the world. If she loses, Lucia dies.'

'Then what do you propose to do?' Asara asked.

'The plans are in place, between ourselves and the Libera Dramach, to ensure the Heir-Empress's safety the only way we can,' Cailin replied. 'We propose to kidnap her.'

TWENTY-SIX

The door crashed inward, wrenched off its hinges with one swing of the short, heavy battering ram that two of the Imperial Guards held between them. Guard Commander Jalis led the way inside, clambering over the fallen obstacle, passing from bright daylight into the gloomy murk of the narrow stone stairway. Already a hue and cry was being raised somewhere beneath. He raced downward, the tarnished white and blue plates of his armour clinking as he descended headlong towards the basement of the tannery. The stench of the place was even worse down here than it had been in the open air, and it crowded him in and almost made him gag. He swallowed the reflex. His heart was pounding, his blood up. Behind him two cohorts of Guards were cramming down the stairway, their rifles and swords clattering. Running blind into who knew what, and none of them cared. They had found the bastards at last, and they were in no mood to go easy on them.

Jalis burst out of the stairwell and into the wide, low ceilinged basement. He had no time to register the details of the room; there was only a flash impression of space, and gloom, and the blur of metal swinging towards him. His sword swept up to meet another man's blade with a ringing of steel. He parried, parried again, then put his weight to his sword and struck, knocking his opponent back as he fended the blow weakly aside. Jalis forced his way into the room, clearing a path for the others to break through and join the combat. Swords clashed in a metallic cacophony, and bodies heaved against each other as battle was joined.

Jalis threw back his attacker with a second push and stabbed. Until that point he had barely seen who it was he was fighting, but now he registered that it was a young man, wearing no armour and plainly no warrior, with his face contorted in an ugly grimace of hate. The unfair odds concerned him not one bit. He ran the young man through, and had his blade out and was fighting with someone else before his enemy's impaled body had hit the floor.

There were dozens of them, outnumbering the Guards in the room; but they were pitifully matched against trained, armoured soldiers. Jalis's arm juddered as he buried his blade in another man's neck, this one no more than eighteen harvests, little more than a boy. The Guards pushed outward from the stairway, allowing more of their number in behind them, and the ferocity of the initial onslaught diminished as more swords arrived to take the strain.

Jalis took a second to sweep the room with his eyes. The basement was massive, and poorly lit, but it took only one glance to realise that their information had been good. Everywhere, tables were laden with tubes of coiled brass, distillation bulbs, disassembled clockwork timers and fuses. All about lay kegs of ignition powder, stacked up against the round pillars that supported the ceiling, secreted in corners behind piles of crates. It was a disorderly clutter at the edges, where odd shapes bulked in the shadows, but the central section was lethally precise, its tables laid in stringent rows so that completed components could be passed along the line to the next worker.

This was the heart of Unger tu Torrhyc's secret army: the bomb factory. Dozens had died at the hands of these fanatics, and hundreds more from the chaos their bombs had sown. He had no pity for them. They were a threat to Blood Erinima, and to the Empire. Each one that fell to his blade made Axekami a better place.

And yet the frenzy with which they threw themselves on to the swords of the Guardsmen surprised even him. These were not fighters, yet not a one of them cowered, or tried to run. Instead they had taken up arms and raced to the attack, and they were hewn down like wheat. Jalis grimaced as a spray of blood gave him a warm slap across the jaw, and wondered what misplaced loyalty possessed them to such fervour.

A moment later, the crack of a rifle jolted his attention, and a Guard to his left fell with a sigh to the ground. It was followed by another, and again. Jalis picked out the source; two men against the far wall, where there was a rack of rifles and ignition powder. Several more had arrived and were taking their choice of weapons. A Guard just behind Jalis was already unslinging his own rifle from his back, but Jalis grabbed his arm roughly.

'Don't be a fool!' he cried. 'Retreat! Get out!'

It had been a risky gamble, to plough blindly into the enemy as they had done, but there was only one way into or out of the basement and they had had no other choice. Now Jalis saw he had underestimated the zeal of the bomb-makers, and it might cost them dearly. Gods, they should know better than to fire rifles down here! The entire place was one enormous bomb waiting to explode! It was suicide!

But perhaps that was exactly their plan.

The Guards pulled back towards the stairway, but the bomb-makers had redoubled the fury of their attack, throwing themselves at the intruders with no heed at all for their safety, choking the passage to freedom. More rifles joined the firefight, shooting friend and foe alike with indiscriminate aim. Jalis tried to push his way back through the ranks, the cloying stench of the tannery suffocating him, sudden panic swelling within; but there was nowhere he could go. He felt a sinking, draining feeling in his chest, and the world slowed to a crawl, and a sinister prescience whispered in his ear that the end was upon him.

He did not hear the rifle ball that ricocheted into a powder keg, nor see the flash. The tannery exploded in a blast that smashed the surrounding streets to rubble, annihilating everything within and sending bricks and flaming timbers looping through the air to hiss and steam as they landed in the river, or to smash through walls and shutters. The earth shook, rattling even the fixtures of the Imperial Keep, and a great dark column of smoke belched upwards from the smouldering remains, to climb skyward and pollute the perfect summer's day.

'You know that my words make sense, Anais.'

The Empress glared at Barak Mos across the low table. They sat on pillows in one of the western rooms of the Keep, an informal meal set before them of fish and rice and crabs from Mataxa Bay. Durun paced back and forth before the pillared arch that let out on to a wide balcony for catching the afternoon sun in spring and autumn. As summer ascended to its zenith, they stayed in the shade; the humidity was hard to bear even there, and scarcely a breath of wind came to relieve them.

'Gods, wife, why don't you listen to him?' Durun cried, his long black hair sweeping as he came to a halt and gestured in exasperation at his spouse. 'It's the only way.'

'Durun, stay out of this!' his father commanded. 'You aren't helping.'

Anais used her tiny silver finger-forks to spear a morsel of slitherfish from her plate, making them wait while she ate it thoughtfully. Durun seethed in the background like a leashed dog in sight of a rabbit. Mos watched her.

'I am not sure I see the need. The single greatest cause of the disruption in Axekami is gone,' she said. 'The threat of Unger tu Torrhyc's army has been removed.'

'Indeed,' Mos agreed. 'But at the cost of two cohorts of your Imperial Guards. You were overstretched already, Anais; now you are worse off. Riots tear through the city; fires rage unchecked. The forces of Blood Amacha and Blood Kerestyn have arrived outside the city, and are squaring up to each other within sight of the walls. Chaos breeds chaos, my Empress; the city is falling apart, and it's beyond the strength of your forces to quell it. Should Amacha or Kerestyn strike at Axekami now, your men would be too busy dealing with the populace to put up any resistance.'

Anais raised an eyebrow. From the usually taciturn Barak, this validation sounded rehearsed. He had obviously been thinking about it for some time.

'Please,' Durun said, unable to resist interrupting again. 'We are next to defenceless here. I won't let our thrones be taken because we were too busy mopping up after the ungrateful cattle down in those streets. Let my family's men do that!'

'Ah,' said Anais. 'So you propose that the forces of Blood Batik will only be deployed for the duties of policing the city?'

Mos cast a furious glance at his son, who was too haughty to have the decency to blush. Instead, he snorted and turned his head away to look out on to the balcony, feigning indifference. He had just given away a potent concession that Mos no doubt had intended to use as his *coup de grâce* in this argument.

'Yes,' Mos grated. 'I'm aware of your caution in allowing any force into Axekami that is not blood-bound to your will, though it puzzles me that you don't seem to see we have the same interests. I have as much to lose as you if Axekami falls to an invader.' He took a breath. 'In order that you don't feel threatened, I propose you withdraw your Imperial Guards to their usual duties of guarding the Keep and securing the walls of Axekami; my troops will be used only in putting down the riots and restoring order to the city, unless you wish otherwise.'

'I may wish to use them in the defence of Axekami in the event of Blood Amacha or Kerestyn making an assault upon the walls. Is that acceptable?'

'Of course,' Mos said. 'My son and granddaughter are here.' Durun snorted again at this, making clear what he thought of Mos calling Lucia his granddaughter. Mos gave him a sharp look, which he ignored, before continuing: 'I would hardly let an invader storm the city while I had any power to prevent it. In fact, to prove my dedication in this matter, I'll stay in the Keep myself, with your permission. Whatever befalls you or Durun or Lucia will befall me as well.'

'This is not a small risk,' Anais replied evenly, her food forgotten before her. 'There would be few of your bloodline left if we were to lose.'

'Ah, but Anais, with my forces and yours combined, and the walls of Axekami protecting us, we *won't* lose. Amacha and Kerestyn *together* would have scarcely a chance of beating us. Squabbling and divided as they are, there is no hope of victory for them.'

Anais thought on it for a moment, returning to her food. He made a convincing argument, and she was aware that her situation was worsening with every passing day. In truth, she already knew in her heart what she would do; she had decided before Mos had called on her. She had to agree; she had no other choice. Yet no matter how trusted the ally, to invite a foreign force into the heart of the capital was dangerous. There were always angles she could not see, vested interests she was not aware of, even with men as plain-speaking and guileless as Mos and Durun.

It was a risk she had to take.

'Very well,' she said. Mos broke into a broad smile. 'But not one of your men shall set foot in the grounds of the Imperial Keep,' she added. 'Not even a retinue for yourself. Are we understood?'

His smile faded a little at the edges, but he nodded. 'Agreed. I will send for my men immediately.'

'You will have to use Vyrrch to contact your Weaver,' Anais said with a wrinkle of distaste. 'Be careful what you say to him.'

'I speak to Weavers as little as I possibly can,' Mos replied.

'I will make the necessary arrangements with my men,' Anais said. She looked at Durun, who looked back at her blandly, his dark eyes piercing on either side of his hawk nose. Typical of him: he had got what he wanted, and yet he acted as if it was his due rather than something granted by his wife. She dismissed him from her mind. She had him under control, anyway. His thoughts and loyalty were dictated by one organ alone, and it was not his brain.

'I'll talk to Vyrrch now,' said Mos, getting to his feet. 'Better to get it over with.'

'And what of the Bloods Amacha and Kerestyn?' Durun asked. The question indicated who was the mind behind this meeting, as if Anais could not have guessed.

Mos flexed his shoulders in the manner of a man relaxing at home, not in the presence of his Empress. Anais almost smiled at his lack of grace. 'Leave them be,' he said. 'Barak Sonmaga tu Amacha will never let the Barak Grigi tu Kerestyn approach the city; and he has not the strength to assault it himself, for that would mean turning his back on the armies of Kerestyn. Let us see if the arrival of a few thousand of our men from the other side of Axekami won't take some of the enthusiasm out of them. My intelligence tells me Sonmaga's ill-equipped for civil war anyway; not enough time to gather troops. And Grigi must know he can beat Sonmaga, but the losses he'd take would mean he'd have no chance of taking Axekami. They're at a stalemate. This might be just the thing to make them cut their losses and go home, and that would be one less problem to deal with.'

Durun stalked over to stand by his father's side. Anais got up from the table and saw them to the doorway of the chamber. 'Then may Ocha bless us and keep us all safe.'

Mos bowed deeply. 'You are wise, Anais, to choose as you have chosen today. The country is in good hands.'

'We shall see,' she replied. 'We shall see.'

The Heir-Empress Lucia tu Erinima knelt on a mat before her pattern-board, her shadow long behind her in the low, bright sun of the evening. She had been there since midday, on the upper terraces of the gardens. There she had settled herself amid the sun-warm beige stones that tiled the floor of this, one of the many tranquil resting places and walkways curving through the greenery. Before her the terraces dropped away in steps until they came to the high perimeter wall of the roof gardens; hidden beyond that was the city of Axekami, the sweltering sprawl of streets surrounded by an even higher wall to separate it from the vast grassy expanses of the plains.

Nuki's eye was descending through the thin streamers of cloud that haunted the distant horizon, and Lucia's eyes flickered periodically from the spectacle before her to the pattern-board and back again. Taking a wide-spaced, soft-bristled circular brush, she dipped it into one of the china bowls of heavy water that rested on the stone next to her and eased it across the pattern-board, leaving a faint mist of pink suspended there in the picture.

The pattern-board was an old art form, practised since before the time of many of the newer bloodlines. It involved the use of a coloured blend of water and paint and sap, thickened to a certain consistency, called 'heavy' water. This was applied to a pattern-board, a three-dimensional wooden cage that held within it a flattened oblong of transparent gel. The gel was part-baked into shape, after which it would always return to its oblong shape no matter what was done to it. This allowed artists to part the gel and paint inside the oblong, in the third dimension. The use of heavy water gave the pictures a curiously feathery, ethereal quality. When the painting was finished, the gel was baked further, becoming a substance like glass, and then displayed in ornate cradles that allowed the picture within to be viewed from all sides.

'Daygreet, Lucia,' came a voice from next to her, deep and smooth. She sat back on her heels, shading her eyes with one hand as she looked up.

'Daygreet, Zaelis,' she said, smiling.

Her tutor crouched down next to her, his lean frame draped in thin silk of black and gold. 'You've nearly finished, then,' he observed, making a languid motion towards the pattern-board.

'Another day and I'll be done, I think,' she said, returning her gaze to the floating swirls of colour before her.

'It's very good,' Zaelis commented.

'It's all right,' she said.

There was silence for a moment.

'Are you angry?' she asked.

'You've been here in the sun all day,' he said. 'And I've spent most of it trying to find you. You know how protective your mother is, Lucia. You should know better than to disappear like that, and you should *really* know better than to sit out in the full glare of Nuki's eye on a day like this.'

Lucia exhaled slowly in what was not quite a sigh. His tone and mode of address showed that he was not angry, but she was chastened all the same. 'I just had to get away,' she said. 'For a little while.'

'Even from me?' Zaelis sounded hurt.

Lucia nodded. She looked back at the sunset, then to the pattern-board, then pushed her fingers a little way into the top of it and pulled open a thin gash in the gel. She made a few quick strokes with a narrow brush, lining the pink of the clouds with red, then withdrew her fingers and let the rift seal itself.

Zaelis watched her, his face impassive. Of course she needed escape. To a girl as sensitive as Lucia was, the tension in the corridors of the Keep bled through even to here. And though he had kept his own concerns to himself regarding her safety, he was sure that even his best efforts at secrecy were useless against her. She knew full well that all the discord, all the deaths, were down to her in one way or another. Zaelis did his best to dissuade her from feeling guilty, but he was not even sure if she *felt* guilty. She had talked before of how she had set all this in motion, and wondered how it might have gone if she had tried to stop it instead of embracing the change. But whether there was regret there, Zaelis could not tell. Lucia's moods were like the deepest oceans, unfathomable to him.

Her head snapped up suddenly, with an urgency that made Zaelis jump. He followed her gaze, not dreamy and unfocused as it usually was but sharp and intense. She was looking to the north, where the white rim of Aurus was just cresting the horizon, foreshadowing the coming night. Her brow creased into a frown, and it trembled there for a moment. The fierceness of her glare shocked him; he had never seen such a look upon her face. Then she tore herself away, staring back into the heart of her painting, seeming to smoulder sullenly.

'What is it?' Zaelis asked. When she did not reply, he repeated: 'Lucia, what is it?' This second question was phrased in a more authoritative mode. He did not usually push her this way, but what he had witnessed a moment ago concerned him enough to try.

'I heard something,' she said reluctantly, still not meeting his eyes.

'Heard something?' Zaelis prompted. He looked back to the northern horizon. 'From whom?'

'No, not like that,' Lucia said, rubbing the back of her neck in agitation. 'Just an echo, a whisper. A reminder. It's gone now.'

Zaelis was staring at the edge of Aurus as it glided infinitesimally higher in the distance. 'A reminder of *what*?'

'A dream!' she snapped. 'I had a dream. I met the Children of the Moons. They were trying to tell me something, but I didn't understand. Not at first. Then . . .' She sagged a little. 'Then I think I did. They tried to show me . . . I don't know if it was a warning, or a threat . . . I don't . . .'

Zaelis was horrified. 'What did they tell you, Lucia?'

She turned to face him.

'Something's going to happen,' she whispered. 'Something bad. To me.'

'You don't know that, Lucia,' Zaelis protested automatically. 'Don't say that.'

She hugged herself to him in a rush, clutching herself close, taking him by surprise. He hugged her back, hard.

'It was just a dream,' he said soothingly. 'You don't need to be scared of a dream.'

But over her shoulder, he was looking to the northern horizon and the cold arc of Aurus's edge, and his eyes were afraid.

Weave-lord Vyrrch rested, his scabrous white flank heaving, the ribs showing through like a washboard. He was naked, his grotesque, withered body pathetic and repulsive to the eye. His scrawny, misshapen arms were gloved in blood; it spattered the melted skin of his face, his thin chest, pot-belly and atrophied genitalia. He looked like something recently born, curled amid the soiled sheets of his broken bed, panting and gasping.

For the object of his recent attention, however, there was no breath to be had. She was an old lady, chosen for the sake of variety in a fit of whimsy after he had sent Barak Mos's requested message to his Weaver. It had vaguely crossed his mind that he was murdering altogether too many people of late; most Weavers only reached that state of frenzy rarely. But then, wherever his servants procured his victims from, they were obviously not being missed. A servant's life was their master's or mistress's to take in Saramyr, and this one lady could not have been anything more than a cook or a cleaner, a servant of the Keep and hence of the Empress. He was sure Anais would not mind, even if she knew. She was aware of the deal when she took on Vyrrch as her Weave-lord; in doing so, she put the low folk of the Keep at his disposal, to satisfy his whims. A small price to pay for a Weave-lord's powers.

The old lady lay in a pool of viscous red, her simple clothes plastered to her body with her own vital fluids. He had been in the mood for the knife today, intending to take his time; but when she had arrived, he had flown into an unaccountable rage and stabbed her, hacking and plunging again and again. She died almost instantly, killed by the shock. It had only increased his fury, and he attacked the corpse over and over until it was almost unrecognisable as human.

Yes, perhaps he had been killing a little too much recently. But he was the spider at the centre of the web, and he needed feeding often.

The Guard Commander who had arrested Unger tu Torrhyc had been a tough one to crack, but Vyrrch had given himself time. As skilled as he was, he dared not simply seize the mind of a man and take control of him. That would require all his concentration, and confine him to his rooms; and there was every possibility that the Guard Commander might realise he had been meddled with once Vyrrch released him. Hasty operations like that were dangerous; he thought back to his recent attempt to sway Barak Zahn, when he was foiled by Zahn's Weaver, and wondered why he had not better considered the risk then.

You're slipping, Vyrrch, he told himself.

With the Guard Commander he had been forced to take a subtler route, implanting small, hypnotic suggestions in his dreams night after night, poisoning him against Unger, convincing him of the rewards he would gain for arresting the thorn in the Empress's side. When Unger tu Torrhyc was taken, Vyrrch had made sure he was with the Empress; that way, she could not accuse him of influencing the Guard Commander. How little she knew of the Weavers' ways.

The bomb-makers were a labour of months. He had been assembling them ever since his first suspicions about Lucia, long before he had persuaded Sonmaga tu Amacha to send the cat-burglar Purloch to confirm the rumour. Steadily wearing at them, turning them in their dreams, ordinary men and women gradually becoming fanatical. More and more time they began to spend in the study of explosives, more and more they became indoctrinated to the idea that any amount of lives was worth a belief. And all the while, they waited for the subliminal trigger: the discovery that the Heir-Empress was an Aberrant. At that signal, they abandoned jobs, homes, families, and became the single-minded bombers Vyrrch had envisioned. They gathered, and began to assemble their instruments of destruction. And when the preparation was done, Vyrrch gave them a new trigger, one that would set them on their destructive course. The arrest of Unger tu Torrhyc.

It was a master stroke. The world at large saw the logic in a man of Unger's charisma and outspoken political views being the leader of a subversive army. Vyrrch had killed Unger himself so he could not contradict the assumption, and that also provided a convenient martyr for the disgruntled citizens of Axekami. Now his own bomb-makers were dead, killing themselves rather than letting themselves be captured, and the circle was closed. There was no evidence to link him to any of it. Axekami was enraged, frightened, maddened; the Empress's eyes were turned outward to the city, and the stage was set for the final part of his plan.

There were more bombs yet to come.

But it had not all been seamless. There was still the niggling itch in the back of his mind that was Ruito tu Makaima, hidden away in some spot where he could not quite scratch it. That the scholar had managed to get into the Lakmar Monastery on Fo was achievement enough. Vyrrch still had no idea how he got hold of a Mask that would get him through the barrier; but he was unlucky enough to trip through one of the invisible triggers on his way out, little Weave-sewn traps that jangled alarm bells in the world beyond human sight. Their agents had shadowed him home, the better to see what his intentions were; but he seemed broken, holed up in the forest, and so they were content merely to keep him there while they decided what to do with him. And so it passed to Vyrrch, as many things did.

He had intended to capture and interrogate Ruito. If he had been able to do that, then he would not be fretting now. But the scholar had outwitted him. The very night Vyrrch struck, he put poison in his family's evening meal, and when they drifted to sleep they did not wake again. Ruito had eluded him.

The shin-shin were hard to entice and harder to control, but it was necessary to ensure no survivors, and no evidence. Human agents were not reliable enough. He needed them to return the Mask without being tempted to use it, and demons told no tales – they could never be traced to him. The employment of such creatures was risky, even for a Weaver of his calibre; but the shin-shin were low demons, and weak, and they had proliferated in the wake of the witchstones' corruption of the land. They felt the power of the witchstones as some kind of benevolent entity, and when the time came they were content to do as Vyrrch asked them. Not that it was as simple as *asking*. With demons, as with any other spirits, communication was muddy and uncertain, passed on in impressions and vague emotions. Without the bridging influence of the witchstones, Vyrrch would not have been able to get through at all.

And then had come the day when the Makaima bloodline met its end. Except, of course, that something went wrong.

He knew there were a thousand reasons why he should not worry about it, and only one why he should. The Mask had gone.

The shin-shin were unable to identify who it was that had escaped; their demon minds worked in ways other than humankind. Their perception did not work on the principles of sight, but rather on ethereal scent-trails and auras beyond the register of mammalian creatures. It made them excellent trackers, but it also made them limited. They could no more differentiate between humans by sight than humans could tell a gull apart from a million other gulls. When Vyrrch had demanded to know who had slipped their grasp, they responded with a confusing identification of impossible markers that meant nothing to him. He was left frustrated.

Who had taken the Mask was yet a mystery, but it had been stolen by two humans. They told him that much. The bodies in the house had been burned to blackened skeletons – making a process of elimination a worthless endeavour – and there were too many servants about the place to make an accurate count, even if Vyrrch had the will to. The shin-shin, at least, had found Ruito's body before the house fell, so Vyrrch could breathe that bit easier. But still, someone had taken the Mask, and he had no idea who. They had chased the trail to Axekami, but the city was no place for demons, and even the shin-shin dared not set foot in that hive of men. There, they lost it.

Yes, a thousand reasons not to worry. What were the chances of anyone realising what they had, or knowing how and where to use it if they did? Most likely it had already been sold to some theatre merchant, his eyes gleaming as he bought what the owners thought was simply an exquisite mask. Scenario after scenario ran through Vyrrch's head, but only one kept coming back to him.

What if they had realised what the Mask was, and used it for its purpose?

No matter, he thought resolutely. In days, a fortnight at most, the jaws of the trap he had set around the Imperial Keep would snap shut. A new power would be ascendant, ruling in conjunction with the Weavers instead of over them. An unprecedented alliance, in which the Weavers would truly be the power behind the throne.

Their time was coming.

TWENTY-SEVEN

'The first step . . .' said Cailin softly. 'The first step is the most important. And the most dangerous.'

The small cave that enclosed them shifted and stirred in the light of a single torch that burned fitfully in its bracket. It was cool here in the bones of the earth, despite the warm summer night outside. Kaiku felt a curiously detached sensation, as if she and Cailin had been cut off from the rest of existence, with this hemisphere of rock forming the limits of their world. The cave was bare and empty, merely a bubble of air within the crushing mantle of stone that pressed in on them. The narrow tunnel that connected this tiny, secluded chamber to the rest of the caves of the Fold was a depthless void, and she wondered what might happen if she were to walk into that blackness, where she might emerge.

She sat cross-legged on a wicker mat in the centre of the chamber, her feathered brown hair damp and inelegantly ruffled, her eyes closed. Cailin walked slowly around her, looming high overhead, almost touching the ceiling. Her boots tapped hollow on the stone of the cave floor. She was talking, but her voice was somehow hypnotic, and Kaiku barely heard the words, absorbing instead the meaning and instruction within.

'Your *kana* is like any wild beast. It is uncontrollable, primal, apt to lash out when angered. Before you can begin to train it, you must first muzzle it, leash it, render it harmless. Or at least as harmless as you can make it.'

Kaiku felt a thrill of unease. For the last week she had been rigorously prepared for this by Cailin; yet now the moment was here, she was afraid. Afraid of what was inside her, of what it might do; afraid of the agony it brought when it boiled up through her veins. Cailin had schooled her in mantras that would calm her mind, warned her of the things she might see and feel, taught her the many things she *must not do* when the procedure was underway.

You will be tempted to resist. Every instinct will tell you to attack me, as if I were an invader. If you do so, I will kill you.

It was not a threat, merely a fact.

'I will sew myself into you, Kaiku,' she was saying, her low voice moving around behind as she walked. 'Were you not talented in the ways of the Weave, you would not even know I was doing it. But you have . . . defences.

I am a foreign element, and your mind and body will try and expel me. You must not let it. You must remain passive, and calm, and let me do my work. I will muzzle the beast within you, but I cannot do so while you resist.'

She had heard it a dozen times before now, but it was all theoretical. Nothing would truly prepare her for the plunge. There was no precedent for this, even in her deepest memories. What if she could not do it?

She knew the answer to that. And yet it never crossed her mind to turn back and give up.

Cailin rested her slim, pale hands on Kaiku's shoulders. 'Are you composed?'

Kaiku took a deep breath and let it out, her eyelids fluttering. 'I am ready,' she lied.

'Then we will begin.'

The beast tore free from its lair with a ferocity and suddenness that was overwhelming. It roared and scorched its way up into her breast like a demon, raging and burning. Her eyes stayed shut, but inside the world exploded into an incomprehensible sea of golden threads, an endless, dazzling vista with no sky, no ground, no boundaries at all. For an instant, she knew nothing but terror as pain racked her, the searing wake of her *kana* fighting to be free.

Then, suddenly, she reorientated. By what instinct she navigated, she could not guess; but in a moment the unearthly complexity of the dazzling junctions and infinite lengths seemed to make sense to her, to *fit* in some indescribable way. These were *her* threads, she recognised. This was herself, her territory within the Weave, the space occupied by her body and mind. She felt the rushing stream of golden blood pumping from the thick knot of her heart, saw it disseminate gradually out through capillaries to feed her flesh. She felt the anxious pre-awareness of incipient life in her ovaries, a cluster of mindless hopes, swarming with potential. She sensed the tide of the air sucking into her lungs, a curling muddle of fine fibres tugged in and spewed out again.

But there was something terribly wrong. A foul, cancerous unknown, a sickening, creeping blight that was seeping into her like blood into a rag, fast, fast, an invasion and violation of the most horrible kind . . .

She saw it then, in her mind's eye, coiling along the golden threads towards her heart, tentacles of light sliding into her territory, into the very fibres of her body, the striations of her muscles. Everything in her wanted to be rid of it, to expel this vileness from her. Her *kana* blazed in response, threading out towards the invader, to burn it out with cleansing fire . . .

No!

It was Cailin. She willed her *kana* to stop, to accept the invader even though every one of her senses screamed against it; and somehow it responded, stalling in its assault. It railed at her attempt to hobble it, but this was different to when it had been unleashed before. This time, the *kana* was still within her body, and had not broken free of the boundaries of her territory. Here, she could master the fire.

She let herself go mentally limp, beginning a mantra over and over. The onslaught continued through her, creeping in towards her core like the paralysing bite of a spider. She felt panic rising within her. What did she know, truly, of Cailin tu Moritat? She was opening herself up to this woman in a way more intimate than making love, giving her the freedom to do *anything* to her, to turn her lungs inside out or burst her heart or rearrange her thoughts so she was a willing slave to Cailin's whims. How could she trust *anyone* that much, let alone this enigmatic Aberrant who was more of a stranger to her than Tane or Asara?

She forced the thoughts down, concentrating on her mantra. Too late now, she told herself. Too late. And yet still the urge grew, to lash out, to expel this invader and be whole and unsullied again. The presence of Cailin was abhorrent, as Cailin had told her it would be. *Your mind will see me as a disease*, she said, and it did; it took all her willpower to stay still while the foulness consumed her.

But the alien threads were quick, slipping into her heart where they were pumped around her body, and with them came a strange, soothing sensation, as of ice put on a burn. Her *kana* quailed, but she sensed that the worst was over. The calm spread through her, swamping her inexorably, its touch bringing peace to the fibres of her body. No longer did it seem a disease that had swallowed her, but a benediction, and distantly, subtly, she felt Cailin begin her work . . .

The Fold was ever ready for battle, a fortress against the dangers of the Xarana Fault. Though there was no true army here, there was a hard core of military expertise culled from the populace, a combination of Libera Dramach and those who had been recruited or drifted their way in. Bandit leaders and strategists for the nobility sat side by side in war councils, the organisational brain behind the defence network of the Fold. And though there were few professional soldiers here, there was no shortage of volunteers to safeguard the newfound freedom that this isolated community offered. Everyone within the valley was expected to hold their own when the time came, and a man who could not shoot a rifle or use a sword or crank a ballista was dead weight. Training was informal, for most of these people were not warriors by nature, and the Fault's terrain was better suited for guerilla tactics anyway; but there were not many here who would be unable or unwilling to fight when the time came. And in the Fault, the time *would* come sooner or later.

Even as night settled into the creases of the world, the work went on by the glow of paper lanterns and bonfires. Fire-cannons were rolled out and cleaned. Ballistae stood silhouetted imposingly on the ridges, backlit by the flames. Mine-carts full of ammunition were rolled along the system of tracks that ran along bridges between the biggest plateaux. Scouting parties slipped quietly back into the Fold, barely noticed. Lifts squeaked and creaked as their pulleys strained against guide wheels and cogs.

Tane sat on the grassy side of the wide, shallow valley that cradled the Fold and hid it from sight. The folk here had warned him not to go out alone at night, but he was unable to reflect and meditate amid all the activity on the steps, so he took the risk and retreated to the darkness. Now he was glad he had.

He looked out over the cascade of the land, a hundred lanterns in bright points tumbling down the dark platforms and plateaux into the valley, pools of light hanging in the deep, abyssal darkness. The windows of the buildings that crowded the steps of the Fold speckled the black with yellow twinkles like grounded stars. High above, only Aurus rode the sky tonight, her vast face looking down on him, the dim white of her skin blotched with patches of pale blue. It was beautiful, to be here, to see this. He gave thanks to Enyu, and felt a strange contentment within.

These last weeks had been a turbulent time for him. It seemed that he had been running to catch up with himself ever since he had first found Kaiku, unconscious and fevered in the Forest of Yuna. It had taken her arrival – and the events that came in her wake – to knock him out of the life he had settled into ever since his mother and sister had left him alone.

His apprenticeship at the temple was a refuge, a restoration for the crime he had committed. He regretted less the fact that he had murdered his own father, but more that his actions had driven away the rest of his family. His mother was ineffectual without her husband's control, incapable of initiative. His sister had been recently raped. The misfortunes that could have assailed them were legion, and he would never know. For weeks he had tried to track them, to find word of them in nearby towns; but they had vanished, like smoke in the wind. Then the guilt had set in, the terrible weight of what he had done. Despair took him, and he languished in his empty home for weeks. After that, he had gone to the temple and offered himself to Enyu. If he could not heal himself, perhaps he could heal others. Grief-stricken, he was not thinking as clearly as he might have been; but the priests accepted him, and there he found order, a routine, and time to piece his life back together.

But it was the wrong life, and he had taken it for the wrong reasons. He had not the temperament nor the discipline nor – he sickened to admit – the raw faith to dedicate his life to serving Enyu in a temple. Kaiku had been the catalyst that had shown him that. He still believed Enyu had spared him from the slaughter at the temple for a reason, but it was not the reason he had first envisaged. She had sent him to walk among the Aberrants.

When he had left Asara in Chaim and gone south, he had sought only to get away from her. He could not bear the thought of Asara's mocking gaze, or what he might say to Kaiku if she ever returned from the mountains. He needed to be alone, to think things through. He had ever been a solitary child, and he was used to his own counsel; now he needed the peace to listen to it.

You believe your journey was ordained by your goddess, that you were spared for a purpose; but there is no greater foulness to Enyu than an Aberrant. Reconcile these things, if you can.

Asara's words haunted him as he took a ship from Pelis, back to Jinka and the mainland. He could not reconcile them. Was this a test of his faith? Was he supposed to help them, or thwart them? Were they not all working towards the same goal: finding the hand behind the shin-shin? Was there a lesson to be learned here, or was he simply not seeing it? Whichever way he turned, he came up against the same block: Aberrants, whether they were inherently evil or not, were perversions of nature, products of the blight that had stricken the land. How could he believe that any path that Enyu set him would coincide with theirs?

He thought about it all the way back to Axekami, where he found the city in turmoil. It was only then that he realised he had given himself no plan, no destination, and that he had nowhere to go. What money he had with him was fast running out, and there was no prospect of getting any more. He had relied on Kaiku and Asara's charity since he had joined them, and payment for the journey back from Fo had sapped the little he had taken from his temple when he left. He thought to find another temple of Enyu, who would not turn away one of their own. Not in Axekami, for it was evident the capital was a seething boil of anger at the moment; but there were others elsewhere, where he could find calm and meditate on his quandary.

Yet he did not go to a temple. That would be going backwards, settling himself into the life that Kaiku had torn him from. And whatever else had come of it, he had not forgotten the feeling of *rightness* he had experienced as he and Asara sailed out of the Forest of Yuna towards Axekami. That feeling told him now that the temple of Enyu was not the answer. Instead, he went to the temple of Panazu.

Getting into the city was not easy, but Axekami had not closed itself off completely. Many folk were leaving in terror as martial law gripped the interior, and a way out was a way in. Tane had not forgotten the note Asara had left him. He was still no closer to an answer than he ever had been, but he had learned that he would never find the truth by leaving the path he had taken. All he could do was follow it and hope things became clearer. That was his reasoning, anyway. He resolutely refused to recognise the tug of his heart in the matter, and he would not think of Kaiku at all.

Now she had returned to him. The news she brought staggered them all, revealing the full extent of the Weavers' evil, showing them finally the source of the sickness in the land. Alone, she had walked into the wilderness, and come back bearing something more precious than all the jewels in the world.

It came to him then as a revelation. In his arrogance, he had always imagined that *he* was the one ordained by Enyu for great things. There had always been beneath his reasoning a selfish centre, considering all events in relation to him. But it was Kaiku who had found the source of the blight, picking up a thread woven by her father and following it to its end. Who knew how far back into time that thread stretched, the accretion of knowledge by scholar after scholar, building into wisdom? It took the courage and guile of one man to find the secret; but it took the strength of his daughter to bring it back. It was not Tane's path that was important, but Kaiku's. All that the priests of Enyu's temples had been working for these past decades, with their prayers and meditation, had been unravelled by an Aberrant, the most cursed of nature.

Then why was he there? As a witness? As one who should guard her? As a representative of Enyu's will? He had not been particularly successful at any of these tasks.

Perhaps you are just here, Tane, he thought. *Perhaps there is no greater plan, or if there is, it is too great for you to see it. You always were too introspective. That is why you never made a good priest. Too many questions, not enough blind faith.*

It was not satisfying, but it would do for now. Whatever the real answers, he had no doubts about Kaiku now. He would follow her where she went. As if his traitor heart would allow him otherwise . . .

'Out of the question,' Cailin snapped. 'She's too valuable.'

'Nobody knows that more than me,' Mishani replied. 'But if you want me to go, she goes too.'

Mishani and Cailin faced each other, locking eyes and wills. Cailin was almost a head taller than the diminutive noblewoman, but Mishani was not in the least cowed by her opponent's size or fearsome appearance. They stood in one of the upper rooms of the house of the Red Order, a long building with a curving, peaked roof which overhung the balconies running around its first floor. In contrast to the somewhat ramshackle nature of its surrounding buildings, this one was tidy and precise, with pennants of red and black hanging from the balcony rail before the entrance.

'You would willingly put your friend in danger, Mishani,' Cailin accused.

'No,' said Kaiku, from where she leaned against a wall boyishly. 'I asked her. I demand to go.'

'So do I,' put in Tane, who was watching from the other side of the room. Asara stood near him, a faint smirk on her face.

'Why?' Cailin asked, her voice cold. 'You are no warrior. Have you killed before? Have you, Kaiku?'

'I made an oath to Ocha,' said Kaiku calmly, ignoring the question. 'My enemy are the Weavers. The Weavers want Lucia dead. I wish to be part of any effort to thwart them.'

'You will be!' Cailin said, anger creeping into her tone. 'You will learn to be a more powerful force than you can imagine. Dying in the Imperial Keep before you grow into your strength is futile.'

'Cailin, she speaks sense,' Asara said. 'The Keep guards will expect warriors, much as those you have already chosen to go. They will not suspect women and priests.'

'She is dangerous still!' Cailin hissed, flinging out a finger at Kaiku. 'She has only begun to learn how to suppress her *kana*. If she should unleash it within the Keep, we would all be killed.'

'Don't be melodramatic,' Asara said. 'You merely wish to protect your investment.'

Anger blazed in Cailin's eyes, but Asara met her gaze with an insouciant stare.

'It is only two more, Cailin,' Mishani said. 'You have asked Asara and I to go because you need us. I am the only noble you have who is willing to set foot in Axekami again; Asara is an experienced handmaiden. But I will not go unless Kaiku goes. And Tane, if he wishes. You said yourself that we four trod a braided path. Perhaps it is braided more tightly than you think.'

Cailin framed a retort, then swallowed it. She rounded on Kaiku. 'Is your mind made up in this?'

Kaiku shrugged, an imitation of her brother from long ago. 'I have no choice. I made an oath.'

'Oaths can be interpreted any way you see fit,' Cailin pointed out archly. 'Very well then. We leave for Axekami tomorrow. All of us. If we do not move soon, we may lose our chance. The danger to Lucia grows daily, and we have little time remaining, if my sources tell me true.' She swept around and stalked out of the room, her black dress trailing behind her. 'We will steal the Heir-Empress from under their noses,' she declared as she left.

Kaiku gave a smile of thanks to Mishani, and wondered what she had let herself in for.

TWENTY-EIGHT

The armies of Blood Kerestyn and Blood Amacha faced each other across the grassy plain to the west of Axekami. The morning sun beat down on them, already cruelly hot and not even close to its zenith. It glinted off swords and rifles, sheening down the edges of pike blades and making men shade their eyes and squint. To the west, Blood Kerestyn, their gold and green standards limp in the windless humidity. To the east, Blood Amacha, a swathe of brown and red mingled with the colours of other, lesser families. Fire-cannons brooded in the swelter, their barrels fashioned into the likenesses of demons and spirits, their mouths open to belch flame. Between the armies was the killing ground, a great strip of untrampled grass where they would meet if it came to conflict.

The sheer weight of numbers was immense. Amacha's army had been swelled to over ten thousand, and Kerestyn had more than that, a wave of soldiers that had washed over the land and now teetered on the edge of breaking. From the city walls, they melted into two huge pools of blades and guns and armour. The front ranks were foot soldiers, horses pawing at the dirt and manxthwa loping back and forth, the soldiers standing ready, hair damp with perspiration. Behind them were riflemen, most in rows but some gathered in little clusters, cleaning and checking their weaponry. Further from the front ranks, the tents began, angular polygons of colour ranging from simple and utilitarian to complex and grandiose. Where the battle lines were still, the rear of the armies was a swarm of activity, a constant shifting of supplies, troops, and information. Tents were being erected; cannons were being repaired; armour was fixed or handed out. To the east, the enormous beige walls of Axekami were a frowning barrier that dwarfed them all to insignificance, stretching to either side of the battlefield and curving out of sight, a bristling mass of guard-towers behind which the jumble of the city's streets could be seen cluttering their way up the hill towards the Imperial Keep, its gold walls paled by distance.

The two vast forces shimmered in the heat haze, waiting.

The armies of Blood Kerestyn had begun their march on the capital some days ago, but they were slow, detouring to amalgamate with other, smaller forces on the way, minor families who had allied themselves with the Kerestyn cause. A further delay was caused by the need to skirt Blood Koli's lands around Mataxa Bay. The Barak Koli had firmly allied himself with Sonmaga, for better or worse.

Blood Kerestyn had been ousted from the throne by Blood Erinima over a matter of dishonour, not warfare. The last Kerestyn Blood Emperor, Mamis, had lied to the council of nobles over a matter of great importance and been discovered. He had done the sensible thing and abdicated, for the council had given a unanimous vote of no-confidence in their ruler after that; Anais's father had filled the void. But though Kerestyn had lost the might of the Imperial Guards, which were sworn to protect the Blood Emperor or Empress regardless of their family, they had retained the vast strength which had won them the throne in the first place. And they had bided their time, waiting for an opportunity just such as this.

Sonmaga tu Amacha was no less ambitious, but his ambition outstripped his means somewhat in this matter. He believed passionately that the Heir-Empress should be removed from the line of succession, even if Anais stayed as Empress. If only that cursed Mishani woman had done what she was supposed to, then all this could have been averted. He didn't want a civil war, principally because he suspected he would lose it. In ten years, when he had enough support, when his plans had come to fruition . . . maybe then would be the time to strike. But getting rid of the Aberrant Heir-Empress would solve all their problems. Kerestyn would no longer have a righteous cause motivating them, and their support would swiftly peel away if they chose to press their suit upon the capital. He wished he'd just had Purloch kill the little bitch when he had the chance, instead of settling for a lock of her hair; but Purloch had disappeared the moment he was paid, and had not been found since.

Sonmaga's tent bulked out of the sea of armour, an island of brown and red surrounded by other smaller, lesser islands. The constant convection of soldiers and horses flowed around them in a grubby tide, relaying messages, reporting from the front line. The smell of rank sweat was overpowering, and the din was a constant background babble, so loud that it was only when people shouted at each other to be heard that they realised how their ears had adjusted to block it out. Sonmaga's tent was near the rear of his forces, his back towards Axekami. He had crossed the Zan and placed himself squarely between the forces of Kerestyn and the capital. He didn't want a civil war, but he'd be gods-damned if he'd let Blood Kerestyn walk into the capital without a fight.

The emissaries from Blood Koli came at mid-morning, twenty soldiers with the hardened leather of their armour dyed black and white. The newcomers arrived on horseback, their eyes narrow beneath the black sashes tied around their heads to avert sunstroke. Heading them was the Barak Avun tu Koli himself, his balding head held high as he rode, his omnipresent expression of weariness temporarily banished for the benefit of appearances.

The forces of Blood Amacha parted to let them through. That he had come out personally spoke of a matter of great importance. They passed through the ranks to the tent of the Barak Sonmaga, and there Avun dismounted and was shown inside.

Barak Sonmaga stood as Avun entered. He had been sitting on one of the woven mats placed around the centre of the tent, studying a map. At the edges were low tables of refreshments, chests of clothes and charts, and a rack where Sonmaga's battle armour hung. It was stiflingly hot in here, but being out of the direct gaze of Nuki's eye was a blessing, and the tent walls somehow managed to muffle the worst of the noise from outside.

'Avun,' Sonmaga said. 'What news?' It was almost insultingly informal, but neither was much concerned with ritual greetings at a time like this.

Avun looked him over, the tired cast returning to his hooded eyes. 'You already know,' he stated.

Sonmaga raised a black eyebrow, impressed at Avun's reading of him. 'Yes, I do. Sit down, please.'

Avun joined him in sitting on another of the floor mats. Sonmaga poured cups of dark red wine for them both. Avun waited until Sonmaga had drank from his before taking a sip.

'The forces of Blood Batik approach the city from the east,' Avun said. 'If they had set out from Batik lands north of Axekami and gone directly south, we would have spotted them long ago. But they crossed the Jabaza and circled round so we would not detect their movement. Now they are almost at the city gates.'

Sonmaga let none of the faint disdain he felt for this man show on his face. Excuses, always excuses. He could not even control his daughter, his own blood; in fact, if his accounts were to be believed, she had fled and was missing even now. For such an allegedly brilliant player of the court, he seemed remarkably inept. His desperation for trade concessions with Sonmaga had revealed the sorry state of affairs at Mataxa Bay; he had even let slip about how ill-maintained the boats of his fishing fleet were, and how they were apt to sink at any time. He had always thought of Blood Koli as one of the most noble of families, an unassailable trading empire; but since circumstances had brought Avun and Sonmaga together, he had seen how hollow that assumption was. Avun was weak, and easily dominated. Sonmaga was content to let it be so. The troops Avun brought to this standoff were a valuable portion of Blood Amacha's army. And if the price he had to pay was to listen to this man's fawning agreement as they discussed their battle plans and strategies, even letting Sonmaga dictate the movements of Avun's soldiers, then it was a small price indeed.

'Do you suppose Grigi knows about it?' Avun asked banally.

'Undoubtedly,' Sonmaga replied. 'They will be at the city tomorrow afternoon. The Empress has evidently decided to let them in. I cannot imagine they are marching on the capital to invade; not with Durun and Mos still in the Keep.'

'You have spies there?'

'It is there for all to see,' Sonmaga said, unable to stop a hint of exasperation. Did this man have no eyes working for him in the most important building in the Empire? 'Everyone in the Keep knows it. If the forces of Blood Batik tried to take Axekami by force, the Imperial Guards would kill Mos and Durun in a moment. Their allegiance is to the *Blood* Empress, not her husband. So we must assume they are approaching with the Empress's consent.'

Avun nodded in understanding. Sonmaga watched him over the rim of his cup as he sipped his wine. 'It appears we remain in a stalemate,' Avun said at length, stating what Sonmaga already knew.

'My only concern is what Grigi might do,' Sonmaga said. 'He must know he'll never get past the walls of Axekami with Blood Batik inside. His only hope is to get inside before they do. That means going through us.'

'Then why not get out of his way?' Avun said. Sonmaga's eyes widened in disbelief. Avun floundered. 'Well, that is to say, isn't what we wanted that the Heir-Empress be disinherited? If we stand in Blood Kerestyn's way, then all we are doing is keeping the capital safe until Blood Batik can move in. Blood Erinima will keep the throne, and the Heir-Empress will come to power.'

'Do you think I am not aware of the situation?' Sonmaga barked. 'Do you think, all this time, I have not been seeking a way to get to the Heir-Empress, to do what your daughter should have done?' Avun cowered before the larger man, whose bulk seemed twice that of Avun's slender frame. 'I do not want Kerestyn on the throne; I want Erinima there, for when Anais's daughter dies – and make no mistake, I *will* get to her, or the people of Axekami will – then I have many more years to prepare before Anais's time is up. And when the Empress dies, childless and barren, then Blood Amacha will be ready to face even the strongest of enemies and claim the throne we have never had! If Kerestyn march into Axekami, with the forces they command, they will rule Saramyr for many decades to come. I cannot rely on another foolish mistake such as had them deposed before. I can only keep them out, and wait. Blood Batik may strengthen the capital now, but a thousand men cannot protect Lucia for ever. I play for time, Avun, for now is not the moment for me to strike.'

Avun's gaze dropped, shamed that he had offended Sonmaga. Sonmaga gave a curt grunt and got to his feet. Avun stayed where he was, head bowed like a servant. Sonmaga rolled his eyes. 'Get up, Avun. We should not quarrel. You know as well as I that we cannot withdraw now. I am committed, as are you. Do not let your courage falter.'

Avun's answer, whatever it was to be, was cut off by a sudden explosion somewhere nearby, a roar and a flare of flame that brightened the thin canvas of the tent. Sonmaga swore a vile oath in surprise, and the world was suddenly a clamour of voices as thousands of men began to shout at once. Another explosion followed, and another, the dull boom of fire-cannon artillery, incendiary bombs that sprayed a burning jelly across a wide area where they hit.

'By the gods, he's attacking us, the bastard!' Sonmaga bellowed. He could hear the distant battle-cry of the Kerestyn forces as they ran as one towards their waiting enemy, an avalanche of swords and pikes and howling throats, as massive and inexorable as the tide. They were joined by the cries of the troops of Blood Amacha, much louder and closer to hand. The generals were sending the front line to engage.

'I didn't think he'd dare,' Sonmaga raged to himself, crossing the tent to pick up his armour. 'The idiot! Doesn't he know this will ruin us both? I didn't think he'd dare!'

He felt suddenly a strong grip on his arm, and he was pulled around to face Avun, who had got to his feet as quick as a snake.

'There were a lot of things you did not think of,' Avun said. A long dagger flashed in his hand, thrusting up below Sonmaga's bearded jaw and ramming through his brain. The larger man gaped in shock. His eyes bulged, reddening with blood; but his life had already left him, cut away by that single stab, and the eyes were sightless. His body went limp, the once-powerful muscles robbed of their strength, and Avun stepped back and released the dagger as Sonmaga fell forward on to his face, smashing his nose to a pulp on the floor.

Avun looked down at the fallen Barak. Spirits, he was gullible. So ready to believe that Blood Koli were willing to be subordinate to him, simply because they had a history of antagonism with Blood Kerestyn. Sonmaga was a man of limited vision, who did not apparently realise that a political ally was most potent when it was kept secret. The façade of enmity between Kerestyn and Koli had fooled all but a clever few. Sonmaga was not one of those few.

He strode out of the tent. Leaderless, the forces of Blood Amacha would be in confusion. The troops of Blood Koli would turn against them when the moment was right, attacking them from within. Grigi tu Kerestyn already knew all Sonmaga's battle plans – which he had been good enough to share with Avun – and it was too late to change them now, as his generals already had their orders. The appearance of Blood Batik had meant time was suddenly short. Sonmaga and his men were an obstacle that had to be removed. With what Grigi knew of Sonmaga's movements, it would be a massacre.

He swept the fold of the tent open and stepped out into the sweltering heat and brightness. All around was a chaos of jostling men, the sound of swords being drawn, horses jockeying for space amid the crush. Flames licked the air nearby, sending choking columns of smoke up towards the sky. A distant crashing, slow and drawn out and immense, heralded the coming together of the two armies on the plains, thousands of blades meeting in a cacophonous mess. He shoved his way to his waiting horse, held by one of his men. Swiftly, he mounted. He saw a soldier entering Sonmaga's tent as he put his heels to the horse, but it was already too late to catch him. Oh, they'd know who the culprit was; but by then the forces of Blood Koli would have turned on them, and they'd be caught in a pincer, like the claws of the crabs of Mataxa Bay that had made his fortune. He thought he heard the cry of outrage as he rode away, and a smile touched his lips.

His only regret in all this was Mishani. If only she had trusted him, as a good daughter should. He had no intention of killing the Heir-Empress. That would have lost him and Blood Kerestyn much of the support they had gained. He had switched the infected nightdress for a harmless one before she had set off for the Keep. He would not risk his daughter and his family's reputation for Sonmaga; he would have simply told the Barak that the illness did not take in Lucia. After all, who knew what an Aberrant's immunities were? But Mishani failed him, turned on him . . . and finally left him. Dead or alive, he cared little. She had proved herself to be without conviction, and disloyal. She was no longer any concern of his. He had bigger plans.

The sound of rising death surrounded him as he rode, and the smile on his lean face widened. How he loved to play these games . . .

TWENTY-NINE

Night fell, but it brought no respite to the people of Axekami. Instead, the darkness bore fear on its back, and panic rode alongside. The western walls of the city were under attack from the forces led by Blood Kerestyn. The air boomed with the sound of fire-cannons, and the ground shook. Men ran back and forth in flaming silhouette along the mighty walls of Saramyr's capital. Guard-towers swarmed. Rifle reports punctuated the constant, low roar of battle. Boiling oil was tipped down on to the invaders in a ponderous deluge, followed by agonised howls from below. Ladders clattered on to the battlements and were flung back again, shedding screaming soldiers as they toppled. Distant voices carried on the hot wind, disembodied barks of command or wails of pain.

In the streets of the city, gangs of men roamed with torches in their hands and makeshift weapons sheening dully in the light of the three moons. All the sisters had come out tonight: massive Aurus, bright Iridima, green Neryn. They occupied different positions in the sky, but it would not be for long. Their next few orbits would bring them into dangerous proximity. A moonstorm was coming.

Nobody slept tonight.

The gates of Axekami were closed, both to keep out intruders and to pen in the frantic populace. Many had taken to the walls themselves, their desire to defend their territory greater than their disgust for their Empress and the monster she intended to rule her people. The white and blue armour of the Imperial Guards mixed and mingled with a thousand different fashions, as men brought their old bows and rifles to bear on the forces of Kerestyn. The weeks of unrest and violence on the streets had heated the blood of the folk of Axekami, and while half of them willingly united against a common foe which was trying to force its way into their city, the other half rioted and looted in protest, demanding that Kerestyn be let in and the Empress give up her throne.

The guards at the eastern gate had been turning away people all day, and continued to do so after nightfall. Traders, frantic relatives, people desperate to salvage or defend their homes; everyone was refused. A small camp of rejected travellers had grown by the side of the road. Only nobles and people of importance were allowed inside the city, and then only after approval from the Keep.

When a simple covered cart rolled up, pulled by a pair of loping manxthwa and driven by a grizzle-jawed young man and his elegant wife, the commander on duty made ready to send them on their way like the others. But when he began to say the words, they came out not quite as intended. And he could not on his life think why he had ordered the gate guard to open up, Keep approval or not; nor why he had not thought to even search the cart. Afterward, he could hardly credit that he had not been dreaming; but the only thing he could really remember with any clarity was the lady's green eyes inside her hooded robe, and how they had suddenly darkened to red.

The tarpaulin was pulled from the cart a little while later, slung back by the young man to uncover the stowaways hidden beneath. They had stopped in a short dead-end alley just inside the city's eastern gates, with tall, deserted buildings rising over them on three sides, blocking out the green-tinted moonlight. They slipped out silently, flexing cramped and numb limbs, and assembled around the cart before the young man and the lady. She was Cailin tu Moritat, surprisingly beautiful without the fearsome makeup of her Order. Her hair was drawn back into a long braid, and her features were sharp-cheeked and catlike. The man was Yugi, the leader of this expedition: a roguish-looking bandit in his late twenties with a devilish smile and dirty brown-blond hair held back from his eyes by a grimy red sash. Despite Cailin's presence, it was quite obvious who was in command. Yugi represented the Libera Dramach, and it was they that held the loyalty of the multitude at the Fold. The Red Order were few in number and, powerful as they were, they were not the driving force here.

Mishani smoothed down her expensive robe and arranged her hair swiftly with the help of Asara. Kaiku glanced at Tane, who raised an eyebrow at Mishani as if to say: *How vain!* Kaiku could not suppress a smile. It was a joke; they both knew that Mishani's appearance was of paramount importance. She had an audience with the Empress in the morning.

'That was the easy part,' said Yugi, addressing them all. 'From here on in you must be on your guard at every moment. Mishani, Asara: in the next street waits a carriage that will take you to a safe house. In the morning, you make your way to the Keep at the arranged time.'

Mishani and Asara nodded their understanding.

'The rest of us have an altogether less pleasant way to spend the night,' Yugi said with a grin. 'We go on foot from here. We have a rendezvous to make.'

Nine of them set out into the city after Mishani and Asara had gone. Along with Kaiku, Tane, Yugi and Cailin were five other men of the Libera Dramach, chosen for their skill at stealth and combat. Just walking the streets was dangerous in Axekami at the moment; strength lay in numbers.

Yugi took them down narrow alleys and through a dizzying maze of back-streets, heading away from the Kerryn. The sounds of the assault on the western wall reached them even here, and the night was full of strange cries and unsettling noises. More than once they heard running footsteps, multiplying suddenly and married with cries of rage as a chase began. The mobs were out tonight, and there was nobody on the streets not looking for violence. Those they passed in side-alleys or huddled in dark doorways – the destitute and vagrant – cowered away from them. Yugi paid them no mind. He was leading them deep into the Poor Quarter.

The buildings seemed to pile up on one another around them, leaning in closer, groaning and warping under their own weight. Timbers bent dangerously, and the labyrinthine streets became cluttered with debris. Shutters hung askew from dark windows. Fire-gutted buildings displayed blackened ribs. Makeshift bridges spanned the diminishing width of the streets, ladders that went from window-ledges to adjacent rooftops. Here it was deserted, but Kaiku felt the unshakeable sensation of being watched. She glimpsed faces retreating from windows as she looked up at them, candles hastily snuffed at the approach of footsteps. Yugi was deliberately keeping them off the main thoroughfares to avoid meeting anyone, but into what danger was he taking them? They had been kept largely in the dark about the details of the plan to kidnap the Heir-Empress, for reasons of security; but it served only to make Kaiku more nervous when she had no idea what lay ahead. She felt the reassuring weight of her rifle against her back, and the sword at her hip, but even they offered her little comfort.

'In here,' Yugi said suddenly, stopping before a doorway in a derelict building that had been covered over with planking and then broken again. He ushered them within, following last after he had seen the coast was clear. This, then, was their destination, Kaiku thought with mingled relief and trepidation. They had been lucky to get this far through the city without coming across any of the mobs; but where were they to go now, from the heart of the Poor Quarter?

Inside, the darkness was deeper still. The green-edged luminescence of the three moons beamed in through chinks and slats in the wooden walls, coming from three directions at once to render the interior in a dim, unsettling light. Whatever this place had once been, it had been abandoned for years. Rubble, broken planks and unidentifiable debris littered the squalid, narrow rooms. Insects droned about in the hot night, exploring the carcass of a dog that had recently expired here.

'Where is he?' Cailin asked sharply, seeming to direct the question at nobody in particular.

'Down,' Yugi said. 'Come on.'

He led them through a series of similarly deserted rooms until he came to a hatch, which he pulled up to reveal a set of wobbly wooden steps. A light burned somewhere below.

'It's us,' he hissed down, before descending. The others followed carefully.

It was a cellar. The warm, damp air tasted of mould, and the stone of its walls looked aged and crumbling in the lantern's glow. The man holding the lantern was murmuring with Yugi as Kaiku came down into the room. He was thin and slightly gaunt, with a worried expression on his brow. His short hair was greying towards his fortieth harvest.

The last man down closed the hatch behind them, shutting them in.

'We're all here? Good,' said Yugi. 'May I introduce the man who will be guiding us the rest of the way. There have been doubts voiced from the start as to whether a group of men – and ladies – such as us could even get *into* the Imperial Keep, let alone to the Heir-Empress herself. But *this* man did it alone, and unaided; and he got close enough to the little Heir-Empress to cut a lock of her hair. This is Purloch tu Irisi.'

The five men of the Libera Dramach burst into amazed exclamations. Kaiku and Tane, who had never heard of him, kept silent and glanced at each other. Tane gave Kaiku a reassuring squeeze on the shoulder. He was just as nervous as she was, yet his presence made her feel a little safer, and she was glad of it.

'Through there,' Purloch said, motioning to a shadowy alcove in the wall. He raised his lantern obligingly, and they saw that a narrow hole had been knocked through it. 'The city's sewer pipes run against this cellar. They also run up the hill, and beneath the Imperial Keep. I used them before to get in, though there's no telling whether they found out and shut off the way. I don't think so. Nobody goes down there unless they have to.'

One of the men went to the hole and peered through, into the dark. 'What's down there?'

'I don't know, and I don't want to find out,' Purloch said. 'But I heard them last time, on my way out.'

'Heard *what*?' the man demanded.

'It doesn't matter what,' Yugi answered sternly. 'Light your lanterns. We're going down there. Ladies, I must apologise in advance for the stench, but—'

'Don't be an idiot,' Cailin said, crippling his gallantry. 'Do not think us frail. Either of us could collapse your heart with a thought.'

Yugi grinned, but there was uneasiness at the edge of it, and he was lost for something to say for the briefest of moments. His eyes flickered to Kaiku, appraising her anew. What Cailin had said was not strictly the truth, at least where it concerned Kaiku; but it gave Yugi pause.

'With such pleasant company, then, this journey will simply fly by!' he declared, recovering admirably.

The dank underworld of the city sewers was not a place Kaiku had ever imagined finding herself. Their world was circumscribed by a wet arc of light that curved over the tunnel walls ahead of them, and beyond it was only a black abyss which threw back a starfield of tiny glimmers as lapping water or moist bricks caught their lanterns' glow. The stench was indescribable. Tane had vomited almost immediately upon entering the sewers, and retched frequently even after his stomach was more than emptied. Several of the other men were similarly afflicted. Kaiku felt permanently on the verge of bringing up her last meal, but somehow the cloying reek never quite made her stomach rebel. Cailin appeared unaffected. Nobody was surprised.

The sewers of Axekami were a network of channels, dams and sluice-gates, flanked by wide stone paths for the sewer workers to use. With the unrest above, they were confident that nobody would be working tonight; but the thought of what they might find instead preyed on their minds.

Kaiku kept her eyes on Purloch as they walked the wet paths with the murky effluent of the city flowing past them. He was plainly terrified, his eyes skittering to every shadow, jumping when a rat scrabbled or a piece of junk in the water bumped against the lip of the path. What had he encountered down here that had scared him so? Had this man really penetrated the Imperial Keep? And if so, then why was he ready to do it again? What had turned him to the cause of the Libera Dramach? It was while musing on this question that she remembered the words of Mishani, on an occasion when Kaiku had asked her the same thing during their time in the Fold.

You only have to see her to know, Kaiku. She will win you with a glance.

Was that it? Had Purloch been so touched by the Heir-Empress? Was she truly such a transcendental creature?

None of them spoke as they walked through the endless dark of the sewers. Existence dwindled to the circumference of their lantern light, and the irregular ticks, patters and splashes of the diseased things that lived here. Purloch was leading them from memory, taking them up slanted inclines, through bottlenecks, over thin metal bridges. The omnipresent nausea that their surroundings induced compounded their misery, but there was nothing to do but plod on. They would be walking till dawn warmed the earth above, so Purloch had told them; but it was necessary to be in place under the Keep by the morning, for that was when the plan would be carried out.

Kaiku was crowded with doubts. Tane walked before her, and her eyes ran over his shaven skull and lean back. The sight of him brought a faint tinge of guilt. She had thrown herself recklessly into this affair, without knowing what she was getting herself into; but that was all right, that was her way. She had ever been headstrong and stubborn. Stubborn enough to walk alone into storm-lashed mountains, anyway. She had never really considered the chances of success then, nor did she now; they were not factored into her way of thinking. Yet her decision to come meant Tane had come too, and that was another matter.

She was not oblivious to what he clearly felt for her. He had followed her since the Forest of Yuna, stood by her side even after he discovered she was the thing he most abhorred. He loved her, she saw that. And she could not deny the desire he provoked in her. It was a heady thing to know that she could have him with a word, that he would come to her bed at her command. And yet it was a dangerous game, to play with men's hearts, and she was not so cruel. It would not be right, not now, not when she was still coming to terms with herself, with her power and her new life as an Aberrant, with Asara . . .

The memories of that night in Chaim caused her to flush. The heat of the moment had been overwhelming, but it had been too brief to make sense of it. Giddy with Asara's assertion that she should unshackle herself from the restrictions men had made for her, she had acted on a foreign impulse and subsumed herself in it. But all too soon the moment had been interrupted by Mamak . . . no . . . by the terrible feeling she had experienced when Asara had kissed her that final time, the awful *hungriness* of her, and how it had seemed her very insides were being wrenched free.

She was too confused to think on it now. Just as she dared not truly consider the implications of what she had learned in the Weavers' monastery. There was too much, too much, and she knew that if she looked at it all at once it would crush her. She would think only of what was in front of her, going one step at a time. It was the only thing she could do.

Her thoughts scattered and her blood froze as an ungodly noise sawed through the silence. For a moment, nobody moved. Everyone was listening. It came again, echoing from a different tunnel this time. A creaking screech like the turning of a vast and long-rusted wheel.

'It's them,' Purloch whispered.

'It's what?' demanded one of the other men. 'It could be anything. A sewer pipe . . . a gate opening . . .'

'No,' Cailin said quietly. 'I sense them. They are coming.' She looked up, her eyes passing down the line to rest on Kaiku. 'We cannot face them here. Run.'

A third screech was her reply, louder than the last and closer. Purloch took flight, his boots skidding on the slippery floor in his haste to get away. The others followed closely, running as fast as they dared. The paths that ran alongside the flow of sludgy water seemed suddenly narrow now. The lantern light swung wildly around them, glinting off the bright, black eyes of rodents and other, less identifiable things that scattered at their approach. The screeches began to come more frequently; inhuman, malevolent sounds that could not have been made by any natural thing. They reverberated through the darkness, seeming to come from all directions at once. Kaiku felt them, a creeping sensation at the base of her neck. Demons.

Shin-shin? she thought, and a sudden wild panic gripped her.

They raced up a set of steps that ascended alongside a series of foul waterfalls. Tane stumbled and retched on his way up, falling to his knees. Kaiku crashed into him from behind, and immediately began pulling him to his feet, fear making her rough. He scrambled up, tangling himself in the rifle slung across his back. The others were already racing ahead, leaving Kaiku and Tane behind, taking the light with them. Neither Kaiku nor Tane carried lanterns.

'Wait!' she cried, as she wrenched Tane's arm out of his rifle strap and righted him. An explosive cacophony of howls sounded from the darkness behind her, terrifyingly close now.

'Come on! Up here!' Yugi cried down the stairway to them, and Tane finally got his feet under him and ran. Kaiku was close on his heels. She heard a scraping sound from behind, as if something were crawling on to the stairs, but she dared not look back. Her breath came in frantic gasps, and Tane could not move fast enough for her.

They burst out into a large, star-shaped chamber into which five tunnels opened. The water here was shallow, and a great circular drain lay in the centre of the floor, its rusty slats open to drink the putrescent water. Between the efforts of the drain and the way the hard stone floor rose up here, the water was only thigh-high. A narrow path ran around the edge of the chamber, but the intruders had already forsaken it and gathered in the water, around the drain, back to back. The creaking wails echoed around them, coming from the dark maws of the tunnels. Kaiku and Tane splashed into the water and joined the others, Tane retching anew at the cold touch of the effluent and the seeping of human waste that soaked his legs.

And then, as one, the wailing stopped. Silence fell, but for the stirring of the water around their feet. Purloch began to mutter a prayer to himself. Swords and rifles were held ready, all eyes on the five passageways. The light of their lanterns seemed to gutter, reminding them of how frail the margin was by which they were allowed their vision. If the lanterns were dropped or extinguished, they would be left in the endless dark, and nothing could save them then.

Kaiku became aware that she was shivering. Not with cold, but with tension. Her *kana* lay quiescent inside her, suppressed by whatever method Cailin had used to stop her being a danger to others; but she wished now that she had at least that to fall back on. Anything, anything to avail her against the things she felt creeping on the edge of the light.

It rose slowly from the water before her, just inside the mouth of the tunnel they had come from. A black, bedraggled shape, hunched over with its filthy hair hanging across its face, dripping putrid water. From its mouldering robe, its hands were curled into claws, white and bloodless and scabbed. A single eye glittered behind the matted curtain of hair, fixing Kaiku with a paralysing gaze. It exhaled a long, rattling breath.

'Gods! There's one here too!' someone cried, and Kaiku tore her attention away for a moment to glance at the second creature that had limped into the light from another tunnel. This one was emaciated and skeletal, a half-rotted corpse with its lower jaw hinged only at one side, and hanging together by a few strips of decaying flesh. It jerked along upright, its head lolling, but the sharp light in its eyes never left the people gathered in the centre of the chamber.

'What are these damned things?' Yugi whispered.

'Maku-sheng,' Cailin replied. 'The spirits of unclean water. They have taken the dead they have found down here and made them their own.'

'Another!' someone cried. It was grotesquely fat and naked, one side of its belly a gaping green wound through which the rotting slither of its intestines was wetly visible.

'And here!'

'Here, too.'

They were surrounded. The demons made no move to approach, only glared at them balefully. A whisper seemed to run around the chamber, a susurrus of hissing. The creatures were conversing at a pitch just outside human hearing. Kaiku was trembling uncontrollably now.

Suddenly, the long-haired demon raised one grimy hand and pointed, an ear-splitting howl coming from her. Her hair fell back from her face, and Kaiku glimpsed a horrifying visage of wrinkled, sagging flesh and long, decaying teeth; then the demons attacked.

All around them, the creatures came through the tunnels, bursting from the darkness and lunging into the chamber, loping and jerking as their atrophied muscles carried them inward. Yugi's rifle roared first, the report of his weapon echoing away in all directions through the sewers. The fat maku-sheng's head exploded in a wet shatter of bone fragments and clotted fluids, and it fell backwards into the water. Those who held lanterns brought their swords to bear, swinging them into the oncoming tide of dead flesh, slicing effortlessly through marrow and sinew. The long-rotted creatures came apart beneath the edges of the blades, toppling into the water; but a moment later the same creatures they had cut in half were coming back at them again, flailing through the murky water while their severed legs twitched uselessly behind them.

'They will not stay down!' someone cried, and a moment later he screamed as one of the things fell on him, its teeth biting into his throat. His scream became a gurgle and his lantern fell into the water with a hiss. The light dropped a notch in the chamber, further cloaking the broken shapes that surrounded them.

Kaiku hastily fumbled her rifle up to fire at the long-haired demon advancing on her, but the shot clicked dead. Her ignition powder had got too damp to light. Baring its foul teeth, the demon lunged at her, and then Tane was there with a cry, his sword stabbing deep into the creature's breast. Kaiku scrambled back, dropping her rifle in the water and wrenching free her own sword; but the demon had already pulled away with a shriek, snapping Tane's blade with the twisting of its body. It retreated a few steps, its eyes glimmering with malice, and a moment later another of them burst out of the water, right in front of Tane. Cold hands clawed at him, and crooked teeth sunk into the meat of his leg.

He cried out in agony, staggering back and swiping downward with the remaining length of his blade; but though he hewed through most of the dead thing's throat, still it held on to him, pawing at his thigh and worrying the chunk of flesh it had in its mouth. Kaiku's sword seemed to elude her panicked grasp, but she somehow swung it down across the thing's shoulder blades, hacking it hard enough for it to make an involuntary shriek and release Tane. As it splashed beneath the water, Tane raised his injured leg and stamped on its head, crushing its skull against the floor in a vile bloom of dark fluid.

Kaiku felt the stir of the Weave around her, and realised suddenly that Cailin had entered the fray. Her eyes were the deep, sulphurous red that heralded the use of her Aberrant power. Three of the maku-sheng went flying to smash bonelessly into the chamber wall, thrown away by her *kana.* The surrounding creatures recoiled, screeching, then attacked with redoubled fury a moment later. The knot of defenders around the centre of the room broke under the assault, splitting apart. The lantern light swung away from Kaiku, plunging her into darkness. Something lunged at her; she parried it, and felt a spray of something cold and foul-smelling across her cheek as her sword bit into dead flesh. Retreating in horror, she tripped against the covering of the drain in the centre of the room. There was a moment of sickening inevitability, and then she felt her balance desert her and she fell. The chill, polluted water closed around her head with a splash.

She flailed, gagging, and broke the surface for the merest of seconds; but then the long-haired demon was on her, its scabrous hands at her throat, forcing her back under into the lightless murk. There was no breath in her to scream. She kicked and thrashed, but the force pressing her down was too strong, relentless. Animal panic seized her. Her lungs burned, reaching for air that was not there. Unconsciousness swarmed at the edges of her vision, a sparkling blanket that encroached further and further towards the centre. She was dimly aware of underwater sounds, the splash and babble of her own weakening resistance, the noise of a rifle shot, the sound of howling as Cailin annihilated another swathe of demons. But it was all fading, receding, and behind her eyes she could see the Weave again, the glittering path that had led her once to the Fields of Omecha and the gatekeeper, Yoru, took her to the Gate but no further. Perhaps this time, she thought, as her struggles ceased . . . perhaps this time . . . she might join her brother on the other side . . .

But in the Weave of her body, something was stirring, thrashing. A knot was fraying. Consciousness fled her, but there was still something awake inside, fighting and twisting, picking at the fibres of Cailin's artistry. Her *kana* had been bounded and suppressed, but not beaten. Even as Kaiku's brain accepted her death, the creature within her fought against it, unravelling its bonds frantically, until with a snap they slipped free—

'Kaiku!' Tane cried. He had been casting about frantically for signs of her, having lost her in the chaos of the battle; but only a single lantern remained, held like a treasure by one of the Libera Dramach men, and it was barely light enough to see on the periphery of the luminescence. Now his eyes settled on the demon, hunched over in the water, pressing down on something; and he caught sight of the limp hand floating on the surface next to it. With a howl of anguish, he leaped at the thing. It raised its head in alarm, but at that moment Kaiku's *kana* finally loosed itself. Tane fell backward, shielding his face, as the demon shrieked and exploded. A blaze of fire threw yellow light across the murky water. The creature's burning, broken husk staggered away a few steps, animated by some shreds of remnant life; then it teetered, and plunged into the water with a hiss.

The other maku-sheng were squealing anew, having felt the force of the blast. Tane paid them no mind, picking himself up and forging over to Kaiku. He dragged her out of the stench and foulness, and her face came up pale, open eyes gazing crimson and sightless, hair plastered to her cheeks.

'Not her! No!' he shouted, though to what god or aspect of fate he addressed his denial he could not say. He sheathed his broken sword, heedless of the demons swarming about in the darkness, and hooked his arms under Kaiku's armpits, towing her through the water to the path at the edge of the chamber.

Cailin was a fearsome sight in the shifting light of the single lantern, her black hair straggled and her eyes burning red. She looked like a demon herself. She flung her hands out again and again, sending her *kana* racing along the threads of the Weave to tear and knot and twist, rending apart the bodies of the maku-sheng. With each one she destroyed, she sensed the demon spirit fleeing invisibly from the now-useless corpse, rippling away through the foul water in search of a new host. Yugi fought stolidly alongside her, guarding her back, his rifle firing again and again, repriming between each shot with remarkable speed.

And then a single, keening howl rose from the demon pack. They halted in their attack, drawing to safe distance from the huddled defenders, glaring at them with their shining eyes from the shadows. The whispers began again, though no mouths moved. Yugi kept his finger tensed on the trigger, Purloch standing close to him. Four of the five men of the Libera Dramach floated amid the putrid mass of re-killed corpses. The last, a man just out of his youth called Espyn, held his lantern high and his gore-streaked sword ready, but the tip trembled perceptibly.

There was a stirring, and the demons retreated, backing out of the light into the shadow as smoothly as they had arrived, being swallowed by the tunnels around the chamber. In moments, they had disappeared.

Yugi breathed out a shaky sigh. 'Gone?' he asked Cailin.

'They will come back. We should not be here when they do.' She looked up suddenly at a movement, and saw Tane heaving Kaiku on to the path at the chamber's edge. 'Gods,' she breathed, and waded through the thigh-high water as fast as she could go. 'Espyn! Bring the lantern!' she commanded, and he scuttled to obey.

Kaiku's lips were blue, her red eyes glazed, her hair lank and sodden. Tane was reaching into her open mouth and pulling out some unidentifiable detritus from her throat as they arrived, haste and fear making him panicky.

'Is she breathing?' Purloch asked, casting quick glances at the tunnels behind them in case any of the maku-sheng should return.

Tane ignored him. 'Can *you* do anything?' he demanded of Cailin.

'She slipped my conditioning, got through my barriers,' Cailin said, with something like wonder in her voice. 'Heart's blood, she has a greater talent than I thought.' She looked at Tane. 'Without her conscious control, her *kana* would rebel if I tried. It would kill her.' She missed the irony of her statement, but nobody felt like making a joke of it.

'Then I will do it,' Tane replied. He crossed his hands and pumped her chest with the heel of his palm, then put his lips to hers and blew breath into her lungs. How cruel that it should be like this, he thought; their first kiss, so cold and foul-tasting and passionless. But then he was at her chest again, pumping, breathing, pumping, breathing, while the others looked at him as if he was mad. None of them knew the technique for reviving drowning victims, but Tane had learned it from Enyu's priests long ago.

'Wake up, for the gods' sake!' he shouted at her, pumping again. 'This is not the end of your path! You have an oath. *An oath.*' Another breath, blowing hot life into her waterlogged lungs. Then pumping. 'You're too damned stubborn to die like this!' he cried.

And as if Omecha himself had reached down and touched the dead woman beneath his hands, she jerked and spasmed into life, rolling on to her side and vomiting bilious sewer water across the path. She retched and retched, cleansing herself agonisingly, as Tane laughed with joy and tears ran down his face and he gave praise to the gods. Yugi clapped him on the back in congratulation, calling him a miracle-worker. Kaiku's retching gradually subsided, and she lay gasping like a landed fish, weak but unhurt.

Cailin shook her head in amazement, a smile on her lips, and wondered how many lives her potential apprentice had left.

THIRTY

Dawn came, and the battle raged on.

The forces of Blood Kerestyn had made little headway in breaching the city walls. The mighty western gates were closed against them, and their ladders were thrown back time and again. Had it been only the Imperial Guards they were facing, they might have overwhelmed the defenders by sheer strength of numbers; but they had been counting on the Guards to have their hands full keeping the riots in the city to a minimum. Instead a large portion of the cityfolk had united in defence of their home, little caring for politics in this matter. Whatever their feelings about the Heir-Empress, it was a point of pride that no one would be allowed to invade Axekami, and so the defenders' numbers had been swollen manyfold. Grigi tu Kerestyn spat his frustration throughout the night, and redoubled his efforts at assault when Nuki's eye peeped over the horizon, but the forces of Blood Batik were marching rapidly from the east, and they would be in the city before nightfall. Once there, they would be immovable, and Blood Erinima's safety would be assured.

Anais sat on her throne next to her husband, icily calm. The sun beamed through the high, unshuttered windows of the room, an unbearable swelter even though the morning had barely begun. Servants fanned air with great ornamental sails, but it did little good; Imperial Guards sweated and itched abominably inside their ceremonial metal armour. The purple and white pennants of Blood Erinima hung slackly against the walls. Braziers leaked perfumed smoke.

Durun was in a foul mood. He had been carousing last night. The Empress had been fighting for the very survival of her family, organising tactics, dealing with reports, and he had stolen away to drink. He had come to her bed and she had spurned him. The memory of their fiery argument combined with the morning's heat, his hangover and the fact that he was wakened so early and dragged to the throne room had all combined to make his temper far shorter than usual.

The doors were opened, and a Speaker announced:

'Mistress Mishani tu Koli of Blood Koli.'

She entered wearing a robe of midnight blue, her immense length of hair tamed with strips of leather in a matching colour. Her pale, thin features were composed in their courtly mask, serene and revealing nothing. Walking behind her and at one side was Asara, dressed in simple white, her hands folded before her in the manner of a handmaiden. The streaks of red that had run though her black hair had disappeared, for they were too ostentatious for a position so humble; and she had artfully shifted the pallor of her skin to take the edge off the remarkable perfection of her features. They walked along the patterned *lach* path that led to the thrones of coiled wood and precious metal, where the slender, fair Anais sat next to her tall, stern and dark-haired husband, who was dressed all in black.

'You have some nerve, Mishani tu Koli,' Durun said, before any formal greetings could be made.

Mishani's eyes flickered to him. None of the frank amazement at his rudeness touched her face.

'Blood Empress Anais tu Erinima,' she said, bowing. Then, to Durun, with a lesser bow, 'Emperor Durun tu Batik. May I know why my presence has caused such offence to you?' She was using the Saramyrrhic mode reserved only for the Emperor and Empress, but Durun's mode was far less polite.

Anais regarded her coldly from her throne on the dais. 'Do not play games, Mishani. It is only because of the special circumstances attending this day that I have agreed to see you. Speak your piece.'

This was wrong, Mishani thought to herself. Terribly wrong. There was something happening here that she did not know about. Her visit to the Empress was ostensibly a friendly one, though its true purpose was more elaborate. She had asked to see Anais immediately upon her arrival, forsaking the usual politenesses, because it was essential to the Libera Dramach's plan that she was not with Lucia this morning. Everything could be ruined if the Empress – and her attendant retinue – were present when they tried to kidnap the child; for secrecy was the most important aspect of this operation, and no one must know who was responsible. Everyone else could be accounted for, but not the Empress; if she chose to visit Lucia today, kidnap would be impossible. There would be too many Guards. Mishani's function, using her noble birth as a lever, was essentially as a decoy.

But what had she done to warrant this hostility? This did not bode well.

'I come to offer you my allegiance,' she said. Durun barked a laugh, but she ignored him. 'When last I visited yourself and Lucia, my intentions were unclear. And though I know my father has opposed you and allied himself with Sonmaga tu Amacha, I would have you know that you may rely on what support I can offer you. Please forgive the urgency of this meeting, but I demanded to see you so that I might tell you this before the scales of this conflict have tipped. Whichever way they go, you and your daughter have my loyalty.'

'Your *loyalty*?' Durun cried incredulously, getting to his feet. 'Gods, I must still be drunk! Here stands the Koli child offering us her strong right arm, when her father not a day past has betrayed Sonmaga and even now assaults the walls of our city! What do you know of loyalty? You yourself are betraying your father by going against his will! His same traitorous blood flows in your veins. What will you offer us, Mishani? Will you call your father away from the attack on Axekami? Answer me! What will you offer us?'

Mishani was shaken. She understood it now, grasping the situation immediately. While her father had been on Sonmaga's side, he had been essentially defending the city by keeping Kerestyn out. If things had been as they were when she set off from the Fold, Anais would have accepted her friendship in good grace. That was all that was necessary. Even now, the Libera Dramach would be inside the Keep and hunting down the Heir-Empress. If all had gone to plan.

But all was not going to plan. Mishani had not known of the secret alliance between her family and Blood Kerestyn; her father had kept that from her. He was one of the invaders, and she was still his daughter in the eyes of the world. She had just stepped into a den of enemies. She glanced about nervously, and saw the Barak Mos by the side of the dais, his arms folded across his broad chest, watching her.

'Speak, Mishani tu Koli,' said Anais, her voice angry and hard. 'Why have you come to us this way?'

Mishani said the only thing she could. 'My father's actions shame me,' she said. She knelt and bowed low, her hair falling over her face, in abject supplication. Asara automatically followed suit, as a good handmaiden should do. 'And they shame Blood Koli. On the one hand, I have my loyalty to my family; on the other, to my Empress. When I learned of his intentions, I turned my back on him. Though he is my father, he is a man without honour. I throw myself on your mercy. I would stand with your daughter against whatever may come, for though I am Blood Koli by name, I am forever apart from them now.'

Anais stood, a frown of disbelief creasing her brow. 'You know better than this, Mishani. The fate of a noble family is bound together. The crimes of the father are your crimes also until retribution is exacted.' She opened her hands. 'You know better,' she said again, almost apologetically.

Mishani did know better. Such an unjust trick of the gods, to put her in this situation. It should have been so easy, civilised, a simple distraction tactic; she would have been gone before the Empress ever realised her child was missing. And now . . . now . . .

Anais shook her head sorrowfully. 'I will never understand what possessed you to come here, Mishani. You were always a shrewd and ruthless player at court.' She sat back down, and waved a hand at her guards.

'Kill them.'

Kaiku's eyes opened to the sound of a metallic creak. She started, scrambling awake from a nightmare of the maku-sheng, dreaming their terrible cries like the squeal of rusty gates echoing through the sewers. Tane caught her, his arms around her shoulders.

'Calm yourself,' he whispered. 'Calm yourself. It was only a dream.'

She relaxed in his grip, listening to her pulse slow. Gradually her surroundings made sense to her again. They were in a small, dank antechamber, lit by the single lantern that lay in the corner. The room stank of their sewage-soaked clothes, and Kaiku had a vile taste in her throat that would not go away. Sodden and dejected, the others were getting to their feet as Kaiku awoke, gathering themselves to go. She did not remember falling asleep. But she remembered the cold tongue of the sewer water forcing itself down her, and the glittering eyes of the thing that held her under . . .

The creak came again, and she realised it was the sound of a key. The door that had blocked their path was being opened. It was time to move.

She recalled an argument, somewhere in the black depths behind them. A conversation about what to do with their dead. Yugi would not leave them for the maku-sheng to have; but they could not bring them either. She thought they compromised by severing their heads from their bodies so the demon spirits could not inhabit them, though that might have been a nightmare too. Tane had argued for taking her back, but something had made her protest that she could go on, and it was a moot point anyway. There was one lantern, and that was going to the Keep.

The maku-sheng had not troubled them again. They had had enough of Cailin's power, and dispersed to seek less taxing prey. Kaiku had staggered on, borne up by Tane's taut shoulders, following the light like a moth. He limped slightly himself, suffering from the pain of being bitten in the leg by one of the foul things; but the bite was not serious, and he had bound it well. She remembered little of the rest of the journey, only an all-enshrouding weariness and misery interspersed with occasional moments of regret. When they had come to the antechamber that she now awoke in, Cailin had declared they were still early.

'I suggest you sleep,' she had murmured. 'In the morning, if all is well, we will be met by the leader of the Libera Dramach. He will take us onward.'

Tane professed his curiosity, for Cailin had mentioned him several times before, and always refused to reveal him for fear of endangering him.

'It does not matter any more,' she said. 'For after today, all deceptions will be over.' And yet, for all that, she had still not told them his name.

Kaiku had slept, but the few hours in the grip of oblivion had seemed only moments. And now Tane was pulling her up and asking meaningless questions about how she felt. But it was Tane who appeared to be suffering more than she was; he looked pallid and shaky, his skin waxy and his eyes bright with fever. He was ill, having picked up some infection from the foul sewer water or the bite of the maku-sheng. Kaiku considered it faintly miraculous that she had not succumbed herself – having swallowed a good deal of the effluent when she was drowning in it – but she doubted that any disease could survive the scouring of her *kana* through her body, and she put it down to that. Besides, she felt so bone-weary and burned-out that she would have been hard pressed to notice even if she *was* sick; she could scarcely feel worse than she already did.

The lock of the iron door disengaged with a clunk, and it swung open, spilling the light from a new lantern in to mingle with their own. Holding it was a middle-aged man, tall and broad-shouldered, with a close-cropped white beard and swept-back hair.

'Cailin. Yugi,' he said by way of greeting. 'What happened to the others?'

'We ran into trouble,' Yugi replied. 'Good to see you.'

'Come through,' the stranger urged, and they did. He shut the iron door behind them. They were in a dank cellar that reeked of disuse, cobwebs and mould. He surveyed the ragtag mob assembled before him. Six were left of the original ten that had entered the sewers.

'We go ahead as planned,' he said. 'Your noble friend entered the Keep safely this morning. Even now the Empress and her idiot husband should be meeting with her in the throne room. The Heir-Empress is wandering the roof gardens, as usual. I have servant clothes ready, and there is a place where you may wash. Your condition would bring the guards down on us in a moment.' He looked Kaiku over. 'I expected only one woman. My apologies. You will have to make do.'

Kaiku was too relieved at the mention of Mishani to respond with more than a nod. Her friend had slipped her mind in the horrors of the sewer, and though she had the safest task of all of them, Kaiku could not help but worry.

'I do not recognise some of you,' the man said. 'Let me introduce myself, then. I am Zaelis tu Unterlyn, tutor to the Heir-Empress Lucia tu Erinima. I am also the founder of the Libera Dramach, and as much a leader as it can be said to have.' He seemed about to say more, to explain himself for the benefit of those who did not know him, but he thought better of it.

'Time is short. Come with me,' he said, and they went.

They were in an old, disused section of the prison dungeons, as it emerged; a long-forgotten place, by the looks of things. Tane wondered how many hundred years it had been since it was sealed off, how many Emperors and Empresses had not known of the small, innocuous iron door that led into the sewers. Time was the greatest concealer of all. He glanced at Purloch, and marvelled at how this man had found it out, had made his way through those sewers alone, with no guide, and had not only broken into the Keep but found his way to its most closely guarded prize. Purloch clearly felt he was pushing his luck too far by bringing them here; but he had brought them anyway, for Lucia. He felt he owed her that. Though Tane did not know it, he blamed himself as the author of the calamity that had seized Saramyr. He had taken Sonmaga's money and exposed Lucia for what she was; but now the weight of his guilt tore at him nightly. He would not be able to live with himself if that serene and unearthly child died because of his greed.

Zaelis led them to a small, dark room that had once been a washroom for guards and prisoners alike. A pair of rudimentary showers belched and splattered water on to the black, slick stone tiles. Clothes were heaped on a low stand in one corner.

'The water still runs, as you see. I managed to make it work; unfortunately I cannot turn it off again. Be quick,' Zaelis instructed.

They showered in pairs, the women first. The water was lukewarm and clean, heated by the sun through pipes high above. Once she had sluiced off as much of the foulness as she could, Kaiku dressed in the clothes of a male servant while Cailin attired herself more appropriately. Kaiku cared little. She fit men's clothes as well as women's, and she doubted it would raise a comment. Attired in simple grey trousers and loose shirt – folded right over left in the female fashion – she emerged from the washroom looking reasonably clean.

The others showered and dressed, and Zaelis instructed them to leave those weapons that could not be concealed behind. There was consternation at this, but Zaelis silenced them with a glare.

'Servants do not carry swords and rifles!' he snapped. 'Our objective is stealth. If it came to a fight in the heart of the Empress's Keep, I very much doubt any of us would survive it, weapons or not. Purloch will look after them.'

Kaiku glanced at the cat-burglar, who seemed almost shamefaced about staying. But he had done his part; he had got them into the Keep, and he would not risk himself further. Zaelis could get into the roof gardens far more easily than he could. Besides, he was their guide out of the Keep, and too valuable to lose. He would wait here, and lead them when the time came, back through the sewers to freedom.

The six who were left made their way out of the disused prison section, finally clambering through a large grille that led into a stockroom full of jars of dried food. The grille was set at ground level, hidden behind a pile of sacks in a corner. Kaiku suspected the entrance to the old prison had been built over long ago, but this sly back way had survived.

'Beyond this point, you are servants,' Zaelis instructed. 'Behave as such. My presence will be enough to deter questions.'

With that, he took them out of the stockroom and into the Keep.

Behind his bronze Mask, the Weave-lord Vyrrch's myopic eyes flickered open.

He was in his chambers. A scrawny jackal roamed about nearby, chewing on what morsels it could find. Vyrrch had demanded he be brought a jackal two days ago now; for what reason he could not remember. The canny creature had managed to stay alive while trapped in here, evading his clutches. He suspected he had brought it in to track down that girl who was still hiding somewhere hereabouts, but it had evidently not been one of his more sensible ploys.

He had not seen the girl for weeks now, and he was reasonably sure he hadn't killed her. He still came across signs of her from time to time, objects moved from their rightful place, food gone missing. She was somewhere in the many rooms of Vyrrch's domain, seeking a way out, finding none. Yet how crafty she was, to have stayed out of sight for this long. He almost respected her.

Another strange shiver in the Weave, and Vyrrch was reminded what had jarred him. Concern flickered across his malformed face, though the expression was unrecognisable on features warped by long exposure to the witch-stone dust in his Mask. Since dawn, he had been preoccupied, spreading his consciousness thinly over the Keep. There were many elements to bring into play here, and he was the overseer of all of them. It was vital that he be ready to correct the slightest slip in this day's events, for the future of the Weavers rested upon them. By nightfall, the Weavers' position would be secured.

And yet there had been stirrings. Last night he had sensed a tugging in the Weave, a foreign thing, like the footstep of another spider on the edge of his web. It was slight, this disturbance; too faint to be a fellow Weaver. He had been asleep at the time, and slow to wake, for he was heavy with the amaxa root he had smoked the night before in a post-Weave craving. By the time he was ready to seek it, it had diminished and disappeared.

He could not imagine what it could be, but it had been close. It gave him cause to worry.

Now he felt something again. Much fainter this time, but because he was actively looking out for it, there was a thrill of recognition; and with it, sudden dread.

Whatever had disturbed the Weave last night was inside the Keep. And it was not the Heir-Empress.

He closed his eyes again, sinking back into the Weave. He searched down the tendrils of the threads, sending his consciousness out, searching, probing; then, like an anemone at the touch of a hand, the presence closed up and was gone.

It had *sensed* him, and concealed itself.

Vyrrch felt his skin grow clammy. Something that was not a Weaver, manipulating the Weave? Impossible! Not even Lucia could manipulate the Weave like a Weaver could; her powers were more subtle, less direct.

But he had felt it. And it knew he was looking for it.

Sudden alarm seized him. There could be only one explanation. Whatever it was, it was sent to thwart him, to meddle with his plans! If it was no artifice of the Weavers, then it must be an enemy. He searched for it frantically, but it had disappeared like a ghost.

His decision was immediate. All around the Keep the last of his bombers waited by the bombs they had constructed. Servants and handymen, their minds skewed gradually in the manner of the army Unger tu Torrhyc had supposedly led, their bombs concealed in baskets, in cupboards, in vents or strapped to their bodies.

He could wait no longer, not with that *thing* inside the Keep. It must be now.

Down the Weave, he sent the command to begin.

*

Zaelis led the intruders through the corridors of the servants' quarters, in the lowest levels of the Keep. In contrast to the elegance above, the servants' quarters were of bare stone and devoid of ostentation. It was unbearably hot and stuffy down here, for there were no arched windows or screens to catch the day's breeze, no bright, open state rooms or *lach* floors. The muggy air from outside found its way in to mingle with the steam from clothes presses and kitchens and the exhalation of a thousand people working. The light came from lanterns that sat in alcoves in the walls, and while they provided enough illumination, they reinforced the closeness of the cramped rooms. This was a part of the Keep that was still underground, buried inside the foundations of the hill; and here was where all the unpleasant and unseemly tasks of running such a vast building were carried out.

They walked with purpose but without hurry, following Zaelis's lead. The servants who squeezed by on errands of their own paid them no mind, beyond a swift bow at Zaelis. The heat and sweat had dishevelled them all enough to make them look like servants – and conveniently disguised Tane's illness – but Zaelis's finery marked him out as a man of importance. Kaiku began to relax a little, content that they would not be instantly decried as intruders. She kept her eyes low as a servant should, and walked on.

She felt the twitching of the Weave at the same time Cailin did, but her perception of it was far more vague. It could only be the Weave-lord Vyrrch. She saw Cailin stiffen slightly, and then felt the slip and sew of her response, hiding herself away within the Weave. Cailin glanced back at Kaiku automatically. The muzzling of her *kana* would have rendered her invisible to the one who was probing them; but it was loose again, and wild, and so Cailin extended her protection to include Kaiku. Kaiku met her gaze, and a flicker of surprise crossed her face. Cailin's eyes had darkened from green to red-brown. If she used any more of her power, they would become the freakish Aberrant red, and the game would be up.

'Zaelis,' she hissed, in a rare moment when no servant was nearby. 'Vyrrch is searching for us. Get me to a safe place. I cannot deal with him here.'

Zaelis's reply was the barest nod. He steered them off the main corridor, into a narrower thoroughfare along a row of rooms where tubs of clothes soaked in hot water, and women stirred them with great pestles. Kaiku felt the creeping sensation of being watched. Did the Weavers somehow know of her? Could they sense the oath she had given to Ocha to avenge herself against them? The very air seemed pregnant with movement now, scurrilous fingers running just beneath the surface of sight, invisible manipulations that registered only to her Aberrant instincts. She could feel herself trying to slip into the Weave, her *kana* stirring in response, and she gritted her teeth and fought to hold it back.

And then time seemed to slow suddenly, a premonition of disaster settling on her shoulders like a leaden shroud. She stumbled, not sure where it was coming from, only that something was about to happen, something inevitable. Her senses had warned her too late, and all she could do was wait with sickening dread for that something to arrive. She saw Cailin turn towards her, moving as if through treacle, and as their eyes met she knew the Sister had felt the same thing.

A moment later, the bombs exploded.

THIRTY-ONE

For one dreadful second, Mishani thought that the Empress's Imperial Guards were going to behead her where she knelt like some common servant, without any of the rituals of execution used to honour a noble adversary. Then she felt rough hands on her, pulling her upright. Asara was being treated similarly. Anais and Durun were sitting on their thrones, looking down. Anais's face was dispassionate, Durun's a smirk. She would be led to the proper place, and there her head separated from her shoulders. She was noble, even if an enemy. She would be allowed to die in a dignified fashion with her handmaiden alongside, and not on the floor of the Empress's throne room.

The Barak Mos stood to one side of the dias, watching her blandly. She met his eyes, and saw nothing there. There would be no help for her, or Asara. Her time had truly come.

Then, chaos.

The sound was a deafening roar that shook the Keep from its foundations up. The Guards who held Mishani and Asara stumbled backward to regain their balance. A moment later, a second bomb exploded, nearer to hand. This one made the room buck, and a scatter of loose stones showered down from a ceiling that had suddenly become spidercracked. The Guard by Mishani went down, and pulled her over with him. Shouts of alarm cluttered the air, suddenly multiplying as a third, more distant explosion rumbled through the room. Durun tried to get to his feet and had to grab on to the arms of his throne for support. The Barak Mos was casting around wildly in confusion, with an expression of what looked like anger on his bearded face.

'What is this?' Anais cried, mingled fear and outrage in her voice. '*What is this?*'

'The Keep is attacked!' someone cried.

The main door to the throne room burst open, and in ran several dozen Imperial Guards, their swords drawn. Mishani, who had squirmed out of the grip of the man who held her, thought for a moment they had come to join the Guards already inside; but it took only that moment to see she was wrong. They were not here to guard anything. They were here to kill.

Swords swung high through the morning sun and smashed through armour, muscle and bone. Those Imperial Guards who had been unbalanced by the blasts did not react quickly enough; they were hacked down before they had even got to their weapons. The throne room erupted into turmoil, Guards running this way and that to take position in defence of the Blood Empress. The man who had held Mishani grabbed her ankle as she crawled away, unwilling to let her go; but in the scramble Mishani kicked him viciously in the face, feeling gristle crunch as his nose broke, and he slumped and went limp. Suddenly Asara was there, pulling her to her feet; her own Guard lay supine, having suffered a similar fate to Mishani's.

Blades were crashing together all around them and men were shouting. They were in the midst of a surging tide of white and blue armour, with no way to tell who were the Empress's and who were the imposters who had stormed the throne room. Mishani shied in fright as someone backed into her and turned automatically, his sword raised to strike. Whether the Guard would have struck or not when he had recognised the noble lady cringing before him was a question never answered; Asara rammed her hand into his throat, fingers rigid, and crushed his oesophagus with a single blow. He collapsed trying to clutch at air that would not come.

'Get out of here!' Barak Mos cried to his son, standing on the steps of the dais with his great, curved sword held before him. His choice of weapon reflected his style of politics: force over finesse. Behind him Anais was calling useless orders, her voice unheard over the tumult. She seemed robbed of her imperial strength now, and all the uncertainty, fear and worry she had suffered since this ordeal began showed on her face. She was betrayed somehow. Someone had got into the Keep. And if they were in the Keep, they might get to—

'*Lucia!*' she cried, as her husband grabbed her arm.

'Come on!' he snapped, pulling her away from the throne. The imposters had broken through the main door, but there was another door at the back for the Emperor and Empress, beyond which were stately rooms where they could arrange themselves in their finery before emerging to give audience. The Imperial Guards who were loyal had formed a defensive barrier, clearing a way to that door for Durun and Anais to escape.

They were hurrying down from the dais when a Guard suddenly broke through the struggling mass, an imposter masquerading as one of the loyal defenders, and ran for the Empress. He met the sword of Barak Mos instead, who leaped to interpose. The man hesitated, taken off-guard by this unexpected opponent, and Mos hewed him down. He fell with an expression of comical surprise on his face.

'Rudrec!' Durun shouted as he led his wife to safety. One of the Guards, wearing the colours of a commander, broke away from the defensive line and ran to him. 'Go!' he hissed, so that nobody but they three would overhear. 'Find Lucia and bring her to the Sun Chamber.'

Rudrec grunted and left without bothering to salute in his haste. He was a hoary old campaigner with little time for niceties, but he was also one of their most trusted men. Anais took some small comfort in that. She clung to her husband, suddenly glad of his strength. She had ever been a formidable woman, despite her pale, elfin looks and slight stature, but she had never been threatened with physical violence in her life beyond the bedroom games she played with Durun. Now he was the one with the power, brandishing his sword in one hand as he led her with the other.

Six men joined them as they hustled out of the door and away, a retinue of bodyguards. Alarm bells were being rung in the high places of the Keep as they fled, and Anais felt a terrible sinking in her heart, a void of uncertainty that whispered her folly to her, ever to think that she could dare to put her daughter on the throne and live through it . . .

Kaiku coughed and choked as she stumbled through the smoke, her boots sliding on loose rubble. Nearby she could hear the rumble and growl of fire, the heat scorching her through the dark pall that filled the corridor. Someone was wailing somewhere; other people shouted orders and instructions, rendered incoherent by the ringing in her ears. She shielded her face with her arm and narrowed her streaming eyes, clambering forward through the hot murk, seeking.

She had lost sight of the others within seconds of the explosion. The bomb had been terrifyingly close, destroying a large portion of the nearby scullery and devastating the surrounding corridors. Kaiku had been knocked flat by the concussion and bruised by rubble that fell from above, and she had been rendered temporarily deaf by the noise. When she had regained her wits, she had found the already unfamiliar corridors in ruin, and disorientation had been immediate. Desperate servants hunted through the burning rooms for survivors; smoke made it impossible to see. Kaiku was picked up and then bustled out of the way when it was clear she was unhurt, pushed into a side corridor and told to make her way upstairs. By the time she knew where she was, she was lost.

The most frightening thing about the explosion was the abject panic it had provoked in the servants. Those running past her were scared out of their minds, unable to understand why their previously stable world had suddenly turned to smoke and fire in an eyeblink. Several were blank-faced and staring, zombie-like with shock, as if the explosion had wiped their brains from their heads. She had never seen people look so utterly *void.*

The fires were becoming too much now; the flames had spread and become fiercer and she could barely approach them without her skin burning. She was beginning to doubt whether she would find any of the others in this madness, much less find her way out; but she kept looking. It seemed the only thing she could do.

Over the squeal in her ears there came the sound of a man screaming. She considered for the briefest second that there was nothing she could do for him, that there was nothing she could do for *anyone* here and she should save her own skin, for her mission was more important than all of them. It did not matter. She could not ignore him.

Doggedly, she forged on into a room with walls ablaze. She kicked away a smouldering chair and ducked low to snatch a breath of lung-scorching air, then headed through the small doorway at the other end.

It had once been a kind of laundry room, she supposed; but the water in the washing troughs was boiling now, and the clothes and sheets heaped here had turned to ash. The far wall was almost totally demolished, and she could see through the smoke to what was left of the rooms beyond: a great disorder of rubble, for the roof had fallen in and the room above had tumbled down on top. She glanced up nervously at the ceiling beams, and saw they were bowing and splitting in the heat.

The scream again, and her tearing eyes picked out a man laid in one of the washing troughs, his skin blackened and one leg a bloody stump. The burns on his body were horrible. He had been caught by the blast, and somehow crawled into the trough, seeking the protection of the water; but the water was boiling, cooking him like a lobster. He went under and surfaced again, shrieking. Kaiku could not help him, but she could not turn her back either. Her eyes welled with fresh tears of sympathy and sorrow.

And then she saw a new movement, at the other end of the room.

She caught her breath at the sight. It was a little girl, dressed in a simple robe. Long, light hair fell in curling tumbles down her back. She had a round face with a curiously lost expression on it. But this was no thing of flesh and blood; she was a spectre, a spirit, that blurred and rippled as she moved as if she were a reflection in disturbed water. She walked across to the man in the trough, heedless of the flames. Kaiku watched, transfixed, as the spectre put her hand in the water, and it stopped boiling instantly like a pan removed from the heat. The man in the trough turned to look at her and on his ravaged face there came an expression of joyous gratitude. Then the spectre laid her small hand on his head, and his eyes closed. With a sigh, he sank beneath the water.

The spectre turned to Kaiku then, her features settling into those of a wide-eyed and dreamy-looking girl.

((. . . help me . . .))

The words seemed to come from far away and were very faint, arriving seconds after the spectre had mouthed them. The roof creaked above her, and Kaiku looked up in alarm. She darted back through the doorway just before the ceiling beams gave up with a tortured bellow, and a rage of stone and flame thundered down into the room, belching hot smoke through the doorway.

Kaiku shielded her face, squinting at the room where the spectre had been buried. There was only rock there now; and the weight was making the walls of this room bulge as well.

'Get out of there!' someone cried, and she turned to see a red-faced man at the other doorway, beckoning her through. He disappeared from sight, leaving a vacant arch; and across that arch, a moment later, walked the spectre.

Kaiku clambered back through the blazing room and out into the corridor beyond. The spectre was a glimpse through the smoke. Coughing, she followed, running close to the floor to avoid the black river of murk overhead. Other people were shouting now, the general theme being that they should get out before the place collapsed. Kaiku ignored them, intent on following where the spectre led. She had a sense that it was very important she should do that, and she was learning to trust her instincts more and more of late.

'Kaiku!' came a voice, and Tane grabbed her shoulder. She clasped his wrist to acknowledge he was there, but she did not take her eyes from the girl, nor slow her pace.

'What is it?' Tane asked, bewildered, hurrying alongside her.

'Can you not see it?' she asked.

'See what?'

Kaiku shook her head, impatient. 'Just come with me.'

'What about the others?'

'They can take care of themselves,' she replied.

The spectre was mercifully leading Kaiku away from the worst of the destruction, and after a few corners the air had become clearer and she could breathe again without pain. Tane walked with her, not asking for an explanation, convinced by the determination on her face. Always the translucent figure was ahead of them, just entering a passageway or flitting across the end of a corridor. They never seemed to catch up. Soon the fire was behind them, and the ways they hurried down were more and more trafficked by running Guards and administrative scholars. None of them saw the phantom girl as she passed among them. By their manner, Kaiku guessed there were other commotions in the castle besides the explosions she had felt, but she had no time to care what. Where the spectre went, she followed.

Cailin, Zaelis and Yugi pushed through the confines of the smoky corridors, away from the fire to where the walls still stood and the fug was thin enough to breathe easily. Most of the servants had fled to whatever imagined shelter they could when the explosions began, so the intruders could travel more quickly here. Cailin found that agreeable enough. Solitude was what she needed.

'In here,' she said, and they followed her into a cramped, windowless kitchen, where a cauldron of stew simmered over a fire and the stone walls seemed to sweat. Iron pots and pans hung untidily from pegs, some of them having fallen to the floor when the blast dislodged them. Cailin looked about. 'This will do,' she said.

'Do for what?' Zaelis asked. 'We should get further away from the fire.'

'I need to be undisturbed. Nobody will come here. We are far enough away from the blaze for the moment.'

'Gods, did you see Espyn?' Yugi coughed, running a hand through his soot-blackened hair. 'What about the other two?'

Cailin had indeed seen Espyn, lying twisted in the rubble, his face bloodied and his body broken. He had caught the fringe of the blast by sheer bad luck, and had not survived it.

'Tane and Kaiku must fend for themselves,' she said coldly. She did not abandon Kaiku lightly, with all the hope she had invested there; but there were more important things to do now.

Zaelis was frantic with worry. 'Bombs? Bombs in the Keep? Heart's blood, what is going on here? This is a disaster.'

'This is Vyrrch's doing,' Cailin said.

She pulled aside some chairs to clear herself a space, and then stood facing the cauldron. They watched silently as she took a breath, relaxing her shoulders. The smell of stew filled the air, and Yugi's skin prickled from the heat, but neither appeared to bother the Sister. She closed her eyes and splayed her fingers out where her hands hung by her sides. Her head bowed, and she let out a sigh; and when she raised her head again and opened her eyes, her irises were the colour of blood, and they knew she was seeing things beyond the reach of their vision.

'I will deal with the Weave-lord. You two go to the roof gardens. Find the Heir-Empress. We are not defeated yet. This confusion may yet serve to aid us.'

Zaelis nodded once, and then he and Yugi were gone, the door slamming shut behind them.

Cailin drifted in an ocean of light, millions upon millions of tiny golden threads shifting in minuscule waves. As always, the euphoria struck her upon entering the Weave, gathering under her heart and lifting it, stealing her breath with the beauty and wonder of this unseen world that surrounded them. She allowed herself a moment to enjoy it, and then her long-practised discipline channelled the feeling away, dispersing it so it could not hook her with its false promises of eternal bliss.

Clear-headed again, she sent her consciousness out among the fibres, picking between them with infinite care, dancing from strand to strand like the fingers of a harpist. She was seeking those fibres which were being twisted out of true, those lines of light that had become marionette strings to the unwitting puppets in the Imperial Keep. Someone was manipulating events here; someone was coordinating from afar. She could sense the corruption of the Weave that surrounded several people in the Keep, and knew they were under the influence of another. They thought they were the instigators of the confusion they sowed, but the *true* instigator was out of their sight. And would remain so until Cailin hunted him down.

And so she darted between the threads, finding this one and that, gathering them up, each string giving her a stronger link to the fingers of the puppeteer. And finally, when she was ready, she began to follow them to their source.

Vyrrch had not moved since dawn from his customary spot, cross-legged on the floor in the centre of his bedchamber. The old lady whom he had chopped into meat had been heaved to the side of the room, from where the enterprising jackal had sneaked a few mouthfuls when it thought it was out of Vyrrch's reach. Of course, it was never really out of his reach; nor was the girl who ran loose somewhere nearby. He could have used the Weave to search for them, to simply stop their hearts or shatter their joints. But that was childishly easy, and Vyrrch was not so unsporting. He was impressed that the girl had been wise enough not to try and attack him when he was Weaving or sleeping, for no matter how comatose he looked, she would have been dead before she got within a yard of him. If she was not cheating, then neither would he. Let her go on with her hide and seek. The only key to the door was around his neck; she could not get out. It would be amusing to see how long she lasted.

Women. They were a crafty breed. Altogether too crafty, if the evidence of the past was to be believed. The Weavers' membership had been exclusively grown men for a reason: children were too undisciplined, and women too *good.* It had become very obvious during the earliest days of the witchstones' discovery that the female talents far outstripped those of men in the manipulation of the Weave. The Weave was the essence of nature, and men could only force nature to their will, clumsily and callously; women were part of it, and it came to them like the cycles of the moons. In those first years of madness, hidden at the settlement in the mountains where the great monastery Adderach now stood, the women had almost surmounted the men in power; but it was a mining village, and women were few in number there. The slaughter was quick. Once the men had felt the witchstones' touch, what lingering consciences they had were swiftly cast aside. From that day forth, only adult males had been accepted into the brotherhood, men who came seeking knowledge or power or sublimity.

It had been the same thinking that prompted the practice of killing Aberrant infants these last centuries, when it was suddenly noticed that girl children were being born with a rudimentary ability to control the Weave. Somehow, through the witchstones' influence on their parents and their parents' diet through the corrupted soil, the foetuses were gaining an instinct that the Weavers had had to learn. And it was as natural to them as breathing. But the Weavers were already well established by then, and the common folk were afraid of the freakish powers the infants displayed: so the practice of murdering Aberrants began. Not just the ones who could Weave, for that would make the Weavers' intentions too plain. All of them had to die, to keep the Weavers' secret.

But he had no time for such musings now. He scoured the Keep with one portion of his consciousness, searching for the anomaly in the Weave that had so alarmed him before. The bombers were out of the picture, annihilated by their own creations. Vyrrch had been forced to take direct control in those final moments, for there remained the possibility that the cat's-paws might balk at suicide. Vyrrch saw that their will remained strong until the fiery end.

The intruder had briefly dropped its guard after the bombs had exploded, but Vyrrch had been busy dealing with other things and, frustratingly, he could not pounce on it. Now he bent all his attention to the task of locating it again. With the Keep in chaos, the rest of the plan would run its course. His most pressing concern was this unknown enemy in their midst.

But Vyrrch had been a Weave-lord too long; he was too used to moving unchallenged, unaccustomed to opposition. He spun and threaded the loom of the Weave, but he did not notice the black widow creeping up the strands of his web until she was almost upon him.

Too late, he realised his mistake. This was no clumsy blundering like that of a lesser Weaver; this was an altogether different class. Even the most powerful of Weavers left tears where they went, snapped threads and tangled skeins; but she was like satin, gliding through the Weave and leaving no trace of her passing. This was a woman's way through that bright world, and Vyrrch saw they had been right to fear it.

He drew himself back suddenly, in terror, knowing that she was inside his defences. Desperately, he struck at her, but she moved like a breath of wind. She feinted and dodged, plucking threads as decoys and then sliding nearer when his attention was elsewhere. The Weave-lord began to panic, trying to recall the old disciplines he had known so well before he became complacent, the arts that would drive her out of him; but madness had robbed them from his memory, and he could not piece his thoughts together again.

'Get away from me!' he shrieked aloud into the silence. The jackal started and fled in a scrabble of claws.

He turned his thoughts inward, feeling her gossamer progress along the threads that linked him with the outside world, the suck and flow of his breath, the touch of his skin against his clothes. Frantic, he began to knot, setting up traps, corrals of fibres that led into labyrinths that would lose her for an eternity. But he could barely feel her, let alone stop her, and all he was doing was delaying the inevitable anyway. He could not afford even the slightest portion of his mind to trace her threads back to their source. He did not know who or where she was; he had nowhere to strike.

And she seemed to come from all directions at once, darting here and there to nip and tug, sending false vibrations thrumming down the glittering fibres of their battleground. He flitted to and fro in the grip of increasing panic, laying tricks and feits for her; but nothing was effective, and he realised in despair that he had no other methods to use. He saw then how one-dimensional his command of his powers were; he, the greatest among the Weavers. For so long had he enjoyed supremacy that his ability to adapt had rotted and fallen away. He could not beat her.

With that realisation, he dropped his defences. This, more than anything he had done so far, caused the intruder to hesitate in uncertainty, and it gave him the time he needed. He drew in the Weave as if he was gathering a vast ball of yarn, sucking it into his breast. Too late, his attacker saw what he meant to do, but by then she could do nothing to prevent it. He threw out the spool, putting every ounce of his strength into it, and it unravelled and spawned a million threads that flew away across the landscape of the Weave, curling and spinning randomly and everywhere. A great clarion call, a deafening broadcast to every Weaver and sensitive in Saramyr and beyond. The intruder reeled with the potency of his cry, a wordless shriek of warning to all his brothers. *Beware! Beware! For women play the Weave!*

But Vyrrch was clever, and amid the uncountable threads was one that was different, one that was tautly focused and directed. And in the depthless dark where they hid from the daylight, four demons of shadow raised their heads as one, eyes blazing like lamps.

The message was simple. An image of Lucia tu Erinima, Heir-Empress of Saramyr, layered with impressions of scent, location, the near-imperceptible vibration that was her presence: all the things the shin-shin needed to track her. And with it was a simple command, phrased not in language but in an empathic blaze of intent.

Kill.

Then Cailin struck, the bite of the black widow coming from nowhere, and he realised she had slipped past his every wall and reached his core. His senses were paralysed, his control of the Weave gone. He was helpless. There was a moment of utter and abject horror as he felt her coiling in his brain, taking the thread of his life in her fingers, toying with it. Then, with a twist, she snapped it.

In his chambers, the Weave-lord screamed, spasmed, and slumped forward on to the floor.

There was silence again. It lasted perhaps an hour before the jackal plucked up the courage to emerge once more from where it had fled. It was another hour or more before the girl appeared, her clothing tattered and torn, her face covered in grime. She peered around the doorway, trembling in fear and hunger. There had been no noise but a soft lapping sound for what seemed an eternity.

The Weave-lord was face down, naked beneath his rags. Thick blood from his nose, eyes and mouth had pooled inside his Mask and run out on to the filthy tiles. The jackal was licking at it still.

She stood there watching, hardly daring to hope. She feared a trick. Only when the jackal began to eat Vyrrch's fingers did she believe it was not. He was dead.

With a sob, she approached him. The jackal retreated with a growl. Around Vyrrch's throat, hidden under the rags, was a brass key. She slipped it off him, ready to run at any moment if he should move. He did not. She stared at him for a while, and finally spat upon him. Then, fearing she had gone too far, she ran away, heading for the locked outer door and freedom, while the jackal returned to resume its meal.

THIRTY-TWO

'Who could do this?' the Empress demanded of her husband, who strode along the high corridors of the Imperial Keep, his long black hair stirring with the movement of his shoulders. 'Who could attack us in our own throne room?'

'Whoever it is, they will suffer,' he said. 'Now hurry.'

Anais had a crawling feeling in her belly. They were in the less-travelled areas of the Keep now, the domain of the scholars and the guest rooms and aged, empty chambers once used for social functions. Six men walked with them, swords drawn, as bodyguards. One, Hutten, she had known for many years, and he was as loyal a retainer as she could imagine. Another, whose name was Yttrys, she did not know so well; but she remembered his face, and she was convinced he was not one of those false guards who had attacked them in the reception room. The rest were familiar also, but she could not remember their names.

Yet despite the Guards, she was afraid. The riots, the explosions, the sudden assault; it was an orchestrated plan, but a plan to what end? Did they seek her life or Durun's? Or was it her precious child they were after? Here, with only six Guards, she felt terribly vulnerable. Whoever had started the trouble down in the city had known exactly what they were doing; the Keep had been drained of most of its soldiers, sent to deal with the mobs or to defend the walls against Blood Kerestyn. Blood Batik's troops would be inside Axekami by nightfall, but it was not yet midday and help seemed a terrifyingly long way off.

'Lucia,' she moaned, unable to contain her concern. 'Where is Lucia?'

'I sent Rudrec to get her; didn't you hear?' he snapped. 'She'll meet us.'

He was right. It wasn't safe where Lucia was. She had been hidden, and hidden well; but too many people knew where. If there was an enemy within, as she suspected, then it was best to have her with her parents, hiding somewhere that *nobody* knew.

She glanced at her husband. Durun was a boor and a layabout, but in his towering anger he was quite impressive. He had repeatedly sworn elaborate revenge on those who had attacked him – though not *her*, she noted – as they had been whisked away from the violence. She believed he would do it, as well, if they crossed his path. She felt an inappropriate stir of ardour.

Sometimes, in his passions, she almost saw a man she could love; but those passions were rare and burned out fast, and then he was the sluggard she had been wedded to for many long years.

Durun drew them to a halt in the Sun Chamber. Anais had almost forgotten this place existed; but even amidst all that was going on, she found herself regretting that she had not come here more often. It was a place of true beauty, a great dome of faded green and tarnished gold, with enormous petal-shaped windows that curved symmetrically down from the ornate boss at the apex. The light of the morning splintered into layers of colour as it spread across the webbed glass, bathing the chamber beneath in a multitude of hues. The floor was a vast circular mosaic, and the walls were lined with three galleries of wood and gold. These had once been where councils had stood while a speaker held court in the centre, or where an audience would look down on performers below. Now, like so many of the Keep's upper levels, the chamber was empty and musty, a ghost of its former glory.

'Where's Lucia?' she fretted. She could hear how she sounded, no longer the Blood Empress but the weak woman they all wanted her to be. She hated herself for it, but she was powerless to stop. The attack on the throne room had shaken her to her core; for the first time she had looked in the eyes of men who intended to kill her. It made her authority seem a joke, a game she had been playing, issuing orders that governed the life or death of her subjects while safely shielded from it all inside her impregnable Keep. Now someone had struck at her, close to her heart, and the mortal terror she had felt was not easily washed away.

Who was it? Vyrrch? Most likely, but then she had a thousand enemies now. The bombs suggested Unger tu Torrhyc's vengeful army. She thought she had wiped them out, but maybe there were more, ready to deal retribution for the death of their brothers . . .

One of the six doors to the room was opened, and in came Rudrec with Lucia. She drifted after him, her eyes far away, bearing that look she always wore, the combination of bewilderment and deep curiosity mixed with a hint that she knew far more about the object of her attention than she should.

Anais gave a cry of joy and ran over to her daughter, kneeling and hugging her in relief. She dared not think what might have happened if the attackers had taken the life of her beautiful child. Trembling, she held Lucia tight, and Lucia stroked her hair absently. The Heir-Empress seemed preoccupied, looking wide-eyed up at the windows above, but Anais was too overcome to notice that her mind was elsewhere.

'Give me news of the battle downstairs,' Durun demanded. They had come up several levels from the throne room. 'What about my father?'

Rudrec frowned, momentarily puzzled. 'I left when you did, my Emperor, and I went directly to the roof gardens to collect Lucia, then to here. I have spoken to no one. I have no news.'

Durun appeared satisfied. 'Good. Then nobody but us knows we are here?

Matters should stay that way until we find out who is responsible for today's outrage.'

'No one knows we are here,' Rudrec affirmed. 'Shall I return to the throne room and search for the Barak?'

'No, stay,' Anais said quickly, getting up. 'We need another guard.'

Durun nodded his assent. Lucia hung on to her mother's dress.

'We should go,' Durun snapped suddenly. 'We can't be sure who to trust until the enemy is found.'

'I suggest we go to the Tower of the North Wind,' said Yttrys. 'There is only one door there, thick and easily barricaded. My Empress and Emperor will be safe until we can gather the Guards and root out the assassins.'

'Agreed,' said Rudrec. 'My Imperial Mistress?' he queried, looking for confirmation.

Anais made a neutral noise that they took as an affirmative.

The Tower of the North Wind could be reached from the Sun Chamber by a long, straight bridge spanning a dizzying drop. The bridge was plated on its side and underneath in a latticework of gold which caught the sun in blinding lines of fire. Its interior surfaces were no less fine, the parapets scattered with murals and the floor veined in dark lacquers. Beneath them was the sloping edge of the Keep, for it stood at the corner where two of the Keep's many-arched sides met; level upon level jumbled up towards them from the ground far below, sculptures lunging out to gaze off over the vast panorama of Axekami's streets. Ahead was the thin finger of the tower, a smooth golden needle rising before them, its tip raking the sky as a monument to the spirit that made the north winds blow. Its sister towers rose behind them, at the west, east and south corners of the Imperial Keep.

They stepped out into the open air, feeling the hot wind rustle their clothes, and there they halted.

The roof of the tower was black with ravens. They perched on the tapering apex, or waited on the sills of the arched windows that pocked its length. Closer to hand, they lined the ornamental parapets on either side of the bridge, and carpeted the floor near the far end, shifting restlessly. Every one of them had its black, bright eyes on the newcomers, watching them with an uncanny avian intelligence.

Anais felt a chill run to her core. She heard Rudrec breathe an oath. Durun cast an accusing glance at Lucia, but Lucia was not looking at him; she was gazing at the birds.

'What should we do?' Yttrys said, addressing Durun.

'Heart's blood!' Durun cried. 'They're just *birds*.' But he sounded less confident than he would have liked, and it came out as bluster.

He took Anais's arm and pulled her ahead with him, leading the group out towards the centre of the bridge. The hot breeze plucked at their clothes as if searching for a grip to throw them off and pitch them to their deaths. To their right, Nuki's eye was a bright, glowering ball, peering malevolently through wispy, slatted clouds.

Durun had evidently been hoping the ravens would scatter at their approach. They did not. They bobbed and shuffled, preened themselves or flexed their black wings, but always they watched.

'This is *your* doing, isn't it?' Durun growled, throwing Anais roughly aside and grabbing Lucia's tiny wrist. 'These are your accursed birds!'

Suddenly he snorted, released Lucia and drew his sword, plunging it into Rudrec's breast before the Guard Commander had time to react. Hutten and Yttrys drew their blades at the same time, but while the former was readying himself to strike at the Emperor, the latter drove his sword under Hutten's ribs. He cried out in surprise and pain, but his voice turned to a gargle as blood welled in his throat, and he slid to the ground with sightless eyes.

The birds began to caw, setting up an almighty and terrifying racket; but Durun had swept Lucia into the crook of his arm, with the point of his sword at her throat.

'You call them off!' he shouted. 'The first bird to take wing will cost your life, you Aberrant monstrosity.'

The ravens' cawing died, and they did not move, but it seemed that the searing summer day suddenly became chill under their baleful regard. Yttrys stepped over to Anais, guarding her with his blade. The other four Guards watched dispassionately. It was evident they were on Durun's side also. Only Rudrec and Hutten had not been in on it, and they had died for their ignorance.

Anais's eyes were fixed on her husband, hate shining through a salt-water sheen. It had happened in only a moment, but now the evidence of her senses had overcome her shock and was pummelling her with the truth. The raw betrayal, the disbelief . . .

Durun. All this time, it had been him. Her own husband.

And she had invited his troops into her city.

Her legs went suddenly weak, and she staggered back a step, her gaze never leaving that of her husband. She saw the whole picture then, and the extent of her ruin crushed her. Barak Mos and his son, working in unison with . . .

'Vyrrch,' she whispered. 'You were working with Vyrrch.'

Durun allowed himself a slow smile. 'Of course I was,' he said. 'The Weavers were most unhappy when you insisted on keeping Lucia in the line of succession. He was only too willing to help. But don't think it started there, wife. How long do you expect it took to find so many men loyal to Blood Batik, to integrate them into your Imperial Guards without anyone finding out? Eight years I've been planning this, Anais. Eight years, since this *thing* was born.' He squeezed Lucia tighter in his grip.

Eight years? Anais felt dizzy, as if the bridge were yawing wildly beneath her, threatening to tip her off. The immediacy of the situation clutched at her, pressing the breath from her lungs. The sheer scale of his bitterness, nursed for eight long years, bled through every word.

'I knew how you felt, Durun,' she said, bewilderment in her voice. 'I knew how you felt. An Emperor in name only, wedded to me for your family's advantage, part of a deal. I knew how frustrated you were, but *this* . . .'

'This isn't about me, Anais,' he replied, glancing at the ravens and then back to her. 'This is about our empire. You'd let us tear ourselves apart for the sake of your little girl.'

'*Our* little girl!' she cried.

'No,' he said. '*Your* little girl. Don't you think I have wenched my way around enough? Strange, then, that there have never been any bastard offspring to bother us, to make their claims to the throne. Strange how we tried so long for an heir, yet you became pregnant only once.'

'What are you accusing me of?' she cried, shamed that this should be aired in front of their subjects, terrified at what would happen to her and Lucia now.

'I have no seed, wife, nor ever had!' he spat. 'This monster in my arms is someone else's spawn, and every sight of her reminds me how I have been cuckolded.'

There it was, then; and suddenly it made sense. Anais felt her eyes welling, angry at herself that she should be weak enough to weep. Nuki's eye glared accusingly at her from behind the thin scratches of cloud in the east: *he* knew what she had done, and here was the long-feared retribution. So long ago, and she thought it had passed into the shadows of history and been forgotten. But Durun had known. And it would cost her and her family dear.

She wiped away the tears, defiant. She had suspected, always suspected . . . but never been sure until now. Well, she would not lie or beg forgiveness; not from him. 'Yes, I slept with another!' she shouted. 'Did you think it easy for me, that the whole castle knew my husband consorted with whores and maids? How was it that I was expected to tolerate your scabid antics, while I was to remain pure and for you only on the occasions when you decided to notice me? I am Blood Empress, curse you! Not some half-educated, placid little fishwife!'

'So who was it?' Durun snapped, silencing her. 'A salesman? A travelling musician?' He looked down at Lucia's face. She was calm, like a doll. 'No, she has noble features. A Barak, perhaps? Someone of high birth, surely.'

'You'll never know,' she sneered. But she did, and Lucia did too. By some instinct she had recognised her father the instant she saw him in the roof garden. And he had recognised her, she believed. The Barak Zahn tu Ikati. A brief affair, a tempest of lovemaking, ended all too quickly. It was as if her womb craved a child, desperate with malnourishment from Durun's empty issue; despite the herbs she had taken to prevent it, she had become pregnant almost immediately. She broke it off as soon as she knew, terrified by the implications. Was it really Zahn's? Or could it be Durun's, for she had made bedplay with him intermittently during the early stages of the affair, driven by a misplaced sense of guilt at deceiving him. What if it *was* Zahn's, and grew to resemble him? What if he tried to lay claim to what was his?

And yet, for all the magnitude of her mistake, she would not end the pregnancy. After trying for so long, a child – *any* child – was too precious to give up, whatever the circumstances. How could she dare to think it was not her husband's? Easier to believe it was his, and say nothing to Zahn. Against the subsequent discovery that the child was Aberrant, her lineage paled into insignificance; and it was surprisingly easy to convince herself that Durun was the father, even to the point where she had forgotten about the other possibility. She resembled her mother, and not Zahn or Durun.

'It does not matter who you prostituted yourself to,' Durun said, and she heard again in his voice the depth of his spite. 'Your polluted bloodline ends here, Anais. A treacherous attack by Unger tu Torrhyc's men, and the Empress and heir lie dead. As the only survivor, I will reluctantly become the *Blood* Emperor, true ruler of Saramyr.' He was beginning to enjoy himself now. The ravens were checkmated; Anais was at last his. So many years as the puppet on the throne, so many years in the shadow of a woman, a cuckolded husband without power. He would not let her die before she knew how totally he had outmanoeuvred her. 'By nightfall, the Imperial Guards will owe their allegiance to me as the only surviving member of the Imperial family, and my family's troops will have the city. Grigi tu Kerestyn can batter himself senseless against our walls, but he'll see it's a hopeless task. The council will accept me as Blood Emperor because they will have no choice. Truth be told, I think they'll be relieved that this whole debacle with you and Lucia is over.'

'And Vyrrch? What did you promise *him*?' Anais cried.

'Vyrrch is dead,' Lucia said quietly.

'Silence,' Durun snapped.

'The dream lady beat him,' she said.

'I told you *silence*!'

The ravens stirred, a black ripple through the blanket of beaks and feathers.

'My Emperor,' said Yttrys nervously. 'Let us be about our business and gone from here.'

Durun was about to reply when his hand exploded.

Anais screamed as hot blood splattered her, but her scream was nothing to the roar of agony that came from her husband as he drew back the blazing stump of his sword arm. Lucia darted out of his grip, her long blonde hair afire, screaming also. At the same moment the ravens took flight as one in a vast black cloud, and the air was filled with the beating and thumping of their wings.

Yttrys was too paralysed by fright at the sight of the birds to pay attention to Anais as she ducked away, grabbing Lucia and slapping at her head to put out the flames. Durun's own hair was alight now, the silken black gloss rilled with licking waves of fire. He beat at himself helplessly. Yttrys, suddenly realising what had become of his prisoner, ran to where Anais was crouched over Lucia. He hesitated for the briefest of moments, constrained by the last vestiges of her authority; then he plunged his sword into the Empress's back with a cry.

Anais screamed, a shriek of pain that overwhelmed the cawing of the approaching ravens. The agony was indescribable, but worse was the sudden, swamping cold that settled on her body like a shroud, numbing her. She barely felt the jerk as the blade was pulled from her, tearing through organs and muscle and skin to come free in a spray of dark arterial blood. She was already sinking into the grey folds of unconsciousness. Desperately she clutched Lucia to her, looking at the pallid face of her child, and tears fell from her eyes as the wet stain on the back of her dress swelled in ugly osmosis.

Yttrys turned to run, but in turning he saw Tane and Kaiku at the other end of the bridge; the shaven-headed man and the young woman with her eyes the colour of blood. The sight caused him to halt, to re-evaluate for a moment. Were they friend or enemy? Could he kill them both? Had they been responsible for what had happened to Durun? It was an automatic soldier's instinct, a second's pause; and that was all it took for the ravens to reach the Imperial Guards.

Yttrys shrieked as they enshrouded him, clawing at his nape and scalp and face, a thousand tiny knives raking and pecking at his flesh. He opened his mouth to shriek again, but they slashed and plucked at his tongue. They tore through his eyelids and gorged on the soft jelly of his eyes. He fell and thrashed and wailed, but they were relentless, attacking every inch of his body until there was no part of him that was not bloodied. The other Guards suffered similar torment before they died.

At the same time the ravens bombarded the Emperor, wings beating at his face, pummelling him, battering his body. Still flailing at his hair to put out the searing torch that was crisping the skin of his back and neck, he stumbled backward, and with a wail of fear he toppled over the parapet and plunged off the bridge. His final scream faded until they could hear it no more.

By the time Kaiku and Tane had run over to the fallen Empress, the quiet had returned. All about was the shifting of wings from the ravens, the soft wet smacking as they devoured the corpses of the Guards. Anais sobbed and gasped, lying across her daughter. Her back was soaked in a great dark patch, and blood had run down her arms and dripped from her sleeves, spattering sinister blooms of red on to the bridge. Kaiku crouched next to her, touched her shoulder with a gentle hand.

'Is she alive?' Kaiku asked.

Anais drew back, her moist eyes never leaving her child. Her face was grey, and seemed to have aged terribly. Lucia lay still, her eyes closed. Her back had been terribly burned through the green dress she wore, the fibres of the clothing having blackened and snapped and curled away from each other. Her breathing was shallow, and a pulse fluttered at her throat, but she would not wake when Anais rocked her.

The spectre that had led them through the Keep, that had brought them here; it was this girl. She had drawn them to her intentionally. She must have known she was in danger.

But it seemed they had come too late.

'Help her. She's . . . my daughter,' Anais gasped. She seemed oblivious to her own mortal wound.

Kaiku nodded, and for the first time Anais saw her, saw the crimson irises of her eyes. She coughed, and blood ran from her mouth. Kaiku felt tears coming. This, the Empress of all Saramyr. For so long she had been an almost mythical creature, holding the power of a vast empire in her hands. Millions would fight and die at her command, armadas would sail the oceans for her; she was as close to godhead as humanity would allow. But in the end, only human after all. She seemed so small now, just a frail dying woman. Kaiku listened to Tane murmuring rites to Noctu and Omecha, final benedictions for the soul of their ruler, and she felt a sense of tragedy overwhelm her.

Suddenly Anais clasped Kaiku's hand in her own, a grip so strong that Kaiku might have been an anchor to keep her from floating away. Her eyes were unfocused, and she was not seeing.

'I am frightened . . .' she sobbed. 'Gods, I am frightened . . .'

Kaiku stroked her hair, smearing a trail of blood into it. 'Shh,' she said. 'Dying is not so bad.'

But whether the Empress heard her or not, she never knew, for the light in her eyes had gone out, and with a final sigh she sagged.

'Good journey,' Kaiku whispered, and tears fell from her lashes. It was only when she looked up again that she saw the ravens, surrounding them in a black tide, a blanket of feathers and beaks and eyes, all turned to the Heir-Empress.

'We must go,' Tane said suddenly. He rolled the Empress ungraciously aside and picked up the child, hefting her easily despite the illness that had weakened him. The ravens fluttered in consternation, but he ignored them. 'I can't help her here. She needs a physician.'

Kaiku did not reply, but she rose to her feet, her gaze still on the dead woman that lay before her. She was beginning to feel the incipient burn of using her *kana*, coming on savagely in response to the effort it had taken to focus her energy on such a small target – the Emperor's hand. What thoughts passed through her then, even she could not say; but then she turned and followed Tane as he ran back into the Keep, the fallen heir to Saramyr couched in his arms.

THIRTY-THREE

The Imperial Keep was in turmoil.

The bombs that had been set to sow chaos and confusion had been more effective than any of the usurpers could have imagined. Scholars raced to save precious manuscripts or works of art from rooms threatened by flame; servants rushed to and fro with water from the pipes to quench the hungry fires; children ran bawling in search of their mothers. The Imperial Guards were in disarray. Since they were unable to trust even their own ranks, they could not mount any kind of coherent operation. The Imperial Family had been taken away into hiding, and none knew where they were. A body had been discovered at the base of the Tower of the North Wind, but it was so flayed by ravens that there was little more than a bloodied skeleton remaining. It would not be for many hours that the rings on the corpse's fingers would be recognised as those of Durun tu Batik, former Emperor of Saramyr. The Empress's body was discovered shortly after; but by then it was far, far too late.

It had all got out of control. The bombs and the madness were necessary to provide a cover so the Empress and her Aberrant spawn could be killed in secret, and their murder credibly blamed on somebody else. Now it worked against its instigators, for amid the confusion nobody stopped for two servants carrying an injured girl. Not many in the Keep had ever seen the Heir-Empress, and few would recognise her in this state if they did, with her clothes burned and her face covered by her hair. Slightly more remarkable was the fact that one of the servants was a woman dressed in man's clothes, and that she stumbled along with her eyes bound by a torn rag of cloth and her hand on her sickly-looking companion's shoulder, evidently blinded by some shard of stone thrown by an explosion. But better the people of the Keep should see that than an Aberrant; for Kaiku's eyes were blood-red in the aftermath of using her *kana*, and would not fade for hours yet. The concentration involved in focusing her power to destroy only Durun's hand had drained her to exhaustion; and even then, she had failed. The Heir-empress lay unconscious and burned because she could not control the force within her well enough, and if she died it would be on Kaiku's head. She did not think she could bear the weight of that guilt.

So they hurried along as best they could, following Tane's memory back to the servants' quarters where Purloch waited for them. They had no time to think what might have become of the others. There was only flight.

((Asara!))

Asara pulled Mishani to a halt, dragging her to the side of the corridor behind a statue of Yoru, guardian of the Gates of Omecha, with his wine jug raised high. The cool, austere thoroughfares of the Imperial Keep had become manic now, and servants and soldiers rushed and clattered by, to and fro, boots clicking on *lach*, shouting commands and questions. They were in one of the interior corridors, where there were no outside windows, and even high-ceilinged and wide as it was, it felt terribly claustrophobic.

Both of them were sweaty and dishevelled. Their escape from the throne room had been a narrow thing, but the Imperial Guards had no interest in a noble lady and her handmaiden while they were locked in combat with each other. The loyal and the traitorous had become mixed and mingled hopelessly, and after Barak Mos had fled the battleground degenerated into a free-for-all. The robed advisors and scribes trapped in the room were ignored, and Mishani and Asara slipped away with them once their route was clear. One Guard had raised his sword to stop them, but Asara had killed him bare-handed in an eyeblink. Mishani still could not credit what she had seen, but astonishment was something that would have to wait. For now, she wanted only to escape this place. The pronouncement of her execution had shaken her enough so that she cared little about the Heir-Empress or the plans of the Libera Dramach at this moment; she needed only safety and sanctuary.

'What is it?' she asked, a little shocked at being roughly taken aside by Asara. She was not accustomed to being manhandled like that by anyone. The Aberrant lady hushed her.

((Asara.))

It was Cailin. This was not the first time the Sister had spoken to Asara from afar, and it did not perturb her now as it had in the beginning.

She concentrated a stream of images, recalling in a jumbled order what had happened to them, making it as clear as she could. There was no way for her to speak directly to Cailin – she did not have the mechanisms in her to send words – but impressions would be enough.

Cailin understood. She replied with another set of images, these ones embedded with instructions and information.

'What *is* it?' Mishani persisted.

Asara blinked, and the contact was gone. 'Cailin,' she said. 'She has done away with Vyrrch, and she has a free hand across the Keep. She is our eyes now.' She turned back the other way. 'We have something we must do.'

'What *must* we do?' Mishani's tone made it clear that she was not moving, and certainly not back towards the heart of the Keep.

'Kaiku and Tane have the Heir-Empress,' Asara said. 'We have to find them. Cailin will lead us there.'

'Kaiku?' Mishani said, and they were on their way.

*

Another explosion rumbled through the Keep, making the walls shake. This one was no bomb, but the stores of ignition powder down in the cellars. Kaiku stumbled and fell as they were crossing an intersection between two corridors, into the path of a frightened group of servant women who almost trampled her. The sound of running feet and the clank of armour came after, and Tane saw with a thrill of horror that a group of Imperial Guards was racing towards them. He shifted Lucia's weight to one arm and used the other to grab Kaiku and haul her to one side, then huddled down with her, shielding the Heir-Empress with his body as the Guards rushed by. They paid him no attention.

Kaiku's eyelids were drooping behind the cloth rag that concealed her eyes, her head lolling forward on to her breast. 'I cannot go on,' she said. 'I am so tired.'

Tane would not listen. The fever that had settled in his bones only seemed to make him more determined not to tire, more unforgiving of weakness; his or hers. Though he sweated and his skin seemed taut and yellowish, he would not allow himself to succumb, and was driving himself ever harder. Relinquishing Lucia for a moment, he dragged Kaiku to her feet. She moaned in protest. 'Be quiet,' he hissed, at the sound of new footsteps. He lifted Lucia up, put Kaiku's hand back on his shoulder, and they went on.

For Kaiku it was a descent into nightmare that was becoming all too familiar. The awful burning, the empty void left inside her after her *kana* had broken free stole her will to do anything but lie where she was and sleep. One day, unless she learned to tame it, it would be the death of her. It might already have been the death of the Heir-Empress, and the hopes of the Libera Dramach. She staggered in Tane's wake, hating him for forcing her to run when she could be asleep, hating herself for being so selfish when there was a child in his arms who could be dying even now.

Tane moved with certainty; after many years of finding his way through forests, the ordered corridors of the Keep presented no problem to him. Under his guidance, they made their way rapidly down into the lower levels, heading for the servants' quarters. Every new person that passed them by brought a fresh dread; every pair of eyes looking them over might recognise the child he carried, and that would be the end for them. But time and again their luck held, and they passed through the confusion unchallenged.

'Tane! Kaiku!'

They jumped at the sound of their names, but trepidation turned to relief as they recognised the voice. They paused on the narrow stairs they were descending, and from behind them came Asara and Mishani. The reek of hot smoke rose from below, but that was to be expected; they were almost into the corridors where Cailin waited.

'Kaiku, are you hurt?' Mishani cried, seeing the binding around Kaiku's eyes. Kaiku slumped, but Asara caught her and bore her up.

'She has used her *kana*,' Asara said. 'It drains her. She just needs sleep.'

Mishani's eyes flickered from her friend to the child in Tane's arms, then to Tane himself. He looked sick; his gaze was grey and bleak. He feared for the Heir-Empress.

'There is no time to waste,' Mishani said, deciding all questions could wait. 'We must go.'

And with that, they plunged down into the depths of the servants' quarters. Poisonous fumes undulated in thin veils along the ceiling. Distant wails and calls for help reached them faintly, even over the dull whine that had muted Kaiku's ears after she had been near-deafened by an earlier bomb. The walls had reverted to rough brick rather than varnished wood or *lach*; bits of rubble were scattered around their feet. People they passed were grimed with smoke and sweat, and the heat was almost intolerable. It was not so cramped here as the first time Kaiku and Tane had passed through it, for those who could escape had already done so, leaving behind only the wounded and those who were willing to try and help them.

They were beginning to hope they might make it back to the old donjon where Purloch waited when they ran into three Imperial Guards.

It was pure bad luck that placed them in the path of the four companions and their supine burden. The Guards had escaped the fighting in the throne room, their courage failing them in the confusion of not knowing who was an ally and who was the enemy, and they had fled down into the servants' chambers to avoid the bloodshed going on above. Their intention – if they were faced with a superior officer – was to offer the explanation of digging out those trapped by the blazing rubble; but ill fortune had brought the kidnappers right to them, and whether they were loyal or traitors, they would not allow the Heir-Empress to leave the Keep if they recognised her.

Tane, in the lead, almost bowled into the Guards as the companions rushed into a plain, square stone room that formed a junction between three corridors. Wooden drying racks hung from the ceiling, and clothes hung from them in turn, now bone-dry and crinkling in the heat. The coarse brown bricks of the walls had cracked in places from nearby bomb-blasts, and the floor was dusted with powder and chips of rock.

They were too surprised by the presence of soldiers down here to keep the guilt off their faces. Mishani was the honourable exception, but her efforts did no good.

'What's that?' one of them said, his rifle already aimed at Tane. The other two raised their own rifles, more in alarm at the violent arrival of the newcomers than in any expectation of a threat. They were jumpy, for it would mean their necks if their cowardice were discovered. The three of them were sweating heavily, baking inside their metal armour, the white and blue lacquer streaked with dirt.

'She is hurt!' Tane cried. 'Let us by!'

'I saw you in the throne room,' said one of the other Guards, his eyes ranging over Asara. They flicked to Mishani. 'You too. The Empress sentenced you to death.'

Neither Tane nor Kaiku reacted to the news. Tane's mind was racing through options of escape, but it was sluggish with fever and would not deliver; Kaiku was almost comatose on her feet.

'And you should be with her, not down here with the servants,' Mishani replied smoothly. 'Unless, that is, you are false Guards, like the other traitors who tried to take our Empress's life.'

Tane quailed inwardly at her boldness, but it made the Guards pause for a moment. They were evidently weighing their loyalties, deciding on the best response to the accusation.

'That girl,' said the Guard who had spoken to Tane. 'Look at her clothes. She's no servant.'

'It's the Heir-Empress,' the second one said, his voice dull with menace.

'It can't be!' said the third.

The second narrowed his eyes. 'I've done duty in the Heir-Empress's chambers before,' he said. 'It's her.'

Tane felt a nausea creep into his gut as the first Guard turned a sickly smile upon Mishani.

'Indeed,' he said. 'Then Shintu smiles on us, for that child is a monster, and she must die.' He put the rifle to his shoulder, pointed it squarely at Tane and pulled the trigger.

Nothing happened. The powder did not ignite. It was a misfire.

The expectation of the shot caused everyone to hesitate; except for Asara. She had covered the distance between her and the nearest Guard in a moment, her elbow smashing into his jaw as she grabbed the barrel of his rifle with her other hand, twisting it out of his grip. It fired with a percussive crack, blasting a spume of grey dust from the stone wall next to his companion's head, causing him to shy back with an oath of alarm. Tane shoved the child into Kaiku's arms, who was too weak to hold her, and the pair of them tumbled to the ground. By then the Guard who had misfired had his sword drawn, his rifle cast aside; but Tane was ready for him. He darted inside the Guard's thrust, grabbing him by the arm and swinging him heavily into the wall. There was not enough force behind it, his fever-burned muscles failing him. The Guard grunted and lashed out with an armoured knee, catching Tane in the gut; it hurt, but it did not knock the breath out of him. Mishani pulled Kaiku out of the way, dragging her into the corner of the smoky room, leaving the unconscious Heir-Empress lying where she had fallen.

Asara's enemy was putting up more of a fight than she had anticipated, and whereas her first blow would have finished most men, this one was particularly resilient. He threw her back, trying to get his rifle in between them, but she knocked it away again. Quicker and stronger than she seemed, she grabbed his forearm and levered it up his back, then tripped him so he fell with his full weight on it. The bone snapped loudly, and his scream of pain was silenced as Asara drove her sandalled foot into his face, smashing the gristle of his nose into his brain.

At the same time, Tane shoved his own opponent away from him, pushing him off-balance towards Asara. He was about to make a follow-up strike while the advantage was his when out of the periphery of his eye he saw the third Guard raise his rifle, and looked to see what he was aiming at.

His first thought was that it might be Kaiku, but she was too weak to be a threat, and her eyes were still bound. Mishani had her in the corner, out of harm's way. It was not them that the Guard was aiming at. It was the Heir-Empress, lying unprotected in the middle of the floor.

Tane howled an oath, sprinting at the Guard; but he was too far away, too late to prevent the trigger from being pulled, the hammer to fall, the powder to ignite. But he was not too late to fling himself in front of it.

The force was like a giant's hand slapping him in the chest, blasting him back to tumble over the small body of Lucia, knocking his breath from him in a white blaze of agony. He was aware of falling, but the air had turned to a cloud of feathers and he seemed to float slowly down; and while the impact of the floor hurt more than he could have imagined it would at that speed, it was overwhelmed by the soft cushion of shock that had settled into him.

He heard someone scream his name, but all he saw was the incomprehensible, idiot shapes of the washing above him, hanging from the drying racks and swaying in the smoky haze.

A gun fired, primed, fired again; two bodies fell. Mishani and Asara jerked about as one to find the source of the sound, and there was Yugi, a rifle in his hand, and Zaelis next to him in the doorway. The last two Guards lay inert on the stone floor. Kaiku had scrambled across the room, tearing off her blindfold, desperation lending her strength from some untapped reserve, and she was screaming Tane's name. Tane could barely hear her. All sounds had become dull, muffled. His body felt numb.

Mishani pulled the child out from under him and handed her to Zaelis. His expression was grim as he looked her over; he exchanged a glance with Yugi. They had feared for the Heir-Empress when they had reached the roof gardens and found that Lucia had been taken away by Rudrec at Durun's command; but hope had returned when Cailin had contacted them and directed them to where the others were. Now he saw how badly hurt Lucia was, and that hope faded again. Things looked graver still.

'Bring him back! Asara, bring him back!' Kaiku was crying.

Asara came to stand over her. She looked down at Tane. His eyes were on something above them, focusing and unfocusing wildly. His tanned skin had gone ghastly and pallid. A bright bloom of black and red soaked his chest, and she could see from the way it ran out from beneath him that the rifle ball had gone right through.

'I cannot,' she said.

'Bring him *back*!' she screamed, picking him up and holding him. If she had possessed an ounce of *kana* she would have used it, no matter what the consequences. To try and stitch his wound, sew up his insides, make him whole again. She had taken him so much for granted, this man; he had been her companion since he had found her in the forest, and she had given him nothing back, closing herself off from him. In that moment when she held him, she knew it was too late to make amends. Though her tears and her voice denied it, she knew his time was come, and no artifice of hers or anyone else's could undo it.

Tane had no breath to speak, even if he had the words. His thoughts were turned inward, spiralling into a void like water down a drain; but those he could snatch and piece together were enough to provide him with the answers he needed. All this time, all this questioning and wondering and uncertainty, and all he needed was to have faith. He had not failed. He had trusted his goddess, against all his doubts and fears.

Why was he here? Why had she spared him from the shin-shin, set him on his path to walk with the Aberrants? He knew now, and the answer was so clear that he marvelled at his ignorance in not seeing it before.

She had sent him here to die, in the place of the Heir-Empress.

I owe the gods a life, he thought, *and at last my debt is paid.*

His eyes focused on Kaiku then, her irises red like a demon's. Aberrant eyes, yet he found them no less beautiful for it. After all, he had sacrificed himself for an Aberrant, to safeguard their futures. And as the clutter of his mind swirled away, what was left was only truth. This was bigger than his beliefs; the Heir-Empress was precious to the world, even to the gods. She was important to them all. If by his life he had saved her, then it was worth giving up.

He drank in the features of Kaiku as she held him, and even contorted in grief as they were he could not look away, not even when they seemed to fade, and beneath them there was a stitchwork of golden fibres, a brightness and an ecstasy such as he had never imagined. He had done his work, and done it well, and the Fields of Omecha waited to receive him in splendour.

And if he might have felt a little resentful at being a pawn in the game of the gods, a sacrifice to be made for another's sake, then at least they let him die in the arms of the woman he loved.

THIRTY-FOUR

They escaped Axekami at nightfall, passing out through the south gate under cover of darkness. It was simple enough. All eyes were on the Keep and the east gate, where the armies of Blood Batik were flooding into the city. Fires still raged unchecked in the great truncated pyramid that brooded on Axekami's highest hill. The rioting had redoubled at the sight of the city's figurehead edifice belching smoke and glowing with flame against the gathering dusk, and Blood Batik's forces had responded savagely. In amid all of this, nobody noticed a covered cart drawing up to the quiet south gate. The sentries had their orders, of course; but oddly, after exchanging a few words with the hooded woman who sat next to the driver, they ignored them. The gates were opened, the cart drove through, and the kidnappers left Axekami behind them to boil and churn in its own anger.

Two miles south of the city, they turned off the road to a disused quarry. There they left the cart and took seven of the twelve fast horses that were being held for them there. The man who had guarded them looked worriedly at the child as she was passed into Zaelis's arms.

'Is it she?' he asked reverently, his eyes glittering in the green-edged moonlight. The air felt charged tonight, and the fine hairs on their skin were standing up. Tomorrow, or the next day . . . it could not be long till the moonstorm struck. They would have to ride hard to outpace it.

'It is,' said Zaelis. 'We must go. Every moment we waste brings her closer to death.'

The man swallowed and nodded, and watched as they rode off through the quarry, heading overland. He returned to the ramshackle hut he had been sheltering in these last few days, previously owned by the foreman of this cheerless place. It was one of several stops along the route the kidnappers would take, to switch horses. Speed was of the essence, for all plans had relied on one factor – that the kidnappers would vanish with the Heir-Empress and leave no clue behind them. Even the tired mounts they left behind would be carefully hidden away until they regained their strength. If their escape was marked and they were followed, the Fold would be placed in great danger, and there were too many innocent lives at risk for that. Most of the populace did not even know of the mission, and were ignorant of the schemes being played out beyond the broken lands of the Fault; the Fold was unprepared and unable to defend itself against the might of the Imperial forces. He was left wondering if they had managed to steal the child without anybody knowing, or if even now there were armies sallying forth from the capital in pursuit.

He tried to sleep, but for most of the night he had no luck. Only towards dawn he began drifting in and out of a drowse, and his dreams were vivid and confusing. When he awoke the next morning, he could not be sure what he had imagined and what had been real; but one image stuck with him, and refused to fade in the manner of nightmares.

He could have sworn to the gods that he saw things moving on the lip of the quarry, just before the dawn. Stilt-legged things with eyes like burning lanterns.

They rode hard, long into the morning. When finally Zaelis called a halt, their horses were lathered, flanks steaming and lips flecked with spittle. They had left the road entirely, racing overland, and were deep in the gently rolling plains and hills of the trackless Saramyr countryside. They took shelter under the vast, ancient boughs of a jukaki tree, which stood alone on a slope, and there they rested. The air hummed with insects and the sun beat down on the grass, brightening the colours of the world. It was an incongruously beautiful day, and it did not match their mood.

Kaiku was asleep the moment she dismounted. She had been driven past endurance, almost falling out of her saddle several times, and she had held back the wave of unconsciousness far too long. Yugi began a fire for cooking. Zaelis laid Lucia on the grass, and he and Cailin crouched by her. Mishani, Asara and Purloch sat in the shade, sore and tired.

They had done it. They had snatched the Heir-Empress out from under the noses of the Imperial family, and nobody had seen them; at least nobody who had lived. Luck had made their timing perfect. The explosions in the Keep and the coup pulled off by Blood Batik, the fact that Durun had intentionally taken Lucia and Anais away in secret so nobody knew where they were when he killed them; it was entirely possible that the Imperial Guards had not even discovered the Heir-Empress was missing yet, and that they still thought she was hidden somewhere in the Keep. In the midst of the shambles, the kidnappers had plucked the child away and left no trail to trace.

And yet it did not feel like a victory, for the child lay there on the grass, hovering between life and death. If it fell to the latter, it would all have been for nothing.

Lucia lay raggedly before them, her breathing shallow. A large portion of her thick blonde hair had gone, and the edges of the surviving fibres were singed black and broke off at a touch. When Zaelis carefully brushed it aside, they saw the terrible burns on her upper back and the nape of her neck, the flesh cracked and oozing.

'Why is she like this?' he asked softly. 'Why won't she wake?'

'The burns go deep,' said Cailin. 'Near the spine.'

'You cannot heal her?'

Cailin shook her head. Even without her sinister makeup, she possessed poise and gravitas. 'I dare not. She is an unprecedented creature. We must hope her strength holds until we get back to the Fold.' She glanced at Kaiku, curled up and asleep. Without her the child would be dead. Yet because of her, the child might still die. Cailin refused to consider the responsibility she would share for allowing Kaiku to come, when she knew how dangerous her powers were.

Mishani was exhausted and miserable, for reasons beyond even her concern for Kaiku and the state of Lucia. She had almost been executed not one day past. Her father's change of heart had caught her in the backwash. Wasn't that what she had once loved about the court, that if you took your eyes away for a moment everything might change? Well, it had, and it had nearly cost her life. It had certainly cost her family. There was no going back, not ever. Not to court, not to Mataxa Bay. She was an outcast.

She looked at Kaiku, her face tranquil in sleep. *But at least I am not alone*, she thought, and found a small measure of comfort in that.

They cooked and ate while they rested, using the supplies provided in the horses' saddlebags. Zaelis drizzled warm honey mixed with milk into Lucia's mouth and was gratified that she reflexively swallowed. He gently prised open her eyes and they reacted to the light. But she saw nothing; she seemed to have gone dead inside, cut herself off in reaction to the pain of the burning. Such a sensitive thing, so fragile . . .

'I have to go,' said a voice at his shoulder. He looked up to see Purloch.

'I understand,' he replied. 'You have my thanks, and hers. You did a brave thing, to lead us back into the Keep and out again.'

Purloch nodded, unconvinced. The journey through the sewers had been harrowing, but mercifully there were no maku-sheng on the return journey. His nerves were frayed and tattered, and he felt strangely empty. If not for him, maybe Lucia would have grown up well, would have learned to disguise her powers and taken the throne. If not for him.

'My debt is paid,' he said. The words seemed hollow, but he said them anyway. There was a limit to his courage, and he had reached it. 'I will retire, I think, and go east. You won't see me again.'

'I wish you luck,' Zaelis replied.

'And I you,' Purloch said, and meant it. He glanced once at the stricken child, and then left to take a horse and ride away across the hills.

Then, too soon, it was time to leave again. They put out the fire and wakened Kaiku, who ate a few morsels of food before mounting up. She was still bone-weary, but the few hours of rest had done her much good. They put heels to their horses and galloped south, towards the Xarana Fault and safety.

*

They changed horses in the evening, and rode late into the night. Kaiku remembered little, for she drowsed in and out of semi-consciousness while her body kept itself barely righted in the saddle. Mishani rode alongside her, constantly concerned that she might fall. It was a dangerous way to go, but they could not afford to have someone lead her horse as Asara had once in Fo, or to have someone ride with her. They could not slacken the pace for anyone.

They camped again in the lee of a low and sheltered rocky outcropping, and there made a small fire, confident it would be invisible from afar. They had no need of the heat against the warm night, but they had to cook and boil water. Yugi had herbs that would either help them sleep deeply or keep them alert and awake, depending on whether they were on watch or not. He drank a large quantity of the latter, knowing he would not sleep until they were back in the Fold. Asara joined him on his vigil, for she needed little rest and could get by perfectly well without it. The others lay out under the triangle of moons that loomed in the northern sky and sank into oblivion.

The journey from the north edge of the Fault to Axekami took several days at normal travelling speed. Zaelis estimated they could make it in two, which put their time of arrival at the broken lands around nightfall the next day. The Heir-Empress was worsening visibly now, becoming feverish and pale, shivering and muttering. If Tane had been here, he might have used his knowledge of herblore to ease the burn, to clean the wound and keep it from becoming infected; but they had no such knowledge, and even Yugi's expertise only extended to a few simple infusions. All they could do was mop the child's brow and tear strips of rags to use as dressings over the burnt flesh at her nape. Cailin sent a message ahead to her Sisters in the Fold, ordering them to have a physician and men to meet them at the northern edge of the Xarana Fault; but looking at the Heir-Empress, she had her doubts if the child could even make it that far.

The next day was plagued with troubles. Mishani's horse broke its leg in a rabbit hole, throwing her off. She was unhurt, but the horse had to be slain. She rode with Kaiku after that, who had become much more her normal self after a night's rest, though she spoke little and sometimes wept in memory of Tane. They were forced to slacken pace a little, but Mishani was very light and the horse was still strong and rested; the difference did not amount to much.

Nuki's eye was abominably intense towards midday, and Mishani became woozy with sunstroke. Zaelis did not stop, even to eat. He himself was beginning to suffer from sunburn across his nose and cheeks, but he drove them on, counting their discomfort a minor thing against the Heir-Empress's life.

As dusk fell, they were hungry and exhausted, and Lucia's breath had become a shallow wheeze. They watched with mounting dread as the dull white disc of Aurus loomed behind them, and small, bright Iridima arced up from the west, chased at a faster pace by Neryn. The air began to tauten and took on a metallic tang. Clouds raced in, drawn seemingly from nowhere, heading north in contradiction to the breeze.

They had reached the periphery of the Xarana Fault when the moonstorm struck at last.

It announced itself with a scream that made the horses whinny and shy, the sound of the air being torn under conflicting gravities. Purple lightning flickered between the clouds as they were shredded in the maelstrom of invisible forces, high up in the atmosphere. The land rose around them suddenly, great shoulders of rock dislodged by the ancient cataclysm that had swallowed the city of Gobinda and the Cho bloodline. Time had smoothed the edges with grass and soil and erosion, but it was still possible to trace the borders with the eye, the point where the unbroken earth suddenly descended into turmoil. They rode into its shelter with the screeching of the moon-sisters in their ears, just as the first spatters of warm rain began to dot the earth. In moments, it thickened to a deluge, and the sky opened to deliver a ferocious payload upon them. Zaelis hastily wrapped a blanket around the child he held in his lap, but he would not let them slow. They darted between enormous rocks, slithering down shallow slopes that were already turning to mud, and disappeared into the maze of the Fault.

Full dark had fallen by the time they pulled to a halt in a clearing surrounded by enormous boulders that hunkered around them like mythical stone ogres. Eerie purple light flickered across the scene, followed by an angry shriek from the sky. Mishani, who was riding with Yugi to give Kaiku's horse a rest, flinched at the sound.

'Why are we stopping?' Kaiku called over the noise of the storm, water dripping from her cheeks and chin.

Zaelis whirled his mount, looking first one way and then the other, his eyes scanning the boulders. 'Cailin?' he queried.

'They are meeting us here,' she confirmed. 'The physician, and stretcher bearers. They know better than to be late.'

'But they *are* late,' he said.

'I know,' she replied neutrally.

The sound of Asara priming the bolt on her rifle framed their concerns neatly enough, without the need for words. Yugi glanced about nervously.

Kaiku's eyes fell to a rivulet of water, gently trickling and dripping into a tiny pool formed by the cup of the rock below. She could not have said what instinct made her narrow her eyes and look closer, but at that moment a flash of eerie lightning flickered across the night, and she saw that the clear rainwater was mingled with something darker, flowing from somewhere behind the rock. In the poor light, it was impossible to tell what it was by sight, but she recognised it by its slow, lazy swirl in the pool. Blood.

'Your men are dead, Zaelis!' she called, as every sense she had clamoured at her to get away from there. 'It is a trap! Ride!'

Perhaps it was the conviction in her voice, or the fact that they were all on edge, but they reacted instantly and without thought to question. It was what saved their lives.

They raced out of the clearing at the same moment as two of the shin-shin leaped from hiding, springing down upon where they had been waiting brief moments ago. The remaining pair of demons were already racing along the rim of the boulders, their blazing eyes fixed on their prey as their spindly stilt-limbs propelled them rapidly over the uneven terrain. Lightning stuttered purple light across them, silhouetting them against the clustered moons, and then darkness fell again, and there were only the twin lamps of their eyes as they came after the Heir-Empress.

'Scatter!' Cailin cried, the reins of her mount gathered in one fist, wrenching it around to avoid sliding on the wet mud and crashing into a looming hunk of rock. The broken stones here provided a thousand routes to follow, and a person might lose themselves forever in this maze; but Cailin was not concerned about that now. Escape was the only option for them. She could not protect them against four shin-shin without her Sisters to help her.

Zaelis wheeled his horse, spraying rainwater from its flanks, and hunching over Lucia he spurred it through a narrow passage between two enormous slabs of granite. Kaiku went that way too. Asara was too late to check her momentum and squeeze through; instead she aimed for a short, muddy slope downward. Yugi followed with Mishani. Cailin went another way.

The sky screamed as if in thwarted fury, and Kaiku hunched her shoulders against its rage as she fought to control her mount. Zaelis was riding at a reckless pace, dodging through the rocks and trees with inches to spare while the rain conspired to blind them with wet gusts. Twice he almost dashed Lucia's brains out against an unforgiving bulge of stone, for she lay clutched to his chest with her head lolling to the side. Kaiku focused only on Zaelis's back, taking her cues from his movements. She scarcely dared to breathe as she whipped through gaps that threatened to smash her kneecaps, and she could not afford a second to look back and see where the shin-shin were.

You'll not get me now, she thought to herself with surprising venom. *I beat you once, and I will do it again.*

They broke out into a short, flat stretch, a strip of sodden grass mottled with patches of stone. Thundering towards a line of trees ahead, Kaiku found a few moment's grace to glance over her shoulder.

There were three of them that she could see; one racing along the ground after them and two darting between the boulders and outcrops that formed the walls of the maze their prey rode through. They were like living shadows, skinny patches of darkness that the eye refused to focus on, lunging through the rain with insectile speed.

She heard Zaelis cry out ahead of her. The fourth shin-shin had appeared from the trees, blocking their path, rearing up on its stilt-legs with a screech. Zaelis's horse brayed and swerved aside to avoid the demon in its path. Its hooves found a patch of slick stone and skidded, and Kaiku watched in horror as it twisted and went down. Zaelis took the brunt of the fall, cushioning Lucia with his body; Kaiku heard the snap as Zaelis's leg went, crushed under the flank of the horse. He bellowed in pain, but Kaiku was already bearing down on him, leaning from her saddle.

'Give her to me!' she called desperately, slowing as much as she dared.

Zaelis, understanding dimly through the fog of agony, lifted the child up as far as he could; and Kaiku snatched her, the weight of the dying girl smacking into her arms and almost pulling her from her saddle. She reined around, righting herself, and came face to face with the shin-shin that had emerged from the trees. She took a single gasp—

– and then Asara's rifle cracked out across the night sky, and the shin-shin was blown aside by the force of the shot. It flailed on the ground, its black stilt-legs pawing spastically. Its three companions looked up at where the shot had come from, and one of them erupted into flame with a howl. Cailin was there, emerging from another gap in the rocks, her eyes blazing red.

'*Go!*' Zaelis roared, his molten voice breaking under the pain as his horse thrashed itself upright and left him lying there.

Kaiku needed no second prompting. She spurred her mount savagely, and it leaped away towards the trees, chased by the sawing shriek of the storm as the moon-sisters watched her go.

She plunged into the dark, wet world of the undergrowth, where every shadow was a hard face of wood and every wrong move promised a sudden end. Her ears filled with the sinister hiss of branches as they waved under the onslaught from the sky, slapping her shoulders as she passed. She was riding one-handed, the other arm crooked around Lucia, the Heir-Empress's head jogging against her chest.

The ground suddenly dropped before her and her horse reacted before she did, turning to take the slope at the best angle it could. Kaiku held on for her life as her mount slid and slipped through the trees and rocks, and it seemed their luck could not hold, that every near-miss and narrow dodge brought them closer to the moment when they would collide with a tree and she would be broken like a twig doll.

And yet somehow the slope gave up before her horse did, and they bolted out into a narrow gully, with a stream running along its bottom. They pounded through the shallow water, throwing splash and spray up behind them. Kaiku knew they were beyond help now. There was no way the others could have followed her down here, much less find her again. She could only hope that the other shin-shin had suffered the same fate as the one Cailin had burned; but she dared not wait around to see. Whether it was her or her burden the shin-shin sought, she fled.

The walls of the gully seemed to narrow, and when the storm shrieked again she shrieked with it, for the sound was amplified and deafening along this corridor of rock. Her eyes were narrowed against the pounding rain, yet she seemed to be able to see almost nothing, and had no idea whether she was heading toward level ground or a cliff that would send her to her death.

It was the latter. Some instinct warned her, some part of her subconscious that recognised the change in turbulence of the stream ahead, and she reined her mount in hard enough to bruise its mouth. The stallion whinnied in pain, scrabbling to a halt. Kaiku leaned back in her saddle and held Lucia tight to avoid being tipped over the horse's neck, down the fatal plunge to moon-washed treetops below. Hooves skidded on wet stones, and Kaiku felt a sickening lurch as she realised that they might not stop in time; but then her mount found its purchase, and they came to rest inches from the precipice. Kaiku gazed out over the dark landscape, so far down, and her stomach churned at the thought of toppling through that endless space, the jagged rocks of the cliff wall rushing by, rains dashing against her face, hurtling towards the ground below . . .

With a rough tug, she pulled the stallion away, looking over her shoulder as she did so. Two of the shadow demons dropped from the treetops into the gully behind, their lantern-eyes trained unwaveringly upon the child in her arms.

'You will not have her!' Kaiku spat into the howling wind. Then her horse tugged left, against the reins, and she saw that the gully had crumbled enough at the cliff edge to form a ragged, unstable slope that they could use to clamber out. The horse wanted to try it, motivated by the terror of the things behind; but Kaiku knew better. Its hooves were not equipped for such uneven terrain. But her feet were.

She swung down off the horse and slung Lucia over her shoulder like a sack. Her arms and legs were aching, and the child needed better care than this, but she had no time to be gentle.

'You will not have her!' she screamed again, and the moonstorm keened in response. With that, she scrambled up the broken slope, inches from the precipice to her right. A thin film of water slipped and hurried past her feet, and twice she stumbled and had to put a hand down to keep her balance, but she gained the lip of the gully, and saw there were trees again, crowding up to the edge of the drop. Her lungs burning, she threw herself into the dark shelter of the branches; though she knew that from the shin-shin they provided no shelter at all.

Her breath came out in pants, her heart thudding in her ears, as she pushed though the dark, dripping netherworld of the trees. She could not outpace them like this; she could only hope to hide until daybreak or until help could arrive. A wild thought came to her. If she could find an ipi, like Asara had that first time she had met the shin-shin . . . but ipi dwelt only in the deep forests, and this was little more than a dense fringe of woodland.

You cannot hide. You cannot outrun them. Think!

Her mind flitted traitorously to her *kana*, the sleeping thing lurking within her that had caused her so much pain. Though she might have used it as a last resort, even knowing it had nearly killed Asara and may yet account for the death of the little girl that jounced and jerked against her shoulder, she knew she did not even have that option now. She had not rested enough since the last time it had burst free; there was nothing inside her to draw on. She had drained herself.

There would be no reprieve this time.

The trees gave up suddenly, discharging her on to a flat table of rain-battered rock that jutted out into the night sky. The three moons glared at her, arrayed directly ahead, their edges overlapping amidst a nest of churning cloud and jagged tines of purple lightning. Their luminescence reflected wetly on the cold stone at her feet. She staggered to a halt.

'No . . .' she whispered, but even from this distance it was possible to see that she had cornered herself. The table of rock ended in another precipice; she could see by the curve of its edge that it ran all the way round to either side of her. She had been fleeing along a steadily narrowing promontory, from which there was only one way out: back the way she had come.

She heard the shin-shin wail from the trees behind, and whirled in terror. That was no option.

Frantically, she fled across the bare rock to its edge. Perhaps there was a way down, perhaps it was not as bad as it seemed, if there was even a lake or a river there then she might dare to jump . . .

But the precipice fell on to a jumble of rocks below, a maw of wet and broken teeth that waited hungrily.

She spun round, the limp form of Lucia still in her arms and wrapped in the sodden blanket, but she knew what she would see before she looked. The shin-shin were there, creeping out of the trees, three of them. The creature Asara shot had not stayed down, and they had escaped Cailin before she could inflict any further damage on them. They came prowling into the moonlight, their bodies slung low between their stilt-legs, yellow eyes glittering like burning jewels.

Kaiku clutched the child tight, feeling Lucia's small heart beat against her breast. The creatures had slowed, knowing their prey was helpless and at their mercy. Kaiku took a shuddering breath and looked over her shoulder at the fall behind her, the rain plunging past to plash on the stone far below.

Dying is not so bad, she thought, remembering her words to the Empress. But she had so much still to do. An oath unfulfilled, a new life to begin. She did not want to die here.

Lucia stirred against her, whimpering.

'Shh,' she murmured, her eyes never leaving the steadily approaching demons. She found the lip of the precipice with her heel. 'I will not let them take you, Lucia.' The wind whipped and teased around her, pulling her, and she thought what it would be like never to feel such a wind again on her face, and wanted to cry.

The shin-shin stiffened suddenly, frozen. They turned their heads to the sky, raising themselves up on their tapering limbs as if sniffing at the air. Kaiku watched them in mingled puzzlement and terror. What was this?

A gust of wind blew a sheet of rain across the rock table, and as it passed something seemed to glimmer within it. It was gone so fast that Kaiku doubted it had been there at all; but the shin-shin reacted, the focus of their gaze shifting to where the glimmer had been. One of them took a hesitant step back, uncertain.

Kaiku looked behind her for the briefest of instants, suddenly convinced there was something over her shoulder that she could not see. But all there was was the massive, blotched face of Aurus, seeming big enough to swallow the sky, and beside her was the white disc of Iridima with the blue cracks and lines that gullied her skin, and hiding behind and between them both, peeping out, was the clear green ball of Neryn.

She turned back, and gasped. For now she *could* see something, a faint iridescence that seemed to hang in the air. Before her eyes, the shimmering coalesced and separated into three. The moonstorm screamed in fury behind her, and the shin-shin's pointed limbs tapped on the stone as they skittered back a few steps, heads bobbing in confusion.

The disturbances were taking on form now, towering to twice Kaiku's height. Slowly the sparkling rain began to gain coherence, knitting shape from the falling droplets of water and merging into a spectral mass.

The very air seemed to go still as the spirits took shape, and Kaiku's breath died in her throat.

They were slender, but great cascades of hair like feathers fell down their backs, and their radiance was a cool, cold light. Long robes, at once magnificent and ragged, tangled around their ankles and wrists, shreds of swirling fabric and strange ornaments swaying as they moved. Their skin was too taut, stretched across them in mockery of human form. They were women in shape, but terrifying of aspect, their features shifting and melting like the moons' reflection in a disturbed pond. They seemed emaciated yet somehow *smoothed*, joints and angles too curved, not prominent enough, like waxworks softened by the sun's heat. Long, hooked fingernails sprouted from thin, cruel hands. They looked down on Kaiku and the child, and in their eyes was a malice, an incomprehensibility of purpose that made Kaiku's body weak and her soul shrivel. It was like looking into eternity, and seeing only the void.

Yet in her terror she knew them for what they were, for there had been legends told of them since long before she was born. They came only on nights like this, sometimes to wreak vengeance, sometimes to bring spite; other times to heal, and protect and save. Their motivations were beyond human ken; they were mad, as the wolves who howled at their mistresses in the darkest nights. The spirits of the moonstorm. The Children of the Moons.

They turned to the shin-shin, and the shadow demons retreated warily, flattening themselves in submission. But the Children of the Moons were not so easily placated. The shin-shin mewled and writhed, and Kaiku was appalled to see the creatures she had so feared abase themselves before these monstrous spirit-women, how much greater the magnitude of the Children's power must be. The shin-shin seemed robbed of their demonic arrogance, cringing helplessly as the spirits approached them. Bright swords slid from beneath shredded, incandescent robes. The shin-shin responded in a frenzy, but like pinned butterflies they could only thrash. They could not escape. The swords glittered, rising in an arc.

The massacre was short, and ugly. The shin-shin jerked and spasmed as they were cut and torn, their bodies rent and dismembered, their blood steaming and turning to vapour as it spewed from them. The Children of the Moons hacked the demons apart, taking them to pieces with their shining, rain-wet blades. Kaiku's view of the killing was obscured by the dreadful sight of the spirit-women, but she could hear the repulsive – and surprisingly human – impact of blade against flesh, the breaking of bone, the crunch of gristle. The joyous, grating shrieks of the Children mingled with the shin-shin's wails and drifted into the storm-torn sky.

In moments it was over, and the demons had faded into nothingness like a dream.

Kaiku shivered in the rain and the wind, the girl still clutched to her, her terror not lessened in the least by the departure of the shin-shin. For the great spirits now turned their ghastly eyes back upon her, and they came close until they loomed over her again. She had nowhere to go, not even an inch she could back away to without plummeting to her death.

She squeezed her eyes shut. Gods, would it have been better to have jumped than to face this? Were these creatures any better than the shin-shin? She felt as if her soul could take no more, racked as it was with fear and pain and weariness. Get it over with, then. Have it done.

She opened her eyes again, and found herself face to face with one of the Children of the Moons.

The spirit was down on one knee, bringing herself to Kaiku's level. Her vast and fearful face was only a foot from Kaiku's own, her nose and cheeks seeming to dissolve and reform with the slight inclinations of her head, her eyes like pits into the aether. Kaiku felt her blood cool and slow as she looked into them.

Then the spirit brought her hand up, and with the long, curved nail of her index finger she touched the bundle in Kaiku's arms, the lightest pressure on the blanket that enwrapped the Heir-Empress. Kaiku felt a shudder run through her, a soft charge of something so sublime that she had no name for it. She felt herself lifted from within, as if her body had become suddenly buoyant, a rush of ecstasy such as she had only felt before when she had touched the hem of death and looked into the Weave. A joyous awe threatened to swallow her whole, and she saw suddenly the nature of these awful beings that stood before her, saw them for the unfathomable, magisterial *vastness* they embodied, so far beyond humankind's understanding that she felt like a mote in the ocean in comparison. She saw into the world of the spirits for an instant, and it humbled her.

And then a gust of wind blew a stinging wave of rain across her face, and she shut her eyes against it. When she opened them again, the Children of the Moons were gone.

She stood on the edge of the precipice, the rain swirling around her and the moonstorm slashing the clouds with lightning in the sky behind. Shakily, she stepped away from the drop, staggering to the safety of solid ground. The trees rustled emptily, a hollow audience to the wonder and terror of the last few moments. She raised her face to the sky and felt the rain lick it with warm spittle, and she could not think of a single thought or word that would sum up the experience of gazing into the face of one of the great spirits, of being touched by it. Stunned with awe, she barely noticed the child in her arms stir, nor did she see when the Heir-Empress opened her eyes. She only noticed Lucia was awake when the child put her arms about Kaiku's neck and hugged her.

'Did you meet my friends?' Lucia asked, and Kaiku nodded and laughed and cried at the same time.

THIRTY-FIVE

Weeks glided into months, and the summer grew old.

The Libera Dramach maintained a perpetual readiness in anticipation of any retaliation from Axekami, their spies ever alert in the streets of the capital and all over the Xarana Fault; but as time drew out they began to believe they had no need of such rigid vigilance, and they relaxed somewhat. The Heir-Empress really had been stolen away unobserved. Saramyr was a vast place, and a thousand men might search for a thousand years and never find her. She had vanished without trace, and out of the sight of the world.

Most of the Fold had no idea who the new girl was. A large proportion of them had taken to this life amid the pleats and valleys of the Fault simply to escape their fetters outside, or to avoid the Weavers. Their interest in the politics of the Libera Dramach was non-existent; they simply had lives to live, and they had found a place to live them. And so it was only the core of the Libera Dramach who knew the secret of the girl in their midst, knew of the power she wielded and who she truly was. For the common folk of the Fold, Lucia was just another new girl, another refugee from one conflict or another, and that was not unusual.

Lucia herself recovered from the burns she had suffered, but she never lost the scars. Her upper back and the nape of her neck were wrinkled and puckered, and though the redness faded over time, they were still an abomination against the clear, unspoilt skin that surrounded them. Lucia, converse to expectations, chose not to grow her hair back to its previous length, but instead had it cut boyishly short. When Zaelis gently pointed out that long hair might hide her scarring, she simply gave him one of her unfathomable looks and ignored his advice.

At first, Zaelis was protective of Lucia and acted as a father to her. His broken leg had healed badly and left him with a pronounced limp, but it did not stop him keeping her apart from the other children and away from harm. Of all people, it was Mishani who finally talked him into letting her run free. Lucia had never tasted freedom, never lived a life outside a gilded cage, always too important to be risked. But on the day of the new Emperor's accession to the throne, Mishani went to Zaelis and spoke with him. She was ever the persuasive one.

'She is not the Heir-Empress now,' Mishani pointed out. 'And she should not be treated like one. You'll make people suspicious.'

Zaelis finally demurred, and allowed Lucia to enrol in the school rather than be taught by him. Kaiku and Mishani took it upon themselves to act as elder sisters to her. She was a strange and distant girl, but there was something about her that drew people in, and within days she had been integrated into the close community of the Fold children, scars or no scars. Zaelis fretted and worried until Cailin pointed out the ravens that had taken to gathering on the rooftops of the buildings lately, and which roosted in the trees in the next valley.

'They will look after her much better than you can,' she said.

For herself, Kaiku found an odd sort of happiness after the kidnapping of the last of the Erinima line. Here she no longer thought of herself as Aberrant. It was a meaningless term now, and one that had lost all the connotations of shame and degradation it had carried for the greater part of her life. For the first time since the Weavers had murdered her family, she could simply be herself, to drift for a while without a pressing purpose to spur her on. Her oath to Ocha was there, of course, always present in the back of her mind; but she had her whole life in which to fulfil it. And besides, she had already struck her enemies a crucial blow. Her discovery that the witchstones were responsible for the blight on the land, for the Aberrants themselves, had caused a furore among the Libera Dramach, and plans were already afoot to deal with the problem. Let them plan, she thought. She found she could hold her cares away for a while in the lazy days of late summer. The Weavers could wait. Their time would come.

But first she had to learn. She applied herself to Cailin's lessons, and those of the other Sisters, who periodically returned from their secretive errands in other parts of Saramyr. Gradually her *kana* became less of an enemy and more of a friend, and she learned not to fear it but to treasure it. Though mastery of her abilities would be a long and arduous journey, she had taken the first steps, and they brought her greater joy than she might have imagined.

She and Mishani shared a house, in one of the middle tiers of the cascade of rocky plateaux that formed the backbone of the Fold. It had stood empty for a long while, so Zaelis gave it to them in recognition of their actions, and they took it and made it their own. The friendship between them was better and stronger now than it had been for years, since Mishani went to the city to learn the ways of court. They supported each other through the days when they felt bleak, when they grieved for the loss of their families or friends. Kaiku remembered Tane often, more often than she would have liked. For someone who had been such a brief episode in her life, he had made more of an impact on her than she would have believed at the time. Only when he was gone did she realise it, and by then it was too late.

Her father's Mask lay in a chest in her house. She took it out once in a while to look at it, and sometimes she felt a tugging, a strange urge to put it on, to have the scent and memories of her father back again. At times it seemed to whisper to her in the darkness of the house at night, calling her to it. Those nights she lay awake, but she never went to the chest. There was something in the call she disliked, something like a craving that she did not want to succumb to. Occasionally she thought of throwing it away, but somehow she always forgot about it soon after.

For Asara's part, she left soon after it became clear nobody was going to follow Lucia to the Fold. The easy days of peace Kaiku and Mishani enjoyed were anathema to her, so one warm evening as they sat on the slopes of the valley she announced to them that she was going. Where she went or when she would return, only she knew. But Kaiku remembered the look that had passed between them as they hugged their goodbyes and kissed each other on the cheek, the moment of uncertainty when it seemed their lips might brush, the awkward swell of repulsion and desire intermingled. Then Asara dropped her eyes, smiled a strange sort of smile and left. That smile haunted Kaiku sometimes. She found she wanted to see it again.

And so it went for them, safe in their sanctuary. The days passed, the summer wore on, and they built themselves new lives and lived them, like the other folk of the Fold. But all were conscious at every moment that there among them was a small bloom of hope, a child upon whom their futures rested. A child who still might take the throne, and change their world for the better.

She was growing. All they had to do was wait.

The new Blood Emperor of Saramyr strode out of the council chamber of the Imperial Keep, the roars of disapproval ringing throughout the corridors. His face was dark as thunder, but he had expected nothing less in reaction to his announcement. The very nobles who had cheered his accession with joyous voices, who had been there as he was proclaimed and all Axekami hailed him, had turned against him today. Yet more potent than the outrage against the laws he had declared was the knowledge that they could do nothing about it. The council was weakened. The nobles teetered, gathering themselves in, fresh from the memory of the recent conflict and keen not to be involved in another one. There was nobody to unite behind against him. Blood Amacha had been all but been annihilated with their defeat outside Axekami. Kerestyn and Koli had expended most of their forces in the attempt on the city, and been forced to retreat empty-handed. They knew better than to show their faces at court now. They hid and licked their wounds.

The Blood Emperor Mos tu Batik swept through a pair of double doors into his private stateroom, and knew there were none left to stand against him.

It was the same room in which he had once met the former Blood Empress, when he had warned her that Vyrrch and Sonmaga were plotting against her. She had little suspected that it was not Sonmaga but he and his son who were conspiring with the Weave-lord. Deception and deceit did not sit easily with a man of Mos's bluntness, but he could rise to the challenge when the occasion demanded.

The room was much as it had been then. It had escaped the fires that burned a portion of the Keep and ruined many precious artefacts. Another consequence of the shambolic execution of their plan. Vyrrch was supposed to have been there to coordinate the dampening of the fires after the coup, using his ungodly powers to help extinguish them. Instead he had been killed, somehow. The door to his chambers had been opened from the inside. And if the Weavers knew anything about it, they weren't saying a cursed thing.

He hadn't wanted this. He had wanted his son to be in his place, the Blood Emperor for the glory of Blood Batik and his family. It wasn't right that it should have gone this way, that the father should take the role of the son, while Durun lay in the catacombs, an unrecognisable corpse. But he would not let Durun's death be for nothing. Blood Batik were the ruling family now, and there would be changes.

He looked about, clearing his head of the bitter thoughts that swirled around it. The enormous ivory bas-relief of two rinji birds crossing in flight dominated one wall; a partition let out on to an open balcony, beyond which the hot breezes rose from the city below. Two couches sat by a low table of black wood. His visitor, as he had expected, had declined to sit on them.

'Emperor Mos,' he said, his voice a slow creak behind the cured-skin Mask.

'Weave-lord Kakre,' Mos replied.

Mos went to the table and poured out a glass of wine for himself, not thinking to offer his guest one. He drank it in one swallow. The new Weave-lord maintained an expectant silence, his face like a corpse amid the ragged bundle of furs and hide that was his robe.

'It's done,' Mos said at last.

The Weave-lord watched him disconcertingly for a time. 'You are a man of your word,' he said. 'Then our pact is complete.'

Mos poured, drained, nodded. 'The nobles can't oppose me. The Weavers will be given all the concessions and honours of a noble family, as if you were all one Blood. You will be allowed to be present at court, and at council. Your vote will carry the same weight as any other noble. You will be allowed to own land on the plains of Saramyr, instead of living up in the mountains where no land laws apply. You are no longer merely advisors and tools for communication, you are a political force in your own right.'

'And, of course, you will not forget the aid the Weavers have given you,' Kakre said. 'You, the Blood Emperor of Saramyr, will not forget who put you on your throne.'

'Heart's blood!' Mos swore. 'We made a deal, and I have my honour! I'll not forget. We have a partnership. See that you do your part, and keep me here.'

Kakre nodded slowly. 'I foresee a long and mutually beneficial relationship between Blood Batik and the Weavers,' he said.

'Indeed,' Mos said, but he was unable to hide the curl of disgust in his voice. Kakre gave no indication that he had detected it. He bade farewell and left Mos to his thoughts.

Mos filled his glass for a third time. He was a big and broad man, and alcohol took a long time to affect him. He took the glass out to the balcony and felt the heat of Nuki's eye on his skin, bathing the streets of Axekami in a balmy evening light. *His* city. He had put it to rights, brought order to the people, and given them a leader they could believe in again. Blood Erinima was ousted, and peace had returned.

He let his eyes range down the hill that the Imperial Keep stood on, over the Imperial Quarter, past the bustling Market District to the docks and the sparkling sweep of the River Kerryn, then beyond, to the plains and the distant horizon.

The body of the Heir-Empress had never been found. She had gone, without a trace, without a trail or a clue. His best men had turned up nothing, and though they searched even now, he doubted they ever would. Like a phantom, a vapour, she had disappeared. There were a thousand ways she might have died in the chaos that had seized the Keep that day. He did not believe any of them.

If only Vyrrch had waited until his troops were in the city, as they had planned. Mos might never know what had caused the Weave-lord to set the bombs off early. He might never know what had happened on that bridge between the Keep and the Tower of the North Wind, from which his son had fallen. They had found the Empress there, stabbed through the back, and while every soldier who lay with her had been picked almost clean of flesh, she lay untouched. Whether some devilry or some grotesque trick, it mattered little. What mattered was who had done it. And what they had done with Lucia.

He looked out as far as he could. Somewhere out there, the disenfranchised heir was hiding, growing, gathering support. He could sense it. She would not be found until she revealed herself.

One day she would return, and that day would shake the foundations of the empire.

THE SKEIN OF LAMENT

ONE

The air, cloying and thick from the jungle heat, swam with insects.

Saran Ycthys Marul lay motionless on a flat boulder of dusty stone, unblinking, shaded from the merciless sun by an overhanging chapapa tree. In his hands was a long, slender rifle, his eye lined up with the sight as it had been for hours now. Before him a narrow valley tumbled away, a chasm like a knife slash, its floor a clutter of white rocks left over from a river that had since been diverted by the catastrophic earthquakes that tore across the vast, wild continent of Okhamba from time to time. To either side of the chasm the land rose like a wall, sheer planes of prehistoric rock, their upper reaches buried beneath a dense complexity of creepers, bushes and trees that clung tenaciously to what cracks and ledges they could find.

He lay at the highest end of the valley, where the river had once begun its descent. The monstrosity that had been chasing them for weeks had only one route if it wanted to follow them further. The geography was simply too hostile to allow any alternatives. It would be coming up this way, sooner or later. And whether it took an hour or a week, Saran would still be waiting.

It had killed the first of the explorers a fortnight ago now, a Saramyr tracker they had hired in a Quraal colony town. At least, they had to assume that he had been killed, for there was never any corpse found nor any trace of violence. The tracker had lived in the jungle his whole adult life, so he had claimed. But even he had not been prepared for what they would find in the darkness at the heart of Okhamba.

After him had gone two of the indigenous folk, Kpeth men, reliable guides who doubled as pack mules. Kpeth were albinos, having lived for thousands of years in the near-impenetrable central areas where the sun rarely forced its way through the canopy. Sometime in the past they had been driven out of their territory and migrated to the coast, where they were forced to live a nocturnal existence away from the blistering heat of the day. But they had not forgotten the old ways, and in the twilight of the deepest jungle their knowledge was invaluable. They were willing to sell their services in return for Quraal money, which meant a life of relative ease and comfort within the heavily defended strip of land owned by the Theocracy on the north-western edge of the continent.

Saran did not regret their loss. He had not liked them, anyway. They had prostituted the ideals of their people by taking money for their services, spat upon thousands of years of belief. Saran had found them eviscerated in a heap, their blood drooling into the dark soil of their homeland.

The other two Kpeth had deserted, overcome by fear for their lives. The creature used them later as bait for a trap. The tortured unfortunates were placed in the explorers' path, their legs broken, left cooking in the heat of the day and begging for help. Their cries were supposed to attract the others. Saran was not fooled. He left them to their fates and gave their location a wide berth. None of the others complained.

Four more in total had been killed now, all Quraal men, all helpless in the face of the majestic cruelty of the jungle continent. Two were the work of the creature tracking them. One fell to his death traversing a gorge. The last one they had lost when his *ktaptha* overturned. The shallow-bottomed reed boat had proved too much for him to handle in his fever-weakened state, and when the boat righted itself again, he was no longer in it.

Nine dead in two weeks. Three remaining, including himself. This had to end now. Though they had made it out of the terrible depths of central Okhamba, they were still days from their rendezvous – if indeed there would even *be* a rendezvous – and they were in bad shape. Weita, the last Saramyr among them, was still shaking off the same fever that had claimed the Quraal man, he was exhausted and at the limit of his sanity. Tsata had picked up a wound in his shoulder which would probably fester unless he had a chance to seek out the necessary herbs to cure himself. Only Saran was healthy. No disease had brushed him, and he was tireless. But even he had begun to doubt their chances of reaching the rendezvous alive, and the consequences of that were far greater than his own death.

Tsata and Weita were somewhere down the valley in the dry river bed, hidden in the maze of moss-edged saltstone boulders. They were waiting, as he was. And beyond them, similarly invisible, were Tsata's traps.

Tsata was a native of Okhamba, but he came from the eastern side, where the Saramyr traders sailed. He was Tkiurathi, an entirely different strain to the albino, night-dwelling Kpeth. He was also the only surviving member of the expedition capable of leading them out of the jungle. In the last three hours, under his direction, they had set wire snares, deadfalls, pits, poisoned stakes, and rigged the last of their explosives. It would be virtually impossible to come up the gorge without triggering something.

Saran was not reassured. He lay as still as the dead, his patience endless.

He was a strikingly handsome man even in this state, with his skin grimed and streaked with sweat, and his chin-length black hair reduced to sodden, lank strips that plastered his neck and cheeks. He had the features of Quraal aristocracy, a certain hauteur in the bow of his lips, in his dark brown eyes and the aggressive curve of his nose. His usual pallor had been darkened by long months in the fierce heat of the jungle, but his complexion remained unblemished by any sign of the trials he had endured. Despite the discomfort, vanity and tradition forebade him to shed the tight, severe clothing of his homeland for attire more suited to the conditions. He wore a starched black jacket that had wilted into creases. The edge of the high collar was chased with silver filigree which coiled into exquisite openwork around the clasps that ran from throat to hip along one side of his chest. His trousers were a matching set with the jacket, continuing the complex theme of the silver thread, and were tucked into oiled leather boots that cinched tight to his calves and chafed abominably on long walks. Hanging from his left wrist – the one which supported the barrel of his rifle – was a small platinum icon, a spiral with a triangular shield, the emblem of the Quraal god Ycthys from whom he took his middle name.

He surveyed the situation mentally, not taking his eye away from the grooved sight. The point where the gorge was at its narrowest was laden with traps, and on either side the walls were sheer. The boulders there, remnants of earlier rockfalls, were piled eight feet high or more, making a narrow maze through which the hunter would have to pick its way. Unless it chose to climb over the top, in which case Saran would shoot it.

Further up the rising slope, closer to him, the old river bed spread out and trees suddenly appeared, a collision of different varieties that jostled for space and light, crowding close to the dry banks. Flanking the trees were more walls of stone, dark grey streaked with white. Saran's priority was to keep his quarry in the gully of the river bed. If it got out into the trees . . .

There was an infinitesimal flicker of movement at the far limit of Saran's vision. Despite the hours of inactivity, his reaction was immediate. He sighted and fired.

Something howled, a sound between a screech and a bellow floating up from the bottom of the slope.

Saran primed the rifle again in one smooth reflex, drawing the bolt back and locking it home. He had a fresh load of ignition powder in the blasting chamber, which he counted as good for around seven shots under normal conditions, maybe five in this humid air. Ignition powder was so cursedly unreliable.

The jungle had fallen silent, perturbed by the unnatural crack of gunfire. Saran watched for another sign of movement. Nothing. Gradually, the trees began to hum and buzz again, animal whoops and birdcalls mixing and mingling in an idiot cacophony of teeming life.

'Did you hit it?' said a voice at his shoulder. Tsata, speaking Saramyrrhic, the only common language the three survivors had left.

'Perhaps,' Saran replied, not taking his eye from the sight.

'It knows we are here,' Tsata said, though whether he meant because Saran had fired at it or not was unclear. He was a skilled polyglot, but not adept enough at the intricacies of Saramyrrhic inflection, which were practically incomprehensible to someone who was not born there.

'It already knew,' murmured Saran, clarifying. The hunter had shown uncanny prescience thus far, having managed to get ahead of them numerous times, guessing their route and ignoring the decoys and false trails they had left. It was only Tsata who had even seen it at all, two days ago, heading after them into the gorge. Neither Tsata nor Saran had been under any illusion that their traps would catch it by surprise. They could only hope that it would simply be unable to avoid them.

'Where is Weita?' Saran asked, suddenly wondering why Tsata was here and not down among the boulders, where he was supposed to be. Sometimes he wished Okhambans had the same ingrained discipline as Saramyr or Quraal, but their anarchic temperament meant that they were never predictable.

'To the right,' Tsata said. 'In the shadow of the trees.'

Saran did not look. He was about to form another question when a dull blast thundered up the gorge, making the trees shiver and the rocks tremble. From the midst of the river bed, a thick cloud of white dust rose slowly into the air.

The echoes of the explosion pulsed away into the sky, and the jungle was silent once again. The absence of animal sounds was eerie; in the months they had been travelling, it had been a constant background noise, and the quiet was an aching void.

For a long moment, neither of them moved or breathed. Finally, the shifting of Tsata's shoe on stone broke the spell. Saran risked a glance back at the Tkiurathi, who was crouching next to him on one knee, hidden against the smooth bark of the chapapa that sheltered them both.

No words were exchanged. They did not need them. They simply waited as the rock dust cleared and settled, then resumed their watch.

Despite himself, Saran felt a little more at ease with his companion at his side. He was strange in appearance and even stranger in attitude, but Saran trusted him, and Saran was not a man who trusted anyone easily.

Tkiurathi were essentially half-breeds, born of the congress between the survivors of the original exodus from Quraal over a thousand years ago, and the indigenous peoples they found on the eastern side of the continent. Tsata had the milky golden hue that resulted, making him seem alternately healthy and tanned or pallid and jaundiced, depending on the light. Dirty orange-blond hair was swept back along his skull and hardened there with sap. He wore a sleeveless waistcoat of simple greyish hemp and trousers of the same, but where he was not covered up it was possible to see the immense tattoo that sprawled across him.

It was a complex, swirling pattern, green against his pale yellow skin, beginning at his lower back and sending tendrils curling up over his shoulder, along his ribs, down his calves to wrap around his ankles. They split and diverged, tapering to points, rigidly symmetrical on either side of the long axis of his body. Smaller tendrils reached up his neck and under his hairline, or slid along his cheek to follow the curve of his eye sockets. Two narrow shoots ran beneath his chin, hooking over to terminate at his lip. From within the tattoo mask that framed his features, his eyes were searching the gorge beneath them, their colour matching the ink that stained him.

It was perhaps an hour later that Weita joined them. He looked sickly and ill, his short dark hair lustreless and his eyes a little too bright.

'What are you doing?' he hissed.

'Waiting,' Saran replied.

'Waiting for what?'

'To see if it moves again.'

Weita swore under his breath. 'Didn't you see? The explosives! If they didn't kill it, then one of the other traps must have.'

'We cannot take the chance,' Saran said implacably. 'It may be only wounded. It may have triggered the trap intentionally.'

'So how long do we sit here?' Weita demanded.

'As long as it takes,' Saran told him.

'Until the light begins to fail,' Tsata said.

Saran accepted the contradiction without rancour. Privately, he was worried that the creature had already slipped up the gorge under cover of the boulders and made it to the treeline, although he counted it unlikely that it could have done so without him catching a glimpse of it. After sunset, it would have the advantage of shadow, and even Tsata's dark-adapted eyes would be hard pressed to pick it out at such a distance.

'Until then,' Saran corrected himself.

But though insects bit them and the air dampened until it took noticeably more effort to breathe, their vigil went unrewarded. They did not see another sign of their pursuer.

Weita's protests fell on deaf ears. Saran could wait forever, and Tsata was content to be as safe as possible in this matter. His concern was the welfare of the group, as it always was, and he knew better than to underestimate their pursuer. But Weita griped and complained, eager to get down among the rocks and see the corpse of their enemy, eager to dispel the fear of the creature that only Tsata had seen so far, the invisible agent of vengeance that had grown in Weita's imagination to the stature of a demon.

Finally, an hour before sunset, Tsata shifted against the trunk of the chapapa and murmured. 'We should go now.'

'At last!' Weita cried.

Saran got up from where he had been lying on his chest for almost the entire day. In the early days of the expedition, Weita had marvelled at the endurance of the man; now it merely irritated him. Saran should have been racked with pain by now, but he seemed as supple as if he had just been for a stroll.

'Weita, you and I will spread out through the rocks and come in from either side. You know where the traps are; be careful. The explosion may not have set them all off.' Weita nodded, only half-listening. 'Tsata, stay high. Go over the top of the boulders. If it tries to shoot or throw anything at you, drop down and head back here as fast as you can.'

'No,' said Tsata. 'It may already be in the trees. I will be an easy target.'

'If it has escaped the gorge, then we are all easy targets,' Saran answered. 'And we need someone up there to look out for it.'

Tsata thought for a moment. 'I understand,' he said. Saran took that to mean he agreed with the plan.

'Do not let your guard down,' Saran advised them all. 'We must assume it is still alive, and still dangerous.'

Tsata checked his rifle, refilled and primed it. Saran and Weita hid theirs in the undergrowth. Rifles would only be a hindrance in the close quarters of the river bed. Instead, they drew blades, Weita a narrow, curved sword and Saran a long dagger. Then they moved out of hiding and went among the rocks.

The heat was worse in the narrow passageways between the boulders. The stifling air was trapped, without wind to stir it. Slanting light cut across the faces of the explorers as they slipped through the sharp dividing lines between bright sun and hot shade and back again. The floor was strewn with rubble, though much of the lesser debris had been washed away in the rainy spells that restored the river to a ghost of its former glory for a few fleeting weeks at a time. What remained was too heavy for the flow to move: ponderous lumps of whitish stone, cracked and smoothed by sun and water.

Saran slid from rock to rock, a succession of blind corners, relying on his sense of direction to keep him going the right way. Somewhere above them, obscured by the boulders, Tsata was keeping to high ground, jumping over the narrow chasms with his rifle held ready, watching for movement. He could hear Weita by the sound of his feet scuffing. The Saramyr man was never capable of being silent; he did not have the grace.

'You are nearing the traps,' Tsata said from overhead.

Saran slowed, looking for the scratched signs they had left in the saltstone, coded signals to warn them where the snares and pits were. He spotted one, looked down, and stepped over the hair-thin wire that hovered an inch above the ground.

'Can you see it?' Weita called. Saran felt a twinge of exasperation. Weita's idea of stealth was pitiful.

'Not yet,' said Tsata, his voice floating down to them. He was already so exposed that he need not worry about endangering himself further by talking.

The boulders did not crowd quite so close here, and Saran caught a glimpse of his Tkiurathi companion, some way distant, picking his way with utmost care.

'Which way should I go?' Weita called again.

'Do you see the boulder to your right? The one that is broken in half?' Tsata asked.

Saran was edging past a concealed pit when he realised that Weita had not answered. He froze.

'Weita?' Tsata prompted.

Silence.

Saran felt his heart begin to accelerate. He stepped to safety and flexed his fingers on the hilt of his dagger.

'Saran,' said Tsata. 'I think it is here.'

Tsata knew better than to expect a response. Saran saw him slip from view and thump to the ground, dropping into the cover of the boulders. Then he was alone.

He brushed his lank hair back from his face in agitation, strained his ears for a sound, a footfall: anything that might give away the location of the creature. Weita was dead, he was sure of that. Not even he would be stupid enough to play a trick on them at a time like this. It was how *silently* he had died that was disturbing.

Better not to stay still. Moving, Saran might at least gain the advantage of surprise. He padded further into the jumble of saltstone boulders, squeezing through a crack where two of them had rolled together. The cursed thing had outwaited them, lured them in here. There was no question of escape now. They would not stand a chance.

He almost missed a coded sign in his mounting trepidation, catching it just in time to avoid setting off a deadfall. Glancing upward, he saw the props balancing a rock above his head. He ducked underneath the chest-high tripwire and stepped over the second one at ankle-height placed just beyond it.

Now he had reached the outskirts of the debris thrown by the explosion. He marvelled that the deadfall had stayed intact. Small stones and dust were scattered underfoot. He went carefully onward.

The quiet was terrifying. Though the sounds of the jungle were loud in the world outside the dim, uneven corridors of light and shade that he stalked through, within it was all stillness. Beads of sweat dripped from his jaw. Was Tsata even alive now, or had the thing caught him too?

A pebble rattled.

Saran reacted fast. The creature moved a fraction faster still. He did not even have time to see it before instinct had pulled his head back and to the side. Its claws were a blur, carving a shallow pair of furrows down the side of his neck. The pain had yet to register before the follow-up strike came, but this time Saran had his blade up, and the thing shrieked and darted backward, coming to rest with its weight evenly spread, momentarily at bay.

Two clawed fingers fell to the ground between the combatants in a puff of white dust.

Saran was stanced low, his blade hidden behind his leading arm so as to disguise his next angle of attack. The wound at his throat was beginning to burn. Poison.

His gaze flickered over his opponent. Its shape was humanoid, and yet not so, as if some manic potter had taken the clay of a man and moulded it into something awful. Its face seemed to have been pulled back over its elongated skull, features stretched, its black shark-eyes set in slanted orbits and its nose flat. Its teeth were perfectly straight and even, a double row of needles the thickness of a quill nib, dark with fresh blood and set into an impossibly wide mouth. Slender limbs were bunched with wiry muscle beneath smooth grey skin, and vestigial frills of flesh like fins ran along its forearms, thighs, and along the monkeylike prehensile tail that curled from its coccyx.

Saran had seen Aberrants in Saramyr that were fouler in shape than this, but they were accidents. This thing had been *made* this way, fleshcrafted in the womb for a fearsome appearance, its attributes altered to streamline it towards one purpose: to be the consummate hunter.

There was a knife in its hand now, a wickedly hooked jungle blade, but it was making no move to attack as yet. It knew it had scored a strike on its opponent, and was waiting for the venom on its claws to take effect.

Saran stumbled back a step, his posture sagging, his eyes drooping heavily. The creature came for him, knife angled to open his throat. But Saran's throat was not where the blade struck; he had already dodged aside, dagger sweeping up towards the creature's narrow chest. Saran was not half so weakened as he had pretended. Taken by surprise, it barely dodged; the tip of Saran's blade sliced a long track down its ribs.

There was not an instant's pause. It came back again, faster this time, less assured of its victim's weakness. Saran parried the strike with a harsh chime of metal and punched at the creature's neck. But his opponent flowed like water, and the blow hit nothing and left Saran dangerously overstretched. The creature grabbed his wrist in an iron grip and flung him bodily over its shoulder; he went sailing through the air for a sickening moment before he crashed into the hard ground, his knife skittering free across the stone. Unable to stop his momentum, he tumbled, feeling a pair of sharp tugs on his body as he came to a halt.

Tripwires.

He pushed off with his feet and backward-rolled a split second before the deadfall smashed to the ground where his head had been. In one smooth motion he was on his feet, but his opponent was springing over the debris of the trap even before the dust had settled, utterly relentless. Saran had barely time to realise that he had lost his dagger; he blocked upward with his hand inside the sweep of the creature's blade, catching it on the inside of the wrist, but already another knife was coming from nowhere, his *own* knife, slicing towards his face. He pulled away fast, the cutting edge missing the bridge of his nose by a whisker, but something caught at his ankle and he toppled backward, his balance deserting him. As he fell there was a harsh hiss of movement, and something blurred past his eyes, stirring his hair with the wind of its passage; then there was a dull, wet impact, and a moment later he crashed flat to the earth, supine and all but helpless against his opponent's killing strike.

But no strike came. He looked up.

The creature stood lifelessly before him, its body limp, supported in the air by the vicious row of wooden spikes that had impaled it through the chest. Saran had literally been tripped by a tripwire, and the bent sapling that was released had passed before his face as he fell backward and caught the creature instead. He lay in a long moment in disbelief, and then began to laugh convulsively. The fleshcrafted monstrosity hung like a marionette with its strings cut, its head lolling, black eyes sightless.

Tsata found Saran dusting himself off and still laughing. The sheer exhilaration of the moment had made him giddy. The Tkiurathi took in the scene with puzzlement on his face.

'Are you hurt?' he asked.

'A little poison,' Saran replied. 'Not enough. I think I will be sick for a while, but not enough. That thing counted on it finishing me off.' He began to laugh again.

Tsata, who was acquainted with Saran's remarkable constitution, did not question further. He studied the creature that had been caught in the spike trap.

'Why are you laughing?' he inquired.

'Gods, it was so fast, Tsata!' he grinned. 'To face something like that and *beat* it . . .'

'I am glad,' said Tsata. 'But we should not celebrate yet.'

Saran's laughter died to an uncertain chuckle. 'What do you mean?' he said. 'It is dead. There is your hunter.'

Tsata looked up at him, and his pale green gaze was bleak. 'There is *a* hunter,' he corrected. 'It is not the one I saw two days ago.'

Saran went cold.

'There is another,' Tsata said.

TWO

The cracked moon Iridima still hung low in the north as dawn took the eastern sky in a firestorm.

It began as a sullen red mound, growing wider and glowering ever fiercer as it slid over the curve of the horizon. Beneath it, the sea, which had brooded under the glow of Iridima and the vast, blotched face of her sister Aurus during the night, took up the sun like a tentative choir picking up a melody. Scattered glints prickled the distance, flashing in rhythm with the tug and ebb of the waves. They began to infect the neighbouring swells, which glittered a counterpoint, lapping to a different time as they were stirred by underlying currents and the memory of the chaotic twin gravities of the moons. The sky overhead began to blend from black into a deep, rich blue, the stars fading by degrees.

The final stages came in a rush. The calm, gradual process collapsed into disorder as it came to crescendo, and the upper rim of Nuki's eye peeped over the edge of the planet, a blazing arc of white that ignited the breadth of the ocean. The light reached past the sea, over the tiny specks of Saramyr junks that plied towards the westward coast, and it spread over the land beyond: a colossal swathe of green as all-encompassing and apparently endless as the sea that foundered on its shores. Okhamba.

The port of Kisanth lay within the sheltered cradle of a lagoon, separated from the sea by a towering wall of ancient rock. The frowning black mass kept the lagoon waters safe from the ravages of the storms that lashed the eastern coast at this time of year, while myriad subterranean channels allowed a plentiful supply of fish through from the open ocean. Uncountable ages of erosion had widened one of these channels until it undermined the rock overhead and caused a section of it to collapse, forming a tall tunnel wide enough to allow through even large commercial trading ships.

The *Heart of Assantua* slid into that cleft, its fanlike sails sheeted close. It passed from the heat of the early morning sun into cold, dank shade, where the ceiling dripped and echoed, where lanterns cast a pitiful glow against the gloom and rope walkways ran along the walls. The interior of the tunnel was just as rough and uneven as it had been all those years ago when it was formed, before the settlers had ever fled here from the burgeoning Theocracy in Quraal, before they had ever discovered what kind of primitive nightmare they were casting themselves into.

Sharp eyes guided their slow way through the eerie half-light. Minute adjustments to the rudder were made as instructions were hollered from the prow. Dozens of men stood on the decks with long push-poles, ready to use their combined weight to avert the course of the bulky junk if it should drift too close to the sides. For a few long minutes, they passed through the strange, enclosed world that linked the port and the ocean; and then the end of the tunnel slipped over them and they were out, the blue sky above them again. The lagoon was still two-thirds in the shadow of the rock wall, but its western side was drenched in light, and there lay Kisanth, and the end of a long journey.

The port sprawled gaudily along the edge of the lagoon and up the steep incline of the forested basin that surrounded it. It was a heady riot of wooden jetties, gangways, brightly painted shacks and peeling warehouses, counting-houses and cathouses. Dirt tracks had been planked over and were lined with inns and rickety bars. Stalls sold foodstuffs from Saramyr and Okhamba in equal measure or combination. Small junks and *ktaptha* glided out from the beaches on the north side, cutting through the wakes of the larger vessels that lumbered towards the spidery piers of the dock. Shipwrights hammered at hulls on the sand. Everything in Kisanth was daubed in dazzling colours, and everything was faded from the scorching rays of the sun and the onslaught of the storms. It was a vivid world of warped boards and steadily flaking signs that tried to disguise its constant state of decay by distracting the eye with brightness.

The *Heart of Assantua* spread its smaller sails for the last, leisurely stretch across the lagoon, found an empty pier and nosed alongside it. The push-poles were gone now, and thick ropes came snaking down to the waiting dockhands, who made them fast to stout posts. The junk came to a standstill and furled itself like peacock.

The disembarkation formalities took most of the morning. Kisanth being a Saramyr colony, there were rigorous checks to be carried out. Robed officials and clerks logged cargo, checked passengers against the list, recorded any dead or missing in transit, asked what the travellers' purpose in Kisanth was and where they were staying or going. Routine though their questions were, the officials carried themselves with a fierce zeal, believing themselves the guardians of order in this untameable land, bastions against the brutal insanity that reigned outside the perimeter of their town. When all was accounted for to their satisfaction, they returned to the dock-master, who would check the list again and then hand it to a Weaver. At the end of the week, the Weaver would pass the information on to a counterpart in Saramyr, bridging the gulf between continents in the span of a thought, and the receiving Weaver would inform the dock-master there of the safe arrival of their dependant merchants' vessels. It was an eminently well-structured and effective system, and typically Saramyr.

Not that it concerned two of the passengers, however, who were travelling under assumed names with falsified papers, and who passed through the multitude of checks without raising the suspicions of anyone.

Kaiku tu Makaima and Mishani tu Koli walked amongst the crowd of their fellow travellers, exchanging goodbyes and empty promises of further contact as they dispersed at the end of the pier and headed away into the wooden streets. After a month aboard ship, legs were unsteady and spirits were high. The journey from Jinka on the north-western coast of Saramyr had shrunk their world to the confines of their luxurious junk. Largely ignored by the busy sailors, and with little else to do, the passengers had got to know each other well. Merchants, emigrants, exiles, diplomats: they had all found common ground in their journey, forming a fragile community that had seemed precious at the time, but which was already collapsing as their world expanded again and people remembered the reasons that they had crossed the sea in the first place. Now they had their own affairs to attend to, affairs that were important enough to spend a month in transit for, and they were forgetting hasty friendships or ill-advised trysts.

'You are far too sentimental, Kaiku,' Mishani told her companion as they wandered away from the pier.

Kaiku laughed. 'I might have known I would hear that advice from you. I suppose *you* feel no regret at seeing any of them go?'

Mishani glanced up at Kaiku, who was several inches the taller of the two. 'We lied to them the entire journey,' she pointed out dryly. 'About our lives, our childhoods, our professions. Did you honestly entertain the hope of meeting them again?'

Kaiku tilted her shoulder in what might have been a shrug, a curiously boyish gesture from a lithe, pretty woman nearing her twenty-sixth harvest.

'Besides, if all goes well we will be away from here within a week,' Mishani continued. 'Make the most of your time.'

'A week . . .' Kaiku sighed, already dreading the prospect of getting aboard another ship, another month back across the ocean. 'I hope this spy is worth it, Mishani.'

'They had better be,' Mishani said, with uncharacteristic feeling in her voice.

Kaiku took in the sights and sounds of Kisanth with fascination as they made their way up steps and along boardwalks, losing themselves in the belly of the town. Their first steps on a foreign continent. Everything around them felt subtly different and indefinably new. The air was wetter, somehow more fresh and raw than the dry summer they had left behind at home. The insect sounds were different, languid and lugubrious in comparison to the rattling chikikii she knew. The hue of the sky was deeper, more luxuriant.

And the town itself was like nowhere she had ever visited before, at once recognisably Saramyr and yet indisputably foreign. The hot streets creaked and cracked as the sun warmed the planking underfoot, which had been laid to keep the trails navigable when the rain turned the sides of the basin to mud. It smelt of salt and paint and damp earth baking, and spices which Kaiku did not even have a name for. They stopped at a streetside stall and bought *pnthe* from the wizened old lady there, an Okhamban meal of de-shelled molluscs, sweetrice and vegetables wrapped up in an edible leaf. A little further on, they sat on a broad set of steps – having observed others doing the same – and ate the *pnthe* with their hands, marvelling at the strangeness of the experience, feeling like children again.

They made an odd pair. Kaiku projected vibrancy, her features lively; Mishani's face was always still, always controlled, and no emotion registered there if she did not desire it. Kaiku was naturally attractive, with a small nose and mischievous brown eyes, and she wore her tawny hair in a fashionable cut that hung in an artfully teased fringe over one eye. Mishani was small, plain, pale and thin, with a mass of black hair that hung down to her ankles in a careful arrangement of thick braids and ornaments tied in with strips of dark red leather, far too impractical for anyone but a noble and carrying all the attendant gravitas. Kaiku's clothes were unfeminine and simple, whereas Mishani's were elegant and plainly expensive.

They finished their meals and left. Later, they found a lodging-house and sent porters to fetch their luggage from the ship. Their time together in Kisanth would be short. In the morning, Kaiku would be leaving to head into the wilds while Mishani stayed to arrange their return to Saramyr. Kaiku hunted down a guide and arranged for her departure.

They slept.

The message that had come to the Fold eight weeks earlier had been of the highest priority and utmost secrecy, and neither Kaiku nor Mishani were even aware of it until the two of them had been summoned by Zaelis tu Unterlyn, leader of the Libera Dramach.

With Zaelis was Cailin tu Moritat, a Sister of the Red Order and Kaiku's mentor in their ways. She was tall and cold, clad in the attire of the Order – a long black dress that clung to her figure and a ruff of raven feathers across her shoulders. Her face was painted to denote her allegiance: alternating red and black triangles on her lips and twin crescents of light red curving from her forehead, over her eyelids and cheeks. Her black hair fell down her back in two thick ponytails, accentuated by a silver circlet on her brow, and where it caught the light it glinted blue.

Between the two of them, they had told Kaiku and Mishani about the message. A coded set of instructions, passed through many hands from the north-western tip of Okhamba, across the sea to Saramyr, and thence to the Xarana Fault and the Fold.

'It comes from one of our finest spies,' Cailin said, her voice like a blade sheathed in velvet. 'They need our help.'

'What can we do?' Mishani had asked.

'We must get them off Okhamba.'

Kaiku had adopted a querying expression. 'Why can they not get *themselves* off it?'

'Travel between Saramyr and Okhamba has been all but choked by the Emperor's ruinous export taxes,' Mishani explained. 'After he raised them, the Colonial Merchant Consortium responded by placing an embargo on all goods to Saramyr.'

Kaiku made a neutral noise. She had little interest in politics, and this was news to her.

'The crux of the matter is, our spy cannot get across the ocean back to Saramyr,' Cailin elaborated. 'A small trade still exists from Saramyr and Okhamba, since the scarcity of Saramyr goods has driven up the price enough for a tiny market to survive there; but next to no ships pass the other way. The merchants tend to travel on from there to Quraal or Yttryx. They are weathering the storm abroad, where the money still flows.'

Mishani, ever the quick one, had second-guessed them by now. 'You have passage over to Okhamba,' she stated. 'But you have no ship back. And for that, you need me.'

'Indeed,' said Cailin, studying her intently for a reaction and getting none.

Kaiku looked from one to the other, and then to Zaelis, who was thoughtfully running his knuckles over his close-cropped white beard. 'You mean she would have to go to the coast? To show her face in a port?' she asked, concern in her voice.

'Nothing so simple,' Mishani said with a wan smile. 'Arranging it from this end would be next to impossible. I would have to travel to Okhamba.'

'No!' said Kaiku automatically, flashing a glare at Cailin. 'Heart's blood! She is the daughter of one of the best-known maritime families in Saramyr! Somebody else can go.'

'That is exactly why she must go,' said Cailin. 'The name of Blood Koli carries great weight among the merchants. And she has many contacts still.'

'That is exactly why she must *not* go,' Kaiku countered. 'She would be recognised.' She turned to her friend. 'What of your father, Mishani?'

'I have evaded him these five years, Kaiku,' Mishani replied. 'I will take my chances.'

'I cannot impress upon you enough the importance of this person,' Zaelis said calmly, squaring his shoulders. 'Nor the information they carry. Suffice to say that since they asked for assistance from us at all, there must have been no other option left to them.'

'No other option?' Kaiku exclaimed. 'If this spy is as good as you seem to think they are, then why can they not make their own way back? There must be *some* ships, even if they are only running passengers. Or why not take the Quraal route? It would take a few more months, but—'

'We do not know,' Zaelis interrupted her, raising a hand. 'We only have the message. The spy needs our help.'

Mishani laid a hand on Kaiku's arm. 'I am the only one who can do it,' she said quietly.

Kaiku tossed her hair truculently, glaring at Cailin. 'Then I am going with her.'

The ghost of a smile touched the taller lady's lips. 'I would hardly expect otherwise.'

THREE

The pre-dawn twilight on Okhamba was a serene time, a lull in the rhythms of the jungle as the nocturnal creatures quieted and slunk away to hide from the steadily brightening day. The air was blood-warm and still. Mist hazed the distance, stirring sluggishly along the ground or twining sinuously between the vine-hung trunks of the trees. Moonflowers which had turned in the night to track the glow of bright Iridima now furled themselves to protect their sensitive cells from the blazing glare of Nuki's eye. The deafening racket of the dark hours trailed away to nothing, and the silence seemed to ache. In that hour, the land became dormant, holding its breath in tremulous anticipation of the day.

Kaiku left Kisanth in that state of preternatural peace, following her guide. The port was surrounded by an enormous stockade wall on the rim of the basin where the lagoon lay, with a single counterweighted gate to let travellers in and out. Beyond there was a wide clearing, where the trees had been cut back for visibility. A dirt road crawled off along the coast to the north, and a thinner one to the north-west, their edges made ragged as the undergrowth encroached on them. A prayer gate to Zanya, the Saramyr goddess of travellers and beggars, stood in the midst of the clearing. It was a pair of carved poles without a crossbeam, their surfaces depicting Zanya's various deeds in the Golden Realm and in Saramyr. Kaiku recognised most of them at a glance: the kindly man who gave his last crust to a fellow beggar, only to find that she was the goddess in disguise and was richly rewarded; Zanya punishing the wicked merchants who flogged the vagrants that came to the market; the ships of the Ancestors leaving Quraal, Zanya sailing ahead with a lantern to light the way. The gate was too weathered to make out what detail had once been there, but the iconography was familiar enough to Kaiku.

She offered a short mantra to the goddess, automatically adopting the female form of the standing prayer posture: head bowed, cupped hands held before her, left hand above the right and palm down, right hand palm up as if cradling an invisible ball. The guide – a leathery old Tkiurathi woman – stood nearby and watched disinterestedly. Once Kaiku was done and had passed through the gate, they headed into the jungle.

The journey to the rendezvous was only a day's walk, a spot chosen –

Kaiku guessed – because it lay almost equidistant from three towns, one of which was Kisanth while the other two lay alongside a river that led shortly thereafter to another sea port. The spy had selected this place to be deliberately vague about their place of departure, in case anyone decoded all or part of the message that had been sent to the Fold. Kaiku found herself wondering about this person she was meant to meet. She did not know their name, nor whether they would be male or female, nor even if they were Saramyr at all. When she had protested at being kept in the dark by Zaelis and Cailin, they had merely said that there were 'reasons' and refused to speak further on it. She was not used to having her curiosity frustrated so. It only piqued her interest further.

From the moment they left the perimeter of man's domain, the land became wild. The roads – heading away to other settlements and to the vast mountainside crop fields – were going in the opposite direction to that in which Kaiku wanted to go, so they were forced to travel on foot and through the dense foliage. The way was hard, and there were no trails to speak of. The terrain underfoot was uncertain, having been moistened by recent rains. Kaiku's rifle snagged on vines with annoying regularity, and she began to regret bringing it at all. They were forced to scramble their way along muddy banks, clamber up rocky slopes that trickled with water, hack their way through knotted walls of creepers with *knaga*, a sickle-like Okhamban blade used for jungle travel. But for all that, Kaiku found the jungle breathlessly beautiful and serene in the quiet before the dawn, and she felt like an intruder as she went stamping and chopping through the eerie netherworld of branches and tangles.

The land warmed about them as they travelled, bringing with it a steadily growing chorus of animal calls, creatures hooting at each other from the meshed ceiling of treetops high above. Birds, with cries both beautiful and comically ugly, began to sing from their invisible vantage points. Frogs belched and croaked; the undergrowth rustled; fast things flitted between the trunks of the trees, sometimes launching themselves across the travellers' path. Kaiku found herself unconsciously dawdling, wanting to soak up the sensations around her, until her guide hissed something sharp in Okhamban and she hurried to catch up.

Kaiku had harboured initial doubts about the guide she had found, but the old woman proved far stronger than she looked. Long after Kaiku's muscles were aching from trudging along cruel inclines and chopping the omnipresent vines that hung between the trees, the Tkiurathi forged unflaggingly onward. She was tough, though Kaiku guessed she must have been somewhere past her fiftieth harvest. Okhambans did not count years, nor keep track of their age.

Conversation was limited to grunts and gestures. The woman spoke very little Saramyrrhic, just enough to agree to take Kaiku where she wanted to go, and Kaiku spoke next to no Okhamban, having learned only a few words and phrases while at sea. In contrast to the excessive complexity of Saramyrrhic,

Okhamban was incredibly simple, possessing only one phonetic alphabet and one spoken mode, and no tenses or similar grammatical subtleties. Unfortunately, the very simplicity of it defeated Kaiku. One word could have six or seven discrete applications depending on its context, and the lack of any specific form of address such as *I, you* or *me* made things terribly hard for one who had grown up speaking a language that was unfailingly precise in meaning. Okhambans traditionally had no concept of ownership, and their individuality was always second to their *pash*, which was roughly translatable as 'the group'; but it was a very slippery meaning, and it could be used to refer to a person's race, family, friends, those who were present, those they were talking to, loved ones, partners, or any of a dozen other combinations with varying degrees of exclusivity.

As the heat climbed and the midges and biting insects began to appear, Kaiku sweltered. Her hardwearing and unflattering clothes – baggy beige trousers and a matching long-sleeved shirt with a drawstring collar – were becoming itchy with sweat and uncomfortably heavy. They stopped for a rest, during which time the guide insisted that Kaiku drink a lot of water. She produced a leaf-wrapped bundle of what seemed to be cold crab meat and a spicy kelp-like plant, and shared it with Kaiku without her asking. Kaiku brought out her own food and shared it with the guide. They ate with their hands.

Kaiku stole glances at the woman as she chewed, eyes roaming over the pale green tattoos that curled over her cheeks and poked from her shirt collar, wondering what thoughts passed through her head. She had not wanted any payment for her services as a guide; indeed, it was an insult to offer any. Mishani had explained that since the guide lived within the town of Kisanth, then at some level that was her *pash* and thereby she would willingly offer her services to anyone within that town who needed them and expect the same courtesy to be offered to her. Kaiku had been warned to be very careful about asking anything of an Okhamban, as they would almost unfailingly oblige, but they would become resentful if their nature was abused. Okhambans only asked for something when they could not do it themselves. She could not pretend to understand their ways, but she thought it seemed a strangely civilised and selfless lifestyle in a people who were generally thought of as primitive in Saramyr.

Night had just deepened to full dark when they arrived at the Aith Pthakath. They came at it from below, following a narrow stream bed until the trees abruptly fell back and exposed the low hilltop hidden in amongst the surrounding jungle. No trees grew on the hill, but in their place were the monuments of ancient Okhamba, built by a dead tribe long before any people's history had begun to be recorded.

Kaiku caught her breath. Aurus and Iridima shared the sky for a third successive night, lighting the scene in a wan white glow. Aurus, pale but patched with darker shades, loomed massive and close to the north. Iridima, smaller and much brighter, her skin gullied with bluish cracks, took station in the west, above and behind the monuments.

There were six of them in all, bulky shadows against the sky with the curves of their faces limned in moonlight. The tallest of them stood at thirty feet, while the smallest was a little over fifteen. They were sculpted from a black, lustrous stone that was like obsidian in quality, set in a loose ring around the crest of the hilltop, facing outward. The largest squatted in the centre, looking over Kaiku's head to the east.

The guide grunted and motioned at Kaiku to go on, so she stepped out of the trees and into the clearing, approaching the nearest of the monuments. The riotous sound of the jungle had not diminished one bit, but she felt suddenly alone here, in the presence of a humbling antiquity, a place sanctified by a long-dead people before any of what she knew existed. The statue she approached was a squatting figure hewn out of a great pillar, features grotesquely exaggerated, a prominent mouth and huge, half-lidded eyes, its hands on its knees. Though the rain of centuries had battered it and smoothed its lines so that they were indistinct, and though one hand had broken away and lay at its feet, it was incredibly well preserved, and its blank, chilling gaze had not diminished in authority. Kaiku felt minuscule under its regard, this forgotten god.

The others were no less intimidating. They were seated or squatting, with swollen bellies and strange faces, some like animals that Kaiku had never seen, some in disturbing caricatures of human features. They guarded the hill, glaring balefully out at the trees, their purpose alien and subtly unsettling.

Kaiku hesitated for a few moments, then laid her hand on the knee of one of the idols. The stone was cool and brooding. Whatever power this place had once seen had not been entirely dispersed. It retained a sacred air, like an echo of distant memory. No trees had encroached here, nor had any animals nested in the crooks and folds of the statues. She wondered if there were spirits here, as there were in the deeper forests and lost places at home. The Tkiurathi did not seem to be pious at all, from the accounts of the travellers she had talked to on the *Heart of Assantua*. Yet here was the evidence that there had once been worship in this land. The weight of ages settled on her like a shroud.

She became conscious that the guide had joined her, and removed her hand from the statue. She had forgotten the reason she came here in the first place. Looking around, it became evident that the spy was not here yet. Well, she was early. The rendezvous was at midnight on this date. They had cut it extremely fine on the crossing, slowed by unfavourable moon-tides caused by some inept navigator's miscalculation of the orbits, but at least she was here now.

'Perhaps we should look around the other side of the hill,' she suggested, more to herself than the guide, who could not understand. She made a motion with her arm to illustrate, and the guide tilted her chin up in an Okhamban nod.

In that instant, a thick arrow smashed through her exposed throat, spun her sideways in a geyser of blood and sent her crashing to the earth.

Kaiku was immobile for a few long seconds, her mouth slightly open, barely certain of what had just happened. Flecks of blood trembled on her cheek and shoulder.

It was the second arrow that broke the paralysis. She felt it coming, sensed it slipping through the air; from her right, from the trees, heading for her chest.

Her *kana* blazed into life inside her. The world became a shimmer of golden threads, a diorama of contours all interlinked, every vine and leaf a stitchwork of dazzling fibres. The pulsing tangles that were the statues of the Aith Pthakath were watching her with dark and impotent attention, aware, *alive* in the world of the Weave.

She swept her hand up, the air before her thickening invisibly to a knot, and the arrow shattered two feet from her heart.

Sense finally caught up with instinct and reaction, and she exhaled a frantic breath. Adrenaline flooded in. She barely remembered to rein her *kana* before it burst free entirely. If it had been a rifle and not an arrow, if it had been her and not the guide that they had aimed at first, would she have been fast enough to repel it?

She ran. Another arrow sliced from the trees, but she felt it going wide of her. She stumbled, her boot sliding in the soil and smearing dirt up the leg of her trousers. Cursing, she scrambled to her feet again, tracing the route of the arrow in her mind. Her irises had darkened from brown to a muddy red, seeing into the Weave, tracking back along fibres torn into eddies by the spin of the arrow's feathered flight. Then – having established the rough location of her attacker – she was racing for cover once more. She slid behind one of the idols as a third arrow came at her, glancing off its obsidian skin. A flood of silent outrage rippled out from the statues at the desecration.

Find them. Find them, she told herself. She wanted to cringe under the weight of the idol's gaze, its ancient and malicious interest in her now that she had stirred the Weave; but she forced herself to ignore it. They were old things, angry at being abandoned by their worshippers and ultimately reduced to observers, incomprehensible in purpose and meaning now. They could not harm her.

Instead she sent her mind racing along the tendrils of the Weave, scattering among the trees to where her attacker was, seeking the inrush of breath, the knitting of muscle, the heavy thump of a pulse. The enemy was moving, circling around; she felt the turbulence of its passing in the air, and followed it.

There! And yet, *not* there. She found the source of the arrows, but its signature in the Weave was vague and meaningless, a twisted blot of fibres. If she could get a purchase on her attacker she could begin to do them harm, but something was defeating her, some kind of protection that she had never encountered before. She began to panic. She was not a warrior; with her *kana* out of the equation, she was no match for anyone who could shoot that accurately with a bow. Shucking her rifle from her shoulder, she primed it hurriedly, tracking the hidden assailant with half her attention as they dodged through the undergrowth without a whisper.

Get away, she told herself. *Get into the trees.*

And yet she dared not. The open space around her was the only warning she had of another attack. In the close quarters of the jungle, she would not be able to run and dodge and keep track of the enemy at the same time.

Who is it out there?

She raised her rifle and leaned around the edge of the idol, aiming at where she guessed her attacker would be. The rifle cracked and the shot puffed through the trees, splintering branches and cutting leaves apart.

Another arrow sped from the darkness. Her enemy had gained an angle on her already. She pulled herself reflexively away as the point smacked into the idol near her face, sending her stumbling backward. She noticed the next arrow, nocked and released with incredible speed, an instant before it hit her in the ribs.

The shock of the impact sent sparkles across her vision and almost made her pass out. She lost control, her *kana* welling within, all Cailin's teachings forgotten in the fear for her life. It ripped up out of her, from her belly and womb, tearing along the threads of the Weave towards the unseen assassin. Whatever protection they wore stopped her pinpointing them, but accuracy was not necessary. There was no subtlety in her counterstrike. Wildly, desperately, she lashed out, and the power inside her responded to her direction.

A long swathe of jungle exploded, blasted to matchwood, rent apart with cataclysmic force and lighting the night with fire. The sheer force of the detonation destroyed a great strip of land, throwing clods of soil into the air like smoking meteorites. The trees nearby burst into flame, leaves and bark and vines igniting; stones split; water boiled.

In a moment, it was over, her *kana* spent. The jungle groaned and snapped on the fringes of the devastation. Sawdust and smoke hung in the air, along with the faint smell of charred flesh from the birds and animals that had been unfortunate enough to live there. The surrounding jungle was silent, stunned. The terrible presences of the idols bore down on her more heavily than ever, hating her.

She teetered for a moment, her hand going to her side, then dropped to one knee in the soil. Her rifle hung limply in her other hand. Her irises were a bright, demonic red now, a side-effect of her power that would not fade for some hours. In past times, when she had first discovered the awful energy within her, she had been unable to rein it in at all, and each use would leave her helpless as a newborn afterward, barely able to walk. Cailin's training had enabled Kaiku to shut off the flow before it drained her to such a state, but it would be some time before her *kana* would regenerate enough to allow her to manipulate the Weave again. She had not unleashed it so recklessly for years; but then, it had been years since she had been in such direct danger.

Kaiku panted where she knelt, scanning the destruction for signs of movement. There was nothing except the slow drift of powdered debris in the air. Whoever had been aiming at her had been in the middle of that. She'd wager there was not much left of them now.

A movement, down the hill at the treeline. She spun to her feet, snatched up her rifle and primed the bolt, raising it to her eye. Two figures burst into the clearing from the south. She sighted and fired.

'No!' one of them cried, scrambling out of the way. The shot had missed, it seemed. Ignoring the ache and the insidious wetness spreading across her side, she reprimed. 'No! Libera Dramach! Stop shooting!'

Kaiku paused, her rifle targeted at the one who had spoken.

'Await the sleeper!' he cried. It was the phrase by which the spy was to have been identified.

'Who is the sleeper?' Kaiku returned, as was the code.

'The former Heir-Empress Lucia tu Erinima,' came the reply. 'Whom you yourself rescued from the Imperial Keep, Kaiku.'

She hesitated a few moments longer, more in surprise at being recognised than anything else, and then lowered her rifle. The two figures headed up the hill towards her.

'How do you know who I am?' she asked, but the words came out strangely weak. She was beginning to feel faint, and her vision was still sparkling.

'I would not be much of a spy if I did not,' said the one who had spoken, hurrying up towards her. The other followed behind, scanning the trees: a Tkiurathi man with the same strange tattoos as her guide, though in a different pattern.

'You are hurt,' the spy stated impassively.

'Who are you?' she asked.

'Saran Ycthys Marul,' came the reply. 'And this is Tsata.' He scanned the treeline before turning his attention back to Kaiku. 'Your display will have attracted anyone hunting for us within twenty miles. We have to go. Can you walk?'

'I can walk,' she said, not at all sure whether she could. The arrow had punctured her shirt and she was certainly bleeding; but it had not stuck in her, and she could still breathe well enough, so it had missed her lungs. She wanted to bind herself up here and now, terrified of the moist stain that was creeping along the fabric under her arm; but something in the authority of Saran's voice got her moving. The three of them hurried into the forest and were swallowed by the shadows, leaving behind the grim sentinels of the Aith Pthakath, the body of Kaiku's guide and the smouldering crackle of the trees.

'What was it?' Kaiku asked. 'What was it out there?'

'Hold still,' Saran told her, crouching next to her in the firelight. He had slid off one arm of her shirt, exposing her wounded side. Beneath the sweat-dirtied strap of her underwear, her ribs were a wet mess of black and red. Unconsciously, she had clutched the other half of her shirt across her chest. Nudity was not something that most Saramyr were concerned about, but something about this man made her feel defensive.

She hissed and flinched as he mopped at her wound with a rag and hot water.

'Hold *still!*' he told her irritably.

She gritted her teeth and endured his ministrations.

'Is it bad?' she forced herself to ask. There was a silence for a few moments, dread crowding her as she waited for his answer.

'No,' he said at last. Kaiku exhaled shakily. 'The arrow ploughed quite a way in, but it only scraped your side. It looks worse than it is.'

The narrow cave echoed softly with the sussuration of their voices. Tsata was nowhere to be seen, out on some errand of his own. The Tkiurathi had found them this place to hide, a cramped tunnel carved by an ancient waterway in the base of an imposing rock outcropping, concealed by trees and with enough of a bend in it so that they could light a fire without fearing that anyone outside would see. It was uncomfortable and the stone was dank, but it meant rest and safety, at least for a short time.

Saran set about making a poultice from crushed leaves, a folded strip of cloth and the water that was boiling in an iron pot. Kaiku pulled her shirt tight around her and watched him silently, eyes skipping over the even planes of his face. He caught her glance suddenly, and she looked away, into the fire.

'It was a *maghkriin*,' Saran said, his voice low and steady. 'The thing that tried to kill you. It got here before us. You are lucky to be alive.'

'Maghkriin?' Kaiku said, trying out the unfamiliar word.

'Created by the Fleshcrafters in the dark heart of Okhamba. You cannot imagine what the world is like there, Kaiku. A place where the sun never shines, where neither your people nor mine dare to go in any number. In over a thousand years since the first settlers arrived, what footholds we have made in this land have been on the coasts, where it is not so wild. But before we came, *they* were here. Tribes so old that they might have stood since before the birth of Quraal. Hidden in the impenetrable centre of this continent, thousands upon thousands of square miles where the land is so hostile that civilised society such as ours cannot exist there.'

'Is that where you have come from?' Kaiku asked. His Saramyrrhic was truly excellent for one who was not a native, though his accent occasionally slipped into the more angular Quraal inflections.

Saran smiled strangely in the shifting firelight. 'Yes,' he said. 'Though we barely made it. Twelve went in; we two are the only ones who came out, and I will not count us safe until we are off this continent entirely.' He looked up at her from where he was grinding the leaves into a mulch. 'Is it arranged?'

'If all goes well,' Kaiku said neutrally. 'My friend is in Kisanth. She intends to have secured us passage to Saramyr by the time we return.'

'Good,' Saran murmured. 'We cannot stay in towns any longer than necessary. They will find us there.'

'The maghkriin?' Kaiku asked.

'Them, or the ones that sent them. That is why I needed somebody to facilitate a quick departure from Okhamba. I did not imagine I could take what I took and not be pursued.'

And what did you take, then? Kaiku thought, but she kept the question to herself.

He added some water to the paste of leaves and then leaned over to Kaiku again, gently peeling her sodden shirt away from the wound. 'This will hurt,' he warned. 'I learned this from Tsata, and in Okhamba there is very little medicine that is gentle.' He pressed the poulticed cloth against her wound. 'Hold it there.'

She did so. The burning and itching began almost immediately, gathering in force and spreading across her ribs. She gritted her teeth again. After a time, it seemed to level off, and the pain remained constant, just on the threshold of being bearable.

'It is fast-acting,' Saran told her. 'You only need hold it there for an hour. After you remove it, the pain will recede.'

Kaiku nodded. Sweat was prickling her scalp from her effort to internalise the discomfort. 'Tell me about the Fleshcrafters,' she said. 'I need to keep my mind off this.'

Saran hunkered back and studied her with his dark eyes. As she looked at him, she remembered that her own eyes were still red. In Saramyr, it would mark her as Aberrant; most people would react with hate and disgust. But neither Saran nor Tsata had seemed concerned. Perhaps they already knew what she was. Saran had certainly seemed to recognise her; but the fact that she was under the tuition of the Red Order – and hence an Aberrant – was not widely known. Even in the Fold, where Aberrants were welcomed, it was best to keep Aberration a secret.

'I cannot guess what kind of things dwell in the deepest darknesses of Okhamba,' Saran said. 'They have men and women there with crafts and arts foreign to us. Your folk and mine, Kaiku, our ways are very different; but these are utterly alien. The Fleshcrafters can mould a baby in the womb, sculpt it to their liking. They take pregnant mothers, captured from enemy tribes, and they change the unborn children into monsters to serve them.'

'Like Aberrants,' Kaiku murmured. 'Like the Weavers,' she added, her voice deepening with venom.

'No,' said Saran, with surprising conviction. 'Not like the Weavers.'

Kaiku frowned. 'You're defending them,' she observed.

'No,' he said again. 'No matter how abhorrent their methods, the Fleshcrafters' art comes from natural things. Herblore, incantations, spirit-craft . . . Natural things. They do not corrupt the land like the Weavers do.'

'The maghkriin . . . I could not . . . I could not find it,' Kaiku said at length, after she had digested this. 'My *kana* seemed to glance off it.' She watched Saran carefully. Years of caution had taught her that discussing her Aberrant powers was not something done lightly, but she wanted to gauge him.

'They have talismans, sigils,' Saran said. 'Dark arts that they trap within shapes and patterns. I do not dare imagine the kind of tricks they use, nor do I know all that the Fleshcrafters can do. But I know they place protections on their warriors. Protections that, apparently, work even against you.'

He brushed the fall of dirty black hair away from his forehead and poked at the fire. Kaiku watched him. Her gaze seemed to flicker back to his face whether she wanted it to or not.

'Are you tired?' he asked. He was not looking up, but she sensed that he knew she was staring. She forced her eyes away with an effort of will, flushing slightly, only to find that they had returned to him again an instant later.

'A little,' Kaiku lied. She was exhausted.

'We have to go.'

'Go?' she repeated. 'Now?'

'Do you think you killed it? The one that attacked you?' he asked, straightening suddenly.

'Certain,' she replied.

'Don't be,' Saran advised. 'You do not know what you are dealing with yet. And there may be more of them. If we travel hard, we can be at Kisanth by mid-afternoon. If we stay and rest, they will find us.'

Kaiku hung her head.

'Are you strong enough?' Saran asked.

'Strong as I need to be,' Kaiku said, getting to her feet. 'Lead the way.'

FOUR

'Mistress Mishani tu Koli,' the merchant said in greeting, and Mishani knew something was wrong.

It was not only his tone, although that would have been enough. It was the momentary hesitation when he saw her, that fractional betrayal that raced across his features before the facade of amiability clamped down. Beneath her own impassive veneer, she already suspected this man; but she had no other choice except to trust him, for he appeared to be her only hope.

The Saramyr servant retreated from the room, closing the folding shutter across the entryway as she left. Mishani waited patiently.

The merchant, who had seemed slightly dazed and lost in thought for a moment, appeared to remember himself. 'My apologies,' he said. 'I haven't introduced myself. I'm Chien os Mumaka. Please, this way.' He motioned to where the study opened onto a wide balcony overlooking the lagoon.

Mishani accompanied him out. There were exotic floor mats laid there, woven of a thick, soft Okhamban fabric, and a low table of wine and fruits. Mishani sat, and Chien took position opposite. The merchant's house was set high up on the slope of the basin that surrounded Kisanth, a sturdy wooden structure raised on oak pillars to make its foremost half sit level. The view was spectacular, with the black rocks of the coastal wall rearing up to the left and Kisanth to the right, lying in a semicircle around the turquoise-blue water. Ships glided their slow way from the docks to the narrow gash in the wall that gave out onto the open sea, and smaller craft poled or paddled between them. The whole vista was smashed with dazzlingly bright sunlight, making the lagoon a fierce glimmer of white.

She sized up her opponent as they went through the usual greetings, platitudes and inquiries after each other's health, a necessary preamble to the meat of the discussion. He was short, with a shaven head and broad, blocky features matched by a broad, blocky physique. His clothes were evidently expensive though not ostentatious; his only concession to conceit was a thin embroidered cloak, a very Quraal affectation on a Saramyr man, presumably meant to advertise his worldliness.

But appearances meant nothing here. Mishani knew him by reputation. Chien os Mumaka. The *os* prefix to his family name meant that he was adopted, and it would stay attached to his natural children for two generations down, bestowing its stigma upon them too, until the third generation reverted to the more usual *tu* prefix. *Os* meant literally 'reared by', and whereas *tu* implied inclusion in the family, *os* did not.

None of this appeared to have hampered Chien os Mumaka's part in his family's meteoric rise in the merchant business, however. Over the last ten years, Blood Mumaka had turned what was initially a small shipping consortium into one of only two major players in the Saramyr-Okhamba trade route. Much of that was down to Chien's daring nature: he was renowned for taking risks which seemed to pay off more often than not. He was not elegant in his manners, nor well educated, but he was undoubtedly a formidable trader.

'It's an honour indeed to have the daughter of such an eminent noble Blood come visit me in Kisanth,' Chien was saying. His speech patterns were less formal than Mishani's or Kaiku's. Mishani placed him as having come from somewhere in the Southern Prefectures. He had obviously also never received elocution training, which many children of high families took for granted. Perhaps he was passed over due to his adopted status, or because his family were too poor at the time.

'My father sends his regards,' she lied. Chien appeared pleased.

'Give him mine, I beg you,' he returned. 'We have a lot to thank your family for, Mistress Mishani. Did you know that my mother was a fisherwoman in your father's fleet in Mataxa Bay?'

'Is that true?' Mishani asked politely, though she knew perfectly well it was. She was frankly surprised he had brought it up. 'I had thought it only a rumour.'

'It's true,' Chien said. 'One day a young son of Blood Mumaka was visiting your father at the bay, and by Shintu's hand or Rieka's, he came face-to-face with the fisherwoman, and it was love from that moment. Isn't that a tale?'

'How beautiful,' said Mishani, thinking just the opposite. 'So like a poem or a play.' The subsequent marriage of a peasant into Blood Mumaka and the family's refusal to excise their shameful son had crippled them politically; it had taken them years to claw back their credibility, mainly due to their success in shipping. That Chien was talking about it at all was somewhat crass. Chien's mother was released from her oath to Blood Koli and given to the lovestruck young noble in return for political concessions that Blood Mumaka were still paying for today. That one foolish marriage had been granted in return for an extremely favourable deal on Blood Mumaka shipping interests in the future. It had been a shrewd move. Now that they were major traders, their promises made back then kept them tied tightly to Blood Koli, and Koli made great profit from them. Mishani could only imagine how that would chafe; it was probably only the fact that they had to make those concessions to her family that prevented them from dominating the trade lane entirely.

'Do you like poetry?' Chien inquired, using her absent comment to steer her in another direction.

'I am fond of Xalis, particularly,' she replied.

'Really? I would not have thought his violent prose would appeal to a lady of such elegance.' This was flattery, and not done well.

'The court at Axekami is every bit as violent as the battlefields Xalis wrote of,' Mishani replied. 'Only the wounds inflicted there are more subtle, and fester.'

Chien smiled crookedly and took a slice of fruit from the table. Mishani exploited the gap to take the initiative.

'I am told that you may be in a position to do a service for me,' she said.

Chien chewed slowly and swallowed, making her wait. A warm breeze rippled her dress. 'Go on,' he prompted.

'I need passage back to Saramyr,' she said.

'When?'

'As soon as possible.'

'Mistress Mishani, you've only just got here. Does Kisanth displease you that much?'

'Kisanth is a remarkable place,' she replied, evading the thrust of the question. 'Very vibrant.'

Chien studied her for a long moment. To press her further on her motives for returning would be rude. Mishani kept her features glacial as the silence drew out uncomfortably. He was evaluating her; she guessed that much. But did he know that the front she presented was a charade?

Her connection to Blood Koli was tenuous at best. Though she was officially still part of the family – the shame in having such a wayward daughter would damage their interests – they shunned her now. Her betrayal had been carefully covered up, and though the rumours inevitably spread, only a few knew the truth of it.

The story went that Mishani was travelling in the east, across the mountains, furthering the interests of Blood Koli there. In reality, her father had been relentlessly hunting for her since she had left him. She was in little doubt what would happen if he caught her. She would become a prisoner on her own estates, forced to maintain the show of solidarity in Blood Koli, to conform to the lie that they had spun to hide the dishonour she had brought upon them. And then, perhaps, she would be quietly killed.

Her nobility was a sham, a bluff. And she suspected that Chien knew that. She had hoped that a merchant trader would not have access to the kind of information that would expose her, but there was something odd about the way he was acting, and she did not trust him an inch. Her father would be a powerful friend, and he would be greatly indebted to anyone who delivered his daughter back to him.

'How soon do you have to leave?' Chien said eventually.

'Tomorrow,' she replied. In truth, she did not know how urgent their departure really was, but it was best to appear definite when bargaining.

'Tomorrow,' he repeated, unfazed.

'Can it be done?' she asked.

'Possibly,' Chien told her. He was buying himself time to think. He looked out over the lagoon, the sun casting shadows in the hollows of his broad features. Weighing the implications. 'It will cost me considerably,' he said at length. 'There will be substantial unused cargo space. No, three days from now is the absolute earliest we can be outfitted and under sail.'

'Good enough,' she said. 'You will be reimbursed. And you will have my deepest gratitude.' How convenient that a phrase like that, implying that he would be owed a favour by a powerful maritime family, could still be true when it meant literally what it said and nothing more. She did have money – the Libera Dramach would spare no expense to get their spy home – but as far as favours went, she had only what she could give, which was not much to a man like Chien. She almost felt bad about cheating him.

'I've a different proposition,' he said. 'Your offer of reimbursement is kind, but I confess I have matters to deal with in our homeland anyway, and money is not an issue here. I'd rather not hold a family as eminent as yours in my debt. Instead, I've a somewhat presumptuous request to make of you.'

Mishani waited, and her heart sank as she listened, knowing that she could not refuse and that she was playing right into his hands.

Later, it rained.

The clouds had rolled in with startling speed as the humidity ascended, and in the early afternoon the skies opened in a torrent. Out in the jungle, thick leaves nodded violently as they were battered by fat droplets; mud sluiced into streams that snaked away between the tree roots; slender waterfalls plunged through the air as rain ramped off the canopy and fell to earth, spattering boughs and rocks. The loud hiss of the downpour drowned the sound of nearby animals hooting from their shelters.

Saran, Tsata and Kaiku trudged through the undergrowth, soaked to the skin. They walked hunched under *gwattha*, hooded green ponchos woven of a native fabric that offered some protection against light rain, but not enough to keep them dry in such an onslaught. Kaiku had been given one by her guide before they set out, and had kept it rolled in a bundle and tied to her small pack; the other two had their own. Setting foot in the jungle without one was idiocy.

The rain slowed an already slow pace. Kaiku stumbled along with barely the strength to pick up her feet. None of them had slept, and they had been travelling through the night. Under ordinary conditions, Kaiku would have found this endurable; however, the long month of inactivity aboard the *Heart of Assantua*, the wound in her side and the detrimental effects of unleashing her *kana* had combined to severely curtail her stamina. But rest was out of the question, and pride forbade her from complaining. The others had trimmed their pace somewhat, but not by much. She kept up miserably, leaving it to Saran and Tsata to look out for any pursuers. Without sleep, her *kana* had not regenerated and her senses had dulled. She told herself that her companions were alert enough for the three of them.

She brooded on the fate of her guide as they made their way back to Kisanth. It saddened her that the Tkiurathi woman had never told Kaiku her name. Saramyr ritual dictated that the dead must be named to Noctu, wife of Omecha, so that she could record them in her book and advise her husband of their great deeds – or lack of them – when they came hoping for admittance to the Golden Realm. Even though the woman had most likely not believed at all, it worried at Kaiku.

Saran and Tsata conferred often in low voices and scanned the jungle with their rifles ready, the weapons wrapped in thick rags and strips of leather to keep their powder chambers dry. The downpour – which would hamper anyone following by obliterating their trail – had not seemed to ease their fears one bit. Despite Saran's reservations, Kaiku was certain that she had incinerated the assassin at the Aith Pthakath. And if there *was* a maghkriin still hunting them, Saran seemed to believe its tracking ability was nothing short of supernatural.

She found herself wondering why this man was so important, what he knew, what was worth risking her life for. She felt galled that her curiosity had not been satisfied yet. Of course, he was a spy, and she should have expected that he would not reveal his secrets easily, but it annoyed her that she should be going through all this without knowing the reason why.

Kaiku had tried to engage Saran in conversation occasionally throughout the morning, but was frustrated by his distractedness. He was too intent on watching out for enemies and jungle animals, which could be deadly even out near the coast where the land was a little more civilised. He barely listened to her. She found that it piqued her unaccountably.

By the time they stopped, exhaustion and the rain had combined to make her fatalistic. If a maghkriin was going to come, let it come. They could do nothing about it.

However, the cause of the halt was not the rest that Kaiku had hoped for.

It was Tsata who saw it first, a little way up the incline which rose to their left, overlooking their route. He darted back in a flash and pointed through the trees. Kaiku squinted through dewed lashes, but she could only see grey shadows in amid the shifting curtains of rain.

'Who is that?' Tsata asked her. Saran was at their side in a moment.

'I cannot see,' Kaiku said. The unspoken question: how should *she* know? She tried to pick out movement, but there was nothing.

Saran and Tsata exchanged a glance. 'Stay here,' Saran told her.

'Where are you going?'

'Just stay,' he said, and he disappeared into the undergrowth with a light splashing of mud. She caught a few glimpses of him heading up the incline towards where Tsata had pointed, and then he was swallowed.

She brushed her sodden fringe back and threw off her hood, suddenly feeling enclosed by it. The warm rain splashed eagerly onto her head and dribbled through to wet her scalp.

When she looked around, Tsata was gone.

The jolt of alarm woke her savagely out of her torpor. Her earlier fatalism was chased away. She drew a breath to call out for her companions, but it died in her lungs. Shouting would be a foolish thing to do.

Hurriedly, she scrambled her rifle off her back and into her arms. The lack of visibility terrified her; she would not have time to react against an attack. She had barely survived when she was out in the open back at the Aith Pthakath, and now she did not even have her *kana* as protection: she was too exhausted to open the Weave.

The pounding rain and constant, disharmonious sounds of running or dripping water masked all but the loudest noises. She blinked and wiped her eyes, glancing around in agitation.

They would be back. Any moment, they would be back, and she would be angry at the way they had deserted her with barely a warning. A branch fell behind her, and she started and whirled, narrowly missing tangling her rifle in a hanging vine. Staring intently into the rain-mist, she looked for movement.

Her sword would be better at close quarters like this, but she had never been much of a swordswoman. Most of the training she had received had built on her natural skills, learned from her constant competition with her older brother back in the Forest of Yuna. They would fight to outride, outshoot, outwrestle each other, for she always was the tomboy; but swords were never a favourite of either of them, and too dangerous to spar with. The rifle was impractical here, but it was comforting. She shifted her grip on the underside of the weapon and scanned the trees.

Time passed, drawing out slowly. They did not come back. Kaiku felt a cold dread creeping along her bones. The effort of waiting here, so exposed, was too much for her. She needed to know what was happening.

Her eyes fell again on the grey shadow that Tsata had pointed out. It still had not moved. She thought on his earlier words. *Who is that?* What did he mean?

Action, any action, was better than cowering in the rain. Even crossing the small distance that would bring her close enough to that half-obscured blot to see what it was. With one last look around, she began to tread warily up the incline, her boots sinking into the mud as she went, rivulets of water diverting to fill up the holes that she left.

The leather wrapped around the powder chamber of her rifle was sodden on the outside. She hoped that none of it had got in to wet the powder, or her rifle would be merely an expensive club. She wiped her hair away with her palm and cursed as it flopped back into her eyes. Her heart was pounding in her chest so hard that she felt her breastbone twitch with each pulse.

The grey shadow resolved all of a sudden, a gust of wind blowing the rain aside like a curtain parting with theatrical flair. It was revealed for only an instant, but that instant was enough for the image to burn itself into Kaiku's mind. Now she understood.

Who is that?

It was the guide, lashed by vines in a bundle as if she had been cocooned by a spider. She hung from the stout lower boughs of an enormous chapapa tree. Her head lolled forward, eyes staring sightlessly down, the arrow still buried in her throat. Her arms and legs were wrapped tight together, and she swayed with the sporadic assault of the rain.

Kaiku felt new panic clutch at her. The maghkriin had left it as a message. Not only that, it had predicted exactly the route its prey would take and got ahead of them. She stumbled back from the horror, slid a few inches in the dirt. Intuition screamed at her.

A maghkriin was here. Now.

It came at her from the left, covering the ground between them in the time it took her to turn her head. The world seemed to slow around her, the raindrops decelerating, her heartbeat deepening to a bass explosion. She was wrenching her rifle up, but she knew even before she began that there was no way she would get the muzzle in between her and the creature. She caught only a sharp impression of red and blackened skin, one blind eye and flailing ropes of hair; then she saw a hooked blade sweeping in to take out her throat, and there was nothing in the world she could do about it in time.

Blood hammered her face as she felt the impact, the maghkriin smashing into her and bearing her to the ground in a blaze of pain and white shock. She could not breathe, could not breathe

– drowning, like before, like in the sewers and a filthy, rotted hand holding her under –

because the air would not get to her lungs, and there was the taste of her own blood in her mouth, blood in her eyes blinding her, blood everywhere

– spirits, she couldn't breathe, couldn't breathe because her throat had been opened, hacked like a fish, her throat! –

Then movement, all around her. Saran, Tsata, pulling the weight off her chest, wrenching away the limp corpse of her attacker. She gasped in a breath, sweet, miraculous air pouring into her lungs in great whoops. Her hand went to her neck, and found it blood-slick but whole. She was being pulled roughly up out of the mud, the rain already washing the gore from her skin and into her clothes.

'Are you hurt?' Saran cried, agitated. 'Are you hurt?'

Kaiku held up a hand shakily to indicate that he should wait a moment. She was badly winded. Her eyes strayed to the muscular monstrosity that lay face-down and half-sunk in the wet earth.

'Look at me!' Saran snapped, grabbing her jaw and pulling her face around roughly. 'Are you *hurt?*' he demanded again, frantic.

She slapped his arm away, suddenly angry at being manhandled. She still did not have enough breath in her to form words. Palm to her chest, she bent over and allowed the normal airflow to return to her lungs.

'She is not hurt,' Tsata said, but whether it came out accusatory, relieved or matter-of-fact was lost amid his inexperience at the language.

'I am . . . not hurt,' Kaiku gasped, glaring at Saran. He hesitated for a moment, then retreated from her, seemingly perturbed at himself.

Tsata reached down into the mud and hauled the maghkriin over onto its back. This one was more humanoid than the last, its clothing burned away in rags to reveal a lithe body slabbed with lean muscle beneath ruddy, tough skin. Only its face was bestial: what of it there was left, anyway. One side was charred and blistered by fire; the other had splintered into bloody pulp by a rifle ball. In between the damage were crooked yellow teeth and a flat nose, and its hair was not hair at all but thin, fleshy tentacles that hung flaccid from its scalp.

Kaiku looked away.

'It was the one that you burned,' said Tsata. 'No wonder it was slow.'

'You shot it?' Kaiku asked numbly, trying to make sense of the confusion. Had he said it was *slow?* The pounding rain had cleansed the blood from her face now, but pink rivulets still raced from her sodden hair. Mud clung to her back and arms and legs. She didn't notice.

Tsata tilted his chin up. It took a moment for Kaiku to remember that this was a nod.

'You left me,' she said suddenly, looking from one to the other. 'You both left me, and you knew that thing was out there!'

'I left you with Tsata!' Saran protested, glaring at the Tkiurathi, who returned with a cool green stare, his tattooed features calm beneath his hood.

'It made sense,' Tsata said. 'The maghkriin would have hunted for you, Saran, as you went away alone. But if we were *all* alone, it would choose the most dangerous or the most defenceless prey first. That was her, on both counts.'

'You used me as *bait?*' Kaiku cried.

'I was hidden, watching you. The maghkriin did not suspect that we would willingly endanger one of our own.'

'You could have missed!' Kaiku shouted. 'It could have killed me!'

'But it did not,' Tsata said, seemingly unable to comprehend why she was angry.

Kaiku glared in disbelief at Tsata, then at Saran, who merely held up his hands to disavow any knowledge or responsibility.

'Is this some Okhamban kind of logic?' she snapped, her face flushed. She could not believe anyone would casually gamble with her life that way. 'Some spirit-cursed primitive matter of *pash?* To sacrifice the individual for the good of the group?'

Tsata looked surprised. 'Exactly that,' he said. 'You are quick to learn our ways.'

'The gods damn your ways,' she spat, and pulled her hood up over her head. 'It cannot be far now to Kisanth. We should go.'

The remainder of the journey was undertaken in silence. Though Saran's and Tsata's alertness had not diminished in the slightest, the danger seemed to have passed now, at least for Kaiku, who nursed her fury all the way to

Kisanth. When they emerged again from the jungle it was in front of Zanya's prayer gate. The sight of the pillars brought a flood of relief and weariness over Kaiku. She walked slowly over to it and gave her thanks for a safe return as ritual dictated. When she was done, she saw that Saran was doing so as well.

'I thought you of Quraal did not give credit to our heathen deities,' she said.

'We need all the deities we can get now,' he replied darkly, and Kaiku wondered if he was serious or making fun of her. She stepped through the gate and stalked onward toward the stockade wall of Kisanth, and he followed.

FIVE

Axekami, heart of the empire, basked in the heat of late summer.

The great city sat astride the confluence of two rivers as they merged into a third, a junction through which most of the trade in north-western Saramyr passed. The Jabaza and the Kerryn came winding their ways across the vast yellow-green plains from the north and east to enter the sprawling, walled capital, carving it up into neat and distinct districts. They met in the centre of Axekami, in the Rush, swirling around a hexagonal platform of stone that was linked across the churning water by three elegant, curving and equidistant bridges. In the middle stood a colossal statue of Isisya, Empress of the gods and goddess of peace, beauty and wisdom. Saramyr tradition tended to depict their deities obliquely rather than directly – as votive objects, or as animal aspects – believing it somewhat arrogant to try to capture the form of divine beings. But here tradition had been ignored, and Isisya had been rendered in dark blue stone as a woman, fifty feet high, robed in finery and wearing an elaborate sequence of ornaments in her tortuously complicated hair. She was gazing to the north-east, towards the Imperial Keep, her expression serene, her hands held together and buried in her voluminous sleeves. Beneath her feet, in the Rush, the Jabaza and the Kerryn mixed and mingled and became the Zan, an immense flow that pushed its way out of the city and headed away in a great sparkling ribbon to the south-west.

As the political and economical centre of Saramyr, Axekami was an unceasing hive of activity. The waterside was lined with docks and warehouses, and swarmed with nomads, merchants, sailors and labourers. On the south bank of the Kerryn, the colourful chaos of smoke-dens, cathouses, shops and bars that crowded the archipelago of the River District were trafficked by outrageously-dressed revellers. To the north, where the land sloped upward towards the Imperial Keep, gaudy temples crowded against serene library domes. Public squares thronged with people while orators and demagogues expounded their beliefs to passers-by, horses crabstepped between creaking carts and lumbering manxthwa in the choked thoroughfares of the Market District, while beneath their bright awnings traders hawked all the goods of the Near World. From the sweat and dust of the roads it was possible to escape to one of the many public parks, to enjoy a luxurious steam bath or visit one of a dozen sculpture gardens, some of them dating from the time of Torus tu Vinaxis, the second Blood Emperor of Saramyr.

North of the Market District, the Imperial Quarter lay around the base of the bluff which topped the hill, surmounted by the Imperial Keep itself. The Quarter was a small town in itself, inhabited by the high families, the independently wealthy and patrons of the arts, kept free from the crush and press of the rest of the city. There, the wide streets were lined with exotic trees and kept scrupulously clean, and spacious townhouses sat within walled compounds amid mosaic-strewn plazas and shady cloisters. Ruthlessly tended water gardens and leafy arbours provided endless secret places for the machinations of court to be played out in.

Then there was the Keep itself. Sitting atop the bluff, its gold and bronze exterior sent blades of reflected sunlight out across the city. It was shaped like a truncated pyramid, its top flattened, with the grand dome of the Imperial family's temple to Ocha rising in the centre to symbolise that no human, even an Emperor, was higher than the gods. The four sloping walls of the Keep were an eye-straining complexity of window-arches, balconies and sculptures, a masterwork of intertwined statues and architecture unequalled anywhere in Axekami. Spirits and demons chased their way around pillars and threaded into and out of scenes of legend inhabited by deities from the Saramyr pantheon. At each of the vertices of the Keep stood a tall, narrow tower. The whole magnificent edifice was surrounded by a massive wall, no less fine in appearance but bristling with fortifications, broken only by an enormous gate set beneath a soaring arch of gold inscribed with ancient blessings.

Inside the Keep, the Blood Emperor of Saramyr, Mos tu Batik, glowered at his reflection in a freestanding wrought-silver mirror. He was a stocky man, a few inches shorter than his width would suggest, which made him barrel-chested and solid in appearance. His jaw was clenched in barely suppressed frustration beneath a bristly beard that was shot through with grey. With terse, angry movements, he arranged his ceremonial finery, tugging his cuffs and adjusting his belt. The afternoon sun angled through a pair of window-arches into the chamber behind him, two tight beams illuminating bright dancing motes. Usually the effect was pleasing, but today the contrast just made the rest of the room seem dim and full of hot shadows.

'You should compose yourself,' creaked a voice from the back of the room. 'Your agitation is obvious.'

'Spirits, Kakre, of course I'm agitated!' Mos snapped, shifting his gaze in the mirror to where a hunched figure was moving slowly into the light from the darkness in the corner of the room. He wore a patchwork robe of rags, leather and other less easily identifiable materials, sewn together in a haphazard mockery of pattern and logic, with stitchwork like scarring tracking randomly across the folds. Buried beneath a frayed hood, the sun cut sharply across the lower half of an emaciated jaw that did not move when he spoke. The Emperor's own Weaver, the Weave-lord.

'It would not do to meet your brother-by-marriage in this condition,' Kakre continued. 'You would cause him offence.'

Mos barked a bitter laugh. 'Reki? I don't care what that bookish little whelp thinks.' He spun away from the mirror and faced the Weave-lord. 'You know of the reports I received, I assume?'

Kakre raised his head, and the radiance of Nuki's eye fell across the face beneath the hood. The True Mask of Weave-lord Kakre was that of a gaping, mummified corpse, a hollow-cheeked visage of cured skin that stretched dry and pallid over his features. Mos had found his predecessor unpleasant enough, but Kakre was worse. He would never be able to look at the Weave-lord without a flinch of distaste.

'I know of the reports,' Kakre said, his voice a dry rasp.

'Yes, I thought you would,' Mos said poisonously. 'Very little goes on in this Keep without you finding out about it, Kakre; even when it's not your concern.'

'Everything is my concern,' Kakre returned.

'Really? Then why don't you concern yourself with finding out why my crops fail year after year? Why don't you do something to stop the blight that creeps through the soil of my empire, that causes babies to be born Aberrant, that twists the trees and makes it dangerous for my men to travel near the mountains because the gods know what kind of monstrosities lurk there now?' Mos stamped across to where a table held a carafe of wine and poured himself a generous glassful. 'It's almost Aestival Week! Unless the goddess Enyu herself steps in and lends us a hand, this year is going to be worse than the last one. We're on the edge of famine, Kakre! Some of the more distant provinces have been rationing the peasants for too long already! I *needed* this crop to hold out against the damned merchant consortium in Okhamba!'

'Your people starve because of *you*, Mos,' Kakre replied venomously. 'Do not apportion blame to the Weavers for your own mistakes. You started the trade war when you raised export taxes.'

'What would you have preferred?' he cried. 'That I allowed our economy to collapse?'

'I care little for your justifications,' Kakre said. 'The fact remains that it was your fault.'

He drained the glass and glared balefully at the Weave-lord. 'We took this throne *together*,' he snarled. 'It cost me my only son, but we took it. I fulfilled my part of the deal. I've made you part of the empire. I gave you land, I gave you *rights*. That was my half of our agreement. Where is yours?'

'We have kept you on your throne!' Kakre replied, his voice rising in fury. 'Without us, your ineptitude would have seen you deposed by now. Do you remember how many insurrections I have warned you of, how many plots and assassination attempts I have unearthed for you? Five years of failing harvests, crumbling markets, political disarray; the high families will not suffer it.' Kakre's voice fell to a quiet mutter. 'They want you gone, Mos. You and me.'

'It's *because* of the failed harvests that this whole damned mess has come about!' Mos cried, choking on his frustration. 'It's this spirit-cursed blight! Where is the source? What is the cause? *Why don't you know?*'

'The Weavers are not all-powerful, my Emperor,' croaked Kakre softly, turning away. 'If we were, we should not need you.'

'There he is!' grinned the Empress Laranya, slipping away from her fussing handmaidens and hurrying across the small chamber to where Mos had just entered. She swept into the Emperor's arms and kissed him playfully, then withdrew and smoothed his hair back from his face, her eyes roaming his.

'You look angry,' she said. 'Is anything wrong?' She smiled suddenly. 'Anything that I could not fix, anyway?'

Mos felt his bad mood evaporate in the arms of his lover, and he bent to kiss her again, with feeling this time. 'There's nothing that you couldn't fix with that smile,' he murmured.

'Flatterer!' she accused, darting out of his grasp with a flirtatious twist. 'You're late. And your clumsy paws have ruffled my dress. Now my handmaidens will have to put it right. Everything must be in order in time to receive my brother.'

'My apologies, Empress,' he said, bowing low with mock sincerity. 'I had no idea that today was such an important day for you.'

She gasped in feigned disbelief. 'Men are so ignorant.'

'Well, if I'm going to be insulted so, I may go back to my chambers and get out of your way,' Mos teased.

'You will stay here and make ready with me!' she told him. 'That is, if you still want to have an Empress by tomorrow.'

Mos acceded graciously, taking his place by his wife and allowing his own handmaidens to see to his appearance. They began spraying him with perfumed oils and affixing the paraphernalia that tradition demanded of his station. He endured it all with a lighter heart than before.

The pomp and ceremony involved in being Blood Emperor taxed his patience at the best of times; he was a blunt man, not given to subtlety and with little time for ritual and age-old tradition. The process of welcoming an important guest for an extended stay was complex and layered in many levels of politeness and formality, depending on the status of the guest in relation to the Imperial family. Too little preparation, and the guest might be offended; too overblown, and they would be embarrassed. Mos wisely left all such matters to his advisers and latterly to his new wife.

The chamber around him was aswarm with retainers clad in their finest robes, Imperial Guards in white and blue armour, servants carrying pennants and elegant courtesans tuning their instruments. Handmaidens ran to and fro, and Mos's Cultural Adviser sent runners here and there to fetch forgotten necessities and make last-minute adjustments. The entrance hall was only the surface gloss to the entire operation. Later, there would be theatre, poetry, music and a myriad other entertainments that were all but interminable to a man of Mos's earthy tastes. Only the feast that would signal the end of the ceremony held any interest for him at all. But despite his own feelings about their visitor, this was Laranya's brother, to whom she was very close, and what made her happy made him happy. He steeled himself and resolved to make an effort.

As the final touches were being made to his outfit, he stole glances at Laranya, who pretended not to notice. How strange the ways of the gods, that they should have brought him a creature as fine as her at this time in his life, approaching his fifty-fifth harvest. Surely divine approval for his assumption of the role of Blood Emperor. Or, he reflected with a twinge of his former black mood, perhaps it was merely redressing the balance for taking his son Durun from him.

It had begun as a simple matter of politics. With his only heir dead and Blood Batik as the high family, Mos needed a child. His first wife, Ononi, was past child-bearing age, so Mos annulled his marriage with her and sought a younger bride. There was no acrimony on either side, since there had been no passion there in the first place; it had been a marriage of mutual advantage, as were most amid the high families of Saramyr. Ononi remained to oversee the Blood Batik estates to the north, while Mos moved into the capital and began to look for potential matches.

He found one in Laranya tu Tanatsua, daughter of Barak Goren of Jospa, a city in the Tchom Rin desert. Forging ties with the eastern half of Saramyr was a sensible move, especially when the mountains that divided them were becoming ever more treacherous to cross and increasingly the only way to communicate between the west and the east was through Weavers. Laranya was eminently eligible and beautiful with it, dark-haired and dusky-skinned, curvaceous and fiery. Mos had liked her immediately, better than the slender, demure and subservient women he had been offered up until then. In a move of outrageous audacity, Laranya had made him come to her, had made him travel all the way to Jospa to assess her suitability for marriage. Even when he had done so, intrigued by her brazen nerve, she had acted as if it were *she* choosing *him* for a suitor, much to her father's chagrin.

Perhaps it was then that she had captured his heart. She had certainly captured his attention. He took her back with him to Axekami, and they were married amid great ceremony and celebration. That was three years ago, and at some point over the intervening time he had fallen in love with her, and she with him. It was unusual, but not unheard of. That she was over twenty harvests his junior was not an issue. Both of them were stubborn, passionate and used to getting their own way; in each other, they met their match. Though their arguments were legendary among the servants of the Keep for their violence, so their affection for each other was immeasureable and obvious. Despite the misfortune that had dogged every step of his way as Blood Emperor, he felt blessed to have her.

There had been only one shadow over their marriage these past years, and the root of most of their fights. Though the physical attraction between them made for energetic and frequent bedplay, no child had come of it. Laranya wanted nothing more than to bear him a son, but she could not conceive, and the bitterness and frustration began to pool like oil beneath their words over time. Unlike his son Durun – who had gone through the same ordeal with his own wife, the murdered former Blood Empress Anais tu Erinima – Mos knew that he was not barren of seed. Yet he knew also that an heir was needed, and Laranya would not graciously step aside as Ononi had to allow him to remarry again. Even if he had wanted to.

Then, miraculously, it had happened. Two weeks ago, she had told him the news. She was pregnant. He saw it already in her manner, the new flush to her cheeks, the secret smiles she kept to herself when she thought he was not looking. Her world had turned inward, to the child in her womb, and Mos was at once mystified and entranced by her. Even now, though she was far from showing her condition, he watched her unconsciously lay a hand on her pelvis, her eyes distant while the handmaidens chattered and worked around her. His child. The thought brought a fierce and sudden grin to his face.

He straightened himself as a horn lowed outside the Keep, and the handmaidens scattered, leaving the Emperor and Empress standing on a low platform at the top of a set of three steps, facing down an aisle of immaculately presented retainers and Guards. The hall whispered with the shuffle of people arranging themselves in their places. The red-and-silver pennants of Blood Batik rippled softly in the hot breeze from the window-arches above the gold-inlaid double doors. Reki had arrived.

Laranya took Mos's hand briefly and smiled up at him, then let it drop to assume the correct posture. The Blood Emperor's heart warmed until it was like a furnace. He thought of the gruelling day ahead, and then of the life growing in his wife's belly.

He was to be a father again, he thought, as the double doors swung open and let in the blazing light from outside, silhouetting the slight form of Laranya's brother at the head of his retinue. For that, he would endure anything.

The coals in the fire-pit at the centre of Kakre's skinning chamber bathed the room in arterial red. Deep, insidious shadows lay all around, cast by the steady glow. At the Weave-lord's insistence, the walls had been stripped down to naked stone and the black, semi-reflective *lach* chiselled away from the floor to reveal the gullied, rough bricks beneath. Overhead, the octagonal chamber rose high above in a lattice of wooden beams, its upper reaches lost in darkness. Chains and hooks hung from there, appearing out of the lofty shadows and hanging down to the level of the floor, where they brushed this way and that in the rising warmth, quietly clinking.

Strange shapes swayed gently between the beams, half-seen things turning slowly and silently. Some of them were hung close enough to the firelight to make out details, underlit in glowering red. Kites of skin, human and animal, stretched across wicker frameworks of terrible ingenuity. Some were mercifully unrecognisable, simple geometric shapes from which it was difficult to determine the donor of the material that surfaced them. Others were more grotesque and artistic. There was a large bird stitched from the skin of a woman; distorted, empty features were still appallingly identifiable over the head and beak, hollow breasts pulled flat between the outspread wings, long black hair still spilling from her scalp. Something that had once been a man hung in a predatory pose, outstretched bat-wings of human skin spread behind him and his face constructed of sewn-together strips of snake scales. A mobile of small animals rotated next to him, each one skilfully peeled on the left side of its front half and the right side of its rear, particoloured sculptures of fur and glistening striations of muscle.

Closer to hand, placed on the walls like trophies, were works in progress or pieces that Kakre was particularly fond of. Black pits that were once eye sockets stared blindly across the chamber from wicker skulls. No matter how changed the form of the being, it was impossible to forget where that dry, stretched surface had been robbed from, and each horror was magnified by the memory. An iron rack stood near the firepit, diabolical in its craftsmanship, capable of being adapted to suit any type of body shape and any size. The stones beneath it were dyed a deep, rusty brown.

Kakre sat cross-legged by the fire-pit, a ragged heap of clothes with a dead face, and Weaved.

He was a ray: a flat, winged shape, infinitesimal in an undulating world of black. He hung in the darkness, rippling slightly, making the tiny adjustments necessary to maintain his position while he probed out along the currents in search of his route. Above and below him and to either side were whorls and eddies, riptides and channels, currents that he could only feel and not see, a violent, lethal churning that could pick him up and dash him apart. He sensed the vast and distant leviathans that haunted the periphery of his senses, the inexplicable denizens of the Weave.

He was blind here in this sightless place, but the water rushed around and through him, over his cold skin and into his mouth, out past his gills or down to his stomach, diffusing into his blood. In his mind, he saw how the currents twisted and corkscrewed and curled in ways impossible for water or wind, tracing each one to where it intersected another, junctions in the chaotic void.

In an instant he had plotted a route of staggering mathematical complexity, a three-dimensional tunnel of currents that flowed in his favour, leading him to where he had to go in the shortest time and with the least effort. Not that physical distance had any bearing in the world of the Weave, but it was a human trait to impose order on the orderless, and this was Kakre's way of understanding a process that could not be understood.

The raw stuff of the Weave was too much for a man's sanity to bear, too alluring and enticing. A proportion of apprentice Weavers were lost every year to the terrifying ecstasy of being opened to the bright fabric of creation, the sheer and overwhelming beauty of it. It was a narcotic beyond anything that the organic world could provide, and in that first rush only the strongest were resilient enough to avoid being swept away, lost to the Weave, mindless phantoms blissfully wandering the stitchwork of the universe while their vacated bodies became vegetative. Weavers were taught from the very first to visualise the Weave in a way that they could cope with. Some thought of it as an endless series of spider's webs; some as a pulsing mass of branching bronchioli; some as a building of impossible dimensions in which any door could lead to any other; some a sequential dream-story in which the process of getting from the start to the finish mirrored the effect that their Weaving was intended to accomplish.

Kakre found it most accommodating like this. More fluid, more dynamic, and never once letting him forget how dangerous the Weave was. Even now, after so many years, he found himself having to rattle hypnotic mantras around in the back of his mind to ward off the constantly encroaching sense of wonder and awe at his surroundings. He knew well that such feelings were merely a sly route to the addiction that would follow if he relaxed his self-control, and once lost he would never be regained.

Now he had the route mapped in his consciousness, and with a tilt of his wings he dropped down into the current beneath him. It threw him forward with a breathless rush, accelerating faster than thought, swifter than instinct. Into a cross-current he dived, riding the maelstrom smoothly, and was flung out again at even greater velocity. Now switching again, more cross-currents, dozens of them coming so rapidly that they were virtually continuous. He was flicking like a spark through the synapses of the human brain, seeing every ebb and flow and countering or riding them with exhilarating grace, quicker and quicker until—

—the world blossomed outwards, sight returning to him, crude human senses replacing the infinitely more subtle ones employed in the Weave. A room; a room built with uneven walls, lines measured by an idiot's hand in a mockery of symmetry. Thin needles of sculpted rock broke through the floor like stalagmites, a forest of strange obelisks marked in nonsense-language. Lamps rested in sconces, some new and burning sullenly, some cold and webbed over. It was dark and shadowy and steeped in an ancient awareness that bled from the walls. He felt the shift and stir of the abominations that haunted the mines far beneath. He sensed the strange delirium of the other Weavers. Here at Adderach, mountain monastery, stronghold and founding-place of the Weavers, the colossal singularity of purpose that united all the wearers of the True Masks resonated more powerfully than ever.

He was a ghost in the chamber, hanging in the air, a hunched and blurred comma. Only his Mask appeared in sharp focus; the hood and rags that surrounded it became progressively less clear with distance. Three other Weavers stood before him, a random trio whom he had never met before. All wore their heavy patchwork robes, their clothing made unique by the lack of rhyme or reason in its construction. They had responded to his summons and awaited him here. They would listen, and advise, with the voice of the entity that was the Weavers, the guiding gestalt presence that even the Weavers themselves, in their insanity, could not identify. These three would then disseminate what information he had to give across the network.

It was time to set things in motion.

'Weave-lord Kakre,' began one them, who wore a Mask of leather and bone. 'We must know of the Emperor and his actions.'

'Then I have much to tell you,' Kakre said hoarsely, his ruined throat making his voice raw and flayed.

'The harvest fails again,' said the second of the trio, whose face was shaped from thin iron, in the shape of a snarling demon. 'Famine will strike. How do we stand?'

'The Blood Emperor Mos loses patience,' Kakre replied. 'He is frustrated at our lack of progress in stopping the blight that twists his crops. He still has no inkling that it is we who are *causing* it. I had hoped that the harvest would hold for longer than this, but it seems the change in the land is more rapid than even we had guessed.'

'This is grave,' said the first Weaver.

'We cannot disguise this,' Kakre said. 'The damage is becoming too pronounced to ignore, and too obvious to hide. Several have already traced the blight to its source; more do so with each passing year. We cannot continue to silence them all. Questions are being asked, and by people that we do not dare to coerce.' Kakre shifted in the air, blurring in and out of focus.

'If it were known that the famine is our doing, it would be the excuse that all Saramyr has been waiting for to destroy us,' said the Weaver with the iron Mask.

'Could they? Could they destroy us?' demanded the first.

'Unlikely,' Kakre croaked. 'Five years ago, maybe.'

'You are overconfident, Kakre,' whispered the third Weaver, wearing an exquisite wooden Mask with an expression of terrific sadness. 'What of the Heir-Empress? What of the presence that Vyrrch warned us of, the *woman* that could play the Weave? You have not found either, in five years of searching.'

'There is no indication the Heir-Empress is alive at all,' Kakre replied slowly, his words crossing the Weave and arriving as a sonorous echo. 'There remains the possibility that she perished in the Imperial Keep and was burned. She may have died after she escaped. I am under no illusion as to how dangerous she is, but she is considerably less dangerous now that we have disposed of her mother and she no longer stands to inherit the throne.'

'She is still a rallying point for discontent,' argued the first and most vocal Weaver. 'And the people may even prefer an Aberrant on the throne to Mos when the famine begins to bite.'

'We would not allow that,' Kakre said calmly. 'The Heir-Empress, and the woman that beat the Weave-lord Vyrrch, are dangers that we can do nothing about now, and unquantifiable. They have evaded our best attempts to find them. Put these matters aside. We must decide what to do *now*.'

'Then what do you propose?' murmured the third Weaver.

Kakre's ghost-image turned to face the one who had spoken. 'We cannot afford to wait any longer. We must embark upon our schemes in earnest. Mos's unpopularity will bring civil war again, and we cannot stand with him without revealing our hand. That we will not do. He has served his purpose; he is worthless to us now.'

There was a murmur of agreement from those assembled.

'Mos's time as Blood Emperor is becoming short,' Kakre continued. 'Blood Kerestyn are rebuilding their forces, and forming secret alliances with the other high families. The people stir in discontent, and superstition is rife. Some believe that the Weavers should never have been given power, that the gods have cursed the land because of it. It is a movement that is gaining much sympathy in the rural areas beyond the cities.' He swept them all with his gaze. 'We must see to our own survival.'

'You have a plan, then?' prompted the bone-and-leather Mask.

'Oh, indeed,' replied Kakre.

SIX

Screams.

Lan hadn't imagined anything so awful could emerge from a human throat, never believed that such a naked shriek of animal terror could be made by an intelligent being. Never dreamed he would be hearing it from his own mother.

It was a perfect day, the occasional sparse train of tiny, puffy clouds freckling what was otherwise a clear blue sky, blending to a turquoise hue near the horizon. The *Pelaska* lazed down the centre of the Kerryn, the huge paddle-wheels at either side idle while the current took the lumbering barge westward from the Tchamil Mountains, heading towards Axekami. They were ahead of schedule, perhaps a half-day east of the fork where the river split and its southward channel became the Rahn, flowing into the wilds of the Xarana Fault. It had begun to seem that nothing would go wrong.

The journey had been a nervous one. Lan had wanted to beg his father not to take the Weaver and his cargo, but he would have been wasting his breath. They had no choice.

And now his mother was screaming.

They had been moored up in the tiny town of Jiji, at the feet of the mountains, loading in metals and ores and surplus equipment from the mines to deliver to Axekami. It was their bad luck that theirs was the only barge there with sufficient capacity for the Weaver's needs.

The Weavers ran their own fleet of barges, which plied the rivers of western Axekami and were viewed with mistrust by all. The barge-masters were cold-eyed, taciturn and strange, and tales circulated up and down the waterways about these damned men who had made pacts with the Weavers in return for riches and power. Exactly where the riches and power came from was unclear: the barges hardly turned a profit, trading enough only to cover their operating costs. For the rest of the time, they passed silently by the ports and rarely docked, running secret errands of their own.

The Weaver commandeered the craft and crew and demanded passage, declaring that he had an urgent delivery to make and that none of the Weavers' own barges were near. Lan's father, Pori, accepted his fate stoically. Their patron would be furious at having one of his barges commandeered;

but being of the peasant class, the barge-folk's lives were a Weaver's to command, or to take.

Lan was terrified of their new passenger. Like most people of Saramyr, he had attended the sporadic gatherings that occurred throughout his childhood when a Weaver arrived in town to preach. The fascination never waned. These strange, fearful, enigmatic men, hidden behind their grotesquely beautiful Masks and clothed in patchwork furs and fabrics, were a sight to see. They talked of Aberrants: evil, deformed monstrosities that desired to subvert the Saramyr way. Aberrants came in many guises. Some wore their deformities on the outside, twisted or crooked, limbless or lame. Others were more subtle and hence more dangerous: those who looked like normal people, but who harboured within them strange and terrible powers. The Weavers taught them how to recognise the taint and what to do when they found it. Execution was the most lenient of recommendations.

Root out the evil, the Weavers urged. Let nothing stop you. Aberrants are a corruption of humanity. It was a message that had been repeated for generations now, and was as ingrained in the Saramyr consciousness as the virtues of tradition and duty that underpinned their society.

But in those gatherings Lan had been one of a crowd, safe in their numbers, able to leave whenever he chose. There had been tales told of the Weavers' terrible appetites, but nobody was sure how much was truth and how much fancy. There was a shiver of danger about them, but nothing more.

Now, however, they were forced to live with a Weaver for at least a week, maybe longer, for they had no idea where their passenger wanted to go and he would not tell them beyond an indication that they were heading downriver. A week spent in fear of some insane whim or demand, trapped within the confines of the barge, avoiding the blank gaze of that dry grey sealskin Mask with its puckered eyes and sewn-up mouth.

And if the Weaver were not bad enough, there was the question of the cargo that he would bring aboard. Instead of loading up at Jiji, they had been informed that they would be stopping along the way. Pori asked where, and had been backhanded across the face for his trouble.

They were forced to set off immediately. Thankfully they already had most of their own goods loaded, mainly barrels of surplus ignition powder from the mines, where it was used for blasting. They were selling it back to the city, where the civil unrest was pushing prices of firearms and powder up as demand increased. The trip might not be entirely wasted; if the Weaver were agreeable they could stop in Axekami to deliver it and fulfil their contract. But then, they had no idea how much space this mysterious new cargo would take up, nor whether they might have to throw out some of their own en route to accommodate it.

The Weaver took the cabin that belonged to Pori and his wife Fuira. That was to be expected; it was the best. Pori was the master of the *Pelaska*. They moved without complaint to the crew's quarters, where Lan slept along with the bargemen and wheelmen. Lan might have been the master's son, but when they were on the river he was no more than another barge-boy, and he swabbed decks with the rest of them.

The first night they were underway, the Weaver brought them to a stop on the port side of the river and made them moor up against the bank. There was nothing there but the trees of the Forest of Yuna crowding in, with the Kerryn carving a trail through what was otherwise a dense wall of undergrowth and foliage. The night was dark, with only one moon riding in the sky, and the current was treacherous there. By the pale green light of Neryn, they managed to secure the craft against the bank with ropes and anchors, and lower a gangplank. When they were done, they glanced at each other and wondered what was in store for them next.

They were not left to wonder long. The Weaver ordered them all below decks, into the crew quarters, and locked them in there.

Lan listened to the griping of the sailors in breathless silence while his father and mother sat calmly next to him on a bunk. Their curses and anger were practically blasphemous. He could not believe they dared to criticise a Weaver; nor did he think it was safe to do so, even out of their target's earshot. But they went on damning the name of the Weavers, pacing their cramped quarters like caged animals. They might have been bound by law and duty to do as the Weaver said, but they did not have to like it. Lan cringed, half-expecting some indefinable retribution to descend upon them; but all that happened was that his father leaned over to him and said softly: 'Remember this, Lan. Five years ago, men like these would not have dared say such things. Look how a mistreated man's anger can make him overcome his fears.'

Lan did not understand. Until this journey, the only thing on his mind had been the upcoming Aestival Week which would mark his fourteenth harvest. He had the sense that his father was imparting some grave wisdom to him, some instinct that told him the comment meant more than it appeared to. But he was only a barge-boy.

It was dawn when the Weaver released them. Most of the bargemen had gone to sleep by then. Those that had stayed awake had heard strange cries from the forest that had made them swear hurried oaths to the gods and make warding signs. The decks were too thick to hear the sounds of the cargo being loaded, but they had to presume that whatever was being put aboard had been brought out of the depths of the forest, and that there were more hands than the Weaver's alone at work. Yet when the lock clicked back and the men were released, there was only the Weaver on the deck, his grey mask impassive in the golden light of the newly rising sun. Despite their furious words of the previous night, the bargemen were less than belligerent as they emerged under the cold gaze of their sinister passenger. None of them dared to ask what had occurred the previous night, nor what kind of cargo now resided in the belly of the barge that was too secret to allow them to lay their eyes on it.

The Weaver took Pori aside and spoke to him, after which Pori addressed the crew, and told them what they had all been expecting. None of them would be allowed to go down to the cargo hold. It was locked, and the Weaver had the key. Anyone attempting to do so would be killed.

After that, the Weaver retreated to his cabin.

The next few days passed without incident. The Weaver stayed inside, seen only when his meals were delivered or his chamber pot was emptied. The sailors listened at the door of the hold and heard scrapes of movement inside, strange grunts and scuffles; but no one dared try to get in and see what was making them. They grumbled, aired their superstitions, and cast suspicious and fearful glances at the cabin where the Weaver had entrenched himself, but Pori hounded them all back to work. Lan was glad of it. Mopping the decks meant he could keep his mind off the baleful presence in his parents' bed and the secret cargo below decks. He found that by not thinking about them, he could pretend that they were not there. It was remarkably effective.

Nuki's eye shone benevolently down over the Kerryn with the pleasant heat of late summer. The air was alive with dancing clouds of midges. Pori walked the barge, ensuring everyone was doing his part. His mother Fuira cooked in the galley, occasionally emerging to share a few words with her husband or give Lan an embarrassing kiss on the cheek. Hookbeaks hovered over the water, floating in the sky on their smoothly curved wings, searching the flow for the silver glint of fish. As time drifted past in the slow wake of the *Pelaska*, it was almost possible to believe that this was a normal voyage again.

Not any more.

The Weaver must have grabbed her as she came to deliver his midday meal. Pori had always been uncomfortable with his wife having any contact with the Weaver at all, but she had told him not to be silly. She handed out the meals to everyone else on the barge; it was her duty to feed their unwanted guest as well. Perhaps he had just finished Weaving, sending his secret messages or completing some other unfathomable task; Lan had heard that some Weavers became very violent and strange after they used their powers. He could imagine her standing there, ringing the brass chime for permission to enter, and the Weaver appearing, all fury and anger, dragging her inside. The Weaver was small and crooked as most of them were, but Fuira would not dare to fight and besides, they had ways to make people do as they wanted.

Then, the screams.

The cabin door was shut, and the bargemen were gathered around it in fear and impotent rage. Lan stood with them, trembling, his eyes fixed on the spilled tray of food on the deck. He wanted to get away from there, to dive off the side of the *Pelaska* and silence her cries in the dull roar underwater. He wanted to rush in and help her. Instead he was paralysed. Nobody could interfere. It would mean their lives.

So he listened to his mother's suffering, numb and detached from the reality of the situation, and did not dare to think what was being done to her in there.

'*No!*' came his father's voice from behind him, and there was a rush of movement as the bargemen hurried to restrain him. '*Fuira!*'

Lan turned and saw Pori in the midst of four men, who were pulling a rifle out of his grip. He was flailing and thrashing with the strength of the possessed, his face contorted in rage. The rifle was torn free and slid across the deck, and then suddenly there was a scrape of steel and the bargemen fell away from him, one of them swearing and clutching a long, bleeding cut on his forearm.

'*That's my wife!*' Pori screamed, spittle flying from his lips. A short, curved blade was in his hand. He glared at them all, his face a deep red, then he plunged through the crowd and shoved open the door of the cabin with a cry.

The door slammed shut behind him, though whether by his hand or some other force Lan never knew. He heard his father's shout of rage, and a moment later something heavy smashed into the inside of the door, splintering the thick wood. There was a beat of silence. Then a new scream from his mother, long, sustained, ragged at the edges. Blood began to seep through the cracks in the door, and crawled slowly down to drip onto the deck.

Lan stood where he was, immobile, as the Weaver went back to work on his mother. He was watching the slow, dreadful path of the blood. Disbelief and shock had settled in, hazing his mind. At some point, he turned and walked away. None of the bargemen noticed him go, nor did they notice him picking up his father's rifle on the way. He did not really know where he was heading, motivated only by some vague impulse that refused to cohere into a form he could understand. He was barely aware of moving at all until he found himself standing in front of the door to the cargo hold, hidden in the shade at the bottom of a set of wooden stairs, and he could go no further.

He raised his rifle and fired into the lock, blasting it to shards.

There was something in here, something that he was looking for, but whenever he tried to picture it he only saw that insidious blood, and his mother's face.

His father was dead. His mother was being . . . *violated.*

He was here for something, but what? It was too terrible to think about, so he didn't think.

The cargo hold was hot and dark and spacious. He knew from memory the dimensions of the place, how high the ribbed wooden ceiling went, how far back the bow wall lay. Crates and barrels were dim shadows nearby, lashed together with rope. Thin lines of sunlight where the tar had worn away on the deck above provided meagre illumination, but not enough to see by until his eyes had adjusted to the gloom from the blinding summer's day outside. Absently, he reprimed the bolt on his father's rifle, taking a step into the hold, searching. There were running footsteps overhead.

Something stirred.

Lan's eyes flickered to the source of the sound. He squinted into the gloom.

It moved then, a slow flexing that allowed him to pick out its shape. The blood drained from his face.

He staggered backward, holding his rifle defensively across his chest. There were *things* down here. As he watched, more of them began to creep from the shadows. They were making a soft trilling sound, like a flock of pigeons, but their predatory lope made them seem anything but benign, and they approached with a casually lethal gait.

Shouts behind him. Bargemen running down the steps to the hold, attracted by the sound of the rifle.

Fuira shrieked distantly, a forlorn wail of loss and agony and fear, and Lan suddenly recalled what he was here for.

Ignition powder. The cargo.

A tidy stack of barrels lay against the stern wall, by the door where the other bargemen had rushed into the hold. They scrambled to a halt, partially because they had remembered the Weaver's edict, mostly because they thought Lan's gun was levelled at them. The darkness made it hard to see. He was aiming at the barrels. Enough there to blast the *Pelaska* to flinders and leave barely a trace of any of them.

It was the only way to end his mother's suffering. The only way.

Behind him, there was the sound of dozens of creatures breaking into a run, and the trilling reached shrieking pitch in his ears.

He whispered a short prayer to Omecha, squeezed the trigger, and the world turned to flame.

SEVEN

The Xarana Fault lay far to the south of the Saramyr capital of Axekami, across a calm expanse of plains and gentle hills. In stark contrast to its approach, the Fault itself was a jagged, rucked chaos of valleys, plateaux, outcrops, canyons and steep-sided rock masses like miniature mountains. Sheer walls abutted sunken rivers; hidden glades nestled in cradles of sharp stones; the very ground was a shattered jigsaw which rose and fell to no apparent geological law. The Fault was a massive scar in the land, over two hundred and fifty miles from end to end and forty at its thickest point, cutting west to east and slanting slightly southwards on its way.

Legend had made it a cursed place, and there was more than a little truth in that. Once, the first Saramyr city of Gobinda had been built there, before a great destruction – said to be the wrath of Ocha in retribution for the pride of the third Blood Emperor Bizak tu Cho – had wiped it away. Restless things remembered that time, and still roamed the hollows and deeps of the Fault, preying on the unwary. It was shunned, at first as a symbol of Saramyr's shame but later as a place where lawlessness abounded, where only bandits and those foolhardy enough to brave the whispered terrors within would go.

But for some, the Fault was a haven. Dangerous though it was, there were those who were willing to learn its ways and make their home there. At first it was a place for criminals, who used it as a long-term base from which to raid the Great Spice Road to the west; but later, more people came, fleeing the world outside. Those under sentence of death, those whose temperament made them too alien to live among normal people, those who sought the deep riches exposed at the bottom of the Fault and were prepared to risk anything to get it. Settlements were founded, small at first but then becoming larger as they amalgamated or conquered others. Aberrants – who would be executed on sight in any lawful town – began to appear, looking for sanctuary from the Weavers who hunted them.

The home of the Libera Dramach was one such community. It was known to its inhabitants as the Fold, both to imply a sense of belonging and because of the valley in which the settlement was built. It was constructed across an overlapping series of plateaux and ledges that tumbled down the blunt western end of the valley, linked together by stairs, wooden bridges and pulley-lifts. The Fold cluttered and piled up on itself in a heap, a confusing mishmash of architecture from all over Saramyr, built by many hands and not all of them skilled. It was an accretion of dwellings raised over twenty-five years to no overarching plan or pattern; instead, newcomers had made their homes wherever they would fit, and in some cases they only barely did.

Off the dirt tracks that wound haphazardly across the uneven terrain, rickety storefronts sold whatever the merchants could get this far into the Fold. Bars peddled liquor from their own stills, smokehouses offered amaxa root and other narcotics for those who could afford it. Dusky Tchom Rin children in their traditional desert garb walked alongside Newlandsmen from the far northeast; an Aberrant youth with mottled skin and yellow eyes like a hawk's kissed deeply with an elegant girl from the wealthy Southern Prefectures; a priest of Omecha knelt in a small and sheltered shrine to make an offering to his deity; a soldier walked the streets, lightly tapping the pommel of his sword, alert for any trouble.

Amid the immediate clutter of houses were the fortifications. Guard-towers and outposts rose above the crush. Walls had been built, their boundaries overrun by the growing town, and newer ones constructed further out. Fire-cannons looked east over the valley. On the rocky rim, which sheltered the Fold from prying eyes, a thick stockade hid between the pleats and dips of the land. In the Xarana Fault, danger was never very far away, and the people of the Fold had learned to defend themselves.

Lucia tu Erinima stood on the balcony of her guardian's house, on one of the uppermost levels of the town, and fed crumbs to tiny piping birds from her cupped hand. A pair of ravens, perched on the guttering of the building opposite, watched her with a careful eye. From within the house, sharing a brew of hot, bitter tea, Zaelis and Cailin watched her also.

'Gods, she's grown so much,' Zaelis sighed, turning away to face his companion.

Cailin smiled faintly, but the black-and-red pattern of alternating triangles on her lips made her look like a smirking predator. 'If I were a more cynical woman, I would think that you engineered the kidnapping of your erstwhile pupil all those years ago just so you could adopt her for yourself.'

'Ha!' he barked. 'You think I haven't been over *that* in my mind enough times?'

'And what did you decide?'

'That I worry far more since I became her surrogate father than I ever did in all the years since I started the Libera Dramach.'

'You have looked after them both admirably,' Cailin said, then took a sip from the small green tea-bowl in her hand.

Zaelis gave her a surprised look. 'That's unusually kind of you, Cailin,' he said.

'I am occasionally capable of being so.'

Zaelis turned his attention back to the balcony where Lucia stood. Once, she had been the heir to the Saramyr Empire. Now she was just a girl a few weeks from her fourteenth harvest, standing in the sun in a simple white dress, feeding birds. Her blonde hair, once long, was cut short and exposed the nape of her neck, from which terrible burn scars ran down her back. He wished she would grow her hair again; her scars were easy enough to conceal. But when he asked her she would only give him that fey, dreamy look of hers and ignore him. She was pretty as a child, and now that the bones of her face and body were lengthening it was already easy to see that she would be beautiful as a woman, with the same petite and deceptively naïve features that her mother had. But in those pale blue eyes there was a strangeness that made her unfathomable to him, to *anyone*. He had known her longer than anyone alive, but he still didn't know her.

'I worry also,' Cailin said eventually.

'About Lucia?'

'Among other things.'

'Then you mean her . . .' – Zaelis searched for a word with an expression of faint disgust – '*followers*.'

Cailin shook her head once, her black ponytails swinging gently with the movement. 'I will admit they are a problem. It is far harder to keep her secret from those who would harm her when rumour spreads from the mouths of those who would keep her safe. Yet they do not concern me overly, and they may eventually prove to serve a purpose.'

Zaelis sipped his tea meditatively and stole a glance at Lucia. Several of the birds were perched on the balcony rail now, looking at her like children attentive to a master. 'What troubles you, then?'

Cailin stirred and stood. At her full height, she was tall for a woman, and of deliberately fearsome appearance. Zaelis, from where he sat cross-legged on a mat by the low table, followed her up with his eyes. She walked a few paces across the room and stopped, looking away from him.

'We are short of time,' she said.

'You know this?' Zaelis asked.

Cailin hesitated, then made a negative noise. 'I feel it.'

Zaelis frowned. It was not like Cailin to be so indefinite with him. She was a practical woman, little given to flights of fancy. He waited for her to continue.

'I know how that sounds, Zaelis,' she snapped irritably, as if he had accused her. 'I wish I had more evidence to present you.'

He got up and stood with her, favouring one leg. His other was weak; it had been badly broken long ago and never quite healed. 'Tell me what you feel, then.'

'Things are building to a head,' Cailin replied after a short pause to marshal her thoughts. 'The Weavers have been too quiet these past years. What have they gained from their alliance with Mos? Think, Zaelis. What moves they had to make, they could have made directly after Mos took power. They had nobody to oppose them then. But what did they do instead?'

'They bought land. They bought land, and shipping companies on the rivers.'

'Legitimate enterprises,' Cailin said, throwing a slender hand up as if to dash the words away. 'And none that turn any kind of profit.' Her frustration was evident in her tone. The Libera Dramach had been unsuccessful at gaining any further information on the Weavers' curious purchases. The Weavers had defences that ordinary spies could not penetrate, and Cailin dared not use any of the Red Order for fear of revealing them. One captured Sister could bring the whole delicate network down.

'This is old news, Cailin,' Zaelis said. 'Why is it bothering you now?'

'I do not know,' Cailin replied. 'Perhaps because I cannot see their plan. There are too many unanswered questions.'

'Yours has been the loudest voice arguing for secrecy these past years,' he reminded her. 'We have been content to consolidate, to build our strength and hide ourselves while Lucia grows. Perhaps we have been too careful. Perhaps we should have been harrying them every step of the way.'

'I think you overestimate us,' Cailin said. 'We hide because we must. To reveal our hand too early would be the death of us all.' She paused, mused for a time, then went on: 'The Weavers *appear* to be consolidating also, but look closer: they knew from the start that their term in power was finite. They knew the very blight their witchstones cause would poison the earth, and they must have known Mos would be blamed for it. Mos is their champion; without him, they will not only be torn from power, but punished for trying to usurp the system. The nobles plot to be rid of him.'

'But who has the strength to do it?' Zaelis asked. 'The only one who even *might* be a contender is Blood Kerestyn, in alliance with Blood Koli. They could stir up an army that would trouble the Blood Emperor. But even they could not defeat him in Axekami, with the Weavers behind him. In a few years, perhaps, but not now. They would not dare attack, no matter what outrages Mos commits. And what chance does an assassin have with Kakre guarding his life?'

'But now there is the famine, and the prospect of poor harvest. The very *people* will rise against Mos sooner or later,' said Cailin. She turned to Zaelis, her gaze cool. 'Do you not see, Zaelis? There was no way that the Weavers could have thought this rise to power was a permanent position, since it is their blight that is undermining their benefactor. They were *buying time*.'

'They have had hundreds of years to do whatever you suspect they are doing,' Zaelis argued, his phlegmy voice as persuasive and authoritative as ever.

'But they have only been able to move freely these past five,' Cailin said. 'They are letting the empire slide towards ruin, because they have no interest in maintaining it. They are up to something, Zaelis. And if they do not play their hand now, it may be too late.'

Zaelis studied his companion. Seeing her so perturbed was profoundly unsettling. She was usually a picture of cold elegance.

'Perhaps our spy from Okhamba will have new insight,' he said to placate her.

'Perhaps,' Cailin said, unconvinced. She looked over at Lucia, who had not moved. 'And in the meantime the spirits in the Fault become more hostile, and we lose more men and women to them than we can afford. They sense the change in the earth and grow bitter. We are being penned in, Zaelis. Soon we will be surrounded by enemies, unable to move within the Fault and unable to leave it.'

This struck closer to Zaelis's heart. Two of his best men had disappeared only last week while scouting west along the Fault. He wondered if this place would soon be too dangerous to inhabit, and what they could possibly do if it became so.

'She can help us,' Zaelis said, following Cailin's eyes. 'She can calm the spirits.'

'Can she?' Cailin mused darkly. 'I wonder.'

The world was full of whispers to Lucia.

It had been that way ever since she could remember. The wind soughed in a secret language, flitting wisps of meaning piquing her attention like catching her name in someone else's conversation. Rain pattered nonsense at her, teasing her with an incipient form that always washed away before she could grasp it. Rocks thought rock thoughts, slower even than the trees, whose gnarled contemplations sometimes took years to complete. Darting between them were the lightning-fast minds of small animals, ever alert, only relaxing their guard in the safety of their burrows and hidey-holes.

She was an Aberrant, a perversion of nature, and yet she was closer to nature than anyone alive, for she had the ability to decipher its many tongues.

She walked along a grassy, well-worn trail that dipped and curved around an overhanging cliff face to her right. To her left, the ground fell suddenly sheer away, leaving her looking out over an enormous canyon half a mile wide or more. On the far side, where the wall was sloped, tall spines of rock and stone pillars stood crookedly, dusty red in the slanting evening sun, casting spindly finger-shadows. The air was dry and hot and smelled of baked earth.

Before her went Yugi and another Libera Dramach guard; behind her, Cailin and Zaelis, and two more armed men. Venturing beyond the lip of the valley where the Fold lay was not a light undertaking these days.

They followed the trail upwards as it bent away from the edge of the chasm and into a long ditch with a thin ribbon of a stream flowing down the middle. Trees meshed tightly overhead. Bees droned in the warm shade, harvesting nectar from the rare flowers that thrived here. Lucia listened to their quiet, comforting industry, and envied their singularity of purpose and unquestioning loyalty to the hive, the simple pleasure they gleaned from serving their queen.

After a short time, they came to a glade, where the ditch ran up against a crumbling rock wall. The trees were driven back here by the pebbly soil, and

Nuki's eye peeped in to brighten it. Water splashed through a narrow gash in the orange stone, pooling in a basin where it overflowed and drained off into a muddy channel that meandered away in the direction they had come.

'You,' Yugi indicated his companion. 'Stay here with me. You two, take station further down the ditch. Call if you see anything bigger than a cat.'

The men grunted and complied, their footfalls thudding away as they departed. Yugi scratched under the sweaty rag that he had wrapped around his forehead to keep his dirty brown-blond hair back from his eyes. He gave those assembled a mischievous grin and said: 'Well, here we are again.'

Lucia smiled. She was fond of Yugi. Though his duties with the Libera Dramach meant that she did not see him as often as Kaiku or Mishani, he was always an entertaining rascal, even though she sensed sometimes that he was not as happy as his manner would suggest. She knew she would only make him uncomfortable if she pried. Whereas once she would have asked the question, now she kept her silence. Wisdom was only one way in which she had grown since they had first met.

Zaelis knelt down in front of her, his calloused hands gripping her upper arms tightly. 'Are you ready, Lucia?'

Lucia held his gaze for a moment and then looked away, to the pool. She gently prised his fingers off her and walked over to it. Crouching at its edge, she stared into the water. It was only a few inches deep, and clear enough to see the eroded curve of the basin beneath. As she watched, a tiny minnow slipped from the cut in the rock and plopped into the pool. It made a few disorientated circuits and then allowed itself to be washed over the pouting lip of the basin, and into the stream that ran along the ditch, little realising that its path would take it plunging over the edge of the canyon in a few short minutes.

Lucia watched it go. She would not have warned it, even if she could and even if it would have listened. Its path was chosen for it, like hers.

Once, she had lived in the Imperial Keep, a prisoner in a gilded cage. Five years ago she had been rescued from that confinement and brought to the Fold, only to discover that it was merely a different prison, and in its way as constricting as the last. Instead of walls, she was suffocated by expectation.

The Libera Dramach had taken that struggling settlement eleven years ago and turned it into a thriving fortress town, using the steadily growing population as recruitment grounds for their own secret cause. It was a carefully organised, well-oiled operation. And it was all for her.

'I saw what would happen,' Zaelis had told her once. 'When you were still an infant, I came to be your tutor, and even then we knew you were Aberrant. You were speaking at six months old, and not only to us. Your mother thought she could hide you, but I knew you couldn't be hidden. That was when I began. I moved in scholars' circles, seeking out those who might be sympathetic with Aberrants, sounding them out; and then, when I was sure, I would tell them about you. It was treason, but I told them. They saw then what you were, what you meant. If you took the throne, if an *Aberrant* ruled the empire, then it would undermine everything the Weavers had stood for. How could the Weavers consent to give service to an Aberrant Blood Empress? Yet to refuse would be to go against all the high families, who would owe you their loyalty. The stranglehold they have on us would be broken.'

And so here she was. Though she was allowed to roam and play free in the valley, there was always someone keeping an eye on her. They had vested all their hopes, all their ambitions in Lucia. Without her as a figurehead, they were merely a treasonous group of subversives. She was their reason to exist. They protected her, hid her, jealously guarding their dispossessed Heir-Empress until she could grow in power and influence, investing their time against the day when she would return to claim her throne.

Nobody had asked her if she even *wanted* to claim the throne. Not in all these years.

'Is everything well, Lucia?' Cailin asked. Lucia looked up at her fleetingly, then returned her gaze to the pool.

'She's probably wishing we had chosen to build the Fold nearer a stream she could talk to,' Yugi quipped. 'I've heard the brooks in our valley curse like soldiers.'

This brought a faint smile to Lucia's lips, and she gave him a grateful glance. He was half right. It was dangerous to go outside the valley, but this was the closest body of water that flowed directly from the Rahn, and its language was less muddied by the ancient ramblings of subterranean rocks and deeper, darker things. She cupped her hands in the water and lifted it carefully, not spilling a drop.

Listen.

Her head bowed, her eyes closed, and the physical world fell quiet to her ears. The rustle of the leaves in the sluggish wind dimmed and the sound of calling birds diminished to a distant staccato. Her heartbeat slowed; her muscles loosened and relaxed. Each exhalation made her sink deeper into unreality. She focused only on the feel of the water in her palm, the trembling of the liquid from the slight movement of her hands, the way it slid into the minuscule gullies in her skin and filled the whorls of her fingertips. She let the water feel her in return, the warmth of her blood, the throb of her pulse.

Everything natural had a spirit. Rivers, trees, hills, valleys, the sea and the four winds. Most were simple, merely an existence of life: an instinctive thing, as incapable of reason as a foetus and yet just as precious. But some were old, and aware, and their thoughts were massive and unfathomable. This water came from the belly of the Tchamil Mountains, flowing along the Kerryn for hundreds of miles until it had split off into the Rahn and travelled southward to the Fault. The great rivers were ancient, but beneath their incomprehensible consciousness they thronged with many more simple spirits. Lucia would not dare try to communicate with the Rahn itself; that was a magnitude of mystery beyond her. But here, at this place, she could sift out something that was within her capabilities. And gradually, while she kept practising like this, she was gaining the control that might one day let her make contact with the true spirit of the river.

She let the water trickle through her fingers, allowing it to carry the feel of her into the pool, tentatively announcing herself. Then, gently, she let her hands rest on the surface, her touch turning it to a chaos of ripples.

Something coming.

Something—

It rushed shrieking at her, a black wave of horror that forced its way into her throat, her lungs, choking. Death and pain and atrocity, washed down-river in the water. And with it something cold, cold and corrupt, a blasphemy against nature, a monstrous clawing thing that rent at her. A terror on the river, *terror on the river*, and the spirits were *screaming!*

Her mind blanked out, overwhelmed by the unimaginable ferocity of the onslaught, and she tipped backwards onto the pebbly floor of the glade without a sound.

EIGHT

The *Servant of the Sea* drifted in an endless black, the lanterns along its gunwale and atop its mast casting lonely globes of light in the abyss. A single gibbous moon stood sentry in the sky overhead: Iridima, her bright white surface spidercracked with blue like a shattered marble. Thick, racing bands of cloud obscured her face periodically, extinguishing stars in their wake.

An unseasonably chilly wind fluttered across the junk, setting the lanterns swaying and making Kaiku hug her blouse tighter to her skin as she picked out constellations on the foredeck. There was the Fang, low in the east – a sure sign that autumn was almost upon them. Just visible through the cold haze of Iridima's glow was the Scytheman, directly above her: another omen of the coming end to the harvest. And there, to the north, the twin baleful reds of The One Who Waits, side by side like a pair of eyes, watching the world hungrily.

It was late, and the passengers were asleep. Those men that kept the junk sailing through the night were quiet presences in the background, their voices low. But Kaiku had not been able to rest tonight. The prospect of arriving at Hanzean tomorrow was too exciting. To set foot on Saramyr soil again . . .

She felt tears start to her eyes. Gods, she never thought she would miss her homeland this much, after it had treated her so badly. But even with her family dead and she an outcast, destined to be shunned for her Aberrant blood, she loved the perfect beauty of the hills and plains, the forests and rivers and mountains. The thought of coming home after two months brought her more joy than she would have ever imagined it could.

Her gaze was drawn to the face of Iridima, most beautiful of the moon-sisters and the most brilliant, and she felt a chill of both awe and fear. She said a silent prayer to the goddess, as she always did when she had a moment like this to herself, and remembered the day when she been touched by the Children of the Moons, brushed by a terrible majesty of purpose that humbled her utterly.

'I thought it would be you,' said a voice next to her, and she felt the chill turn to an altogether more pleasant warmth that seeped through her body. Turning her head slightly, she favoured her new companion with an appraising glance.

'Did you?' she answered him, making it less of a question and more an expression of casual disinterest.

'Nobody else wanders the decks at night,' Saran replied. 'Except the sailors, but they have a heavier tread than you.'

He was standing close to her, a little closer than was proper, but she made no move to lean away. After a month of seeing each other every day, she had given up trying to conceal her attraction, and so had he. It had become a delicious game between them; both aware of the other's feelings to some extent, neither willing to give in and be the one to make the next move. Waiting each other out. She suspected that part of it was the allure of the message he carried, the implied air of mystery which it lent him. She was desperately curious about the nature of his mission, yet he always evaded her probing, and the frustration only added to how tantalising he was.

'You are thinking of home?' he guessed.

Kaiku made a soft noise in her throat, an affirmation.

'What is there for you?' he persisted.

'Just home,' she said. 'That is enough for the moment.'

He was silent for a time. Kaiku suddenly realised that she had been callous, and misinterpreted the pause. She laid a hand on his arm.

'My apologies. I had forgotten. Your accent has improved so much, sometimes you seem almost Saramyr.'

Saran gave her a heartbreaking smile. As usual, he was immaculately dressed and not a hair out of place. He might have been vain – something Kaiku had learned over the past weeks – but he certainly had something to be vain about.

'You should not apologise. Quraal is not my home, not any more. I have been away a long time, but I do not miss it. My people are blinkered and reluctant to leave their own shores, afraid that mingling with other cultures is offensive to our gods, afraid that the Theocrats might accuse them of heresy. I do not think that. Those Quraal that do deal with foreigners stay aloof, but I find beauty in all people. Some more than most.'

He was not looking at her as he delivered the final sentence, nor was it weighted any more that its predecessors, but Kaiku felt a blush anyway.

'I thought that way once,' she said quietly. 'I suppose I still do, but it is not so easy nowadays. Mishani tells me I need a harder heart, and she is right. To think too much of someone only makes a person vulnerable. Sooner or later, one will disappoint or betray the other.'

'That is Mishani's opinion, not yours,' Saran said. 'And besides, what of Mishani herself? You two seem close as kin.'

'Even she has wounded me in the past, and that hurt went deeper than any had before it,' Kaiku murmured.

Saran was silent for a time. They stood together, listening to the sussurant breathing of the sea, looking out over the darkness. Kaiku had more she wanted to say, but she felt she had already said too much, revealed too great a portion of herself to him. She kept her inner self guarded; it was her way, and experience had taught her that there was little point in trying to change it. Somehow, whenever she let her defences down, she always chose the wrong person; yet if she kept them up, she drove people away from her.

She had fallen into two relationships since she had lived in the Fold, both fulfilling at the time but ultimately proving empty. One man she was with for three years before realising that she stayed with him to alleviate the guilt she felt over the death of Tane, who had followed her into the Imperial Keep out of love and had died there. The other lasted six months before he revealed a terrible temper, made worse by the fact that he could not physically overpower her since she was an apprentice of the Red Order. She did not see the rage building until it burst out. He hit her once. She used her *kana* to crush the bones in his hand. Unfortunately, despite his other failings, he had been a skilled bomb engineer and a great asset to the Libera Dramach, but Kaiku's actions had put paid to that. She felt more sorry about causing trouble for Zaelis's organisation than about maiming him.

But there was one other, who had got under her skin a long while ago and would not be dislodged, persistent as the whispers from her father's Mask that sometimes woke her in the night with their insidious temptations.

'I miss Asara,' she said absently, her eyes unfocused.

'Asara tu Amarecha?' Saran said.

Kaiku's head snapped around to meet his gaze. 'You know her?'

'I have met her,' he said. 'Not that she was going by that name, but then, she never did keep to one identity for too long.'

'Where? Where did you meet her?'

Saran raised a sculpted eyebrow at the urgency in Kaiku's voice. 'Actually, it was in the very port that we are docking at tomorrow. Several years ago, now. She did not know me, but I knew her. She was wearing a different face, but I had intelligence of her arrival.' He smiled to himself, enjoying Kaiku's attention. 'I made contact with her. We are both, after all, on the same side.'

'Asara is on nobody's side,' Kaiku said.

'She chooses her allegiances to suit herself,' Saran said, then turned away from her and into the wind, flicking his hair away from his face with a flourish. 'But you of all people should know that she is helping the Red Order and the Libera Dramach.'

'She *was*,' said Kaiku. 'I have not seen her since Lucia was—' She stopped herself, then remembered that Saran already knew. Brushing her fringe back in an unconscious imitation of him, she continued more carefully. 'Since Lucia came to the Fold.'

'She spoke highly of you,' Saran told her, pacing slowly about the foredeck. He stood too rigid, too straight, and Kaiku felt that his movements and speech were pretentiously theatrical. He annoyed her when he became like this. Suddenly, now that he knew he had information she wanted, he was showing off, making the most of his advantage. She should have deflated him and feigned disinterest, but it was too late. Quraal were legendarily arrogant, and Saran was no exception. Like many people who were naturally beautiful, he did not feel he had to cultivate the finer points of his personality since women would fall at his feet anyway. What irked Kaiku more than anything was that she *knew* that, and yet she still kept coming back to him.

Saran wanted her to ask what Asara had said about her, but she would not give him the satisfaction this time.

He leaned on his elbows against the bow railing, the moon at his shoulder, and studied her with his dark eyes. 'What were you two to each other?' he asked eventually.

Kaiku almost felt that she did not want to tell him; but tonight she felt reflective, and it did her good to talk.

'I do not know,' she said. 'I never knew who she was, or *what* she was. I knew she could . . . shift her form somehow. I knew she had watched over me for a long time, waiting for my *kana* to show itself. She could be cruel, or kind. I think maybe she was lonely, but too obsessed with being independent to admit it to herself.'

'Were you friends?'

Kaiku frowned. 'We were . . . more than friends, and less than friends. I do not know what she thought of me, but . . . there is a piece of her still in me. Here.' She tapped her breastbone. 'She stole the breath of another and put it into me, and some of her went with it. And some of me went into her.' She became aware that Saran was watching her coolly, shook her head and snorted a laugh. 'I do not expect you to understand.'

'I think I understand enough,' Saran said.

'Do you? I doubt it.'

'Did you love her?'

Kaiku's eyes flashed in disbelief. 'How dare you ask me that?' she snapped.

Saran gave an insouciant shrug. 'I was merely asking. You sounded like—'

'I loved what she taught me,' she interrupted him. 'She made me accept myself for what I am. An Aberrant. She helped me to stop being ashamed of myself. But I couldn't love *her*. Not as she was. Deceitful, selfish, heartless.' Kaiku checked herself, realising that she had raised her voice. She flushed angrily. 'Does that answer your question?'

'Quite adequately,' Saran said, unruffled.

Kaiku stalked to the other side of the foredeck and stood with her arms crossed, glaring at the moon-limned waves, furious with herself. Asara was still an open wound that refused to heal. She had told Saran far more than she intended. It would be better to cut her losses and leave now, but she stayed.

After a moment, she heard him walk over to her. His hands touched her shoulders, and she turned around, her arms unknitting. He was standing close to her again, his dark eyes piercing in the shadowed frame of his face, heavy with intent. She felt her pulse quicken; a salty wind blew between them. Then he bent to kiss her, and she turned her mouth away. He drew back, hurt and angry.

Kaiku slipped from his grasp and turned her back again, her arms once more folded beneath her breasts. She could feel his frustrated confusion prickling at the back of her neck. She countered with a coldness in the set of her shoulders, an impassable resolve. Finally, she heard him leave.

Kaiku stood alone again, watching the stars, and added another brick to the barrier around her heart.

They arrived at Hanzean early in the morning of the next day. The harbour town was bathed in a pink light. Far to the east, the Surananyi was blowing, great hurricanes throwing up the red dust of the Tchom Rin desert to tinge Nuki's eye.

As was customary, the sailors enacted a small ceremony around a tiny shrine that they brought up from its usual place belowdecks, and made offerings of incense to Assantua, goddess of the sea and sky, for their safe passage. All the Saramyr folk attended, but Saran and Tsata were notably absent.

Hanzean was less hectic than Jinka to the north, which took most of the traffic from Okhamba, but though the journey was slightly longer it was the home port of Blood Mumaka's fleet. It was the most picturesque of the western coastal towns, and the oldest, being the first Saramyr settlement ever on this continent. Ninety miles to the southwest stood the Palexai, the great obelisk that marked the point where landfall was first made. Though Hanzean had never blossomed into Saramyr's first capital – the cursed Gobinda had held that title – it remained an influential place, steeped in its own history.

Mishani had visited Hanzean several times, in the days before her estrangement from her family. She was fond of its quiet alleyways and ancient plazas; it reminded her of the Imperial Quarter in Axekami, but a little less carefully kept, a little rougher around the edges. Somehow more *real.* Now, however, the sight of the smooth stone towers and the red skirts of ornamental guttering around the market-dome made her feel a strange mix of relief and trepidation. Their journey had been bought at a price, but what kind of price she could not yet tell. Chien had not been interested in money; instead, he had exacted a promise from her, one that courtesy demanded she grant in such a situation, even if it was not in return for such a heavy favour as the merchant had done them.

'You must be my guest at my townhouse in Hanzean,' he said.

On the surface, it seemed innocent enough; but surfaces, like masks, covered over the truth beneath. Though no time had been set, etiquette demanded that Mishani stay for at least five days. And in that five days, anything could happen. She was far too close to Blood Koli's estates in Mataxa Bay for her comfort.

She examined all the angles, looked for hidden meaning in everything. It was a necessary habit with Mishani, and she was particularly talented at it.

Chien was not an idiot; he could have negotiated great advantage for himself out of the deal. She knew what she would do in his shoes. If he truly had heard about the rift in her family, then he was aware that she had nothing to offer him, and he probably knew that Barak Avun was secretly searching for his daughter. He would simply trade her into the arms of her enemy.

Then why am I letting him? she asked herself, as she mouthed the words of the mantra to Assantua and paid attention to the sailors' ceremony with only a small fraction of her mind.

Because she had made a promise. It was her refusal to compromise her honour that had made her an outcast in the first place; she would scarcely abandon it now. Chien knew she could not refuse his invitation without insult, and it would have revealed that she suspected him. He was probably just as puzzled about her motives as she was of his. What had she been doing on Okhamba? Why risk herself that way?

She had told him nothing, though they had talked often on the journey. His uncertainty was her advantage, and she had to keep hold of it. When they got to his townhouse, then she would see what could be done about her situation.

She had not shared her fears with Kaiku. Though Kaiku had initially had the same suspicions as Mishani, she had been calmed by assurances that Chien was trustworthy. It was, of course, a lie, but Kaiku was in no position to help anyway. She had to take Saran and his Tkiurathi companion back to the Fold, and her passionate outbursts would be counterproductive to Mishani's intrigues.

Kaiku was content to let it drop, in the end. Mishani's intention had always been to head south when they returned from Okhamba, anyway; Kaiku knew that. Mishani was next to useless in the Fold, except when Zaelis or Cailin called on her for advice or Lucia needed a sisterly hand. No, she had other errands to run, assuming she had liberty to run them after Chien was done with her. She was going to Lalyara, to meet with the Barak Zahn tu Ikati. Lucia's true father.

They disembarked on Chien's private jetty, after which he insisted that they come to his townhouse and dine with him before they set off. Saran appeared reluctant to Mishani's practised eye, but he made no complaint. Kaiku, who was eager to put off her farewells to her friend, was happy to accept. Tsata and Chien exchanged a few words in Okhamban – in which the merchant was apparently fluent – and then he, too, acquiesced. Not being bound by Saramyr manners, Kaiku had feared he would say something rude; but Chien knew how to deal with Tkiurathi.

They were met at the jetty and taken by carriage through the quiet streets of Hanzean. Slender cats watched them curiously from rooftops; sun-browned women stepped aside as they passed, and then returned to sweeping the dust away from their doorsteps with reed brooms; old men sat outside streetside restaurants with cups of wine and cubes of exotic cheese; startled birds took flight from where they bathed in ancient fountains. Kaiku was rapt, enjoying the simple glory of being back in Saramyr and off that ship.

Mishani wished she could do the same. She had noted that the carriage was taking a very indirect route to wherever it was going, heading down narrow, winding thoroughfares and doubling back on itself several times. The others had not noticed, or appeared not to; but for one who knew Hanzean well, it was obvious.

Chien's townhouse was not particularly ostentatious. It was a squat, three-storeyed building like a crushed pagoda, with scalloped tiling on its skirts and a sculpted effigy of a spirit on each corner serving as a gargoyle. Enclosed within was a small garden, with colourful rockeries arranged with typical care and forethought. The grounds were small and tidy, merely a lawn within the compound wall and a few cultivated areas of flowers and trees, where stone benches were placed and a small brook ran. It was located in a wealthy district, on a street of compounds that were a similar size, and it stood out not at all from its neighbours.

The theme continued on the inside. While he was a man of undoubted wealth, Chien had chosen comfort and simplicity over opulence, and the only real displays of his merchant prowess were the rare and valuable Okhamban stone icons that rested on pedestals in some of the rooms. Kaiku shivered at the sight, remembering the dreadful awareness of the idols at the Aith Pthakath.

The meal was exquisite, and doubly so after the preserved food that they had been getting on board the ship. Pot-cooked slitherfish, seasoned saltrice in delicate cakes wrapped in strips of kelpweed, a stew of vegetables and grilled banathi, and – most delicious of all – jukara berries, that only flourished in the last few weeks of the harvest, and were ruinously hard to cultivate. They ate and talked and joked, united in the common relief of being back on dry land. Laughing, reminiscing about the journey, they cut and speared food with silver finger-forks worn on the second and third digit of the left hand, and their counterpart finger-blades on the right. Occasionally they switched to delicate spoons, held between the unencumbered thumb and forefinger. Neither Saran nor Tsata appeared to have any trouble with the technique, nor with the rituals of politeness at the table. Mishani guessed that the quiet Tkiurathi was a lot better educated than she had initially thought.

Finally, the meal was over. Chien, as was expected, asked Mishani's companions to stay and they, as was equally expected, regrettably refused. Chien did not insist; but he did offer to put a carriage at their disposal to take them out of the town.

They went out to the small lawn of the compound together, strolling idly in the muggy heat of the afternoon. The cooling breezes of approaching autumn had died off and left the air still and humid. Mishani walked ahead with Kaiku, the former as poised as ever, the latter as casual.

'I will miss you, Mishani,' Kaiku said. 'It is a long way to the Southern Prefectures.'

'I shall not be gone for ever. A month, two at most, if my errands are well.'

She gave her friend a wry smile. 'I thought after this trip you would have had enough of me.'

Kaiku returned the smile. 'Of course not. Who else would keep me out of trouble?'

'Cailin tries, but you do not let her.'

'Cailin wants me as a pet,' Kaiku said derisively. 'If she had her way, I would spend every day studying, and by now I would have been putting on that ghoulish make-up and that black dress as part of the Red Order.'

'She does have a lot of faith in you,' Mishani pointed out. 'Most masters would not put up with such an errant pupil.'

'Cailin looks after her own concerns,' Kaiku replied, shading her eyes and squinting up absently into the sun. 'She trained me to harness what I have inside me – for that, I will always be grateful – but I never agreed to spend the rest of my life as one of her Sisters. She does not understand that.' Kaiku dropped her gaze. 'Besides, I am pledged first to a higher power than her.'

Mishani laid a hand on her elbow. 'You have done much to help the Libera Dramach over these past years, Kaiku. You have played an important part in many of their operations. Everything you do for them hurts the Weavers, even in a small way. Do not forget that.'

'It is not enough,' Kaiku murmured. 'My family are still unavenged; my promise to Ocha unfulfilled. I have waited, and waited, but my patience is growing thin.'

'You cannot defeat the Weavers on your own,' Mishani told her. 'Nor can you expect to undo two and a half centuries of history in half a decade.'

'I know,' said Kaiku. 'But that does not help.'

They said their goodbyes, then Saran, Tsata and Kaiku departed in a carriage, leaving Mishani with Chien.

'Shall we go inside?' he offered, after they had left. Mishani acquiesced politely, and went with him, more aware than ever now that she was alone, and very likely walking into a trap.

NINE

Mos sat in the Chamber of Tears, and listened to the rain.

He had never been to this room before. That was not unusual; many of the upper levels of the Imperial Keep were almost entirely empty. It had been built as a somewhat impractical gesture of appeasement by the fourth Blood Emperor of Saramyr, Huita tu Lilira, in recompense to Ocha for the hubris of his predecessor. But not even the Imperial Family needed a building of the sheer size and complexity of the Keep. Even if Mos had summoned all his distant relatives to live there – which was hardly possible, since it was always necessary to have bloodline scattered about the country to oversee the diverse affairs of Blood Batik – they would have had trouble filling all the rooms. When the great fire of five years ago had destroyed large areas of the interior, the inhabitants had simply moved to new sections and carried on quite comfortably while the repairs were made.

The upper levels, where Mos had found the Chamber of Tears, were the least practical to get to, and their *lach* corridors held only hollow echoes. Laranya had said once that there could be people living up here, a whole community of lost wanderers that might have gone undiscovered for centuries. Mos had laughed and told her that she was being fanciful. Though they were deserted, they were not covered in dust or neglected, and he suspected that one of his advisers' duties was to ensure that servants did not let any part of the Keep go to ruin.

The sound of falling water had brought him here as he wandered, seeking solitude, carrying his third bottle of wine. It was a wide, circular chamber with a domed roof, in the centre of which was a hole through which the rain fell onto the tiled floor and drained away through small grilles. The floor was slightly slanted towards the centre to keep the water there, so that it was possible to sit just outside the curtain of droplets and remain dry. A crafty system of guttering on the roof funnelled water down through secret channels to the statues that stood in alcoves at the periphery of the chamber, and tears ran from their eyes and down their faces, collecting in stone basins at their feet.

It was dusk, and no lanterns had been lit. The room was gloomy and sultry with the remainder of the day's heat. The rain was unusual for this time of year, but it suited Mos's mood, and he was drawn to it. He sat in one of the many chairs that formed a circle around the room, and watched the column of droplets come down, the carpet of tiny explosions they made as they struck the shallow pool in the middle of the chamber. The only light was the fading glow of Nuki's eye, coming through the hole in the dome, outlining Mos's brow and bearded jaw and the edge of the bottle he held. He took another swig, without finesse, a bitter and angry draught.

'You should not be alone,' croaked Kakre from the doorway of the chamber, and Mos swore loudly.

'Gods, you are the *last* person I want to see now, Kakre,' he said. 'Go away.'

'We must talk,' the Weave-lord insisted, coming further into the room.

Mos glared at him. 'Come closer then. I'll not talk to you while you're lurking over there.'

Kakre obliged, shambling into the light. Mos didn't look at him, watching the rain instead. The vaguely cloying scent of decay and animal fur reached him even through the haze of the wine, like the smell of a sick dog.

'What must we talk about?' he sneered.

'You are drunk,' Kakre said.

'I'm never drunk. Is that what you had to say to me? I have a wife to scold me, Kakre; I don't need you for it.'

Kakre bridled, a wave of anger emanating from him that made the hairs of Mos's neck stand on end.

'You are too insolent sometimes, my *Emperor*,' Kakre warned, loading the title with scorn. 'I am not one of your servants, to be dismissed or mocked as you choose.'

'No, you're not,' Mos agreed, taking another swig from his bottle. 'My servants are loyal, and they do what they're supposed to. You don't. It makes me wonder why I even keep you around at all.'

Kakre did not reply to that, regarding him in malicious silence instead.

'What do you have to tell me, then?' Mos snapped, casting Kakre an irritated glance.

'I have news from the south. There has been a revolt in Zila.'

Mos did not react, except that his frown deepened and his brow clouded.

'A revolt,' he repeated slowly.

'The Governor has been killed. It was a mob, mainly peasants and townsfolk. They stormed the administration plaza. One of my Weavers sent me the news, before he too was killed.'

'They killed a Weaver?' Mos exclaimed in frank surprise.

Kakre did not see any need to answer that. The spatter of the rain filled the void in the conversation while Mos thought.

'Who is responsible?' the Emperor asked eventually.

'It is too early to say,' rasped the Weave-Lord. 'But the peasants were organised. And my agents in Zila had been reporting a rise in sympathy for that somewhat persistent cult that has been a constant diversion of our resources these past few years.'

'The Ais Maraxa? It was *them*?' Mos cried in sudden fury, flinging his bottle across the room. It smashed against one of the weeping statues, mixing red wine into the rainwater that collected in the basin at its feet.

'Perhaps. I have warned you often that they would manage something like this eventually.'

'You were supposed to prevent this kind of thing from happening!' The Emperor stood up violently, knocking his chair away behind him.

'They know about the harvests,' Kakre said. He was not intimidated, even though he was physically dwarfed by the larger man. 'Here in the north west we can disguise the damage somewhat, but Zila lies on the edge of the Southern Prefectures. Down there, they see the blight destroying their crops before their very eyes; and all bad news travels through Zila on its way up the western coast. The Weavers are powerful, my Emperor, and we have many subtle ways; but we cannot see all plans, not when the very country turns against us. You should have let me tackle the Ais Maraxa when we first heard of them.'

'Don't shift the blame, Kakre!' Mos raged. 'This is *your* fault!' He grabbed the Weaver roughly by his patchwork robe. 'Your fault!'

'*Do not touch me!*' Kakre hissed, and Mos felt his body seized, his chest gripped as if by an iron hand. The strength flooded out of him, replaced by sudden panic. His hands spasmed open, releasing the Weave-lord, and he staggered backward, his throat bubbling with phlegm and his breath short. Kakre seemed to loom, becoming huge and terrifying in his mind: a hunched figure with emaciated white hands clenched into claws, held over him like the hands of a puppeteer over a marionette. Backing away, Mos slipped and fell into the column of rain, splashed into the shallow pool where he cringed, whimpering. Kakre seemed to fill the room, his Mask shadowed and cadaverous, and the very air seemed to crush Mos down to the floor.

'You overstep your boundaries,' said the Weave-lord, his voice dark and cold as the grave. 'You will learn your place!'

Mos cried out in fear, unmanned by Kakre's power, his natural courage subverted by the insidious manipulation of his body and mind. The rain fell, soaking him, dripping from his beard and plastering his hair.

'You need me, Mos,' Kakre told him. 'And I, regrettably, need you. But do not forget what I can do to you. Do not forget that I hold the power of life and death over you at every moment. I can stop your heart with a thought, or burst it within your breast. I can make you bleed inside in such a way that not even the best physicians could tell it was not natural. I can drive you insane in the time it takes for you to unsheathe your sword. *Never* touch me again, or perhaps I shall do something more permanent to you next time.'

Then, gradually, Kakre seemed to diminish, and the terrible energy in the air slackened. Mos found his breath again, gasping. The room returned to what it once had been, gloomy and spacious and echoing, and Kakre was once again a small, twisted figure with a bent back, buried in badly sewn rags and hide.

'You will deal with the revolt in Zila. I will deal with its causes,' he rasped, and with that he departed, leaving Mos lying on his side in the rain, overlit by the fading dusk, angry and fearful and beaten.

The Empress Laranya and her younger brother Reki collapsed through the elliptical doorway, wet and breathless from laughing. Eszel raised a theatrical eyebrow as they blundered into the pavilion, and said wryly to Reki: 'Anyone would think you had never seen rain before.'

Reki laughed again, exhilirated. It was not far from the truth.

The pavilion lay in the middle of a wide pond, joined to the rest of the Imperial Keep's roof gardens by a narrow bridge. Its sides were carved wood, a thin, hollow webwork of leaf shapes and pictograms that allowed those inside to look through them and out over the water. Baskets of flowers hung from the drip-tiles on the sloping roof, and at each corner were stout stone pillars painted in coral red. Eszel had lit the lanterns that hung on the inner sides of the pillars, for night had newly fallen outside. It was small, but not so small that eight people could not sit in comfort on its benches, and with only the three of them there was plenty of room.

Reki flopped down and looked out through the wooden patterns, marvelling. Laranya gave him an indulgent kiss on the cheek and sat beside him.

'Rain is something of a novelty where we come from,' she explained to Eszel.

'I gathered as much,' Eszel replied, with a quirk of a grin.

'Spirits!' Reki exclaimed, his eyes flickering over the dark and turbulent surface of the rain-dashed pool. 'Now I know what Ziazthan Ri felt when he wrote *The Pearl Of The Water God*.'

Eszel looked at the young man with newly piqued interest. 'You've read that?'

Reki became shy all of a sudden, realising that he had been boasting. Ziazthan Ri's ancient text – containing what was generally recognised as some of the greatest naturalistic writing in the Empire – was extraordinarily rare and valuable. 'Well . . . that is . . .' he stammered.

'You precious thing! You must tell me about it!' Eszel enthused, rescuing him. 'I've seen copied extracts, but never known the whole story.'

'I memorised it,' said Reki, trying to sound as modest as possible. 'It is one of my favourites.'

Eszel practically squealed: 'You *memorised* it? I would *die* to hear it from beginning to end.'

Reki beamed, the smile lighting up his thin face. 'I would be honoured,' he said. 'I have never met anyone who has even heard of Ziazthan Ri before.'

'Then you haven't met the right people yet,' Eszel told him with a wink. 'I'll introduce you around.'

'Now wait there,' Laranya said, springing from Reki's side to sit next to Eszel. She grabbed his arm possessively, dripping all over him. 'Eszel is mine!

I'll not have you stealing him away from me with your dry book-learning and conversations about dead old men.'

Eszel laughed. 'The Empress is jealous!' he taunted.

Laranya looked from her brother to Eszel and back. She held great fondness for both of them. The two could not be more different, yet they seemed to be getting on better than she had hoped. Reki was grey-eyed and intense, his features oddly accentuated by a deep scar that ran from the outside of his left eye to the tip of his cheekbone. His chin-length hair was jet-black, with a streak of white on the left side from the same childhood fall that had marred his face. He was quiet, clever, and awkward, never seeming to quite fit the clothes that he wore or to feel comfortable in his own skin.

Eszel, in contrast, was flamboyant and lively, very handsome but very affected; he seemed like he belonged in the River District rather than the Imperial Keep, with his bright eye make-up and his hair dyed in purple and red and green, tied with ornaments and beads.

'Perhaps a little jealous,' she conceded mischievously. 'I want you both to myself!'

'Rank has its privileges,' Eszel said, standing up and making an exaggerated bow. 'I am yours to command, my Empress.'

'Then I demand that you recite us a poem about rain!' she said. Reki's eyes lit up.

'I do so happen to have one in which rain forms something of a key element,' he said. 'Would you like to hear it?'

'I would!' said Reki. He was somewhat awed by Eszel, who Laranya had told him was a brilliant poet. He was a member of the Imperial Court on the suggestion of Mos's Cultural Adviser, who believed that with a few years' patronage Eszel would be turning out poems good enough to make him a household name in Axekami, and a prestigious figure to be associated with the Imperial family.

Preening himself outrageously in the lantern-light, Eszel took up position in the middle of the pavilion and cleared his throat. For a few moments, the only sound was the hiss and trickle of the rain, and he basked in the rapt attention of his audience. Then he began to speak, the words flowing across his tongue like molten silver. High Saramyrrhic was a wonderfully complex language, and lent itself well to poetry. It was capable of being soft and sibilant or jarring and sharp, layered with meanings that could be shifted and manipulated in the mouth of a wordsmith to make them a sly puzzle to unlock and a joy to hear. Eszel was extremely talented, and he knew it; the pure beauty of his sentences entranced the listener.

The poem was only obliquely about rain, being rather the story of a man whose wife had been possessed by an achicita, a demon vapour that had stolen in through her nostrils as she slept and was turning her sick inside. The man's heartbreak made him mad, and in his madness he was visited by Shintu, the trickster god of luck, who persuaded him to carry his wife outside their house and lay her in the road for three days, at the end of which time

Shintu would drive out the demon. Then Shintu asked his cousin Panazu to bring three days of rain, to test the man's faith, for his wife was already weak and would likely not survive three days of being soaking wet. After the first day of sitting by his wife in the rain, the villagers, thinking the man insane, locked him up and put his wife back to bed, where she continued to sicken.

Shintu, having played his trick, thought it was over and promptly turned his attention to something else. He forgot about the whole affair, at which time it came to the attention of Narisa, goddess of forgotten things, who saw how terrible and unjust it was that this couple should suffer so. She appealed to Panazu to put things right, since he too had played a part in this. Panazu, who loved Narisa – and whose love would later draw Shintu's attention and result in the birth of the bastard child Suran by Panazu's own sister Aspinis – could not refuse her, and so he relieved the wife of the achicita and sent lightning to break open the man's jail cell. Freed and reunited, they were both pronounced cured, and found their happiness together once again.

Eszel was just coming to the end of his tale, and was gratified to see tears standing in Reki's eyes, when suddenly Mos came stamping in out of the rain. The poet faltered at the sight of the Blood Emperor, whose face was like a thunderhead. He stood there dripping, surveying the scene before him. Eszel fell silent.

'You all seem to be enjoying yourselves,' he said, and even Eszel could tell that he was spoiling for a fight, and wisely remained quiet. The Blood Emperor did not like him, and made no disguise of the fact. Eszel's somewhat effeminate ways and showy appearance offended a man of his earthy nature. In addition, it was plain that Mos resented the friendship between Eszel and Laranya, for she often sought him out when Mos was too busy with affairs of court to attend to her.

'Come and join us, then,' said Laranya, getting up and holding out her hands for Mos to take. 'You look like you need some enjoyment.'

He ignored her hands and glowered at her. 'I have searched for you, Laranya, because I thought I might find some solace from my wife after the ordeal I have suffered. Instead I find you . . . soaking wet and playing childish games in the rain!'

'What ordeal? What are you talking about?' Laranya asked, but in amid the concern there was already the spark of anger that had ignited in response to the Emperor's tone. Eszel sat down unobtrusively next to Reki.

'Don't concern yourself,' he snapped. 'Why is it that whenever I have to track you down, I find you with this abhorrent peacock of a man?' He waved a dismissive gesture at Eszel, who took the insult meekly. He could scarcely do any different. Reki looked in horror from Mos to Eszel.

'Do not take out your frustrations on your subjects, who cannot answer you back!' she cried, her cheeks becoming flushed. 'If your grievance is with me, then say so! I am not at your beck and call, to wait in your bedchamber until you decide you need *solace*.' She twisted the word to mock him, making him seem needy and ridiculous.

'Gods!' he roared. 'Am I to face hostility from all sides? Is there not one person with who I can exchange a kind word?'

'How persecuted you are!' she retorted sarcastically. 'Especially when you blunder in here like a banathi and begin insulting my friend, and embarrassing me in front of my brother!'

'Come with me, then!' Mos said, grabbing her wrist. 'Let me speak to you in private, away from them.'

She pulled her arm back. 'Eszel was reciting a poem,' she said, her voice taut. 'And I will stay to hear it finished.'

Mos glared balefully at the poet, almost shaking with rage. Reki could almost feel Eszel's heart sink. His sister meant well, but when incensed she was not subtle. In providing a reason to refuse Mos, she had turned his wrath back onto her defenceless friend.

'And how would you feel if your treasured poet was suddenly to find himself without a patron?' he grated.

'Then my treasured husband would find himself without a wife!' Laranya fired back. Once she had dug her heels in, she would give no ground.

'Does he mean so much to you, then?' Mos sneered. 'This half-man?'

'This *half-man* is more a man than you, since he can keep his temper, as a noble like you should be able to!'

This was too much. Mos raised his hand suddenly, a reflex of pure anger, drawing back to hit her.

She went suddenly cold, her passion taking her beyond mere fury and into a steely calm. 'I *dare* you,' she said, her voice like fingernails scraping on rusted metal.

The change in her stopped him. He had never raised his hand to her before, never lost control this way. Trembling, he looked into her eyes, and thought how achingly beautiful their arguments made her, and how much he loved and hated her at the same time. Then he cast one last glare of pure malice at Eszel, and stormed out of the doorway and onto the bridge, disappearing into the rainy night.

Reki let out a breath that he did not know he had been holding. Eszel looked miserable. Laranya's chin was tilted arrogantly, her breast heaving, fiercely pleased that she had faced her husband down.

The mood was spoiled now, and by unspoken consent they dispersed to their chambers. Later, Laranya would find Mos, and they would fight, and reconcile, and make frenetic love in the embers of their anger, unaware that then, as now, Kakre would be watching from the Weave.

TEN

Kaiku, Saran and Tsata arrived in the Fold in the early morning, having ridden hard from Hanzean. They had made their way along secret routes into the Xarana Fault under the cover of darkness and slipped into the heart of the broken land without alerting any of the hostiles that lived there. Their return was greeted with great activity by those who knew of Kaiku's mission and guessed who her companion was. By midday, an assembly of the upper echelons of the Libera Dramach and the Red Order had gathered to hear what their spy had to tell them, and Kaiku was included, both at Saran's insistence and at Cailin's. She felt a certain amount of relief. After giving two months of her life – and almost losing it – to bring this man back, the thought that the information he carried might be too sensitive to trust her with was too cruel.

They met on the top floor of a semicircular building that was unofficially the nerve centre of the Libera Dramach. It stood on one of the highest tiers of the Fold, its curved face looking out over the town and into the valley below. The uppermost storey was open to the view, with pillars to hold up the flat roof and a waist-high barrier of wrought iron running between them. The whole storey was a single room, used for congregations or occasional private theatrical performances or recitations, and like most of the buildings in the Fold it was functional rather than elegant. Its beige walls were hung with cheap tapestries and there was wicker matting to cover the floor, and little else except a prayer wheel in one corner and some wind chimes ringing softly in the desultory breeze, to ward off evil spirits. It was a quaint and ancient superstition that seemed somehow less comical here in the Xarana Fault.

There was no real formality about the meeting, but basic hospitality demanded that refreshments be served. The traditional low tables of black wood were scattered with small plates, and metal beakers of various wines, spirits and hot beverages were placed between them. Kaiku was sitting with Cailin and two other similarly attired members of the Red Order, neither of whom she had met before, since the membership seemed to be constantly shifting and only Cailin provided any permanence. She was excessively paranoid about letting the numbers of the Red Order be known, and kept them scattered so that they might not all be wiped out at once by any disaster. Nearby sat Zaelis with Yugi, who was virtually his right-hand man. Yugi caught her look and gave her a reassuring grin; startled, she smiled back. Tsata sat on his own, away from the tables at the edge of the room.

Kaiku watched him for a moment. She had to wonder what the Tkiurathi was doing here at all. Why had he accompanied Saran so far? What was the relationship between them? Though her anger at the callous way he had risked her life had been ameliorated by the intervening month, she had learned little about him and Saran was strangely reluctant to fill in the details, claiming that it was Tsata's business and that he would tell her if he wanted. Kaiku could not decide if Saran was being diplomatic out of respect for his companion's foreign beliefs, or if he was just being obtuse to vex her.

Her thoughts turned from Saran to Lucia. She wished she had been given time to visit the former Heir-Empress before the meeting, but she supposed there would be time later. Still, something chewed annoyingly at her about the matter. When Kaiku enquired after her health to Zaelis, he had responded with a breezy comment and changed the subject; but thinking back on it, he never had answered her question. If she had been Mishani, she might have thought it suspicious; but being Kaiku, she assumed that it was her own fault for not pressing him.

Then silence fell, and Saran stood with his back to the railing, framed against the far end of the valley and outlined by the sun. It was time to learn what she had risked her life for, and to determine whether it was worth it.

'Only a few of you here know me,' he began, his voice clear and almost entirely free of Quraal inflections now. In his tight, severe clothes he looked like a general addressing his troops, and his voice had a similar authority. 'So I will begin with an introduction. My name is Saran Ycthys Marul. I have been a spy for the Libera Dramach for several years now, travelling far afield with one objective in mind: to discover all I could about the Weavers. My mission has taken me to the four countries of the Near World: Saramyr, Okhamba, Quraal and distant Yttryx. If you will indulge me, I will tell you now what I have found.'

He paused dramatically, and prowled left and right, sweeping the assembly with his gaze. Kaiku flinched inwardly at his grandstanding. It occurred to her suddenly that by delivering his message personally to so many people he was endangering himself in the future. The more people that knew he was a spy, the more likely he was to be discovered. She wondered what had brought on this recklessness; surely it was not that he was so conceited that he was willing to take the risk in exchange for this moment of glory?

'Saramyr has forgotten its history,' he said. 'So proud were you to settle this great continent that you did not think about what you were sweeping aside. In hunting the Ugati aboriginals to extinction, you wiped the slate clean, and lost thousands upon thousands of years of this land's memory. But other lands still remember. In Okhamba, tribes have lived untouched by outside civilisation for centuries. In Quraal, the repression of doctrine and the rewriting of history by the Theocracy was not thorough enough, and still there persists evidence from the darkest depths of the past, if a person knows where to look for it. And in Yttryx, where the constant internal wars have shifted the epicentre of power so often, documents have become so scattered that it is both impossible to find them all and impossible to destroy them all. History persists. Even here. And it seems we would do best not to forget it, for we never know when the events of the past may emerge to change the present.'

Some of the assembly shifted uneasily at the impertinence of this Quraal upbraiding them for their history, when it was the Quraal who had driven them to Saramyr in the first place; but Kaiku noted that Cailin wore a faint smile on her painted lips.

'I will be brief, and begin with the good news,' Saran continued, flicking back his hair and fixing Zaelis with a haughty eye. 'Later, I am sure, I will have an opportunity to give a more detailed account to those who wish to hear it.' He made an expansive gesture with his arm to encircle the assembly with his account. 'In all my travels throughout the Near World, I was looking for three things: firstly, evidence of the corruption that is spreading through your own land, that we now generally believe is a side-effect of the Weavers' witchstones; secondly, the Weavers themselves, or beings analogous to them; and finally, the witchstones, since these are the source of the Weavers' powers.'

He began stalking back and forth again, his features profiled in the sunlight from outside. 'I am pleased to report that on two counts, I found nothing at all. Nowhere did I find any kind of blight that could not be accounted for by insect plague or other natural explanation, and none that possessed the insidious persistence of the one that affects Saramyr. And nowhere did I find anything that might be described as a Weaver, except those few that reside in distant colonies on other continents. Certainly, there are those who possess abilities unusual to the common folk; our own priests are an example, having learned to communicate in a rudimentary fashion with the spirits of our land. The honourable Kaiku tu Makaima, here present, was witness to the abilities of the Fleshcrafters of Okhamba; and there are worse things even than Fleshcrafters in the hidden world of the deep jungle. In Quraal there are the Oblates, in Yttryx the Muhd-Taal. But however these talents are attained, it is through processes either natural or spiritual. Even the Aberrants, who were born from the corruption that the Weavers create, do not actively participate in its spreading.' He paused, ran a finger along his cheekbone. 'I found no Aberrants outside your own shores. There were the deformed, and lame, and crippled, but these are not Aberrants, merely the way of nature. In this land, most people do not differentiate any more; though if I may say, those in this room provide the exception to that rule, and I applaud you for it.'

Kaiku watched him as he held court, her mind wandering to the lean physique that she imagined underneath his strict black Quraal clothing. Why had she rejected him, anyway? It did not have to mean anything, to share a bed with him for a night. Why allow her mistrust of her own emotions to get in the way of enjoying herself?

She realised that she was drifting, caught herself and returned to the matter at hand.

'From this, we can surmise that the blight is responsible for Aberrancy,' Saran was saying. 'This we had already guessed, but now I believe it proven beyond doubt. There is no blight outside of Saramyr, and hence no Aberrants. But there *are* witchstones.'

This brought general consternation to the assembly. Kaiku ate a spiced dumpling and kept quiet, her eyes flickering over the suddenly animated audience.

'He plays his crowd well,' Cailin whispered, leaning over to her.

'He craves the attention, I think,' Kaiku murmured. 'It flatters his vanity.'

Cailin gave a surprised laugh and subsided with an insinuating glance at her pupil. Kaiku ignored it.

'But if the witchstones cause the corruption in our land, how is it that there are witchstones abroad, but no blight?' someone called.

'Because they have not been *found* yet,' Saran said, raising a finger. The assembly hushed. 'They lie deep in the earth. Dormant. Waiting. Waiting to be woken up.'

'Then what wakes them up?' asked the same man.

'Blood,' Kaiku said. She had meant to say it to herself, but it came out louder than she had intended and the assembly heard it.

'Blood. Indeed,' said Saran, giving her a disarming half-smile. 'Of all of us here, only Kaiku has seen a witchstone. She has witnessed the human sacrifice that feeds them. She has seen the heart.'

Kaiku felt suddenly embarrassed. Her account of her infiltration into the Weavers' monastery in the Lakmar Mountains on Fo was a subject of some scepticism among the Libera Dramach. Many argued, quite reasonably, that what she had seen in the chamber where the witchstone was kept could have been a hallucination. She had been weak from exhaustion and starvation, and had been wearing a Weaver's Mask for days, which was dangerous to anyone's sanity. But for all that, Kaiku knew what she saw and stuck by it. She had seen the great branches of stone that reached from the witchstone's main mass into the walls of the cavern, too organic to be formed by pressure or any other geological force. She had seen *into* the witchstone as it fed, seen the bright veins running through the rock, seen the pulsing core at its centre. Whatever the witchstones were, they were more than just inert matter. They were alive, like the trees were alive. They *grew.*

'How do you know the witchstones are there if they haven't been found?' Yugi asked Saran.

'At least one *has* been found, in Quraal, five hundred years ago or more,' Saran said. 'It is mentioned in texts I stole from the Librum of Aquirra's own vaults, which I brought here at great peril to myself. These texts tell of an incident in a rural province wherein a small mining village began exhibiting sudden and violent behaviour. When soldiers were sent in to quell the disturbance, they were overwhelmed, with survivors reporting strange bouts of insanity and displays of unholy abilities by the villagers, such as being able to move objects without touching them and killing men from a distance without using weapons. The Theocrats sent in a much greater force to stamp out the heretics, and they triumphed with heavy losses. In the mine beneath the town, they found evidence of an altar upon which blood sacrifices had been made. The soldiers later said how they had been drawn to the altar by evil temptations and promises, but their faith was strong enough to resist, and with explosives they destroyed the altar and pounded it to dust, then sealed the mine.' He tossed his black hair and looked around the room. 'I am certain that what they found was a witchstone.'

'So they can be destroyed?' Zaelis asked.

'If the account is to be believed, yes,' Saran replied.

'You said that *at least* one has been found,' another member of the assembly asked. 'Do you imply that there are others?'

'Consider this,' Saran said. 'There are four witchstones that we know of in Saramyr, and all of them the Weavers have built monasteries on. Two in the Tchamil Mountains: one beneath Adderach and one beneath Igarach on the edge of the Tchom Rin desert. Another in the Lakmar Mountains on the isle of Fo. The last in the mountains near Lake Xemit. We know that the witchstones are there, thanks to the efforts of Kaiku and her father Ruito, because these are the epicentres of the surrounding corruption. That is four in Saramyr alone. Why should our continent be the only one to have them?'

'Why shouldn't it?' asked Yugi. 'Unless you know what they are and how they came to be there, then who knows how they are distributed over the lands?'

'But I *do* know,' Saran said. He turned his back on his audience a moment, walking over to the railing, looking down onto the shambolic rooftops of the Fold, the narrow streets through which children ran, the bridges and pulleys and stairways. 'This may be hard for you to hear.'

Kaiku sat up straighter, a thin shiver passing through her. A subdued mutter ran around the room.

Saran turned and stood leaning on the railing. 'I found records of a fire from the sky,' he said, his handsome face grave. 'Many thousands of years ago, in Quraal, back when our language was young. A cataclysm of flaming rocks, annihilating whole settlements, boiling lakes, smashing the earth. We believed it a punishment from our gods.' He tilted his head slightly, the sunlight shifting to add new accents to his cheekbones. 'I found pieces of the same story in Okhamba, where there is no written history, only their legends. Tales of destruction and burning. The same in Yttryx; more coherent documents this time, for theirs was the first alphabet. There is even talk of primitive paintings somewhere in the Newlands of Saramyr, where the Ugati made their own records of the catastrophe. Every ancient culture in the Near World has their version of the event, it seems, and they all correspond.' His eyes darkened. 'Then, following the advice of a man I met in Yttryx, I returned to Okhamba and went deep into it, to its centre, and there I found this.'

He walked quickly over to a table, where he picked up a roll of what looked like parchment. He knelt on the wicker matting in the centre of the room and smoothed it open. The assembly craned for a closer look.

'Careful,' he said. 'This is over two thousand years old, and it was copied from a document even older than that.'

This drew a collective gasp from the audience. What had seemed to be parchment was in fact animal skin of some kind, cured by some forgotten technique and in remarkably good condition considering its incredible age.

'I will, of course, pass it to our allies in the Red Order to verify its authenticity,' Saran went on. 'But I myself am convinced. The Fleshcrafters of the tribe I stole it from certainly were. It cost the lives of ten men to bring that here to you.' He exchanged a look with Tsata, who was watching him expressionlessly, his pallid green eyes blank.

Kaiku moved around to get a better view. The picture itself was enough to make her uneasy. The main characters were all but unidentifiable, stylised and jagged horrors that might have been men dancing or animals rutting. There was a fire in the central foreground, its flames time-dimmed but still visible. Kaiku found herself marvelling at the preservation methods that had carried it through all the ages. If it were not for Saran's promise to let the Red Order verify it – which they could easily do, at least as far as telling how old it was – then Kaiku would have not believed it could be so ancient.

She looked around its border, which was inscribed with many strange patterns, searching for the clue that Saran wanted them to find. At the top, in the centre, was the blazing lower half of the sun, and below that, in a crescent shape, were the moons.

The moons!

'There are four moons,' Yugi said, before anyone else could.

Kaiku felt something deep shift inside her, an unpleasant stirring that made her feel slightly nauseous. He was right. There was Aurus, biggest of them all; Iridima, with her cracked skin; Neryn, the small green moon; and a fourth, the same size as Neryn, charcoal black and scratched with dark red lines like scuff marks. Kaiku's skin began to crawl. She frowned, puzzled at her own reaction, and then noticed that Cailin was looking at her inquiringly, as if she had noted Kaiku's discomfort too.

Saran folded his arms and nodded. 'There were clues. I found several references to an entity called Aricarat in Yttryx, and one in Quraal to Ariquraa. I had assumed they were different versions of the same root word, but I could not imagine to what they referred. Even though they were almost always used in conjunction with stories of the other moon-sisters, I did not guess. After all, it was always referred to as male. Then I found an old Yttryxian creation myth that made reference to Aricarat as being born from the same stuff as the other moons, and it suddenly made sense.' Saran bowed his head. 'Aricarat was the fourth moon. He disappeared thousands of years ago. The moon-sisters, it seems, had a brother.'

If Saran had expected a barrage of abuse or denial, he was disappointed. The Saramyr pantheon had never held anything but three moons, and the genealogy of the gods was something taught to all children at an early age. To accept what he was suggesting ran counter to more than a thousand years of belief. But the assembly looked merely dazed. A few belligerent dissenters said loudly that his idea was ridiculous, but soon quieted, finding little support. Kaiku had sat down, overwhelmed suddenly by a terrible, creeping dread that made her lightheaded and faint.

'Are you unwell?' Cailin asked.

'I do not know,' Kaiku said. 'Something . . . there is something about Saran's account that is troubling me.'

'You think he is wrong?'

'No, I think he is *right.* I am certain of it. But I do not know *why* I am certain.'

Zaelis stood up. 'I believe I understand,' he said, his molten voice commanding attention. 'You think the fourth moon . . . Aricarat?' Saran tilted his head in a nod. 'You think that Aricarat was destroyed somehow back when the world was young, and that it fell to earth in pieces. And these pieces are the witchstones.'

'Exactly,' Saran said.

'This is a wild theory, Saran.'

'I have evidence to support it,' the Quraal man said, unruffled. 'But that will bear close examination, and will take time. There are dry tomes and parchments that require translating from dead languages.'

'You will permit me to see this evidence?'

'Of course. I am convinced of its authenticity. Anyone who wishes can study it.'

Zaelis limped in a slow circle around Saran, his brow furrowed, his hands linked behind his back. The wind chimes rang softly into the silence. 'Then I will reserve judgement until I have done so; and I would urge you all to do the same.' This last was addressed to the general assembly. He returned his attention to Saran, stopped pacing, and put a curled forefinger on his white-bearded chin. 'There is one thing that puzzles me, though.'

'Please,' Saran said, inviting his inquiry.

'If pieces of the moon rained down all over the Near World all that time ago, then why are they only found in the mountains? Why not the deserts and the plains?'

Saran smiled. He had been anticipating this.

'They *are* in the deserts and the plains,' he said. 'You are looking at the matter from the wrong angle. First, we should be asking how we know where the witchstones are at all. It is only through the Weavers. How do the Weavers *find* them? That I do not know. But until five years ago, the Weavers were not allowed to own land in Saramyr; the only places they could inhabit were the mountains, where no land laws applied as there were no crops to be had. It is not easy for them to mine something out from so deep underground and keep it a secret; yet in the mountains, behind their shields of misdirection that our spies cannot penetrate, they have leisure to do so. The reason that the only witchstones we know of are in the mountains are because they are the only ones the Weavers have been able to *get* to.'

'But not any more,' Zaelis concluded for him.

'No,' Saran agreed. 'Now the Weavers have bought land all over Saramyr and guard it jealously, and on that land they erect strange buildings, and not even the high families know what they do there. But I believe *I* know. They are mining for witchstones.'

There was a grim attentiveness fixed on him now. It was not a new idea to them, but in conjunction with what Saran believed he had discovered about the origin of the witchstones, it made for an uncomfortably neat fit.

'But why seek out new witchstones?' Zaelis asked. 'They seem to have enough for the Edgefathers to make Masks.'

'I do not pretend to know that,' Saran said. 'But I am certain that they are seeking them. And that is not the worst of it.' He spun around melodramatically from Zaelis to face the audience again. 'Extrapolate from this. Since they first appeared, the Weavers have infiltrated society and made themselves indispensible. You pay a terrible price for their powers, but you cannot be rid of them. Now that they are part of the empire itself, they are even harder to dislodge. All of us know that the Weavers must be removed; all of us know that they desire power for themselves. But I ask you, what if the Weavers' sole purpose is to find these witchstones? What if they grow to dominate all of Saramyr? Even if they somehow subverted your entire continent, they would be stuck. No other land would permit Weavers onto its shores in any number; we have a healthy and sensible mistrust of them. So what then?'

'They invade,' Cailin said, standing up herself. All eyes turned to her. She walked slowly into the centre of the room to stand by Zaelis, a tower of darkness against the noon sun. 'Perhaps you extrapolate too far, Saran Ycthys Marul.'

'Perhaps,' he conceded. 'And perhaps not. We know nothing of the motives of the Weavers other than what history has shown us; and in that, they have proved to be as aggressive and acquisitive as they have been able while still at the mercy of the high families. But I believe soon the high families will be at the *Weavers'* mercy, and then there will be no stopping them. And there would be no stopping an invading army backed up by Weavers, either. No other country has any kind of defence against that.' He looked to Tsata again; Kaiku caught the brief glance. 'This is not only a threat to Saramyr; this is a shadow that could fall on the whole of the Near World. I would have you aware of that.'

His report concluded, Saran walked to where the tattooed Tkiurathi was and sat next to him. It had been a lot for the audience to digest, and it was uncomfortable for them. He could see some of them already dismissing his findings as ridiculous speculation: how could he make guesses like that, with the little they knew of the Weavers? But they were the voices that would bring down the Libera Dramach if they were allowed to prevail, for Saran knew better than to allow the Weavers even an inch of leeway, to let them have the benefit of any doubt.

'Saran's information sheds a somewhat more foreboding light on another piece of news I received this morning,' said Zaelis. 'Nomoru, please stand.'

It was a young woman of perhaps twenty winters who responded. She was wiry and skinny and not particularly attractive, with a surly expression and short, blonde-brown hair in a ragged, spiky tangle. Her clothes were simple peasant garb, and her arms were inked with pictures, in the manner of street folk and beggars.

'Nomuru is one of our finest scouts,' Zaelis said. 'She has just returned from the westward end of the Fault, near where the Zan cuts through it. Tell them what you saw.'

'It's what I *didn't* see,' Nomoru said. Her dialect was clipped and sullen, muddied with coarse Low Saramyrrhic vowels. Everyone in the room immediately placed her as being from the Poor Quarter of Axekami, and weighted their prejudices accordingly. 'I know that area. Know it well. Not easy to cross the Fault lengthways, not with all that's in between here and there. I hadn't been there for a long time, though. Years. Too hard to get to.'

She appeared to be uncomfortable talking to so many people; it was obvious in her manner. Rather than be embarrassed, she took on an angry tone, but seemed not to know where to direct it.

'There was a flood plain there. I used to navigate by it. But this time . . . this time I couldn't find it.' She looked at Zaelis, who motioned for her to go on. 'Knew it was there, just couldn't get to it. Kept on getting turned around. But it wasn't me. I know that area well.'

Kaiku could see what was coming, suddenly. Her heart sank.

'Then I remembered. Been told about this before. A place that should be there, but you can't get to. Happened to her.' She pointed at Kaiku with an insultingly accusatory finger. 'Misdirection. They put it around places they don't want you to find.'

She looked fiercely at the assembly.

'The Weavers are in the Fault.'

ELEVEN

The Baraks Grigi tu Kerestyn and Avun tu Koli walked side by side along the dirt path, between the tall rows of kamako cane. Nuki's eye looked down on them benevolently from above, while tiny hovering reedpeckers swung back and forth seeking suitable candidates to drill with their pointed beaks. The sky was clear, the air dry, the heat not too fierce: another day of perfect weather. And yet Grigi's thoughts were anything but sunny.

He reached out and snapped off a cane with a twist of his massive hand; a puff of powder burst out from where it was broken.

'Look here,' he said, proffering it to Avun. His companion took it and turned it slowly under his sleepy, hooded gaze. There were streaks of black discolouration along its outer surface, not that Avun needed such a sign to tell it had been blighted. Good kamako cane was hard enough to be used as scaffolding; this was brittle and worthless.

'The entire crop?' Avun asked.

'Some can be salvaged,' Grigi mused, waddling his immense frame over to the other side of the dirt path and breaking off another cane experimentally. 'It's strong enough, but if word gets out that the rest of the crop is afflicted . . . Well, I suppose I can sell through a broker, but the price won't be half what it could be. It's a gods-cursed disaster.'

Avun regarded the other blandly. 'You cannot pretend that you did not expect as much.'

'True, true,' said Grigi. 'In fact, half of me had hoped for this. If the harvest had picked up this year, then some of our allies would be having second thoughts about the side they had chosen. Desperation makes weak links in politics, and they're easily undone when times turn.' He tossed the cane aside in disgust. 'But I don't like seeing thousands of shirets in market goods going to waste, whatever the cause. Especially not mine!'

'It can only strengthen our position,' Avun said. 'We have made preparations against this. Others are not so fortunate. They will see that the only alternative to starvation is to oust Mos and put someone who knows how to run the empire on the throne.'

Grigi gave him a knowing glance. There was something else that they did not say, that they never spoke of any more than necessary. Getting Grigi on the throne was only part of the plan; the other part was getting the Weavers away from it. Neither of them had any particular animosity towards the Weavers – no more than any other high family had, anyway, in that they resented the necessity of having them – but they sensed the popular mood, and they knew how the common folk felt. The peasantry thought that the Weavers were responsible for the evil times that had befallen the empire, that their appointment as equals to the high familes was an affront against tradition and the gods. Avun did not know whether that was true or not, but it really didn't matter. Once Grigi was Blood Emperor, he would have to cut the Weavers down to size, or the same thing that was happening to Mos would happen to him.

But it was a dangerous game, plotting against the Weavers under their very noses. For like all the high families, Grigi and Avun had Weavers in their own homes, and who could tell how much they knew?

They walked on a little, until the dirt track emerged from the forest of kamako cane and curved left to follow the contours of a shallow hill. Below them, Grigi's plantation spread out like a canvas, uneven polygons of light brown tessellating with fields of green, where the cane had not yet been stripped and still retained its leafy aerial parts. In between were long, low barns and yards where harvesting equipment was left. Men and women, genderless beneath the wide wicker hats that protected them from the sun, moved slowly between the rows, cutting or stripping or erecting nets over the unblighted sections to keep off the persistent reedpeckers. From up here, all looked normal, and faintly idyllic. An untrained eye would not guess that there was poison in the earth.

Grigi sighed regretfully. He was being philosophical about his loss, but it still made him sad. Waste was not something he approved of, a fact evidenced by his enormous frame and ponderous weight. In Saramyr high society, it was usual to prepare more food than was necessary, and let diners pick and choose as they would; people ate only as much as they wanted and left the rest. That lesson had never taken with Grigi, and his fondness for fine meals and his reluctance to leave any on the table had made him obese. He wore voluminous robes and a purple skullcap, beneath which his black hair was knotted in a queue; a thin beard hung from his chin to give his fleshy face definition.

To look at him, it would not be easy to guess he was a formidable Barak, and perhaps the only contender to the throne since he had annihilated Blood Amacha's forces. He appeared rather as a pampered noble, gone soft on luxury, and his high, girlish voice and passion for poetry and history merely corroborated the illusion. But gluttony was his only vice. Unlike many of the other Baraks, he did not indulge in narcotics, bloodsports, courtesans or any of the other privileges of rank. Beneath the layers of fat there was hard muscle on a broad skeleton well over six feet in height, a legacy of a ruthless regime of wrestling and lifting heavy rocks. Much like his companion Avun, whose languid, drowsy manner hid a brain as sharp and unforgiving as a blade, he was often underestimated by those who assumed that the weakness of character that led to such excess hinted at a weak mind.

If he had any fault, it was the one that his entire family shared: he was bitter about the twist of fate that had dethroned his father and allowed Blood Erinima to become the high family over a decade ago. If not for that, Kerestyn would still have been the head of the empire. It was his bitterness that led him to make an ill-advised assault on Axekami during the last coup; ill-advised because, despite his clever disposal of Blood Amacha, he had not counted on the cityfolk uniting to repel his invading force, and they kept him out long enough for Blood Batik to enter the capital at the east gate and take the throne themselves.

Now the people of Axekami wished they had let him in, he thought darkly.

But if it was fate that had torn Blood Kerestyn from the Imperial Keep, then it was fate that would put them back there. His father was dead now, and his two older brothers carried away by crowpox – so called because nobody ever survived it, and crows gathered around in anticipation of a meal. The mantle had passed to him, and now things were turning his way again. Nobles and armies flocked to his banner, supporting the only real alternative to the Blood Emperor Mos. This time, he vowed, he would not fail.

They ambled in the sun for a time, walking along the side of the hill to where the trail began to take them back through the fields of kamako cane, towards the Kerestyn estate. It was one of several that the family owned, and he and Avun had been using it as a base for the diplomatic visits they had been conducting among the highborn of the Southern Prefectures. The Prefects were gone now, rendered unnecessary by the Weavers, who made it pointless to appoint largely independent governors over distant lands when instantaneous communication meant that they could be overseen from the capital, and thus power kept with the Imperial family. But the Prefects' wealthy descendants remained, and they were appalled at seeing their beloved land rendered barren by the blight. They were eager to make promises to Grigi, if he could stop the rot in the land. Of course, he had no idea *how*, but by the time they knew that it would be too late.

'What news of your daughter, Avun?' he asked eventually, knowing that the Barak would walk in complete silence all the way back to the estate unless he spoke first.

'Her ship should have arrived several days ago,' he said offhandedly. 'I expect to learn of her capture very soon.'

'It will be something of a relief to you, I imagine,' Grigi said. He knew the whole truth behind Avun's rift with his daughter; in fact, he had been instrumental in spreading the smokescreen to save face for Blood Koli. 'To have her back, I mean.'

Avun's lip curled. 'I mean to ensure that she does not embarrass her family this way again. When I return to Mataxa Bay, I will deal with her.'

'Are you so confident that you have her, then?'

'Her movements have been known to me ever since she arrived in

Okhamba,' he said. 'And my informant is extremely reliable. I do not predict any difficulties. She will be in very capable hands.'

When Kaiku arrived at Zaelis's study, she found Cailin already there. It was a small, close room with thick wooden walls to dampen sound from the rest of the house. One wall was crammed with ledgers, and a table rested in a corner with brushes scattered haphazardly across it and a half-written scroll partially furled. The shutters were thrown open against the afternoon sun, and the air was hot and still. Zaelis and Cailin were standing near the windows, their features dimmed by contrast to the bright external light. Birds peeped and chittered on the gables and rooftops below.

'How could I have guessed *you* would be first to offer your services?' Cailin said wryly.

Kaiku ignored the comment. 'Zaelis,' she began, but he raised a seamed palm.

'I know, and yes you may,' he replied.

Kaiku was momentarily wrongfooted. 'It appears that I have become somewhat predictable of late,' she observed.

Zaelis laughed unexpectedly. 'My apologies, Kaiku. Do not doubt that I am grateful to you for the good work you have done for us these past years; I'm glad that you still have the enthusiasm.'

'I only wish she were so eager to apply herself to her studies,' Cailin said, arching an eyebrow.

'This is more important,' Kaiku returned. 'And I have to go. I am the only one who can do it. The only one who can use the Mask.'

Cailin tilted her head in acquiescence. 'For once, I agree.'

Kaiku had not expected that. She had been ready for an argument. In truth, half of her *wanted* them to argue, to forbid her to go. Gods, just the thought of it made her afraid. Crossing the Fault was bad enough, between the terror of the spirits and the murderous clans and the hostile terrain; but at the end of it waited the Weavers, the most deadly enemy of all. Yet she had no option, not in the eyes of Ocha, to whom she had sworn an oath of vengeance. She did not want to throw herself into danger this way. She merely had to.

Zaelis stepped away from the window, out of the dazzling light. 'This may be more important than you imagine, Kaiku,' he murmured in his molten bass.

Kaiku had the impression that she had come in at the end of a grave conversation between the two of them, and she was unsure what she had missed.

'The Xarana Fault has always been our sanctuary,' he said. 'It has hidden us and protected us from the Weavers for many years now . . .' He trailed off, then looked up at her, his gaze shadowed beneath his white eyebrows. 'If the Fold has been compromised, all may be lost. We must know what they are planning, and we must know now. Go with Yugi and Nomoru; find out what the Weavers are hiding at the other end of the Fault.'

Kaiku made an affirmative noise, then looked expectantly at Cailin.

'I will not try and dissuade you,' Cailin said. 'You are too headstrong. One day you will realise the power you have and how you are squandering it with your negligence; then you will come back to me, and I will teach you how to harness what you have. But until then, Kaiku, you will go your own way.'

Kaiku frowned slightly, suspicious at this easy capitulation; but she did not have a chance to question it before Zaelis spoke again.

'It is all connected somehow, Kaiku,' he said. 'The Weavers in the Fault, the strange buildings they have constructed all over Saramyr, the information that Saran brought, what happened to Lucia . . . We have to act, Kaiku, but I do not know which direction to strike in.' He looked at Cailin. 'I think sometimes we have hidden too long, while outside our enemies have strengthened.'

But Kaiku had caught something in his explanation that chilled her. 'What *did* happen to Lucia?'

'Ah,' said Zaelis. 'Perhaps you had better sit down.'

Mishani lay awake in the guest bedchamber of Chien os Mumaka's townhouse, and listened to the night.

The room was simple and spacious, as Mishani liked it. A few carefully placed pots holding miniature trees or flowers stood on tall, narrow tables. Prayer beads hung from the ceiling, tapping softly against each other in the warm stir of the breeze that stole around the edges of the sliding paper screens. They were supposed to be left open, to provide a view of the enclosed garden beyond, but Mishani had kept them shut. Her attention was not on the external sounds of Hanzean: the distant hoot of an owl, the ubiquitous rattle of chikkikii, the occasional snatch of distant laughter or the creak of a cart. She was listening for sounds within the house: for a footstep, for the quiet hiss of a partition being drawn aside, for a dagger drawn from its sheath.

Tonight was the last night she was going to spend at Chien's hospitality. One way or another.

She had slept little and lightly these past four days. When Nuki's eye was in the sky it was almost possible to forget the danger she was in; Chien was an excellent host, and despite everything she had even begun to enjoy his company. They dined together, they had musicians perform for them, they wandered the grounds or sat in the garden and talked. But it was when the sun went down and she was alone that the fear came close enough to touch her. Then the immediacy of her situation struck home, and the air was full of whispered doubts. There were too many things wrong. Why so suspiciously generous in offering to provide passage from Okhamba? Why the convoluted route of the carriage from the jetty to the townhouse? And why did he never take her outside the walls of his compound, in all of these five days? In Hanzean there was theatre, art, spectacles of all kinds that a host was virtually obligated to show a visitor; and yet Chien had not offered any. On the one hand, Mishani was relieved at not being forced to parade around a port town, for any public exposure was dangerous; but the fact that Chien seemed to know that did not bode well for her.

If Chien was to make his play, she knew it would be tonight. This evening she had gone through the ritual of informing him of her departure on the morning of the morrow. It was perhaps a little inelegant to seem in such haste to leave after staying for the bare minimum of time that etiquette required, but her nerves had frayed enough so that she did not care. If she got away from this, she was unlikely ever to come across Chien again anyway. He was too well connected in the maritime industry to risk it. He had not seemed offended; but then, he was still frustratingly hard to read.

Tonight, she resolved, she would not sleep at all. She had asked one of the handmaidens to make her a brew of xatamchi, an analgesic with a strong stimulant side-effect usually taken in the morning to overcome menstrual pains. The handmaiden had warned her that she would be up all night if she took it so late in the day, but Mishani had said that she was willing to take that risk, and only xatamchi would do.

The handmaiden had not been exaggerating. Mishani had never taken xatamchi or anything similar before – her cycles were mercifully gentle, and had been all her life – but she knew now why she had been advised against it. She could not imagine being further from sleep as she was now, and she felt marvellously aware despite the late hour. In fact, the inactivity of lying on her sleeping-mat was chafing at her, and she longed to go out and stroll around in the garden at night.

She was just considering doing so when she heard a soft thud through the paper screens on the other side of the room. Someone else was in the garden, she realised with a thrill of fright; and she knew with a sudden certainty that her enemies were coming for her at last.

Her ears strained as she lay there, seeking another sound. Her heart had become very loud in her ears; she felt the pressure of her pulse at her temples. A whispered voice: a short, terse command from one to another, too quiet to make out. It was beyond doubt, then. Now she could only wait to hear the dreadful sound of the paper screens sliding back, to pray to the gods that they would pass by, change their minds somehow, just leave her where she lay.

Her eyes were closed, feigning sleep, when it happened. A whisper of wood sliding against wood, slow and careful so as not to wake her. A soft breeze from outside, carrying with it the fresh, healthy smell of the trees in the garden; and another smell, a faint metallic tang of sweat. Then, overwhelmingly, the stink of matchoula oil, a few breaths of which would render a person unconscious.

The creak of leather as one of them crouched down next to her mat.

She screamed at the top of her lungs, throwing her blanket aside in one violent movement and flinging the handful of red dust that she had kept gathered in her palm. The intruder, surprised, jerked back in alarm, and the dust hit him full in the face: abrasive bathing salts that she had smuggled into her bedroom. He cried out in pain as the scratchy crystals got into his eyes and bubbled on his tongue and lips, fizzing with the moisture there. The second shadow in the room was already lunging at her, but she had rolled off the mat and got to her feet. She was wearing an outdoor robe instead of nightclothes, and her curved dagger sheened in the wan moonlight.

'You tell your master Chien that I will not be taken so easily!' she hissed, surprising herself with the strength in her voice; then she cried: '*Intruders! Intruders!*' as loud as she could manage. The gods knew what good that would do – she doubted it would bring any aid, since it was the master of the house that had sent these men – but she was not going to allow herself to be stolen away in the night without making it known to everybody she could.

The one who was not blinded ran at her, oblivious to his companion's cries. He was wielding a pad of cloth that reeked of matchoula oil. They wanted her alive then, she thought, through the cold panic that was gripping her. That gave her an advantage.

She backed away as he came at her, and slashed wildly with her blade. She was no fighter: she had never been threatened with genuine physical violence in her life beyond the occasional slap from her father, and did not know how to react to it. The intruder swore as the dagger cut into the meat of his forearm, then he smacked her hand aside, and numbing force of the blow sent the blade skidding away. Though slender in build, he was much bigger and stronger than her, and she had no hope of overmatching him. She tried to run, but he grabbed at her, only half-catching her wrist; she spun and tripped on her hem, and in a flail of hair and robes she crashed through the paper screens and fell down the two short wooden steps to the townhouse's central garden.

She landed on the path that ran around the inside edge of the house, the paper screens falling around her. The impact was enough to bring tears to her eyes. She scrabbled to free herself from the light wooden frames of the screens. Her ankle-length hair was tangled and caught in everything, and she kept kneeling on it and having it wrench painfully at her scalp.

Then the screens were torn away from her, and there was her attacker. In the warm, moonlit night, she could see him better. He was dressed in bandit clothes, and his hair was unkempt, his face swarthy and angry. She slipped out from under his grip, another scream rising from her to wake the household. She got only a few paces across the garden before he caught her, hooking his foot under hers so that she tumbled again, rolling into a flowerbed and cracking her wrist on a rock. Then he was on her, pinning her hands with one arm while she thrashed and kicked.

'*Get off me!*' she cried through gritted teeth, and she felt the impact as one of her kicks connected and the man grunted. She thought for a moment that he might release her, but instead he knelt one leg agonisingly hard on her stomach, driving the breath from her, and he wadded the matchoula-soaked cloth in one hand and brought it to her face. Then she was being smothered, and his relentless palm was moving with the shaking of her head and would not be dislodged. The stinging reek was in her nostrils, on her lips, and her lungs burned for oxygen. She bucked and twisted in panic, but she was small and frail and she did not have the strength to get him off her.

Then, a shriek from somewhere in the house, and running feet thumping across the turf. The pad was pulled away suddenly, the knee released, and Mishani gasped as she sucked in the air, wild-eyed.

But the man who held her had only dropped the pad to pull a knife, and it was already driving towards her throat. Something deep and faster than thought made her shift her shoulders and shove with her knees, now that she had the purchase to do so. She bucked him forward enough so that he automatically put out his arms for balance, his knife-stroke arrested; and an instant later an arrow took him through the eye, the force of the shaft throwing him off her and sending him tumbling into a shallow pool at the base of a rockery.

She scrambled to her feet before he had come to rest, sweeping up the knife that he had dropped and brandishing it as she turned to face the ones who were running across the garden. Panting, dishevelled, her mass of black hair in a muddy mess, she glared at the shadows that came for her and held her blade ready.

'Mistress Mishani!' said Chien, the foremost of them. Behind him were three guards, one carrying a bow. At the sound of her name, she raised the dagger to throat-height, daring him to come closer. He scrambled to a halt with his hands raised placatingly before him. 'Mistress Mishani, it's me. Chien.'

'I know who you are,' she told him, an unforgivable tremble in her voice from the shock of being attacked in such a way. 'Stay back.'

Chien seemed confused. 'It's me,' he repeated.

'Your men have failed, Chien,' she said. 'If you want to kill me, you will have to do it yourself.'

'*Kill* you? I . . .' Chien said, lost for words. Behind her, she heard a guard call out. Chien looked over her shoulder. 'Are there more?' he asked her.

'How many did you hire?' she returned.

The second attacker was dragged out behind her into the garden. He was limp. Poison, she guessed. His employer would want no evidence left.

'Mistress Mishani . . .' he said, sounding terribly wounded. 'How could you think this of me?'

'Come now, Chien,' she said. 'You did not get to where you were without seeing all the angles. And nor did I.'

'Then you have not considered the right ones, it seems,' Chien said. He sounded desperate to convince her, almost wheedling. 'I had nothing to do with this!'

Mishani glanced around. There were no escape routes; guards were everywhere now. She could not fight her way out of here. If they wanted her dead, they could simply shoot her.

'Why should I believe you, Chien?' she asked.

'Put down the blade, and I will *tell* you why,' he said. 'But not here. Your business and mine is between us.'

Mishani felt a great weariness suddenly. She tossed the dagger away with an insultingly casual gesture, then gave the merchant a withering look. 'Lead on, then.'

'May we drop the façade now?' Mishani demanded, when they were alone.

They stood in Chien's accounting office, a sombre room heavy with dark wood and weighty furniture. Scrolls cluttered the shelves and lay across the desk where the merchant usually worked, heaped untidily against stacks of leather-bound tally books. The Blood Mumaka crest hung on one wall, a curving pictogram rendered in gold-edged calligraphy against a grey background. Chien had lit the lanterns in their brackets, and now the room was alive with a soft, warm glow.

'There is no façade, Mistress Mishani,' Chien said, then blew out the taper he was holding and put it back in the pot it had come from. He turned to her, and there was new strength in his voice all of a sudden. 'If I wanted you killed, I could have done it many times by now, and by subtler means. If I wanted to give you up to your father, I could have done that, too.'

'Why are you still playing this game?' Mishani said quietly. She might have been muddied and bedraggled, but her poise and gravitas had returned, and she seemed formidable for such a slight woman. 'Your words betray you. You know the state of play between myself and my father. You have known from the start. If you do not mean me any harm, then why insist on inviting me to stay at your pleasure? You have been well aware of the uncertainty and doubt I have suffered these past days. Does it give you joy to torment me? Your maliciousness shames you. Do with me as you will, since you seem to hold all the cards here; but give up this sham, Chien, for it is getting tiresome now.'

'You forget who I am and who you are, that you can throw insults around so lightly!' Chien snapped, his temper igniting. 'Before you waste another breath on calling me honourless, then listen to me. I *did* know that you were estranged from your father, and that he wanted you back. I also knew that your arrival in Okhamba had been marked by merchants in the Barak Avun's employ. You got away from Saramyr without being seen by his people, though the gods only know what luck you must have had; but the moment you showed up in Kisanth you were spotted. They were going to wait until you returned to Saramyr, watch what ship you were travelling on, and have someone there to meet you when you disembarked. Those were your father's men. I'm not. In fact, I've made a considerable risk on your behalf, and he most likely now counts me one of his enemies!'

Mishani was pleased that she had rattled him. She did seem to have a way of getting under his skin; she had learned that in the time they had spent together.

'Go on,' she said. This was suddenly interesting.

Chien took a steadying breath and stalked to the other side of the room. 'I had a carriage meet us at the docks, and brought you and your friends here before your father's men could get to you. It was necessary to take a circuitous route through Hanzean in case we were followed; I imagine you noticed that. The location of my townhouse isn't generally known.' He waved a hand to dismiss the point. 'I saw your friends to safety, but you I knew would not be safe. You said you were heading south. I couldn't let you. Not until I'd found out who your father had hired and what they knew. They would have been on you before you got ten miles down the Great Spice Road.' He gazed at her earnestly. 'So I have kept you here, under my protection, for these past days, while my men have been trying to divine just how much trouble you're in.'

'This was your *protection?*' Mishani said softly. 'I was almost killed, Chien. You will forgive me if my faith in you has been shaken somewhat.'

Chien looked pained. 'That is my shame. Not what you would imagine, Mistress Mishani. I have not tormented you or betrayed you. I have tried to safeguard you, and I failed.'

Mishani regarded him coldly. His explanation fitted, at least, but it seemed to her frankly unlikely. Still, she could not think why he would waste the effort on making it up, nor why, if he meant her harm, he had not done it to her by now. Why kill his own men? She supposed that it could be a trick – kill his men to win her trust; she had seen cleverer ploys than that in her time at court – but what advantage would that win him? She considered asking him why he was protecting her at all, then thought better of it. Any answer would likely be a lie. What was there that he thought she could do for him, what *point* was there in his winning her favour? He knew she was politically impotent.

'I didn't tell you before,' Chien said. 'If you realised that I knew about you and your father, you would have tried to get away from me as soon as you could. That would have only got you caught faster.'

Mishani had surmised this already, just as she had guessed why the intruders started off trying to kidnap her and ended up trying to kill her. Their orders were simple: alive if possible, dead if necessary. She was not in the least surprised at her father's ruthlessness.

Chien looked at her levelly, his blocky features even, the lantern light limning one side of his shaven head. 'Mistress Mishani, you may believe me or not, but I was going to tell you all this in the morning to try and prevent you from leaving. I left it too late, it seems. Your father's men found you, and nearly had your life.' He walked over to her. 'If there is anything I can do to atone for my failure to protect you, you have only to name it.'

Mishani studied him for a long moment. She *did* believe him, but that did not mean she trusted him. If he was in alliance with her father, or even if he wasn't, there was something down the line that he wanted from her, something that she did not even know she had in her power to give. Chien's attempt at an explanation had made him more puzzling than ever. Was this an elaborate trap, or something entirely unexpected? Was he telling the truth about her father's men?

It didn't matter. He owed her now, and she needed him.

'Take me south,' she said.

TWELVE

The Fold was alive with celebration. The paths between the houses thronged with revellers in the heat of the late afternoon. The morning rituals were over, the noontime feast had been cooked and consumed, and now the people had taken to the streets, sated and merry and many of them already drunk. In the cities there would be fireworks as night drew in, but here in the Fault it was too dangerous to broadcast their presence with such fancies. Still, there would be bonfires, and another, more communal feast, and the revelries would go on past dawn.

Aestival Week had begun.

It was the biggest event in the Saramyr calendar: the last farewell to summer, the festival of the harvest. Since Saramyr folk counted their age in the amount of harvests they had lived through rather than the date on which they were born, everyone was a year older today. On the last day of Aestival Week, a grand ritual would see out the season, and autumn would begin with the next dawn.

The morning had seen a ceremony conducted on the valley floor for the whole town, by three priests of different orders. The denomination did not matter in any case, since Aestival Week was about thanking the gods and spirits alike. The bulk of the ceremony was an expression of gratitude for the simple joy and beauty of nature. Saramyr folk were particularly close to their land, and they had never lost their sense of the magnificence of the continent that they lived on. Everyone attended, for while most Saramyr picked and chose their godly allegiances piecemeal and prayed or attended temples as much as their conscience dictated, there were certain days when even the least pious person would not risk staying away if they could help it. And if there were some shreds of bleak and bitter irony in celebrating the harvest this particular year, they did not spoil the excitement that marked the beginning of the revels to come.

The midday feast was as much a tradition as the morning rituals, though its content differed wildly from region to region. The Fold's enterpreneurial importers had been stretched to their limit to fulfil the many and varied orders over the preceding weeks, and charged accordingly. Gazel lizards from Tchom Rin, lapinth from the Newlands, coilfish from Lake Xemit, shadeberries and kokomach and sunroot, wines and spirits and exotic beverages: one meal in the year had to be perfect for everyone, and this was it. Most people gathered in groups with family and friends, with the prestige of creating the meal going to best cook among them. Afterwards, small gifts were exchanged, vows between couples were renewed, promises were made between families.

Now the valley floor was a mass of preparations as tables and tents and mats were set for the enormous feast after dark. Bonfires were being built, pennants hung, a stage erected. But around the valley rim, the guards had been doubled, and they looked outward over the Fault, knowing that they dared not be caught off guard even now.

Kaiku walked with Lucia through the crowded, baked-dirt streets, along one of the higher ledges on which the town was built. It was a little quieter up here, and the streets were not yet so crammed that it was difficult to move. A few temporary stalls sold favours and streamers, or hot nuts, and groups of singing revellers would sweep by them every so often; but most people that they passed were either coming up from the main crush on the lower levels of the valley slope or going down to it. The two of them idled, sated with the memory of the wonderful meal cooked for them by Zaelis, who had revealed a somewhat startling culinary talent. They had shared their celebration with Yugi and a dozen others. Cailin was not to be found, and Saran and Tsata were also elsewhere, having not been seen since the day they arrived. They were not missed, though Kaiku did find herself glancing at the doorway every so often, expecting to see the tall, stern Quraal man there. She supposed that he and his Tkiurathi companion did not observe Aestival Week.

It had been a warm time, and their troubles had been forgotten in the uncomplicated atmosphere of happiness there. Kaiku sought to preserve that, and so she had wandered away before conversation could turn to weightier matters, and taken Lucia with her. Later, Lucia would undoubtedly find friends of her own age – despite her quietness, she had a magnetism that made her popular among the other children of the Fold – but for now, she was wonderful company for Kaiku, who felt contemplative and not a little emotional. Such a precious child. Kaiku could not imagine what she would have done if . . . if . . .

Lucia caught Kaiku looking at her fondly, and smiled. 'Stop worrying,' she said. 'I only fainted.'

'You fainted for *two days*,' Kaiku returned. Heart's blood, two days! When Kaiku had learned of her strange experience with the river spirits, she had been frantic with concern. It was only because Lucia appeared to be fully recovered now that Kaiku had been placated. She dreaded to think what worse consequences could have come from Lucia's interfering in the unknown. Thank the gods that she seemed alright now.

'It was just something bad,' Lucia said, shedding no light on her ordeal at all. 'Something happened on the river. The spirits didn't like it. It gave me a shock.'

'I just want you to be careful,' Kaiku told her. 'You are still young. There is plenty of time to learn what you can and cannot do.'

'I'm fourteen harvests today!' Lucia mock-protested. 'Not so young any more.'

They came to a wooden bridge that arced between two ledges, vaulting over the rooftops of the plateau below, and there they rested, leaning their arms on the parapet and looking out into the valley. The whole haphazard jumble of the Fold was spread beneath them, and the raucous sounds of merriment drifted up from below. A few revellers on the rooftops saw them and waved. Nuki's eye looked down on it all from a cloudless sky that gave no hint that summer was ending.

'You're still worrying,' Lucia observed, looking sidelong at her friend. She was uncannily perceptive, and it was not worth hiding the truth from her.

'It is what Zaelis said that worries me,' Kaiku explained.

Lucia seemed to sadden a little. They both knew what she referred to. Earlier, Zaelis had toasted Lucia's recovery, and asked her when she would be ready to tackle the spirits again. Kaiku had responded somewhat irately on Lucia's behalf, telling him that Lucia was not some tool to be sharpened until she was useful enough to wield against an enemy. She had already suffered some unknown trauma that even she did not understand; Kaiku admonished Zaelis for even thinking about pushing her further. It had cast a momentary pall over the midday meal; but then Yugi had defused the situation with a well-chosen comment, and both Kaiku and Zaelis had dropped the matter. In retrospect, Kaiku felt that she had been overprotective, a reaction fuelled by her anger at the fact that she had not been told of Lucia's ordeal until after the assembly. Yet she could not stop fretting about it.

'Do not listen to him,' she said. 'I know he is like a father to you, but only you know your capabilities, Lucia. Only you know what you are willing to risk.'

Lucia's pale blue eyes were far away. She was not too much shorter than Kaiku these days. Kaiku's gaze flickered over the burns on the back of her neck, and she felt the familiar jab of guilt. Burns that Kaiku had given her. She wished that Lucia did not wear them so openly.

'We need to know,' Lucia said quietly. 'About what happened on the river.'

'That is not true,' Kaiku responded, her tone sharp. 'Heart's blood, Lucia! You know as well as anyone that the spirits are not to be trifled with. Nothing is worth risking yourself like that. Start small again, if you must. Work up to it.' She paused, then added: 'Zaelis is sending spies to investigate. Let them do their work.'

'We may not have time,' Lucia said simply.

'Are those Zaelis's words, or yours?'

Lucia did not give a reply. Kaiku felt her mood souring a little, but she was unwilling to let this go. She tried to keep the stridency out of her tone in the spirit of the occasion.

'Lucia,' she said softly. 'I know the responsibility you have to bear. But even the strongest backs bend under the weight of expectations. Do not let anyone push you. Not even Zaelis.'

Lucia turned to Kaiku with a dreamy expression on her face. She had heard, even if she seemed inattentive. A part of her was listening to the wind, and the ravens who watched her from their perches on the rooftops.

'Do you remember when Mishani came to you in the roof gardens of the Imperial Keep, carrying that nightdress for you?' Kaiku asked.

Lucia nodded.

'What did you think? When she offered it to you?'

'I thought it would kill me,' Lucia said simply.

'Would you have taken it?' Kaiku asked. 'Would you have worn it, even knowing what it was?'

Lucia turned away slowly, looking back out over the town. A clamour of drunken men staggered across the bridge behind them, hollering bawdy songs. Kaiku flinched in annoyance.

A silence stretched between them.

'Lucia, you are not somebody's sacrifice,' she said, her voice becoming gentle. 'You are too unselfish, too passive. You are not a pawn here, don't you see that? If you do not learn that now, then what will you be like in the years to come, when people will look to you with even greater hope in their eyes?' Kaiku sighed, and put her arm around Lucia's slender shoulders, hugging her companionably. 'I think of you as a sister. And so it is my job to worry about you.'

A grin touched the corner of Lucia's mouth, and she returned the hug with both arms. 'I'll try,' she said. 'To be more like you.' The grin spread. 'A big, stubborn loudmouth.'

Kaiku gave a gasp of spurious disbelief and pulled away from the hug. 'Monster!' she cried, and Lucia fled laughing as Kaiku chased her off the bridge and up the street.

Night fell over the Xarana Fault. Fires were started and paper lanterns were lit in warm constellations. The darkness lay muggy and sultry around the periphery of the celebrations, but within the light all was merriment. The communal feast was well underway. Many people had already left the table to make room for others, and had gone to watch the actors performing on the stage, or were dancing to an impromptu orchestra of six musicians who were improvising their way around old folk melodies. The mismatched instruments and varying skill of the players made for a controlled raucousness, raw-edged and visceral. The low, sawing drone of the three-stringed miriki was counterpointed by the glassy, plucked chimes of the reed harp and the mournful double-barrelled melodies of the two dewhorns. The rhythm was dictated by a swarthy man and his animal-skin drum, while over it all played the true talent of the group, a lady who had once been a courtesan for the Imperial family before the last coup. She played the irira, a seven-stringed instrument of leather and bone and wood that produced a hollow and fragile keening, and her achingly sweet touch on the strings almost made the air glimmer.

Kaiku, red-cheeked with wine and heat and laughter, danced a peasant dance with the young men and women of the Fold. It was much more energetic and less elegant than the courtly fashion, but far more fun. She spun and whirled from one man's arms to another, and then found herself with an Aberrant boy, whose skin was clammy as a dead fish and whose blank eyes were bulbous and blind. After the initial moment of surprise, she led him through the wild motions until someone else took his hand and they parted. Exhilarated and not a little drunk, she let the music sweep her up, and for once her cares were forgotten in the movement and the motion of the dance.

The song ended abruptly as she was being passed from one dancer to another, and she was surprised to find Yugi before her as the revellers rested in the pregnant silence between tunes. They were both breathing hard from the exertion, and exchanged a guilty grin.

'My timing is as good as ever, then,' he said. His eyes were very bright, his pupils huge. 'May I have the honour?' He held out his hand, inviting her to partner him for the next dance.

But Kaiku had seen a figure watching her on the edge of the lantern light, leaning against one of the wooden poles that held up the overhead banners.

'My apologies, Yugi,' she said, kissing him on his stubbled cheek. 'I have someone I have to see.'

And with that she left him, the music started up again behind her, and he was gathered up by a pretty Newlander girl and drawn into the heart of the dance. Kaiku left the noise and the warmth, walking out to where the darkness and quiet held ready to invade, and where Saran was waiting.

'Do you dance?' she asked, tilting herself flirtatiously.

'Regretfully not,' he replied. 'I do not think we Quraal have such loose joints as your folk seem to.'

It took her a moment to realise that it was a joke, delivered as it was in a tone dry as dust.

'Where have you been?' she asked. She wavered slightly, but the flush in her cheeks and her more inviting manner only heightened her allure to him.

'This is not my celebration,' he said, his features dark against the moonless night.

'No, I mean: where have you *been*?' she persisted. 'It has been days since the assembly. Have you forgotten me that soon? Could you not even muster a goodbye? Spirits, I am leaving the day after tomorrow to cross the Fault!'

'I know,' he said. 'Tsata is going with you.'

'Is he?' Kaiku asked. That was news to her. 'And what about you?'

'I have not decided yet.' He was silent for a long moment. 'I thought things would be awkward,' he said at last. 'So I stayed away.'

Kaiku regarded him for a time, then held out her hand. 'Walk with me,' she said.

He hesitated, studying her intensely; then he took it. Kaiku tugged him gently away from the pole he had been leaning on, and they made their way around the edges of the celebration, back towards the town. To their left, the valley was like a void, only defined by the lighter night sky that surmounted its rim. To their right, there was fire and laughter and feasting. They walked the line of the limbo in between, where the two sides met and blended and neither could quite find dominance.

'Part of me . . .' Kaiku began, then stopped, then began again. 'Part of me is glad to be going. I have been idle too long, I think. I have been helping the Libera Dramach in my own small way over the years, but these subtle increments of progress do not satisfy me.' She looked up at Saran. 'Nor do they satisfy Ocha.'

'The gods are patient, Kaiku,' he said. 'Do not underestimate the Weavers. You were lucky once. Most people do not get a second chance.'

'Is that *concern* I hear from you?' she teased.

Saran released her hand and shrugged. 'Why would you care for my concern?'

Kaiku's expression fell a little. 'I apologise. I did not mean to mock you.' She had forgotten how tender his pride was. They walked a little further.

'It is the Mask I fear,' she said, feeling it necessary to give a little to rekindle the moment that had existed between them. 'It has been five years since I wore it last, but it still calls to me.' She shivered suddenly. 'I have to wear it again, if we are to get past the Weavers' misdirection.'

'You are cold,' Saran said, unclasping his cloak and putting it around her shoulders. She wasn't, but she let him anyway, and as he fixed the clasp at her throat she put her hand over his. He paused, prolonging the contact, before drawing away.

'Why not have a Sister unravel the barrier?' he said. 'Why you?'

'Cailin dare not risk a fully-fledged Sister being discovered,' Kaiku said. 'And it would be unsafe to let anyone else use the Mask. The Weavers know nothing of the Red Order, and she would have it stay that way. The Mask is a Weaver device, and so the breach it causes in the barrier should raise no alarms.'

'But you have no idea if the Mask will even work this time,' Saran argued. 'Perhaps it was made only to work at the monastery on Fo.'

Kaiku made an expression of resignation. 'I have to try,' she said.

Saran brushed his sleek black hair behind his ear. Kaiku watched him sidelong, studying the lines of his figure beneath the severe cut of his clothes. A cautionary voice was warning her against what she was doing, but she ignored it. The pleasant glow of the wine she had drunk kept her mind resolutely in the present and refused to allow it to construct consequences.

Saran caught her looking, and she was a little too obvious in her haste to look away.

'Why is Tsata coming with us?' she asked, suddenly needing something to say. Then, realising that it was something she actually wanted to know, she added: 'What is he to you?'

Saran was silent a while, thinking. Kaiku could never decide if he was merely weighing his words or if he added these pauses in a conscious attempt at drama or gravitas. It was difficult to tell with Saran, whom she found annoyingly affected at times.

'He is nothing to me,' Saran said at last. 'No more than a companion. I met him in Okhamba, and he came with me into the heart of the continent for reasons of his own. By the same token he came to Saramyr. I do not know why he has asked to go with you across the Fault, but I can vouch for his worthiness. Of all those who I travelled with on my journeys across the Near World, there was none I would more readily trust with my life.'

By now they had reached the edge of the town, where it spilled onto the valley floor. The lowest steps formed a natural protective barricade, into which lifts had been built and gated stairways cut. The gates would be closed in times of war and the lifts drawn up to prevent enemies getting in.

They made their way upward along the less-travelled routes. Lanterns spilled bright islands into the darkness. They passed townsfolk kissing or singing or fighting, and once they almost walked into a parade which had gathered up hundreds in its wake and was marching them on a sinuous path to an uncertain destination. At some point, Kaiku took Saran's hand again. She thought she could detect him trembling slightly, and smiled secretly to herself.

'Do you have any doubts?' she said. 'About what you found?'

'The fourth moon? No,' Saran replied. 'Zaelis is convinced, too, now I have shown him the evidence and the Sisters have verified it. I had thought, perhaps, that the idea would be too outlandish for your people to accept; after all, you are the only people in the Near World who still worship the moons.' He flicked a strand of hair away from his forehead in a curiously effeminate manner. 'But it seems that I was wrong. In only the last thousand years, there have been other gods forgotten and lost in antiquity; it is only natural that you should not know of one that died before your civilisation was founded.'

'Perhaps he did not die,' Kaiku murmured. 'Perhaps that is the problem.'

Saran made a questioning noise.

'It is nothing,' Kaiku said. 'Just . . . I have an ill suspicion about all this. I was touched by one of the Children of the Moons; did you know that? Indirectly, anyway. It was Lucia they were helping.'

'I knew,' said Saran.

'This affair with Aricarat, it makes me . . . uneasy.' She could not put it better than that, but there was a faint nausea, a trepidation like the warning rumble of the earth before a quake, whenever she thought of that name. Would she have felt it if she had not once brushed against the unfathomable majesty of those spirits? She could not be sure.

'But more than that,' she continued. 'My friend Tane died trying to live out what he believed his goddess Enyu thought he should do. I almost shared that fate on Ocha's behalf, and tomorrow I set off to risk the same again. The Children of the Moons themselves intervened for Lucia. And now you tell me that the source of the Weavers' power, the true reason for this land's affliction and misery, are the remnants of another moon, a forgotten one?' She made an unconscious sign against blasphemy before continuing. 'I begin to believe that I have stumbled into a game of the gods, willingly or not; that we are part of some conflict beyond our power to see. And that we are all of us expendable in the eyes of the Golden Realm.'

Saran considered this for a moment. 'I think you put too much stock in your gods, Kaiku,' he said. 'Some people mistake their own courage for the will of their deities, and others use their faith as an excuse to do evil. Be careful, Kaiku. What your heart dictates and what your gods tell you may one day be in opposition.'

Kaiku was frankly surprised to hear such words from a Quraal, whose upbringing within the Theocracy generally made them rigid in their piety. She would have responded then, but she found herself suddenly before the door of the house that she shared with Mishani. It stood on one of the middle tiers of the Fold, a small and unassuming place with the rough edges of its construction smoothed over by some artful use of creepers and potted plants. Since it was hardly possible to recreate the elegant minimalism of the dwellings they had grown up in among all the surrounding chaos, they had decided to try and beautify it as much as possible. It was all Mishani's work, as was the interior, for Kaiku was hopeless at decorating; it was a very feminine art, and she had been too busy competing with her older brother to learn it.

There was a moment of shared intent, when Kaiku and Saran met each other's eyes and neither really considered saying goodbye to the other, when both feared that any advance might be rebuffed even though their senses told them it would not. Then Kaiku opened the door, and they both went inside.

The threshold that they crossed was more than physical. Kaiku had barely closed the door before Saran was kissing her, and she responded with equal fervour, her hands on his cheeks and in his hair, a warm flush seeping through her body as their tongues touched and slid. He pressed her against the wall, their lips meeting and parting, the hot gusts of breath the only sound between them. Kaiku moved her hips up against him, felt with lewd pleasure the bulge at his crotch. The cautionary voice had been swept away to the corners of her mind now, and there was no question of stopping what was going to happen.

Her hands were already working at his tight jacket, fumbling with the unfamiliar Quraal catches. She laughed at her own clumsiness; he had to help her with the last few before he slid his jacket off to reveal the bare torso underneath. She pushed him back from her a little way to see what she had uncovered. He was lean and muscled like an athlete, not an ounce of fat on his body. She ran her hands over the landscape of his abdomen, and he shivered in pleasure. She smiled to herself, coming in closer to place wet, languorous kisses on his neck and clavicle. His lips were in her hair, on the lobe of her ear.

Kaiku steered them over to a long settee and fell on to it, pulling him down on top of her. The night was close and shadowy, for the lanterns in the room had not been lit. The shutters were closed, muting the revelries outside. They kissed again, moving against each other, her hands running down the ridge of his spine to his lower back.

He stripped her blouse from her with fluid expertise, leaving it rumpled and discarded; then, without pause, he slipped off her upper undergarment, which caused Kaiku a twinge of disappointment. He was getting hasty in his ardour, and she liked her lovemaking to be slow and gradual. Anxious to interrupt him – for his hands were already moving towards her waist – she tipped him gently off the settee and onto the floor, rolling with him so that she came out on top.

Straddling his hips, she kissed his cheeks and forehead, and he leaned upward to take her breast in his hand and bring his mouth to her nipple, the hot, wet touch of his tongue sending minute trembles of delight through her. She reached behind herself and began to massage his erection through the fabric of his trousers with the heel of her hand. He was becoming excited, his breathing fast and shallow, and while part of her found it flattering that she elicited such a reaction in a man so rigidly calm and controlled, she was again a little concerned that he was getting too overeager. She sucked in her breath through her teeth as he bit her nipple hard enough to hurt.

He shifted her weight suddenly, turning her over so that he was on top now, and she saw that his face had become red and straining and ugly. Her heat faded, underpinned by something unpleasant that she saw in his eyes, an animal lust that went beyond the coupling of man and woman.

'Saran . . .' she began, not knowing what she would say, whether she would ride this out and hope that it was but a passing moment or if she would disappoint him and stop this. She was afraid of how he might react if she dared to do that. She did not want to hurt him, but she would if she had to.

He silenced her with a hard and savage kiss, one that bruised her lips with its ferocity, and suddenly there was a shift in the nature of the kiss, turning it from passion to something else.

Feeding.

Her *kana* uncoiled like a nest of snakes, bursting from her groin and her womb and tearing through her almost before she knew what was happening. There was a moment in which she felt something trying to pull free from her insides, as if her organs would rip from their tethers and crowd through her mouth and into Saran's, and then there was a blast of white and Saran was thrown back across the room, slamming into the opposite wall and landing in a heap.

It was just like last time. She had felt that hunger before.

'No . . .' she murmured, tears standing in her eyes as she got up. She had gathered her blouse across her breasts protectively. Her fringe fell over her face. 'No, no, no.' She whimpered it like a mantra, as if she could deny the magnitude of the betrayal she felt.

Saran was getting to his feet, his face a picture of anguish.

'Kaiku . . .' he began.

'No, no, *NO!*' she screamed, and the tears spilled over and down her cheeks. Her lip trembled. 'Is it you? Is it you?'

Saran did not speak, but he shook his head a little, not in denial but because he was begging her not to ask the question.

'Asara?' she whispered.

His expression tightened in a stab of pain, and that was all the answer Kaiku needed. She fell to her knees, her features crumpling as she began to cry.

'How could you?' she sobbed, then suddenly she found her anger and she shrieked: '*How could you?*'

His gaze was aggrieved, but they were Asara's eyes. He opened his mouth to speak, but there were no words. Instead, he picked up his jacket and walked out into the warm night, leaving Kaiku on the floor of the room, weeping.

THIRTEEN

Dawn came to the Xarana Fault, a bleak and flat light muted by a blanket of unseasonable cloud that haunted the eastern horizon. Morning mists wisped in the hollows of the Fold, stirring gently among the creases and pits of the valley. The town was eerily silent, and not a soul walked the crooked streets except for an occasional guard, the creak of their hardened-leather armour preceding them along the empty passageways and dirt alleys. Aestival Week had begun two days ago now, and that first night the whole town had celebrated long past the dawn and into the morning. Last night, the festivities had been less raucous: people slept and recovered, and they would still be in bed for a long while yet.

But there were some whose purpose even Aestival Week could not be allowed to delay. They had gathered on the uppermost tier of the town, where a sheer wall of rock rose up on the western end of the valley, riddled with caves bored by the same ancient and long-dried waterways that had cut the plateaux and ledges below them. Blessings and etchings had been carved into the stone around the cave mouths, and small alcoves had been cut into the rock to serve as shrines. Even now, the musky smell of smouldering kama nuts and incense reached them faintly, the remnants of yesterday's offerings. Small hanging charms clacked and chimed.

Kaiku sat on the grass, her face pale and her eyes dark from sleeplessness, and gazed bitterly over the valley and into the east. She was vaguely aware of the other three behind her. They were tightening the belts on their backpacks, chambering ammunition in their rifles, murmuring softly as if loth to disturb the stillness of the dawn: Tsata, Yugi, and Nomoru, the surly scout whose report had inspired this expedition. Today they set out to cross the Fault, heading along it lengthwise to where the Zan cut through near its western end, and there to investigate the anomaly that Nomoru had found. There to seek out the Weavers once again.

She should have felt something more than this. After so long champing at the bit, the prospect of coming up against the Weavers, the murderers of her family whom she was oath-bound to oppose, should have fired something inside her. If not excitement, then at least fear or trepidation. But her heart felt dead in her breast, an ashen lump like a fire burned out, and she could not even summon the enthusiasm to care.

How could she not have known about Saran? How could she not have recognised the source of her attraction? Gods, she had stood there on the bow of Chien's ship and *told* him about how Asara brought her back from the brink of death, how that act had bonded them on some deep and subtle level, and all the time it had been that very bond that was drawing them together. All the time it had been Asara she had been talking to.

Spirits, Kaiku hated her. She hated her deceit, her trickery, her unbearable selfishness. Hated how she had allowed Kaiku to believe she was Saran, to dupe her into talking about Asara while Asara herself watched from behind those dark Quraal eyes; and then, worst of all, to allow Kaiku to seduce him, to make love to him, thinking he was a real person and not some cursed *counterfeit.* It made no difference that they had not completed the act. The betrayal was in the intention, not in the result: and it was total.

Kaiku knew now that her decision to sleep with him had not been one based on simple lust and the desire to enjoy him; she had been fooling herself there. She had opened herself to him, and in her mind the consummation would have been more than just bedplay but an affirmation of the feeling that she thought had grown between them. Not that she admitted it to herself, of course. She had never been an honest judge of her own emotions. It was only by the savagery of her grief that she realised how much she had secretly invested in Saran, and by then it was too late.

She had made herself vulnerable, and once again she had been cut to pieces. Staring balefully into the middle distance, she promised herself grimly that it would never happen again.

'It's time, Kaiku,' said Yugi, laying a hand on her shoulder.

She looked up at him slowly, hardly seeming to see him; then she got wearily to her feet, picked up her pack and rifle and shouldered them.

'I am ready,' she said.

They passed through the fortifications on the rim of the Fold and headed westward. Nuki's eye rose above the louring clouds to warm the canyons and valleys of the Xarana Fault. For a long while, nobody spoke. Nomoru led them into narrow pleats that angled down to the lower depths, where they could pass unobserved through the wild land about them. The jagged and bumped horizon was consumed by high walls of scree-dusted rock, rising before and behind and to either side. They passed out of Nuki's sight, and into the cool shadow.

The western side of the Fold was guarded by a tight labyrinth of fissures and tunnels known as the Knot. Here, ages ago, the same springs that had flowed east from the lip of the valley to sculpt the land on which the town was built had also flowed westward, gnawing through the ancient stone. As time passed the water would undermine some vital support, or the earth would be shaken by the tremors and quakes that ran through the Fault from time to time, and the rock above it would collapse and divert some of the tunnels elsewhere. Now the water was gone, but the paths remained, a maze of branching dead-ends that led tortuously downward. It was possible, and much faster, to go over the top of the Knot, where there was a bare hump of smooth stone a mile wide, like a horseshoe around the western edge of the Fold; but up there was no kind of cover and anyone attempting to cross it would be visible for miles around. In the Fault, secrecy was the watchword.

The dawn had grown into a bright morning by the time they emerged from the Knot. They clambered out of a thin crack onto the floor of a ravine, sloping gently upward ahead of them. Kaiku caught her breath as she saw it, and even through the weight of misery that she carried she felt a moment of awe.

The walls of the ravine rose sheer to over a hundred feet above their heads, a weathered mass of creases and ledges on which narrow swatches of bushes grew where they could find purchase. The floor was an untamed garden of trees and flowers, leaves of deep red and purple mixed in amid the green. A spring fed into a series of small pools. The sun was blazing over the rim at a shallow angle, throwing its light to the far end of the ravine and leaving the near end in shade. Bright birds nested in the heights, occasionally bursting out to swoop and tumble, chattering as they went. The air was still and hazed with a dreamlike glow. They had stepped into a secret paradise.

'This is the edge of our territory,' Nomoru said. It was the first anyone had spoken since they set out, and her harsh and ugly Low Saramyrrhic vowels jarred against Kaiku's mood. 'Not so safe from now on.'

The Xarana Fault was an ever-shifting mass of unacknowledged borders, neutral ground and disputed areas. The political geography of the place was as unstable as the Fault itself. Like gangs, each faction held their territory jealously, but from one month to the next entire communities might be sacked or overthrown, or defect to join a more powerful leader. The Fold was at constant war to keep its routes open to the outside world, and bandits preyed upon the cargoes that were smuggled in to supply the Libera Dramach. Other forces had other agendas: some were relentlessly expansionist, pursuing the hopeless ideal of dominating or uniting the Fault; others wanted merely to be left alone, and poured their efforts into defence rather than aggression; still others simply hid. The business of knowing what their neighbours were up to was a perpetual drain on the time and resources of Zaelis and the Libera Dramach, but it was vital for survival in the cut-throat world that they had settled in.

They headed onward with renewed vigilance. The terrain was hard, and Nomoru seemed to choose difficult routes more often than not, for the most inaccessible ways were often the safest. Within hours, Kaiku had utterly lost her sense of direction. She glared resentfully at the wiry figure leading them, blaming her for their ordeal; then she caught herself and realised how unfair that was. If not for Asara, she would have been glad to come on this expedition. If not for Asara.

She found herself lapsing into dark thoughts again in the absence of conversation. Yugi was unusually subdued, and Tsata rarely said anything unless it was worth saying, content instead to observe and listen with an alien and faintly unsettling curiosity. Had *he* known? Had he known that Saran was not who he appeared to be? What about Zaelis and Cailin; surely *they* had known? Cailin would have, certainly: she could sense Aberrants merely by looking at them. All the Sisters could.

In the aftermath of her discovery, in the rage that came after grief, she had wanted to face Cailin and Zaelis and demand to know why they had not told her. But it was useless; she already knew their arguments. Asara was a spy, and it was not their place to reveal her. Kaiku had spoken little enough to anyone but Mishani about Asara, and said nothing at all about her attraction to Saran. Why should they intervene? And besides, she would only be feeding Cailin ammunition for her demands that Kaiku apply herself to the teachings of the Red Order. If she had attended to her lessons instead of restlessly combing the land, she would have sensed Asara's true identity herself.

And yet she had not suspected. How could she, really? She had no idea of the extent of Asara's Aberrant abilities. She had witnessed her shift her features subtly, change the hue of her hair, even seen a tattoo on her arm that faded away; she had seen her repair the most horrendous burns to her face. But to change not only the form of her body but her *gender* . . . that had been beyond even Kaiku's notion of possibility. What kind of creature could do that? What kind of thing?

And what kind of thing can twist the threads of reality to shape fire or break minds? she asked herself pitilessly. *She is no more impossible than you. The world is changing faster than you imagine. The witchstones are remaking Saramyr, and all that once was is uncertain now.*

'You're brooding, Kaiku,' Yugi said from behind her. 'I can feel it from here.'

She smiled apologetically at him, and her heart lifted a little. 'Talk to me, Yugi. This will be a long journey, and if someone does not do something to lighten the mood then I do not think I will last the day.'

'Sorry. I've been a little remiss as the provider of good humour,' he said with a grin. 'I was suffering somewhat from last night, but the walk has cleared my head.'

'Over-indulged yourself, did you?' Kaiku prodded.

'Hardly. I didn't touch a thing. No wonder I feel so awful.'

She laughed softly. Nomoru, up ahead, glanced back at them with an irritable expression.

'You're troubled,' Yugi said, his voice becoming more serious. 'Is it the Mask?'

'Not the Mask,' she said, and it was true: she had entirely forgotten it until now, obsessed as she was with nursing the hurt Asara had done to her. It lay wrapped in her pack, the Mask her father had stolen and died for. She felt it suddenly, leering at her. For five years it had been hidden in a chest in her house, and she had never put it on again, for she knew well enough the way the True Masks worked, how they were narcotic in nature, addicting the wearer to the euphoria of the Weave, granting great power but stealing reason and sanity. Yet the insidious craving was undiminished, the tickle at the back of her mind whenever she thought of it. Calling to her.

Sometime in the afternoon, they rested and ate on a grassy slope beneath an overhang. They had passed out of the ravine and were skirting a sunken plain of broken rocks, bordered on all sides by high cliffs. Some of the rocks had thrust their way up from below in shattered formations like brutal stone flowers, their petals lined with quartz and limestone and malachite; others had fallen from the tall buttes that jutted precariously into the sky. The travellers had been darting from cover to cover for over an hour now, and while the progress they made was faster than it had been through the ravines, it was harder on the nerves. They were too exposed for comfort here.

'Why did we come this way? We're not in so much of a hurry,' Yugi asked Nomoru conversationally, as he ate a cold leg of waterfowl.

Nomoru's thin face hardened, taking umbrage at the comment. 'I'm the guide,' she snapped. 'I know these lands.'

Yugi was unperturbed. 'Then educate me, please. I know them too, though not so well as you, I'd imagine. There's a high pass to the south where—'

'Can't go that way,' Nomoru said dismissively.

'Why not?' said Tsata. Kaiku looked at him in vague surprise. It was the first he had spoken that day.

'It doesn't matter why not,' Nomoru replied, digging her heels in further. Kaiku was taken aback by the rudeness of her manner.

Tsata studied the scout for a moment. Hunkered in the shade of the rock, the pale green tattoo reaching tendrils over his arms and face, he looked strangely at home here in the Fault. His skin, which had been sallow in the dawn light, now seemed golden in the afternoon and he appeared healthier for it. 'You have knowledge of these lands, so you must share it. To withhold it hurts the *pash*.'

'The *pash?*' Nomoru sneered, uncomprehending.

'The group,' Kaiku said. 'We four are now travelling together, so that makes us the *pash*. Is that right?' She addressed this last to Tsata.

'One kind of *pash*,' Tsata corrected. 'Not the only kind. But yes, that is what I was referring to.'

Nomoru held up her hands in exasperation. Kaiku noted Nomoru's own tattoos on her arms as her sleeves fell back: intricate, jagged shapes and spirals, intertwining through emblems and pictograms symbolic of allegiances or debts owed and honoured. It was the tradition of the beggars, thieves and other low folk of the Poor Quarter in Axekami to ink their history onto their skin; in that way, promises made could not be broken. In poverty, need drove them to perform services for each other, a community of necessity. Mostly, their word was their bond; but occasionally, for more important matters, something greater was required. A tattoo was an outward display of their undertaking. Usually it was left half-drawn, and finished when the task was done. The Inkers of the Poor Quarter knew all faces and all debts, and they would only complete a tattoo once they had word the task had been fulfilled. An oathbreaker would soon be exposed, and they would not survive long when others refused to aid them.

How strange, Kaiku thought, that the need for honour increased as money and possessions decreased. She wondered if Nomoru had been an oath-breaker; but the meaning of the tattooes was incomprehensible to her, and any words she could see were written in an argot of Low Saramyrrhic which she did not know.

'Territories change,' Nomoru said, relenting ungraciously at last. 'But the borders aren't defined. Between territories, it's uncertain. Scouts, warriors sometimes, but no proper guards, no fortifications. So I've been taking you between the territories. Not so well guarded, easier to slip through.' She tilted her head in the direction of the rock-strewn plain. 'This place is a battlefield. Look at the terrain. Nobody owns it. Too many spirits here.'

'Spirits?' Kaiku asked.

'They come at night,' Nomoru said. 'Lot of killing here. Places remember. So we come in the day. Keep our heads down, we stay safe.'

She scratched her knee beneath her trousers, and looked at Yugi. 'The high pass got taken a month ago. There was a fight; someone lost, someone won.' She shrugged. 'Used to be safe. Now you'd be killed before you got a yard into it.' She raised her eyebrow at Tsata. 'Satisfied?' she asked archly.

He tipped his chin at her. Nomoru scowled in confusion, not knowing that it was the Okhamban way of nodding. Kaiku did not enlighten her. She had already decided that she disliked the tangle-haired scout.

It was late evening when their luck ran out.

The sky was a dull and glowering purple-red, streaked with shades of deep blue and ribboned with strips of translucent cloud. Neryn and Aurus were travelling together tonight, and they were already hanging low in the western sky, a thin crescent of green peeping out from behind the vast waxing face of the larger sister. Nomoru was leading them along a high spine of land, rising up above the surrounding miles of thin ghylls and narrow canyons. The ground here was broken into a jigsaw of grassy ledges which rose and fell alarmingly, so that they often found themselves having to climb around dark pits or clamber up thin, dizzying slopes with a terrible drop on either side. As hard as it was, it did have one advantage: they were well hidden within its folds, and nobody was likely to see them unless they ran into them.

They had almost reached the far end of the spine, where the land loomed glowering to meet them again, when Nomoru suddenly held her hand up, her fingers curved in the Saramyr gesture for quiet. It was something that all children learned, generally from their parents who used it often on them. Tsata either knew or guessed its meaning, but his movements were utterly silent anyway.

Kaiku strained to hear anything, but all that came to her were distant animal cries and the rising chorus of night insects. They had seen no evidence of human life so far, whether by chance or by Nomoru's skill, and only the occasional glimpse of a large predator in the distance had kept them from relaxing. Now the presence of danger tautened her, her body flooding with chill adrenaline, sweeping her brooding thoughts away.

Nomoru glanced back at them, indicating for them to stay. A moment later, she had flitted up the side of the rock wall that faced them and disappeared over the top.

Yugi crept up alongside her in a crouch, his rifle primed in his hands. 'Do you sense anything?' he whispered.

'I have not tried,' she said. 'I dare not, yet. If it should be a Weaver, he might notice me.' She did not express her deeper fears on the subject: that she had never faced a Weaver in the battlefield of the Weave, that no Sister had except Cailin, and that she was terrified that one day the moment might arrive when she had to.

It was then she noticed Tsata was gone.

The Tkiurathi kept himself low, hugging close to the stone bulk rising to his left. On a level so basic that it did not even need conscious thought, he was aware of what angles he was exposed from and where he was covered. The thorny brakes to his right guarded his flank, and he would hear anyone coming through them, but there were shadowy spots high up on a thin finger of rock beyond that might provide a hiding place for a rifleman or an archer. He had gone to the right around the rise of stone where Nomoru had gone left, hoping to encircle the bulk and meet her on the other side, or clamber over the top if he could not get past it.

It was simple sense to him, born of a logic shaped over thousands of years of jungle life. One scout could be bitten by a snake, fall into a trap, break a leg, or be captured and be unable to warn the rest of the *pash* when enemies inevitably tracked back to where the scout had come from. Two scouts, taking different routes but still watching each other, were much harder to surprise, and if misfortune befell one then the other could rescue them or go for help. Above all, it was safer for the group.

Tsata was confounded over and over by the incomprehensible thought processes of foreigners, Quraal and Saramyr alike. Their motives baffled him. So much was not said in foreign society, a mass of implications and suggestions meant to hint at private understandings. Their loveplay, for example: he had watched Saran and Kaiku fence around each other for weeks aboard Chien's ship. How was it that it was somehow unacceptable to say something that both of them knew, to admit their lust for one another, and yet it *was* acceptable to make it just as obvious through oblique means? Every one of them was so secretive, so locked into themselves, unwilling to share any part of their being with anyone. They hoarded their strength instead of distributing it, building themselves through words and actions for personal advancement rather than using what they had gained to benefit their *pash*.

And so, instead of a community, they had this wildly unequal culture of many social levels in which inferiority was bestowed by birth, or by lack of possessions, or by the deeds of a man's father. It was so far beyond ridiculous that Tsata did not even know where to begin.

He felt some affinity with Saran, because Saran had been willing to sacrifice every man that accompanied him into the jungles of Okhamba to get himself out alive. That, at least, Tsata could understand, for he was working for the good of a greater *pash*, that of the Libera Dramach and the Saramyr people. The others on the expedition were merely interested in monetary gain or fame. Only Saran's motives seemed unselfish. But even Saran, like all of them, was so hidden in intention, and often tried to tell Tsata where to go and what to do. He had thought of himself as the 'leader' of their group, even though Tsata had taken no payment and joined of his own free will.

It was too much. He put it from his mind. Time to muse on these puzzling people later.

The stone bulk on his left was not showing any sign of rounding off and allowing Tsata's path to converge with Nomoru's, so he decided to chance climbing over it. It would leave him dangerously exposed for a few moments, but there was no help for that. In one lithe movement, he rose from his running crouch and sprang up to grip the rough sides of the rock, using his momentum and his dense muscles to pull himself up. He found a toehold and boosted himself to the top, spreading himself flat on the lumpy roof of stone. In the jungle of his homeland, his jaundiced skin and green tattoos served to camouflage him; now he felt uncomfortably visible. He crawled swiftly over the rock to the other side, staying close to what sparse vegetation grew up here. The waxing moons glared down at him as the light slowly bled from the sky to be replaced by a pale, green-tinged glow.

He was atop a long, thin ridge. Below and to its left, a ledge ran close, following the ridge's contours until it dropped away suddenly to a small clearing, which was hemmed in on three sides by other shoulders of land.

He could hear them and smell them even before he saw the men moving along the ledge towards where Kaiku and Yugi waited.

There were two of them. They were dressed in a curious assemblage of loose black clothing and dark leather armour, and their faces were powdered unnaturally white, with bruise-coloured dye around their eyes. Their clothes, hair and skin were dirty and striped with a kind of dark blue war-paint, and they were unkempt and stank of an incense that Tsata recognised as ritasi, a five-petalled flower which he understood the Saramyr often burned at funerals. They carried rifles of an early and unreliable make, heavy and grimy things, and there were curved swords at their waists.

Tsata shifted his own rifle, slung on a strap across his back, and loosed his *kntha* from his belt. *Kntha* were Okhamban weapons, made for close combat in jungles where longer weapons were unwieldy and likely to snag on creepers. They comprised of a grip of bound leather with a steel knuckle-guard, and two kinked blades a foot long, protruding from the top and bottom of the grip. The blades bent smoothly the opposite way from each other, about halfway along their length, tapering to a wicked edge. *Kntha* were used in pairs, one to block with and the other to slash, making a total of four blades with which to attack an opponent. They required a particularly vicious fighting style to use effectively. The Saramyr folk had a name for them that was easier for them to remember than the Okhamban: gutting-hooks.

He dropped down to the ledge like a cat, his landing soundless. Tkiurathi disdained any kind of ornamentation that might make a noise, for their skill was in stealth. The two men, intent on their own inept creeping, did not hear him come up behind them. They were easy prey.

He took them by surprise, sweeping at the neck of the rightmost, putting enough of his body weight behind it to behead the man cleanly. With his left hand he slashed out at the other one as he turned into the blow; it caught him square in the throat, not hard enough to decapitate him but enough to plough through thick muscle and lodge in his spine. As the first man fell, Tsata pressed his hide shoe into the second man's chest and used it as leverage to wrench his gutting-hook free. A spume of steaming blood came with it, followed by a belch of gore from the wound that spilled down his victim's chest. Tsata stepped back and watched him slump to the ground, his body still not seeming to realise that he was dead, his heart spasmodically pumping as he went.

Satisfied that the greater part of his *pash* was safe, his thoughts immediately turned to Nomoru. He wiped the blood off his blades and his sleeveless hemp waistcoat so as not to provide any scent-warning to an enemy, and then headed along the ledge in the direction the men had come from.

He found her in the sunken clearing at the end of the ledge. She was backed against a wall, facing him. There were two more with her, one with his knife pressed up under her chin, the other wielding a rifle and scanning the rim. In the last light of the day, Tsata was all but invisible as he watched from the shadow of the rocky ridge. He checked quickly for signs of any others nearby, but there was nothing, not even any sentries or lookouts on the high points surrounding the clearing. These were not warriors, however much they swaggered.

His priority was the man with the knife to Nomoru's throat. He would have liked to try and do it in silence, but the risk was far too great. Instead, he waited until neither of them were looking at him, then took aim with his rifle. He was just weighing the possibilities of taking the man out without him reflexively stabbing Nomoru when the scout spotted him with an infinitesimal flicker of her eyes. A moment later, she looked back at him again, hard. Purposefully. The man guarding her frowned as he noticed. She glared wide at Tsata, her eyes urging him.

Tsata held his fire. Clever. She was trying to turn her enemy's attention from her.

'Stop mugging, you fool,' the man hissed. 'I'm no idiot. You won't make me look away.' And with that, he slapped her. But he had to take his knife away a few inches to do it, and the instant he did so Tsata blew his brains out of the side of his head.

The last man turned with a cry, raising his rifle; but Tsata was already leaping down upon him, driving the butt of his weapon into the man's jaw. His enemy's rifle fired wild as he fell, and a second blow from Tsata stove his skull in.

The echoes of the gunshots rang across the Fault and into the gathering night.

There was a pause as Nomoru and Tsata looked at each other in the gloom, and then Nomoru turned away and scooped up her rifle and dagger, which had been taken from her.

'They'll be coming,' she said, not meeting his eye. 'More of them. We have to go.'

FOURTEEN

The echoes of the hunt floated distantly across the peaks.

Upon her return with Tsata, Nomoru had led them off the spine of land that they had been following, taking a north-westward route that descended hard. They were bruised and scratched from sliding down steep slopes of shale, and the exertion had tired them, for Nomoru had set a reckless pace for more than an hour. She seemed furious, though whether at herself or at them it was difficult to tell. She pushed them to their limits, guiding them down into the depths of the Fault, until the dark land reared all around them.

Finally, she called a halt in a round, grassy clearing that seemed to spring out of nowhere amid the lifeless rock that bordered it. A dank mist lay on the ground, despite the night's warmth, a sad pearly green in the light of the crescent moons. The clearing slid away down a narrow hillside to the west, but whatever was there was obscured by the contour of the land.

Yugi and Kaiku threw themselves down on the grass. Tsata squatted nearby. Nomoru stalked about in agitation.

'Gods, I could sleep right here,' Yugi declared.

'We can't stay here. Just take a rest,' Nomoru snapped. 'I didn't want to go this way.'

'We are going on?' Kaiku asked in disbelief. 'We have been travelling since dawn!'

'Why break our backs over this? There's no hurry,' Yugi reminded them again.

'They are tracking us,' Tsata said. When Yugi and Kaiku looked at him, he motioned up to where they had come from with a tilt of his head. 'They are calling to each other. And they are getting closer.'

Yugi scratched the back of his neck. 'Persistent. That's annoying. Who are they?'

Nomoru had her arms crossed, leaning against a wall of rock. 'Don't know their name. It's an Omecha cult. Not like in the cities. These are very extreme. They think death is the point of life.' She waved a hand dismissively. 'Blood sacrifice, mutilation rituals, votive suicide. They look forward to their own deaths.'

'I expect Tsata was something of a pleasant surprise for them, then,' Yugi quipped, grinning at the Tkiurathi. Tsata laughed, startling them all. None of them had ever heard him laugh before; he had seemed utterly humourless until now. It was inexplicably strange to hear. Somehow, they had expected his expression of mirth to be different to a Saramyr laugh.

Nomoru did not appreciate the comment. She was already angry at herself for being captured, and perversely she was also angry with Tsata for rescuing her. 'They weren't supposed to be there,' she said churlishly. 'There were different ones there a week ago. We could have got past them. They didn't pay much attention.'

'Perhaps that was why they got driven off,' suggested Yugi.

She scowled at him. 'I didn't want to come this way,' she said again.

Kaiku, who was eating a stick of spicebread from her pack to replenish some energy, looked up at her. 'Why not?' she asked round a mouthful of food. 'What is this way?'

Nomoru seemed about to say something, a haunted look in her eyes; then she clammed up. 'Don't know,' she said. 'But I know not to come here.'

'Nomoru, if you have heard something about this place, then tell us!' Kaiku said. Her reticence was more alarming than if she had spoken out.

'Don't know!' she said again. 'The Fault is full of stories. I hear them all. But there's bad rumours about where we're going.'

'*What* rumours?' Kaiku persisted, brushing her fringe back from her face and giving Nomoru a hard look.

'Bad rumours,' said the scout stubbornly, returning the glare.

'Will they follow us in there?' Yugi asked, trying a different tack.

'Not if they have any sense,' Nomoru said; then, tiring of questions, she told them to get up. 'We have to go. They're getting close.'

Yugi looked to Tsata, who confirmed it with a grim tip of his chin. He hauled himself to his feet, and offered a hand to Kaiku to help her do the same. Their legs were aching, but not so much as they would be tomorrow.

'We have to go *now*!' Nomoru hissed impatiently, and she headed off down the narrow grass slope to what lay beyond.

The slope tipped gently into a broad, flat marsh; a long, curving alley flanked by walls of black granite that trickled and splashed with thousands of tiny waterways. The air was inexplicably chill; the travellers felt their skin pimpling as they descended. Humps of grass and ragged thickets rose like islands above the dreary, funereal ground mist. Strange lichens and brackens streaked the dark walls or straggled from the mire, swathes of sombre green and red and purple. Under the mournful glow of Aurus and Neryn, it lay dismal and quiet, disturbed only by the occasional shriek or croak of some unseen creature.

The terrain underfoot became steadily wetter, and water welled up in their bootprints. By the time the slope had levelled off enough to become the marsh floor, Yugi was expressing concerns over whether they could cross it at all. Nomoru ignored him. The sounds of their pursuers calling to each other in some dark, sacred cant provided all the reply she needed to give. Though the air around them seemed to dampen sound and foil echoes, it was evident that the cultists were not far away.

They forged on into the marsh, and the disturbed mist wrapped around their legs and swirled sullenly up to their knees. Already, the water had found ways in through their boots, and their feet squelched with every step. They trudged in single file, the mud sucking at them in an attempt to rob them of their footwear. Tsata took the rear, his rifle in his hands, glancing often back at the slope to the clearing, where he expected at any moment to see more of the dirty figures appear.

'We are too exposed here,' he said.

'That's why we're hurrying,' Nomoru said tersely, then stumbled and cursed. 'They'll never hit us if we're too far ahead.'

It was too late to argue the call now, so they laboured through the doleful marsh as fast as they could, following Nomoru's lead. She seemed uncannily sure-footed, and though a misstep often landed them in the watery sludge that lay to either side of the paths she chose, as long as they walked in her footprints they found relatively solid ground there.

Suddenly, Tsata clicked his tongue, a startlingly loud snap that made Kaiku jump. 'There they are,' he said.

Nomoru looked back. On the crest of the slope: four men and a woman, two with rifles. They were calling to companions out of sight. As she watched, one of the riflemen aimed and fired. The sharp crack was swallowed by the thick marsh air. Kaiku and Yugi ducked automatically, but the shot went nowhere near them.

Nomoru slipped back along the line to where Tsata was, unslinging her rifle. For the first time, Kaiku noticed how incongruous the weapon was in comparison with the woman that carried it. Whereas Nomoru was scrawny and scruffy and uncouth, her rifle was a thing of beauty, with a sleek black lacquer on its stock and body, inscribed with tiny gold pictograms, and a swirling silver intaglio along the length of its barrel.

'Stop worrying,' she told Kaiku and Yugi, as another cultist fired and they cringed from the shot. 'They'll never hit us. We're out of their range.'

'So what are you doing?' Yugi asked. Standing still in the open while somebody shot at them, no matter how distant, was fundamentally unnerving; yet he did not dare move without Nomoru leading them, for he had already gained a healthy respect for the dangers of the marsh.

Nomoru settled her rifle against her shoulder, took aim, and squeezed the trigger. A moment later, one of the cultists collapsed, shot through the forehead.

'They're not out of *my* range,' she said. She pulled the bolt back into position to reprime the rifle, swung the barrel fractionally to the left, and fired again. Another cultist went down.

'Heart's blood . . .' Yugi murmured in amazement.

The remaining cultists were hurriedly retreating now, back into the clearing and out of view.

'Now they've got something to think about,' Nomoru said, shouldering her rifle. 'Let's go.'

She made her way to the head of the line and trekked onward. The others followed her as best they could.

It was not long before Kaiku began to sense a change. At first, it was too subtle for her to identify, merely a feeling of unease. Gradually it grew, until it made the fine hairs on her arms prickle. She glanced at the others to see if anyone shared her discomfort, but nobody showed any sign. She had the slightly unreal sensation of being sealed off from her companions, of existing on a level apart from them, as if she was a ghost that they were powerless to see or touch or interact with. Her *kana* stirred within her.

The sensation was emanating from the marsh, from the very ground that they walked on. A feeling of steadily intensifying awareness, as if the land was slowly waking up around them. And with that awareness, malevolence.

'Wait,' she said, and they stopped. They were midway through the marsh, stranded far from any place of safety, and still the sensation grew, the colossal, rank *evil* that seemed to bleed from the air. 'Gods, wait. The marsh . . . there's something in the marsh . . .' Her voice sounded thin and weak and trancelike, and her eyes were unfocused.

As if her warning was a signal, there was a sudden gust of foul-smelling wind, whipping the mist at their feet high above their heads. The wind passed, dying as quickly as it came; but the vapour stayed hanging there, a white, hazy veil that turned the world around them to grey shadow. From being able to see the length and breadth of the marsh, they found their vision sharply curtailed, and the sensation of being shut in was alarming.

'What had you heard about this place, Nomoru?' Tsata demanded suddenly.

'It was the only way we could go,' she snapped defensively. 'They were just rumours. I didn't know they—'

'*What had you heard?*'

The quiet Tkiurathi's voice was rarely ever raised, but his frustration at Nomoru was getting too much. She was a complete loner, disappearing on her own without telling anyone why, stashing nuggets of information instead of sharing them so that she could keep control of the group, meting out what knowledge she had as it suited her. It was anathema to Tsata. And now her evasions were endangering the *pash*, and that could not be borne. If necessary, he would threaten her to find out what she knew.

There was a silence for a moment, a battle of wills between the two of them. Finally, it was Nomoru who relented. 'Demons,' she said resentfully. '*Ruku-shai.*'

A distant rattling sound cut through the mist, like hollow sticks being knocked together, rising to a crescendo and then dropping away. Yugi let out a breath, turning it into an unpleasant oath.

'It was the only way we could go,' Nomoru said again, more softly this time. 'I didn't believe the rumours.'

Yugi ran his hand through his hair in exasperation, adjusted the rag tied around his forehead, and shot her a disgusted look. 'Just get us out of here,' he said.

'I don't know which way *out* is!' she cried, sweeping a hand to encompass the murk that surrounded them.

'Guess!' Yugi shouted.

'That way,' said Tsata calmly. He had kept his bearings, for he had not turned or moved since the mist came down.

'They're coming!' Kaiku said, looking around in a panic. Her irises had darkened from brown to a deeper, richer shade of red.

They did not waste any more time. Nomoru took the lead, following Tsata's direction, and she headed across the marsh as fast as she dared. The mist was not thick enough to make it impossible to see nearby objects, but the accumulation of it over distance rendered anything beyond twenty feet away as an indistinct blur. They waded through the muck in long strides, eyes and ears alert. The rattling came from all around them now, a rhythmic clicking noise that swayed from slow and sinister to rapid and aggressive. The mist ruined any hope they had of pinpointing it. They went with guns ready, knowing that the iron in a rifle ball was the only weapon they had against demons, knowing also that it could do no more than deter them.

'Kaiku,' said Yugi from behind her. She did not seem to hear him; her gaze was on something beyond what they could see. 'Kaiku!' he said again, putting his hand on her shoulder. She looked up at him suddenly, as if shaken from a dream. Her eyes were wild, and she trembled. She was remembering other demons, and the terror she had suffered at their hands.

'Kaiku, we need you,' Yugi said, staring hard at her. She did not seem to comprehend. He smiled suddenly, unexpectedly, and brushed her hair back from where it lay over one side of her face. 'We need you to protect us. Can you do that?'

She searched his face for a second, then nodded quickly. His smile broadened encouragingly, and he gave her a companionable pat on the upper arm. 'Good girl,' he said, using an affectionate diminutive that Kaiku would have found insultingly patronising in any other situation. Now, however, she found it strangely heartening.

'Come on!' Nomoru barked from up ahead, and they hurried to catch her.

Kaiku was in a different world to the others. She had slipped into the Weave, maintaining herself on a level midway between the realm of the senses and the unearthly tapestry that ran beneath human sight. But her heightened perceptions made her open to more sensations than the simple fear that the others had to deal with. She brushed against the enormity of the demon minds, the dimensionless pathways of their thoughts, and it threatened to crush her. She fought to shut it out, to keep herself from slipping off that knife-edge into the yawning void that waited if she should try to understand it. This was of a different order to the moment when she had glimpsed into the world of the Children of the Moons. Kaiku had been overwhelmed then by her own insignificance, how unimportant she was to that incomprehensible consciousness. The ruku-shai were not even close to the power of those terrible spirits, but they *hated*, and she quailed at the force of it. Their attention was bent upon her now.

Saramyr legend had it that demons were unclean souls cursed to corporeal form for their terrible offences against the gods in life; neither living nor dead but condemned to the torment of limbo. But in that moment, Kaiku knew that it was not true, that her people would never know their origins, for they were so far from human that it was impossible to believe they had ever walked the earth, that they had loved and lost and smiled and cried like she had.

She could see through the mist, through the lazily swirling threads of glittering gold; and there she watched the demons pulling themselves up from the mire, their shapes a black, knotted tangle against the purity of the Weave. She could not make out details, but their forms were clear to her. Their bodies were sinuous and snakelike, ending in sharp, cord-like tails. Six slender legs radiated from their underbellies, thrusting upward and outward and then crooking down at a spiked knee joint. They crept onward slowly, high-stepping with exaggerated care, placing their two-toed forefeet delicately. And all the time, there was that horrible rattling as they clicked together the bones in their throat, communicating in their dreadful language.

'Three of them,' she said, then stumbled and went thigh-deep into a brackish pool of foul-smelling water. Tsata caught her under her arm before she could topple in any further, and lifted her out as if she weighed nothing at all. 'There's three of them,' she repeated breathlessly.

'Where?' Tsata demanded, urging her into motion once again.

'On our left.'

Yugi looked over automatically, but there was only the grey shroud of the mist. Nomoru was forging on, almost too far ahead to see.

'Nomoru, wait!' he cried, and there was an explosive oath of exasperation from up ahead. When they caught her up, she was furious; but it was obvious by now that the anger was merely a thin sheen to contain the raw fear that bubbled underneath and threatened to spill over. As soon as they were close enough, she headed off again, setting a cruel pace.

'How far are we from the edge of the swamp?' Yugi asked Kaiku.

'Too far,' she said. She could sense the demons prowling unhurriedly towards them, content to let them wear themselves out, like dogs hunting antelope. They had been on their feet since dawn, and it told in their tired steps and frequent stumbles. The ruku-shai only had to wait, and pick their moment.

And with that realisation, she halted. She had run from other demons in the past, from the relentless shin-shin. She had spent days and nights hiding from Aberrants in the Lakmar Mountains on Fo, creeping and huddling. She had slunk through the corridors of a Weaver monastery in terror of discovery. Always running, sneaking, shying from the notice of beings more powerful than she was. But those were the days before she had been taught to use her *kana* by Cailin, before her schooling had made it a weapon she could wield instead of a random and destructive thing. She was not so defenceless any more.

'What *now*?' Nomoru cried.

Kaiku ignored her, turning her face to the blank mist and the demons beyond which were approaching with their languid, mincing gait. Her irises darkened to blood-red, and a wind stirred her hair and ruffled her clothes, momentarily blowing back the gloomy vapour.

'I will not run,' she said, heady with a sudden recklessness. 'We have to stand.'

Her *kana* burst out from her, a million fibrous tendrils winding away into the golden diorama of the Weave, invisible to the eyes of her companions. The barrage smashed into the nearest of the ruku-shai, and Kaiku's consciousness went with it. It was like being plunged into freezing, foetid tar. For a few fractions of a second – though in the world of the Weave they seemed like minutes – she was suffocating, her senses encased in the cloying foulness of the demon, flailing in panic at the unfamiliar brutality of the sensation; and then her instincts took over, and she found her bearings and oriented herself. The demon had been as confused and unprepared for the attack as Kaiku was, but the advantage was lost now, and they tackled each other on equal footing.

Nothing in the Sisters' training could have prepared her for this. Nothing in her carefully orchestrated sparring had come close to the frantic sensation of meeting another being in combat within the Weave. Some part of her had thought that she could simply rip the demon apart, tear its fibres in a blast of flame as she had done to several other unfortunates that had crossed her path in the days after her power awakened; but demons and spirits were not so easily despatched.

They met in a scrabbling mesh of threads, bursting apart and arcing in on each other again like a ball of serpents chasing one another's tails. The demon fought to track the threads back to her body, where it could begin to do her damage; she strove to foil it while simultaneously attempting the same thing. Suddenly, she was everywhere, her mind fractured and following a thousand different tiny conflicts, here knotting a strand to block the oncoming blackness that slipped along it, there skipping between fibres and probing weaknesses in the demon's defences. She used tricks Cailin had taught her, finding to her surprise that they came to her as if she had known them all her life. She broke and fused threads to form loops which turned the ruku-shai's advance back on itself; she created stuttered tears in the fabric of their battleground which her enemy was forced to work around while she sent darts of *kana* to harry at its inner defences.

She feinted and probed, now drawing all her threads into a bundle, now scattering them and engaging the demon on many fronts at once. With each contact she felt the hot, dark reek of her enemy, the frightening singularity of its hatred. Again and again she was forced to retreat to sew up a gap that the ruku-shai had opened, to corral its quick advances before it could get to her and touch her with the awful energy that composed it. She shrank before it, rallied and drove it back, then was driven back in turn by its sheer presence. It used maneouvres unlike anything that the Sisters had schooled her in, patterns of demon logic that she could never have thought of.

And yet, they were evenly matched. Their struggle swayed one way and another, but essentially they were at a stalemate. And gradually, Kaiku became accustomed to the conflict. Her movements became a little more assured. She felt less like she was floundering, and more in control. If the demon had thrown all its strength at her in the beginning, she might have been defeated; but she was learning its ways now, for its methods were few and often repeated. She found with a fierce delight that she could spot the demon's tricks and prevent them. The ruku-shai's inroads into her defences became less frequent. She realised that, untested as she was, she was quicker and more agile on the strings of the Weave than the creature she faced, and only her inexperience had allowed it to hold her back thus far.

She began to think she could win.

She gathered the threads under her control into a tight ribbon and went spiralling skyward, dragging her enemy with her like the tail of a comet. She took the demon dizzyingly high and fast, keeping it snared with hooks and loops, and it was bewildered by this strange offensive and slow to react. Dogging it with swift attacks, she drew its attention far from the core of its consciousness; then, nimbly, she cut it loose and plunged, skipping onto different threads and racing back towards the demon's body, circumventing the battle front entirely. The ruku-shai, realising that it had been lured away from the place it was meant to be defending, followed as rapidly as it could. But Kaiku used all her speed now, and her enemy was not quick enough. She crashed up against its inner defences like a tidal wave, utilising the full force of her *kana*, and they crumbled. Then she was in, racing through the fibres of the ruku-shai's physical body, scorching through its muscles and veins, suffusing herself into every part of its alien physiology.

There was no more time for subtlety. She simply planted herself inside it, and tore apart the black knot of its being.

The demon emitted an inhuman clattering from its throat as it ruptured from the inside. A cloud of fire belched from its mouth, its limbs and belly distended, and then it exploded into flaming chunks of sinew and cartilage. Kaiku felt the rage and pain of its demise come washing over her as she withdrew her *kana*, an aftershock across the Weave that stunned her with its force. She snapped back into reality, her *kana* retreating into the depths of her body again, recoiling from the backlash of the demon's ending.

She blinked, and suddenly she was no longer seeing the Weave but the grey mist, and her companions staring at the muted bloom of flame that had suddenly lightened it on one side. Perhaps a second had passed for them, if that; but Kaiku felt as if she had fought a war singlehanded.

Her momentary elation at being the winner of that war disappeared as she heard the rhythmic gallop of the approaching demons. She had beaten one, but its companions were enraged, and they were no longer content to wait on their prey. Their rattling took on a harsher pitch that hurt the ear. The dank curtains of vapour coalesced into two monstrous shadows. She did not have time to gather her *kana* again before the ruku-shai were upon them.

They burst from the gloomy haze, their six legs propelling them in a strange double-jointed run. They were seven feet high from their wickedly hoofed toes to the knobbed ridge of their spines, and over twelve feet in length, a drab green-grey in colour. Their torsos were a mass of angles, plates of bony armour covering their sides and back. It grew in sharp bumps and spikes like a coat of thorns, smeared with rank mud and trailing straggly bits of marshweed. Their heads were similarly plated around their sunken yellow eyes and forehead, and when they opened their jaws a cadaverous film of skin stretched across the inner sides of their mouth.

They smashed into the group, catching them off-guard with their unexpected speed. Kaiku threw herself aside as one of them thundered past her, lashing its tail in a blur at her head. She fell awkwardly, tripping on a clump of long grass and going down full-length into a vile slick of sucking mud. Her attacker pulled up short, rearing on its back four legs, and drew its front ones up like a praying mantis, spearing her with a deadly regard. Then a rifle sounded, and the ball sparked off the armour on its cheek. The demon recoiled, and Kaiku felt Yugi's arm on her, pulling her back to her feet.

She found her balance just in time to catch sight of the other ruku-shai over Yugi's shoulder. It had also reared in a mantis position, and as Kaiku watched in horror it jabbed a blow at Tsata with its hoofed foreleg, faster than the eye could follow, sending the Tkiurathi reeling back in a spray of blood to collapse against a marshy hillock. An instant later, it came for them.

'Yugi! Behind us!' she cried, but she was too late. The demon's cord-like tail whipped Yugi across the ribs as he turned to respond to her warning. He sighed and fell forward onto Kaiku, his muscles going slack all at once. She caught him automatically; then she heard another rifle shot, and the angry, clattering snarl of a demon. She threw Yugi's limp weight down, registering momentarily that the demon who had stung him was now flailing in agony at a wound in its neck where Nomoru's rifle had pierced its armour.

But the ruku-shai who had first attacked them was looming over her now, its forelegs held before it and its mouth open, crooked and broken fangs joined by strings of yellow saliva as they stretched apart. A sinister rattle came from deep in its throat.

She had only an instant to act, but it was enough. With an effort of desperate will, she marshalled her *kana* from within, and throwing out her hand at the demon she projected herself into a furious attack. The Weave erupted into life around her as she narrowed her energies into a tight focus, driving into the demon's defences like a needle through stitchwork, leaving nothing back to protect herself. The ruku-shai was not quick enough to mount an effective counter, overcome by the suicidal audacity of the maneouvre, and Kaiku lanced into its core in the space of an eyeblink and ripped it apart.

The force of the explosion scorched her muddied face as the demon was destroyed. Somewhere behind her, Nomoru was swearing, foul curse words in a gutter dialect thrown at the last demon as she fired again and again, repriming between each ball as she pumped shot after shot into the creature. Ignoring Yugi, Kaiku turned from the flaming remains of her victim and stumbled to the scout's aid.

Nomoru was standing over the prone form of Tsata on the hillock, holding the ruku-shai at bay. Each time she hit it, the creature writhed in pain as the iron in the rifle ball burned its flesh; but each time it came for her again, and Nomoru's ammunition could not last forever.

Kaiku cried out in challenge. She was wading through the marsh towards it, her irises a deep red and her expression grim. The sight of her approach robbed the demon of the last of its spirit, and with a final rattle it plunged away into the mist.

Nomoru squeezed the trigger for a parting shot, and her rifle puffed uselessly. Her ignition powder had burned up. She glanced at Kaiku with a flat expression, revealing nothing; then she crouched down next to Tsata, and rolled him over.

'Get the other one,' she said to Kaiku, not looking up.

Kaiku did as she was told. The air was becoming less oppressive, the evil departing like an exhaled breath, the mist thinning around them. She felt numb. The demons were gone, but she was racked with tiredness, and the sudden departure of adrenaline from her system left her trembling.

Yugi lay sprawled face-down, his shirt torn open where the tail of the ruku-shai had hit him. Blood welled through from beneath. Kaiku knelt down by his side, her heart sinking. She pulled off his pack, then turned him over and shook him. When that produced no response, she shook him again, his head lolling back and forth as she did so.

Puzzlement turned to alarm. He had not been hit hard. What was wrong with him? She had no training in herbcraft or healing; she did not know what to do. The cushioning folds of exhaustion were not enough to suppress the new horror rising up inside her. Yugi was her friend. Why was he not waking up?

Omecha, silent harvester, have you not taken enough from me already? she prayed bitterly. *Let him live!*

'Poison,' said a voice by her shoulder, and she looked round to see Tsata crouching by her. His face was bloodied with a deep gash, and his right eye was swollen shut. When he talked, his bruised lips made a smacking noise.

'Poison?' Kaiku repeated.

'Demon poison,' Nomoru said, from where she stood over them. 'The ruku-shai have barbs in their tails.'

Kaiku remained staring at the face of the fallen man, which was turning steadily a deep shade of purple as they watched.

'Can you help him?' Kaiku said, her voice small.

Tsata put his fingers to Yugi's throat, feeling for a pulse. Kaiku did not know to do that. It was not part of a high-born girl's education. 'He is dying,' Tsata said. 'It is too late to remove the poison.'

The mist had almost sunk back to the ground now, and in some peripheral part of her mind Kaiku realised that they were three-quarters of the way through the marsh. The cultists on the other side were gone.

'You get it out,' said Nomoru. It took Kaiku a moment to realise who she was addressing.

'I do not know how,' she whispered. She did not trust the power inside her enough. Suddenly she felt a crushing regret for all those years she had spurned Cailin's advice to study, to learn to master her *kana.* Wielding it as a weapon was one thing, but to use it to heal was a different matter entirely. She had almost killed Asara with it before, and later she had almost killed Lucia, all because of her lack of control. She would not have Yugi's death on her hands, would not be responsible for him.

'You're an apprentice,' Nomoru persisted. 'An apprentice of the Red Order.'

'I do not know *how*!' Kaiku repeated helplessly.

Tsata grabbed her collar and pulled her towards him, glaring at her with his good eye.

'*Try!*'

Kaiku tried.

She threw herself into Yugi before her fear could overwhelm her again, placing her hands on his chest and squeezing her eyes shut. The veined film of her eyelids did nothing to block the Weave-sight as the world turned golden again. She plunged into the rushing fibres of his body, knitting past the striations of muscle and into the weakening current that kept him alive.

She could sense the poison, could *see* it as it blackened the golden threads of his flesh. The slow thunder of his heart throbbed through her.

She did not know where to start or what to do. She had hardly any formal knowledge of biology and none of toxicology. She did not know how to defend against the poison without destroying it and Yugi with it. Indecision paralysed her. Her consciousness hung within the diorama of Yugi's body.

Learn from your surroundings. Mould yourself to them.

The words that came to her were Cailin's. A lesson taught long ago. If all else failed, go limp and let the flow of the Weave show you how to move.

Yugi's body was a machine that had run efficiently for over thirty years now. It knew what it was doing. She only had to listen to it.

She began a mantra, a meditation designed to make her relax. Against all odds, it began to ease her, and the rigid form of her consciousness began to disseminate, to melt like ice into water. Kaiku was startled by how easily her *kana* responded to her command. What had moments ago seemed an impossible task became simple. She allowed herself to be absorbed into the matrices of Yugi's body, and let nature instruct her instincts.

It made perfect sense: the circulation of the blood, the flickering of the synapses in his brain, the tiny pulses through his nerves. By becoming part of it, she found his body as familiar to her as her own. She found that she knew what to do on a subconscious level rather than a conscious one, so she let her *kana* guide her.

The poison spread like a cancer, with even the tiniest part blooming out evil threads of corruption if left unchecked. Kaiku was forced to move within the fibres of Yugi's body with the precision of a surgeon, tracking the dark coils amid the glowing tubes of his veins and capillaries, defending his heart from the insidious inward progress of the invader while simultaneously cleansing the befouled blood that passed through it with every weakening beat. The mental strain of trying to keep Yugi alive while neutralising the poison was immense, and more so because she had little idea of what she was doing; but she found herself gaining the upper hand, her *kana* working with a mind of its own, seeming to be only nominally under her control.

She chased the poison. She knotted and looped it to arrest its progress. She gently excised corrupted threads and sent them elsewhere, discharging harmlessly into the swamp around her. She erected tumorous barriers that it could not pass, and then took them down when the danger had gone. Twice she thought she had beaten it, only to find that a tiny shred of poison had been overlooked and was creeping inward again. Exhaustion threatened to overwhelm her, but her will held strong. She would not let him die. She would *not.*

Then, unexpectedly, it was done. Her eyes flickered open, irises deep crimson, and she was back in the marsh once again. Tsata was looking at her with something like awe in his gaze; even Nomoru bore an air of grudging respect. Yugi was breathing normally, his pallor back to its usual hue, sleeping deeply. She felt disoriented; it was a few moments before she realised where she was and what had happened.

Gods, she thought to herself in stark disbelief. *I did not realise. I did not see what I could do with the power inside me. Why did I not let Cailin teach me?*

A sense of elation more deep and profound than any she could remember touched her. She had saved Yugi's life. Not by bearing him out of danger, or protecting him in battle, but by physically drawing him back from the brink of death. She knew well enough the perilous euphoria of the Weave, but this was a different ecstasy, purer somehow. She had used her power to heal instead of to destroy; and what was more, she had done it without ever being taught how. A smile spread across her face, and she began to laugh with relief and joy. It was some time before she realised she was crying also.

FIFTEEN

The Blood Emperor Mos woke with a shout from a dream. He gazed wildly around, his meaty hands clutched tight to the gold sheets of his bed; then sense returned to him as he realised he was awake. But the dream lingered: the humiliation, the sorrow, the rage.

It was too hot. Past midday, he guessed, and the Imperial bedchamber was stifling despite the open shutters. The room was designed to be wide and airy, with a floor of black *lach* and a single archway leading to a balcony high up on the north-eastern side of the Imperial Keep. Smaller, oval windows flanked the archway, beaming painful brightness into the room.

Mos lay on the bed that formed the centrepiece. Most of the other furniture was for Laranya – dressing-tables, mirrors, an elegant couch – but this was his, a gift from an emissary of Yttryx that he had received near the start of his reign. At each corner of the bed, the ivory horns of some colossal Yttryxian animal formed the bedposts, six feet long and curving outward in symmetry, ringed with gold bracelets and studded with precious stones.

The room smelled of sour alcohol sweat, and his mouth tasted of old wine, befouled by the dry mucus in his throat and on his tongue. He was naked amid the tangle of covers that his nocturnal thrashing had displaced.

His wife the Empress was not in the bed with him, and by the absence of her perfume he knew she had not slept there the previous night.

Recollection came sluggishly. Aestival Week was still young. He remembered a feast, musicians . . . and wine, a lot of wine. Vague images of faces and laughter scattered across his mind. His head throbbed.

An argument. Of course, an argument; they seemed to be doing that more and more of late. When two firebrands clashed, sparks flew. But he had been in a conciliatory mood, still feeling faint tatters of guilt for that moment in the pavilion when he had almost struck her. He had made it up to her somehow, and they had celebrated through the night. Feeling that their temporary peace was fragile, he had even tolerated the terrible company she attracted, forsaking his more stolid and interesting companions for his wife's repellantly gaudy and theatrical friends.

Of course, Eszel was there, and her brother Reki. The bookworm seemed to have found his element among Laranya's lot. Mos remembered swaying drunkenly, not saying much, while they talked gibberish about inconsequential matters that seemed designed to exclude him from the conversation. What did he know of the ancient philosophers? What did he care for classical Vinaxan sculpture? Beyond occasional attempts by Laranya to rope him into the conversation, like throwing scraps to a starving dog, he had absolutely nothing to contribute.

He frowned as bits and pieces slotted into place. A feeling of resentment, that they were not paying attention to him, their Blood Emperor. Satisfaction that his presence was making both Reki and Eszel very uncomfortable. Ardour . . . that was very strong. He remembered wanting Laranya, a deep stirring that needed satisfaction. Yet he would not ask his own wife to come to bed with him, not in front of the peacocks she was mingling with. It offended his sense of manhood. She should come with him when he told her to; he would not beg. Heart's blood, he was the Emperor! But he feared an embarrassing rejection if he commanded her, and she was too wilful to be sure of a yes.

He wanted to go, and he wanted her to come with him. He did not want to leave her here. Sometime during the night, in a moment of drunken clarity, he realised that he did not want to leave her with Eszel. He did not trust what they might do, once he was gone.

Dawn was the last thing he could recall. By then, unable to keep awake beneath the smothering blanket that wine had laid over his senses, he announced loudly and awkwardly that he was going to bed, gazing pointedly at Laranya as he did so. The peacocks all bade him farewell with the usual graceful rituals, and Laranya kissed him swiftly on the lips and said that she would be there soon.

But she did not come. And Mos's dreams had been bad that night, and uncommonly vivid. Though he could recall only one, he could not shake the feelings it had evoked. A dream of hot, red rutting, of walking invisibly into a room and finding his wife there, fingers clawing the back of the man who thrust between her legs, gasping and moaning the way she did when Mos was with her. And he was powerless in his dream, impotent, unable to intervene or to see the face of the man that was cuckolding him. Weak and pathetic. Like that moment when Kakre had loomed over him, cowed him like a child.

He lay back down in his bed, his jaw clenched bitterly. First the Weave-lord, now his own wife? Did they conspire to humiliate him? Sense told him that Laranya was probably still where he left her, still celebrating with the inexhaustible zest for life that was one of the things he loved in her. But he would never know what had gone on in those lost hours since dawn, and his dream tormented him as he waited angrily for her return.

The townsfolk of Ashiki had learned to fear the coming of the night.

Aestival Week had been a cursed time for them. There were no celebrations now. They were only a tiny community, and new to the Fault. Scholars and their families, mainly, though their personal wealth had been used to hire soldiers as guards. In the past few years, there had seemed to be more and more people fleeing to the Xarana Fault to escape the oppressive atmosphere in the cities, the sense of slowly rising tension. The Weavers' eyes were everywhere except here, and the scholars and thinkers who had founded Ashiki had feared persecution for their radical ideas more than they feared the tales they heard of the Fault.

They had not heard the right tales.

Their arrival in the Fault had been blessed with good luck. Guided by Zanya or Shintu or both, they had happened upon a secluded vale near the east bank of the Rahn, at the foot of the great falls. Initially it had appeared to be an ill omen, a charnel-house of corpses that horrified them; but they were pragmatic people, and not superstitious, and soon they realised what had happened here and understood that it was the perfect place for a town. Here, two warring factions had wiped each other out fighting over one another's territory, and the remainder had scattered. The land was unclaimed, and so the scholars claimed it.

They did not know the extent of their fortune. Most new arrivals in the Fault did not last a week before some other force, already well entrenched, consumed them. But the great battle had emptied the land for a mile in every direction, and they managed to create a small community unhindered and unnoticed, hiding in their picturesque vale while they built crude fortifications and homes.

This was to have been their first Aestival Week in the Fault, and despite the hardships they felt like explorers on a new frontier, and they were glad.

Then, on the second night of Aestival Week, people started to disappear.

Lulled by their apparent safety, the revellers in Ashiki had allowed their security to become lax amid the celebrations. Four people were nowhere to be found by the morning. Their absence was hardly noted at first; when it was, it was thought that they had fallen asleep somewhere, drunk. By nightfall, their families and friends were concerned, but the rest of the town were not worried enough about a few missing people to curtail their festivities. In all probability they had simply gone off to find themselves a place to couple or to get a much-needed break from the community at large. It was not unknown.

That night, six people disappeared. Some of them from their beds.

This time the town took notice. They sent out search parties to comb the surrounding area. When they returned, they were two men short.

Now, as night came on the fourth day of Aestival Week, nobody slept. The silent demons and spirits that were stealing them away had made them mortally afraid, and they clustered in their houses or hid behind their stockade walls and dreaded what the dawn might bring. They did not know that their demon had done its work, and departed now. It had all the victims it needed.

The entity that Kaiku knew as Asara brooded in a cave, still wearing the shape of Saran Ycthys Marul. Kaiku would not have recognised him, however. He was massive and swollen, his skin a webwork of angry red veins that hung loosely off him in folds as if all the elasticity had gone out of it. His strict Quraal clothes lay discarded at his side, next to a different set of clothes that he had stolen for the purpose of his new guise. The once-muscular body was grotesque and sagging now, spilling over his folded knees. His eyes were filmed with white and speckled with shards of dark iris which floated freely around in myopic orbs. The components of his body were breaking themselves down, reordering themselves in a genetic dance of incredible precision, changing bit by bit to ensure that all functions kept working while the miracle of metamorphosis occurred. He was altering his very structure, being reborn within his own skin.

The cave was dank and pitch-black, well hidden. By firelight, it would have been a small, pretty grotto, dominated by a shallow pool surrounded by stalagmites, its walls glinting with green and yellow mineral flecks. But he had lit no fire, for he needed no heat. He had chosen the cave for its inaccessibility, and had made sure it was well away from any settlement in the Fault. It reeked of a choking animal musk. The occupant had been killed and removed by Saran a few days ago, but the stink would serve to keep other animals away. He had barricaded the entrance with stones, to be sure.

In the days it would take him to change, he was vulnerable. His muscles had already wasted to the point where he could barely move. He was effectively blind and deaf. Alone in the dark, there was only the gradually slowing tide of his thoughts to keep him company, decelerating towards the hibernation state in which he would spend the bulk of his transformation.

What thoughts still swirled around in the bottom of his mind were bitter dregs.

Asara had taken on the body of Saran Ycthys Marul with entirely innocent intentions. It had been a necessary guise to facilitate her mission in Quraal. Under the rigidly patriarchal Theocracy, women were not allowed to move between provinces without special dispensation, and foreign women were not even allowed to set foot in the country. Taking on the form of a Quraal male was the only realistic way of performing any kind of investigation there. It was distasteful to her, but not entirely unpleasant. She had spent a few years as a man before, during her years of wandering and searching for the sense of identity that had ever eluded her. This time around, she found she was better accustomed to it, and she fit easier in her own skin. Still, she could not help sometimes feeling that she was acting as she thought a man should, rather than the behaviour coming naturally to her. Such moments manifested themselves as moments of grandiose gravity or flair that, unbeknownst to her, seemed somewhat forced and ridiculous.

He had kept the guise for that last visit to Okhamba. Partially it was because he had got used to it, but it was also because it would be easier to gather men for a dangerous trip if he himself was a man: there would be no tiresome issues of gender, whether in preparation for the journey or during it. Men were apt to either feel disdain towards a woman who sought to risk herself – thinking arrogantly that she was trying to measure up to a man by doing so – or they felt protective, which was worse. They were as predictable as night and day.

But there was another, more important reason. To effect a change of his entire body meant that he was forced to glut himself, to steal the breath and the essence of others until he was gorged to the limit of endurance. The forge of change, the organ that he felt nestling between his stomach and spine – which he imagined as a coil, though he really had no anatomical comparison to draw against – had to be stocked with fuel enough to keep it burning throughout the metamorphosis. That required many lives of men and women.

Not that Saran felt guilt about taking what he needed. He had long since learned that he was unable to feel more than a passing regret in killing, no more than a butcher would in slaughtering a banathi. But he had lived to eighty-six harvests by being careful, and a dozen deaths in quick succession would always arouse terror and suspicion among the survivors. Sometimes they thought it was a mysterious plague, the Sleeping Death that they had heard of, for his victims were found dead without a mark on them as if they had simply stopped breathing; but other times, they sought a scapegoat, and if they found him in mid-transformation, they would tear him apart.

Usually he did not change his whole body any more than he absolutely had to. But this time was an exception.

A violent loathing had taken him. This form, this skin, was tainted now. Saran Ycthys Marul would be sloughed away, and with it perhaps some remnant of the responsibility for the memories it bore.

How could he have known that they would send Kaiku to meet him? Of all people, why her? Though they had been separated for five years, the same cursed attraction existed between them in whatever form he took, and now it was strengthened by the simplicity of being between man and woman. He wished he had never saved Kaiku's life now. It had exacted a heavy price on one who prided himself on his utter independence.

Yet for a time, he had believed that fortune had turned his way. Why tell her? he had thought. He did not owe her the knowledge. It was his prerogative to change his identity whenever he pleased, and he did not feel that he was betraying a trust if he chose to lie about his past. Then, after Kaiku had told him what she thought of Asara, his mind had been made up. Better to begin again. Kaiku would never have to know.

And then came the time, the moment of joining; but his body betrayed him as Asara's had done before him. The desire to take her, to be inside her, was stronger than the act of making love could satisfy. At a primal level he wanted to *consume* her, to reclaim the lost part of himself and to assimilate her very being in the process. Once again, he had lost control.

Now he had ruined everything. He knew Kaiku too well: she was as stubborn in her grudges as in everything else. She would not forgive him, ever. His deception, which had seemed justifiable at the time, now seemed abhorrent when mirrored through Kaiku's eyes. What a pitiful vermin he was, taking on shapes to reinvent himself over and over, to erase past mistakes with different faces. A being with no core, and no soul, stealing his essence from others, vapid inside.

He had gone to Cailin, and they had spoken of a new task for him, one that would require him to take a new form. He was only too glad to take it.

He could bear himself no longer. It was time to change.

Zaelis found Lucia sitting with a young boy her own age in the lee of a rocky jut that protruded from the side of the valley. It was midday, and Nuki's eye was fierce overhead, pummelling the world in dazzling light. Lucia and the boy lay in what little shade the rock provided, he on his back, she on her belly reading, kicking her legs absently. Several small animals busied themselves nearby, strangely nonchalant in their activities: a pair of squirrels dug for nuts, darting quickly about but never straying far; a raven prowled up and down the jut like a lookout; a black fox sat worrying at its brush, glancing back occasionally at the two adolescents who lounged under its protection.

Zaelis halted for a time, watching them from downslope. His heart softened at the sight. It was like a painting, a moment of childhood idyll. Lucia's posture and manner were more girlish than he had ever seen. As he thought this, she turned to the boy and said something about the book she was studying, and he burst into explosive laughter, startling the squirrels. She grinned at him in response; a carefree, genuine smile. Zaelis felt gladdened, then suddenly sad. Such moments were too rare for Lucia, and now he came to ruin it for her. He almost turned back then, resolving to talk to her later; but he reminded himself that there was more at stake than his feelings or hers now. He limped up the hill towards them.

He knew that boy, he realised, as he got closer. His name was Flen; the son of one of the few professional soldiers that the Fold possessed. His father was a Libera Dramach man. Zaelis remembered meeting him once or twice. Of all the people that Lucia spent her time with, Flen was the one she preferred; or so his informers told him, anyway. Caution had driven him to keep a watch on the former Heir-Empress's activities as she grew.

He found himself disliking the boy already. He had warned Lucia against making her abilities overt, for fear of revealing herself. Even though nobody knew the Heir-Empress of Blood Erinima was even alive, much less the strange affinity with nature that she bore, it was too great a risk. Yet she did not conceal them around Flen. Only Flen. Out of all her friends, what made *him* special?

Careful, Zaelis, he told himself. *She is fourteen harvests old now. No longer a little girl. No matter what you may prefer to think.*

Flen noticed him then, though the animals – and hence Lucia – had spotted him a long time ago. They did not scatter as animals should, but held their ground with a peculiarly insolent air.

'Master Zaelis,' he said, getting to his feet and bowing swiftly in the male-child fashion, hands linked behind his back.

'Flen,' he replied, with a mere dip of his head. 'May I have a private word with Lucia?'

Flen glanced at Lucia as if to seek her approval; it irritated Zaelis inexplicably. But she was still reading her book as if neither of them were there.

'Of course,' he said. He seemed about to say some words of farewell to Lucia, but then decided against it. He walked away hesitantly, unsure of whether he should stay nearby or leave, and then made a decision and struck out towards the town.

'Daygreet, Zaelis,' Lucia said, not looking up. It was the first time they had met today, for she had left the house before he had awoken, making the pleasantry an appropriate one.

He sat down next to her, his damaged leg out straight before him. He could manage the traditional cross-legged position when he needed to, but it made his knee ache. His eyes wandered over the puckered and grooved skin on the nape of her neck, the appalling burn scars revealed by her short hair. She looked up at him over her shoulder, narrowing her eyes against the glare of the sun, and waited expectantly.

Zaelis sighed. Talking to her was never easy. She gave so little back.

'How are you feeling?' he asked.

'I'm fine,' she said casually. 'And you?'

'Lucia, you should really be using a more formal mode by now,' he told her. Her language had subtly evolved into a hybrid of girl-child form and woman-form, which was usual for adolescents as they became embarrassed about using a diminutive mode and began to copy adults; but the dialect she had picked up from the mass of influences among the people of the Fold did not seem appropriate for the child of an Empress.

'I am quite capable of adopting a far more elegant mode, Zaelis,' she said, in crisply elocuted, chilly syllables. She sounded eerily like Cailin. 'But only when I need to,' she finished, reverting to her usual style.

Zaelis abandoned that line of conversation. He should never have brought it up.

'I see you have been communicating with the wildlife of the valley again,' he said, indicating the black fox, which glared at him.

'They come to me whether I talk to them or not,' she said.

'Does this mean that you are well recovered from your incident with the river spirits?' he asked, absently running his knuckles over his close-cut white beard.

'I told you I was,' she replied.

Zaelis looked out across the valley, framing his next sentence; Lucia, surprisingly, spoke up first.

'You want me to try again,' she said. It was a flat statement.

Zaelis turned back to her, his expression set as a grim affirmative. There was no point evading it; she was far too incisive.

Lucia got up and sat cross-legged, arranging her dress over her knees. She seemed so tall and slender suddenly, Zaelis thought. Where was the little girl he had tutored, the little girl he had built a secret army around?

'It will do no good,' she said. 'What happened on the river has been forgotten now, at least by any spirits that I could contact.'

'I know that,' said Zaelis, although he really hadn't for sure until Lucia told him. 'But *something* happened there, Lucia. I sent spies to investigate, after what happened to you. The river towns are talking of nothing else.'

Lucia studied him with her fey blue eyes, her silence prompting him to continue.

'A barge was destroyed on the Kerryn,' he said, shifting himself awkwardly. 'Carrying explosives, apparently, and they must have gone off and blown it to pieces. But there were . . .' He hesitated, wondering if he should share this with her. 'There were bits washed up, bits of the people that had been on the barge. That, and bits of *other* things. That barge was carrying something when it exploded, and it wasn't human.'

Still Lucia did not speak. She knew he was getting to his point.

'Cailin believes that things are building to a head. The failing crops, Blood Kerestyn's armies, Saran's report, the thing you sensed on the river, the Weavers in the Fault. I have grown to believe her. We have little time left.'

He intentionally left out the revolt in Zila, though intelligence had reached him long ago about that. He tried to keep the doings of the Ais Maraxa as far from Lucia's ears as possible.

He laid a hand on his adopted daughter's knee. 'I have come to realise that we have no clear idea of what we are truly facing, and ignorance will kill us. We have to know what is going on *now*,' he said. 'We have to know what we are dealing with. The source of all of this.'

Her heart sank as she felt the inevitability of what was to come.

'Lucia, we need you to tell us. To go to Alskain Mar, contact one of the great spirits. We need to know about the witchstones.' He looked pained as he said it. 'Will you do it?'

You are not a pawn here. Kaiku's words came back to her then, spoken on the first day of Aestival Week. But they seemed hollow, brittle under the weight of necessity. She knew in her heart that she was not capable of a meeting of minds with a spirit such as dwelt in Alskain Mar, and that she would be placing herself in grave danger by trying; and yet, how could she refuse? She owed her life to Zaelis, and she loved him dearly. He would not ask her if it was not a matter of utmost importance.

'I will,' she said, and the day seemed suddenly a little darker.

SIXTEEN

Aestival Week passed, but for Mishani there had been no celebration this year. For seven days now she had been riding through the Saramyr countryside, and for one not used to long journeys on horseback it was a gruelling test. Yet despite saddle-sores and fatigue, and the endless watchfulness, she never made a complaint, never let her mask slip even a little. Though she was surrounded by men whom she mistrusted, though she headed south in secret to an uncertain end, though her own father was trying to have her killed, she was calm and serene. It was her way.

They had left Hanzean soon after the attempt on Mishani's life, timing their departure to coincide with the beginning of the harvest celebrations so as to take advantage of the confusion and slip away unnoticed. Chien had insisted on personally accompanying her as escort, to make reparations for the shame of allowing assassins to menace his guest. Mishani had expected no less. Whatever Chien's plans for her, she was sure that he would want to be present to see them carried out.

Nevertheless, their journey was far from safe, despite the retinue of eight guards who went with them; the merchant put himself at considerable risk by travelling with her. Transport by sea was not an option, since all boats would be watched by Barak Avun's men and their arrival logged in their destination port. That left land travel, which was more fraught with minor perils but which would make evading her father a much simpler task. Anyone seeking them from Hanzean would have no idea which way they went, since nobody knew their destination but Mishani.

Still, the need for secrecy carried its own disadvantages. Mishani was accustomed to travelling by carriage; but they were forced to stay off the roads, and that meant horses, and camping under the stars. Though Chien expended every effort to make her comfortable, providing her with sheets and an elegant tent which the grumbling guards had to put up for her each night, it was still somewhat irksome for the child of a Barak. Mishani liked her little luxuries, and she did not share Kaiku's readiness to forsake them. But at least she still had her luggage with her from her trip to Okhamba, so she had her clothes and scents, and plenty of diversions.

They had struck out south from Hanzean for several days before turning south-east to meet the Great Spice Road below Barask, which ran almost exactly a thousand miles from Axekami to Suwana in the Southern Prefectures. They did not dare use the Han-Barask Highway, one of only two major routes out of the port, and even when they found the Great Spice Road they stayed well off it, keeping to the west of the thoroughfare until the northern reaches of the Forest of Xu began to loom to their left, and they were forced to join the road to take the Pirika Bridge across the Zan. There they were warned about the revolt in Zila and told to go back if they could and find another route to their destination.

Few heeded the warning: there was no other way. The vast and fearful forest crowded them to the east, spirit-haunted and ancient, while to the west was the coast. There were no ports of a size capable of supporting passenger craft unless they went back to Hanzean, and to go around the forest would require a detour of some nine hundred miles, which was insanity. Instead, most travellers were heading off the road, skirting the Forest as closely as they dared and passing to the east of Zila. With no option left to them, Mishani and her retinue took that route also.

By nightfall of their seventh day of travel, they were camped twenty-five miles to the south-east of the troubled city, near a shallow semicircle of black rocks that knuckled out of the flat plains. It was the last day of summer, and in Axekami the final ritual of Aestival Week would be at its height, welcoming in the autumn. There was no question of hiding out here, unless they cared to go within the borders of the forest which glowered a mile to their east. But their camp was anonymous among many scattered across the plains: other travellers heading south like them and forced to brave the bottleneck that Zila commanded.

Mishani sat cross-legged on a mat near the fire, her back to the rocks that ran along one edge of their campsite, and watched the guards building her small tent nearby. A slender book lay closed on the ground next to her. One of her mother's. It was a gift from Chien: the latest volume of Muraki tu Koli's ongoing series of fictions about a dashing romantic named Nida-jan and his adventures in the courts. Muraki's creation had made her moderately famous among the high families, and her stories had spread by word of mouth to the servant classes and peasantry as well. Handmaidens would beg their masters and mistresses to read them the tales of Nida-jan, which were printed in High Saramyrrhic, a written language taught to high-borns, priests and scholars but incomprehensible to the lower classes. They would then eagerly pass the stories on to their friends, embellishing here and there, and their friends would do the same for *their* friends.

Nida-jan was everything Mishani's mother was not: daring, adventurous, sexually uninhibited and confident enough to talk his way out of any situation, or able to fight his way out if words failed. Mishani's mother was quiet, shy, and fiercely intelligent, with a strong moral compass; she lived her life in her books, for there she could shape the world any way she saw fit instead of having to deal with the one that was presented to her, a place that was often too cruel and hurtful for a woman so sensitive.

Mishani took after her mother in appearance, but her father in temperament. Muraki was a lonely woman, too introverted to connect with those around her, and though she was pleasant company, it was easy to forget that she was there at all. When her father Avun began grooming Mishani in the ways of the court, Muraki dropped out of the picture almost entirely. While Mishani spent all her time in Axekami with her father, Muraki stayed at their Mataxa Bay estates and wrote. When Mishani had fled to exile in the Xarana Fault, she had not considered her mother's feelings at all. Muraki showed them so rarely that it simply did not occur to Mishani that they might be affected.

Now Mishani had finished the book, and a deep sorrow had taken her. The stories were not the usual Nida-jan fare; instead, they were melancholy and tragic, an unusual turn for the irrepressible hero. They concerned Nida-jan's discovery that one of his courtly liasons had produced a son, who had been hidden from him, and whom he only learned of when the mother confessed it to him on her death-bed. But the boy had gone to the east, and had disappeared there some months before. Nida-jan was tortured by love for this unknown son, and set out to find him, becoming obsessed with his quest, spurning his friends when they told him it was hopeless. He set out on foolhardy adventures to seek clues to the boy's whereabouts. Finally he faced a great demon with a hundred eyes, and he blinded his enemy with mirrors and slew it; but as it died, the demon cursed him to wander the world without rest until he found his son, and until his son called him 'Father' and meant it.

So the book ended with Nida-jan condemned, his soul racked and his quest still incomplete. Loss bled from every line. Each story had, directly or indirectly, been about a parent's yearning for their child. Mishani's mother may have been introverted, but she had not been cold. She poured out her pain on to the pages, and Mishani grieved to read it. Suddenly, she missed her mother like a physical ache in her stomach. She missed her father too, the way he had been, before she made herself an enemy to him. She wanted desperately to wipe away the years that separated them, to return to the time when she was her father's pride, to embrace her mother and tell her how sorry she was that they had never been closer, that she had not realised how Muraki felt.

All the years of hiding bore down on her, living in fear of being recognised, terrified of her own family. She would have cried, had she been alone.

She was looking up at the moonless sky when Chien sat down next to her. The air, though warm, seemed unnaturally clear and brittle tonight, and the light of the stars was sharp and hard.

'You're thinking of your mother, aren't you?' Chien said, after a time.

Mishani supposed that was a guess based on the book lying by her side. She did not wish to answer him, so she avoided the question.

'The Grey Moth is out tonight,' she said, gesturing upward. Chien looked.

'I don't see it,' he said.

'It is very faint. Most nights it cannot be seen at all.'

'I only see the Diving Bird,' the merchant said, counting off nine stars in the constellation with one stubby finger.

Mishani lowered her head, her hair falling forward over her shoulder with the movement. 'It is there,' she said. 'Hidden to some and visible to others. That is part of its mystery.'

Chien was still trying to find it, eager to be included in her experience. 'Is it an omen, do you think?'

'I do not believe in omens,' Mishani replied. 'I merely find it appropriate to my mood.'

'How?'

Mishani looked up at him. 'Surely you know how. Do you not remember the story of how the gods created our world?'

Chien's blocky face was blank. 'Mistress Mishani, I was adopted. They don't teach adopted children the finer points of religion, and academia hasn't played a great part in managing my family's shipping business. I know about the tapestry, but nothing about moths.'

Mishani studied him, sidelit as he was by the fire of their camp. He seemed earnest, at least, but she half-suspected he was feigning ignorance simply to engage her in further conversation. He was sometimes hard work to be around, since he had none of the ease of spirit which allowed most people to sit in comfortable silence with each other. He always had to talk when he was with her, always had to have something to say. She could feel him squirming awkwardly when he did not.

'The story goes that the gods were bored, and Yoru suggested they weave a tapestry to amuse themselves,' Mishani began. 'This was in the time before his enforced vigil at the gates of the Golden Realm, before Ocha discovered his affair with Isisya and banished him there.'

'That part I *do* know,' Chien said with a crooked smile.

'Each god or goddess would stitch their own piece,' Mishani continued. 'But they had nothing to make it out of, so Misamcha went to her garden and gathered caterpillars. The caterpillars made silk at her touch, and she wrapped them up into skeins and gave them to the gods, who made their tapestry. When the work was done, all agreed that it was the most wonderful tapestry they had ever seen, the richest and the most detailed. Since they liked it so much, Ocha decided to give it life, so they could watch their tapestry grow. Each god or goddess became reflected in their favourite aspect. Some took physical things: the sea, the sun, the trees, fire and ice. Others took less tangible matters: love, death, revenge, honour. And so the world was created.'

'You've told me of caterpillars now,' said Chien, 'but not of moths.'

Mishani looked back up at the night sky, where the Grey Moth hung, seven dim stars surrounding an abyss of perfect void. 'The gods wanted the tapestry to be perfect. But after it was sewn and the world made, the caterpillars changed into beautiful coloured moths. All but one, and that one was grey and sickly. For no thing is utterly perfect, not even that which the gods create, not even the gods themselves.'

She turned her gaze to the fire, and it danced in the pupils of her eyes. 'The grey moth had produced a silk that was corrupt, a thread that the gods had used along with all the others to make their tapestry, interwoven with the other threads. And in that silk was all the evils of the world, all the jealousy and hatred and foulness, all the sadness and grief and hunger and pain. Once the gods saw what had been done, they were appalled; but it was too late to undo their work. They loved the world a little less after that.' She paused for a time, considering. 'They called the silk of that caterpillar the Skein of Lament, and then they put the image of the Grey Moth in the night sky as a reminder.'

'A reminder? Of what?' Chien asked.

'A reminder that we should never relax our vigilance. That even the gods could not make something perfect without it becoming corrupted, and humankind is more fallible than they. If we cease to be watchful, then evil slips into our lives, and it will undermine us and bring us down.' She met Chien's gaze, and she let her eyes show her weariness, and a fraction of her melancholy. 'I do not think we have been watchful enough of late.'

Chien regarded her strangely for a few moments, his plain features blank with incomprehension. Mishani did not feel inclined to elaborate any further. Presently, Chien began fiddling with the hem of his cloak, a sure sign that he was becoming uncomfortable. She let him suffer until he spoke again.

'We've passed Zila,' he said, 'and the way south widens again. Perhaps it's time you told us where you're going now. We need to decide if we have to stop for supplies and choose the best route.'

Mishani acceded with a tilt of her head; Chien would, after all, be unable to do anything about it now, even if he had wished to betray her somehow.

'I will go to Lalyara,' she said. 'There you may leave me, and I will count your obligation fulfilled with honour.'

'Not until I have you safely delivered to your ultimate destination, Mistress Mishani,' Chien insisted. 'Into the care of someone who will take responsibility for your welfare.'

Mishani laughed. 'You are kind, Chien os Mumaka; but there is nobody in Lalyara who will do that. My business must remain my own, and I am bound by other promises not to tell you.'

Chien bore the news well enough. She had expected him to be crestfallen – he was curiously childlike at times – but he smiled faintly in understanding. 'Then I will treasure these last days we will spend in each other's company,' he said.

'As will I,' Mishani replied, though more because it was expected than because she meant it. In truth, against her better judgement, she did like Chien. It was wise not to feel affection for a potential opponent, but that tension was the part of their relationship that she found most interesting, and she had to admit that he had grown on her. He had a quick brain and a sharp wit, and Mishani could not help but respect his achievements: how he had overcome the stigma of being adopted into a disgraced family to help raise Blood Mumaka back to power through his devious mercantile skills.

Still, for all that, it would be a great relief to be rid of him. She was constantly on edge, waiting for his hidden agenda to manifest itself.

But would her destination be any better?

He excused himself and got up to go and talk to his men, leaving Mishani to her thoughts. She found them wandering ahead of her, to what she had to do once he was gone.

She was to meet Barak Zahn tu Ikati, Lucia's true father. And if things went well, she was to tell him that his daughter still lived – and that Mishani knew where she was.

It would be a terribly delicate thing to achieve, and it would test her diplomatic skills more sorely than at any time past. The risk was immense, and the responsibility placed in her hands was greater still. Mishani dared not reveal that she knew anything about Lucia until she was sure that the Barak would react in the way that they wanted. If she misplayed her hand, she could find herself a hostage, held and interrogated, at the mercy of Zahn's Weaver. Zahn might demand to have his daughter brought to him, or he might marshal his troops and storm into the Fold, and that would be catastrophic.

His mental state over the last few years had been more and more distracted and lugubrious if accounts were to be believed. He had let the affairs of his family slip and retreated to one of his estates north of Lalyara. Popular rumour had it that he was mourning the death of his friend – and lover, so the gossips said with unwitting accuracy – the former Blood Empress Anais tu Erinima. Mishani knew better.

Zaelis had witnessed the moment when Zahn met Lucia for the first time in the roof gardens of the Imperial Keep, and both father and daughter had known at that moment what Anais had kept concealed all those years.

But if Zahn had ever intended to make a claim on his daughter, he missed his chance. The Blood Empress was slaughtered, and in amongst the confusion the little Heir-Empress disappeared. Though her body was never found, it was assumed that she had died in the fires and explosions that raged through the Keep on that day, her corpse charred beyond recognition. In reality, she had been snatched away by the Libera Dramach, but not even Zahn knew about that.

Zaelis had charged Mishani to make the decision whether to tell him or not. It was a heavy burden to bear. But they could not keep Lucia a secret for ever, and if they could get Zahn onto their side, then they would gain a powerful ally. It would take time to prepare the moment when Lucia would emerge from the shadows, years of planning; and it began here, with Mishani. After Zahn, she would approach Blood Erinima, who also had a vested interest, for Lucia was a living child of theirs that they had thought dead, and ties of blood were the strongest of all.

But first, Barak Zahn. One trick at a time.

A stirring in the camp brought her out of her musing. A few of the guards had got up hurriedly from around the fire, and were looking into the darkness over her head, past the shallow semicircle of black rocks. She felt a vibration in the ground, and a moment later the sound reached her ears. Hooves, pounding on the plains.

Approaching fast.

The first volley of shots cut down four of the eight men that Chien had brought to protect them. The defenders' night vision was destroyed by the fire, and the attackers were firing from the outside in, so Chien's men were easy targets while the newcomers were impossible to see. Mishani scrambled into the shelter of the rocks a moment before six horses came leaping over them, one thundering to the ground mere inches from where she lay and trampling over the mat where she had sat. The attackers rode into the camp, swords chiming free, and cut down another of the guards; then they galloped through Mishani's tent and off into the dark again.

'*Put out that fire!*' Chien screamed. He kicked the blaze into burning clumps of wood and stamped on them. One of the other guards threw a pan of water across the embers, soaking Chien's boots in the process, while the remaining two had got their rifles up. Somewhere beyond their circle of vision, their attackers were repriming their weapons, ready to shoot again. The light dimmed suddenly as the fire was dispersed, and darkness took the camp.

'Mistress Mishani! Are you hurt?' the merchant cried, but Mishani did not reply. She had already clambered over the low rocks to the other side, keeping them between her and where she imagined the attackers to be, hiding her from the camp. Her heart was hammering in her chest with that same horrible nervous fear that had gripped her when the assassins came for her at Chien's townhouse. Were these more of the same? Was it her they wanted? She had to assume so.

'Mishani!' Chien called again, a tone of desperation in his voice; but she did not want them to find her. Right now, they were in the open, and they were the targets these new killers would go for. That gave her a chance.

She heard an anxious blast of breath, and suddenly remembered the horses. They had been tethered to a post on the near side of the camp. She could almost make them out if she squinted, ghostly blue shapes jostling in alarm. By Shintu's luck, they still wore their tack; the guards had been told by Chien to put up Mishani's tent each night before unsaddling their mounts. Her disdain for sleeping rough just might save her life.

'Mishani!' Chien cried again. Mishani was happy to let him carry on doing so. He was drawing attention to himself. Through a gap in the rocks, she could see that Chien and his remaining guards had adopted a defensive stance now, grabbing what cover they could, their guns pointed outwards. But the riders were not attacking yet. Dousing the fire had made the assassins' job of picking targets a lot harder. Mishani thanked the moon sisters for their decision to stay out of the sky tonight, and then crept to the horses.

The twenty feet that she had to cross felt like a mile, and she had the terrible intuition that at any moment she would feel the brutal smack of a rifle ball and know no more. And yet, to her mild disbelief, the moment never came. She slipped the tethers of her horse from the post and swung into the saddle with a stealthiness that surprised even herself.

That was when the second attack began.

They came in from three sides this time, in pairs. One of each pair had a rifle raised, the other a sword. They fired as they galloped in, and Chien's men fired back at the same time. By good fortune or poor aim, the defenders came off better: none of them were hit, but they managed to kill one of the horses as it bore down on them, striking it directly between its eyes so that it crashed to the ground and rolled over its rider with a cracking of bones.

And then there were swords, crashing against rifle barrels or the guards' own hastily drawn blades, and the cries of men as they fought desperately. Mishani, who had stayed motionless since the attack had begun for fear of drawing attention to herself, put heels to her mount. At her signal, it bolted, and the acceleration took her breath away. The cool wind caught her great length of hair and blew it out in a streamer behind her, and she plunged away into the concealing darkness.

Then, seemingly from nowhere – her eyes were still labouring to adjust to the night – there were other horses alongside her, blocking her in, and a hand grabbed the reins she was holding and pulled her horse to heel. All around, there was a percussion of hooves as they slowed hard and came to a halt, and guns were trained on her. Other men went racing away towards the camp, where Chien and his guards fought a losing battle.

A tall, broad-shouldered man – the one who had stopped her horse – studied her. She could not make out his face, but she glared at him defiantly.

'Mistress Mishani tu Koli,' he said, his voice a deep Newlands burr. Then he chuckled. 'Well, well, well.'

SEVENTEEN

The town of Zila stood on the southern bank of the River Zan, grim and unwelcoming. It had been built at the estuary of the great flow, where the waters that had begun their six-hundred-mile journey in the Tchamil Mountains blended into the sea. It was not a picturesque place, for its original purpose had been military, as a bastion against the Ugati folk who had occupied this land before the Saramyr took it, guarding the bottleneck between the coast and the Forest of Xu while the early settlers raised the city of Barask to the north. It had been here for over a thousand years now, and though its walls had crumbled and been rebuilt, though there was scarcely a building or street left that had existed back then, it still exuded the same brooding presence that it had possessed in the beginning. Cold, and watchful.

It had been constructed to take advantage of a steep hill, which sloped upwards from the south and fell off in a sharp decline at the riverbank. A high wall of black stone surrounded it, which curved and bent to accommodate the contours of the land. Above the wall, the slanting rooftops of red tile and slate angled backwards and up towards the small keep at the centre. The keep was the hub of the town; in fact, the whole of Zila was constructed like a misshapen wheel, with concentric alleyways shot through by streets that radiated out from the keep like spokes. Everything was built from the dense, dour local rock, quite at odds with the usual Saramyr preference for light stone or wood. There were two gates in its wall, but they were both closed; and though there were pockets of activity on the hills outside the silent town, they were few and far between. Most people had drawn back within the protection of the perimeter, and made what preparations they could for the oncoming storm. Zila waited defiantly.

The Emperor's troops were coming.

It was early morning, and a soft, warm rain was falling, when Mishani and her captors arrived. They rode in along the river bank, down to the base of the sharp slope between the walls of Zila and the Zan. Docks had been built there, and steep, zigzagging stairs to link them to the town itself. But no craft were moored; they had been scuttled or cast adrift and floated out into the sea, to prevent the enemy seizing them.

The riders dismounted, and a man broke away from the dozen or so who milled about and walked over to meet them.

'Bakkara!' said the man, making the gesture of greeting between adults of roughly equal social rank: a small dip of the head, tilted slightly to the side. 'I wondered if you'd be back in time. We're closing the last gate at noon.'

The man he had addressed – the man who had captured Mishani's horse, and the leader of the party – gave him a companionable blow on the shoulder. 'You think I'd let myself get locked out and miss the fun?' he cried. 'Besides, there's probably more food in there than in the rest of Saramyr, my friend. And a soldier fights on his stomach.'

'Might have known you'd be where the meal is,' replied the other, grinning. Then, catching sight of Mishani, he added: 'I see you brought back more than just supplies.' He glanced over at Chien, who was battered and bloodied in his saddle. 'That one has seen better days.'

'He wouldn't have seen any more of them if we hadn't arrived when we did,' Bakkara said, casting a look at the merchant. 'Bandits. These two were the only ones that got out alive.'

'Well, I hope they're suitably grateful,' replied the man; then he looked at Mishani meaningfully and winked at Bakkara. 'One of them, anyway.'

Mishani gazed at him icily until the humour faded from his face. Bakkara bellowed a laugh.

'She's a fearsome thing, isn't she?' he roared. 'It wouldn't do well to mock her. These are nobles we've got here.'

The man glared at Mishani sullenly. 'Get inside, then,' he said to the group in general. 'I'll take care of your horses.'

Mishani and Chien were forced to walk up the stone steps from the dock to the city. Chien was struggling because of his injuries, so their captors made allowances for him, and their progress was slow.

Mishani looked up at the towering walls above them. They were being brought into a city in revolt, and forced to weather it with them against the might of the armies of the empire. She did not know whether to thank the god of fortune or curse him.

The men who had attacked them had undoubtedly been her father's, though she had certainly not told Barakka that. She did not believe that bandits would choose a party of armed guards rather than any of the other dozens of unarmed travellers that had been scattered across the plains last night. Besides, they were too singleminded in purpose, and too few. Bandits would never attack an enemy which outnumbered them.

She had no idea how the men had tracked them this far, but it had shaken her that they had managed to get so close to her once again. What if she had been in her tent when they rode through it? It was plain now that her father did not care whether she came back to him alive or dead. She felt a slender knife of sadness slide into her gut at that. It was a terrible thing to admit to herself.

Then Bakkara and his riders had turned up. Perhaps she could have got away if not for their intervention, but the point was moot now. They had slaughtered Avun's killers by weight of numbers, in time to save Chien's life but not those of his guards. And then, instead of setting them free, they had asked Mishani and Chien to accompany them. It was phrased as a request, but they were in no doubt that they were captives. And besides, Chien needed medical attention, which they offered at Zila. Mishani acceded, to spare herself the humiliation of being tied and taken anyway.

Despite their purpose, they did not treat her like a prisoner. They were talkative enough, and she learned a lot from them during their journey, and the short camp they made on their way back. Most of them were townsfolk from Zila, peasants or artisans. They had been despatched to raid supplies from the travellers passing south down the bottleneck – without harming anyone, they took pains to emphasise – and bring them back to bolster the stocks in the city for the oncoming siege. Their scouts had reported several armies due to reach them the next evening to crush the revolt, and they were by turns fearful and excited at the prospect. Something had sparked an unusual zeal in them, but Mishani could not divine what. They seemed more like folk with a purpose than desperate men fighting for their right to feed.

But it was Bakkara that Mishani spent most of the journey with. An ingrained sense of political expedience dictated that she should not waste time with the foot-soldiers when she could forge relations with their leader; and he, apparently, was as happy to talk as his subordinates. He was a big man: swart, with small dark eyes, a stubbled lantern jaw and a squashed nose. His black hair was bound into ropes and tied through with coloured cord, swept back from his low forehead to hang down to his nape. Though he was nearing his fiftieth harvest, his bearish physique made him more than a match for most men half his age. In his voice and his eyes were a weary authority, a soldier who had seen it all many times before and had resigned himself to seeing it again.

It was through Bakkara that Mishani learned how they had known who she was, and why his men's reaction to their impending fate was so optimistic.

'It's not my habit to rescue noble ladies,' he had said with a rough grin, in response to her question. They had been riding through the early hours of the night, and the atmosphere had a surreal and disjointed quality, as if their group were alone in an empty world.

'Then what prompted you to break with tradition and kidnap me?' she asked.

'Hardly kidnapping, Mistress,' he said. He used the correct title, though the mode he spoke in was anything but subservient. 'Unless you want your man back there to ride the rest of the way to your destination in that state.'

Mishani angled her head, and the faint starlight caught the sharp, thin planes of her cheek. 'We both know that you would not let me ride away now,' she said. 'As for Chien, I care little for him. And he is certainly not my *man*.'

Bakkara chuckled. 'I'll be straight with you,' he said. 'Anyone else, we'd have let them go on their way. But not you. On the one hand, Ocha forbid harm should come to you; and I wouldn't like to let you go riding on your own any further south. Things are getting worse down there.' His face creased in a twinge of regret. 'On the other, you're an asset too valuable to pass up, and Xejen would kill me if I did. We may need you at Zila. So I'm afraid that's where you're going.'

Mishani had already worked out what her situation was before he mentioned Xejen's name and confirmed it.

'You're Ais Maraxa,' she said.

He grunted an affirmative. 'Aren't you lucky?' he said sarcastically.

Mishani laughed.

'You're something of a legend in the Ais Maraxa, Mistress, as I'm sure you know,' Bakkara continued with a wry tone. 'You were one of those who saved our little messiah from the jaws of death.'

'Forgive me, but you do not sound like the foaming zealot I would have expected of a man in your position,' Mishani said, provoking a bellow of mirth from the soldier.

'Wait till you meet Xejen,' he returned. 'He should match up to your standards much better than I.' His laughter diminished a little, and he gave Mishani a strange look. 'I believe in Lucia,' he said eventually. 'Just because I don't spout the dogma doesn't make my strength of conviction any the less.'

'But you understand it is rather harder for me to see the point of view your organisation espouses,' Mishani explained. 'For you, she may represent an ideal, and objects of worship I find are more effective when worshipped from a distance; but for me, she is like a younger sister.'

'*Worship* is a strong word,' said Bakkara uncomfortably. 'She is not a goddess.'

'That much I am certain of,' said Mishani. She found Bakkara curious. He did not seem entirely at ease with his professed allegiance, and that puzzled her.

'But she's something more than human,' the soldier continued. 'That much *I* am certain of.'

Mishani brought herself back to the present, and back to the frowning walls of Zila that rose above them as they climbed the steps, helping the wounded merchant. She was recalling all that she knew of the Ais Maraxa, remembering old conversations with Zaelis and Cailin, mining titbits of information from the past like diamonds from coal. It had been too long since she had paid attention to the Ais Maraxa; she had never given them as much credit as she should have. Now she had been away and out of contact for over two months, and in her absence the Ais Maraxa seemed to have showed themselves at last to the world at large. She would never have thought them capable. It was what everyone close to Lucia had feared.

They had begun as nothing more than a particularly radical and enthusiastic part of the fledgling Libera Dramach. Stories among the peasantry concerning a saviour from the blight were already rife long before the name of Lucia tu Erinima was heard. It was a natural reaction to something that they did not understand: the malaise in their soil that could not be checked. Though the Libera Dramach strove for secrecy, there were still those among them who talked, and stories spread. The tale of the imprisoned Heir-Empress became mingled with the already established webwork of vague prophecies, hope and superstition, and fitted in perfectly. In their eyes, the appearance of a hidden Heir-Empress who could talk to the spirits was a little too coincidental with the spread of the blight. It made sense that she had been put on Saramyr by the gods to engage the evil in the land. Certainly, there could be no other reason why Enyu, goddess of nature, would allow an Aberrant to be born into the Imperial family. Suddenly, the peasants talked not of a god or a hero who would save them, but a little girl.

Still, the organisation that would become the Ais Maraxa remained nothing more than a mildly over-enthusastic splinter of the Libera Dramach. Until the Heir-Empress was rescued.

The presence of their figurehead in the Fold was the incitement that they needed. Lucia's preternatural aura and her seemingly miraculous escape from death convinced them that the messiah they had dreamed of was here at last. They had become more vocal in their dissent, arguing that total secrecy was not the answer; they should spread the news that Lucia was alive throughout the land, to gather support for the day when she would lead them. Much of the peasantry had seen their faith crushed when the Imperial Keep fell, and telling them of the child's escape would only redouble their joy.

Zaelis had forbidden it outright, and eventually the dissenting faction had quieted. Several months later they had left without warning, taking with them some of the most eminent members of the Libera Dramach. It was not long after that reports began to filter back of an organisation calling itself the Ais Maraxa – literally 'followers of the pure child' in a reverent dialect of High Saramyrrhic – that was spreading uncannily accurate rumours far and wide.

Zaelis had fretted and cursed, and Cailin had sent her Sisters to divine the extent of the danger the Ais Maraxa posed; but it seemed at least that their worst fears had not been realised. Those few who had split from the Libera Dramach to form the Ais Maraxa had kept the location of the Heir-Empress a secret. Only a very select number knew where Lucia was. The rest of the organisation knew only that she was hidden, and passed that information on to others. It did little to reassure Zaelis, who thought them reckless and irresponsible; yet it had seemed for years that they were content to spread their message, and in the end Mishani had begun to discount them as virtually harmless.

Now the gates of Zila stood before her, and she walked at Bakkara's side into a town that was soon to close itself up for a siege. She wished she had paid more attention to Lucia's fanatical followers, for the oversight might yet cost her dearly.

*

The estate of Blood Koli lay on the western side of Mataxa Bay, on a cliff overlooking the wide blue water. Far beneath it were white beaches and coves, unspoilt stretches of sand that dazzled the eye. Several small wooden villages of huts, jetties and walkways built on stilts sprawled from the feet of the cliff out into the bay, and tiny boats and junks bobbed against their tethers. Several massive shapes bulked out of the sea in the distance, enormous limestone formations covered with moss and bushes, their bases worn away so that their tops were wider than their bottom ends, like inverted pinecones. The fishermen glided around them, stirring pole-paddles, and cast nets in their shadow.

The Koli family house was built close to the edge on the highest point of the promontory. It was a coral-coloured building, constructed around a circular central section with a flattened and ribbed dome atop it. The uniformity of its surface at ground level was broken by a square entrance hall that poked out like a blunt snout, facing away from the bay. Two slender wings encompassing stables and servants' quarters ran along the cliff edge. Cut in steps into the cliff itself was an enormous three-tiered garden, its lowest tier balconied and jutting out over the drop to the beach below. All kinds of trees and plants were cultivated there, and carved pillars of rock had been left in strategic places to maximise the aesthetic pleasure in the fusion of stone and greenery. On the highest tier was a small conservatory, a skeletal framework of tall arches and curved pillars, where Mishani's mother Muraki would sit to write.

She was there now, Barak Avun suspected, though he could not see from where he lounged on the lowest tier with Barak Grigi tu Kerestyn. No doubt concocting more of her stories, he thought with distaste. Sharing her family's problems with the empire. In all things she obeyed him, except in this. He had been furious when news of her latest book had reached him; it fuelled scandalmongers the breadth of the land. There was enough rumour about their missing daughter without her adding to it. But she would write what she would write, and she defied him to censor her.

Still, the damage could be minimised. If all went well, then soon he would have his daughter back, one way or another, and then they could concoct a cover story that would put all that dishonour to rest. If all went well . . .

'Gods, it's not so bad, is it?' said Grigi, who was lying on a couch and looking over the balcony to the bay. 'Up here, you can forget about the problems of the world, forget about the blight. Nuki's eye still shines on us, the sea still ebbs and flows. Our problems are small, when you look at them from this height.'

Avun regarded him with vague contempt. The obese Barak was drunk. Between them was a table scattered with the remnants of the food Grigi had devoured, and empty pitchers of wine. Avun was ascetic in his tastes, but Grigi was a glutton, and he had gorged himself all afternoon.

'They are not small to me,' Avun said coldly. 'The sea still ebbs and flows, but its fish are becoming twisted; and those fish paid for the food you have eaten. My fishermen have taken to holding back some of their catch for their own families. Preserving them against the famine. Stealing from me.' He turned his hooded eyes outward, to where the distant cliffs of the eastern side of the bay were a low, jagged line of deep blue. 'It is easy to pretend that nothing is wrong. It is also foolish.'

'No need to be so dour, Avun,' said Grigi, a little disappointed that his ally did not share his expansive mood. 'Heart's blood, you know how to bring a man down.'

'I see nothing to be cheerful about.'

'Then you don't see the opportunity that this famine brings us,' Grigi said. 'There is no stouter warrior than a man fighting for his life, and the lives of his family. All they need is someone to unite behind. That person will be me!' He raised his goblet clumsily, spilling a little wine onto the slabs of the balcony.

'There goes the Barakess,' said Avun, languidly indicating a brightly coloured junk that was slipping out of the harbour far below them, making its way through the clutter of fishing vessels.

Grigi shaded his eyes against the glare of the sun and looked down. 'Do you trust her?'

Avun nodded slowly. 'She will be there when the time comes.'

The afternoon's work had been satisfactory. Emira, a young Barakess of Blood Ziris, had visited them at her request. She had talked with them about many things: the threat of famine, the Blood Emperor, the plight of her own people. And, in her sly and roundabout way, she had wondered whether Blood Kerestyn intended to make a play for the throne, and whether they might need Blood Ziris's help when they did.

It was ever this way, in the game of the Imperial courts. Families backed each other in the hope that the one they supported would gain power, and in turn that family would elevate the ones that had helped them get there. As Mos's ineptitude became clearer, and with Blood Kerestyn the only realistic alternative, the high families were flocking to Grigi's banner without him even having to call them. With Blood Koli at his right hand, he was a powerful figurehead, and the strength of the empire was gathering itself to him.

But always there had been the problem of the Emperor's strength of numbers. With the Weavers at his side, and the Imperial Guards at his command, he was a near-invincible force. While Kerestyn forces had been smashed during the last coup, Blood Batik had walked unopposed into the city, and had grown since then. Even with overwhelming support from the other high families, Grigi knew it would be a close call. He had broken himself on the walls of Axekami once before; he would have to be very sure of himself before he would try it again.

Avun had brought him the solution to that problem this very day.

'I have a new friend,' he had said, as they walked through the chambers of the family house that morning. 'One very close to the Emperor. I was contacted not long ago.'

'A new friend?' Grigi had asked, raising an eyebrow.

'This person tells me that something is going to happen, very soon. We must be ready.'

'Ready?'

'We must assemble our support, so we can march on Axekami at a day's notice.'

'A day! Ridiculous! We would have to tell all the families well in advance, gather their forces here.'

'Then we shall do so, when the time is right. There will be a signal. And when it comes, we must act swiftly, and have our allies ready to do the same.'

Grigi had adjusted his purple skullcap on top of his head. 'That's a little too much to take on trust, Avun. Tell me just who this new friend of yours is.'

'Kakre. The Emperor's own Weaver.'

EIGHTEEN

'It's time, Kaiku,' said Yugi.

Darkness was falling. The sky was a soft purple in the east, the harbinger of oncoming night. Iridima stood alone at half-moon amid a thick blanket of dim stars, pallid and ghostly in the dusk. The heat of the early autumn day was fading to a warm night, and a gentle breeze dispersed the muggy closeness of the previous hours.

They had found the Weavers' barrier, the edge of the secret that they had crossed the Fault to uncover. Nomoru had announced that they were nearing the point where she had lost her way on her previous visit, and an hour later they returned to the same spot, despite having headed steadily westward. If that was not enough, Kaiku's senses had begun to crackle; she was certain that she knew exactly where the barrier cut across the landscape, and when they had been turned around. She had been very careful to keep her *kana* reined tight as they passed into it. She did not want to try and tackle the barrier without the help of her father's Mask.

The four travellers sheltered in a dell for a few hours to wait for the cover of night. Kaiku spent them sat against a tree, holding the leering, red-and-black face before her, looking into its empty eyes. When Yugi spoke to her, she barely heard him. He had to shake her arm before she looked up at him sharply, annoyed; then she softened, and smiled in thanks. Yugi's eyes mirrored uncertainty for a moment, and he retreated.

Her mind flitted back, skipping over days of hard journeying, alighting eventually on the gloomy, doleful marsh where Yugi had lain dying. The battle to extract the demon poison was etched in Kaiku's memory; every probing fibre, every twist and knot were mapped onto her consciousness in shining lines. Despite herself, she felt a small grin of triumph touch her lips, and her spirits rose. But then her gaze fell on Yugi, who was shouldering his pack, and her grin faded a little.

Ever since he had awoken, Yugi had been *different* somehow. She had sensed something when she had been inside him, a faint wash from his mind that hinted at something dark and unspeakably ugly. She could not guess what it was, only that it lay deep and hidden, and unconsciousness had loosened it from where it was fettered. She watched him, and wondered.

Yugi tried not to notice, but he could feel her eyes on his back. His brush with the demons had sobered him, that much was certain. The proximity of death had reminded him of a previous life, before he had joined the Libera Dramach. Days of blood and blade and mayhem. He began to play with the dirty sash wrapped around his forehead; a totem of those times, times that he wanted desperately to forget but never could.

He pushed the thoughts away as the travellers got to their feet and made ready to breach the Weavers' barrier. The immediacy of the situation focused him. Their trip across the Fault had not been an easy one, but it would get worse from here on in.

'Is that going to work?' Nomoru asked doubtfully, motioning to the Mask in Kaiku's hand.

'We will know soon enough,' Kaiku said, and put it on.

Dreadfully, it felt like coming home. The Mask warmed to her skin, and she fancied that she felt it mould itself to the tiny changes in her face since the last time she had worn it. She felt a great contentment, a nostalgic warmth such as she felt as a little girl asleep in her father's lap. She could hear the comforting whisper of Ruito's voice, a phantom of his memory brushing against her, and tears sprang to her eyes.

She blinked them back. The Mask felt like her father because it had robbed him of some of his thoughts and personality when he had worn it. He had been killed for this piece of wood. The Masks were cruel masters, taking and taking in return for the power they gave, addicting their users until their victims could not live without them. Until they were Weavers. She would not let herself forget that.

Spirits, what would happen if a Sister of the Red Order became a Weaver?

'You look ridiculous,' said Nomoru, her voice devoid of humour. 'What's this going to achieve?'

Kaiku gave her a contemptuous glance. Strangely, she did not feel in the least bit ridiculous, wearing this Mask with its knowing leer. In fact, she felt that it suited her perfectly, and made her appear more impressive.

'What it will *achieve* is to get us through that barrier when you could not,' Kaiku replied airily. 'Let us be quick. I do not want to wear this thing a moment longer than necessary.'

She thought, as they departed, that those words felt curiously hollow. She had spoken them because she thought she was supposed to, rather than because she actually meant them.

The last light had fled the sky when they came up against the barrier. Topping a gentle rise in the land between two peaks of hulking stone, Kaiku felt the Mask become hot against her cheeks.

'It is here,' she said. 'Tie yourselves to me.'

Tsata produced a rope, and they did as she instructed. It was difficult to tell how much the Tkiurathi believed in the necessity of what they were doing, but he acceded to the will of the group without complaint.

Kaiku proceeded tentatively, holding her hand out before her. The Mask grew hotter still, rising in temperature until she thought it might burn her; and then her fingers brushed the barrier, and it was unveiled to her eyes.

She could not hold back a gasp. The glittering Weave-sewn tapestry swept away to either side of her, six metres high and six deep, curving up and over the steep contours of the Fault. It was a churn of golden spirals and whirls, spinning and writhing slowly, curling around each other and taking on new forms, stretching and flexing in a dance of impossible chaos. Like an eddy in the waters of reality, perception was turned around and thrown out on a new course in this place, and Kaiku marvelled anew at the complexity of the Weavers' creation.

'What is it?' asked Yugi. 'Is it the barrier?'

Kaiku realised by the tone of his voice that he was asking why she had stopped, not what the thing before them was. It was invisible to everyone but her. For a brief moment, she felt a smug and selfish glee at being the only one privy to this wonder; then, surprised at herself, she cast it aside.

'Hold hands,' she told them, and she gave her hand to Yugi. The others did the same.

She stepped into the barrier, and was consumed by the Weave. The first time it had happened, back on Fo, she had been tempted to let herself be swept away in the unutterable beauty of the golden world that surrounded her. This time she was ready for it, and her heart was hardened against its charms. In a few strides, she was through, pulling Yugi with her; but the sensation was a cruel wrench, and the return to reality made everything seem grey and bland by comparison.

Yugi came stumbling through backwards and tripped as he did, disoriented at finding himself turned around. He had let go of Nomoru, the next in line, and as he fell to the ground the rope around his waist tautened. She was tugging the other way. Kaiku could see her now: the barrier had faded from her sight as soon as she was past it. Nomoru was trapped in the invisible zone of disorientation, blank-faced, labouring to drag herself back in the direction they had come and seemingly unable to understand why she could not get there. Tsata was in a similar state nearby, his face a picture of childlike confusion.

'Pull them through,' Kaiku told Yugi, and though he was still bewildered as to where he was, he did as he was told. Between them they dragged their companions across the barrier and onto the other side.

It took the better part of ten minutes for their thoughts to become coherent again, by which time Kaiku had removed the Mask and stashed it back in her pack. She studied them with fascination as they gazed glassy-eyed at each other like babies, or looked around at their surroundings as if completely unable to process where they were. No wonder that nobody could penetrate the barrier without a Mask. What a masterpiece of Weave-manipulation it was.

Once they had collected themselves, Nomoru was still unable to remember this area which she had once professed to know. So it was Kaiku who took the lead, as Nomoru's sense of direction seemed to be still suppressed, making her hopeless at navigation.

'We have to get away from this place,' Kaiku said. 'I am not convinced that it is safe to pass the barrier, even with the Mask. We may have alerted those who set it here.'

With that, they set off into the broken landscape to their right, skirting the inside of the barrier. Kaiku relied on her senses to let her know when they were brushing too close to the invisible perimeter, and using that as a guide, they lost themselves in the dark rills and juts of the Xarana Fault, and Iridima watched them go with half a face.

When they were far from the point where they had entered the domain of the Weavers, Nomoru called a halt.

'It's hopeless,' she said. 'Doing it this way. We'll never get there in the dark.'

The others wearily agreed. For a time, it had seemed like they were making progress; but then the night sky clouded, shutting out the glow of the stars and the single moon, and now they could barely see at all. They had been wandering amid a stretch of uneven gullies and scrub ground for some time now, scratching themselves on thorny bushes and probably going in circles. Their frustration was multiplied by the fact that they did not know exactly what they were looking for. Seeking out evidence of Weaver activity was a broad and vague objective, when they had no idea of the extent of their enemies' capabilities, nor what form such evidence might take. Now they were walking down a trench of baked mud, with steep sides rising up over their heads: an old ditch, long dry, and infested with weeds.

'We should rest,' said Yugi. 'We can go on when the sky clears, or when dawn comes.'

'I am not tired,' Kaiku said, who did indeed feel strangely energised. 'I will keep watch.'

'I will join you,' said Tsata, unexpectedly.

They threw their packs down at the base of the ditch; Nomoru and Yugi unrolled mats, and were asleep in minutes.

Kaiku sat with her back against the trench wall, her hands linked around her knees. Tsata sat opposite her, silently. It was eerily quiet; even the raucous drone of night insects was absent. Distantly, she heard the unpleasant cawing of some bird she could not identify.

'Should one of us go up to the top, to look out for . . .' she trailed off, realising that she had no idea what she expected might come for them.

'No,' said the Tkiurathi. 'We cannot see far, but there may be things that can see us in the deep darkness. It is better to be hidden.'

Kaiku nodded slightly. She had not wanted to go up there anyway, and it felt sheltered here.

'I wish to talk,' said Tsata suddenly. 'About Weavers.'

Kaiku brushed her fringe back from her face, tucked it behind one ear. 'Very well.'

'I have learned about them from Saran, but I still do not know how your people accept them,' he said.

The mention of Saran made Kaiku's eyes narrow. That was something that the encounter with the Omecha cultists and the ruku-shai had driven entirely out of her head.

'I am not sure I understand what you are asking,' said Kaiku.

'Let me say how I see it, and you may correct me afterward. Is that acceptable?'

Kaiku tilted her chin up, then realised with some embarrassment that she had used an Okhamban gesture rather than a Saramyr one.

'Once your civilisation was dedicated to great art and learning, to building wonderful architecture and long roads and incredible dwellings,' Tsata began. 'I have read your histories. And though I do not share your love for stone cities, or for the way you gather in such numbers that *pash* becomes meaningless, I am aware that all ways are not my ways, and I can accept that. I can even accept the terrible divide between the nobles and the peasant classes, and how knowledge is hoarded by one to keep the other in ignorant labour. That I find nothing less than evil, for it is so counter to the nature of my people; yet if I began to talk about that, we would be here a lot longer, and it is the Weavers I wish to speak of.'

Kaiku was mildly taken aback, both by his bluntness – which verged on rude – and his eloquence. She had rarely heard Tsata say more than a few sentences at a time; but his evident passion for this subject seemed to have overridden his usual quiet reticence.

'When the Weavers came, your ancestors took them in,' he said at length, his pale green eyes steady in the darkness. 'They were dazzled by the power they might command with a Weaver at their side. Your nobles had so long been accustomed to treating lesser men like tools, that they thought they could use the Weavers in the same way, not knowing how dangerous a tool they were. For to accept the Weavers into your world was to make a pact; a pact that your ancestors made knowing full well the terms that they were agreeing to.' His head hung in sorrow. 'Greed ruined them. Perhaps they had noble causes at first; perhaps they thought that with the Weavers on their side, they could expand the empire and make it greater and more invincible. But sometimes the price is too high, no matter what the reward.'

Kaiku noticed that his hands were clenched in fists, the yellow skin taut around his knuckles.

'You invited the Weavers into your homes, and you fed them with your children.'

That shocked her. But though she drew breath to protest, she found that she could not. He was right, after all. It was a noble family's duty to supply their Weaver with whatever they wanted during their post-Weaving mania. She knew well enough some of the awful perversions that those creatures were capable of. As the backlash from using their Masks set in, like the withdrawal symptoms of a narcotic, they had no conscience in the face of their irrational, primal lusts and needs. Nothing was too depraved where the Weavers were concerned. Rape, murder, torture . . . these were only some of the desires that the Weavers demanded be satisfied. She knew of others. Blood Kerestyn's Weaver was reportedly a cannibal. Blood Nira had one who ate human and animal faeces. The current Weave-lord apparently had a penchant for skinning victims alive and making sculptures from them. Though not every Weaver's mania was harmful to others – some would do things as mundane as painting or merely hallucinate for hours – a lot of them were, and while they did not need to sate themselves every time they went Weaving, most Weavers still accounted for dozens of lives each. And as they become more insane and addicted and raddled with disease, the quantity increased.

She felt suddenly ashamed, remembering the simple joy she had felt in Hanzean at returning to her homeland from Okhamba. Saramyr was a place of beauty and harmony that she felt lucky to live in, and yet it was built on the bones of so many. Before the Weavers, there had been the systematic extermination of the native Ugati, a death toll that must have reached into millions. None of this was new to Kaiku – and still, it seemed so distant and so unconnected to her that she could not really identify with it – but hearing it put in such a straightforward way reminded her what a thin veneer civilisation was, a crust on which the dainty feet of the highborn walked, while beneath their soles a sea of disorder and violence seethed.

But Tsata was not finished. 'You are not to blame for the crimes of your ancestors,' he said, 'though often your society punishes sons for their fathers' mistakes, it seems. But now the Weavers despoil the very land you live on. That is the final joke. Your people have come to rely on them to the extent that you cannot bring yourselves to get rid of them, even though they will destroy all the beauty that you once loved. You have invested so much in making your empire bigger and better that you are destroying the very foundation that it is built on. You have built a tower so tall and so high that you have begun to take bricks from the bottom to put at the top.' He leaned closer to Kaiku. 'You are killing the earth with your selfishness.'

'I *know* that, Tsata,' Kaiku said. She was becoming angry; this seemed a little too much like a personal attack at her. Even though she was aware that Tsata did not subscribe to the evasions and politenesses of her society, she still found his manner of speaking too confrontational. 'What do you think we are doing here now? I am trying to *fight* them.'

'Yes,' he said. 'But are you fighting them for the right reasons? You fight for vengeance. Saran told me that much. Now the people of your land rise up, for their food is becoming short; but until then, they were content to let the blight creep, thinking that somebody else would deal with it. None of you fight for the good of the many. You only decide to struggle when it is in your personal interest.'

'That is the way people are,' Kaiku snapped.

'It is not the way *my* people are,' Tsata countered.

'Perhaps, then, that is why you still remain living in the jungle, and your children eaten by wild beasts,' she returned. 'Perhaps civilisation is built on selfishness.'

The Tkiurathi took the implied insult without offence. 'Perhaps,' he said. 'But I am not intending to compare my culture to yours, to judge the merits of one against the other.'

'That is what you seem to be doing,' Kaiki told him sullenly.

'I am telling you how your land looks through my eyes,' he said simply. 'Does honesty make you so uncomfortable?'

'I do not need to have you pointing out the failings of my people. Perhaps my reasons are not selfless enough to fit your taste, but the fact remains that I *am* doing something about the Weavers. I choose not to accept the way things are, for I know they are wrong. So do not lecture me on morality.'

Tsata watched her quietly. She calmed a little, and scuffed her heel in the dirt.

'I have nothing to teach you about the Weavers,' she admitted eventually. 'Your understanding of the situation is correct.'

'Is it a product of your culture, then?' Tsata asked. 'Because each of you strives for personal advancement rather than for that of the group, you will not act against a threat until it is in your interest to do so?'

'Possibly,' said Kaiku. 'I do not know. But I do know that much of our acceptance of the Weavers is born of ignorance. If the high families had proof that the Weavers were the ones responsible for despoiling the land, they would rise up and destroy them. That is what I believe.'

'But it's not true, Kaiku,' said Yugi. They looked over at him, and saw him sit up. He adjusted the rag around his brow and gave them an apologetic smile. 'Difficult to sleep with you two setting the world to rights,' he explained.

'What do you mean, it is not true?' Kaiku asked.

'I probably shouldn't tell you this, but I suppose it doesn't matter,' he said, getting to his feet and stretching. 'There are a lot of dealings high up in the Libera Dramach that we don't reveal; we made sure we checked your father's theory about the witchstones. When we were sure he was right, we . . . well, we made it known to some of the nobles. Subtly. Hints here and there, and when those didn't work, we actually presented them with proof and challenged them to check it themselves.' He scratched the back of his neck. 'Obviously, this was all through middlemen. The Libera Dramach was never really exposed.'

Kaiku waved a hand at him, indicating that he should get to the meat of the issue. 'How did it end, then?'

He wandered over to where they sat and looked down on them. 'They didn't do anything. Not one. Very few of them even bothered to verify the facts we gave them.' He laughed bitterly. 'All this time the Weavers have been kept in check by the fear of what might happen if the high familes rose up against them. Well, we tried to make that happen, and they ignored us.'

Kaiku was aghast. 'How can that be? When they can see what the Weavers are doing?'

Yugi put a hand on Tsata's bare shoulder. 'Our foreign friend here is right,' he said. 'It's not in their interest. If one or even a dozen high families acted on the information, they would lose their Weavers, and the other families who *did* have Weavers would crush them. There are too many enmities, too many old wounds. There'll always be someone trying to get the upper hand, thinking only about the short-term, seizing any chance they can get. Because people are selfish. The only way anything fundamental will change is if *everyone* decides to change *at the same time*.' He shrugged. 'And the only way that will happen is if there's a catastrophe.'

'It is true. You will have to wait until this land is so ruined that it can barely be lived on before it is in everyone's interest to act,' Tsata said. 'And by then, it may well be too late.'

'Is that the way of it, then?' Kaiku demanded, feeling unfairly outnumbered. 'That people have to die before anything changes?'

Yugi and Tsata merely looked at her, and that was answer enough.

The clouds cleared towards dawn, and they set off again to take advantage of Iridima's glow. By now Nomoru's sense of direction seemed to have returned, and by estimating the curvature of the barrier, she established a route inward that would take them towards the centre of the area that the Weavers had cut off from the world. It seemed reasonable to assume that whatever they were looking for lay there.

They had not travelled far before the land dropped steeply away before them, and they found themselves looking down a boulder-riven slope at the darkly glinting swathe of the River Zan. Its sibilant murmuring drifted up to them through the silence.

'Are we still upstream of the falls?' Yugi asked.

Nomoru made an affirmative noise. 'This way,' she said, turning them southward. Kaiku doubted if the scout had any more idea of where they were going than she did, but one way was as good as another when they were all lost.

The sky was beginning to lighten when Yugi stopped them suddenly. They had been on the alert for any signs of life, but nothing had appeared as yet. In fact, it was eerily empty. Even the animals seemed to have deserted this place.

'What is it?' Kaiku whispered.

'Look,' Yugi said. 'Look at the tree.'

They looked. Standing on a rocky rise above them in silhouette was a crooked tree, its branches bare and warped, its boughs twisted in a corkscrew and curling at strange angles. It hunched there like a foreboding signpost, a warning of things to come if they should proceed.

'It's blighted,' Yugi supplied redundantly.

'They have found another witchstone,' Kaiku said. 'And they have woken it up.'

'*Woken it up?*' Nomoru sneered. 'It's a *rock*, Kaiku.'

'Is that all it is?' Kaiku returned sarcastically. 'Then what are the Weavers hiding it for?'

Nomoru gave a snort of disgust and walked onward, heading downriver. The others went after her.

It was just past dawn when they found what they had been looking for; and it was far, far worse than they had imagined.

The ridge of land that they had been following began to curve away from the Zan below, and a great stretch of flat land opened up between the river's eastern bank and the high ground, a grassy and fertile flood plain. Their view of the plain was obscured, for they had been forced to retreat from the lip of the slope by a suddenly hostile terrain of broken rocks, but finally Nomoru picked them a route back to the edge so that they could command a good view of the land to the west, and that was when they saw what the Weavers had been hiding all this time.

The slope had steepened into an enormous black cliff overlooking the plain, and when Nomoru reached the precipice she ducked down suddenly and motioned that the others should do the same. The burgeoning daylight was flat and devoid of force, lacking yet the strength to imbue the world with colour. The sky overhead was a drab grey, and the solitary moon was heading towards obscurity behind the jagged teeth of the Fault. They scrambled on their bellies to where Nomoru lay, and looked over.

Kaiku swore under her breath.

On the far side of the flood plain, near the river bank, hulked a massive construction, a glabrous hump like the carapace of some monstrous beetle. It was a dull, rusty bronze in colour, formed of immense strips of banded metal. Around its base, smaller constructions clustered like newborn animals clamouring for their mother's teats. There, strange wheels of spiked metal rotated slowly, chains rattled as they slid on pulleys that emerged from narrow shafts in the earth, and stubby chimneys emitted an oily black smoke. From within came faint clattering and clanking sounds.

The observers gazed aghast at the edifice. It was like nothing they had ever seen before, something so alien to their experience that its very presence seemed out of kilter with the world. A dirty, seething horror, foul to the eye.

But that was not all. There was a more immediate and recognisable danger. The plain was awash with Aberrants.

The sheer number of the creatures that milled down there was impossible to estimate, for they were in no order or formation, and it was difficult to tell where one clot ended and another began. It was made worse by the variety of shapes and forms: a phantasmagoria of grotesqueries that seemed to have spilled whole from the imagination of a maniac. Thousands, perhaps; maybe tens of thousands. The horde carpeted the ground from the foot of the cliffs to the banks of the Zan, clustered in groups or imprisoned within enormous metal pens. Some stalked restlessly along the river, some slept on the ground, some squabbled and scratched.

Kaiku felt a pat on her shoulder, and she looked to see Nomoru proffering her a spyglass. It was a simple, portable affair – two glass lenses wrapped in a conical tube of stiffened leather – but it was effective enough. She took it with an uncertain smile of thanks. It was probably the first time Nomoru had ever volunteered any good will to any of them. Evidently the scale of what they had discovered had caused her to lay aside her petty surliness for the moment.

She put it to her eye, and the spectacle below sprang into noisome detail. Everywhere, the forms of nature had been twisted out of true. Dark, loping things like elongated jungle cats snarled as they prowled, their faces curious hybrids of canine and lizard; demonic creatures that might once have been small apes hung from the bars of their pens, lips skinning back along their gums to reveal vicious arrays of yellowed fangs; hunched, boarlike things with furious visages and great hooked tusks rooted in the dirt, compact barrels of tooth and muscle. Kaiku felt an uncomfortable thrill of recognition at the sight of a roosting-pen of enormous birds, with keratinous beaks and kinked, ragged wings with a span of six feet or more: gristle-crows, which she had last seen on the isle of Fo several years ago.

And yet there was a pattern in amid the chaos. The presence of the gristle-crows had alerted her to it, and now as she scanned the plain again she saw, in the bleak light of the dawn, that each Aberrant was not unique. There were perhaps a few dozen different types, but these types recurred over and over again. The same features cropped up, the same forms. These were not random offshoots of the witchstones' influence. These were discrete species. Though they were horrible to look at, there were no redundant features, no evolutionary characteristic that might hamper them. No deformities.

'Not there,' Nomoru said impatiently. She grabbed the end of the spyglass and turned it. 'There.'

Kaiku spared her an annoyed glance for her rudeness before she looked through it again. When she did, her blood ran cold.

There was a figure walking slowly through the horde, apparently heedless of the predators that surrounded it. At first, she thought it must be a Weaver; but if it was, it was like no Weaver she had ever seen. This one was tall, seven feet at least, and rake-thin. It walked with an erect spine instead of the hunch that Weavers seemed to adopt as their bodies became more riddled with foulness. Its robe was not patchwork like a Weaver's, but simple black, with a heavy hood; and though it wore a mask, it was a blank white oval, perfectly smooth except for two eye-holes.

'A new kind of Weaver?' she breathed.

'Don't know,' Nomoru replied.

Yugi took the spyglass and looked.

'What is it I'm seeing here?' he said, slowly panning across the horde. 'What are they doing?'

'Some kind of menagerie?' Kaiku suggested. 'A collection of Aberrant predator species?'

Nomoru laughed bitterly. 'That's what you think?'

Tsata's expression was grim. 'It is not a menagerie, Kaiku,' he told her. 'It is an army.'

NINETEEN

At the same time that Kaiku and her companions were gazing down on the horde of Aberrants by the River Zan, Lucia and her retinue were arriving at Alskain Mar.

It lay almost one hundred and fifty miles away from Kaiku, east and a little south of her position, on the other side of the Xarana Fault near the River Rahn. Once, it had been a magnificent underground shrine, in the days before the cataclysm that rent the earth and swallowed Gobinda over a thousand years ago. Then its entrances had collapsed, and the roof had fallen in on it, and uncounted souls had been buried in the quake. Now it was a haunted place, the abode of something ancient and ageless, and even the most savage of the factions in the Fault stayed well away from there. A great spirit held sway in Alskain Mar, and the spirits guarded their territory resentfully.

But into that place Lucia was to go. Alone.

Her escort on the journey from the Fold was a small group of the most trusted warriors of the Libera Dramach, accompanied by Zaelis and Cailin. The leader of the Libera Dramach, the head of the Red Order, and the girl on which all their endeavours rested. It was risky for them to venture out of the Fold together, but Cailin insisted on coming and Zaelis could not let his adopted daughter face this trial without his support. Guilt lay heavy on his heart, and the least he could do was walk with her as far as he could.

Cailin had been furious when Zaelis had told her what he had done. Though he had implied to Lucia that he and Cailin were in agreement about asking her to go to Alskain Mar, it had in reality been his idea entirely. Cailin was in violent opposition, and not afraid to tell him so. She had faced him at his house, amid the quiet, cosy surroundings of his study.

'This is idiocy, Zaelis!' she had cried, a tower of black anger. 'You know what happened to her last time! Now you would send her up against a spirit unfathomably stronger! What possessed you?'

'Do you think I made my decision lightly?' Zaelis retorted. 'Do you think I enjoy the idea of sending my daughter into the lair of that *thing*? Necessity forces my hand, Cailin!'

'There is nothing so necessary as to risk the life of that girl. She is the lynchpin of everything we have striven for.'

'We will *lose* everything we have striven for if the Weavers find the Fold,' Zaelis said, stalking agitatedly around the room. The raised voices seemed to discomfit the still air. Lanterns cast warm shadows across the hardwood floor. 'It is easy for you to judge: you have the Red Order. You can disappear in a day, go into hiding, leave all of this behind. But I have a responsibility to what I have started! Every man and woman in this town is here because of what I created; even those who are not of the Libera Dramach have come because of the ideals that we represent.' He dropped his eyes. 'And they look to me as their leader.'

'The day will come when they look to *Lucia* as their leader, Zaelis,' Cailin said. 'Was that not the plan? How, then, can you dare risk her this way?' She paused, then added a final barb. 'Quite aside from the fact that she is, as you say, your own daughter.'

Zaelis's bearded jaw tightened in pain. 'I risk her because I have to,' he said quietly.

'Wait for the scouts to get back,' Cailin advised. 'You may be worrying needlessly.'

'It's not good enough,' he said. 'No matter what they find, the fact remains that the Weavers are in the Fault. They could have been there for *years*, don't you see? It is only because Nomoru is so good at what she does that she even noticed the Weavers' barrier. How many of our scouts have passed through that way and not even realised that they had been misdirected?' He looked up accusingly at Cailin. 'It was *you* that told me how those barriers worked.'

Cailin tilted her head. The raven feathers on her ruff stirred slightly. 'You are correct. The nature of the barriers are subtle enough so that most minds are fooled into thinking that they have got *themselves* lost.'

'Then what else might the Weavers have under our very noses?' Zaelis asked. 'We only found this one through blind luck.' He threw up his calloused hands in exasperation. 'I have been suddenly and shockingly faced with the fact that we are all but defenceless against the very enemy we have been fighting against. We have relied on hiding from them. But now I realise that they *will* find us, whether by accident or design, sooner or later. They may already have found us. We have to know what we are up against; and only the spirits can tell us that.'

'Are you sure, Zaelis?' Cailin asked. 'What do you know of spirits?'

'I know what Lucia tells me,' he said. 'And she believes it is worth trying.'

Cailin gave him a level gaze. 'Of course she does. She would do anything you asked of her. Even if it killed her.'

'Gods, Cailin, don't make this worse for me than it is!' he cried. 'I have made my choice. We are going to Alskain Mar.'

Cailin had not argued further, but as she was leaving she had paused at the threshold of the room and looked back at him.

'What was the purpose of all this in the beginning? What did you do this for? You created the Libera Dramach out of nothing. One man inspired all of that. But who inspired *you?*'

Zaelis did not reply. He knew it was a leading question, but he did not wish to be led.

'Which is more important to you now?' Cailin had asked softly. 'The girl, or the secret army you lead? Lucia, or the Libera Dramach?'

The memories echoed bitterly in Zaelis's thoughts as the company picked its way through the brightening dawn towards the ruined shrine. They had travelled overnight from the Fold for the sake of stealth. The going had been slow, as they had been forced to accommodate Zaelis's limp, and Lucia – who had never in her life had to walk on a journey of more than a few miles at a time – became exhausted quickly. The clouds that troubled Kaiku far away had not reached this far east, and they had the light of Iridima to guide them through the plunging terrain of the Fault.

As the first signs of day approached, they had come to a wide, circular depression in the land, a mile or more in diameter. It lay on a long, flat hilltop, thick with dewy grass and shrubs and small, thin trees. On the eastern side, the Fault began a disjointed but steady descent down to the banks of the Rahn. At the centre of the depression was a deep, uneven hole, a toothed shaft into the vast cavern beneath, where Alskain Mar lay.

They halted at the edge of the dip. Soul-eaters had been set in a rough circle around the perimeter, their surfaces weathered and their paint fading. They made a loud rattling as the wind brushed them, old knucklebone charms and stones of transparent resin tapping against the rock. Several of them were cracked, and moss had grown in the fissures. One had broken in half, and its upper section lay next to the stump.

Cailin cast a disparaging eye over the soul-eaters. They were superstitious artifacts cannibalised from the Ugati: slender, elliptical stones daubed in a combination of blessings and curses and hung with noisy and primitive jewellery. The stories went that when a spirit came near to a soul-eater, it would be terrified by the sound of the charms, and both repelled by the blessings and disgusted by the curses; then it would flee back to where it had come from and hide. They did not work, and had been dismissed as quaint bits of folklore by the Saramyr for hundreds of years; and yet these examples were recent, no more than fifty years old. Who could guess who had put them there, and what they had hoped to achieve? Maybe they had thought that an ancient method would work to pen an ancient spirit. In the Xarana Fault, the usual rules of civilisation did not apply.

They rested outside the depression as the sun climbed into the sky. Lucia curled up on a mat and slept. The overnight walk had been hard on her. She may have had plenty of energy, but for that she was still frail, having been sheltered all through her childhood. The guards ate cold food nervously, warily scanning the quiet hilltop. They were safe enough from any human danger here, for no settlements thrived this close to Alskain Mar; but the presence of the spirit could be felt by the least perceptive of men, and it made their skin crawl. Even the heat and light of the day did not dispel the chill. They kept catching flitting movements among the bushes out of the corner of their eyes; but whenever they investigated, there was nothing there.

Zaelis and Cailin sat together. Zaelis was regarding his sleeping daughter with concern; Cailin was silently studying the hole at the centre of the depression.

'There is still time to turn back, Zaelis,' the Sister said.

'Don't,' he said. 'The decision is made.'

'Decisions can be unmade,' Cailin told him.

Zaelis's brow was furrowed deeply, his eyes pained as he watched the rise and fall of Lucia's slender back. 'Not this one,' he said.

Cailin did not reply to that. If she had dared to stop him, she would have; but she could not jeopardise her own position or that of the Red Order by risking it. She found herself wishing that Kaiku or Mishani were with them. Perhaps they could have swayed Zaelis. A wild idea occurred to her, that she might use the Weave to manipulate him subtly; but Lucia would know, even if Zaelis did not, and the act would be a terrible betrayal of trust. She could not afford that.

So she had to watch as he sent all their hope into Alskain Mar, and wait to see if it came out again.

'What of Asara?' Zaelis said at length, starting a new subject suddenly. 'Have you heard from her? We may need her again very soon.'

'She is gone,' said Cailin. They both still referred to her as Asara, though they had known her as Saran in the brief time she had spent at the Fold. The identity of the spy they had sent away to scour the Near World for signs of the Weavers had always been known to them, but they had not known what guises she might take. 'She went just before Kaiku left. I suspect they had something of a disagreement.'

Zaelis raised an eyebrow.

'I do keep a very close eye on my most errant pupil,' she said. She looked east, to the autumn morning sky. 'I do not think we will be seeing Saran Ycthys Marul again, though. She is changing her identity.'

'Have you spoken to her, then? What do you know?'

Cailin's black and red lips curled in a faint smile. 'She is running a small errand for me. I managed to convince her that it was . . . in her interests.'

'An errand?' Zaelis repeated, his molten voice becoming suspicious. 'What errand, Cailin?'

Cailin looked at him sidelong. 'That is our business,' she said.

'Heart's blood! You just sent away my best spy and you won't even tell me why? What are you up to?'

'She is not *your* spy,' Cailin reminded him. 'If she is anyone's, she is mine. And she is abroad on matters of the Red Order now.'

'The Libera Dramach and the Red Order are supposed to be working together,' Zaelis said. 'What kind of co-operation is this?'

Cailin laughed quietly. 'If this were a *co-operative* effort, Zaelis, then we would certainly not be bringing Lucia anywhere near Alskain Mar. If I had the power, I would veto it. No, the Libera Dramach rule in the Fold, and well you know it. We owe you nothing. We may be helping you, but we are not beholden to you. And I have other interests to attend to before all this is over.'

Lucia woke in the afternoon, ate a little food, and made her preparations to do what had to be done. She did not speak to anyone.

After a time, she walked past the ring of soul-eaters to the edge of the hole that lay in the centre of the depression. The afternoon sun warmed her from behind, but on the nape of her neck and upper back – where the scarring was – her dead nerves felt nothing. Her gaze was distant, focused on the speckling of tiny clouds in the eastern sky, where the deep azure blended into shades of purple.

She let herself relax, and listened. The wind whispered sibilant nonsense at her, and the slow, stirring thoughts of the hilltop grumbled along so slowly as to be incomprehensible. There were no animals here: they had been driven away by an instinct that warned them of whatever lurked at the bottom of that hole in the earth. Lucia felt it too, all around her but concentrated mostly underground; it was like the distant soughing of some enormous animal, asleep but still aware of them. The air seemed taut, and tricked the vision with half-seen movements.

Zaelis appeared next to her with Cailin, and gave her an entirely unconvincing smile of reassurance. The Sister stroked the hair on the side of her head in a gesture of surprising tenderness.

'Remember, Lucia,' she said. 'Nobody is forcing you to do this.'

Lucia did not reply, and after a moment Cailin gave a slight nod of understanding and retreated.

'I am ready,' she told them, though she really wasn't.

Several of the guards who had travelled with them had brought the components for a cradle, which they had assembled as Lucia slept. It was little more than a lightweight chair made from interlocked pieces of kamako cane, and a system of ropes, both to secure Lucia into the chair and to provide a way of lowering it down into the cavern. They tied her into it awkwardly, for they regarded her with reverence and did not want to hurt her, yet they did not dare make their knots loose in case they should slip. When it was done, two of them picked her up while the remainder of the guards took up the slack of the long rope and secured it at its end to one of the more sturdy-looking soul-eaters. The two guards who carried her slid her gently out over the edge of the pit, allowing their companions to take her weight gradually. They did so without straining; she was slender enough that any of them could bear her without too much trouble. Finally, she was hanging over the shaft, the back of the chair resting against one wall.

Zaelis looked down on her, a final war of indecision going on behind his eyes. Then he crouched. 'Come back safely.'

She merely gazed at him with that strange, distracted look on her face, and said nothing.

'Let her down!' one of the guards called to his companions, and Lucia's descent began.

The first few metres were not easy. The men at the lip of the hole were forced to lean out as far as they dared to lower the rope, and Lucia had to fend off the black, wet rock of the shaft to stop her scraping against the sides. It took only a minute, but in that time Lucia's hands and legs were bruised and scratched all over.

Then the shaft opened out and she was hanging in a void above Alskain Mar, a tiny figure in a cradle dangling within the immensity of the subterranean cavern. The reality of her situation crowded in on her then, the terror of her predicament; and worse, the disbelief that her father had allowed it to happen. She realised only then that a part of her had been expecting Zaelis to change his mind, to tell her that she did not have to go, that he would not blame her if she backed away. Yet he had not. He had never even provided her an opportunity for second thoughts. How could he have done that to her? How *could* he?

The light of Nuki's eye was the only illumination here, a dazzling beam that drenched Lucia from above, limning her blonde hair and her back in unbearable brightness and casting her face into sharp shadow. Beneath her was water, a lake that glittered harshly where the sun struck it, so perfectly clear that it was possible to see the debris that cluttered its bottom. There were remnants of ancient stonework there, and hunks of broken rock eroded by time, grown over with lichens and aquatic plants. Islands were scattered about the lake, humps of pale cream rising above the waterline that had once been arches or the flanks of mighty pillars. She could see one wall of the cavern, but its rough curves faded into darkness on either side and left the rest of the chamber an unguessable abyss. Vines and greenery hung from the mouth of the shaft, straggling downward as if seeking the lake below. It was cold and dank here, and the only sound was the echoing drip of water and the occasional splash of a fish.

Most of the superstructure of the shrine was still standing, a thousand years after the earth had fallen in on it. It rose around Lucia in all its melancholy grandeur, colossal ribs of stone that thrust from the lake and arced up the curved sides of the cavern to broken tips. Huge pictograms were carved on the ribs in a language too old for Lucia to recognise, a dialect left behind in the evolution of society; their shapes suggested to her a grave and serious tone, resonant and wise.

Other sections of the shrine remained, too. Below her was the skeleton of a domed chamber, its floor raised enough so that the water lapped around its edges but did not swallow it. Fractured pieces of other rooms gave hints to the layout of the building before its destruction. On the wall before her, there was a massive section of stonework supported between two of the ribs, a piece of what had once been the original roof of the shrine. Angular patterns scrawled along its surface, a tiny glimpse of the majesty that this place had once possessed when it was intact. At the periphery of the light, she could see other structures, too dim to make out but evoking an impression of breathtaking size.

She felt suddenly, awfully small and alone. Alone, except for the presence that waited in Alskain Mar.

They lowered her towards the ruin of the domed chamber, and her creaking chair descended in steady increments, pausing between each gentle drop. Thankfully, she had no fear of heights, but she was dreadfully afraid of the chair or the rope giving way, even though she had been assured that they had taken every possible precaution and that the cradle was sturdy enough for someone six times her weight. She listened to her heart thumping, and tried to endure as she slowly neared the bottom of the cavern.

Then, finally, she was passing through the curled, broken fingers of the shattered dome, and her cradle bumped to the stone floor. She untied herself hurriedly, desperate to be out of it, as if they might haul her back up into the abyss again at any moment.

'Lucia?' Zaelis called from the shaft above, where the heads of the observers were dark blots against the blinding sunlight. 'Are you well?'

His voice rang like a blasphemy against the eerie peace of the cavern, and the air suddenly seemed to darken, to become thick with an overwhelming and angry disapproval so palpable that it made Lucia shy and whimper. The others felt it too, for she heard the guards exclaiming frightened oaths, and Cailin snapped something at Zaelis, after which he was quiet and did not shout any more.

The light swelled in the room again gradually, the tension easing. Lucia breathed again, but her hands trembled slightly. She looked back at the tiny, fragile cradle which was her only lifeline out of this place, and realised just how far from help she truly was. Standing on the edge of the slanting sunlight, she was just a willowy girl of fourteen harvests, wearing a scuffed and dirty pair of trousers and a white blouse.

Lucia, you are not somebody's sacrifice. Kaiku's words, spoken to her on the first day of Aestival Week. And yet here she was, in the lair of some unguessable entity, like a maiden offered to a mythical demon by her own father.

She willed herself to relax once again. The voices of the other spirits that she heard every day – the animals, the earth, the air – were silent here. It made her nervous. She had never been without them before, and it only intensified the loneliness and abandonment that she felt.

The occupant of the shrine was paying her little more attention now than it had been before. It was dormant and uninterested. If she had to rouse it, she would have to do it *very* gently.

The time had come. She could not put it off any longer. She walked to the edge of the platform, facing the darkness, and knelt on the cool stone. She placed her hands flat on its surface and bowed her head. And she listened.

The process of actively communicating with a spirit was not as simple as language. Animals were easy enough for Lucia, but most spirits were largely ignorant of the world that humans saw and felt. There was no real lexicon through which humans and spirits were capable of understanding each other, since they did not share the same senses. Instead, they had to connect on a level far beneath reason, a primal melding which could only be achieved by becoming one with the nature of each other. A tentative, dim unity had to be formed, like that between a baby in a womb and its mother.

Now Lucia let herself become aware of the stone beneath her palms, and let the stone become aware of her. At first, the sensations were merely physical: the cold touch against her skin, the pressure of her flesh against the surface. They became sharpened and more acute as she slipped further into her trance, so that she became aware of the infinity of pores and creases in the skin of her hands, and could sense the microscopic cracks and seams in the stone that she knelt on.

By now she was entirely still, her breathing slowed to a languorous sigh, her heartbeat a dull and lazy thump.

Next, she let the sharing of sensation spread beyond the point of contact, expanding her awareness to include her whole body: the gush and pump of her blood, the net of follicles on her scalp, the snarled and dead tissue of her scars, the mesh of muscle in her back. She opened to the stone her knowledge of the steadily gathering potential of her ovaries and womb, which would soon become active; of the gradually lengthening bones in her limbs; all the processes of life and growth.

And with that, she let herself sink further into the essence of the stone, skimming its ancient, grinding memory. She felt its structure, its flaws; she sensed its origins, where it had grown and where it had been hewed from; she knew of its hard, senseless existence. There was no real life in a stone that had been separated from its mountain, cut from the greater entity of the land it was formed in; but there was still an imprint of things that had occurred here, an impression left by time on the character of the place.

Then, all at once, the shrine woke up around her. She almost lost her trance as her perception widened in one dramatic sweep, and she was feeling not just the stone but the entire structure of the shrine, a millennium of existence revealed to her at once. She sensed the pride and power of this place in its youth, felt its bitterness at its abandonment. This had been a site of great worship once, and it had not forgotten the days when men and women praised in its halls and burned sacrifices on its altars. Then she knew of a long emptiness, and of the coming of the new inhabitant, and the shrine was a place of power once again, though a wan and hollow shadow of its former self.

She began to tentatively probe, reaching toward this new inhabitant, to make it aware of her. Despite her trance, she was becoming fearful again. Even the oblique sensations she had received about the spirit that dwelt here had been massive and daunting, as if she were an insect brushing up against the flanks of some enormous beast.

Slowly, the spirit of Alskain Mar roused.

Lucia felt the change in the air around her with her finely attuned senses. The cavern was darkening, a blackness like smoky ink billowing into the light and defeating the glare of Nuki's eye. She could hear, distantly, Zaelis's exclamation of horror as the sight of her was obscured. The small heat that the beam of sun had provided faded away, and the temperature plummeted. She started to shiver; her breath came out in slow jets of vapour. The discomfort was causing her to slip back out of her trance again, and she retreated from the spirit to master herself, to relax.

But the spirit came after her. Her contact had stirred it, and it would not let her go without knowing something of the nature of the intruder in its lair. Lucia had a moment of terror at its sudden aggression before it engulfed her mind, melding forcefully with her in one cruel deluge.

There was the briefest instant where she was brutally faced with an immensity impossible to fathom with her human structures of thought. Then she died of shock.

And kept living.

Her eyes fluttered open. She lay face down on the floor of the ruined chamber. Her cheek and breasts hurt where she had fallen forward. There was light, pale blue and ethereal.

She raised herself up on her arms.

The illumination was coming from beneath the lake, underlighting her face eerily. The entire cavern was aglow. It was bigger even than her initial glimpses of it had suggested. The water cast shining ripples onto the walls and the remnants of the shrine. Overhead, the darkness was total, and no sight of the shaft through which she had entered Alskain Mar could be seen.

As her consciousness reassembled itself, she realised that the spirit of the shrine was still melded with her. She could feel it, tentative now. It sent a wash of knowledge, a recapitulation and something that she interpreted as an apology. The spirit had accidentally killed her, but only for moments. It had taken that long to absorb the nature of the girl, and to reactivate her biology, to repair the damage done to her sanity. Though she had died, she had not missed more than a couple of beats of her heart; her blood had barely time to slow.

Lucia realised with amazement that she was *communicating* with it. Or rather, it was communicating with her. She had known that it was hopelessly beyond her capabilities to make herself understood to a thing that was so alien, but she had never considered that the spirit might be able to simplify itself enough to descend to her level. Yet, in absorbing her nature, it had gained knowledge of her limitations and capabilities, and a rudimentary contact was achieved and held.

She crawled weakly to the edge of the platform, driven by a half-heard motivation, and knelt by the edge. Then she looked down into the water, and saw it.

There was no bottom to the lake any more. Though still as clear as crystal, it now plunged away to endless depths, from which the strange glow came. And down there, at some unguessable distance, the spirit looked back at her.

It had no form. It was like a dent in the water, hovering at the edge of Lucia's sight, more a suggestion of a shape than a physical entity. Somewhere within it two oval formations that approximated eyes watched her with a frightening intensity. It flickered with the invisible convection of the lake, sometimes jumping for a fraction of a second to another place before returning to its original location, flitting fitfully about while remaining perfectly still. It seemed at once small and looming to Lucia's eyes. She could not trust her perspective; it was as if she could reach into the water and touch it, though it appeared further away than the moons. Despite its best attempts at a manifestation she could comprehend, it still bent her senses just to look at it; yet look at it she did, for she knew that was what it wanted.

Awe and joy and raw terror clashed within her. She would never have believed she could ever achieve an understanding with a spirit such as this; but now that she had, she was committed to that contact, and there was no telling what kind of force she was dealing with. It could annihilate her mind in a fit of whimsy; it could keep her trapped here for an eternity as a companion; it could do something entirely beyond her imagination. She was still stunned and fragile from the mental impact of the spirit's first touch, from her momentary skip across the surface of death; she did not know if she was strong enough to deal with what was to follow.

But there was no other recourse now. She had questions to ask. Slowly, she spread her hands and laid them onto the cold surface of the lake. She exhaled a long, shivering breath, and a plume of vapour rose around her.

Then she began.

TWENTY

'I will not go back!' Kaiku said, stalking around the rock-lined hollow where the travellers hid. 'Not yet. Not while we still know nothing about those creatures down there.'

'It's *because* we know nothing that we have to go back,' Yugi argued. He glanced up at Tsata, who was on lookout, crouched on the lip of a flat stone. 'We have no idea what kind of defences they can muster. And we're certainly not equipped to try and infiltrate them. What is it exactly you're planning to *do*, Kaiku?'

'It is not enough for us to return to the Fold with news of an Aberrant army hiding in the Fault,' Kaiku said. 'Why are they here? Who are they intended for? Is it the Libera Dramach, or somebody else? We need answers, not a report that will only breed more questions.'

'Keep your voices down,' Nomoru told them coldly.

They had observed the Aberrants and the strange Weaver-like newcomers for several hours before retreating from the edge of the cliff that overlooked the flood plain. Fearing the brightening day, they had pulled back to a less exposed spot where they could chew over their options. Nomoru had found them a pebbly dip between a cluster of tall rocks that leaned together, shutting out most of the sky. Despite the relative ease with which they had penetrated this far into the Weavers' protected area, they were all becoming increasingly nervous. The lack of any form of guards could be explained by the barrier they had passed through: as with the monastery on Fo that Kaiku had infiltrated in the past, the Weavers believed their barrier was infallible, and did not trouble themselves with security. But still, they had begun to feel that their luck was running thin, and something had to be done.

'If we stay and try to find out more, we run the risk that we are captured or killed,' said Yugi, running a hand through his hair before readjusting the rag around his forehead. He had dark circles under his eyes, and his stubbled cheeks made him look haggard and weary; but he was the leader here, and he spoke with authority. 'Then nobody gets *any* answers, and no warning of what the Weavers are planning.'

'But what *are* they planning?' Kaiku said. She was unusually agitated. 'What do we know?'

'We know that they have a horde of several different species of Aberrant,'

Yugi said. 'All predator species or specialised in some way. And they're all pure-bloods; no freaks.' Yugi shrugged. 'That means they've either selected them very carefully from their natural habitat, or bred them that way. This is what they have been moving in secret with their barges. This is what Lucia sensed on the river.'

'They're under control,' Nomoru said. She was sitting on the slope of the hollow, her face striped with the shadow of the rocks overhead, cleaning her exquisite rifle. 'Should have been fighting each other. They aren't. So they're under control.'

'Can they do that?' Yugi asked Kaiku. 'Can a Weaver influence that many creatures like that?'

'No,' Kaiku said. 'Not even a Sister could keep a constant check on all those minds at once. Not even a hundred Sisters, and they're a lot more . . . *efficient* with their use of the Weave than men are.'

'Maybe you're wrong,' said Nomoru. 'Maybe the Weavers *can* do it.'

'I am *not* wrong,' Kaiki returned. 'I would have sensed it, even if they could. Whatever was going on down there, it was too subtle to be Weavers controlling those creatures.'

'Then what about those black-robed people?' Yugi suggested. They had seen dozens of them, wandering between the scabrous masses of Aberrant beasts. 'Are they the keepers of the menagerie?'

'Perhaps,' said Kaiku. 'Perhaps not.'

'Could you find out?'

'Not by the method you mean. I do not know what I would be facing,' she said. 'If they caught me using my *kana*, the consequences could be disastrous. For all of us.'

'What about that building?' Nomoru said, squinting down the barrel of her rifle. 'Don't have any idea about that. Need to get closer.'

'It's a mine,' said Yugi. 'Surely that's obvious? The fact that the blight is present here means they've got a witchstone down there. It also means that it's been awake long enough to start corrupting the land.'

'I think the presence of the building is enough to indicate that they have been here a long time,' Kaiku pointed out. 'Yet they have not made any move to attack the Fold. So we can presume—'

'It's a flood plain,' Nomoru interrupted, continuing her original train of thought. 'How do you dig a mine on a flood plain? It would *flood*.'

Tsata had been listening to the conversation patiently. It had been obvious to him what to do since the start, but he knew that simple survival logic did not work on Saramyr; they insisted on complicating things. Now that they had argued their way around the subject enough to satisfy themselves, he decided the time was right to interject.

'I have a solution,' he said.

The others looked up at where he crouched, his pale green eyes flitting among the broken rocks that surrounded them.

'Two of us stay and investigate,' he said. 'Two of us go back.'

'Only Nomoru knows the way back,' Yugi pointed out.

'I know the way back,' Tsata said. After a lifetime of navigating his way through dense jungles, the relatively open terrain of the Fault was simple to remember. He could retrace their route easily, and avoid the dangers that they had passed through on their journey here.

'Nobody's staying,' said Yugi.

'*I* am,' Kaiku shot back.

'You're the only one who can get us out through that barrier,' Yugi reasoned.

'Then I will accompany you to the other side and then come back,' said Kaiku.

'I will stay with her,' Tsata put in. 'I would be more use here.'

'You're both in a real hurry to get killed,' Nomoru said with a nasty smile. 'I don't mind. I'll go with him.' She thumbed at Yugi. 'Safer.'

'We're all going back *together*,' Yugi said. 'We almost didn't make it here with four of us. With just two—'

Kaiku cut him off. '*You* almost did not make it here,' she said. 'Need I remind you to whom you owe the fact that you are here at all?'

Yugi sighed. 'Kaiku, I won't let you do this. And certainly not out of gratitude for saving my life.'

Kaiku brushed her fringe back from where it hung across her face. She had ever been a stubborn one, and now she had her heels firmly planted. 'It is not your choice,' she said. 'I am here as a representative of the Red Order; you do not have rank over me. And Tsata is under allegiance to no one.'

'You're not even *in* the Red Order! You're still an apprentice! Gods, Kaiku, don't you understand the *threat?*' Yugi cried. 'What happens if you're caught? You know how paranoid Cailin is about exposing any of her operatives; what do you think will happen if a Weaver gets hold of you? You'll jeopardise the whole of the Sisterhood! And besides,' he finished, his voice dropping to a hiss as Nomoru shushed him, 'you both know where the Fold is.'

Kaiku was unconvinced. 'Someone needs to stay and let everyone know if this army begins to move. Only I can do that; only I can get a warning to the Fold instantly if the Weavers start to march.'

'Correct me if I'm mistaken, but hasn't Cailin forbidden long-distance communication between Sisters?' Yugi pointed out.

'She has not *forbidden* it,' Kaiku replied. 'She has merely made it clear that it is only to be used when absolutely no other option is available. As now.'

'And you think you are qualified to decide that? You think she would be happy for an apprentice to take that responsibility?'

'I do not care what makes her happy or otherwise,' Kaiku said dismissively. 'I am not her servant.' She paused for a moment, then continued. 'Why do you think she let me go to Okhamba with Mishani? She needed someone who could thread the Weave. In case we could not get the spy away, I was to send her the information he held. That was how important she considered it. This is how important *I* consider *this.* It is our only chance to find out what the Weavers are up to.' She swept her hand in a gesture of frustration. 'All this time, we've been too careful. *Cailin* has been too careful. And look at the result. The Weavers have an army under our noses! The Red Order should have been looking for this kind of thing, but Cailin is too afraid of any of them getting caught. If we do not find out *now* what is happening, it will be too late!' She met Yugi's eyes earnestly. '*We* are here and they are not, and if I return, Cailin will never let me get close enough again to make a difference.'

And there it was. That was the truth of it. If they retreated now, Cailin would not let her risk herself again, and they would have missed a potentially crucial opportunity to discover the Weavers' plans. She could not turn her back on this. Not with her oath to Ocha still smouldering in her mind, and her family's deaths unavenged.

Ocha looked after me once, she thought, recalling her frozen trek through the Lakmar Mountains many years ago. *He will do so again.*

'You'll make a difference, I've no doubt of that,' Yugi said, but he sounded defeated, and Kaiku knew that he would not argue any further. 'Whether it is a triumph or a catastrophe, time will tell.' He shrugged again. 'I can't stop you, Kaiku. Not by force or by reason. I just want you to know how many lives you're playing with.'

'For too long we have been too afraid of the Weavers,' Kaiku said. 'We have not dared to take a risk. We cannot hide forever.' She put a hand on his shoulder. 'I will be careful.'

'You'd better be,' said Yugi, then flashed an unexpected grin. 'I need you to come back safely to the Fold. So I can kill you for making me worry like this.'

The humour was forced, and nobody took it up.

'Are you finished?' Nomoru said drily. 'Can we go?'

Kaiku gave her a poisonous glance, then leaned close to Yugi's ear and breathed: 'I do not envy your company for the trip back.'

Yugi groaned.

Reki tu Tanatsua, younger brother of the Empress of Saramyr, had begun to regret ever visiting his sister at all.

He sat on the wide stone shelf of a window-arch in his chambers, curled up with the soles of his shoes resting against one end and his back against the other. He was looking out northward over the mighty walls of Axekami and the plains beyond, with the sparkling Jabaza curving in from the left side of the panorama, heading for the horizon and the mountains. It had been a hot and sultry day, and the very land seemed to laze in the burnished light as Nuki's eye sank to the west. Soft strips of cloud hung drowsily at the high altitudes, barely moving. Reki's head was resting against the arch, his arms crossed, a study in thoughtfulness lit in gentle fire and warm shadow.

When he had learned that his request to travel to the Imperial City had been granted, he had been ecstatic. Not only because it would be his first opportunity to travel there unaccompanied by family – he was seventeen harvests then; eighteen since the beginning of autumn – nor because he loved his sister dearly and had missed her since she had gone to live in Axekami. No, most of his happiness was because he could finally get away from his father, Barak Goren, whose constant disappointment at Reki was wearing more and more at the boy's nerves.

The age difference between Reki and Laranya, who was thirty-three harvests, was due to the fragility of their mother. Despite having a fierce strength of mind, she had a weak constitution. Giving birth to Laranya had nearly taken her life, and Goren, who cared for her deeply, would not ask her to try for another child. But though she saw how proud he was of his daughter, she knew that he wanted a son. Not as a matter of lineage, for Laranya was eminently suitable to become Barakess, and in Saramyr titles were passed down to the eldest regardless of gender, unless special dispensation were made to bestow it upon a different child. Rather, it was because he was the kind of man who needed to prove his virility through his offspring, and a strong son would make him proud in a way that even a firebrand like Laranya could not.

After many years, she could bear it no longer; she stopped drinking the herbal brew that prevented pregnancy, and she gave him Reki. And this one *did* take her life.

Goren was not so unfair as to blame Reki for the death of his wife; but as Reki grew, it soon became clear that there were other reasons for Goren to be resentful. Whereas Laranya had the robust constitution of her father, Reki inherited his mother's frailty, and the rough-and-tumble of growing up always ended with him being hurt. He became shy and introverted, a lover of books and learning: safe things, that were not apt to turn on him. His father had little time for it.

The white streak in his hair and the scar running from the side of his left eye to the tip of his cheekbone were from childhood, a fall from some rocks where he hit his head and face. He knew even then not to go to his father about it, but simply huddled miserably until the pain and concussion went away.

His relationship with his father had never got any better, and Reki had long since ceased trying to please him. The opportunity to travel here from faraway Jospa was a relief to all concerned. But it was fast turning sour, and Reki began to wonder if he was not better off back at home in the desert. And whether Laranya might not be too.

The Blood Emperor's behaviour was becoming terribly unbalanced. It seemed that scarcely a day passed by without some terrible argument between Mos and Laranya. Arguments for them were nothing new, of course, but these had a surpassing savagery; and after witnessing that moment in the pavilion when Mos had almost struck his pregnant wife, Reki was afraid for her.

Reki was Laranya's confidant in these matters, and she passed on every detail. What he heard deepened his concern more and more. The Blood Emperor was suffering strange dreams that he talked about obsessively, even using them as accusations against his wife. Several times he had asked Laranya if she was being unfaithful to him. Once, he had asked her whose baby she carried; for they had tried for so long for a child, and it was no coincidence in Mos's eyes that she had become such close friends with Eszel around the time she had miraculously conceived.

What Laranya did not know, and Reki did, was that Mos had already drunkenly threatened Eszel when the poet was unfortunate enough to be present during one of his rages. Eszel had confessed his fears for his life to Reki; but Reki had not passed them on to Laranya. He knew his sister too well. She would use it as ammunition to confront Mos, and get Eszel into deeper trouble.

Reki had told Eszel that the best thing to do would be to make himself scarce for the time being, and Eszel had taken his advice. He had gone on a long trip to 'gather inspiration' for his poetry, and wisely left no address where he could be contacted. Reki was not sure whether Mos had heard about this yet or not, but Laranya certainly had, and was bitterly hurt by his desertion.

It was not only the Blood Emperor's personal life that was falling to pieces, however. His advisers hardly dared advise him, but they dared not act without his approval, either. Nothing was being done about the mounting crisis and the reports of famine in the far settlements of the empire. The high families' cries went unheard.

Reki wanted to leave, and he wanted Laranya to come with him. It was not safe here for her, and not good for her child. But she would not go; she would not forsake the man she loved. And she begged him to stay with her, for she had nobody else to turn to.

How could he refuse? She was his sister, the only person who had loved him unconditionally all his life. There was nobody more precious to him.

His dark thoughts were interrupted by a chime outside the curtained doorway. He cursed softly and looked around the room for the small bell he was supposed to ring to indicate permission to enter. It was not a custom in the desert, and he found it annoying. Eventually he decided that he would not bother with formality, nor with moving from the window-shelf where he lounged.

'Enter,' he called.

The young woman who brushed aside the curtain was breathtaking. She was utterly beautiful in every aspect: her features were small and flawless, her figure perfect, her grace total. Her dusky skin and her deep black hair – drawn back tightly across her scalp and passing through a complex junction of jewelled pins and ornaments before twisting down her back in three braids – marked her as being from Tchom Rin, like Reki. She wore soft green and blue cosmetics around her almond-shaped eyes, and a subtle gloss on her lips; a necklace of carved ivory rested against her collarbone. She was dressed desert-fashion, in an elegant white robe clasped at one shoulder with a round green brooch, leaving one of her shoulders bare.

'Am I interrupting?' she asked, in a voice like thick honey.

'No,' he said, suddenly very conscious of the insolent way he was lazing on the window-shelf. He slid clumsily down from his perch. 'Not at all.'

She slipped into the room and let the curtain fall behind her. 'What were you doing?' she asked.

He considered inventing something grand, but his courage failed him. 'Thinking,' he said, and blushed at the way it sounded.

'Yes, Eszel said you were a thinker,' she smiled, disarming him completely. 'I admire that. So few men seem that way these days.'

'You know Eszel?' Reki asked, unconsciously brushing back his hair with one hand. Then, remembering his manners, said: 'Would you like to sit? I can call for some refreshments.'

She looked over at the couches and the table he had indicated. There was a *lach* pitcher there on a silver tray, and several goblets of silver and glass, etched with swirling patterns. A selection of small cakes were arranged around the pitcher. 'You already have wine,' she said. 'Might we share it?'

Reki felt the heat rising in his face again. There were always refreshments at his table; it was a courtesy provided to him as an important guest. The servants periodically replaced the pitcher to keep it cool, even though he never touched it. He had found it vaguely irritating to begin with, but he felt it would be rude to ask them to stop bringing it. He had got so used to their unobtrusive visits by now that he had quite forgotten the wine was there.

'Of course,' he said.

She arranged herself on the couch, lying sideways with her legs folded and tucked underneath her. Reki sat on another, awkwardly. The simple presence of this woman was excruciating.

'Shall I pour?' she asked.

He made an indication that she should do so; he did not trust his tongue.

She gave another flicker of a smile and picked up the pitcher. Her eyes on the wine as she tipped it, she said: 'You seem nervous, Reki.'

'Does it show so much?' he managed.

'Oh yes,' she replied. She offered him a glass of the delicate amber liquid. 'But that is why Yoru gave us wine. To smooth the edges of a moment.'

'Perhaps you had better hand me the pitcher, then,' Reki said, and to his delight she laughed. The sound ignited a bloom of warmth in his chest.

'One glass at a time, I think,' she said, then sipped her drink, regarding him seductively.

For Reki, the momentary pause seemed an endless silence, and he struggled to fill it. 'You mentioned that you knew Eszel . . .' he prompted.

She relaxed back into the couch. 'A little. I know a lot of people.' She was not making this easy for him. She seemed, in fact, to be enjoying his discomfort. Just being this near her was making his groin stir, and he had to adjust himself so that it would not show.

'Why have you come to see me?' he asked, and then inwardly winced as he realised how blunt it sounded. He took a swallow of wine to cover it.

She did not appear to be offended. 'Ziazthan Ri. *The Pearl Of The Water God.*'

Reki was confused. 'I do not understand.'

'Eszel told me that you had read it, and that you gave him a very accomplished recitation of the story.' She leaned forward a little, her eyes bright. 'Is that true?'

'I memorised it,' Reki said. 'It is only short. The accomplishment was the author's, not mine.'

'Ah, but it is the passion of the speaker, the understanding of verse and melody, that can bring the heart from a story read aloud.' She looked at him with something like wonderment. 'Have you really memorised it? I suspect it is not as short as you pretend. You must have an exceptional recollection.'

'Only for words,' Reki said, feeling that he was coming uncomfortably close to bragging.

'I would be very interested to hear it,' she purred. 'If you would recite it to me, I would be *very* grateful.'

The tone in her voice forced Reki to shift position again to conceal his gathering ardour. He was blushing furiously now, and for a moment he could not think of anything to say.

'Let me explain,' she said. 'I subscribe to the philosophy of Huika: that everything should be experienced once in the interests of a completeness of being. I have spent fortunes for a glimpse of the rarest paintings; I have travelled long and far to see the wonders of the Near World; I have learned many arts unknown to the land at large.'

'But you are so young to have done so much . . .' Reki said. It was true; she could not have been more than twenty harvests, only a little older than him.

'Not so young,' she said, though she sounded pleased. 'As I was saying, I met Eszel before he left the Imperial Keep, and he told me about you.' She leaned over, reached out and stroked her hand lightly down his face, whispered: 'Ziazthan Ri's masterwork inside your head.' Then she let him go, and he realised he had been holding his breath. 'There are so few copies in existence, so few uncorrupted versions of the story. There is little I would not do to experience something so rare.'

'My father possesses a copy,' Reki said, feeling the need to say something, 'in his library.'

'Will you recite it to me?' she said, slipping off the couch and getting up.

'Of . . . of course,' he said, furiously trying to summon it to mind. His memory seemed to have become jumbled. 'Now?'

'Afterwards,' she said; and she put out her hands for him to take, and lifted him to his feet.

'Afterwards?' he repeated tremulously.

She pressed herself gently against him, one finger tracing the line of the scar on his eye. The softness of her breasts and body make his erection painful. He felt drunk, but it was nothing to do with the wine.

'I believe in a fair trade,' she said. Her lips were close enough to his so that he had to resist the almost magnetic pull of her. Her breath was scented, like oasis flowers. 'An experience for an experience.' Her hand slipped to the brooch at her shoulder, and she twisted it; her robe fell away like a veil. 'Unlike any you have ever had before.'

Reki's heart was pounding in his chest. A voice was warning him to caution, but it went unheeded. 'I do not even know your name,' he whispered.

She told him just before her mouth closed on his.

'Asara.'

The man screamed as the knife slipped under the warm skin of his cheek, slicing through the thin layer of subcutaneous fat to the wet red landscape of muscle beneath. Weave-lord Kakre rode the swell of the scream like an expert, angling the blade to account for the distortion in his victim's face. He sheared upward to the level of the eye socket, then cut towards the back of the skull, gliding through the soft tissue until a bloody triangular flap peeled away. At the sight, he felt a deep peace, a fulfilment that never seemed to wane no matter how many times he sated himself. The post-Weaving mania was upon him, and he was skinning again.

His skinning chamber was windowless, hot and gloomy, lit only by the coals of the fire-pit in the centre of the room. Underlit in the red glow were his other creations, arranged on the walls or hanging on chains in the heights: kites and sculptures of skin gazing at him from empty eyes, watching him at his craft. His latest victim was placed on the iron rack which was his canvas, tilted upright in a spread eagle. This particular piece he had been carving since dawn, and now it was a patchwork, a frame of muscle with jigsaw skin and half the pieces missing.

Kakre felt inspired today. He did not know if he would get a kite out of this one or if it would simply be therapeutic, but the joy of cutting rendered it immaterial. It had been too long since he had worked at his art, too long; but the rigours of his Weaving had lately increased, and his appetite had increased with it.

He realised that he had been standing admiring the flap of skin he had peeled for some time, and in that time the man had fainted again. Kakre felt a pang of annoyance. He was usually so good at keeping his victims awake, with herbs and poultices and infusions. His knifework was shoddy as well, he noticed suddenly. He glared at his withered, white hand. His joints pained him constantly. Could that be a contributing factor? Was he losing his skill with a blade?

It was an idea too horrible to contemplate. Even though, distantly, he knew that his Mask was eating him from the inside as it had eaten its previous owners, the actual implications of that had never occurred to him. How strange, that a mind as sharp as his might miss something as obvious as that.

A moment later, he had forgotten about it again.

He put his bloodied blade listlessly on a platter with all his other instruments, and wandered to the edge of the fire-pit before easing himself into a sitting position. As always, he was planning.

Already the deceptions were being drawn. Blood Kerestyn and Blood Koli were gathering a formidable army, but it was not formidable enough to challenge the might of Axekami yet. In a few more years, maybe. But in those years, the source of the blight might be discovered by the people at large. He had heard of rumours, extremely accurate rumours, that were being repeated quietly in the courts of the high families. They worried him. Soon the famine would bring the country to the point of total desperation, and those rumours might be enough to make the high families turn their wrath from Mos onto the Weavers.

He did not have time to wait. Therefore, Kakre intended to tempt Mos's enemies closer.

His overtures to Barak Avun tu Koli had been well received; but Avun was a treacherous snake, as likely to bite the one who handled him as the one he was set upon. Had Avun believed him? And could he convince Grigi tu Kerestyn to believe him as well?

You must strike when I say! he thought. *Or this will all be for nothing.*

More distressing than that, though, was a message that had come from the Imperial Keep itself, one sent by courier that he had failed to intercept. He was not sure who had sent it, but he knew Avun had received it, and he was anxious to know what it said. Another doublecross? But who was making deals behind his back?

It worried at Kakre's mind even as he worried at the Blood Emperor's.

At night, when Mos fell into a drunken sleep, Kakre wove dreams for him. Dreams of infidelity and anger, dreams of impotence and fury. Dreams calculated to tip him in the direction Kakre needed him to go. It was a dreadful risk, for if Mos began to suspect him, all would be lost. Even the best Weavers could be clumsy – he thought of his aching joints, and wondered if his skill in the Weave had suffered also – and they might leave traces of themselves behind that would fester, until the victim eventually realised what had been done to them. If Mos were not drinking too much and already beleaguered with stress, Kakre might not have dared it; but the Blood Emperor had become unbalanced long before the Weave-lord had begun to interfere with his mind.

Lies, deceit, treachery. And only the Weavers matter.

He sat in his ragged robes of badly-sewn hide and fur and little pieces of bone, rolling that phrase around in his head. Only the Weavers mattered. Only the continuation of their work. And it was Kakre's job – no, his *calling* –

to manipulate this crisis to ensure their survival. There was only one way out of it that he could see, but it required a game to be played so skilfully, so subtly, that the slightest miscalculation could mean disaster.

The pieces were in place. But the board was anyone's yet.

TWENTY-ONE

The besieged town of Zila sat grim and cold in the twilight, a crooked crown atop a lopsided hill. Hundreds of yellow lights burned in the narrow windows of its buildings, gathering up towards the keep at its tip. To the north, where the hill was viciously steep, the Zan was a black, restless torrent, dim fins of drab lime glinting on its surface. Neryn had taken early station high in the sky tonight, even before the stars had begun to show; she commanded the scene alone, bathing it in funereal green.

The soldiers ringed the town, just out of bowshot and fire-cannon range, which was some considerable distance. Seven thousand men, all told, representing four of the high families. Tents were being erected and mortars assembled. Campfires dotted the dark swathe of the siege-line like jewellery. Fire-cannons of their own had been set up on either side of the Zan where the ring cut across it, to prevent any attempt to escape by water either upstream or down. The absence of any visible boats at the docks did not concern them. They were taking no chances. Nobody was getting out.

Mishani looked out from a window in the keep, surveying the forces arrayed against the town, calculating.

'There are not so many as I would have expected,' she said at last. 'The muster is poor.'

'It's more than enough to take this town,' Chien said darkly.

'Still,' she said, turning away from the window. 'The high families have spared only a small fraction of their armies. They keep their true strength to guard their own assets against the coming conflict. And there are no Imperial Guards at all, nor Blood Batik troops. Where is the Blood Emperor when one of his own towns defies him?'

The room they shared was a little stark, with its bare stone walls and floor, but Mishani considered that she could have done much worse for a prison. There were two sleeping-mats, a coarse rug, and cheap, heavy wall-hangings emblazoned with simple designs. There was also a table, with smaller mats for sitting on, and the food they had been getting these last few days was bland but palatable. The heavy wooden door was locked, but there were a pair of guards outside who would escort them to the appropriate room when they needed to make toilet or get dressed. They were not treated badly by any means, but for the simple fact that they were confined to their room.

There were other excursions, beyond the necessities of privacy. Bakkara had visited several times, and twice had escorted Mishani around the keep. He was not subtle at disguising his motivation: he wanted to hear about Lucia, and Mishani suspected that beneath his tough exterior he was somewhat awed to be in the presence of someone who knew her personally. Mishani played up to the reflected glory. It got her out of that room, and besides, she had to admit to herself that she found Bakkara strangely attractive. The sheer, overwhelming *manliness* of him, which her cynical side found faintly amusing in a pitying kind of a way, was also what made him so appealing: his lack of social graces, his jaded air that suggested he was above bothering to please anyone, his brawny physicality. It was a contradiction that she did not even attempt to reconcile; she knew well enough that matters of intellect and matters of the heart were independent of each other.

Chien was not fit enough to leave the room for long periods. His injuries had been treated, but he had developed a bad fever, probably due to the overnight ride to Zila. He spent most of the day lying on his sleeping-mat, dosed into near-unconsciousness with analgesic tinctures and febrifuges, occasionally rousing himself to complain about the lack of information they were getting, or to protest on Mishani's behalf that a noble lady should be allowed her own room. Mishani wished it were so. Chien was beginning to annoy her. He did not take inactivity well.

The siege had been slow in coming. Troops arrived at different times, and co-ordinating them all efficiently took a long while. It had been three days since the first of the forces appeared, bearing the banner of Blood Vinaxis. They had been the first family ever to hold the Imperial throne, but they had diminished now, and were weak. Their holdings were directly in the midst of the blighted Southern Prefectures, and most of their money came from crops which passed through Zila on their way to Axekami. A lot of those crops were hoarded within the walls of the town. Small wonder, then, that Barak Moshito tu Vinaxis was first on the scene to get them back.

Mishani had learned from Bakkara that the Governor of Zila had been stockpiling a great deal of food against the coming famine, confiscating portions from the trade caravans that passed over nearby Pirika Bridge. He had been intending to keep enough only for the Town Guards and the administrative body, and to sell the surplus at extortionate rates to the high families when the starvation began to bite. The townsfolk would be left to get by as they could. It was the exposure of his plan by Xejen, leader of the Ais Maraxa, that had triggered the revolt; and now the townsfolk were sitting on a store of food that would last them through the winter and long beyond, with careful rationing. As long as their walls held and they kept the enemy out, they would be a tough nut to crack.

After Blood Vinaxis had come Blood Zechen, though Barakess Alita had sent generals in her stead; then a token force from Blood Lilira, who could afford many more, and whose Barakess Juun was similarly absent.

Last to arrive had been Barak Zahn, from his estates north of Lalyara, leading a thousand mounted Blood Ikati warriors and a thousand on foot, the green and grey standards of his family stirring limply in the faint wind as they approached. Mishani could appreciate the irony. It was Zahn whom she had been on her way to see, Zahn the reason that she had been captured; and now he came to her, and they found themselves on opposite sides of an uprising. The gods were nothing if not perverse.

There were a few quick thuds on the door, and Bakkara opened it without waiting for permission. Mishani could never get used to the doors in this keep; they seemed such an impediment. She supposed their purpose was defensive, but they stopped breezes getting through to lighten the humidity of the hot days. Luckily, the draughty stone walls compensated well enough.

Mishani was still standing by the window when the old soldier entered. Chien was sitting upright on his sleeping-mat, his face swollen from bruising and sheened with fever. He glared at Bakkara. The merchant seemed to have taken a strong dislike to the soldier, presumably because of the older man's rough tongue.

'You're wanted, Mistress Mishani,' he said.

'Am I?' she said dryly, an imperious tone in her voice that suggested she was not about to be ordered anywhere.

Bakkara rolled his eyes and sighed. 'Very well: I am here to request your presence at an audience with Xejen tu Imotu, leader of the Ais Maraxa, mastermind of the Zila revolt and maniacal foaming zealot. Is that better?'

Mishani could not help but laugh at the bathos. 'It will do,' she said.

'And how are you feeling?' he asked Chien.

'Well enough,' Chien replied rudely. 'Are you going to let us out of here now?'

'That's up to Xejen,' Bakkara said, scratching the back of his neck. 'Though I can't see your hurry. If we let you out of here, you'll still be stuck in Zila. Nobody's getting past that wall, one way or another, for a very long time yet.'

Chien cursed softly and looked away, breaking off the conversation.

'Are you coming?' Bakkara asked Mishani.

'Of course,' she said. 'I have been waiting to talk to Xejen for quite some time now.'

'He's been very busy,' Bakkara said. 'You may have noticed a little disturbance outside Zila that's causing us all some concern.'

They left Chien to his rest; he bade them a sullen farewell as they departed.

Bakkara took Mishani along a route that they had not walked before, but the surroundings were little different from any other part of the keep. It was dour and utilitarian, with narrow corridors of dark stone and little ornamentation or consideration for the natural flow of the elements.

Bakkara told her that it was built to the original plans, drawn up over a thousand years ago, which explained its miserable lack of soul. It was a military building constructed in a time when the recently-settled Saramyr folk were still using Quraal architectural ideas, where the weather was harsher and where ruthless practicality was far more important than the frivolity of aesthetics. As Saramyr evolved its own identity, the people began to explore the freedom of religion and thought and art that had been suppressed in Quraal by the rise of the Theocracy, and which had led them to choose exile. The blazing summers and warm winters made the stuffy and close Quraal dwellings uncomfortable to live in, and so they invented for themselves new types of housing, ones that accommodated their environment rather than shutting it out. Many old settlements still bore traces of the Quraal influence in some parts, but most remnants of that era had been torn down as they crumbled and replaced with more modern buildings. Saramyr folk had little love for ruins.

Xejen tu Imotu, leader of the Ais Maraxa, was pacing his chamber when they arrived. He was a bland-looking man of thirty-three harvests, thin and full of nervous energy. A mop of black hair topped his head, and he had sharp cheekbones and a long jawline that made his face seem narrower than it was. He was dressed in simple black clothes that hugged his wiry figure, and he scampered across the room to meet them as Bakkara knocked and entered.

'Mistress Mishani tu Koli,' he said, his speech rapid. 'An honour to have you here.'

'With such a gracious invitation, how could I refuse?' she said, glancing at Bakkara.

Xejen did not seem to quite know how to take that. 'I hope your confinement has not been too terrible. Please forgive me; I would have seen you earlier, but the task of organising Zila into a force capable of defending itself is taking up all of my time.'

He resumed his pacing around the room, picking up things and putting them back down, adjusting bits of paper on his desk that did not need adjusting. This room was as spartan as the rest in the keep: a few mats, a table, a desk and a small settee. Glowing lanterns depended from ceiling hooks, and outside the single window the twilight was deepening to darkness. If his headquarters were anything to go by, then Xejen could not be accused of the same abuse of power that the erstwhile Governor had.

Mishani decided to be blunt. 'Why was I brought here?' she asked.

'To my chambers?'

'To Zila.'

'Ah!' He snapped his fingers. 'Part charity, part misunderstanding. Bakkara, why don't you explain?'

Mishani turned to the soldier with a patient expression, as if to say: *Yes, why don't you*? It had been one of the few things he had refused to talk about; he had been waiting for Xejen's permission, it seemed.

'Well, first there was the matter of your friend Chien,' he said, scratching his stubbled jaw. 'Even if you hadn't been there, we couldn't leave him in the state he was in. Then—'

'That's the charity part,' Xejen broke in. 'And as for you, well, Bakkara made the entirely understandable mistake of assuming you were still well connected in the high families, and that you may prove very useful in attracting Blood Koli to come to our defence, to heighten the profile of our plight.'

Bakkara looked abashed and gave an apologetic shrug, but Mishani was not concerned with that. She did not take it personally.

'By the time you had come to my attention, the gates had been shut and we could not very well let you out,' Xejen chattered on. 'Of course, I realised immediately that you did not possess the worth that Bakkara imagined – excuse my plain speaking – because I knew that you and your father were very much at odds. And since you are, after all, something of a heroine to the Ais Maraxa, I would hardly use you as a bargaining chip and deliver you to him.'

'I am relieved to hear it,' Mishani said. 'Am I to take it, then, that my relationship with my father is known to the Ais Maraxa?'

'Only myself and a few others,' Xejen replied almost before she had finished her sentence. 'Many of us were part of the upper echelons of the Libera Dramach, don't forget; and we were there when you came to the Fold. But your secret is safe. I understand you have been a great help to the Libera Dramach by trading on the illusion that you are still a part of Blood Koli.'

'I still am, as far as I am aware,' Mishani said. 'Legally, at least. My father has not cut me off yet.' Though he *had* tried to kill her twice, she added mentally.

'Your mother's latest book has not helped matters in your case, I imagine,' Xejen commented.

'That remains to be seen,' Mishani said. Truthfully, she had not even begun to consider the implications that Muraki tu Koli's latest collection of Nida-jan tales might have.

Xejen cleared his throat, wandering restlessly to the other side of the room. Mishani found his constant motion dizzying.

'I'll not dance around the issue, Mistress Mishani,' he said. 'You'd be a great asset to our cause. One of Lucia's rescuers. Someone who knows her intimately.' He looked up at her sharply. 'You'd do wonders for the morale of these townsfolk, and lend the Ais Maraxa a good deal of credibility.'

'What are you asking me to do?' she prompted.

Xejen stopped for a brief instant. 'To support us. Publicly.'

Mishani considered for a moment.

'There are things I would learn first,' she said.

'Ah,' said Xejen. 'Then I will do the best I can to answer any questions you have.'

'What are you doing here in Zila?' Mishani asked, her keen eyes studying him from within the black mass of her hair. 'What purpose does it serve the Ais Maraxa?'

'Notoriety,' came the reply. 'It has been some years since we first learned of the sublimity of the Heir-Empress Lucia, some time since we broke away from the Libera Dramach whose more . . .' he waved his hand, searching for the word, '*secular* appreciation of her was blinkering them to the wider picture. In that time the Ais Maraxa have striven to spread the news that there exists one to deliver us from the evil of the Weavers, to end the oppression of the peasantry and to turn back the blight that ruins our land.'

Mishani watched him carefully as his rhetoric became more heated. She knew Bakkara had meant his comment about Xejen being a zealot as a joke, but she was conscious that there was a grain of truth in what the soldier had said, and now that she met him she suspected that Bakkara was not entirely at ease with his leader.

'But spreading the word is not enough,' Xejen continued, wagging a finger in the air. 'The Heir-Empress is a rumour, a whisper of hope, but the people need more than rumours to motivate them. We need to be a threat that is taken seriously. We need the high families talking about us, so that their servants see they are worried . . . so that they see that even the most noble and powerful are afraid of the followers of Lucia. Then they'll believe, and they'll come to her when she calls, when she returns in glory to take the throne.'

He was gazing out of the window into the night now. Mishani cast a glance up at Bakkara, who caught it. He looked skyward briefly in spurious exasperation, and the corner of his mouth curved into a faint smile.

'But even with our best efforts, we couldn't make the empire sit up and take notice,' Xejen went on. 'Until now. We've been working at Zila for a long time, and the onset of famine has given us just the climate we need to make our move. The fact that the Governor has stockpiled all our provisions for us . . . it's as if Ocha himself has given us his blessing. We can hold out for a year within these walls. By that time, there won't be anyone in the empire who hasn't heard of the Ais Maraxa and learned of our cause.'

'Are you not concerned about Lucia?' Mishani inquired. 'After all, if her name becomes so notorious, you can be sure the Weavers will be searching for her harder than ever. It is because she is presumed dead and her abilities are not generally known that we have managed to hide her so long.'

'The Weavers will still think she's dead,' said Xejen dismissively. 'They'll think we're just wasting time fostering rumours. Besides, they'll never find her. But what preparations are the Libera Dramach making for when she comes of age? None! We are building her an army, an army of common folk, and when she reveals herself they'll suddenly discover that their rumour of hope is real, and they'll come flocking to her banner.'

Mishani's inclination was to argue: what banner? If this was all about building Lucia an army, then he was making an extraordinary assumption in assuming that Lucia *wanted* one. She wondered if he would talk this way if he knew Lucia as she did. Not as some glorious general, nor as some beatific child assured of her own destiny. Just a young girl.

But she had no illusions about changing Xejen's mind, and she wanted to stay on his good side, so she held her tongue.

'But what of the siege?' she asked. 'How do you plan to deal with that? You will run out of food eventually.'

'You know what's going on in Axekami, Mistress Mishani,' he said, again clipping the end off her sentence in his rush to speak. 'The high families will have a lot more than us to worry about in this coming year. You can see yourself how little enthusiasm they have for a fight. Look at that army!' He made a sweeping gesture to the window. 'We have ways of communicating with our operatives outside Zila. They are already talking about our plight and what we represent. Word will spread. A lot may change in a year, but whatever comes, everyone will know the name of Lucia tu Erinima before we are done.'

Xejen crossed the room to face them, his thin features wan in the lantern light. There was an intensity in his eyes now, a fire ignited by his speech. Mishani had no doubt that he was a formidable orator when faced with a crowd. His conviction in his own words was indisputable.

'Will you help us, Mistress Mishani?'

'I will consider it,' she said. 'But I have a condition.'

'Yes, you wish to have your confinement ended,' Xejen finished for her. 'Done. A sign of good faith. It would have been sooner, but I had too many other things to worry about. I don't want you as a prisoner, I want you as an ally.'

'You have my thanks,' said Mishani. 'And I will think on your proposal.'

'I need not tell you, I suppose, that your freedom only extends to the walls of Zila,' Xejen added. 'If you try and leave the town, you will regrettably be shot. I am sure you will not attempt anything so foolish.'

'Your advice is noted,' Mishani said, and with that she made the requisite politenesses and left, telling Bakkara that she could find her own way back.

Chien was asleep when she returned, murmuring and stirring in the grip of a dream. She shut the door of their room quietly behind her and sat on a mat to think. A plan was forming in her mind. It was like the old days at court. The principal players had been introduced; now she just had to work out how best to exploit them.

But *this* man, she did not yet understand. There was a piece of the puzzle missing here, and had been since the start. Until she knew what it was, until she knew whether Chien was an enemy or a friend, she dared not act.

She studied him closely, trying to find an answer in the broad angles of his face. He muttered and turned away from her, rolling over on his mat and gathering the blankets around him tighter. He was shivering despite the warmth of the night.

'What *is* your secret, Chien?' she murmured. 'Why are you here?'

After a time, she got up and extinguished the lantern, undressed in the moonlight and slipped beneath her own covers. She was just drowsing when Chien began to sing.

She felt a smile touch the corner of her lips. He was dreaming, his voice a tuneless drone, too soft to vocalise the words properly. She listened, and listened, and then suddenly she sat up in bed, staring across the dark room at him.

He continued, oblivious, singing his fevered song.

Mishani's breath was a shudder. She felt her throat close up, and then she slowly sank down to her pillow and faced the wall, stifling her sobs with her blanket. Tears came and would not be held back, sliding over the bridge of her nose and dripping into the fabric.

She knew that song, and it all made sense now.

TWENTY-TWO

The Blood Emperor Mos tu Batik stormed through the marbled corridors of the Imperial Keep, his brow dark with fury. His beard, once close and tidy, had grown unkempt, the patches of grey more pronounced. His hair was a mess, hanging in draggles over his eyes and damp with sweat. Wine had spilled on his tunic, and his clothes were wrinkled and pungent.

There was madness in his eye.

Days and nights had blended into one, an endless half-consciousness swamped in alcohol. Sleep brought him no rest, only terrible dreams in which his wife rutted with faceless strangers. His waking hours were spent in a constant state of suspicion, punctuated by sporadic outbursts of rage, directed either at himself or at anyone else near him. He was spiralling slowly and inexorably into mania, and the only escape from the torture was intoxication, which provided a small surcease but only made him more bitter afterward.

He had taken enough. Now he meant to have it out, once and for all. He would not stand by while he was cuckolded.

There would be a reckoning.

It had started long ago, before Eszel the flamboyant poet. He had come to realise that, in the long nights he had spent alone while spite gnawed at his soul. He remembered other times, when Laranya had wanted to pursue her interests and he his, and how he had indulged her in whatever she wished. Times when he had been disappointed that she was not waiting for him when he returned from a particularly harrowing day in the council chamber. Times when she had laughed and joked with other men, who seem attracted like moths to a candle, drawn by the brightness and vivacity of her. He remembered the jealousy then, the seeds of resentment burrowing into a soil made moist by his natural inclination for domination. Among the delusions and venomous slanders that he had persuaded himself to believe in those lonely hours, he had found nuggets of truth.

He had come to realise that he wanted Laranya as two different people, and that she could not be both. On the one hand was the fiery, wilful and entirely insubordinate woman he had fallen in love with; on the other, the dutiful spouse, who would be there when he wanted her and be absent when he did not, who would make him feel like a man because a man should be able to control his wife. One of the reasons he had fallen in love with her – and stayed in love with her – was because she would not bend to his will, would never be meek and submissive; it was because she galled him that she challenged him and kept his interest. His first wife Ononi had been the model of how a woman should be, but he had not loved her. Laranya was impossible, would never be tamed no matter how he tried, and she had both captured his heart and poisoned it.

It was the child that had turned things bad. For years, Mos had forgotten those fleeting moments of mistrust and disappointment, the feelings erased as soon as he saw Laranya's face again. But now he brought them all back to pick over them like a vulture at a carcass. All that time, and no child; but now, suddenly, she was pregnant.

He remembered when she had told him, what his first reaction had been, an instant of doubt that he had swept away, feeling guilty for ever having thought it.

Just like Durun. Just like my son, and his scheming bitch wife, letting him raise a child that wasn't even his own.

History was repeating itself. But this time, Mos was ahead of the game.

It was late as he stalked towards the Imperial chambers. His sleep patterns were erratic and took no account of the sun or the moons, and he had begun to fear the nightmares so much that he would do anything to put them off. He had been awake for more than forty hours now, dosed up with herbal stimulants to counteract the soporific lull of the wine, thinking in tighter and tighter circles until there was nothing left but a white-hot ball of fury that demanded release.

Oh, she had come to him to plead, or to demand, or to shout. Different approaches to the same end: she wanted to know what had possessed him, why he was acting this way. As if she did not know.

There were others, too. Kakre loomed in and out of his memory, croaking reports and meaningless observations. Advisers came and went. In some dim fashion, he had been aware of the other affairs of state which he was supposed to be attending to, but everything had become transparent to him in contrast to the one overwhelming matter of Laranya. Until it was resolved, he could not care about anything else. Reason had failed. The spies he had set to watch his wife had failed.

But there was another way; the only resort he had left.

He threw aside the curtain and stamped into the Imperial bedchamber. The violence of his entrance startled Laranya out of sleep. She sat up with a cry, clutching the sheets to her chest in the warm dark of the autumn night. Something moved in the pale green moonlight, by the archway that led to the balcony beyond: a figure, blurred, gone in an instant. Mos blundered across the room in pursuit, roaring in anger.

'What is it? Mos, *what is it*?' Laranya cried.

The Blood Emperor's hands were clutched on the stone balustrade; he was glaring down the north-eastern side of the Imperial Keep where it sloped away in a clutter of interlocking sculptures and carvings. He cast about, looking up, then to his left and right, then leaning far out as if he might see underneath the balcony. It was no good. There were too many folds and creases in the ornamentation, too many looming effigies and archways where the intruder might have hidden himself. Gods, he was so quick! Mos had barely even seen him.

Laranya was at his elbow, in her nightdress, her touch fearful on his arm. 'What *is* it?' she asked again.

'I saw him, whore!' Mos bellowed, flinging her arm away. 'You can't pretend any more! I saw him with my own eyes!'

Laranya was backing away into the room. Some emotion midway between enragement and fear had taken her, and did not seem to know which way to resolve itself. There was a new edge to Mos tonight, and she was not at all sure what he might do.

'Who? Who did you see?'

'Shouldn't you know? Was it that effeminate poet? Or is there someone else I should know who enjoys my bed?'

'Mos, I have told you . . . I cannot prove it to you any more than I already have! There is no one!'

'*I saw him!*' Mos howled, stumbling after her, his face distorted and haggard. 'He was just here!'

'There was nobody here!' Laranya cried. Now she *was* afraid.

'Liar!' Mos accused, advancing, looming in the green-tinted shadows.

'No! Mos, you are drunk, you are tired! You need sleep! You are seeing phantoms!'

'*Liar!*'

She reached the dresser, knocking into it and tipping bottles of perfume and make-up brushes over. There was no further she could retreat.

'A man cannot rule an empire when he cannot rule his wife!' Mos snarled. 'I will teach you obedience!'

She saw in his eyes what he meant to do, even before he had raised his fist.

'Mos! No! Our baby!' she pleaded, her hand going defensively to her belly.

'*His* baby,' Mos breathed.

Laranya did not have time to ask who he meant before the first blows fell; nor did she find out afterward, when he left her alone on the floor of the bedchamber with her body aching and her face bruised and blood seeping from between her legs as their child died inside her.

Reki was woken by a servant calling his name outside the curtain of his room. Asara was already awake, watching him. She lay next to him in his bed, and as he saw her it seemed that the pallid green moonlight caught her at an odd angle, and her eyes were two saucers of reflected illumination, like a cat's. Then she looked to the curtain, and the moment passed.

His gaze lingered on her shadowed face for an instant, unable to draw away from the beauty there. She had indeed, as she had promised, given him an experience unlike any he had had before; but though he had repaid her with a flawless rendition of *The Pearl Of The Water God*, she had not gone away as he had feared, never to see him again. To his delight, she had barely left him since the moment they had met. A sweet recollection of lazy days and passionate nights flitted across his consciousness. And if it seemed too good to be true, then he was loth to shatter his fragile happiness by questioning it.

'What is it?' he called, his throat tight from sleep.

'The Empress!' the servant replied. 'The Empress!'

The tone in her voice made him sit up with a jolt of alarm. 'A moment,' he said, and slid naked out of bed to put on a robe. Asara did the same. He was too preoccupied to even glance at her sublime form. Though she had shared his bed for several nights now, and he already worshipped her like a goddess, it was all dashed away in that dreadful instant.

'Enter,' he called, and the servant hurried in, speaking as she came. It was one of Laranya's handmaidens, a servant of Blood Tanatsua rather than one of the Keep servants.

'The Empress is hurt,' she babbled. 'I heard her . . . we all heard them fighting. We went in after the Emperor had gone. We—'

'Where is she?' Reki demanded.

'The Imperial chambers,' the servant said, but she had barely finished before Reki swept past her and out of the room.

He ran barefoot through the corridors of the Keep, the *lach* floor chill on his soles, heedless of how ridiculous he looked sprinting in a bedrobe.

The Empress is hurt.

Imperial Guards in their blue and white armour stood aside for him; servants hurried out of his way.

'Laranya,' he was murmuring breathlessly to himself, his voice like a whimper. 'Suran, let her be all right. I will do anything.'

But if the desert goddess heard his plea, she did not answer.

His quarters were not far from his sister's bedchamber. The life of the Keep went on all around as if nothing had happened. Cleaners were polishing the *lach* and dusting the sculptures, night-time activities carried out unobtrusively when most people were asleep. By the time he reached the door to the Imperial chambers, he knew that all the servants here must have heard what the handmaiden heard; yet they pretended otherwise. Since Saramyr houses rarely ever had interior doors due to the need for breezes in the scorching summers, codes of privacy had arisen in which it was extremely rude to eavesdrop or to pass on anything that was inadvertently learned. That Laranya's handmaiden had broken that silence was an indication of how serious she felt it was.

He heard Laranya sobbing before he shoved the curtain aside, and though the sound made him feel as if his heart would break, he was desperately relieved that she was still capable of making it.

She was on the bed, on her hands and knees, in amid a tangle of golden sheets stained with thin smears of blood that looked black in the moonlight. She was weeping as she pawed through the sheets as if searching for something.

She looked up at him, framed between the curving ivory horns that were the bedposts, and her eyes were blackened and swollen.

'I cannot find him,' she whispered. 'I cannot find him.'

Reki's eyes welled. He rushed over to hold her, but she shrieked at him to stay back. He shuddered to a halt in uncomprehending misery.

'I cannot find him!' she howled again. Her battered face was made ugly by bruises and tears. He had never seen her this way before. Whenever she had cried in the past, it had been only a cloud across the sun; but suddenly she seemed like a shade of herself, all the vigour and spirit gone from her. She looked like someone he did not know.

'Who are you searching for?'

She grubbed around in the bloodied sheets again. 'I felt him come out, I felt him *leave* me!' she cried. 'But I cannot see him!' She picked up something tiny that looked like a dense clot of blood, holding it up to the light. Threads of sticky liquid ran through the gaps in her fingers. 'Is that him? Is that him?'

With a sickening wrench, Reki realised where all the blood had come from, and what she was looking for. He felt suddenly dislocated from reality, one beat out of time with the world. He could barely breathe for the horror of seeing his sister this way.

'That is not him,' Reki said. The words seemed to come from elsewhere. 'He is gone. Omecha has him now.'

'No, no, no,' Laranya began to whine, rocking back and forth on her knees. She had discarded the clot. 'It is not him.' She looked up at Reki, her eyes imploring. 'If I find him, I can put him back.'

Reki began to cry, and the sight brought Laranya to new grief. She reached out for him with bloodied hands, and he slumped onto the bed and embraced her. She flinched as they hugged and he let her go reflexively, knowing that he had hurt her.

'What did he do to you?' Reki said, and Laranya wailed, clutching herself to him. He dared not hold her, but he let his hands rest lightly on her back, and tears of fury and grief angled down his thin cheeks.

After a time during which they did not speak, Reki said: 'He needs a name.'

Laranya nodded. Even the unborn needed names for Noctu to record them. It did not matter that they had no idea of the sex of the child. Laranya had wanted it to be a son, for Mos.

'Pehiku,' she muttered.

'Pehiku,' Reki repeated, and silently commended the nephew he would never see to the Fields of Omecha.

That was how Asara found them when she arrived. She had taken a little time to dress, though she wore no make-up and her black hair hung loose over one shoulder. She slipped inside the curtain without asking permission to enter, and stood in the green moonlight silently until Reki noticed her.

'I will kill him,' Reki promised, through gritted teeth. His eyes were red and his nose streaming, forcing him to sniff loudly every so often. Ordinarily he would have been mortified to be seen like this by a woman he found so attractive, but his grief was too clean, too justifiable.

'No, Reki,' Laranya said, and by the steadiness in her voice he knew that sense had returned to her. 'No, you will not.' She raised her head, and Reki saw a little of the old fire in her gaze. 'Father will.'

Reki did not understand for a moment, but Laranya did not wait for him to catch up. She looked to Asara.

'Look in that chest,' she said, motioning to a small, ornate box laced in gold, that lay against one wall. 'Bring me the knife.'

Asara obeyed. She found amid the folded silks a jewelled dagger, and brought it to the Empress.

Reki was faintly alarmed, unsure what his sister intended to do with the blade.

'You have a task, brother,' she said, her swollen lips making repulsive smacking noises as she spoke. 'It will be hard, and the road will be long; but for the honour of your family, you must not shirk it. No matter what may come. Do you hear?'

Reki was taken aback by the gravity in her voice. It seemed appallingly incongruous with the disfigured woman who knelt on the bed with him. He nodded, his eyes wide.

'Then do this for me,' she said, and with that she twisted her long hair into a bunch at the back of her head and put the knife to it.

'*Don't!*' Reki cried, but he was too slow; in three short jerks it was complete, and Laranya's hair fell forward again, cut roughly to the length of her jaw. The rest had come free in her hand.

He moaned as she held the severed hair up in front of him. She tied it into a knot and offered it.

'Take this to Father. Tell him what has happened.'

Reki dared not touch it. To take the hair would be to accept his sister's charge, to be bound by an oath to deliver it which was as sacred as the oath she had made by cutting it off. To the folk of Tchom Rin, the shearing of a woman's hair meant vengeance. It was done only when they were wronged in some terrible way, and it would take blood to redress the balance.

If he gave this to his father, Blood Tanatsua would be at war with the Emperor.

For the briefest of instants, he was dizzyingly aware of how many lives would be sacrificed because of this one act, how much agony and death would come of it. But an instant was all it was, for there were higher concerns here than men's lives. This was about honour. His sister had been brutally beaten, his nephew murdered in the womb. There was no question what had to happen next. And in some cowardly part of his soul, he was glad that the burden ultimately would not fall to him, that he was only a courier.

He took his sister's hair from her, and the oath was made.

'Now go,' she said.

'Now?'

'*Now!*' Laranya cried. 'Take two horses and ride. Switch between them; you'll go faster that way. If Mos finds out, if Kakre hears of this, they will try and stop you. They will try and cover this up with lies, they will play for every moment and use it to arm themselves against our family. Go!'

'Laranya . . .' he began.

'*Go!*' she howled, because she could not bear the parting. He scrambled off the bed, cast one last tearful look at her, then stuffed the hair into the pocket of his bedrobe and fled.

'Not you,' Laranya said quietly, even though Asara had shown no sign of leaving. 'I need your help. There is something that must be done.' Her tone was dull and flinty.

'I am at your command, Empress,' Asara replied.

'Then let me lean on you,' she said. 'And we will walk.'

So they did. Bruised and battered, her nightrobe bloodstained around her thighs, the Empress of Saramyr limped out of her bedchamber on Asara's arm, out through the Imperial chambers, and into the corridors of the Keep. The servants were too amazed to avert their eyes quickly enough. Even the Imperial Guards who stood station at the doorways stared in horror. Their Empress, well loved by all, reduced to a trembling wreck. It was not the done thing for a woman so abused to show herself in public, but Laranya did not shrink from it. Her pride was greater than her vanity; she would not play the game of the servants' silence, would not cower in secret and pretend that nothing had happened. She wore Mos's crimes on her body for all to see.

The Keep was asleep, and there were few people in the corridors and none that dared to detain her; but even so, the route to the Tower of the East Wind was a long and arduous ordeal. Laranya could barely support herself, and though Asara was uncommonly strong, it was a struggle. Her world was a mass of pain, yet still she was conscious of the eyes that regarded her with fear and disbelief as she staggered through their midst. Asara bore her stoically and in silence, and let Laranya direct her.

The Tower of the East Wind, like all the other towers, was connected to the Keep by long, slender bridges positioned at the vertices. It was a tall needle, reaching high above the Keep's flat roof, with a bulbous tip that tapered to a point. Small window-arches pocked its otherwise smooth surface. Far above, a balcony ringed the tower just below where it swelled outward.

The climb was hard on Laranya. The spiral stairs seemed endless, and she would not pause at any of the observation points where chairs were set by the window-arches to view the city. Only when they reached the balcony and stepped out into the warm night air did Laranya allow herself to rest.

Asara stood with her, looking out over the parapet. Close by, the city of Axekami fell away down the hill on which the Keep stood, a multitude of lights speckling the dark. Then the black band of the city walls, and beyond that the plains and the River Kerryn, flowing from the Tchamil Mountains which were too distant to see. The night was clear and the stars bright, and Neryn hung before them, the small green moon low in the eastern sky, an unflawed ball floating in the abyss.

'Such a beautiful night,' Laranya murmured. She sounded strangely peaceful. 'How can the gods be so careless? How can the world go on as normal? Does my loss mean so little to them?'

'Do not look to the gods for aid,' said Asara. 'If they cared in the least for human suffering, they would never have allowed me to be born.'

Laranya did not understand this, did not know what manner of creature she was talking to: an Aberrant whose form shifted like water, whose lack of identity made her a walking shell, loathsome to herself.

Asara turned to the Empress, her beautiful eyes cold. 'Do you mean to do it?'

Laranya leaned over the parapet and looked down to the courtyard far, far below, visibly only by pinpricks of lantern light. 'I have no choice,' she whispered. 'I will not live so . . . diminished. And you know Mos will not let me leave.'

'Reki would have stopped you,' Asara said quietly.

'He would have tried,' the Empress agreed. 'But he does not know what I feel. Mos has taken from me everything I am. But my spirit will strike at him from beyond this world.' She took Asara's arm. 'Help me up.'

The Empress of Saramyr clambered onto the parapet at the top of the Tower of the East Wind, and looked down on all of Axekami. With an effort, she stood straight. Her soiled nightrobe flapped about as the breeze caressed her. She breathed, slowly. So easy . . . it would be so easy to stop the pain.

Then, a gust, rippling the silk against her skin, blowing her newly shorn hair back from her face. It smelt of home, a dry desert wind from the east. She felt a terrible ache, a longing for the vast simplicity of Tchom Rin, when she had not been an Empress and where love had never touched her nor wounded her so cruelly. Where she had never felt her child die inside her.

And with that scent came a new resolve, a strengthening of her ruined core. It felt like the breath of the goddess Suran, revivifying her, imbuing new life. Why throw herself away like this? Why let Mos win? Perhaps she *could* endure the pain. Maybe she could survive the dishonour. She could revenge herself upon him in a thousand different ways, she could make him rue the tragedy he had brought upon himself. The worst he could do was kill her.

If her father declared war, he would be casting himself into a nearly hopeless battle for her sake. Dignity would demand it. All those lives. Yet, if she turned back now, she could send Asara to catch Reki, to stop him. She could seek retribution in ways far more subtle and effective.

'The wind has changed,' said Laranya, after standing there for some minutes, an inch from that terrible drop.

'Doubts?' Asara asked.

Laranya nodded, her eyes faraway.

'I think not,' said Asara, and pushed her.

There was an instant when the Empress of Saramyr teetered, a moment of raw and overwhelming disbelief in which the thousands of routes fate held for her collapsed down to one single dead-end thread; then she tipped out into the dark night and her scream lasted all the way until she hit the courtyard below.

TWENTY-THREE

One hundred and seventy five miles away from where the Empress was falling from the Tower of the East Wind, Kaiku and Tsata hunted by the green light of Neryn.

The Tkiurathi slunk along the shadowed lee of a row of rocks, his gutting-hooks held lightly in his hands. Kaiku was some way behind him; she could not move at the speed he could and still remain quiet.

The cocktail of fear and excitement that Kaiku felt when on the hunt had become almost intoxicating now. For days they had been living on their wits and reactions, staying one step ahead of the beasts that wandered inside the Weavers' invisible barrier. The paralysing terror that she had experienced almost constantly at first had subsided as they had evaded or killed the Aberrant predators time and again. She had learned to be confident in Tsata's ability to keep them alive, and she trusted herself enough to know she was no burden to him.

The shrilling was somewhere to their right. She could hear it, warbling softly to itself, a cooing sound like a wood pigeon that was soft and reassuring and decidedly at odds with the powerhouse of muscle and teeth and sinew that made it. She and Tsata had begun to name the different breeds of Aberrant by now for the sake of mutual identification. They had five so far, and that still left an uncertain number of species that they had only glimpsed. Aside from the gristle-crows and the shrillings, there were the brutal furies, the insidious skrendel, and most dangerous of all, the giant ghauregs. Tsata had named the latter two in Okhamban. The sharp and guttural syllables seemed to suit them well.

On the other side of the row of rocks, a narrow trench cut through the stony earth, scattered with thorny, blight-twisted bushes and straggling weeds. The shrilling's paws crunched on loose gravel and shale as it walked. Its steady, casual gait disturbed Kaiku. As with the other creatures they had encountered, she could not get used to the eerie sensation that it was *patrolling*. Not looking for food or marking its territory or any other understandable animal instinct, but acting as a sentry. It went slow and alert, and if they followed it for long enough Kaiku was certain that it would come back to this spot, treading the same path over and over until it returned to the flood plain and another Aberrant would appear in its stead.

They were not acting like animals. It should have been carnage down on the plain, with that many violent predators in close proximity, but an uneasy peace existed as of enemies forced to be allies by necessity. Skirmishes and squabbles broke out, but never more than an angry snap or scratch before both parties retreated. And then there were the perfectly regular patterns of the gristle-crows' flight during the day, and the curiously organised patrols at night. No, there was something unnatural here.

Tonight, Kaiku meant to find out for sure what that was.

She kept her eyes on the stealthy Okhamban ahead of her. When he was like this, he seemed half-animal himself, a being of primal energy capable of shocking viciousness; it was a bizarre alter-ego to the quiet and contemplative man who had accompanied them across the sea, with his strange and alien mind-set.

A little way ahead of him, a hazy splash of pallid green moonlight spilled through a gap in the rocks. He looked back at her, making an up-and-over motion with one tattooed arm. She took his meaning. Adjusting her rifle on its strap across her back, she slipped up to the dark face of the barrier to their right. She listened: the gentle trill of the Aberrant drifted back to her, the scrape of its paws. With a deliberate tread, it passed the spot where she crouched.

In one quick motion, she pulled herself onto the top of the row and jammed her feet into the uneven folds to brace herself. She swung her rifle around and sighted down into the trench. Her ascent was not as quiet as she would have liked, but it made little difference. Shrillings navigated like bats, blatting a series of frequencies which were picked up and sorted by sense glands in their throat, building up a picture according to which frequencies returned to them and how long they took. It made them exceptional night hunters in their element, but it had the side-effect of limiting their field of perception to what was in front of them. Kaiku had her rifle trained on it squarely, but it kept steadily walking away from her down the trench, towards the gap in the rocks where Tsata waited.

She did not fire. Squatting in the light of Neryn and uncomfortably exposed, she held her nerve and her trigger finger. She was there as a back-up only, in case the worst should happen. The report of a rifle would alert everyone and everything within miles to their presence.

The shrillings were lithe and deadly beasts, an uncomfortable blending of mammal and reptile, preserving the most advantageous aspects of both. Their size, bone structure and movements were like a big cat, but their skin was covered with tough, overlapping scales of natural armour. Elongated skulls curved to a long, smooth crest. Their upper jaws were lipless, and rigid and beaklike, but from beneath them dark red gums sheathed killing teeth. They walked on all fours, though they could stand on two legs for a short time while balancing on their tails, and their forepaws each held a single outsized claw which could unzip flesh and separate muscle effortlessly. They were efficient carnivores who had climbed to the top of their rapidly shifting food chain in the blighted areas of the Tchamil Mountains, using their night-seeing capabilities to pinpoint animals that hid at the sound of their warbling. Fast, streamlined and deadly.

But so was Tsata.

He waited until the creature had just passed the gap in the rocks before he sprang. Movement so close to its body was picked up by some peripheral sense, and it curved its spine to meet him, its jaws gaping wide. But he had predicted it, and swung to one side, so that its teeth snapped shut on nothing but air. He rammed one end of his gutting-hook into its outstretched neck, behind its crest. It spasmed once, but in that time Tsata had swung onto its back, using the embedded gutting-hook as a lever, and buried his second blade into the other side of its throat. Its legs collapsed beneath it and it started to thrash before Tsata wrenched both blades upward, tearing them through the muscle of its neck and severing its vertebrae in a gout of blood and spinal fluid. The shrilling flopped. It was all over in an instant.

Kaiku scrambled down from her perch and slid into the trench. Tsata's gutting-hooks were laid aside, and he had turned the Aberrant's head so as to move its crest out of the way. Its black eye reflected his face as he felt amid the pulses of gore that ran down its neck.

'Have you found it?' Kaiku asked as she hurried up to him. His bare arms and hands were dripping with noxious blood, black in the green moonlight.

'Here,' he said. Kaiku met his glance. 'Can you do this?'

'I have to risk it,' she said. 'For the *pash*.'

He grinned. 'One day I will teach you how to use that word properly.'

The fleeting moment of camaraderie was too brief to enjoy. She put her hands where his were, and felt the repellent skin of the black, wormlike creature attached to the arch of the shrilling's neck, just above the point where Tsata's blades had cut. This was the fourth Aberrant they had killed between them, and every time they had found one of these nauseating things in the same place, deep in the flesh, dead.

This one was not dead yet, but it had only seconds left, its body failing as its host's systems ceased. Seconds were enough.

Kaiku touched it, and opened the Weave. Tsata watched her as her eyes fluttered closed. The dark gush of the Aberrant's blood over the wrists and hands became a trickle as the heart stopped pumping.

The link was easy to follow, once she was inside it. The slug-thing's fading consciousness was like an anchor in the body of the Aberrant beast. Small tendrils of influence were retreating as it died, the hooks it had buried into its deadly host; but the strongest link arced away across the Fault, connected to some far destination like an umbilical cord. She followed it, and it led her to a nexus where dozens of other similar links converged like ribbons around a maypole, wafting in the flow of the Weave.

She read the fibres, and the answers came to her.

The nexus was one of the tall, black-robed strangers. They were not Weavers; they could not shape and twist the Weave. Rather, they were the hands that held a multitude of leashes, and the leashes tethered the Aberrants through the vile entities embedded close to their spines. They were the handlers.

That was how the Aberrants were under control, she realised. Carefully, she probed further. She was not sure to what extent the link operated: did the handlers actively know what the Aberrants know? Did they see through the beasts' eyes? No, surely not, for if the handlers were linked mind-to-mind with the beasts then they would know of Tsata and Kaiku's incursions, and the Weavers would have reacted with much more alarm. She gave up trying to guess; it was useless to speculate at this point.

Her eyes flicked open, and the irises were deepest crimson. She stepped back.

'As we thought,' she murmured. Her gaze went to Tsata's. 'We should go. They will be coming.'

The two of them slipped up the trench, disappearing into the shadows. Tsata led with practiced ease; Kaiku followed, alert for danger. Distantly, a yammering and howling had begun, but by the time the other Aberrants arrived at the scene of the death, the perpetrators had long fled.

Kaiku's glance strayed to the Mask that lay on the ground beside her. Tsata, hunkered down next to her in the glade, intercepted the look.

'It is wearing you down,' he said softly. 'Is it not?'

Kaiku nodded slightly. She picked up her pack and threw it on top of the Mask, obscuring its mocking expression.

The night was warm, but a cooler breeze hinted at the promise of distant winter. Chikkikii cracked and snapped like branches in a fire from the darkness, a staccato percussion as they clicked their rigid wing-cases, underpinning the melodic cheeping of other nocturnal insects and the occasional hoot of some arboreal animal. Neryn's smooth face glowed through the gently swaying network of leaves overhead, dappling the small clearing in restful light, playing across the arches of tough roots that poked out of the ground and the colonies of weeds and foliage that had made their home here. A spray of moonflowers nodded lazily, their petals open in drowsy grey stars, questing up toward the life-giving illumination.

The glade lay beyond the Weavers' barrier of misdirection, a mile east of the point where it began. They never rested inside the danger area, especially not now that the enemy was on the alert. Ever since the first Aberrant sentry had surprised them and they had been forced to kill it, the patrols had been more intense, and gristle-crows scoured the sky during daylight hours. They had only barely escaped that time, for they had wasted precious minutes examining the strange, slimy thing attached to the sentry's neck, and only Tsata's instincts had warned them in time to evade the dozen other Aberrants that came running. It had been just another part of the puzzle: how did the creatures know when one of their own had died?

Since then Kaiku had been forced to shield them more than once from the malevolent attention of a Weaver, hiding them as an unseen presence swept across the domain in search of the mysterious intruders. The Weavers suspected that something was amiss, and the occasional death of one of their creatures must have caused consternation by evidence of the increased security; but they could not find the cause of the disturbance.

They were limited in their thinking. They imagined a rogue tribesman from elsewhere in the Fault had somehow got inside and was now trapped and causing them minor inconvenience. They had not considered the fact that someone was passing freely through their barrier, and so they never looked outside it. Nor, of course, did the Aberrants stray beyond those boundaries. Kaiku and Tsata took advantage of that, to sleep and plan in relative safety.

'I wish to apologise,' Tsata said, out of nowhere.

'Yes?' Kaiku said mildly.

'I was ungenerous in my judgement of you,' he said. He shifted position to a more comfortable cross-legged arrangement: it was one of the few mannerisms that Saramyr and Okhamba shared.

'I had forgotten about it,' Kaiku lied, but Tsata knew her people's ways well enough not to be fooled.

'Among the Tkiurathi it is necessary to say what we think,' he explained. 'Since we do not *own* things, since our community is based on sharing, it is not good to keep things inside us. If we resent someone for taking too much food at every meal, we will tell them so; we do not let it fester. Our equilibrium is maintained by approval or disapproval of the *pash*, and from that we determine the common good.'

Kaiku regarded him evenly with dark red eyes.

'I said that you took on this cause for selfish reasons, and it is still true,' he went on. 'But you are unselfish in your pursuit of that cause. You make many sacrifices, and you ask of nobody what you would not do yourself. I admire that. It runs counter to my experience of Saramyr folk.'

Kaiku could not decide whether to feel praised or insulted by that, for he had complimented her at the same time as deriding her countrymen. She chose to take it in a forgiving spirit.

'You *are* brutal in your honesty, and frank with your opinions,' she said with a weary smile. 'It takes a little time to get accustomed to it. But I did not hold myself offended by what you said.'

His reaction to that was impenetrable. She watched him for a short while. She had become quite used to him now, from the sap-stiffened orange-blond hair that swept back over his skull to the unusual pallor of his skin and the curves of the pale green tattoos over his face and down his bare arms to his fingertips. He no longer seemed foreign, only strange, in the way Lucia was strange. And he was certainly not hampered by the language barrier. He had improved since he had arrived on the shores of her homeland, and his Saramyrrhic was virtually flawless now. In fact, he was uncommonly articulate when he wanted to be.

'What do you think of us, Tsata?' she asked. 'Of Aberrants like me?'

Tsata considered that for a time. 'Nothing,' he replied.

'Nothing?'

'We cannot help the circumstances of our birth,' he said. 'A strong man may be born a strong child, may always outmatch his friends in wrestling or lifting. But if he only uses his strength, if he relies on it alone to make him acceptable, he will fail in other ways. We should only be seen by how we utilise or overcome what we have.'

Kaiku sighed. 'Your philosophies are so simple, and so clear,' she said. 'Yet ideals sometimes cannot weather reality. I wish that life were so uncomplicated.'

'You have complicated it yourself,' Tsata said. 'With money and property and laws. You strive for things you do not need, and it makes you jealous and resentful and greedy.'

'But with those things come medicines, art, philosophy,' Kaiku answered him. 'Do the wrongs in our society that we have to suffer outweigh the benefits of being able to cure plagues that would decimate less developed cultures like yours?' She knew he would not take this as a slight; in fact, she had picked up some of his indelicacy of speech, for only days ago she would have phrased her meaning much more cunningly.

'Your own scholar Jujanchi posited the theory that the survivors of such a plague would be the ones best able to carry on the race,' he argued. 'That your goddess Enyu weeds out the weaker elements.'

'But you would allow yourself to be culled by the whims of nature,' Kaiku put back. 'You live within the forest, and let it rule you like it rules the animals. We have dominated this land.'

'No, you have subjugated it,' he replied. 'More, you have annexed it from the Ugati, who by your own laws had the rights to be here. You did not like your own country, so you took another.'

'And on the way, we stopped at Okhamba, and the Tkiurathi came of that,' she reminded him. 'You cannot make me feel guilty for what my ancestors have done. You said yourself: I cannot help the circumstances of my birth.'

'I do not ask you to feel guilty,' he said. 'I am only showing you the price of your "developed" culture. Your people should not feel responsible for it; but it terrifies me that you ignore it and condone it. You forget the lessons of the past because they are unpalatable, like your noble families ignore the damage the Weavers are doing to your land.'

Kaiku was quiet, listening to the night noises, thinking. There was no heat in the argument. She had gone past the point of feeling defensive about Saramyr, especially since her culture had long ago ostracised her for being Aberrant. It was merely interesting to hear such a coldly analytical and unfavourable point of view on ways of life she had always taken for granted. His perspective intrigued her, and they had talked often over the last few days about their differences. Some aspects of the Tkiurathi way she found impossible to believe would work in practice, and others she found incomprehensible; but there were many valid and enviable facets to their mode of living as well, and she learned a lot from those conversations.

Now she turned matters to more immediate concerns. She brushed her fringe away from her face and adopted a more decisive tone.

'Matters are beyond doubt,' she said. 'The Weavers have a way to control the Aberrants. We do not know exactly how, but it is connected to the creatures that we have found on the back of the Aberrant's necks.' She rolled her shoulders tiredly. 'We can assume that every Aberrant down there has one.'

'And we know now that it is not the Weavers who control them,' Tsata added. 'But the *other* masked ones.'

'So we have that much, at least, to aid us,' she said, scratching at some mud on her boot. 'What is next?'

'We must fill in the gaps in our knowledge,' Tsata replied. 'We must kill one of the black-robed men.'

The next day dawned red, and stayed red until late morning. History would record that the Surananyi blew for three days in Tchom Rin after the Empress Laranya's death, striking unexpectedly and without warning. The hurricanes flensed the deserts in the east, sandstorms raged, and the dust rose like a cloud beyond the mountains to stain Nuki's eye the colour of blood. Later, when the news of Laranya's tragic suicide had spread across the empire, it would be said that the tempest was the fury of the goddess Suran at the death of one of her most beloved daughters, and that Mos was forever cursed in her eyes.

But Lucia knew nothing of this beyond a vague unease that settled in her marrow that morning, and did not abate until the Surananyi had ceased. She sat by a rocky brook on the northern side of the valley where the Fold lay, and looked to the east, and imagined she could hear a distant howling as of some unearthly voice in rage and torment.

Flen sat with her. He was tall for his age, gangly with sudden growth, possessed of a head of dark brown hair that flopped loosely over his eyes and a quick, ready smile. He had not smiled all that much this morning.

Lucia had changed.

She had not told him about the trip to Alskain Mar until after they had returned, and then only in the barest terms. Of course none of the adults thought he was important enough to know, but it was Lucia's decision to keep it a secret that hurt him. It was not entirely a surprise: nothing Lucia did was too unusual, for she had always seemed to operate on some level quite apart from everybody else, and it made her strange and fascinating. But it troubled him deeply that she was *different* now, and he was frightened that she was becoming more detached.

It was not something he could describe; only a feeling, in the instinctive way that adolescents navigated their way through the passage to adulthood. Like the sly, forbidden self-assuredness of a newly shed virginity that the inexperienced unconsciously deferred to; like the constantly switching hierarchy of friendships and leaders and scapegoats that was ingrained in pubescents without them knowing who gave them the rules or even that they were following rules at all.

There was a new distance in her pale blue eyes now. Something had been shed, and a new skin grown underneath; something lost, something gained. She had talked to a creature that was one step down from a god. She had *died*, however briefly, and it had shifted her perspective somewhere that Flen could not follow. She seemed to have aged, not outwardly but in the measure of her responses and her tone. And all Flen could think was that he was losing his best friend, and how unfair it was.

They sat together for a long time on the edge of that rocky brook, leaning against a boulder. Tall grasses rose all around them, tickling the backs of their knees. The brook trickled through a chicane of broken stone from the valley rim, and dragonflies droned about, moving in jerky little spurts to hover before their faces, studying them uncomprehendingly. The sky was pink, and the cascading tiers of houses to their right had a sinister and brooding quality in that light, no longer homely but a jumble of jagged edges and smoothly rounded blades.

Below them, on the flat valley floor, a herd of banathi was grazing, watched over by a dozen men and women on horseback. Flen watched them shamble idly about, cropping the grass with their wide, rubbery mouths. They were huge creatures but very docile, beasts seemingly destined to exist only to feed predators. Though the bulls possessed enormous curving horns, they only ever used them in the mating season when competing for females. In ancient times, they had roamed freely across the plains; now they were almost entirely bred for meat and milk.

It was while Flen was musing on the lot of the banathi that Lucia finally spoke, as he knew she would.

'Forgive me,' she said quietly.

Flen shrugged. 'I always do,' he said.

She took his arm and leaned her head on his shoulder. 'I know what you think. That things are different now.'

'Are they?'

'Not between us,' she replied.

Flen adjusted himself so that they were both more comfortable. He had bony shoulders.

'You understand, though,' she said. 'There are things I can't explain. Things there are no words for.'

'You live in a place different to me,' he said. 'It's like . . . you live beyond a door, and I can only see through the cracks around the edges. You see what's inside the room, but I can only catch a glimpse. It's always been that way.' He put a hand on her thin forearm, her delicate wrist. 'You're alone, and everyone else is shut out.'

She smiled a little. How like Flen, to turn around her apology to make it seem as if it were she who deserved sympathy.

She drew herself upright again. 'I shouldn't tell you this . . .' she said, her voice dropping in volume.

'But you will,' he grinned.

'This is very important, Flen,' she told him. 'You can't let anybody else hear of it.'

'When have I ever?' he asked rhetorically.

Lucia regarded him for a moment. She had a way of seeing into people that was frankly uncanny; but she did not need to doubt him. She knew that Flen counted her the most important person alive, and not because of any expectations of healing the land or ruling the empire. It was simply because she was his best friend.

There was one thing that she had never quite been able to puzzle out about him, though: why did he *want* to be with her? Not that she thought herself unpopular: on the contrary, she had a wide circle of friends, who seemingly came to her without any effort on her part, attracted by some magnetism of personality that she did not really understand since she was by no means the most lively or social of people. But Flen had been virtually inseparable from her since the day they had met. He had always sought her out before any others, had always possessed a seemingly endless patience for her quirks and oddities. She had given virtually nothing back for a long time. She enjoyed his company, and allowed him to be with her, but she was in a world of her own and she had learned by then that it was useless inviting anyone to join her there.

Yet he had persisted. He was a popular boy himself, and she often wondered why he did not spend his time with someone whom he did not need to make such an effort for; but she was always his priority, and gradually, *gradually*, she became used to him. Of all the people she had ever known, he was the one closest to understanding her, and she loved him for it. She loved his guileless, unselfish heart and his honesty. Though they made a strange pair, they were friends, in the purity of that state that only exists before the complication of adulthood corrupts it.

'I'll tell you what I learned in Alskain Mar,' she said.

'Spirits, I thought you'd never get round to it,' Flen said mischievously. She did not laugh or smile, but she knew it was his way to joke when he was nervous or uncertain, and he was suddenly both. Lucia's expression was grave. She was remembering the horror on Zaelis's face as she passed on to him the things the spirit had showed her, the coldness in Cailin's eyes.

'Maybe *learn* is the wrong word,' she corrected herself. 'I didn't learn as if someone was teaching me. It was . . . as if I was remembering and prophesying at the same time; as if it was a memory and a prediction of a future that had already come to pass. At first it was hard to understand . . . it still *is* hard for me to think on it. The things I know now aren't clear.' She looked down at the ground and began to fiddle with a blade of grass. 'It was like hanging onto the fin of a whale, and having it plunge you down further than you can imagine to the wonders at the bottom of the sea. Except that your eyes can't focus underwater, so it's all a blur. You can't open your mouth to speak. And sooner or later you remember that the whale doesn't need to breathe as much as you do.'

'What did it show you?'

'It showed me the witchstones,' she said, and her gaze seemed suddenly haunted.

When she did not elaborate for a time, Flen prompted her: 'And what did you see?'

She shook her head slightly, as if in denial of what she was about to say. 'Flen, I am part of something much bigger than anyone thought,' she whispered. She clutched his hands and looked up to meet his stare. 'We all are. This isn't just about an empire; this isn't a matter of who sits on the throne, no matter how many thousand lives are at stake. The Golden Realm itself watches us with the keenest intent, and the gods themselves are playing their hand.'

'You're saying that the gods are controlling things?' Flen asked, unable to keep a hint of scepticism from his voice.

'No, no,' Lucia said. 'The gods don't *control*. They're more subtle than that. They use avatars and omens, to bend the will of their faithful to do their work. There's no predestination, no destiny. We all have our choices to make. It's *us* who have to fight our battles.'

'Then what . . .'

'Kaiku always said that the witchstones were alive, but she was only half right,' Lucia explained, uncharacteristically hurried. The words were trembling out of her and she could not stop them. 'They're not just alive, they're *aware*! Not like the spirits of the rocks in the earth; not like the simple thoughts of the trees. They're intelligent, and malevolent, and they are becoming more so with every passing day.'

Flen barely knew whether to credit this at all, but he did not have the chance to decide.

'The Weavers are not our true enemies, Flen!' Lucia cried, her face an unnatural red in the dust-veiled morning sun. 'They believe themselves the puppet masters, but they are only the puppets. Slaves to the witchstones.'

'This is—' Flen began, but Lucia interrupted him again.

'You have to hear me out!' she snapped, and Flen was shocked into silence. For the first time he began to appreciate the depth of Lucia's terror at what she had found out in Alskain Mar. 'The witchstones *use* the Weavers. They make them think that they are operating to their own agenda, but no Weaver really knows who sets that agenda; they believe it part of a collective consciousness. That consciousness is the will of the witchstones. The Weavers are only the foot-soldiers. They are *addicts*, trapped by their longing for the witchstone dust in their Masks, not even knowing that in gaining their powers they are subverting themselves to a higher master.'

She looked around, as if fearing someone was listening; and indeed it seemed that way, for the dragonflies had quieted and departed, and the wind had fallen. 'That first witchstone, the one beneath Adderach . . . it ensnared the miners who found it. It was weak then, starved for thousands of years, but they were weaker. They took the dust, driven by some compulsion they did not understand. They learned to give it blood in the same way. It grew, and as it grew its power grew, and it sent the Weavers out into the world to be its eyes and ears and hands. It sent them to find more witchstones.'

'But what *are* the witchstones?' Flen asked.

'The answers were in front of us, but nobody wanted to believe it,' Lucia whispered. '*I* would not have believed it, except that what the spirit of Alskain Mar showed me was more than truth or lies or fact or fiction. Even that spirit was not old enough to have witnessed what happened all that time ago, but it told me what it knew.'

She closed her eyes, squeezed them tightly shut, and when she spoke she was using a more formal mode of speech, used when referring directly to the gods.

'The gods fought, in an epoch when civilisation had barely left its cradle. In that time, the entity we call Aricarat, youngest of Assantua and Jurani, made war in the Golden Realm, for reasons lost to history. He almost overthrew Ocha himself, but in a last stand his own parents led an army that slew him, in a battle that tore the skies. At his death, his own aspect in the tapestry of the world – the fourth moon that bore his name – was destroyed, and pieces of the moon rained down onto the world in the cataclysm that Saran told us about.' She squeezed his hands harder. 'But he was not dead,' she whispered. 'Not while a part of him remained in the tapestry . . . in *our* world. The moon came down in pieces, and some of those pieces survived. In each of them, a tiny fragment of Aricarat's spirit remained. Dormant.'

'Fragments?'

Lucia nodded and released his hands, lifting her head. 'Fragments of a shattered god. They have lain there for thousands of years, until chance unearthed one again in the spot where Adderach now stands. Now it uses the Weavers to reach out to other fragments, unearthing them, awakening them with blood sacrifice. They are linked, as the Weavers are linked, like a web. Each one that they dig up makes the whole stronger; each one gives the Weavers more power. They are the fractured pieces of Aricarat; and each one they rescue is one step closer to his resurrection.' Her eyes filled with tears, and her voice became quiet and fearful. 'He's so angry, Flen. I felt his rage. Right now he is still weak, only a shadow of his former self, impotent; but his hate burns so brightly. He will dominate this land, and he will dominate all the lands. And when enough of the witchstones have been awoken, he will return, and wreak his vengeance.'

Flen did not have a response to that. The bloody light of Nuki's eye seemed infernal, bathing the valley in dread.

'Already his power works against Enyu and her children, the gods and goddesses of natural things,' Lucia continued. 'His very existence poisons the land, twists the animals and the people who eat of its crops. If he wins here, he will take the battle to the Golden Realm, against the gods themselves. That is why we have to stop him. For if the Weavers and the witchstones are not destroyed now, they will engulf the world like a shroud. And that will only be the beginning.'

A single tear slid from her eye and coursed down her cheek. 'It is a new war of the gods, played out here in Saramyr. And all of Creation is at stake.'

TWENTY-FOUR

Over Zila, grey clouds blanketed the sky, turning midday into a muted, steely glower. A horseman in Blood Vinaxis livery rode from the massive south gate of the town, down the hill towards where the lines of troops waited, overlooked by tall siege engines. Behind him, the gate boomed shut.

Xejen watched him go from the window of his chamber at the top of the keep, hands clasped behind his back, drumming his fingertips nervously on his knuckles. When the rider was out of sight, he swung around to where Bakkara stood scratching his jaw. Mishani reclined on a settee against one wall, her hair spilling over her shoulder, her eyes revealing nothing.

'What do you think?' Xejen asked them.

Bakkara shrugged. 'What difference does it make? They're going to attack us anyway, whether we give them a "gesture of good faith" or not. They just don't want the embarrassment of dealing with a bunch of minor noble families who'll be angry if their sons and daughters get killed during the liberation.'

'Liberation?' Xejen said, with a high laugh. 'Spirits, you talk like you're on their side.'

'They'll call it a liberation if they win,' he said equably. 'Besides, what's the choice? We can hardly send them out any hostages. The mob had them when we took this town.'

'That news will not win you any friends,' Mishani pointed out.

'So we just refuse, then,' Xejen concluded, snapping his fingers at the air. 'Let them believe we have the hostages. As you say, they'll attack us anyway, sooner or later. But I have faith in Zila's walls, unlike you.' He finished with a sharp look at the grizzled soldier.

'I would not advise that,' Mishani said. 'A flat refusal will make them think you are stubborn and unwilling to parlay. Next time, they will not trouble themselves. And you may need to fall back on negotiation if things do not go according to your plan.'

Bakkara suppressed a smile. For such a small and dainty thing, she was remarkably self-assured. It was evidence of her skill at politics that she had, over the last few days, installed herself as Xejen's primary adviser while still never giving him a straight answer as to whether she would declare her support for the Ais Maraxa or not. Xejen was pathetically eager for her help, for Bakkara's help, for anyone who was more decisive than he was. In matters concerning Lucia, his mind was sharp and clear and inflexible; but now he had won himself a town, he appeared increasingly unsure of what to do with it. He may have been a powerful motivator, but he knew nothing of military matters, and left most of it to Bakkara, whom he had declared his second-in-command in Zila after the revolt.

'What would you do, then, Mistress Mishani?' Bakkara asked with exaggerated reverence. She ignored the tone.

'Send them Chien,' she said.

Bakkara barked a laugh in surprise, then shut his mouth. Xejen glared at him.

'Is there some joke I'm missing?' he asked.

'Apologies,' Bakkara said wryly. 'I'm merely touched by the noble sacrifice Mistress Mishani is making. She could have pleaded her own case, after all.'

Mishani gazed evenly at Xejen, disregarding the soldier's jibe. She had no intention of pleading her own case. If she went out there, news of her presence would be everywhere within a day, and she would be an easy target for her father's men. Besides, she knew perfectly well that Xejen would not allow her to leave. She was too precious an asset to him, and she remained so by making him believe that she shared the same goals and beliefs as he.

'Send them *one* hostage as a gesture of good faith,' she said. 'He does not know that the other nobles have died; for all he is aware, there could be many more imprisoned in the donjons of the keep. Chien is useless to you anyway, and what is more, he is very ill and your physician has been unable to do anything to help him.' She glanced at Bakkara. 'He is innocent, and does not deserve to be here.'

'He will tell them of the strength of our forces,' Xejen said, stalking around the room. 'He will name names.'

'He has barely been outside the room you put him in,' Mishani replied. 'He knows nothing of your forces.'

'And as to naming names,' Bakkara put in, 'isn't that what we *want* to happen?'

'Exactly,' Mishani agreed. 'Chien is a major player among merchants and maritime industries. If he starts talking, his ships will carry the word across the Near World.'

Xejen twiddled the fingers on one hand. He was obviously persuaded, but he was making a great show of deliberation. Evidently he thought someone like Mishani might be fooled by that, and he would not seem quite so eager to agree with her.

'Yes, yes, it could work,' he muttered to himself. 'Will you talk to him, Mistress Mishani?'

'I will talk to him,' Mishani said.

As it turned out, it was not quite as easy as Mishani had thought.

'I will not leave you alone here!' Chien raged. 'You can't ask me to do this!'

Mishani was as impassive as always, but inside she was frankly shocked at the sudden fierceness of his emotion. He had been moved to more comfortable quarters after his confinement had ended. It was no different from the rest of the drab keep, comprising a few heavy wall hangings, rugs, a comfortable bed in consideration of his weak state and a few odds and ends like a table and a chest for clothes. She had not exaggerated the severity of his fever to Xejen; but he obviously felt well enough to get angry, even if he was still too weak to stand up.

'Calm yourself!' she snapped, and the sudden harshness in her voice quieted him. 'You are acting like a child. Do you think I would not rather come with you? I want you to go because you must do something for me that only you can do.'

His hair had grown out a little during his confinement, a black stubble across his broad scalp, and he had evidently not been inclined to put a razor to it yet. He gave her a reluctantly mollified look and said: 'What is it, then, that only I can do?'

'You can help save my life,' she said. It was calculated to stall the last of his indignation, and it worked.

'How?' he asked. Now he was ready to hear it.

'I need you to take a message for me,' she told him. 'To Barak Zahn tu Ikati.'

Chien watched her suspiciously. 'The Barak Zahn who is besieging this town?'

'The same,' she said.

'Go on,' Chien prompted.

'You must ask to meet him alone. You cannot let anyone else know I am here. If you do, my father's men will be waiting for me upon my release.'

'And what will I tell him?'

Mishani lowered her head, the thick, braided ropes of black hair swaying with the movement. 'Tell him I have news of his daughter. Tell him she is alive and well and that I know where she is.'

Chien's eyes narrowed. 'The Barak Zahn doesn't have a daughter.'

'Yes, he does,' Mishani said levelly.

Chien held her gaze for a moment, then sagged. 'How can I leave you here?' he asked, more to himself than her. 'There is an army outside, waiting to assault this place, and it is defended by peasants and tradesmen.'

'I know your honour demands that you stay, Chien,' Mishani said. 'But you will be doing me a service greater than all the protection you can offer if you leave Zila and take my message. That is all I ask of you. Barak Zahn will do the rest.'

'Mistress Mishani . . .' he groaned. 'I cannot.'

'It is my best chance at surviving this siege, Chien,' she told him. She walked over to his bedside and looked down. 'I know who sent you, Chien,' she said quietly. 'She swore you to secrecy, did she not? My mother.'

Chien tried to conceal his reaction, but against Mishani it was hopeless. The flicker in his eyes told her everything she needed to know.

'I will not ask you to break your oath,' Mishani said. She sat on the edge of his bed. 'She must have had word of me when I passed through Hanzean on my way out to Okhamba. I can only thank fortune that it was her people and not my father's who spotted me. During the month I was at sea, she contacted you; I imagine it was through a Weaver, but I doubt it was our family's. She asked you to safeguard me against my father.'

She felt tears threatening again, but she forced them down and they did not show. Her mother, her quiet, neglected mother, had been working behind the scenes all this time to protect her daughter. Gods, what if Avun had found out? What would have happened to Muraki then?

Chien was watching her silently, refusing to speak.

'She offered you release,' Mishani said. 'The bonds that tie you to Blood Koli have been all that have held your family back these long years, the marriage price of your mother, who was a fisherwoman in my father's fleet. If you were free of your debt, you would no longer need to offer my family the best price, the best ships to distribute their produce. You could rule the trade lane between Saramyr and the jungle continent.' She studied him closely for confirmation, although she was already certain that she was right. It all fitted at last. 'You would risk much for that, to free your family. My mother offered it to you. She is the only one other than Avun with the power to annul the contract. And she would do it, whatever the cost to herself, if you would keep me safe on my journey.'

Chien's eyes dropped, ashamed. He wanted to ask how she knew, but to do so would be to admit that she was right. Mishani did not wish to torture him. She understood now. All the time, she had been looking for his angle, trying to determine what he hoped to gain from her; but she had never considered *this.*

'There was one more thing,' Mishani said softly, pushing her hair back over one shoulder. 'My mother gave you a sign, in case there was no other way to persuade me. She knew how suspicious I would be. It was a lullaby, a song which she herself wrote. She used to sing it when I was young. It was about me. Only she and I knew the words.' She got up, her back to him. 'You sang it in your fever dream last night.'

Chien did not say anything for a long while; then finally, he spoke: 'If I do this for you, you will tell her that I fulfilled my oath?'

'I swear it,' Mishani said, not turning around. 'For you have acted with honour. Forgive me for mistrusting you.'

Chien lay back in his bed. 'I will do as you ask,' he said.

'My thanks,' Mishani said. 'For everything.' And with that, she left.

They did not see each other again before Chien was carried out of the gates and down to the waiting army. Mishani did not watch him go. She stood with her back to the window, alone.

*

Later, she offered herself to Bakkara, and they coupled urgently in his room.

She could not have said why she felt moved to do so then; it was entirely against her character. She should have waited, should have ensured that the moment was right. She found him appealing, and sensed that he felt the same towards her, but that was as far as it went; beyond that, there was only politics, and the fact that it made good sense to lie with him. She had ascertained by now that Xejen was not the leader his reputation made him out to be, and that Bakkara was eminently more suitable for the position. And she knew well the power a woman's art could have over a man, even one to whom she was merely an interesting and pleasurable diversion.

Yet, in the end, it had been something else that had driven her to him, to discard subtlety for immediate gratification. The episode with Chien had made her ache with a loneliness she had not imagined she could feel, a throbbing void that was too much for her to bear, and she wanted rid of it any way she could. The ethereal touch of her mother in her affairs had reminded her how adrift she was, how much she had given up to oppose her father. But she could not afford to grieve here. There was too much at stake.

She was not foolish enough to think that she could bury the pain permanently amid the throes of orgasm, but she could at least push it aside for a time.

Afterwards, when the treacherous glow had faded that sometimes made her say unguarded things, she lay alongside the soldier and ran her tiny hand over his scarred chest, curling her fingertips in the coarse hair between his pectoral bulges. His arm was around her, dwarfing her, and though she was bony and angular and thin she still felt soft against him. The warmth of a man's body was something she had almost forgotten that she missed.

'You do not think Xejen can do this, do you?' she said quietly. It was a statement.

'Hmm?' he murmured drowsily.

'You do not think he is capable of running this revolt and winning.'

He sighed irritably, his eyes still closed. 'I doubt it.'

'So why—'

'Are you going to keep asking questions all night?'

'Until I get some answers, yes,' she smiled.

He groaned and rolled over a little so that they were face to face. She gave him a little kiss on the lips.

'Every man's nightmare,' he said. 'A woman who won't shut up after she's been seen to.'

'I am merely interested in my chances of surviving the situation *you* put me in,' she said. 'Why are you here at all?'

He picked up a handful of her unbound hair that had fallen between them and rubbed it idly with his calloused fingertips.

'I come from the Newlands,' he said tangentially. 'There was a lot of conflict there when I was young. Land disputes, merchant wars. I was a boy, poor and hardworking and full and anger. Being a soldier was the best I could hope for, so I joined the Mark's militia, a tiny little village army. It turned out I was good at it. I got recruited into the army of a minor noble, we won a few battles . . . Gods, I'm even boring myself now.'

Mishani laughed. 'Do go on.'

'Let me skip all that. So many years – *many* years – later, I ended up a general in Blood Amacha's army, on the other side of the continent. I was something of a mercenary by then, not blood-bound to any master since my original Barak had managed to get himself killed and his family wiped out. I was there at the battle outside Axekami five years ago.'

Mishani stiffened fractionally.

'Don't worry,' he chuckled. 'I hardly blame you for what your father did. Especially after what Xejen told me about you and he.' His mirth faded, and he became serious. 'A lot of men I'd known died in that battle. I was lucky to get out alive.' He was silent for a moment, and when he continued his tone was resigned. 'But that's the way of it as a soldier. Friends die. Battles are won and lost. I do the best for myself and my men, but in the end, I'm just one part in thousands. A muscle. It's the brain that directs us all. It's those higher up who take the responsibility for a massacre like that. Sonmaga was a fool, and your father was treacherous. And many people were killed for both of them.'

Mishani was not sure what to say to that. She was suddenly terribly conscious of how strong he was. He could snap her bones like twigs if he just tightened the arm that he had around her shoulders.

'After that, I said I was done with soldiering,' he went on. 'But soldiering wasn't done with me, I suppose. Thirty years and more I've spent fighting other men's wars, sitting round fires with people and not knowing whether they'll be alive in the morning, living in tents and marching all over Saramyr. It may not sound like much, but it's hard to give up. There's a feeling between fighting men, a bond like you can't imagine that doesn't exist anywhere else. I tried to settle, but it's too late for me; I'm a soldier in the blood now.'

Mishani relaxed a little now that he had strayed off the more dangerous subject of her family's crimes. She began to idly trace lines on his arms as she listened.

'So I drifted. Couldn't find a purpose. I'd never needed one till then. I was drinking in a cathouse when I heard about the Ais Maraxa. Don't know why, but it caught my interest. So I started to investigate a little, and soon they heard about it and they found me.'

'You had something to believe in,' Mishani supplied for him.

His face scrunched as if in distaste. 'Let's just say it was a cause I thought was worthy. I'm a follower, Mistress Mishani, not a leader. I might command men, but I don't start wars, I don't change the world. That's not for people like me; that's for people like Xejen. He might not know a thing about war, but he's a leader. The Ais Maraxa would die for him.'

'Would you?'

'I'd die for Lucia,' he said. 'Seems much more sensible than any of the other causes I've been willing to die for in the past. Which were mostly to do with money.'

Neither of them spoke for a time. Bakkara was drowsing again when he felt Mishani's face crease into a smile.

'I know you're going to say something,' he said warningly. 'So have it over with.'

'You never answered my question.'

'Which one?'

'Why did you help take Zila if you thought that you couldn't hold it?'

'Xejen thought we could. He believes. That's enough.' He considered for a moment. 'Maybe the tide will turn yet.'

'So you don't take any of the responsibility? Even thought you think it's foolishness, you're following him.'

'I've followed greater fools,' he muttered. 'And responsibility is a matter for philosophers and politicians. I'm a soldier. Hard as it may be to imagine, I do what I do with no clearer motive than because I do it.'

'Or maybe you do not see your own motive.'

'Woman, if you don't shut up right now then I will be forced to do something to you to shut you up.'

'Oh?' Mishani said innocently. 'And what might that be?'

Bakkara showed her, and after that she let him sleep; but she was awake, and thinking.

She could not leave Zila: Xejen would not let her. And she certainly had no intention of remaining trapped in here for the next year. Instead, she had concocted a plan to invite Barak Zahn into the town in order to sound him out about Lucia, to make the negotiations she had wanted to make in Lalyara. To try and recruit him to the Libera Dramach with the news that they had his daughter. In Zila, she would bargain from a position of advantage, and Zahn would have to listen to her. But again, Xejen was the problem; he would stop her as soon as he knew what she was up to.

Xejen was an obstacle that had to be removed. Bakkara was not only the better leader, and the person most able to keep Zila in order and safe from their enemies, but he was also more malleable. Therefore, she would slowly work on both Bakkara and Xejen, undermining the one with the other to bring Bakkara – and hence herself – out on top. Once Bakkara had the primacy, she could manipulate him into her way of thinking, but Xejen was too intransigent, too rigid in his zeal.

This was her aim, then. She only needed time . . .

It was dark where Mos was.

The air stank of blood. Monstrous shapes loomed half-seen to either side and overhead. A quiet clanking came from above, the tapping of chains as they stirred in the heat. The only light was a sullen red glow from the embers of the fire-pit.

Into that light came a dead face, a corpse-mask of emaciated flesh in a ghastly yawn, hooded and shadowed. Mos looked at it across the fire-pit. His own features were haggard and drawn, his eyes swollen with weeping, his features slack.

Above them, Weave-lord Kakre's kites of skin gazed down emptily from the blackness.

'He is gone, then?' Kakre croaked.

'He is gone,' Mos replied.

'You have sent men to search for him?'

'He will not get far.'

'That remains to be seen.'

Mos looked down into the embers, as if there might be some solace there. 'What possessed me, Kakre?'

The Weave-lord did not reply. He knew well what had possessed Mos; but even he had not expected the Empress to commit suicide. It would have been enough for her to be beaten so that Laranya's father could learn of it and be incited to gather the armies of the desert in outrage. This was a better result than he could have hoped. And having Mos kidnap Reki in order to minimise the damage was just perfect; all it would take was a small leak of information, arranged by Kakre, and Tchom Rin's response would be assured.

Kakre had gone to Mos after the beating and found him weeping and pathetic, pleading for help – as if Kakre was someone he could confess to, who might offer succour. It had been made to look like coincidence, but very little that Kakre did was without forethought. While he was with the Emperor he could not Weave, for Weaving required all his concentration and Mos would know.

He had not been able to witness Laranya's last moments; but he had been provided with a perfect alibi that exonerated him from any suspicion of a hand in the Empress's death. Even Mos – poor, poor Mos – had never even thought of the possibility that the dreams that sent him mad had been coming from Kakre. Kakre had been too sly; he had cut away that line of reasoning from Mos's mind, so that it never got to flower.

'Barak Goren tu Tanatsua will hear of his daughter's death long before Reki reaches him,' Kakre rasped at last. 'And he will know the circumstances. Laranya was not discreet about her condition.' He stirred, his hood throwing his face into shadow. 'Her hair was cut, Mos. You know what that means.'

'Perhaps if we have Reki, his father may pause and listen to reason.' Mos's words were empty of feeling. He did not really care either way. He was merely going through the motions of being Emperor, because he had nothing else left now.

'Nevertheless,' Kakre said, 'preparations must be made. With your marriage to Laranya, the desert Baraks were pacified for a long time; but now that link is severed, they will react badly. They have ever been the troublesome ones. Too autonomous for their own good, within their trackless realm of sand.'

Mos gazed blankly at Kakre for a time, sweat creeping from his brow in the heat of the skinning-chamber.

'If they come to Axekami, they will encourage the other discontented Baraks,' Kakre told him. 'Imagine a desert army marching through Tchamaska and up the East Way, intent on demanding satisfaction for Laranya's death. Imagine how powerless that will make you seem.'

Mos could not really picture it.

'You should send men to Maxachta,' the Weave-lord advised. 'Many men. If you must meet them, meet them in the mountains at the Juwacha Pass. Contain them there. Prevent them from coming into the west.'

'I need all my men here,' Mos replied, but there was no strength in his voice.

'For what? For Blood Kerestyn? They have made only noises and taken no action. It will take them years to become strong enough to challenge you. Axekami is unassailable by any force in Saramyr at the moment; unless the desert Baraks join with those in the west, that is.'

Mos thought on that for a little while.

'I will send men,' he said, as Kakre had known he would. Mos had not been listening to his advisers, and Kakre had carefully underestimated the size of the forces that were being ranged against the Emperor in the wake of the gathering starvation. The signal would be sent tonight to Barak Avun tu Koli, advising him to begin the muster of the armies. The Imperial forces were dividing, and many thousands would be marching far from Axekami to meet the potential desert threat, leaving the capital weaker for their absence.

The game begins, Kakre thought, and behind his mask his ruined face twisted into a smile.

TWENTY-FIVE

Kaiku slid recklessly down the shale slope, her boots pluming dust in the sharp white moonlight. Tsata had already reached the bottom and was levelling his rifle back up it, to where the undulating rim was framed against Aurus's huge, blotched face. At any instant, he expected to see the silhouette of their pursuer blocking out the light, for it to come raging down after Kaiku.

The ghaureg roared, a sound that was a cross between a bear and a wolf cry. It was closing on them fast.

Kaiku fled headlong past him as he covered the point where he guessed the Aberrant monster would emerge. The land around her was virtually devoid of vegetation, just a broken tangle of rocks and hard, stony soil. She made for a spot where the land slipped lower and a ridge rose up on the left. Maybe cover could be found there. Or maybe the ghaureg would just use it to jump down on top of them.

Then Tsata was with her, taking the lead. They ran at a crouch down the decline, the ledge screening them from view. The ghaureg bellowed again, terrifyingly close. Over the thump of her heart and the scuff of their footsteps she heard the creature loping nearer, its heavy tread reminding her of the sheer mass that their pursuer possessed. If they got within reach of those arms, those rending hands, they would be ripped to pieces.

The apparent disappearance of its prey gave the Aberrant pause. Tsata and Kaiku took advantage of that to put distance between them and it. The decline became shallow and fractured, depositing them into a wide, flat-bottomed trench scattered with rocks. On the far side, a natural wall rose to higher ground, pale and grim in the combined light of Aurus and Iridima, whose orbits had lately begun to glide closer, threatening the prospect of a moonstorm if the third sister joined them in the nights to come.

Kaiku struck out for a cluster of rocks. They were too exposed here. If they could get out of its sight for long enough, she was sure it would give up the chase. Though the ghauregs were brutal and dangerous, they were not the most intelligent of the predator species that the Weavers had collected.

But Shintu was not on her side that night. They had almost gained the shadow of the rocks when the Aberrant appeared on the ridge. Kaiku caught a frightened glance of its shape, its head low between its hunched shoulders as it surveyed the trench. Then it saw them, its eyes meeting Kaiku's and sending a shiver down her back. With a howl, it leaped from the ridge down to the floor of the trench, a clear twenty feet; Kaiku felt the impact of its landing through the soles of her boots.

Ghauregs. They were the largest of the Aberrants that Kaiku and Tsata had yet encountered in the Fault, and by far the most vicious. But they were also the most disturbingly akin to humans, and that struck Kaiku worst of all. When she had first heard their roars and seen their shaggy outlines in the night, she had found them unsettlingly familiar; it was only days later when she realised that she had hidden from those very creatures in the Lakmar Mountains on Fo, huddling and shivering in the snow during her lone trek to trace her father's footsteps back to the Weaver monastery. Then, they had been ghostly, half-seen things, glimpsed against white horizons; now they were brought into relief, and she found that they were worse than she had imagined.

They stood eight feet high, though their habitual slouching posture meant that they would be even taller if fully upright. They were somewhat apelike in appearance and though they could run on all fours, their back legs were thick and large enough to allow them to stand on two legs, and they tended to walk that way, contributing to their grotesquely human-like appearance. Their skulls were huge, dominated by enormous jaws that were heavy enough to account for their slouch. The jaws were like steel traps, bearded with shaggy fur and full of omnivore teeth, blunt at the sides and sharp at the front. Small, yellow eyes and a snub snout were little more than mechanisms for locating what to eat next.

Their bodies were covered in a thick grey pelt, but their hands and chests and feet were bare, and the skin beneath was a wrinkled black. Though they did not have the natural weaponry of some of the other predator species, they made up for it in sheer size and power: their strength was truly appalling. And they were not slow, either.

Kaiku froze for the shortest of seconds as it landed in the trench and began to pound towards them on all fours, paralysed by the sheer size of the beast. Then Tsata was pulling her again, and she fled.

Her *kana* boiled inside her, fighting for release, as they raced across the trench. She dared not let it go. She had only been able to get away with using it before, on the dead shrilling, because she had employed it in an extremely subtle way. If she did something as violent as attacking the Aberrant, the Weavers here would detect it and spare no effort to find her.

Yet they were fast running out of other options.

'Here!' Tsata cried suddenly. 'This way!'

Tsata sprinted past her in a burst of speed and changed direction, heading up the trench to where a section of the far side had split and cracked, making a shallow fissure in the rock. Tsata reached it at a run and clambered up. Kaiku reached the sheer wall a moment later, her rifle clattering painfully against her back as she threw herself up at the fissure. She was no stranger to rock-climbing – it had been one of the challenges she and her brother Machim had competed at when they were children – but she could afford no purchase on her first try. Fear made her waste a second looking over her shoulder. The ghaureg was racing towards her, galloping on its knuckles, its matted hair flapping against its massive body.

'Climb!' Tsata shouted, and she did so. This time she found something to grip on to, wedging her fingers inside the fissure, and she pulled herself high enough to get a foothold. Tsata's hand was reaching down to her. Too far away. She found another purchase, took the strain on that and scrabbled for another, higher spot to put her free boot.

'Kaiku, *now*!'

The toe of her boot dug in, and she propelled herself with it, her hand reaching for his. He caught her with a grip like a clamp and wrenched her upward, the veins standing out on his tattooed arm. She was pulled over the lip and into his arms an instant before the ghaureg reached her, and its hand missed her ascending ankle by inches.

There was no time for relief. Kaiku extricated herself from her companion's grip and they ran again. The ghaureg could jump, but it was too heavy to get much height. The top of the trench wall was out of its reach, but it would not be long before it found an alternative way up.

Things had become too dangerous. Whatever the truth about the relationship between the Aberrants and the strange, masked handlers – which Kaiku had dubbed Nexuses – it was obvious that the Weavers knew something was amiss inside their protected enclosure, and had determined to remedy it. Kaiku and Tsata's forays through the barrier had become progressively more risky. The blighted, bleak land that surrounded the flood plain where the Aberrant army was stationed now swarmed with sentries. Time and again they had been forced to retreat without getting anywhere near the plain, let alone managing to find one of the Nexuses. Tsata's suggestion that they should kill one of the black-robed figures so that Kaiku could try and divine their nature was looking increasingly impossible; and it was becoming apparent to both of them that they could not keep on trying with things the way they were. Sooner or later they would be caught or killed.

The ghaureg was just bad luck. Normally they were easy enough to avoid, for they were hardly silent creatures and not particularly skilled hunters, relying on brute strength to dominate the food chain in the snowy wastes they had been gathered from. But Kaiku and Tsata had been avoiding a furie that had picked up their trail, and in their haste to get out of that Aberrant's path they had accidentally ran into another. It was the kind of slip that Kaiku had begun to think Tsata incapable of making, but it appeared that even the Tkiurathi was fallible.

She just hoped that discovery would not cost them their lives.

'Which way is it?' she panted, as they raced over the uneven ground.

'Ahead,' he replied. 'Not far.'

Not far turned out to be a lot further than Kaiku imagined, and by that time the ghaureg was on them again.

It spotted them from a rise in the land as they headed across a slice of flat terrain, and howled as it gave chase. Kaiku observed that it seemed to be the way of the ghauregs to go to high ground when trying to spot prey, for they were without natural predators and hence unafraid of revealing themselves out in the open. She noted it in case they ever had the misfortune to deal with one again. Staying low and close to obscuring walls was the best policy when trying to avoid this species.

But it was too late now. The beast was thundering down after them. They scrambled up a shallow slope, dislodging rocks and soil in little tumbles as the ground shifted beneath their feet. At the top was a withered clump of blighted trees, stark in the moonlight, which Kaiku recognised. They were at the edge of the Weaver's territory.

'The Mask, Kaiku!' Tsata urged, glancing back along the flat ground that they had just crossed. The ghaureg burst into sight, galloping relentlessly after them.

They ran again as Kaiku pulled the Mask out from where it was secured to her belt. But she had secured it too well, and in her haste the lip snagged on her clothing and the Mask spun from her hand, clattering to the stone, its mischievous face leering emptily.

She swore in disbelief. Tsata had his rifle out in a moment, tracking the approaching Aberrant as Kaiku ran over to where her Mask had fallen. The ghaureg had covered the distance between them fast, and Kaiku was not exactly sure how far the barrier was from here, and whether they would get to it in time.

It was the last, fleeting thought that crossed her mind before she scooped the Mask up and put it to her face.

The warm, sinking sensation of mild euphoria was stronger this time, more noticeable than it had ever been before. The intimation of her father's presence was stronger too; the smell of him seemed to emanate from the grain of the wood, gentling her as if she were a child in his arms again. The Mask was a perfect fit for her face, resting against her skin like a lover's hand on her cheek.

'*Run!*'

Tsata's voice shattered the timeless instant, and she was back to the present. The Mask was hot against her: the barrier had to be close. She fled, and Tsata dropped his arm and fled with her. The ghaureg bellowed as it raced up the treacherous incline, unhindered by the sliding soil, its hands and feet digging deep into the earth and throwing out stony divots behind it.

'Give me your hand!' Kaiku cried, reaching back for Tsata. The barrier was upon them, suddenly, and she realised it was *too* close, for if Tsata was not with her then he would not get through.

He reacted almost before she had finished her sentence, springing toward her and clamping his hand tight around hers. The ghaureg was mere feet away from them now, blocking out the moons with its bulk, its teeth dripping with saliva as it roared in anticipation of the kill.

The Weave bloomed around Kaiku, the world turning to a golden chaos of light as she plunged headlong into the barrier. She felt Tsata loose his grip instantly, felt him tug to the right as his senses skewed and he tried to change direction; but she had his hand, and she would not let it go. She pulled him as hard as she could, felt him trip and stumble sideways as his body went in a direction that all his instincts told him not to. His balance held for several steps before the two of them fell out of the other side of the barrier, and the Weave slipped into invisibility behind them.

Tsata was on his hands and knees, the familiar listlessness and disorientation in his eyes. Kaiku ignored him, her attention on the ghaureg. The creature had turned around and was racing away from them at an angle, pounding back into the heart of the Weaver's territory as if unaware that its prey was no longer in front of it. She kept her gaze on it until it had disappeared from sight behind a fold in the grey land.

Tsata recovered quickly, by which time Kaiku had reluctantly taken off the Mask. She had begun to feel guilty about doing so of late, as if it were some sort of betrayal, that by doing so she was disappointing her father's spirit somehow.

The Tkiurathi's brow cleared; he sat down on the rock and looked at Kaiku.

'That was an extremely lucky escape,' he said.

Kaiku brushed her fringe aside. 'We were careless,' she said. 'That is all.'

'I think,' said Tsata, 'the time has come to give up. We cannot get close to the Weavers or the Nexuses. We have to return to the Fold.'

Kaiku shook her head. 'Not yet. Not until we find out more.' She met his gaze. 'You go.'

'You know I cannot.'

She got to her feet, offered her hand to him. He took it, and she helped him up.

'Then it seems that you are stuck with me.'

He regarded her for a long moment, his tattooed face unreadable in the moonlight.

'It appears so,' he said, but his tone was warm, and made her smile.

Chien os Mumaka lay on a bed in the infirmary tent outside Zila, hazing in and out of consciousness. Sleep would not come to him, though his body ached and it felt as if the ends of his bones were rubbing against each other. The tent was empty apart from him. Several rows of beds lay waiting to be filled when the conflict began. It was cool and shadowy, and he was surrounded by the muted sounds of a military camp: subdued voices rising and falling as they passed near, the snort of horses, the crackle of fires, unidentifiable creaks and taps and groans. Out here near the coast, on the plain south of the fortified town, the night insects were not so numerous or noisy, and the dark seemed peaceful.

He had been taken into the care of a physician as soon as he had arrived at the camp, who had given him an infusion to drink, in order to bring down his fever. Chien had demanded weakly that he see the Barak Zahn. The physician had dismissed him at first, but Chien was insistent, declaring that he had a message of the gravest importance and that Zahn would be very unhappy with whoever delayed him. That gave the other man pause for thought. Chien knew well enough from his time as a merchant that people were more likely to do what they were told if they believed that they would be held responsible for the consequences of inaction. Yet the physician did not like to be ordered about within his own infirmary, and Chien was very ill, and Zahn was already abed by that point.

'In the morning,' the physician said, snappishly. 'By then you will be well enough to have visitors. And I will *ask* if the Barak wishes to see you.'

Chien was forced to be content with that.

Once alone, Chien was left to think about the events of the day. Gods, that Mishani was a sharp one. He did not know whether to feel ashamed or philosophical about how she had outguessed him in the end. It was not as if he could help what he said in dreams. In fact, he was inclined to think it was the will of the gods, or more specifically of Myen, the goddess of sleep, who had more than a little of her younger brother Shintu's trickster blood in her. In which case, who was he to feel bad about it?

And she was right: he had to grudgingly admit that. Leaving her was the best way he could help her. He had failed to protect her twice; it was only by the narrowest margin that she had survived the attentions of her father's assassins. He did not know what kind of game she was playing with Zahn, but he was glad that he would be out of it once his message was done. His obligation would be fulfilled then. As long as Mishani survived, Muraki would be honour-bound to release Blood Mumaka from their ties to her family.

He managed a small smile around the pain of the fever. His whole life, he had been fighting an uphill war, overcoming the prejudice of being an adopted child. It had not helped that his parents had subsequently managed natural children, though physicians had given them no hope of it. Every day he had been forced to prove himself against his siblings. But though he might not be elegant or subtle or educated, as his younger brothers were, he could hold his head with pride. As if it were not enough that he had been instrumental in raising up his family from the disgrace his parents had put them in, he was now going to free them from the debt they had incurred by choosing love over politics.

Unconsciousness slipped towards him, bringing respite from the fever; but he came awake again suddenly as something moved at the tent flap. He raised his head with some effort, peering into the darkness. His eyes refused to focus properly.

He could not see anyone, but that did not lessen his certainty. There was someone in here with him. The sensation of a presence crawled across his skin. He got himself up on his elbows, cast around again, trying to find the elusive shadow he had glimpsed. His head went light. A hallucination? The physician had warned him that the infusion might have side-effects.

'Is someone there?' he said at last, unable to bear the silence any longer.

'I'm here,' said a voice at Chien's bedside, and the surprise made him start violently. A black shape, made fuzzy by the drug in his system, standing next to him.

'You've caused my employer a great deal of trouble,' the man hissed, and as he did so Chien felt a gloved hand smothering him, holding his nose, and a wooden phial shoved between his lips before he could close them. He thrashed, tried to cry out and gagged on the liquid in his mouth a moment before another hand clamped over his face, preventing him from spitting it up. He swallowed reflexively to clear his airway; and only then did he realise what he had done.

'Good boy,' the shadow said. 'Drink it down.'

He stopped thrashing, his eyes wide in mute terror. A new drowsiness was spreading through him, turning his muscles to lead. His limbs become too heavy to lift; his head lolled back onto the pillow. A dreadful sleep descended on him, too fast for him to resist.

In seconds, he was still, his eyes open, pupils saucers of black staring at the roof of the darkened infirmary tent. The intruder took his hands away from Chien's face, watched as his breathing became shallow gasps and finally stopped altogether.

'I commend you to Omecha and Noctu, Chien os Mumaka,' the assassin murmured, closing the merchant's eyes with his fingers. 'May you have more luck in the Golden Realm.'

With that, the shadow was gone, slipping out into the camp to resume his guise as a soldier in Barak Moshito's army. Barak Avun tu Koli may have been far to the north, but his reach was long.

Chien lay cooling in the darkness, a death that would be attributed to fever in the morning, and his message remained undelivered at the last.

Reki tu Tanatsua, brother-by-marriage to the Emperor of Saramyr, huddled in the corner of an abandoned shack and wept into his sister's hair.

He had crossed the Rahn at sunset, having ridden headlong from Axekami all through the previous night. The bridge on the East Way had been far too dangerous, but he had found a ferryman without any trouble: a small mercy, for which he should have been grateful, if he had been capable of feeling so. But there was no room in him for anything but grief, and so he sobbed in the shadows of the old field-worker's hut that he had found to shelter in, amid the smell of mouldy hay from the pallet bed and rusted sickles leaning against the thin plank wall. The horses whickered nearby, uncomfortable at being kept in such close quarters; but he had not dared leave them outside, and they were too exhausted to be restless. They munched oats from their feed-bags, and ignored him.

He had ridden all day and most of the night, but sleep could not have been further from his mind. He did not care if he never slept again. He did not believe that this overwhelming sorrow and bitterness and pain would ever go away. How cruel the world could be, that just when he had found a searing happiness in Asara, it was all torn away and he was flung into the night, forced to abandon his sister and charged with a terrible responsibility. He could not bring himself to recall the pitiful state Laranya had been in when he had found her. It was a blasphemy against the person she had been, had *always* been until Mos had beaten her like that. The agony seemed too great to allow him to draw breath; the physical ache in his chest and stomach doubled him over.

Then, he had no idea that his sister was already dead.

They would be looking for him, she had said. They would try and stop him. Mos had crossed a line, and there was no telling what he might do now. Reki did not really understand: he had not known what his sister intended to do, how she had exposed her humiliation to the servants of the Keep so that rumour would be unquenchable, how she had meant to take her own life to ensure that vengeance would come from the desert. He did not think Mos would dare capture him and keep him against his will. As abhorrent as his actions were, kidnap was another order of magnitude.

None of that mattered though. He had his sister's black hair twisted around his fist. She had charged him with delivering it to their father. Honour bound him, as it would bind Blood Tanatsua. And Blood Tanatsua, one of the most powerful of the Tchom Rin families, would call on the other families in the name of Suran to aid them. Reki had no doubt his father could and would raise a great army to his banner.

The desert folk were traditionally insular, dealing with affairs within their own territories and not involving themselves in the politics of the west. The Emperors and Empresses were happy to let them do so. Even with Weavers at their command, the desert was a difficult place to administer, and those who lived in the fertile lands on this side of the Tchamil Mountains had little knowledge of the complex ways of the Suran-worshippers. Though they were all part of the Empire, in a land as vast as Saramyr it was possible for neighbouring cultures to be as foreigners to each other.

Reki held war in his hand. It was a responsibility he did not want. And yet to shirk it would be to betray his sister, who had suffered terribly at the hands of the man she loved. His own grief was nothing compared to hers, but that was no comfort to him. It seemed the crying would never stop, a racking spasm like vomiting, bringing up a bottomless void of shame and guilt and hate and woe.

He was so consumed by his own misery that he did not hear the door to the shack open and close, nor the newcomer walk over to him. It was only when he felt a touch on his shoulder that he suddenly scrambled away, pressing himself up against the corner of the shack, cringing from the shadow who stood over him.

'Oh, Reki,' said Asara.

He whimpered at the sound of her voice and threw his arms around her legs, his weeping beginning afresh. She knelt down next to him, allowing him to hold her and she him. There in the darkness he clung to her as if she were the mother he had never known, and she soothed him. For a long time, they stayed like that. The horses murmured to themselves, and the autumn wind rattled the shack door against its latch.

'Why are you here?' he managed at last, touching her face with beatific wonder as if she were some deity of mercy come to rescue him.

'Do you suppose you can do this alone?' she asked. 'I followed your trail as easily as if you had left me a map. If I did, so can others. Without me, you will be caught by next moonrise.'

'You came after me,' he sobbed, and embraced her again.

She pushed him away gently. 'Calm yourself,' she said. 'You are not a child any longer.'

That stung him, and his tear-blotched face showed how wounded he was.

'We must go now,' she told him, her voice firm. She was a sleek outline in the shadows, but her eyes glittered strangely. 'This place is too dangerous. I will take you by roads quicker and less travelled. I will see you discharge your sister's oath.'

Reki clambered to his feet, and Asara rose with him. His eyes burned and his nose ran. He wiped the back of his hand across his face, ashamed.

'You could be executed if you are caught,' he whispered.

'I know,' she replied. 'I will ensure we are not caught.'

He sniffed loudly. 'You should not be here.'

'But I am.'

'Why?' he asked again, because she had never really answered him the first time.

She kissed him swiftly on the lips. 'That, you will have to work out for yourself.'

They led the tired horses out to where Asara's own horses were, and headed away into the night. Later, she would tell him of his sister's suicide. But for now, it was enough to get him to safety, and to guard him on his long trek south-east to his father's lands. She would ensure he delivered Laranya's hair into the hands of Barak Green. She would make certain that he started the civil war that had to come.

As they travelled across fields and fens, Asara's eyes were flat. She was thinking on the murder of the Empress.

She had not originally intended to assassinate Laranya. In truth, she had been sent by Cailin only to keep an eye on developments within the Imperial family, for word of Mos's growing insanity was leaking out and Cailin believed that something would happen soon. She wanted Asara there to deal with it when it did. Asara had infiltrated the Imperial Keep only days before Mos's little disagreement with his wife.

As a spy she was peerless, and getting into the Keep – and into a shy young man's bed – was easy for a creature such as her. She was old, despite her appearance, and she had seen much and studied much. It was simple to charm her way into the company of the poets and playwrights and musicians that Laranya surrounded herself with. She had a greater wealth of knowledge than most of them, which was remarkable in a woman of such apparent youth. From there, gossip about Eszel and Laranya had led to Reki, and so she had formed her introduction. It had not been difficult. He was still a boy, still inexperienced in the way of women. It was simple to seduce him.

Then, the Empress. Reki had told her about the dreams Mos had been having. Asara had put the piece together with the massing armies of Blood Kerestyn, the approaching famine and what she had learned of the Weavers in her guise as Saran Ycthys Marul, and come to only one conclusion. The one she would have suspected anyway. The Weavers were driving Mos mad with jealousy. They meant him to harm his wife.

They *wanted* to draw the desert families into the conflict. And therefore, so did Asara. When opportunity came her way, she did not hesitate.

If there was one thing that Asara knew for certain, it was this: the Libera Dramach could not beat the Weavers as things stood. Not now, not in ten years' time, and probably not ever. The instant that Lucia revealed herself and made her claim to the throne, she would be killed, the Libera Dramach annihilated by the full force of the Weavers. Lucia could not win the Empire.

But with a little help from Asara, the Weavers could.

TWENTY-SIX

The assault on Zila came in the dead of night.

The clouds that had been stroking Saramyr's western coast had consolidated into a dour blanket by sunset, and when the darkness came it was almost total. No stars shone, Aurus was entirely invisible, and Iridima was reduced to a hazy smear of white in the sky, her radiance choked before it could reach the earth. Then the rain began: a few warning patters, insidious wet taps on the stone of the town before the deluge came. Suddenly the night was swarming, droplets battering down from the sky, hissing on torches and smacking off sword blades.

It was a painful, aggressive downpour, forcing its way through the clothes of the men who stood armed and on watch, their eyes narrowed as they watched the distant campfires of the besieging armies. They flickered in a ring around the hill upon which Zila sat, beacons of light in otherwise total darkness, illuminating nothing. Eventually, they went out, doused by the rain.

The onslaught kept up for hours. Zila waited, a crown of glowing windows and lanterns hanging suspended in rainswept blackness.

The man who first noticed that something was amiss was a calligrapher, an educated man who, like many others, had found himself swept up in the events that had overtaken his town and did not really have any clear idea how to swim against the tide. He had been assigned to the watch by some structure of authority he did not understand, and had unquestioningly obeyed. Now he was soaked and miserable, holding a rifle he did not know how to use and expecting at any moment to be struck in the forehead by an arrow from the abyss beyond the walls of the town.

It was, perhaps, this fearful expectation that made him more attentive than the others on the watch that night. They had settled themselves in, after several nights of inactivity, for a long period of negotiation and preparation before any actual combat would occur. The heat of the revolt had cooled in them now, and most had resigned themselves to a long autumn and a long winter trapped inside Zila. What choice did they have? They did not like the idea of throwing themselves on the mercy of the armies, even if they could leave. Some were wondering whether it might not have been better just to let the Governor keep hoarding his food, and take their chances with the famine;

but their companions reminded them that they were thinking from the luxury of a full belly, and if they had been starving now, they would not be so complacent. There was food in Zila, more than they would have outside.

Like the calligrapher, many wondered now how they had got into this mess, and what they could possibly do to get out of it with their skins.

It was while chewing over these very thoughts that the calligrapher began to hear noises over the constant tumult of the rain. The wind was switching back and forth in fitful gusts, spraying him with warm droplets, and when it came his way he thought he heard an occasional creaking sound, or the squeak of a wheel. Being a timid man, he was reluctant to embarrass himself by pointing these out to any of the others on the watch, so he chose to do nothing for a long while. And yet time and again he heard the sounds – very faint, blown on the breeze – and gradually a certainty grew in his breast that something was wrong. The sounds were fleeting enough to be imagination, except that he had none. He was level-headed, practical, and had never been prone to phantoms of the mind.

Eventually, he shared his concerns with the next man on the wall. That man listened, and after a time he reported to his officer, and so it came to the commander of the watch. The commander demanded the calligrapher's account of what he had heard. Other men joined in: they had heard it too. They stared hard into the darkness, but the shrouded night was impenetrable.

'Send up a rocket,' the commander said eventually. He did not like to do it: he thought he might unduly alarm the troops and the enemy both. But he liked less the crawling trepidation that was ascending his spine.

A few minutes later, the night was torn by a piercing shriek, and the firework arced into the sky, trailing a thin stream of smoke. Its whistle faded to silence, and then blossomed into a furious ball of light, a burning phosphorescence that lit the whole hillside.

What they saw terrified them.

The base of the hill was aswarm with troops, frozen in the false sun like a bas-relief. They were draped in tarpaulins of black over their leather armour, disguising their colours, and under that camouflage they had advanced from the campfires, crossing in secret a potential killing field where the folk of Zila might have been able to shred them with bowshot and fire-cannon. Beneath the tarpaulins, they looked like a slick-backed horde of grotesque and outsize beetles, creeping insidiously up to the walls of the town, dragging with them mortars and ladders and fire-cannons of their own. The very suddenness of the image was horrifying, like pulling back a bandage to find a wound swarming with maggots.

Perhaps three thousand men were climbing the muddy hill towards Zila.

There was a great clamour as the firework died, both from the town and from the troops below. They cast off their tarpaulins in the last light of the rocket, and tugged them away from the sculpted barrels of the fire-cannons, which were shaped like snarling dogs or screaming demons. Then blackness returned, and they were hidden once again; but Zila was speckled in light, and could not hide.

Alarm bells clanged. Voices cried out orders and warnings. Men scattered dice or bowls of stew as they scrambled to the weapons that they had left carelessly leaning against walls.

Then the fire-cannons opened up.

The darkness at the base of the hill was lit anew with flashes of flame gouting from iron mouths, briefly illuminating the troops as they broke into a charge. Shellshot looped lazily up and over the walls, black orbs leaking chemical fire from cracks in their surfaces as they spun. They crashed through the roofs of houses, shattered in the streets, tore chunks out of buildings. Where they impacted hard enough, they burst and sprayed a jelly which ignited on contact with air. Blazing slicks raced along the cobbled roads of Zila, and the rain was powerless to extinguish them; dark dwellings suddenly brightened from within as their interiors turned to bonfires; howling figures, men and women and children, staggered and flailed as their skin crisped.

The first salvo was devastating. The second was not long in following.

Bakkara was out of his bed before the first screech of the rocket had died, and was strapping on his leather armour when the shellshot hit. Mishani had woken at the same time, but she had not understood what the firework might mean. At the sound of the explosions, however, she was in motion herself. While Bakkara was at the window, throwing open the shutters, she was slipping into her robe and winding her hair in a single massive plait which she knotted at the bottom.

Bakkara cursed foully as he looked down onto the rooftops of Zila, saw the flames already rising.

'I *knew* they'd do it like this,' he grated. 'Gods damn them! I knew it!'

He turned away from the window to find Mishani putting her sandals on. Ordinarily it took her a long while to make herself ready, but when elegance was not an issue she could do it inside of a minute.

'Where do you think you're going?' he demanded.

'With you,' she said.

'Woman, this is not a time to be a burden, I warn you.'

The room shook suddenly to a deafening impact, a tremor that made Bakkara stumble and catch hold of a dresser to steady himself. The keep had been struck. A fire-cannon's artillery would not penetrate walls this thick, but there was a flaming rill left on the keep's flank that dripped down into the courtyard below.

'I am not staying here; it is the most prominent target in Zila,' she said. 'Go. Do not concern yourself with me. I will keep up.'

She could not have said why she felt the need to accompany him, only that to be wakened in this way had frightened her, and she did not want to be left alone to wonder at what fate might befall the town.

'No, you're right,' Bakkara said, sobering for a moment. 'I have a safer place to put you.'

Mishani was about to ask what he meant by that, but she did not have the chance. Xejen burst into the room, jabbering frantically. He had evidently been awake, for he was not sleep-mussed and his hair was neat; in her time observing the leader of the Ais Maraxa, Mishani had established that he was a chronic insomniac.

'What are they doing, what are they *doing*?' he cried. He registered Mishani's presence in the room, then looked at Bakkara with obvious surprise on his face. He had evidently not known that they were sleeping together. 'Bakkara, what are they—'

'They're *attacking* us, you fool, as I *told* you they would!' he shouted. He pushed past Xejen and out of the door. Xejen and Mishani followed him as he hurried through the keep, adjusting his scabbard as he went. Outside, the staccato crack of rifles had begun as the men on the walls organised themselves enough to mount a defence.

'We were negotiating!' Xejen blustered, running to keep up with Bakkara's strides. 'Don't they care about the hostages? Are they intending to burn an Imperial town to the ground?'

'If that's what it takes,' Bakkara replied grimly.

As a soldier, he was used to the frustration of suffering for a leader's incompetence, and accepted it. In a chain of command, even if one man thought he knew better than the one above him, he still had to accept his superior's orders. Bakkara had not, in his heart, thought that the Baraks Zahn tu Ikati and Moshito tu Vinaxis would dare a ploy like this, but he had warned Xejen of the possibility.

Xejen had not heeded him. He believed, as he had always believed, that troops of the Empire would try and wait them out. They would waste time with diplomacy, letting the people become bored and complacent and dispirited, hanging on until the rebels' morale slipped. Then they would make offers to the people themselves, to try and incite a coup from within. At the very worst, they would assault the walls, and Xejen believed that they could be held back easily from the advantage of high ground. The Empire's hands were tied to some extent: they would not want to cause any more damage to the town itself than they had to, and the Emperor would not want to kill thousands of Saramyr peasant townsfolk, especially when things were so volatile.

If Xejen knew anything, he knew how to play people, how to inspire them or make them doubt. And he had intended to use the time spent in negotiation to spread the doctrine of the Ais Maraxa, to give the people of Zila something to believe in, a purpose that would keep them unshakable. He had banked on the generals being unenthusiastic about the fight, seeking to preserve their strength for the civil war that was brewing.

Xejen thought only in his own terms, and he assumed – fatally – that everyone else of education thought that way too. After all, sense was sense;

surely anyone with a mind could tell that? He had thought it would come to a battle of wills. He was wrong.

They burst out of the keep into a tumult of rain and screams and flame, then ducked reflexively as shellshot came rushing over their heads to explode across the far side of Zila, spewing burning jelly onto the rooftops. Bakkara cursed roundly and raced down the stone steps towards street level, his hair sodden in an instant. The streets were alive with people running and calling to each other, seeking any kind of shelter in their panic, frightened faces sidelit by fire.

The steps of the keep folded back on themselves twice before they reached the surrounding plaza. Several guards stood at the bottom, professional soldiers who knew better than to desert their posts even under an assault like this. Bakkara clapped one of them on the shoulder.

'Get more men!' he said urgently. 'Sooner or later these people are going to end up thinking the only safe place in Zila is the keep, and they'll want in. You need to hold them back. We don't want them taking sanctuary; we want them out there fighting!'

The guard snapped a salute across his chest and began giving orders. Bakkara did not wait. He was heading for the southern wall, where the sounds of battle were beginning already.

Those with military training in the Ais Maraxa had known it would be a tall order to co-ordinate peasantry and artisans into an effective defence force, but even they had not expected quite such spectacular disorganisation. The Baraks' battle plan had been perfectly pitched to sow confusion, sending Zila into a panic by its sheer callous brutality. Fire-cannons rained shellshot indiscriminately upon the town, taking no care to aim. Mortars pitched bombs through the air, destroying chunks of masonry and doing real damage to the walls of the keep. The men of Zila had been ready for a fight, but this was no fight; this was a massacre.

Or so it seemed. Actually, as men like Bakkara knew, there were far fewer casualties than the level of destruction would suggest. The intent was to make the damage look worse than it was. The rain was stopping many of the fires spreading too far, and the outer wall of the town was as strong as it always had been. But the townsfolk saw only that their houses were being burned and their families were fleeing in terror, and many of them ran from their posts to try and save their loved ones from whatever danger they imagined them to be in.

It took a long time, too long, for Zila's own fire-cannons to open up, blasting flaming rents in the lines of the attackers, sending them scattering. Fireworks whistled into the sky and turned into blazing white torches, lighting a scene of labouring ghosts at the foot of Zila's wall as the soldiers clambered through mud and bowshot and rifle fire, shields locked above their heads. Shields were rarely used in Saramyr combat except for such purposes as this, and so they were fashioned from thick metal to make them heavy enough to deflect rifle balls. Men fell at the flanks of the formations, but the core remained strong as ladders were passed under the canopy of shields. Distantly, the sinister creaking of the siege engines could be heard approaching through the night, and reinforcements who had not been part of the first assault were arriving.

But the worst consequence of the disorganisation was this: all eyes were on the south, and nobody was looking north, to the river.

The darkness and rain and cloud that had concealed the Baraks' armies so effectively had done the same for the soldiers that had crossed the Zan and ascended the steep side of the hill, filing up the stairs from the docks to the small gate at the top and then fanning out along the wall.

The men on the north side had not lessened in their vigilance, but under the conditions it was impossible to see anything, and the chaos of the bombardment had put the more nervous men into a panic. The watch commander's request to have fireworks sent up on the north side of the town got lost somewhere in the muddle, and while he was waiting for a reply that never came, disaster struck.

Four soldiers guarded the small northern gate on the inside. It was massively thick, studded with rivets and banded with metal, practically unbreachable due to its width and compact size. The angle of the slope beyond, which plunged down to the south bank of the Zan, made foolish any attempt to assault it. Men would have to use the stairs – for the grassy sides were just too sharp an incline, especially in this rain – and they would be easy targets for anything the defenders cared to drop on them from above. Any attackers would be forced to huddle close to the tiny margin of level ground by the walls, where burning pitch could be poured on them, while a few soldiers fruitlessly battered at the gate. There was not even enough clearance between the gate and the edge of the slope to manoeuvre a ram effectively.

Giri stood in the lantern-lit antechamber with his three companions on duty, listening to the destruction of Zila going on outside. He was a soldier by trade, but he did not have the temperament for it. He did not enjoy fighting, nor did he revel in the camaraderie that other soldiers thrived on. Most of his time was spent trying to get himself posted in the place where there was least likely to be any danger of him losing his life. He believed himself lucky this time. This was probably the safest place in the town.

He only began to suspect that something was wrong when his head began to throb. At first it was nothing alarming, just a slight, dull pain which he expected to pass momentarily. But it increased rather than diminishing. He squinted, blinking his right eye rapidly as it started to get worse.

'Are you unwell?' one of the other guards asked him.

But Giri was very far from well. The agony was becoming unbearable. He pawed at his right eye with his fingertips, wanting by some perverse instinct to touch the area that hurt; but it was inside his head, like a small animal scrabbling within his skull. He could see another guard frowning now, not at

Giri but at something else, as if a sudden thought had occurred to him that was too important to dismiss.

They had all taken on that expression now, a curious attentiveness as if listening to something. Then the guard who had spoken turned back to him, his sword sliding free from its sheath.

'You're not co-operating, Giri,' he said.

Giri's eyes widened in realisation. 'No, stop! Gods! It's a Weaver! They've got a Weaver out there!'

The blade plunged into his chest before he could get any further.

One of the three remaining guards, those who had not had such an adverse reaction to the Weaver's influence, doused the lanterns and unbarred the gate. They drew it open to the rain and darkness outside. Barely visible was a Mask of precious metal cut into angles, a splintered, jagged visage of gold and silver and bronze. Behind the hunched figure, soldiers in black tarpaulins waited with swords drawn. They rushed past and slew the unfortunate puppets, then crowded into the antechamber.

Stealthily, they crept onward into Zila.

'Report!' Bakkara roared over the crashing of burning timbers and the shattering din of the explosives.

'They're all over us!' the watch commander cried. He was a man of middle age with a drooping moustache, now lank with moisture. 'They've got to the walls and they're putting up ladders. A third of the men have left their posts already; they're running around like idiots inside the town.'

'You didn't stop them?' Bakkara was incredulous.

'How? By killing them? Who would kill them? The townsfolk won't, and if the Ais Maraxa get sword-happy, what pitiful defence we have left will collapse.' The commander looked resigned. 'Men won't fight if they aren't willing. We started a revolt; we didn't create an army.'

'But they'll be killed if they *don't* fight!' Xejen blurted.

He, like the others, was sheltering beneath the wooden awning of an empty bar near the southern wall. People ran by on the street, intermittently lit by flashes. Mishani listened to the exchange with half her attention elsewhere. She was scared rigid beneath her dispassionate exterior. The pummelling tumult all around her, the knowledge that they could be incinerated at any moment, was shredding her nerves. She wanted desperately to turn back to the keep; she wished she had never left it. Looking up through the rain, she saw it rising in the centre of the town. Though its sides were scored and scorched, and chunks had fallen free, it still seemed many times safer than where she was now. Fear had driven her towards where the action was, for she had no wish then to remain in a tower that was being bombarded. But she knew nothing of war, and was shocked by its ferocity. Twice they had almost been hit by shellshot; several times they had passed by burnt and blasted corpses. Mishani had seen atrocities like this before, when she had been a victim of subversive bombing in the Market District of Axekami; but that had been one terrible moment of danger, and then the horrifying aftermath. Here, the bombs kept coming, and sooner or later one of them had to hit her.

The commander was looking at Xejen gravely. 'They're saying the men will be spared if they surrender. We can hear Barak Moshito down there somewhere.'

'Impossible!' Xejen cried.

'Weavers,' Bakkara said. 'They can make a man's voice carry. They used to do it when generals were addressing troops, back when I fought in the Newlands. There would be two thousand men there, but every one could hear as if the general was right in front of them.'

'Weavers?' Xejen repeated nervously.

'What did you expect?' he grunted.

'We need you on the wall, Bakkara,' the commander said. 'It's a shambles up there. They don't know how to deal with an all-out attack.'

'Nobody is surrendering!' Xejen snapped suddenly. 'Tell the men that! Whatever Moshito says!' He snorted. 'I'll go to the wall and tell them myself.'

The commander looked uncertainly at Bakkara. 'You mean to lead the men?' he asked Xejen.

'Since I must, yes,' he replied.

'Xejen . . .' Bakkara began, then subsided. But Mishani would not let him defer to Xejen, not here. Even amid her fear, she saw that they were at the fulcrum of the balance of power; and the time had come to throw her own weight into the fray.

'Gods, Xejen, let him do his job!' she snapped, imbuing her voice with a crisp and disparaging tone. 'He is the man to lead the battle, not you!'

Bakkara's brows raised in surprise. His eyes flicked from Mishani to Xejen. 'Go to the safehouse. There's nothing you can do here.'

'I have to be here!' Xejen protested immediately.

But now it was a matter of pride; as much as he would not have admitted it to himself, Bakkara would not be overridden in front of his woman, however inaccurate that term might be. Mishani had judged him aright.

'You will do Lucia no good if you get killed!' Bakkara barked. 'And you, Mistress Mishani, this is not your fight. If you're caught up in the fray, they'll kill you, noble or not.'

'Ladders!' someone cried in the distance. 'More ladders coming!'

The commander glared at Bakkara urgently. 'We *need* you!' he repeated. 'They're trying to scale the wall!'

'*Go!*' Bakkara shouted at Xejen, and then he turned and ran, following the other soldier.

Xejen and Mishani stood together under the awning, the rain splattering off it and onto the cobbles. Bakkara did not look back. Xejen seemed momentarily bereft of direction. Mishani, noting his expression, guessed that things would be different if they managed to weather this battle. Bakkara, without even intending to, had taken a great step towards becoming the head of the Ais Maraxa, and Xejen had been diminished. It would serve Mishani well.

'We should do as he says,' Mishani suggested. She surprised herself by how calm she sounded, when all she wanted to do was flee towards what little sanctuary she could find. Bakkara had mentioned the safehouse once before: a small, underground complex of chambers that the Ais Maraxa had discovered while rooting through the usurped Governor's notes. A retreat where they would be protected from the bombs and shellshot.

Xejen spat on the ground in frustration and stalked away in the direction they had come. 'Follow me!' he said, his long jaw set.

They hurried through the grim, steep streets of Zila. The tall buildings crowded in on them threateningly as they slipped off the main thoroughfares and through the narrow lanes that ran between the spoke-roads. Flaming rubble had blocked many routes, and some buildings had fire licking from their windows, burning from the inside out. People pushed past them in the other direction. Some of them recognised Xejen. A few pleaded with him, as if he had the power to stop this. He told them to get up on the wall and fight, if they had any pride in their town. They looked at him in confusion and ran on. As far as they were concerned, things were hopeless.

The analytical part of Mishani's mind was studying Xejen even through the fear. He was enraged by the turn of events, betrayed by the weakness of the townsfolk and by Bakkara; and yet she saw by his manner that he still had supreme faith in his plan, that no matter how bad it looked the walls of Zila *would* hold. He cursed as he went, muttering in fury at the sight of men shepherding their families away from the blazing buildings, genuinely unable to believe that they did not see the best way to keep them safe was to fight for their town.

That was when she realised unequivocably that his belief in his cause had blinded him, and that was why they would be defeated. The Ais Maraxa were dangerous, not only to the Empire but to the Libera Dramach as well. Zaelis had known that from the start. They were a liability, driven by their fervour to act without caution and to stretch themselves beyond their abilities. Fortune had put them in this town at a time when it was ripe to overthrow its inept ruler, but it had not given them the resources or experience to govern it, and certainly not to face two very competent Baraks and a multitude of war-tested generals.

She had been working towards a way to resolve this mess in her favour, a route to safety; but events had turned on her too quickly. Where was Zahn? Had he chosen to ignore her message? Gods, did he not realise how important she was to him? If she survived the night, she told herself, she might still have a chance of getting out of Zila alive. If she survived the night.

She was thinking just that when the mortar bomb struck the building next to her with a deafening roar, and the whole frontage came slumping down into the street.

It was only Xejen's perpetually keyed-up reactions that saved her. He had seen the projectile an instant before it hit, and he darted into the open doorway of the building opposite, grabbing the cuff of Mishani's robe as he went. At the instant she was stunned by the noise and light and the blast of concussion that physically pushed her backwards, she was also pulled hard through the doorway, and she fell over the step as the street where she had just been turned into an avalanche of stone and timber.

A billow of dust blew into the room, forcing itself into Mishani's lungs and making her choke. Through tearing eyes she could vaguely make out the shape of Xejen. Then she heard the sound of splitting wood and the terrible, ominous groan of the house all around them. She had barely realised that she had evaded death by a hair's breadth before she heard something crack overhead, and knew that she had not evaded it at all. Her stomach knotted sickeningly as she heard the last of the beams give, and then the ceiling came in on top of her.

Bakkara's blade swept in a high arc, shattering the soldier's collarbone and almost removing his head. His victim's grip went loose on the ladder and he fell, crashing onto the men beneath him and dislodging several, who went screaming towards the upturned shields of their companions below. Bakkara and another man got the end of the ladder and pushed away; it swung back, teetered, and then pivoted in a quarter-circle and tipped over, shedding the last of the men on its back as it crashed onto the heads of the troops that assaulted Zila's southern wall.

'Where *is* everyone?' he cried in exasperation, racing to where another ladder was already clattering ominously against the parapet. They could have held this position with a tenth of the men attacking it, but there was barely even that. It was all the defenders could do to keep the troops from getting over the wall. In the back of his mind, he noted that Zila's fire-cannons had gone silent, and the Baraks' troops attacked fearlessly now.

It was an Ais Maraxa man who answered him, a soldier as weathered and weary as he. 'They fled the wall, the cowards,' he grated. 'Some to their families, some because they want to surrender. They'll hide 'till this is through, gods rot them.'

Bakkara swore. This was a disaster. The townsfolk had all but given up, demoralised utterly by the sight of their homes burning and the apparently overwhelming odds. They could have held out, if they had stayed together. But that required unity and discipline, and Xejen's ragtag army of peasants had neither.

He had no time to think further, for he was already at the new ladder, where two Blood Vinaxis men had spilled onto the stone walkway and were running at him. His sword swung up to meet the ill-advised overhead strike of the first, then he stamped on the side of the man's foot, feeling the joint give under his heel. His enemy shrieked and clutched his ankle reflexively, and Bakkara beheaded him while his guard was down. He slumped to the ground, blood gushing from his severed neck to be washed away by the pouring rain.

The Ais Maraxa soldier, whose name was Hruji, had despatched his opponent with similar efficiency, and the two of them tipped the ladder back before any others could get to the top.

Bakkara glanced grimly up and down the wall. There were too few men here, too few. Almost all of them were Ais Maraxa. The peasants had left them to it. In the lantern-light, he saw small clots of soldiers rushing back and forth, desperately engaging the encroaching troops. But the troops were endless, and his men were flagging.

There were not enough to keep the enemy at bay over such a perimeter.

'Bakkara!' someone cried, and he turned to see a dishevelled man come racing along the walkway towards him. He knew the face, but memory failed at the name.

'Give me some good news,' Bakkara warned, but at the man's expression he knew what news he had to give would certainly not be good.

'They've got in through the north gate! They've taken the north wall. The peasants are surrendering . . . some are even *helping* them in the streets up there. Our men are fleeing south, towards the centre.'

That was it. There was no more time for procrastination.

'We fall back to the keep,' Bakkara said, the words like ashes in his mouth. 'The town is lost. Meet at the rally point. We go from there.'

Hruji and the messenger both saluted and ran to spread the order. Bakkara turned flat eyes to the scorched and damaged building that rose above the burning streets of Zila, and wondered if his decision would do them any good at all, or if he was merely delaying the inevitable. He suspected the latter.

A moment later, a horn sounded a shrill, clear note that echoed into the battle-tainted night: the signal to give up the wall.

The retreat was as disorganised as the rest of the defence had been. The Ais Maraxa had been the last to give up their posts, but not all of them were soldiers, and the withdrawal turned into a rout as enemy troops began pouring over the vacated wall and into the town. Booted feet splashed through streets that had turned into shallow rivers of murky water, fearful glances were cast over shoulders at the tide of swords and rifles and armour cresting Zila's parapets. The Ais Maraxa ran headlong through the glow cast by the street lanterns, flicking from shadow to light and back again, fleeing to gather in a dour square that stood at the crossing of a spoke-road and a side street.

Bakkara stood at the square's north end as the ragged fighters poured in from all sides, surveying them bleakly. Their expressions were disbelieving, their faith in their cause tattered. For so long they had worked in secret, and they had thought themselves invincible, righteous crusaders for a cause blessed by the gods. But the moment they had stepped into the light they had been smashed by the power of the Empire. It was a cruel lesson, and

Bakkara considered what would become of the Ais Maraxa if they managed to get themselves out of this.

Now sufficient numbers had crammed into the square for him to call the order to head for the keep. Through the fires of the shellshot that were still bursting all around them, he led the crowd at a run up the steep, cobbled spoke-road that headed towards the looming structure at Zila's hub. Maybe there they could at least give the enemy pause. New strategies could be mooted, new plans made.

But who would make them?

He dashed the rain from his eyes, casting his doubts away as he did so. Regroup and defend. That was the next thing he had to do, and he did not think beyond that. He had never thought beyond his next objective. That was his nature.

They came to the end of the spoke-road, and it opened out into the great circular plaza that surrounded the keep. Bakkara slowed to a halt, and so did the men who ran with him. The stillness spread backwards, until even those at the rear of the crowd who could not see had ceased jostling, subdued by a dreadful trepidation.

Ranked before them, at the foot of the keep, were more than a thousand men; double the amount that Bakkara had mustered.

Bakkara took a breath and assessed the amount of trouble they were in. The space between the Ais Maraxa and the enemy troops was all but empty, a dark, slick expanse of crescent-shaped flagstones. A pair of large fires to their left – where shellshot jelly still burned against the downpour – cast multiple yellow glints across the divide. The troops were a mixture of all the Bloods who had arrayed themselves against the revolt; but he also saw peasants there, townsfolk of Zila, eager to buy their own lives by abetting the invaders. He tried to feel disgust, but he could not. It seemed petty now.

There above them, on the steps leading to the keep, he picked out the dimly shining Mask of a Weaver. The face of precious metals was an obscenity against the ragged robes that he wore. Bakkara did not need to look up any further to know that the keep had already been breached.

Men were murmuring in fear behind him. The very thought of facing a Weaver was enough to make them balk. Yet the enemy forces that had scaled the southern wall were catching up to them with every wasted moment. Bakkara sensed that he had to act now, or he would lose them.

Their lives were forfeit if they were captured. He knew that, with the certainty of a man who had seen war over and over. He also knew that there were worse things than dying.

'Ais Maraxa!' he roared, his voice carrying over the crowd. It sounded like someone else's voice, someone else's words. 'For Lucia! *For Lucia!*'

With that he raised his sword high and cried wordlessly, and as one the men that followed him did the same, their instant of weakness passing at the sound of Lucia's name, reminded of the faith that had brought them here in the first place. Bakkara's chest swelled with an emotion so glorious that he could not put a name to it, and he swung his sword forward to point at the enemy who waited to receive them with better weapons, better guns, and greater numbers.

'*Attack!*' he bellowed.

Rifles cracked and swords rang free of their scabbards as the last of the Ais Maraxa surged forward to the death that awaited them, and in his final moments Bakkara knew what it was like to be a leader at last.

TWENTY-SEVEN

When Nuki's eye rose over the eastern horizon, it looked down on a very different Zila.

The Surananyi in Tchom Rin, the rage of the pestilent goddess of the desert at the murder of the Empress, had blown itself out by now, and left the successive mornings with a brittle and crystalline quality. It was such a light that fell across the broken crown of Zila, its rooftops blackened and timbers open to the sky, trailing dozens of streamers of thick smoke into the air where the gentle wind blew them northward. No longer grim and defiant, it was a carcass of its former pride, and those townsfolk that walked its streets went shamefaced and terrified of the consequences of their insurrection.

Everywhere was the slow, lazy movement of an aftermath, like tired revellers cleaning up after a festival. As the sun climbed to its zenith, camps were being broken and repitched closer to the hill. Some troops were departing altogether, their presence urgently needed elsewhere. Corpses of the shot, impaled or incinerated were cleared away from the foot of the town wall, and a steady stream of carts rolled from the south gate carrying the dead from within.

The process of restoring order and meting out punishment would not be short. Zila had defied the Empire, and an example had to be made. That was Xejen's downfall, in the end. He had not accounted for the Baraks' ruthless determination to keep the status quo in these times. A famine was coming, was already biting at the edges of Saramyr and gnawing its way inward. Society teetered on the brink of chaos. In such a climate, any dissent had to be stamped on as hard as possible. Only with rigid order could the Empire make its way through the hard times ahead. The peasants had to learn that revolution was impossible. And so the high families had assaulted Zila with force far beyond anything Xejen or the townsfolk had expected, caring nothing for the sanctity of non-combatants or the structural damage to one of Saramyr's most important settlements. If they had not been able to breach the wall, they would have burned Zila to embers or smashed it flat with explosives.

Rebellion was unacceptable. The people of Zila had learned that now, and they would learn it again and again over the next few weeks. The message would carry. The Empire was inviolable.

But to the Barak Zahn tu Ikati, it felt like trying to blow life into a cadaver. The Empire, to him, had died long ago. He had been instrumental in the planning of last night's attack, but his contribution had been emotionless. He did not burn with zeal for the preservation of their way of life like Barak Moshito tu Vinaxis did, or the generals sent by the other high families.

Yet he had felt that way once. Before Mos usurped the throne, before Anais tu Erinima was killed. Before his daughter died.

It was midday when he walked from the doors of the scorched keep, down into the plaza where the last of the Ais Maraxa dead were being cleared away, their slack limbs and gaping faces sundered by scabbed wounds. The congealed blood on the crescent flagstones was cooking in the fierce heat, a sticky and sickly-sweet odour that cloyed in the back of the throat. The grey and shattered streets of Zila had dried already, and now they were dusty and quiet, a maze of bright sunlight and harsh black shadow in which cowed men and women skulked and would not meet his eye.

He was a lean, rangy man, with spare features and pox-pitted cheeks that had become lately gaunt and hollow. His trim, prematurely white beard hid most of it, but not around his eyes, where the toll of his long suffering was easy to see. Over fifty harvests had passed him by, but none had been as hard as the last few. Not since Lucia was lost.

The moment of their meeting was engraved upon his memory as if it had happened yesterday. He had lived it every day since, recalling over and over the fundamental shift that he had experienced when he first laid eyes on the Aberrant child. Suddenly he had been aware of a level of feeling that he had not known existed, something deeply primal and irresistible in force, and he knew then what a man must know when he watches his wife give birth: an overwhelming introduction into the mysteries of the wonderful and terrible bond between parent and child. He saw her, and he *knew*. Every instinct blared at him at once: *she is yours.*

She knew, too. It was in the way she threw her arms around him, and he saw it in those pale eyes, and in the gaze of pure betrayal she gave him as tears welled in them.

Where were you? they asked, and they tore his heart into pieces.

The fact that he had not known he had a daughter did not make it any easier for him. Of course, her age and the time of her birth corresponded with the short, tempestuous affair he had conducted with the Blood Empress all those years ago, but then he had known that Anais had still been sleeping with her husband during that period, and when it was announced that she had become pregnant it had simply seemed impossible that it might be his. The idea had occurred to him only briefly, and then been dismissed. If she suspected it was Zahn's issue, he was certain that she would have either told him, or poisoned it in the womb without ever letting anyone but her physician find out that she was with child. They were the only politically expedient courses of action. When she did neither, Zahn reasoned that it was nothing to do with him: he had already surmounted the bitterness that he had felt when she had broken off their dangerous relationship, and was happy to be out of it now that an heir had become involved. Children were simply something that Zahn had no interest in. Or so he thought.

But in that instant when they had met, the grief and loss and regret crushed him. He felt like he had abandoned her at birth.

He had retreated from the Imperial Keep, stunned by what had happened, but he had not intended to retreat for long. He would have confronted Anais, even amid all the civil unrest that was going on at the time, even though he had no proof beyond the simple certainty that he was right. He would have demanded to know why she kept Lucia from him. He would have done all sorts of reckless things, like a hot-headed youth, if Anais and their daughter had not been killed first.

Something had withered inside him at the news, and had never grown back. Some crucial part of his soul had shrivelled and blackened, and robbed the colour from the world. He tried to tell himself that it was ridiculous for him to be so affected by this. After all, he had been content in ignorance for years, and he had only known his true connection to Lucia for a very short time. How could he feel loss for something he had had so briefly?

But the words were hollow, and their echoes mocked him, and he stopped trying to apply sense to senselessness.

Misery spread like a cancer, killing other parts of him. Food no longer gave him joy. His companions found him saturnine and melancholy. He took little interest in the affairs of his family and his estates, delegating many tasks that should have been his to younger brothers and sisters. He was no less competent as a Barak, but he was disinterested, stripped of ambition. He maintained his family's holdings well enough, but he had no passion for the political games and the jostling for status that were an integral part of Saramyr high society. He was merely treading water.

But something was to happen this morning that would ignite a flicker of something long forgotten in his breast, something so foreign to him now that he struggled to recall its name.

Hope. Foolish hope.

A woman had been detained by Blood Ikati troops after she had been found unconscious in the ruins of a building, having been struck on the head by a falling beam as the ceiling above her came down. That same beam had saved her life, for it had collapsed at an angle and sheltered her from the bricks raining around her. She had been uncovered by peasants who had begun to dig for survivors, and turned over to Zahn's men along with a much greater prize: Xejen tu Imotu, whom the peasants eagerly denounced as the leader of the Ais Maraxa.

Though nobody knew who she was, her noble attire and hair were enough to mark her as not being of Zila, and her proximity to Xejen when she was found was damning. She was kept under guard and nursed until she awoke, at which point she demanded to see Barak Zahn tu Ikati, claiming that she was Mishani tu Koli.

'I will see her,' he had told the messenger who brought him the news. Then, remembering himself, he added: 'Have my servants bathe and dress her first, if needs be. She is high-born. Treat her as such.'

And so he strode through the newly hushed streets of Zila, to where Mishani waited for him.

Mishani met him by her sickbed, but not in it. She was weak from breathing dust and badly bruised all over, and she had suffered a terrible blow to the back of her head that was causing her eyes not to focus properly. The physicians would not let her leave her room; indeed, they hovered about in case she should faint from the exertion of getting out of bed. The knowledge that she was noble and important to their Barak had turned them from imperious and haughty men into fawning servants. When Zahn chimed and entered, he dismissed them with a flick of his hand.

The physicians had commandeered a row of undamaged houses for their base of operations, and filled the beds with injured soldiers and townsfolk. Mishani, whether by chance or by virtue of her dress, had been put in the master bedroom of some wealthy merchant's abode. The bed was plainly expensive, and the walls were decorated with charcoal sketches and elegant watercolours. In an ornate bone cradle there was a pattern-board depicting a seascape, the washes of colour suspended within a three-dimensional oblong of hardened transparent gel. Zahn idly wondered if the person who possessed all of this had been killed at the hands of the townsfolk during the revolt, in last night's bombardment, or if they were still alive now and simply thrown out on the street. Revolution was an unpleasant business.

Mishani tu Koli was standing by her bed, dressed in borrowed robes with her voluminous hair combed and loose. She appeared to be entirely unhurt, but Zahn knew well enough that she was simply not letting it show. There were clues: she was wearing her hair in a style that covered her cheeks, to hide scratches on her ear; there was a faint patch of blue on the back of her wrist where the cuff of her robe did not hide it; then there was the telling fact that she had not strayed far from the edge of her bed, in case her strength failed her. He had met her several times before in the Imperial Court when she was younger, and her poise had always been remarkable.

'Mistress Mishani tu Koli,' he said, performing the correct bow for their relative social rank. 'It grieves me to hear that you have been injured in this calamity.'

She returned the female form of the same bow. 'By Ocha's grace, I have not suffered as much as I might have,' she said. None of the weakness of her condition bled into her voice.

'Would you like to sit?' Zahn offered, gesturing at a chair. But Mishani was not about to take any concessions.

'I prefer to stand,' she said levelly, knowing that there was only one chair and no mats in the room. He was well over a foot taller than her; if she sat then he would be looking down on her at a steeper angle than he already was.

'My servants have told me that you wished to see me,' he said.

'Indeed,' came the reply. 'I have been wanting to see you ever since I was detained in Zila by the Ais Maraxa. Though in the end you had a somewhat violent way of bringing our meeting about.'

Zahn gave her a hint of a smile.

'May I ask you a question?' she said.

'Of course.'

'What has become of Xejen tu Imotu?'

Zahn considered that for a moment. 'He lives, barely.'

'Might I know where he is?'

'Are you concerned for him?'

'I am concerned, but not for the reasons you imagine,' she told him.

Zahn studied her for a moment. She was a sculpture in ice.

'I let Barak Moshito deal with him,' Zahn said. He linked his hands behind his back and walked over to the pattern-board, studying it. 'Moshito will undoubtedly turn him over to his Weaver. I cannot say I feel sympathy. I have little love for the Ais Maraxa.'

'Because they remind you of your daughter,' Mishani finished. 'They make you believe in the possibility that she is still alive, and that is a raw wound indeed.'

Zahn's head snapped around, his eyes flashing angrily.

'Forgive my bluntness,' she said. 'I was heading to Lalyara to find you with the intention of divining your feelings towards her. Now I cannot afford the time to be delicate.' She fixed him with a steady gaze. 'Her life hangs in the balance. Xejen tu Imotu knows where she is.'

Zahn made the connection immediately. If Xejen knew, then the Weaver would get it out of him. And if the Weavers knew . . .

This was too fast, too much to believe. If he accepted that, then he accepted his daughter was still alive. He shook his head, running his fingers down his bearded chin.

'No, no,' he murmured. 'What is your agenda, Mishani tu Koli? Why were you here, in Zila?'

'Did Chien not tell you this?' she asked.

'Chien? Ah, the hostage. I am sorry to say he died the night he was brought out of Zila.'

Mishani's face showed nothing. She felt no grief for him: he was merely a casualty. What did concern her was that it meant her father's men were aware she was in Zila, and they would be very close indeed. She had to win Zahn's trust now, in any way she could. It was imperative that she got out of the town in secret, and the only way she would do that would be under Zahn's protection.

'So, will you answer my question?' he prompted. 'Why were you in Zila?'

'Misfortune,' she said. 'I was waylaid as I travelled to find you. Although it seems the gods have brought us together anyway.'

'That is too convenient,' he said. His tone had become a lot less polite now. 'You know that your being here is enough to have you beheaded. And you certainly were not a prisoner; you were found with the leader of the Ais Maraxa.'

Mishani had feared this. If she had been able to meet him at Lalyara, then his suspicions would not have been aroused; but circumstances had forced her into a position in which any play she made would seem like bargaining for her life.

'You are correct,' she said. 'I was brought here against my will, but they did not keep me as a prisoner. I am something of a heroine to their cause because I helped to save your daughter. It does not mean I endorse it.'

'Stop these *lies*!' Zahn cried suddenly, grabbing the pattern-board and tipping the cradle. It hit the floor and smashed into coloured shards. 'Lucia tu Erinima died five years ago and more. Her father was Durun tu Batik. I do not know what leverage you think you have over me, Mistress Mishani, but you are sorely misguided if you believe you will win your freedom by trying to resurrect a ghost.'

Mishani's triumph did not show on her face, but she knew she had the advantage now. A man such as Zahn did not abandon his dignity easily; his skills at negotiation had kept Blood Ikati a major player in the courts, and his display of rage showed how sensitive the subject of Lucia was to him.

'You could have me executed,' Mishani said, her voice cold. 'But then you will only learn that I was telling the truth when the Weavers kill your daughter. Could you live with that, Zahn? You have not been living with it well these past years.'

'Heart's blood, you do not know when to stop!' Zahn cried. 'I will not hear any more of this!'

He was heading for the curtained doorway when Mishani spoke again.

'Zaelis tu Unterlyn was there on the day you met your daughter,' she snapped, her voice rising. 'It was he who organised the kidnapping of Lucia. On the very day that Blood Batik overthrew Blood Erinima, we stole the child and hid her. No corpse was ever found because there *was* no corpse, Zahn! Lucia is alive!'

Zahn's shoulders were hunched, his hand on the curtain. She had not wanted to bring the leader of the Libera Dramach's name into this, but matters were too critical. She could not let him leave.

He turned back to her, and his face was suddenly haggard again.

'You *know* you believe me,' she said. A sudden rush of lightheadedness took her, but she fought against it. It was stiflingly hot; she did not know how much longer she could go without sitting down.

'I cannot believe you,' Zahn croaked. 'Do you understand?' He knew how clever Mishani could be, he knew the ways of the court, and though he wanted more than anything to think that Lucia could be alive, he would not be manipulated. He was no friend to Blood Koli, and he had no reason to trust one of them. He would not lose his daughter again, by allowing himself to think he might regain her and then to discover it was a bluff. He could not go through that. He had been numb so long that it had become a shield against the world, and when it came to the moment, he found that he was afraid to discard it.

He turned to go again. This kind of torment could not be borne.

'Wait,' Mishani said. 'I can prove it.'

Zahn had almost dreaded to hear those words.

'How?' he said, his head bowed.

'Xejen will be interrogated,' she said. 'You must attend.'

'What good will that do?'

'He knows where she is, as I do. Sooner or later, we will talk. The Weaver will try to keep it secret; he will try to obtain the information for his kind alone. He will scour Xejen's mind and then decide what to tell you. You must not let him. *Make* him share what he learns *as he learns it.* Have him make Xejen speak only the truth, and ask Xejen yourself. The Weaver cannot refuse you if you order him.'

Zahn was silent, his back to her. Mishani knew that this was a desperate play, but it was all she had. The lives of thousands depended on her. If she was unable to prevent the Weavers finding the Fold, then at least with Zahn on her side she might be able to get them a warning in time to do something about it. It was a slim chance, but better than none at all.

'You will learn the truth at the same time as you condemn her to death,' Mishani said. 'But if I cannot persuade you to stop this, then that must be the price we all pay. If you will not believe what your heart knows, then you will hear your daughter's name on the lips of a Weaver.'

'Pray that I do,' Zahn replied. 'For if not, I will be back, and I will have you killed.'

'I pray that you do not,' Mishani said. 'For I would give my life in exchange for all those who will die to convince you.'

Xejen tu Imotu thought that his story was over when the ceiling came down on him, but he regained consciousness to find that there was an epilogue, and it was full of agony.

He woke on a bed in the donjon of the keep, and woke screaming. The pain from his shattered legs propelled him out of oblivion, an idiot, senseless roar of breathtaking brutality. His trousers had been cut away above the knee. His legs were massive and blue-purple, obese with swelling and the terrible bruising of drastic trauma. Both of them kinked unnaturally in several places. No attempt had been made to set them, and the snapped ends of bone made bulges against the blotched skin.

He screamed again, and screamed until his throat was raw. At some point, he blacked out.

When he awoke again, it was to a new horror.

He felt himself pulled into awareness, his mind hooked like a fish and dragged out of the protective cocoon where it sheltered from the inconceivable pain. His eyes flickered open. Afternoon light misted in through the dusty air from a barred window high on one wall, scattering across his ruined legs and the bare stone cell. Figures surrounded him, but one leaned closer than the others. A Mask of angles, sharp cheeks and jutting ridges of chin and forehead, some of gold and some of silver and others of bronze; a mountainous metal landscape, crafted by a master Edgefather, surrounding the dark, black pits of the eyes.

A Weaver.

He sucked in a breath to shriek, but a pale, withered hand passed over him, and his throat locked.

'Be silent,' hissed the voice behind the Mask.

There were two others here. He recognised the Baraks: Zahn, tall and rangy and gaunt; Moshito, stocky and bald and grim-faced. They looked down on him pitilessly.

'You are Xejen tu Imoto?' Moshito asked. Xejen nodded mutely, his eyes tearing. 'Leader of the Ais Maraxa?' He nodded again.

Zahn shifted his gaze to the Weaver. This one was in the employ of Blood Vinaxis, a particularly vicious and sadistic monster if Moshito's accounts were to be believed. His name was Fahrekh. Zahn's own Weaver he had left back at his estates at the disposal of his family; he detested Weavers, especially since he suspected that the last Weave-lord, Vyrrch, had been responsible for the coup in which Lucia had disappeared.

He caught himself. Already he was amending his beliefs to suit Mishani. In which Lucia had *died*, he forced himself to think. Blood Koli was an enemy, Mishani was an enemy, and however they might have learned of his weakness, he would not let her exploit it.

But gods, what if she *was* telling the truth? If Xejen talked, then neither the Weavers nor the Emperor would rest until Lucia was hunted down. Was there any way to stop this? Was there?

He bit down on his lip. Idiocy. Foolishness.

Lucia was dead.

'Are you sure he will do as you told him?' Zahn asked Moshito, motioning at the bent and hooded figure crouching over the bed.

'I have heard my Barak's command,' Fahrekh said, with a curl of disdain in his voice. 'Nothing will be hidden. You will ask him your questions. I will ensure he answers and speaks true.'

Xejen's eyes roved from one to the other in alarm.

'It is as he says, Zahn,' Moshito replied. 'What's got you so suspicious?'

'Weavers always make me suspicious,' Zahn replied, trying to keep the uncertainty and indecision out of his voice. Yet he wondered whether the Weaver might not simply scour Xejen's mind in secret and take what he wanted, and whether there was any way they could tell. Heart's blood, how had it fallen this way: that the only method he had to prove Mishani right would also put that same knowledge in the hands of those who would desire Lucia's death?

It came down to a matter of faith. Could he believe Mishani? Could he believe his daughter was alive? Once, perhaps. But his faith had died along with the other parts of his soul, and he had to know. Belief was not enough. He had to *know*.

'Begin,' said Moshito.

Fahrekh turned his gleaming face slowly toward the broken figure on the bed, the afternoon light skipping from plane to plane in triangles of brightness.

'Yes, my Barak,' he muttered.

As the Weaver bored into his thoughts and will like a weevil into the bole of a tree, Xejen found his throat free to scream again. Fahrekh found that he worked better when his victims were responsive.

TWENTY-EIGHT

The science of predicting the orbits of the three moons was ancient. Though moonstorms came at apparently random intervals, over hundreds of years it was possible to see a pattern of unwavering regularity. Astronomers could now tell almost exactly when the three moons would be in close enough proximity to spark a moonstorm. Navigators relied heavily on their ability to plot the course of the moons so that they could assess what effect each would have on the world's tides. Though it was only the learned who knew just when a moonstorm would hit, usually rumours carried far enough among the peasantry to make almost everyone aware of it.

None of which was any help to Kaiku and Tsata, who were out in the open when the moonstorm struck.

There had been developments since the night when they had narrowly escaped the ghaureg, and all thoughts of turning back for home had been cast aside. Though they had previously abandoned any hope of catching or killing one of the Nexuses, they had resolved to observe the flood plain and see if any more information could be gained about the foul, seething building that crouched near the banks of the Zan. They kept themselves at a distance, where the sentries were sparse enough to avoid. Getting close to the plain was impossible now, for it was too well guarded.

Kaiku's determination to stay was rewarded sooner than she thought. The very next night, the barges began to arrive.

She had theorised that the river must have been the method for getting all these Aberrants here in the first place, and that they must be transporting food from the north which they had stockpiled in the strange building for their army of predators. Kaiku and Tsata had witnessed several mass feedings, in which great piles of meat were brought out on carts driven by the same docile midget-folk that had served the Weavers at the monastery on Fo. She called them *golneri,* meaning 'small people' in a Saramyrrhic mode usually applied to children. She should have expected that they would be here: the Weavers were notoriously incapable of looking after themselves, afflicted as they were by a gradually increasing insanity as a result of using their Masks.

Still, for all that, they had never seen any evidence of river travel until now; but when the barges arrived, it was in a multitude.

They had appeared during the day, so when Kaiku and Tsata breached the barrier that night they found them already waiting. They crowded the banks of the river on either side, a clutter of more than three dozen massive craft along the edge of the flood plain. For two nights a steady stream of carts went back and forth in the moonlight and the golneri swarmed to unload great bales and boxes. Suddenly the Weavers' apparently random barge-buying enterprises over the last five years made sense: they had been moving the Aberrant predators along the rivers, gathering them together, assembling their forces. Kaiku wondered what kind of influence the Weavers had over the barge-masters that walked the decks, to trust them with the knowledge of this secret army. It had to be something more than money.

On the third night, the boarding began.

The initial shock at finding the flood plain half-empty when they arrived just after dusk was quickly surmounted by what was happening on the river. The Aberrants were being herded up wide gangplanks into the holds of the fat-bellied barges, a steady stream of muscle and tooth parading meekly onto the cargo decks under the watchful eyes of the Nexuses. There were so many barges that they could not all berth along the bank at once, and they queued northward to receive their allocation of the monstrosities, and headed upstream when they were done. It seemed that the barrier of misdirection did not cover the river; but then, nobody came this far down the Zan anyway, for the great falls were just to the south and no river traffic could pass that. Kaiku and Tsata watched in amazement at the sheer scale of the logistical maneouvring.

'They are on the move,' Tsata said, his pale green eyes shining in the moonlight.

'But where are they moving to?' Kaiku asked herself.

As dawn broke, and the last of the barges departed, Kaiku and Tsata retreated beyond the barrier to rest; but sleep would not come easily that day, and they spent their time restlessly chewing over the implications, and whether they should risk warning Cailin via the Weave. This was what they had remained behind for: to raise the alarm if the Weavers should make a move towards the Fold. But the barges were not heading that way. They were going towards Axekami, and from there they could travel to any point along the Jabaza, the Kerryn or the Rahn.

Tsata pointed out that it was possible they could re-enter the Xarana Fault via the latter river. The Fold was only a dozen miles or so to the west of the Rahn. But Kaiku did not dare to send word unless it was absolutely necessary, and they did not know enough of where those barges were going.

Eventually, they agreed that they would stay two more nights. If no other information had come to light by then, they would head east for a day to get as far from the Weavers as they might, and Kaiku would send her message. What perils that would bring, she had no idea. Perhaps the Weavers would not notice her at all, and Cailin's edict against distance communication was simply her being overcautious. Or perhaps it would be like a waterfowl trying to sneak through a roomful of foxes.

The next night brought the moonstorm.

It was because they had been out of contact with the world for so long, existing in their own little society of two, that they did not expect it. They had crossed the Zan and were watching from a bluff on the western side, where the sentries were much fewer. There, the high ground reached like fingers towards the edge of the river, cutting off suddenly in sheer cliffs as it came to the water. Wide open-ended valleys lay between the cliffs, nuzzling gently against the banks. Kaiku and Tsata had hidden themselves in a brake of blighted undergrowth that fringed a tall promontory, and were lying on their bellies watching the inactivity below through Nomoru's spyglass. She had reluctantly consented to leave it with them in amid sullen threats as to what would happen if they did not bring it back intact.

The moons had risen from different horizons – Aurus in the north, Iridima in the west, and Neryn from the south-west – so that there was no warning until they had almost converged, directly overhead.

Kaiku felt the sharpening in the air first, the strange plucking sensation as if they were being gently lifted. She looked at Tsata, and the golden-skinned man with his green tattoos looked corpselike and unearthly in the moonlight. The rustling of the tough bushes in which they sheltered seemed a rasping whisper. Her senses tautened, picking up a sensation of unseen movement like rats in the walls of a house.

She looked up, and felt a thrill of alarm as she saw the three orbs, all half-shadowed at a diagonal angle across their faces, crowding towards each other in the sky. Clouds were boiling out of nowhere, churning and writhing under the influence of the muddled gravities.

'Spirits,' she muttered, glaring down at the plain. 'We need to get to shelter.'

They barely made it.

The moonstorm began with a calamitous shriek just as they found the shelter they were searching for. It was a deep and wide shelf in a hulking accretion of limestone, with a broad overhang for a ceiling, as if some enormous beast had taken a bite out of the smooth side of the rock. The bottom sloped up towards the top so that it narrowed as it went further in, but even at the back there was enough space for Kaiku and Tsata to huddle under, he cross-legged, she with her arms around her knees.

The rain followed that first unearthly cry, coming down all at once, and suddenly the previously quiet night was a wet roar of pummelling rain, bowing the gnarled stalks of the blighted foliage and spattering furiously against unyielding stone. Kaiku and Tsata found that they were quite dry in their little haven. Though the lip of the shelf became quickly soaked, they were well clear of the storm's reach.

Tsata broke out some cold smoked meat and split it with Kaiku, as he always did, and for a time they sat in silence, watching the rain and listening to the saw and scrape of the sky tearing itself to pieces. The desolate scene flickered purple in the backwash of the eerie lightning that attended the phenomenon.

Kaiku felt uneasy. Moonstorms had always frightened her, even as a child; but events in her past had rendered them heavy with bad memories. Her family had died in a moonstorm, poisoned by her own father to save them from what the Weavers would do to them. And both that moonstorm and the subsequent one had seen her fleeing for her life from the shin-shin, the demons of shadow that the Weavers had sent to claim first her and then Lucia.

There was concern in Tsata's eyes as he regarded her.

'It will be brief,' he said reassuringly. 'The moons are only passing each other; they have not matched orbits.'

Kaiku brushed her hair away from where it hung across one side of her face and nodded. She felt a little awkward as the recipient of his sympathy. Why had she told him about her family, anyway? Why had she talked of her past to him? It was strange, that one as guarded as she was should have done so: and yet, somehow, to speak of such things with him did not seem as hard as it did with anyone else. With anyone Saramyr.

Kaiku had lost track of the time that had passed since she had left the Fold. A month? Had it been that long? The beginning of Aestival Week and her betrayal by Asara in the guise of Saran seemed distant memories now; she had been too busy to dwell on it. The land was beginning to feel autumnal, the mugginess of summer dispersed by cooler breezes even if the heat of the daytime had not diminished by much. The food they had brought with them had been eaten long ago, so they hunted animals outside the Weavers' barrier when they were not sleeping, or gathered roots and plants to make stews. There was a kind of cleanness to the way they had been living since Nomoru and Yugi had departed. The diet was rough and had far too much red meat in it for Kaiku's liking, but she felt oddly close to the land, and that made her happy.

By night, they braved the Aberrant sentries, and Kaiku was becoming very good at the lessons Tsata taught her. He no longer had to worry about keeping an eye on her when they were sneaking through the rucks and pleats of broken land. Rather, he had begun to rely on her, making her more of a partner and less of a pupil. She had become stealthy and adept at hiding, more observant and competent than she had been a few short weeks ago. And in those weeks they had come to know one another very well, in a way that they never had on the confinement of the ship from Okhamba to Saramyr.

Kaiku had disliked him for a long time after he had risked her life as bait for the maghkriin back in the jungles of his home continent; but now she understood him better, and it made perfect sense through his eyes. She knew it was probably a transient thing, like her friendships with the travellers who had accompanied them on the junk the first time she had crossed the ocean; but for the moment, she felt closer to him than anyone she could remember in recent years. The constant companionship, the weeks of doing everything as a pair, reminded her of the relationship she had shared with her brother Machim, back in a time before she had ever known true loss.

But for all that, there were still barriers; it was just that they were in different places to the usual ones. She had surprised herself by telling him about her family, yet he had never spoken of his own. She knew why well enough: because she had not asked. He would not refuse her if she wanted to talk about him – Okhambans, she had learned, were notoriously co-operative – but it was that very knowledge that prevented her. She felt that by asking him she might be forcing him to speak of something he did not want to, and that he would be bound by his nature to suffer that for her. She still did not wholly comprehend his mentality, and was wary of being as rude to him as he unwittingly was to her at times.

Perhaps it was the strange, faintly unreal atmosphere of the moonstorm, or the sudden feeling that she had been cheated out of her secrets while he still kept his, but she decided then to risk it.

'Why are you here, Tsata?' she asked. Then, once the first step was taken, she said with more conviction: 'Why did you come to Saramyr? Gods, Tsata, I have been with you practically every moment for weeks now and I still know nothing about you. Your people seem to share everything; why not this?'

Tsata was laughing by the time she had finished. 'You are truly an amazing people, your kind,' he said. 'I have been tormenting you all this time and you have resisted your curiosity so.' He smiled. 'I was interested to see how long you would hold out.'

Kaiku blushed.

'Forgive me,' he said. 'You are so obsessed with manners and formality that you have not dared ask me about any information I did not volunteer first. With all you have learned about me and the Tkiurathi, have you not guessed the value of openness yet?'

'It is *because* you are so open that I did not want to ask you about things you had not mentioned,' she replied, feeling embarrassed and relieved at the same time.

He laughed again. 'I had not expected that. I suppose it makes a kind of sense.' He gave her a wry glance. 'It seems that I am not as familiar with your ways yet as I thought.'

The skies screamed overhead, and a jagged shaft of vermilion lightning split the distant horizon, making Kaiku cringe unconsciously.

'Saran was the same,' Tsata said. 'He never asked me my motives, was content in ignorance. He believed that it was my business, I suppose, and not his.'

'Hers,' Kaiku corrected bitterly. Kaiku had told him about Asara, though not about how she had almost coupled with her. Tsata had not been in the least taken aback by the deception, or by the idea of an Aberrant that could take on other forms and other genders. There were frogs in Okhamba that could change sex, he had told her, and insects that could rebuild their bodies in cocoons. She was not without precedent in nature, only in humanity.

Tsata became thoughtful for a moment. 'The answer to your question is simple,' he said at length. 'Saran told me of his – or her – mission, and of the danger the Weavers posed to Saramyr. He also spoke of what he believed might happen if they won this continent. They would invade others.'

Kaiku nodded at that: it ran concurrent with what she had already guessed.

'I went with him to the heart of Okhamba to see if his theories bore weight. I returned convinced.' He rubbed absently at his bare upper arm, fingers tracing the green swirls of the tattoo that covered him. 'I have a responsibility to the greater *pash*, that of all my people. So I determined to come to Saramyr and see the threat for myself, to observe what your people's reaction would be and to carry the news back home if I could. I will need to tell my people as Saran told yours. That is why I came here, and that is why I will have to leave.'

Kaiku felt abruptly saddened. It was no more than she had expected, but she was surprised at her own reaction. Their time in this isolated existence was limited, and his words were a reminder that it would have to end soon. The return to the real world, with all its attendant complications, was inevitable.

'That is what I had surmised,' Kaiku said, her voice not much louder than the hiss of the rain. 'It seems I am learning to predict you also.'

Tsata gave her an odd look. 'Perhaps you are,' he mused. He looked out over the bleak, rain-lashed landscape for a short time, listening to the horrible racket of the moonstorm.

Kaiku stiffened suddenly. She scrambled to the edge of the rock shelf and looked about.

'Did you hear something?' he asked, appearing next to her in a crouch.

'The barrier is down,' she said.

Tsata did not understand her for a moment.

'*The barrier is down!*' she said, more urgently. 'The shield of misdirection. It is gone. I can sense its absence.'

'We should get back to the flood plain,' Tsata said.

Kaiku nodded, her expression grim. The barrier had come down. The Weavers were not hiding any more.

She dreaded to think what that might mean.

Cailin tu Moritat's eyes flicked open, and her irises were red as blood.

'Kaiku,' she breathed, aghast.

There were two other Sisters in the conference chamber with her. It was one of the upper rooms of the house of the Red Order, its walls painted black and hung with pennants and symbols of crimson. They had been sitting on mats around the table in the centre of the room, talking softly over the maelstrom that howled and battered at the shutters like some hungry and thwarted beast. The glow of the lanterns and the sinuous path of the scented smoke from the brazier that sat between them had taken on a malevolent quality under the warping influence of the moonstorm, and their identically painted faces seemed narrow and shrewd with conspiracy.

The other two looked at Cailin. They did not need to see her red eyes to know that something had happened; they had felt it stroking past them, a whisper in the Weave that could only have been one of their own.

Cailin stood up suddenly, rising to her full height.

'Gather our Sisters,' she said. 'I want every one of us that resides in the Fold to be here in this house in an hour's time.'

She left the room before the others could rise to obey, stalking away and down the stairs, out onto the muddy, makeshift streets. It was barely midnight. Zaelis would still be awake. Not that she would have hesitated to rouse him anyway; this was far too important.

She passed along the deserted ways of the Fold, a tall and thin shadow slipping through the rain, seeming to slide *between* the droplets, for as heavy as the downpour was it only dampened her slightly. She was furious and afraid all at once, and her thoughts were dark as she went.

Kaiku. Gods, how could she be so reckless? Cailin did not know whether to applaud her or curse her. She had been in an almost constant state of worry since Yugi and Nomoru had returned with news of the Aberrant army massed on the banks of the Zan, and of Kaiku's refusal to return. If Kaiku had been captured during that time, the Weavers would have flensed her mind and gleaned everything they would need to know about the Red Order. Now, Kaiku had used the Weave to send a message more than a hundred miles, spooling a thread across all that distance. It only took one Weaver to sense it, to catch that thread and piggyback to its destination or track it to its source, and all the Red Order's years of secrecy would be undone. Bad enough that the Weavers knew there was *one* Aberrant woman who could beat them at their own game – the previous Weave-lord Vyrrch had warned them of that just before she killed him – but one was only a freak occurrence, a lone misfire of nature like Asara was. Two of them communicating hinted at much greater things, at collaboration, at organisation. If the Weavers caught even the slightest indication of the Red Order's existence, they would dedicate all their efforts to wiping them out.

The Red Order were the single biggest threat to the Weavers, maybe even greater than Lucia herself, because against them the Weavers did not have the superiority afforded them by their Masks. The Red Order could Weave too, but their power was inherent and natural to them, and that made them better at it than men, who needed clumsy devices to penetrate the realm beyond the senses.

But the Sisters were few, too few. And Cailin dared not expose them unless it was absolutely necessary.

Now, perhaps, that time had come. For as angry as she was with Kaiku for taking such a risk, Cailin was equally disturbed by the message. Matters had taken a very grave turn. Action was needed, and soon; but it might not be in the way that Zaelis imagined. Cailin's overwhelming priority was the survival of the Red Order. Beyond that, very little mattered.

Though the journey between her house and Zaelis's was a short one, the rain had stopped and the skies quieted by the time she got there. The moons were gliding apart again, and the raging clouds now drifted listlessly, thinning and dispersing. The storm had been quick and savage, and its ending was as abrupt as its beginning.

The dwelling that Zaelis shared with his adopted daughter Lucia was an unremarkable one, nestling on one of the Fold's upper tiers amid several other houses that had been built to the same design. It was a simple, two-storey building of polished wood and plaster, with a balcony on the eastern side to look out over the valley, and a small shrine by its door with carved icons of Ocha and Isisya surrounded by burnt incense sticks and crushed flowers and smooth white pebbles. A single paper lantern burned outside, illuminating from within the pictograms of welcome and blessing it offered to visitors. Next to it hung a chime, which Cailin struck with the small hammer that hung alongside it.

Zaelis was at the door almost immediately, inviting her inside. It was a humble room, with a few mats and tables, potted plants nodding drowsily on stands, some ornamental weapons on the wall and an oil-paint landscape from a Fold artist whose work Zaelis seemed to admire, though the appeal had always escaped Cailin. A single lamp hung from the ceiling, putting the epicentre of illumination overhead and casting flattering shadows on everyone within. Lucia sat cross-legged on a mat in her nightgown, drinking a herbal infusion from a ceramic mug. She looked up as Cailin came in, her eyes blandly curious.

'She couldn't sleep,' Zaelis explained. He noted absently that Cailin's twin ponytails should have been dripping with water, the raven feathers of her ruff lank with moisture, her make-up smudged; yet none of these things were true. 'The moonstorm.'

Cailin did not have time for niceties. 'Kaiku has contacted me across the Weave,' she said. Zaelis's face fell at her tone. Lucia, unperturbed, continued to regard the Sister over the rim of her mug, as if she was merely relating something that the girl had known all along.

'Is it bad?'

'It is very bad,' she replied. 'The Aberrants are most certainly under the Weavers' control, through the medium of those beings that Yugi reported, which she calls Nexuses. Several nights ago most of them departed northward by barge up the Zan, but thousands were still left. Now all but a few of those have departed as well. The Weavers have dropped their barrier, and the Aberrants are on the move.'

'Where?' Zaelis demanded.

'East. Across the Fault. Towards us.'

Zaelis felt a pit open in the bottom of his stomach. 'How long?'

'They travel fast,' Cailin said. 'Very fast. She estimates we have four days and nights before they are upon us.'

'Four days and nights . . .' Zaelis repeated. He looked dazed. 'Heart's blood.'

'I have matters to attend to in the wake of this news,' Cailin said. 'I imagine you do too. I will return in a few hours.' She gave Lucia a peremptory tilt of her head. 'I doubt any of us will sleep tonight.'

With that, she was gone as fast as she had come, walking back towards the house of the Red Order, where she would prepare for the arrival of her brethren. Around her, the first gently glittering flakes of starfall had begun, tiny crystals of fused ice drifting down in the green-tinted light of the triple moons. It would fall sporadically for the next day or so. She ignored it, for her mind was on other things. She did indeed have matters to attend to, and a decision that might well be the most important she ever had to make.

The Fold had been compromised, and the Weavers were coming. She knew as well as Zaelis that four days and nights was not enough time to try and evacuate the population of the Fold across the hostile Fault, and even if he did, they would be caught on the run and killed. Where would they go? What would they do? He would not abandon all he had worked for, all his weapons and supplies and fortifications; nor would he abandon the townsfolk. He would be forced to make a stand here, at least until an alternative could be made feasible.

Her choice was simple. Zaelis and the Libera Dramach were bound to this place, but she was not. Should the Red Order stand with them against the Weavers, or should they leave them to their fate?

Yugi arrived at Zaelis's house shortly afterward. Lucia had dressed, and returned to her spot on the mat. She should have been asleep by now, but she did not appear to be tired in the slightest.

Zaelis had been too preoccupied to disapprove. His mind was full of dark musings in the wake of Cailin's news. He was thinking of Weavers, and gods, and Alskain Mar. Did the Libera Dramach even stand a chance, if what the spirit had shown Lucia was true? If this was indeed some conflict of the gods, what hope did they have of resisting the tides? Were they like some cork bobbing on a stormy ocean, powerless to act, merely staying afloat? He had a depressing sense that his life's work had been merely an illusion, an old man's folly, creating a resistance that could not, in the end, resist anything. He blamed Cailin, bitterly, for bringing them to this: for holding them back, for advising secrecy when action was needed. And now, finally, their cover had been somehow torn away, and they were exposed. They were not strong enough to fight the Weavers head-on, Zaelis knew that. Yet the alternative was to give up, and that he could never do.

He realised immediately that Yugi had been smoking amaxa root. It was in the sheen of his eyes and his dilated pupils, and the pungent smell still clung to his clothes.

'Gods, Yugi, I need you clearheaded!' he snapped in lieu of a greeting.

'Then you should have called for me in the morning,' Yugi retorted cheerily. 'As it is, I'm here. So what do you want?' He saw Lucia and gave her a little bow. Lucia returned it amiably with a dip of her head.

Zaelis sighed. 'Come inside and sit down,' he said. 'Lucia, would you brew something strong for Yugi?'

'Yes, Father,' she replied, and obediently went to the kitchen.

Zaelis sat opposite Yugi on the floor mat and studied him, gauging how far gone he was and whether he would take in anything that was said. Yugi's recreational use of amaxa root had always been a source of worry, but he had been doing it ever since Zaelis first knew him, and despite the dangers it had never bloomed into addiction. Yugi seemed to possess an unusual resistance to its withdrawal symptoms, and he insisted that he was able to take it or leave it as he chose. Zaelis had been sceptical for a long time, but he had been forced to accept after a while that Yugi was right. He was able to go without for weeks and months at a stretch, and it had never affected his reliability. He said that he used it to 'cope with the bad nights'. Zaelis was unsure what this meant, and Yugi would never talk about it.

It was simply an unfortunate moment that Zaelis had caught him at, and despite his annoyance he could not expect Yugi to be ready for action every moment of every day. Eventually, Zaelis decided that he was only mildly intoxicated, and that he would still be sharp-witted enough to understand what was being said to him. He had become adept at judging his friend's state over the years. And so he began to explain to Yugi what had occurred.

Shortly afterward, Lucia came back with a brew of lathamri, a bitter black infusion that promoted awareness and stimulated the body. She paused at the threshold of the room, looking at the two men sitting locked in conversation. Her father, white-bearded and rangy beneath his robe, his swept-back hair seeming thinner than she remembered and the lines of his face etched a little deeper. Yugi, scruffy as ever in a shirt and trousers and boots, with the omnipresent rag tied around his forehead, penning the unruly spikes of his brown-blond hair. She was assailed suddenly by a terrible sense of the gravity of the situation, that these two men were discussing life and death for hundreds or even thousands of people, and it was all down to her.

They are coming for me, she thought. *Everyone that dies here will die because of me.*

Then Yugi noticed her, and smiled, and ushered her over. He took the mug from her with a grateful nod and then said to Zaelis: 'She should hear this. It concerns her.'

Zaelis grunted and motioned for her to sit down.

'We need to get you to a safe place, Lucia,' he said, his voice a rumble in the back of his throat. 'There's no way we can get the people out of the Fault in any number at short notice, and they would be too many to hide. But a few, a dozen or so . . . an escort . . . we could send you north-east. To Tchamaska. There are Libera Dramach there who can hide you.'

Lucia barely reacted. 'And you will stay here and fight,' she said.

Zaelis looked pained. 'I have to,' he said. 'The Libera Dramach practically built this place. After we took it over all that time ago . . . well, the stockpiles alone are worth defending. If we can hold off this attack, we can buy time to move them out, to start again.' He laid his hand on her arm. 'People came here because *we* drew them here, even the ones who aren't a part of the organisation. I'm responsible.'

'You're responsible for me too,' Lucia said. Yugi looked at her in surprise. He had never heard Lucia use such an accusatory mode with her father.

Zaelis was plainly hurt. He drew his hand back from her. 'That's why I'm sending you out of harm's way,' he said. 'It will only be for a short time. I will come and find you afterward.'

'No,' said Lucia, quite firmly. 'I will stay.'

'You can't stay,' Zaelis told her.

'Why not? Because I might be killed?' She leaned forward, and her voice was a furious hiss that shocked him. 'You'll abandon me, but you won't abandon them! Well, neither will I! All these people, all my friends and my friend's families, all of them are going to die here! Because the Weavers want *me*! Most of them will never even know why. And you want me to leave them, to go and hide again until the Weavers hunt me down and *more* people die?' She was shouting now. '*I'm* responsible for these people as much as you are. You made me responsible when you promised them a saviour from the Weavers. You tied all their lives to me and you never once asked me if I *wanted* that!'

Her last words rang into silence. In all her life, they had never heard her raise her voice in anger. The force of it, coming after fourteen years of placid calm, stunned them.

'I will not go,' she said, her voice dropping again but losing none of its steel. 'I will stay here and live or die with you, and with the people to whom you bound me.'

Yugi looked from Lucia to Zaelis and back again. Suddenly, she no longer looked like a child, and he caught a glimpse of her mother's fire in her glare. Zaelis was dumbstruck. Finally, he swallowed, and he dropped his eyes from the fierce and unfamiliar girl who had taken the place of his daughter.

'So be it,' he said, his mode formal and distant. 'Do as you will.'

Yugi felt the moment become excruciating, even softened as it was by the pleasant fuzz of the amaxa root.

'Remember that army of Aberrants coming our way?' he said with forced flippancy. 'If anybody's interested, I have a plan.'

Asara sat with her arms around one knee and the other leg tucked beneath her, and watched the starfall drifting down over Lake Sazazu. The grass was sodden, and the moisture soaked through her clothes to dampen her skin.

The water still rocked with the memory of the storm, flashing fitful arcs of moonlight from shore to distant shore. Night-birds swooped back and forth, plucking at fish that were attracted to the surface to nibble at the tiny ice-flakes, thinking them to be food of some kind. The sensation of unreality was fading now, returning the world to normal.

Alone, she gazed out over the lake, deep in thought.

Reki slumbered back in the shelter they had made. He was so exhausted he had slept through the chaos. The thought brought a twitch of a smile. Poor boy. His grief and misery had destroyed him, but she still found herself with a strange affection for the bookish young Heir-Barak. Where she would have been disgusted at the weakness of someone else for wallowing so in their agony, for him she made an exception. It was, after all, her fault.

The last few days had been curious. She had expected pursuit, but Mos's men were either criminally inept or were not searching for them at all, and she found that very odd. It worried her more than if they had been hot on Reki's trail. Surely they knew what he carried, and what it meant for the Empire? And yet Asara had stayed effortlessly ahead of the game. Such good fortune was frankly suspicious.

Reki had not taken the news of his sister's death at all well, and they had been forced to rest a while here, for he was in no state to go on. His lamentations would draw attention to them. Even when he was silent, he bore such a shattering sorrow in his eyes that people would remember him. In retrospect, Asara thought that she should probably have kept Laranya's suicide quiet until they were in a safer place; but what was done, was done. He would have felt betrayed if she had kept it from him any longer, and she wanted him smitten.

She left him to sleep, to heal himself of tragedy. Asara had watched many dramas like this over the course of her long life, and they bored her in the main; but she was curious to see how Reki would fare under this test of his mettle. Though he was as easy to manipulate as any man, he had innocence and inexperience as his excuse, and she found those qualities appealing enough so that she did not have to entirely fake her interest in him.

But she herself could not sleep. She was thinking of an argument, weeks ago, and of Kaiku.

After her deception had been revealed, after she had fled from Kaiku in shame, she had gone to Cailin. It was ever her way: to run from what hurt her, to change herself and hide again. Cailin would provide her with an excuse to leave, something that she could tell herself was the *real* reason she was going, and not Kaiku at all.

But somehow it had descended into an argument. Cailin was just that little bit too haughty, taking her for granted, *telling* her that she had to go to the Imperial Keep.

'I am not your servant, Cailin!' Asara had spat, whirling around the black-and-red conference chamber of the house of the Red Order. 'You would do well to remember that.'

'Spare me these half-hearted attempts at independence,' the Sister had replied coldly. 'You know you can leave at any time. But you will not leave, will you? Because I can grant what you desire most in the world.'

Asara had glared at her furiously. 'We had a deal. I did not agree to be your subordinate!'

'Then we are equals, if you prefer,' Cailin said. 'It changes nothing. You will do as I ask, or you may break the deal. But until then, you will help me get what I want. And then, I will give you what *you* want.'

'*Can* you?' Asara had accused. 'Can you do it?'

'You know I can, Asara, and you know I will. You have my promise.'

'And you have *my* promise,' she returned savagely, 'that if you trick me I will be avenged. You would not want me as an enemy, Cailin.'

'Stop these threats!' Cailin had snapped. 'The deal stands. It requires a certain measure of trust on both our parts, but you knew that from the beginning.'

Trust. Asara could have laughed. Trust was an overrated commodity. But Cailin knew what it was that Asara longed for, what she would risk almost anything to get. And so Asara worked for the Red Order, partly because they had the same goals, mostly because it was the only way she could imagine her wish might be granted.

An end to the loneliness, to the emptiness, to the void inside her. It was almost too precious to imagine.

TWENTY-NINE

The sun was setting on the Xarana Fault, igniting the western horizon in clouded bands of red and silver and purple. In the golden light of the day's end, Yugi and Nomoru crouched on a bluff overlooking a land riven with ghylls and canyons, from which flat-topped plateaux, rocky hills and buttes thrust upward unevenly.

Below them, hidden within the creases of the Fault, men and women were dying. The sounds of gunfire and occasional detonations echoed into the calm sky. Wisps of smoke seeped like fumes from the cracks. Fleeting glimpses of movement caught their eyes from time to time: swiftly retreating figures, pursued by dark and terrible shapes. At several points over the last few hours, the battle had spilled up out of the shadow and into the open, skirmishes across hillsides or areas of scrubland. Yugi did not recognise half of the factions that he saw, but he was sure they were not Libera Dramach or folk of the Fold.

'Getting close,' Nomoru said, her tone suggesting that she did not care one way or the other about it.

'We're not slowing them by much,' Yugi observed distractedly.

'What did you expect?'

Yugi shrugged at that. He did not want to deal with Nomoru's surly pessimism now. He had more pressing concerns.

Kaiku's estimation of the Aberrant army's speed had been accurate. Three days had passed since the night of the moonstorm, and their rate of advance had been steady and rapid. A force of thousands were swarming through the Fault at roughly twice the speed that Yugi and his band of three companions had traversed it in the other direction. In a place like the Fault, that was a recklessness verging on insanity. He wondered if their strength of numbers had been enough to overcome the dangers that they would have faced: the clan armies, the canyons bristling with traps and deadfalls, the swamps that belched poison miasma, the haunted places. For a force so big, there was no safe route. How many had they lost? And would it matter, in the end?

The Libera Dramach scouts – Nomoru included – had brought back scattered reports, but the army were simply moving too fast. They learned most of what they knew from other friendly clans, driven before the invaders, and the intelligence they had gleaned had come too recently to really do anything about it. The army had smashed through any settlements that had got in their way, overwhelming them in a tide and then ploughing onward. The clans and factions in or near the path of the Aberrants were in turmoil. Some were fleeing eastward, towards the Fold; word had been spread that it would be a last stronghold against the enemy, and it would welcome any clans who would unite with them there. A frankly dangerous gamble, to invite any of the other people of the Fault inside their fortifications, but Yugi knew that Zaelis had no other choice now.

Other communities – the vengeful remnants of those that the army had passed through, or simply those who recognised the threat – were harrying the flanks and tail of the horde. The Xarana Fault was made for hit-and-run manoeuvres, and these people had lived there the better part of their lives and knew every trick. But the Aberrants ignored the attacks nibbling at their fringes, forging onward unstoppably towards the Fold with no consideration for casualties.

Yugi's mood was dark. How did they know? How did they find out where Lucia was? He cursed the Weavers and their ungodly methods. Heart's blood, it could only have been a matter of time, but why *now*? In a few more years Lucia would have been of an age to take the throne, and they could have begun to gather real armies to support her, could have come out of hiding and challenged Mos and the Weavers.

He caught himself, remembering her shocking tirade on the night of the moonstorm. They had so long been used to Lucia being dreamy and passive, like a veil drifting on the winds, that they had not considered what she wanted at all. They had assumed that she would have objected by now if she had any objections to make. Her detachment went so deep that they had ceased to think that opinions were something that applied to her. Yugi felt a solemn guilt at how they had taken her for granted. Whatever else she was, she was also a fourteen-harvest girl, with all the associated complications, and her patience and tolerance were not endless.

He dared not think what it might mean if she developed a stubborn streak like Kaiku had. So much relied on her.

A particularly loud explosion, near at hand, brought his mind back to the present. Nomoru rubbed a hand through her thatch of hair and scowled.

'You're cutting it fine,' she warned.

'Let's go,' he said.

They headed away from the bluff, down a narrow slope bulwarked on either side by root-split walls of earth. There was a man there at the bottom, tensed to run, looking at them expectantly.

'They're coming!' he called. 'Be ready!'

The man sketched a salute and fled, scrambling up another slope that looped off to their right. Yugi and Nomoru carried on down without pause, their rifles clattering against their backs. They passed two more runners on the way, despatching them to their respective destinations with orders. Yugi found himself thinking how much easier, how much faster this might be if they had the women of the Red Order as relays; but Cailin had refused to commit them to the advance forces, insisting that the element of surprise was vital in their deployment. She would keep them at the Fold. Privately, Yugi wondered if she would deploy them at all.

They sprinted out into the open, running low, and the wall to their left fell away to spit them out onto a colossal shelf overlooking a barren, dead-end canyon. Sheer walls of sandy rock, banded with the striations of countless epochs, plunged down hundreds of feet to a dusty floor of churned earth. Birds rode the thermals below them in the slowly reddening light. Yugi felt a vertiginous moment at the sudden exposure to the chasm; the hot wind of the failing day blustered around him. Then they were hunkering down amid dozens of riflemen who hid behind a heap of stone further along the shelf, and he was grateful that the drop was hidden from sight.

'Any activity down there?' he asked.

'Nothing,' said a scarred young man named Kihu, whom Yugi had left in charge. 'Can't expect it yet though. Sun's still out.'

'No, you're right,' Yugi mused. 'You, you, and you,' he picked out two men and a middle-aged woman, all Libera Dramach. 'Stay here and watch; I want to know if anything moves in this canyon before we get back. Everyone else, into position. They're on their way.'

His orders were obeyed immediately and without question. It was what they had been waiting for. With a grim eagerness, they broke cover and headed further along the enormous rock shelf. It slanted down for some way, finally joining a greater outthrust mass that jutted out away from the cliffs they had been hugging to their right.

The vista broadened dramatically. The canyon they had been watching over was only one branch of a fork, the southernmost arm of a great junction. To the west, there was a breathtaking trench that crooked out of sight amid a clutter of buttes. East, the trench continued on, narrowing slightly. Yugi and the riflemen were running along the divider between the southern canyon and the eastern one, a steadily tapering promontory that collapsed at its tip into a series of ledges fringed with tough bushes and wretched trees.

As they ran, Yugi caught sight of one of the runners signalling across the canyon, catching the last rays of Nuki's eye with a hand-mirror. A moment later, flashes returned in acknowledgement from concealed positions along the opposite ridge. The junction was crawling on all sides with Libera Dramach, hidden among the broken landscape.

Yugi felt a surge of fierce pride. Nothing had stopped the relentless onslaught of the Aberrants so far, but then nobody had been given a chance to prepare until now. He remembered how he had doubted the wisdom of Kaiku's decision to stay with the army. Now he had cause to be thankful for it. It was only because of the risk Kaiku took that they had been given enough warning to organise. The Weavers had charged heedlessly through the Fault, oblivious to their casualties; but Yugi planned to give them pause for thought here.

'Gristle-crows!' someone called, and Yugi looked up to see the first of the huge black Aberrant birds soaring overhead. They scrambled down the sloping tip of the divider, concealing themselves among the ledges and the dry foliage that clung there. Nomoru slid down next to him in a billow of dust, her exquisite rifle clenched in her thin hands, and the two of them crouched together amidst a brake of bushes. The walls of the eastern and western canyon were not so high as the southern arm, and the floor rose up too, so that they were perhaps seventy feet above it by the time they had dug in. They waited motionless, listening to the harsh caws of the gristle-crows as they circled, scouting ahead of the main mass of Aberrants that were pouring towards them.

'Is this going to work?' Nomoru whispered.

'If it doesn't, at least there'll be nobody left alive to tell how we failed,' he replied.

Nomoru cackled quietly and primed her rifle. She motioned up at the birds with her eyes. 'Want me to bring them down?'

Yugi shook his head. 'You've got your targets. Until then, you don't fire a shot.'

He settled himself, watching the mouth of the western canyon, from which the Aberrants would come. The enemy army had spread out somewhat but the Fault bottlenecked here, several routes converging into this one canyon, and it would be driving a good portion of the Aberrants this way. The alternative was to clamber up to the open high ground, but Yugi was sure they would not take that route. The reckless speed of the army meant only one thing: they wanted to surprise the Fold, so that the Libera Dramach would not have a chance to spirit Lucia away. Equally, that was why they went along the Xarana Fault rather than travelling the smooth plains on its outskirts. They would not expose themselves if they could help it, either to their intended victims or to the world at large.

Yugi wondered suddenly why they were using such a bludgeoning force instead of sending assassins, or Weavers, to quietly pick off the dispossessed Heir-Empress. Perhaps, he thought, they simply did not have time. He thought of the *other* army, that had departed northward in barges. The Weavers' eyes were elsewhere, it seemed. They had matters even more important than Lucia to attend to.

The sun had almost disappeared, and the last of the red was fading from the sky, when the first sounds of the army were heard. The gristle-crows had departed now, as Yugi had expected. Kaiku had informed them about the various types of Aberrants she had encountered, and what strengths and weaknesses she had been able to learn. Gristle-crows never flew at night; she guessed that their vision in the dark was very poor.

The steadily growing noise prompted a trickle of dread in Yugi's chest. It was a distant cacophony to begin with, but it swelled with alarming speed, a clash of gibbering and yammering, of bellows and snarls, becoming an overwhelming blanket of chaos and madness. Gunfire from the Libera Dramach and other clanfolk that were picking at their sides provided sporadic punctuation.

Yugi gripped the stock of his rifle tight, and felt the first inklings of real doubt. It was like waiting at the breakwater for a tsunami.

The horde came thundering into sight, turning into the western canyon, and he paled as he saw them spread like oil to flow between the buttes and around the rocks, a fluid mass of corruption that took his breath away. He was not prey to the prejudice against Aberrants that all Saramyr had been brought up with – indeed, it was almost possible to forget that such a thing existed in the liberal world of the Fold – but he was unable to suppress his disgust and fear at the sight of the monstrosities that now came towards him. Nature twisted out of true, a collision of species and traits, changes accelerated by the Weavers' blight and making a mockery of Enyu's plan.

How can these things and Kaiku be the same? he asked himself.

They were travelling at a pace akin to a jog, a speed at which they were tireless and could travel day and night with very little rest. There was no organisation in their formation, and yet somehow they managed not to trample each other as they went. Massive ghauregs towered over galloping, boarlike furies, lumbering along as the smaller Aberrants pushed past them and clamoured onward. Spidery-limbed skrendel scuttled at the fringes, monkeylike things with long fingers that kept out of the way of the larger beasts by leaping nimbly up the sides of buttes, where they hissed at each other. Shrillings slid between their clumsy allies with sinuous grace. In amongst them were others, too hard to identify at such a distance, shrieking and growling as they plunged down the canyon.

'Gods,' murmured Nomoru. 'If they get to the Fold, we're all dead.'

'So many dogs, but who's got the leash?' Yugi said, peering through the bushes. 'Where are the Nexuses? Where are the Weavers?'

The army poured out of the western canyon, into the junction where their route forked. There was no indecision: they headed east. The gristle-crows' advance reconnaissance had already determined that the southern fork was a dead end, and they communicated that knowledge to the Nexuses by the strange link they shared through the nexus-worms. Yugi and the other riflemen who hid amid the ledges at the tip of the promontory hardly dared to breathe as the horde swept by beneath them and to their right, the rumble of thousands of feet, paws and claws shaking the earth.

'There they are,' whispered Nomoru, more to herself than to Yugi. She was gazing down the canyon with a calm and intense focus, and he followed her eyes to where the first of the Nexuses had come into view.

They were some way back, hidden amidst the mass, riding on beasts that looked like manxthwa except that they were hairless, and much faster. The sight of a Nexus, even so far away, brought a dreadful nausea to Yugi's gut. They were too much like Weavers in their cloaks and their blank masks. As another came into view, he noticed that they were surrounded by a retinue of ghauregs that never strayed far from them, shielding the Nexuses with their massive bodies.

'They're protecting the Nexuses,' Yugi said, raising his voice over the din of the Aberrants passing them by. 'Can you do it?'

Nomoru gave him a disparaging look, but if she had been about to offer some snide reply, she missed her chance. At that moment, the air was shattered by a tremendous explosion, making the ground shudder violently. Yugi and Nomoru ducked instinctively as a scatter of pebbles and loose earth sloughed down on them from the ledge above.

The detonation was incredible, echoing the breadth of the Fault, destroying enormous sections of rock in a billowing cloud of dust that blasted up and down the canyon and plumed high into the sky. The Libera Dramach had placed explosives all along both sides of the eastern canyon, just beyond the junction. The initial concussion rained stones and rocks and boulders on the front line of the Aberrant army, bringing them stumbling to a sudden halt as they were battered by falling debris. But that was only the start, for a moment later came the grinding roar of collapsing rock, a monolithic rumbling that pounded the ears, and the canyon sides came down.

The Aberrants squealed and howled and stamped each other underfoot as they dissolved in confusion, but it was too late to avoid the avalanche of stone that slumped upon them. It smashed into their disordered ranks with unstoppable force, pulverising bone and rending bodies, crushing them to mangled dolls or ripping them limb from limb. Those who were not caught directly beneath the incomprehensible weight of rock were driven into it by the ranks behind, and the life squeezed from them. The dust that filled the canyon reduced visibility to almost nothing, only a yellow and stinging world filled with animal shrieks. Still the Aberrants pushed onwards, swept up in their own tide, unwittingly propelling more of their kind into the rock barrier where they bent and snapped like twigs.

Yugi raised his head and gave Nomoru a grin. 'Now let's show them what kind of fight they have on their hands,' he said.

The riflemen opened fire.

There were almost a hundred of them positioned all around the junction, high above the invaders. Though the seething dust stung their eyes and made it impossible to see down to the canyon floor, the Aberrants were packed so closely that it was harder to miss than to hit. They shot indiscriminately, pulling back the sliding bolt on their weapons after each report, pausing only when their ignition powder burnt out or when they needed to reload. A murderous and inescapable crossfire turned the air into a hail of rifle balls, shredding the Aberrants that were caught within it. It punched through chitinous armour and ripped through skin and fur and flesh, fountaining blood in its wake. The canyon resounded with the agonised cries of the beasts as they flailed under the assault, seeking enemies and finding none.

Yugi, closer to the ground than the men and women on the canyon rims, was firing with the rest of them. Kihu and the other riflemen who were hidden among the ledges kept up an uneven staccato of weapon reports above and below. Occasionally, one of the agile skrendel rose out of the dusty murk, trying to climb the sides of the canyon to escape the bloodbath, but Yugi had two men down there whose job was to shoot them if they tried, and they never got close to the Libera Dramach position.

Amid all of that, Nomoru was as still as a statue, her hand around the barrel of her black-lacquered rifle, tracing the silver intaglio there. The dust was steadily clearing, blown down the canyon by the evening breeze as the land cooled. The writhing, panicked shapes of the Aberrants were becoming visible again, dim shadows in the faint glow of the recently departed sun. The sky overhead was a deep blue, so dark that it was almost black now.

'They're turning!' someone cried. 'They're turning!'

It was true. The Aberrants, desperate to escape the killing zone and realising that their way east was blocked, had begun to flood down into the southern canyon. Yugi felt a surge of bitter triumph, wondering whether the Nexuses had lost control of their troops or if they themselves had instigated it. Either way, the result would be the same.

'Hold this position!' Yugi cried. They were beginning to run out of ammunition and ignition powder now, but he did not want them to let up yet. Not until Nomoru had her chance.

As if responding to his thought, she lifted her rifle to her shoulder, sighting through the bushes. The dust was settling, and the scene on the canyon floor was unveiling itself to the eyes of the ambushers. The ground was littered with shattered bodies, but it was barely possible to see them beneath the stampede of grotesqueries that trampled them.

Yet even as they saw the disorder they had sown, they noticed the Aberrants beginning to slow. The rifle fire from overhead was petering out now as guns overheated and powder punches emptied. The panic seemed to be diminishing with uncanny speed, decelerating the headlong rush into the southern canyon.

'Nomoru,' Yugi warned, realising now that he had an answer to his own question. 'They're getting control back.'

Nomoru ignored him. She had her eye to the sight, her body poised with a grace entirely at odds with her appearance or her character.

Down in the canyon, the Nexuses were gathered together, surrounded by their bodyguard of ghauregs. No expression could be seen behind their masks, but Yugi could almost feel their intent, their *will*, dominating the animals that they commanded.

She fired; the ball missed the shoulder of a ghaureg by an inch and hit one of the Nexuses in the face, smashing the blank white mask inward in a bloody spidercrack. The Nexus lurched, swayed and fell from its saddle.

The reaction among the Aberrants was immediate. A small section of them flew into a rage, different breeds attacking one another, and the hysteria spread swiftly. The riflemen concentrated their assault on the surrounding beasts.

Nomoru fired again. Another Nexus was pitched backward and fell from his mount.

Then someone from one of the canyon rims tipped an explosive package down into the fray, a bomb on a sizzling fuse, and when it went off pandemonium ensued. The stalled rush of the Aberrants became a charge down the only exit left to them: the southern canyon. Nomoru, unperturbed, took down a third Nexus. The ghaureg bodyguards were in disarray now. Two of them were tearing apart one of the Nexuses' mounts. Chaos spread as the Nexuses' guiding minds winked out like candles. The other Nexuses were retreating, forging back through the crush as best they could. As the last of the light drained from the sky, Nomoru put up her rifle and said: 'Out of range now.'

Yugi clapped her on the shoulder in congratulation. She scowled at him.

'Time to go,' he said. 'It's not over yet.'

Accompanied by the rest of the riflemen in their group, they climbed back up to the top of the promontory and retraced their steps as swiftly as they could, heading along the lofty ledge that overlooked the southern canyon. Gunfire was still pocking the air behind them, sharp raps resonating emptily. As they got higher, they could see the vista across the Fault had turned a secretive blue-black in the twilight, and that the edge of Aurus was just rising in the north. It was cooling fast by the time they reached a vantage point and crouched at the lip of the ledge.

Below them, the Aberrants had swarmed in, and the vanguard had almost reached the end of the canyon and were slowing hard, realising that there was nowhere for them to go. But with no guiding force behind them they had no way to communicate to the hundreds who were coming after, and those that slowed were forced underfoot by the ones who had not yet seen the danger. The Aberrants piled up against the end of the canyon, the broken bodies of their kind forming a brake like earth before a plough. Still more crammed in behind them, seeking to escape the gunfire at the junction. Finally, when the immutability of their situation became apparent, they slowed and stopped, having packed the canyon with the dead and living.

The remaining explosives detonated at that point.

The Aberrants howled in fear as the mouth of the canyon collapsed, tons of rock hammering down, forming a wall with crushed corpses as its mortar. Sealing off their only escape, trapping hundreds of them there.

There was a pregnant pause, an expectancy that even the twisted animals felt. They prowled and paced, snapping at each other, clawing at the unyielding rock. Snarling struggles broke out. The rifles had fallen silent across the Fault.

It was difficult for those above to see in the fading light, but some of them had spyglasses, and they looked down and waited.

Whether the ghaureg was the first one to go or merely the first one they noticed, nobody could be sure. But as they watched, suddenly and without warning, the enormous beast disappeared into the earth.

The Aberrants were milling uneasily now, sensing that something was amiss here. Another one, this time a furie, was swallowed up by the ground. It had time to let out a distressed squeal and then it was gone.

'Gods,' murmured Kihu, who was hunkered next to Yugi. 'This is going to be a slaughter.'

And then it was happening all over the canyon. Aberrants were disappearing, simply dropping into the earth as if the ground beneath their feet were suddenly gone. At first it was one at a time, and then several began to vanish at once, and moments later there were dozens being sucked under. The animals began to panic afresh, rearing and shrieking and roaring, attacking each other in their confusion. The skrendel, by far the most intelligent of the predator species, were trying to climb the canyon walls; but while they could get themselves off the deadly ground that way, the stone was too smooth for them to escape the trap. The canyon was emptying fast, as living and dead alike were swallowed by the churned earth of the canyon floor.

Those with spyglasses began to see the swift wakes of things speeding just below the surface, shallow humps that arrowed towards their targets. Even in the darkness, it was possible to spot the insidious swatches of blood that soaked upward from the earth, the ground too glutted to hold it all in. The Aberrants ran and scuttled on soil made damp with the fluids of their own kind, attempting a hopeless evasion as the things that hunted them swarmed about in a multitude. The skrendel were snatched from the walls by sudden profusions of thin tendrils that burst from the ground and enwrapped them, pulling them under in the blink of an eye, like a chameleon's tongue picking off a fly.

By the time true dark had fallen, and Aurus was some way into her ascent, the canyon was quiet again. The only sign that the Aberrants had ever been there was the glistening of the moonlight on the canyon floor, where the blood of the dead creatures gradually soaked back into the earth.

Yugi let out a low whistle. There had been stories told about this place ever since he had arrived in the Fault, and several people who had not listened to those stories had provided more concrete proof of their veracity by dying here. But he had never imagined the sheer voraciousness of the *liha-kiri* – the burrowing demons.

A woman came racing down from further up the ledge to stand before them. 'They're heading back, Yugi,' she said breathlessly. 'They're retreating.'

There was a cheer from those assembled, and Yugi was pounded by companionable slaps on his shoulder and back. He grinned roguishly.

'They'll not be in quite such a hurry to get to the Fold now,' he said. 'Well done, all of you.'

He would allow them a few moments of self-congratulation before he would urge them to withdraw. They deserved that much, at least. They had struck the Weaver army a terrible blow today, but the Weavers would not be so reckless a second time. Despite the hundreds they had killed, they had not done more than dent the enemy's numbers. The Weavers, whatever else they were, were not tacticians, and they had fallen into a trap that any experienced general would have avoided; but their insanity also made them unpredictable, and that was dangerous.

He caught Nomoru's eye, the only person not celebrating, and knew that she was thinking the same as he was. They had won a small respite, but the real battle would be at the Fold. And it might very well be a battle they could not win.

THIRTY

Nuki's eye had risen and set since the massacre of the Aberrants, and Iridima held court in the cloudy sky far to the west of the Fold. Kaiku and Tsata stood on the western bank of the Zan in the moon-shade of a thicket of tumisi trees that had somehow resisted the blight emanating from the nearby witchstone. The warm night was silent, but for a cool autumn breeze that stirred the leaves restlessly.

Across the river sat the bizarre building that dominated the flood plain, the strange grublike hump of banded metal that they had wondered about for weeks now. It seethed a foul-smelling, oily miasma, and it groaned and squeaked with the rotation of the massive spiked wheels that turned slowly at its sides. Smaller constructions were clustered around it, as indeterminate of purpose as the central edifice. Slats of metal in their sides sometimes lit up brightly from within, accompanied by a bellow as of the sudden roar of a furnace; chains would unexpectedly clank into life, rattling along enormous pulleys and cogs that strung like sinews between the buildings; mechanisms would jitter fitfully and then fall silent. From this side, it was possible to see the mouths of the twin pipes that ran underground the short distance to the riverbank, half-submerged grilles peeping over the gently flowing surface of the Zan.

Kaiku watched the building closely, her eyes hard. She hated it. Hated its incomprehensibility, hated its alienness, its unnatural noise and its stench. It was like the blight made manifest, a thing of corruption that belched poison. And more, she hated it because it was keeping her here while her friends and her home were in desperate peril back in the Fold, and even though she could not be with them, would never have got there in time, it clawed at her heart that she had not at least tried.

But it seemed as if that gods-cursed Okhamban way of thinking had rubbed off on her in the time she had spent with Tsata, that curious selflessness of surrendering themselves to the common need over personal desires. On that night under the moonstorm when the barrier had gone down, when they had watched the predator horde swarming away from the flood plain and heading east towards the Fold, she had wanted nothing more than to go after them. No matter that they moved far too fast to catch up with, and that she would be only one among thousands even if she *could* get to the Fold in time. The old Kaiku would have gone anyway, because that was her nature.

But she had not gone. She knew what Tsata was thinking, and she was surprised to find that she was thinking the same. The flood plains were all but empty now, only a skeleton guard remaining to supervise the Weavers' base here in the Fault. And they were the only ones in a position to take advantage of such an oversight.

The only ones who could get to the witchstone.

Tsata did not even need to talk her round. A chance like this might never come again. Whatever the outcome of the battle to the east, they owed it to their companions to make use of the opportunity that had unwittingly been provided. They were going into the Weavers' mine.

'There,' muttered Kaiku, as a deep growl came from within the bowels of the building. There were a series of loud clanks, and a moment later the pipes in the riverbank spewed forth a torrent of brackish water, blasting the hinged upper and lower halves of the grilles open. The torrent continued for several minutes, carrying with it chunks of rock and organic debris and other things impossible to identify in the moonlight, depositing it all for the Zan to sweep away southward towards the falls. Finally, the roar of the water subsided to a trickle, and the grilles swung closed, no longer forced apart by the pressure. There were a few more heavy thumps from within the brooding building, and then the only noise was the steady rush of the river.

Kaiku and Tsata emerged from the thicket and crawled through the long grass to the water's edge. The banks of the Zan were not as barren as the surrounding high ground, being provided with a plentiful supply of fresh water, and the foliage was welcome cover. The two of them went on their knees and elbows to where a log lay some distance upstream, a warped thing that corkscrewed midway along its length. They had rolled it there the previous night in readiness. The tree had been weak enough to topple when they wrapped rope around its top and pulled it down. After that they had been able to tear the branches off by hand, and fashion a very good float with which to cross the river.

They watched the flood plain for some time. There were shapes there in the dark, perhaps a hundred spread over the whole expanse. Some were wandering idly, but most were asleep. The patrols, what few there were now, were largely on the eastern side of the river; the intruders had little fear of the occasional sentry they had encountered on the western side. The cliffs rose behind the plain, a frowning black wall. Kaiku remembered when they had first lain on that edge and looked down at the enormous army the Aberrants had assembled, terrified of the sheer power that had been gathered here. Now the plain seemed so deserted that it was almost ghostly.

Once satisfied that nothing was paying attention to the river, they waited for Iridima to hide her face behind a cloud. Kaiku was thankful that they had not had to delay any longer than this for the right conditions in which to attempt their infiltration of the mine; the inactivity, combined with her fears for her friends, had frayed her nerves. But the season was with them: though the weather throughout the year in Saramyr did not vary all that much, due to its position close to the equator of the planet, autumn and spring were generally cloudier and rainier than winter or summer. The habit of dividing the year into seasons was something they had brought with them from temperate Quraal and never really shaken off.

A feathery blanket of cloud slid across the face of the moon. Kaiku and Tsata glanced at each other once for confirmation and then rolled the log quietly into the river and dropped in after it.

The water was surprisingly warm, heated over and over by the sun during the many hundreds of miles it had run from the freezing depths of the Tchamil Mountains. Kaiku felt its sodden embrace swamp through her clothes and over her skin. She gauged the tug of the current. The river was sluggish here, gathering itself before the rush towards the falls to the south. She got the log under her armpits and waited for Tsata to do the same; then, when they were balanced, they kicked out into the river.

The crossing was completed in silence and darkness, with only the plangent lap of the water against the log as they glided towards the eastern bank. They had struck out at an angle upstream, trusting the current to carry them down to where the hulking carapace of the mine brooded sullenly. Their estimation was good, and their luck held, for Iridima stayed hidden and the night remained impenetrable. They bumped against the far side a few dozen feet from the mouths of the pipes, and there they grabbed hold of the bars of the grille and let the log drift away. It was too dangerous to tether their float here; it might be seen when the sun rose.

The weeks they had spent observing the flood plain had borne fruit in the end. Though Kaiku had been frustrated by their inability to get close to a Nexus or the mysterious Weaver building, they had gleaned much about the comings and goings that went on here, and made many theoretical plans. But the one that had obsessed Kaiku the most involved the rhythmic evacuation of water through those pipes. She was unable to gauge exactly how long it was between each deluge, for she had no means accurate enough, but both she and Tsata agreed that it was more or less regular, and that there were several hours at least separating one from the next. The water was coming from somewhere, she reasoned. As long as they timed their entry right, they would be able to crawl up one of the pipes and investigate. Presumably the grilles were there to stop debris or animals from the river getting in; and that meant that there would be somewhere for them to get *to*.

It was only now that she looked into the mouth of one of the pipes, sheltered from the sight of the plain by the rise of the riverbank, that the reality of her plan hit home. Once in there, she would be trammelled, hemmed in by the cold sides of the pipe, with nowhere to go but forward or back. She felt a fluttering panic in her belly.

Tsata put his hand on her wet shoulder and squeezed, sensing her hesitation. She looked back at him, his tattooed face almost invisible in the dark.

She could feel the determination in his gaze and took a little of that for her own.

Between them, they pulled down the lower half of the grille. There was some kind of spring mechanism on it to help it close against the push of the river, but it was weak and rusted from lack of maintenance. Kaiku went first, taking a breath and ducking under the upper grille to emerge on the other side, looking back through the bars at Tsata with her hair plastered across one side of her face. The pipe was big enough to stand in if she hunched over; the river water came up to her waist. Tsata followed her through, letting the grille close behind him after checking that there was no apparent locking mechanism.

'If it comes to that,' Kaiku said, reading his thoughts, 'I'll blow them apart.'

Tsata knew what she implied. It had been enough of a risk to send the warning to Cailin; even though the Weavers had not caught her, they might well be more alert now if they had detected it. To use her *kana* in here would be a virtual death sentence; but for all that, she would use it if she had to. She was merely making that clear to him, and to herself. Whatever Cailin advised, her power was her own, to use as she would.

Tsata found himself smiling. If ever she took the robes of the Red Order, Cailin would have a fight on her hands to keep this one in line.

They made their way into the pipe, the gentle splashes as they forged the water aside echoing amid the sussurance. Other sounds came to them, distant grindings and irregular clumps and scrapes, made eerie by reverberation. Darkness closed about, utter blackness, with only the faint slitted circle of the pipe mouth providing any kind of touchstone to their location. Once they had gone inward for some way, they stopped. Tsata began unwrapping the candle that he had tied in a waterproof bag on his belt.

'Wait,' Kaiku whispered.

'You need the light,' he said. He did not need to point out that he did not, at least not yet. He had vision like an owl's, an inheritance from the purestrain Okhambans that had bred with the refugees from Quraal all that time ago and produced the Tkiurathi.

'Wait,' she said again. 'Give me time.'

Her eyes were adjusting to the darkness fast enough that she could actually see shapes appearing out of the blackness: the blank curve the pipe, the shifting contours of the water.

'I can see,' she said.

'Are you sure?' Tsata asked, surprise in his voice.

'Of course I am sure,' she said, amused. 'Put the candle away.'

He did so, and they went onward. They had guessed that the pipe would not be very long, since the buildings they fed from were set close to the riverbank, and Kaiku found it was not so much of a trial as she had expected. The claustrophobia of her situation did not bother her as she had thought it might, as long as she did not dwell on the possibility of all those tons of water smashing into them. But she was confident enough in the unwavering regularity of the evacuation, and confident enough in herself that she was not plagued with her usual doubts and fears.

With a faint hint of wonder, she realised how much she had grown since Aestival Week: since she had been tricked by Asara and outmatched demons in the Weave; since she had healed a dying friend by instinct alone and spent weeks living on her wits, killing Aberrants, relying only on herself and this foreigner with his barely comprehensible ways. She was fundamentally the same as she always had been, but her attitude had changed, matured, bringing with it a self-assuredness that she never knew she had.

She found that she liked herself that way.

Presently, the sporadic clanks and groans became louder, enveloping them, and chinks of what seemed like firelight began to appear in the pipe, minute rust-fractures hinting at what lay beyond. Then, as they rounded a bend so slight that they had barely noticed it, they came in sight of the end.

Kaiku blinked at the brightness. The pipe appeared to widen as it neared its termination, joining with the second pipe that ran alongside it to make one huge oblong corridor. Its floor sloped upward so that it was above the level of the river water that they had been wading through. Beyond it she could only see what looked like a wall of dull, bronze-coloured metal.

She glanced at Tsata. He murmured something in Okhamban, his eyes on what lay ahead.

'What does that mean?' she whispered.

Tsata seemed faintly taken aback that she had heard him. He had not meant to say it aloud. 'It is like you might say a prayer for protection,' he replied.

'But you have no gods in Okhamba,' Kaiku said. 'And you do not believe in your ancestors living on in anything but memory.'

'It is addressed to the *pash*,' he said. For the first time, she saw him embarrassed. 'I was asking for your protection, and offering you mine. It is merely a custom.'

Kaiku wiped the sodden hair back from her face. 'And how am I supposed to respond?'

'*Hthre*,' he said. Kaiku repeated it, unsure of her pronunciation. 'It means you accept the pledge and offer your own.'

She smiled. '*Hthre*,' she said, with more conviction this time.

He looked away from her. 'It is merely a custom,' he repeated.

They crept out of the water and along the widening pipe. After so long in night and darkness, the warm, fiery glow at the end made them feel uneasy. Their progress was wary, hugging the walls as they flattened out, their fingers running over rusting panels fused together by some craft that neither Kaiku nor Tsata knew. As they neared the light, they saw that it was not a wall at the end but a steep slope, like a chute, which they were at the bottom of. They peeked out of the end of the pipe, but there was nobody there. Above them, they could see only darkness, and around them were the walls of the chute that fed into the pipe where they emerged. The source of the glow was similarly obscured.

But there was a ladder, made of metal, fixed against one side of the chute. Kaiku climbed. There was nothing else to do, and no other, more subtle way up. Tsata remained at the bottom, his hide clothes dripping and forming a puddle around his shoes. She wished suddenly that there had been some way to waterproof her rifle and bring it along. It would have comforted her, even if she knew it would be little help in the event that they were discovered.

She reached the top of the ladder, and her stomach fell away as she saw the true immensity of the Weavers' mine.

The humped roof of the building was not, as she had expected, the ceiling of some kind of dwelling; rather, it was the cap of a colossal shaft that plunged down into abyssal depths. The shaft was not a straight drop; the blackness at its bottom was obscured by stone bulges where the sides narrowed and jags of rock that projected into the centre. Vast ledges scarred it, and pillars rose up like blunt needles, made small by comparison to their surroundings.

The chute that Kaiku had clambered out of was set on the edge of a great semicircular sill. Its lower lip continued up above her to an enormous dump-tank which sat upright in a cradle of curled iron. A pair of spiked wheels rotated slowly behind it, huge cogs dragging up scoops affixed to rattling chains which tipped water into the dump-tank and then headed monotonously downward again to collect more.

Kaiku, peripherally aware that the immediate vicinity appeared to be deserted, clambered out of the chute and stood there gawking, awed by the sheer size and strangeness of the place.

The illumination that she had seen from the bottom of the chute was provided by metal torches and pillars which burned with flame; but it was not like any normal flame, being more similar to combusting vapour. They billowed clouds of smoky fire that trailed upward and then dissipated, turning to noisome black fumes which floated away to collect at the top of the shaft. She realised that the darkness above her was not through lack of light, but that it was a churning pall of smoke which slowly vented itself into the clean air outside through pores in the cap.

The multitude of ledges and pillars were linked with a network of precarious walkways, rope bridges and stairways that hung like spiderwebs across the shaft. Walls were scabbed with props and joists of wood and metal, delineating pathways for mine carts to travel, and caves opened all over the shaft, glowing from within. Paternosters groaned and steamed in the depths, furnaces blazing at their heart as they rotated in idiot procession. Iron cranes jabbed out into nowhere, still carrying loads, abandoned. Thin waterfalls plunged endlessly, issuing from cave mouths to fall into nothingness, or to strike a rock ledge further down in a mist of spray before running off and down again. Kaiku saw small, ramshackle wooden huts clustered together, sometimes built on the tip of a pillar and linked only by a single bridge to the rest of the mine. It was hot in the shaft, and reeked; there was an unpleasant tinny taste that caught at the back of the throat.

Kaiku stared in wonder and terror at the thing the Weavers had created. She had never seen so much metal in her life, nor seen it wrought in such quantity. What kind of forges must the Weavers have? What had been going on for over two hundred years in the heart of their monasteries where the Edgefathers crafted their Masks? What kind of art had created those strange torches, or those hissing and steaming contraptions that moved without anything apparent to power them?

She felt a touch on her upper arm and jumped, but it was only Tsata.

'We are too exposed,' he said, his eyes flickering over the scene with a glint in them that might have been disgust, might have been anger.

She was glad to tear herself away from it.

They retreated along the sill to the sides of the shaft, where the enfolding darkness lurked. The huge metal torches were only sparsely placed about the mine, and though the area they illuminated was much greater than a normal torch or lantern would be, it still left areas of deep shadow. From here, Kaiku and Tsata carried out a more thorough observation of their surroundings, looking for movement. There was none. The shaft appeared to be deserted.

'Your eyes,' Tsata said after a time, motioning at her.

Kaiku frowned, making a querying noise.

'They have changed. Your irises have more red in them than before.'

She gave him a puzzled look. 'Before?'

'Before we entered the pipe.'

Kaiku thought on that for a moment, remembering the surprise in Tsata's voice when she had refused the illumination he had offered.

'How dark was it in there?' she asked.

'Too dark for you to see,' he replied.

Kaiku felt a thrill of unease. Had she . . . *adapted* herself? Had she been using her *kana* without even knowing it, the tiniest increase in her senses to compensate for her lack of vision? She did not even know how she would go about doing that, but her subconscious certainly seemed to. Just like with Yugi, cleaning him of the raku-shai's poison. The more she used her *kana*, the more it seemed to use her, making her a conduit rather than a mistress. Was that what it was like for all the Sisters? She would have to discuss it with Cailin when she returned.

If there was anything left to return to.

She strangled that thought as soon as it arrived. There was no time for doubts now. The Aberrant horde would almost be upon the Fold, and there was nothing in the world she could do about it. She could only hope that her warning had given them enough time to prepare or to get away from there.

They headed along the sill and onto a walkway that hugged the sides of the shaft, curving round to the entrance of a tunnel. The walkway was made of iron, supported by joists driven into the rock and hanging over an unfathomable drop. Kaiku did not want to touch the railing with her bare skin. Railings in Saramyr were made of carved wood, or occasionally polished stone; never a metal like this, rusting and flaking in the updrafts of steam, spotted with brown decay.

It was a relief when they came to the end of the walkway. Stone she could trust.

The tunnel led inward and down, and they took it warily. It was scattered with debris – rocks and pebbles, mouldering bits of food and broken hafts and chips of wood – but it was as empty as the rest of the place appeared to be, and there was little evidence here of any actual mining being done. The walls were uneven and ancient.

'This is natural,' Tsata said quietly, with a short indicative sweep of his hand. 'Like the shaft. There is no artificial framework here, nor any shoring up of the sides. What they have built, they have built on top of what was already there.'

'Then they did not mine all of this out?' Kaiku asked. Her clothes had dried in the heat now, and rubbed her uncomfortably.

'No,' he agreed. 'This place had stood for a long time before the Weavers came to it and built their devices.'

Kaiku found some comfort in that. Initially she had been stunned by the thought that the Weavers could have carved out something so massive in only a few years. Tsata's observation made the Weavers seem a fraction more mortal.

But still, as they descended, and the tunnel branched and led them through chambers that were makeshift kitchens and storerooms piled with food in barrels and sacks, they found the place eerily, utterly deserted.

'Do you think they have gone?' Kaiku whispered. 'All of them?'

'What about the small men?' Tsata asked. 'Would they have left?'

The small men: it took Kaiku a moment to realise that Tsata was talking about the diminutive servants of the Weavers. He had taken the name she had given them – golneri – and mistranslated it with the incorrect gender. His Saramyrrhic was excellent, but he was not beyond making mistakes now and then. It was not his mother tongue, after all.

The golneri. That was another mystery, to go with the Nexuses, the Edgefathers and the imprisoned, intelligent Aberrants that she had witnessed in the monastery on Fo. Heart's blood, this was all connected somehow. For so long, the Weavers had been such a dreadful and inextricable part of the people of Saramyr, and yet so little was known about them. How many more surprises had they been keeping in the depths of their monasteries these past centuries, stewing in their own black insanity while they hatched their plots?

What had the people of Saramyr allowed to happen, right under their noses?

Kaiku shook her head, as much to dismiss the enormity of her own question as to reply to Tsata's. 'The golneri will still be here.' A thought struck her. 'I think it is so empty because the Weavers did not expect the army to have to leave,' she said. 'That would explain the stockpiled food also.

Most of the army went north, and the rest remained to guard this place. But the Weavers here found out about the Fold somehow, after the main mass had left. Whatever the barges are doing is too important to turn back from; instead, the Weavers sent all that they had left here to the Fold. There are still enough Aberrants outside to deter casual attackers, and remember: nobody knows this place is here. The Weavers believe it is an acceptable risk. The second army will be gone for two weeks at the most – time to get to the Fold, decimate it, and come back – and when it returns the barrier will be up again and this place will be impregnable once more.'

'Kaiku, they may not take the Fold,' Tsata muttered. 'Do not give up yet.'

'I am simply guessing what they are thinking,' Kaiku told him, but there was a tightness to her voice that told him he had struck a nerve. She closed herself off to the visions of what might be happening even now in her adopted home.

'Their forces are stretched,' Tsata said. 'That gives us hope. If they had to leave themselves all but defenceless to get at Lucia, then they must have their attention elsewhere, on something more important.'

Kaiku nodded grimly. It was small comfort. She could venture a guess where those barges were headed: to Axekami, to the aid of Mos's troops. The Weavers were going to use Aberrants to secure Mos's throne, and to keep themselves in power throughout the oncoming famine. Shock troops that would make men's hearts quail and their knees buckle just before they were ripped to pieces. A show of force to bring the nobles and peasantry of Axekami back into line.

The Weavers were making their move in the game for control of Saramyr, and Kaiku could not imagine anything that could stand against them. The coup that had been brewing ever since Mos had allowed the Weavers to hold rank and land like one of the high families was destined to fail. Gods, it was as if everything had been set up just to make it harder for the Libera Dramach. If the Weavers consolidated themselves around the throne they would become immovable.

Kaiku found herself becoming angry. If only Cailin had not been so cursedly paranoid, keeping the Red Order reined and secret, not allowing them to challenge the Weavers. Because of that, the Weavers had spread unchecked, and the secrets they held remained secret, so that nobody could plan against them.

Cailin. So in love with her precious organisation, like Zaelis was with his. So afraid to endanger herself, to fight for her cause. She would not commit the Red Order against the Weavers; she was selfish, like Zaelis was, like *everyone* was, hoarding her power, biding her time, waiting until it was too late. Why had she held back so long? Why had a woman so shrewd, so commanding, allowed matters to get so out of hand?

Kaiku caught herself. Where was all this coming from?

But the answer had presented itself almost as soon as she posed the question. She *suspected* Cailin. She had suspected her from the beginning, from their very first meeting, when she had mistrusted her Sister's apparently altruistic invitation to join the Red Order. So much time had passed, and she had almost forgotten, almost become used to Cailin's ways; but nothing had changed, not really.

It was her encounter with Asara that had reminded her, the deep and fundamental deception that she had been subjected to. Cailin *knew* who Saran really was, and yet she had kept the secret, even though she must have suspected Kaiku's feelings for him. It had been Asara that had watched her for two years in the guise of her handmaiden, waiting for Kaiku to manifest her *kana.* Asara who had brought her to Cailin. Now Asara who had given five years of her life to glean clues buried by thousands of years of history all over the Near World.

Yet no matter what Tsata thought, Asara was not working for the greater good; she was selfishness personified. Whatever she was up to, it was for her good and hers alone. She and Cailin, locked in a conspiracy of two, hidden behind veils of misdirection and always, always working towards *something.* Something that Kaiku had not been let in on.

Machinations, wheels turning within wheels. She was not like Mishani. She sickened of deceit.

They were forced to cross the shaft again as they descended, for the tunnel branches that they chose looped around and spat them back out into the open. They endured a passage across an immeasurable void on a thin metal bridge anchored by spidery struts to the surrounding rock. On the way, they came so close to one of the curiously beautiful waterfalls that Kaiku might have reached out and touched it if she were not unreasonably afraid that her interference in the flow might trigger some sort of alarm.

When they regained the safety of the tunnels, and the massive weight of the stone closed in around them once more, they began to come across the long-expected signs of life. This tunnel had been adapted from its original form, which was probably too uneven or obstructive to be viable as a corridor, and it was braced with a metal framework. The torches that burned here were of the usual kind, not the strange contraptions belching inflammable gas that were present in the enormous dark of the shaft.

It was the golneri. The smell of cooking meat and the sound of muttering voices alerted the intruders. They instinctively drew back into shadow, listening to the jabber of the golneri's incomprehensible dialect. Kaiku wondered where they had come from, how they had come to be so enslaved by the Weavers. A pygmy tribe, hidden in the depths of the Tchamil Mountains, subjugated all those years ago when the first Weavers' baptism of slaughter was over and they disappeared into the uncharted peaks of Saramyr? Certainly, it was not beyond possibility. Between her home in the Forest of Yuna and the Newlands to the east, the mountain range was three hundred miles wide. From Riri on the southern edge to the northern coast which abutted them, they stretched for over eight hundred miles, dividing Saramyr into west and east with only two major passes along that whole length. There were unexplored areas of the Tchamil Mountains so vast that an entire civilisation could have thrived there and nobody in Saramyr would be the wiser. Even after more than a thousand years of settlement, the land was simply bigger than they could swell to fill it; and in those empty places the spirits still held sway, and resented the encroachment of humankind.

She would probably never know. Whatever the golneri were or had been, now they were merely appendages to the Weavers, to feed them and care of them when their masters' insanity took hold. Kaiku tried to pity them, but she had precious little pity left, and she saved it for her own kind.

They crept onward until the tunnel became a small cavern, hot and smoky and redolent with the scent of crisping flesh. The tunnels were by no means smooth and straight, their sides a mass of folds and natural alcoves, and the haphazard placement of torch brackets throughout the mine left enough gaps between the light for them to conceal themselves to some extent. They crouched near the mouth of the cavern and looked in.

Animals turned on spits; vegetables boiled in vats. Strips of red meat hung on hooks over smoking embers, and elsewhere great fires blazed. Fish were being decapitated and eviscerated, their guts tossed aside to slither in the accumulated filth that carpeted the floor. Dozen of the tiny beings were here, their faces screwed up into wrinkled clutters, eyes vacuous and expressions strangely immobile. They were swarthy and skinny, looking like resentful children, their features set in permanent scowls as they rapped orders at one another in their unfamiliar language. Kaiku watched them with a fascination, mesmerised by their ugliness, until with a start she noticed that several of them were looking back at her. The shock of being discovered made her heart leap in fright.

'Tsata . . .' she murmured.

'I know,' he said quietly. 'They have sharp eyes.'

They kept very still. Now the first ones who had spotted them were returning to their work, and others were noticing them. Their presence did not seem to excite any kind of alarm. After a time, they were entirely ignored. Kaiku breathed again. She had half-expected that reaction from her experiences with them when she had penetrated the Weavers' monastery on Fo, but her relief was still profound.

'They do not seem concerned,' Tsata observed, wary of a trick.

Kaiku swallowed against a dry throat. 'Then that is our good fortune,' she said. 'The Weavers have never had much need for guards. Their barriers have kept everything and everyone out for hundreds of years. They have not needed to fear for so long, they have forgotten how to.'

She stood up, and walked out of hiding. The golneri paid her no attention. Slowly, Tsata joined her, and they crossed the underground kitchen together, expecting at any moment for a clamour to be raised. But the golneri's indifference was total.

'I would not rely on that, Kaiku,' Tsata said. 'I think they will be guarding their witchstone very closely, and they will not entrust these small men or Aberrants with the task.'

Indeed, Kaiku thought, and his words reminded her of something that she had been trying to push to the back of her mind since they had taken on this task. There were still likely to be Weavers here. She might have beaten a demon with her *kana*, but they were lesser things. She dared not match herself against even a single Weaver. The stakes were too high, even for her.

Yet they had to know. Had to know whether the stories Asara had brought back from the other continents were true. Had to know if the Weavers had any vulnerabilities at all. For her oath to Ocha, for her dead family, for her friends who might even now be dying at the other end of the Fault, they had to strike a blow.

Somehow, they had to destroy the witchstone.

THIRTY-ONE

For the second time in his life, Barak Grigi tu Kerestyn sat on horseback in the midst of an army and looked upon the city of Axekami.

It was beautiful in the light of the early morning. Nuki's eye was rising directly behind it in the east, the brilliance carved into rays by the spires and minarets of the capital, casting a long shadow like reaching fingers towards the throng of thousands who came to possess it. The air had a hazy, beatific quality, a fragile shimmer that made promises of the winter to come, where the days would be warm and still, and the night skies clear as crystal.

Axekami. Grigi could feel the desire kindling in his heart just by shaping the word in his mind. Those towering beige walls that had thwarted him once before; the jumble of streets and temples, libraries and bath-houses, docks and plazas. A chaotic profusion of life and industry.

His eyes travelled up the hill to where the Imperial Quarter lay, serene and ordered beneath the bluff that the Keep sat on, its far side aflame with sunlight and its western face in shadow. His gaze lingered on it, drinking in the sight of its magnificence, roaming over the temple to Ocha that crowned it and the Towers of the Winds that rose needle-thin at its corners. The Jabaza, distantly visible, wound in from the north, and the Zan headed away to the south, junks and barges waiting idly near the banks. Axekami had been sealed tight since the night before, as it always was in times of threat, and no river traffic was getting in or out.

How he wanted that city, craved it as if it were a mistress long denied him. The throne had slipped from Blood Kerestyn before, but now he was here to restore his family to the glory they deserved. He felt an elation, a certainty of the righteousness of his cause. The revolt in Zila had showed just how weak Mos's hold was on his empire. The fact that he had left the matter to local Baraks and sent none of his own troops only made things look worse for him. How the people of Axekami would welcome Grigi this time, instead of uniting to fight against him as they had before.

And the only thing standing against him was the twenty thousand men camped between him and his prize.

'History repeats itself,' he grinned, flushed with the proximity of his dream. 'Except that five years ago in summer, you were on *that* side.'

'Briefly,' Barak Avun said, the reins of his mount gripped in one bony fist. 'Let us hope that history is kinder to us this time.'

'After today, we will *write* history,' Grigi said expansively, and pulled his horse into a canter.

The two of them rode together along the rear of the battle lines, one huge and obese, the other gaunt and ascetic. Their Weavers were not far away, keeping pace, hunched ghoulishly in their saddles. They were on hand to co-ordinate instructions between the multitude of Baraks and Barakesses whose forces stood as allies.

The high families had flocked to Kerestyn's banner as the alternative to the ineptitude of Mos. If there had been any doubt, it had been dashed when the Empress Laranya fell from the Tower of the East Wind. Rumours of Mos's state of mind had reached them long before, but his wife's apparent suicide in response to the beating he delivered her was the final evidence that the Blood Emperor was insane. Grigi trusted that they would stand firm simply because there was no other option. None of the other high families, including Blood Koli, had the support or the power to make a play for the throne. Even if one or all of them betrayed him now, the families would simply fracture into an evenly-matched and self-destructive squabble, and they knew that. It was Grigi, or Mos.

The armies stood on the yellow-green grass of the plains to the west of Axekami, where so much blood had been spilt before. The sheer numbers present defeated the eye, thousands upon thousands, an accretion of humanity too vast to take in. Each man a different face, a different past, a different dream; yet here they were anonymous, defined only by the colours dyed on the leather of their armour or the hue of the sashes that some wore tied around their heads. Great swathes of warriors, sworn by blood to the families that ruled them. Each one a weapon for their nobles to wield, and in their hands a weapon of their own. Divisions of riflemen, swordsmen, riders of horses and manxthwa, men to operate fire-cannons and mortars; they stood in formations according to their allegiance or their speciality, their discipline utter, their dedication total. For these were soldiers of Saramyr: their lives were subordinate to the will of their masters and mistresses, and disobedience or cowardice was worse than death in their eyes.

The defenders were predominantly attired in red and silver, the colours of Blood Batik. Those wearing other colours were the few whose dogged loyalty to the Imperial throne had blinded them to Mos's faults, or whose hatred of Blood Kerestyn had led them to join against him. The Imperial Guards he had kept within the city, but Mos had sent the remainder of his forces out onto the battlefield. Mos knew that if he allowed the usurpers to lay siege to the city, with the onset of famine and his unpopularity among the people he ruled, then it would only be a matter of time before the end.

Mos would not let himself be cornered. Instead, he chose to meet his enemy head on. Even weakened by splitting his forces, he possessed an army not much smaller than the combined might that Kerestyn had brought against him.

But Grigi had a trick up his sleeve. He had the Weave-lord.

Gods, the treachery was spectacular. Grigi could not even begin to imagine how Kakre had arranged the Empress's death, but it had weakened Mos just enough. All the time Kakre had been conspiring with Grigi and Avun tu Koli, spinning secret deals, plotting to get rid of the unpopular Mos and install a new, powerful ruler in the shape of Grigi. Like a rat leaving a sinking ship, and swimming to a new one.

Of course, such untrustworthiness made them dangerous. And Weavers were not the only ones who could be sly. Once he was firmly in his rightful place, Grigi would use Kakre's betrayal of Mos as an excuse to get rid of the Weavers once and for all. The people would demand it. Grigi had no wish to have his own ship sunk under the weight of the rats that clambered aboard.

He looked at Avun, his small eyes agleam amid the folds of his face. Avun returned the gaze unblinkingly. As if summoned, the two Weavers rode up alongside, one with the visage of a grimacing demon, one with an insectile face of gemstone, a Mask of incalculable wealth.

Avun nodded imperceptibly at Grigi. Grigi's voice was trembling with excitement as he turned to the Weavers and spoke.

'Begin.'

The rising roar of the armies as they closed on each other floated high into the sky, reaching to where Mos stood on a balcony of the Imperial Keep and looked down over the distant battle. His eyes were hollow and his beard thin and lank; a soft breath of air from the city below stirred his hair where it hung limply against his forehead. His flesh seemed to hang off his broad, stocky frame now, and he held a goblet of dark wine in one hand, nursing it as tenderly as if it were the child he had killed. But his gaze was clear, and despite the grief written so plainly on him, he seemed more his old self than in recent days.

How ridiculous it seemed, he thought. The plains surrounding Axekami were so flat that there was no real terrain advantage to be had, so Kerestyn had simply marched up to the city, Mos had sent his men out, and they had stood there waiting to kill each other. An idiotic civility. If there had been any passion involved, the enemy forces would have torn into each other on sight; but war was passionless, at least from where he stood. So they lined up their pieces in preparation for a charge, and only commenced when everyone was ready. It was enough to make him laugh, if he had any laughter in him.

The charge looked strangely surreal, like homing birds released from their cages. The front ranks simply dissolved into a mad dash as the signal to attack was given, and were matched by their counterparts on the other side. The distant report of fire-cannons preceded flashes of flame as sections of the charging troops were immolated. Riflemen were firing, reloading, firing, switching guns when their powder burned out. Horsemen swung out to the flanks. Manxthwa-riders powered through the foot-soldiers, their mounts turned from docile beasts of burden to angry mountains of shaggy muscle in the heat of combat, kicking out with their spatulate front hooves, their sad and misleadingly wise-looking faces turned to snarls. Up here, it was possible to see the formations moving in a slow dance, arranging themselves around the great central mass where the foot-soldiers hacked each other into bloody slabs in a dance of exquisite bladework.

'You do not seem at all concerned, my Emperor,' Kakre said, stepping out onto the balcony. Mos's nose wrinkled slightly at the sick-dog smell of him.

'Perhaps I simply don't care,' Mos replied. 'Win, lose, what does it matter? The land is still blighted. Perhaps Kerestyn will kill me, perhaps I will kill him. I don't envy him the task he takes on with my mantle.'

Kakre regarded him strangely. He disliked the tone in Mos's voice. It was entirely too light. Since the death of Laranya, Kakre had ceased twisting the Emperor's dreams, trusting his own despondency to make him pliable without the risk of manipulating his mind directly. For a time, it had worked: he had barely questioned Kakre when he had advised that an army should be sent to forestall the desert Baraks, had not even checked the size of Kerestyn's army for himself. And yet now, despite his words, that despondency seemed to have fallen from him. Perhaps he was simply being fatalistic, Kakre reasoned. He had good reason to be, oh indeed.

Kakre's mind went elsewhere, to another battle, where at the very same moment the last remaining thorn in the Weavers' side was about to be removed. How things had shifted in their favour, that the Ais Maraxa should be foolish enough to expose themselves by inciting a revolt in Zila. Kakre had promised Mos that he would deal with the cause of that revolt and he had meant it. He had contacted Fahrekh, Blood Vinaxis' Weaver, and all the others in the vicinity and given them one simple instruction: take one of the leaders alive, and strip their mind raw. Chance had delivered them Xejen tu Imotu, but it could as easily have been one of a half-dozen others. The Ais Maraxa had been troublesome for so long: they were too well hidden, and Kakre did not have the time to ferret them out, especially as their connection with the Heir-Empress might have been a false lead. But their zeal had been the end of them, and now it would be the end of their divine saviour. For Lucia *was* alive, and furthermore, Fahrekh had found out where she was.

The timing was fractionally inconvenient. Kakre would have liked to send an even greater number of Aberrants to the Fold than they had mustered, but the bulk of their force had been needed elsewhere. Even so, there were more than enough; enough to weather the occasional mistakes and setbacks, such as the massacre of the Aberrants in the canyons west of the Fold.

Kakre did not want to take the risk of simply killing the Heir-Empress and then have the Libera Dramach use her as a martyr. He wanted the Libera Dramach too, to smash that last resistance, to capture their leaders and force them to give up their co-conspirators until all sedition was stamped out. And if he was fortunate, more fortunate than he dared hope, he might even find that Weaving bitch that had killed his predecessor.

Today, in the span between sunrise and sunset, all the Weavers' troubles would be removed.

He had all but forgotten about his suspicious mood when he felt the mental approach of another of his kind. Fast as the flicker of a synapse, he dived into the Weave to meet him, flashing along the currents of the void until the two minds joined in a tangle of threads, knotting and mingling, passing information, then pulling away into retreat. Kakre was back into himself in moments, rage bursting into life inside him. He turned his attention to the battle again, looking hard at the tiny figures that fought and died down there.

A mile north-west of the combat, a vast clot of red and silver had appeared, moving fast towards the rear of the Blood Kerestyn forces. Eight thousand Blood Batik troops, as if from nowhere. From the Imperial Keep, they could see fifteen miles to the horizon, and there had been no sign of the troops until now.

'Mos!' he croaked. 'What is this?'

Mos gave him a dry look. 'This is how I beat Grigi tu Kerestyn,' he said.

'*How?*' Kakre cried, his fingers turned to claws on the parapet of the balcony.

'Kakre, you seem discomfited,' Mos observed, mockingly polite. 'I'd advise you not to take out your aggressions on me as you did before. I may be Emperor for a very long time yet, despite your best efforts to the contrary, and it would be well not to make me angry.' He smiled suddenly, a mirthless rictus. 'Do we understand each other?'

Kakre had been listening in disbelief, but now he found his voice again. 'What have you done, Mos?' he demanded hoarsely.

'Eight thousand cloaks, matched to the colour of the grass on the plains,' he said. He sounded nothing like the broken man that he had seemed to be only a few short hours ago. Now his voice was flat and cold. 'I didn't send my men to meet the desert Baraks. And I didn't send them after Reki either. I had them all double back. I had something of an intuition that Kerestyn might hear of this opportunity, and that he might come in greater numbers than I expected. Before dawn, I sent them out and had them hide under their cloaks and wait. You'd never see them unless you were close.'

Kakre's eyes blazed within the black pits of his Mask. 'And what about the desert Baraks?' he hissed.

'Let them come,' Mos shrugged. 'They'll find Kerestyn shattered and me ruling in Axekami with nobody to challenge me. And of course, my loyal Weavers by my side.' This last was delivered in an insultingly sardonic tone. 'Sometimes it's best not to let anyone know everything, Kakre. A good ruler realises that. And don't forget I helped make Blood Batik great long before I met you.'

'I am your Weave-lord!' Kakre barked. 'I *need* to know everything!'

'So you can turn it against me? I think not,' Mos said, his voice quiet and deadly. He was a man who had nothing left to lose, and even the terror of the Weavers had no hold on him now. The Imperial Keep had cast them both in shadow, but Mos's rage made him seem darker still. 'I'm no fool. I know what you're doing. You treat with Koli and Kerestyn to get rid of me.' His eyes filled with tears of sheer hatred. 'You should never have let go, Kakre. You should never have stopped the dreams.' He leaned closer, breathing in the stench of corrupted flesh, showing his enemy that he was not afraid.

'*I know it was you*,' he whispered.

The gaping death-mask of Kakre looked back at him emptily.

'I can kill you in a moment,' the Weave-lord said, the words issuing from the cavernous black mouth dripping with venom.

'But you daren't,' Mos said, leaning back and away from him. 'Because you don't know who will be Emperor by nightfall now. And you won't use your cursed mind-bending power on me, because you can't be sure it will work. You slipped up once, Kakre. You didn't cover your tracks when you left.' He was almost shaking with disgust. 'I *remember*. I remember your filthy fingers inside my head. The memories came back; you didn't bury them deep enough.'

He turned away, back to the battle, the tears still standing in his eyes. 'But I still need you, Kakre. Gods save me, I need the Weavers. Without you, there's no way to get in touch with Okhamba and the Merchant Consortium fast enough to avert this famine. There's no way to keep this land together when people begin to starve. It will be chaos, and riots, and slaughter.' He took a shuddering breath, and the tears spilled at last, twin tracks losing themselves in the bristles of his beard. 'To expose you, to call the noble houses to rise up and throw you out, would cause the death of millions.'

Kakre's reaction was unreadable. He faced the Emperor for a long while, but the Emperor would only look at the battle below. Eventually, Kakre turned his attention back that way also.

'Watch closely, Kakre,' Mos said through gritted teeth. 'I still have one trick left to play.'

The noise of the battle was immense, a thuggish, constant bellow underpinned by the boom of artillery and counterpointed by the scrape of steel on steel, the screams of the dead and the dying, the bone-snap reports of rifles. In the killing ground at its centre, men struggled and fought in amidst a crowd of allies and enemies, a world of disorder where every angle could bring a new attack, the survivors owing their continued life to luck as much as skill. Arrows smacked into shoulders and thighs like diving birds plunging after fish. Swords carved through flesh, causing death in ways far more brutal than fiction or history would present. The neat beheadings and swift killing strokes were few; blows glanced, slicing meat from the forearm or hacking halfway through a man's knee, splitting someone's face from left cheek to right ear in a spray of shattered bone or chopping into an artery to leave the wounded man bleeding white on the grass of the plains. Flame sprang up in slicks as shellshot burst, burning jelly sticking to skin and cooking it, men flailing and shrieking as their tongues blackened and their eyeballs popped and ran sizzling down their faces. The air was smoke and blood and the sick-sweet smell of charred bodies, and the battle raged on.

'I need the Bloods Nabichi and Gor back here *now*!' Grigi was demanding of his Weaver. His high, girlish voice made him sound panicky, but he was far from that. Grigi was very hard to rattle, and the seemingly inexplicable appearance of eight thousand Blood Batik troops behind them was merely a clever move to be countered. Already he had a force moving up to delay them while he could get his fire-cannons turned around and aimed. It was going to make this fight more costly, but he could still win it with shrewd leadership.

'That fool Kakre is going to pay for this,' he promised, reining his horse around. He did not care that other Weavers were within earshot, both Blood Kerestyn's and the gemstone-Masked Weaver of Blood Koli. 'Why didn't he warn me about the extra troops? And where's this *intervention* he promised?' He glared at Barak Avun, blaming him for Kakre's mistakes; after all, it was through Avun that Kakre had contacted him.

Avun, who had been watching the battle with his hooded, drowsy eyes, turned and gave Grigi a bland stare.

'There will be an intervention,' Avun said. 'Just not as you imagine.' He flicked a gesture at his Weaver.

The stabbing pain in Grigi's chest took his breath away. His multitudinous chins bunched up as he gaped, clutching at his leather breastplate. A sparkling agony was spreading along his collarbone to his left arm, numbing his hand. His eyes were wide with disbelief. They flicked to his own Weaver, desperate supplication in their gaze, but the grimacing demon looked at him pitilessly. Grigi gasped half a curse as the strength drained from his limbs.

'History does repeat itself, Grigi,' Avun said. 'But it appears that you do not learn from it. You had me betray Blood Amacha last time we were here; you should have known that I cannot be trusted.'

Grigi's face had reddened, his eyes bulging as he fought for air that would not seem to come. His heart was a bright star of agony in his chest, sending ribbons of fire through his veins. The sounds of the battle had dimmed, and Avun's voice was thin in his ear as if from far away. He clutched at his saddle as realisation struck like a hammer: he was dying here, now, surrounded by these three impassive figures on horseback. Gods, no, he wasn't ready! He hadn't done what he needed to do! He was within sight of his prize, and it was being snatched from him, and he could not even make a sound to voice his defiance at his tormentor.

His Weaver. His Weaver was supposed to defend him. They were always loyal, *always*. The very fabric of their society depended on it. If a Weaver did not serve his master in all things, then the Weavers were too dangerous to exist. They even killed each other in the service of the family that supported them. But this one was letting him die.

How had Avun won round his Weaver? *How?*

'You will find that the orders you sent did not get through to their intended recipients,' Avun was saying languidly. 'And they will most likely be quite surprised when my troops turn on them, and they are sandwiched between Koli and Batik men to the west and Mos's main force to the east. It will be quite a slaughter.' He raised an eyebrow. 'You, of course, will not live to see it. Your heart gave out in the heat of battle. Small wonder, for one so fat.'

The pain in Grigi's body was nothing compared to the pain in his soul, the raw and searing frustration and anger and terror all mixing and mingling to scald him. His vision was dimming now, turning to black, and no matter how he fought against it, no matter how he struggled to cry out and make a sound, he was mute. Men of Blood Kerestyn were only metres away, and yet none of them marked him, none of them saw what the Weavers were doing, reaching an invisible hand inside him to squeeze his heart. To them, he was merely in conference with his aides, and if his expression was distressed and gawping, something like a landed fish, then they were not close enough to notice.

He looked to Axekami, and it was dark now, the shadowed fingers of its spires reaching out across the carnage to enfold him. Twice he had sought it; twice been denied. Unconsciousness was a mercy. He did not feel himself slump forward and then slide from his saddle, his mountainous body crashing to the earth; did not hear the cries of alarm from Avun, false words to Grigi's men as they gathered; did not see him and his Weaver slip away from the crowd, to turn the battle with perfidy. There was only the growing golden light, and the threads that seemed to sew through everything, wafting him like fallopian cilia towards what lay beyond oblivion.

Kakre's hood flapped about his Masked face in a flurry of wind as he watched the battle unfold. Nuki's eye had risen overhead now. It was hot in the direct sun, and Kakre's sweltering robe was entirely inappropriate, but he did not retreat. Neither did Mos. Reports came to them both: to Mos through his runners; to Kakre through the Weave. The morning had passed, and the forces led by Blood Kerestyn were decimated. The armies of some of the most prominent high families in the land had been cut to pieces. Kerestyn themselves, who had dedicated almost all their troops to this venture, would not be able to rise again for decades, if ever. Weakened, they would be unable to continue fighting in the vicious internecine dealings of the nobles, and would be torn apart.

Avun tu Koli had been clever. Whatever deals he had made, he had managed to execute them without Grigi finding out. It was not only Blood Koli that turned on Kerestyn, but several other families as well, tipping the balance far enough in the Emperor's favour to make it virtually impossible for Blood Kerestyn to turn the tide back. Ragged armies were fleeing in retreat now, Grigi's allies deserting him as their cause became hopeless. Kakre noted that Blood Koli troops were almost entirely intact; Avun tu Koli had drawn them out of the conflict, letting the others take care of the battle, content to watch from the sidelines and preserve his men.

'It was you,' Kakre said at last. 'I remember now. I had learned of a message to Avun tu Koli, sent from the Keep, but I failed to intercept it.' He felt a pang of concern that he had forgotten about it until this point.

'Avun tu Koli has always been an honourless dog,' Mos replied. 'And that makes him reliable. He'll always choose the winning side, no matter what his previous loyalties. I just had to convince him that I would win. Look at him, holding his men back. Blood Koli will be the most powerful family behind Batik after this, and he knows it.' He scratched at his beard, which had gone scraggy and heavily scattered with white as if withered by his grief. 'You tried, Kakre, and it was a cursed good try. But you are stuck with me, and I'm stuck with you. No matter what you've done, we need each other.'

The words almost caught in his throat: *no matter what you've done.* As if he could dismiss the murder of the woman he loved so easily. As if he could ever love again, or feel anything but sorrow and hatred and shame. Locked with the Weavers in a symbiosis of mutual loathing, he saw nothing but evil in his future; but evil must be endured, for the sake of power. He had lost a son, a wife, and an unborn child now. Such things could drive better men than him to ruin. But he had nephews, and other relations that could take the reins of the Empire when he was gone; and he had a duty to his family, to Blood Batik. He would not give up the throne while he still breathed.

'You are mistaken,' said Kakre, his voice a dry rasp. 'And your runners come now to tell you why.'

An urgent chime outside the door of the chamber behind them made Mos whirl. He stepped into the room, out of the sun to where the coloured *lach* of the walls and floor and pillars kept the air cool. He stopped halfway to the curtained doorway, and looked back at where Kakre was coming through the archway after him.

'What is this, Kakre?' he demanded. Suddenly, he was afraid. 'What is this?'

The bell chimed again. Kakre's scrawny white hand emerged from the folds of his robe and gestured towards the doorway.

'Tell me!' Mos roared at the Weave-lord.

The runner thought that this was an invitation to enter, and he drew the curtain aside and hurried in, blanching as Mos swung a furious glare on him and he realised his mistake. But he was terrified already, and he blurted out his message recklessly as if by delivering it he could expel its meaning from him and purge the horror that his words carried.

'Aberrants!' he cried. 'There are Aberrants all over the docks. Thousands! They're killing anything that moves!'

'*Aberrants?*' Mos howled, swinging back to Kakre.

'Aberrants,' Kakre said, quite calmly. 'We sailed bargeloads of them into Axekami last night, and then you shut the gates and locked them in. You'll find that many more are deploying on the west bank of the Zan now and heading towards the soldiers outside Axekami. They will slaughter anyone not wearing the colours of Blood Koli.'

'Koli?' Mos was choking on the sheer enormity of what Kakre was saying. Aberrants? In Axekami? The most dreadful enemy of civilisation at the very heart of the empire? And the Weavers had *brought them here*?

'Yes, Koli,' Kakre replied. 'Quite the treacherous one. Ever ready to step over the corpses of his allies to victory, like a true Saramyr. He has been on my side all along.'

Mos had the terrible impression that Kakre was grinning behind his Mask.

'Let us not delude ourselves, Mos,' he croaked. 'The Weavers see the way that Saramyr is turning. Soon, you would try to get rid of us. The people would demand it. Grigi tu Kerestyn was plotting to do the same. That cannot happen.'

The runner was rooted to the spot, trembling, a young man of eighteen harvests witnessing an event of an importance far beyond anything he could ever imagine being privy to.

'At this time, Aberrants are pouring from the mountains, from our mines, from dozens of locations where we have collected them and hidden them from your sight. You were kind enough to be part of the process of demolishing the standing armies of the nobles with this charade being played out beyond Axekami's walls. Our Aberrants will take care of the rest.'

For an instant, Mos was too stunned to take in what the Weave-lord was telling him. Then, with a strangled cry of rage, he lunged, a blade sliding free of the sheath where it had been hidden at his belt. Kakre put up a hand, and Mos's charge turned into a stumbling collapse as his muscles spasmed and locked. He went crashing to the ground in a foetal position, his face contorted, jaw thrust to one side, his fingers jutting out at all angles, his wrists bent inwards and his neck twisted, as if he were a piece of paper screwed up and discarded. His eyes rolled madly, but he could only make a hoarse gargle emit from his mouth.

The Weave-lord stood over the Emperor, small and hunched and infinitely lethal. 'The time of the high families is over,' he said. 'Your day is done. The Weavers have served you for centuries, but we will serve you no longer. The Empire ends today.'

He waved his hand, and Mos burst. Blood splattered explosively from his eyes, ears, nose and mouth, from his genitals, from his anus. His belly split and his sundered intestines coiled out in a gory slither; his vertebrae shattered from skull to coccyx.

In an instant, it was over. The ruined corpse of the Emperor lay amid a blast-pattern of his own fluids on the green *lach* floor of the room.

Kakre raised his head, the corpse-Mask fixing on the messenger. The shock and disbelief on the young man's face was comical. He dropped to his knees, haemorrhaging massively.

There was silence in the room; but outside, in the streets of the city, rifle fire could be heard. Bells were tolling. An alarm was being raised.

The brightness of the sunlight on the balcony made the room seem dim in comparison. Kakre studied the bodies of the men he had killed. An Emperor and a servant, both just husks in the end.

The Aberrant predators in Axekami would rampage through the city, crush all resistance, bring the populace savagely to heel. All over northern Saramyr, huge armies of beasts were sallying forth from the Tchamil Mountains and along the rivers, an accumulation of decades of planning and five short years of unrestricted movement within the empire. Monstrous hordes, blossoming out from within like spreading cancers under the auspices of the Weavers and the Nexuses.

Messages begging for help would not get to where they were sent. Weavers would disappear, their masters murdered. So long had the nobles of Saramyr relied on the power of the Weavers to communicate that they would not know what to do. So long had they accepted the Weavers' servitude that they could not imagine rebellion. Suddenly, they would be alone, isolated in the midst of a massive country, separated by huge expanses from anyone who could help them. By the time they adapted it would be too late. The high families would be overthrown.

The game was done, and the Weavers had won.

Kakre walked slowly from the room. When Mos's corpse was discovered, the Imperial Guards would draw the obvious conclusion. But by that time he would be back in his chambers, and the door was thick enough to withstand the Imperial Guards long enough for the Keep to fall, if they should hunt him down.

Besides, he had a celebratory titbit waiting there, brought to him last night for just this occasion. A young woman, smooth as silk, lithe and beautiful and perfect. And such skin she had, such skin.

The Juwacha Pass lay between Maxachta and Xaxai, bridging the Tchamil Mountains where they narrowed, reaching from the fertile west to the desert of Tchom Rin in the east. Apart from the Riri Gap on the south coast, it was the only major crossing-point between the two halves of the divided land. Legend had it that Ocha himself had parted the mountains with one stamp of his foot, to open Tchom Rin and the Newlands to his chosen people and give them licence to drive the aboriginal Ugati out. More likely it was some cataclysmic shifting of the earth that had carved the sinuous route between the peaks, one hundred and fifty miles long, as if the upper and lower parts of the range were simply drawn apart and the ground between had stretched flat.

At its widest point it was two miles across, though it narrowed to half a mile at the western end, where its mouth was guarded by the sprawling city of Maxachta. What obstacles had been strewn across it on its discovery – boulder formations, glassy hulks of volcanic rock, massive jags of black stone: imperfections thrown up in the violence of its creation – had been destroyed with explosives and levelled long ago. The mountains had many passes for the agile, but for an army the Juwacha Pass was the only feasible way across without heading five hundred miles south to Riri.

Reki tu Tanatsua reached the summit of the mountain ridge at mid-morning, with the sun low and clear and sharp, shining directly in his eyes. Reki's thin face was bearded now, the hair growing surprisingly thick for such a young man. His black hair had become shaggy, the streak of white dyed to make it invisible. His finery had gone, traded away for sturdy peasant travelling-clothes, and his gaze was flintier and wiser, less that of a child and more that of a man. He laboured up the last few yards to the top, crunching through autumn snows that dusted the ground lightly at this altitude, and there he stopped and looked back.

Asara came up behind him, clad in a fur cloak, her clothes as simple and hardwearing as his. She wore her hair down, and her face was unadorned, but even without effort she was strikingly beautiful. The exertion of the climb had not even tired her. Beyond her, over the peaks, Maxachta spread across the yellow-green plains, tiny domes and spires shining as they came out of the frowning shadow of the mountains. They had passed it the day before yesterday and given it a wide berth, shunning habitation, just as they now chose a mountainous trail to the south of the Juwacha Pass rather than risk meeting anyone on it. It was a harder road, but a safer one, for all ways had become dangerous now.

Reki offered a hand to her, and she took it with a smile. He helped her the last few steps to the tip of the ridge, and there they walked to the far side and looked down.

The mountain ridge that they had climbed lay ten miles in from the western end of the pass, at the point where it curved slightly northward. From its heights, it was possible to see a long way in either direction. Asara had judged it a prudent point to take stock of where they were and anticipate any dangers ahead; Reki had submitted without argument. He had long learned to trust her in these matters. She had kept him alive thus far, and she was astonishingly capable for a woman her age. He desired her and was in awe of her at the same time.

But there was another motive behind their ascent. Asara had a suspicion which she was unwilling to share with Reki, and she wanted to be certain of it before she continued. Her Aberrant eyes were exceptionally sharp, and the tiny wheeling dots that she had spied from afar had set her to thinking. Now she saw her suspicion confirmed.

The mountains shouldered together to the east, forming a narrow, grey valley. It was carpeted in dead men and Aberrant beasts. Carrion birds plucked and pulled flesh so fresh that it had hardly even begun to decompose, or circled silently overhead, as if spoilt for choice and unable to decide where next to feast. From where they stood, the corpses were one incoherent jumble, bodies upon bodies in their thousands.

Thousands of desert folk. Men and women in the garb of Tchom Rin.

Asara shaded her eyes and scanned the pass, picking out broken standards and faded colours. She saw the emblems of the cities of Xaxai and Muio, in among those of other high families. It took her only moments to find the one she was looking for.

Blood Tanatsua, tattered and torn, lying across several bodies like a shroud. The emblem of Reki's family. And she knew enough of desert lore to realise that the standard was only raised above an army when the Barak himself was present.

The desert families had marched quickly at the news of Laranya's suicide. Had Kakre's Weavers been setting things up here too, playing the families as Kakre was doing in Axekami? Certainly, it seemed that this army had moved with uncanny speed, even assuming that news of the Empress's death had been communicated instantly by Kakre to his foul brethren in the desert. A vanguard, perhaps? A show of might? The desert cities would not declare war on the strength of what they had heard. It would take the token that Reki carried to make them do that. But now, it seemed, his errand was redundant.

She glanced at him. His vision was not as good as hers, but he saw enough. He stared down on the scene for a long time in silence, his face still but tears welling in his eyes.

'Is my father down there?' Reki asked.

'Who can say?' Asara replied, but she knew that he was, and Reki caught it in her tone. She could only imagine what had happened: how these men had been ambushed by Aberrants, how even this massive force had been outnumbered by the tide of monstrosities pouring from the mountains. Yet how could the Aberrants be so organised, so numerous, so purposeful? Could this, too, be some dark result of the Weavers' ambitions? It seemed impossible, yet the alternatives were even more impossible yet.

Reki wiped his eyes with the back of his hand. He did not grieve for his father, to whom he had been a source of endless disappointment; he had enough residual bitterness to pretend that he did not care. He wept instead for the death of his people. He wept at his first sight of the cost of war.

They made a fire on the summit of the ridge, careless of the consequences, and there Reki took out the sheaf of hair that had been his sister's, and burned it. The acrid stink carried up on the thin trail of smoke into the morning sky, the ends of the hair glowing, curling and blackening. Reki knelt over it, gazing into the heart of the blaze at the last part of his sister he had as it smouldered into ash. Asara stood at his shoulder, watching, wondering how he would feel if he ever knew that his sister's murderer was the woman by his side. Wondering what would happen if she was ever on the receiving end of his promised vengeance.

'The responsibility passes to me,' he said, eventually. 'What was to be my father's cause is now mine.'

Asara studied him. He stood up, and met her eyes. His gaze was steady, and there was a determination there that she had never seen before.

'You are a Barak now,' she said quietly.

His gaze did not flinch or flicker. Finally, he turned it eastward, looking over the peaks, as if he could see past them to the vast desert beyond where his home lay. Without a word, he set off that way, heading down the far slope of the ridge. Asara watched him go, noted the new set to his shoulders and the grim line of his jaw; then, with one final look to the west as if in farewell, she followed him.

THIRTY-TWO

Yugi sprinted along the barricade, the air a pall of acrid smoke and his face blackened and grimed with sweat. The sharp clatter of rifle fire punctured the cries of men and women. Aberrants roared and squealed as they were mown down in their dozens, and still they kept coming.

Yugi slung his rifle over his shoulder and drew his sword, leaping over the corpse of someone whose face had been ruined by shrapnel – they had let their weapon overheat and it had exploded – and racing towards where a skrendel had slipped over the barricade and was struggling with Nomoru. She was holding her lacquered rifle between them to fend off its scorpion-like tail-lashes, her head ducking back as the creature bared long, yellowed fangs and snapped at her. It sensed Yugi's approach and scampered off in a flail of spindly limbs, realising it was outnumbered; but Nomoru was faster, and she caught it by its ankle, tripping it so that it sprawled in the dust. It was all the time Yugi needed to plunge his sword into its ribs. It screamed, spasming wildly, raking claws at the two of them; but Yugi put his weight on the sword and pinned the creature to the ground, and Nomoru got to her feet, aimed calmly and blew its head to fragments.

'Are you hurt?' Yugi asked breathlessly.

Nomoru gazed at him for a long moment, her eyes unreadable. 'No,' she said eventually.

Yugi was about to say something else, but he changed his mind. He raced back to the barricade, sheathing his sword and priming his rifle, and joined the rest of the defenders as they shredded the creatures surging up the pass towards them. A moment later, Nomoru appeared alongside him, and did the same.

But the Aberrants were endless.

The fighting had begun at dawn. The efforts of Yugi and several other Libera Dramach traps and ambushes had slowed the advance of the Weavers' army, but only enough to buy them an extra night of preparation. Still, that night had given several clans, factions and survivors of previous Aberrant attacks time to get to the Fold and join the Libera Dramach in their stand. Since sunrise, Yugi had fought alongside some of the very Omecha death-cultists who had tried to kill them several weeks ago. He had also battled next to warrior monks, frightened scholars, crippled and deformed Aberrants from the nearby village in which non-Aberrant folk were not allowed, spirit-worshippers, bandits, narcotics smugglers, and any of three dozen other types of person that had either been cast out from society or had chosen to separate themselves from it.

The Xarana Fault, for all its diversity and constant infighting and struggles for territorial power, was united in one thing: they all lived in the Fault, and that made them different. And now the factions had put aside their differences to struggle against an enemy that threatened them all, and the Fold was where they would turn back the tide or die trying.

They had engaged the Aberrants in the Knot, the labyrinth of killing alleys that guarded the Fold to the west. There, the creatures could not get through more than a few at a time, and the spots where the way opened up enough to get more than two or three abreast had been trapped with explosives or slicewires or incendiaries. More defenders were positioned on top of the Knot, to pick off the cumbersome gristle-crows that acted as lookouts for the Nexuses and to cover the horseshoe of flat stone that abutted the western side of the valley, in case the Aberrants chose to forsake the narrow defiles and come over the top. In the Fault, it was necessary to think three-dimensionally in battle.

By mid-morning, the paths of the Knot were choked with Aberrant dead, but the defenders had been driven back steadily. Reports had come to Yugi of the fight to the north and south of the Fold, where the enemy were trying to circumvent the Knot entirely to attack the valley from the eastern side. It was the first tactical move that they had made. Yugi took a little heart from that. The Weavers did not know the first thing about how to fight a war; they had simply thought to sweep aside everyone in their way, caring nothing for the casualties they sustained. Thousands of Aberrant predators lay as testament to their ineptitude.

And yet it still seemed that in the end, they would be proved right in their assumption that they could simply trample down the opposition by weight of numbers. Ammunition was running very low now, and it was not getting to some of the places that needed it. The defenders' death toll had been light thus far, but when they lost the advantage of ranged weapons and had to close in hand-to-hand, the Aberrants would even the balance.

In all this, there was no sign of the Nexuses, nor of the Weavers. Nor, Yugi noted, the Red Order. Where in the Golden Realm was the help Cailin and her painted kind were meant to provide? Just to have them on hand to facilitate communication between groups of fighters would have been a huge help; but they were nowhere to be found.

Heart's blood, if she's run out on us, I'll kill that woman myself, he thought.

They had held this pass for over two hours now. There were only a limited number of ways out of the Knot, and each one had been fortified with one or more fire-cannons, as well as hastily constructed stone walls and earth banks. The sides of the defile rose sheer on either side, and the Aberrants were being forced to crowd uphill along an uneven surface of blood-slick stone to get to the barricade at the top. The sun had been slanting down into the enemy's eyes all morning, dazzling them, though it had now risen overhead and would soon begin to do the same to the defenders.

Rifles were fired dry, then swapped with loaders who refilled the chambers of the weapons and then swapped back when the next one was done. A small stack of guns steamed in a shadowed alcove, cooling so that the heat of repeated shooting would not make the ignition powder explode all at once. Three men attended to the fire-cannon behind the barricade, which was fashioned in the shape of a demon of the air, its body streamlined and mouth agape to spit flame. Half of the defile was ablaze from shellshot, sending thick black clouds of smoke up towards the defenders and making them squint. Yugi had been forced to limit use of the fire-cannon for fear of unwittingly providing the Aberrants with too much cover. The hot reek of bubbling fat and blackening flesh had resulted in vomiting behind the barricade, and in the midday heat the stench of warming stomach acids was appalling.

'They're trying again,' Nomoru said, setting her rifle stock under her armpit and sighting. She took her eye away to glance at Yugi. 'Wish I'd stayed with Kaiku now,' she deadpanned. Yugi laughed explosively, but it came out with a manic and desperate edge to it.

Despite the fact that the Nexuses had not been seen yet, their presence was still much in evidence in the way the Aberrants acted. They would attack in number, return and regroup in a very military fashion, and their strikes became more careful and organised as the day progressed. Yugi suspected that the Nexuses were hanging back after snipers like Nomoru had taught them that it was dangerous to show themselves, but their influence could still be observed.

There had been a short pause in the attacks after the skrendel had managed to slip over the barricade. That had been a lucky run, a product of too many people swapping weapons at once, combined with the speed and agility of the creature. Now the Aberrants were coming again, dark shapes running around the flames and through the swirling smoke. Rifles cracked once more, pummelling iron balls into the attackers at high velocity, smacking through flesh and shattering bone.

But this time, the Aberrants did not fall.

It took the defenders too long to realise that the creatures were still coming. The riflemen and women had paused, expecting the Aberrants to collapse and provide a clearer shot at the ones behind. By the time Yugi had yelled at the fire-cannon crew, and another salvo of bullets had failed to stop the rush, Nomoru had realised what was going on.

They were using their dead as shields.

Out of the smoke came a half-dozen ghauregs, each with another one of their number propelled before them: limp bags of muscle that jerked like dolls as they absorbed the hail of rifle balls. The monstrous, shaggy humanoids were powering over the heaped corpses of their companions, forming a line across the defile behind which a horde of other Aberrants pressed forward. Nomoru picked off two of them by dint of her skill with the rifle, and another one had its legs shot out from under it by some quick-thinking defenders, but they had no sooner stumbled than they were borne up again by another ghaureg, lifted and presented as targets so that the creatures behind could push on. The fire-cannon roared, but it was fired in haste before the operators could decline the elevation enough; it blasted the middle of the horde to flaming ruin and prevented any more from getting through, but that still left too many, who discarded their burdens as they reached the barricade and began to clamber over.

Guns were thrown aside and swords drawn as the defenders crowded to counter the assault. Yugi saw a ghaureg pick up an Aberrant woman by her leg and fling her into the side of the defile; he heard the breaking of her bones as she hit. Then he was in close, ducking a swipe from the creature's enormous arm, his blade lashing out to sever the hand at the wrist. The beast roared in pain, then jerked as two men came from behind it and buried their weapons in its back. Its huge jaw went slack and the light went out in its eyes, and it slumped to the ground with a bubbling sigh.

He cast about for Nomoru, but the wiry scout was nowhere to be seen. The warble of a shrilling warned him an instant before it leaped from the top of the barricade towards him. He dodged the first pounce, but it reared up on its hind legs and slashed a sickle-claw, which cut a furrow through his shirt and missed his skin by the width of a hair. His counterstrike was pre-empted by a rifle shot from his left, which smashed through the creature's skull armour and dropped it to the dusty ground. He glanced at his saviour, already knowing who it would be. Nomoru had retreated to a nook further up the pass and was crouching there, picking off Aberrants one by one. She was no hand-to-hand fighter; she was much more deadly from a distance.

Reassured now that he knew where she was, he swung back to the fray. The barricade had collapsed under the weight of the ghauregs that lumbered over it. Already the ground was cluttered with the fallen, attacker and defender alike. The Aberrants were heavily outnumbered, and their reinforcements were cut off by a wall of flame further down the defile, but they took three for every one of them that died. Yugi vaulted a man whose throat had been torn out and ran to the rescue of another who was facing a furie alone. He recognised it from Kaiku's description: like some demonic boar, its multiple tusks huge and hooked, its trotters like blades, its back tufted with spines and its face warped into a snarl. His attempt at intervention was foiled as something appeared as if from nowhere in front of him, an awful, shrieking creature with tentacles whirling around a circular maw and a body black, hairless and glistening. It was already wounded, maddened with pain; he finished it off in moments, but by the time he returned to his original objective, the man had been stamped underfoot by the furie and lay bloodied and dead in a rising haze of dust.

He was about to chase after the beast, motivated by some illogical sense of responsibility at allowing the man to be killed, when he heard the rising wail of the wind-alarms from behind him, an eerie, mournful howl coming from the east. More of them joined in, the Libera Dramach lookouts spinning tubes of hollow wood on long ropes around their heads to create a noise that could be heard for miles. It was an idea stolen from the Speakers at the Imperial councils, who used smaller versions to call for order among the assembly. Yugi had been dreading to hear it ever since that morning.

Somewhere along the defensive line, the enemy had broken through. They were at the Fold, and behind the Libera Dramach positions. The retreat had been sounded.

He went for the furie anyway. The fight was not yet over here, though the Aberrants were few in number and were being whittled down at great cost to the defenders. If there were going to be any folk left to retreat at all, there would need to be more Aberrant blood spilt. Thinking of the streets of his home being trampled under the feet of these predators, he let his anger and frustration fuel him, and with a cry Yugi threw himself into the battle.

The rim of the Fold was a mass of fortifications, and no more so than on the western side. Enemies coming down from the north, south or east slopes could be engaged on the valley floor, where the defenders would have the advantage of height, being able to attack from the plateaux and rain death down on any invaders. But anyone surmounting the western end would be above the town, critically negating the Libera Dramach's ability to use artillery for fear of hitting their own buildings. The invaders could spill over the cave-riddled cliffs like a river over a waterfall, flooding down through the steps and levels of the town. Because of this, the western edge was guarded most fiercely of all; and since it was directly in their way, that was where the Aberrant army struck hardest.

The primary defence was a stockade wall, a triple layer of tree trunks driven into holes bored into the stone. The effort it had taken to dig out the foundations had been enormous, but in the Xarana Fault security was the most important priority. Kamako cane scaffolding had been built up behind the wall, supporting walkways and small pulleys, a jumble of ladders and ropes. Now it was aswarm with men and women, vibrating beneath the weight of running feet. Fire-cannons bellowed from their positions atop the wall; ballistae threw rocks and explosives, lobbing them in languid and deadly arcs against the clear blue sky. The sound of rifles was a deafening and constant rattle, interspersed with the sinister hum of bowstrings, and the air stank of burnt ignition powder and sweat.

Zaelis tu Unterlyn clambered up the last ladder to the top of the wall, his lame leg making the climb awkward. His heart was racing: the chaos all around him terrified him. He was no general. He knew little of the arts of combat and had never been this close to conflict before. The defence of the Fold he had left in the hands of men like Yugi, who knew what they were doing. For his own part, he felt suddenly demoted and useless. It was a hard thing for him to surrender the reins of an organisation he had built from the ground up, even temporarily. Between that and his daughter's sudden and entirely unexpected rebellion against his will, he felt more like an old man than he ever had before. He feared he was not taking it well.

The last few days he had been either interfering in the battle plans of men who clearly knew their business better than he did, or clashing with Lucia. Having never had to discipline her before, he had no idea what to do. She was not like other children he had tutored in years past. To some extent, he dared not punish her at all because he relied so much on her as the uniting force behind his organisation, and to estrange her would be divisive to the Libera Dramach.

Were they right, Lucia and Cailin? Did Zaelis truly care for the Libera Dramach more than he cared for his own daughter? Had he adopted her simply to keep his most important asset under his control? Gods, he did not even want to think what that said about him, but he could not wholly dismiss the idea either.

Alskain Mar. It had all started at Alskain Mar, when he had pushed Lucia into using her powers again, had lowered her into the lair of a creature of unimaginable power and unguessable intent. Because he was afraid of what might happen to the people of the Fold, he had risked her. Heart's blood, what had possessed him? Even when he had been agonising over his choice, had it been because he had been weighing the danger to his most precious figurehead, not to his *daughter* as he should have been? She had been so passive and pliable for so long that he had almost forgotten there was a person behind those distant eyes. No wonder she felt betrayed. No wonder she turned on him.

He could see her drifting closer to Cailin day by day. Since Alskain Mar. But he could not allow the Red Order to have Lucia's heart; they were too influential by half as it was, and they shared little of the Libera Dramach's dedication of purpose. They were looking to their own advantage, their own survival. And they were secretive. Cailin had not shared her plans concerning the invasion with Zaelis, and had refused to participate in collaborative strategies. Now she had disappeared entirely when he needed her most.

One thing he feared more than losing Lucia was losing her to Cailin. But once again, the question scratched at him: *whom do you love, your daughter or the people you gathered to follow her?*

He was still thinking it as he climbed onto the walkway and looked out over the stockade wall and to the west, but the sight there chased it from his mind as the blood drained from his cheeks.

The Aberrants were everywhere, a vast black swathe pressed up against the stockade wall, a terrible horde of tooth and muscle and armoured skin that gnashed and raged with bloodlust. They had poured out of the labyrinth of thin defiles and ravines that led down into the Knot and thrown themselves against the stockade walls to be massacred. Black columns of smoke billowed upward, where shellshot had made flaming ruin of the attackers. Explosions scorched the stone and sent broken bodies flying as ballistae found their mark.

At the base of the wall, hundreds lay crushed and dead, and still more piled on top to add their corpses, forming a steadily growing slope of blood and gristle. They were concentrating their efforts in several spots, seeking to make a mound big enough to get over the wall. Their suicidal singularity of purpose was horrifying; but worse, it was unstoppable.

Next to Zaelis, four men took a cauldron of molten metal that had been winched up from the ground and tipped it onto those creatures that were clamouring beneath them, but their animal screams only signified new additions to the slippery heap that was already halfway up the stockade.

'Burn them!' someone was shouting. 'Bring oil and burn them! *Keep* them burning!'

Zaelis looked along the wall at the man who was striding along the walkway towards him. Yugi. He was dirtied and gore-smeared, his hair in its usual disarray behind the rag around his forehead, but he broke into a grin as he saw Zaelis, and greeted him warmly. He sent a runner down the line of the stockade to spread the order, which had come from the general in command of the western defences, and then looked Zaelis over.

'Heart's blood, you look terrible,' he said.

'No more than you,' Zaelis countered. He scratched his bearded neck, which was itching with sweat. 'I'm glad to see you got back behind the wall in one piece.'

'Zaelis, what's happening? Where are the Red Order? We *need* them to organise ourselves. It's taking too long for word to get from one place to another.'

'I know, Yugi, I know,' Zaelis said helplessly, moving aside as someone jostled past them with a murmured apology. 'But you've dealt with their kind.'

Yugi nodded grimly. 'Where's Lucia?' he asked.

'Hidden,' Zaelis said. 'Guarded. She would not leave. That was all I could do.'

'She's your *daughter*!' Yugi was aghast.

'I could hardly force her,' Zaelis replied. 'She is not like a normal child.'

'That's *exactly* what she's like,' Yugi said. 'She's fourteen harvests of age, and every one of those things out there is baying for her blood! Don't you think she's scared? You need to be with her, not out here.'

Zaelis was about to protest, but Yugi overrode him. 'Show me where she is,' he said, grabbing the older man's arm.

'You have to stay!' Zaelis said.

'If she's going to be guarded, *I'll* guard her.' He was propelling them both towards a ladder now. 'There are Weavers about, Zaelis. If I've learned one lesson from this whole mess, it's that you can't keep *anything* hidden from them for long.'

*

The cellar of Flen's house was hot and dark. What light there was came from imperfections in the fit of the floorboards overhead, thin lines of warm daylight spilling through to stripe the faces of the two adolescents that were concealed there.

As with most Saramyr cellars, the air was too dry for mildew or damp, and though plain it was kept neat and presentable with the same fastidiousness as the rest of the house. The wooden floor and walls were sanded and varnished. Barrels and boxes were neatly stacked and secured with hemp webbing. Bottles of wine lay in racks, half-seen outlines in the gloom.

A set of steps ran up to a hatch in the ceiling, which had been closed on them an hour ago. Since then, they had sat on floor-mats down here, whispering to each other, taking occasional sips from the jug of berry juice that they had been provided with and ignoring the parcel of food wrapped in wax paper that came with it. Overhead, the creaking footsteps of the guards went to and fro, sometimes blocking the light so that it seemed as if a great shadow crossed the cellar.

They hid, and waited, and listened to the reverberations of the fire-cannons in the distance.

'I hope he'll not be hurt,' Flen said, for the dozenth time. His train of thought had been returning to the same subject over and over again, whenever enough silence had passed.

Lucia betrayed no sign of impatience, but she did not respond. She had feared he might bring it up again. A few minutes ago Lucia had experienced an unpleasant intuition that Flen's father – the object of his musing – had been killed. She could not say for sure, but it would be far from the first time her instincts had informed her of something she could not possibly have known otherwise. Perhaps she had unconsciously picked it up from the indecipherable sussurus of the spirit-voices that surrounded her, some half-gleaned shred of intention or meaning that hinted at revelation. She had, after all, been giving Flen's father a lot of thought on her friend's behalf.

Flen looked up at her, expecting her to reassure him; but she could not. Hurt flickered in his eyes. She hesitated a moment, then slid nearer to him and hugged him gently. He hugged her back, looking over her shoulder into the darkness that surrounded them, and the two of them embraced in the dim island of illumination for a time, the lines of sunlight from above moulding to the contours of their shoulders and faces.

'They're all being killed,' she whispered. 'And it's my fault.'

'No,' Flen hissed before she had even finished. 'It's not your fault. What the Weavers did isn't your fault. It's *their* fault you were born with the abilities you have; it's *their* fault. You didn't do anything.'

'I started this all,' she said. 'I let Purloch take that lock of my hair. I let him go back to the Weavers with proof I was an Aberrant. If I hadn't done that . . . Mother might still be alive . . . nobody would be dying . . .'

Flen clutched her harder, his own troubles forgotten in the need to reassure her. He stroked her hair, his fingers running onto the burned and puckered skin at the nape of her neck, gliding over its nerveless surface.

'It's not your fault,' he repeated. 'You can't help what you are.'

'What am I?' she said, drawing back from him. Had it been any other girl, he would have expected tears in her eyes, but her gaze was fey and strange. Did she feel remorse or guilt as other people did? Did it make her truly sad? Or had what he had taken as self-recrimination simply been a statement of fact? So long he had known her, and he would never understand her properly.

'You said it yourself. You're an avatar.'

Lucia studied him carefully, and did not reply, which prompted him to explain himself.

'It's like you told me,' he said. 'The gods don't want Aricarat back, but they won't interfere directly. So they put people like you here instead. People who can change things. Remember how the Children of the Moons saved your life when the shin-shin were after you? Remember how Tane gave his life up for you, even though he was a priest of Enyu and he was supposed to hate Aberrants?' He wrung his hands, not sure that he was articulating himself properly. He imagined that Lucia did not like to be reminded of Tane's sacrifice, though he told himself that she did not always react as he thought she should. 'He must have known that his goddess wanted you alive, even though you stood against everything he believed in. Because Aricarat is killing the land, and the Weavers serve Aricarat, and even though you're an Aberrant – *because* you're an Aberrant – you're a threat to the Weavers. Just like the moon-sisters wanted you alive, so you could help fight against their brother.'

He took her hands earnestly, trying to make her see what seemed so clear to him. 'If you hadn't been born the way you are, there'd be no Libera Dramach. There'd have been no Saran, and we'd have never known about Aricarat at all until it was too late. The gods might have been fighting this war ever since the Weavers first appeared, but it's only now that we know what we're fighting *about*.'

'Maybe,' she conceded. She smiled faintly, but there was no amusement in it. 'I am no saviour, Flen.'

'I didn't say you were a saviour,' he replied. 'I just said you were put here for a reason. Even if we don't know what that reason is yet.'

She seemed about to reply, her lips forming a response for her friend, when her expression changed. She snapped him the curved-finger gesture for quiet, her eyes wide; at the same moment, there was a sigh and a slump from overhead. Flen looked up, then blinked and flinched as something dripped onto his cheek through the gaps in the floorboards. He wiped it automatically from his face, and gave a tiny noise of terror as he saw blood on his fingertips.

'*Weavers*,' Lucia whispered.

There was another slump from above, then several more. The sound of the guards falling. Flen could only imagine how the Weavers had got here, what dreadful arts they had used to slip into the heart of the Fold while the Aberrants pounded at the perimeter. Had they twisted the minds of the soldiers to make their appearance different? Had they been able to walk with impunity through the streets of the Fold, cloaked in illusion? Who knew what the Weavers could really do, what they had practised for centuries in secret, what particles of knowledge their reawakening god had taught them?

But speculation was useless. They were here now, and here for Lucia.

'Don't be scared,' he said to her, though he was far more frightened than she was. They huddled against the wall opposite the stairs, trapped there in the grille of light with hot darkness crowding all around.

Something was shifted from above the hatch. A rug was rolled back. Concealment was pointless; they knew exactly where she was.

A rectangle of light opened at the top of the stairs, silhouetting three figures against the blinding brightness of the day. Motes drifted in the sunbeams that pushed past them, but they were ragged heaps of shadow.

'Lucia . . .' whispered a hoarse voice.

She got to her feet. Flen got up with her. His attempt at a defiant posture was laughable; he could barely stand for fear.

The Weavers came down the steps, moving slowly, their arthritic and cancer-ridden bodies making them ungainly and weak. Gradually she saw them as they moved from the dazzle into the gloom: three Masks, one of coloured feathers, one of bark chips, one of beaten gold.

'I am Lucia tu Erinima,' she said, her voice low and steady. 'I am the one you have come for.'

'We know,' said one of the Weavers; it was impossible to tell which. They had reached the bottom of the stairs now. Flen's eyes flickered around the cellar, probing the darkness as if searching for escape. He was almost sobbing with fright now. Lucia was a statue.

The feather-Mask Weaver raised one white and sore-pocked hand, unfolded a long fingernail towards Lucia.

'Your time is done, Aberrant,' he whispered.

But the threat was never carried out. As one, the Weavers shrieked and recoiled, whirling away from Lucia and Flen. The children backed off as the creatures writhed and spasmed, wailing in sudden torment, their limbs seizing spastically. There was a nauseating crack as a Weaver's arm broke, the bone pushing a lump through his patchwork robe; a moment later, his legs snapped, the knees inverting with appalling violence and sending him screaming to the floor. One of the others was lying on his side and bending backward, pushed as if by some invisible force, howling as his vertebrae clicked, one by one, until finally his spine gave way. The Weavers jerked and twisted as their bones fractured and broke again and again, over and over in hideous torture. Blood seeped from beneath their Masks and they soiled themselves, but still they screeched, still they lived. It was many minutes before it ended, by which time they were not even recognisable as humanoid, merely bloodied, jagged pulps like piles of sticks beneath their mercifully concealing robes and Masks.

Flen had turned away in horror, crouching in the corner, his hands over his ears; Lucia had watched the scene dispassionately.

Cailin tu Moritat stepped into the light from the hatchway, her irises a deep crimson in amid her painted face. From their positions of concealment, the other Sisters emerged: ten of them in total, all with the red-and-black triangles on their lips, the red crescents across their eyes and down their cheeks. All wearing variations of the black dress of the Order.

Cailin looked down on Lucia, her face half-hidden by shadow, limned in the light from outside. Her expression could not be seen.

'You did well, Lucia,' she said.

Lucia did not reply.

The Weavers had walked into a trap, following Lucia's Weave-signature. Had they known what the late Weave-lord Vyrrch had known, they would have realised that Lucia was usually undetectable, that her power was too subtle to pick up on their trawls across the infinity of golden threads. But with the Sisters' help, she had made herself visible to them. It was too tempting for them to resist.

The Sisters were elated now, casting glances at each other in mutual congratulation. Among them, only Cailin had ever faced a Weaver before. Now they were blooded. The instant of conflict that had ended in them taking control of the Weaver's bodies and cracking their bones like sticks had been a long and arduous struggle in Weave-time. What had seemed less than a second to Flen and Lucia had been an eternity to them. Even though they greatly outnumbered their foes, it had been by no means an easy match. Yet they had won through unhurt, and the shattered corpses at their feet bore testament to their abilities to face these creatures and win.

Lucia was listening to the harsh and agitated thoughts of the distant ravens. They had been sent away so that their presence would not reveal Lucia's position or deter the Weavers, and were going frantic at what might have happened. She had been forced to command them in this instance, something she rarely did. She sent them a wash of reassurance, and their turmoil eased like water taken off the boil.

'You *all* did well,' Cailin said, raising her voice to include the Sisters. 'But this was not your true test. We kept them from alerting their kind; that means we still have the element of surprise, at least for a short time. Let us not waste it. Now the real battle begins!'

The Sisters murmured in approval and headed up the stairs, through the hatch. They heard running feet overhead, and voices.

'Zaelis and Yugi are here,' Cailin said. She glanced at Flen, who was still cowering in the corner, the horror of the Weavers' death too much for him.

'You have my deepest gratitude, Cailin,' Lucia said, sounding older than her fourteen harvests. 'You did not have to stay and fight for the Libera Dramach.'

Cailin shook her head slowly, then bent down to Lucia's level, which was not so far now. 'I fight for you, child,' she said; and with that, she kissed Lucia on the cheek in a gesture of tenderness utterly at odds with her character. Then she straightened and swept up the stairs and away.

There were a few words exchanged, out of sight, and Yugi and Zaelis appeared, slowing as they descended the steps, aghast at the ruin of the Weavers below them.

'You're late, Father,' Lucia said coldly.

He had no chance to reply to that, for at that moment the mournful howl of the wind-alarms began for the second time that day. The breath he had drawn to respond was exhaled as an oath.

The wall had been breached. The Aberrants were inside the Fold.

THIRTY-THREE

Kaiku and Tsata had been lost for hours by the time they came across the worm-farm.

The mine beneath the flood plain was bigger than they had imagined, a maze of tunnels and caverns running off the vast central shaft that looped and split and joined with no rhyme or reason in its structure. Some parts were entirely abandoned, or appeared to have never been inhabited or used at all; other parts were cluttered with stores and tools and all manner of mining equipment, yet they were nowhere near anything that was being mined. They had stolen explosives from these stockpiles, of which there were plenty, piled dangerously high and kept without care, left to sweat volatile chemicals. They had expected to find explosives eventually – indeed, they had relied on it, for it was the only way they had to destroy a witchstone as far as they knew – but not in this state. It would only take a spark in one of those rooms to bring half the mine down. Kaiku did not want to think about that happening while they were inside. They gingerly wrapped what they needed in rags and stowed it in a sack which Tsata carried.

They saw golneri from time to time, but the diminutive folk always ignored them and went about whatever business they had. They found several dead ones as well, horribly mutilated, victims of the Weavers' appetites. Other evidence of the Weavers appeared as they descended further and further into the groaning, steaming darkness of the mine. There were strange sculptures chiselled out of the rock, depictions of some inner madness that Kaiku could not guess at. Tunnels were scrawled with pictograms in all kinds of languages and some that appeared to be entirely made up, swirls of gibberish in which sometimes a horrible moment of sense could be made out, hinting at dark and twisted musings. One particularly disturbing cave was hung with dozens of female golneri, swinging by their ankles from a system of pulleys and ropes and eyelets, their throats cut and blood staining the ground below in a flaky brown patina. Kaiku found herself thinking that not only were the golneri forced to see this slaughter every time they passed through the cavern, but that it must have been them who assembled the complex system of ropes in the first place. Like making prisoners tie their own nooses. She wondered what the golneri had once been, and how their pride had been so destroyed that they could suffer atrocities like this and apparently not care.

They had come across a Weaver not long afterward.

Kaiku sensed him before they saw him. He was Weaving, though not in any structured way that she could recognise. Instead, his consciousness was streaming like a flag tied to a railing, anchored at one end while the other was tattering and rippling in the flow of the Weave. Later, they heard him mumbling and shrieking, a thin, reedy sound that floated down the tunnels to their ears. Though Kaiku was not sure there was any need, they back-tracked to avoid him. She had seen that kind of Weaver at the Lakmar monastery. Their minds had been lost, eroded by their Masks, and they spent their time wandering, their thoughts flapping free in the bliss of the Weave, tethered by one last cruel thread of sanity to their bodies.

Kaiku was sure it was daylight outside, but they were far underground now, and there was no way to tell. As they descended, they found more mysteries. Great chambers of fuming contraptions that clanked and pistoned. Massive black furnaces that filled the caverns with red light. Golneri scuttled to and fro, feeding the flames with coal, their faces grimed and streaked with sweat. The noise was deafening, abhorrent, and made Tsata and Kaiku cover their ears and flee. They passed immense paternosters leading up into the darkness, splashing water as it tipped over the edge of the bucket-scoops and fell endlessly into the abyss below. The inflammable-gas torches rumbled menacingly at them from the walls of the larger caverns, or from metal posts, belching gouts of smoky flame from their tips. Occasionally they came across mining operations, where golneri stood on metal scaffolds, chipping and chiselling. Chains rattled and pulleys shrieked as the loads were moved around the scaffolding, lowered to the ground or dumped slithering down chutes. Coal to feed the furnaces. But what were the furnaces for?

Kaiku had wondered why a place so massive should be so empty, but then she reasoned that this place was not a monastery or a stronghold. The Weavers only wanted one thing out of this mine: the witchstone. And that was buried deep, deep under the earth. There were simply not enough uses for all the multitude of caverns and miles of natural tunnels in between. They needed to stockpile the vast amounts of food required to supply their standing army, to house the golneri and the Weavers and the Nexuses, to mine the fuel for the furnaces and to accommodate all the machinery and contraptions; but even that only accounted for a fraction of the total size of the subterranean network. And on top of that, the place appeared to have been virtually deserted when the army headed off north and east.

But there was one thing she had not accounted for: where had the nexus-worms come from? She found her answer in the worm-farm.

They came into the cavern on a shadowed metal gallery, little more than a rusting walkway bolted against one wall to form a bridge between two apertures in the stone. The roof of the cavern was low and wide. Illumination came from gas-torch poles linked by strange metal ropelike things that snaked between them. The intruders hunkered down and looked upon the scene below them, the curve of their cheeks and the lines of their forearms and knees lit a soft amber.

The cavern was carpeted in squirming black, a constant and nauseating movement accompanied by a sound like the wringing of wet and soapy hands. Nexus-worms: uncountable thousands of them. Raised earthen banks cut through the mass with a typically Weaver-esque lack of order or pattern, and along these travelled dozens of golneri, who occasionally plunged into the crush of slimy bodies to sow some kind of powdery food among the worms, or throw buckets of water across them. But the golneri were not the only ones who walked along the banks; there were Nexuses there too, accompanied by loping shrillings, who trilled and warbled softly as they followed their masters at heel like dogs. The flaming poles cast flickering glints on the moist backs of the worms, thousands of reflected crescents like an oily sea at sunset.

'Gods . . .' Kaiku breathed, mesmerised.

As they stared, it became apparent that there were not only nexus-worms in amid the crush. From their observations of the Aberrants they had killed, Tsata and Kaiku had determined that the worms were smooth and almost featureless, except for a round, toothless mouth for ingestion – fringed with little bumps – and an opening for excretion at the other end. The creatures secreted some kind of acid spittle which allowed them to burrow into the skin of their victims, where they affixed themselves with hundreds of hair-thin filaments extruded from the bumps around the mouth. Tsata had discovered that when he tried to pull a dead one free from its host and found it inextricably attached by a thick mass of these fine threads. Saramyr lore was nowhere near advanced enough to understand what they did next; but the result was obvious enough. They subverted the host's will to their own, which was in turn under the command of something else – the Nexuses.

Yet now they saw other types of creature. There were several flat, narrow things with short tails. Tiny tendrils waved in the air above them like a cloud, occasionally descending to stroke the worms that clustered around them. They were about the length and width of a man's forearm, and the worms behaved as piglets to a sow, writhing over one another in an attempt to get close.

There was a third type, too, much bigger than the other two: sluglike creatures, two or three feet high, with blotchy stripes of venomous orange against the glittering black. These things appeared to be little more than enormous rubbery maws surrounded by a sphincter of muscle, so that they resembled bags with drawstring necks. Some were obesely large while others looked starved and withered. Tsata spotted the flat, narrow creatures oozing into and out of the mouths of the fat ones, though never the thinner variety. They went right *inside*, deep into whatever passed for its innards, and were later vomited out on a slick of steaming bile. Kaiku witnessed another phenomenon too: one of the thinnest of the sluglike things belched out a thrashing heap of minuscule worms, like black maggots, which immediately began to squirm around in their own fluids and then headed off in search of the powdery food the golneri were sowing.

They spent some time on that walkway in the shadows, observing, before Tsata spoke quietly.

'I have it,' he said. 'Three sexes.'

Kaiku looked at him quizzically.

'We have something similar in Okhamba,' he told her. 'Watch what happens. The nexus-worms are the males. They clamour to inseminate the females, which are those longer ones. The third sex is essentially a womb. The females crawl into its mouth and deposit the fertilised eggs. The eggs hatch inside and feed off whatever sustenance the thing provides; the fat ones have great stores of it inside them, and they get thinner as the pregnancy advances and their reserves are depleted. Then they give birth by vomiting up the larvae, each of which grows into one of the three sexes, and the cycle continues.'

Kaiku blinked. She had never heard of a three-sex system on Saramyr. Although, she reminded herself, these things were probably *from* Saramyr. Some kind of unrecorded creature, warped by the witchstones' influence into this new configuration? Or had they always been there, hidden within the vast tracts of unexplored land in the mountains, found and exploited by the Weavers decades or centuries ago?

'I would guess that the females share a link with the males,' Tsata theorised. 'A kind of hive-mind with many queens. The males are like the drones.'

Kaiku did not need any more. She could imagine how these things worked: the males crept up on sleeping animals or Aberrants in the wild, affixing themselves, taking them over, making them slaves. The males and the womb-things appeared to be mindless enough, but the females moved with purpose. The males were merely there to create the link to the females, through which the *females* controlled the subjugated animal. What better kind of defence for a creature's nest than to use relatively massive and expendable proxies as guards? Or what better hunter-gatherers, since the nexus-worms themselves were physically helpless? She found herself marvelling at the sinister ingenuity of these parasites.

But the Nexuses controlled the males now. How was that possible? Certainly not through the Weave. It was vital that they knew, if they were to have any hope of disrupting them.

Kaiku's thoughts fled as a warbling shriek sounded from the floor of the cavern, ascending in pitch until it hurt the ears. An instant later, it was joined by another, and another. The shrillings were all looking at the spot where Kaiku and Tsata crouched; and now the Nexuses had turned their blank white faces that way too.

'They have seen us!' Kaiku hissed, remembering too late that the shrillings did not need to *see* at all, that darkness was no obstacle for their sonic navigation system.

'Time to be elsewhere,' Tsata muttered, and they ran.

It was a measure of their determination, perhaps, that they both chose to run onward rather than back, picking unfamiliar territories over caverns they had already passed through. They raced along the walkway, their feet clanging on the metal, and burst into the tunnel on the far side. The wailing of the shrillings was echoing from all directions now. The alarm was spreading.

'Hold this,' Tsata said, shoving the small sack of explosives into Kaiku's arms. She whimpered at the rough treatment it was suffering.

They headed down a bare and featureless tunnel, lit by occasional torches in wall brackets, most of which had gone out. The gas-flames were only generally present in the larger caverns and in areas where normal torches would not provide enough illumination. Shadows flickered by against the rough angles of the rounded walls, some ancient lava tube from an ancient cataclysm. Tsata ran ahead of Kaiku, and she saw that he had his gutting-hooks drawn, one in each hand. Gods, she wished she had her rifle now. She only possessed a sword which she was pitifully ineffective at using. That, and her *kana*, which would bring every Weaver in the mine down on top of her.

The shrilling leaped out of nowhere, reaching Tsata as the tunnel kinked right and obscured their vision any further. But Tsata's reactions were honed by generations of life in a jungle where a man would get less warning than *that* before he died. He dropped and rolled under the shrilling's pounce, his blades scything across its unarmoured belly and unzipping it from throat to tailbone. It hit the ground at Kaiku's feet in a slick of its own guts, pawing the ground helplessly in its death throes.

But the shrilling had not been alone. Two more of its kind ran into view, accompanied by a Nexus. Kaiku felt a slow chill as she looked upon the thing, seven feet tall and rake-thin, robed and cowled in black with its featureless mask hiding it completely. She put down the stack of explosives and drew her sword.

'Stay back,' Tsata said, without taking his eyes off the enemy. He was in a fighting crouch now. 'You would do no good here.'

He was right; and yet she felt terrible having him face three enemies alone without her, a deep and wrenching fear and guilt that surprised her in its intensity. Subconsciously, she was already preparing her *kana*. Whatever the cost, she would not let him die at the hands of these creatures.

The two shrillings came at him at once, moving with the fluidity of jaguars. One of them reared up on its hind legs to strike with the sickle-claws on its forepaws; Tsata used that moment to dart out of its reach and engage the second shrilling, which snapped at his belly with its fanged jaws. He barely evaded the bite, and the smooth bony crest of the creature butted him in the thigh, knocking his counterstrike awry and causing his blade to glance off the scales on its back instead of finding the soft spot where the throat joined the long skull. The first shrilling lashed out with its other claw, overreaching itself in the attempt; Tsata grunted as it tore into his arm, but he turned inside the strike and drove his gutting-hook into the rearing beast's chest. Its ululating death-cry was deafening, and it appeared to confuse the other shrilling, which suddenly went still as its frequency-sensitive glands were overloaded. The first shrilling had barely hit the floor before Tsata was on the second one, driving both his gutting-hooks into the back of the creature's neck, slicing through the nexus-worm affixed there. The Aberrant shivered and went boneless, collapsing in a heap, borne down by Tsata's weight.

Kaiku had seen the Tkiurathi fight enough times during the last few weeks, but his deadly grace never ceased to amaze her. He faced the Nexus now over the corpses of its shrillings, his bare left arm pumping blood over his golden, tattooed skin to run down the lower edge of his forearm and drip from his wrist.

There was a moment of hesitation. The Nexus was an unknown quantity. They had no idea of its capabilities.

Tsata's good arm snapped out and sent his gutting-hook spinning through the air. The Nexus was either not fast enough to get out of the way or simply chose not to; either way, the blade buried in its body with a sickening impact, and its knees buckled. It fell silently to the floor.

The Tkiurathi did not waste any time. The cries of the other shrillings were getting nearer. He pulled the gutting-hook out of the Nexus as Kaiku ran up to him.

'You're bleeding,' she said.

Tsata gave her one of his unexpected smiles. 'I had noticed,' he replied. Then he reached down and tore off the mask of the Nexus, and Kaiku caught her breath at what was uncovered.

Its face was dead white, cracked with thin purple capillaries, its expression as blank as the mask Tsata had thrown aside. The mouth was a thin slash, hanging open and toothless. Its eyes were large and pure black, reflecting Kaiku as she peered into them with an expression of horror.

But for all that, it was the face of a child.

Beneath the veined skin, a multitude of thin tendrils sewed over the forehead and across the sunken cheeks, terminating at the lips and ears and eyes and throat, dozens of tiny bumped lines radiating along the contours of the skull.

Tsata raised the Nexus's head and pulled back its hood. Buried in the flesh of the scalp, sunken into the skin, was one of the nexus-worm females, a glistening black diamond shape. Its tail ran down the nape of the neck and disappeared between the shoulder blades, diving into the spine.

'Now we know,' Tsata said.

Kaiku sheathed her sword and squatted by the fallen thing, appalled to the point of disbelief. The Nexuses were human symbiotes, their will joined with the nexus-worm females who shared their body. The females in turn controlled the males, who controlled the Aberrants. The Weavers must have been capturing predators for years in the mountains, perhaps subduing them with their Masks before implanting them with worms, building the superstructure of their army. No civilised humans would fight for the Weavers, so they had built a force of killing beasts, monsters spawned by the blight that the Weavers themselves had created. And they controlled them with the Nexuses.

But *children*? They affixed the female worms to children? Was that the only way to achieve the necessary integration, to implant them early? Did that explain the freakish way they had developed?

Kaiku gritted her teeth in rage, feeling tears come to her eyes.

It had no tongue. The stump was still there.

They did this to children.

Tsata grabbed her arm. 'There is no time to grieve for them, Kaiku,' he said, bringing her to her feet and handing her the sack of explosives.

Then they were running again. The shrillings' cries were coming from before and behind now. The tunnel ended in a three-way junction, cluttered with discarded metal components of some kind of half-built contraption. Tsata did not hesitate, choosing a tunnel and heading into it, apparently oblivious to the wound that was streaking blood down his arm. There was not so much noise from that direction, and the tunnel was uneven and rough. It bore the signs of a passage rarely used, and that meant it was less likely that anything would be coming down it. Torches became infrequent, so Tsata snatched one and carried it with him. Kaiku hung back, conscious of letting the flame near the dangerous burden she was carrying.

The sensation of Weaving crackled over her in a wave, a dark and malevolent interest sweeping the mine. Someone was looking for them. Kaiku carefully made them invisible to the seeker, blending their signatures into the Weave. It was one of the first things Cailin had taught her to do after she had got her power under control, and as bad a pupil as she had been, after five years of practice it was a discipline she was very good at. The Weaver's attention prickled across them and away, searching the tunnels and caverns. Kaiku did not drop her guard. Now she knew that there was at least one Weaver here sane enough to be a danger.

She looked back. The sounds of pursuit were echoing up the tunnel from the junction now. She did not think the shrillings were good trackers, but there were few places to hide in these tunnels, and Tsata needed to stop so he could tend to his wound. It was pumping out a worrying amount of blood and leaving a very obvious trail.

She began to be afraid. Beating the demons in the marsh, healing Yugi, hunting for weeks with Tsata: all these had combined to make her feel somewhat invulnerable of late, more mistress of her abilities and herself, more confident in her choices. But now she became suddenly aware of their situation, and it hit her that they were in the midst of a Weaver lair, surrounded by enemies, and that they might very well not get out again. Her *kana* was next to useless since she did not dare take on a Weaver; and despite Tsata's martial skill he tended to rely on surprise to win his battles. He might have killed three shrillings and a Nexus, but it had been a near thing, and despite his uncomplaining nature he was hurt badly.

Ocha, what have I got myself into? Should I have gone back to Cailin when I had the chance?

But that thought only reminded her of what might be happening at the Fold now, images of slaughter and terror.

She pushed her indecision aside. It was too late for regrets or second-guessing.

Tsata came to a sudden halt. Kaiku caught him up, her gradually reddening eyes flickering nervously over the torch in his hand.

'Down there,' he said, pointing. There was a gash in the rock at ground level, through which something was moving, throwing back his torchlight in rapid firefly glimmers. It took Kaiku a moment to realise that it was water.

The tightness of the cleft made her hesitate, a moment of claustrophobia assailing her; but then the trilling of their pursuers sounded again, closer than ever, and her mind was made up. Leaving the sack of explosives, she slid feet-first into the gap. It was too dark to see what was below, but the water hinted at where the ground would be. She slipped as far into the cleft as she could, until her legs were dangling through, and then dropped.

There was a blaze of pain as something ripped up her lower back, and then a moment of falling. She hit the ground with a jarring impact that buckled her knees. The water was only an inch deep.

'Kaiku?' Tsata's voice came through from above.

She put her hand to her back, and it came away wet.

'It is safe,' she said. 'Put out the torch. And watch the rocks; they are sharp.'

Tsata carefully handed the sack of explosives to her and then slipped through. Once there, he doused the torch in the water, plunging them into darkness. The sound of the shrillings and hurrying feet seemed suddenly louder.

'Can you see?' Tsata whispered.

'No,' Kaiku said, wondering if her eyes would adjust as they had last time. 'Lead me.'

She felt his hand in hers, the clasp wet and warm. Blood trickled over his wrist and into their grip, across the gullies of her palm, welling between her slender fingers. He was using his good arm to carry the explosives; this was his wounded one. The sensation did not repulse her. Instead it seemed a strange intimacy, cementing their link with his life fluids. She felt an entirely inappropriate rush of pleasure at the sensation.

Then they were moving. He led her into the blackness, splashing softly as he went. The air was cold and dank down here, the breath of the deep earth, and it took Kaiku a moment to realise that there was a breeze, and that Tsata was heading into it. She was surprised to find that her lack of vision did not perturb her. She was not alone here, and she trusted Tsata absolutely. Once, she would not have even entertained the idea of putting her faith in this man, this foreigner with his foreign ideas, who had once used her as bait for a murderous hunter without a second thought. She wondered if he would do the same thing now. Would the closeness that had grown between them make him loth to risk her life so casually again? She could not say. But she understood his ways better now, his subordination of the individual to the greater good, and she knew that as things stood he would never abandon her down here, would give his own life for hers if it was better for the both of them. There was something touching in the raw simplicity of that.

She began to make out the edges of the tunnel, and the rippling of the water that ran past their feet. At first it was so gradual that she could not tell whether her mind was tricking her, but then it became too pronounced to discount. The world took shape steadily in a flat monochrome, until she could see as well as if Aurus were in the sky above them.

After a time, when the sounds of pursuit had faded behind them and it seemed as if they were all alone in the mine again, Tsata drew to a halt at a spot where the tunnel wall pulled away from the stream and the floor rose above the level of the water. Kaiku could feel the Weaver still searching for them, but his probing was far away.

'There is a dry section here,' he said.

'I can see it,' Kaiku replied.

Tsata looked back at her, then for an instant glanced at their linked hands. Kaiku belatedly realised that for some while he had been leading her when she had been perfectly capable of leading herself. She had simply not wanted to surrender that reassuring touch.

'I need to treat this wound,' he said. 'It is not closing.'

The next few minutes, more than any other, taught Kaiku how different the stock of their two continents were, how the Okhamban environment had bred tough and resilient folk while in Saramyr luxury had made the nobles soft. She watched him perform surgery on himself in the darkness, biting her lip as he used the tip of his gutting-hook to scrape out a shard of claw that had broken in the wound, cringing as he used a thin needle of smooth wood and some kind of fibrous thread to stitch the edges together. He refused her help – though she had made the offer with no idea how she *could* help – and efficiently sewed himself up, with no indication of the pain beyond an occasional hiss of breath across his teeth.

When he was done, he took a tiny jar of paste from a pouch at his waist and applied it to the still-bleeding slash. His body tensed violently, making Kaiku jump. His features screwed up in an expression of intense pain; the veins of his arm and throat stood out starkly against his skin. A faint wisp of evil-smelling smoke was rising from the wound.

Kaiku was suddenly reminded of Asara's words, coming from the lips of Saran Ycthys Marul: *in Okhamba there is very little medicine that is gentle.* The paste seemed to be literally scorching the wound shut.

She watched helplessly, listening to Tsata gasp at the shocking agony of the healing process, but finally his breathing steadied. He washed off the paste with water from the stream. His wound no longer bled, instead there was an ugly, puckered scar.

Kaiku was about to offer some words of comfort when they heard the warbling cry of a shrilling echo down the tunnel. The Nexuses had not given up the pursuit. They had found their quarry again.

Kaiku hauled Tsata to his feet, hefted the sack of explosives, and they ran once more.

The tunnel curved downward, and the water gathered pace on its descent, making the floor slippery. The noise of the shrillings had multiplied now. Evidently they had followed Tsata's trail of blood to the gash where she and the Tkiurathi had slipped through, and surmised where the intruders were. Suddenly, the Weaver's attention roved over them again, like a cruel and terrible glare; she was almost caught unawares, and she concealed them only just in time. It was because she was so intent on keeping them hidden that she barely noticed the new light at the end of the tunnel, and it was only when the Weaver's mind was elsewhere that she came back to herself and realised that Tsata was slowing.

The tunnel ended in a grille, bronzed with rust, an impassable line of thick square columns through which the water sluiced away to the cavern beyond. A foul, uneasy glow bled through from the other side, bathing them in strange light. They could hear the clanking of the Weavers' contraptions. On either side of the tunnel there were several vertical cracks and openings, all of them barred and dark.

Tsata had stopped, casting a look back up the tunnel, where the clamour of the chase continued to grow. Kaiku ran past him to the grille. She knew that appalling, unnatural illumination. It was branded on her memory, a nightmare that refused to fade.

She looked through the grille, and there was the witchstone.

They had been brought at last to the bottom of the shaft, the hub of the network of subterranean corridors which the Weavers had taken for their own. The tunnel mouth opened high in the shaft wall, over a massive underground lake, its surface still and black. Two narrow waterfalls plunged from above, throwing up low clouds of mist that hazed the scene. Bare, rocky islands hunched sullenly there, and tapering skewers of limestone thrust upward towards the dizzying heights, where distant fires burned at the tips of the metal gas-torches.

The noise of the machinery was all about, and everywhere was movement. Huge cogs, half-submerged, drove scoops which rotated steadily, drawing the water from the lake to dump it in catch-tanks somewhere above. Pipes were set vertically in the shaft walls, rising from beneath the surface to disappear into boxy buildings of black iron which steamed and roared, blazing an infernal red from slats in their sides. From there, further pipes went upward, into the darkness. Sluice-gates had been built into the sides of the shaft. Small huts sat on the flatter islands. Everywhere there were walkways of metal, a precarious three-dimensional web that connected the islands and the machines, and the golneri scuttled around between them on incomprehensible errands.

In the centre, on an island of rock all its own, the witchstone lay. It was vaguely spherical, perhaps twenty feet in diameter, heavily scarred with deep pits and pocks and lined with thousands of tiny gullies. But like the one she had seen before, this one appeared to have *sprouted* in a way that no rock could have done. Dozens of thin, crooked arcs of stone reached from its side into the water, or drove like roots into the surrounding earth; they branched out towards the distant walls of the shaft, questing, or formed bridges to the nearby islands. It looked grotesquely like a rearing spider, and its luminescence made Kaiku queasy and cast disturbing shadows onto the walls.

She understood now. The great scoops descending and ascending, the pipes that evacuated into the river, the machinery and the furnaces and the horrible, oily smoke. Nomoru had unwittingly struck on the answer long ago, but it was only now that Kaiku looked upon the lake that she realised it.

How do you dig a mine on a flood plain? It would *flood.*

This mine was not about mining, it was about water. The Zan was constantly leaking into the shaft through the thin wall that separated it from the river; when it flooded, the leakage was even worse. This whole place had probably been underwater for thousands of years, ever since it was formed. These machines were a massive drainage system, a way to move the water up the shaft and back out into the river so the Weavers could get to the witchstone that had been down here all this time. It was a constant battle to pump the river out of the shaft faster than it could leak through or flood over, to keep the witchstone above water where they could feed it blood sacrifices. Those furnaces and clanking contraptions had to be what gave power to the process, through some evil art that Kaiku did not understand.

Gods, the sheer *scale* of their determination staggered her.

'Kaiku . . .' Tsata murmured.

She looked back at him, and followed his gaze.

In the side-tunnels, behind the bars, figures were moving. Distant howls and moans had begun, and strange cackling and gurgling noises. From the direction in which they had come, the shrillings were calling louder than ever, nearly upon them now. And at their backs was the grille.

'Kaiku,' he said softly. 'We are trapped.'

THIRTY-FOUR

The defenders were losing the battle for the Fold.

Though the western end still barely held out, the fortifications on the northern side of the valley had been overwhelmed. What little chance they had of keeping back the Aberrant army was lost when the Weavers appeared on the battlefield. They spread their insidious fingers of influence among the men and women of the Fault, twisting their perceptions so that they saw enemies wherever they looked. The defenders began to fight among themselves. Brothers slew one another; members of different clans and factions fractured and became embroiled in bloody internecine squabbles. Some fled in fear, thinking that the Aberrants had already breached the fortifications. It was not long before their mistaken assumption became fact.

With the defenders in disarray, the nimble skrendel swarmed over the stockade wall and began to kill and maim with their long, strangling fingers and vicious teeth. Somewhere in amid the chaos, a few of them found their way to the small northern gate, where most of the guards already lay dead. With their nimble digits they filched the keys from a corpse and opened the gate. The ghauregs were first through, roaring mountains of muscle, and they tore the remaining defenders limb from limb in a frenzy of bloodlust terrifying to behold.

The Aberrants flooded down into the valley, and the Fold's *real* artillery opened up.

The advantage of having the town of the Fold built on a narrow slope of steps and plateaux was that it was highly defensible on three sides out of four. The landscape funnelled the invaders to the valley floor, which lay east of the buildings, and an enemy attacking from that direction was at a disadvantage, for they were fully exposed to the Fold's entire battery of weapons.

The slaughter was breathtaking.

Several dozen fire-cannons released a fusillade into the horde as they pooled at the bottom of the valley, igniting the flammable oil that had been spread there. A section of the valley floor erupted in an inferno, turning everything within it into a flaming torch. The air resounded with a cacophony of animal screams. The charge became a blazing wreck of bodies squirming and thrashing as flesh cooked and blood bubbled. Twenty ballistae fired, flinging loose packets of explosives that came apart in mid-flight and fell randomly on to the horde, geysering broken corpses in all directions.

The Aberrants came up against the eastern edge of the town, where the rise of the bottommost steps formed a natural and impenetrable wall, cut through only by gated stairways. The lifts that were used for transporting things too large for the narrow stairs were raised up and out of the predators' reach. Two hundred riflemen and women were arrayed along the lip of the massive semicircular steps, and they cut the Aberrant predators down like wheat. The Aberrants threw themselves at the wall, at the gates, but the wall was too high, and the gates were so solid that they would not give under any amount of weight. A black pall of smoke churned into the sky, rising out of the valley, as the fire-cannons and ballistae smashed burning holes in the ranks of the Aberrants. Gristle-crows circled and swooped overhead, cawing raucously. At some point, the defences on the southern edge of the Fold collapsed too, and even more Aberrant creatures swarmed in to be massacred.

But the Fold was surrounded now, and still they kept coming.

The Weavers, from their vantage points, extended their influence once again. They did not care about the losses they were suffering. The creatures were expendable, and they were confident that any barrier could be overcome from within by turning the minds of the defenders as they had earlier.

But their confidence was misplaced. This time they were met by the Sisters of the Red Order.

The first contact was nothing short of an ambush. The Weavers were brazen, accustomed to a lifetime of moving unopposed through the Weave. In fact, were it not for the strange and distant leviathans that glided on the edge of consciousness, always out of reach, then they might have believed that the glittering realm was their domain alone. But they were arrogant. Their control of the Weave was clumsy and brutal in comparison to the Sisters, wrenching nature to their will through their Masks, leaving torn and snapped threads in their wake. In contrast, the women were like silk.

Cailin and her Sisters had spiralled along the Weavers' encroaching threads, tracing them to their source, and were unravelling the stitchwork of defences before the Weavers even knew what was happening. They frantically withdrew, marshalling their powers to repel this new enemy, but the Sisters had struck in force and were at them like piranhas, nibbling from every direction at once, feinting and tugging, unravelling a knot here, picking loose a thread there, seeking a way through into the Weavers' core where they could begin to do real, physical damage. Cailin darted and jabbed, dancing from fibre to fibre and leaving phantom echoes of her presence to confuse and delay the enemy. She cut threads, excised knots, opened pathways for her brethren to exploit.

The Weavers desperately repaired the rents that the Sisters opened, batting them away, but it was hopeless. The Sisters worked as if they were one: an effortless communication existed between them that allowed them to co-ordinate themselves perfectly. They were aware of each and every ally in the battle, where they were and what they were doing. Several of them would mount attacks on unassailable positions so that others could quietly work at boring through less protected spots while the Weavers were distracted. Others harried the enemy by confusing them with ephemeral vibrations while their brethren knotted nets to catch the Weavers out.

Cailin evaded the grasping tendrils of the Weavers' counterattacks with disdainful ease, slipping away from them like an eel. She struck at them fearlessly: she had killed one of their number before, and these were no comparison to him. Yet she spared a concern for her Sisters, whose experience was less than hers. She would defend them from the Weavers' attacks, spinning barriers of confusion or clots of entanglement to slow them if the enemy assault should chance to come too near.

The collapse, when it came, was total. Cailin had been carefully weakening sections of the Weave, so carefully that the enemy was not even aware of her, and at her command the Sisters hit those sections all at once. The Weave gave way before them, opening gaping maws in the Weavers' defences. The Sisters swarmed through the Weavers' sundered barricades, sewing into the fabric of their bodies, ripping apart the bonds that held them together. The Weavers shrieked as they burst into flame, a half-dozen new pyres lighting simultaneously across the battlefield to join the blaze that was consuming sections of the valley floor.

But the Sisters' advantage of surprise had been used up now. At least two of the dead Weavers had had the foresight to send calls of distress across the Weave, flinging threads that were too scattered to intercept. A silent plea for help to their brothers who fought elsewhere in the Fold, and a warning.

The swell of outrage was almost palpable, a fury among the remaining Weavers that there should exist *anything* to challenge their authority in the Weave. Fury, and fear. For they remembered the final cry of the Weave-lord Vyrrch before he died, five years ago and more:

Beware! Beware! For women play the Weave!

Threads snaked out across the invisible realm, seeking, seeking. And while men and women and Aberrants both human and animal fought and struggled and died all along the valley, battle was joined in a place beyond their senses. The Red Order had revealed itself at last.

On the western side of the Fold, the stockade wall groaned under the weight of the corpses piled against it.

It was hard to breathe for the stench of burnt and burning meat. Nomoru's eyes teared as she aimed her rifle; she blinked several times and finally gave up. The air was a fog of black smoke and flakes of carbonised skin. The Aberrants' attempts to create ramps of their own dead had been stalled for a time when the folk of the Fold had begun pouring oil over them and setting them alight, but the pause had not lasted for long. The creatures resumed their climbing, squealing and howling as they were immolated.

Some of the corpse-heaps were high enough for the invaders to get over the wall now; they burst through in flames and fell off the walkway to smoulder on the ground below, or came flailing onto the swords of the Libera Dramach. But their sheer relentlessness was keeping the defenders occupied, and the oil was not getting to the fires where it was needed. Blazes were already dying, and some Aberrants were beginning to surmount the wall without setting themselves alight in the process.

Further down the line, several dozen creatures had managed to overwhelm some of the men and escape into the streets of the Fold before more swords arrived to seal the gap, and other breaches were happening more and more frequently. The Aberrant army seemed to have no interest in fighting the men and women on the wall: they only wanted to get into the heart of the town.

The line would not hold for long. Nomoru sensed that with a chilling certainty.

She knew what the key to this was. The Nexuses. She remembered how the beasts had stampeded back in the canyons when she had shot several of their handlers. But the Nexuses had learned their lesson from that, and they stayed out of sight now, co-ordinating the battle from afar. Shooting these foot-soldiers was a waste of her ammunition. She had to get to the generals.

An Aberrant man with a bulbous forehead and nictitating membranes across his eyes rushed past her, paused, and turned back. She gave him a rudely expectant look.

'Why aren't you fighting? Out of ammunition? Here, take some.' He handed her a pouch of rifle balls, then ran on without waiting for the thanks she was not going to give anyway.

Nomoru followed him with her eyes, ignoring the constant din of gunshot and screams and the crackle of flames. Aberrants fighting against Aberrants. If only the people in the cities and the towns might see this, then they might think twice about the deep and ingrained prejudices they bore for the victims of the Weaver's blight. The Weavers, the very ones who had instilled that hatred in the first place, were now using the fruits of their creation to kill other Aberrants. The defining line was not between human and Aberrant, it was between human and animal. The only ones that did not qualify as either were the Weavers. They might have been human once, but they had sloughed off their humanity when they put on their Masks.

Nomoru had no special love for Aberrants, but nor did she hate them. She hated the Weavers. And through that hatred, she rejected all of their teachings, and that made the Aberrants and the Libera Dramach her natural allies. Had she only known it, she had a lot in common with Kaiku, and many other men and women throughout the Fold. She fought for revenge.

Her body was inked with many tattoos, marking moments of a childhood that was as dirty and ragged as she herself was. A baby born to a gang in the Poor Quarter of Axekami, her mother an amaxa root addict, her father uncertain. She was brought up by whoever was around, part of a community of violence in which members came and went, where people were recruited or killed daily. Stability was not a part of her life, and she learned to lean on no one. Everyone she had let herself care about died. Her first love, her friends, even her mother to whom she had some illogical loyalty. It was a vicious, insular world, and only her talents for travelling unobserved and exceptional sharpshooting kept her from becoming another victim of the narcotics, the inter-gang wars, the illness and starvation that led people to thievery and the donjons.

The tattoos marked deals she had made, debts she was owed and had collected, and denoted solidarity with the members of her gang. They sprawled in complex profusion all up her arms, across her shoulders, down her calves and shins. But there was one more prominent than all in the centre of her back, more important to her than anything before or since. That one represented a loathing so pure it burned her every day, a promise of vengeance more powerful and binding than the most sacred lover's oath.

A True Mask, half-completed, with one side inked only as an outline to be filled in when she had completed her vendetta against the Weavers. The bronze visage of a demented and ancient god. The Mask of the Weave-lord Vyrrch.

And had she but known it, the face of Aricarat, the long-forgotten sibling of the moon sisters.

She had been only a little older than Lucia was now when she had been abducted. Those kind of disappearances happened all the time in the Poor Quarter. They were a part of life, and usually went unnoticed except by those close to the one who was taken. The nobles had to feed the monsters that lived in their houses, to keep them appeased, and so they chose the destitute, the poor, the people they saw as worthless. She had believed she was clever enough to stay ahead of them, but that night she had overindulged in amaxa root – little caring that she was going the way of her mother – and she had been shopped to the Weavers' agents by a man she thought she could trust. She had awoken bound up in the chambers of the Weave-lord Vyrrch, deep in the Imperial Keep.

She had no idea what kind of fate had been planned for her. But the knots had been badly tied, and she had slipped free and spent day after terrifying day evading the Weave-lord, searching for a way out of his chambers. Competing for discarded food with the hungry jackal that prowled the rooms, scrabbling a feral existence to prevent herself starving to death or dying of thirst in the swelter. And all the time listening for the key in the door, the *only* door, knowing that if the Weave-lord caught her she would be subjected to unimaginable tortures. She had never known such constant and unrelenting fear.

It had only ended when the Weave-lord dropped dead in amidst the explosions that rocked the Imperial Keep. She later discovered that his death had been the work of Cailin tu Moritat, but that had not concerned her then. She had taken the key from his corpse and escaped the Keep in the confusion of the coup, while Lucia was being rescued by Kaiku and her companions.

Nomoru had gone back to the Poor Quarter only once after that, but she was unable to locate the man who betrayed her. Instead she went to see the Inker, who had put the Mask on her back, and a smaller symbol on her upper arm for the man that had sold her to them.

She left Axekami, shunning the people she had once known. Being delivered to the Weavers had been the last straw. She would not trust anyone again. And so she had wandered, and heard rumours, and eventually followed them to the Libera Dramach and the Fold, where people lived who wished harm to the Weavers. That, at least, was a common cause.

She blinked rapidly as a choking cloud of smoke wafted across her face, her quick mind flitting over options and discarding them. She'd be gods-dammed if she was going to die here in the Fold with so much left undone. There had to be an answer, some way to get to the Nexuses and disrupt their hold over their army. But they were simply too far away, and too well hidden.

A gust of heated air blew aside the smoke and let the sun shine through. She shaded her eyes and looked up. In the sky above the Fold, wheeling and turning, the gristle-crows cawed. She stared at them for a long moment.

The gristle-crows. They were the key.

Slinging her rifle over her shoulder, she ran along the walkway and began to clamber down the ladders towards the ground. The western wall could not stand for much longer. She only hoped it might stand for long enough.

Yugi hurried through the Fold, his rifle at the ready. Every crooked alleyway, every curve in the packed-dirt lanes was a threat to them now. Behind him went Lucia, Flen and Irilia, one of the Sisters of the Red Order, a narrow-faced, blonde-haired woman left by Cailin as an escort. Bringing up the rear was Zaelis, limping awkwardly on his bad leg, a rifle of his own in his hand.

Predators ran loose in the streets. They had met and killed one already, and passed several maimed and wounded men and women who bore further testimony to the news. Though the defences had not fallen, the creatures had leaked in over the western wall, and that meant there was no sanctuary any more among the plateaux and ledges of the town.

Contingency plans had been laid, but they were being put into effect far too late. The children were being herded into the caves at the top of the Fold, where a network of tunnels housed stockpiles of ammunition and supplies. Yugi had argued that they should have done this before the attack even began, but Zaelis would not hear of it. There were too many entrances and those too large; it was impossible to defend, and once inside the children would be trapped. He had wanted to keep the option open to flee along the valley to the east and scatter into the Xarana Fault, hoping that the army would be content with taking the town and would not disperse to hunt individuals. That in itself was dangerous enough, for the Fault was not a place for children to wander alone; but it was better than the certainty of being massacred. It was a measure of their desperation that they were considering last resorts like these.

The breaching of the barricades to the north and south had made that plan impossible now, for the Fold was surrounded. Sending the children to the caves was only delaying the inevitable, but they had to do *something* to protect their young.

Yugi led them across a wooden bridge that arched over the rooftops of a cramped huddle of Newlands-style buildings, passing a family of Aberrant townsfolk who were inexplicably going the other way. The otherwise clear sky was almost totally hidden by roiling clouds of dark smoke. Lucia coughed constantly, hiding her mouth with her hand, while Flen hung close to her and gave her worried glances. The Sister followed with half her attention elsewhere: the air around her was crawling with the resonance of the battle being fought by her companions, and she was both afraid and yet longing to join them. Cailin would have guarded Lucia herself, but she was needed to lead the fight against the Weavers, so she had left one of her less experienced brethren to look after the disenfranchised Heir-Empress. Irilia was fresh from her apprenticeship, but she had talent, and it would be easily enough to deal with any Aberrant creatures that came their way.

They hurried up a wide stone stairway to a higher tier, turning into a thin and winding street where the haphazard clutter of dwellings leaned in close. Shrines smoked gently with incense and were piled with offerings. Most of them had a small cluster of people praying around them, looking to divine deliverance as the only way to avert the inevitable.

As they headed down the street, a long-limbed, six-legged thing sprang from an alleyway before them, a spidery, emaciated horror with a face that was at once simian and disturbingly human. Yugi had levelled and fired in an instant, but his shot went wide, and the Aberrant disappeared into another alley as quickly as it had come. The people at the shrines scattered, running for what shelter they could find.

Zaelis looked about in dismay, a great weight settling on his heart. For the first time, he was faced with the utter ruin of all he had worked for. All these years spent gathering people, organising and uniting them; all the years those people themselves had spent, building these houses, living their lives. Aberrant folk worked side-by-side with those who were predisposed to hate them, yet the differences had been overcome, prejudices had been torn down, and the Fold had thrived. The people here were fiercely proud of what they had done, the community they had constructed, and Zaelis was too. This place was a monument to the fact that there *was* another way outside of the Weavers and outside of the empire.

But it was all coming down around him. Even if they survived this day, the Fold was over. Now that the Weavers knew where it was, they would be back again and again until it was destroyed. The thought brought a lump to his throat that was painful to swallow.

And then there was Lucia. He felt her actions as a betrayal. How could she have conspired with Cailin to lay a trap like that for the Weavers, to use herself as bait? She would listen to the Red Order, but she would not listen to the man who had brought her up these past years. She could very well die here, all because she had refused to be taken to safety. Was she doing it only to torment him? Was this merely the rebellion of an adolescent girl? Who could tell with Lucia? But he knew this much: she was punishing him for sending her into Alskain Mar, punishing him because she believed he valued the Libera Dramach above her, that he saw her as a means to an end rather than as a daughter.

Did he deserve that? Maybe. But by the spirits, he had not imagined it would hurt so much.

They made their way up to another tier, nearing the top where the caves were. Women were hurrying their children along frantically, on the edge of panic. As if the caves would provide succour when the walls fell . . .

The Sister came to a sudden halt in the middle of the street, and Zaelis almost went into the back of her. Yugi stopped as well, holding out a hand to indicate that the younger ones should do the same. They were smoke-grimed and sweaty, and all but Yugi were panting with exertion.

'What is it?' Yugi asked, sensing something in the Sister's manner that made him uneasy.

She was scanning the balconies of the houses on either side, their dirtied pennants flapping. The very air seemed to have stilled and quieted, the din around them fading to a distant buzz.

'What *is* it?' Yugi hissed again. A dreadful foreboding was building within him.

The Sister's eyes fell upon a ragged woman and a child walking slowly towards them, and her irises darkened to red.

Zaelis never even saw the furies. They cannoned out of an open doorway and charged right through him, butting him aside and knocking him off his feet to crash in a heap on the ground. Yugi whirled on them with a cry, his rifle already levelled. The massive, boar-like monstrosities were bearing down on him; he squeezed the trigger and took one of them directly between the eyes. Its charge turned into a roll as its legs went limp, but its momentum was too great to check and it barrelled into Yugi. He tried to jump it, but he was not fast enough; it clipped his boots and he somersaulted, landing on his back with a force that winded him.

The second furie was not going for Yugi. It went for Flen instead. The boy was paralysed, too late to run, too weak to fight. The creature was many times his weight and almost as tall as him at the shoulder. It thundered into him, a compact mass of brutality fronted by a tangle of long, hooked tusks, and smashed him down. He went skidding across the dusty street in a chaos of loose limbs, rolling over and over and coming to rest with his unkempt brown hair covering his face.

The furie turned its small, black eyes to Lucia. Lucia looked back at it calmly.

The air erupted in a screaming, shrieking mass of movement, feather and beak and claw. The ravens tore into the Aberrant beast, diving out of the smoky sky and bombarding it, latching on with their talons and stabbing with their beaks. The creature had a thick hide, but its eyes were ripped out in moments and its snout plucked to bloody ribbons. It thrashed and squealed as it was buried beneath a mass of beating wings, finally slumping to the earth where it lay wheezing.

And then, as one, the ravens dropped dead.

Yugi was stunned. He could not credit what his eyes had seen, even as the last few birds hit the ground. They had all died instantaneously, simply falling out of the air. As the breath returned to his lungs and he got up, he took in the scene: Zaelis, struggling to his feet; Flen, lying motionless on the ground; two furies, one dead and one flayed to point of death; Lucia, standing there with a calmness on her face that was somehow worse than the horror she should have been showing; and scattered around, dozens of raven corpses.

Then he looked for Irilia, and he realised that it was not over yet.

She was sprawled a short distance away, her head twisted backwards on her neck. Next to her lay a filthy-looking child, blood streaming from its eyes and nose. And coming towards Yugi now was the woman that he had seen moments ago, a shuffling, hobbling beggar.

As he watched, something happened to his vision, a sudden and violent shift of perspective; and he saw in the woman's place a Weaver, his Mask a shimmering mass of lizard scales that sheened like a rainbow. The dead child had become a Weaver too. Irilia had been overmatched by the two of them, but she managed to take one of them with her. One, however, was not enough, and not even Lucia's ravens could save them now. The people in the street – who had not reacted fast enough to intervene when the furies attacked – ran at the sight of the figure in their midst.

Yugi's blood turned to ice. The Red Order were not infallible, it seemed, and the Weavers were cleverer than they imagined. Somehow these two had slipped past the Sisters.

He heard Zaelis's indrawn breath. Lucia, standing amid all that death, was watching the Weaver.

The Weaver looked back at her, a hidden gaze beneath his patchwork cowl.

Yugi saw Zaelis move on the periphery of his vision. The older man's rifle swung up.

'Zaelis, *no*!' he cried, but it was much too late. The Weaver's Mask turned to the leader of the Libera Dramach, and one hand thrust out, white fingers curled into a claw. Zaelis's attempt to aim was arrested as suddenly as if someone had grabbed the end of the barrel. Yugi felt his muscles lock rigid at the same time. Every part of him cramped agonisingly, rooting him to the spot. His eyes were wide and staring, but his body would not respond, not even to scream.

Zaelis was turning the rifle towards himself. It was clear by the expression of utter and awful horror on his face that the movement was not of his volition, but the muzzle of the weapon was slowly and steadily turning towards him anyway. Yugi, frozen, could do nothing but watch. Lucia stood there, her gaze faraway, and did not move.

The pulse at Zaelis's throat was jumping with the effort of resisting, but it was no good. He had angled the rifle so that the muzzle was pressed into his bearded throat, beneath his chin.

He can't reach the trigger, Yugi thought, with a flicker of futile hope. *The rifle's too long.*

The trigger began to move slowly of its own accord. The Weaver's fingers curled into a fist.

'Gods curse you, you inhuman bastards,' Zaelis croaked, and then the rifle fired and blew his brains out.

The shot rang across the streets and was lost in the distant sounds of battle. The cry of grief that sounded in Yugi's mind was trapped in his throat. Lucia was still and silent. Flecks of her adopted father's blood had ribboned her face. She was trembling, her eyes welling, her mouth open a little.

Zaelis fell to his knees, and then pitched sideways to the ground. A tear broke from Lucia's lashes and raced down her grimy cheek.

The Weaver ignored Yugi, turning his scaled face back to the girl now.

'Tears, Lucia?' he croaked. 'No good. No good at all.'

Yugi made a strangled noise: *Not her! Take me!* But no amount of will could undo the Weaver's power. He wanted to shriek at his own helplessness, but he was not even permitted to do that.

The Weaver took a step towards her; and his Mask shattered.

The report of a rifle reached them an instant later. The Weaver stood blankly for a few seconds, thin blood welling through the cracked fractions of his face, and then he tipped backward and collapsed in a heap.

Yugi's muscles unknotted themselves at once, sending him gasping to his knees. A gust of wind blew a thick cloud of smoke over him, turning the street to a fuggy pall, and he coughed ralingly; but the sheer relief from the pain of the Weaver's grip brought tears to his eyes that were nothing to do with the polluted air. He sobbed once, the shock and terror and grief of the last few moments swamping him; then he swallowed, hitched a shuddering breath, and wiped his eyes with the edge of the rag around his forehead.

Lucia.

The wind changed then. The smoke blew up and away as if sucked back skyward, and there was Nomoru, slowing to a halt from a run as she neared Lucia, her ornate rifle cradled in one arm. She surveyed the scene dispassionately and raked a hand through her messy hair.

Yugi went slowly over to them, his body and mind numb and aching. He met Nomoru's gaze as he came.

'Followed the ravens,' she said.

He stared at her, unable to find words; then he crouched down in front of

Lucia, put his hands on her shoulders. She was shaking like a leaf, looking past him, tears running down her face.

'Is that Zaelis?' Nomoru said.

Yugi flinched at her insensitivity. 'The boy. See if he's alright.'

Nomoru did as she was asked. Other people were coming down the street now, running to help, gasping at the sight of the dead Weavers, far too late to do anything. *Where were they when we needed them?* Yugi thought bitterly.

'Lucia?' he prompted. She did not look at him, nor did she appear to have heard. 'Lucia?' he said again.

Then Nomoru was back. He looked up at her: she shook her head. Flen was gone.

Yugi bit his lip; the grief was almost too much to keep inside. He got up and turned away, fearful of losing control in front of Lucia. He was no stranger to murder; there were many things in his past he would rather forget. But gods, all this *killing* . . .

He heard Nomoru behind him.

'Lucia? Lucia, can you hear me? Are there more birds? Are there more ravens?'

He was about to whirl and shout at her to leave the poor child alone, she'd suffered enough; but then he heard a small voice in reply.

'There are more.'

Yugi turned back, saw the scout standing there awkwardly, and the slender, beautiful girl looking up at her with a depth of sorrow written on her features that made him want to cry.

'We need them.'

'Nomoru . . .' Yugi began, but she held up a hand and he subsided.

Lucia pushed gently but forcefully past Nomoru. She walked over to where Zaelis lay and looked down on him. Then she stepped over the corpses of birds to where Flen's broken body was, now turned face-up and staring sightlessly into the afterlife. For a long time, her eyes roamed him, as if expecting him at any moment to get up again, to breathe, to laugh.

She looked over her shoulder, her tear-streaked face unnaturally calm, as if a glaze had been painted over her expression.

'The ravens are yours,' she said, and her voice was chill as a knife. 'What would you have me do?'

THIRTY-FIVE

((Let us out))

Kaiku looked automatically towards the source of the sound, before realising that there had *been* no sound. The voice was coming from inside her head, a form of Weave-communication alike to the sort that the Red Order practised, but much cruder.

Tsata stanced ready to receive the approaching shrillings, which were coming down the tunnel, their warbling preceding them. He could see only a dark, stony maw: his night vision had been destroyed by the putrescent light of the witchstone that glowed through the grille at their backs.

'Kaiku, if you have any ideas, now is the time,' he said with a hint of black humour.

((let us out))

The voice was an insistent whisper, hoarse and cracked. It was coming from the creatures that moved behind the bars in the side-tunnels. They stayed just on the edge of the light, allowing hints of their form but no more. The hints were disturbing enough. There was no regular form to them: their shapes were asymmetrical, twisted, some with many limbs and some with tentacles or claws, some with spines or vestigial fins. Most of them had appendages she could not even recognise.

I know them, she thought to herself. *I have seen them before.*

In the Weavers' monastery, deep in the Lakmar Mountains, she had come across creatures similar to this, and similarly imprisoned. They had tried to attack her, thinking she was a Weaver, for she had been disguised as one. Much speculation had been made in the Fold as to what these things were, but theories were all anyone could come up with.

She backed away instinctively from the creature that spoke to her. Her Weave-sense had allowed her to pinpoint the direction. It was coming closer.

But in retreating from one side, she neared the other, and the tunnel was narrow here. Something cold and slimy wrapped around her hand in a tight grip.

She shrieked and spun; the grip loosened, and a thin tendril retreated between the bars. Tsata turned at the sound, to see her staring at the place where it had disappeared. Something was moving closer to the bars now, some small, wrecked thing.

The light fell across it, and Kaiku went pale.

It was a monstrosity, a warped clutter of legs and arms attached around a central torso that was barely recognisable as such. Its yellowed skin was stretched across a hopelessly mangled skeleton, and it jerked and move spasmodically, its multiple limbs waving. There was a kind of neckless head somewhere in the middle of it, little more than a bulbous lump, upon which something like features sat.

But the face it wore was Kaiku's.

The shock of it made her stagger. It was like looking in a distorted mirror, or a sculpture of herself that had been pulled out of shape and half-melted. Flesh drooped from the eye sockets, the mouth was tugged to one side as if by an invisible hook, her teeth in multiple rows . . . but it was still, unmistakably, an approximation of *her.*

((let us out)) the voice came again, insistent.

((What are you?)) she responded, disgust making her forget about the dangers of using her *kana.*

The thing that had copied her face had retreated into the shadows now, and she turned back to the one who was somehow speaking to her. It had come up to the bars, a pathetically runty thing with a flaccid sail of spines and all of its limbs drastically different in size. Gummy odd-coloured eyes fixed her from within a lopsided face.

((What are you?)) she demanded again, needing to make some sense of this.

((Edgefathers)) it replied, and Kaiku was bombarded with images, sights and sensations that hit her all in a disorientating mass, flashing through her mind in an instant.

Edgefathers. The ones who created the Masks for the Weavers to wear. She picked up confused recollections of forges and workshops, deep underground in the monasteries, built to the Weavers' insane ideas of architecture; then, further back, a memory of a family – *gods, this had once been a man, an artisan* – and he was taken, the Weavers coming in the night like evil spirits, stealing him away from his tiny village in the mountains; now he was working, working, crafting the Masks alongside other men – never women – artists and woodworkers and metalsmiths, and always the dust, the dust, the witchstone dust which they put into their work to give it the power the Weavers wanted; and looking around him and seeing what the dust was *doing* to all those men, what it was doing to *him,* beginning as a scaly patch on the heel of his hand, and then some kind of growth on his back, and the changes, the terrible corruption that came from handling raw, untreated witchstone dust day after day; and when they had changed too much they were taken away and not killed – *heart's blood why weren't they killed?* – but imprisoned while they kept changing, even away from the dust; and sometimes like now their prisons overflowed and they were taken elsewhere to be imprisoned because too many together was dangerous, because some *like this one* could do things, strange things brought on by the relentless and unending mutation, and others *like that one* could steal parts from others and copy them and couldn't help it and

((LET US OUT!!!))

The mental force of the sending made Kaiku reel. Torment flooded her in an empathic wave.

'Kaiku!' Tsata said urgently. The shrillings were almost upon them.

She made her decision. Her irises darkened to deep red with the full and unshielded release of her *kana*, her hair stirring around her face as if by some spectral wind. Power leaped eagerly from her, knitting through the golden threads of the air, sewing into the metal of the grille that separated them from the witchstone. With a wrench, two of the columns tore away and went spinning into the lake below, making a gap big enough for a person to pass through. The Edgefathers began to howl.

((NO! NO! LET US OUT!!!))

'Tsata! This way!'

The Tkiurathi had turned at the sound of the tearing metal; now, seeing an escape route, he ran to it, pausing for a moment in front of Kaiku. Their eyes met; his pale and green, hers a demonic Aberrant red. She shoved the sack of explosives into his arms.

'You first,' she said.

He did not question. He simply jumped out into the air, trusting to luck that the water beneath would be deep enough to receive him.

Kaiku heard the splash as he hit. The first of the shrillings raced around the corner of the tunnel, sprinting towards her with its catlike gait. Several more followed a moment later.

She waved her hand, and the bars of the side-tunnels ripped off, clattering to the stone floor. The Edgefathers howled in exultation, pouring out of their prisons; but by that point, Kaiku had already jumped, and was falling towards the lake. The shrillings tore into the Edgefathers, who responded with a mob savagery and overwhelming numbers, careless of their own lives, a furious and insane mass. The rest of the shrillings and the Nexuses that arrived after them found themselves facing dozens of grotesqueries baying for blood.

Their end was as unpleasant as the Edgefathers' lives had been.

The victors rampaged up the tunnel, spreading out into the caverns, sowing havoc where they went. They sought death and vengeance in equal measure, and left destruction in their wake.

The temperature of the water drove the breath from Kaiku's lungs. The cries of the Edgefathers became suddenly bassy and dim as she plummeted into the lake, and her ears were filled with the roar of bubbles; then, as her downward momentum dissipated, she kicked upward towards the foul luminescence of the witchstone. She broke the surface with a gasp, her hair plastered across one side of her face. The tumult seemed suddenly deafening again.

Tsata was already swimming away from her, one arm clutched around the sack of explosives. She called his name, but he did not stop, and so she struck out after him. Behind her, the shrillings were wailing as they were torn apart by the things she had released. Some of the grotesqueries were spilling out from the sundered grille, falling gracelessly through the air into the lake where they swam or sank, depending on the severity of their mutation and the configuration of their bodies. Two of them had clambered out and were crawling up the sides of the shaft like spiders. Golneri were fleeing in all directions, terrified by the sight of the Edgefathers, their boots clattering on the walkways that crisscrossed overhead. What Nexuses and Aberrants there had been here at the bottom of the shaft had gone, following the alarms raised by the sighting of Tsata and Kaiku back in the worm-farm; nobody was here to protect the diminutive creatures, and they panicked. Pandemonium reigned.

Kaiku was a better swimmer than Tsata was, and she caught him as he was clambering out onto a small, rocky hump from which a precarious bridge crossed the water to the central island, where the witchstone lay glowering. Huge scoops continued their procession into and out of the lake in the background, and massive pipes sucked water nearby. She grabbed his good arm as he made to run, and he turned back to her, his tattooed face grim in the eerie light.

'We've got to—' she began, but he shook his head. He knew what she would say: they had to hide, to get away from this place before the Weavers arrived, drawn by her *kana*. But there was no hiding for him.

He clicked his tongue and pointed. Hobbling along a walkway high overhead, a cowled and Masked figure in ragged robes.

'Hold him off,' Tsata said, and then he sprinted across the bridge, towards the witchstone, carrying with him the sodden bag of explosives.

Kaiku had no time to protest, not even time to consider whether the warped Edgefathers that splashed in the water were as much a threat to her and Tsata as they were to anyone else. The Weaver, seeing the Tkiurathi approaching the dreadful rock, sent out a mass of tendrils across the Weave to rip him apart. Kaiku reacted without thought, and her *kana* burst forth to intercept. Their consciousnesses collided, and all became golden.

She was a spray of threads, crashing and entangling with the Weaver's own, using the fractional advantage of surprise to penetrate as deep as she could before the Weaver twisted and closed up like a fist, burying them both in a ball of scurrying combat. Knots appeared before her as she sought to untangle herself and drive onward, insoluble junctions that she sometimes picked at, sometimes avoided. Her mind had split into a jumble of countless consciousnesses, an army of her thoughts each fighting a personal battle amid the churning tapestry of light. The Weaver's fury swamped her, not as intense as the unfathomable malice of the ruku-shai but more personal: woman had invaded man's realm, and her punishment would be extraordinary.

And then suddenly, shockingly, her vision inverted and the diorama went dark. She was in a corridor: a long, shadow-laden corridor. Purple lightning threw bright and rapid illumination through the shutters, flashing strange patterns onto the wall. Moonstorm lightning, like there had been on the last day she ever saw this place. Vases of guya blossoms stood on tables, dipping and nodding in the stir of the breeze. It was raining, though she knew it not by the sound but by the warm moisture in the air. The silence ached in her ears; only the roar of blood could be heard in its stead.

It was her father's house in the Forest of Yuna. The house where her family had died, and where the demon shin-shin had stalked her. She had never quite shed the nightmares from which she would wake up sweating with a diminishing memory of corridors and unseen, stilt-legged things hiding behind doorways and around corners.

But this was no dream; this was impossibly real.

She looked down at herself, and she confirmed what she already knew: she was a child again, in a nightgown, alone in an empty house. And something was coming for her.

She felt its black presence approaching, nearing her rapidly, a thing of rage and wrath. Something that would be on her in moments, a beast so enormous it would engulf her and swallow her whole.

She was a child, and so she ran.

But the night was like tar, thick and cloying, dragging her limbs down. She could not run without turning her back on the approaching monstrosity, but she could not outpace it. And yet she fled anyway, for the terror of that invisible malice was beyond belief, making her want to beg and weep and plead for it to go away, yet suffocating her with the knowledge that nothing she could do would avert it.

Her barefoot sprint was agonisingly slow. The guya blossoms turned their petal-hooded faces towards her, watching her pass with sinister interest. The end of the corridor seemed to be retreating one step away from her for every two she took. Behind her, the creature was coming closer and closer, thundering through the dream-maze of her house, and it seemed perpetually that it must take her at any moment, that it could not *get* any closer without reaching her, yet always the sensation of awful nearness grew, until tears streaked her face and she screamed without noise. And still she fled, and the corridor's end neared with a patience intended to thwart her of her life.

The Weaver! It is the Weaver!

Her thoughts freed themselves from the child-form where they had become momentarily muddled. She reminded herself forcefully that she was in the Weave, that her body stood dripping wet on an island in an underground lake at the bottom of a great shaft in the earth. And yet where was the golden world she had known, the landscape that her *kana* navigated by? Where were the threads?

It struck her then. The Weaver had changed the rules of play. Cailin had told her how the Weavers chose visualisations of the Weave, adapting it to some form that they could understand and deal with, because unlike the Sisters they could not handle the raw element without losing their minds to the dangerous, hypnotic bliss. Her opponent had jacketed her in a visualisation of her own nightmare, had picked up the leaking subconscious fears she was too inexperienced to curb and turned them to his advantage. She was trapped here, a weak and helpless child facing a monster of unimaginable potential.

How could she fight him here? How could she beat a Weaver? It was suicide to face one of them! They were masters of this realm, whereas she had only a few rudimentary techniques and her instinct to guide her. How could she beat her enemy when it was he that was setting the game, he that made the rules?

Despair took her, despair at being a little girl lost in a nightmare, an adult trapped in a hopeless battle. The Weaver would catch her, and it would kill her or worse. And after that, it would kill Tsata.

It was that thought and no other that braked her downward slide into submission.

I cannot run. It is not only my life at stake here.

The purity of that realisation strengthened her. It was no mere attempt at self-persuasion; it was a matter of what she utterly, unarguably *had* to do. Sometime over these last days she had stopped thinking of herself and Tsata as a team, as companions, even as friends; in fact, she was not sure that *friendship* was entirely accurate to describe the bonds that had grown between them, the strange and tentative understanding of each other, the unthinking trust necessary to survive the deadly Aberrant predators that they had hunted and been hunted by. Some subtle osmosis of words and actions had bled from him to her, and she had begun to think of them as a symbiote, a state of existence in which one could not do without the other – a single entity, fused of two independent beings. If she died here, he died. He had placed his life in her hands when he had charged her to hold off the Weaver while he tried to destroy the witchstone. Kaiku had no idea how much time had passed in Tsata's world – she was too deeply immersed in this one – but every moment she could give him might make the distinction between his life and death, between completing their task and failing.

This was *pash*, the Okhamban concept of togetherness and unselfish subversion of personal desires to the greater good. She understood it now, and it put steel in her spine.

She slowed to a stop. The end of the corridor seemed to spring towards her invitingly, urging her onward. The Weaver's advance faltered, and now she was conscious of his presence directly behind her, close enough to touch, making the fine hairs of her back and neck prickle with the intensity of its hunger. She was nearly there, nearly at the corner that would obscure her from that hateful gaze.

But she turned away from it. And as she turned she grew, passing through twenty years in an instant, and it was an adult Kaiku with her irises an arterial red that looked upon the creature the Weaver had become.

It filled the whole of the corridor, an enormous, slavering, six-armed man-beast that loomed over her, its hot and rotten breath stinking of carrion. Its feet and hands were clawed, but the rest of its body was humanoid, lumpen with muscle and covered with thick black hair across the chest and groin. Its skin was red and glistening with sweat, and its face was all snout and horn and fang. Noxious vapours leaked from between its sharp teeth, wreathing it in smoke. Small eyes glimmered fiercely.

It was a demonic exaggeration of one of her most prominent childhood fears, based on the icon of Jurani her father had kept in his study. The six-armed god of fire had two depictions, and statuettes of him were always crafted in pairs – one as a benevolent life-giver, source of light and warmth, and one as a raging creature of destruction. Kaiku had been scared of the latter statuette as an infant, ever since her mother had told her that Jurani lived in Mount Makara and its perpetual smouldering was the steam from the god's nostrils.

It was the Weaver's mistake. Fear of the gaping dark, of empty corridors filled with nameless dreads . . . that was something that had always been with her, a subtle and primal instinct that followed children into adulthood and old age. But she had surmounted her fear of Jurani when she was young, and his appearance here was incongruous and jarring. The Weaver was manipulating her fears, but it was only picking up resonances and memories, and this was one that was long dead.

She threw herself into the beast, grappling it, and the world burst into a rush of golden fibres again. The Weaver's illusion was shattered.

But she saw now what her enemy had been doing while she was distracted by his ploy. He had used the time she had wasted in fleeing to press the advantage, sewing through her defences, gnawing away knots until the barrier holding him from Kaiku's physical body was threadbare and ready to break. Frantically, she shored them up, spinning new stitches across the battlefield, dancing from strand to strand. The Weaver pressed aggressively, a flurry of jabs and feints intended to distract her from the real damage he was doing; but Kaiku guessed its trick and ignored the false vibrations, skipping rapidly here and there, rebuilding, fashioning knots and traps and tangles to tire and confuse her opponent.

The world shifted again, becoming a long, dark tunnel at the end of which something was tearing towards her, but she knew it now for what it was and she wrenched her perception back into the Weave again, dispelling the scene. Here, she was not hampered by the need to interpret the realm as the Weaver was. She could deal with the raw stuff instead. It gave her an advantage, made her faster than her opponent.

But she was still woefully inexperienced in her art, and the Weaver was clever. She was on the defensive, and quick as she was she could not keep him out indefinitely. The idea of counterattacking was unfeasible while he dogged her like this.

You need only buy time, she thought.

Then she saw it: an opening, a gap in the Weaver's barrier that had frayed from lack of maintenance, pulled apart by the stretching of the strings around it. The Weaver's attention was fixed firmly on her, heedless of defending himself. He was worrying his way towards an insoluble labyrinth that Kaiku had set up to delay him. That would keep him busy long enough for Kaiku to—

She had no time for further consideration. Marshalling her consciousness to a point, she arrowed it past the glittering tendrils of the Weaver's influence and into the gap.

By the time she saw that it was a snare, she was too late. The gap closed behind her, dropping a curtain of chaotic tangles to prevent her from pulling out. The surrounding fibres pulled tight like a net, constricting her. She struggled desperately, but the bonds were slow to break, and new ones were enwrapping her all the time, like a spider cocooning a fly. In another part of her mind, she sensed the Weaver dodging out of the trap she had set, and realised that he had sensed it all along and had been merely giving her an opportunity to rush into his own trap. He began to bore into her defences again, unpicking them steadily, and she could not disentangle herself to deal with it. She had gone in too eagerly, fallen for an amateurish trick, and there was no way she could get out in time to stop him now. It was a mistake that would cost her her life.

She flailed and screamed soundlessly, fighting to be free, as the Weaver threaded past the last of the obstacles she had laid and sent awful tendrils into her body, into her *flesh.*

Then the fibres of the Weave flexed mightily, a tsunami smashing through them, a wordless, idiot cry that swept both Kaiku and the Weaver up in a riptide and left them spinning in the eddies of its aftermath. Kaiku felt the Weaver's tendrils snapping away from her as she was torn free of her cocoon, all defences blasted aside by the force of the disturbance. She was dizzied and uncomprehending, waiting for her instincts to translate the blare that had stunned them.

The witchstone. *The witchstone!*

It was in distress.

The Weaver was paralysed, battered by the force of the cry and simultaneously drawn to it. His priority was, and ever had been, the welfare of the witchstone in his keeping. It was more than simply a task, it was the very purpose of his being. He did not understand the source of the compulsion that drove him, did not know the source of the group-mind that directed the Weavers. He did not know that what he guarded was not only the fount of the Weavers' power, but also a fragment of the moon-god Aricarat. At the witchstone's cry he was like a mother whose child is threatened, and nothing else but saving it mattered. Not even defending himself.

He did not even realise Kaiku was attacking him until she had burst through the tatter of his barricades and into his core. She was a spiralling needle that tracked along the diorama of the Weave, blooming inside him, anchoring herself until she had the kind of grip she needed.

Even from the start, she had always been able to use her power for one basic purpose: to destroy. She rent the Weaver apart.

Her vision flicked back to reality in time to see the cowled figure explode in a shower of flaming bone and blood on the walkway, burning shreds of robe and Mask and skin sailing through the air to fall hissing into the dark water of the lake. A terrible weakness drenched her, and she was pulled to her hands and knees by its weight, her sodden hair falling across her face, her back rising and falling with heaving breaths. Something felt broken inside her, some remnant damage that the Weaver had managed to cause. The violation of his touch made her vomit, spattering the meagre contents of her stomach across the slick rock between her hands. Dimly, she was aware of the roar of the plunging waterfalls, the echoing moans and howls of the Edgefathers, the clatter of boots on metal as golneri tried to escape up the shaft.

Then it came to her, a thought that rang with triumph and disbelief equally. She had faced a Weaver, and she had won.

But the moment of joy was fleeting. She had drained herself in doing so, overextended her power in the way she used to do before Cailin had taught her moderation. Her *kana* was all but burned out, and her body with it; she was pathetically vulnerable now, and still in the direst danger. She could barely raise her head to gaze at the central island where the witchstone lay, at the foul thing that had unwittingly saved her life.

It was crawling with Edgefathers, chipping at it with rocks and tools and scraping with bare claws. They had snapped teeth and nails on its surface, and bloodied fists and maws bore testament to the insane fury of their assault. The damage they were doing was far greater to themselves than to the witchstone, which was suffering only negligibly under their attacks. She could still sense its wail, resonating across the Weave, carrying over unguessable distance to summon aid. If there were any Weavers left here, they would be rushing to the chamber even now; and Kaiku could not withstand another one.

Then she found Tsata. The Tkiurathi was crouched at the base of the witchstone, jamming explosives beneath it and tamping them with mud from below the waterline. The Edgefathers appeared to be ignoring him, and for his part he seemed focused on nothing else. Had he even noticed the struggle she had been through to save his life? Kaiku felt a surge of resentment at that, and she rode it to her feet, using it as a crutch to overcome the tiredness that had settled upon her.

Somewhere above, Edgefathers and shrillings and Nexuses were fighting on the network of walkways. She was too exhausted to think about anything but stumbling across the bridge towards the central island, towards Tsata. The scoops rotated and the pipes sucked and the furnaces steamed and hissed and rumbled, heedless of her plight, endless in their purpose. The witchstone seethed its foul light, and the very air seemed to crawl as she approached; her stomach shrivelled and began to churn. She staggered to her companion's side, trusting that the Edgefathers would not hinder her, and knelt heavily down next to him. His pallor was even more jaundiced than usual; it was plain that the vile proximity of the witchstone was affecting him too. He spared her a sideways look, then returned to his task.

She knew his ways by now. The most important thing for them all was to destroy the witchstone. That made everything else secondary for Tsata. But spirits, did he even realise what she had just *done*? A word of congratulation, of thanks, even of relief at seeing her . . . that would have been all that was needed. But he was too focused, too rigid in his priorities.

'The fuses are wet,' he said, as the last of the explosives were put into place. 'They will not light.'

Kaiku took a moment to process that, and a further moment for the implication to hit her. What anger she had felt at his uncaring demeanour was swept aside under the force of a new emotion.

'No, Tsata,' she said, aghast. She knew what he was thinking. She knew what a Tkiurathi would do.

'You have to go,' he said, looking over at her. 'I will stay, and make certain the explosives work.'

'You mean you will stay and *die* here!' she cried.

'There is no other way,' Tsata said.

She clutched him by the shoulders, hard, and turned him towards her. His orange-blond hair lay in wet spikes across his forehead, his tattooed face strangely calm. Of course he was *calm*, she thought, infuriated. All his choices had been made for him. That same gods-cursed philosophy of selflessness that had helped to save her life meant that he was going to throw away his, because it was *for the greater good*.

'I will not let you die this way,' she hissed at him. 'A man was killed five years ago because he followed me into something he should not have been involved in, and I still bear his death on my conscience. I will not have yours too!'

'You cannot prevent me, Kaiku,' he said. 'It is simple. If I go, we cannot destroy the witchstone, and all this is for nothing. This is not about us. It is about the millions of people in Saramyr. We have the chance to strike a blow, and my life means nothing compared to those it might save.'

'It means something to *me*!' she cried, and almost instantly regretted it. But it was said, and could not be unsaid.

She fell silent immediately. Something in her wanted to go on, to explain what she felt welling up in her, that in this man she saw a person she could trust utterly, one who was incapable of betraying her as Asara had, someone whom she did not need to fear laying herself bare to. But the healing of her heart after so many wounds was not to be completed in a moment, and as much as she knew that she could not stand the pain of letting him sacrifice himself like this, she knew also that she dared not let herself say it.

He regarded her tenderly. 'There is no time,' he said, and there was something like regret in his voice. 'Go!'

'I cannot go!' she said, swallowing bile as her stomach reacted to the emanations of the witchstone. 'I am too weak. I need you to help me.'

A flicker of doubt crossed Tsata's pale eyes, then disappeared as resolve firmed them. 'Then you must stay too.'

'No!' she shrieked. 'Spirits, this selflessness you hold so dear sickens me sometimes! I will not sacrifice myself for this, and you will not make that choice for me! You are the only one who can carry the message of the danger the Weavers pose back to your people; they will not believe a Saramyr. To kill yourself here is *selfish*! You are thinking of my *pash*, and not of your own, not of your *people*! If they are not told of this, they will be next after Saramyr falls, and you are the only person alive who can warn them! We do not know what destroying this witchstone will do, but we *do* know what the Weavers will do to your land when they get there, and if the Tkiurathi are unprepared then they will all die! The world is *not* so black and white, Tsata. There are many ways to do what you think is right.'

Tsata's expression showed that he was wavering, but when he spoke it brought tears of exhausted frustration to her eyes.

'I have to stay,' he insisted. 'The fuses are wet.'

'*I can do it!*' she screamed at him. 'I am a gods-damned Aberrant! I can ignite them from a distance.'

Tsata searched her eyes, probing her. He was wise enough to know that she would say anything to get him away from there.

'Can you?'

'Yes!' she replied instantly. But could she? She had no idea. She did not know the range of her abilities, nor if there was enough *kana* left inside her. She had never tried anything like it before, and she was at the lowest ebb of her power. But she gazed into his eyes, and she lied to him.

I will not lose you. Not like Tane.

'Then we must go,' Tsata said, springing to his feet and pulling Kaiku up with him. She gasped in both relief and pain – whatever the Weaver had done to her twinged at the movement – and allowed herself to be propelled across to the water and then into it. She had barely the strength to swim, but Tsata supported her with one arm, striking out with the other. She let him take her, not caring where they were going, only that they were getting out, that he had believed her. Whether she could do what she had promised or not was another matter, but she did not allow herself to worry about that now. She clung to him, and he held on to her.

The sounds of the shrillings were all about as they fought with the rampant Edgefathers across the walkways. Some were almost at the central island now. The roaring of machinery filled her ears, getting louder, and she looked up and saw Tsata's reckless plan.

Several metres ahead of them, the massive water-scoops were rising out of the lake, heading upward into the darkness of the shaft. Tsata was swimming right towards them.

'Do not be afraid,' he murmured, seeing her expression; and then one of the scoops passed right in front of them and up and away, and with a few sturdy strokes Tsata pulled them into the patch of water it had just vacated.

Kaiku went limp. She trusted him. There was nothing left to do.

She felt a dip, then something collided with her ankles from beneath, tipping her into the great metal cradle that rose around her. She was submerged and flailed for an instant, banging her hand on something hard, and then righted herself and burst free. They were ascending, the lake falling away beneath them, splashes of water slopping over the lip of the scoop to plunge back to their source. Already, other scoops were following them upward. The awful sinking feeling of being lifted made Kaiku want to panic, but she felt too precarious to dare, and instead she froze.

They were rising past the webwork of walkways, past Edgefathers fighting with predators, past bellowing constructions and glowing furnaces and enormous cogs rotating. A Nexus fell silently from above to smash into a railing, thence to pitch broken-backed into the lake. A shrilling was savaging a golneri, the creature gone wild after the death of its handler. All was chaos, and nobody noticed the scoop and its passengers heading toward the abyss overhead and the beckoning clouds of distant flame from the gas-torches.

She felt Tsata next to her, his steadying hand on her shoulder.

'Now, Kaiku,' he said.

She closed her eyes, searching inside herself for what energy she had left. She would only need a spark, only that. She racked her burning body, eking out reserves, gathering her *kana.*

Just this time, she pleaded, and she realised that it was Ocha she was addressing, Emperor of the Gods, to whom she had sworn the oath that had put her on this road in the first place. *I just need a little help.*

And there it was. She found it, felt it burning in her womb and belly, and she forced it up into her chest and free from her body, a meagre glimmer of energy that seared her on its way out. Her eyes flew open and she drew a shuddering breath, and the world was once again the Weave. She saw the convection of the threads in the lake, the swirl of golden, fibrous blood on the walkways, the curling clouds of steam from the machines. She picked a thread and followed it, down into the lake and then along, and there she found the witchstone.

It was a black, seething knot, a heart of corruption so terrible that she could not bear to look on it. It seemed to writhe in restless anger, and its wail of distress cut across the Weave like a hurricane. And it was *alive*, malevolently alive, its hate radiating out from it, the rage of a crippled god.

But it was powerless to stop her. A last swell of courage sent her onward, finding the mud packed at the witchstone's base, passing through it into the tightly sealed bars of explosive. The threads were coiled and deadly within, throbbing with potential energy.

She found her spark, and threw it.

THIRTY-SIX

The battle in the Fold had been carried into the sky. The ravens had launched from the rooftops, from distant trees, from rookeries among the stony nooks to the east, rising in a cloud as thick as the smoke that billowed from the valley. In their small animal thoughts Lucia's call was like a clarion. She regarded them as her friends, and until now she would have done nothing to risk them; but matters had changed, and now she called on her avian guardians and sent them with a single, simple command: kill the gristle-crows.

Black shapes wheeled and shrieked in the ash-darkened afternoon, harrying the much larger and stronger Aberrant birds. The ravens were legion, outnumbering the Aberrants by many times. The gristle-crows slashed and snapped, banking and swooping on their ragged wings; but the ravens were more agile, and they dodged near and raked with talons or beaks before darting away again, reddened with their enemy's blood. Gory clots of feathers plunged through the air to smash onto the uneven rooftops of the town; and for every three of the ravens went a gristle-crow, falling stunned from the air with a bone-splintering impact as it hit.

Cailin tu Moritat was peripherally aware of the conflict going on over her head, but her attention was taken up by the greater conflict in the Weave. She stood on the edge of one of the higher tiers, flanked by two of her Sisters and guarded by twenty men who watched anxiously for predators. Below them, the ledges and plateaux of the town cluttered down towards the barricade and the horde beyond, who were senselessly throwing themselves at the eastern fortifications while the fire-cannons and riflemen destroyed them in their hundreds. Smoke rendered the vista in shades of obscurity, occasionally allowing a glimpse of the streets, where more and more Aberrants ran. The western wall was failing, and the creatures leaked in steadily to prey on those women and children who had not yet found sanctuary in the caves.

The battle in the sky found its mirror in the Weave. The Sisters swooped and struck like comets, evading the Weavers' more cumbersome attempts to strike back. They spun nets of knots, working in co-operation with an ease and fluidity that their male counterparts could not hope to match. The Sisters outnumbered the Weavers now, and the fight had turned to their advantage.

The more experienced Weavers had held out desperately until the great disturbance had swept over them. Cailin knew with a fierce joy what that disturbance was: a witchstone's cry of distress. After that, the Weavers began to make mistakes, distraction ruining the attention to detail that was necessary to keep the Sisters out. Two of them fell in quick succession, erupting into flame as the Sisters dug into them and pulled their threads apart.

Another Weaver was on the verge of crumbling when Cailin felt a terrible chill upon her, like a presentiment of her own death. She braced herself an instant before the shockwave hit them, an immensity of force that dwarfed the witchstone's distress-call. The very fabric of reality flexed and warped, a rolling hump of distortion blasting outward from the epicentre, passing over them and leaving them suddenly becalmed. Instinctively, Cailin quested, tracking the fibres strewn by the blast back to their source.

West. West, where Kaiku was.

It hit her in a moment of triumph. The witchstone in the Fault had been destroyed. She sent a rallying cry to her brethren and they plunged in to attack.

But the Weavers had given up. The souls had gone out of them. Like faint ghosts, their minds drifted, stunned, bewildered by the calamity that had overcome them. The Sisters hesitated, fearing a trick, expecting opposition; but the hesitation lasted only a moment. Like wolves to wounded rabbits, they tore their enemies to pieces.

And then it was done. The Sisters drifted alone in the Weave, disembodied among the gently stirring fibres. Alone, except for the leviathans that glided at the edge of their perception, their movements strangely agitated now. They had felt the shockwave and been perturbed by it.

Gradually, Cailin began to feel strange sensations passing along the Weave. It took her some time to understand what this new phenomenon was. Echoes of their alien language as they called to one another, dull bass snaps and pops that reverberated through her being. She listened in amazement. Never before had the distant creatures ever given a hint that they were even aware of humans in the Weave, other than their seemingly effortless ability to stay constantly out of the reach of the inquisitive; but now they were reacting to the death knell of the witchstone.

Cailin laughed breathlessly as her senses returned to the world of sight and sound. She had wanted to remain there, to listen to the voices of the mysterious denizens of the Weave, but there was far too much to do yet. Though they had defeated the Weavers here in the Fold, it might have been too late to turn the tide.

She looked at the Sisters to her left and right, saw the barely suppressed smiles on their painted lips, the fiery glint in their red eyes, and she felt pride such as she had never imagined she could. These few in the Fold represented only a fraction of the total strength of the network, for she had kept it scattered and decentralised out of fear for her fragile, nascent sorority. Yet here, they had proven themselves as worthy as she had hoped, finally revealing themselves to the Weavers and beating them at their own game. She felt a true kinship then, to all of them, every child that had been born with the *kana*, each one rescued from death. She had always believed they were greater than humans, a superior breed, an Aberration that had surmounted the race that spawned them; and now she *knew*.

Kaiku, precious Kaiku. It was she, perhaps, who had saved them all. Cailin's faith had not been misplaced, in the end.

She sent a flurry of orders across the Weave, distributing her Sisters to where they would be needed the most, and then she swept away. An insidious worry that was growing in her mind, souring her elation. While she had been fighting, she had not the spare time to notice; but now she realised that the Sister Irilia, whom she had left guarding Lucia, was not communicating any more.

The last few gristle-crows were being shredded on the wing when Lucia turned to Nomoru and said: 'What now?'

Yugi gave her a look of grave concern. She was not reacting at all as a fourteen-winter child should. Her father and her best friend had just died in front of her – spirits, she was still splattered with Zaelis's blood, which she had made no attempt to wipe off – but her brief tears had dried and her soot-grimed face was an icy mask. Her eyes, so often dreamy and unfocused, were like crystal shards now, piercing and unsettling.

He cast a quick glance around the street. They were still in the spot where the Weavers had attacked them. The corpses of Flen and Zaelis lay untouched alongside the dead furies, the Weavers, the Sister Irilia and dozens of ravens. Lucia stood in the midst of the charnel-pit. She had ignored Yugi's pleas to get to a safer place, which had been made half out of sympathy for her loss, half because he could not bear to look on his friend and leader Zaelis lying in the dust. Eventually, other soldiers had arrived and Yugi had stationed them all around her position. If she would not move, then he would have to protect her.

He had guessed what Nomoru was doing, even though she had been typically reticent when he asked her. The gristle-crows had taken no part in combat until now, always remaining out of reach, circling high above. With hindsight, it was obvious what their purpose was. They were the Nexuses' eyes. That was the thinking behind Nomoru's plan, anyway. Blind the Nexuses by tearing out their eyes. Put them at a disadvantage. And then . . .

'Find them,' Nomoru said flatly.

Lucia did not respond, but overhead the pattern of the ravens' flight shifted. Those that were not occupied with mopping up the Aberrant birds scattered in all directions, spreading over the battlefield. Searching for the Nexuses.

Lucia listened to the jabber of the ravens, her eyes closed. Nomoru watched her anxiously. A runner came from the western wall, reporting that sections of it were on the verge of collapse, weakened by fire and the weight of the corpses leaning against it.

Yugi bore the news grimly. If the wall fell, it was all over. Even if they could find the Nexuses, he had little hope of getting to them. Perhaps one last, concerted charge might be able to penetrate the Aberrants and reach their handlers, but he doubted it. Still, it would be better than waiting here for death, cowering behind collapsing walls, hiding until the enemy tide came to drown them in a wave of claws and fangs.

Rifles clattered to shoulders as a black shape emerged at the end of the street, but it was only Cailin, striding as tall and unruffled as ever. The guards lowered their weapons, and Cailin passed them without so much as a glance. She took in the scene and then fixed her red gaze on Yugi.

'Is she hurt?'

'She's not hurt,' Yugi said.

Lucia's eyes opened.

'Cailin,' she said, using an imperative mode she had never used before. 'I need your help.'

Cailin walked over to her. 'Of course,' she said, and just for a moment Yugi looked from one to the other and they could have been mother and daughter, so close were they in voice and posture. 'How can I help you?'

'I have found something.'

'The Nexuses?' Nomoru asked eagerly.

'I found *them* some time ago,' she said, with a nasty smile that looked shockingly out of place on her beatific features. 'I have something better.'

The Nexuses, unlike the Sisters of the Red Order, had no fear of clustering together. They had taken station some way to the south of the Fold, away from the main battle, and surrounded themselves with a bodyguard of a hundred ghauregs that made them unassailable by any force the Fault could muster. Occasional attacks from small, rogue groups were swiftly repelled, and the only army with sufficient number to threaten them was trammelled in the Fold. Nevertheless, they had learned the merits of keeping their distance, and so they hid at the limits of their control-range and directed the battle from afar.

The loss of the Weavers was not a concern to the Nexuses; they did not have the emotion necessary to respond to the death of their masters. What was more perturbing was the massacre of the gristle-crows, for those beasts had been specialised as lookouts. The Nexuses were not directly linked to the vision of all their beasts, but it was possible to see through the eyes of *some* of them. They prioritised their links; there was, after all, only so much information it was possible to deal with at a time.

They had now switched to skrendel and sent them climbing as high as they could to observe the battlefield, but it was a poor substitute for the gristle-crows.

The spot that they had chosen was a sunken crescent of grassy land banked by a hilly ridge to the west, south and east. They were sheltered from sight from those directions, and as long as they kept their ghauregs off the ridge then they were confident that nobody of importance knew they were here at all. Almost two hundred Nexuses were gathered, an eerie crowd of identical black, cowled robes and blank white faces, looking northward. When the army had first embarked they had been at the limit of their capacity to control the Aberrant predators, for there was only a finite amount that each Nexus could handle. However, as the predators' numbers had been brutally cut down, so the workload had eased. They were comfortably in command now. The ghauregs prowled restlessly around the silent figures, walking low to the ground with their shaggy arms swinging.

The ghauregs were not the most sensitive of creatures, and nor were the Nexuses, which was why they did not think to react to the steadily growing rumble from the south until it was too late. By the time the ghauregs began to look to the ridge with quizzical grunts, the sound was already beginning to separate into something discernible, and a moment before a new and unexpected enemy came into view, they realised what it was.

Hooves.

The mounted soldiers of Blood Ikati burst over the ridge, a battle-cry rising from their front ranks. Barak Zahn was in the midst of the green and grey mass, his sword held high, his voice rising above the voices of his men. The ghauregs' lumbering attempts to consolidate some kind of defence were woefully slow. The riders thundered down towards the enemy, firing off a volley of shots from horseback that decimated the Aberrant line. They switched to blades as they swept into the creatures. The two fronts collided: hairy fists smashed riders from their mounts, blades hacked into tough hide and opened up muscle beneath, horses had their legs broken like twigs, rifles cracked, men fell and were trampled. The ghauregs were fearsome opponents, and the attack became a chaos of hand-to-hand fighting, with the massive Aberrants tackling down the riders.

Zahn danced his horse this way and that, pulling it out of the reach of the beasts and cutting off any hand that came near. In his eyes was a fervour such as nobody had seen in him for years. His gaunt, white-bearded cheeks were speckled with blood, and his jaw was set tight. The riders outnumbered the ghauregs three to one, but the ghauregs held, protecting their black-robed masters who still looked northward as if oblivious to the threat.

Then the second front crested the western ridge, seven hundred men who swept into the sunken crescent of land and crashed into the flanks of the ghauregs. The beasts were faced with overwhelming odds now, and they had no way of preventing the attackers from circumventing them and reaching the Nexuses. The riders hewed the silent figures down from horseback, beheading them or hacking across their collarbones or chests, and the Nexuses stood mutely and allowed themselves to be killed. The men of Blood Ikati did not question their good fortune: they simply massacred their unresisting victims, and drenched themselves in their enemy.

The effect on the ghauregs was immediate and obvious. All coherence in their resistance dissolved. They became frenzied animals, seeking wildly for a way out of the forest of slashing blades and jostling warriors, concerned only for their own survival. It had the opposite effect, making them more vulnerable. They were chopped into bloody meat in minutes.

Finally the last of them had fallen, and the carnage was done. Barak Zahn sat panting in his saddle, surveying the corpse-littered scene. Then, with a breathless grin, he held his sword to the sky and let out a cheer that all his men echoed in one enormous swell of savage triumph.

Mishani tu Koli watched from her horse on the ridge, her ankle-length hair blowing in the breeze, her face, as ever, impassive.

Without the Nexuses, the Aberrants collapsed into disorder. Animals they had been, and animals they became again. On the western side of the Fold, where the stockade wall bowed dangerously inward and where the walkways on the rim were scattered with the dead of both sides, the creatures stopped their suicidal charges and turned on each other, maddened by the smoke and the smell of blood. They left their brethren impaled on the sharp tips of the wall and fell back from the flames, attacking anything that moved in a frenzied panic. The defenders, exhausted and ragged, stared in amazement as the beasts that had been on the verge of breaking through suddenly retreated in the most incredible rout they had ever seen. Someone was hysterically shouting thanks to the gods, and the cry was taken up down the line; for only the gods, it seemed, could have turned back an enemy such as this at the very last minute. They stood on the wall, their swords and rifles hanging on slack arms, and did nothing but breathe, and live, and enjoy the simplicity of that.

The scene at the eastern edge of the town was much the same, but there the Aberrants were penned in by the valley sides and the upward incline discounted it as an easy escape route in the minds of the maniacal beasts. They had no straightforward place to run, and they were still being pounded by fire-cannons and ballistae and rifles. Without the steadying influence of the Nexuses, they went utterly insane amid the explosions, some of them gnawing at their own limbs, others burying themselves under piles of smoking dead, still others simply lying down as if catatonic and being trampled or ripped to pieces by the horde. Some of them managed to escape up the valley, but most stayed at the bottom, trapped in a whirlpool of death until their turn came, by fire or rifle ball or claw.

By dusk, the Fold was quiet again. Smoke drifted into the reddening sky, and Nuki's eye glared angrily over the western peaks of the Xarana Fault. The foul stench in the air had become imperceptible to the survivors of the conflict, so long had they suffered it. Men and women and children wandered the town, battle-shattered and glazed, or roused themselves to slothful and exhausted activity in the knowledge that there was much to be done and little time to do it. Wives wept at the news that their husbands would never return; children screamed for parents who lay sundered in the dust somewhere, and were hastily gathered in by other mothers. Aberrants temporarily adopted non-Aberrants and vice versa, not knowing that their responsibility would become permanent as the dead were identified.

The predators were all killed or scattered, and hunting parties were chasing those that still prowled in the wilds nearby or who hid in houses within the Fold. Against impossible odds, the town had held out; but there was no sense of triumph here, only a weary and broken resignation, a numbness brought on by more horror than they could have imagined. The valley was drowned in gore, choked in corpses. The cost in grief and misery was appalling. And on top of all that was the knowledge that even in triumph they had won only a pyrrhic victory. They had their lives, but the Fold was forfeit. Nobody could stay here now. The Weavers would be coming again, and next time they would not be so reckless. Next time, all the luck in the world would not be enough to save the town.

A dozen troops of Blood Ikati rode slowly into town, with Barak Zahn and Mishani tu Koli at their head. They were as weary as the townsfolk, but for different reasons. Their gruelling ride from Zila had been days of hard travel, pushing their mounts to the limit of their endurance. When Xejen tu Imotu had given up the location of Lucia to the Weaver Fahrekh, Zahn had been finally convinced of the truth behind Mishani's claim. He had taken a thousand mounted men that he had brought to Zila and made all speed to the Fault, following Mishani's lead. They had passed east of Barask, skirted the terrible Forest of Xu on its northern edge, and entered the Fault south of the Fold, where Mishani took them through trails that their horses could travel. Usually, such ways would have been dangerous in the extreme, guarded as they were by hostile factions; but the Fault had given up its petty territorial squabbles in the face of a more extreme danger, and they had made good speed and arrived, it seemed, just in time.

Yet there was no hero's welcome for them in the town. Few even realised that they were responsible for the enemy's ruin. They passed through stares that ranged from curious to accusatory: why were soldiers on horseback here *now*? Where were they when they were needed?

It took all Mishani's strength to retain her composure. With each new corpse she expected to see Kaiku or Lucia or somebody else that she knew. Several of the dead or bereaved she did recognise vaguely, but she dared not allow them sympathy, for she did not yet know how deep her own hurt would be. The sight of her home town destroyed was bad enough, but to Mishani a place was just a place, and she was not so sentimental. However, she dreaded the thought of asking after her friends, what she might hear in response. If she knew Kaiku, she would have been in the thick of it. She always was a stubborn one, who would not back down from anything. Mishani dared not think of what she would feel if Kaiku was dead.

She barely knew where she was leading Zahn's men, only that she had a definite sense of where she should be, a lingering instruction left in her head by Cailin. The shock of having the Sister speak in her thoughts had still not worn off, hours later. She understood how the chain of events had come about – how Lucia's ravens had spotted them from on high, how Cailin had used her *kana* to speak to Mishani and tell her where the Nexuses were and what they had to do – but the sheer narrowness of their margin of victory terrified her. Gods, if the Weavers had been a little quicker off the mark in sending their army here, or if Zahn had wasted any more time with doubt and disbelief . . . if Fahrekh had suspected what Zahn was up to and had kept Xejen's knowledge of Lucia a secret, if Mishani had not been 'rescued' by Bakkara from her father's men . . . if Chien had not insisted she stay at his townhouse in Hanzean . . .

She shivered at the possibilities.

Thinking about Chien brought an image of his face back to her, his blocky features and shaven scalp. She felt little more than a passing regret for his death. He had been a good man, in the end, but she had learned that good men died as readily as evil men. She suspected her father's hand in it, of course; but the assassins were far behind her now, for she had been smuggled out of Zila with all secrecy. At the last, Chien had not managed to fulfil the task she set him, so she did not count herself held to her promise of ensuring his family would be released from their ties to Blood Koli. In other times, she might have been more generous; but she had her mother's welfare to think about, and for now it was best that the pact died with Chien. The world was cruel, but Mishani could be cruel too.

They turned onto a dusty street, and there Mishani saw what lay at their destination. The troops halted, and she dismounted and walked slowly onward, through the carpet of dead ravens and past the corpses of Weavers and furies and the body of the dead Sister. Standing in their midst was Cailin, like a black spike at the hub of all this killing. And crouched over the body of Zaelis was Lucia, her burned neck bent downward and her head hung, face in her hands.

Mishani stopped in front of Cailin and looked up at her, black hair sloughing back from her cheeks as she met the gaze of the taller woman. Cailin's irises had returned to their usual green by now.

'Mishani tu Koli,' the Sister said, with the appropriate bow. 'You have my gratitude.'

Mishani was too agitated to respond with the correct pleasantries. Instead, she asked: 'Where is Kaiku?'

Cailin did not reply for a moment, and Mishani's heart jerked painfully in her chest.

'I am not sure,' she said at length. 'She was on the other side of the Fault. She destroyed the witchstone we found there. It was she, as much as you, that turned this battle around. If the Weavers had still been fighting us, I would not have been able to contact you to direct you to the Nexuses.'

Witchstone? Mishani thought, but did not say. Much had occurred in her absence.

'I cannot reach her,' Cailin continued after a moment. 'She does not respond to my attempts. What that means, I do not know.'

Mishani digested that, processing the implications and coming out only with uncertainty.

Cailin glanced towards Lucia. 'She has not moved for hours. She will not let us take the bodies away. I fear she has taken a wound that she might never recover from.'

Mishani was about to reply, but then a footstep behind her made her look back, and she saw Zahn there, picking his way through the bodies, his eyes only on one person, on—

'Lucia?'

She raised her head at his voice, but no more than that.

'Lucia?' he said again, and this time she turned to him, her face and hair smeared red. He took a shuddering breath at the sight of her. She got slowly to her feet and faced him.

They stood gazing at each other.

Then she raised her arms, palms wet with Zaelis's blood held out to him. Her lower lip began to shake, and her face crumpled into tears. He covered the ground between them in a rush and gathered her up in an embrace, and she hugged him back desperately, her slender body racked with sobs. They stood there, amid smoke and grief and death, father and daughter clutched to each other with a force born of years of secret longing.

For the moment, it was enough.

THIRTY-SEVEN

Kaiku stirred and opened her eyes, squinting against the midday brightness. Her body ached in every part, and her clothes felt stiff against her skin. Nearby, there was the soft murmur of a fire, and smells of cooking meat. She was lying on stony soil, in a shallow depression surrounded by rock on three sides, a narrow step in the uneven land. Her pack was rolled beneath her head as a pillow. The air was curiously dead and silent; no insects hummed, nor birds flew. She had become used to it over the weeks. It meant that they were still close to the witchstone, still within the range of the blight.

She sat up urgently, wincing as her battered muscles protested their ill-use. Tsata was there, crouching by the fire. He looked over at her.

'Do not exert yourself,' he advised. 'You are still weak.'

'Where are we?' she asked, and found her throat was parchment-dry and she could only manage a thin croak. Tsata handed her a water-skin, and she gulped from it, gasping as she finished. She repeated herself more audibly.

'Several miles west of the mine,' he said. 'I think we are safe, at least for a short while.'

'How did we get here?'

'I carried you,' he said.

She rubbed at her forehead as if to massage life back into her mind. It did seem now that she could recall moments, half-dream and half-waking, dreams of water and being towed through rushing blackness, of being carried like a slain deer across his shoulders.

'We got out the way we came in?'

Tsata nodded. 'We rode the scoops as high as we could, and I ran with you the rest of the way. There were no Aberrants near the top of the mine.' He smiled at her warmly, the tattoos on his face curving with the movement. 'I do not think you noticed, though. That last effort was a little too much for you.'

She snorted a laugh.

'Are you hungry?' he asked, indicating the scrawny thing spitted over the fire.

She tilted her chin at him with a grin. He brought the spit over to her, settling himself by her side. Both of them were bedraggled, having been soaked and dried several times over the last few hours. Tsata tore off a chunk of flesh with his fingers; Kaiku brushed her errant fringe out of her eyes and took the proffered meat. They sat and ate for a time in companionable silence, their thoughts far away, Kaiku happy for the joy of being alive, of the sun on her face and the taste of the meal.

She felt a deep sense of validation, a relaxing of some tension inside her that she had not even known was there. They had destroyed a witchstone; they had struck the Weavers a blow that nobody in Saramyr had ever managed before. It was still a long, long way from the vengeance demanded by her oath to Ocha, but it was enough for now. She had been chafing at her inactivity for so long, driven to *do* something instead of playing this interminable waiting game that Zaelis and Cailin favoured. She could ask no more of herself for the moment. She felt worthy again.

But there was more, even than that. She was not the Kaiku that had set off broken-hearted from the Fold all those weeks ago. That Kaiku had been marvellously naïve, unaware of the potential of the power inside her, content to wield it like a club and control it only as far as preventing it damaging herself. Yet circumstances had forced her to stretch herself again and again, to use her *kana* in ways she had never dared before, and she had risen to the challenge every time. Without adequate schooling, without any experience whatsoever, she had faced down demons, had cleansed a man of poison and saved his life, and most incredible of all, she had beaten a Weaver. Granted, the victory had been a terribly near thing, but it was still a victory.

She had wondered often about why Cailin was so cursedly persistent with her, why she tolerated a pupil so errant that most tutors would have given up. Now she knew. Cailin had told her time and time again, but she was too stubborn to listen; it was only after all this, only after she had learned it herself, that she realised Cailin was right. Her talent with *kana* was extraordinary; her potential was limitless. Spirits, the things she could do with it . . .

She had been too impatient to devote herself to years of study and the Red Order, and so she had squandered her talents on small missions that could have been done by other people. But these past weeks had made her realise at last that her *kana* was more than a weapon. And she also realised that possessing a power and not knowing how to use it well was worse than not possessing it at all. What if she had not been able to save Yugi's life? Or to have destroyed the witchstone? How heavy would the guilt have weighed on her then? She would keep on finding herself in situations where she was forced to use her *kana*, and one day she would not be equal to the challenge, and it would cost lives.

She saw now that the quickest path to fulfilling her oath to Ocha was not the one she thought. Cailin had always said she must go slowly to reach the end faster: that she must master herself to become a more effective player in the game. It had seemed like specious reasoning at the time, but now it made perfect sense. She cursed herself as a fool for not seeing it before.

And in that moment, she came to a decision. She *would* let Cailin teach her. When she returned, she would make her apologies, and ask to begin again as a pupil; and this time, she would hold nothing more important. Her resolve was firmer than ever now that her burning urge for vengeance was temporarily sated. She would join the Red Order. She would become a Sister. And through them, she would fight the Weavers with the abilities that she had once thought a curse, that had once made her outcast.

If, of course, there was any Red Order left when she returned. But curiously, she could not find it in herself to worry about that, nor about the Fold or Mishani or Lucia. She had strange, elusive memories of her time in unconsciousness, of a voice calling to her, and whatever that voice said set her heart at ease. With no clear reason why, she knew that all was not lost, the Weavers had not crushed the last hope, and that both Mishani and Lucia still lived. With that, she was content.

'What will you do now?' she asked Tsata.

'I will return with you to the Fold, then I will make my way back to Okhamba,' he said. 'I have to tell my people what has happened here.' He hesitated a moment, then looked at her. 'You could come with me, if you so chose.'

And just for a moment Kaiku saw how simple that would be, how wonderful, that they might prolong this time that they had spent together, that she would not have to return to the world she knew. How it might be to be with him, this man whom she trusted utterly and whom she believed incapable of guile or deceit or treachery. For that moment, she wavered; but it was only a moment.

'I would like nothing more,' she said, smiling sadly. 'But we both know I cannot. And we both know you cannot stay.'

He nodded, Saramyr-fashion. 'I wish that it were otherwise,' he said, and Kaiku felt a painful squeeze in her chest at his words.

After that, there was nothing that could be said. They finished their meal, and rested for a time, and when Kaiku was strong enough to walk he helped her up. They shouldered their packs and their rifles, and together they set off east, back towards the Fold, and whatever lay afterward.

The temple to Ocha on the top of the Imperial Keep was the highest point in Axekami, excepting the tips of the towers that stood at the vertices of the colossal golden edifice. It was ornate to the point of excess, a circular building supporting a wondrous dome, chased with mosaics, filigrees, intaglios, and inlaid with precious metals and reflective stones so that the sheer wealth it exuded stunned the eye. Eight exquisite statues of white marble broke the dome at the points of the compass, each a representation of one of the major deities, both in their rarely-depicted human forms and with their earthly animal aspects at their feet: Assantua, Rieka, Jurani, Omecha, Enyu, Shintu, Isisya and Ocha himself standing over the entrance, a rearing boar before him. The boss of the dome was most magnificent of all, a cluster of iridescent diamonds visible only from the top of the Towers of the Four Winds, representing the one star, Abinaxis, that had created the universe and birthed the gods and goddesses in the beginning. When Nuki's eye looked upon it, the diamonds blazed like their namesake. That sight was intended for the gods above, in recompense for the arrogance that had led to the downfall of Gobinda all those centuries ago.

It was no less resplendent within, though redecoration had updated it over the years to make it less gaudy than the exterior and more in keeping with the elegance of Saramyr architecture. Here, tall *lach* sentinels stood in alcoves in the walls, and an ivory bas-relief twisted across the interior of the dome like convoluted vines. The air was cool and moist in contrast to the heat of the day. A raised path was laid from the entrance to the grand altar at its centre, but all else was water, a clear, shallow pool with submerged mosaics and clusters of polished stones arranged artfully to please the eye. No fish swam in the pool, and it was still as glass and restful.

Avun tu Koli knelt on the circular central island, before the ivory altar, a cluster of incense sticks in his hand and his balding head bowed. He mouthed a silent mantra, over and over, time and again. He had unconsciously begun to rock to the rhythm, his body swaying slightly with the imagined cadence of the words. It was a ritual of thanks offered to Ocha, who apart from being the ruler of the Golden Realm was also god of war, revenge, exploration and endeavour. Thanks to the god who had delivered him and his family safely through the fall of the empire.

Once again, Avun had guided Blood Koli into the most terrible peril and brought them stronger to the other side. Blood Batik would be extinguished, without mercy; already none bearing that name lived in Axekami. With its standing army gone, its holdings would soon be seized, and any remaining members of the line hunted down. For five brief years they had held the throne, and Blood Koli had been outcast; but in the end it was Avun that knelt in the temple of Ocha, and Mos who was crushed.

There would be many changes in the weeks to come. Kakre had explained it all to him. The Weavers were too hated to rule, the Aberrants too fearsome to keep order in any way other than by terror. A terrified populace was not a productive one. And so they had needed him, a figurehead. He would be the human face to the Weaver's regime; his men would replace the decimated Imperial Guards with a new peacekeeping force. Once order was established in Axekami, then the Aberrants' presence would be diminished, moved elsewhere where it was needed more. And gradually, the people would come to understand that this was the new way, that their world of courts and tradition and nobility was dead and gone, that *family* meant nothing any more. Avun would be the Emperor in all but name, only subordinate to the Weavers. They would call him Lord Protector, and his men would be the Blackguard.

All it had cost him was his honour. But honour was a small thing compared to victory. Honour had driven his daughter from him.

He thought on Mishani. She was only a face to him now; there was no parental love left in him for his absent child. He had to assume that she had evaded his attempts upon her life, for he had received no word of success. It brought a faint smile to his face. She was her father's daughter in that, at least. Tough to kill. Well, let her do as she would now, for she shamed him no longer. Now that the elaborate politics of the Saramyr courts meant nothing, she had no power to cause him disadvantage. The news of a disobedient child could harm him as a Barak, but it could not harm the Lord Protector, who had no peers to jostle with. He would not waste his time trying to be rid of her now. He would simply forget about her.

He only wished his wife Muraki would see sense and do the same, but it was a minor annoyance.

Footsteps from behind him heralded the arrival of the Weave-lord Kakre, and he finished his round of mantras and stood to bow deeply to the altar. When he was done, he turned to face his new master.

'Prayers, Lord Protector?' Kakre rasped. 'How quaint.'

'The gods have favoured me,' Avun replied. 'They deserve my gratitude.'

'The gods have deserted this land,' Kakre said. 'If ever they existed to begin with.'

Avun raised an eyebrow. 'The Weavers bow to no gods, then?'

'From this day, we *are* your gods,' the Weave-lord said.

Avun studied the corpse-faced grotesquerie in front of him, and made no response.

'Come,' said Kakre. 'We have much to talk about.'

Avun nodded. There was plenty to be done. Even the Weavers could not conquer a land as vast as Saramyr in a day, or a year. They had cut the head off the empire, and seized its capital and several major cities, but the nobility and populace were too widely scattered to easily subjugate, even with the overwhelming numbers that the Weavers possessed and the armies of most of the high families destroyed. The north-west quarter of the continent would be entirely under Weaver control within the month. After that, it would be a matter of sweeping away the disoriented remnants of the nobility, powerless without their Weavers, blinded and crippled. Consolidating and then pushing southward, until all the land was theirs and there was no one to oppose them.

Whether it would be as easy as that, Avun had no idea; but he had a knack for picking the winning side, and in this case he would far rather be with the Weavers than against them.

Kakre's own concerns ran deeper than troops and war and occupation. His thoughts were on what might have happened in the Fault, the loss of so many Weavers, and most abhorrently the destruction of a witchstone. He felt its death like a physical wound, and it had aged him, making him more bent and pain-racked than ever before. What had become, then, of the Fold, and of Lucia?

And what of the entities that had fought his Weavers, the women who dared oppose them in the realm beyond the senses? That was a danger beyond anything he had yet encountered, the most potent threat he could imagine now. If he had been able to spare enough of his forces, he would have sent them rampaging toward the Xarana Fault; but even then, he suspected he would find that his targets had gone back into hiding. How long had they been there? How long had they spread and grown? All these years of killing Aberrant children had been precisely to prevent something like this from happening, and yet despite their best efforts it had happened anyway. How strong were they now? How many did they number?

He thought of the Sisters, and he feared them.

They walked slowly down the raised path across the pool towards the entrance to the temple, where blinding sunlight shone through the doorway. They spoke as they went, of triumph and failure, their voices echoing in the silence until they faded, leaving the house of the Emperor of the gods empty and hollow.

The sun was setting in the west as Cailin watched, a sullen red orb glaring through the veil of smoke that still rose from the valley of the Fold. She stood on a high lip of land, a grassy shelf jutting out over a splintered hillside of dark rock. She had been here for some time now, thinking. There were many plans to make yet.

The remainder of the Sisters were scattered around the Fold, helping in the dispersal. The Libera Dramach was breaking up, spreading out, making itself an impossible target; they would regroup at a rendezvous in several weeks' time. The people of the Fold were doing what they could: most were intending to rejoin the others, putting their trust in the leaders who had seen them through good times and tragedy. Others were going their own way, amalgamating into other tribes and factions or heading out of the Fault altogether. The unity of the Fold was shattered, and would never be regained.

Messages had been flashing across the Weave all day, from other cells of the Red Order elsewhere. News of Axekami, of massacres in the northern cities, of the Weavers' daring and unstoppable coup. News of the fall of the Emperor, and with him the empire. The Sisters knew that the game was up now, that the Weavers were aware of them at last, and their silence was broken.

There was a soft tread behind. Cailin did not need to turn to know it was Phaeca. The red-headed Sister walked to the edge of the precipice and stood beside her. She was clothed in black, as all the Sisters were, and she wore the intimidating face-paint of the Order; but her dress was a different cut to Cailin's, her hair worn in an elaborate style of braids and bunches that bore testament to her River District upbringing.

For a time, they were silent. Nuki's eye was slipping towards the horizon, turning the sky to coral pink and purple, marred by the drifting smoke.

'So many dead,' Phaeca said at last. 'Is this how you planned it?'

'Hardly,' Cailin said. 'The Weavers finding out about the Fold was an unfortunate happenstance brought about by a mob of foolish and misguided zealots.'

Phaeca's silence was response enough. Cailin let it drag out.

'Did we cause all this?' Phaeca persisted at length. 'Hiding, refusing to act, all these years when we could have done something . . . is this the price we pay?'

Cailin's voice was edged with annoyance. 'Phaeca, stop this. You know as well as I why we have not acted these long years. And the lives lost here will be nothing to the lives that will be lost in the months to come.'

'We could have stopped them,' Phaeca argued. 'We could have stopped the Weavers taking the throne. If we had tried.'

'Perhaps,' Cailin conceded doubtfully. She turned her head slightly, looking sidelong at her companion. She was seeking a salve to justify herself. Cailin had none to give. 'But whyever would we do that? There is no sacrifice too high, Phaeca. Do not let your conscience prick you now; it is too late for regrets. This is only the beginning. The Sisters have awakened. The war for Saramyr has commenced.' A sultry breeze stirred the feathers of her ruff. 'We *wanted* the Weavers to take the throne. That is why we have held our allies back, that is why we preached secrecy and told them to hide, that is why we refused to use our abilities to aid them. They can never be allowed to know that. They would call it a betrayal.'

Phaeca nodded in reluctant understanding, her gaze fixed on the middle distance.

'If this is only the beginning,' she said, 'I fear what is to come.'

'As well you should, Sister,' Cailin told her. 'As well you should.'

They said no more, but neither did they leave. The Sisters stood together for a long while in the fading light of the dusk, watching the rising smoke from the valley as the colours bled from the sky and darkness covered the land.

THE ASCENDANCY VEIL

ONE

They loomed through the smoke, shadows in the billowing murk. In the instant before they came charging into the hall, they seemed as demons, their forms huge and vaporous. But they were not demons. The demons were still outside.

The pitiful scattering of defenders met the assault with grim stoicism. Some had taken up station on the balcony that ran around the room, but most were arranged at ground level behind a barricade they had assembled from toppled statues, plinths and the few small tables they had found. The Saramyr tendency towards minimal furniture had not worked to their advantage here. Still, they took what cover they could, aimed their rifles, and filled the air with gunfire as the ghauregs came pounding towards them.

Once, the entrance hall had been exquisite, a cool and echoing chamber intended to impress dignitaries and nobles. Now it had been stripped of its finery and ornaments, and the walls were scorched. The floor had been cracked by the same explosion that had set fire to the hangings and tapestries near the doorway. A dozen or so monstrous corpses were scattered there. One well-timed bomb had dealt with the first wave of creatures; the rifles would take care of a portion of the next. But beyond that, the defenders' cause was hopeless.

The ghauregs thundered across the wide open space at the centre of the hall and were cut down, their thick grey pelts ribboning with red as the rifle balls punched through them. But for each one that died there was another behind it, and several that fell got up again, their wounds only enraging them further. Eight feet high at the shoulder and apelike in posture, they were savage ogres of fur and muscle. Pain and death meant nothing to them, and they raced through the crossfire with suicidal fury.

The defenders managed to reprime fast enough for a second volley before the creatures crashed into the barricade and began tearing it apart, clambering over the top to reach the men behind. Rifles were dropped and swords drawn, but against the sheer size and power of the ghauregs there were too few blades. They knew this, and still they fought. They had been ordered to hold the administrative complex and they would do so with their lives. Saramyr soldiers would take death before the shame of disobeying orders.

The ghauregs punched and grabbed at their targets. Where the defenders were not quick enough to evade, they were bludgeoned to pulp or snatched up to be flung through the air like broken mannequins. Those who dodged away struck back with their swords, slashing at tendons and hamstrings. In moments, the floor was slippery with blood, and the cries of men were drowned by the bellowing of the beasts.

The soldiers on the balcony picked their targets as best they could in the melee, but they had problems of their own now. For behind the ghauregs had come several skrendel: slender, nimble things with long, strangling fingers that swarmed up the pillars. What little support the soldiers could give the men below dissipated swiftly as they struggled to keep the newcomers away.

The beasts had destroyed the barricade now and were sowing mayhem. Outsize jaws bit and snapped, crunching through bone and gristle; enormous shoulders strained as they rent apart their small and frail prey. In less than a minute, the remaining half-dozen ghauregs had decimated the tiny force holding the entrance hall, and only a few soldiers were left, their deaths merely an afterthought. But as the ghauregs' small yellow eyes fixed on the final, defiant dregs of resistance, one of their number burst into flames.

The two Sisters of the Red Order swept into the hall from the back, an arrogant lethality in their stride. Both wore the sheer dark dress of the Order, both the intimidating face-paint of their kind: the black and red shark-tooth triangles across their lips, the twin crimson crescents curving over their eyes from forehead to cheek. Their irises were the colour of smouldering coals.

The other ghauregs shied away from the heat of their burning companion, and in that moment of hesitation the Sisters took them apart. Two of the beasts fell, spewing blood from every orifice; two more burst into white flames, becoming pillars of fire and smoke and bubbling fat; the last was picked up as if by some invisible hand and pulverised against the wall with enough force to shatter the stone. The skrendel began to scatter, winding back down the pillars and making for the entranceway. One of the Sisters made a casual gesture with a black-gloved hand and maimed them, popping and cracking their thin bones and leaving them flailing weakly on the floor.

In seconds, it was done. All that was left in the wake of the conflict was the restless industry of the flames, the mewling of the dying skrendel and the cries of wounded men. The remnants of the defenders regarded the Sisters with ragged awe.

Kaiku tu Makaima surveyed the scene before her. Her vision was poised on the cusp of the world of natural light and that of the Weave, overlaying one on top of the other. She looked past the battered and bloodied figures gazing at her, past the corpse-strewn hall to the doorway where smoke from the fire plumed angrily into the room. But beneath that veneer of reality she saw a golden diorama of threads, the stitches and fibres of existence: the whole hall rendered in millions of tiny, endless tendrils. She saw the inrush and exhalation of the stirred air as the living drew it into their lungs; the curl and roll at the heart of the smoke; the stout, unwavering lines of the pillars.

She flexed her fingers and tied up the frantic threads of the flame, wrapping it tighter and tighter until it choked and extinguished itself.

'Juraka has fallen,' she said, her voice ringing out across the hall. 'We retreat south-west to the river.'

She felt their disappointment like a wave. She had not wanted to tell them this. Their companions lay dead around them, dozens of lives sacrificed to defend this place, and she was the one who had to inform the survivors that it was all for nothing. Perhaps they hated her for doing so. Perhaps, in their breasts, they harboured a bitterness that she had arrived and made their struggles meaningless, and they thought: *filthy Aberrant.*

She cared little. She had greater concerns.

She left her companion, Phaeca, to explain matters in more sensitive terms while she walked through the dispersing smoke of the snuffed-out fire and out into the warm and bright winter's day.

Juraka had been founded on a hillside overlooking the shores of the colossal Lake Azlea, an ancient market town that had begun as a stop-off point for travellers making the long trek from Tchamaska to Machita along the Prefectural Highway. In time, it had evolved a fishing and boatmaking industry, and sometime during the bloody internecine wars following the death of the mad Emperor Cadis tu Othoro it had been fortified and garrisoned. Latterly, it had become a vital part of the line which the remnants of the Empire had held for years against the Weavers and the hordes at their command.

But by the time Nuki's eye sank below the horizon today, it would be in the enemy's hands.

Kaiku swore under her breath, an unladylike habit picked up from her long-dead brother and never shed. She knew that the stalemate would have to end sooner or later, that eventually one side would devise an advantage over the other. She just wished the Weavers had not got there first.

The administrative complex was a sprawling, walled enclosure of several grandiose buildings in a circular formation. To her right, houses ran up the hill to the fringe of a small forest; to her left, streets and tiny plazas fell away in a clutter of ornamental slate rooftops to the vast expanse of the lake, which glittered sharply in the crisp daylight until it was lost to the haze of distance. Ships were battling out there in a slow dance, the sporadic crack of gunfire and the bellow of cannons drifting up to her. The shore was crowded with jetties and warehouses, most of which were smashed and burning now. Smoke rose in indistinct columns, cloaking the lower streets in a fug.

Kaiku's gaze roamed across the town, across the broken shrines and sundered houses, the streets where men and women fought running skirmishes with shrillings and furies and worse. Gristle-crows soared high on the thermals overhead, providing a literal birds-eye view for their Nexus masters.

But these were enemies she knew, creatures she had dealt with many times in the four years since this war had begun. She turned her attention to the authors of the town's downfall.

There were two of them, one down by the shore and another rearing over the treeline on the hilltop. *Feya-kori*: 'blight demons' in the Saramyrrhic mode used for speaking of supernatural beings. They were forty feet high: drooling, lumbering, foetid things in a mocking approximation of human shape, distorted figures with long, thick arms and legs, that walked on all fours and seethed a dire miasma as they moved. They were formed of some kind of noisome, roiling sludge that dripped and spattered, and where it touched it spread fire and rot, causing leaves to crinkle and wood to decay. They had no faces, merely a bulge between their shoulders, in which burned incandescent orbs that trailed luminous gobbets. They moaned plaintively to each other as they went about their destruction, their mournful cries accompanying the slow, idiot savagery of their actions.

As Kaiku watched, one of them waded out into the lake. The waters hissed and boiled, and a black patina began to spread from where its limbs plunged. She felt her stomach sink as she saw its intention. It forged its way towards one of the Empire's junks, and with a doleful groan it raised one stump of a hand and brought it crashing down onto the vessel, breaking it in half and setting men and sails aflame. Kaiku closed her eyes reflexively and turned away, but even then she could feel the force of the demons' presence through the Weave, a blasphemous dark pummelling at her consciousness.

The other feya-kori was surging out of the forest, leaving a vile scar of browning foliage and collapsing trees in its wake. It smashed an arm into the nearest rooftops, wanton in its malice. Five of Kaiku's Sisters had already died attempting to tackle the feya-kori. All over Juraka the order to retreat was spreading, and the forces of the Empire were pulling back to the south-west.

Then she sensed the spidery movement of a Weaver down in the streets below, heard the distant screams of soldiers, and the rage and sorrow in her heart found a target.

If I cannot stop this, she promised herself, *I will at least take one of them in payment.*

She stalked away from the administrative complex, out through the prayer gate with its eloquent paean to Naris, god of scholars, and into the narrow, sloping streets beyond.

Blood ran in chain-link trickles between the cobbles, inching slowly downhill from the bodies of men and women and the foetally curled corpses of Aberrant predators. Kaiku experienced a moment of bitter humour at how Aberrants, which were created by the Weavers in the first place, were simultaneously their greatest resource and their greatest opponents. She and all the other Sisters were a product of the same process that had spawned monstrosities like the ghauregs. She was certain that the gods, watching from the Golden Realm, never tired of laughing at the way events had turned out.

She passed swiftly between the newly scarred buildings, little fearing the creatures that ran amok in the alleys. Wooden balconies and shop-fronts gaped emptily as if in shock at how they had been deserted. Carts and rickshaws were left where they had been abandoned in the rush to evacuate the townsfolk. A crackle of rifle fire sounded up the hill as dozens of soldiers wasted their ammunition in a futile attempt to hurt the demon that was battering its way towards the lake from the treeline.

The screams she had heard were louder now. She sensed the stirring of the Weave like coiling tentacles, the Weaver's ugly manipulation of the invisible fabric beneath the skin of the waking world. She hated them, hated their clumsiness in comparison to the Sisters' elegant sewing, hated their brutal way of forcing nature to their will. She fed her rage as she approached, concealing her presence from the Weaver with a few deft evasions.

The street opened out into a junction of three major thoroughfares. The heart of the junction was a cobbled area in which stood a bronze statue of a catfish, depicted as if swimming upward towards the sky, its torso curved and fins and whiskers trailing. It was the animal aspect of Panazu, god of rivers, storms and rain and – by extension – lakes. An appropriate choice for a town on the shore of the greatest lake on the continent. Two-storied buildings leaned in close, their shutters hanging open, cracked plant pots outside and wooden walls riven by holes from rifle balls.

This had been one of the critical defensive points of Juraka, and had been fortified accordingly with barricades and a pair of fire-cannon. But such measures were useless against Weavers. Without a Sister of the Red Order to counter him, the Weaver had muddled the soldiers' minds and thrown them into rout. Aberrants had overrun the unmanned positions and were tearing into their panicking prey. The Weaver was nowhere to be seen.

Kaiku did not waste time considering how this predicament had come about. There should have been a Sister here to protect the soldiers, but the Red Order was in disarray across the town. Instead she stood brazenly at one end of the junction and opened up the Weave. The air stirred around her, rippling her dress and ruffling her tawny hair where it lay across one side of her face. She surrendered herself to the ecstasy of Weaving.

The pure joy of disembodiment, of witnessing the raw stuff of creation in an endless profusion of glittering threads, was enough to drive the untrained to madness. But Kaiku had been there many times, and she had mantras and methods of self-control that anchored her against that first tidal wash of narcotic harmony. She saw the tears and rents left by the Weaver's passing, felt his influence extending into the golden stitchwork dolls that were the soldiers, twisting their perceptions, making them confused and helpless.

He was unaware of her yet, and she used that. She slipped closer, winding along fibres, darting from strand to strand so that the emanations of her approach would be subtle and widely spread, faint enough to be missed in amongst the throb of the demons' presence. She could locate him with ease: he was in the upper storey of an old cathouse overlooking the junction. This Weaver was young and careless, for despite his power he did not notice her until she was close enough to strike him.

She did not strike him, however. Even angry as she was, she knew the risks that facing a Weaver entailed. Instead, she slid into the fibres of the beams that held up the roof of the cathouse, securing herself along their length to obtain the necessary mental leverage. The best way to kill a Weaver, she had found, was to do it indirectly.

In one violent twist, she ripped the beams apart.

The explosive detonation caused by shredding the fibres of the Weave created enough concussion to blow the shutters of the cathouse off their hinges. Flame billowed from the topmost windows; boards splintered and went spinning end over end through the air. The roof caved in, crushing the Weaver beneath it. The reverberations of the death flashed out across the Weave in a frantic pulse and slowly faded away.

One less of you, then, Kaiku thought, as the Weave faded from her vision.

The soldiers were coming to their senses, disorientated at finding themselves in the midst of an attack. Some were too slow to react, and were cut to pieces by the Aberrants that swarmed among them; but others were faster, and they brought their swords to bear. There were enough remaining to put up a resistance yet, and they did so with sudden and fierce anger.

Kaiku walked among them, slaying Aberrants as she went. With a wave of her hand she burst organs and shattered bone, tossed the creatures away or burned them to tallow and char. The soldiers, shouting hoarse rallying cries to one another, fought with renewed heart. Kaiku joined the cry, venting a deep and nameless hatred for what had been done to her, to her land, to these people; and for a time she steeped herself in blood.

Presently, there were no more enemies to fight. She came to herself as if from a vague and shallow trance. The junction was quiet now, a charnel house of bodies rank with the stink of gore and ignition powder. The soldiers were congratulating themselves and watching her warily, suspicious of their saviour. One of them took a step towards her, as if to offer her thanks or gratitude, but his step faltered and he turned aside, pretending that he was shifting his feet. She could see them arguing quietly as to who should do the honourable thing and acknowledge her help, but the fact that no one would do it of their own free will rendered it hollow. Gods, even now she was *Aberrant* to them.

'We should go,' said Phaeca, who had appeared at her shoulder. When Kaiku did not respond, the Sister laid a hand gently on her arm.

Kaiku made a soft noise of acknowledgement in her throat, but she did not move. The feya-kori from uphill was coming closer, its funereal moans preceding the jagged sounds of the destruction it was wreaking.

'We should go,' Phaeca repeated, quietly insistent, and Kaiku realised that she had tears standing in her eyes, tears of raw fury and disappointment. She wiped them with the back of her hand and stalked away, overwhelmed by a prescient feeling that the desperate war they had been fighting for their homeland had just turned fundamentally, and not in their favour.

TWO

Sasako Bridge lay a little over thirty miles south-west of Juraka, spanning the Kespa as part of the winding Prefectural Highway. The terrain was hilly and forested right down to the banks of the river, and the road skulked its way between great shoulders of land that, in days gone by, had provided perfect points of ambush for bandits and thieves preying on the trade caravans which used this route in times of peace. The bridge itself was a hidden treasure: an elegant arch of white, supported by a fan of pillars that emerged from the centre of the river on either side of the thoroughfare like the spokes of two skeletal wheels. It had been worked from an extremely hard wood that had weathered little with time, and the careful etchings and votive iconography on the pillars and parapets were still clear after many centuries, though some of the scenes and characters and beasts they depicted had been lost to all but the most scholarly minds.

Now, with the retreat at Juraka, Sasako Bridge had become the key point in holding the eastern line against the armies of the Weavers.

The rain began at dusk, soaking the canvas tents of the army of the Empire. Sasako Bridge was the fallback point if Juraka was lost. A defensive infrastructure had been built here long ago against just this eventuality. Stockade walls and guard-towers were already in place; fire-cannons and mortars lay hidden among the folds of the hills. Sasako Bridge was the only spot where an army could cross the Kespa, unless they cared to head seventy miles south to Yupi Bridge – similarly guarded – or even further into the swamps, where the city of Fos watched over the Lotus Arch. If they were coming – and they undoubtedly were – then they would be coming through here.

Kaiku stood in the songbird-house, high up on the flank of a forested slope, and looked out over the hills to the river. The embroidered wall-screens had been opened to the west, for the cool breeze was blowing the rain against the opposite side, and the pale light of the moon Neryn bathed the view in spectral green. Lanterns glimmered down there among the glistening boughs, evidence of the sprawling camp hidden below the canopy of the foliage. The Kespa was just visible through the overlapping flanks of land, making its way steadily from Lake Azlea in the north towards the swamp-lands in the south and the ocean beyond. The air was alive with the restful hiss and patter of the downpour, and the insects had fallen silent under the barrage.

The troops of the Empire had found the songbird-house abandoned when they first began to set up fortifications here, and taken it as their own. It was a tender memory of days that already seemed impossibly distant, when the high families' domination of the Empire was unchallenged, as it had been for a thousand years until the Weavers had usurped them and thrown them into a savage war to preserve their own existence. Then, noble families often owned a songbird-house, a secluded love-nest bedecked with romantic finery – including songbirds – which was employed by newlyweds or young couples, or parents who wanted a little peace from their offspring.

Kaiku gave a small, involuntary sigh. It had been four years since the war began; but her war had begun almost a decade ago. Would she have even recognised herself if she had met the woman she was to become? Would she have ever imagined she might be wearing the make-up of the Red Order? She remembered a time when she had found it ghoulish. Now she enjoyed painting it on. It gave her a new strength, made her feel as fearsome as she appeared. Strange, the effect that wearing such a Mask could have; but if she had learned one thing in these ten years, it was that there was power in Masks.

She thought of the True Mask that had once belonged to her father, its leering face blazing in her mind like the sudden appearance of the sun. It came to her unbidden, as it always did, but as she forced it away it tugged at her with promises that would not easily fade.

Needing to distract herself, she turned back to face the room, where others were gathering for conference. It was wide and spacious, empty of furniture but for a low, oval table of black wood in its centre, upon which vases of guya blossoms and silver trays of refreshments were set. The screens were adorned with depictions of birds in flight and landscapes of lakes and mountains and forests, and mats for sitting on were laid across the polished wood floor. Servants hovered in the corners of the room, where twisting pillars cut from tree boughs held charms and superstitious knick-knacks. Even at a hurriedly assembled meeting such as this the rules of etiquette were not ignored.

She could identify most of the people here. It was the usual mishmash of generals sent by different Baraks, a scattering of Libera Dramach, a few representatives of other high families. She sought out the people she knew well: Yugi, clapping someone heartily on the shoulder and laughing; Phaeca, talking gravely with a man that Kaiku did not recognise; Nomoru, sitting alone at one side of the room, looking as scruffy as ever and wearing an expression that indicated she would rather be elsewhere.

When all were present, they seated themselves around the table, except for Nomoru, who remained on the periphery. Kaiku gave her a scowl. She was unable to understand why Yugi always included her in gatherings like this. Nomoru was so unrelentingly rude that Kaiku felt embarrassed being around her. Even now she radiated surliness and drew the gazes of the generals and highborns, who wondered what she was doing here but were too polite to ask.

The man at the head of the table was General Maroko of Blood Erinima. He was thickset and bald-headed, with a long black beard and moustache that hung down to his collarbone and made him look older than his forty-five harvests. He was in ultimate command of the forces that had been stationed in Juraka, elected through the usual process of squabbling and jostling between the high families that attended such matters.

'Are we all here, then?' he asked, a little informally considering the occasion.

'There is one more,' said Kaiku. She had barely finished her sentence before the latecomer's arrival was heralded by a stirring in the Weave. The air thickened, and Cailin tu Moritat manifested herself at the opposite end of the table from Maroko.

She was a ghostly haze in the air, a white smear of a face atop a long streak of black that tapered away to nothing several inches above the floor. The vague impression of features could be made out, but they blurred and shimmered. Kaiku sensed the unease of those who looked upon her and allowed herself a private smile. Cailin could make herself appear in perfect clarity if she liked, almost indistinguishable from the real thing. But she loved her theatrics, and she was much more menacing as an oblique, half-seen entity hanging vulture-like over the proceedings. She preferred to frighten people.

Kaiku announced her for those who did not already know, adding the correct honorific: Pre-Eminent of the Red Order. She was the official head of the Sisterhood now, having taken the title when the Sisters declared themselves publicly in the wake of the Weavers' great coup. Though the Red Order had never operated as a hierarchy, Cailin had long been their leader in all but name, and she declared it necessary to sanction her position if they were to be taken seriously. Kaiku could not argue with her logic, but as with much that Cailin did, it left her with an uneasy suspicion that what seemed apparently spontaneous had in fact been set up long before, and was merely part of a greater plan of which she was not aware.

Maroko went curtly through the pleasantries of greeting and welcome, then settled to the matter at hand. 'I have read your reports, and I know of our losses,' he said. 'I am not interested in apportioning blame or merit at this point. What I want to know is: what in Omecha's name were those *things* in Juraka, and how do we beat them?'

It was clear that the question was addressed to the Sisters. Kaiku was the one to reply.

'We call them feya-kori,' she said. 'I say *we* call them that because we dubbed them ourselves: they are not like any demon we have heard of, in living memory or in legend.'

'You knew of them *before* they attacked us?' jumped in one old general. Kaiku remembered him: he was ever quick to throw accusations at the

Sisterhood. Did he distrust them because they were Sisters, or Aberrants, or both? He would be far from alone in any case.

'No,' she said calmly. 'Our information reached us only during the assault. Sadly, the intelligence came too slow, or the Weavers moved too fast, for us to forewarn you. Even so, I think you will agree that the loss of five of our number is ample evidence that we were taken as much by surprise as you were.'

'Ample,' agreed Maroko, with a pointed glare at the general. 'Nobody here questions the loyalty of the Red Order.' He looked back to Kaiku. 'What information do you have?'

'Very little,' Kaiku admitted. 'Much of what we have is speculation. The Weavers have summoned demons before, but nowhere near the magnitude of the feya-kori. Even with the new witchstones they have awoken these past years, none of us had imagined that their abilities had increased so much.'

'Then how have they managed to do it?' asked another general, leaning forward on his elbows in the lanternlight. 'And how can we stop them?'

'To both questions, I have no answer,' she replied. 'We know only that they came from Axekami.'

'*Axekami?*' someone exclaimed.

'Indeed. These demons did not come from the depths of a forest, or a volcano, nor any other wild or deserted place where their kind might usually be found. These came from the heart of our capital city.'

There was consternation at this. The generals began to argue and theorise amongst themselves. Kaiku and Phaeca used the time to communicate with Cailin. Some of the generals threw them distasteful glances, noting the telltale coloration of their irises as they strung and sewed the Weave. The Sisters constructed patterns of impression and intent and flashed them across the four hundred miles that separated them from their Pre-Eminent. Kaiku took care of the security of their link, monitoring the vibrations of the threads for roaming Weavers who might listen in, but nothing threatened them that she could find.

'I think the first and most obvious thing we should do,' Yugi was saying, 'is to send someone to Axekami.'

His proposition silenced the murmurings that were going on across the table. Though he had no power in any official capacity, he was the leader of the Libera Dramach, the organisation founded to protect the disenfranchised Heir-Empress Lucia tu Erinima. The fact that both Lucia and the Red Order were closely tied in with them made them as much a force to be reckoned with as any of the high families of the Empire.

'I'm sure you are aware of how dangerous such an undertaking would be,' General Maroko said; but as he did so, he was stroking the end of his drooping moustache with his fingertips, a habit which indicated he liked what he was hearing. 'The capital is deep in the Weavers' territory, and reports indicate that it has . . . changed quite drastically.'

Yugi shrugged. 'I'll go,' he said.

'I doubt that we can afford to risk you,' Maroko replied, raising an eyebrow.

Yugi had expected such a response. 'Still, somebody must,' he said, absently taking a sip of wine from the cup on the table before him. 'These feya-kori represent the greatest danger we have faced since this war began. We have no idea how to deal with them. They're too powerful for the Red Order, and artillery seems to have little effect if the assault on Juraka is any measure. Someone needs to go to Axekami and find out what these creatures are and where they are coming from.'

'I agree,' Maroko said. 'But such a decision is not under my authority. Our responsibility is to hold the eastern line. However, we can pass our suggestion back to the councils at Saraku . . .'

'We need answers, not more arguments!' someone called, to which there was a smattering of laughter and a grim smile from Maroko.

'Then I'll handle it myself, as a Libera Dramach matter,' said Yugi. 'With your permission, of course,' he added, even though he had no real need of it.

'See to it,' Maroko replied. 'Inform us of your findings.'

Kaiku was forming a request to Cailin when she received the pre-emptive response. Cailin knew her prize pupil well.

((Go with them. Both of you))

Kaiku and Phaeca went to see Yugi after the conference had disbanded. They found him in his tent, which had been pitched in the grounds of the songbird-house, where paths wound between weed-choked ponds and overgrown gardens. The boughs nodded with the impact of the rain, drizzling thin ribbons of water from their leaves onto the soldiers below as they hurried back and forth busily like ants in a nest. It took some effort to locate the tent among the crowded grounds, but once outside they knew that they had the right place by the lingering scent of burnt amaxa root that clung to it.

There was no chime nor any method of gaining the attention of those within, so Kaiku simply opened the flap and stepped inside, with Phaeca close behind her.

Yugi looked up from the map spread on the table before him. He was sitting cross-legged on a mat. The rest of the tent was a clutter of possessions that he had not yet unpacked. In the wan light of the paper lantern above him, Kaiku thought how old he looked, how deep the lines on his face and how haggard his cheeks. He had not coped well with the pressures of leadership. Though his exterior was still as roguish and bluff as it had always been, inside he was deteriorating fast. His amaxa root habit had increased in proportion to his decline, the symptom of some inner turmoil the exact nature of which Kaiku was unaware. For long years, even before she had known him, he had smoked the narcotic in secret and it had never got in the way of his efficiency as a member of the Libera Dramach. He had always been able to take it or leave it, a biological quirk or facet of his character that allowed him to somehow sidestep the addiction that snared most users of the drug. But now, more and more often, she found him with that slightly too-bright edge in his eyes, and smelt the lingering fumes in places where he rested, and she feared for him.

There was an instant of incomprehension on his face as he looked upon the two black-clad Sisters, who had come in from the rain and yet were not even damp. Then the grin appeared, a somewhat sickly rictus in the jaundiced light. 'Kaiku,' he said. 'Come to volunteer?'

'You sound surprised,' she observed.

He got to his feet, running a hand through the brown-blond quills of his hair. 'I would have thought Cailin would not let you go.'

'We have more than enough Sisters to defend a single bridge against the Weavers. And as to the feya-kori . . . well, you know as well as I. One Sister or a dozen will make little difference there.'

'I meant that I didn't think she would let *you* go,' he said. 'You are something of a valued possession of hers nowadays.'

Kaiku did not like the implication of that phrase, but she deflected it with a smile. 'I do not often do what I am told anyway, Yugi. You know me.'

Yugi did not take up the humour. 'I used to,' he murmured. Then his eyes went to Phaeca and he made a distracted noise of acknowledgement. 'You too?'

'It'd be nice to see home again,' Phaeca said.

He paced slowly around the periphery of the tent, deep in thought. 'Agreed. Three of you, then. That will be enough.'

'Three?' Kaiku asked. 'Who is the third?'

'Nomoru,' he replied. 'She asked to go.'

Kaiku kept her expression carefully neutral, allowing neither her dislike of the wiry scout nor her surprise that Nomoru had volunteered to cross her face.

'She's from the Poor Quarter,' Yugi said. 'She knows people. I want to test the water there, make contact with our spies. Those poor bastards in the capital have been living under the Weavers for four years now. They were happy enough to rise against Lucia taking the throne; maybe a little taste of the alternative has taught them the error of their ways. Let's see if the conditions have kindled any of that old fire.'

'A revolt?' Phaeca prompted.

He gave an affirmative grunt. 'Test the water,' he said again.

There was a silence for a moment, but for the dull percussion of the rain on the canvas.

'Is that all?' he asked.

Kaiku gave Phaeca a look, and Phaeca took the hint. She excused herself and slipped out of the tent.

'Ah,' Yugi said wryly, scratching under the rag around his forehead. 'This seems serious. Am I in trouble?'

'I was about to ask you the very same thing,' Kaiku replied. 'Are you?'

'Only as much as all of us,' he replied, looking around the tent at everything but her. He picked up a scroll case and began absently fiddling with it.

She hesitated, then tried a different approach. 'We have not seen each other as often as I would like these past years, Yugi,' she said.

'I imagine that's true of most of those you once knew,' he returned, glancing at her briefly. 'You've been otherwise engaged.'

That was a little too close to the bone for Kaiku. She knew her old friendships had suffered neglect, partly because of the war, mostly because she had devoted herself to Cailin's tutelage, which allowed time for little else. Lucia had become distant and alien, worse now than when she was a child. Mishani was ever absent, always engaged in some form of diplomacy or another. She had heard nothing of Tsata since he had departed for his homeland just after the war began. And Asara . . . well, best for her not to think about Asara. As much as Kaiku hated her, she was haunted in the small hours of the night by an insidious longing to see her erstwhile handmaiden again. But Asara was far to the east now, and likely would remain there, and that was best for both of them.

'The war has changed many things,' she said quietly.

'And none more so than you,' Yugi replied with a faintly snappish edge to his tone, looking her over.

She was hurt by that. 'Why attack me so? We were friends once, and even if you do not believe that any more, we are certainly not enemies. What has turned you into this?'

He laughed bitterly, a sudden bark that made her start. 'Gods, Kaiku! It's not as it once was between us. I look at you now and I see Cailin. You're not the woman I knew. You're different, *colder*. You're a Sister now.' He waved a hand at her in exasperation. 'How do you expect me to confide in you when you're wearing that damned stuff?'

Kaiku could barely believe what she was hearing. She wanted to remind him that she had become a Sister to fight for *his* cause, that without the Sisters the war would have been over in a year and the Weavers victorious. But she held her tongue. She knew that if she opened her mouth, she would begin an argument, and she would likely destroy whatever slender bridges still existed between them. Instead, she swallowed her anger with a discipline which the trials of the Red Order had instilled in her.

'I suppose I cannot,' she said calmly. 'Please let me know the arrangements for our departure to Axekami.'

With that she left, stepping out into the rain where Phaeca waited for her, and the two of them walked through the crowded grounds of the songbird-house, back towards the river. For the first time in some while, Kaiku noticed how the soldiers unobtrusively moved aside to let them pass.

THREE

The triad of moons hung in a sky thick with stars. Two of them had matched orbits low in the west, descending towards the crooked teeth of the Tchamil Mountains, the flawless green pearl of Neryn peeping out from behind the huge blotched disc of her sister Aurus. Iridima glowered at them from the east, her white skin marbled with blue. Beneath, from horizon to horizon, lay the desert of Tchom Rin, an eternity of languid waves desiccated on the point of breaking. A cool wind brushed across the smooth, shadowy humps, dusting their crests. It was the only sound that could be heard in all the vastness.

Saramyr was riven north to south by the spine of the Tchamil Mountains, dividing the more populous and developed lands to the west from the wilder places in the east. The south-eastern quadrant of Saramyr was dominated by the continent's only desert, stretching over six hundred miles from the foot of the mountains to peter out a little short of the eastern coast. It was here that the settlers had come over seven hundred years ago, to begin the colonisation of the eastern territories.

Stories of those pioneer days were rife in Tchom Rin legend: tales of those who chose to stay while others went on to the more fertile Newlands to the north, those who made a pact with the bastard goddess Suran to live in her realm and worship her in return for being taught the ways of this cruel new world. Suran was kind to her followers, and she showed them how to thrive. In the wasteland of the desert, they built sprawling cities and gargantuan temples, and they chased out the Ugati and their old and impotent gods. The settlers took the desert as their own, and the desert changed them, until they had become like a people unto themselves, and the ways of the west seemed distant.

One of the greatest of the cities that the early settlers founded was Muia. It lay serene and peaceful in the green-tinged moonlight, in the lee of an escarpment that stretched for miles along its western edge. Tchom Rin architecture, so popular history told, had been invented by a man named Iyatimo, who had based his constructions on the bladed leaves of the hardy chia shrub, one of the few plants capable of surviving in the desert. Whatever the truth of it, the style proliferated, and the buildings of the Tchom Rin became renowned for their smooth edges and sharp tips. Bulbous bases flowed into needle-like spires; windows were teardrop-shaped, tapering upward; the walls that surrounded the city were made impressive and forbidding with rows of knife-like ornamentation. Though the lower levels of the complex, twining streets rose in orderly stepped rows of broad dwellings, the upper reaches were a dense forest of spikes, a multitude of stilettos thrust at the sky. Everything was drawn into the air as if the gravity of the moons overhead had sucked the cities of Tchom Rin out of shape and made them into something new and strangely beautiful to the eye.

Muia slept beneath the fearsome auspices of a statue of Suran some two hundred feet high. She was seated in an alcove carved out of the cliff face, a lizard coiled in her lap and a snake wrapped around her shoulders to symbolise the creatures that fed her in the desert cave where she was abandoned by her mother Aspinis. The belief in western Saramyr that it was arrogant to depict deities in any way other than through oblique icons or animal aspects had never taken in Tchom Rin, and so Suran was portrayed as the legends told her to be: as a sullen and angry adolescent, her hair long and tangled, with one green and one blue eye picked out in coloured slate. She was dressed in rags and holding a gnarled staff around which the snake had partially wrapped itself.

Suran did not have the grandeur of the majority of the Saramyr pantheon, nor the benevolence. The people of Tchom Rin had chosen a goddess that needed to be appeased rather than simply praised, a tough and bitter deity who would overcome any adversity and believed vengeance to be the purest of emotional ends. It suited their temperament, and they worshipped her with great fervour and to the exclusion of all others, scorning the passive and elastic religious beliefs of their ancestors. Though those outside the desert saw her as a dark goddess, the bringer of drought and pestilence, those within adored her because she kept those evils from their door. She was the guardian of the sands, and in Tchom Rin she reigned supreme.

Tonight, the city slept peacefully in the blessed respite from the heat of the day. But here, as anywhere else, there were those who needed the darkness of night for their business, and one such was on his way to assassinate the most important man in Tchom Rin.

Keroki flowed like quicksilver along the rope that stretched taut between two adjacent spires, heedless of the fatal drop onto the flagged and dusty streets below. Vertigo was a weakness he could not afford to have, and like the other minor frailties that he had possessed as a child, it had been beaten out of him during his cruel apprenticeship in the art of murder.

He reached the end of the rope, where it looped around the pointed parapet of a balcony, and slipped onto solid ground again. He allowed himself a flicker of humour: Tchom Rin architecture was pretty enough, but it did provide a lot of places to snag a rope. He left it where it was, strung between the two thin towers and invisible against the night sky. If all went well, he would be returning this way. If not, then he would be dead.

He was a short and thickset man, his appearance at odds with the grace with which he carried himself. His features were swarthy and his skin tanned dark by the desert sun. He was dressed in light green silks which hung loosely against his skin, tied with a purple sash: the attire of one of the servants of Blood Tanatsua. Often the simplest disguises were the best. He marvelled at how often he had heard of assassins masked and dressed in black, advertising their profession to anyone who saw them. His life had been saved more than once by the simple expedience of an appropriate costume for his task.

There were three guards inside the tower, but all were dead at their posts. His employer had promised it would be so. He had another man on the inside, for whom poisons were something of a speciality.

Blood Tanatsua's Muia residence was not an easy place to get into. In fact, had it not been for the virtually limitless resources of Keroki's employer and the amount of time they had had to prepare, it would have been impossible. He had already evaded or despatched at least a dozen sentries and avoided numerous traps on his way up the tower from which he had reached this one. The only way he had a hope of getting to his target was via this most circuitous route, and even then he was relying on the removal of some of the obstacles in his path.

But he was not a man to consider the possibility of failure. No matter what the difficulties and dangers that Keroki had to face, Barak Reki tu Tanatsua would meet his end tonight.

He slipped into the tower, through the rooms where the guards were slumped, victims of a slow-release venom that was so subtle they had not even realised what was happening to them, much less connected it with the meal they had eaten hours before. In contrast to the unadorned exterior of the tower, the chambers he passed through were lavish and ornate, with lacquered walls, lintels of coiled bronze, and wide mirrors duplicating everything. Globular lanterns of gold-leaf mesh hung from the ceiling, casting intriguing shadows.

Keroki did not appreciate the subtleties of the decor. His sense of aesthetic appreciation had gone the way of his vertigo. Instead, he listened for sounds, and his eyes roved for clues that things were not entirely as they should be: a pulse at a guard's temple to indicate he was only faking death; a screen positioned to conceal an attacker; evidence of the bodies being disturbed by someone who had happened upon them and gone to raise the alarm. As an afterthought, he considered cutting the throats of the three men so that suspicion would not fall upon the poisoner, but he reasoned that they would not bleed enough to fool anyone with their hearts long stopped, and he dismissed the idea. Let the poisoner take his chances. He would undoubtedly have covered his own trail well enough.

Keroki headed down the stairs. The tower was made up of a succession of circular chambers, apparently innocuous, decorated as small libraries, studies, rooms for relaxing in and enjoying entertainment and music. Keroki's practised eye saw through the disguise immediately. These were false rooms, which nobody used except those guards who had spent weeks learning where the multitude of lethal barbs and alarms were hidden. They were placed here to protect the heart of the residence from thieves entering the way he did. Embroidered boxes on elaborate dressing-tables promised jewellery within, but anyone opening them would have their fingers scored with a poisoned blade or caustic powder puffed into their face to eat their eyes away. Valuable tapestries were attached by threads to incendiary devices. Stout doors – much more common here than in the west, where screens and curtains were used instead – were rigged to explode if they were not opened in a certain fashion. Even the stairs between the rooms were constructed with occasional breakaway steps, where the stone was a crust as thin as a biscuit and concealed spring-loaded mantraps beneath.

Keroki spent the best part of two hours descending the tower. Even with the information provided by the insider, detailing the location and operation of the traps, he was forced to be excessively cautious. He had not lived to thirty-five harvests by trusting anyone with his life, and he double-checked everything to his satisfaction before risking it. Additionally, there were some secrets which the insider had not been able to obtain, and certain traps which could not be simply avoided but had to be puzzled out and deactivated with his collection of exquisite tools.

He thought on his mission during that time, picking it over in the back of his mind as he had done for weeks now, examining it for anything which might compromise him. But no, it was as straightforward now as it had been when he first received the assignment. The morning would bring the great meeting of the desert Baraks, the culmination of many days of negotiations, treaties signed and agreements made. Presiding over all would be the young Barak Reki tu Tanatsua. It would be a unification of the Baraks of Tchom Rin; and with it, the cementing of Blood Tanatsua's position as the dominant family among them.

But if Keroki succeeded tonight, then the figurehead of the unification would be dead, and the meeting would collapse into chaos. His employer – the son of a rival Barak – believed that it shamed the family for his father to submit to Blood Tanatsua in this matter. And that was where Keroki entered the equation.

He had just made his way clear of the last of the false rooms when he heard voices.

His senses were immediately on alert. There should not have been guards here at the foot of the tower: the ones at the top and the gauntlet of lethal chambers in between were more than enough protection. A last-minute doubling of security? A failure on the part of his informant? No matter now; he was committed.

The men were beyond the door that he listened against. They were static, and judging by the tone of their voices and their conversation they were not particularly alert. But still, they presented something of an inconvenient obstacle.

He lay down with his eye close to the floor and drew out two tiny, flat mirrors attached to long, thin handles. By sliding them under the door and angling them in sequence he was able to obtain a view of the room. It was a large atrium with a domed and frescoed ceiling and a floor of clouded coral marble, overhung by a balcony which created a colonnade all around its edge. In the day, they would be lit by the light shining through the teardrop apertures in the walls, but at night they were cool and dark. Perfect cover.

Now that he had judged it was safe to dare, Keroki was able to ease open the door without a sound, lifting it on its hinges so that they would not whine. Once there was enough space to fit his head through, he peered out. Three guards, talking amongst themselves in the centre of the atrium, dressed in baggy silks of crimson and with nakata blades at their belts. The lanterns that hung from slender golden chains in the central space cast a dim and intimate illumination. The edges of the room were brightened with free-standing lamps of coiled brass, but it was not enough to dispel the patches of shadow.

Deciding that the guards could not see the doorway well enough to notice that it was slightly ajar, he slipped out and behind one of the broad pillars of the colonnade. His heartbeat had barely sped up at all with the proximity of danger; he trod with the calm ease of a jungle cat. The guards' voices echoed about the atrium as he glided from pillar to pillar, timing his crossings to when their talk would become particularly animated, or one of them would laugh, so as to cover even the slightest noise he might make. He knew how to move in such a way that he could evade the eye's natural tendency to be drawn to an object in motion, so that unless they were looking directly at him they would not detect him passing along the dim recesses of the cloisters.

His intention was to skirt the room and leave undetected through the door on the other side, which would bring him near to Barak Reki's bedchamber. In all probability he would have managed it had he not triggered the pressure plate that was hidden behind one of the pillars.

He felt the infinitesimal give in the stone beneath his foot, the fractional slide and click as he depressed it. His body froze, his pulse and breath going still.

Nothing happened.

He exhaled slowly. He was not foolish enough to think that trap had malfunctioned, but it appeared to be designed in such a way that it triggered when it was released. Standing on it merely primed the mechanism. Stepping off would activate it. Most people would not even have noticed the tiny shift that betrayed its presence; but Keroki was sharper than most people.

He cursed silently to himself. The colonnade had been left dark to tempt an intruder, and at its most inviting point a trap had been laid. Keroki's informer had known nothing about it. He should have realised that it was too easy.

Despite himself, a chill sweat began to form on his brow. He assessed his predicament. He was safely concealed from the guards, but he was also stuck here. Taking the weight of his foot from the pressure plate would undoubtedly not be pleasant for him. But what kind of trap was it? He could not imagine it would be anything fatal or overly dangerous, since this was a functional room and hence visited by people who would not know about the trap. Perhaps it was only rigged at night? Even so, he found it hard to believe that anyone would run the risk of accidentally killing a guest. An alarm, then; most probably a loud chime struck by a hammer that was cocked by putting weight on the pressure plate. But an alarm was just as fatal to him, for he had little chance of escaping alive if his presence was discovered.

The sweat inched down his cheek, and minutes crawled by against the background murmur of the guards. He had already wasted enough time negotiating the deadly false rooms in the tower; he could not afford to lose any more. Too soon the dawn would be upon them, and he had best be gone by then if he wanted to see another one.

He was still searching for an answer when the tone of the guards' voices warned him that they were ending their conversation. Then they fell silent, and he heard their soft footsteps heading away in different directions. It took him an instant to realise what they were doing.

They were splitting up and patrolling the colonnade.

He felt a dreadful flood of adrenaline, and mastered it. Years of brutal training had made him ruthlessly disciplined, and he knew when to take advantage of his body's reflexes and when to suppress them. Now was not the time for excitement. He needed to be calm, to think. And he had only seconds in which to do it.

When the guard found him, he was lying flat on his back and in such a way that the shadow of the pillar and the dim light combined to make him hard to see. The guard did not spot him until he was several feet away, and then he had to squint to be sure. It appeared to be a house servant by the garb, unconscious at the base of the pillar as if laid low by an intruder. And if the servant's foot happened to be still pressing down hard on the invisible pressure plate, then the guard was too surprised to notice.

He gave a peremptory whistle to his companions and leaned closer to investigate. Foolishly, he did not imagine any threat from the prone figure. He assumed that the threat had already passed on and left this poor servant in its wake. The assumption cost him his life.

Keroki twisted his body, bringing the small blowpipe to his mouth and firing the dart into the guard's throat. The poison was so fast-acting as to be nearly instantaneous, but even so, the man had a moment to let out a grunt of surprise before his vocal cords locked tight. By the time he had thought to draw his sword, the strength had left his body, and he was slumping. Keroki shifted to catch the falling guard's arm, pivoting on the foot which was still holding down the pressure plate. He pulled the man's weight so that he fell towards his killer, and Keroki muffled the sound of the impact with his own body. The guard was dead by the time Keroki pulled him onto the pressure plate. He sent a silent prayer to his deity Omecha that the mechanism was not especially sensitive, and then slipped his own foot off the plate.

There were no alarms.

The other two guards were calling in response to their companion's whistle now. Keroki slipped another dart into his blowpipe. Looking round the edge of the pillar, he saw one man starting across the atrium from the colonnade, and another in the shadows who had not reacted quite so decisively. Keroki aimed an expert shot and fired across the width of the chamber. The dart flitted invisibly past the first guard in the gloom and hit the man behind him, who slid to the floor with a groan. The sound was loud enough to make the remaining guard turn around. He saw his collapsed companion, swung back with his sword drawn, and took Keroki's third dart just below his eye. He managed a few seconds of defiant staggering before he, too, went limp and thumped to the ground hard enough to crack his skull.

Keroki stepped out from behind the pillar, glanced around the room, and clucked his tongue. The inside man who had provided the poison for his darts really did have a remarkable talent.

He dragged the corpse of the last guard behind the colonnade and used a piece of fabric to wipe away the smeared trail of blood and hair that he left behind him. Then, satisfied that the bodies would not be seen if anyone should casually enter the room, he headed onward. Dawn was pressing on him, and he still had to get back out through the trap-laden false rooms before the household awoke.

He found no more holes in his informer's knowledge. He negotiated the opulent corridors of the residence without another mishap, though twice he had to conceal himself to avoid a patrol of guards, and at one point he needed the assistance of a cleverly stashed key to allow him through a certain door that was always locked. Mirrored figures slunk alongside him in the silent corridors, where the cool air hung still as a dream, bereft of moisture. The night's hue became a deeper green as Neryn glided out from behind her larger sister and cast her full glow. Statues of Suran regarded him from spiked niches in the lacquered walls. Once a cat padded past, keeping to the corners, on its own mission of subterfuge.

There were no guards on the door of Barak Reki's bedchamber. His wife, so it was said, could not abide the idea of armed men so close as they slept. It was a foible that Keroki thought she would have cause to regret.

He put his hand to the door, resting it against the patterned surface, his other hand reaching for the blade of his knife. He got no further.

It was not the needle-bladed dagger that drove into his arm which truly stunned him, nor the hand that clamped around his mouth and drew his head roughly back. Simply, it was the fact that he had not heard them coming. He was tripped to the floor before he had a chance to react, and he hit the cold marble with enough force to take his breath away.

Now he found himself lying flat on his back once again, looking up at the ceiling, with a terrible numbness spreading like ice through his body. He tried to move, but his mind had been divorced from his muscles and his thoughts did not translate into action. Poison on the blade. Real panic filled him for the first time since childhood, a terror of paralysis that was raw and fresh and untested, and it pummelled him and made him want to scream.

Standing astride him in the darkness was a woman of almost supernatural beauty, with dusky skin and deep black hair, clad in a thin veil of a dress that was belted with silk. Keroki had purged all thoughts of lust from himself a long time ago, but even so a creature like this would have been enough to shatter his resolve, had the situation been different. But he felt far from ardour now.

She knelt down over him, straddling his waist with her hips. Delicately, she plucked the dagger from his arm and laid it aside, then brought her face close to his. Her breath smelt of desert flowers.

'Your friend with the poisons is outstanding, is he not?' she purred. 'Before I killed him I persuaded him to give me the one you are enjoying at the moment.' A slow smile, cruel and mesmerising, touched her lips. 'I thought perhaps I would handle this matter myself. No need to trouble Reki; there would be so many . . . repercussions. And besides,' she added, her voice dropping to a whisper, 'I like my prey alive. And I am so very hungry tonight.'

Keroki, believing himself to be in the clutches of some demon, tried anew to scream; but all he could force from his body was a whimper.

She laid a finger on his lips.

'Sssh,' she murmured. 'You will wake my husband.'

That was when Keroki finally realised who his assailant was. He had not recognised her at first, for he had never seen her face, and artistic renderings did not do her justice. Reki's wife. Asara.

She put her lips to his and sucked, until he felt something wrench free inside him and the rushing, bright flow of his essence came sparkling and glittering from his mouth into hers. His last thoughts as he felt the tidal pulses of his life retreating into darkness were strangely unselfish. He wondered what would be the fate of his land, the land that he loved although he had never known it till now, if a monster such as this stood at the right hand of the most powerful man in the desert.

FOUR

The unification of the Baraks of Tchom Rin was made official at mid-morning, in the western courtyard of the Governor of Muia's residence. It was a suitably grand venue for a day so momentous, set high up above the surrounding houses, protected by a wall whose top had been moulded into spiked cornices. The white flagstones and the pillars that ran around the edge of the interior were dazzling where the sunlight struck them. Verdant troughs of lush flowers were arranged around the central space; vines dangled through the wooden trellis that reached from the top of the pillars to the outside wall, forming a roof for the shaded portico. Steps went up to a dais at the western side, where the treaty was laid out, and beyond that it was possible to see to the cliffs where the enormous seated figure of Suran watched over proceedings with her odd-eyed gaze.

It was a remarkably sedate affair considering the importance of the occasion: merely a half-dozen speeches and a little pomp as the Baraks filed up with their retinues to sign the agreement. But then few people felt that this was truly a cause for celebration. Pride had been swallowed and old enmities grudgingly put aside, and the sting of it was bitter. Even as whole portions of Saramyr were overrun by the Weavers, even when Aberrants poured from the mountains to threaten their own homes, they had still squabbled and jostled between themselves for four years before finally accepting that they needed to band together for mutual survival in the face of the greater threat. It was not an easy matter to put their differences aside; they were buried deep in the grain.

One person who *was* celebrating was Mishani tu Koli. She stood near the back of the sparse gathering, holding a glass of chilled wine, as the last of the signatures were put to the treaty and Reki delivered the final speech. The rays of Nuki's eye slanted across the courtyard and the clean heat on her pale skin was pleasant and soothing. She felt lighter of spirit than she had in a long time. The treaty was completed, and her work was done here.

She had been in the desert almost a year in an ambassadorial role, for the Libera Dramach specifically and the western high families generally. Not that the time had darkened her complexion at all, but it had given her a taste for Tchom Rin fashion. Her dress was airier than she would have worn back home, a deep orange-brown like the last minutes of the sunset. Her black hair had been coiled and arranged with jewelled pins to fall in a multitude of braids down to the backs of her knees. She wore a dusky eye shadow, and small silver ear-ornaments. If not for her skin, she could have passed as a woman of the desert.

'Mishani,' said a soft voice in greeting. Mishani turned her head to see Asara standing next to her, watching the events on the dais draw to a close. As always, it took a fraction of a second to connect her with the Asara that she had known in the past. Even after all the time they had spent in each other's company trying to arrange the treaty that was being signed today, she could not reconcile this woman with the one who had been Kaiku's handmaiden. Something fundamental and instinctive in her rebelled against it, and had to be mastered by intellect. After all, they were physically *not the same.* Nothing by which she might recognise the old Asara existed in this new form.

Had she not known better, she would have said she was looking at a purebred Tchom Rin woman from the noblest desert stock. Her skin was tanned and flawless, her hair – blacker even than Mishani's – tied back in a simple ponytail that accentuated the elegant bones of her face, and drew attention to her almond-shaped eyes whose natural hue had been complemented by sea-toned eye shadow. Her pale blue robe was clasped at one shoulder with a brooch and clung to her figure, fluttering slightly in the warm breaths of wind that came from the west. She had dressed with the minimum of ostentation so as not to outshine her husband on this day, and yet all it served to do was to highlight how beautiful she really was.

But it was a false beauty. Mishani knew that, even if nobody else here did, except the Sister of the Red Order that observed from one side of the dais. Asara was an Aberrant, able to change her appearance to suit her desires. Her talent was unique among her kind, and Mishani was thankful that it was so. One of her was dangerous enough.

'You must be proud, Asara,' Mishani commented.

'Of Reki?' she appeared to consider this for a moment. 'I suppose I am. Let us just say I still find him interesting. He has come a long way since I met him.'

That was something of an understatement. Though they had never met, Mishani had heard accounts of Reki as an adolescent: bookish, timid, lacking the fire of his older sister the Empress. Yet when he returned to Jospa to take the title of Barak after his father's death, he had been a different person. Harder, more driven, ruthless in the application of his natural intelligence and cunning. And in four years he had not only made Blood Tanatsua into the strongest high family in the desert, but today he had succeeded in bringing the other families under his banner.

Mishani sipped her wine. 'You must be proud of yourself, also.'

'I do have a way of landing on my feet, don't I?' Asara smiled.

'You have heard, I suppose, about the events at Juraka?'

'Of course.' The Sister by the dais had told them both about it, having received the message from other Sisters who were present at the fall of the town.

'This treaty comes not a moment too soon,' Mishani commented. 'We cannot afford to be divided now.'

'You are optimistic, Mishani, if you think that the unification of the desert tribes will benefit the west,' Asara told her. 'They will not go to your aid.'

'No,' she agreed. 'But while the Weavers divert their resources in their attempts to conquer the desert, their full attention is not on us. And with this treaty and the collaboration of the desert Baraks, they might never take Tchom Rin.'

'Oh, they will, sooner or later,' Asara said, plucking a glass from a servant who was passing with a silver tray. 'They have the entire northern half of the continent and everything in the south-east outside of the desert. We hold the Southern Prefectures – barely – and Tchom Rin. We are encircled, and we have been on the defensive ever since this war began. Behind their battle lines, the Weavers have leisure to put into practice any scheme they can imagine. Like these . . . feya-kori.' She made a dismissive motion with her hand.

'I do not share your fatalism,' Mishani said. 'The Weavers are not in such a strong position as it would seem. Their very nature undermines their plans. Their territories are famine-struck because of the influence of their witch-stones, and we hold the greatest area of cropland on the continent. They must feed their armies, and their armies are carnivorous, and need a great deal of meat. Without crops, their livestock die, and their armies falter.'

'And what of your own crops?'

'We have enough to feed the Prefectures,' Mishani said. 'The fact that we are driven into a corner means we have enough food to go around; if we had the whole continent to take care of, we would be starving. And since the fall of Utraxxa, I am told the blight is lessened slightly.'

'Is that so?' Asara sounded surprised. This was recent news, and she had not heard it, wrapped up as she was in foiling the inevitable attempt on her husband's life. 'That implies that it may retreat altogether. That the land might heal itself if the witchstones were gone.'

'Indeed,' Mishani said. 'We can only hope.'

Mishani and Asara stood side by side as the speech ended and the nobles and their retinues mingled and talked among themselves. The usual machinations and powerplays seemed subdued now, although there was an unmistakable wariness in the courtyard. Asara made sure the man who sent last night's assassin knew she was looking at him, then stared coolly until he broke the gaze.

'Will you be travelling west again, now that the treaty is signed?' Asara asked Mishani, looking down over her shoulder at the diminutive noblewoman.

'I must,' Mishani replied. 'I have been away too long. There are others here who can take my place. Yugi needs my eyes and ears among the high families in the Prefectures.' In truth, she was reluctant to leave, though she could not deny a keen pang of homesickness. But the journey across the mountains would be dangerous, and the memories of her trip here were not pleasant.

'I almost forgot,' Asara said. 'I have a present for you. Wait here.'

She slipped away, and returned a few moments later with a slender black book, its cover inlaid in gold filigree that spelt out the title in curving pictograms of High Saramyrrhic.

Mishani's time in the courts of Axekami had taught her how to conceal her reactions, to keep her face a mask; but it would be rude not to let her delight show at such a gift. She took it from Asara with a broad smile of gratitude.

'Your mother's latest masterpiece,' Asara said. 'I thought you might like it. This is the first copy to reach the city.'

'How did you get it?' Mishani breathed, running her fingertips over the filigree.

Asara laughed. 'It is strange. We have shortages of so many things that cannot get through to us due to the war, and yet Muraki tu Koli's books seem to find their way everywhere.' Her laughter subsided, but there was still an amused glimmer in her eye. 'I know of a merchant who smuggles fine art and literature, most of which I suspect he steals from the Weaver-held territories where they have scant need of it. I asked him to look out for your mother's works.'

'I cannot thank you enough, Asara,' Mishani said, looking up.

'Consider it a fortuitously-timed reward for helping us achieve what has passed today,' Asara returned. 'At least now you will have something to read on your way home.'

Asara caught somebody's eye then, and excused herself to go and talk to them, leaving Mishani alone with the book. She stared at it for a long while without opening it, thinking about her mother. After a time, she left the courtyard unobtrusively and made her way back to her rooms. Her appetite for celebration had suddenly deserted her.

Reki and Asara made love in the master bedchamber of the Muia residence, mere feet from where Asara had killed a man the night before. The silver light of the lone moon Iridima drew gleaming lines along the contours of her sweat-moistened back as she rode him to completion, gasping murmurs of affirmation. After they both had peaked, she lay on his stomach, face to face with him as she idly twisted his hair through her fingers.

'We did it . . .' she said softly.

He nodded with a languid smile, still luxuriating in the satisfaction of the afterglow. She could feel his heart thump a syncopation to hers through his thin chest.

'We did it,' he echoed, raising himself up on his elbows to kiss her.

When he had laid his head back on the pillow, she resumed stroking his hair, her fingertips tracing the white streak amid the black, then down his cheek to where the deep scar ran from the side of his left eye to the tip of his cheekbone.

'I like this scar.'

'I know,' Reki said with a grin. 'You never leave it alone.'

'It is interesting to me,' she offered as an explanation. 'I do not scar.'

'Everybody scars,' he returned.

She let it drop, and for a long while she just looked at him, enjoying the heat of their bodies pressed together. He was no longer the boy she had seduced back in the Imperial Keep years ago. The loss of his father and sister, the sudden impact of responsibility upon him, had broken the chrysalis of adolescence and revealed the man inside. No longer able to hide from the world in books, nor under the repressive disapproval of Barak Goren or overshadowed by the vivacious Empress Laranya, he had been forced to cope and had surprised himself and everyone else with how well he had done so. The boy whom most had perceived as a weakling, while still not physically strong, had a fortitude of will beyond that which anybody had expected; and all his time spent in books had made him crafty and learned. His confidence in himself had multiplied rapidly, helped not least by the breathtaking woman who – to his bewilderment – had stayed with him through all his trials and supported him tirelessly. He was wondrously, madly in love with her. It was impossible not to be.

Of course, he still had no idea that she had murdered his sister Laranya and, by doing so, precipitated the death of his father Goren. Nobody knew that but Asara, and she, wisely, was not telling.

Blood Tanatsua had always been one of the strongest of the Tchom Rin high families, even after the slaughter in the Juwacha Pass that had claimed Barak Goren's life. The small advance force that had lost their lives there had not crippled the family, for the bulk of their armies had still been in Jospa, unable to respond fast enough to the news of Laranya's death. But under Reki's astute guidance, they had risen over the space of four years to the prime power in the desert.

It was not, however, all his doing. Circumstance had worked in his favour. The desert had remained a hard territory for the Weavers to conquer because the Aberrant predators that formed their army were not adapted to the sands and were at a great disadvantage there. But in recent months, a new type of Aberrant had appeared, one which might have been born for the desert, and it had begun decimating those territories near the mountains. Jospa, the seat of Blood Tanatsua, was in the deep desert and had yet to be threatened by this, but the other families had suddenly realised just how much danger they were in, and it was this that had spurred the sudden desire to unify. Blood Tanatsua had not been weakened by these attacks as their rivals had.

Then there was Asara. More than once a stout rival or an insurmountable obstacle to Reki's ascent had disappeared quietly and mysteriously. In the desert the use of assassination as a political tool was a little more overtly acceptable than in the west – hence their more thorough security – and Asara was the perfect assassin. Reki knew nothing of this: she took care to spend time away from him often, so that it would not occur to him that these instances of good fortune always coincided with her absences. Nor did he notice the occasional vanishing of a servant or a dancing-girl from their lands. He lived in ignorance of the nature of his wife; but then, he was far from the first man to ever do so.

'Reki . . .' Asara murmured.

'I recognise that tone,' he said.

She sighed and slid off him, lying on her back and looking up at the ceiling. He rolled onto his side, his hand on her smooth stomach, and kissed her softly on the neck.

'You are going away again,' he said.

She made a noise low in her throat to indicate he was correct. 'Reki, this will not just be for a week, or even several weeks,' she said. She felt him tense slightly through his fingers on her skin.

'How long?' he said, his voice tight.

'I do not know,' she replied. She rolled onto her side to face him; his hand slid over to her hip. 'Reki, I am not leaving you. Not in that way. I will be back.'

She could see his distress, though he fought to hide it from her. She even felt bad about it, and guilt was not something that Asara was used to feeling. Like it or not, this man had got under her skin in a way nobody but Kaiku ever had before. She could not have said if she loved him or not – she was too empty and hollow to find that emotion within herself – but she did not despise him, and that to her was as good as love considering that she secretly despised almost everyone.

'I have to go with Mishani to the Southern Prefectures. To Araka Jo,' she said.

'Why?' he asked, and in that one word was all the pain of the wound she had just dealt him.

'There is something I must do there.'

It was as blunt an answer as he had learned to expect from her. Her past was off-limits to him, and he had been forced to accept that before they married. Though she seemed little older than him, she had a wealth of knowledge and experience far beyond her years, and she forbade him to pry into how she had obtained it. It was a necessary stain on their relationship. Even Asara might be caught out with a lie if she had to invent a watertight past for her new self and maintain it over years of intimacy. The truth was, she was past her ninetieth harvest; but her body did not age, renewing itself constantly as long as it was fed with the lives of others. To admit that was to admit that she was Aberrant, and that would ruin everything she had worked to achieve even if it did not result in her immediate execution.

Reki was bitterly silent. After a few moments, she felt she had to give him something more.

'I made a deal, a long time ago. It is something that we both want, Reki.

But you must trust me when I tell you that you *cannot* know what it is, nor how much it means to me.' She ran a sculpted nail along his arm. 'You know I have secrets. I warned you that one day my past might affect our present.' Her fingers twined in between his and held his grip. 'Please,' she whispered. 'I know your frustration. But let me go without anger. You are my love.'

Tears were in her eyes now, and answering tears welled in his. He could not bear to see her cry, and Asara knew it. The tears were a calculated deceit; they melted him. He kissed her, and the sobs turned to panting, and they joined again with something like desperation, as if he could salve the grief in his breast by dousing it in her throes.

By the time they were spent, he had already resigned himself to sorrow. She could always make him do as she wished. She had his heart, even if sometimes he suspected that he did not have hers.

FIVE

Nuki's eye was rising in the east as the barge lumbered downstream, following the river Kerryn towards Axekami. Paddle-wheels churned the water, driven by the groaning and clanking mechanism deep in the swollen belly of the craft. Vents on either side seethed a heavy black smoke that tattered and dispersed in oily trails. Once, there had been wheelmen to drive the paddles, swart and muscular folk who would labour below decks during those times when the barge headed against the flow or when the current was not strong enough to carry it. But their day was passing; many of the vessels that plied the three rivers out of Axekami had replaced the wheelmen with contraptions of oil and brass, pistons and gears.

Kaiku stood on the foredeck, the morning wind stirring her hair, watching the land slide by with a sickened heart. She was no longer dressed in the attire of the Red Order; her clothes were simpler now, unflattering and tough, made for travelling in. Her face was clean of the Sisters' paint. The cares of the past decade had not seamed her skin, though they told in the bleakness of her gaze sometimes. And it was bleak now.

The world had lost its colour. The plains that stretched away to the horizon on either side were not the sun-washed yellow-green she remembered. Even in the pale light of the dawn, she could see that they had been drained of something, some indefinable element of life and growth. Now they were doleful, and the occasional trees that grew in copses seemed isolated in a dull emptiness. Even the hue of the river water was unsettlingly altered to her eyes: once a blue so deep it was almost purple, it now seemed greyer, its vigour robbed. In days gone by birds would have circled the barge and settled in its rigging in the vain hope that it was a fishing vessel; but here there was not a bird to be seen.

This is how it begins, she thought. *The slow death of our homeland. And we do not have the strength to prevent it.*

She looked to the west, along the river, and there she saw a dim smear on the horizon and realised what it must be. She had heard the tales from their spies and from the refugees who had made it to the Prefectures from the Weaver-held territories. But nothing could prepare her for the sight of what Axekami had become.

The once-glorious city was a louring fortress, shadowed under a gloomy veil of fumes. The great walls bristled with fire-cannons, and other devices of war which Kaiku had never seen before. A huge metal watchtower squatted outside the south-east gate, dominating the road and the river alike. Scaffolding and half-constructed buildings patched the exterior of the capital. Kaiku remembered how she had been thrilled as a child to see this place, the wonder of their civilisation, the cradle of thought and art and politics. She was appalled to find it turned so, a forbidding stronghold steeped in a dark miasma that drifted slowly up to sully the sky.

The shanties of the river nomads on the approach to the city proper were deserted, their stilt huts empty. The nomads were gone. No longer would they crowd the banks and squint suspiciously at the barges passing by, no longer would they sew or string beads or pole out into the river for fish. The roofs of their huts were collapsing, crushed by the slow grip of entropy, and the supports on their rotting jetties tilted as they sunk into the mud. The clatter and growl of the barge's mechanisms disappeared into the silence as it slid by.

'What's been done to this place?' murmured Phaeca, who had joined her on the foredeck while she had been lost in reverie.

Kaiku glanced at her companion, but did not reply. She always found it strange to see Phaeca bereft of the accoutrements of the Order. Perhaps it was because she was more used to seeing her with the make-up than without it, but Kaiku thought it suited her better when she was painted. It shifted the emphasis of her face favourably; when it was not there, she looked too thin, and forfeited some of her mystery and character. Still, what she lost she more than regained through her natural style. She had grown up in the River District of Axekami, and had a flamboyancy about her that Kaiku faintly envied. Her hair was always a masterpiece, her deep red locks twisted through elaborate arrangements of hair ornaments, here hanging in a tress, there coiled or bunched or teased into a curl. Her clothes were outrageous in comparison to Kaiku's, and though she had toned herself down today so as not to attract too much attention in the city, she still trod the thin line between elegance and gaudiness that characterised the fashions of the River District.

'Where is Nomoru?' Kaiku asked distractedly.

Phaeca made a noise that indicated she did not really care. Nomoru had, predictably, failed to endear herself to the Sister on their long journey from the Southern Prefectures. Even Phaeca, who was the soul of tolerance, had grown to dislike the scout's unremitting rudeness.

'Be aware,' Kaiku said after a time. 'The Weavers may be searching. Do not let your guard rest until we are out of the city again.' She looked again at the grim cloud seeping upward from the city and felt nausea roll in her stomach. 'And do not use your *kana* if you can possibly help it, except to hide yourself from their attention. It will draw them down onto us.'

'You're nervous, Kaiku,' Phaeca smiled. 'There's no need to remind me what to do; I know well enough.'

Kaiku gave her an apologetic look. Phaeca's ability to see through people was second only to Lucia's; she had an extraordinary talent for empathy. 'Of course I am nervous. What kind of fool would I be if I was not?'

'The kind of fool who volunteered for the mission in the first place,' Phaeca said dryly. Kaiku could not muster the humour to laugh. Her spirits had been too depressed by the ghastly shape of the unfamiliar city that loomed up before them.

The enormous stone prayer arch that had straddled the gate where the Kerryn flowed into the city was chiselled blank, the blessings gone. The grumbling, fuming barge took them steadily towards it. Kaiku feared to think what would be beyond that smooth maw, what she would find when they were swallowed.

If it had been a matter of preference, she would not have set foot on the barge at all. But the roads were carefully guarded by Weavers, and it was easier to slip into the city undetected at a crowded dock, so they had left their horses in a small town on the south bank of the Kerryn and taken this route. She despised every moment she spent aboard this craft with its mechanical core. It was a Weaver contraption, and Weavers created with no thought for consequence. She watched the greasy smoke venting from the barge with flat and desolate eyes.

Yet even they are not the real enemy, Kaiku reminded herself, *only puppets of a greater master.*

'Kaiku,' Phaeca murmured suddenly, a warning in her tone. 'Weavers.'

She had already sensed them, their consciousnesses purposeful as sharks, slipping beneath the surface of the world. They were hunting for Sisters, seeking any disturbance in the Weave that might indicate the presence of their most dangerous foes. The chances were slim that Kaiku and Phaeca would be noticed, but it was never wise to rely on chance. The Weavers' abilities had been unpredictable of late. Each witchstone they awakened increased their powers, and they had surprised the Red Order more than once. The feya-kori were only the latest example of that.

Phaeca and Kaiku sewed themselves into the Weave, blending with the background, becoming as inert to the Weavers' perception as the boards of the deck beneath their feet. Such a technique was second nature to them, and required only a small amount of concentration and a minuscule exertion, not enough even to trigger the darkening of the irises that came as a side-effect of *kana* usage. They stood together as the Weavers passed over them, unseeing, and faded away to search elsewhere.

The barge slid beneath the desecrated arch and into the city proper, and Kaiku felt her chest squeeze tight in anguish at the sight.

Axekami had *withered.* Where once the sun had beat down on thronging thoroughfares, on gardens and mosaic-addled plazas, on shining temple domes and imposing galleries and bathhouses, now it filtered onto a place that Kaiku would not have thought was the same city had it not been for the familiar layout of the streets. A funereal gloom hung over the scene, a product of something deeper than the smoke that shrouded Nuki's eye. It exuded from the buildings themselves, from their shuttered windows and discoloured walls: a sense of exhaustion, of resignation, of defeat. It bore down on the Sisters like a weight.

The temples had gone. Kaiku searched for them, seeking out points of recognition from long ago, and found that where once the gaudiest and grandest buildings had stood there were strange carapaces of metal, humped monstrosities that sprouted pipes and vast cogs and vents seeping fumes. As her gaze travelled up the hill to their right towards the Imperial Keep at the top, she saw that the stone and gold prayer gate which had once marked the entrance to the Imperial Quarter had been pulled down. Even the small shrines in the doorways of the riverside houses were gone, the wind-chimes taken away. Without the religious clutter that adorned their façades, they seemed hollow and abandoned.

To their left, the archipelago of the River District was a shell of its former brightness and vivacity. Kaiku heard Phaeca suck her breath over her teeth at the sight of what her home had become. The great temple of Panazu had been destroyed and left to ruin. The cathouses and narcotic dens were empty, and those few people who walked its narrow paths or poled boats between the splintered islands were drab and went with their eyes lowered. The bizarre and whimsical architecture of the houses had not changed, but now it seemed foolish rather than impressive, a folly like an old man's last, sad snatch at youth.

Kaiku heard the catch in Phaeca's throat as she spoke. 'I think I'll go and change,' she murmured. 'Even this dress is too much for a city so dour.'

Kaiku nodded. It was a wise enough decision, but she suspected it was really an excuse to retreat and compose herself. Phaeca's sensitivity to emotions was a double-edged sword, and she was undoubtedly feeling the oppressiveness of this place far more than Kaiku was. She departed hastily.

'Find Nomoru,' Kaiku said absently after her, and Phaeca made a noise in acknowledgement before she was gone.

By the time they reached the docks, the fug in the air was thick enough so that it was palpably unhealthy to breathe, and Kaiku felt dirty just standing in it. The streets were crowded around the warehouses. Barges and smaller craft unloaded at piers amid the hollering of foremen; carts and drays pulled by manxthwa creaked by, heaped with netted crates and barrels; merchants argued and haggled; scrawny cats wound in and out of the chaos in the hope of spying a rat or two. But for all the industry, there was no laughter, no raucousness: cries were limited to instructions and orders, and the men worked doggedly with their attention on what they were doing. Heads down, concentrating only on getting through their tasks, as if existence was an obstacle they had to surmount daily. They were simply enduring.

Nomoru joined them as they disembarked. There were formalities: a passenger register to be signed with false names, faked papers of identification to be shown, a search for weapons. An officer of the Blackguard asked them their business, and reminded them of several rules and regulations that they were to abide by: no private gatherings of more than five people, no icons or symbols of a religious nature to be displayed, a sunset curfew. Phaeca and Kaiku listened politely, half their attention on shielding themselves from the Weavers who lurked nearby and monitored the docks. Nomoru looked bored.

They found their contact in the Poor Quarter as arranged. Nomoru led them, having grown up among the endless gang warfare that consumed the shambolic, poverty-stricken alleyways of this section of Axekami. Even here, the change in the city was evident. As squalid as it was, its occupants had always been angry, their tempers quickly roused, railing against their conditions rather than meekly submitting to them; but now the alleyways were quiet and doors were kept closed. Those people that they saw were thin and starving. The famine was biting even in the capital, and as always, the underprivileged were the first to suffer.

The sight made Kaiku think of Tsata, with his alien views on her society, and she wondered what he would make of all this. The memory of him brought a twinge of sadness. He had almost entirely slipped her mind over the years, buried as she was in studying the ways of the Red Order under Cailin; but his influence had lasted, and she often found herself trying to think of things from his viewpoint to lend herself a measure of objectivity. It was because nobody questioned the way things were that the Empire was in this situation in the first place: the ingrained belief that society could not do without the Weavers had allowed them to wrest the Empire from the hands of those who created it. Tsata had helped her see that, but then he had left her, returning to his homeland to warn his people about what was happening in Saramyr. As they walked through the dereliction of the Poor Quarter, she wondered vaguely if he would ever come back.

Their contact lived on the second storey of a tumbledown building, and they had to climb a set of rickety steps propped up with makeshift kamako cane scaffolding to get to the door. Kaiku's uneasiness had grown during their journey. Distantly she could hear the rumble and clank of one of the Weavers' beetle-like buildings in the eerily subdued quiet. The atmosphere here was an effort to breathe and tasted foul. If it were not for the fact that she knew her body was subtly and instinctively neutralising the poisons she was inhaling, she would have worried what damage it might be doing to her. Gods, what must it be like to *live* in this miasma?

Nomoru struck the chime and the door was opened by a sallow, ill-looking man. His eyes widened in recognition as he saw the scout. After an awkward instant, they exchanged passwords and he let them inside. He took them into a threadbare room where tatty mats lay on the floor. Sliding doors were left half-open to expose cupboards of junk crockery and chipped ornaments, and thin veils were draped over the window-arches, obscuring the view and making the room dim. An imposing, shaven-headed figure had moved one of the veils aside a little and was peering out at the street below. As they entered, he let the veil fall and turned to face them. He was ugly, with thick lips and a squashed nose and a brow that fell in a natural scowl.

'Nomoru?' he said. 'Gods, I never thought I'd see *you* again. You haven't changed a bit.'

Nomoru shrugged without replying.

He looked at the Sisters. 'And you must be Kaiku and Phaeca then. Which is which?'

They introduced themselves properly, despite his informality, bowing in the correct manner for their relative social stations.

'Good,' he said. 'I imagine you've guessed me by now. Juto en Garika. And that's Lon in the doorway. There's more of us, but we don't gather here. For now, you deal with me and Lon, and that's all.'

Kaiku studied him closely. His accent and manner all bespoke a life in the Poor Quarter. Like many here, he had no family name, but he took in its place the name of his gang, and the Low Saramyrrhic *en* prefix meaning literally 'a part of'. His sheer physical presence was intimidating. Ordinarily, Kaiku would not have felt threatened by that – not now she was a Sister of the Red Order – but the shock of seeing how Axekami had fallen and the fact that she could not use her powers within its walls had combined to make her feel on edge.

He sat down cross-legged on a mat without inviting anyone else to, but Nomoru sat down anyway and the Sisters followed her lead. Lon slipped unobtrusively away. The room was haphazardly set out with no thought to aesthetics, which mildly offended Kaiku's highborn sensibilities, but she told herself not to be priggish. If this was as much as she had to deal with during her time in Axekami, she would count herself blessed by Shintu.

'Let's get to it, then,' Juto said. He cast a glance at the Sisters. 'First thing, though: we all know who you are and your particular . . . abilities.' Kaiku was pleased to note that the familiar note of disgust when referring to her Aberrant powers was absent in his tone. 'It'd be best if none of us mentioned them aloud. Plots and schemes come and go, but anyone catches a whiff of you and they'll trip over themselves to sell you to the Blackguard.' He caught Phaeca's glance towards the doorway. 'Lon knows. You can trust him. Nobody else, though.'

'Do you two know each other?' Phaeca asked, referring to Juto and Nomoru. Kaiku had been wondering the same thing ever since Juto had first spoken.

Juto grinned, exposing big, browned teeth. 'We don't forget our own.'

'You were part of the same gang?' Phaeca prompted her. Nomoru just gave her a sullen glare in reply.

'Some time ago now,' Juto said. 'We'd given her up.' His gaze flickered to Nomoru. 'I went looking for you. Tracked you to the Inker that did you last. He said you—'

'Juto!' she snapped suddenly, cutting him off. 'Not their business.'

His eyes blazed for a moment, and then an expression of dangerous calm settled on his face. 'You haven't been Nomoru en Garika for a long while,' he said with an unmistakable threat in his voice. 'You be careful how you speak to me.'

She just stared at him, a challenge in the set of her shoulders, a scrawny creature with hair in spiky tangles levelling with somebody twice her bulk. There was no fear in either of them.

'How are things in the city?' Kaiku asked, in an attempt to break the stalemate. It worked better than she intended, for Juto bellowed with laughter and shook his head.

'Were you wearing blinkers on the way here?' he asked in disbelief. 'The people are crushed. The Lord Protector has the city under his boot heel and he'll keep on grinding until all that's left is powder and bone. Axekami is the lucky recipient of most of the remaining food in the north-west and still hundreds starve to death every day. The only good thing I can say is that at least we don't have the nobles siphoning all the supplies as we would have done under the *magnificent* government of the Empire.' His sarcasm was obvious and scathing. 'The workers get the food. And the Blackguard and the Weavers' damned Aberrant army, of course; that goes without saying. But the Poor Quarter suffers as ever, because some of us would rather die than go to labour in those gods-cursed constructions they've built in place of our temples.'

'And what do they do in there?' Phaeca asked. The Sisters had never been able to establish the purpose of the Weavers' buildings in the cities.

Juto curled his lip. 'No idea. Each worker only knows his own task, and what all those tasks amount to, nobody seems to be able to work out. They don't seem to *produce* anything. That's the cursed mystery of the things.'

He got to his feet and went to the window-arch again, looking out past the veil. When he spoke again, it was more measured. 'Then there's this murk. Old men cough themselves to death, mothers miscarry, the sick don't get better and cuts gets infected. What kind of people take over a city and then poison their own well? What idiocy is that?'

The question did not seem directed at any of them, so they stayed silent. He turned around and leaned against the wall with his arms crossed. 'They've outlawed the gods,' he went on. 'All of them. They're crippling any chance of rebellion by not allowing us to gather and coordinate. That's the reason everybody thinks they took down the temples. But heart's blood, it doesn't make sense! Letting the people have their faith would keep them calm, *discourage* revolt.' He scratched his ear and snorted. 'Some say they just want us to know that we haven't any hope. I don't believe that. I just think they hate the gods. Either that, or they're afraid of them.'

'And has it worked?' Kaiku asked. 'Do you think Axekami could be persuaded to rise against their oppressors?'

Juto sat down again, shaking his head as he did so. 'You could march an army up to the gates and they wouldn't dare to open them. It's not only a matter of spirit, though there's little enough of that left. We're weak and sickly. The Blackguard are fed and strong and there's more of them each month because people join up all the time. They see their families dying and their principles fade like mist in the morning sun. Then you've got informers and spies, all working to fill their bellies. The Weavers seem to know everything, whether by the cursed powers they possess or by the folk who've sold themselves. As fast as rumours start spreading about a new leader there are rumours that they've died or disappeared. And on top of all that, there's the Aberrants. The Weavers just have to say the word and the streets are full of them.'

'What about Lucia?' Nomoru interjected. 'Could rouse them then. If Lucia came.'

'Lucia?' Juto mocked. 'I won't deny the people would welcome *anyone* in place of the Weavers, Aberrant or not, but a legendary figure's no good if they're not here. I won't believe she's real till I see her with my own eyes, and even then she'd have to be in golden armour with the gods themselves singing her praises from the skies before I'd count myself safe enough to turn on the Weavers.' His tone was becoming bitter now. 'You think you can even *get* to Axekami with an army? I don't. The Weavers would crush you before you got north of the Fault.'

Kaiku took the disappointment stoically. She had expected such a response anyway. It did not take someone of Phaeca's skills to divine that Yugi's faint hope of picking up the scent of revolt would be thwarted; Kaiku had guessed that as soon as they entered the city. She did not think he had seriously entertained the possibility anyway.

'Enough of our troubles,' said Juto, hunkering forward and giving them a smile that was more like a snarl. 'What about yours? How goes the battle in the south?'

'That is a puzzle,' Kaiku said, brushing her hair behind her ear. 'It is much as we left it almost a fortnight ago. The Weavers have occupied Juraka, but there has been no move to cross the river as yet, and the feya-kori seem to have disappeared.'

'Ah, there's the meat of it,' said Juto. 'The feya-kori.'

'They came from Axekami,' Phaeca said. 'Do you know where?'

'I have my suspicions,' Juto said. 'But I've been waiting for you to arrive so we can take a look.'

'When can we go?'

'Tonight,' he said. 'After curfew.'

Kaiku considered this for a moment, then a small frown crossed her brow. 'What exactly do the Blackguard do to enforce this curfew?'

Juto grinned nastily. 'They let the Aberrants out.'

SIX

The Lord Protector Avun tu Koli trod warily through the chambers of his home. Despite Kakre's assurances that he would not be harmed, he could never be even slightly at ease in the areas that the Weave-lord had taken to inhabiting. The upper levels of the Imperial Keep had become an asylum.

The great truncated pyramid stood atop a bluff on the crest of the highest hill in Axekami. It was a masterpiece of architecture, arguably still unsurpassed since the fourth Blood Emperor Huira tu Lilira began building it more than a thousand years ago. The complex sculptures of gold and bronze that swarmed across its tiered sides had stunned visitors for a millennium with their intricacy and power, while the four slender towers that stood at its corners, linked to the main body of the Keep by ornate bridges, were as impressive now as they were all that time ago.

Throughout history, there had always been large sections of the Keep that were empty, simply because no high family had enough members to fill a building so huge, nor needed a retinue so large as to take up the spare room. Avun wondered distastefully what his ancestors might make of things now that the new occupants had arrived, and the Keep was finally filled.

The route to the Sun Chamber took him through room after gloomy room of depravity and madness. Weavers gibbered and rocked in clusters, hunched together, their Masks iridescing subtly as they shared the ecstatic bliss of their unseen world. Walls were smeared in blood and excrement, or scrawled with arcane languages which had sprung whole from the subconscious of the author. Abstract mathematics and diagrams, nonsense mingling with insights of staggering genius, were scored into priceless marble pillars or daubed across artwork that was hundreds of years old. The flyblown corpse of a servant, his lips and jaw eaten away by a roaming dog, lay in the centre of a room surrounded by strange clay sculptures, each precisely a foot high. An exquisitely clean and orderly bathing-chamber was guarded by a lunatic Weaver who spent his time obsessively tracing the grains of the wooden floor with his eye, and who screamed and flailed at anyone who entered.

Yet among these horrors other Weavers shuffled and limped, younger ones who had not yet fallen prey to the insanity of their kind. They were Kakre's lieutenants and aides, an assortment of bizarre figures who maintained their own private domains amid the chaos of the upper levels. Their own depravities only emerged after Weaving, when the trauma of withdrawal would trigger their particular manias, which were as varied and repulsive as imagination would allow.

The Weavers had always been careful to conceal the true extent of the damage that their Masks did to them, hiding away their worst casualties in their mountain monasteries; but here the inexorable and terrifying erosion of their minds was appallingly obvious. At least, Avun thought, the famine had provided plenty of victims for those Weavers who liked to kill or rape. He tried not to waste his trained servants when he could help it, preferring to use peasants or townsfolk culled from the Poor Quarter, but the necessity of navigating through this bedlam to attend to the whims of the Weavers had claimed the lives of many of them. It seemed that Kakre's decree of protection extended only to Avun, and anyone else was fair game.

The Sun Chamber had once been beautiful. The roof was a dome of faded gold and green, with great petal-shaped windows following its contours down from the flamboyant boss at its centre. It was rare enough to see glass in Saramyr windows anyway, but these were magnificent creations of many different colours whose designs had caught the light of Nuki's eye in days past and shone down onto the enormous circular mosaic on the floor. Now the light was weak and grim and flat, and what it fell on made Avun wish for darkness.

Kakre had taken the Sun Chamber for his own, and decorated it with the products of his craft. In the three galleries of wood and gold, where in ancient times councils had stood to attend to a speaker or watch a performance on the floor below, malformed and disturbing shapes hid in the gloom. Avun tried not to think about them. Here was where Kakre came to display some of the appalling art he made in his chambers many levels below. Every creation here was sheathed in skin taken from men and women and beasts while they were still alive, arranged as if in audience.

They had been moved around since last time Avun visited, and he unconsciously sought out the figures that had stuck most in his mind: the hunched figure whose left side was stitched from the skin of a man and whose right side from a woman; the winged being whose feathers were made of tanned and leathery sinew; the shrieking man from whose gaping mouth another face peered. There were animals and birds too, and other things not humanoid, frames overlaid with patchwork epidermis of many shades to form strange geometric shapes, or forms so repellent to the eye that they could not be classified. The accumulation of torture and pain and terror this room represented was more than even a man as cold as Avun could bear to consider. The faint shrieks of the tormented Weavers in nearby rooms only served to disconcert him further.

The Weave-lord Kakre was there, of course. He seemed to have lapsed into some sort of trance, standing immobile just off-centre of the mosaic that covered the floor. Avun approached quietly, watching him for any sudden movements. He had learned to be careful around the Weave-lord of late.

Kakre's mental health had taken a dangerous slide in recent months, and Avun never quite knew where he stood with his master these days.

He studied the hunched figure before him. Like all his kind, the Weave-lord was clad in heavy, ragged robes sewn haphazardly together from all manner of materials – including hide and skin, in Kakre's case – and hung with ornaments: knucklebone strings and twists of hair and the like. The voluminous cowl partially covered the stretched, ghastly corpse-face that was his True Mask; the Mask concealed the even fouler visage beneath. Avun had never seen Kakre's real face, and never wished to.

'Kakre?' he prompted. The Weaver started a little and then slowly turned his dead face to the Lord Protector.

'You have come,' he wheezed, a faintly disorientated and dreamlike tone to his voice. Avun wondered whether he had accidentally interrupted Kakre's Weaving.

'You asked to see me,' Avun pointed out.

Kakre paused for a little too long, then shook himself and recovered from whatever befuddlement had been upon him. 'I did,' he said, more decisively. 'The feya-kori are ready once again. What is your advice?'

Avun regarded Kakre with his drowsy eyes. His permanent expression of disinterest belied a mind of uncommon ruthlessless. He did not look the part of the most important non-Weaver in Axekami, with his gaunt frame and balding pate, but appearances could deceive. He had rode the chaos of the Weavers' coup to make Koli the only high family to come out on top while the others went under, and in a short time had worked his way from being a mere figurehead for the Weavers – the human face of their reign – to becoming utterly invaluable to them.

'Zila,' he said.

'Zila?' Kakre repeated. 'Why not attack? Go straight for their core, straight for Saraku?'

'They expect you to move on and try to take the Sasako Bridge, to push towards their heartland from Juraka. Do not do so. Let them know we can harry them all along their front. They will be forced to divide their armies, not knowing where the next assault will come from. Attack Zila with the feya-kori, take it, and fortify.'

'What good will that do?' Kakre asked impatiently. 'To chip away at them one town at a time?'

'War is not conducted in a headlong charge, Kakre,' Avun said. 'I would have thought you had proved that yourselves by now. Remember the early days, Kakre? That first sweep across the country after taking Axekami? Your only strategy was to fling as many troops as possible at your targets, counting your numbers as unlimited. You were beaten back time and again by forces one tenth your size. Because they used *tactics*. They knew how to fight wars.' He raised an eyebrow. 'As do I.'

He could feel the hatred in Kakre's glare from behind the shadowed eyes of the Mask. It was necessary to remind the Weavers of his worth now and again, lest they forget, but it was a risky business. Kakre was apt to lose his temper, and the consequences for Avun were usually painful.

'Tell me the details,' Kakre said eventually, and Avun felt the tightness in his chest slacken a little. He began to explain, recalling troop locations and the size of armies from memory, laying out the plan for his master. And if, long ago, he might have felt a twinge of guilt at betraying his fellow man this way, he felt nothing of the sort now.

The beginning of the war had not gone at all the way the Weavers had wanted it to. They had envisioned a complete collapse of the Empire, allowing them to overwhelm the disorganised opposition with their superior numbers and suicidal troops. But they had known nothing of the Sisters. With the Red Order knitting themselves across the gap that the Weavers had left and protecting the nobles from the Weavers' influence, the high families put up an unexpectedly efficient resistance. They were quick to recognise that their opponent had no knowledge of military strategies, and capitalised on it. The Weavers had the advantage in numbers; but the skilful generals of the Empire, well-studied and practised in the art of war, made them pay dearly for every mile gained. In time, it became obvious that even the apparently endless armies of the Weavers could not support such losses, and the Empire began to counterattack.

That was when Avun stepped in to lend his services. The Weavers were not generals: they were erratic, most of them were borderline maniacs, and they had no interest in history and so had not learned its lessons. Avun was shrewd and clever, and under his direction the armies of the Weavers became suddenly far more effective, and the Empire's counterattack was battered into a stalemate.

But by then the advantage had been lost. The forces of the Empire had retreated to the Southern Prefectures and held it tenaciously. The damage caused by the Weavers' ineptitude and the vast areas that they now had to keep occupied meant that the Aberrant armies were stretched thin, and the breeding programmes would take years to catch up. Time was both on their side and against them, for every witchstone unearthed made the Weavers stronger, but it accelerated the blight that was killing the crops.

The Weavers were impatient. They were afraid of their armies starving. Avun could understand that. But what he could not understand was what method lay in the Weavers' madness. A desire to conquer he could appreciate. The thirst for power through Masks and witchstones he could sympathise with. But the witchstones were *causing* the blight. It had been a secret for so long, but only the blind could fail to see the connection now. What use was a poisoned land to the Weavers? Even they had to eat.

Kakre would provide no answers, Avun was sure of that. But for his part, as ever, he would seek advantage for himself and his own, and as long as he was Lord Protector he had leisure to manoeuvre. Let the other nobles fight their hopeless battle against the Weavers' tide. Avun had made betrayal a science, and it had served him well. When the time came, he would betray the Weavers too.

But for now, he spoke his soft words of advice, teaching Kakre the best way to kill those he had once counted as allies, while distantly there came the hoot and gibber of the inmates of the madhouse that surrounded him.

He found his wife in her chambers. It was hardly a surprise to him. She almost never left them.

Muraki tu Koli was quiet, pale and petite, an elegant ghost whose voice was rarely raised above a whisper. Her long black hair fell in an unadorned centre parting to either side of her face, and she wore an embroidered lilac gown and soft black slippers because she did not like the noise that shoes made on the hard *lach* floors of the Imperial Keep. Her quill was scratching as Avun entered the room, inking vertical chains of symbols on a paper scroll.

She appeared not to notice Avun. That, too, was hardly a surprise. She spent a great deal of her time in her fantasies, and when she was there it was as if the real world did not exist. She had once told him, back when they were in something approximating a normal marriage, that she could not tell what her hands were doing when she was in that fugue state, that they set down words with a will of their own, as if she were a medium and others were speaking through her. He did not pretend to understand. He had marvelled at his wife's gift back then. Now it infuriated him. She used it as a retreat, and more and more she refused to return.

'Is it going well?' he asked, referring to what she was writing. He did not need to ask the nature of it. It was a Nida-jan book. It always was.

She ignored the question while she finished off a line and then put down her quill and glanced at him briefly through her curtains of hair.

'Is it going well?' he asked again.

She nodded, but gave no more answer than that.

He sighed and took a seat nearby. Her writing room was small and stuffy and lantern-lit, with no windows to the outside, only small ornamental partitions on the top edge of the wall to provide a throughflow of air. It was exactly the opposite of the kind of open and sunny place she liked to work. She hated this room, and resented working here. Avun knew that, and she knew he did. She was martyring herself in protest at being forced to remain in Axekami when she wanted to be home in Mataxa Bay. In such indirect ways she expressed her displeasure to him.

Avun regarded her for a time. She was not looking at him, but was staring into the middle distance. 'Are you sure you would not be more comfortable in a larger room?' he asked at length.

'The local air does not agree with me,' she replied softly. 'Did your meeting with Kakre go well?'

He told her about what had been said, pleased to have something to converse about. Muraki usually took little interest in anything he did, but they could talk politics at least. Or rather, he could talk to *her* about it; she never gave anything back. But she listened. That was better than nothing.

He exhausted that topic and, feeling the conversation was going unusually well, he went on with a new one.

'This cannot continue, Muraki,' he said. 'Why are you so unhappy?'

'I am not unhappy,' she whispered.

'You have been unhappy for ten years!'

She was silent. Contradicting him twice in a row would be too much for her, and she was plainly lying anyway. He knew exactly why she was unhappy, and wanted to draw her into a discussion. She did not like confrontations.

'What can I do?' he said eventually, seeing that she was not rising to the bait.

'You can let me go back to Mataxa Bay,' she replied, meeting his eye at last. Then she broke his gaze and looked intently down at the paper before her, fearing she had gone too far.

But Avun was cold-blooded as a lizard and slow to anger. 'You know I cannot do that,' he said. 'You would be in danger there. You are the wife of the Lord Protector; there are many who could kill or kidnap you, use you as a bargaining chip against me.'

'Would you bargain for me, then?' she murmured. 'If I was captured?'

'Of course. You are my wife.'

'Indeed,' she said. 'But we have no love.' She glanced at him again, her face half-hidden by her hair. 'Would you sacrifice for me?'

'Of course,' he said again.

'Why?'

He gazed at her strangely. He could not see why she was finding this difficult to understand. 'Because you are my wife,' he repeated.

Muraki gave up. She had learned long ago that Avun's views on marriage and fatherhood had nothing to do with the finer points of emotion. Their own joining was one of political advantage, like many in Saramyr high society. There had been an element of attraction at the start, but that had long died, and they had been virtually strangers ever since.

Yet there was no possibility of annulment, even now, when the political advantage had become meaningless since the courts of the Empire had disbanded. She would not ask, and he would not countenance it. It would be shameful to him, a failure on his part. Just as he still refused to cut off Mishani from Blood Koli, even so long after he had driven her away. He would not admit to the dishonour of a wayward daughter, and yet he certainly would not reconcile with her.

'I am in the midst of writing,' she said after a time. 'Please let me finish.'

Avun took the dismissal with weary resignation. He got up from his seat and walked to the doorway. Once there he paused and looked back to where his wife was already freshening the ink on her quill.

'Will you *ever* finish?' he asked.

But she had already begun scratching her neat rows of pictograms, and she did not reply.

More than six hundred miles to the southeast, high in the Tchamil Mountains, Mishani was reading her mother's words.

She sat sheltered in the lee of a rock, wrapped in a heavy woollen cloak with the wind blowing her hair across her face. She had put it into one enormous braid for the journey, tied through with blue leather strips, but some errant fronds had escaped and now tormented her. She brushed them away behind her ears; they worked free and came back.

Asara was nearby, feeding the manxthwa while the others went off and hunted. They jostled for their muzzle bags, nudging her with their heads. Mishani was surprised to hear her laugh at their impatience, and she looked up from her book as Asara playfully berated one of them. A smile curved Mishani's lips. The manxthwa's drooping, ape-like faces made them look mournful and wise, but they were in reality docile and stupid. They stared at Asara in incomprehension before beginning to butt her again.

The manxthwa had carried them from Muia, across the rocky paths of the desert and up into the mountains. They were seven feet high at the shoulder, incredibly strong and tireless, with shaggy red-orange fur and knees that crooked backwards. Since their introduction to Saramyr, they had become the most popular mount and beast of burden in Tchom Rin. Their spatulate black hooves, wide and split, dealt with smooth or uneven ground just as easily, and spread the manxthwa's weight well enough for them to walk on the dunes; they had evolved in the snowy peaks of the arctic wastes where the ground was soft and treacherous. Though slow, they were nimble enough for narrow passes, they could go for days without rest as long as they were fed often, and they could survive extremes of heat without discomfort even beneath their thick pelts.

Once Asara had fixed on all their muzzle bags, she sat down next to Mishani and began rummaging in her pack. She was wearing furs, for winter at this altitude was cold even in Saramyr. Presently, she pulled out a small, round loaf of spicebread, tore it down the middle and offered one half to Mishani. Mishani put her book aside, accepted it with thanks, and the two of them ate companionably for a time, looking out across the hard, slate-coloured folds to where Mount Ariachtha rose in the south, its tip lost in cloud.

'You seem in high spirits,' Mishani remarked.

'Aren't you enjoying this?' Asara replied with a grin, knowing full well that Mishani hated it. She had been born a noble, and unlike Kaiku she disliked giving up the luxuries of her position.

'I can think of better ways to spend my day. But you seem glad of the journey.'

Asara lay back against the rock and took a bite of spicebread. It was baked with chopped fruit inside, and made a refreshingly sweet snack. 'I have been in the desert too long, I think,' she said. 'I need a little danger now and again. When you get to be ninety harvests, Mishani, you will know how jaded the old thrills can get; but risk is a drug that never gets dull.'

Mishani gave her an odd look. It was not like Asara to be so effusive. She usually avoided mention of her Aberrant abilities, even with those, like Mishani, who already knew about them. 'The gods grant I get to ninety harvests at all,' she said. 'Still, we have been fortunate so far. Our guides have kept us out of trouble. We may yet cross the mountains without running into anything unpleasant.'

'The Tchamil Mountains are a very big place, and I think there are not so many Aberrants out there as the Weavers would have us believe,' Asara said. 'But I was thinking of the danger at our destination.'

'That cannot be the only reason you chose to come with me,' said Mishani. 'There is danger enough in the desert.'

Asara gave her a wry smile. 'It is not the only reason,' she replied, and elaborated no more. Mishani knew better than to persist. Asara was extremely good at keeping secrets.

'Do you like my present?' she asked, out of nowhere.

Mishani picked up the book again and turned it in her hand. 'It is strange . . .' she said.

'Strange?'

Mishani nodded. 'My mother's books . . . have you ever read any?'

'One or two of her early works,' Asara said. 'She is very talented.'

'Her style has changed,' Mishani went on. 'I have noticed it over the previous few books. For one thing, she now produces much smaller tales, and has them printed faster, so that it seems a new Nida-jan book arrives every few months rather than every few years as before. But it is not only that . . .'

'I have heard they have become much more melancholy since your disagreement with your father,' Asara said. 'There are few that doubt she is expressing her own woe at your absence.'

Mishani felt tears suddenly prick at her eyes, and automatically fought them down. Her conditioning at the Imperial Court was too deep to allow her to show how Asara's comment affected her.

'It is not the subject but the content,' Mishani explained. 'Nida-jan has taken to poetry to express his sense of loss in his search for his absent son; but the poetry is ugly, and nonsensical in parts. Poetry was never her strong suit, but this is very crass.' She turned the book over again, as if she could find answers from another angle. 'And the books seem . . . hurried. She used to take such time over them, making every sentence exquisite. Now they seem hasty and haphazard in comparison.'

Asara chewed her spicebread thoughtfully. 'You think it reflects her situation,' she stated. 'Her writing became sad when you left. Now it has changed again and you do not know why.' She drew out a flask of warming wine and poured some for Mishani, who took it gratefully.

'I fear that something awful is happening to her,' Mishani admitted. 'And she is so far away.'

Asara settled herself next to Mishani again. 'May I offer you some advice?'

Mishani was not used to Asara being this friendly, but she saw no reason to refuse.

'Take wisdom from one who has been around a lot longer than you have,' Asara said. 'Do not always seek cause and effect. Your mother's words may not reflect her heart in the way you think. Forgive me for saying this, but you cannot help her. She is the wife of the most dreaded man in Saramyr. There is nothing you can do.'

'It is *because* there is nothing I can do that I lament,' Mishani replied. 'But you are right. I may be concerning myself over nothing.'

Asara was about to say something else when they heard the sound of scraping boots and voices from upwind, heralding the return of the guards and guides that were crossing the mountains with them.

'Be of good cheer,' Asara said, as she got up. 'In a few weeks you may be reunited with your friends. Surely that is something worth looking forward to?' Then she headed away to meet the men.

Mishani watched her go. She did not trust Asara an inch; her eagerness to travel west only made Mishani wonder what kind of business she had there. From what she knew of Asara's past, she had an unpleasant suspicion that it would be something to do with Kaiku.

SEVEN

The curfew in Axekami was heralded by an ululating wail from the Imperial Keep that set the teeth on edge and sawed at the nerves. Its source was the cause of much grim speculation among the people of the city. Some said it was the cry of a tormented spirit that the Weavers had trapped in one of the towers; others that it was a diabolical device used to summon the Aberrants from their slumber and to send them back when dawn came. But whatever the truth of it, there was no questioning that it was dreadful, both in itself and in what it represented. After the curfew, anyone found on the street who was not a Blackguard, a Nexus or a Weaver would be killed. There was no reasoning with the Aberrant predators, no pleas for clemency that would stay them in their purpose. They attacked on sight.

Juto cinched tight the straps on his boots and looked up to where the others waited by the doorway. They seemed nervous. Even Lon seemed nervous, and it had been his idea, his information that they were acting on tonight. Obviously wishing he had kept quiet about it now, Juto thought. Only Nomoru did not seem affected by the prevailing mood. She was slouched against one wall, checking the rifle she had borrowed, occasionally casting surly glances at the group in general. The newcomers had not been able to smuggle weapons into the city, so they were forced to use what was provided. Nomoru was clearly unhappy about it.

Juto stood up and studied the ragtag assembly. Gods, he was glad he was getting paid well for this. Patriotism, liberation, revolution: fools' games. Whatever agenda a man cared to operate under, Juto had found nothing put steel in the spine like the papery crinkle of Imperial shirets. If not for that, he would have been content to batten down and ride out the storm. But he needed money to survive in these hard times, and if there was one thing the forces of the old empire were not short of, it was money. As one of their best-placed informers in Axekami, he demanded his share of that wealth. It was unfortunate that sometimes he had to risk his neck in the interests of his continued employment, but that was the way of things.

They waited for the remnants of Nuki's light to draw away over the horizon, for the city's smoky shroud to choke the streets into darkness. Outside the silence was eerie. No footstep sounded, no cart creaked, no voices could be heard. Axekami was a tomb.

To break the silence, Juto suggested that Lon bring the newcomers up to date on events. 'And stop acting so gods-damned jumpy,' he added.

'Right, right,' Lon murmured, his eyes flickering over the assembled group. 'You all know the content of the communiqué I sent?'

'That's why we're here,' Phaeca replied. 'There was some confusion as to the author, though. Our information usually comes from Juto.'

Juto grinned, an expression which looked hideous on him coupled with his omnipresent scowl. 'Lon was very keen to claim the credit on this one,' he said. 'He wants to be sure I don't forget whose work it was when the money comes.'

'I was the one that saw them,' Lon protested in rough and ugly Low Saramyrrhic tones. He turned back to the sisters, as if seeking their support. 'And it was me who found out where they live as well.'

'Where they *live*?' Kaiku prompted, looking at Juto.

He nodded. 'That's where we're heading tonight. Out to the pall-pits.'

Kaiku's brow crinkled at the unfamiliar term.

'You'll see,' Juto promised, laughing.

'You said they lived there . . . ?' Phaeca inquired of Lon.

'I saw them. After they left Axekami and I sent you that message, after that they came *back*. After they'd been to Juraka.'

Kaiku did not trouble to ask how he knew about that. 'And you saw them?'

'I was right near the pall-pits. They bring a murk with them; it covers everything so you can't see, so they can move in secret. It covered the city, worse even than what we have now. But I was close enough; I saw them go to the pits. *Into* the pits.'

'There wasn't any . . . *murk* at Juraka,' Phaeca observed to Kaiku.

Kaiku shrugged. 'It would have hampered their own troops in Juraka. Perhaps they *wanted* us to see them. To let us know what we were up against.' She turned her attention back to Juto. 'And that is where we are going? These pall-pits?'

'Unless you have any other suggestions?' Juto replied.

'We will need to get close if we are to determine the veracity of Lon's information.'

'My lady, I can get you so close you can jump right in if the mood takes you.'

She let his irreverence slide off her. 'Have the feya-kori emerged again since you saw them return?' she asked Lon.

He shook his head and coughed ralingly into his fist.

Juto leaned out of the window and looked down into the street. A few lanterns burned in the depths of the houses, but none outside. Shadows were thickening. 'It's nearly time.' He turned back to them and gave them another of his nasty grins. 'Whatever gods you've got, pray to them now and hope they can still hear you in Axekami.'

The night was shockingly dark. With moonlight blanketed by the miasma that the city seethed, and without street lighting, it was difficult to see anything at all. What illumination there was came from the feeble candle-glow that leaked from the buildings of the Poor Quarter.

Juto took them up onto the flat roof of the building, which was cluttered with debris and bricks, and made them stop there while their eyes adjusted. For the Sisters, there was no such need: their *kana* modified their vision, without any conscious thought on their parts, until they could see as well as cats. They waited for the others to catch up.

Beyond the Poor Quarter the hillside was crowded with pinpricks of brightness, topped by the clustered windows of the Imperial Keep. It might have been possible to look on such a sight and imagine the Axekami of old, but even at night the Weavers' influence was evident. The streets were black and quiet where once they had teemed with people in the lanternlight, and around the city the Weavers' buildings were islands aglow in their own industry, a red illumination from within that seeped through slats and vents: the glare of the furnaces. They stood out like sores, angry coronas limning the surrounding buildings that they hid behind. The air tasted of metal, thick with corruption. It did not seem to bother the others, but the Sisters found it made them claustrophobic, penned in by the threat of suffocation.

'I'm worried, Kaiku,' Phaeca said quietly.

'As am I,' Kaiku replied.

'No I mean . . . about *them*.' She motioned with her head to indicate the others; they had drifted a little way apart from the group.

'Juto and Lon?'

'And Nomoru.'

'Nomoru?' Kaiku was surprised. 'Why?'

'There's something between them. Something they don't want to reveal to us.'

Kaiku was inclined to agree. While Cailin's teaching left her less and less time to see her friends, it brought her into closer contact with the other Sisters, and of them Phaeca was her natural ally in temperament. Through sharing the trials of the Red Order's apprenticeship, they had come to understand one another very well, and Kaiku knew better than to dismiss Phaeca's intuition where people were concerned.

'They used to be in a gang together,' Kaiku murmured. 'It could be anything.'

'They're not pleased to see Nomoru.'

'Who is?' Kaiku returned dryly.

'But Nomoru volunteered . . .'

'Which is entirely unlike her.'

'Exactly,' Phaeca said, clapping her fingertips against the heel of her other hand. 'They didn't know she was coming, but she knew that they would be here. There's a history between them, that much is certain. And it's Nomoru who has chosen to dredge it up.'

Kaiku sighed, rubbed the back of her neck. 'We must be careful.'

'You ready?' Juto said, walking over to them. 'We'd better go. It will take us most of the night.' Behind him, Lon was manhandling a plank into place with Nomoru's help, lowering it to form a bridge across the narrow alley to the next rooftop.

Juto caught Kaiku's gaze and smiled. 'We're not going down to street level until we don't have any other choice. Not scared of heights, are you?'

Lon scampered across the plank and secured the other side as they approached. Kaiku looked over the lip of the alleyway into the empty street below. Nothing moved.

'Get on with it,' Nomoru hissed.

Kaiku gave her a disdainful stare and stepped up onto the plank. It was thick and solid, wide enough so that she would have thought nothing of walking its length if it were not suspended above a bone-breaking drop. Taking careful steps, she crossed the alleyway and stepped past Lon onto the next rooftop, which was similarly flat. The others followed without mishap, and then Juto and Lon hefted the plank between them and went to the other side of the roof.

'There, that wasn't so bad, was it?' Juto grunted as he passed. 'We're great improvisers here in Poor Quarter.'

In that way, they began to head round the hill on its westward side. Juto's preparations were certainly thorough. Though most of the rooftops were not flat but made of patchy slate, he had mapped out a route that meant there was always one adjacent roof or balcony that they could use. It was circuitous and indirect, certainly, but caution was needed over speed, and his method did not require them to touch the ground for the greater portion of their journey. The buildings of the Poor Quarter were crowded close enough that it was often possible to jump the alleys without needing the plank, and they began to spot other people doing the same thing as them, passing by stealthily in the distance.

As they went, Juto explained how this kind of travel had evolved in response to the curfew, and was used all throughout the Poor Quarter, which was the only place in Axekami where there were enough flat roofs to make it viable.

'It's a sort of truce,' he murmured, as they darted quietly across another dark expanse littered with derelict shacks. Men idled there, watching them as they passed. 'There's people who live in these buildings who'd cut my throat in the daylight; but at night, they give us free passage, and our gang will do the same for them. We might be dirty bastards, but we'll be gods-damned if we'll let the Weavers imprison us in our own territory.'

'Could we not have got closer to the pall-pits during daylight, and gone from there?' Phaeca asked. 'We would not have had so far to travel then.'

Nomoru snorted a laugh. Juto's lips twitched in response.

'You don't know the Poor Quarter,' he said. 'Believe me, that dump where you met us was as close as any of our gang could safely get. The pall-pits aren't far; it's just slow going.'

And it got slower, for the Aberrant predators were appearing in numbers now. More and more often Juto froze as if in response to some signal, and they crept to the edge of their rooftop or balcony to see the dark, sleek shape of a shrilling loping through the street below, its soft pigeon-warble drifting up through the night to them. Eventually Kaiku realised that the clicks and taps that she had thought were the sounds of boards settling in the night were being made by the men and women who lounged on the rooftops: they were lookouts, communicating in code, warning each other when Aberrants were nearby. She found herself marvelling that such a disparate group of antagonists could be so united in purpose against a greater enemy. It was like the battle for the Fold, when the people of the Xarana Fault had joined against the Aberrant army. Perhaps Juto was wrong; perhaps there *was* hope for an uprising, if the folk of the Poor Quarter were willing to put aside their differences and resist their new despots.

Eventually they came to the great thoroughfare that delineated the western edge of the Poor Quarter. They rested on the rooftop, overlooking the wide street, a river of deep shadow separating them from the more affluent districts on the other side.

'That was the easy part,' said Juto, hunkering down close to them. 'From here on in we have to go through the streets. We have to be fast, and quiet; and *don't* fire your rifles unless you have absolutely no other choice. Understand?'

'Is that it over there?' Phaeca asked, looking west to where an infernal red glow leaked into the sky, underlighting plumes of slowly roiling smog.

'That's it,' Juto said. 'We're close. But it only takes one Aberrant to see us, and it's over. Now you all know about shrillings, right?'

'Echo location,' Nomoru said. 'Helps them see when it's too dark for their eyes. Only forward, though. Can't see behind them.'

'It's mostly shrillings we'll be dealing with, though there's skrendel out here too, and they're hard to spot. Not so dangerous, but they'll put up a racket if they see you. Maybe ghauregs, but they can't see too well without any light. Chichaws, feyns. Assorted other types.'

Kaiku felt a strange thrill. She and Tsata had christened those creatures, among others, back in the Xarana Fault; it made her feel unaccountably dislocated to hear those names used here, hundreds of miles away. She found herself in a fleeting recollection of the Tkiurathi man with whom she had shared that feral existence for a time. They had seemed sweeter days, somehow.

They slipped down to ground level via a series of unsteady ladders and balconies on the north side of the building, after checking that the thoroughfare was clear. Kaiku felt her pulse begin to accelerate as soon as she touched the street. Suddenly the rooftops seemed a haven which she was reluctant to forsake. She clutched the barrel of her rifle, but it gave scant comfort, for like her *kana* it was a weapon of last resort and more likely to cost their lives than to save them.

'Stay here,' Nomoru hissed to the group at large. 'I'll go ahead.'

Lon made a noise of protest, but before he could speak Juto grabbed her arm. 'You won't,' he said. 'We stick together.'

She shook him off, her thin face angry, eyes glittering. 'I'm a *scout*,' she snapped. 'Wait for my signal.' Then before he could say another word, she flitted across the thoroughfare and disappeared into the black slash of an alley.

Lon swore in frustration. Juto motioned the others back against the wall, and slid to the corner of the building where he could get a better view of anything approaching. The clicks and taps of the lookouts were fainter here, but Kaiku still had the distinct impression that Juto was listening to them keenly, keeping track of the beasts that stalked their streets.

Time passed, marked by the thump of Kaiku's heart. She glanced at Phaeca, who managed a wan smile of reassurance and clutched her hand briefly. The night was full of small movements: rats scuttled along, hugging close to the buildings; part of a wall would crumble in a soft patter of dust, seemingly of its own accord; a stone bounced into the street from a rooftop, making them jump in fright.

'Enough,' said Juto. 'She'll find us. Let's move. It's too dangerous to stay here.'

Nobody protested. They slipped out of the Poor Quarter and across the street, where they were swallowed up by the alleys on the other side.

Lon took the lead now, moving with a purpose. They hurried through the narrow ways that lay between the main thoroughfares, pausing at every corner, scrambling into cover at the slightest hint of motion. There were more lighted windows here, but they were shuttered tight and only a tiny glow fought through to brighten the night. No lookouts aided them now; each turning could bring them face to face with the beaklike muzzle of a shrilling. Periodically they would stop and listen for the telltale warbling that the creatures made, which might give them a few moments' warning; but that did nothing to counter the threat of the other Aberrants who prowled more silently. Kaiku found her hands trembling with adrenaline.

'Back! Back!' Lon was whispering suddenly, and they flattened against the wall. They were in the middle of a long and narrow lane between residential houses, façades blank and featureless without the shrines and votive ornaments that they used to display. Dead plants straggled from clay pots, poisoned by the atmosphere.

A soft trilling coming from the end of the alley. Lon looked in alarm the other way, but it was too far to run. Kaiku felt a sinking feeling in her stomach, and gripped her rifle hard enough to bleach her knuckles.

'Here!' Juto snapped, and they scrambled behind a set of stone steps that descended from the porch-front of a house. It was pitifully inadequate as a hiding place: the four of them could barely cram behind it. Then Kaiku saw what Juto was up to. There was a cross-hatched grille there, covering the opening to the house's basement. He was pulling at it frantically.

Phaeca drew her breath in over her teeth. She was peering down the alley, where the lithe shape of a shrilling was silhouetted against the lighter street. It paused, head swinging one way and then the other, deciding which way to go next. The seconds it took making up its mind were agony for the Sister, who was praying to all the gods at once that it should go on its way and leave them alone.

But the gods, if they heard her, were feeling malicious that day. It turned towards them, and into the alley.

'It's coming,' she warned.

Lon cursed. 'Get that grille off!' he urged Juto, who gave him a roundly offensive oath as a reply. He had given up trying to pull and was shaking it instead, trying to work it loose from its setting. He had made some progress, for the stone was crumbly and weak, but it was still firmly in place.

'How close?' he murmured.

'Close,' Phaeca replied.

'*How* close?' he hissed.

'I don't know!' she said. She had never been good at judging distances.

Kaiku began to look over the edge of the step, but Lon pulled her down, and Phaeca with her. 'It'll see you!'

The warbling they could hear was merely the lower end of the aural spectrum of the shrilling's calls, which rebounded from objects and were picked up and sorted by sense glands in their throat, in a manner analogous to that of bats. The Sisters had captured live specimens in the past and studied them well.

Juto had freed up the grille a little, but not enough. The warble of the shrilling was becoming louder. He shook the grille hard. It was breaking away the stone bit by bit, scraping out dust and tiny pebbles, but it was still not coming free.

'Sweet gods, come *on*,' he pleaded. The shrilling was almost upon them now, they could hear it, as if it were standing right beside them . . .

Phaeca grabbed his arm.

And they were still, all of them, like statues hunkered together. A moment later, the shrilling's head appeared, its long skull curving back to a bony crest, its sharp teeth bared beneath its rigid upper jaw. It came slowly forward, bringing its scaled, jaguar-like forequarters into view, and there it stopped, cooing softly, looking up the length of the lane.

The creature was mere feet away from where they crouched motionless in the shadow of the steps. They could see the rise and fall of its flanks, hear the hiss of its breath. They were paralysed, some ancient and primal biological response freezing them to the spot like a mouse in sight of a cat. It seemed ridiculous that the thing was *right in front of them* and it had not yet pounced.

But it did not see them. The darkness was too deep for its peripheral vision to pick them out, and its echo location system was too directional to detect them. At least, until it turned its head.

Still it did not move. The outsize sickle-claws of its forepaws tapped softly on the cobbles. Some animal intuition was pricking it, a sensation of being watched, of the nearness of other beings.

Go, Kaiku urged silently. They were close enough so that she could see the glistening black nexus-worm buried in its neck. *Heart's blood, go!*

She could sense Lon reaching for his dagger, moving slowly, slowly. She wanted to tell him to stop, but she dared not make a noise, fearing that even the movement of her lips or the disturbance of her exhaled breath would tip the balance here and bring the creature down upon them. Her *kana* was on a hair-trigger, coiled inside her, ready to burst free in an instant.

The shrilling padded onward.

Kaiku could barely believe it. They watched it go, prowling up the lane, its sinuous form exuding a deadly confidence, its tail dragging behind it. She thought it was a trick at first, and she kept thinking that right up until the point where the Aberrant turned out of the end of the lane and was lost from view.

They sagged with ragged sighs of relief.

'I think we all owe Shintu a year's worth of thanks for that one,' Phaeca murmured, invoking the trickster deity of luck.

Lon was chanting a mantra of swear-words that were lurid enough to make even Kaiku uncomfortable.

Juto, visibly rattled, got to his feet and kicked the grille he had been trying to loosen. It broke free and fell into the basement.

'Come on,' he said in disgust. 'The sooner we're out of this gods-damned place, the sooner I get paid.'

They came upon the pall-pits not long afterward.

Nomoru had still not returned, and Kaiku was worried despite herself. She did not like the surly scout – nobody liked her, as far as she could fathom, though she and Yugi did seem to have a tacit connection – but she had become used to her, enough so that her disappearance made Kaiku concerned for her well-being. Phaeca was more pragmatic: she was only hoping that Nomoru had not got herself caught or killed and alerted the enemy to their presence. But the Weavers seemed quiet now; in fact, there was a curious absence of them, for when Kaiku and the others first arrived in the city there had been periodic sweeps across the Weave to look for Sisters or other anomalies, and in the last few hours there had been none.

The pall-pits were set into the hillside at a slight angle, and from where the intruders hid at the edge of the housing district they could see the whole terrible scene. A great swathe of the city had been levelled to make space for the pits, and rubble still surrounded them, half-standing walls and split beams and spars of metal piled in heaps or leaning against each other to form bizarre and discomfiting sculptures of ruin.

Beyond the waste ground the disorder ceased: the pall-pits themselves were built with ruthless precision. They were two sets of concentric circles side by side, enclosed by a wall of metal. Each circle was stepped lower than the last as they progressed inward to the gaping holes at the centre, colossal black maws that exuded turgid, oily smoke in vast columns. Wide, smooth ramps led from the inner pits to their outer edges. The red light of furnaces blazed along the tiers, trapped behind grilles and slats and vents, painting the pits the colour of dirty blood. It sheened across a grimy warren of pipes.

They paused for a time in the shadow of the houses, surveying the cluttered waste ground. The glow from the pall-pits pushed back the darkness; they would be exposed when they broke out into the open. Lon was more nervous than ever now, glancing here and there, his fingers twitching as if playing some invisible instrument. He kept on choking back coughs, occasionally eliciting an annoyed glare from Juto.

'We'll never make it across that,' he murmured. Then, tangentially: 'Where *is* that *bitch?*'

Kaiku felt irritated that he should be abusing a companion of hers, no matter how disliked she was; it made her feel cheap and disloyal to tolerate it. 'Will you be quiet?' she hissed sharply, and he gave her a resentful glare and held his tongue.

'We'll make it,' Juto said, responding to Lon's first comment. 'The fog's coming. Let's wait a while.'

Juto was right. There was indeed a thickening in the air, the murk drifting down in veils too heavy to stay aloft. The rank taste in Kaiku's mouth that had been there since they had arrived in the city became more pronounced, an unhealthy metallic tang.

'Could have done with this earlier,' Juto observed, scrunching up his face.

'Does it happen often here? The fogs?' Phaeca asked.

'Once in a while. Not often. Seems we really do have Shintu on our side tonight.'

The haze sank into the streets quickly, concealing the pall-pits and turning the waste ground into a red mist, in which shadowy shapes hulked like the carcasses of wrecked ships. At Juto's signal, they scuttled out into the disconcerting light, running low towards a heap of rubble and rusty iron beams. They skidded into cover in a scramble of loose stones, and Juto was just scanning to be sure all was clear for their next run when Lon grabbed his arm.

'We can't go,' he whined.

'What?' Juto said. 'Why not?'

'The fog. It's the demons. It's the *demons!*'

A spasm of disgust passed across Juto's face. Lon was cringing, his eyes darting about.

'Don't be an idiot,' Juto snarled. 'It's just fog. It doesn't mean it's the feya-kori's doing.'

'It's the demons!' Lon cried, trailing off into a strangled whimper as

Juto grabbed him by the throat and pulled him closer, so that they were eye to eye.

'It's just fog,' he said menacingly. There was a moment when they held each other's gaze, and then Lon looked down and away. Juto released him. 'You're the one who knows the way into this place. Get moving, or I'll shoot you myself.'

With that, he broke cover, dragging Lon with him. The Sisters followed close on their heels. They charged through the dense red miasma, hid, looked around, ran again. Once Phaeca saw a dark shape lumbering at the limit of their vision, a mist-ghost that she swore was a ghaureg; but it did not appear again, and they had no choice but to go on. There would never be any better conditions for an infiltration.

Eventually they reached the wall of the pall-pits. It loomed out of the red fog before them, resolving into detail as they neared, a grotesque hybrid of stone and plates of metal. With Lon in the lead, they skirted round the curve of the wall, eyes straining for any sight of Aberrant guards in the swirling murk.

But fortune was with them once again: they reached Lon's secret entrance without being spotted. It was a square hole in the wall, where a panel had either come loose or been ripped off, hidden behind a pile of rubble and joists. Lon paused at it, looked pleadingly at Juto.

'It's the demons,' he whispered.

'Get inside!' Juto snapped, and they crawled through and into the pall-pits.

EIGHT

The murk was so heavy inside the pits that it was all Kaiku could do not to retch. Her eyes teared and became bloodshot, and her skin crawled. Her *kana* was ridding her body of the impurities she was breathing, and it was literally seeping out of her pores. She wanted nothing more than to be gone from here; but she had a task to complete, and there was no turning back now.

The tiers were mazed with huge pipes, or cut through with trenches. While it made picking their way to the centre a complicated task, it also kept them well hidden as long as they crouched. It was barely possible to see the next tier down anyway, and the pits themselves were only visible as a fierce red haze. They headed to the right side of one of the ramps that ran from the edge to the smoking abyss. While it would provide the most direct route, it was too exposed to travel on, and they found themselves wondering why it was so smooth and featureless when every other part of the pall-pits was so densely packed.

Lon knew his way, it seemed, however reluctant he was to follow it. He led them between bellowing furnaces that made the Sisters shy away; down steps of metal that clanked underneath their shoes; past slowly rotating cogs that rumbled threateningly. Kaiku had been near Weaver machinery before, but the din threatened to overwhelm her. She would have clapped her hands over her ears to shut it out, if she thought it would have done any good.

The murk seemed to be getting thicker as they descended, and with it a steadily growing sense of something . . . *other.* The Sisters exchanged a glance; they both felt it. Lon had not been lying: there were demons here. Even keeping their *kana* reined tightly, it was impossible not to register their presence in the Weave. It became more pronounced as they neared the centre of the pit; a vast and infantile malevolence, beyond human understanding, brooding in the depths. The feya-kori.

'They're here,' she said quietly.

'As promised,' Juto replied.

Phaeca was getting as jumpy as Lon now; Kaiku could see her out of the corner of her eye, starting violently whenever a swirl in the fog suggested the shape of an enemy. Despite her nausea and the fear of her surroundings, Kaiku was more experienced at this kind of thing than Phaeca was, and she held her nerve more steadily.

'Be calm, Phaeca,' she murmured. 'I will do the work. You have only to conceal me.'

'Gods, there's something wrong,' Phaeca replied, her angular face rendered sinister by the light. 'There's something wrong.'

'I know,' Kaiku replied. 'Let us do what we have to and be gone.'

They clambered down a ladder onto the lowest tier, and their surroundings opened out fractionally. There were fewer pipes here, only a few hulking metal chambers of some kind, and just visible across a short expanse of metallic flooring was a railing, beyond which a raging torrent of red smoke churned upward. The bellow of the furnaces all around the interior edge of the pit was deafening.

'Close enough for you?' Juto cried over the noise.

Kaiku gave him a look and disdained to respond. She walked to the railing, Phaeca trailing at her heels, and looked down. The smoke stung her eyes abominably. She blinked and turned away to Phaeca.

'Are you ready?'

Phaeca nodded.

'Then let us begin.'

They eased into the Weave together, subtle as a needle into satin.

This time, there was little of the euphoria that usually attended entry into the golden stitchwork of reality. Instead, a cold ugliness swamped the Sisters, emanating from all around, dimming the shine of the threads that sewed through their surroundings. The pall-pit before them was a black abyss of corruption, a dreadful tangle of fibres that sucked and boiled, concealing all within. Here in the Weave, the presence of the demons was more terrifying still: immense, dormant monstrosities just below the surface of their sight.

Dormant, and yet becoming less so. For now the Sisters realised that their growing awareness of the feya-kori had not been because they were getting nearer to their targets. It was because the demons were waking up.

'Oh, gods, Kaiku,' Phaeca said aloud.

((Stay with me)) came the reply across the Weave, phrased without words. *((We have time))*

Phaeca, despite her terror, did not falter. She knitted the Weave around them, blending them into its warp and weft, deadening the faint emanations of their presence. Kaiku was going to have to use her *kana* if they were to learn anything about the demons, and while she would make every effort to be as delicate as possible, it would still draw Weavers. Phaeca's job was to disguise them as best she could.

Kaiku fought to keep her composure amid the swelling awareness of the feya-kori. A part of her was sorting the implications of their situation even as she sent her *kana* into the pall-pit. The feya-kori could not have known they were here; they were not even using their powers to any appreciable degree when the murk began to descend. She refused to believe that the creatures were waking up in response to the Sisters' presence. Part of her thought that it was a trap, that the demons knew they were coming; but who could lay such a trap? Certainly not Lon, who was plainly terrified, and not Juto, who was in as much danger as all of them if the demons emerged before they had time to get away.

Nomoru?

She did not dare to think about it further. Gently, she subsumed her consciousness in the greasy plethora of the pall-pit. It cloyed and stroked at her, making her feel befouled. She ignored the discomfort and concentrated on reading the threads, following thousands of them at once, mapping the contours of their movements, picking them apart to understand their composure and purpose. She could feel Phaeca's presence behind her, brushing away her trail with consummate artistry. And in the depths, she could sense something massive stirring, and prayed it was only a murmur in the demon's sleep.

The belching smoke in the pall-pit was heavy with metals and poison. Kaiku set herself to tracing it, seeking out its source. She slid through vents, down black, churning pipes, spreading out across the city. Phaeca sent her a warning resonation, indicating that she would not be able to disguise Kaiku if she dispersed her *kana* so widely. Kaiku drew back, limited herself to following only a dozen or so routes. She felt suddenly irritated that she had been checked by her companion: she had a scent, and a suspicion was growing in her mind that she was eager to prove.

She followed it back to the factories, the grub-like buildings of the Weavers where men laboured, uncertain as to what they were producing. But Kaiku saw now. What they were producing was the smoke. It was piped from the buildings to the pall-pits, into a steam-driven system of gates and vents and airlocks and furnaces that regulated pressure and heat and refined the raw pollution into an even more concentrated form. And what ended up in the pall-pits was not like normal smoke.

It was *congealing.*

The awakening of the feya-kori was sudden and terrible. Kaiku felt the Weave bunch around her, drawing inward around the pall-pit, and a huge and baleful mind uncovered itself as if an eye had blinked open, drenching the Sisters in a wave of hostility. Kaiku pulled away, caring nothing for subtlety now, only wanting to escape the pall-pit before her *kana* became ensnared in the demon. She could not be sure whether they had noticed her or not, so minuscule was she to its attention; but their course was clear either way. They had to go. The smoke in the pit was thickening to a solid, and the feya-kori were coming.

She and Phaeca returned to themselves at the same moment. Perhaps seconds had passed in the world of human perception: Juto and Lon were still watching them expectantly. The Sisters twisted away from the barrier, their *kana*-reddened eyes wide in alarm, and in that instant a colossal arm of rank and foetid sludge reared out of the pall-pit behind them. Kaiku saw the horror on the faces of the two men, felt the sickening weight of inevitability as the arm descended . . .

It crashed down on the edge of the pall-pit, several metres to their right.

Kaiku did not even have time to feel relief that it had missed her. The need to escape was overwhelming. She could hear the hissing as the demon dripped and spattered over the metal, could sense the force of its presence emanating from the pall-pit. It was climbing out.

Juto and Lon had already turned to run, but they stopped still even as the Sisters did. Someone was blocking their escape.

Nomoru.

She stood at the foot of the ladder to the next tier, her rifle at her shoulder, trained on Lon. Thin and dishevelled as she was, the hateful expression on her face in the red light convinced them that hers was not a threat to be taken lightly. Juto's own rifle was up in a heartbeat, trained on the scout.

'What's this?' he demanded.

'Nomoru!' Kaiku cried. 'We have to get out of here!'

'Not him,' she said, tipping her head at Lon. 'The rest of you go.'

Behind them, a dreadful moan issued from the depths of the pit. The blunted arm-stump of the demon compressed as it took the weight of the body below. From the second pall-pit, away to their right, an echoing answer came.

'Heart's blood, Nomoru, we will all die here! Deal with this later!'

'Won't be a later,' she said, her voice steely calm, her tangled hair flapping around in the updrafts. 'Weavers and Aberrants everywhere. He knows.' She narrowed her eyes as she looked at Lon. 'Sold us out. Like he sold me out before.'

Kaiku went cold. Lon staggered, his knees suddenly going weak.

'Thought I didn't remember?' Nomoru called over the bellow of the furnaces. 'Thought I was too drugged on root to realise? You *gave* me to them.'

'Put it down, Nomoru!' Juto said through gritted teeth. 'Whatever you think he's done, if you fire that rifle, you'll be dead before he hits the ground.'

'Never thought you'd see me again, did you?' Nomoru continued, ignoring Juto, focused only on Lon. 'Didn't expect me back. Thought maybe you'd be able to get rid of me. At the same time you got rid of all the others. Juto included.'

'Nomoru . . .' Juto warned.

'Fixed the obstruction in my rifle,' she said to Lon. 'It'll fire now without blowing up and killing me. Thought you should know.'

'It didn't happen like that!' Lon cried. 'They came for *me!* I got away, but you were too drugged. You'd smoked too much! I never sold you.'

Phaeca jumped with a shriek as another of the feya-kori's massive arms crashed onto the lower tier of the pall-pit. Through the murk they could see the second one as an enormous silhouette, swelling from the ground as it pulled its body up. The position of the nearer demon's hand-stumps showed that it was clambering out to their right, far too close. At the bottom of the ramp which, they realised in a belated flash, was the the feya-kori's way in and out of the pit.

'Come on!' she shouted at Kaiku over the din. 'Let's go!'

'Not without her,' Kaiku replied, her hair lashing about her face.

'What do you care about *her?*' Phaeca howled.

'She is one of us,' Kaiku said simply.

'Put it down!' Juto roared, even as Lon tried again to explain to Nomoru what had happened that day, when she had been taken as an adolescent and brought to the Weave-lord Vyrrch, whom she had evaded for days before fortune allowed her to escape during the kidnapping of Lucia from the Imperial Keep.

'You want proof?' she said to Juto. 'Had to wait till I had proof. Went looking around. Weavers are hiding here. Waiting for his signal. He led us to them.'

'No, no!' Lon cringed, almost in tears. '*He* sold you! *He* did!'

He was pointing at Juto, whose face was a hideous rictus of anger. 'Why you gods-damned cur! You'd lie to save your own skin?'

'He's not lying,' Phaeca said.

'What do you know, you cursed she-Weaver?' he hollered over his shoulder.

'You're not a good liar. It's in your eyes,' she replied. 'He's telling the truth.'

A great, dreary moan rose from the pall-pit, and metal screeched as it took the strain of the demon beneath. Nomoru's gaze had moved from Lon for the first time, and was on Juto now. Kaiku dared not look away, but she could sense the massive shape of the feya-kori rising from the pall-pit over her shoulder, could smell its abominable stench.

'You?' Nomoru hissed.

Juto deliberated for an instant, then decided that pretence was not worth it any more. 'You were becoming a root addict, just like your mother. A liability. We could spare you, and it never hurts to be on the Weavers' good side.' He grinned. 'And since your friends over there can't use their powers without giving themselves away, and their rifles are useless like yours was, I think that gives me the advantage.' And with that, he squeezed the trigger and fired.

Kaiku did not even think. Time crushed to a treacly crawl. She was in the Weave before the ignition powder had sparked, was flashing across the distance between them before the ball had left the end of the barrel, and had caught it and torn it apart before it reached Nomoru.

She only just made it. The ball exploded a few inches from the side of Nomoru's face, peppering her in burning fragments of iron and lead. The shot that had fired from her gun towards Lon suffered no such intercession: it hit him dead centre in the forehead and blew out through the back of his head in a crimson spray.

Time snapped into rhythm again. Nomoru flailed backward into the ladder, her hand flying to her face, one side of which was a lashwork of blood. Lon fell to the ground. Juto looked shocked, unable to understand why his target was still on her feet. Then he turned to the Sisters in realisation.

And from above them, a doleful groan, and the Sisters looked up to see the feya-kori towering to their right, half-out of the pit, a slimy mass in the suggestion of a humanoid shape, with a mere bulge for its head in which two yellow orbs fizzed and blazed. Those eyes were turned upon them now.

'Gods,' Phaeca whispered. '*Run!*'

Nobody needed another prompt this time. Juto shoved Nomoru aside and clambered up the ladder and away; Nomoru scrambled after him in enraged pursuit, and the Sisters followed. They ran low, hiding themselves in the maze of obscuring pipes, shrinking under the dread regard of the demon. Nomoru was screaming at Juto, who was darting away ahead of them; she was still bent on revenge, apparently careless of the danger they were all in.

The feya-kori dragged its hindquarters out of the pall-pit, emerging from the column of red smoke, rising to its full height of forty feet at the shoulder. Its companion gave a cry, and it responded; then, with a slow and langourous movement, it swept one enormous arm down to crush the four little humans that fled from it.

They felt it coming, sensed the fog sucked away to either side as the stump came towards them, and they scattered. Nomoru threw herself beneath some enormous pressure chamber that was like a barrel of metal in a cradle; the Sisters flattened themselves against a rack of pipes; Juto ran on, seeking to outdistance the blow. The hand slapped down, spraying its acid vileness across the tier. It crashed into furnaces that buckled with the force and blasted steam and burning slag out in furious plumes. But its aim was poor, for they were hidden and it was only guessing where they were; though iron was bent and melted mere feet from Kaiku and Phaeca, they were unharmed.

The Weave was suddenly alive, heavy with activity. Nomoru had not been wrong: it was an ambush. Weavers were here, close by. Phaeca and Kaiku had not noticed them till now, since they were reining in their *kana* and the Weavers were hiding themselves. The Sisters knitted themselves into their surroundings, trying to become invisible to the searchers; but Kaiku's violent use of the Weave in saving Nomoru had given the game away, and they could not hide for long when the Weavers were on the scent.

Yet across it all was the huge and disorientating presence of the feya-kori, throwing the Weave into disarray. They were simply too massive to work around; they influenced everything with an overwhelming force, confusing the Weavers and the Sisters equally.

The Sisters did not dare to move. They could feel the feya-kori searching for them, like a piqued child looking for ants to squash, its gaze sweeping the pall-pits. Kaiku's heart pounded in an agony of expectation.

Then she saw Juto, spotted him through the buckled pipes before them. He was climbing up to the next tier, still running from the demon. And there at the top of the steps Kaiku saw a pair of Weavers, their Masks turning as they scanned for their quarries. If there had been any doubt as to Nomoru's story, it was dispelled by the sight of Juto heading up towards them, hailing them as he went.

The feya-kori lumbered past them to their right, its steps accompanied by a shriek of metal as it stamped the landscape of the pall-pit flat. It had stepped off the ramp and onto the tiers. Heading for Juto.

He looked back in alarm, clambered up the last of the stairs so he was standing near the Weavers. It was evident that he thought it would provide some kind of sanctuary. He was wrong. The feya-kori's stump crashed down onto him in a geyser of sludge, turning Juto and the Weavers alike into burning pulp.

The Weavers' death-cry rolled across the Weave like thunder. Kaiku and Phaeca used its wake to dig themselves deeper into concealment, evading the frustrated minds that searched for them. The Weavers were distressed by the loss of two of their number. Kaiku found strength in that. She remembered Lon's reaction to the descending fog, and Juto's strange and mistaken certainty that it was nothing to do with the feya-kori. Matching that with the circumstances of the Weaver's ambush, she could only draw one conclusion. Neither the men who had betrayed them nor the Weavers who lay in wait had known that the demons were going to emerge.

Still they did not dare to move. They could sense the feya-kori waiting for them to show themselves. The Weavers had turned their attention to it now, lulling it, cajoling it in some fashion that Kaiku did not understand. After an agonising minute, the Sisters heard it turn and climb back onto the ramp. Kaiku dared a glimpse through the piping at their back, and saw it retreating into the red smoke. The second demon was visible as a ghostly blur beyond it. They were heading up the ramp, towards the Emperor's Road, a wide thoroughfare that led to the west gate. Gradually, the stench of their presence began to diminish, and with it their violent influence on the Weave.

'We have to go,' Kaiku said. If they did not take advantage of the Weavers' disarray now, it would be too late.

Phaeca was shivering, her pupils pinpricks in her red irises. She jumped at Kaiku's touch, startled back into the real world. Kaiku repeated herself, and Phaeca nodded tersely. They got to their feet and hurried to where Nomoru had hidden; but when they arrived, there was no sign of her, except for a rusty spattering of bloodstains.

'She can take care of herself,' Phaeca murmured. When Kaiku hesitated, her companion gripped her arm hard. 'She *can*, Kaiku. It's us they're after. She's safer on her own.'

Kaiku realised that they were still carrying their rifles, and she threw hers aside. She would not dare to fire it after what Juto had said. Phaeca did the same.

The steps that Juto had climbed had been melted by the touch of the demon, so they headed around the tier to find another way up. Without a guide, their path was tortuous, and they found dead-ends more often than not. As the demons retreated, the Weavers were returning to their search in earnest, but the Sisters were harder to find now that they had moved on. It was not only the Weavers they had to worry about, however: through a break in the miasma they spotted the tall, black-robed shape of a Nexus on a higher tier, and that meant there were Aberrants hunting for them too.

But the feya-kori's fog worked in their favour. As foul as it was, it was keeping them hidden. They made their way up two tiers in quick succession without encountering anything, and with distance the Weaver's probing grew less accurate.

Kaiku gave her companion a nervous glance. In the red light, without her make-up and dressed in dowdy peasant clothes, she barely recognised her friend. Nor did she recognise the expression of abject terror on her face. Kaiku, frightened as she was, had been hunted before, and she had survived then as she was determined to survive now. But this was new to Phaeca, and her talent for empathy made her mentally frail. The unrelenting expectation of running into a Weaver or an Aberrant – both of which would result in an excruciating death – was pushing her into the edge of something like shock. Her Weaving was suffering too, becoming clumsy and distracted; she was not disguising herself well.

Kaiku grabbed her suddenly, pulling her aside into the niche between two sets of pipes. She was only just fast enough. Her eyesight was better than the ghaureg's, and she had spotted its silhouette in the mist before it had registered hers. Kaiku clutched her friend close to her as the massive Aberrant trod slowly towards them, then on and past, leaving only a fleeting glimpse of a shaggy, muscular body and oversized jaws packed with teeth. Phaeca's breath fluttered as she released it, and Kaiku saw that her eyes were squeezed tightly shut.

'We will get out of this,' she whispered. 'Trust me.'

Phaeca managed a nod, her red hair falling untidily across her face. Kaiku brushed it back, unconvinced.

'*Trust* me,' she repeated with a smile, and through her fear she actually felt confident. They would not die here. She would see to that, even if she had to take on every Weaver in the area.

She pulled Phaeca into motion, and they slipped away in the direction the ghaureg had come from. The air crawled with the attention of the Weavers, the threads of the Weave humming with their resonance. They were sending vibrations between themselves, throwing a net for the others to catch and hold, hoping that the Sisters' presence would interfere with the pattern. It was a technique Kaiku had never seen before: ineffective, to be certain, but it meant that the Weavers had begun devising ways of working together, and that was dangerous.

The Sisters cringed as something jumped across the aisle right in front of them, a shadow darting out of the murk and away. They froze, but it did not come back; it had not seen them. Phaeca was a wreck after that, but Kaiku urged her up another set of steps and onto a higher tier. They were hopelessly lost, navigating only by the brighter glow in the mist that was the pall-pit's centre. The plaintive wail of the feya-kori came to them distantly.

Kaiku said a quick prayer to Shintu – she could not decide whether he was on their side or not tonight, but with what she knew of the god of fortune it was probably both and neither – and an instant later she turned a corner and almost ran into the outer wall of the pit.

She blinked in surprise.

'It's the wall . . .' Phaeca said, a slowly dawning hope in her voice.

Kaiku gave her a companionable squeeze on the arm. 'See? Have faith.' She looked up at it. It was only nine feet high. Scalable. They would not have to waste time looking for the way in that Lon had provided for them.

'Help me up,' Kaiku said. Phaeca glanced around, seeing only the swirling mist – which was gradually beginning to lift with the departure of the demons – and the dark bulk of the Weaver contraptions that hummed and tapped. Convinced that there was nothing immediately nearby, she made a stirrup with her hands for Kaiku to step into. Kaiku boosted herself up onto the wall, and Phaeca jumped as her friend unexpectedly shrieked. Her fingers came loose and Kaiku fell back down, landed on her heels and collapsed onto her back. She scrambled to her feet, and her forearms were running with blood.

Phaeca was frantic. The Weavers' attention had devolved upon them suddenly, drawn by the scream.

'Again,' Kaiku said through gritted teeth.

'But it's—'

'Again!'

For she knew that her cry had given them away, and if they did not get out of there now they were not getting out at all. Phaeca hurriedly knitted her fingers again and Kaiku threw herself up before her instinct for self-preservation could stop her. The thin bladed fins atop the wall cut into her arms in a dozen different places, slicing across the existing cuts, bringing tears to her eyes. Her *kana* was racing to repair the damage, awakening without her volition; she forced it down, for it would bring the Weavers more surely than her scream had. She lifted her weight, driving the blades deeper into her flesh, tiny razors that ribboned her skin agonisingly. She got one foot to the top of the wall, holding her body clear, and then she stood in one convulsive movement. The blades slid clear of her, and the pain was so exquisite that she almost fainted.

'Kaiku!'

It was Phaeca's cry that brought her back from the brink. She staggered, and the blades cut through the sole of her boot and pricked into her heel. With a moan, she bent down, holding her arm out, and only then did she catch sight of the thing thumping towards Phaeca from the right. It was a feyn, an awful collision between a bear and a lizard, with the worst features of each. Phaeca's expression was desperate, frantic: she saw Kaiku leaning down and she jumped. Kaiku braced just in time, her adrenaline pumping, and she caught Phaeca and hauled her up and over the wall. Phaeca's legs dragged across the blades as she went, carving through her trousers and darkening them in red, but she somehow got them under her again in time for Kaiku to drop her over the other side of the wall.

Kaiku had one last glimpse of the enraged monstrosity before she pulled her foot free and jumped down next to Phaeca, who was picking herself up, tears blurring her eyes. She was whimpering; Kaiku, whose wounds were much worse, was silent. They staggered across the waste ground towards the city, and the fog swallowed them, leaving the fruitless questing of the Weavers behind them like the buzzing of angry wasps.

Kaiku did not remember the journey back to the Poor Quarter, and the sanctuary of the rooftops. She did not know what Phaeca said to the men that they found there. She remembered rough faces and an ugly dialect, questions which frightened her; and then dirty bandages, mummifying her arms and enwrapping her feet. They were little more than strips of cloth. At some point her ability to suppress her *kana* had slipped: she could feel her body healing itself restlessly.

She never exactly lost consciousness, but she slipped out of the world for a time, and when she came back to it she was in a bare room, and a grey dawn was brightening outside. Her head was on Phaeca's breast, and she was being held like a baby. Her arms burned. She became aware that Phaeca was Weaving, concealing the activity within Kaiku's body as the power inside her repaired the damage done to its host. She felt hollow, as if there was a vacuum in her veins where the lost blood should be. But she was alive.

'Kaiku?' Phaeca's voice came simultaneously from her mouth and reverberantly though her breastbone.

'I am here,' she said.

There was a silence for a time. 'You faded away for a while.'

'It takes more than that to kill a Sister,' she replied, with a faint chuckle that hurt too much to continue. Then, because the bravado felt good, she added: 'I told you to trust me.'

'You did,' Phaeca agreed.

Kaiku swallowed against a dry throat. 'Where are we?'

'The building belongs to a gang. I don't know their name.'

'Are we prisoners?'

'No.'

'Not even . . . did they see our eyes?'

'Of course,' Phaeca said. 'They know we're Aberrants. I could scarcely conceal it from them.'

Kaiku sat up slowly and felt lightheaded. Phaeca put out a hand to help her, but Kaiku waved her off. She steadied herself, took a few breaths, and raked her tawny hair back.

'What will they do? What did you tell them?'

'I told them the truth,' said Phaeca simply. 'What they will do is up to them. We're in no state to do anything about it.'

Kaiku frowned. 'You are very calm.'

'Should I be scared of *men*? After what we saw in the pall-pits?' Phaeca's face was wry. 'I think they already knew of us. I believe they believed me. Aberrants are the least of their worries here in the Poor Quarter. And now we are not the scapegoat for all the world's ills, people like these have found somewhere new to put their hate.'

Kaiku looked around the room. It smelt of mildew. The wooden walls were greened with mould, and the beams were dank. A few dirty pillows were thrown in one corner, and a heavy drape hung across the doorway. No lantern burned here; they must have been sitting in the dark.

Kaiku noticed then the bandages around her friend's legs, beneath the bloodied tatters of her trousers. 'Spirits, Phaeca, you're hurt too.' She remembered what had happened as she said it.

'Not as badly as you were,' she replied, and there was something in her eyes, some depth of gratitude that words were inadequate to express. She looked away. 'I'll deal with it later. Until then, you rest.'

Kaiku sagged, and Phaeca put her arm round her friend again, letting her rest her head. 'I am tired,' Kaiku murmured.

They heard footsteps, and the drape was pulled back. Kaiku did not even rouse herself from Phaeca; her muscles were too heavy. Two men came in: one was very tall and thickly bearded; the other had shaggy brown hair and a rugged, pitted face, and when he spoke Kaiku saw that his teeth were made of brass.

'We've been talking,' he said, without introduction or preamble.

Phaeca looked at him squarely. 'And what have you decided?'

The brass-toothed man squatted down in front of them. 'We've decided that you look like you need a hand.'

NINE

Yugi tu Xamata, leader of the Libera Dramach, awoke in his cell at Araka Jo to find Lucia standing at the window, looking out onto the lake. His head was thick with amaxa root. His hookah stood cold in the corner, but the sharp scent remained in the air, evidence of another night of over-indulgence. He sat up on his sleeping-mat, the blanket falling away from his bare shoulders. It was chilly in winter at these altitudes, and there was no glass in the windows, but he had been burning up with narcotic fever last night.

He blinked, frowning, and squinted at Lucia. Whether by a trick of the morning light or his own mind, she looked ethereal, her slender form transparent, her thin white-and-gold dress a veil. Yugi had never known Lucia's mother, but he was told that she resembled Anais strongly in her petite, pretty features and the pale blonde colour of her hair. But there the similarity ended: the hair was cut short and boyish, revealing the appallingly trenched and rucked scar-flesh at the back of her neck, and her light blue eyes told a story that nobody else could share. She was eighteen harvests of age, and the child he had watched grow had gone, replaced by something beautiful and alien.

He coughed to clear his throat of the taste of last night's excesses. When Lucia did not react, he dispensed with politeness. 'What are you doing here, Lucia?'

After a long moment, Lucia turned her head to him. 'Hmm?'

'You're in my room,' Yugi said patiently. 'Why are you in my room?'

She seemed puzzled by that for a moment. She glanced around the cell as if wondering how she got there: great blocks of weathered white stone draped with simple hangings, a wicker mat covering the floor, a small table, a chest, other odds and ends scattered about. Then she gave him a smile as innocent as an infant's.

'We want to see you.'

'We?'

'Cailin and I.'

Yugi sighed and sat up further, the blankets sloughing to his waist. His upper torso was almost smooth of hair, but several long cicatrices tracked over the skin, old wounds from long ago. He did not like the way she phrased her words, the implication that Lucia and Cailin had decided to summon him together. Cailin was held in altogether too high a regard by this girl, and that was dangerous. He knew what Cailin was like.

'What's this about?'

'News from Axekami,' she said, and did not elaborate. 'We'll be by the lake.'

Yugi decided not to bother asking her any more questions. 'I'll come and find you.'

Lucia gave him another smile, and turned to leave. As she did so, the hookah overturned with a crash, spilling ash and charred root onto the mat. Yugi jumped.

'He doesn't like the way you make his room smell,' Lucia said, and then went out through the drape.

Yugi got up and dressed himself. The cold chased off the tatters of sleep. He set the hookah back upright and tidied the ash away, annoyed. The spirit had never managed anything quite so violent before. He could sense it there, a tall black smudge just on the edge of his vision, but he knew that if he looked at it directly, it would be gone. It was a peripheral thing, seen only from the corner of the eye. A weak ghost, like the hundreds of others that haunted Araka Jo, clots of congealed memory that dogged the present.

Outside his cell was a walkway of the same ubiquitous white stone that formed the bones of the complex. On one side was a long row of cells like his own, simple rectangular doorways; the other was open to the view.

It was something to wake up to, he had to admit that, even though the dregs of last night were somewhat blunting his appreciation. The ground sloped down to a wide road, again of white and aged stone, and beyond that it swept up, to where the scalloped slate roofs of the temples showed among the jagged green treetops. The swoop and swell of the mountainside hid dozens of them, all linked by dirt paths or flagged walkways that wound through the pines and kijis and kamakas. They were solid and crude in comparison to modern temples, but their form gave them a gravity that was primal and brooding, and the bas-relief friezes on their entablatures depicted scenes heavy with forgotten myth.

Araka Jo was ancient and in partial ruin, several of the temples little more than outlines of their original floorplan surrounded by mossy rubble. Despite the unfamiliar presence of inhabitants again – it had become the Libera Dramach's home these past few years – it still felt as if they were intruders there. The spirits never let them forget it.

There was a stone basin near his doorway, from which he splashed icy water on his face to wake himself. Once he was done, he removed the dirty rag from his forehead and wet his hair, smoothing it back into untidy spikes before reattaching the rag. He had slept in it, as usual.

That done, he went to find some lathamri. People were up and about even at this early hour, travelling to and fro along the roads of the complex, on visits and errands and business. Several people he greeted on his way, the cheery façade snapping into place automatically. Everyone knew him as the leader of the community. Unlike their previous hideout in the Fold, the Libera Dramach did not operate in secret in Araka Jo. Everybody here knew about Lucia, and the organisation that had been built around her. Everybody here was Libera Dramach by allegiance. Anybody who had not been able to stomach that had gone elsewhere in the Southern Prefectures.

He turned off the thoroughfare to where a side-road was lined with wooden stalls, feeling exhausted even by that short journey. The tiredness was not physical – he had always been healthy as a mule – but a weariness of spirit that weighed him down. His smile felt false now, more so than ever before: he was forced to use it too much. The people needed him to be positive, looked to him as an indicator of their fortunes. He could not afford to show weakness. He could not afford to let them know that he did not want to lead them any more.

Between the stalls were rows of stone idols, strange crouching things that had been smoothed by centuries of rain and wind. Their slitted, blank eyes stared across the side-road at each other, over the heads of the people who milled between them. Some kind of guardian spirits? Nobody knew. Araka Jo had been built in the early years after landfall, the result of a splinter religion taking advantage of the new freedom to explore their beliefs. They must have been particularly numerous and industrious to have created a complex of temples the size of a small town. Perhaps it was a mountain retreat, a place of prayer and meditation. But its purpose and its creators had been lost to history, and it had been abandoned. The folk of Saramyr were not interested in ruins.

Yugi bought a mug of lathamri from a merchant and drank it while staring at the statues. Frightening how easily the past could be forgotten. He wondered how the previous inhabitants might have felt, labouring towards what they thought was a great work, if they knew that mere centuries later nobody would know or care what they had done it for.

Perhaps they would have appreciated the irony, he thought. It was Saramyr's blithe ignorance of its past that now threatened its future.

The hot, bitter drink awakened him enough to face dealing with Cailin and Lucia, so he returned the mug to the merchant with a coin inside it and left. It was an old tradition: if the drink was not drained then the coin would be wet, so it was only polite to finish it all. Strange, Yugi thought as he walked away, that traditions linger long past the time that their origins had been lost to memory, yet the lessons of history can fade in a generation.

He headed back towards the building where his cell was, and over to the other side, where the lake lay. It was a bracingly cool and crisp day, and while there was no dew on the grass the air felt moist. He slept in what had once been the living-quarters of the worshippers who had built the place. There were about twenty of that type of building scattered around the complex, identically white and rectangular, differentiated by the carvings and sculptures on their corners. They were spartan and austere inside, being merely corridors and cells with a central atrium for cooking and washing, but Yugi did not overly mind. Some days he thought about moving down into the village that had been built around the lower slopes of the complex to house the overflow, but to do so would cause gossip, and now was not the time for rumours. Everything he did was political, whether he wanted it or not. He wished he had Mishani's faculty to enjoy that kind of life.

Beyond the building there was a long, grassy slope down to the shore of Lake Xemit. A dirt path led to a large boathouse from which fishermen issued across the water. Trees encroached in copses here and there, but not enough to obscure the magnificent view. Folk were scattered about, some talking, others on their way from one place to another. It was easy to forget the famine even existed here, in the heart of the Southern Prefectures. Life went on, regardless.

Yugi spotted Cailin and Lucia and made his way towards them. As he went, he looked out over the lake to the horizon. Lake Xemit was colossal: forty-five miles across and nearly two hundred and fifty long. It was the second largest inland body of water in Saramyr after Lake Azlea, cradled between two mountain ranges.

He had been to the other side once before, during the assault on Utraxxa. It had been one of the most famous victories of the last four years. An ancient Weaver stronghold, deep in the heart of the Southern Prefectures. Though cut off from the other Weavers after the forces of the Empire had consolidated, it still exuded its foulness into the earth, still spawned more Aberrant predators to harry the troops of the Empire from within. Protected by the mountains, it took two years before the high families, led by Barak Zahn, managed to penetrate the monastery. Though the Weavers destroyed everything of value, even the witchstone itself, it was a triumph in the eyes of the people.

It was that, more than any other incident, that gave the men and women of the Empire the strength to fight on through the long years of war. The Weavers, who for so many generations had been held as mysterious and unfathomable beings by the common folk, were only mortal. They could be beaten. The fight could be won.

They needed another victory like Utraxxa, Yugi thought. *He* needed one.

Lucia and Cailin were walking together slowly, talking. It irked him that Cailin was the only one whom Lucia ever seemed attentive to; with most people she had a frustrating air of distraction. Yugi could not help noticing the odd behaviour of the wildlife as he approached: the way the ravens in the trees never stopped watching her, the cat that unobtrusively tracked her from downslope, the rabbits who would hop and hide, hop and hide, yet always keeping abreast of her. Natural enemies, yet with Lucia about they were not interested in each other.

Cailin noticed him coming and they stopped to let him catch up. She was a little taller than he was, her face painted like those of all the Sisters, her black hair drawn back through a jewelled comb into twin ponytails and a thin silver circlet set with a red gem placed around her forehead. Her sheer black dress and ruff of raven feathers lent her a somewhat predatory aspect, adding to the air of cool superiority she exuded. Yugi wondered how well her arrogance would stand up in bed, whether her icy exterior would shatter in the throes of orgasm; then he caught himself, and forced the thought away.

'Daygreet, Yugi,' Cailin said. 'Did you sleep well?'

It was a weighted question. Yugi made a neutral noise to evade it. 'Lucia said there is news.'

'Kaiku has made contact.'

'She is safe, then?' Yugi asked. Despite their estrangement, he had been worried for her these past weeks; it was only now, at the point of discovery, that he realised how worried.

'She is safe,' Cailin said. 'Though she very nearly did not make it out at all.'

'Where is she now?'

'Heading down the Zan towards Maza.'

'And the others?'

'Phaeca is with her. Nomoru is gone.'

'What do you mean, *gone?*'

'She disappeared. They do not know where she is.'

Yugi held up a hand. 'Start from the beginning, Cailin, and tell me what Kaiku told you.'

So Cailin relayed the story of the investigation of the pall-pits, of their betrayal and how Nomoru had second-guessed it, and how they had escaped the city.

'A gang from the Poor Quarter helped them?' Yugi repeated in frank disbelief.

'Smuggled them aboard a barge.'

'And what did they want in return?'

'Apparently nothing.'

Yugi grimaced. 'Gods, they were lucky, then.'

'Perhaps so. But the people of the Poor Quarter are not stupid. The Sisters may be Aberrants, but even we are not so despised as the Weavers. Things are turning, Yugi. They know we are on their side.'

'Are you really?' Yugi said skeptically.

Cailin did not reply, and Yugi left it at that. He glanced at Lucia, who was looking away across the lake, apparently oblivious to their conversation.

'My Sisters learned a lot from the pall-pit,' Cailin said at length. 'The implications are grave indeed.'

Yugi felt a cold eel of nausea turn gently in his stomach, a remnant of last night's excesses. He did not want to hear any bad news now.

'The Weavers have modified the old sewers into a pipe network. They are channelling the miasma that their buildings produce.'

'Into the pall-pits,' Yugi guessed. He scratched his stubbled cheek. 'Why?'

'Because that is where the feya-kori are.'

'Because that is *what* the feya-kori are,' Lucia corrected, over her shoulder.

Yugi cocked his head at Cailin, expecting elaboration.

'They are composed of the Weavers' miasma,' Cailin said. 'Without it, they are formless. They draw it around them like a shroud, and build their shape from it. When we called them blight-demons, we did not know how right we were.'

Yugi was quick to latch on to a potential upside. 'Would that explain why they returned to Axekami after the assault on Juraka? That they need to . . . replenish themselves? Like a whale can dive for hours, but has to come up for air?'

'Exactly,' Cailin said, raising an eyebrow. 'An apt analogy.'

'Could that be the reason the Weavers are poisoning Axekami in such a way?'

'Perhaps,' came the careful reply. 'But let us not tie all our threads to a single revelation. There is much we do not understand yet.'

'But this gives us hope, surely?' Yugi said. 'The feya-kori have a limit, a weakness.'

'You do not yet see the grander scale,' Cailin replied. 'It is not only Axekami that the Weavers are choking. There are pall-pits in various stages of completion in Tchamaska, Maxachta and Barask. More are being built on the north side of Axekami, and in Hanzean to the west.' A chill wind off the lake rippled through the grass and hissed through the trees. 'These two feya-kori are only the first. The Weavers will bring more. We cannot stand against them.'

Yugi sighed and rubbed at his eye. 'Gods, Cailin, does it get any worse?'

'Oh yes,' she said. 'Two nights ago, the feya-kori left Axekami again.'

The fortified town of Zila had seen its fair share of conflict. Since the time it was built over a thousand years ago it had weathered assaults from the native Ugati, from renegade warlords, and from the Empire itself; and still it stood, grim and dark upon a steep hill to the south of the River Zan. It was a strategic linchpin, commanding both the estuary and the thirty-five mile strip of land between the coast and the western edges of the Forest of Xu, a thoroughfare vital for travel between the affluent northwest and the fertile Southern Prefectures. Now it had become a bastion against the Weavers, denying them the passage along the Great Spice Road.

Barak Zahn looked over his shoulder at the town, a crown of stone, the roofs of its houses sloping back to the narrow pinnacle of the keep at its tip. That wall had never fallen to an enemy, not in all the history of Zila. Not even when the town was overrun, when Zahn himself had been one of the invaders; they had surmounted the wall, but they had not breached it. Then, he had left Zila smoking and battered. It was in considerably better shape now: the ruined houses had been rebuilt, the keep repaired, the streets set back in order. Troops of the Empire walked behind its parapets; fire-cannons looked out over the river. But its air of invulnerability was gone, its power diminished.

His horse stirred beneath him, and he turned his attention back to the estuary, where four huge junks swayed at anchor. The wind was brisk and the light crisp and sharp: they were heading into midwinter now, and though it was still warm the breeze off the sea could be biting.

He was a lean man, his hair grey and his stubbled cheeks uneven with pox-scars. He wore a brocaded jacket with its collar turned up, and his eyes were narrow as he stared across the water. Around him and before him were hundreds of mounted men in the colours of their respective houses. Most of them were his own Blood Ikati, clad in green and grey. To his right, wrapped in a fur cloak, the head of Blood Erinima sat in her saddle, plump and wizened. Lucia's great-aunt Oyo.

It was over a week since Kaiku and Phaeca had escaped Axekami, but Zahn knew nothing of that. He had, however, heard the news that the feya-kori were on the move again. The Red Order were few in number and stretched thin, but Cailin tried to ensure that there was at least one in every frontline settlement. The warning had spread within minutes. Not that it concerned Zahn overly: the feya-kori, like the Aberrant armies, moved too fast to keep up with, and the news that they had been deployed simply meant they were at large again, and Saramyr was a very big place. They could be up to anything. Besides, he had more immediate concerns.

The first was the woman next to him. It seemed that even in the face of the greatest threat the Empire had encountered since its inception, the wranglings of the courts went on. Though they were all ostensibly united against the Weavers, the old powerplay of concessions and arrangements and oaths continued. Oyo was annoyingly persistent, even following him up to Zila where the greater portion of his armies were garrisoned along with those of Blood Vinaxis. Her demands were simple: she wanted his daughter.

Zahn had known it would be impossible to keep Lucia's parentage a secret forever. She was so obviously affectionate towards him, and that coupled with the rumours of the Emperor Durun's infertility and Zahn's close relationship with the Empress Anais was all that anyone needed to draw the correct conclusion. Once he had become convinced that it was hopeless concealing it any longer, he let it be known that he was the father, and hoped to have done with it. But Blood Erinima – the mother's family – were not satisfied. They disputed his claim. They wanted her back, to bind her to Blood Erinima where they believed she belonged.

Zahn did not want to trouble himself with it. He believed their loyalty towards their kin was genuine – and indeed, he had never prevented them seeing Lucia – but it was also painfully transparent that they were thinking towards the outcome of the war, for if victorious then Lucia was by far the most likely candidate for the throne, and Blood Erinima wanted to ride with her to power again. However, Zahn's claim on her complicated things immensely, for as the only surviving parent she was legally his child before the family of the deceased mother. If that claim could be proved to be genuine.

But Zahn was not the biggest problem: Lucia was. She had no interest in such matters. She was happy to acknowledge her relatives, but she would not talk politics with them. Zahn was her father; it was that simple. As far as matters of Blood went, she needed neither Blood Ikati nor Blood Erinima. The Libera Dramach were at her beck and call, an army to rival any of the great houses and independent of them. She did not care about becoming Empress. She did not care about being a leader, or a figurehead, or anything at all of that nature. It was difficult to tell *what* she cared about. That frustrated women like Oyo immensely, and they fumed and said that the child did not realise what was good for her, and that she should be with her family. But Zahn knew his child, as well as anyone *could* know her, and he believed her a thing apart from the grubby machinations that Oyo wanted to drag her into. He loved her, and he let her go her own way. But he would not renounce his fatherhood, no matter how Blood Erinima cajoled and promised and threatened.

A rowboat was sliding across the estuary towards the southern shore; it was time to deal with the second and more recent concern. Zahn spurred his horse through the ranks of his men and trotted down the shallow incline at the base of the hill. Oyo watched him go with an unfriendly gaze. A small guard of twenty fell in behind at the command of one of his generals. A Sister joined them, appearing unobtrusively at his side like a shadow, her face still. They passed through the army to the stretch of clear grass where the water ended, and there they stopped.

The rowboat had reached the shore now, and the newcomers were dragging it out of the water, all four of them together. Zahn tried to establish which one of them was the leader, but it was hopeless. They were all dressed in simple hemp clothes, their hair varying in colour from blond to black; all had the same yellowish skin tattooed head to foot in curving tendrils of pale green. Tkiurathi, from the jungle continent of Okhamba, so his aides informed him. Savages, they said.

The question was, what were the savages doing in Saramyr?

The boat secured, one of them approached Zahn, walking fearlessly towards the forest of soldiers. Zahn glanced up at the junks. They were of Saramyr make. The gods knew how many other Tkiurathi were in there, but they had better hope they could swim: one signal from him and Zila's fire-cannons would blow them to flinders.

The stranger stopped a short way from Zahn. His orange-blond hair was smoothed back along his skull and hardened there with sap. Okhamban *kntha* – called 'gutting-hooks' in Saramyrrhic – hung from either side of his belt: double-bladed weapons with a handle set at the point where they met, each blade kinked the opposite way to the other.

'Daygreet, honoured Barak,' said the Tkiurathi, in near-flawless Saramyrrhic. 'I am Tsata.' He bowed in an ambiguous manner, in a style used between men who were unsure of their relative social standing to each other.

Zahn could not decide if it was arrogance or accident. The name was faintly familiar to him, however.

'I am the Barak Zahn tu Ikati,' he said.

Tsata gave him a curious look. 'Indeed? Then we have a mutual acquaintance. Kaiku tu Makaima.'

Zahn's horse crabstepped with a snort; he pulled it firmly back into line. Now he knew where he had heard the name before. This was the man who had travelled with the spy Saran into the heart of Okhamba to bring back the evidence of the Weavers' origins; the man who had helped Kaiku destroy a witchstone in the Xarana Fault. He looked down at the Sister who stood to his right.

'Can you confirm this?'

Her irises had already turned to red. 'I am doing so.'

Zahn regarded the foreigner with frank suspicion on his face. 'Why are you here, Tsata? This is not a good time to be visiting Saramyr.'

'We come to offer you our aid,' said Tsata. 'A thousand Tkiurathi, to fight alongside you against the Weavers.'

'I see,' Zahn said. 'And what would you do if we did not *want* your aid?'

'We would fight anyway, whatever your wishes,' Tsata replied. 'We come to stop the Weavers. If we can do it together, so be it. If not, we shall do it alone.'

'He is who he says he is,' the Sister said. 'I have contacted Kaiku tu Makaima.' She bowed to Tsata in the appropriate female mode. 'She sends you greetings, honoured friend. The Red Order are pleased that your path has set you upon our shores again.'

Zahn felt a twinge of irritation at being undercut. His unfriendly stance was somewhat robbed of force now that Tsata had the Sisters' approval. The Red Order considered themselves above political loyalty; they knew they were invaluable, and took advantage of it. They might have been easier on the eye than the Weavers were, but they were not so different as they liked to think.

He slid down from his horse and handed the reins to a nearby soldier. 'It seems I have been ungracious,' he said, and bowed. 'Welcome back.'

'I am only sorry I could not come sooner, or bring more of my people,' Tsata said, dismissing the apology. 'Ten times this many would have come, if we had the ships.'

'I had not known the Tkiurathi were a seafaring folk,' Zahn said, embedding an implied question in an observation.

Tsata smiled to himself. Such a Saramyr thing to do, to be so indirect. 'The ships came from Blood Mumaka, as did the crew.'

'I thought they had fled Saramyr when the war began.' What Zahn thought of that was evident in his voice.

'To Okhamba, yes. They sailed their fleet away. But they still desire to help their homeland in such ways as they can. Mishani tu Koli came to me before I left and asked me to pass on news of Chien os Mumaka's death to his mother. I found them only hours before they left Hanzean, ahead of the

Aberrant armies that were spreading through the northwest. In return for my news they allowed me to travel with them back to Okhamba. I have kept in contact with Blood Mumaka ever since; when the time came, they offered their aid.'

'Four ships?' Zahn said disparagingly.

'They need the others to conduct their trade with,' Tsata replied. 'The rest of the Near World goes on as ever, no matter what the state of matters here. They cannot see that if Saramyr falls, they will be next. But my people can. I have shown them.'

Zahn considered the Tkiurathi for a moment. On the one hand, any aid was welcome in these times, and he was not such a fool as to turn away a genuine ally; but on the other, it was difficult to believe that a thousand men – *ten* thousand, if Tsata was to be believed – would willingly sail to another continent to fight for people they had virtually no contact with.

'Our ways are not your ways, Barak Zahn,' Tsata said, his expression serious. He had guessed the other man's thoughts. 'We will not wait at home until it is our turn to be attacked. The Weavers threaten the whole of the Near World. We will stop them at their source, if we can.'

Zahn was about to reply when the Sister touched him on his arm. She was looking to the north, over the river. The line of the horizon was hazed. Zahn's eyes went to the junks: they seemed ghosted slightly, blurred at the edges. He blinked, feeling faintly myopic.

'Is it usual for fog to come so quickly in these parts?' Tsata asked, as the air thickened around them.

TEN

The walls of Zila had held back the enemies of the Empire for a thousand years and more. The feya-kori went through them like children kicking over mudcastles.

They approached under the cover of the fog, but nobody was deceived. Kaiku had warned the Sisters about the demons' methods, and the murk had gathered too quickly and smelt too foul to be natural. Yet, somehow, knowing that they were coming only made it worse: the sickening inevitability of their arrival weighed on the defenders' hearts.

The troops had already begun to prepare the town for evacuation by the time the feya-kori appeared. They lunged suddenly out of the miasma, emerging as if from nowhere within a few dozen metres of the wall. Men howled as the demons loomed up towards them; the sharp slope to the north of the town made them seem as if they were coming from below, surfacing from a sea of mist. They grabbed hold of the lip of the wall, the stump-ends of their arms smashing down onto the stone in a hissing mass of black ooze, crushing and dissolving those soldiers not quick enough to get out of the way. Then, with a long, protracted groan, they hauled, and the top third of the wall gave way in an avalanche of bodies and bricks and mortar.

Alarm bells clanged from the murk; men fought to decline their fire-cannons far enough to hit the enemy. But the feya-kori were too close. They punched and tore and smashed, their movements slow and massive, destroying a great section of the wall in minutes while rifles and arrows pocked them ineffectually.

They lumbered into the town, crashing through buildings as if they were made of sticks and paper. The Aberrant predators and Nexuses were not far behind them.

Tsata raced through the ruined streets left in the demons' wake. A dozen Tkiurathi were with him, their gutting-hooks held ready, eyes darting about for signs of the enemy. Behind them they could hear the cries of the feya-kori, disembodied moans drifting through the swiftly thinning fog; before them, distantly, was the sound of combat, where the troops of the Empire had knitted across the gash in the wall and were putting up a bloody resistance against the Aberrant horde. Tsata was concerned with neither: his purpose was the area in between, where the smoking, charred trail of the demons had left houses collapsed into rubble, with men and women and children trapped and maimed or out of their wits with fear.

The Tkiurathi dispersed at his suggestion, fracturing into groups of two and three and hurrying in different directions. They filtered off into the narrow spoke-roads and cross-alleys of the town, heading away from the main swathe of destruction – where nothing was left alive, and the cobbled thoroughfares were a melted quagmire – to the edges, where there were people to be helped.

Tsata tasted bile: the very air was bad here. The sight of the feya-kori still burned in the forefront of his mind. For the month that it took to cross the sea from his lands, he had been experiencing a steadily growing elation at the thought of returning to Saramyr. Four years he had been gathering his people, tracking them down and persuading them to his cause; four years of hunting through deep jungle, of tireless diplomacy, of bringing together men and women who had scattered over hundreds of miles of nearly impenetrable terrain. And though he might have only managed four ships to carry them, those four could go back and forth as many times as was necessary to transport all the Tkiurathi to Saramyr.

But he had been here mere hours before he witnessed how much worse things had become in his absence, and now he wished he had listened to his heart instead of his head and got here sooner.

He scrambled over a slope of rubble, where the dusty guts of a building had spilled out across the street, to where a pair of women were heaving at a beam to uncover the supine man beneath. He did not give them time to react to his appearance, to act on the flicker of fear and uncertainty at the sight of him. He grabbed the beam and lifted, and after a moment's hesitation the women added their strength to his, and two more Tkiurathi appeared and joined in. The beam moved, and the man scrambled free, delirious with agony, his foot crushed inside his boot. One of the women helped him stand one-legged.

'Find a crutch and get away from here,' Tsata told them. 'Through the south gate.' Then he rapped a few words in guttural Okhamban to his companions and they were running again.

The mist had faded to a fine haze, burnt off by the sharp light of the winter sun. The demons were abandoning their concealment; they had no need of it now. One of them had reached the town's keep, the highest and most central point, hub of Zila's wheel-like layout. Burning and broken buildings traced the creature's path from the gap in the north wall to where it was smashing into the keep's brickwork. The other one had rampaged towards the western wall.

Tsata hoped the ships had got away. There had barely been time for the Tkiurathi to gather their communal belongings and swim for shore; he had last seen the junks turning in the estuary, their prows pointing towards the open sea. A few Tkiurathi men had stayed, along with the crew. They would return and tell others what they had seen today. What the Weavers were now capable of.

For the Tkiurathi who were on Saramyr, the protection of their *pash* was now the priority. Okhambans did not think in the way Saramyr did: they had no concept of personal ownership, and their society had evolved around a group dynamic which meant, at its most basic level, that they considered individual needs less important than those of the many. *Pash* was their name for whichever 'many' they were involved with at the time, a fluid and multilayered concept of overlapping priorities which was how the Okhamban people – including the Tkiurathi – assigned importance to a situation. At this moment, at this time, their *pash* included the people of Zila; and so they had headed into the town without a second thought, to help with the retreat, to save lives when they could, heedless of any risk to themselves.

A cry for help drew them into a small square where one side had collapsed inward. The façades of the buildings had shaken away from their superstructures and opened the rooms to the sky. Smoke was seeping from beneath the rubble on the ground floor of what had once been a cobbler's shop, where something was ablaze. An old, bearded man was frantically working to clear away the stones there. He caught sight of Tsata and his companions, wasted a moment on uncertainty, then called to them.

'There's someone under here!'

They joined him in his work, hefting the heavy, uneven stones and flinging them away. There was a frantic knocking noise coming from beneath.

Tsata's survival instincts kept him fitfully glancing about as he laboured, honed by generation upon generation of jungle life. Without even thinking about it, he knew where the feya-kori were by their dreary, yawning voices; they were too far away to be a threat. He could tell by the cadence and timbre of the battle to the north that the forces of the Empire were still holding out. But there were Aberrant predators loose in the city, those that had slipped through the gap in the wall before it could be sealed. He had seen their handiwork, and one or two of their corpses.

They had just uncovered the corner of a trapdoor, from which the smoke was coming, when something moved in the square.

The three Tkiurathi were on their feet, gutting-hooks in hands, before the pair of ghauregs even noticed them. They ran out from the cover of the building and into the square, drawing the eyes of the beasts, leading them away from the old man. The Aberrants snorted at the sight of prey, growling deep in their chests. One of them bellowed a challenge, shaking its head, its grey shaggy pelt flailing with the movement; then slowly they advanced.

Tsata circled around the square, keeping his gaze on the predators. His companions were fanning away from him, treading soundlessly across the rubble-strewn cobbles. Coherent thought had fallen away, succeeded by the quicker and more direct reactions of a hunter. The ghauregs clacked their jaws together with a bony snap like a crocodile's, wary of their opponents. Their muzzles were streaked in blood.

There was a banging from the trapdoor, louder and more urgent than before now that it was not muffled by so much rubble, and the ghaureg's heads snapped around to fix on the old man who crouched there. He paled.

The three Tkiurathi moved together, taking advantage of the instant of distraction to cross the distance between them and the predators. Their hide shoes were so soft and their tread so light that the ghauregs did not hear them coming; they turned back only just in time to react to the attack.

Tsata saw the fist swiping towards him early enough to duck beneath it. He rammed one of his gutting-hooks into the ghaureg's ribs with as much force as he could muster. It bit deep, but the thick muscles of the beast were too tough to cut easily, and the blade wrenched free of his hand as he darted past. The ghaureg overswung, roaring in pain, and one of the other Tkiurathi took its hand off at the wrist with a brutal downward stroke; but he had been too eager at the sight of an inviting target, and he did not see the ghaureg's other hand until it grabbed his shin in an unbreakable grip. He slashed across the beast's muzzle, slicing through its lip, but the blade jarred against bone and glanced off. It flung him away, whipping him by his leg with a cracking of bones to send him flailing through the air. He crashed in a heap against the rubble, but even before he had landed Tsata had made his second strike. Occupied with one enemy, the ghaureg had no time to deal with the other, and Tsata plunged his second gutting-hook into the creature's back with all his strength.

This time he found something vital. His enemy lurched away spasmodically for a few steps, trying to paw at its back but unable to reach; then it collapsed, and blood ran over its lower teeth with its last bubbling breath.

Tsata had never lost sight of the second ghaureg in the time it took to despatch the first one. That one was still engaged with the remaining Tkiurathi. He did not spare a moment to check on his fallen comrade, but instead he carefully approached the body of the ghaureg, ready to leap away if it should move. He wrenched his weapons free and then went to the aid of his beleaguered kinsman.

That man – his name was Heth – had been fighting tactically. Instead of going up alone against a stronger enemy he had been drawing it after him to allow the others time to finish off the first ghaureg. Now he saw Tsata coming, and the advantage turned his way. He switched to the offensive, ducking in low to hack across his enemy's knees. The strike was inexact, hitting its calf instead, but it was enough to send a flood of red soaking through the grey fur. Heth pulled back faster than the counterpunch could follow, and in that moment Tsata got in behind the beast, close enough to chop a deep blow into its tricep before retreating out of its reach. Enraged, it swung back to snap at him, and once again Heth slipped inside its guard and raked a cut along its thigh.

They harried it for several minutes, each time leaving a wound, each time escaping its grasp. Finally, when its pelt was drenched crimson and blood loss had made it sluggish, Heth took advantage of an ill-executed lunge to take it through the throat, and it went down without another sound.

Tsata exchanged a breathless smile with Heth. 'We must be quick,' he said in their native tongue. 'Others may come.'

They sheathed their blades. Heth went to see to their companion, who was beginning to scream as the shock wore off. Tsata went for the trapdoor. Fumes were coming thickly from beneath it now. The knocking had stopped, and the old man was long gone. Tsata cleared away the remainder of the debris and pulled the trapdoor open, keeping it between himself and the hatchway. Flame billowed out, then retreated and settled to an insidious purr.

He took a breath, held it, and looked down into the hatchway. His eyes began tearing immediately: the smoke was too hot to bear for long. Unable to see, he instead reached in, trusting to his senses to tell him if he was getting too close to the fire. His hand touched fabric and muscle. He found a purchase, guessing it to be the upper arm of the person who had been knocking, and pulled.

The man was surprisingly light for his size, but even so Tsata had trouble with the dead weight. He dragged the limp figure across the rubble a little way and laid him down, but by then it was already apparent that he was too late.

Tsata looked down on him for a moment. His skin was white, his features so small as to be almost vestigial. There were little gill-slits at his neck, and his glazed eyes were bulbous, with pupils like crosses. An Aberrant.

He had been hiding in the city, perhaps sheltered by the cobbler. Tsata had heard that Aberrants were no longer executed on sight as they had been before the civil war began. Priorities had changed now, and with both the Red Order and Lucia fighting on their side, it seemed inappropriate to allow the killing any longer. But prejudice could not be erased as easily. Though it was unlawful to murder them, they were still reviled in the main, still forced to hide or to take shelter in their own remote communities. People like the Red Order were the lucky ones; they had the outside appearance of normality, at least. This man would have been treated as a freak.

Tsata's eyes tightened in disgust at the thought. There was so much hate in this once-beautiful land. He wondered if this man had had a family, for unlike Tsata's home, pair-bonding and the exclusive possession of offspring was the way in Saramyr. Then he glanced over at the hatchway, where flames were licking out. He decided that he would rather not know.

Barak Zahn sat on horseback near the south gate of Zila, overseeing the rabble of townsfolk fleeing for their lives. He was flanked by several bodyguards, and nearby a group of Blood Vinaxis soldiers fought to herd the crowd and keep them calm. Like panicked animals, they were liable to stampede. The noise was terrible, and the air still lingered with the smell of the feya-kori's fog, mingled with the infectious odour of fear.

He looked up the hill at where one of the demons had almost finished smashing the keep to rubble. The other one was tracking about at random, pounding houses and shops and warehouses to pieces with slow and methodical blows. The sound of tumbling stone and the demon's cries rolled across the town.

His blood burned: he was furious at his own impotence. Gods, it felt so fundamentally *wrong* to abandon a strategic outpost like this. He had men ranged along the riverbank and along the walls, but they were only putting up as much resistance as was necessary to evacuate everyone they could, keeping the Aberrants out for as long as possible. This was a lost battle the moment the feya-kori appeared. There simply was no defence against them. And this is what it would be like in the next town they attacked, and the next, until the Southern Prefectures had fallen and the Weavers had swallowed the land.

Still, even in the face of such abject defeat, he salvaged what positive aspects he could to pass on to his allies. They were holding back the Aberrants along the river to the west and east with relative ease. Apparently the attack had relied on the feya-kori breaking down the wall and the Aberrants flooding over the water north of the town. But the feya-kori had broken through and then gone on a rampage, and the troops of the Empire were quick enough to seal the breach behind them. If there had been any kind of tactical thought applied by the demons, they would have made a bigger hole, or at least stayed there to ensure that enough Aberrants had got through to keep the passage open. Zahn doubted that the Weavers had more than a rudimentary control over their terrible creations, and that, at least, was something worth knowing.

He looked up at where the gristle-crows circled high above, out of rifle range. As always, the Nexuses were nearby, hidden and protected, directing the battle from afar. The gristle-crows were their eyes, the Aberrant predators their puppets. If they could get to the Nexuses they could throw the animals into disorder; but the Nexuses had learned to stay scattered since Zahn had routed them at the battle of the Fold, years ago. And even if they did, even if they slew every Aberrant here, they still could not win. It came back to one immutable fact: they had no weapon against the blight demons.

A rider drew up before him: a young and handsome man with a thick head of brown hair, wearing Blood Ikati colours.

'What news of our allies?' Zahn asked. He remembered this man; he had sent him into the town to keep tabs on the Tkiurathi. He had been uneasy about letting them leave their ships, but in the chaos that followed the gathering of the demon fog he had been loth to spare the men necessary to prevent them. Now they were loose in the town, and though they appeared to be a help rather than a hindrance, long experience had taught him to mistrust such apparent altruism.

But the young man's report shed no new light. The Tkiurathi were indeed doing their best to speed the retreat, rescuing the injured and aiding stragglers, hunting down those Aberrants that were loose in the streets. Some of them were dying in the process. Perhaps a ploy to win his trust, then?

The young man was coming to the conclusion of his report, but Zahn was not really listening any more. He was gazing up at where the feya-kori rose seething above the slate rooftops of the town, thinking about the strange folk from the jungle continent. It was probably what saved his life.

He saw the rifleman in the upper window of a ramshackle house an instant before the muzzle flash, and only because he happened to be looking that way. It gave him that extra minuscule fraction of a moment which was the difference between the ball hitting his heart or his shoulder. The force of it knocked him out of his saddle, sending him crashing to the ground, his feet tangled in his stirrups. His horse neighed and bucked wildly; he was dragged thrashing across the cobbles. The horse's hooves clattered as it stepped back over him. Shock swamped his senses, making everything distant and slow and remote. He was dimly aware of a man lunging for him, the young messenger, a knife in his hand; but then the messenger's hand was gone, and a moment later his head, as the swords of Zahn's bodyguards cleft through him. Another stroke, and the stirrups that tethered Zahn to the horse were severed. Suddenly, he saw the sky again; the horse danced away, kicking, and someone shot it.

There were men surrounding him, and angry cries as others rode towards the building to flush out the sniper. But the sniper would be already dead, having taken his own life. Nobody would know who had sent him, nor the messenger that had been the backup; but Zahn knew. Of course he knew.

As he lay there panting and white with his men looking into his eyes and speaking incoherently to him, he cursed the name of Oyo tu Erinima, who wanted her grand-niece back.

ELEVEN

Kaiku spun and sewed, looped and knotted, moving on a thousand fronts at once as she darted through the labyrinth of the Weave. Her opponent was fast as she, *faster*, blocking her, confusing her, burrowing into her stitchwork defences; but Kaiku would not relent, would not allow even the most fractional lapse of concentration. For every gain her opponent made, they lost an equal amount. Tangles frayed, nets were strung, traps laid and avoided; a scurrying combat like an army of tiny spiders warring on a golden web so complex that it stunned the mind.

Kaiku used every trick she knew, and improvised some she didn't. Sink-holes that sucked threads into an insoluble muddle; scatter-stitch that created an endless and disorientating array of possible routes across the battlefield, ultimately heading nowhere. She plucked strings like a harp and meshed them with other resonances to set up interference patterns, disguising her movements. Sometimes her methods were effective, sometimes not; but then, the same applied to her opponent's attempts. This battle had raged for long minutes in the world of human senses. In the Weave, it seemed like it had been going for years, and still neither combatant flagged, neither wavered. They were evenly matched. Stalemate.

Then, finally, her adversary withdrew. Kaiku did the same. They hung there, disembodied, exhausted and wary, like bloodied tigers at bay. On the edge of her perception, she sensed the shift and glide of the leviathans that haunted this glittering world, ever elusive, unreachable. They were calling to each other in their fashion, concussive pops and creaks passing back and forth along the Weave. Kaiku knew that her senses were only interpreting the sounds to accommodate her human mindset, for there was no sound at all in this place; but even so, it was eerie and magical to hear. The leviathans spoke more and more often now.

At the signal, she drew her *kana* back, retreating into herself like the tentacles of an anemone, and opened her eyes. She was kneeling on a wicker mat in the centre of a wood-panelled room. A paper lantern hung overhead, casting shadows in the cool gloom, half-illuminating the charcoal etchings that hung on the wall, the tiny tables with their vases of dark blossoms. An incense burner filled the room with the scent of kama nuts, bitter and fruity and smoky all at once. Opposite Kaiku was Cailin, regarding her approvingly, her irises a rich red. Both were breathing hard, their skin glistening with sweat in the lantern-light. Both wore the attire of the Order.

Cailin smiled. 'Congratulations,' she said.

Kaiku could not suppress a short laugh of exultation. She had fought her tutor to a standstill for the first time ever. She had taken on the most powerful Sister alive, the Pre-Eminent of the Red Order, and not been beaten by her. It felt magnificent.

Cailin stood up, and Kaiku with her. 'Walk with me,' she said.

Kaiku was a little unsteady, but she obeyed, flushed with success. They walked through the building that housed those Sisters who lived in the village downslope of Araka Jo, and went out into the night.

The village was haphazard and a little ramshackle, as had been the town of the Fold where most of its inhabitants had come from. The Libera Dramach had taken Araka Jo as their own after being driven from the Xarana Fault, since nobody else appeared to want it. The nobles and high families, used to their luxury, had retreated to cities like Machita and Saraku; the latter had become the unofficial capital of the Empire's territories while the war raged.

They followed dirt paths between stilt-legged dwellings. Lights glowed on porches in the darkness; candles flickered in small shrines of stone and metal. Chikkikii popped and cracked in the bushes; mountain rodents sang to each other as they darted in quick bursts from shadow to shadow. Aurus hung high and full in the east, massive and looming.

They did not speak for a time, except to acknowledge the occasional hail from the villagers. The Sisters were well regarded here, and Kaiku enjoyed the attention. Eventually, the houses became sparser, the trees crowded close to the paths, and the gentle sound of the village faded behind them and left only the sounds of the night, riotous and yet strangely restful.

'You have been something of a trial, Kaiku,' Cailin said, then looked at her. 'I hope you see now why I persevered with you.'

'You were right,' she said. She had to admit that, at least. 'It took me a long time to understand, but you were right.'

The taller woman smiled indulgently. 'You have no idea how it felt to let you go, knowing what a talent you had. To watch you throwing yourself into anything and everything with scarce an inkling of your abilities. The gods forbid I ever have children, if they cause me such worry as you.'

Kaiku laughed softly. 'Muleheadedness is one of my less admirable traits.'

They walked on for a time.

'Would you?' Kaiku asked. 'Have children, I mean?'

'None of us should,' Cailin replied. 'Not yet.'

'None of us? You mean the Red Order?'

'We do not know what might happen if we did. We dare not think what might come of it.'

'But surely someone has tried? An accident, even?'

'Nobody has tried. Accidents have occurred, but they have been dealt with.' She saw the expression on Kaiku's face, and added: 'They chose to do it. They knew that now was not the time.'

Kaiku did not like what she was hearing. Children were something that had barely even occurred to her – she assumed herself lacking in the maternal instinct – but to have the choice taken away from her was not something she would condone. Cailin sensed that, and attempted to explain.

'We are long-lived in the Red Order, Kaiku. We are few, but we are tightly knit. More so, perhaps, than any other faction in Saramyr. The nobles continue their internecine squabbling even in the face of famine and destruction. Look at what has happened to Barak Zahn. But the Red Order remains united, and that is because our highest priority is *ourselves*.'

'Then perhaps we are the most selfish of all, then,' Kaiku murmured.

'That is your Tkiurathi friend talking,' Cailin snapped. The warmth had fled from her now. 'Need I remind you that not even ten years ago any of us would have been killed for manifesting the abilities we possess? That most of us died through burning ourselves alive or committing suicide for shame at what we had become? This is *still happening* in the Weaver territories, Kaiku. Children are still manifesting *kana* and dying for it, and we can only get to a small fraction of them. Were it not for our selfishness, you would not be here and nor would I, and the Weavers would have had this land long ago.'

Kaiku lapsed into angry silence. She could not argue with that, but Cailin's tone made her furious. The mention of Tsata only made things worse: it reminded her of the news they had received from Zila, which told only of the destruction of the town and the fact that the Tkiurathi were there, but not whether Tsata had survived it. Beneath her carefully suppressed exterior, she was frantic.

'We are a breed apart,' Cailin went on in a softer tone. She laid a hand on Kaiku's shoulder to stop her walking. 'The first of an upward step in humanity. It is our duty to preserve ourselves, our purpose to make a world in which we can live. That is why we fight the Weavers. When that threat is gone, when this land is stable and we have found our place in it, then perhaps children will come. But until then, Kaiku, they are too uncertain.' She sighed, bowing her head, and closed her painted eyes. 'Look how dangerous we are; it is only through the Red Order that we even know how to cope with the gift we have been given. What if our offspring possess power greater than ours? What if they begin to manifest that power from birth instead of adolescence? A child who could annihilate half a town in a fit of pique? What would we do with such a creature? Kill it? *Could* we? And what would the mother say to that?'

Kaiku would not meet her eyes. She would not concede, though she saw the sense in the argument. But nobody would choose for her on a matter such as this, not even Cailin.

'We have enough troubles to contend with for now,' Cailin said. 'We remain focused and united, and nothing must jeopardise that.'

'Enough!' Kaiku replied tersely. 'You have made your point. I do not wish to discuss it.'

The triumphant glow of their battle had faded now and left her feeling irritable. She began to walk again, not caring whether Cailin came with her or not; but the Pre-Eminent joined her after a few steps.

'I have something to show you,' she said.

'Indeed?'

'You have earned it, I think.'

This caught Kaiku's interest. She brushed her hair back from her face and gave Cailin an expectant look.

'Not here,' she said. 'Come with me.'

They walked on a little way. The path they were taking turned and sloped upward. Kaiku knew where they were heading: a small and remote building that had presumably been some kind of temple in past ages, hidden amid the trees in a tiny dirt clearing. There was a dry stone font at the entrance to the clearing, and beyond was a mound-shaped structure with sealed doors at each point of the compass, topped with a cone of concentrically tapering discs that ended in a small gold bobble at the tip. Around its base were fashioned symbols in a dialect of High Saramyrrhic too old for Kaiku to understand.

'This?' Kaiku asked. She had often wondered what was inside. It exuded a faintly watchful emanation.

'No,' Cailin replied. 'I only wanted to be sure we were alone. I would have it that we kept what I have to show you between ourselves. Only a select few know of it.'

'More secrets?' Kaiku asked wearily. Deception did not sit easily with her; it went against her character.

'It is better to always have something with which to surprise those who might turn on you,' Cailin said. 'Look at the Weavers. They must have spent centuries developing their crafts, and still we have not the barest idea of what may yet lie unrevealed.'

'We are not the Weavers,' Kaiku replied.

'Do not be obtuse, Kaiku.' Cailin's velvety voice was frosting over again. 'I ask that you keep this matter secret. Even from Phaeca. It is a small favour, but important to me. Do we understand each other?'

'I understand,' Kaiku said, but she fell diplomatically short of agreeing.

'Watch, then.' Cailin closed her eyes and took a long, slow breath.

Kaiku felt the Weave stirring, tiny currents across the unseen realm. Her sensory powers had increased dramatically since she had applied herself to her studies, and now she was always aware of the Weave even when she was not actively Weaving. Like her Sisters, she could tell an Aberrant just by looking at them, and she could perceive the trails left by spirits and the imprints of strange places that most people could only feel as a kind of sixth-sense unease, if at all. With a little more effort, she could sense bonds between family and friends and even enemies, charting the physical and emotional response between their bodies.

Cailin had once told her, Tane, Asara and Mishani that they walked a braided path, that they were fated to be drawn back together no matter how far they were apart. Kaiku had asked her then how she knew; now she had the answer. Cailin had seen the insoluble ties: Kaiku's friendship with Mishani; Tane's love for her; the link that existed between her and Asara through sharing breath. But Cailin did not know all, it seemed. Tane had died, and none of the Sisters' vaunted powers could do a thing to predict that.

Then, before her eyes, Cailin disappeared.

She blinked. It was if a shadow had passed before the moon across the tall, thin figure of the Pre-Eminent, and when it was gone, so was she.

And yet . . . and yet she was *not* gone. Kaiku could still feel her there, her imprint on the Weave. Her eyes were just not seeing her.

She slipped into the Weave herself, and there was Cailin, contoured in innumerable strings of light.

((How?)) She was aghast with wonder.

((There is more. Touch me with your hand))

Kaiku did so, reaching slowly towards the Pre-Eminent, using her Weave-imprint to see her. She rested her hand on Cailin's shoulder: but where she should have found flesh and bone, there was nothing. She inhaled a sharp breath in surprise. Again she tried, again she failed. She passed her arm through where Cailin's body should be, and apart from a faintly glutinous drag on her fingertips, she touched only air.

((Impossible . . .)) Kaiku felt foolish as soon as she had transmitted the thought, but she could find no other way to express it. Cailin was in the Weave, and *only* in the Weave; her physical body was . . . *gone.*

((We have arts of which you have only scratched the surface, Kaiku)) Cailin's communication came without words, phrased instead in a semantic blaze. *((New techniques of manipulation that we have laboured on in secret for decades. You are ready to begin learning the inner mysteries of the Red Order))*

The Weave warped, flexing inward and knotting into a singularity that existed for the slenderest of instants before bursting back into shape; and there was a leviathan.

Its very presence was enough to stun them. Distance had no meaning in the Weave except in how human minds interpreted it, but until this moment the leviathans had been far, far away, unfathomably aloof. Now one of them appeared in such close proximity that the backwash almost scattered the Sisters' consciousnesses, shaking them out of coherence. They regrouped, overwhelmed; but the entity was still now, and calm descended.

Its size, its sheer *impact* on the Weave was colossal. The Sisters were motes in its presence: it dominated utterly the world of golden threads. It was a white void, an aching, blazing split that burned the eye with its brilliance. There was no shape to it, for it seemed to exist in many shapes all together; yet the human mind could not allow that, and so they put their own shape to the leviathan, fixed it in their perception. It was vast and smooth and streamlined, something like a whale in form but so alien to any creature they knew that analogy was impossible; and they were plankton against its flanks.

They regarded it in utter terror, not daring to do anything but hang there, motionless, while their Weave-senses fought to cope with what was happening.

It regarded them, too. They felt its attention brushing them as the hull of some dark, gargantuan ship sliding past, a crushing force missing them by inches. It could destroy them with the weight of that scrutiny. Kaiku had once faced the Children of the Moons, spirits so old that it was not within humanity's grasp to comprehend them; yet they were children indeed compared to this. This was a factor of magnitude so far beyond those spirits that sanity would not hold long enough to consider it.

A moment passed, and then, without warning, the Weave furled like a flower into a knot of infinite density, and then sprang back. The leviathan was gone, but the resonation of its passing rang like a bell.

Kaiku and Cailin left the Weave together. Cailin was visible again. For a long minute, they stood listening to the banal night, breathing, feeling the touch of the wind on their faces and in their hair.

Questions were lancing back and forth beneath the skin of reality. The other Sisters had sensed the leviathan. But neither Cailin nor Kaiku could respond. They stared at one another, and did not say anything. They did not have the words.

A few days later, Mishani arrived at Araka Jo.

She found Kaiku by a small lake a little way east of the temple complex. She was standing at the edge of a wooden viewing-platform, looking out across the carpet of lily pads and floating blossoms of white and red. The lake was surrounded by kamaka trees, their leaves hanging over the water in long drowsy chains. Nuki's eye had that peculiarly sharp winter's quality; it was pleasantly warm in his gaze, but where the shade obscured it there was a faint chill.

Kaiku was not wearing the attire of the Order. She had dressed in a thick robe, purple and blue and lavender, belted with a green sash. To Mishani, who was used to her friend's tomboyish tendencies, it was an unexpectedly feminine choice of clothing. Mishani watched her for a time from the end of the viewing-platform, simply enjoying the sight of her in contemplation.

'I know you are there, Mishani,' she said, a smile in her voice. 'I am long past the stage where you could sneak up on me.'

Mishani laughed, and Kaiku turned around to embrace her.

'Gods, I am glad to see you safe,' she murmured.

They talked for a long while, for they had much to tell. It had been over a year since they had last met, just before Mishani departed for Tchom Rin. Kaiku's talk was mostly of her training, for she had not travelled so far as her friend had. Mishani carried the bulk of the conversation; Kaiku was eager to hear all about the desert cities.

'And look at you now!' Kaiku said, plucking at Mishani's sleeve. 'You look like a desert noble yourself!'

'I will confess a certain fondness for the fashion,' Mishani grinned. Then she sobered and said: 'I have to tell you this, Kaiku: Asara is here.'

Kaiku's mirth flickered like a guttering candle. 'Asara?' For an instant, she was reliving that moment in the Fold, when she had seduced a man named Saran Ycthys Marul, not knowing that it was Asara in another shape. The sheer *betrayal* still scorched her. Then her smile returned, a little forced now. 'She can wait. Come, let us walk.'

They followed a trail around the edge of the lake, a dirt path scattered with worn stones that had mostly sunk into the ground with the passing of centuries. Ravens and jays hopped about the undergrowth, or took off in a startled flap of wings, blasting leaves and twigs in their wake. Most of the foliage in Saramyr was evergreen, but the people held some residual genetic memory of the time when their ancestors dwelt in temperate Quraal, and even more than a thousand years after they had come to this land there was a faintly disjointed feel to the wintertime. A sensation that something should be, and was not. The majority of the trees here never bared themselves, and that jarred with old instincts.

Kaiku felt happy to be with her friend again. There was an ease between them that nobody else in her life shared. As always, she was surprised that she could forsake that feeling so easily, that she could forget how it was when they were together; and yet she knew that when they were next parted, she would forget anew.

As they walked, Mishani told Kaiku of her journey back across the mountains.

'My impression was that the peaks were swarming with Aberrants, but we saw scarcely any, and those at a distance,' she said. 'Even when we got to the plains, and we had to cross the South Tradeway and skirt north of the marshes, our journey was unhindered. I had thought I was fortunate not to have encountered any trouble when I first crossed into the desert, but I am beginning to think that fortune had nothing to do with it.'

'Our scouts report the same,' Kaiku agreed. 'The Weavers are concentrating their forces in the cities, and fewer of them are roaming the countryside. There is speculation that even they do not have the numbers to stretch adequately across all that territory. They lost hundreds of thousands in the early months of the war, before they learned to fight tactically. Maybe they cannot breed enough, or capture enough – or however they are replenishing their armies – to cover the shortfall.'

'In that, at least, we can take heart.'

There was a pause, filled with the soft tread of their shoes and the rustling of the leaves, long enough to elicit a new subject.

'I read your mother's new book,' Kaiku said.

'So did I. Several times.'

'There is something odd about it. About those last lines, especially.'

Mishani nodded sadly. 'The words Nida-jan says to the dying man? They are the first stanza of a lullaby she used to sing to me, one that she wrote herself. We were the only ones that knew it in its entirety.'

'*I* know it,' Kaiku said. 'You sang it to me once, when you were telling me how you discovered Chien was working for your mother.'

'You remember that?' Mishani asked in surprise. She had not thought of the unfortunate merchant for a long time now. He had been poisoned by her father's assassins during the siege at Zila; but not before Mishani had found out that he had been charged by her mother in secret to protect her from those same assassins.

Kaiku's lip twitched at the edge. 'She does have a gift for words. It sticks in the mind.' She kicked at a branch that lay across their path. 'After I read those lines, I could not shake the sensation that she meant something by them.'

'That is plain enough,' said Mishani.

'So I began to read her earlier books. The ones since her style changed, since your father became Lord Protector. Trying to divine what her intention might be, what she was trying to express.'

'And did you come to any conclusion?' Mishani was fascinated by this, that her friend should have been thinking along exactly the same lines as her.

Kaiku tilted her shoulders in a shrug. 'Nothing, beyond a certainty that there is something there. The answers remain impenetrable.'

Mishani felt a twinge of disappointment. She had hoped her friend might have some kind of resolution for her.

'Tsata is back,' Kaiku said, apropos of nothing.

'Here?'

'In Saramyr. He is coming to Araka Jo with the Tkiurathi.' Kaiku had charged the Sister present at the attack to find out whether Tsata had survived. It had taken several days, for the Tkiurathi had departed from the main army some time before, and the Sister had other things to do; finding someone who remembered one man amid an army of people who looked identical to her eyes was not an easy task. But the answer had come that morning.

Kaiku had been almost giddy with relief: she had not realised how tautly she was wound until the tension inside her slackened.

'Strange days indeed,' Mishani said wryly, looking up at Kaiku, who was several inches the taller.

'Do not use that tone!' Kaiku laughed. 'I know what you insinuate.'

'He has crossed an ocean to come back to you, Kaiku,' Mishani pointed out.

'He has crossed an ocean to fight the Weavers,' she replied. 'You know his kind; it was the only logical course of action to him.'

'I do *not* know his kind,' said Mishani. 'Their ways are hard for me to understand. Not for you, though, it seems.'

Kaiku made a prissy little *moue* at her friend. 'Perhaps I should be the ambassador, then, instead of you.'

'Ha! You? We would be at open war within the day!'

And so it went. They meandered along the lakeside in the bright light of the winter's day, and for a time they forgot their cares in the simplicity of companionship. Such moments were all too brief, for both of them.

In the Imperial Keep at Axekami, the evening meal was served.

The Lord Protector Avun tu Koli knelt opposite his wife at the small, square table of black and red lacquer. Between them were woven baskets which steamed gently, separate ones for shellfish, saltrice, dumplings and vegetables. Little bowls of soup and sauces, tall glasses of amber wine. The servants ensured everything was satisfactory and then retreated through the curtained archway, leaving their master and mistress alone.

They sat in silence for a time. The room, though not so large, seemed cavernous and hollow; the sound of their breathing and their tiny movements were amplified by the empty space. It was not yet late enough to merit lanterns, but the murk over the city choked the sunlight that came in through the trio of floor-to-ceiling window-arches in the western wall and left only a drab gloom. Vases and sculptures were positioned in alcoves, but the central space was open, and only they were there, kneeling on their mats with the table and the food between them.

'Will you eat?' Avun said eventually.

Muraki did not respond for a few seconds. Then she began to slip on the finger-cutlery. Avun did the same, and they took food from the baskets and put it onto their plates.

'Did your writing go well today?' he asked.

'Well enough,' she replied quietly, an unspoken accusation in her voice.

'I thought you should get away from that room,' Avun said. 'It is not good for your health, to shut yourself away like that.'

Muraki glanced up at him through the curtains of her hair, then looked meaningfully out of the window and back to him. *Healthier than breathing this air*, her gaze said.

'I am sorry for having interrupted you, then,' he said, pouring a dark sauce over the shellfish, holding the bowl with his unencumbered thumb and forefinger. 'I wanted to have a meal with my wife.'

She did not reply to that. Instead, she began to eat, cutting portions with the tiny blades and forks set on silver thimbles that she wore on the middle and ring fingers of her right and left hand, taking small and delicate bites.

'The feya-kori are on their way back from Zila,' Avun said. He needed to say something to breach his wife's wall of silence. When she did not respond, he persevered: 'The troops of the Empire were driven out with barely any resistance at all. The Weavers are pleased with their new creations; more will join them soon, I think.'

The quiet became excruciating once again, but Avun had given enough to expect something in return. Eventually, Muraki asked: 'How soon?'

'A matter of weeks. It is uncertain.'

'And then?'

'We will overrun the Southern Prefectures, and after that we will turn to Tchom Rin.'

'And will you turn their cities into places like this?'

'I cannot see why the Weavers would do so,' he replied. 'There will be no need for feya-kori once they have control of the continent. And so, there will be no need for this miasma.'

'Will there be a need for us, do you think?' she asked softly. 'When they have control of the continent?'

Avun smiled gently. 'I am no fool, Muraki. I do not think they would keep me as Lord Protector out of gratitude. I will be invaluable to them still. The people need a human face upon their leader. They will never trust a Mask.'

'But they will trust you?'

'They will trust me because I will give them their skies back,' Avun said. He took a sip of wine. 'I do not want to live under this murk any more than you do; it is unnatural. But the sooner we are rid of the opposition, the sooner we can dispense with the feya-kori and dissemble the pall-pits.'

'And the temples?'

Avun was lost for an answer for a moment. His wife had a way of pricking his sorest spots in a tone so submissive that he could not take umbrage. 'The temples will not return. The Weavers do not like our gods.'

Muraki's silence was more eloquent than words. She knew he still prayed in the dead of night, in the empty interior of the temple to Ocha on the roof of the Keep. The dome still remained in all its finery, though the statues of the gods that had ringed it were gone, and the altars and icons stripped away. It had an appallingly wounded feel to it now, and Muraki would not go near it. But Avun did.

Muraki wondered how he reconciled his actions to himself: he was not the most pious of men, but he would not forsake his gods, even though he would tear down their temples. Did he expect forgiveness? She knew of no deity so divinely gracious as to provide him with that, after the crimes he had committed against the Golden Realm.

Avun dodged the subject in the end, returning to his previous point. 'In the end, the world will be as it was. The blight can be contained once the Red Order are overthrown, for the Weavers will not need so many witchstones. The miasma will be gone. And the land will be united once again.'

'That is what the Weavers say? I had not heard that before now.'

'I met with Kakre this morning. I persuaded him to divulge. It was not easy.' Avun seemed proud of himself; she had no trouble believing that it was a courageous thing to do. She knew what had happened to him in the past when Kakre was displeased.

'Why?' she asked, puzzled. 'Why did you do it? You have been content in ignorance until now.'

He gazed at her levelly. 'Because my wife does not like the air here,' he said. 'And I had to be able to tell her it would be pure again one day.'

Muraki's eyes flickered to his, and then back to her plate. It was the only outward sign of the flutter she felt in her breast. For a long while, she said nothing.

'Do you believe them?'

'It is the only way I can make sense of it. The alternative is to continue to poison the land. To do that would kill their own people, their own army. There is not enough food, and the famine will get worse.'

'Or perhaps we do not see the Weavers' greater plan,' she whispered, her voice softening with the terror of contradicting him. 'Perhaps Kakre is merely mad.'

Avun nodded. 'He is mad.'

Muraki looked at him in surprise.

'I have been watching his decline most carefully,' Avun said. 'It has steepened since he awakened the feya-kori. I think the effort of controlling them has hit him the hardest. His sanity is eroding fast.' He took a bite of a dumpling, chewed for a moment and swallowed, as if what he was saying was just idle conversation and not something he might be executed for. 'I suspect he would not have told me the Weavers' long-term plans if he had not been quite so addled.'

'But if the Weave-lord is mad,' Muraki breathed, 'who will direct the Weavers?'

'That,' he said, raising his glass, 'is the question.'

TWELVE

The desert city of Izanzai sprawled over an uneven plateau that rose high above the dusty plains. It was a forest of dark spikes, its buildings cramming up to the lip of the sand-coloured cliffs. Needle-thin towers speared towards the pale sky; bulbous temples tapered to elegant spires as they ascended; bridges looped above the hot, shadowy streets. At its southern edge there was a vast earthen ramp that was the only road up to the top of the plateau, built through years of toil and costing many lives.

Izanzai commanded an impressive view of its surroundings. To the south and east the plains were gradually swallowed by the deep desert, and in the distance it was possible to see the beginning of the enormous dunes that humped across central Tchom Rin. To the north and west the land was starker still, dry flats and mesas streaked with swatches of muddy yellow and deep brown, then suddenly rising hard, becoming the great barrier of the Tchamil Mountains. The mountains loomed grey and bleak, their sides flensed of life by hurricanes, innumerable peaks ranked one behind the other and stretching to infinity.

At their feet, men fought and died.

Barak Reki tu Tanatsua sat on manxthwa-back on the lip of a mesa, overlooking the battle. The warm wind plucked at his hair and clothes and ruffled the pelt of his mount. His eyes were narrowed, studying the form and movement of both sides, calculating strategies. The fight was all but over, and the desert forces were the victors, but he would not count it done until every last one of the enemy were dead. To his right and left, also on manxthwa, were a Sister of the Red Order and Jikiel, his spymaster. Other bodyguards waited at a distance, keen and alert, though they were far from anything that could harm them.

The latchjaws had arrived in greater numbers than ever this time. Had they come up against the armies of the families of Izanzai alone, they would have crushed them. But the unification of the Baraks had changed things, and with old enmities laid aside, Reki had been able to direct a much larger force to defend the city. The alliance had come not a day too soon, it seemed.

But the battle had been costly. Those cursed Aberrant beasts were tough to kill, and more often than not they took a few men with them when they went. Unlike the majority of the predator species that the Weavers had deployed thus far, they needed little water or food and were all but immune to the heat. They dealt with shifting sand or hard stone with equal ease; and their deadly natural armour meant that the desert warriors' manic, close-up fighting style was effectively rendered suicidal. Too many were falling to them, snatched up in the mantrap-like jaws that gave them their name. Gods, if he didn't think it impossible, he would have believed that the Weavers had tailored this species for exactly this purpose: to overrun the desert.

It *was* impossible, wasn't it?

'Your men in the mountains have located some of the Nexuses,' the Sister murmured suddenly, relaying the information passed from her companions nearer the battle.

Reki made a noise of acknowledgement. He could have guessed that anyway. A section of the shambling monstrosities down on the plain had suddenly gone berserk, a sure sign that their masters had been killed. No longer under the control of the Nexuses, they reverted to being animals again, and animals were liable to react badly at finding themselves in the midst of a pitched battle of thousands.

'It seems that this day is ours,' Jikiel observed.

Reki looked askance at his spymaster. '*This* day,' he said. 'But how many more can we win?'

Jikiel nodded gravely. He was old and bald, brown and wrinkled as a nut, with a thin black beard and moustaches hanging in three slender ropes down his chest. He was robed in beige, with a nakata, the hook-tipped sword worn by the warriors of Tchom Rin, belted to his hip. 'Perhaps we should take action against the source,' he suggested.

'I was thinking the same,' said Reki. 'Each time they come, there are more. We are forced to spread ourselves thin, for the borders of the mountains are vast. By bringing the Baraks together, we have won a respite; but that is all. They will overwhelm us in time.'

'What are your orders, my Barak?'

'Assemble as many men as you need. Send them into the mountains. I want to know where these things are coming from.'

'It shall be done.'

They watched the battle for a little longer. The Nexuses were falling, and with them went their troops, collapsing into disorder and being shot down by the desert folk. The manxthwa stirred and grumbled, shuffling from side to side and scraping their hooves. The Sister delivered reports from time to time.

Half of Reki's mind was on the battlefield, but half had drifted elsewhere, to his wife. It always seemed to. She had been gone over a month now, but the anxiety of separation had not faded. He still yearned for her. And he still burned at the way she had left him: without an explanation, with only cryptic hints and emotional blackmail left in her wake. He was furious at himself for letting her go without demanding more. He wondered what she was doing now, what was so important as to take her over seven hundred miles to the west. In the time she had been gone, he had tormented himself with innumerable invented histories; but in the end, how could he guess? What did he really know about Asara's past? She was a mystery to him, as much as she had ever been.

And yet, was there really anything to fear? Was there anything he could not forgive her for, anything that might stop him loving her? He could not believe that. And he could not bear the torture of possibilities when there were the prospect of certainties that he could deal with and overcome.

'Jikiel?' he murmured, turning himself so that he was out of the Sister's earshot.

'My Barak?'

'Find out about my wife.' It felt like the most exquisite betrayal, and for a moment he considered taking it back; but it was a risk he had to take. If Asara did not trust their love, then he would have to take matters into his own hands. 'Find out *everything* about her.'

A smile touched the corner of Jikiel's mouth. 'I thought you'd never ask.'

Asara came to Cailin in the small hours of the morning, in the house of the Red Order at Araka Jo. Cailin was drinking bitter tea, looking out through the sliding panels at the dark trees, watching owls.

'Asara,' she purred. 'It was only a matter of time.'

Asara was already inside the room, having glided through the drapes without a sound. 'Why else do you suppose I would come this far, if not to see you?'

Cailin put aside the delicate bowl that she was drinking from, stood up and faced her visitor. 'Kaiku, perhaps? You never did seem to be able to keep away from her for long.'

Asara did not rise to the bait. 'I saved Kaiku's life for *you*,' she said calmly. 'I have paid a price for it ever since. I expect a measure of gratitude for that.'

'Ah, gratitude,' Cailin replied. 'Why would I owe you that, Asara? You did what I told you to. You will get your reward when our deal is complete.'

Asara stepped a little further into the room. It was dark; there was no light but the white glow of the two larger moons. She stood there in the shadows, a disdainful arrogance in the tilt of her chin. She wore a white dress fastened with a brooch, delicate jewellery on her wrists and in her hair. Every inch the desert Barakess.

'Things are different now,' Asara said. 'I am no longer the woman I once was.'

'You think you have *changed?*' Cailin said in disbelief. 'You can change all you want on the outside, Asara, but inside you are just as empty as you have always been.'

'It is my situation that has changed.' Her tone had become edged with venom now. 'As well you know.'

They regarded each other across the room. It was the same one in which

Kaiku and Cailin had been Weaving several nights before, on the second storey of the Red Order's house. The vases stood empty now, the incense burner cold. The charcoal etchings on the wood-panelled walls seemed to creep in the darkness.

'I must congratulate you,' Cailin said at length. 'Your seduction of the Heir-Barak showed impressive foresight. How you must have grieved when both his sister and his father died, making way for him to become head of his family.'

'His sister was ineligible to become head of the family, since she was wed to the Emperor,' Asara replied levelly. 'Her demise benefitted you more than me. You wanted the Weavers to succeed in their coup, you *wanted* them to take this land. And now you have your wish.'

'And you had nothing to do with her death, I suppose?'

'Maybe so, and maybe not,' Asara replied. 'If the former, it would have been another example of how I have given more on your behalf that anyone has a right to ask, and received nothing in return.'

'Such is the nature of our agreement, Asara. You will be paid in full when the time comes.'

'Then I am altering our agreement.'

Cailin raised an eyebrow. 'You are? How amusing.'

'I am the wife of a Barak now, Cailin,' Asara said, bridling a little. 'I hold the most powerful man in the desert in the palm of my hand. You cannot sweep me aside as you might once have done.'

Cailin's red-and-black lips were set in a mocking smirk. 'I see. And you think that because you have fooled a callow boy into marriage that you can use it as leverage to bully me? I had thought better of you, Asara.'

'I have been over a *decade* in your thrall, Cailin,' Asara spat, sudden rage igniting within her. 'Kept tied by your promises. You realised what I needed – the gods know how; your filthy *kana*-games, no doubt – and you have exploited me ever since. And all this time I have chased a dream that I am not even sure you are capable of fulfilling! Now I have the power in the desert, and I can turn Tchom Rin against you and your kind. I know what *you* desire, and I can make it much more difficult for you if you do not give me what I want *now!*'

'Enough!' Cailin snapped. 'What is ten years, twenty, *fifty* to such as us? We will not age, Asara. We do not run out of time as others do. Where is your patience?'

'I have been patient,' came the reply. 'But there is a line between patience and foolishness. Should I be your slave for another decade, and another, until you decide to release me? And even then, could you grant me what you say you will? *Would* you? One woman's word is a slender thread to hang such a weight from. And you have hardly been a paragon of trustworthiness in the years I have known you.'

Cailin laughed, the sound high and bright. 'Poor Asara,' she said. 'Poor, murdering Asara.' Her laughter faded, and her voice grew dark. 'You want sympathy? I have none. The Red Order's cause is as much in your interests as ours—'

'I doubt that,' Asara interrupted.

'—and however unwillingly, you are fighting for yourself when you fight on our side. We will make a world where Aberrants can live without fear. And you *will* aid us in that, whether you want to or not.'

'You are avoiding the issue,' Asara said, stalking closer. 'Give me what I want.'

'Release you from our compact? Hardly. You are, despite your faults, an extremely useful ally.'

'*Give me what I want!*' Asara cried.

'Or *what?*' Cailin shouted. 'What will you do, Asara? You think you can turn the desert against us? You think you can *stop* us? Your best efforts would be nothing more than a mosquito bite to the Red Order. We could kill you a thousand times over before you could even get back to your beloved Barak. And even Reki is not such a fool as to forsake the powers we lend him when the Weavers are even now trying to invade Tchom Rin. Yours is a poor bluff, Asara, and you tire me now.'

'It ends here, then!' Asara returned. 'It all ends here. If you cannot prove to me that you can do what you say, then I—'

Cailin cut her throat.

It was a swift, dismissive gesture with her hand, a disgusted flick of her fingers in the moonlight. She did not touch the other woman; they were too far apart. But Asara's neck opened from side to side in a red slit, as cleanly as if Cailin had been holding a sword.

Asara staggered backward, her eyes wide, making damp noises in her chest. Blood gushed, pulsing down the front of her dress, staining it a glistening black in the moonlight. Cailin watched impassively, sidelit by the moonlight, her irises gone crimson.

Asara tried to make a sound, but none would come. She tried to draw breath, but not even a gasp would make it through her severed windpipe. Panic swamped her, a terror like nothing she had ever known before: she was dying, dying unfulfilled, and when she was gone it would be as if she had never been here. Her legs went weak, her muscles leaden. She fell to her knees, clutching her throat with one hand, the other feebly propping her upright, her splayed fingers sliding in her own fluids. Her head was becoming light. So much blood, so much blood, and nothing she could do would staunch it.

Not like this, was all she could think with the last dregs of her reason. *Not like this.*

Cailin made a vague waving motion with two of her fingers, and Asara's throat sewed shut, fibres and tissues knitting seamlessly from side to side as if zipped. Eager nourishment slammed from her heart to her brain, and she hauled in a huge, sobbing breath. She had never felt such a divine sensation as the relief she experienced then, nor a hatred so pure as that which she had for the one who had hurt her this way. Still gasping, her dress sodden black, she raised her head and fixed Cailin with a gaze of utter malice.

The Pre-Eminent of the Red Order looked down on her coldly. 'Satisfied?' she asked, then walked out of the room, leaving Asara kneeling in a pool of her own blood.

An hour's walk northeast of Araka Jo, deep in the forested mountains, lay the glade of an ipi.

It was a place of preternatural stillness and tranquillity, a cavernous sanctum with a roof of interlaced branches and leaves through which the winter sun shone in bright, slanting shafts of light. Gently rolling hillocks and tuffets cradled pools as motionless and transparent as glass; rocks smooth and white like bleached bone hid half-buried in the earth. In the midst of the glade stood the ipi itself: a colossal tree, its bark black as char, rucked and gnarled with age. Its uppermost branches meshed with the canopy overhead, while the lower boughs reached out across the clearing like crooked arms, fingers shaggy with pine blades.

Lucia knelt at the base of the tree, her head bowed, clad in a belted robe of dark green. She was meditating, communing with the spirit of the glade. To talk to an ipi was easy for her these days. Her power had grown at a frightening rate since she had emerged from the shrine of Alskain Mar back in the Xarana Fault, and all but the most ancient spirits were open to her now. Yet with every step she took into the world of the spirits, she took one away from the world of humanity, and she was becoming more like them by the day.

Kaiku watched her from the edge of the glade. Somewhere in the trees, out of sight, were her Libera Dramach bodyguards. But in this place, in the ipi's serene presence, Lucia might have been alone in all the world. And it was true, in a sense. For there was no one like Lucia, nobody who could imagine what it was like to be as she was, poised halfway between two worlds and belonging to neither any more.

It pained Kaiku to see her so isolated. Mishani's visit had reminded her of Yugi's stinging words, how he had accused her of neglecting her friends while she subsumed herself in the teachings of the Red Order. Once, Lucia had been like a younger sister to her; now, Kaiku was not so sure.

Eventually, Lucia lifted her head and stood. She picked her way barefoot along the knolls, retrieved her shoes from where she had left them at the edge of the glade, and then joined Kaiku.

'Daygreet,' she said with a beatific smile, and then hugged Kaiku impulsively. Kaiku, faintly surprised, returned it.

'Gods, you are the same height as me now,' she said.

'Growing like a weed,' Lucia laughed. 'It's been too long since you came to see me, Kaiku.'

'I know,' Kaiku muttered. 'I know.'

Lucia put her shoes on and they began to walk back towards Araka Jo.

Kaiku dismissed the bodyguards and sent them ahead: their charge would be safer with her than with twenty armed men, and they recognised her even without the makeup and attire of the Order. She and Lucia ambled along the narrow forest trails. Lucia chattered happily as they went. She was in an unusually ebullient mood, certainly not the state of dreamy detachment that Kaiku had come to expect from her.

'The blight is retreating,' she said out of nowhere, interrupting herself in the process of telling Kaiku about her day.

'It is?'

'The ipi can sense it. Since the witchstone beneath Utraxxa broke. The land here is recovering, little by little.' She watched a bird arrowing through the treetops as she spoke. 'We are not too far gone to go back. Not yet.'

'But that is wonderful news!' Kaiku cried. Lucia gave her a sidelong grin. 'No wonder you are so cheerful today.'

'It is wonderful news,' she agreed. 'And I hear you have news also.'

Kaiku nodded. 'Though I am not so sure whether it is good news or bad.' And she went on to tell Lucia about her and Cailin's encounter with the leviathan. The *Weave-whale*, as Cailin had come to call it.

'I am afraid of them,' she admitted. 'For too long we had ignored them as they ignored us, assuming them forever out of our reach. But we have attracted them now, I think. They have noticed what was once beneath their notice. Our meddling in the Weave is drawing creatures to which the Weavers' capabilities for destruction pale in comparison.'

'But what are they?' Lucia asked.

'Perhaps they are gods,' came the reply.

Lucia did not comment on that, but it sobered her. They walked on a short way in silence through the sun-dappled forest. A raven hopped from branch to branch overhead.

'Lucia, I truly am sorry,' Kaiku said at length. 'I have neglected you for some time now. I was so caught up in learning how to use what I have that I . . . forgot what I had.'

Lucia took her hand. It was a gesture from the old Lucia, the child, before she became a young woman.

'It is the war,' she said. 'Do not be sorry, Kaiku. You are a weapon, as am I. What good is a weapon if its edge is not sharpened?'

Kaiku was shocked at the fatalism in her tone. 'Lucia, no! We are *not* merely weapons. If I taught you nothing else, I taught you that.'

'Then you believe we have a choice? That we can turn away from all this now?' She smiled sadly, and relinquished Kaiku's hand. 'I can't. And I don't believe you can, either.'

'You *have* that choice, Lucia!' she insisted.

'Do I?' Lucia laughed again, and this time it was bitter and made Kaiku uneasy. 'If I wanted to duck the expectations the world has of me, I should have done it long ago. Before the Libera Dramach reorganised; before the battle at the Fold, even. Too many people have died in my name now. I cannot go back. That time has passed.' She looked down the trail, and her eyes became unfocused. She was listening to the rustle of the forest. 'I've become what they wanted of me. I've become their bridge to the spirits, for what good it will do. I am a weapon, and a weapon is useless if it is not wielded. I cannot stay useless for very much longer.'

'Lucia—' Kaiku began, but was interrupted.

'You think I don't know about the feya-kori? How we have no defence against them, no way to strike back? How long before you all call on me, then? Your last resort? Your only hope?' They had stopped walking now, and Lucia looked fierce. 'Do you know how that is, Kaiku? To spend your whole life knowing that your options are narrowing day by day, that eventually you must deliver on this promise that you *never made!* They look to me as their saviour, but I don't know how to save anyone!'

'You do not have to,' Kaiku told her. 'Listen to me: you do *not* have to.'

Lucia looked away, not remotely convinced.

'In my life I have known people who are so selfish that they would sacrifice anything and anyone to bring advantage to themselves,' Kaiku said, putting her hand on Lucia's arm. 'And I have known a man so selfless that he was willing to throw away his life too cheaply for the good of others. I believe the right path lies somewhere in between. I have told you before, Lucia: you need to be a little more selfish. Think of yourself for once.'

'Even at the expense of this land and everyone in it?' Lucia replied scornfully.

'Even then,' said Kaiku. 'For as much as you think it might, the fate of the world does not rest on your actions.'

Lucia would not meet her gaze. 'I'm afraid, Kaiku,' she whispered.

'I know.'

'You *don't* know,' she said, and her expression revealed a depth of something that made Kaiku scared to see it. 'I'm *changing*.'

'Changing? How?'

Lucia turned from her, staring out into the forest. Kaiku's attention fell upon the burn scars on the nape of her neck. The stab of guilt at the sight would never go away, it seemed.

'I realise I am distracted sometimes . . . *most* of the time,' she said. 'I realise how hard it is to talk to me. I do not blame you for not coming to see me so often.' She raised a hand to forestall Kaiku's protest. 'It's true, Kaiku. I can't pay attention to anything any more. Everywhere I go, there are the voices. The breath of the wind, the mutter of the earth; the birds, the trees, the stone. I do not know what silence is.' She turned her face sideways, looking over her shoulder at Kaiku, and a tear slid down her cheek. 'I can't shut them out,' she whispered.

A lump rose in Kaiku's throat.

'I'm becoming like them,' Lucia said, her voice small and terrifying in its hopelessness. 'I'm forgetting. Forgetting how to care. I think of Zaelis and Flen, of my mother . . . and I don't *feel*. They died because of me, and sometimes I can't even recall their faces.' Her lip began to tremble, and her face crumpled, and she rushed into Kaiku's arms suddenly and clutched her so tightly that it hurt. 'I'm so *lonely*,' she said, and began to cry in earnest then.

Kaiku's stomach and heart were a knot of grief that brought tears to her own eyes. She wanted to reach Lucia somehow, to do something to make things better, but she was as helpless as anyone. All Kaiku could do was to be there for her, and she had been sadly remiss at that these past years.

And as they held each other on the narrow forest trail, the leaves began to fall. First one, then two, then a dozen and more, drifting down from the evergreens to settle on their shoulders and pile around their feet. Lucia was weeping, and the trees were shedding in sympathy.

THIRTEEN

The Tkiurathi appeared one morning soon afterward, on a slope south of Araka Jo. By the time anyone noticed them, they had already made cook-fires, strung up shelters of animal hide, and dozens of them were sleeping in the boughs like cats. A makeshift village of yurts and hemp hammocks had sprung up overnight amid the tree trunks. To all appearances, they might have been living there for weeks.

Tsata was sitting in the crook of a tree, where the branch met the bole, one leg dangling. He was idly sharpening his gutting-hooks on a whetstone, his attention elsewhere. From his vantage point at the north side of the village he could see up the dirt trail towards Araka Jo. He believed at first that he had chosen this spot at random, but he decided in the end that he was fooling himself. He was keeping an eye on the trail. Waiting to see if Kaiku would come to him.

A Tkiurathi woman called from below. She raised her blade, and he tossed her down the whetstone, which she plucked from the air with a grin of thanks before wandering back towards the centre of the village.

Tsata slipped his gutting-hook back on to the catch at his belt and relaxed, watching the activity around him. It was exciting to be here in Saramyr again, and the better because this time he was not alone, but surrounded by his people. They took the strangeness of the land in their stride. They were brothers and sisters, insulated within their *pash*, comforted by the knowledge of community. Tsata found himself smiling.

At the base of the trees, traditional three-sided yurts called *repka* had been built. They were communal places for living and sleeping, with splayed, tunnel-like arms around a large hub construction with a chimney-hole through which curls of smoke rose. Other fires had been made outside: the hunters had already caught some of the local wildlife, and Tsata had been busy indicating foods that were safe to eat. He was recognised as the authority on Saramyr within the *pash*, having been here before and having studied its language and its customs long before that.

It was the way among the Tkiurathi that they were all teachers, each one sharing what unique knowledge or abilities they had. It had been one such man who had taught Tsata Saramyrrhic, a man who had travelled and lived here for decades before returning to his homeland. Tsata had a particular gift for languages – he had already learned a good deal of Quraal, which was the lingua franca of the trading settlements dotted around the Okhamban coast – and he had been bewildered and fascinated by stories of Saramyr. He applied himself to learning Saramyrrhic with a singularity of purpose that impressed his teacher, and within a few years he was as skilled at it as any foreigner could be. The months he had spent here had improved his command of the language vastly, but even now he was not entirely fluent in the overwhelming multitude of modes and inflections, the tiny subtleties of High Saramyrrhic that only those born to it could hope to master.

When he looked away from the settlement and back to the trail, Kaiku was there. She was regarding him impishly, a wry expression on her face.

'Are you coming down here, or shall I come up there?' she called.

He laughed; he knew her well enough to tell that she was not bluffing. With monkey-like grace, he slipped off the branch and swung from it to the ground ten feet below. There was a moment of awkward hesitation as they met, as each tried to determine whether to greet the other in their native fashion or that of the foreigner; then Kaiku stood on tiptoes, kissed him on the forehead and embraced him. Tsata was warmly surprised: it was an unusual gesture of extraordinary intimacy for a Saramyr to bestow.

'Welcome back,' she said.

'It is good to be here,' he said. 'I wish all welcomes had been as pleasant.'

'The feya-kori,' Kaiku murmured, nodding slightly. 'I fear you could have timed your arrival a little better.'

'Perhaps we have arrived at just the right moment,' he countered. 'From what I have learned, there have been no darker days than these. And there is no further need to convince my people of the threat to us; the men who return to Okhamba will spread the word. Seventy-five of us lost their lives the day we landed, but the remainder will fight harder for their sacrifice.' His face cleared suddenly. 'But we can talk of such things later. Let me show you our new home. And you must tell me what has occurred in my absence.'

It was as if they had never been apart. They fell easily into the rhythms of conversation that they had established during their long period of isolation, when they had lived and hunted together in the shattered wilderness of the Xarana Fault.

He talked of the many obstacles he had faced in his mission to alert his people to the danger of the Weavers. Kaiku spoke of her induction into the Red Order and her training. She told him also of Lucia and Mishani; he had met them briefly before his departure from the Fold, but he knew them primarily through Kaiku's stories. And she spoke of her fears for Lucia, and about the Weave-whales, and the plight of the beleaguered forces of the Empire.

They wandered the village as they talked. Kaiku had chosen travel clothes over the attire of the Order for her visit to the Tkiurathi village, for she did not wish to appear intimidating. Now she was glad that she had. Amid the informality of the Tkiurathi, she would have felt self-conscious in her make-up.

The people were muscled and lean, their skin tough and their hands seamed through the rigours of their lifestyle. She often found herself identifying them as much from the unique pattern of their tattoos as by their features, for it was difficult to see past them at first: they were such an overwhelmingly prominent facet of their appearance. The women were strong and physically unfeminine by Saramyr standards, having little softness about them, though Kaiku found in some a kind of wild beauty that was appealing. They sat as equals with the men, their long hair bound with cord or left loose, wearing sleeveless garments of hemp or hide and trousers of the same.

Tsata sat with her around one of the campfires that had been built out in the open, along with a dozen other Tkiurathi who were eating. The men to either side of them handed them bowls and tipped a portion of their own bowls into those of the newcomers. It was a typically Okhamban gesture of sharing. Kaiku did not know how she was supposed to respond, for she had nothing to give back; but Tsata motioned to her not to worry, no response was needed, and he began to fill the remainder of both their bowls from a pot of stew that hung over the fire. It was the meat of some local animal mixed in with vegetables and unfamiliar spices: it smelt delicious, though not so delicate as Saramyr food, more laden with heavy flavour. By the time he had finished, they had been handed chunks of bread from others in the circle, torn from their own loaves. Kaiku could not help but thank them, even though she knew almost nothing of their language.

'You do not need to thank them,' Tsata told her. 'You do so by allowing them to share in *your* food, when *you* have some and they are hungry.'

'I know,' she said. 'But it is difficult to break the habits of a lifetime. Just as I would find it odd if some of your people turned up at the door of my house expecting to be fed.'

'It does not quite work that way,' he laughed. 'But I can tell there will be many such misunderstandings between your folk and mine in the days to come.'

One of the women, who had been studying Kaiku, said something to her in their rough, guttural dialect. She looked uncertainly at Tsata.

'She says your language is very beautiful,' he translated. 'Like birds singing.'

'Should I thank her for that?'

He smiled. 'Yes. *Ghohkri.*'

Kaiku repeated the word to the woman, by chance pronouncing it perfectly to murmurs of approval from round the fire. Encouraged by her response, others started to ask her questions or make observations, which Tsata translated rapidly back and forth. Presently Kaiku was drawn into the conversation around the circle, with Tsata murmuring condensed explanations in her ear as people spoke to each other in Okhamban. She began to interject with a few comments of her own, to which there was always a slightly uncomfortable moment of incomprehension until Tsata could provide the Okhamban; but they were polite and patient, and Kaiku began to enjoy herself greatly. They were clearly fascinated by her, and they thought that even the shabby travel clothes she wore were incredibly exotic.

'Gods, they should see the River District in Axekami,' Kaiku commented to Tsata, then remembered that Axekami was not as it once was, and saddened a little.

Eventually, they left the circle and wandered around the rest of the camp. Everywhere Kaiku looked, she found something out of the ordinary, whether it was the way the Tkiurathi fashioned their tools, the smell of their strange meals or the startling way they slept in the trees.

'It is an old instinct,' Tsata explained. 'There are many things on the ground that cannot reach us in the branches. Some people still prefer it, even in a safe forest like this one. The rest of us sleep in the *repka*.'

'No forest is truly safe,' Kaiku said. 'The animals have become steadily more violent as the blight has encroached on our land.'

'In the jungles that we come from, Saramyr animals would not last a night,' Tsata said. 'We are used to worse predators than bears or wolves. I doubt you have anything that would trouble us much.'

'Ah,' said Kaiku. 'But we have Aberrants.'

'Yes,' Tsata said, who had gathered a good deal of experience at hunting them on his last visit. 'Tell me about them. I hear things are different now.'

So Kaiku told him about the latchjaws in the desert, and about other new breeds they had identified and named. Nobody was sure if these species had recently appeared or if they had simply not been seen frequently enough to be noticed in the past. Certainly, there always seemed to be a few reports of Aberrants that nobody recognised, in among the usual ghauregs and shrillings and furies.

Then Tsata told her about the Aberrant man he had tried to rescue in Zila, and they were off on a new tack.

'Of course they still hate us,' Kaiku said, as they walked around the edge of the village. 'People have always been susceptible to the fear of difference. But things are progressing at a different pace in different areas. Aberrants who are outwardly freakish are despised more than those who look "normal." I do not think most people even think of Lucia as Aberrant any more: they have elevated her into something else, some nebulous and divine saviour to suit their purposes, and the high families appear content to encourage it. They need a figurehead, and if the price of winning back their Empire is to have Lucia on the throne, then so be it. At least she is of noble blood. Plus she has Blood Ikati and Blood Erinima on her side, and the Libera Dramach. Between them they form the strongest alliance by far, and nobody wants to be divisive and oppose them.'

'And what of the Red Order?' Tsata asked.

A brief look of frustration passed over her face. 'The high families do not like us, despite the fact that we saved them from destruction, despite the fact that we are the ones who protect them from the Weavers, who could otherwise simply reach into their heads from Axekami and kill them.' She snorted. 'The Red Order is mistrusted, as if we were another kind of Weaver.'

'And aren't you?'

She should not have been surprised: he was ever blunt. 'No!' she said. 'The Weavers killed Aberrants for centuries to cover the evidence of their own crimes. Their post-Weaving whims still account for more deaths than I would like to think. And they have taken the land from us.'

'As your people took it from the Ugati,' Tsata reminded her. 'I know the Sisters are not so foul nor so cruel as the Weavers, but you seek to fulfil their role within the Empire. Will you be content as servants? The Weavers were not.'

'The Weavers never intended to be. They always meant to dominate, whether they knew it themselves or not. The god that pulls their strings demanded it. It was the only way they could get to the witchstones.'

'You have not answered the question,' he chided softly.

'I do not *know* the answer,' she replied. '*I* do not intend to be a servant of the high families when this is done, but I do not know what plans Cailin has made. I have an oath to fulfil, and that oath requires the destruction of the Weavers. If I can make it that far, I will die content.'

'You must consider the consequences of your actions, Kaiku,' Tsata said, though it was evident by his tone that he meant it as general advice rather than referring specifically to the Sisters. 'You must look ahead.'

'What point is there in that?' she asked. 'There is no alternative. We have but one path in this matter. The Red Order are trying to help people achieve that.'

'This land has been stung once before by placing their trust in beings more powerful than they,' Tsata said. 'It is understandable that they are wary of you.'

She let it drop at that. Tsata was a questioner, and she admired that in him – he made her examine herself, to scrutinise her own choices and opinions – but he was also tenacious, and she did not want to get into an argument now. Instead their talk drifted to other things. Surrounded by Tkiurathi, she found herself wondering about Tsata's childhood, and began to ask him about it. She was surprised that she had never done so before, but she had always been afraid to pry for fear of making him reveal something he did not want to: Okhambans were unfailingly obliging, but they did not like their generosity abused. He was perfectly open, however.

'We do not have parents in Okhamba.' He saw the smile growing on her face, and corrected himself. 'I mean, we do not assign responsibilities to the ones who give birth to us. The children are raised equally as part of whatever *pash* they are. Everyone takes a hand in child-rearing. I do not know which of them were my parents, though I had an inkling. The biological bond is discouraged. It would lead to favouritism and competition.'

They talked of gods and ancestors also. Kaiku had learned in the past that Okhambans did not revere deities, but rather pursued a form of ancestor-worship similar to Saramyr folk, if much more extreme. Whereas Saramyr respected and honoured their ancestors, Okhambans had a more ruthless process. Those who had achieved great things were treated as heroes, with stories told about them and legends spun so that their deeds might be passed on to inspire the younger generation. Those who had not were forgotten, and their names were not spoken aloud. Okhambans believed that a person's strength and courage, ingenuity and wit and inspiration came from themselves alone; that they were responsible for all that they did, that there was no deity to make reparations to or to blame when things went bad. Tsata saw deities as a kind of cushion against the brutal and raw realities of existence.

Kaiku, on the other hand, could not believe how an entire continent of millions could not see what every Saramyr saw: that the gods were all around them, their influence felt everywhere, that they might be capricious and sometimes terrible but that they were undoubtedly *there*.

'But Quraal has different gods,' he had said once. 'How can you both be right?'

'Perhaps they are merely different aspects ascribed to the same entities,' Kaiku had countered. 'We put our own faces on our gods.'

'Then who would they side with in a war between Quraal and Saramyr?' Tsata had returned. 'How do you know who is right if you do not know what they want?'

But Kaiku could only think how empty her life would be if she believed that the world as she perceived it was all that there was. She knew otherwise. She had looked into the eyes of the Children of the Moons. Tsata's ruthless practicality and realism failed to take into account the spirits that haunted both their lands.

'Spirits are beings that cannot be explained,' he had said, 'but we do not worship them, or ask them for forgiveness.'

'If you cannot explain spirits,' Kaiku had replied, 'then how much else can you not explain?'

'But what if your gods are merely spirits of a much greater magnitude?'

So it had gone on. But that was a debate that she had no wish to revisit, so she steered away from contention. She talked about her own beliefs, hopes and fears, and was surprised anew by how easy it was. For such a guarded soul, she found it remarkably effortless to lower her defences to this man. He was so honest that she could not believe him capable of deception, and deception was what she feared the most: she had been duped too many times in her life. So caught up was she that she did not notice Nuki's eye slipping westward through the trees. When she did, she gave a start and clutched his arm.

'Heart's blood, Tsata! It's late. I'd forgotten the other reason I came to see you. Will you come back to Araka Jo with me? Yugi has called a meeting, and he asked if you would attend.'

'I will come,' he said. 'May I bring others?' In response to Kaiku's puzzled frown, he said: 'I am not their leader, merely their . . . favoured ambassador. Others should come, to hear and decide. I will keep the number small. There will be three, including myself. Is that acceptable?'

'Three, then,' Kaiku said. 'We convene at sunset.'

The meeting was held in the rectangular central hall of the largest temple in the complex. It was open to the air, for what once had been a magnificent roof had crumbled under the pressure of ages, and the early-risen Iridima looked into the hall from overhead as Nuki's light turned the sky to copper and gold. It was built of the same white stone as the rest of the complex, and from that stone were carved a dozen enormous idols which lined the walls, four on each of the long sides and one at each corner. The roof had protected the idols for centuries from the worst of time's assaults before it fell, and they were better preserved than most: disconcerting, imposing beings that spoke to something subconscious in the viewer, some ancient memory long lost that still lingered in wisps in the deepest chasms of the mind. Their eyes were uniformly bulbous and slitted horizontally, exuding a dark hunger, and their forms were amalgamations of mammal and reptile and bird.

Lanterns had been placed in newly-set brackets, and an enormous wicker mat dyed with fine designs had been laid in the centre of the otherwise featureless floor, on which the debaters would sit. When Kaiku and Tsata arrived, most were already there, kneeling or cross-legged with their shoes or boots neatly set behind them, just beyond the edge of the mat. She recognised them all: Cailin, Phaeca and several other Sisters, Yugi, Mishani, Lucia, Heir-Barak Hikken tu Erinima, Barakess Emira tu Ziris, and assorted folk of the Libera Dramach. Kaiku was relieved to note that Asara was not present: she had been avoiding her ever since she received news of her arrival. Then she wondered if she *was* here, and Kaiku simply did not recognise her.

There were few nobles present, since most were content to stay in the cities, and this was primarily a Libera Dramach gathering. Hikken was here because he never strayed far from his niece Lucia, hovering like a vulture, and Barakess Emira had been at Araka Jo on a visit. She was an enthusiastic supporter of the Libera Dramach, but she was not powerful, having unwisely backed Blood Kerestyn during the last coup and suffering the loss of most of her army.

Kaiku led Tsata into the hall along with the two other Tkiurathi – a brown-haired, thickset man named Heth who spoke some Saramyrrhic, and the woman who had complimented her on her language back at the village, whose name was Peithre. Beyond the mat where the principle participants would sit, there were a few dozen others lining the walls to observe. Then she spotted Nomoru.

Kaiku's heart jumped in surprise as their eyes met. There she was, in the flesh, scrawny and unkempt and surly, half her face in shadow. Kaiku had almost given up on seeing her again, assuming that she had died in Axekami.

How she had got out of the pall-pits and out of the city, Kaiku would probably never know. But she was tough as a rat, this one, and she had come through once again.

As Kaiku stared, she tilted her head, and the light from nearby fell on the side of her face that had been hidden. Kaiku caught her breath. Nomoru's skin was crisscrossed with scars, thin raised tracks like ploughlines streaking her from cheek to ear and along her neck. It occurred suddenly that Nomoru was *showing* them to her. She looked away, perturbed by this new thought. Did Nomoru hold her responsible? Kaiku had not thought fast enough when she saw Juto squeeze the trigger to shoot Nomoru: she should have killed the momentum of the rifle ball in the air instead of blowing it apart. Even though Kaiku had scarred her in the process of saving her life, did Nomoru blame her for her disfigurement? Gods, she did not want that woman as an enemy.

But then she was slipping her shoes from her feet and kneeling on the communal mat, and Tsata indicated to his companions that they should do the same. She was in full Red Order garb now, and it armoured her against the stares of the people in the hall, against the resentful presence of the idols and the restless flitting of the spirits that whirled invisibly in the recesses, stirred by the unwelcome crowd.

The appearance of the Tkiurathi caused some whispering around the room, but they seemed oblivious. When the meeting began and formal introductions were made for the benefit of all assembled, Kaiku stood and named the Tkiurathi, explaining their presence and apologising in advance for the necessity of translating. Heth murmured her words in Okhamban to Peithre.

Refreshments were laid between them as the formalities went on, small lacquered tables of drinks and silver bowls of finger-food. Heth immediately reached for one of the morsels but was arrested by a negative glare from Tsata, and retreated. The welcomes were done as the last light bled out of the sky and left Iridima hanging in a star-speckled winter night, and it was Yugi, leader of the Libera Dramach, who put forward the reason why they were all here.

'The question before us today is simple,' he said. 'What do we do now? The stalemate has been broken, and the Weavers have the advantage. If we do nothing, they will create more of the feya-kori, and they will sweep aside our forces as they have at Juraka and Zila. As yet we have established no defence against these demons, and though we have learned something of their nature it hasn't yielded any way to hold them back. It's only because they are forced to return to their pall-pits and recuperate that they have not been able to invade the Southern Prefectures with impunity; but though we have a little time, we don't have much of it. Soon, other pall-pits in other cities will be operational. If we can't stand against two feya-kori, what chance do we have against ten or more?'

And so the debate began. Opinions were put back and forth. Yugi mooted the option of marshalling their forces for a full-scale attack on Axekami, more to get it out of the way than because he believed it was a viable option. It was quickly dismissed by the council as foolhardy and pointless: even if they succeeded, it would leave them overstretched and vulnerable. Axekami was not the Weaver's power base, but the old Empire's, and hence it would not be a fatal blow to them; additionally, they still could not hold the city against the feya-kori, and it could be easily retaken.

'If Axekami is to be won, it must be won by the people!' Hikken tu Erinima declared, at which point Yugi called Kaiku and Phaeca to give an account of their recent movements in Axekami and how they gauged the mood of the people. It was not encouraging. Other spies that had reported to Yugi corroborated their opinion.

'We cannot allow ourselves to hope for revolt,' Cailin said. 'The scale is too big, and there is little hope against the Weavers. They can eliminate agitators at will. Without the Red Order to defend them, the people would not have a chance to organise, and there are barely enough of us to protect the forces of the Empire, let alone its citizenry as well.' Her eyes glided over the assembly. 'Passive resistance is the best we could hope for, and even then it is a slim hope. Disseminating the message would not be an easy task, and it would have to be done without the Red Order, for we dare not operate in the Weavers' cities. We cannot even allow Lucia to use her talent for dreamwalking to spy for us there. The risk is too great.'

'Then what do you propose?' Hikken demanded, barely hiding his contempt. 'Should we do nothing?'

'That is not so inadvisable as it sounds,' put in the Barakess Emira. She was a plain-faced woman somewhere near her thirtieth harvest, with dark brown hair worn long and straight. 'The Weavers' forces have seemed thinner of late. It is possible that their armies are starving due to the effects of their own blight. They are short of time, as we are. The question is, whose will run out first?'

'But our spies have been unable to confirm that their forces really are less than before,' Yugi pointed out. 'And we don't know the extent of their supplies. At best it's a guess.'

'However, if we could find some way to hold them off, to delay them, it might be enough to turn the tide,' Emira persisted.

'We *have* no way to hold them off,' Cailin said. 'That is the crux of the matter. The only limitation on the speed they can demolish our cities is their own need to revivify.'

'Perhaps a retreat to the mountains, then?' suggested a Libera Dramach man. 'If we cannot stand against them, we could disperse and strike at them like bandits.'

Yugi nodded. 'That's a last resort, perhaps. But I think that would be the end of us as surely as if we stood up to the feya-kori with only swords and cannon. And if the Weavers do to the Prefectures what they are doing to the territories they have already taken, then the famine will get far worse, and in the mountains there will be no food at all.'

'There is another alternative,' said Cailin. 'To strike at the witchstones.'

'It has been tried,' Hikken said. 'At Utraxxa. And it failed.'

'No,' Cailin replied. 'At Utraxxa we underestimated the Weavers. But their reaction indicates that we *would* have succeeded if we had been given a chance.'

'Perhaps you could explain for the benefit of our guests and our audience?' Kaiku prompted politely. The Tkiurathi had not spoken, except to mutter translations to each other. They knew little about the state of affairs in Saramyr, and were content to listen and learn.

Cailin inclined her head in acknowledgement. 'When we finally mustered the strength to assault the Weaver monastery that lay in the mountains west of here, across Lake Xemit, the Red Order had another plan in mind beyond simply destroying the witchstone there and ridding us of the blight. We intended to engage the witchstone, to learn about it. Through our own observations of how the Weavers' power grew with each stone awakened, and the information Lucia gleaned from the spirit of Alskain Mar in the Xarana Fault, we had determined that all the stones were connected in a manner similar to a net or a web. We believed that we could exploit that link, trace it to the other witchstones and destroy them, too. Instead of one victory, we would win them all at once.'

The assembly did not make a sound; only the faint sussuration of the wind could be heard. The temperature was dropping now that Nuki's light had fled the sky, settling towards a level that was cool but not unpleasant.

'We never got the chance. Just before we penetrated the chamber where the witchstone lay, it was destroyed. We can only assume that the Weavers used explosives. It was something we would never have expected them to do: they had always prized the witchstones' welfare above even their own lives. They were protecting the network by removing our way in.' She swept her gaze across the assembly then, and her tone became fiercer. 'But I say it was *not* a failure. We were close enough to glimpse the witchstone's nature as it came apart. Two years have passed since then, and we have not wasted that time. We have studied what we learned at Utraxxa, and we are more ready than ever now to engage a witchstone again. And this time we will destroy them all.'

Kaiku felt a thrill at the determination in her voice. Gods, the promise of action after so long in hiding or retreat or stalemate was enticing to her.

'And how do you propose to stop yourself becoming . . . cut off, as before?' Mishani asked.

Cailin settled herself again. 'The Red Order have reconstructed the network we observed between the witchstones and examined it. There is no stone that cannot be sacrificed, but there is one which will seriously damage the structure if it falls: the hub, if you will. As the Nexuses are the anchor for the beasts they control, so this stone is the anchor for the other stones. The

Weavers had plenty of time during our long assault on Utraxxa to prepare explosives. But I think they will be much more reluctant to destroy their hub, the most powerful node of them all. And if we catch them by surprise, they may not have *time* to destroy it. If we can get to it intact, we can use it as a way in to the network, and reach all the witchstones in one swoop.'

Kaiku's skin prickled at the thought. Was there a chance, even so slim, that they could end this? She had not been at Utraxxa, having been reluctantly kept back by Cailin, but she had heard of the horrors that her brethren had experienced within. Could it be done? To go through the veins of their power structure, spreading like a virus?

'Do you *know* this, or is it merely conjecture?' Hikken asked. He was a prickly middle-aged man, with a deeply-etched face and prematurely grey hair, and his manner of speaking was aggressive and confrontational.

'It is conjecture,' Cailin admitted, spreading her hands to indicate helplessness. 'But it is based on very educated guesswork. We have *seen* how these stones operate. This is not a wild theory, nor would be be rushing at this blindly. If it were to be done, it would be our second attempt, and we would not make the same mistakes twice.'

'Where is this . . . anchor-stone?' It was Tsata who spoke.

'It is the first stone that was awakened,' Cailin replied. 'The one that started it all. It lies beneath the mountain monastery of Adderach.'

Hikken laughed rudely. 'And how do you propose we *get* to Adderach? Even if it were not deep in the mountains, it is surely the most fiercely guarded stronghold the Weavers have!'

'That is also conjecture,' Phaeca put in. 'We have no idea what awaits us at Adderach. Nobody has ever been there. I may remind the council that several times we have found the Weavers rely too much on their shields of misdirection and not on physical guards.'

'Those were in the days before the Red Order became known to them,' Mishani said.

'But they may think themselves protected by the mountains,' Phaeca argued. 'They may not be able to get enough food to such a remote place to sustain an army. Who knows what the Weavers think?'

'There are many ways to Adderach,' said Cailin. 'But none of them are easy.'

'And you think the Weavers will not notice an army marching towards Adderach?' Hikken cried. 'How exactly *do* you intend to do it?'

'We go quietly,' Cailin replied. 'And we—'

'This is pointless!' Lucia said suddenly. She had been customarily distracted up until this point, but she appeared entirely focused now. At the sound of her voice, everyone in the hall fell silent and looked to where she knelt.

'Pointless,' she repeated, softer this time. When she spoke, it was with surety and conviction, and she sounded like her mother the Empress. 'Even if we did attack Adderach, even if we succeeded, in our absence the Weavers would cut a swathe through the Prefectures and cause such murder as would make any victory too costly. And if the Weavers discovered our plan, they need only send one of the demons to defend Adderach and all would be lost. Whatever our other intentions, we need to be able to tackle the feya-kori. And the only way to stop an entity like that is with a similar entity.'

She stood up, and when she spoke, her voice was stronger than Kaiku would have believed possible from such a slip of a woman.

'It has been ten years since I was taken from the Imperial Keep in Axekami. Ten long years, and in that time there has been more blood shed for me than I dare think of. You have placed such hope in me and I have given you nothing in return but death. Now the time has come to live up to your expectations.'

She paused for a moment, and Kaiku noticed that even the spirits had quieted, and the ancient attention of the idols was on her. *Do not say it, Lucia*, she thought. *Do not do this.*

'A friend once told me I was an avatar, placed here by the gods to do their will,' she continued. 'I do not know. But I know this: we can face these demons and beat them, but we can only do so with the aid of the spirits. The entities that have lived in this land since long before we ever came here. If the Weavers can raise an army of such beings, then so can I.' She took a breath, and there was an infinitesimal tremor as she drew in the air, the only flicker of uncertainty that she showed.

'I will go to the oldest and most powerful spirit that our lore knows, deep in the heart of the Forest of Xu. I will speak with that spirit, and rouse it to our banner. The soul of the land will rise to its own defence.' Her voice was rising to a crescendo now. 'We shall make such war as the gods themselves will tremble to see it!'

The explosion of noise from the crowd was earsplitting. Cheers and cries of support rang around the hall and floated up into the night sky. This was the sign they had waited for all this time: the call to arms, the moment when their saviour would enter the fray and turn the tide. They did not care whether such a plan was even feasible; all that mattered was that Lucia had taken a hand, and with that, she had become the leader they had so desperately needed.

But though the people around her rejoiced, Kaiku was silent. She knelt where she was, and looked up at where Lucia stood, so terribly frail in the face of this riotous adulation. A battle had been lost today. Lucia was theirs now, irrevocably; she had forsaken her last chance of turning away.

As if sensing her thoughts, Lucia's eyes met hers, and in them was such sorrow as made Kaiku want to weep.

FOURTEEN

After that, there was little else to say.

The assembly dispersed with a sense that things had been left unfinished. Lucia's announcement had effectively ended the conference. Kaiku saw Cailin muttering into Yugi's ear, and she suspected that the seeds of action put forward today had only just begun to germinate. But diplomacy was not her strong suit, and she was content to leave it to people like Mishani, who appreciated the subtleties. She looked around for Nomoru, still worried about the scout's intentions, but could not find her in the crowd. Instead, she led Tsata and the Tkiurathi out of the temple and into the cool night beyond.

'We will go with you, if you will have us,' Tsata said to Kaiku, as they came to the edge of the complex where the trail ran back towards the Tkiurathi village.

He was assuming that she would not let Lucia follow this course alone. And what was worse, Kaiku reflected, was that he was probably right.

'Xu is no ordinary forest,' Kaiku said. 'The spirits hold sway there, and have done since before my people ever set foot on these shores.' Her eyes were grave. 'There is no more dangerous place in all of Saramyr for our kind.'

'The more reason for you to take us,' said Tsata.

Kaiku felt too weary to try and argue. She thanked them all – though she suspected by Tsata's expression that she did not need to – and bade them farewell, leaving the offer open. She was not the one to make such decisions, and she had no intention of bearing the responsibility for their deaths inside the Forest of Xu. Only the gods knew what awaited them in there.

It occurred to her, as she walked back to her house in the Libera Dramach village downslope of the temple complex, that she was already thinking about the journey in terms of *when* she went, rather than *if*.

Heart's blood, where did all my choices go? she thought in a morose moment, then snorted with disgust at her own self-pity.

She shared a house with Mishani here at Araka Jo as she had in the Fold, though the two of them were rarely there at the same time, as turned out to be the case tonight. She presumed Mishani had gone elsewhere with other members of the assembly to continue their discussions privately. The house was near the building where the Red Order met and where most of the Sister had their rooms, but Kaiku had not felt comfortable with the idea of living there as Phaeca did: it felt too much like surrendering a part of herself. The place was relatively nondescript and a little cold in the wintertime, but Kaiku had given up on the idea of having a stable home at least until the war was over, and as long as she had a roof and a private space she was happy.

It felt empty tonight. She slid the outer door closed behind her and listened to the darkness for a time. Outside, night-insects were chirruping and clattering. She walked through to her bedroom. The glow of the lanterns rose gently as flames kindled in their wicks at her passing, sparked by a small and frivolous use of her *kana*. Cailin would have disapproved. Kaiku didn't care.

Her bedroom was small: she only came here to sleep. There was a comfortable mat of woven, springy fibres, upon which was laid a thick blanket, and then a further blanket on top of that. Simple, unadorned, utilitarian. On the wall facing the curtained doorway was a mirror, an old one of Mishani's; she caught her reflection, and thought how well the make-up of the Order hid the melancholy mood that had descended on her. Even now, she projected a certain aura of authority and aloofness. On the far side of her sleeping-mat were a pair of chests flanking a dressing-table with another mirror, and on one wall hung a scroll with a verse from Xalis, another donation from Mishani. Kaiku was terrible at decorating: it seemed so unimportant to her. Her interest was not in material things.

She had sat down at her dressing-table and was preparing to remove her make-up when she spotted the Mask. She saw it over the shoulder of her double in the small vanity mirror, leering at her from where it hung on the wall, and it startled her so badly that she jumped with a yelp and sent little wooden pots of lip-paint scattering noisily to the floor. She stared at it, meeting its empty gaze in the mirror. It stared back at her.

Her skin crawled. She could not remember putting it up there.

She got up and slowly walked over to it. Its face of red and black lacquer was mischievous, mocking.

'Gods curse you,' she whispered to it. 'Leave me be.'

She took it down from where it hung on the wall. The contact of her hand brought a faint sense-memory of her father, the indefinable warmth of his presence. She bit back tears and put the Mask back in its chest.

Why couldn't she just destroy it? Why put up with that malevolent, insidious lure night after night? She could not have said herself. Perhaps because it was the last piece of her father she had. Perhaps it was the practicalities involved: she had used it twice before to breach the Weavers' barriers, and since the Weavers were still no wiser as to how she had done it, there was no reason it could not be used again. Cailin had made a brief stab at studying it, but there was little to learn beyond what the Sisters already knew. As True Masks went, it was young and weak and unremarkable, but no Sister dared probe too far into the workings of a True Mask, even one such as this. That way lay insanity.

Perhaps she kept it to remind her of what she was fighting against, and why she was fighting them. For this Mask had started it all for her: it had cost the lives of her family and set her adrift in the world. Until she found the Red Order; until she found another red and black mask to wear.

She caught herself. Thinking like that was not a good idea in her current state of lassitude. Seeing Lucia give herself up to her followers had drained her somehow, and she felt beaten and defeated. What was worse, she was resigned to going to the Forest of Xu, because *someone* that Lucia trusted had to be there, and she was the only option: Yugi was too valuable to go, and Mishani would be no use as part of such an expedition. Her talents lay elsewhere.

So Kaiku would be leaving Mishani again, after so short a time. She swore bitterly. This war was taking everything from her, little nibbled increments of her soul being swallowed as the harvests passed by, leaving her with just enough hate and determination to go on surviving. Her own side did not even appreciate her sacrifices. Her friends were torn away from her again and again. And it seemed they had not gained ground on the Weavers once since this whole affair began, since the death of the Blood Empress Anais. The best they had managed was to stall their retreat temporarily.

Something had to give. She could not continue this way for another ten years.

Take heart, then, a sardonic inner voice told her. *The way things are going, the Weavers will have us all before the summer.*

The chime sounded outside the door of the house. Kaiku looked up. For a moment, she considered not answering, but the lanterns were lit so her visitor knew she was in. Eventually curiosity got the better of her. She arranged herself quickly in the mirror, walked to the door and slid it open.

It was Asara. Kaiku recognised her even though she wore the form of a stranger, a dusky-skinned Tchom Rin woman with black hair in a loose ponytail hanging over her shoulder. She was wearing a robe of silver-grey.

'What do you want?' Kaiku asked, but she could not muster the effort to put any venom in her voice. It all seemed so pointless suddenly.

'Am I to take it, then, that you still resent me after our last encounter?' Asara guessed by Kaiku's tone that she had surmised her identity.

'A grudge worth holding is a grudge worth keeping alive,' she replied.

'May I come inside? I wish to talk.'

Kaiku thought about that for a moment, then she turned away and went into the house. Asara followed and slid the door shut behind her. Kaiku stood in the centre of the room, and did not invite Asara to sit.

'The attire of the Red Order does not suit you,' Asara said. 'It makes you into something you are not.'

'Spare me the criticism, Asara,' she said dismissively. 'If I had been a Sister when last we met, you would not have been able to deceive me as you did.'

'Perhaps that would have been better for both of us.'

'It would have been better for *me!*' Kaiku snapped, finding her anger.

But Asara did not rise to it; it seemed to slide off her. 'I came here to apologise,' she said.

'I am not interested in your apologies. They are as false as that skin you wear.'

Asara looked faintly amused. 'This skin is my own, Kaiku. It just happens that I can change it. I am Aberrant, just like you. How is it that you can celebrate your own abilities and despise mine?'

'Because I do not use mine to deceive other people,' she hissed.

'No, you use them to *kill* other people.'

'Weavers and Nexuses, demons and Aberrant animals,' Kaiku returned. 'They are not what I would call people. They are monsters.' She missed the hypocrisy of Asara's statement, for she had no knowledge of the lives that had been given to feed her, to fuel the metamorphic processes in her body.

'You killed several men on Fo; have you forgotten?'

'That was *your* fault!' Kaiku cried.

Asara raised one hand in a placating gesture. 'I am sorry. You are right. I do not want this to become an argument. But I would have you listen, even if you do not believe me.'

'Speak, then,' Kaiku said; but her arms were crossed beneath her breasts, and it was clear that nothing Asara said would appease her.

Asara regarded her for a moment, her gaze unreadable, made smoky by her eyeshadow.

'I have never meant to be your enemy, Kaiku. I did deceive you in the past, but I did not intend to harm you. Even that last time.' Her voice dropped a little. 'I would have stayed as Saran Ycthys Marul. You would never have known. We could have been happy.'

Kaiku opened her mouth to speak, but Asara stopped her.

'I know what you would say, Kaiku. It was foolish of me. I thought I could create myself anew, spin a new past: to wipe the slate clean. And you were ready to love Saran. You *were*, Kaiku.' She overrode Kaiku's weak protest. 'You would not love me, but you would love him.'

'He was not real,' Kaiku said in disgust.

'He was as real as Asara was. As I am now.'

'Then *you* are not real either,' Kaiku returned. 'The Asara I knew was only the face you wore, the role you took on, when first I met you. Is that who you are? How many faces had you worn before that? Do you even know?'

Asara saddened. 'No,' she said. 'No, I do not. Have you an idea what it is to be me? I do not even know what I should *look* like. Counterfeits are all I have.'

'You will get no pity from me,' Kaiku laughed scornfully.

Asara's face became stony. 'I do not want pity from anyone. But sometimes . . .' She looked away. 'Sometimes I do need help.'

This shocked Kaiku more than anything Asara had said so far. Asara had always been fierce in asserting her independence; this was a terrible admission for her. Despite herself, she softened for a moment. Then came the memory of Saran Ycthys Marul, looking at her with Asara's eyes as Kaiku, half-clothed, wept with the shame of betrayal.

'You do not deserve my help,' she said.

Asara glared across the room, her beautiful face cold in the lantern-light. 'I do, Kaiku. Honour demands that you discharge your debts, and you owe me your *life*. I did not merely save you from dying. I brought you back from the dead. Nothing you have done for me has ever come close to repaying that.' Her voice was flat with menace now. 'You nearly killed me, and I have never held you accountable. I watched over you for years before your *kana* emerged, and I rescued you from the shin-shin when they would certainly have had you. You think me so deceitful and cruel, but I have been a better friend to you than you realise. I have forgiven you everything, and asked almost nothing in return.'

Kaiku was unmoved. Asara tossed her head and made a noise of disgust. 'Think on what I have said. You count yourself honourable; well, honour does not extend only to your friends and your loved ones. The time has come to pay me back what is owed. Then we will be even, and I will leave you forever.'

With that, she walked to the door and slid it open. On the threshold, she looked back.

'I am going with you into the forest. We shall resolve this later.'

Then she was gone, and Kaiku was alone again.

Sometimes, when the fumes of the amaxa root had swaddled him in their plush and acidic folds, Yugi thought he could glimpse the spirit that haunted his room. It hid in the corner where the ceiling and two of the walls met, a spindly thing all bones and angles, black and beaked and half-seen. It was never still; instead it was in constant jittering motion, shivering and twitching with a rapidity hard for the eye to follow, making it blurred and unfocused. Yugi would study it while he lay on his sleeping-mat, puffing at the mouthpiece of his hookah. It was a part of the night to him, and night was where he found his peace, where he could be left alone and the jagged rocks of his memory could be blanketed in a narcotic fog.

He had been watching the spirit, lost in a haze, when he noticed a movement at his doorway. It took him a moment to establish who his visitor was. She came and squatted down next to him, laying her rifle aside.

'Bad habit,' she murmured.

'I know,' he replied. His mouth was dry and the words felt thick in his throat. He felt her hand grip his jaw gently, move his head left and right, looking into the cracked whites of his eyes.

'You're under,' she said. 'Thought you could handle this.'

'Want some?'

'No.'

She took the pipe out of his hand and put it back in its cradle on the hookah, where a wisp of smoke drifted up towards the white stone ceiling. Yugi tried muzzily to focus on her.

'I'm sorry about your face,' he mumbled.

Nomoru shrugged her narrow shoulders. 'Never the prettiest kitten in the box anyway. Besides, it makes Kaiku nervous. Can tell she thinks I want to kill her. Funny.'

Yugi grinned widely, then faltered, not sure whether it was appropriate. His hand came up, seemingly belonging to someone else, moving into his vision to touch her scarred cheek. At the moment of contact his fingertips exploded into sensation, bypassing his numb arm and going straight to his brain, islands of exquisite sensitivity free-floating before him. He felt the rayed tracks of the cicatrices that marred her skin, his face a comical picture of childlike wonder.

'It's a beautiful pattern,' he murmured.

Nomoru grunted a laugh. 'You're under,' she said again. 'You'd think mud was beautiful.'

Yugi did not appear to be listening. He took his hand away, suddenly unable to get comfortable on his mat. The curvature of his spine was annoying him. He got up into a cross-legged position with some difficulty, only to find that his knees were now causing him bother and he had merely shifted the ache from his upper back to his coccyx. He reached for the hookah, but Nomoru caught his arm and guided it back to his lap.

'Don't,' she said. 'Not going to watch you end up like my mother.'

'Come under with me,' he said, his pupils huge and bright though his face was slack.

She shook her head. 'You know what happened last time.'

'Weavers won't get you here. You can trust me.'

She looked away from him. 'I don't trust anyone.'

He was hurt by that. For a moment, there was nothing to say.

'Where did you go? In Axekami,' he asked at length. Sparkling shapes were whirring about the floor like translucent wriggling eels. 'I was worried.'

'No you weren't,' she said. She leaned back on her hands. 'Easier to get away on my own. Had to see an Inker.' She drew up her sleeve, where a freshly completed tattoo of a hookah with a dagger in it stood out against the paler pictures surrounding it. 'Paid the debt I owed Lon. Or Juto. Doesn't matter which.'

He was getting more lucid now. Amaxa root was short-lived in potency, and required a constant topping-up from the hookah to remain effective. The spirit that lived in the corner of his room was nothing more than a grey smear now, if ever he had seen it at all.

Suddenly he reached out and slipped his arm round Nomoru's waist, drawing her to him. He lay back as she moved with the pressure, uncrossing his legs so that she could slip onto his chest, her thin, hard body resting down the length of him. Her face was close enough to his so that he could feel her breath on his face, the sensation narcotically amplified to a rolling cloud of fire on his stubbled cheek. He studied the newly cut contours in her skin, his eyes flicking across them in fascination. Then he put his lips to hers. Her tongue was small and she tasted sour and kissed too hard, but it was familiar to him and he liked it. The amaxa root sent sparkling bursts from his mouth throughout his body.

She pulled away from him. 'Take that off,' she said, touching the trailing end of the rag tied round his forehead. 'Feels strange.'

'I can't,' he said, with a tired sigh. They had been through this before.

She was cooling again. 'She's dead. It's done. Take it off.'

'I *can't*.'

She looked down at him a moment, then shrugged. 'Worth a try,' she said, and fell to him once more.

The roof gardens of the Imperial Keep had withered and died. Where once they had been verdant and lush, planted with trees and flowers gathered from all over the Near World, now they were a brown, skeletal wasteland. The flowerbeds were a mush of detritus and spindly crinkles that were the remnants of bushes. The trees sloughed bark and oozed sap, and the leaves were all gone. It was a doleful and tragic place, and few came here now. The murk closed it in, a smoky grey canopy, and a bitter wind chased sticks and twigs across the flagstones.

Avun met the Weaver in a small paved area screened by a dense tangle of branches on all sides. At its south end, a double set of steps flanked by small statues of mythical beings led to paths set higher and lower in the gardens. There was a carved wooden bench, dull from lack of care, but Avun did not sit. He stood with a heavy cloak wrapped around him, for the lack of sunlight and the wind made it as cold as he could ever remember being in his life. The branches rattled a macabre and erratic rhythm as they tapped against each other.

The Weaver came slowly up the steps from below. He was young, not so raddled as others of his breed, and he moved with a slow and controlled gait. His Mask was all angles of gold, silver and bronze, his cowl hanging loosely over it. The patchwork robe was stitched and patterned crazily; there seemed to be some kind of order there, but Avun could not grasp it. He gave up looking. Perhaps it would be best not to work it out.

'Lord Protector,' he said, the voice made tinny by the metal Mask.

'Fahrekh,' Avun replied.

'I assume you have heard about Kakre's injudicious choice of victim today?'

Avun blinked languidly. 'He was a useful general.'

'He may still be alive,' Fahrekh said. 'Though I doubt he will be good for much any more.'

'He had been with Kakre too long before I found out,' said Avun. 'There is no point antagonising the Weave-lord now. My general would not lead the Blackguard so well without half his skin.'

'And without half his sanity, I suspect.'

Avun did not care to think about it. 'This has become intolerable,' he muttered.

'Indeed.'

There was a silence between them. Each was waiting for the other to say what they both thought. In the end, it was Fahrekh.

'Something must be done.'

'And what do you have in mind?' Avun said carefully, though he knew full well what it was. They had fenced around this before. Avun had no idea about Fahrekh's feelings, but he was gods-damned if he was going to incriminate himself by being the first to speak it out aloud.

'We will kill him, of course,' Fahrekh said.

Avun regarded the Weaver with hooded eyes. Could he trust this one? He still had a suspicion that Fahrekh was only faking complicity, that this was some test of loyalty by the Weavers. If he went along with it, would they treat him as a betrayer?

'You would kill one of your own?' he asked.

'It is necessary. We must cut off the spoiled right hand to save the arm.' Fahrekh's voice was an even and measured monotone. 'Kakre is a liability. For the good of the Weavers, he must be removed.'

'Will he stand down?'

Fahrekh chuckled. 'No Weave-lord has ever stood down before. Besides, he is too irrational now. He will not see things as we do. The Weavers need a new and clear-sighted leader, or our ambitions will go unfulfilled.'

Avun thought about this. He had learned a lot about the Weavers in his time as Lord Protector, through observation and conversation and by listening to Kakre's periodic fugues. Discovering the power structure of his allies was an important goal for him: their strength lay in secrecy, and Avun was determined to uncover them.

How was it that the Weavers were so united in purpose? And how could that be squared with the way they would kill each other in times past at the behest of their masters? At first he had believed that there was a coterie of Weavers in Adderach dispensing orders, but that was not good enough. In two hundred and fifty years he would have expected at least a few coups, power struggles, *something* like that. Yet there was no evidence of such. There were certainly disagreements about the way things should be done from time to time, but never about the ends, only the means.

Avun had not been able to understand it to his satisfaction, but he had established some things. The Weavers did not appear to know themselves where their direction came from: it was simply an instinctive drive towards the same goal. Whatever provided this goal was vague and indistinct, not an absolute dictator or an entity that was in complete control of the Weavers; it was simply a *knowledge* that all of them accepted and did not question.

There had never been a usurper in the Weavers before; but then, they had never needed one until now. Weave-lords had become liabilities to their patrons in the past, but they had been mere inconveniences. Kakre was the first Weave-lord who had *command*: command of the Aberrant armies, the feya-kori, and through Avun, the Blackguard. And a commander who was insane worked against the best interests of the Weavers.

Avun had to decide: was Fahrekh genuine, or was this all a trick?

'How would you do it?' he asked.

'I will catch him after he has Weaved. During his mania, when he is vulnerable.' Avun could feel the Weaver studying him from behind his Mask. 'I will need you to help me,' he said.

This was what Avun had feared. To commit himself would mean his death, if Fahrekh was false.

'What would you have me do?'

'We must contrive a reason for him to Weave. Something very difficult. I will supply you with the task; you must persuade him to take it up. Once exhausted, I will strike.'

'And after he is dead? I suppose you will be the new Weave-lord?'

'For the good of the Weavers,' Fahrekh said. 'I shall expect your immediate support.'

The branches rattled as the two of them faced each other beneath the iron-grey sky. Avun knew there was no way to be sure of the creature before him. Who could tell what kind of madness lurked beneath that surface? But he also knew that Kakre was a liability, and becoming more so by the day, and sooner or later he might take it into his head to get rid of his Lord Protector. There was risk in both action and inaction, and in the end, he had to trust his intuition. And he was an expert betrayer.

'I will do as you ask,' he said.

Fahrekh nodded slowly, once. He turned and departed without a word. Avun watched him go, and then clutched his cloak tighter around him. It really was cold out here; he had begun to shiver.

FIFTEEN

Nuki's eye rose on a clear, chilly day, the grass trembling with dew; but Kaiku, Lucia, and their companions were up long before, and as they ate a cold breakfast, their eyes were on the trees. The endless wall of trees.

They had camped within sight of the southern edge of the Forest of Xu, on the north bank of the River Ko. Few of them had slept much that night. Those that did woke unrested, complaining of ill dreams. There were twenty-five of them in all: Kaiku and Phaeca, Lucia, Asara, the three Tkiurathi, and eighteen other men and women of the Libera Dramach. They were here to face the Forest, and to find that which lurked at its heart: the Xhiang Xhi, most ancient and powerful of all the land's spirits.

Kaiku returned to the camp, having washed in the river. Her teeth should have been chattering, but the autonomic reaction of her *kana* had raised her body temperature enough to cope. She was taking such things for granted now, her sense of wonder having faded over time. Perhaps she could not yet bring herself to believe Cailin's screed about how the Sisters and certain other Aberrants were superior to those who had not been changed by the Weavers' blight; but she could not resist a private smirk of amusement at the sight of the other soldiers hopping and flapping to warm themselves after dunking their stripped upper bodies in the freezing water.

She stood on the crest of the river bank and debated for a moment whether to dress herself as a Sister or to remain in her tough, sexless travelling attire. She decided on the latter, in the end. It felt somehow false to put on the face of the Red Order to go into the forest. The forest would not be fooled.

She stared grimly at the trees, the border between humanity's realm and that of the spirits. They stretched from horizon to horizon east to west, and rose upon hills in the northern distance. The Forest of Xu was the single largest feature of Saramyr west of the mountains, almost three hundred miles north to south and two-thirds that in width, bigger even than the colossal Lake Azlea which neighboured it. The only information about what lay within were rumours and legends, and none of them pleasant. The Saramyr folk had learned long ago that their land was big enough to live in without disturbing the spirits, and the Forest of Xu was the densest concentration of spirits in the land. Half-hearted attempts at exploration had been made, in advance of a foolhardy plan to build a road through the trees to facilitate trade between Barask and Saraku. Few who went in there had ever come out. Those that did escape left their sanity behind.

It would be suicide, then, to set foot in such a place. But this time, they had something new. This time, they had Lucia. And on her slender shoulders rested all their lives.

As if sensing her thoughts, Lucia appeared at her side. Kaiku glanced over at her, then back at the forest.

'It hates us,' Lucia whispered.

'I know,' Kaiku murmured. 'It has a right to.'

A line creased Lucia's brow. 'We are not the enemies, Kaiku. The Weavers are.'

'The Weavers were like us once,' Kaiku said.

'But it is their god that makes them what they are,' Lucia said. She sounded frail, ready to shatter, and part of Kaiku did not even want to respond to this. But she had to now.

'Their god never made anyone *join* the Weavers. Not after those first ones. The rest came of their own free will. He never made them put on the Masks. That was ambition, and greed, and the need to control and dominate. There is no depravity they commit that was not already there inside them. It is only that their consciences have withered.' She brushed her hair back from her face. 'They are just men. Men who wanted power, the way all men do.'

'Not all men,' said Lucia.

Kaiku looked over at where Tsata was sitting cross-legged, talking with his two companions. She nodded slightly. 'Not all men.'

'Don't despair,' Lucia said, laying a hand on her arm. 'Please. You have always been stronger than me. I can't do this if you don't believe.'

'Then do not do it,' Kaiku replied, turning to her. 'Go back, and I will go back with you.'

Lucia's smile was sad. 'You have always thought of me over everybody else,' she said. 'Even if it cost the world, even if it cost the Golden Realm itself, you would have me prize my own safety before others.' She embraced Kaiku. 'You, and you only.'

Kaiku felt a slow tightening in her heart; she knew by Lucia's tone that there was no dissuading her.

Lucia released her and looked into her eyes. 'Nobody is safe any more, Kaiku.'

They made ready to leave as the dawn light grew. Little was said. There was a palpable air of foreboding among them. A pair of manthxwa had been brought as pack animals, but like the ravens that had accompanied Lucia on her journey from Araka Jo they refused to go nearer to the forest than they already were. In the end the travellers were forced to distribute their supplies as best they could and turn the creatures loose. Only the Tkiurathi did not seem intimidated.

Kaiku caught Asara looking at her strangely. Asara did not break the gaze;

in the end, Kaiku did. Gods, it was bad enough going in there at all, but with Asara's black hints at some debt to be discharged, she was not sure whether that woman was to be trusted. Why had she come? She was never one to recklessly endanger herself. What price would she demand of Kaiku in return for saving her life?

There was only one reason why the Aberrant spy was here, risking her life with the rest of them. She had unfinished business.

When they were ready, they gathered at the edge of the trees. Beyond, the forest was a tangle of boughs and bushes, the ground knotted with hillocks and roots. Birds chittered, insects droned, distant animal cries could be heard. There was nothing out of the ordinary that they could see; but some prickling sense on the fringe of perception warned them against stepping past the ranked trunks of the border, something deep and primal.

They were waiting for Lucia. She wore no armour like the soldiers, only some time-stained peasant clothes that did not suit her frame and made her seem small. She carried a pack as the rest of them did, at her own insistence, though they had loaded it lightly. She stood with her head bowed, her short blonde hair hanging forward, the burned skin of her neck exposed. They wanted her to turn and rouse them, to give them some of that fire that had blazed during the assembly at Araka Jo; but she had none to give them. Instead, she hitched up her pack to make it sit more comfortably on her shoulders, looked up, and walked into the forest. Without a word, the others followed.

At Lucia's first step beyond the barrier of the trees, the forest fell silent. It spread outward in a wave, as if the tread of her foot had triggered some great ripple like a pebble dropped in a pond. As the ripple passed, the birds stopped singing, the insects quieted, the cries of the animals died in their throats.

The intruders found themselves subject to a hush so profound that it was unnerving. The creak of leather armour and the rustle of their clothes were the only sounds they could hear, beyond the faint stir of the wind across the plains and the distant hiss of the river. They felt subtly fractured from reality, bereft of the spectrum of background sounds which had surrounded them to some degree all their lives. The silence ached.

They went on. If they had harboured any doubt that the forest was aware of them, it had been discarded now.

The trees thickened as they went further inward. The bulk of the companions travelled in single file, threading their way around the rise of tuffets and rocks, hopping over dry ditches. The Tkiurathi took alternative routes, spreading out, reading the land. Though Lucia was their navigator they would not let her take the lead. She walked in front of Kaiku, occasionally shouldering her pack anew as it began to chafe. She was not strong: a sheltered childhood and adolescence had given her no experience of physical hardship. But though she struggled, she did not complain.

Nobody spoke for what must have been an hour at least. The sense of oppression in the air was heavy, and getting heavier. Kaiku could feel the presence of the spirits here; they pervaded the place like the scent of disuse in a vacant house. They were waiting, breathless with malice and appalled that these humans would dare to enter their realm.

Kaiku hoped that Lucia knew what she was doing. She was certain that Lucia could communicate with these spirits easily enough, but whether they would listen to her was another matter. And when – *if* – they got to the Xhiang Xhi which hid at the heart of the vast forest, would Lucia's abilities be up to the task?

She recalled trying to reason with her back at Araka Jo. Why here? she had asked. Why this? Of all the spirits in the land which inhabited the deep and high and empty places, why choose the Xhiang Xhi?

'Because the other spirits hold that one in awe,' she had replied, half-listening. 'Because no other could rouse them. This one dwarfs all the spirits in Saramyr. Even the Children of the Moons fear the Xhiang Xhi.'

At one point, Kaiku dropped back to talk to Phaeca. She had somehow managed to imbue even her drab travelling clothes with a touch of flair, and her red hair was as immaculately arranged as ever. Small details like this gladdened Kaiku; they helped to stave off the steadily growing sense of hostility and isolation.

'Why don't they get it over with?' she hissed, as soon as Kaiku was nearby.

'Have faith, Phaeca,' Kaiku said. 'Lucia will protect us.'

Phaeca gave her a quick look of disgust. 'Don't spin me such platitudes,' she snapped. 'You're as afraid as I am.' Almost immediately, the anger was gone, and she was aghast at her own reaction. 'Forgive me,' she murmured. 'This place is hard on my nerves.'

Kaiku nodded. Phaeca's particularly sensitive nature was both a blessing and a curse here. She wondered whether Cailin had been wise to send her; she suspected the Pre-Eminent had done so only because Kaiku was going, and Phaeca was her closest companion within the Red Order.

Phaeca, Asara, and possibly Tsata and the two other Tkiurathi were all here because she had come. And she had come because she could not let Lucia make this journey without her. Both she and Lucia, by risking themselves, had dragged others in their wake and put their lives in danger. Selfishness out of selflessness. There was no way to win. She thought she understood a little of Lucia's sense of being crushed by responsibility now.

The change, when it came, was sudden.

Phaeca cried out in fear at the sensation. It was like a thick tar that gathered in from all directions to engulf the mind. The Sisters spun defences automatically to preserve themselves; but the other members of the party had no such recourse. They were swamped by a glowering prescience of doom that manifested all around them. The sunlight that leaked through the leaf canopy thinned and died as if a cloud had passed before Nuki's eye; but then it began to darken beyond even the drabbest day, blackening to deepest night and worse, until all light was excluded and even those with the ability to see in the dark were rendered blind.

Panic ensued. The darkness was bad enough, but the terror they felt was out of proportion even to that. Their senses screamed danger at them: there were *things* nearby, and while their eyes were useless their imaginations took charge. Monstrous, fanged beings, hanging in the air or slinking along the ground, black creatures who could only be envisioned by the gimlet gleam of their claws and teeth. The only sound was the desperate voices of the party, somebody shouting that they must protect Lucia, men who wanted to run but did not dare.

It took Kaiku a few paralysed seconds before she had the presence of mind to switch her vision into the Weave. The darkness was merely physical, and had no power there. The world blazed into light again, the stitchwork contours of golden threads outlining the forest and the people within. She could see them stumbling, their arms out, eyes open but unseeing, pupils like saucers. Some had drawn swords, and were standing rigidly, listening for the approach of the enemy. The Tkiurathi had dropped into crouches, making themselves small targets; they appeared calm, though the pounding of their hearts and the rush of blood around their bodies told a different story. The threads of the Weave were churning, confirming Kaiku's suspicion: this terror was an artificial thing, a projection.

But it was not without cause. For the spirits were coming, manifesting in the air all around them, forming into shapes that mimicked the party's fears. They were vague and indistinct yet, but gaining coherence with every passing moment, their blurred forms separating into limbs, jaws, talons. Dozens of them. She and Phaeca could not hope to fight them all.

'Lucia!' she cried, but Lucia was not listening. She was kneeling on the ground, her hands buried into the grassy dirt, her head hung. Somebody shrieked, a voice that faded rapidly as if carried away at speed; Kaiku tried to locate them, but it had happened too fast for her. She cast about helplessly, unable to act. Lucia was talking to them. She could only hope that whatever she said was enough.

The spirits were bleeding from the air, slinking from the treetops, knotting and sewing into shape with deadly purpose. The blinded humans in their midst flailed, aware that something was coming for them and having no way to prevent it. Kaiku's *kana* was raging within her, desperate for release; but the enemy were too many, and there was nowhere to send it that would have any effect. She felt Phaeca across the Weave, felt her struggle to keep control against the choking terror. She could see, as Kaiku could. One of the Libera Dramach narrowly missed impaling a companion on the point of his drawn sword as he staggered about; another almost tripped over Lucia, his hands held out before him, eyes unfocused.

'Stand still, all of you!' she shouted, putting as much authority as she could muster into her voice. They did so, clinging to her words as a lifeline to control.

'What's happening?' someone called to her, fraying with hysteria.

'Lucia will see us through,' she replied, with more conviction than she felt. 'Wait.'

She glanced back at where Lucia knelt. There was another shriek somewhere among the trees, cut short. She squeezed her eyes shut – which did nothing to block her Weave-vision – and prayed. The spirits were looming now, nightmare caricatures of childhood terrors, prowling between the trunks of the trees, stalking the humans. Kaiku desperately wanted to lash out; maybe she could ward them off, make them think twice about their prey. But to do so would mean the death of them all, for whatever Lucia was saying to them, her negotiations would collapse at the first sign of hostility from Kaiku.

'Stand still and wait!' she said again, because she could not bear the silence. The Tkiurathi had not moved. Asara was nowhere to be seen. And seeping towards them like mist came the spirits, their forms now shifting and warping as they moved, bending perspective to become elongated, then suddenly two-dimensional, now folding around a tree at an angle that had not seemed possible a moment before.

Closer, closer. Close enough to kill any one of them.

Something slackened, some constriction in the air that went loose. The oppressive hatred of the spirits seemed to retreat. Kaiku looked to Lucia, but there was no outward reaction from her. The spirits hung where they were. Some of them had risen up by their intended victims like malevolent shadows about to snatch the bodies that formed them. She dared not breathe. Here, at this instant, was the balance. If it tipped one way, they would all live; if the other, she would have no option but to fight, and there would be no hope for them then.

Then the forest sighed, and the spirits began to float backwards and away, bright eyes still fixed on the humans as they slipped between the trunks of the trees. Kaiku let out the breath she had been holding. The horrifying shapes were losing coherence now, dissipating into the Weave. And with their passing, the sense of malice and danger faded and the light returned. Slowly and by degrees, vision returned to them. It was like waking from a dream.

They stared at one another gratefully, their eyes thirsty for sight. Guilt and confusion flickered across their faces as they were revealed: some were caught still cringing, others brandished swords inches from their companions. All were ashamed of their fear. Those who had moved about or fallen over reoriented themselves, blinking. The Tkiurathi rose slowly to their feet. Asara reappeared, stepping into view from where she had hidden herself.

The forest had lightened back to normal now; Nuki's eye glowed through the canopy, and the world was green and brown and sane again. The silence was as great as before, but the spirits were gone.

Lucia stood up slowly, her hands still dirty. She looked around, but her gaze passed over them as if they were not there.

'They will give us passage,' she said simply.

Phaeca began to cry.

They went on, for there was little else to do; but their fragile confidence was shattered, and they crept like skulking children beneath the louring boughs of the forest.

Two of the soldiers had been lost in the darkness, vanished without trace. Had Lucia not been there, none of them would have been alive now. Far from reassuring them of their faith in their appointed saviour, the incident had reminded them of just how slender their chances really were. Even the Weavers were better than this: at least they were a physical enemy. In the Forest of Xu, they were allowed to survive only because the spirits chose not to kill them. If anything happened to Lucia, they would never leave this place.

Kaiku's thoughts were darker still. For she knew something the others did not, and it made matters worse than they already were.

'We're still not safe here,' Lucia had said in response to her prompting, once they were back on their way. 'These spirits suffer us to pass, but there are others that won't.'

Kaiku checked that there was nobody else within earshot. 'What are you saying?'

'As we go further towards the heart, we will find older spirits,' Lucia replied. 'They will not be so easily pacified.'

Kaiku was observing the shaken expressions on the faces of the party.

'Perhaps you had better keep that to yourself for now,' she muttered, hating herself for advocating dishonesty. 'For a while, at least.'

Lucia made a distracted noise, and seemed to forget that Kaiku was there at all.

Kaiku had walked with Phaeca for a time: she was affected worst of all of them. It hurt to see her in such a state, but some callous part of Kaiku wished that she had not been so indiscreet about her distress. Heart's blood, she was supposed to be a Sister. These people *needed* to believe that she was indomitable. Her own weakness was infecting the others, undermining everyone. She was concerned that Phaeca might pick up some of the impatience in her manner, but if she did, she said nothing.

As the day aged through evening to dusk, the forest became strange.

The change was slow and gradual. At first it was only an occasional incident: an unfamiliar flower, or a tree that looked odd. Then they found a remarkable rock that poked from the turf, a brilliant silvery lump of some kind of metallic mineral. Later they came across a cluster of dark magenta blossoms which nobody could identify, and a tree whose branches wrapped through the branches of other trees, twisting like vines. The green of their surroundings deepened and became mixed with purple and platinum.

Heading deeper into the forest, they began to see animals, silent and watchful, some unlike anything they had ever observed before. One of the soldiers swore that he had seen a white creature like a deer, out in the trees.

Asara spotted a long-legged spider, carapaced like a crab and as high as a man's knee, sidling from its burrow. The terrain became rougher, hills and cliffs rising, ghylls and ditches deepening into chasms.

The sky was a sullen crimson when the leader of the party, a middle-aged Libera Dramach man known as Doja, called for a camp. The spot he chose was on the grassy lip of a stony gorge, where the trees drew back and left a fringe of clear ground, a gentle slope between the forest and the dizzying drop, where there was mercifully no canopy to hem them in. Iridima was visible through the translucent veils of colour still hanging across the ceiling of the night. On the other side of the gorge there was a narrow and immensely high waterfall. The water was carved into three uneven streams by red-veined rocks, and plunged in thin, misty strings, joining together again halfway down in their rush to the river below.

When the camp was made, Kaiku stood on the edge of the precipice and looked down into the gorge. What river was this? A tributary of the Ko? Where was the source, and where did it end? Had anyone in living memory ever looked upon it until now? This river had flowed here, perhaps for thousands of years, and nobody had known it. If not for Lucia, it might have flowed for thousands more, untroubled by humanity.

She gazed into the middle distance, saddened by the indifference of the world. How small they were in the eyes of creation, how petty their struggles. The spirits guarded their territories, the moons glided through the skies, the seas remained bottomless. Nature did not care for the plight of humankind. She began to wonder if Lucia's task was not an impossible one after all. Could she really rouse the spirits, even to protect themselves? Did even the gods take notice of how they fought and died?

She turned away from the gorge. Such thoughts would only make her despair. And yet the idea of returning to the camp held no attraction for her, either. The party was subdued, still reeling from how easily they had been overcome. Asara was there; Kaiku was avoiding her as best she could. Phaeca was a wreck that she did not want to deal with. She did not feel like talking to Tsata or the Tkiurathi, either: somehow, what she felt was too private to try to explain to them.

She was deciding whether to get some rest when she spotted Lucia walking into the trees.

She blinked. Had she really seen what she thought she saw? She headed up the grassy slope towards the treeline. Her doubt evaporated as she went. Of course Lucia had slipped away on her own: it was just like her to disappear like that. Probably the people in the camp thought she had gone to sleep. Lucia needed solitude more than any of them, and she had the least to fear from the forest spirits.

The thought did not comfort Kaiku. She skirted the camp and reached the point where she had seen Lucia enter the trees. A pair of sentries were watching her from where the tents were clustered, evidently wondering what she was up to. She let them wonder. Better if she could get Lucia back without anyone noticing. On the heels of that thought came another: how had Lucia got away without being seen?

The forest seemed funereal in the moonlight. The silence and the still air gave it a tomblike feel, and the unfamiliar foliage put everything subtly off-kilter. Though Iridima's glow rendered everything in monochrome, these plants still reflected a kind of colour, some hue that she found hard to identify. She listened for a moment, and faintly she heard a tread heading away from her.

She was about to follow when something moved in the darkness, a shifting of some vast shadow. She paled. It was massive, as big as a feya-kori but wider, filling the space between the roots of the forest and its canopy. She could see it only as glimpses, obscured as it was by the boles of the trees in between; but glimpses were enough. Some colossal four-legged thing, there in the forest. Watching her.

She went cold as she found its eyes. Small and yellow, impossibly bright, and set far apart on a head that must have been bigger than she was.

It could not be there, her rational mind told her. It would knock over trees whenever it moved. It could not be there because it could not *fit*.

But yet she saw it, in defiance of sense, a hulking shape among the trees, wreathed in dark. If she set foot in the forest, it would come for her. And yet, if she did not, she left Lucia to its mercy.

The sentries were staring at her oddly now, as she stood transfixed on the edge of the clearing. She did not notice. She was caught by the gaze of that dreadful beast.

Lucia, she thought. She took a step forward, and the beast was on her.

Mishani shivered suddenly at her writing desk. She frowned and looked over her shoulder. At the edges of the lantern-light the room was cool and empty. The unease persisted for a moment or two, but Mishani was too level-headed to give much credit to phantoms of the mind, and she was soon immersed in her task once more.

She was kneeling on a mat in the communal room of the house at Araka Jo which she shared with Kaiku. Before her, spread across the table, were rolls of paper, inkpots and quills and brushes, a glazed-clay mug of lathamri and a stack of books. She was dressed in a warm sleeping-robe and soft slippers, but she had no intention of sleeping just yet.

Her interest in her mother's books had become an obsession these past weeks. She was desperate to understand, dogged by the certainty that there was something she should *know* through these words, some message her mother was trying to communicate to her. It had been a growing suspicion for some time now, but with the publication of the last book she had realised that it was indisputably more than fancy on her part. The final lines that Nida-jan spoke were the first half of a lullaby that had been a private song between mother and daughter. Her mother had used it once before, with the merchant Chien, as a way to identify him as an ally to Mishani if all else should fail. Now she was using it again.

But to what end? That was the puzzle. And no matter how Mishani pored over the books, she could not see what it was she was supposed to work out.

She took a sip of lathamri and stared at the paper before her. After exploring several theories, she had returned to the area of the books that bothered her the most: the awful poems that Nida-jan had taken to reciting. Their appearance seemed to coincide with the point where her mother had begun producing smaller books at a faster rate, and her exquisite prose had become sloppy. Mishani had written out one of them with a brush on the paper before her, large calligraphic pictograms painted in black ink. As if by increasing their size they would give up their secrets. She had tried making anagrams for hours now, scratching the words she built from the symbols in tiny script at the bottom of the paper, but it all came out as nonsense.

She tutted to herself. She was getting frustrated, and it was late. She had drunk too much lathamri which was making her jittery, for she had a small frame and was not used to it. And she could not concentrate properly while she had the knowledge in the back of her mind that Kaiku and Lucia had most likely reached the Forest of Xu by now. Gods, she hoped their trust in Lucia was well founded. If she did not come out of there alive, all their hopes were gone. And if she did not come back, then Kaiku would not either . . .

Such thoughts bring you no profit, Mishani, she told herself. *Make yourself useful.*

Indeed, making herself useful was something she really should have been doing; but she did not want to leave Araka Jo until she had unlocked the mystery of Muraki's books. She had returned from the desert to lend her political skills to the Libera Dramach in the Southern Prefectures, but most of the nobles were in Saraku or Machita, and seldom visited here. She had heard about the assassination attempt upon Barak Zahn during the rout at Zila, and suspicion naturally fell upon Blood Erinima. She wondered what kind of retribution Zahn had in mind, and whether she should go to him and offer her help. Division was the worst thing at this time, and yet it did not surprise Mishani in the least that the nobles could not cooperate even in the face of such an overwhelming enemy. Blood Erinima sought advantage for themselves, just like every other high family. They were not thinking of the wider consequences, only the chance to win themselves the throne. Such was the way of politics.

She could sense the proximity of an answer in the pages before her. She knew she was close, but the solution still eluded her. Though she did not know what to focus on, where to look, she believed that if she persisted, the picture would gradually become clear. If only through sheer force of will.

An owl hooted outside. She stared at the paper. For a long time, she did not move; she was entirely consumed by the workings of her mind, turning possibilities over and over. Absently, she picked up her mug, took a sip, and put it back again.

The slight movement in her peripheral field of vision, the way the mug did not seem to sit quite right against her fingers as she replaced it: these were the tiny warnings that told her she had misjudged where to set it down, that the lathamri was tipping off the edge of the desk. She snatched at it, catching it before it could fall, and in doing so the trailing edge of her other sleeve caught the ink pot and tipped it over. She hurriedly set the drink down and righted the ink pot, but by that time a slick of black had spread in an ellipse over a section of her calligraphy.

She huffed out a breath, annoyed by the waste of ink. Her sleeping-robe was stained at the cuffs too. She reached to roll up the paper and discard it, but she was arrested halfway. Slowly, she drew her hand back and stared at the paper again.

The ink had spilled across several lines, but the one that caught her eye had escaped with only minor damage. Only two pictograms in the middle of a four-syllable word had been obscured. But what had caught Mishani's eye was that there was a new word made by taking out those two symbols. The first and the last, when contracted together, created a new meaning.

Demons.

Excited, she looked to the book where the original poem had been, identified the missing symbols. Doing so shed no new light, but it did not diminish her sudden momentum. She laid aside the stained parchment and copied out the poem anew, then put two strokes across the two syllables to make *demons* again. On a whim, she hunted down any other instances of those pictograms. There was only one. She crossed it out, and it made the word senseless. Yet still she refused to believe that the appearance of *demons* was coincidence. She stared at the word she had mutilated. In its entirety, it meant *perhaps.* After a moment, she put a stroke through another of the pictograms. Now it said *by*, in the chronological sense. She studied the word for any other combinations that might make a meaning, but found none. She looked through the poem for other pictograms like this third one she had struck off, but it did not occur again. She examined the other words for symbols she might remove to make new meanings, but the possibilities were too many, and some words could not be contracted.

She was confounded once more, but the elation of progress would not let her stop. After a moment of listlessness, she began flicking through the books to find other poems, copied them out, and crossed through the three pictograms whenever she could find them. *Demons* appeared again, formed out of the same word as last time. It was nothing conclusive, but it was the possibility that was tantalising.

Finally, as night drew on, she found the word she needed. It was five pictograms long, and three of them were the three symbols she had marked for deletion. With quick strokes, she cut them out and looked at the result.

Mountain.

She was fractionally disappointed, having hoped for something more definite, something that could not possibly have been a random coincidence of syllables. But the disappointment lasted only a moment. It was a word, at least.

She needed to know more symbols to strike out. She needed a key to solve the code. Where would she find such a key?

The answer came to her immediately. She had had it all along; it was only a matter of asking herself the right question. The lullaby.

Snatching up a new roll of paper, she scribbled the lullaby down, then located the original poem she had been working on. Notes spilled from the edge of the desk, displaced by frantic activity. She went through the poem symbol by symbol, crossing out whenever she found a pictogram that matched a pictogram in the lullaby. And slowly, words began to emerge there. Some of them were nonsense, and some were impossible to contract at all, but these she ignored. She read only those words that she had altered to form a new meaning, and when she did so, she found the message.

New demons attack Juraka by midwinter.

She sat back on her heels, gazing at the page. For some time, she was blank, her mind scattered in the aftermath of revelation. Then she began to draw her thoughts together.

Mother, she thought in disbelief. *All this time . . .*

It had started not long after the war had begun. The poems, the bad writing. She had become sloppy because she was writing too fast. The books were short because she had to distribute them quickly enough for the information contained to be relevant. The poetry was terrible because it was hampered by the need to embed messages in it, and because she wanted to draw attention to it.

All this time, Muraki had been their spy in the heart of their enemy's camp, and they had not known it till now. *Mishani* had not known it till now. For it was only she who could have broken the code, only she – and Kaiku, though her mother did not know that – who possessed the necessary knowledge. But Muraki must have noticed that her warnings were doing no good, and finally, in her latest book, she offered a broad hint to her daughter, whom she must have believed was reading. For anyone else to decipher it meant death for Muraki. That was why it was only the first stanza of the poem: without both stanzas, the code was still gibberish.

Now Mishani thought back. There had been other clues. References to lullabies; Nida-jan's meditations on how his poetry had the cadence of a parent singing to their child; a passage where Nida-jan considered composing a song for his lost son, one that only they would know, which he would sing when he found the boy at last. Heart's blood, how many lives might have been saved, how many battles won, if Mishani had been clever enough to decipher this earlier? It was so obvious in hindsight that she could not believe she had been so dull-witted.

Her mother had been risking her life to help the Empire, drawing information from her husband the Lord Protector and passing it on through her writing. And nobody had realised.

Once Mishani had thought her mother weak, weak and uncaring. She felt tears pricking her eyes at the shame of her ungraciousness.

Spurred by that feeling, she went to work on the other poems. There would be no sleep for her tonight.

SIXTEEN

Kaiku awoke from a vivid dream of sweat and heat and sex, memory tattering with wakefulness, leaving only the face of the man who had been taking her. Tane.

She felt suddenly embarrassed as her eyes flickered open, and she saw the others in the tent, kneeling nearby. Asara and Tsata. Had her dream showed outwardly, in moans or in the languid movement of her body? She was still fully clothed, but no blankets had been laid on her, which made her feel exposed. And gods, why Tane? She had not thought of him for a long time.

Then she remembered the beast.

She jerked upright in alarm. Tsata held up his hands in a placating gesture.

'Be calm, Kaiku. No harm has come to you,' he said.

'No harm?' she repeated. 'And Lucia?'

'Lucia is perfectly safe. Why would it be otherwise?' Asara said.

Kaiku stared at her for a moment. She was remembering how the thing had *flitted* at her, a charge broken up into a thousand tiny and discrete increments: flash impressions of shadow, each one larger than the last as it neared, enacted in a fraction of an instant. It was so fast she had not even time to rouse her *kana*. It should have battered aside dozens of trees as it came. Then darkness, and dreaming.

Asara handed her a cup of water. She took it with a suspicious glance at the desert lady. Watching over her while she slept was far too compassionate an act for Asara: she cared only because Kaiku still owed her, and she intended to collect.

Asara sensed her mood, perhaps, for she rose into a crouch then. 'I am relieved that you are well,' she said. 'I must help with the preparations. We leave soon.' And she left, ducking through the flap.

Kaiku began to arrange herself, a little self-conscious at being seen straight out of bed with her hair mussed and eyes puffy with sleep; then she remembered the weeks she had spent in the wild with Tsata back in the Xarana Fault, and laughed at herself for her vanity. He had already seen her at her worst; it was scarcely worth concerning herself over.

He responded to her laughter with a look of bewilderment. 'You seem in good spirits,' he observed.

She sighed. 'No, it is not that,' she said. She thought about explaining, but decided it was not worth the effort. Tsata would not understand.

He let it drop. 'What happened to you?' he asked.

So Kaiku explained about the beast in the trees. She made no mention of why she had strayed from the camp. She meant to have a word with Lucia about her dangerous wanderings as soon as circumstances would permit.

Tsata listened as she talked. In contrast to Lucia, he had a wonderfully grave expression when listening, as if the object of his attention was the only thing in the world. Kaiku had found it mildly intimidating at first, but now she enjoyed it. When she spoke, she knew he thought her words important. It made her feel better about herself.

When she was done, he shifted himself so that he was sitting cross-legged. Tkiurathi could never kneel for long; it became excruciating for them after a while, unlike the folk of Saramyr.

'It appears that you were fortunate indeed. We lost two more soldiers last night. We can presume that they met the same creature that you did.'

'We *lost* them? How do you mean?'

'They are gone. Tracks lead into the forest, but beyond that all trace has disappeared.'

Kaiku rubbed her hands over her face. 'Gods . . .' she murmured. 'Lucia said that the spirits' agreement to let us pass was no guarantee of safety. I had hoped to keep that from the rest of the group, at least until our morale was better.'

'That was foolish,' said Tsata. From anyone else, it would have been rude, but Kaiku knew how he was. 'Perhaps we would have been more careful if we had been told.'

'More careful than we were? I doubt it.' She would not shoulder the responsibility for their deaths. 'Everyone was frightened last night; they were watchful, despite what Lucia had told them.'

'They are more frightened now,' Tsata observed.

'As well they should be,' Kaiku replied.

There was a beat of silence between them.

'You were writhing in your sleep. Who were you dreaming of?' he asked suddenly.

Kaiku blushed. 'Heart's blood, Tsata! There are some politenesses my people employ that you would do well to learn.'

He did not look in the least abashed. 'I apologise,' he said. 'I did not realise you would be embarrassed.'

She brushed her hair behind her ear and shook her head. 'You should not ask a lady such things.' She met his gaze, his pale green eyes devoid of guile, strangely like a child's. For a moment she held it; then she looked away.

'Tane,' she said with a sigh, as if he had forced it out of her. 'I dreamt of Tane.'

Tsata tilted his chin upward: an Okhamban nod, in understanding. 'I appreciate your honesty. It is important to me.'

'I know,' she murmured. Then, feeling she needed to apologise herself, she took his hand in both of hers. 'It was only a dream,' she said.

He seemed surprised by the contact. After a moment, he squeezed her hand gently and let go. 'We all dreamed last night,' he said. 'But you, it seems, were the only one who dreamt anything pleasant.'

'I am not so sure it was pleasant at all,' she said. Though she could remember nothing for certain except that Tane was in it, she was unsure whether the dream-congress was entirely consensual on her part. In fact, she had an uneasy intuition that he had been raping her. She looked up. 'What did you dream of?'

Tsata seemed uncomfortable, and did not reply. 'We should go; the others will be waiting for us.'

'Ah! You will not get away so easily,' she said, grabbing his arm as he made to rise. 'Where is your honesty now?' she chided playfully.

'I dreamt of you,' he said, his tone flat.

'Of me?'

'I dreamt I was gutting you with a knife.'

Kaiku stared at him for a moment. She blinked.

'I see your studies of Saramyrrhic have not yet encompassed the art of telling a woman what she wants to hear,' she said, and then burst out laughing at his expression. 'Come. We should be on our way.' When he still seemed uneasy, she said again: 'It was only a dream, Tsata. As was mine.'

They emerged from the tent to a crisp dawn. It was early yet, but from the faces of the group Kaiku guessed that few had slept well, if at all. They were wearily taking down the camp, wandering in pairs or eating cold food – no fires were allowed in the forest, on Lucia's advice. The silence that surrounded them was as oppressive as it had been the day before. It made the whole forest seem dead. Asara had packed her tent up and was sitting on the grass, watching Kaiku across the camp. Kaiku dismissed her with a glance. She did not want to worry about that one for now.

A sudden commotion from the treeline drew her attention. People were getting to their feet, running up towards where two men were emerging with a third being dragged between them.

'Spirits, what now?' Kaiku muttered, and she headed that way herself, with Tsata close behind.

They had dumped the man face down on the grass by the time she arrived, and soldiers were jabbering over the corpse. 'Who is this?' she demanded, putting enough of the Red Order authority into her tone to silence them. 'What happened to him?'

'He's one of those who went missing last night,' came the reply. 'We went to look for them. Didn't find the other.' He exchanged glances with his companion. 'As to what happened to him, your guess is as good as ours.'

With that, he tipped the body over with his boot, and it came to lie on its back with one arm awkwardly underneath it. The soldiers swore and cursed.

Though he seemed otherwise untouched, his eyes were milky white, no pupil or iris visible. The skin around them was speckled with burst blood vessels, and brilliant blue veins radiated out from the sockets, starkly protuberant. The man's expression was slack, his jaw hanging open in an idiot gape.

'I think you were more fortunate than we had guessed,' Tsata muttered, 'if this is what your beast does to its victims.'

Kaiku turned away, crossing her arms over her stomach, hugging herself. 'Then why did it spare me?'

She began to walk; the sight of the dead man was more than she could take at the moment.

They travelled round the gorge and onward, following Lucia's directions. She was their compass, for she could sense the Xhiang Xhi and headed unerringly towards it. The group were jumpy now. The forest had a way of tricking the eye, inventing movement from nothing, so that people would start violently and look down at their feet, or out into the trees, thinking something had scurried past. They began to hear noises in the silence now, strange taps and clicks from afar. The first time they occurred, Doja – the leader of the soldiers – called a halt and they listened for a while; but the sounds were random and monotonous, and eventually they tried to ignore them. It did little good. The tapping began to wear at them, much as the silence had before it.

The forest continued to change, darkening as they penetrated further. Purple was predominant now, as of deciduous leaves on the late edge of autumn, and the canopy thickened overhead so that they walked in twilight. A strange gloom hung in the air. The taps and clicks echoed as if they were in a cavernous hall, unnaturally reverberant.

The group threaded its way through terrain that became increasingly hard, up muddy slopes and through tangled thickets with branches they dared not hack aside for fear of retaliation. They went with swords and rifles held ready, in the faint hope that they would be any use.

Kaiku and Phaeca walked together, keeping close to Lucia. Phaeca seemed better today, despite having barely slept. Whenever she had closed her eyes she had been pitched into the same nightmare, something so horrible that she refused to speak of it. Still, she had artfully made herself up and disguised the shadows under her eyes, and it did not show on her. Kaiku had been concerned about how well she might hold up in this environment, but she felt a small relief at seeing her friend recovered.

'How is she?' Phaeca murmured, gesturing at Lucia.

Kaiku made a face that said: *who can tell?* 'I do not think she even knows where she is at the moment.'

They observed her for a time, and indeed, she had the look of a sleep-walker. She drifted along without paying attention to anything or anyone nearby.

'She is listening to them,' Phaeca said. 'To the spirits.'

'I fear for her, Phaeca,' Kaiku admitted. 'She said things to me, back at

Araka Jo . . .' She trailed off, deciding that to speak of it to Phaeca would be breaking a confidence. 'I fear for her,' she repeated.

Phaeca did not pry. 'What is she, truly?' she mused.

'She is an Aberrant, the same as you and me.'

Phaeca looked unconvinced. 'Is that all she is, do you think? I'm not so sure. It's her nature more than her abilities. And her uniqueness.' She glanced at Kaiku. 'Why aren't there more of her? There were many with our powers: the Sisterhood only accounts for a fraction of the total, those that were not killed or who did not kill themselves. Yet have you ever heard of anyone with Lucia's talent?'

Kaiku did not like where this was going. It came uncomfortably close to suggesting that Lucia was divine, and she had thought Phaeca above that. 'What are you saying?' she asked.

Phaeca shook her head. 'Nothing,' she replied. 'Just thinking aloud.'

Kaiku lapsed into silence, wondering about this. She had tried to talk to Lucia earlier in the day about her late-night excursion into the forest, but alarmingly she found it impossible to get through. Lucia was not only paying no attention, but she could not bring herself to focus enough to make any sense of Kaiku. She stared right through her as if she were some puzzling phantom, then her eyes would slide away elsewhere.

Whatever was happening to Lucia, she was, as ever, facing it alone. Kaiku was entirely shut out. She could do nothing but worry.

Another one of them fell by mid–afternoon.

It was Tsata's cry to his kinsman that alerted them. They did not catch the meaning, phrased as it was in Okhamban, but they understood the tone. Several men clustered around Lucia; the others hurried into the trees towards the source of the sound. Kaiku directed Phaeca to stay, haste making her peremptory, and then went after them. She clambered up a steep rise of land, using roots as handholds and odd gold-veined rocks as steps, and ducked through the foliage and past a thicket of tall, straight trees to where she could see the soldiers' backs in a circle. They made way for her as she arrived.

It was the Tkiurathi woman, Peithre. She lay in Tsata's arms, breathing in thin, rasping gasps, her skin pale. Heth broke through the circle a moment later, and demanded something of Tsata in their native language. Tsata's reply was clear without translation: he did not know what was wrong with her.

'Let me,' said Kaiku. She crouched down in front of Peithre. The ailing woman's eyes fixed on her, a mixture of desperation and pleading. Tsata looked around, searching for the source of what had done such harm, but nothing was evident.

'Tsata, tell her to be calm. I will help her,' she said, not taking her gaze from Peithre's. Tsata did so. Then Kaiku put her hand on Peithre's bare shoulder, and as the soldiers watched her irises changed from brown to bright red.

'She is poisoned,' Kaiku said immediately. She held her hand cupped beneath Peithre's chin, and a dozen tiny flecks, like bee-stings, popped from the skin of the jaw and throat and collarbone and fell into her palm, where they ignited in tiny pyres. 'That plant,' she pointed behind her, at where a patch of curved, thin reeds with bulbous tips rose out of the bank of a tiny brook.

One of the soldiers brandished his sword and took a step towards them.

'Do not touch them!' Kaiku snapped. 'You will kill us all. We will not harm the forest, even if the forest harms us.'

'Can you save her?' Tsata murmured.

'I can try,' she replied; and for a moment they were back in a fog-laden marsh in the Xarana Fault, and it was Yugi and not Peithre who lay dying. But then she had been a clumsy apprentice; now she was a seamstress of the Weave. She closed her eyes and plunged into the golden world, and the Tkiurathi and soldiers could do nothing but wait. Heth muttered to Tsata in Okhamban. They watched the patient closely, observers to a process too subtle for them to understand. Peithre began to sweat, giving off an acrid stink: Kaiku was hounding the poison from her body. Then gradually her breathing slowed. Her eyes drifted closed. Heth exploded into a guttural tirade, but Tsata held his hand up for silence. Kaiku was concentrating too hard to reassure him. Peithre was not dying, not now; but she would have to sleep.

Minutes passed before Kaiku's eyes flickered open again. The soldiers murmured to each other.

'She will live,' Kaiku said. 'But she is very weak. The damage the poison has done is too widespread and too deep for me to repair entirely.'

Heth spoke up in Saramyrrhic. 'I will carry her.'

'It is not that simple. She needs rest, or she may not survive. Her body is at its limits already.' She met Tsata's gaze. 'The poison was very strong,' she said. 'It is a miracle she lived long enough for me to get to her.'

She looked up, and caught sight of Asara standing there, watching her through the trees with singular interest. Then she turned away and was gone, leaving Kaiku faintly perturbed.

'Make her comfortable,' Kaiku said to the Tkiurathi. 'I will speak with Doja.' She got to her feet.

'You have my gratitude,' Heth said uncertainly, glancing at Tsata for approval. He found Saramyr customs as difficult as she found theirs.

'And mine,' Tsata said.

'We are *pash*, you idiots,' she said tenderly. 'No thanks are needed.'

'You mean we're staying here?' one of the soldiers called in disbelief. All eyes looked to him. He was a black-haired man around his twenty-fifth harvest. She knew him: his name was Kugo.

Kaiku fixed him a hard stare, made harder by the demonic colour of her eyes. She could feel the momentary warmth of cameraderie drain from her. 'That is what I am going to talk to your leader about.'

'We can't stay here!' he said. 'Heart's blood, four of us are dead already;

you yourself were nearly a fifth; she was a hair's breadth from being number six. This is only our second day! How long do you think we're going to survive if we just wait around in the forest?'

Kaiku could feel herself tensing, readying for a confrontation. She should have just walked away from this, swept him icily aside. But something inside her would not allow her to let it go, because she knew where this was coming from, and she wanted to hear him say it.

'What would you have us do, Kugo? Abandon her? What if it were you?'

'It's *not* me. And if it were, or if it were any of these men, I'd stay with them whatever the consequence. We would not abandon our own.' There was a murmur of approval at this. 'But these are not our own,' he said. 'I won't risk my life for foreigners.'

Tsata and Heth did not react to this, but Kaiku did.

'Have you learned *nothing?*' she cried, walking up to Kugo until she was facing him. 'Why do you think we are fighting this war, you fool? Because we were so ready to let the Weavers scapegoat Aberrants that we never thought to question them! We let them kill children for more than two centuries because we held jealously onto the prejudices that they instilled in us! People like you joined the Libera Dramach to change that. And now, now that Aberrants like me have *saved your empire*, now that we are *following* an Aberrant into the heart of the most gods-damned dangerous place on the continent, now you say that these people who are willing to die alongside us are *not our own?*'

She was in a fury now such as she had rarely been, and the air tautened around her, the tips of her hair lifting in the palpable aura of her rage. Kugo's face was a picture of shock.

'This division is what kills us! Do you not see? You cannot throw away one set of arbitrary prejudices and still maintain another! You cannot decide to accept Aberrants like me and still regard foreigners as lesser than you! Your ignorance condemns us to repeat the same cycle, war after war until there is nothing left! Heart's blood, if your kind ran out of enemies you would start killing your friends! These people,' she gestured at Tsata and Heth, 'could teach you something about *unity*.'

She grabbed the side of his head with one hand; he was paralysed with fright now. Her voice dropped.

'You will afford the Tkiurathi the same respect you give these other men, or you will have me to deal with.'

With that, she shoved him roughly away and stalked into the forest. Silence reigned in her wake. Tsata watched her leave, his tattooed face unreadable; but he stared at the point where she was lost to the undergrowth for a long time after she was gone.

She went to see Doja when she had calmed down, and he agreed that they should stop here for the night and evaluate Peithre's condition anew in the morning.

'But if another of my men goes missing, we're leaving,' he warned.

'You must do what you will,' she said. 'But I am staying. And in the end, it is Lucia's decision whether you will leave or not: you would not last an hour in this place without her.'

Doja was angry, she could sense that, though he suppressed it well. He was a square-jawed man with a cleft chin covered in wiry black stubble, a sharp nose and small eyes. Kaiku respected him immensely as a leader, but she had undermined him and he resented that. Threatening one of his soldiers had not done her any favours in his estimation, and now her intransigence was a direct challenge to his authority. The relationship between the Libera Dramach and the Red Order had become more and more strained of late. Whereas before the Red Order had been an extremely useful secret weapon for their cause, now that they were out in the open they were too powerful to be trusted, and there was a general suspicion that they only fought on the side of the Empire because it coincided with their own agenda.

'I give you one night,' he said. 'After that, we will ask Lucia.'

A clamour arose before Kaiku could reply, coming from the direction where she had left Peithre. She broke off their conversation without another word and hurried back to that spot, and there she found the soldiers with their rifles ready, spread in a loose circle, aiming outward between the trees. Someone, made jumpy by his surroundings, sighted on her as she approached; she ducked instinctively, but thankfully he did not fire. She swept past him with a corrosive glare and he cringed away from her.

'What is it?' she asked Tsata. He and Heth knelt by Peithre, their own guns ready.

'Out in the trees,' he said, motioning with his head.

She looked, and as she did so, she glimpsed something. It was a flash of white, darting between the vine-strewn maze of trunks.

'Do not fire on them!' she said, raising her voice to include the whole group. 'Remember where we are! Shoot only if they attack.'

The soldiers muttered sarcastically between themselves. She glanced down at Peithre, still asleep on the forest floor with a blanket as a pillow, and then out into the trees again. Another movement caught her eye, but it was too quick, gone before she could find it.

((Are you with Lucia?)) she asked Phaeca, and received an immediate affirmative. *((Bring her here))*

'There's one!' someone cried.

'Do not fire!' Kaiku shouted again, fearful of the excitement in the man's tone, as if he had just spotted game and was about to take it down. Kaiku saw where everyone else was looking, down a corridor of boles and bushes to where one of the things had frozen, caught in their eyes, watching them watching it.

It was beautiful and terrifying all at once. Its short fur was perfectly white, but for where shadows delineated the hollows of its ribs. It had elements in it of deer and fox – a brush for a tail; stubby, sharp antlers; a certain furtiveness of movement – and yet its musculature and bone structure were disturbingly human, as though it were a lithe and elongated man standing on all fours. Its face had something of the fox's narrow cunning, and something of the deer's alarmed docility, but its features were more mobile than either, and when it skinned back its lips it showed an array of close-fitting, daggerlike teeth that betrayed a carnivorous diet.

'Aberrant,' someone hissed.

'It is no Aberrant,' Kaiku murmured in reply. Even if she could not sense it by their Weave-signature, she would have known anyway. There was something about these creatures, some linearity of structure that bespoke an entirely natural evolution. They were somewhere between spirit and animal, a hybrid of the two.

Then it was gone, launching itself back into the trees. Phaeca appeared a few moments later, leading Lucia and a group of soldiers who acted as her bodyguards. Asara arrived, her own rifle ready.

'Lucia,' Kaiku said. She did not respond: her eyes were far away. '*Lucia!*'

She focused suddenly, but almost immediately began to drift again. 'What are these things?' Kaiku demanded. 'Can you talk to them? Do they mean to harm us?' She shook Lucia's shoulder and said her name again. '*Listen* to me!'

'Emyrynn,' Lucia murmured, staring over Kaiku's shoulder into the trees. 'They're called emyrynn in our tongue. They want us to follow them.'

'Follow them? Is this some kind of trap?'

Lucia made a vague negative noise in her throat. 'We have to follow them . . .' she said, and then she had slipped beyond rousing again, lost in some dreamwalk where Kaiku could not reach her. Kaiku bit her lip to kill the frustration at seeing her this way. This forest was too much for Lucia, overwhelming her, making her more distant than ever before. It was agony to watch, for Kaiku had no way of knowing if she could ever come back from this, or whether every moment within the borders of the forest was making her worse.

Doja was quicker to decide than she was, and his faith in Lucia was evidently greater. 'We can't move this woman yet. Three men, go with them. Come back and fetch us when you find whatever it is they want us to see. And heart's blood, *be careful*.'

'I will go,' Kaiku said, because she would do anything not to be around Lucia a moment longer.

'And I,' said Tsata.

Asara volunteered also. Doja was happy to accept: it meant he did not to have to risk any of his soldiers. Kaiku felt a flicker of uncertainty at the thought of having Asara along, but she had Tsata at least, and in him her trust was total.

'Where are they? Where are you seeing them?' she asked the group in general, and several men pointed, all in roughly the same direction. They set off into the trees; Tsata warned Asara about the reed that had poisoned Peithre, and she nodded in acknowledgement, not taking her eyes off Kaiku.

Rifles held close, they forged through the undergrowth, while ahead of them the emyrynn led onward, annoyingly elusive and yet never quite out of sight. None of them spoke; their concentration was bent on seeking out danger, waiting for the jaws of a trap to spring shut, hoping to predict it in time to evade.

But their journey was not a long one. They had not been travelling for more than ten minutes before they found what it was the emyrynn wanted to show them, and there they stood dumbfounded, and wondered what kind of beings they had stumbled upon in the depths of the Forest of Xu.

In the upper levels of the Imperial Keep, where the Weavers' lunacy had made it dangerous to tread, the dust lay thick and spiders webbed the windows.

Kakre's preferred room for Weaving was not the Sun Chamber that he had populated with his kites and mannequins of skin. He found the noise of the other Weavers distracting. Instead, he took himself to a section where he could be alone, a morose and silent place too out of the way for the Weavers or the frightened servants to trouble themselves with. The floor was rucked with wide, overlapping trails, paths carved in the powdery dust by the threadbare hem of his robe as he wandered. Weak daylight filtered through the miasma that cloaked the city, and the air was heavy and oily.

Avun had been here for three hours now, talking with spectres. Seven Governors of the major towns and cities within the Weavers' territory hung in a circle around the centre of the empty room, blurred apparitions, with Avun the only solid one among them. They were discussing the interminable minutiae of their respective situations, the state of the land, the course of the famine. Kakre was the link that held them all together, a junction through which all eight participants could see each other as murky avatars. Avun had insisted that it be so, for drawing eight people together in a country the size of Saramyr was impractical at best, especially as some lived in the distant Newlands to the east.

Kakre was getting angry. He had allowed himself to be persuaded to achieve this feat, and yet so far he had heard nothing that could not have been done by individual conferences, which were far less taxing. If he did not believe that Avun had been sufficiently cowed by past punishments, he would have thought the Lord Protector was beginning to take his masters for granted.

The conference dragged out while the light of Nuki's eye began to fade. Kakre was the greatest among the Weavers – certainly in his own estimation, anyway – but the strain of maintaining so many links for so long was beginning to wear on him. Pride forbade him to buckle, but he cursed Avun's name inwardly, and began to think of myriad discomforts he might wreak upon the man when this was done.

Finally, Avun began to wrap up the proceedings, enacting elaborate rituals of farewell to each of the participants in turn. Kakre cut the connection when Avun was finished with them, and the spectres faded away. At last it was over, and only Avun remained. Kakre staggered slightly, his knees weak. Avun's quick glance indicated that he had noticed, but he wisely forbore to mention it.

'You have my deepest gratitude,' Avun said. 'A face-to-face conference, or as near as we can get it, makes all the difference in government. Many valuable ideas can be mined when our heads are put together.'

Kakre was not convinced anything had come out of that meeting beyond a few status reports and vague allusions to methods of progress, and Avun's thanks sounded facile. But he was not in a very coherent state of mind at the moment, and he mistrusted himself. The mania would surely strike him after such a long and strenuous period of Weaving; he could already feel himself itching for the knife he kept beneath his robes.

'You would be best to leave now,' Kakre snarled. 'If you wish to avoid being harmed. I shall have words for you later. Oh, indeed.'

Avun bowed and left. Kakre shakily sat down on the floor; dust rose in a languid puff around him. He was thankful now that he had insisted Avun come to him for the conference, instead of holding it in a state room. At the time, it had been a whim, a reminder that Avun was his servant and not vice versa; but now he found his solitude a balm, for there was nobody to see his weakness.

The post-Weaving mania was spreading slow tentacles through him like blood dripped into water. He wanted to do some skinning, but he felt too weak to procure himself a victim, and he had used up his last canvas a few days ago. The urge and the lethargy were growing at the same pace, putting him in an impossible situation. He breathed a cracked curse and gritted what was left of his teeth. He would have to ride this one out, at least until he had the strength to do something about it. He briefly fantasised about torturing Avun, but in the face of his growing need the visions he conjured seemed pallid and childish.

Instead, he was blinded by a rare window of clarity upon himself, a moment in which he saw what he had become, free of delusion and madness. His bladework had been steadily deteriorating for years now. Most of the sculptures that he kept had been cut in the days before the Weavers shattered the Empire. His arthritic hands trembled as they held the knife, and he was more a butcher than a surgeon of late. But it was not only his coordination: his mind had rotted too. The effort of summoning and controlling the feya-kori had battered the frail mush of his physical brain, turned him addled and senile, and he saw now the damage it had wreaked and how much more it would do next time he roused the blight demons from their pall-pits.

For a short time, he knew what he was, saw the ruin he had visited on his body and mind, and he screamed and cried and clawed himself; but it passed, and the thoughts became too hard to hold on to, and dissipated like smoke.

Fahrekh found him like that: curled up, a heap of rags and hide, the dead-skin Mask pressed to the floor, caked with grey dust. He stood in the doorway for a time, his angular face of bronze, silver and gold expressionless.

'Weave-lord Kakre,' he said. 'You seem unwell.'

'Get out,' Kakre croaked.

'I think not,' came the reply. He walked into the room, until he was standing over the Weave-lord, who strained his neck to look up at the younger Weaver.

'Get out!' he hissed again, and was racked with spasms.

'We have matters to discuss, you and I,' Fahrekh said slowly. 'Matters of succession. Specifically, mine.'

Kakre's head snapped up, suddenly lucid. Fahrekh's impassive Mask gazed back at him.

They plunged into the Weave together, and battle was joined.

It was in the abyss that they met, the endless, watery dark which was Kakre's preferred visualisation of the fabric of reality. Whether by accident or design, it was Fahrekh's too, and he was equally happy with the interpretation. As they attacked each other, their interactions with the Weave took on the form of fish to fit their surroundings. Thousands of individual strings of thought became shoals of piranhas, riding the invisible cross-currents which flowed in mazy twists all around them. On either side of the fray, the masters of the conflict floated, maintaining their positions amid the whip and slide of the Weave. Kakre was a ray, Fahrekh a massive black jellyfish, its tentacles deadly purple streamers. These were the representations of their physical bodies, the core of their presence in the Weave. The piranhas were their fighters, a dizzying multitude of mind-strands that darted through the space between them, seeking for a way through the enemy shoal. They savaged one another, bursting into bright blooms of scrabbling gold threads as they hit, illuminating the darkness with brief globes of light that knotted inward to infinity and collapsed.

The squabbling of the piranhas was enacted faster than the eye could follow. They arced and looped in squads of dozens, thrusting or retreating or laying decoys. Smaller fish darted around the periphery of the thrashing battlefield, trying to circumvent the conflict and reach the enemy: some would be caught by their opponent's defences, others dashed to pieces in the cross-currents. The Weavers had innumerable tricks: using fish to shield other fish, slingshotting off the edge of invisible whirlpools, laying sluggish bait which would explode into an insoluble labyrinth of tangles when engaged. It was a dizzying tableau of astonishing viciousness, hidden beneath a thin skin of illusion to protect the minds of the combatants from the raw and maddening beauty of the Weave.

And Kakre was losing.

Though less than a second had passed in the world outside the Weave, where time was governed by the sun and the moons, the private battle had passed through a multitude of shifts and phases, as of a military campaign enacted at extreme speed. Kakre was canny, and had tricks learned from long experience; gaining mastery of the feya-kori had taught him some things that Fahrekh had yet to fathom. But he was making mistakes. Little slips, infinitesimal blank spots in his mind where once a reaction would have been instinctive, sinister patches of forgetfulness that drifted across his psyche, robbing him of focus. Fahrekh was young and burning with energy; his vigour made up for his relative lack of finesse. Kakre's shoal was losing ground, becoming tattered. Holes were opening in his defences faster than he could stitch them shut.

But there was worse. Kakre was exhausted. His physical body was tearing itself apart under the stress of the combat. He could feel his systems wrecking themselves in an effort to provide him with the strength to fight, and there would soon be nothing left for him to draw on. Fahrekh, who would have been a difficult opponent even when they were on equal footing, had caught him at his lowest ebb. Kakre could not win; he was only delaying the inevitable.

Well, if that was so, it was so. Kakre would never relinquish himself. He would fight till his dying breath.

His moment of defiance was his last thought before Fahrekh outmanoeuvred him totally. His enemy had been gathering forces behind a knitted ball of decoys, and now they suddenly shot out and round, engulfing Kakre's shoal like a hand closing into a fist. Kakre abandoned them immediately, knowing they were lost, and began creating a new shoal; but he had no vitality to give them, and they were sickly and slow. Fahrekh's ravening horde swept them aside and tore towards Kakre's unprotected ray to rip him apart.

And in that instant, the Weave-whale appeared.

It burst out of nothingness, filling the black abyss, overwhelming them with its sheer scale. The impact of its arrival blasted across the Weave like a detonation, scattering Fahrekh's shoal, buffeting them with a shockwave. Fahrekh managed to hold his coherence, but Kakre tattered away, losing his grip on the Weave, dissipating back into his physical body again.

It was sheer insane fury that saved him. There was no confusion as he was wrenched back to the world of human senses, no hesitation, and no conscious thought involved. Riding a wave of rage, a scream ripping from his throat, he lunged at Fahrekh, drawing his skinning knife from his belt. Fahrekh, stunned by the Weave-whale, was not fast enough to react. Kakre drove the blade beneath his metal Mask, ramming it deep into the soft flesh under his chin, through his palate and up into the front of his brain. The force of it took Fahrekh off his feet, and he collapsed to the floor in a billow of dust with Kakre on top of him. Still screaming, Kakre plunged the knife into Fahrekh's throat and chest again and again, drawing spurts of blood into the air, hacking flesh to moist ribbons. Finally, in one last, disgusted motion, he tore off Fahrekh's Mask and buried the knife up to the hilt in his eye; and after that, he was done.

He slid off the corpse of his enemy, his patchwork robe wet with blood, and lay there for some time, the only sound the laboured wheeze of his breath, slowing and slowing until he fell asleep.

SEVENTEEN

There was a village inside the Forest of Xu.

At least, when they had first laid eyes on it, they had *assumed* it was a village. They still were not entirely certain even now, as dusk approached on their second day in the forest. It was something so utterly alien to their experience that they had no adequate parallels to draw.

It was built around the existing trees with no apparent boundaries, sprawling up the trunks into the canopy and spreading along the ground in a curiously organic fashion. The constructions were formed of a glistening substance, hard as rock and smooth to the touch, predominantly an icy blue-white, but sometimes shaded brown or green. It had a subtle iridescence and a maddening quality that was not quite translucence but more a chameleon-like mimicry of colour: it seemed to change its hue to whatever lay behind it, depending on where the viewer stood. When Kaiku laid her hand on it, she left a hazy pink imprint which faded after a time.

Tsata, particularly, had been fascinated by how this strange village had been built, and it was he that found the key, and uncovered the secret at least partially. The substance was sap, bled from the trees and hardened through some unknown art into a multitude of shapes. Every construction, no matter how remote, was eventually linked to a tree bole at some point, though no evidence of cutting could be found. And now that they had established this, it was possible to see a certain flow to the architecture, a kind of glacial creep around which offshoots had been moulded with exquisite artistry. Kaiku had the uncomfortable sensation that the village was still growing; indeed, she found evidence of channels in which glistening sap still lay, oozing with excruciating torpidity towards the tips and edges of the existing constructions, which were wet with the stuff. She guessed that this would be moulded and hardened too, in time, to form another offshoot.

The village was an exhibition of dizzying variety. Wide discs buried in the bark of the trees were set in irregular patterns, sometimes growing in size as they ascended, sometimes diminishing. Spiky sprays erupted into the air. Gossamer threads were stitched through the branches, or formed twisting, unsupported bridges that defied physics. Some of the dwellings were like uneven pagodas, others smooth semicircular domes, still others jagged starbursts of colourful sap. Many of them had no visible means of entry.

Some were up in the trees: inverted cones of three-quarter circumference growing out from the trunks. Venous tubes like tunnels ran between them, sometimes fracturing into smaller capillaries that tapered away to nothingness as they ran like shatter-cracks along the bark.

Different building styles were evident in different parts of the village, one graduating into another as the eye followed the lines of the dwellings. Some had been sculpted like coral, hulking accretions of sap that branched and overlapped in a dozen different formations and colours; others were thin and needle-like, white clusters of stalagmites rising high overhead; still others were cloudlike and billowing, rounded shapes heaped together like a pile of snowballs.

Kaiku, Asara and Tsata were the first to see it, and it was only afterwards that Tsata pointed out they were probably the first humans ever to have done so. The impact of that had made Kaiku lightheaded, and she had to sit down for a short while.

They had to assume that it was built by the emyrynn, but their only basis for that was the way the creatures had led them here. Once Kaiku and her companions had arrived, the emyrynn disappeared entirely. Upon exploration, there was no sign of life here, nor any indication that anyone or anything had ever occupied these bizarre abodes. Either that, or the inhabitants had deserted this place on their approach, taking everything with them, leaving it preternaturally spotless.

Tsata returned and led the rest of the party to the village. Lucia seemed to believe the spirit-beasts were trustworthy, and they had little alternative but to take her word for it. If that was the case, then had they been provided this place for shelter, somewhere to rest their wounded? Was it possible that these creatures were benevolent rather than hostile? Though many of them suspected a trap, for spirits were notoriously tricky, they settled themselves for the night. The disconcertingly alien surroundings were made more ominous by the eerie quiet and failing light. Doja insisted that they camp in the open and not sleep inside any of the sap-buildings. His men were only too glad to comply.

Neryn was waxing tonight, casting a soothing green light through the interknit branches overhead. Aurus was low in the northern sky, visible only by her glow on the edges of the leaves. Kaiku wandered through the camp amid the restless murmur of the troops, distracted by the architecture. The troops cast unfriendly glances at her. She was alone, and content to be so. Lucia was asleep; Phaeca had also retired, complaining that she felt ill; Tsata and Heth were tending their fallen comrade and would not leave her side.

Kaiku had spotted Asara earlier that evening, leaning against the side of one of the emyrynn dwellings, watching her while she absentmindedly cleaned her rifle. Kaiku, suddenly tired of her manner, had strode over to her to have this out; but she had picked up her rifle and gone before Kaiku got there. Obviously she did not want to talk then.

But now, suddenly, she appeared at Kaiku's side. 'I wish to speak with you,' she murmured.

'And I with you,' Kaiku replied.

'Not here,' said Asara. 'Come with me,'

Kaiku followed as Asara led them away from the camp. The village spread and towered around them, the silent edifice of an unknown species, aloof and impenetrable. They went some way from the camp, until they were sure there was nobody around, and there Asara stopped. For a moment, she did not turn; her shoulders were tight with suppressed emotion. Then she seemed to make a decision, and she faced Kaiku.

Kaiku studied her expectantly. The almond-shaped eyes painted in soft green, the dark skin, the achingly exotic beauty of her all belonged to a stranger, but under that she was still Asara; wonderful, treacherous Asara, whom she loved and hated in equal measure. The woman who had given her life, and taken for it a piece of Kaiku's essence and left a piece of her own, little splinters of desire that had lodged in their hearts and never quite worked free. Each wanted what the other had: that sliver of themselves that had been lost in the transaction.

Eventually, for Asara seemed so uncertain, it was Kaiku who spoke first. 'What is my debt, Asara?' she asked. 'What would you have me do to redress the balance between us?'

'You admit that you owe me, then?' Asara said quickly.

'I do owe you,' Kaiku said. 'But do I owe you enough to do as you ask? I will hear what you have to say before I decide.'

'Very well.' Asara still seemed wary. 'But you must swear first that what I have to ask you will never be repeated by you to anyone. To *anyone*. Whether you agree or not.'

'You have my oath,' said Kaiku, for she knew that Asara would go no further without it, and she wanted this done.

Asara regarded her carefully in the darkness, her eyes glittering. Debating whether to trust her.

'Asara,' Kaiku snapped, impatient. 'You have followed me this far. Do not fool yourself into thinking you are making a choice; you made it some time ago. You have shadowed my footsteps too long. What do you *want*?'

'I want a *child*,' Asara hissed.

There was silence between them. Asara retreated, spent by the effort of the admission. Kaiku stared.

'I want a child,' she said again, quieter. 'But I cannot bear one.'

'Why not?' Kaiku asked, slightly dazed. *This* was her secret longing?

'I do not know why not,' Asara replied. 'I can . . . change myself, but only to an extent. I can take on the forms of men and women, but not of beasts, nor of birds. I can alter my skin and my shape, but I have limits. What I can do, I do by instinct. I do not know how it happens. I cannot see inside myself. I cannot *fix* myself.'

It made sense to Kaiku then. 'You want me to make you fertile.'

'You can do this!' Asara said, and there was naked hunger in her voice. 'I have heard of the deeds you and your kind are capable of. I have seen Sisters bring men back from the brink of death, healing with their hands. I watched you save that Tkiurathi woman's life just hours ago! You have the power to repair whatever is wrong with me.'

'Perhaps,' said Kaiku.

'*Perhaps?*' Asara cried.

'I am not a god, Asara,' Kaiku said. 'I cannot create what is not there. I do not know what kind of changes Aberrancy has wreaked in you. What if you have no womb? I cannot give you one.'

'Then look! Look inside! You can tell me!' Asara was desperate now; her hopes had been vested in this for so long that the possibility of them being dashed was too much for her to take. For so long, lonely and empty; ever outcast, ever unable to fill the void that yawned inside her. There were none like she was, even among the Aberrants. In all ninety of her years, she had never found another. And it was Shintu's cruellest trick indeed to make her ageless and yet rob her of the power to procreate.

But Kaiku's brow was creased in a frown. 'I will have to think on this, Asara.'

'You *owe* me,' Asara spat, her fear turning to fury. 'I gave you a life; now you give me one!'

'And what would you do with it, Asara?' Kaiku asked. Her hair hung across one eye, but the other one regarded Asara steadily. 'What would I be unleashing if I allowed more creatures like you into the world?'

'It is the right of every woman! I was denied!'

'*Are* you even a woman?' Kaiku asked. 'Were you one to begin with? I wonder.' She had lapsed into the tone she used when she wore the make-up of the Sisterhood: stern, authoritative. 'Perhaps the gods had a reason to deny you. Perhaps one of you is enough.'

'Do not pronounce moral judgements upon me!' Asara raged. 'Not when you and your Red Order plot and scheme towards the throne. Your conscience is not unstained, Kaiku. Ask Cailin why your kind let the Weavers take the Empire. Ask her if hundreds of thousands, if *millions* of lives were worth sacrificing so that the Sisterhood could rise!'

Kaiku gazed at her levelly. 'Perhaps I will,' she said, and she turned and walked away. She could sense Asara's hateful glare prickling against her nape, and was half expecting the spy to attack her out of sheer thwarted anger; but Asara let her go.

Kaiku let the quietude of the forest envelop her, broken only by the sinister ticks and taps in the distance. Once her mind was still, she began to consider what Asara had said.

They spent an uneasy night within the emyrynn village, but when dawn came they were still all there. None of them were in good shape, however. Terrifying dreams haunted them, and the early watches had been punctuated by the shrieks of waking men. Most gave up trying to sleep, too afraid of what lurked just beneath the skin of unconsciousness. Those that persevered caught snatches of slumber, a few minutes at a time, before awakening in a worse state than they had been before. Tempers were fraying among the men. They resented the forest and the spirits and so, lacking targets, they snapped at each other.

What was worse, it became clear soon afterward that they would not be going anywhere that day. Peithre had improved a little, but Phaeca had become sick. Kaiku talked with Doja, who admitted that it was foolhardy to go on with one of the Sisters down and the other one determined to stay. He broke the news to his men, sweetening it by pointing out that he believed they were safe from the forest in the emyrynn village.

Kaiku was dubious about this last statement, but it served her purpose. The soldiers accepted their fate with stoic expressions, though later there would be dissent amongst them. The spirits were bad enough, but the sleeplessness was getting to them too. There was something in this place that poisoned the mind, and they did not want to linger a moment more than necessary. She knew how they felt. There was no telling how much longer it would take them to get to the Xhiang Xhi, and every day there was a day back.

She visited Phaeca. Against Doja's wishes, Phaeca had moved herself out of her tent and inside one of the emyrynn dwellings, where she had unrolled her sleeping-mat. It was warm and oddly sterile there, an irregularly shaped room with the curve of a tree bole as one wall. Protuberances of sap were moulded from parts of the floor and ceiling, things that could have been sculpture or which might have had a mundane and utilitarian purpose. A thin tunnel, too small for anything bigger than a mouse, opened out into the room. From what Kaiku could determine, it wound all the way up the tree until it was lost in the branches, but she could not imagine what it was for.

Phaeca was making little sense. She was babbling as if feverish, but she had no temperature, and though she was agitated she was not sallow. She slapped Kaiku's hand away when it was laid on her cheek, and muttered unpleasant things about her as if she was not in the room. Kaiku knelt by her for a time, deeply concerned. There was no healing possible: she had defences to keep others out, even other Sisters. Besides, the more she studied her companion, the more Kaiku worried that the affliction was not physical at all. Her shrieks had been the loudest last night. Like Lucia, the forest was battering her, and Kaiku did not know how well her sanity would hold.

Gods, why did we ever come to this cursed place? she thought to herself, but she already knew the answer to that one. They came here because it was their last chance.

She glimpsed the emyrynn a few times that day, flitting among the trees in the distance. Each time, she stared out into the blue and green folds of the forest and wondered about the nature of their curious hosts. She went to see Peithre, who was very weak but awake, and spoke with Tsata for a time. But he seemed odd to her today: there was something in his manner that she could not fathom, and eventually she gave up on trying and left him alone. The atmosphere in the camp depressed her, but she was stuck here, as they all were.

She took to wandering around the village, to give herself space to think. The charge laid on her by Asara was a heavy one. At least she knew now why Asara had followed her into the forest: she had an investment to protect. But even if Kaiku could do it, the question was: *should* she? Did she dare allow a being like that to procreate?

It was not the same to her as being asked to stop Asara having children. That she would never do. That was taking something away from her. But giving her the ability to breed seemed another matter entirely. It was action rather than inaction: every deed of her offspring, every result would be because of Kaiku.

What if they all grew with Asara's abilities? What if they were all as deceitful as their mother? How could they fail to be? Gods, she would be making Asara the progenitor of a new race. A race of beings who could take on any face, any human form; the perfect spies, lethal mimics, with unguessable lifespans. Only the Sisters would be able to penetrate their disguise.

She caught herself. Her imagination was running away with her, perhaps. There was no guarantee that Asara's offspring would inherit her gift. And even if they did, there was no reason why they should become the beautiful and dreadful creatures that Kaiku envisaged. Asara's nature would not necessarily be theirs.

But the possibility was there. She could not deny that.

She wanted to talk it over with Tsata. It was frustrating that he was so close by and yet she was oath-bound not to speak of it. She admired his incisive mind and his honesty. He would have been able to help her untangle the knots. He would have told her that action and inaction are the same in this matter, that if she was prepared to deny Asara the gift of fertility for fear of creating a race of monsters then she should be prepared to prevent her from conceiving too, and vice versa. He would have cut through the deceptions that she made for herself, the double standards and smokescreens of etiquette and belief. He would have told her that the real reason she was debating this was because she did not want the responsibility of having to make that choice.

She knew all this, but it did not make the deciding any easier.

Night stole across the land again, and this time there were no moons to leaven it.

The soldiers had come to dread the darkness. The prospect of sleep was worse than the exhaustion of being awake, and many were too afraid to even try; yet always they were dragged down towards unconsciousness. Sentries nodded at their posts; heads lolled, and their owners were startled awake with a cry as the nightmares leaped hungrily upon them. The forest was a place that tricked the eye anyway, but deprived of sleep as they were, they were constantly seeing movement and fleeting hallucinations.

'We have to set out tomorrow,' Doja had growled at Kaiku. 'These men can't take this any longer. We'll carry Phaeca and the Tkiurathi woman if necessary.'

Kaiku had not flatly forebade it, but she was reluctant. In the end, she agreed that if Peithre's condition improved overnight enough to safely move her, then they could fashion stretchers and set off again. She, too, was concerned about the state of mind of the party. Her *kana*-ministered metabolism meant that she was not so exhausted as the others, but she feared that accidents were bound to happen if there was much more of this. There were altogether too many rifles and jumpy trigger fingers in this camp.

But there was one ray of hope among it all: just after the last of the dusk had fled the sky, word came to Kaiku that Lucia was awake and lucid. Kaiku hurried to her, and found her outside her tent. She gave Kaiku a fleeting smile and invited her to walk. They wandered a little way from the camp, among the nacreous wonders of the emyrynn, and Kaiku was relieved to see that she was indeed clear-headed and attentive.

'The Xhiang Xhi is not far,' Lucia said.

'Is that so?' Kaiku asked in surprise. 'We cannot have penetrated very deep into the forest yet.'

Lucia cast her a slyly amused look. 'This is a place of spirits,' she said. 'We could walk forever and never reach the other side, or we could emerge there within an hour's march. Distance is fluid here. Don't you think it a coincidence that this village happened to be so close to where Peithre fell? In a forest this size, wasn't that extraordinarily convenient?'

'It had occurred to me,' Kaiku admitted.

'If the Xhiang Xhi did not want to be found, we would never find it,' Lucia said. 'But it does.'

'Then why does it not appear? Why put us through this?'

'I don't know. The ways of the spirits are strange. Perhaps it's testing us. Perhaps it's curious about me, and wishes to study me first.'

Kaiku did not like that thought. 'You could still turn back, Lucia,' she said. 'It is not too late.'

Lucia gave her a sorrowful look. 'Oh, it is. *Far* too late.' She looked away, out of the village through the dark trees and unfamiliar foliage. 'Besides, if we turned back now we would never get out of the forest. The Xhiang Xhi wants to see me. It's intrigued, I think. If not for that, we would not have survived even this long.'

'If it wants to see you, why is it allowing us to be harmed?' Kaiku asked rhetorically.

Lucia answered anyway. 'It wants to see *me*,' she replied. 'The rest of you are expendable, perhaps.'

Kaiku felt a slow chill creep through her.

Lucia turned with a suddenness of movement that made Kaiku stop walking. The younger woman gazed at her with an unfamiliar purpose in her eyes.

'Lucia, what is it?'

'There are things I must say to you,' she said. 'In case I never again get the chance to speak them.'

Kaiku frowned. 'Do not talk that way.'

'I'm serious, Kaiku,' she said. 'I don't know if I'll ever be this clear-headed again.'

'Of course you will!' Kaiku protested. 'Once we get out of the forest, you will—'

'Let me speak!' Lucia snapped. Kaiku was shocked into silence. Lucia softened. 'Forgive me. Let me say this. That is all I ask.'

Kaiku nodded.

'I want to thank you. That is all. You and Mishani. I want you to know that . . . I appreciate everything you have done for me. For being like sisters to me. And you have always, always been on my side. When all this is done, I . . .' She trailed off. 'I just wanted you to know. You have my love, and you always will.'

Kaiku felt her eyes welling, and she gathered Lucia up in an embrace. 'Heart's blood, you make it sound like a farewell. We will come through this, Lucia. You will live to tell Mishani that yourself.' Lucia clutched her closer. 'I will protect you, even if it means my life.'

'There are some things that even you cannot protect me from,' Lucia whispered. And then she looked up, over Kaiku's shoulder, and some aspect of her body language told Kaiku there was somebody there. She turned, and it was Heth.

'Is Tsata with you?' he asked without apology or preamble.

The tone in his voice killed the caustic reply Kaiku was about to make. 'I have not seen him,' she replied instead.

'But he left to go after you,' Heth said, his features animate with confusion as he wrestled with the unfamiliar Saramyrrhic syllables. 'Into the forest.'

'I have not been out of the village,' Kaiku said.

'He saw you leave,' Heth persisted. 'I was with him. I did not see you, but he did. He said he must talk with you.'

An odd foreboding was settling into Kaiku's marrow. 'When was this?'

'A few minutes ago. Peithre has worsened; I came to fetch him.'

Kaiku looked at Lucia. 'Three nights past, the night I was attacked by the spirit in the trees . . . I saw you walk out into the forest, and I went to follow you.'

Lucia looked blank. 'I didn't leave my tent that night. I was asleep, and there were guards outside.'

'Gods!' Kaiku hissed. 'Go back to the camp! Heth, show me where he went!'

Heth obeyed without hesitation, while Lucia hurried away, alarmed. Kaiku followed the Tkiurathi for a short distance, until he stopped and pointed. 'That way.'

Kaiku's irises turned red. She would never be able to track a Tkiurathi through conventional means, even if she had the necessary skills; but in the Weave she could still hunt him. She could see his scent-trail, the faint agitation of air in his wake, the memory of his breath and the reverberation of his heartbeat.

'See to Peithre,' she murmured. 'You cannot help me now.'

And with that, she plunged into the forest.

It swallowed her eagerly. Hanging vines and tendrils of blue plants brushed at her as she ran. The ground was treacherous, a tangle of roots and glittering rocks; it rose and dipped and twisted, making her speed reckless. But she read the ground as she read the air, predicting its contours through the threads of the Weave, and she was sure-footed.

She cursed herself as she went. If only she had pushed Lucia a little more, if only she had thought to investigate further the incident when she had seen her walking away from camp. But Lucia had been impenetrable, her mind elsewhere, and Kaiku had not wanted to cause more trouble among the soldiers before she heard the story from Lucia's own lips.

Now she knew that there was no story. Lucia had not gone anywhere. Whatever it was she had been following that night, it was not Lucia. And Tsata had fallen for the same trick.

If he died because of her stupidity . . .

She was genuinely, utterly terrified. Not for herself, but for the incomplete half of that thought. She was afraid of the void that would be left in the wake of his passing. Adept at armouring her own heart, she had not realised how much she had missed him while he was away, how much it gladdened her to talk with him, to fence with his foreign mind-set, to simply have him near her. Not until now, not until she thought she might be about to lose him again, and permanently this time.

She accelerated to a sprint, following his invisible trail, her boots sliding on the ground, her shoulders clipping trees that she failed to dodge entirely. There was a panic welling within her, something that threatened her with madness. She dared not think about what would happen if she found him dead, his eyes milky white and his face a map of swollen veins like the other man they had found. Even if she had to face down that massive shadow, that half-seen beast that had attacked her before, she would not falter.

The sound of her passing was loud in the silence of the forest, the lashing of fronds against her body and the dull sound of her boots on the dirt. Something was whispering to her, some premonition that told her every second was precious, every instant she delayed could be the crucial one, the difference between facing the awful emptiness of Tsata's death and the joy of finding him alive and well. Fighting her way through the golden tapestry of the forest, she cried out his name, hoping to warn him somehow, praying that he could hear her and that it was not too late.

And then she burst through a screen of leaves and into a tiny patch of open ground, and there was Tsata, his outline a million glowing threads, turning towards her in surprise. And over his shoulder she saw *something*, some black and twisted entity that shared her shape in the physical world but not here in the Weave: a spirit that mimicked others, leading its victims away to kill them. Its illusion failed it then, and it turned its face upon her, and she saw there a doorway to the secrets of the spirit realm, a sight so incomprehensible that it would turn a man's mind inside out and slay him on the spot. But she was a Sister of the Red Order, and she had seen things that no man had.

'*Do not look at her!*' she screamed, grabbing Tsata's head and pulling it down into her shoulder. Her other arm she threw out at the spirit, and her *kana* burst free and tore into it. It howled, an unearthly shriek as Kaiku shredded through its defences and ripped into its essence, and then it was rent into tatters.

The silence returned, and there was only the two of them. Kaiku became suddenly conscious of the nearness of their bodies. She released Tsata's head and he raised it, a question in his pale green eyes. Though he did not understand, he knew by what he had heard that Kaiku had saved him from something. Their faces were a fraction too close still: he had not drawn away past the point where proximity could still pull lips and tongues together. They trembled there for an instant, on the cusp of that; and then she kissed him, and he melted into her, his arms sliding around her back.

For a time, there was nothing but the sensation of it, the rhythm of their mouths meeting and parting, the pressure of their contact. Then, as their kisses became shallower until they were mere brushes of the lips, thought began to intrude once again. Kaiku opened her eyes – still blood-red in the aftermath of her *kana* – and saw Tsata looking back at her. Her gaze roamed him uncertainly, afraid of the blow that would shatter the fragile state they had found themselves in. She traced the lines of the tattoos on his cheeks, the orange-blond sap-stiffened hair, the line of his jaw; and she saw in him the antithesis of all she hated in her life, all the deceit and subterfuge and secrecy that had killed her family and torn her world apart. And yet she waited in terror for him to break the spell, to tell her that this was only a mistake of passion, that his brutal self-honesty would not allow him to go on with this if his heart was not in it.

He seemed about to speak; but in the end, he moved to kiss her instead. She pulled away fractionally, and he stopped, confused.

'Peithre has worsened,' she murmured. 'You should go to her.'

His pale green eyes flickered across her face. Then he was gone, disappearing without a word into the forest, leaving Kaiku alone.

When Nuki's eye next rose in the east, it found Mishani sitting on the shore of Lake Xemit, looking out over the water.

It was a cold dawn, and around her she had a heavy crimson shawl, embroidered in gold. Her hair pooled on the cloth that she had laid down to prevent her dirtying her hem. She had been here most of the night, thinking, chasing herself in ever tighter circles until she was left with a conclusion. It was an unwise course, one that she dreaded to take, and she did not want to accept it; yet she knew in her heart that it was inevitable, and her protests were weak and failing fast.

Presently she heard the tread of approaching feet on the dewy grass slope that led down from the temple complex of Araka Jo. She guessed it to be Yugi even before he walked into her line of sight.

'Daygreet, Mishani,' he said. 'May I join you?'

'Daygreet, Yugi. Please do.' She moved across to make space for him on the cloth, and he sat down heavily next to her.

'No sleep for you, then?' he said.

'Nor for you, it seems.' She studied him. He looked dishevelled as ever, and he reeked of amaxa root. It was obvious what had kept him up.

'I begin to wonder how many more nights I have left,' he said. 'Sleeping seems such a waste of precious time.'

'That sounds a fast route to madness,' Mishani said, half-seriously.

Yugi scratched the back of his neck. 'This whole land is in the grip of madness, Mishani. If I were mad, I might at least have a chance of understanding it.'

They looked out across the lake for a time, before Yugi spoke again.

'There is word that your mother will publish another book soon. Cailin speaks of plans in the wake of the information you have given us,' he said, and coughed. 'She's still agitating for an assault on Adderach when Lucia returns. Depending on what news comes from this latest tale.'

'Foolish,' Mishani said with a sigh. 'An army would be cut to pieces in those mountains.'

'Perhaps,' Yugi replied.

She glanced at him. He was unshaven and gaunt. 'You are overfond of the root, Yugi,' she said. 'Once you controlled it; now it controls you. You are the leader of many men and women. Their lives are your responsibility. Stop this idiocy before you lose your judgement.'

Yugi seemed a little surprised, apparently deciding whether to take umbrage or not. Then he sagged, and merely looked weary. 'You're far from the first to tell me that. It's not so simple.'

'Cailin could help you overcome the addiction, perhaps,' Mishani suggested, brushing her hair over her shoulder.

Yugi snorted a laugh. 'I'm not addicted, Mishani. I smoked amaxa root for years and it never got a hold on me. The root is only a symptom of the cause.'

'What, then, is the cause?' she asked.

He did not answer for a while, debating whether to tell her or not. Mishani was no confidante of his. But she waited patiently, and finally he shrugged and sighed.

'I was a bandit, once,' he said. 'I imagine you know that.'

'I had surmised as much from things Zaelis said,' she admitted.

'Did you also know that I had a woman back then?'

'A wife?'

'As near as can be. We had little use for marriage, and no priests.'

'That I did not know.'

Yugi was tentative, ready to abandon this conversation at the slightest hint of sarcasm or mockery from Mishani. She gave him none. This was important to him, and that made it important to her, for he was the leader of the Libera Dramach and any knowledge about his state of mind could be advantageous.

'Her name was Keila,' he said. He opened his mouth to say more, perhaps to describe her to Mishani, perhaps to talk of what he felt for her; but he changed his mind. Mishani understood that. Words seemed mawkish that were most deeply felt.

'What happened to her?' Mishani asked.

'She died,' Yugi said. He looked down at the ground.

'Because of you,' Mishani said, reading his reaction.

He nodded. 'There were perhaps a hundred of us at our height. And we had a reputation. We were the most feared bandit gang from Barask to Tchamaska.'

'And you led them, back then?' Mishani guessed.

Yugi nodded. 'Gods, I'm not proud of some of the things I did. We were bandits, Mishani. That made us killers, thieves, and worse. Every man had his morals, every man had . . . things he wouldn't do. But there was always someone who would.'

He gave Mishani a wary glance. She watched him steadily, showing nothing. He was searching for condemnation from her, but she would not condemn him. Her own past was hardly unstained.

'A man can . . . detach himself,' Yugi murmured. 'He can learn to see people as obstacles, or objects. He can learn to shut out the crying of women and the look in his enemy's eyes as he dies. They are just animal reactions, like the thrashing of a wounded rabbit or the twisting of a fish on a hook. A man can persuade himself to the necessity of anything, if he has the will to.' The lake was grey and still in the dawn light. He gazed into it. 'The world of bandits was a ruthless one. We had to be more ruthless still.' He smiled faintly, but it was bitter and there was no joy there.

'Does it disturb you?' he asked. 'To know that the leader of the Libera Dramach is a thief and a murderer?'

'No,' said Mishani. 'I ceased to believe in innocence long ago. A bandit may kill a hundred men, but those we choose to govern us kill many times that number with their schemes and policies. I learned of such things at court. At least your way of murder is honest.' She watched a bird winging its way across the lake, south to north. 'I cannot speak for others, but I do not care about your past. I did not know those you harmed, and to be outraged at you would be false sentiment. We are all of us guilty of things that make us ashamed. Good men do evil deeds, and evil men can become good. I care only what you do now, Yugi, for you hold the reins of many lives.' The bird disappeared at last, vanishing in the distance, and she shifted herself where she sat and turned her eyes to him again. 'Go on with your tale.'

'We made enemies, of course,' Yugi said after a time. 'Other bandit gangs wanted to topple us, but none of them had a chance against our strength. I became overconfident.' He began to pick at the cloth between his knees. 'There was word of a gathering of our rivals. I led my men out to ambush them. But it was a trick. One I should have seen coming.'

'They ambushed you?'

'Not us. They raided our camp, where we had left our women and children. There were only a dozen fighting men there. I didn't think they knew where we hid, didn't think they'd dare to attack us even if they did know. Wrong on both counts.' His eyes tightened. 'Gods, when we got back . . .'

Mishani was silent. She pulled her shawl a little tighter around her to fend off the cold.

'She wasn't quite dead when I found her. I'll never know how she held on that long. But she waited for me, and . . . we . . .' His voice failed him. He swallowed. 'She died in my arms.'

He stared furiously out across the lake, taut with a festering anger. 'And do you know what my first thought was after she had died? My very first? I'll tell you. I *deserved* it. I deserved for her to die. Because I realised then that every person who died on my blade had a mother or a brother or a child who felt the grief that I was feeling. And I tore a strip from the hem of her dress and I wrapped it around my head, and I swore I'd wear it always to remind me of what I'd done, and who I'd lost because of it.' He touched the dirty rag around his forehead. 'This.'

'And what happened afterward?' Mishani asked. She did not offer sympathy. She did not think he wanted any from her, nor would she have given it if he had.

'The others were already screaming for revenge,' he said. 'But I knew how it would be. Our retribution would spark other retributions, as it always had and always would. Running around in circles, getting nowhere, an endless back and forth of blades and bleeding bodies. And so I walked away from there. They thought to give me space, to let me grieve for my woman. They thought I would be back.' His eyes were flat. 'But I never came back.'

Mishani knew the rest from Zaelis: how Yugi had drifted into the Libera Dramach; how his natural leadership skills and experience had made him more and more invaluable until he had become Zaelis's right-hand man; how, after Zaelis had died at the Fold, he had become the head of the Libera Dramach. And she understood him now.

'You do not want to lead these people, do you?' she asked.

Yugi looked at her for a long moment, then tilted his head in affirmation. 'I'm no general like Zahn. I don't have the vision and ambition that Zaelis had. I led a hundred men and I led them well, but in the end I failed and it cost me the only thing I ever . . .' He looked away. 'Ah, what use is talking?'

'You could step down,' said Mishani.

'No, I couldn't. Because I'm still the best gods-damned leader they've got. Zaelis may have picked his men well, but he couldn't get generals, he couldn't get war-makers. They belong to the noble houses, and the moment one of them get near the Libera Dramach, the moment *politics* becomes involved, then it's over for us. They all want Lucia.'

Mishani nodded. 'There is sense in what you say. Even Zahn would be a danger. But can you lead thousands to war, Yugi? Your skills were of great use in the Fold, but then you were fighting as bandits fight. It may come to a moment when you must be a general, and your choices on the battlefield will cost many lives. Will you be able to make those choices? Or will you hide in your drugged dreams?'

Yugi looked grim. 'If it's my punishment that I must suffer to lead these men and women, then I'll bear it because I have to. The gods certainly have a sick sense of humour, to make revenge on me for my past misdeeds by giving me *more* lives to ruin.'

'They do indeed,' said Mishani.

Yugi got to his feet then. Nuki's eye had risen a little more by now. The lake was blue, and the air was warming. 'Thank you for hearing me out, Mishani. I don't know why I chose to talk to you of all people, but I'm glad I did.' He looked up the slope, to where the white temples of Araka Jo stood crumbling. 'How is it that our past dictates our future?' he wondered aloud. 'Where's the sense in that?'

And then he was gone, walking away from her, and she was alone again.

She sat for a long time and thought on what he had said. Then she returned to her house and began to pack what things she needed.

She was going to see her mother.

EIGHTEEN

Few slept in the forest that night, but for Kaiku it was not out of fear of dreams.

She wandered the emyrynn village alone after Tsata had left her, traipsing listlessly between the iridescent columns and swirls and spikes that clung to the trees and sprawled along the ground. Fretfully replaying the moment in her mind when they had kissed, picking it apart to find what meaning she could therein. What had been in his eyes when she had halted him? Would it have been better to have let him kiss her again before giving him news of his ailing kinswoman? Did he interpret it as an excuse for rejection? And indeed, in Kaiku's intention, had it been that? Did she shy from him on purpose, using Peithre as an excuse to get herself out of it? Gods, she did not even know herself what she had wanted then; but retrospect was a hard eye to cast upon her actions, and she was full of regrets and uncertainties.

She had achieved no resolution by the time dawn came, and she heard Phaeca's scream.

Her meanderings had almost brought her back to the camp when the sound reached her. It took longer to process than it otherwise would, for the sleeplessness was beginning to tell. She wasted a second on incomprehension before breaking into a run, sprinting around the tent cluster where others were getting to their feet. She reached the alien dwelling where Phaeca had been resting, pushed aside the soldiers who crowded around the entranceway and went inside.

Phaeca was still screaming. She was hunkered against the tree bole that formed one wall of the room, her possessions and bedding scattered across the floor. Blood ran from the walls and lay in pools on the floor, smeared at the edges where her heels had slipped in them. Chunks of smoking flesh and blackened bone were strewn about. Some of them were whole enough to still have the fur on. White fur, soaked in red.

Kaiku stared at the scene, aghast. 'Phaeca, what have you done?' she breathed. Her voice rose in anger and disbelief. 'You *killed* one of them? You killed an emyrynn?' She crossed the room and grabbed hold of Phaeca's shoulders, shaking her roughly. 'Why? *Why?*'

'It was trying to kill *me!*' Phaeca shrieked. 'It was in my room! I woke up and it was in my room!'

Kaiku squeezed her eyes shut. The scene as it might have happened played across the darkness: Phaeca, awakening from a nightmare to find an unfamiliar creature before her, lashing out with her *kana*. She was already in a state of questionable sanity, driven to raving and feverish mutterings by the malevolence of the forest. The sight of the emyrynn must have been too much for her. Or maybe it *had* attacked her. Maybe she was telling the truth. It didn't matter, in the end. She had killed one of them.

'This is not *your* room,' she said, her voice quieter now. 'You were sleeping in its home.'

A cry of alarm went up in the camp, and those soldiers at the doorway turned back to look. 'There's something moving out in the trees!' came the shout.

'Do you know what you have done, Phaeca?' Kaiku said, her tone heavy with despondency. 'Your actions will be the death of us all.'

At that, Phaeca's face twisted into a snarl, and she launched herself at Kaiku.

Kaiku did not expect it in the least. Perhaps, had she thought on it, she would have been more careful in her words. She knew how fragile her friend was in this place. But though she had worried about Phaeca's state of mind over the past few days, she had never once thought that she might become violent. Even in the wake of what she had just discovered, she assumed the killing of the emyrynn was an accident, a reaction rather than a premeditated act. The sight of the Sister's face twisting into a contortion of such utter hatred made her quail; and then she was being carried out of the doorway of the dwelling by the weight of the attack, scattering the soldiers there, and she fell onto the blue-green grass outside with Phaeca atop her.

The savagery of Phaeca's assault stunned her; she only resisted at all because instinct drove her to. Phaeca raked her face with her nails, slapped and punched at her head, shrieking and screaming oaths and curses in a coarse Axekami dialect that was entirely unlike her usual mode of speech. Two of the soldiers, unable to credit what they were seeing, reached down to pull the crazed Sister from her victim; they were flung back and away by an invisible force that flattened the grass and cracked the sap wall of the emyrynn dwelling.

It was the outrush of Phaeca's *kana* that brought Kaiku to her senses. The wrenching of the Weave sparked an answer in her own body, a surge of energy that she fought to curtail before it broke out of her, fearful of hurting her friend.

She should not have done so. It took her too long to realise that Phaeca's *kana* was not only directed at the soldiers, it was also directed at her. Phaeca was attacking her in the Weave, and that made her intent lethal.

She surrendered herself to the will of her *kana*. Time decelerated to a crawl in the world of the five senses, while beneath its skin the Sisters clashed at blinding speed. Kaiku's fractional hesitation had afforded Phaeca an advantage. Only when she had cast aside all doubts and had realised that her friend really meant to kill her, that this was a fight for her very life, did she lend her will to the conflict and begin resisting in earnest.

But by then it was too late. Phaeca had undermined her, laid traps that foiled her attempts at constructing defences. Kaiku constructed labyrinthine tangles only to have them come apart at a single tug. She built snares to delay her opponent and watched them fall to pieces when they were sprung. By the time she had got her barriers up, Phaeca was already behind them, and Kaiku was forced to abandon them and back away further. The assault was relentless, furious; she crumbled under it. Phaeca was not as good as Cailin, but she was still better than most Weavers, sliding and shuttling like a needle. And Kaiku had been taken totally by surprise, had still refused to believe it even when she *had* realised what was happening.

Phaeca burst through the holes in Kaiku's stitchwork and reached into her body, grasping, encircling her heart, sewing into muscle and bone. Kaiku screamed in horror, a wordless mental anguish at the violation, the knowledge that she had no way to fight back now and that this cry would be her last.

Then the pain hit her. Phaeca was tearing her apart. She had done it to others before, and always wondered what it must have felt like, the kind of agony they would suffer in the instant before they died. Now she knew. It was as if her every vein and nerve were being pulled forcibly from her flesh, sucked out like tendrils through her skin to be cast away. The torture was incredible, overwhelming . . .

. . . and suddenly gone.

She was alone in the Weave. Phaeca had disappeared, with only an aching pulse of sadness left in her wake.

Her mind settled again, reorientating her senses. She left the Weave, her *kana* turning inwards and scouring her for damage. Her red eyes refocused and the light of dawn in the forest filtered back.

There was a weight atop her. A booted foot braced against it and shoved it off. Asara. She reached down and helped Kaiku up.

'I had no choice,' Asara said. 'It was her or you.'

She forced herself to look at Phaeca. The Sister lay face-down, her hair bloody. Shot through the neck.

'It was her or you,' Asara said again.

Asara's voice was dim and tinny in Kaiku's ears, cushioned by a numb blanket that had settled on her. Her vision had narrowed, the periphery hazed. She felt fractured from her surroundings, barely aware. Around her, gunshots and cries, denting the whine of the blood in her ears. She could not reconcile the figure lying before her with the woman she had known. The fact that this husk of flesh was here did not equate with the certainty that she would never see nor speak with Phaeca again.

'Kaiku, we have to go,' Asara was saying to her. Then, turning her so that she was looking into her eyes. 'Do you hear? We have to go *now!*'

She could see over Asara's shoulder, into the trees that surrounded the village. Of course, of course. The retaliation. From the foliage, white shapes were slinking, muzzles wrinkled and teeth bared. The emyrynn were coming. Their hospitality had been abused.

'Where is Lucia?' someone cried. 'Where is Lucia?'

It was that name that brought Kaiku out of her daze. With a whimper, she moved to flee into the camp and search, thinking only of the need to protect her. Asara grabbed her arm.

'She is there,' Asara said, pointing. And indeed she was, with Doja and a half-dozen soldiers clustered around her. Tsata and Heth were approaching, Peithre carried in Heth's arms. Kaiku saw him and motioned towards Lucia, then ran that way herself, with Asara following.

Phaeca . . .

Kaiku shoved the grief away. She could not allow herself to think on it now. There were others whose lives would depend on her. Lucia was all that mattered.

The emyrynn were coming from all around the village, but they appeared in greatest number at the point where the camp lay against the outermost edge. They sprang through the leaves, sleek and graceful, their white fur pristine. Such beautiful creatures, but their faces were sharp now, grinning in animal rictus, and there was deadly purpose in their steps. The soldiers were firing into the undergrowth, rifle balls clipping purple stems and ricocheting off tree trunks with a splintering of wood. They hit nothing. The emyrynn appeared in glimpses, and each glimpse showed them to be ever closer to their prey.

'Fall back!' Doja cried. 'Protect Lucia!'

'Which way?' Asara called, addressing Lucia, who was gazing into the middle distance. 'Lucia, which way do we go?'

'They're so angry,' she whispered.

Kaiku wiped her eyes with the back of her hand and moved Asara aside. 'Which way, Lucia?' she asked, gently. 'We have to leave.'

At the sound of her voice, Lucia's focus shifted to her. She trembled for a moment, then flung her arm out and pointed into the trees. 'That way.'

'Fall back!' Doja cried again to the soldiers who were retreating towards them, loosing shots into the trees. And with that, Lucia and her retinue ran, away from the village, and the forest closed around them.

The emyrynn broke cover with a harmonic cascade of piercing howls. They burst out into the open, sprinting on all fours, moving like liquid. Their curious musculature gave them a disconcerting gait, rippling them left and right in a sinuous charge towards the men who were covering Lucia's retreat. Those who still had powder in their chambers fired off what shots they had, but all of them missed. Some turned and took flight at the sight of the creatures; some stayed and fought. The outcome was the same. The emyrynn tore into them with surpassing savagery, gouging at faces with their small, sharp antlers, ripping at throats with their blade-like teeth. They bounded onto their prey, bore them to the ground like hunting cats, then shredded them while they were helpless. Their white fur became stained dark red, their muzzles wet with blood. They revelled in the slaughter.

Lucia and Kaiku hurried into the forest, the centre of a stumbling cluster of soldiers who fought to protect them from every side. There were perhaps ten soldiers left now including Doja; also with them went the three Tkiurathi and Asara. Kaiku's eyes were blurring with tears that fell from her lashes with the jolting of her feet on the ground, but she did not notice. She was seeing past them. The forest could not obscure her vision; it had turned to a transparent mass of golden sinews, and within it she saw the emyrynn stalking. Hundreds of them, converging on the village.

'Kaiku, can you see them?' The voice was Asara's.

'Yes.'

'Are they coming after us?'

Kaiku looked. She had dared to hope that vacating the village might curb their wrath, that the emyrynn merely wanted their unwelcome visitors gone. But now she saw, as the last of the soldiers who had stayed behind were killed, that some of the emyrynn had set off in pursuit, following the trail Lucia and the others had left.

'Yes,' she said.

There were scattered emyrynn ahead of them and to either side as well. Some were moving away, either ignorant of their presence or uninterested. Others lay in wait in hollows or in the branches of trees, plainly hoping for their victims to come near. Though some of the creatures seemed content to leave them be now that they were driven off, others had decided to hunt them. There was no way they would be able to escape without further bloodshed.

'Can you speak to them, Lucia?' Kaiku asked. 'Can you explain?'

Lucia did not hear her. She was sobbing and panting, propelled along by Doja's strong arm, tripping on branches and roots. She seemed seized by some fear that she could not identify, gazing around wildly like a madwoman, fleeing without hope of escape.

Kaiku breathed a curse. They had no choice but to go where Lucia led them, and abandoning the village had robbed them of any place to make a stand, however futile. The low, slanting light of Nuki's eye forced its way dimly through the canopy, but the trees were too dense here to see far, and only Kaiku could spot the emyrynn as they darted nimbly through the trees. The forest still resounded with the fading echoes of their comrades' screams, and the only other sound was the scraping of twigs, the thump of boots and the rush of exhaled breath as they raced away from the emyrynn village. That, and the endless, monotonous tapping in the distance that had plagued them for days.

Gods, what were they hoping for, anyway? That the emyrynn would turn around and give up? That was a slim chance indeed. They would run, they would fight, and after that they would die. The odds were impossible. But there was nothing else left to do.

'There are two of them, ahead and to our left,' Kaiku called, as she sensed their approach. The soldiers shifted their blades, ready to receive the creatures; but Kaiku got to them first. Though there was something of the spirit world in them, they were not as hard as demons or Weavers to overmatch; but they were awkward and unfamiliar, and it took time to engage them, longer than she would have liked. She would be unable to deal with more than a few at a time.

She used her *kana* to reach inside their minds and stun them into unconsciousness. She was reluctant to kill them if she could help it.

'They have been dealt with,' she said.

'Any more?' Asara asked, as they scrambled up an incline thick with bluish bracken, shepherding Lucia awkwardly onward.

'Three from behind,' Kaiku said. Her heart sank as she saw them arrowing through the forest. 'They will catch us in a few moments. Three from the right. Two ahead.' She grimaced. 'I cannot protect you from all of them.'

'Then you take the ones that are following,' Doja said tersely. 'We'll handle the rest.'

The soldiers had slung their rifles back over their shoulders and drawn swords by now, for ranged weapons were useless in the confines of thick undergrowth. Despite Kaiku's warning, they were still not prepared for the emyrynn when they attacked. They expected to be able to hear the stirring of leaves, the rustle of bracken as their enemies neared; but the emyrynn were like ghosts, and made no sound at all. They sprang as if from nowhere, took down two of the soldiers, ripped out their throats in a single bite and were gone before anyone could lay a blade to them.

'Keep going!' Doja cried, as some of the soldiers faltered. The wounded men were still flailing, gurgling out their last. 'We cannot stand here!'

In the forest behind them, three bright blooms of fire ignited. Kaiku turned back to Doja, her eyes hard. Now that they had shown their intentions beyond all doubt, she would not be merciful to these creatures any longer.

The five remaining emyrynn attacked all at once. The soldiers had a few seconds to prepare at Kaiku's cry, and then the enemy were among them in a blur of white and a flurry of teeth. Asara, faster than most, ducked under the leap of one of them and divided it neatly in half along its midriff; Kaiku incinerated another. Between them, the soldiers took down a third, but as the remaining two disappeared they left behind one man dead and another with a stump for an arm, spewing blood. There was a scramble to get a tourniquet on the wound, during which the group's onward motion collapsed: they would not leave one of their wounded behind when there was still a chance of saving them.

'More! All around us!' Kaiku barely had time to shout before the emyrynn were among them. They had seemed to appear out of nowhere, even to her Weave-sight, a dozen of the creatures flitting suddenly into existence. She saw Tsata slashing with his gutting-hooks, darting between the emyrynn's antlers, protecting Heth and his burden Peithre. She saw Asara dodging and slashing, her movements fluid, honed by ninety years of practice and a perfect metabolism. And she saw the soldiers fighting, and Doja being savaged, and Lucia fallen to the ground where another of the creatures was about to pounce on her . . .

Kaiku was about to obliterate the threat to Lucia when she was knocked aside, crashing into a tree trunk with the weight of an emyrynn, its teeth fastened in her shoulder at the collar. Too many of them; she hadn't seen it coming. She screamed with the pain. Blood pumped between her attacker's teeth as it bit deeper into her flesh. Then her *kana* reacted, seizing the creature and flinging it away from her with enough force to break its back against a thick bough. She clutched her torn shoulder, blood pulsing through her fingers. Her body was already repairing itself, but it was sapping vital resources she needed to protect others, and she was already looking to Lucia, a terrible fear gripping her heart. She would be too late, too late to save her from the emyrynn now.

But then a new sensation bore down on her, a terrible, crushing presence that drove her to her knees with its fury. She looked up, and blanched as she saw it.

The beast. The vast shadow that she had met a few nights ago was back, its colossal bulk swelling up to the treetops. Its bellow, midway between a roar and a screech, shook the earth and blasted a hurricane through the forest, sending men and women and emyrynn alike tumbling and scrambling. The trees hissed and rattled as the wind wailed through their branches. Kaiku was blown back into the base of a tree, the breath squeezed from her lungs, her hair whipping around her face. She gritted her teeth against the agony from her shoulder, eyes shut tight, fighting down the urge to shriek. The creature was a black wall of rage in the Weave, a power that Kaiku could not hope to match. Her *kana* recoiled from it, retreating, curling up inside her.

Silence. The hurricane died all at once, faint skirling gusts chasing away through the trees to nothingness. Leaves drifted slowly earthward, spiralling clumsily.

Kaiku opened her eyes. The site of the ambush was strewn with bodies, men and emyrynn alike. Bloody swatches of white fur lay alongside torn corpses. She saw Asara getting to her feet, her blade hanging loose in her hand. Tsata and Heth crouched protectively together over the prone Peithre. A few soldiers were stirring, but not many. The emyrynn were gone.

At the edge of the carnage stood Lucia, staring up into the face of the beast. Its shape was hidden from sight by the trees, and by the darkness that it exuded like smoke, but it was still possible to make out its size. Small, glittering eyes regarded her. She was a tiny morsel to it, minute and insignificant; yet she stood there alone, and it glared down on her, the heavy soughing of its breath faintly audible, as slow and massive as waves on a beach.

Gradually, the survivors of the massacre rose, their gazes pinned to the monster. All except the Tkiurathi. Kaiku stumbled over towards Lucia, her hand clutching her shoulder where her wound was sealing itself, but as she neared Tsata he looked up at her, and his eyes were wet. The shock of that stopped her for a moment. She had never seen him weep before. Then she glanced down at Peithre, and saw that she was dead. They had protected her from the emyrynn, but in her weakened state the exertion of being carried so violently had proved too much. Heth was bent over her, his shoulders shaking. Kaiku met Tsata's gaze once again, but her eyes were bleak and she had nothing to give him; then she staggered away, towards Lucia.

Lucia was swaying slightly as Kaiku came to stand near her. She did not dare get too close, afraid of breaking whatever spell held the beast in check. Lucia's eyes were rolled up in her head and flickering with movement.

'Gods, what has happened here?' she whispered, though she said it more to herself than to anyone else, and expected no response.

Lucia surprised her. 'It is an emissary,' she said, the words barely formed as if she spoke them in a dream.

Kaiku thought for a moment. 'Of the Xhiang Xhi?' she asked.

'Leave our dead,' Lucia murmured, 'and follow.'

Kaiku closed her eyes. She had been sure to memorise the names of each and every man and woman in the party before they set off into the forest, for she had believed that many would not live to leave it and they would need to be commended to Noctu after their deaths. As long as she had their names, the place where their bodies lay meant little.

She raised her head and met the expectant faces of the survivors, Doja was among the fallen, and those who believed in leaders looked to her now.

'We leave our dead,' she said, her voice almost breaking as she spoke. 'We leave our dead and follow.'

It was several hours later that they came across the entrance to the Xhiang Xhi's lair.

Kaiku remembered little of the intervening time. She trudged dazedly through the forest with the rest of them, in something like a state of shock. The beast led them, always ahead, a colossal shadow that was never quite seen, a fraction too distant to make out in detail.

She wept as she went, mainly for Phaeca but also for the other men who lay behind them and Peithre, whose body Heth carried and refused to leave. She had kept herself at a distance from the soldiers, out of habit – she was a Sister, and she could no longer easily mix as she had in the past – but the suddenness of their deaths, the frightening savagery of the emyrynn, had shaken her badly. She knew enough of war and killing, but she was not inured to it entirely.

Other thoughts had briefly intruded on her misery. Thoughts of the beast that they followed, and how it had not been attacking her that day but that it had for some reason been *protecting* her from the spirit that had taken Lucia's shape. It had prevented her from being lured away; her, and her only, for the other soldiers had been left to their fate. Why was that? Why had *she* been treated differently?

Then there were the memories of the moment she had shared with Tsata, and her argument with Asara. Both were decisions she had to face, matters of huge importance to her; and yet for now she could not bring herself to care about them. All she wanted to do was to get away from this gods-cursed forest and never look back.

But there was one more challenge yet, and it was Lucia who had to face it.

They would have known when they came to the boundary of the Xhiang Xhi's domain even if Lucia had not told them. The air was thick with the presence of the great spirit, a charge in the air that made the fine hairs on their bodies stand on end. It came from a tunnel mouth sunk into a hillock, on either side of which stood twisted old trees like pillars. The beast crouched atop the hillock, obscured by undergrowth, sapping the day's light from the air.

'You can go no further,' Lucia said to them all. She appeared sharper now, her mind clear. 'It is up to me now.'

Nobody argued, not even Kaiku. She knew it would come to this. Lucia made no ceremony about it, merely looked over her shoulder at the seven ragged figures that remained of the twenty-four that had followed her into the forest. Her eyes lingered on Kaiku's for a moment, and she tried a smile; but it felt false, and it faltered, so she turned away and walked into the tunnel. They watched as the darkness consumed her, and then she was gone.

At first they were listless, unsure what to do or what to say. Then they began to settle themselves to wait: the three surviving soldiers together, Tsata and Heth with their burden, Kaiku and Asara both sitting alone.

After a time, Kaiku got to her feet and joined the Tkiurathi.

NINETEEN

There was no light in the tunnel, and Lucia was forced to feel her way along it. Her fingers trailed over the moist soil of the tunnel wall, bumping occasionally against protruding roots. It was silent. The babble of the spirits and the animals was quiet. Nothing existed except the Xhiang Xhi.

She wished she could stay here, in the peaceful dark, where there were no voices to plague her. To rest, to sleep in this precious hush just for a single night, would be a prize beyond anything she could ask for. To be this clear-headed forever, not to be burdened with the knowledge that outside this oasis of calm lay chaos, and that even if she survived this she would have to return to it. A place where her thoughts were fogged and a thousand whispers clamoured for her attention, and to even interact with humankind was a struggle to focus.

But it was only a wish. There was no sanctuary for her. She went on through the tunnel, until a short way onwards she saw a ragged oval of grey, with roots hanging across it like a curtain. She pushed through them and stepped into the domain of the great spirit.

It was a gloomy dell that she found on the other side, a hollow surrounded by thick forest which leaned overhead to make a roof of tangled branches. The ground was marshy; ridges of turf rose out of the water, dividing it into brackish pools full of weeds, and thin mists hung in the cold, still air or slunk close to the earth. An occasional tree grew in the dell, ancient and knotted, its leaves brown and dead.

She could sense the spirit here, a vast and brooding melancholy, its attention fixed upon her. The force of its presence was oppressive, the magnitude of its power beyond comprehension. She had spoken with many of the land's oldest spirits since that day when she had descended into Alskain Mar, deciphering the ways of their kind; but this was a thing apart, older than the rocks, older than the rivers, older than the forest it dwelt in.

She waited. Though she was afraid, she was armoured by fatalism. Her life had led to here, and she was as ready as she could possibly be. If it all came to nothing, then that was the way it would go. She could do no more.

Nothing stirred.

After a time, she took off her shoes and walked forward, picking her way from the edge of the dell along a bank of earth towards a tuffet that poked out of the marsh. Chill water welled up between her toes as the soft grass sank beneath her feet. When she reached the tuffet, she knelt there, and laid her hands upon the ground. She bowed her head and let her breathing slow, readying herself to enter the trance-like state necessary for communication with the spirits.

((There is no need, Lucia. I am not as the others are))

She tensed. The voice had been like the sigh of a dying man, a breath of air through a dusty temple. In all her life, a spirit had never *spoken* to her before. Contact had always been achieved without language, a primal, empathic exchange. It was a meeting on the most basic of levels, because it was the only way beings utterly alien to each other could reach some sort of understanding.

((I understand you)) said the Xhiang Xhi. Her thoughts were as transparent to it as if she had said them out loud. *((They are as children to me, and lack wisdom. They do not know how to think as you do))*

She felt dizzied. Children? Heart's blood, this being saw the other spirits as children? What kind of fool had she been, thinking that she was ready for the Xhiang Xhi? She dared not consider what might happen if she had tried to meld with it as she had with the others.

Slowly, she opened her eyes and looked upon the spirit. It hung in the air before her, a slender wraith of mist, an elongated wisp of humanoid form like a shadow cast at sunset. It had hands, with spindly, attenuated fingers, and something that might have been a head, but it shifted and blended with the stir of the murk, so that Lucia could see only impressions of it. Perspective was skewed: it appeared near and far all at once, tiny and massive, and its aspect shifted with its movements and frustrated her efforts to decide. It was ever the way with the spirits: they could not manifest themselves in ways that human senses were entirely comfortable with.

((Stand)) it said to her. *((Do not abase yourself before me. I have no need of worship or respect))*

She did so.

((You need not fear to speak, Lucia))

And indeed she did not fear it, not in the way she had some of the other spirits, the ones who were angry and capricious and who had met her with malice or resentment. What she did fear was its terrible sorrow, the heartbreaking sense of tragedy that seeped from it. She was afraid that it might let her know the source of that sorrow and pass its grief on to her, and that was something she would not be able to bear.

'How old are you?' she said eventually. She wanted to test its responses before she asked what she had come to ask, even though she was sure it already knew her purpose. But there was a way for things to be done, and she would bow to that.

((I existed before the first of you stood upright, before the land was formed, before the moons were born. I existed when this world was but dust, and before that. There is no measurement I can give you that would have meaning. I am

not like the other spirits you know: they were formed of this land, but I was not. I came from elsewhere, and I will go elsewhere once again when this world is swallowed in fire and its moons turned to ash))

Its voice, like the stirring of dry leaves in her skull, arrived amid fleeting images, spectral glimpses of star-studded void with gargantuan spheres of breathtaking colour turning slowly, and bright, bright flame swelling to consume them. Then, as quickly as they flitted across her consciousness, they were gone, leaving her wide-eyed, her breathing quick, her pulse fluttering. The Xhiang Xhi swirled restlessly in the mist.

'Are you a god?' Lucia asked at last.

((I am not a god)) it replied. *((What now you call gods you may come to call by other names. Some you will lose to myth; others may be more real than you imagine. It is not my place to reveal them. There can be no understanding for you of the things you speak of, though that may come with the passing of ages. For now, you have only interpretation, and that will change as you change, sometimes taking you closer to truth, sometimes further away. Your race is young, Lucia; and like infants you cannot fully comprehend what you see))*

Lucia accepted this with a slight nod of her head. Her mind had gone blank. Now that she was here, in the presence of the great spirit, she found that words were eluding her. For long seconds she stood mute, a slight figure in torn and muddied travelling clothes, her blonde hair in disarray.

((There are things you need to know, Lucia)) the spirit said at last. *((You seek to make war to save your homeland, but you do not yet realise the threat. I will show you))*

'Show me,' Lucia murmured, and the dell and everything around her disappeared.

She was standing on a vast plain of black rock, rucked with ridges of shattered stone and scattered with smouldering rubble. The air rippled with heat, scorching her lungs, shrinking her flesh. Wind screamed past her, throwing dust and pebbles and pushing boulders end over end, making her clothes flap furiously against her body. It stank of sulphur and poison. At her feet, a massive chasm roiled with magma, underlighting the contours of her face in infernal red. Other chasms scratched their way across the plain, and the earth shook sporadically like the shivers of some sleeping leviathan.

Lucia was shocked by the panorama and the chaos of the gale. She knew, somehow, that she was not really here, and she believed it had no power to harm her; but her instincts said otherwise, and she stumbled away from the chasm, gazing wildly around for a rescuer.

The lava ran from a distant range of volcanoes, so broad and high that their tips were lost above the thick blanket of brown vapours that roofed the world. Muted red glows blazed up there, amid thunderous concussions as the volcanoes erupted endlessly. Other mountains, seemingly dead and cold but just as gigantic, loomed around her, and where she could see across the plain to the horizon it seemed much too near. Lightning flickered in the clouds and struck the earth, faster than she had ever seen, a dozen times a second and more.

'What is . . . what is this place?' she said against the howl of the wind.

((This is the home of your enemy, thousands of years ago, before it was destroyed. This is the moon which you call Aricarat))

The Xhiang Xhi's voice came from inside her head like a rattle of twigs.

((It is not a place for your kind. The air here would choke you. The temperature would melt the flesh from your bones. The wind would pick you up and dash you to pieces. The very atmosphere would crush you like an egg))

'Why have you brought me here?' Lucia gasped, her eyes beginning to tear in horror.

((To show you)) the spirit said again.

'Show me what?'

((Your enemy))

Lucia looked around helplessly. 'I see nothing.'

((You are hampered by the limits of your senses. Use the ability that makes you unique. Listen))

And so she did. With some effort, she began calming herself, sinking slowly down into a trance of stillness. Practice had made it possible, even amid the maelstrom that whipped around her, to turn herself inward and create a core of quietude to retreat to. She sank to her knees, only now noticing that her feet were still bare. She laid her hand on the hot rock, and listened to the heartbeat of the moon.

As careful as she was, the sheer violence of Aricarat was still overwhelming: the burning veins of lava tubing, the swirling core, the constantly changing surface that crumbled and was remade by earthquakes and volcanoes. The raging fury of creation stripped raw and made terrible. She retreated, drawing herself away in fear of being destroyed by the power of the sensation. She could not allow herself to be subsumed in that.

Delicately, she sank back into the trance and began again, and this time she was more tentative. Among the roar and screech of this awful place, she began to make out thoughts. Thoughts as slow and massive as continents, drifting beneath her, processes too colossal and complex for her to even begin to fathom. The ruminations of a god.

'I hear him . . .' she said hoarsely, tears spilling from her eyes. 'I hear him . . .'

((Now, look)) the Xhiang Xhi urged, and she cast her eyes upward to where a white glow was growing rapidly behind the clouds, speeding from horizon to horizon, growing from dim to unbearably bright in the span of a second.

'The spear of Jurani,' Lucia whispered to herself. Then something burst through the clouds, a sun flung from the sky, and there was a sound like the end of the world. Lucia screamed as the fireball of its impact hit her.

When she came to her senses, she was lying on the tuffet in the Xhiang Xhi's dell, her face and hair dirty where she had fallen. After a moment to orient herself, she stood shakily, facing the spirit once again. It still hung in the mist before her, veiled from clear sight, a long-fingered wisp like some childish sketch of a nightmare. Drifting, shifting, its dreary emanations oppressing her.

She took a few breaths to compose herself, then raised her head.

'That was the moment when the gods destroyed Aricarat,' she said. 'When the army led by his parents, Assantua and Jurani, made war on him; and his own father, the god of fire, destroyed him with his spear.'

((That is your interpretation. Muddled with myth, but holding a core of truth, as many legends do))

She frowned. 'But I was told of it by the spirit of Alskain Mar.'

((The spirit of Alskain Mar is not old enough to remember nor wise enough to understand. Spirits know much, but their experience is narrow))

This was new. It had never occurred to Lucia that spirits could be wrong. She knew them to be wilful liars at times, but she had always had faith in their superior lore. To hear that even *they* were deemed benighted by this entity shook her deeply.

'And what is *your* interpretation?' she asked, almost fearing an answer.

((You would not understand mine. Your knowledge is built on the knowledge of your ancestors, slowly accreting towards truth. That is the way of your species. At all times you believe you know all there is to know, and that which you do not know you explain in other ways. Yet later generations will laugh at your ignorance, and do the same, and be laughed at in their turn. Understanding must be reached gradually, Lucia. What answers I would have for you, you would not believe even if you could comprehend them))

'Then what can you tell me?' Lucia asked, spreading her hands in supplication. 'What is it I must know?'

((You have learned much already, but not enough)) the spirit replied. *((You know that the fragments of Aricarat that fell onto your planet carried with it fragments of the entity that resided there. You know that this being had enough remnant influence to create the Weavers, and that they carry out its work with no knowledge of what controls them. But you do not understand the Weavers' intentions. You think they want to conquer. But conquest is not their aim, merely a stage in Aricarat's plan. They will not spread beyond Saramyr. They will not have to))*

Lucia waited in dread. So many certainties were falling into ruin around her. The Xhiang Xhi loomed in the mist, becoming darker.

((They are changing your world, Lucia. They are making it more like their master's home. They are preparing it for his arrival))

Lucia saw again, suddenly, the blasted plain and brown clouds, tasted the sulphur in the air, and a weakness swept her. The buildings that the Weavers had erected, the machines, the pall-pits: these were the tools by which they would make the world dark and poisonous. From Saramyr they would spread a miasma over the whole of the Near World, and across the great oceans that none had ever crossed except the mysterious explorers of Yttryx; then even the strange and distant lands beyond would be swallowed, and

Nuki's eye would never again gaze down on the world, for it would be forever concealed from his sight.

((There is no word in your language for what they are doing)) the Xhiang Xhi was saying. *((Other cultures in other places far, far, from here have a name for the process, but it would be meaningless to you. You need know only this: if you do not stop the Weavers, one way or another, your world will end))*

Lucia's pale eyes were cold as she looked into the mist. 'Whether by Aricarat's plan, or by that of the other gods.'

((You are perceptive for one of your kind. The spirit of Alskain Mar was right in that, at least. Once, Aricarat was powerful, a great presence in the Weave. If he returns he will again make war on what you call gods. They fear him. The spear of Jurani may strike this planet too))

Lucia's jaw clenched. It took some time for her to realise that she was furious.

'Then the gods are spiteful,' she said, 'that they should make us pay for their ineptitude. They should have made certain of their enemy the first time.'

((Even gods make mistakes)) the Xhiang Xhi replied. *((Your people have a story, of the Grey Moth and the Skein of Lament, that attests to your belief in that))*

'And where are the gods now?' Lucia cried.

((To that I have no answer)) it said. *((Their ways are beyond me, just as mine are beyond you. All things are transient, all things dwarfed by matters of greater scale. Perhaps your war is beneath contempt in the eyes of such beings. Perhaps the acts you commit in the name of your gods go unnoticed. Or perhaps they watch your every move, and they wait for reasons of their own. I do not know. The gods do not interfere unless they must))*

Lucia bit down on her frustration. Anger was an emotion that was almost foreign to her, but she felt it now. So many had died to bring her to this point, the culmination of her purpose, and now she learned that all their strife was to correct an error of judgement made by the gods themselves, and that the gods might not even be present to see them.

No. She would not believe that. When she was a child, the moon sisters themselves had sent their children to save her from the shin-shin. More than once she knew Kaiku had been spurred by the Emperor of the gods into actions she would not otherwise have committed.

And yet . . . what if the moon sisters were merely spirits that had no connection with the goddesses of the moon at all? It was entirely possible that they had saved Lucia for reasons of their own. Spirits were capricious in general, and the Children of the Moons were insane by human standards. What if Kaiku's dreams were only that: dreams, evoked by faith?

The gods don't control. They're more subtle than that. They use avatars and omens, to bend the will of their faithful to do their work. There's no predestination, no destiny. We all have our choices to make. It's us who have to fight our battles.

Her own words, spoken to her friend Flen back when he was still alive. And there was the crux: avatars, omens, subtlety. Never allowing certainty, never allowing their believers to know for sure, never providing anything that could not be accounted for in other ways, as coincidence or delusion. Heart's blood, did they *purposefully* shroud themselves? Did they enjoy the torment of anxiety and bewilderment that their inconclusiveness caused in their followers? Was it better to be like the Tkiurathi, to worship no gods at all but the memories of their distinguished ancestors?

Or were the gods like distant parents, allowing their children to make their own mistakes and solve their own problems? Teaching them that they could not rely on anyone but themselves, intervening with only a guiding nudge here and there? Even when there was *everything* at stake?

But then, thought Lucia with a vertiginous plunge as her perspective shifted, perhaps theirs was not the only world that the gods ministered. Perhaps they were only a tiny, insignificant mote among the stars, one of uncountable cultures, each one squalling for attention in the emptiness.

The cruelty of that drove her to her knees.

((You can never know, Lucia)) said the Xhiang Xhi. *((One way or another, certainty would destroy you))*

She stared at the wet grass of the tuffet.

'Tell me,' she said eventually. 'What hope is there?'

((There is hope)) the spirit replied. *((For Aricarat's plans have gone against him in some ways. He did not expect the Sisters. He did not expect you))*

'But we are Aberrants. We came from the blight he created. A disease of the land, that kills crops and twists children in the womb.'

((The blight is not a disease of the land. It is a catalyst of change. Aricarat does not want to kill all life on the planet; he needs you still, and will for a long time yet, until he is entirely restored. People and plants and animals will die, but some will adapt and survive and recover. He is changing the flora of Saramyr, and he is changing your people))

'Changing us?'

((Changing you so that you can live in the new world he will make. So that you can breathe the air that is poison to you now. The Sisters can already do it to a limited degree. Over time, the change will accelerate. More of you will be born Aberrant. As the air turns more hostile, only those Aberrants who can breathe it well will survive, and their children will inherit that ability. Eventually, only the Saramyr will remain: the blight will be what saves you. All other countries will die, and the witchstones there will be excavated at leisure. By your people))

Lucia closed her eyes, and saw the images as the spirit spoke. A tear ran from the edge of one eye.

'Then how does that offer hope?' she asked.

((You offer hope. The Sisters offer hope. He did not know what he was unlocking when he meddled with your kind. His interference has provoked changes that would not have otherwise occurred for millions of years, if ever))

'Then what are we?'

((You are the next stage. You have torn the veil of ascendancy: the divide between the base world of the physical and the world beyond the senses. In the eyes of the gods, it is the line that marks the end of your infancy. You achieve this in one way, the Sisters in another. It matters nothing. Beyond that point, you are no longer as you were. You are the first of the true transcendents of humanity))

'Cailin was right,' Lucia whispered. 'All this time, she was right.'

((Indeed)) the spirit replied. *((I would have ensured safe passage for you and the Sisters, though I extended no such courtesy to those who had not breached the veil. One of you fell, however, and I could not prevent that))*

She raised her head. 'What about the Weavers?'

The Xhiang Xhi seemed to recede in her vision, melting into the mist. *((They are not as you are. Their abilities come from their Masks. From Aricarat))*

'But if Aricarat created the Aberrants, then why were the Weavers killing them?' Lucia protested. She did not want to believe any of this, and was fighting to find holes in the spirit's logic.

But the Xhiang Xhi was relentless. *((It was necessary, to safeguard their rise to power, to prevent beings such as you and the Sisters from existing. They failed at that, in the end. They will stop killing Aberrants in time, and begin breeding them selectively instead))*

'How do you *know* this?' she cried.

((Because it is the only course of action that makes sense)) the spirit replied, and she was defeated. She could not argue with such an entity, something older than recorded history, which dwarfed her understanding so completely that she was fighting to assimilate even the limited snatches of information it fed to her. She dared not think of how much it was not telling, how much lay outside her experience. Maybe, if she knew, she would be as sorrowful as it was. Perhaps ignorance was better. How small they all were, in the final analysis.

She got to her feet, dishevelled and haggard, and stared into the mist at the vague and swaying shape of the Xhiang Xhi.

'I beg you,' she said. 'Help us. Help us stop all this coming to pass.'

She felt the Xhiang Xhi regarding her, there in its chill and gloomy dell.

((I will help you)) it said. Then, after a pause of moments that felt like hours: *((But there is a price))*

It was dusk when Lucia emerged from the tunnel.

Nobody noticed her at first. They had sunk into grief, and sat wearily on the forest floor beneath the unwavering gaze of the shadow-beast that hunkered atop the hillock. Most of them had fallen into an exhausted slumber, for here, in the presence of the great spirit, the nightmares were held at bay.

Kaiku awoke to the touch of Tsata's hand on her shoulder. She looked up at him. Sometime over the past hours, she had cried herself to sleep with her head on his thigh where he sat. She raised herself, brushing her hair back behind one ear, and followed his eyes to where Lucia stood.

Then she was scrambling to her feet and rushing over. She gathered Lucia in a tight embrace; but the words of relief that were forming were never spoken. Lucia remained rigid, her arms by her sides. Kaiku backed away, searching her face quizzically.

'Lucia?'

The three soldiers were getting to their feet now, coming closer, warily, as if afraid of her. Asara had stood also, but she watched from a distance.

'It is done,' Lucia said, her gaze shifting minutely to meet Kaiku's. Her voice was flat and expressionless. 'We have been granted passage out of this forest. The beast will guard us.'

'Lucia?' Kaiku said again, the word a question. She tried to smile, but it faded into uncertainty. 'Lucia, what happened?'

'The spirits will aid us when the time comes,' Lucia said bitterly. 'That is what you wanted, is it not?'

Before Kaiku could protest, Lucia addressed the group, overriding her.

'We must return to Araka Jo. I do not wish to stay in this place an instant longer.'

Her tone precluded any further questions, and she did not give anyone the opportunity anyway. She walked away from Kaiku, leaving her bewildered and hurt, and headed into the trees. With nothing else they could do, the remnants of her retinue followed, one by one, as night fell across the Forest of Xu.

TWENTY

The great city of Axekami loured in its own miasma.

The exhalations of the Weavers' constructions had a strange weight to them, a persistency unlike that of smoke. The main bulk of it rose above the city in a roiling cap, slanted by the breeze across the plains so that it leaned eastward; but it also sank to mist the earth, and to spread outward along the ground. At its edges it was a diffuse haze, but still it appeared to permeate the air from horizon to horizon, a suspicion of something amiss that was too subtle for the eye to define. There were always clouds around Axekami now, which was unusual for winter when the skies were traditionally clear. Occasionally they unleashed a brown rain which smelt powerfully of rotten eggs.

The Imperial Quarter was a spectre of its former glory now. Its gardens went untended, its fountains murky and unclean. Its trees had shed their leaves and they decayed on the flagstones and cobbles. The townhouses that had once been occupied by the nobles and high families of the Empire had been gutted, their fineries long since stripped, occupied now by swarms of the destitute. The wide thoroughfares were all but empty of traffic, and shuffling vagrants meandered in the overgrown parks or the scummed water gardens.

Yet though the heart of the place was gone, small sections of its past remained. Shops and wholesalers stayed open, eking a living from what they could get into the city to sell, barely able to afford the guards that prevented them from being robbed. A thin trade from the rest of Axekami kept them alive. The alternative was to abandon their property and move, but few had the money or the opportunity now. They weathered the troubles as best they could, and hoped for better days.

One such shop was owned by a herbalist, who once had enjoyed a reputation as the best in the land. His father and grandfather before him had been appointed as suppliers to the physicians of the Imperial family, as had he in his turn. After the Weavers had taken Axekami, and the Imperial family was no more, he had refused to give up his ancestral premises. Even when the physician to the Lord Protector and Blood Koli offered him a place in the Imperial Keep, he had refused. Apart from his determination to keep his shop, he had little love for the Weavers, and he trusted them not at all.

So he remained here in the Imperial Quarter, and the physician came to him to buy what he needed, arriving in a black carriage gilded in gold, escorted by guards with rifles. The guards took station outside the shop while he went within.

The physician, whose name was Ukida, was thin and frail, with lank white hair combed across a balding pate and rheumy blue eyes. Despite the infirmity of his appearance, he moved like a man half his age and his hands and voice were steady and sure. His robe hung awkwardly on his spare frame as he walked up to the counter of the shop, passing rows of jars and cloth bags half-full of powdered roots. Most of the shelving was bare. The lanterns lit to aid the grim daylight only served to add to the depressing atmosphere, for they reminded Ukida that there should have been no need for them at such an hour.

He and the herbalist – a stout, rotund man with a whiskery moustache and a brisk, efficient manner – exchanged a few friendly words before a list was passed between them, and the herbalist disappeared into his preparation room to grind the necessary quantities. Ukida waited, tapping his fingers on the counter, looking idly about the shop.

'Master Ukida,' said a voice. 'You are looking well.'

The sound of his name startled him: he had thought the shop empty. He located the owner of the voice, appearing from a doorway that led into the back of the shop. She walked towards him, and his eyes widened in recognition.

'I have been waiting a long time for you,' she said. 'Three days.'

'Mistress Mishani!' he exclaimed in a hiss, too shocked even to bow. 'What are you doing here?'

'I have come to ask a favour of you,' she replied, her narrow face sallow in the bad light. She was not dressed in her usual finery. The robe she wore was battered and dirty, made for travelling, and her hair was worn in an unadorned ponytail and tucked into the back of her robe to disguise its length, the deception concealed by a voluminous hood. Tied tight against her small skull, it made her look faintly rodentine and not at all noble.

'You will be killed if they find you,' Ukida said, then added: 'I could be killed for just talking to you.' He glanced nervously over the counter, where the herbalist had been.

'He knows,' Mishani said. 'He remembers the days of the Empire, and he is loyal to them. I guessed you would come here eventually, so I asked him to let me wait for you.' She gave him a wry smile. 'This was always the only place you would come to for supplies. You were most insistent, even with my father, that you would settle for nothing but the best.'

'Your memory is good, Mistress, but I fear your judgement is not. You are in great danger in Axekami. Did you walk through these streets alone? Such madness!'

'I know the risks, Ukida. Better than you do,' Mishani replied. 'I have a letter for you to deliver to my mother.'

Ukida shook his head in alarm. 'Mistress Mishani, you would risk my life!'

'There is no risk. You may read it, if you wish.' She drew the letter from the sash of her robe and held it out to him. It had no seal.

He looked at it uncertainly. Mishani could tell he was deciding where his loyalties lay in this situation. On the one hand, he was blood-bound to Mishani's family, and that meant her as well; she was still officially part of Blood Koli. On the other, all the retainers knew that Mishani was no longer welcome within that family, and her father would most likely have her executed if he caught her. At the very least, she would be imprisoned and interrogated. Her involvement in the kidnapping of Lucia was generally known now, though never officially ratified, as was her hand in the revolt at Zila several years later. The Weavers would show her no mercy if they found her, nor anyone who had abetted her.

'Take it,' she urged him. She was recalling how he had nursed her through childhood illnesses, tended to her scratches and grazes. He would not betray her; of that she was sure. The question was whether he would help her.

Reluctantly, he took the letter and unfolded it. There was no indication of the recipient or the sender, only a dozen vertical rows of High Saramyrrhic pictograms.

'It is a poem,' he said. *And not a very good one*, he added mentally.

'That it is,' said Mishani. 'Please, give that to my mother. You need not even say it was from me. Nobody will know.'

'The Weavers will know,' he said. 'There are no secrets from them.'

'Do you really believe that?' Mishani asked him. 'I would not have thought you prone to their scaremongering.'

'They can pluck the guilt from a man's mind,' Ukida said.

'Only if they have reason to look there,' she replied. 'Trust me, Master Ukida. I have lived alongside the Red Order a long time. I know what the Weavers are capable of, and what they are not. There is a risk, but it is small. You are my only hope.'

Ukida studied her carefully, then folded up the letter and bowed to her. 'It shall be done,' he said tightly.

'You have my deepest gratitude,' Mishani said. And with that, she returned his bow, purposefully choosing a more humble attitude than she should have. She knew him: arrogance would not play well, even though he was still her servant. He seemed faintly shamed by her action.

She departed through the doorway to the back of the shop as the herbalist returned, his timing impeccable. Ukida paid for his supplies and left, the letter carefully concealed in his robe.

Muraki tu Koli sat at her writing desk in her small room, her quill scratching and jerking in the light of a lantern. The lack of windows meant that she took no account of day or night, and she had little desire to see the murk-shrouded disc of Nuki's eye anyway. Aside from the occasional meals that she took with her husband, she rarely left this room. She was nearing the end of her new volume of the adventures of Nida-jan, and she was lost in the world she had created, spurred along by the unstoppable momentum of the story. A part of her still felt bitter at the necessity of haste, for she took great pride in her work and she resented that matters of the real world had conspired to make her rush it; but though unpolished, her tales still had an energy all their own, and she lived for that.

She did not hear Ukida's chime outside the curtained doorway, nor did she notice him enter uninvited. Her retainers had learned not to wait for her to reply, for she never did. He simply entered, bowed, and placed a letter on the edge of her writing desk. He cast an appraising eye over her, noting that she was very pale and looked consumptive. Bad air, bad eating habits, no exercise, no sunlight. She would sicken soon. He had told her so, and had dared to tell Avun too, but he had been politely ignored. With another bow, he withdrew.

Muraki continued writing. It was several hours before she stopped to ease the cramp in her hand, and then she noticed the letter and wondered how it had got there. She picked it up and unfolded it, read what was within. There was a short interruption in her breathing, a soft intake of surprise. She read it again, crossed out several of the pictograms, read it once more and then burned it to ash in the lantern. Then she sat back at her desk and stared at the page that she had been writing.

After an hour, she got up and went to find Ukida, her soft shoes whispering as she went.

Avun tu Koli entered his study with a wary tread. It was dim and cool in here, the swirled *lach* floors sucking what warmth there was from the room. There was little furniture but a huge marble desk before a row of window-arches that looked out across the shrouded city, and a few cabinets for storing paperwork and stationery. He kept his private space orderly and spartan, like his life.

He glanced around the room, unconsciously furtive in his movements, then, satisfied that it was empty, he slipped inside and let the curtain fall behind him.

'Welcome back, Avun,' Kakre croaked, and Avun jumped and swore.

The Weave-lord was standing behind his desk, but Avun had somehow not seen him there. His eyes had skipped over the intruder, a blind spot in his mind.

'You seem unusually nervous today,' Kakre observed. 'You have good reason to be.'

'Do not try anything foolish, Kakre,' Avun warned, but there was little strength in his voice. 'Fahrekh's actions were nothing to do with me.'

'Convenient, though. Oh, indeed,' the Weave-lord replied, shuffling around the edge of the desk. 'What excellent timing he possessed, to strike just after you had done your level best to exhaust me.' He cocked his head to one side, the gaping corpse-Mask tipping in a grotesque parody of curiosity. 'Where have you been, my Lord Protector?'

Avun calmed himself, regaining his composure. Like his daughter, he valued the ability to control the expression of emotion, and it was a measure of how scared he was that Kakre had noticed his fear.

'I went to Ren to discuss the construction of a new pall-pit there,' he said.

'And was that not something you could have left to an underling?'

'I wanted to be there personally,' Avun replied, walking further into the room to assert that he was not afraid, that he had nothing to be afraid for. 'It is well to keep myself involved in small matters as well as large. It helps me to keep perspective.'

'Here is your *perspective*,' Kakre hissed. He cast one withered hand towards Avun, and the Lord Protector's insides wrenched as if twisted. The agony made him stagger, but he gritted his teeth and did not scream as he wanted to.

'You thought my anger might calm if you got out of my way for a few days?' Kakre snarled. 'You thought I would *forget*, perhaps? That my addled mind would not remember what you had done when you returned? Like Fahrekh, you underestimate me greatly.' His fist clenched, and Avun did cry out this time, and dropped to one knee. His pate was sheened with sweat and his face taut with pain.

'I knew . . . you would make . . . the wrong assumption,' Avun gasped.

'I think I know you well enough, Avun, to be confident that you were conspiring with Fahrekh to kill me,' Kakre said. 'Treachery is second nature to you. But you chose the wrong victim this time.'

'I . . . it was not . . . I . . .' Avun could barely manage a breath now. Kakre was increasing the pain, and it was like knives had been shoved into his guts and were slowly revolving.

'More denials? I could search your thoughts to find the truth, if you would prefer,' the Weave-lord offered. 'Though I am not as precise as I used to be. The results could be . . . unfortunate.' His dead face stared passionlessly from beneath the shadow cast by his hood. 'It would be easier just to kill you.'

'You *cannot* kill me,' Avun spat. Loops of crimson spittle hung from his narrow chin.

'Would you like me to try harder?'

Avun's teeth were pressed together so tightly that it was an effort to force them apart to speak. 'The Weavers . . . die with me . . .'

Abruptly the pressure on his organs loosened. Not much, but enough to let him breathe precious air easily again. He sucked in great lungfuls, on his hands and knees now. Blood dripped from his mouth onto the floor.

'Interesting,' Kakre said, his tone flat. 'And what did you mean by that, my Lord Protector?'

Avun delayed his answer for a moment, savouring the respite, choosing his words carefully. They meant the difference between life and death. He wiped his mouth with the back of his hand and glared up at the hunched figure who stood over him.

'There is nobody else who can lead your armies,' he said.

'Is that the best you can do?' Kakre mocked. 'Pitiful. There are many subordinates, generals of the Blackguard who would be eager to take your place.'

'And who chose those generals? I did. And I have been systematically removing all the *good* ones from positions of power for years now.'

Kakre was silent. Avun got one foot beneath him and rose unsteadily, clutching his thin stomach with one hand.

'Search their records, if you wish,' Avun said. 'None of them have any real experience of mass warfare. They are peacekeepers, men whose expertise is policing our cities. The old generals were useless since we had Aberrants and Nexuses to fight with, so I got rid of them. You did not pay close enough attention to that, Kakre. It is well to keep yourself involved in small matters,' – he managed a red-stained grin – 'as well as large.'

Still the Weave-lord said nothing, merely regarding him from within the dark pits of the Mask's eye-holes. Avun stumbled to his desk and leaned one arm on it, supporting himself. He felt like he had swallowed broken glass.

'Remember the first months of this war? Remember how your armies were slaughtered by the generals of the old empire? That is how it will be again, if you kill me. There is nobody to take my place.'

'We can find one,' Kakre said darkly, but he sounded uncertain.

'Can you? Do you know what to look for in a leader?' Avun shook his head dismissively. 'No matter. It would take time for them to familiarise themselves with your forces, to assemble a power structure. Time you do not have. Your breeding programmes fail to provide you with enough Aberrants to both control your territories and attack new ones. And the more you produce, the faster your armies starve. You need the Southern Prefectures, and you need them before Aestival Week. We will be hard pressed to do so as it is. If you get rid of me, your chances drop to nothing. And then begins the slow decline of your forces, and the Empire will take you apart, piece by piece, feya-kori or not. You can invade a city with your blight demons, but you cannot occupy it. For that you need armies. For that you need *me!*'

He raised himself to stand erect again, keeping the pain from his face, and turned his dull, reptilian eyes upon the Weave-lord.

'The new pall-pits are operational. The feya-kori are ready to be called. We need to work together or your precious monasteries will fall like Utraxxa did.'

With that, he walked boldly out of the room. The few steps it took him to get to the curtained doorway of his study were heavy with terror: he expected to be struck down and tortured. But then he was at the curtain, and through it, and though he felt Kakre's seething frustration and anger like a palpable thing, he knew he had won this round.

TWENTY-ONE

Kaiku slid the screen closed on the celebrations throughout Araka Jo and looked across the room at Cailin.

'They are in rare spirits tonight,' Cailin observed.

'They are idiots,' Kaiku said rancorously. 'Like goats, blindly trusting in their herders.'

It was dusk, and the night insects were beginning their discordant chorus in the undergrowth, all but smothered by the cheers and raised voices and fireworks that arced over the rim of the mountains. The house of the Red Order was quiet in comparison. Most of the Sisters were out in the village or up at the temple complex, overseeing the festivities that had erupted at the news of Lucia's return.

'You are angry,' Cailin said.

'Yes,' Kaiku replied. She was not wearing the attire of the Order: she had come here directly after their arrival, having found the folk of the Libera Dramach waiting for them, warned by scouts of their approach.

'About them?' Cailin motioned beyond the screens.

'Among other things,' Kaiku replied.

Cailin was standing, lantern-light falling on one side of her painted face. A table sat against one wall with mats tucked underneath it, but she did not bring it out or invite Kaiku to sit. There was a hostility to her that Cailin did not like.

'They think this is a triumph?' Kaiku snapped. 'They think we return in splendour? We straggle back, only a handful of survivors, and all they care about is that Lucia has returned, and with her she brings some . . . *promise.* That is all. No word of elaboration, nothing that might justify all those deaths, *Phaeca's* death. She will not speak a word of what went on in that forest, except to say that the spirits will aid us when the time comes.'

'She means hope to them,' Cailin replied softly. 'They do not care about the cost. They feared to lose their figurehead. Their saviour. They may be foolish, but they are desperate too. If we had lost her, we would have lost the hearts of the people.' She watched Kaiku suspiciously. 'I am grateful to you, Kaiku. Once again you have excelled yourself. You brought her back alive.'

'I am not certain I care for your gratitude,' Kaiku said.

Cailin descended into icy silence. She would not rise to that. Let Kaiku say what she wanted to say; Cailin would not trouble herself to draw it from her.

'You should not have sent Phaeca with us,' Kaiku said eventually. But her tone was quieter, and Cailin surmised that even this was not the true cause of her ire.

'You should not have agreed to have her along,' Cailin countered. 'I note you did not protest overly at her inclusion.'

'She was too sensitive,' Kaiku murmured. 'It drove her mad. Maybe she would have recovered when we got out of that gods-cursed place. But she should not have been there at all.'

Cailin let this go past. She did not have anything to say to it. None of them had any idea about what the Forest of Xu was like before Lucia and the others had entered. Placing blame was useless. Cailin felt Phaeca's death as keenly as Kaiku did, though for different reasons: she grieved to lose one of her precious Order, Kaiku grieved to lose a friend.

'And Lucia?' she asked. 'How is Lucia?'

'Different,' Kaiku said, pacing restlessly around her side of the room. 'Cold. Taciturn. But since she visited the Xhiang Xhi, she has been clear of mind. She is no longer dreamy or unfocused. If she is unresponsive, it is because she wants to be. I do not know which way I preferred her: they are equally bad.'

The agitation of her body language was increasing. Cailin knew that she would soon come to her point, that she was delaying the moment. She was afraid to speak her mind, perhaps. But Kaiku's nature would drive her thoughts into the open eventually.

'I must know,' she said suddenly. 'The Red Order. I must know.' She stopped pacing, faced Cailin and said bluntly: 'What are we doing?'

'We are saving Saramyr.'

'*No!*' Kaiku voice was sharp. 'I want the truth! What happens afterwards?'

Cailin's tone was faintly puzzled. 'You know this, Kaiku.'

'Tell me again.'

Cailin studied her for a moment, then turned away from the lantern. 'We take the place that the Weavers have occupied. We become the glue that holds our society together.' She turned her head to meet Kaiku's eyes. 'But there will be no conflict between us. We are not as the Weavers. We would not kill each other at our masters' behest, nor would we use our abilities to assassinate our masters' rivals. We would have no masters.'

'And in such a way could you hold the whole of Saramyr to ransom,' Kaiku said.

Cailin regarded her steadily. 'Is that what you think we will do?'

Kaiku gave a short, humourless laugh. 'What does it matter what I think? The nobles will think that. The Empire cannot be run when its power lies in the hands of the Red Order. Are the nobles to believe that we would act out of charity? That we would dedicate our lives to being their mouthpieces, their messengers? We are not blood-bound to anyone, and hence we can do as we choose. Do you think they would stand that for long?'

'They would have little option,' Cailin said. 'Granted, we would be able to extract certain concessions, but not more than the Weavers took. We do not need lives as the price of our power.'

'No, Cailin. They are too clever to fall for that, and you know they are. That is not security enough. Eventually, their fear of us would make them depose us. And I will wager that whatever plan you have for the Sisterhood is geared towards making that eventuality impossible. Even if it means deposing *them* first.'

'Your accusations are becoming insulting, Kaiku,' Cailin warned. 'Remember to whom you speak.'

Kaiku shook her head. 'I have heard you talk about how the Sisterhood are higher beings than men. I do not for one instant think that you would willingly be a servant to anyone. You are lying, Cailin. You have an agenda.' She brushed her hair back behind her ear. 'Otherwise, you would not have let the Weavers take the throne. You would not have let Axekami fall into ruin. You would not have let all those people die.'

Cailin was a thin, severe line of black against the blue light of the night that glowed through the paper screens. 'You have been speaking with Asara, I see.'

'No,' said Kaiku. 'I speak to her as little as possible. I have been thinking, though. It is all very obvious if I proceed from the premise that you – like everybody else in this damned world, it seems – are merely out for your own advantage.

'If we had resisted the Weavers at the first, if we had warned the nobles and lent our strength to their cause, they might have stopped all this from happening. But what would we gain? The nobles would have averted a terrible danger, and, once their lesson was learned, they would never let beings such as the Weavers – beings such as *us* – anywhere near a position of power again. Aberrants would still be Aberrants: despised, outcast and hunted. Lucia would have been executed.

'But what if it were different? What if the Weavers shattered the Empire? What if they were allowed to become a threat so terrible that *anything* would be preferable to them? What if the only way the Empire could be saved was by an Aberrant empress and by the Red Order? How could they refuse to let us be part of their new world then? Everyone already accepts that Lucia will be Empress if we win this war; and you have been making very certain that she holds you in the highest regard all these years. The Red Order will rise as she does. I imagine that the Red Order would rise even without her now. You have played your hand well.'

Kaiku stared hard at the Pre-Eminent. 'The Weavers had to crush the people so that they would accept us, and we let it happen. Maybe we even helped it along.'

Cailin gave a dismissive flick of her fingers. 'Of course we helped it along. Do you really think the Libera Dramach could *ever* have resisted the

Weavers? Even with Lucia on our side, we would have gone the way of the Ais Maraxa, cut down as soon as we showed ourselves. The high families needed to be united against the Weavers, and that would never happen unless they were under real and direct threat. So yes, we wanted the Weavers to take the throne, no matter how many lives it cost. It was the only way to get the nobles on our side, to make them see what was good for them. Such is the art of politics, and its results are not measured in lives but in who gets to write the history books.'

'So we manipulate them as the Weavers did,' Kaiku said, and lowered her head. 'We are the lesser of two evils, Cailin. But we are still evil.'

Cailin laughed bitterly. 'Evil! What do you know of evil?' Her laughter faded, and her face took on a hateful expression, her voice deepening. 'Evil is a village stoning a seven-harvest child and leaving her for dead in a ditch. Evil is being left to fend for yourself when you are afraid of even going to sleep in case the fires come, wandering from town to town, a slave and later a whore because you have no home, because each time the burning comes you have to run, you have to run into the wilderness and scrabble for roots and starve or the men with knives will come and kill you! Evil is the look in their eyes, those ignorant bastard *cattle* who populate this land, as they despise you for being Aberrant!' Her voice had risen to a shout, but now it dropped, and was hard with scorn. 'They can despise me, Kaiku. But they will fear me also.'

Kaiku was silent for a long time. The two of them faced each other across the room.

'I will help you destroy the Weavers,' said Kaiku. 'And after that, it is over. I want no part of you or your Order, Cailin. I see now that you are not what I was looking for all this time.'

She slid the screen open and left, shutting it behind her. Cailin stood alone, listening to the celebrations outside.

Barak Zahn found his daughter sitting on the roof of a temple.

It was a flat roof, made of white stone. Figures guarded the corners, eroded away to mere lumps; it was otherwise featureless. A stairway led up from beneath. Lucia was sitting inches from the edge, with her arms wrapped around her legs and her knees drawn up to her chin, looking out into the night.

When Zahn emerged and saw his daughter like that, he was momentarily at a loss for what to say. When he did speak, the words came awkwardly.

'The guards below told me I might find you here,' he said, redundantly.

She turned to look at him and smiled over her shoulder. 'Father,' she said. 'Come sit with me.'

Puzzled by this response, which was at odds with the one he had been expecting from the accounts of those who had spoken with her recently, he did as she bade, and settled his rangy frame next to her, dangling his legs over the edge of the roof.

'Everyone is happy tonight,' she said. The lights from the lanterns below were glowing strings in the pale blue of her eye. The dirt paths of the temple complex were bright and stalls were busy. People talked and drank or wandered down the slope on their left, towards the lake. Music drifted up to them from an unseen band.

Not knowing what to say to that, Zahn looked at the moons. Aurus was full in the north, dominating the sky, and Iridima peered out from behind it like a sharp white blister.

'I am glad to see you are recovered,' she said. 'I missed you.' Gods, she was a beautiful creature, so much resembling her mother. It made him proud to think that she was his child.

'Your relatives will have to do better than that to get you from me,' Zahn said, his lips twisting into a grin.

'I have spoken with Oyo,' she said. 'It will not happen again.'

Zahn blinked. 'You did what?'

Lucia gave him an innocent look.

'But you did not even know it was her!' he exclaimed. 'Even *I* am not certain.'

'I knew,' she said calmly. 'It was obvious.'

'And you accused her? You have only been back a few hours!'

'I did not accuse her,' Lucia said, unfolding her legs and dangling them alongside his. 'I said to her that if you should die in the future, in any manner I found suspicious, I would disown Blood Erinima.'

Zahn was open-mouthed for a moment, then he laughed heartily and shook his head in disbelief. He had never known Lucia to be this assertive. 'Heart's blood, you really *are* getting to be like your mother. Whatever happened in that forest, it certainly lit a fire in you.'

'Yes,' she said quietly, her eyes drifting to the horizon, to the north, where the Forest of Xu lay beyond the mountains and beneath the moons. 'Yes, it did that.'

Asara came to Kaiku's house in the dead of night. Kaiku had known she would. Kaiku was waiting for her.

'Sit down, Asara,' she offered as an invitation, motioning to the mats she had laid in the centre of the room. There was a table next to them, with bitter tea and wine and other spirits, as well as several snacks and small cakes. A proper reception for a guest; something that Kaiku rarely bothered with, if ever, and doubly strange to Asara since she had turned up unannounced. Trebly so, since she was under the impression that Kaiku hated her.

Asara stood just inside the door for a moment, caution evident on her face. Then she knelt on one of the mats, arranging herself elegantly. She had bathed and dressed and reapplied sparse touches of eyeshadow, and she looked perfect, as ever. Kaiku wore a simple black robe of silk belted with gold, her hair damp and raked through with her fingers, as casual as if Asara were her sister and had dropped around for a gossip.

Asara looked frankly uncomfortable as Kaiku offered her tea. She had wine instead. Kaiku had the same, then sat cross-legged on the mat opposite.

'What is all this?' Asara asked.

Kaiku tilted her shoulder in a shrug. 'I felt like it.'

Asara's unease was not abated at all by that.

'I envy you sometimes, Asara,' she said conversationally. 'I envy the way you can change. How you can start again at any time. That is a wonderful gift, I imagine.'

'Are you mocking me?' Asara asked. It was impossible to tell by her tone.

'No,' Kaiku said. 'I mean it.'

'Then you have nothing to envy,' she replied. 'We do not learn from our mistakes. Age lends no wisdom, only removes the enthusiasm for foolishness. You could change yourself a thousand times and you would still dig yourself the same holes to fall into.'

Kaiku's eyes lowered to her glass. 'I was afraid you might say that.' She took a sip.

'Kaiku, are you in some kind of trouble?' Asara could hardly believe that those words had come from her mouth, but there was something in Kaiku's manner that moved her.

Kaiku raised her eyes, and her lashes dislodged a tear from each eye to run unevenly down her cheeks. Asara almost reached across the gap between them to touch her arm in comfort, then stopped herself.

'Everything is falling apart, Asara,' she whispered, her throat tight. 'I cannot hold it together. I cannot hold anything together any more.'

Asara, shocked, could not think of a thing to say.

'I watch my friends die and I am powerless to prevent it,' she said. 'I have been fighting for almost ten years and it has gained me nothing. What good is victory? All I will succeed in is removing the only reason I have had to keep living ever since my family died. I will destroy the Weavers and be left with nothing. Nobody I can trust, nothing I can believe in. Everyone proves false in the end, every ideal is a sham. I am not fighting to make my life better, I am just fighting to stop it becoming *worse*.'

'This is not like you,' Asara said at last. 'You are stronger than this.'

'Am I not allowed *limits*?' Kaiku cried. 'Gods, how much am I expected to take before I go the way of Phaeca?'

Asara did not comment on that. She was not sure whether Kaiku blamed her for the death of her friend or not.

Kaiku wiped her eyes with the sleeve of her robe. 'Oh, this is ridiculous,' she murmured to herself. 'I can hardly expect you to care.'

'But I have . . . contributed to your sorrow,' Asara said, wringing her hands in her lap. 'Forgive me.'

Kaiku shifted herself so that she was kneeling, and she put her arms around Asara and held her closely. Asara, still perturbed by Kaiku's mood, returned the embrace. After a moment, it stopped feeling unnatural.

'I cannot hold you in enmity, Asara,' she said. 'You have been a friend to me, in your way.'

Asara let out a sigh, battling down an emotion that she did not wish to experience again. She held Kaiku for a long while, until she was sure she had herself under control, and then said: 'I will not hurt you again. I promise you that. I am selfish and cruel – more than you know – but I will not hurt you again.'

She heard a sob from Kaiku, and then she drew away; and Asara saw that Kaiku's eyes were red, and not only from weeping.

'It is done,' she said.

Asara's heart jumped a beat. She stared at Kaiku, not daring to believe.

'A small thing,' Kaiku said, 'Some kind of process that was not working as it should. I made it work.' Her face saddened a little. 'There has been too much death in this world. I would take this one chance to bring life. It is all I can do.'

When Asara still appeared stunned, Kaiku sobbed a laugh and wiped her eyes. 'Do not just sit there gaping. You are fertile. Go back to your husband.'

Asara exhaled a shuddering breath, and her eyes filled and spilled over. 'Promise me,' she whispered. 'Promise me you will never tell anyone of this. Of what you have done.'

'You have my promise.'

'I will never forget this, Kaiku,' Asara said tremulously. 'In all the emptiness of this world, you will always have me, for what that is worth to you.'

'It is worth much,' Kaiku said, then reached over and stroked her cheek, wiping a tear across her skin. 'I have never seen you cry,' she said thoughtfully.

Asara caught her hand and held it against her cheek, her eyes fluttering closed. Then she got to her feet and went to the door. She slid it open, looked back, and was gone, closing the door behind her.

An hour later, she had stolen a horse and was riding east, to the Tchamil Mountains and the desert beyond.

TWENTY-TWO

The gate of the Imperial Keep stood open during the day to allow in and out the traffic necessary to keep such a vast building running. Carts of food, heavily guarded against the starving masses outside, rattled in and returned empty. Others came with jars of wine and spices, vats of cleaning fluid, bolts of cloth; and not a few of them with unconscious men, women and children concealed inside, slender vagrants from the Poor Quarter to be delivered for the Weavers' delectation.

There were Blackguard and a pair of Weavers at the gate, as always. They watched over the traffic, the Blackguard checking permits, the Weavers looking for any more subtle dangers: concealed bombs and the like. They stood hunched on either side of the wide entranceway like ragged gargoyles, immobile as they went about their invisible task.

Inside his carriage, the physician Ukida fidgeted nervously as they approached the gate.

'They have removed the blessing on the arch,' Mishani commented, staring out of the window. The arc of gold above the gate had indeed been smoothed clean.

Ukida made a vaguely questioning noise out of politeness; he was not listening to her, obsessed as he was with his own fear. Mishani looked away from the window and over at him.

'You will give us away, Master Ukida, if you do not control yourself,' she said sternly.

That stung him, and he made an effort at composing his demeanour, which made his state more obvious rather than less. He wished he had never taken the letter from Mishani in the first place. He should have just refused her. What could she have done? Taken him to face Imperial justice? Ha! There was no empire, and certainly no justice, and she would be arrested herself if she tried. Why had he not thought of that before, instead of clinging to his old notions of honour and ties of allegiance? If he had done so, his Mistress Muraki might not have commanded him to set up this deception, and he might not be in great peril of losing his life.

Hindsight was a cruel thing, and it crowed and gloated at him now as they drew up to the gate and one of the Blackguard approached the door of the carriage.

'Master Ukida,' he said in acknowledgement. He was a good-looking young man, wearing the dark bandana and leather armour that was the uniform of the Blackguard. 'Who is this?' he asked, his eyes shifting to Mishani, who sat meekly in the back of the carriage.

Ukida glanced nervously over the Blackguard's shoulder to the Weaver there, whose coral Mask was turned towards them.

'An assistant,' he said, brandishing a sealed roll of paper which he handed to the guard. 'Just temporary, you understand. Mistress Muraki is ill, something quite unusual, and has need of this one's special knowledge of such conditions.'

Mishani met the Blackguard's inquiring gaze calmly.

'May I?' he asked, indicating the seal. Ukida motioned hastily for him to do so. He broke it open and began to read.

Mishani waited, her anxiety carefully internalised. Ukida was plainly jittery. She could only hope that the guard would not think matters suspicious enough to act upon: to call the Weaver, maybe, or to detain them while he checked the validity of the permit he held. It was written and signed and sealed by Muraki tu Koli herself, granting entrance to the Keep for Ukida's new assistant.

'Mistress Muraki is not too ill to write, I see,' the Blackguard said. A taut beat of silence passed as he looked from Ukida to Mishani. 'That is good news,' he finished, and the tension slackened. He handed the permit back to Ukida and made a small bow to them both. 'Master Ukida. Mistress Soa. Please go on in.'

Ukida was perhaps a little gushing in his thanks, but the Blackguard was not paying attention now. He waved their driver on and was already heading toward the next cart in line.

Mishani allowed herself a moment of relief as they passed across the courtyard. That was one obstacle down. Now she had to contend with the possibility of being recognised, and the certainty of meeting another Weaver before she could get to her mother. If Shintu smiled on them, they might just make it through with her mother's permit. If not . . .

She looked out of the window. The courtyard was busy as always: men and women hurried to and fro; manxthwa lowed and nuzzled one another; arguments and exchanges went on at the feet of the double row of obelisks that led from the gate to the Keep. At least here it was not as downtrodden and dreary as the rest of the city, though there was something of a fierce industry in the manner of the people who came and went, as if they were eager to be done with their task so that they might get away. In the gloom of the overhanging miasma, the golden, sculptured slope of the south wall towered above them, intimidating in scale. They passed down a gentle ramp into a wide bay swarming with attendants, and there they disembarked and went through a guarded doorway reserved for nobles and important retainers which circumvented the subterranean servants' quarters. The guard barely glanced at them.

They ascended a set of stairs and entered the corridors of the Keep proper, a multitude of elegant *lach* passageways and many rooms, from huge and grandiose halls and galleries to tiny and exquisite chambers. Ukida led and Mishani followed, adopting an attitude appropriate to her rank as a physician's assistant. She felt curiously buoyant despite her fear, in a literal sense as well as an emotional one. She had been forced to alter her appearance beyond wearing the correct dress to make herself convincing in her role. She had cut her hair.

She had thought it would be much more of a wrench than it turned out to be. Her hair had been long since she was an infant, and ankle-length since adolescence. It was the feature she was most proud of. It lent her gravitas, for its sheer impracticality bespoke a noble existence, and she had thought it as permanent as her small nose or her thin eyebrows. But nobody would believe a physician's assistant would have hair so long: for one not born to nobility, it was immodest.

And so it became an impediment to her seeing her mother, and in such a light expendable. Mishani was always deeply pragmatic and little given to sentiment. Though she barely recognised herself in the mirror now, she knew that to be a good thing. With her hair worn up, her whole aspect was changed, and at a glance she seemed a completely different person. Some artfully applied make-up, shifting the emphasis of her eyes and cheeks and mouth, completed the deception.

We all wear our masks, she had thought to herself as she had put on the final touches.

She had not realised the weight of her hair till now, and the sense that came from her neck and scalp that there was something amiss was fractionally irritating. She wondered if she would get used to it, in time. It was shoulder-length when worn straight, but it was too similar to her old style that way, so she had arranged it with pins and combs so that it piled up and around her head in a style associated with educated women of low birth.

There would not be many in the vastness of the Keep that would know who she was, even without the changes she had wreaked upon herself. Still, as they neared the Imperial chambers, there would be more and more retainers of Blood Koli, and the danger would increase.

But first, they had to face the Weaver. She could only hope that her mother's plan would work.

Mishani had to chide Ukida for hurrying several times as they made their way through the corridors. He was sweating and plainly agitated, and Mishani cursed his inability to conceal his terror. It did not take a Weaver to know that something was wrong; if anyone asked, she had advised him to put it down to his anxiety at Muraki's condition. Ukida had assured her that her mother had feigned illness these past few days, and his own false diagnoses had confirmed it. Muraki had left strict instructions that she was not to be disturbed today by anyone but Ukida and the assistant he would bring. The retainers and the Weavers had been informed, so there would be no surprise at Mishani's arrival.

And yet it would take only the smallest thing to go wrong, and disaster would befall them. It was not only Mishani's life and Ukida's that were at stake here. Mishani knew far too much about the plans and dealings of the Libera Dramach and the high families in the south, and if she were caught those secrets would be ripped from her mind by a Weaver. What she was doing was selfish and irresponsible, but she did not care. She was going to see her mother. Whatever the cost.

They made their way up several sets of stairs, taking less travelled routes whenever they could. Once Mishani had to grab Ukida's arm and feign interest in an ornamental vase that was set in an alcove, so as to avert her face from a woman she thought she recognised. But most of the servants here were those who came with the Keep when Blood Koli took it over, so they did not know her; and the corridors were quiet, for there were no nobles or their retinues to populate them. The Imperial Keep was all but empty of guests now, though Ukida spoke darkly of the upper levels where the Weavers lived.

'We are nearing the section where the Imperial chambers lie,' he muttered at one point. Shortly afterward, they saw a boy of fourteen harvests or so, who spotted them and ran away in the direction they were heading.

'I was afraid he would not be there,' Ukida said, taking what solace he could. At least so far, the plan was working well.

They dawdled for a while, pretending to examine a tapestry but ready to move if anyone should come; then, when Ukida judged that enough time had passed, they continued down the corridor to where the Weaver would be.

The Imperial chambers were guarded much more strictly than the rest of the Keep. It was impossible to maintain maximum security in such a huge building, when the day-to-day running of the place required ingress and egress on such a scale. But the Keep was designed so that certain sections could only be accessed by a small number of entry points, and these were where the vigilance was greatest. Each entry to the Imperial chambers was watched over by a Weaver, and Weavers could steal the thoughts from a person's mind.

The corridor ended in a stout door. Before it stood a Weaver with a Mask of silver, fashioned in the countenance of a woman. Mishani sent silent thanks to the gods that it had not been Blood Koli's own Weaver; but then, why should it? Weavers did not belong to families any more.

Just as the Weaver came into view, the door behind him opened and Muraki tu Koli appeared, supported by the boy they had seen earlier. Ukida sped up and hurried towards her. Mishani hesitated a moment at the sight – *Mother!* – then followed him.

'Mistress! What are you doing out of bed?' he cried as he approached.

'Ukida,' she said in a voice barely above a whisper. 'I am so glad you are here. I felt ill . . . I had to take some air.'

'I have brought the assistant you asked for,' he motioned at Mishani, but Muraki did not even look at her. 'Come now, back to your bed. I will take you.'

Ignoring the Weaver, they headed past him and into the Imperial chambers.

'Wait,' rasped the voice behind the silver Mask. It was turned towards Mishani.

'What is it?' Ukida said, and by good fortune his fear made his words come out as authoritative snap. 'She has to rest; she should not have been wandering.'

'I do not know this one,' the Weaver said, meaning Mishani.

'I asked for her,' Muraki said. 'Let her pass.'

'A moment . . .' said the Weaver, and Mishani knew with a sinking feeling in the pit of her stomach what would come next.

She felt the Weaver's influence brush her mind, detestable tentacles slithering over her thoughts. She shuddered. He could not fail to see her as she really was, to dredge up memories of her life in Blood Koli. Frantically she tried to hide her past beneath a muddle of images, but the images that came to her were the junks in the harbour at Mataxa Bay, or pictures of Lucia and Kaiku and incidents that would only make her identity more obvious. She stared, transfixed, into the black slits of the silver Mask, the woman-face hiding its disfigured owner; heard the wheeze of his breath and was touched by the decay of his mind.

Then the sensation was gone. 'Enter,' the Weaver said, and Ukadi put his hands on her shoulders and led her away swiftly. The door closed behind them.

'Heart's blood . . .' she murmured to herself. 'He did not see . . . he did not see . . .'

She kept her head lowered as they turned a corner and went along a short way. Fortune was with them and they saw nobody. Ukadi held aside a curtain and ushered Muraki and Mishani through, and when he let it drop they were alone together.

The room was a small bedchamber, with only a single bed near to a window-arch that looked out past the arm of one of the great stone figures that lunged from the Keep's sloping walls. A veil had been hung across it, muting the already muted light. There was a table with a slender book on it, and two chests of drawers in a matched pair.

A difficult silence passed as mother and daughter looked upon each other for the first time in a decade. The resemblance between them was remarkable.

'You cut your hair,' Muraki whispered.

'I had to,' Mishani said. 'It matters nothing. I can grow it back.'

Muraki reached out and touched it carefully. 'It looks odd. But it suits you.'

Mishani smiled and turned her head away. 'I look like a peasant. I will be taking it down as soon as I possibly can.' Studying the veiled window-arch, she said: 'I read your books. All of them.'

'I knew you would,' her mother replied. 'I knew it.'

'The Weaver . . .' Mishani began, a question on her face.

'They are there to root out those who mean harm to the Imperial family. You, apparently, do not. Not even towards your father. They read no further into a person's thoughts than that. To do so would be . . . violation. It is dangerous. They have accidentally killed guests that way, or driven them mad, until Avun forbade it.' She glanced uneasily around the room. 'I would not have let you come if I had been able to leave myself. But I cannot leave. Your father sees to that.'

'I told you I would not take refusal,' Mishani said. 'I would have tried anyway, with or without your help. The risks are acceptable to me.'

She motioned to the bed, and they sat down on its edge next to each other.

'There are things I want to say to you,' Mishani replied. 'Things that must come from my lips, not from a coded poem. We are on two sides of a war now, Mother, and one side or the other must win eventually. Whichever of us is on the losing side will not survive, I think. We are both of us too involved.'

Muraki was silent, her hair hanging across her face. She had always hidden behind her hair: straight and centre-parted, it concealed her, leaving only a narrow gap for her eyes and nose and mouth.

'I have wanted to see you for so long,' Mishani said. 'I pictured throwing my arms around you, laughing with joy. But now that I am here, I find that it is as it always was. Why are we this way with each other?'

'It is our nature,' Muraki said quietly. 'And no amount of time can change that.'

'But I saw you in your writing, Mother,' Mishani said. 'I saw your heart in that. I know you feel as deeply as anyone, *deeper* than most. Deeper than Father.'

Muraki could not meet her gaze. 'My writing can express my soul better than my words or actions ever could,' she said. 'There is comfort there. I am not afraid there.'

'I *know* that, Mother,' Mishani said, laying a hand on Muraki's. It was clammy and cold. Startled, Muraki looked at her daughter's hand as if it were something that might bite her. Mishani did not remove it. 'I know now. There are many things I did not see before. Like the code in your poems, they took me too long to understand.'

The words came quickly from them both: there was a sense of haste in their meeting, the knowledge that the danger was far from past. They could not waste time when it was so short and precious. Neither of them had ever spoken this directly to the other before.

'I am older now than then, and much has passed in between,' Mishani said. 'When I was young, I thought you weak and distant. You were a shadow of a woman in comparison to my father. I did not even think of you when I went to Axekami to join him at the courts. It did not occur to me that you would care.' She met her mother's eyes briefly, before Muraki became uncomfortable and broke the contact. 'I was a callous child. You deserved better.'

'No,' said Muraki. 'How could you have realised that? Do we not judge everyone by how they act towards us? You cannot be blamed for my failings, daughter. If you thought me aloof, it was because I did not hold you as a child, because I did not touch you or speak with you. If you thought me weak, it was because I did not make myself heard. There is . . . passion in my imagination, passion in my books . . . but there I can shape the world as I will it. The world outside . . . is stultifying, and awkward, and I am shamed when I speak and afraid of people . . . I am embarrassed by attention . . .' Realising that she had trailed into a mumble, she recovered herself. 'These are my failings. They have been with me since I was a child, since I can remember. It is not what I want for myself – that is in my books – but it is how I am.'

Mishani squeezed her hand gently. 'But every book you have written has made me feel more that I have wronged you. So I came to you now to make amends. To ask you to forgive me. And to tell you that I am proud of you, Mother.'

Muraki's expression was one of incomprehension.

'Do you not see what you have done?' Mishani said. 'You dared to make yourself a spy for us, you risked yourself by sending Chien to protect me all those years ago.' Muraki put her hand to her mouth at this. 'Yes, I surmised that much before he died. Father's men got to him. But in the end, if not for him, if not for *you*, thousands of lives would have been lost in the Xarana Fault. Things could have turned out very differently. In your quiet way you have contributed more than we could ever ask.' She took her hand away. 'And yet still we remain in two different worlds, and soon one of them will end. That is why I am here, that is why I risk all this. There are some things that must be done, at any cost. My spirit could not rest if either of us died and . . . you did not know.'

'I had not realised my child could be so reckless,' Muraki whispered, but a smile touched the edge of her lips.

'It is a new experience for me too,' Mishani grinned. She felt as if a heavy stone had been lifted from her chest. Even if she was caught now, it did not matter so much. It was done, and could not be undone. 'Perhaps nature *can* change with time.'

'Perhaps,' said Muraki, then got up and went to the window-arch. She brushed aside the veil and looked out.

'Daughter, I love you,' she said, her back to Mishani. 'I always have. Never doubt that, though I may not show it, though we may never have the opportunity to speak again. I am glad you came so I could tell you. We should not have left these matters so late.'

Mishani felt tears start to her eyes. She knew how much it had cost her mother to say those words, and to hear them for the first time in her life was ecstasy.

'Now listen to me,' she said, turning away from the window-arch and letting the veil drop. 'I have much to tell.'

And she spoke then of Avun's plans and schemes, of hints he had given and the intentions that he had expressed. She told of his failed plot to unseat Kakre, of the imminent creation of more feya-kori; of the true numbers of the Aberrants and the dire situation that the Weavers were in, how they faced starvation unless they could take the Prefectures by the next harvest. Mishani did not interrupt, filing every word in her memory, and as her mother went on she realised that her visit could turn out to be far more valuable than even she might have guessed: for this was information only days old, reaching her without the delay of months that was necessary in the publication of a book. She was staggered how much her mother knew. Avun discussed everything with her, it seemed, and the little snippets she had managed to secrete in her stories were only those few long-term events that she thought might still be relevant by the time they reached the hands of those she meant it for. In five minutes Muraki told her more than the entire spy network and the Sisterhood put together had managed to learn in four years.

'Lord Protector!' Ukadi suddenly cried from outside the doorway, and mother and daughter froze. Mishani went numb with the force of the sadness that struck her. Being discovered by her father was one thing, with all the lives that would be cost by her foolishness in coming here; but what was worse at this moment was the knowledge that now she and her mother had to part, that they would likely never meet again, that these precious handful of minutes out of ten years were all they would ever have.

'Go!' Muraki hissed, and Mishani hesitated, taking her mother's hands, gripping them. 'Go!' she urged again, terror in her eyes.

'I heard she was walking about,' said Avun. 'I must see her!'

'She is being attended by my assistant,' Ukadi was saying beyond the curtain. 'Please, it would be best if you . . .'

Mishani leaned forward quickly, kissed Muraki on the cheek, and whispered in her ear: 'You were the strongest of us all, Mother. My heart will always be with you.'

Then she got up and swept towards the doorway, just as Avun came through the curtain. Mishani made a deep bow, still walking, and passed by her startled father with her head down as he held the curtain aside for her. Due to the difference in height, he only saw the back of her head. It was an incredibly rude thing to do, and Avun's shock prevented him from reacting for a moment; then, as he opened his mouth to call her back, Muraki cried: 'Avun! Avun! Come here!'

The volume of his wife's voice, which was never more than a whisper, made him forget the servant immediately and hurry into the room, where Muraki embraced him and kissed him with an affection he had not witnessed in years, and she did not let him go. She drew him down onto the bed, and there she made love to him for the first time in longer than he cared to remember.

So surprised and pleased was he that he entirely forgot about the physician's assistant until long after she had left the Imperial Keep; and yet later he found he could not shake the insidious feeling that, even though he had not seen her face, he knew her from somewhcre. But he could never recall quite where.

TWENTY-THREE

Word from Mishani reached Araka Jo a day later, via a Sister who operated secretly out of Maza. She was an important relay for the spies in Axekami, and Mishani went straight to her after leaving the capital. Her news caused great commotion. Nobody had known where Mishani had gone, only that she had departed Araka Jo some time before, saying that she was attending to business of her own. When the upper echelons of the Libera Dramach learned what she had done, she was denounced as being reprehensible for placing them all at such risk; but it was Cailin who defended her, who pointed out that great risk had brought great reward, and the information she had given them was priceless.

A meeting was called immediately, and plans were put forward, many of which had been fermenting over the previous weeks and had been discussed in other meetings beforehand. Finally consensus was reached. There was no more room for delays. The time for action had come.

It was the morning after that meeting when Kaiku made her way down the trail to the south of Araka Jo, and found the Tkiurathi village in a state of busy preparation. They had conducted their own meeting last night, in the wake of the one with the Libera Dramach. Each individual had been asked to make their own choice as to whether they would follow the course suggested by the council. Kaiku had come to find the results of that.

She wandered through the Tkiurathi village, exchanging gestured greetings with a few men and women that she recognised. It was not hard to guess how the decision had gone. Blades were being sharpened, rifles cleaned, supplies made ready. They were packing for a journey.

There was a simplicity to this place that Kaiku liked: the smell of the cookfires, the *repka* yurts which looked like huge three-armed starfish lying between the trees, the sense of ease in the interaction of the tattooed folk. They seemed so untroubled in their daily lives, even now, even knowing that they were heading into something that they might well not come back from. Laughter came easily to them when they were together. Some of them were breakfasting, taking from a communal pot, exchanging food from their plates. Even this small act of sharing made a difference, something so natural to them that they must have long ceased to think about it.

She remembered a conversation she had had with Tsata long ago, in which he said that the Saramyr way of life resulted directly from their development of cities and courts and all the things Kaiku associated with civilisation; Tkiurathi shunned all that. Now that she had seen them, the way they interacted as a group, she wondered whose philosophy was better in the end.

Kaiku asked after Tsata by making his name a question, and was directed towards a rough circle of Tkiurathi who sat talking and drinking from wooden cups shaped somewhat like pears or pinecones. There was a large bowl in the centre from which they took refills. Heth was there, too; he noticed her first, and hailed her by name. The circle broke to leave a space between Tsata and Heth, and she smiled her gratitude as she sat down and was immediately handed a cup by a woman she did not recognise. The woman took a new one and filled it for herself.

She managed a general greeting in Okhamban in response to the one she received, then took a sip of the liquid. It was warm, and spicy and fiery on her tongue.

'Daygreet. Have I interrupted?' she asked Tsata, but her presence had cause barely a lull in the conversation, and they were already back to their discussion.

'We are working out final details of our departure,' Tsata said. 'It is not anything of great importance.'

'They agreed, then?'

'Without exception,' Heth said on her other side.

'There was little doubt they would. It is a matter of *pash*,' Tsata explained.

'Gods, it seems such a short time since we came back,' Kaiku mused, then she glanced at Heth. 'How are you?'

'I grieve,' he said. 'But Peithre has been returned to her people. I am thankful for that.'

Kaiku nodded, closing her eyes. In the Forest of Xu, Heth had refused to relinquish Peithre's body until he had brought her back to the village. In the end, he and Tsata had gone separately from the others, for her corpse, even wrapped as it was, had begun to reek of decay. But still Heth would not bury her or burn her. Kaiku did not know what the rites of honouring the dead were in Tkiurathi culture, but she was sure that there had been something beyond mere companionship between Heth and Peithre.

'Our course is set, then,' she said. 'One way or another, I think we come to the last movement of our war.'

The meeting of the day before had been coordinated, via the Sisters, with Barak Reki tu Tanatsua and several other desert Baraks in Izanzai. Mishani's information had been shared among all, though its source had been kept carefully secret for fear of compromising Muraki. Its most pertinent and pressing aspect was this: that the Weavers planned a massive surprise assault upon Saraku in the near future. Saraku, the centre of debate and administration, formed the heart of the Empire's resistance as well as being where most of the nobles and high families resided. If Saraku were to fall then the Weavers would have an all but unassailable foothold deep behind the frontline. From there, they could strike at Machita or Araka Jo, or demolish the marshland cities to the east. Once the Prefectures were secured, they could overwhelm Tchom Rin at their leisure.

But there was hope as well. For if the Weavers could be kept out of the Prefectures until the harvest could be gathered, then the tide might turn.

'But we will not be able to keep them out,' Cailin had said. 'Not even with the information we have. We may be able to turn back the assault on Saraku, but they will strike at us again elsewhere before the summer. Unless they are forced to devote some of their forces to defending their territories. We must prove to them that nowhere is safe. We must attack Adderach.'

Cailin had been the loudest voice advocating an attack on Adderach since Kaiku's visit to Axekami, but now she found she had support at last. Lucia's return had given them hope, a belief that they could face down the previously invincible feya-kori. And with their morale so restored, they were a little more inclined to consider the prospect, however uncertain or unlikely, of ending the war in one strike. They knew now that the Weavers' forces did not number as many as they had believed, and that the Aberrants and Nexuses were disastrously overstretched: the Weavers were using them as an attacking force and relying primarily on the Blackguard to keep order in the cities. It was entirely possible that Adderach would only be lightly defended, for it sat deep in enemy territory and was undoubtedly protected by the Weavers' shields of misdirection. The Weavers had consistently shown themselves to be inept at tactical thinking, and Adderach was one place they would certainly not have let the Lord Protector look after. Cailin had cleverly slanted her pitch so that the chance to get at the Weavers' witchstones – which was her primary concern – was barely mentioned. Whether they were successful in that or not, the idea of destroying their enemy's most prized fortress was too tempting to pass up. And there was an even sweeter aspect to the plan for the high families of the western Empire. None of their troops would be going.

Thus the decision was made and agreed: a three-pointed attack upon the Weavers. The forces of the Libera Dramach and the western Empire would deal with the Saraku assault. Meanwhile, the warriors of Tchom Rin and the Tkiurathi, along with a number of Sisters, would make their way to Adderach. The desert folk would have the most arduous task: a trek along the mountains lengthwise to reach Adderach from the south. The Tkiurathi and Sisters would go by sea, passing through enemy-held waters to land north of Mount Aon. If all went well, the Weavers would be looking south, to the army of desert warriors; and they would not see the attack from the north until it was too late.

But first there was the problem of getting the ships. Lalyara, to the west, was the only feasible option if they wanted to get to Adderach at roughly the same time as the desert folk. There were ships there enough for the Tkiurathi. But a week ago, the port had been blockaded by Weaver vessels. They made no move to attack, only to prevent anything entering or leaving. The Libera

Dramach had guessed what the Weavers were up to even before Mishani confirmed it.

The Weavers' next target was Lalyara. And if they got there before the Tkiurathi did, then half of the assault on Adderach had failed before it had begun.

Later, Kaiku and Tsata walked together in the forest. Kaiku needed some activity to keep her mind off their imminent departure. She knew that time was short, and she was chafing to be away; but organising supplies and equipment to send nearly a thousand men and women to war was not an easy matter, and would take more than a few hours.

It was bright and still and cool, and their feet crunched on twigs as they wandered. They talked idly about things of little importance. Kaiku was trying not to think about the possible consequences of making Asara capable of breeding, and she had fretted about Lucia for so long that she was getting tired of her own voice. They did touch on her feelings about Mishani's disappearance and her subsequent revelations, but Kaiku was not overly concerned about her friend. Since she had not known Mishani was in danger until she was out of it, she experienced nothing more than a vague sense of relief. It certainly went against Mishani's character to do something like that, but the fact that Kaiku had not seen it coming only served to remind her how little contact she had had with her friend these past few years, and that saddened her.

Kaiku was acutely aware that this was the first time that she and Tsata had been together alone since their kiss in the Forest of Xu. After that, the death of Phaeca and Peithre and the terrible events surrounding them had made any amorous notions seem wan and forceless amid all the grief. But there was something in Tsata's manner today, some coiled tension, that expressed itself in quick glances and half-taken breaths to start sentences that never came. There was an urgency in the air, a sense that this might be the last few moments of peace before the storm broke and swallowed them all, and there were things that had to be said between them that would not wait.

Eventually they found a spot where the land humped up and met the lake shore, dropping a dozen rocky feet to the water, which glittered in the sharp winter light. Distant junks cut slowly towards the horizon, and hookbeaks hovered on the thermals, questing for fish. Kaiku and Tsata sat side by side on a fallen tree that had been partially claimed by moss, and beneath the gently waving leaves of the evergreens they came to the moment they had been putting off.

Tsata looked at his hands, caught in an agony of indecision that was so plain that Kaiku had to laugh a little. It broke the tension: he smiled in answer.

'Your kind are never good at hiding your feelings,' Kaiku said. 'Say it, then.'

'I am afraid to,' he replied, then looked up at her uncertainly as if to gauge her reaction to this. 'I fear I still do not know your ways, and you Saramyr place such store by etiquette.'

'Most of us do. I seem to find it less important than they. Mishani is always telling me how uncultured I am.' She looked at him with tenderness in her eyes, both wanting and not wanting to hear what he would say. 'Honesty is better.'

'But that is one of the things I cannot understand about your people. Though you say you want honesty, you seldom do. You are so in love with evasions that honesty makes you uncomfortable.'

'Stop hedging, Tsata,' she said, not unkindly. 'It does not suit you.'

Eventually he shook his head, as if ridding himself of some annoyance, and clasped his hands together. Kaiku noticed how the pale green tendrils of tattoo that ran along his fingers meshed beautifully when he did so.

'I cannot do this your way,' he said. 'If this were—'

Kaiku ran out of patience. 'Tsata, do you want me or not?'

The bluntness of this surprised even him. He turned towards her, and in the instant before he spoke she fixed the image of him there, preserving the final moments of flux before certainty solidified their relationship one way or another. This picture she would keep in her mind, as insurance against his reply.

But the reply, when it came, was: 'Yes.'

A breath passed.

'Yet it is not that simple for you,' he continued. 'Is it?'

Kaiku's head bowed a little, her hair hanging down across the left side of her face, screening her from him. 'Simplicity is something that my people do not do well,' she said.

She felt betrayed by herself, suddenly angry. Gods, had she not waited for this moment for long enough? She knew how she felt about him. She had known it, without admitting it to herself, since those weeks they had spent together in the Xarana Fault four years ago, hunting Aberrants and spying on the Weavers. It had not been a sudden thing, but something so gradual that she had trouble identifying it. In the time he had been away across the sea, she had almost managed to dismiss it as a fancy. Almost. Since he had come back, since that kiss in the forest, she knew it for what it was. Yet in some matters he was so hard to read, and she could never be certain if that feeling was reciprocated. Not until now.

But it was nothing like she had imagined. Instead of a flood of joy, relief, *release*, she felt only an awful weariness, a sour negation of possibilities. Now she knew beyond doubt that he wanted her, she came up against all the barriers that she had carefully constructed in her heart over the years, shoring them up each time she had been wounded. She found that she had built them so well that they would not come down easily.

'Tsata, I am sorry,' she said. 'You deserve a better response than this.'

He looked down at his hands again. She straightened, brushed her hair back behind her ear and turned to him, taking one hand and clasping it in both of hers. She tried to find words that would not be mawkish or hurtful, but she had never been good at expressing herself in this way.

'I want you also, Tsata,' she said. 'I *do.* That is small comfort to you now, I think, but I want you to know it. Do not doubt that, whatever else.' She was lost again for a moment, before beginning on a new tack. 'Since the beginning, everything I thought good and stable has collapsed. My family, my friends, my . . . relationships. The Sisterhood has failed me, too. Perhaps even the Libera Dramach cannot be trusted now; I cannot let myself be sure.' She gripped his hand harder, willing him to understand. 'I was beginning to feel love for Tane when he was taken from me; I was betrayed by Saran – by *Asara* – just as I had allowed myself to believe that there could be something between us. There were men in between, whom I did not love so fiercely, but they, too, ended in betrayal or disappointment.'

He had raised his head now, and was looking at her.

'Each time I let something or someone close to my heart I am left with a new scar,' she said, a pleading note in her tone, seeking to make him forgive her. 'I want to be alone, to need nobody; and yet I see Asara, and what that has made of her, and I know that is no way to go either. But I cannot bear another wound, Tsata. I cannot bear to let myself love you, and then have you killed in the conflict to come, or to return to your homeland and leave me, or to find another woman. Your people do not believe in exclusive pair-bonding.'

'No,' he murmured. 'But you do. And for me, that would be enough.'

She frowned. 'What do you mean by that?'

'It is hardly unheard of,' Tsata said. 'My people have lived near Saramyr settlements for a thousand years. Tkiurathi have paired monogamously with Saramyr before. Some have even married. It is a matter of personal choice, of redefining the *pash.*'

'And you would do that for me?'

'I would,' he said. He stared out across the lake. 'I had been . . . unsure for a long time. I would have spoken of these feelings then, even when I did not know if I wished to do anything about them. But that is our way, and it is not yours. I knew it would cause you confusion and in all probability would have driven you away, so I stayed silent. I did not know if we could ever be together; I thought our cultures too fundamentally different. But then, in the forest, when I saw you defend us against the soldier, when you refused to leave Peithre fallen . . .' he trailed away, and then turned and looked back at her. 'That was when I knew.'

And now she felt it, like a physical pressure spreading outward from her chest, a warm swell that filled her. It struck her so suddenly that she had to exhale, a short huff of air that turned into an involuntary smile. But it lasted only a moment, for she forced it down again, knowing what it meant, knowing what it would lead to.

But do I have a choice? she thought. *If I turn this man away, this man whom*

I know I can trust more than anyone not to deceive me, how will the rest of my life be?

She bit the inside of her lip gently and closed her eyes. Could she live that way, ever guarded, secure and numb? Or was that the beginning of a downward slope from which there was no return? If she came through this war she faced a long, long span of years. Not even the Sisters knew how long. Maybe forever.

And if you let this man into your heart, could you stand to watch him age when you do not?

She would not face that question now. It had occurred to her before in a more general sense, but it was too vast to deal with. What was the alternative? Again, there could be only one: to shut herself off, to be alone forever, barriered against the world. Cloistered, with the Red Order the only safe company, who would be similarly ageless. That was no option, either. All ways led to pain in the end; it was only a question of time.

'Time,' she murmured softly, so quietly that Tsata barely heard it. Puzzlement showed on his face. 'Give me time . . . to think about this.'

He was about to speak again, but he thought better of it. Instead, he withdrew his hand and got to his feet, and she rose with him. They stood together, caught in an instant of prolonged parting and neither wanting to leave it that way; then Kaiku kissed him swiftly on the lips and withdrew into the forest, leaving him behind. She did not look back. She did not want him to see the tears gathering in her eyes.

The Tkiurathi travelled fast and light. By evening they had stripped their village of everything they needed for their journey to Lalyara. Cailin had arranged for the ships at their destination to be stocked with the provisions necessary for what would come afterward. In less than a day, the village was hollow and empty, the fires doused and the *repka* tied closed, awaiting their return. They were gathering in a valley north of the temple complex, ready to depart at dusk. Dozens of Sisters would be travelling with them, including Cailin herself. Kaiku was going too.

After seeing Tsata she spent the rest of the day hurrying around her house, finishing last-minute preparations and ensuring all was in order. She did not know whether Mishani would return soon or not, so she had to prepare the place for a possible period of vacancy. She cleaned and tidied, packed and repacked, prayed briefly at the house shrine, prepared food and ate it in quick, nervous bites. In truth, she needed to be doing something to stop her thinking. Her course was chosen now. She would not turn from it. She was heading to Adderach, the birthplace of the Weavers. Her oath to Ocha, taken long ago, demanded that she do so. Everything else – *everything* – could wait. Her business was with the Weavers, and if there was any chance of ruining them, of breaking their power, then she had to take that. Her family's spirits would not forgive her otherwise.

In a fit of bitterness, she debated whether or not to take the dress of the

Red Order with her or just burn it there and then. But when it came to the choice, she was reluctant to destroy it. Though it represented an allegiance she no longer felt, she could not deny the sense of authority and power it conferred on her, and she would need all the courage she could get in Adderach. In the whole length of the war, she had never been into battle without it.

Very well, then, she thought. *I will wear it again. Until the Weavers are gone.*

The last thing to take was the Mask from the chest where it lay. She snatched it up in one swift, disgusted motion and stuffed it in her backpack. Then she shut the pack and secured it.

She was about to depart when she heard a chime outside, and went to open the door. It was Lucia, with two Sisters behind her as guards.

'May I come inside?' Lucia asked. Kaiku invited her, waited to see if the Sisters intended on coming also, and when they did not, she slid the door shut. The room was all but bare, the minimal furniture having been put away. Lucia crossed the floor, stood with her back to Kaiku for a moment, and then turned around decisively.

'You are leaving?' she asked. 'Now?'

'I was about to,' Kaiku said.

'I only heard about it a short while ago,' Lucia said.

'You were at the meeting,' Kaiku said. 'You knew the Tkiurathi were going.'

'I did not know *you* were going,' Lucia replied. 'Were you intending to leave without telling me?'

Kaiku studied her. Lucia's light blonde hair was growing out a little, after years of her keeping it boyishly short. Kaiku wondered what this meant, or if it meant anything at all, or if anything meant anything any more.

'I did not think you would be interested,' Kaiku said truthfully, and was surprised at how cruel it sounded.

The look on Lucia's face showed plainly how deep she felt the barb. 'That is unfair, Kaiku.'

'Is it? You have not seemed to want to know me since your visit to the Xhiang Xhi. What had I done to deserve such treatment?'

'You should know more than anyone that I have . . . *matters* to deal with,' Lucia replied. 'I would expect a little more latitude.'

Kaiku was bewildered by her tone: she sounded nothing like the Lucia she knew. She was much more strident.

'Forgive me, then,' said Kaiku, tossing her a casual apology that had no weight to it. 'But how am I meant to know when you will not talk to me? Before we entered the forest, you were at least *you*, even when you were not lucid. But since then you have changed. I am not sure who you are or what you want now.' Her voice softened as she realised she was being harsh; the emotional rigors of these last days and her nervousness at the prospect of leaving had made her callous. 'What happened to you in there?'

It was the concern in the question that caused Lucia to crumble. Abruptly she seemed to shed her thorny exterior and become once again the Lucia of old. She told Kaiku of what the spirit had said to her, of the true purpose of the Weavers and the veil of ascendancy. But she made no mention of the price that the spirits' aid would entail.

Kaiku listened. It all seemed curiously unimportant to her, and revelations that should have shocked her barely penetrated. The scale was too large: it did not interfere or impact upon her sworn purpose. But Lucia's evasions were obvious, and when she was done, Kaiku said: 'There is something else you are not telling me.'

'That is between myself and the Xhiang Xhi,' Lucia replied.

That brought them to an impasse for a time.

'I am sorry for being rude,' Kaiku said eventually, with sincerity this time. 'You are under a great deal of strain, and you cannot or will not share the burden. It was ungracious of me to leave without saying farewell.'

'Let us forget all this,' said Lucia. 'I want you to know that I did not mean to treat you badly these last few days, and that all I said to you in the emyrynn village still holds true. You have always cared for me, and I for you. I do not wish our last goodbye to be tainted with rancour.'

'What makes you think it is our last?' Kaiku asked. The question was phrased with enforced lightness, to counter the thrill of dread at Lucia's words.

Lucia did not answer: instead she approached Kaiku and embraced her gently. It was worse than any reply she could have given.

'Lucia, what is it?' Kaiku whispered, suddenly terrified. 'What do you know that you are not telling me?'

Lucia released her, and her pale blue eyes were full of sorrow and pity.

'Goodbye,' she whispered, and then she walked away.

Kaiku wanted to call after her, to demand an answer to her question, but she could not think of a single thing to say that might change Lucia's mind. Some part of her did not want to rupture the purity of the moment with anger and shrill entreatments. She felt crushed by the pressure of something invisible and inevitable that she did not understand, and by the time she had recovered herself the door had slid shut and Lucia was gone.

Kaiku stood in the emptiness of the house for a time. It felt like a tomb now, and she could not bear to be here. She snatched up her pack and shouldered it, and she left her house to head to the valley where the Tkiurathi were meeting.

As she walked away up the dirt street, she was suddenly conscious that it might be the final time she ever saw the place. She did not look back.

TWENTY-FOUR

The journey from Araka Jo – around the north edge of Lake Xemit and west, skirting the south of the Forest of Xu – was made with all haste, but even with Mishani's information they had no certain date when Lalyara would be attacked. It was clear by their actions that the Weavers intended to destroy the fleet trapped in the harbour. The Tkiurathi hoped to get there in time to fight their way through the barricade of Weaver ships and away. Then warning reached them several days from their destination that the Weaver force had been sighted, and was moving quickly towards Lalyara. The rest of the journey was taken at a punishing pace; but the Tkiurathi were extraordinarily fit, hardened by the dangers of their homeland, and they covered ground fast when they needed to. They reached Lalyara a mere hour before the fog began to descend, and preparations commenced immediately to launch the vessels waiting in dock.

But quick as they were, they were not quick enough.

Explosions. The creak of timber and the turbulent slap of water against the stone of the dock. Men and women calling to each other, hurrying past Kaiku; the sense of huge movement as one of the enormous ships pulled away from its pier to her right, the deep splash as the discarded gangplank plunged into the sea. An uneven pattern of gunfire speckling the distance. Salt in the air, cold spray on her face, the scent of burning and blood and everywhere the terrible, choking fog.

The feya-kori had arrived.

The docks were in chaos. Sailors clambered along the shadowy rigging of their vessels, obeying hollered instructions. The junks were looming silhouettes in the haze. Tkiurathi clattered up gangplanks, cramming onto the decks of the ships while dockhands hacked hawsers free and the coastal wind caught rising sails to belly them outwards. Kaiku steadied herself against the buffeting flow of men and women and looked to the north with red eyes, penetrating the murk.

There they were, on the crest of a distant slope, rising over the northern wall of the city with all the inexorability of a tidal wave. Two of them, the same two that had demolished Juraka and Zila, their forms black, seething tangles of Weave-threads. Their drear moans drifted across the rooftops as they pounded the wall to rubble. And though she could not see, she knew that the Aberrants were swarming in.

Something rushed overhead and she flinched; it hit a warehouse a few streets away and obliterated one of its walls. Out to sea she could hear the sounds of fire-cannon. The coastal batteries were shelling blind, foiled by the feya-kori's miasma. Weaver ships had drawn in closer now, no longer content to be a blockade and with little fear of the guns; their Weavers were their eyes, and they rained destruction on the city, using a new kind of artillery that was heavier and more explosive than the kind the Empire had used in years past.

But less than half the junks had set out yet, and there were still many to go.

Kaiku sensed the incoming shellshot from a fire-cannon, instinctively calculated its trajectory and realised that it would hit square on the docks. She was about to deal with it when one of the other Sisters got there first: its momentum dissipated in mid-air and it dropped into the waves.

Another one, and another: two of them coming in at once. She took one out in the same way as her companion had, careful not to break the shell and scatter the jelly within, which would ignite on contact with air. The second one was similarly repulsed.

Two more; and two more on top of that. The Weaver ships had got their range now.

Three of the missiles dropped harmlessly; the fourth did not. In haste, one of the Sisters braked it as it looped over a ship that was almost ready to set sail. It dipped and smashed into the mast, blowing it to splinters. Sailors and Tkiurathi on the deck fell clutching their faces and bodies as they were pierced by shards of burning hardwood; the mast collapsed in a slow topple, trailing smoke from its blazing sails. The men beneath did not have space or time to get out of its way. The ship descended into confusion: some evacuated, some fought to help the wounded, and meanwhile more artillery was coming in, whispering through the fog with deadly speed.

((This cannot stand)) said Cailin to Kaiku privately. *((The Aberrants are approaching fast. We cannot defend against both them and the cannons))*

((Then we should get out there and give those ships something else to deal with)) Kaiku thought fiercely, the message expressed in a blaze of images: burning ships, dying men, blistering hands and melting Masks.

((Agreed, I want you on the next ship. The first of our vessels are already beginning to engage the enemy on the sea))

Kaiku sent her a defiant jumble of emotions in response, indicating that she would go when she was gods-damned ready and that she would not be ordered by Cailin. But in her heart, she would be glad to get off the dock where she was little use for anything but intercepting the enemy's missiles. Defence was not her style.

((Then I am asking *you, Kaiku))* Cailin said irascibly. *((Will you take the next ship?))*

((I will)) she said, because at that moment she spotted Tsata racing up a jetty, and her last reason for staying was removed.

She pushed her way through to the ship that Tsata had boarded. To the north, the feya-kori were engaged in their usual mindless destruction of anything and everything around them, but they were cutting a very definite swathe towards the docks. Shellshot cut through the air overhead, but it was going long and none of the Sisters were interested in stopping it. It smashed into the domed roof of a temple and stove it in with a blaze of smoke and flame.

Another missile got through the Sisters' defences, this time because the sheer volume of artillery was too much for them. It hit the docks in the midst of a swarm of people, most of them Tkiurathi. The explosion ripped bodies apart, sending mutilated limbs skidding across the cracked flagstones, men clawing at their blinded eyes and women flailing on the ground, waving cauterised stumps of flesh that used to be arms and legs.

Kaiku squeezed her eyes shut for a moment, appalled, but she had no time to spend on horror or sympathy, and she pushed on through to the gang-plank. Men stumbled past her, supporting the wounded from the burning ship. She smelt the reek of suffering, mixed with the vile, poisonous odour of the feya-kori's miasma, and she used it to fuel her hatred. Breaking free of the crowd, she slipped up the jetty and on to the junk.

There was little space to move on the deck. The sailors were shouting at the Tkiurathi to get below, but few of them obeyed. They were not seafarers, and they did not like the idea of being trapped in a box of wood which was in danger of sinking at any moment. She sought out Tsata, but it was hopeless amongst the mass of tattooed and camouflaged folk.

Other ships were being freed from their moorings up and down the dock now. The remaining craft were filling fast, and Kaiku guessed they would depart close together, for the sailors knew they could not afford to wait any more. The report of cannons bellowed through the air, seeming nearer now than before.

And then suddenly the docks were alive with gunfire as the soldiers of Lalyara opened up on the first of the Aberrants. Sailors on board Kaiku's ship roared the order to cast off, and the sails unfurled along the mast as ropes pulled tight. Tkiurathi on board sought targets for their rifles as the Aberrants appeared.

Massive ghauregs led the charge, smashing into the defenders on the north side of the docks and throwing them aside like broken dolls. Shrillings tore in after them, warbling in their throats as they pounced here and there, taking down men and savaging them; and skrendel slipped between, biting and strangling. They overwhelmed the primary defences by sheer suicidal force. Even after four years, Saramyr soldiers found it hard to stand against an enemy that cared nothing for their own lives. Then the Tkiurathi on the ships opened up, and the predators were cut to pieces in a shredding hail of rifle balls. But the range was long, and some of them survived to engage the remainder of the soldiers. A dockside cathouse, empty now, took a direct hit from one of the Weaver cannons and vomited fiery rubble from its façade. Swords were drawn, rifles barked, and the soldiers fought as best they could, but they knew their cause was hopeless. They were giving their lives so that the ships could get away. They had been ordered to hold this spot and they would die doing so.

Now Kaiku could feel the slow, massive movement of the junk as it caught the wind and the last of its hawsers were cut free. She shoved through the crowd, her mind divided between the communication of the Sisters and the incoming missiles. She let her *kana* seek Tsata out, following the link between them, the bonds of emotion that existed in a palpable sense within the Weave.

She found him refilling the ignition powder in his rifle from a pouch, just as the pier began to slide away. Another boat to their right had launched ahead of them, a huge, swaying shadow in the murk as it gathered speed. Tsata did not see her as she approached; he was intent on priming and aiming again, picking off the Aberrants that were invading the docks.

One of the junks was not fast enough to escape the tide of teeth and claws, and the creatures swarmed up the gangplank onto the ship; but then it began to move, and the plank fell free, pitching the creatures into the sea. Those few on board were killed, but they took three times their number with them.

Kaiku frowned as she bent her concentration towards a fresh volley from the Weaver ships. There were fewer missiles coming in now, as the Weavers turned their cannons to the junks that were trying to run the blockade; but one of the feya-kori had accelerated in its rampage towards the docks, smashing through the buildings of the city. Though slow, it was not slow enough for Kaiku's liking, and it seemed to know that the ships were escaping and was heading right for them.

Then the pier was behind them and they were out in the harbour. Some of the Aberrants were throwing themselves at the junks, bouncing off their hulls and into the water, where they swam raggedly away. Others were pushed over the edge of the docks by the headlong rush of those behind them.

But they were out of the Aberrants' reach now. The last of the ships had pulled away, and those soldiers that were left on the docks – including several dozen Tkiurathi who had not made it aboard in time – were cut to meat by the Weavers' creatures. The sight was mercifully shrouded by the fog, which gathered ever thicker as they gained distance on the carnage.

There was a moment's respite in the bombardment from the sea, during which Kaiku laid her hand on Tsata's bare shoulder. He was wearing a sleeveless waistcoat of grey hemp, as ever, stitched with traditional patterns. He did not turn, but he laid the hand of his other arm across hers as he stared at the fading outline of the dock.

A burst of alarm across the Weave shocked her out of her brief calm, and she turned her attention to it. It was one of her Sisters, noting that the approaching feya-kori had changed direction, and was no longer heading for the docks but had angled itself out into the sea. Kaiku heard the furious hiss from the fog, the angry boiling and bubbling of the salt water as the feya-kori touched it. A wave rocked the junk to their left, and then Kaiku felt the swell pass underneath their vessel too.

She went cold as she saw the black Weave-shape of the demon ploughing through the waves. It was going to intercept them.

A mournful groan came from the mist, terrifyingly close, and it spread panic across the deck. The ship that had left dock ahead of them was still close on their starboard side. The mist thinned in a swirl of wind and the vast shape of the demon reared out of the water, trailing spray and steam and drooling poison. It rose up, its yellow eyes muted and baleful in the haze, and raised both its enormous arms above its head; then it came down with a thunderous rush of air, onto the junk next to Kaiku's.

She could not help joining in the cry of horror from her ship as the feya-kori smashed the hull of their neighbour in half, breaking its back in one great lunge. The noise was tremendous; the water detonated as the demon's arms plunged through the junk and into the waves, blasting spume and spray in a great cloud. A wave humped under their vessel, tipping it sickeningly. Kaiku grabbed the railing, thinking that they would capsize; several people were knocked overboard. Then the tipping slowed, and with a vertiginous plunge it pitched the other way with enough momentum to fling a few more shrieking into the sea. Kaiku was crushed against the railing by the people sliding across the mist-wet deck behind her. She could not take her eyes from the ruin of the junk as its two halves keeled towards each other, its sails burning from the touch of the feya-kori, shedding blackened bodies and live men and women as its horrible, inexorable tilt steepened.

The bow half did not have time to sink; the feya-kori reared up again, and smashed it to flinders with sullen brutality.

Kaiku looked away; but she could not avoid the sight, for it was there in the Weave, and she was aware of everything around. The death-cries of the three Sisters that had been on board pulsed over her.

Their own junk levelled out, cutting through the waves, leaving the demon behind in the midst of the wreckage. She could hear the bellowing of the captain as he shouted incomprehensible commands at his crew, bullying them into action. The wind was tugging them onward, out towards the harbour mouth, and they were picking up speed. The feya-kori made no move to follow. They had reached water that was too deep for it. Instead, it turned towards the dock with a long, low moan, and was slowly swallowed by the fog.

The Tkiurathi on deck fell silent. The wind whipped around the rigging, flapping the edges of the fanlike sails. There was no question of going back for survivors. The feya-kori could still be about, and they would not be able to outrun it a second time. A dawning grief settled on the ship,

But the silence did not last long, for the cannons began again somewhere ahead of them, and incoming shellshot began to splash into the sea.

'Cannons ready!' the captain bellowed.

((Find and engage the Weavers)) instructed a Sister who stood at the captain's side. *((Blind their ships))*

Kaiku could see the ragged line of vessels now, strung out across their path, beacons of golden light in the Weave. Some of the Sisters' ships were already on the other side of the line, some slipping through, and at least one sinking in flames. The closest enemy was waiting in the water ahead of them: they would pass it to their starboard side if they kept on this tack. It was flinging cannon fire with spectacular inaccuracy in their direction.

There was no Weaver on board.

((This one has already been dealt with)) Kaiku informed her Sisters. *((Instruct the captain))*

She offhandedly destroyed shellshot that was looping near, then returned her attention to the enemy ship. The men on board were aware of them: the captain's voice had carried even through the fog, and the creaking of the ship as it hauled its massive weight across the waves could be heard. But the fog hid everything.

Kaiku held her breath as they cut alongside it. It loomed close, so close that Kaiku, with her Weave-sight, could not believe that the enemy did not see them. She could pick out the individual men on the ship, could sense their anxiety as they gazed out into the murk to catch a glimpse of their adversary. Others were busy loading cannons.

Then, a skirl of wind, and the mist parted; and she saw their anxiety turn to horror as they caught sight of the huge shadow gliding past them.

'Starboard cannons!' the captain shouted. 'Fire!'

The junk's artillery engaged with a deafening multiple roar, and the side of the enemy ship erupted. Grapeshot riddled the hull, scoring a long and splintered scar down its flank. The fire-cannons threw flaming slicks along its deck, into its sails, sending the crew into a shrieking panic as their hair and skin was coated in burning jelly. There was an enormous explosion on the far side of the ship, blasting a rain of splinters outward and leaving a gaping wound there. In one point-blank broadside the enemy was fatally damaged, and what retaliation they might have made was abandoned in the futile rush to save their craft.

Kaiku's ship slid by and away, leaving their opponents listing hard and already beginning to sink, fading in the gloom.

'Are we out of danger?' Tsata murmured to Kaiku.

'Not yet,' she replied, 'Two more are moving to intercept us. These two have Weavers with them. They can see us.' She paused for a moment. 'One of them is changing direction toward another one of our craft.' She checked the waters again, listening to the reports of those Sisters that were through the line. Distant explosions boomed through the fog. 'Once we have tackled this one, we will be out and in open sea.'

'Can we evade it?'

'I think not,' Kaiku replied. 'We are laden more heavily. Spread the word; we may need rifles ready.'

Tsata tipped his chin and passed on her words in rapid Okhamban to those nearest to him, who then began to do same to their neighbours.

'Do not disturb me now,' Kaiku said, feeling the approach of the Weavers. 'I need to concentrate.'

She abandoned her senses almost entirely, leaving only enough to maintain a vague awareness of her surroundings, and sewed her consciousness fully into the Weave. She meshed with two other Sisters who were on board with her, constructing defences, fortifying their position with traps and barriers and labyrinths in preparation. They worked with a beautiful and unthinking concinnity. Kaiku found herself suddenly thinking that she would miss that when she abandoned the Red Order for good.

Then the Weavers were upon them, and battle was joined.

While the invisible conflict was conducted on a plane beyond their abilities to register, the men and women on board the junk peered into the fog. One of the Sisters had not entered the fray, for she was the captain's eyes, and she relayed to him the position of the enemy. A distant creaking could be heard now, and the rustling of sails. The captain's brow was taut. He knew that to come through this with any hope of surviving the long sea journey ahead, they could not afford to be greatly damaged. There would be no port between here and there to effect repairs. They had to win this match outright.

Seconds crawled slowly by on the ship, but in the Weave they lasted much longer. Kaiku darted back and forth in flurries, harrying the three Weavers with spirals and tangles while the other Sisters spun new defences in front of the old. They were gaining ground steadily, bewildering the enemy and forcing them to retreat, then consolidating their position and pushing forward again. One of the Weavers was a weak link, and Kaiku attacked him mercilessly. She guessed that he was retaining a portion of his consciousness to instruct his captain. They did not have the luxury of a spare combatant. It was that Weaver whose inefficient mazes Kaiku went for, tearing them to shreds, chasing him back towards his own vessel, which left his companions exposed unless they retreated themselves. By unspoken consent, she was the aggressor here, and her Sisters lent her cover and support. Slowly but surely, the Weavers were being beaten back.

'They are angling for a broadside,' murmured the Sister who accompanied the captain.

The captain cursed under his breath. He struggled for inspiration, but none came. Since each captain knew where the other was, they might as well be tackling each other in daylight. There was nowhere to run and hide. With what he knew of the Weaver ships, he guessed that he had a roughly equal chance of winning out in a broadside, but he doubted he could come away from it without wounds to his junk that would sink it sometime during the subsequent voyage. The artillery was loaded, the men ready. All he could do was wait and hope.

Though she was occupied almost entirely with the slip and sew of the combat in the Weave, Kaiku was peripherally aware of the two golden ships, their outline drawn in millions of threads, that were gliding steadily closer to each other. Kaiku had guessed what the captain knew: they would not get away from this without damage and loss of life.

By now she had the measure of these Weavers. They were young and clumsy and arrogant, making foolish mistakes which she exploited. The ships were lining up with one another, excruciatingly slow in Weave-time. Soon they would be level, and firing would commence.

It was time to abandon caution. She sent an instruction to her Sisters, and the Weave erupted in response, a blizzard of threads lashing everywhere, random and impossible to follow. The Weavers recoiled, having never encountered this tactic before, unsure of how it might harm them.

But it was not meant to harm; it was meant to distract. Quick and subtle as a blade, Kaiku slid towards them.

'Enemy to port!' hollered the lookout, as the hulking ship emerged from the mist. It was coming in at a distance, too far away to allow boarding, its flanks bristling with sculpted fire-cannon like gaping metal demons. It hove alongside, approaching from the opposite direction, a rapid succession of portholes and shadowy figures holding rifles. Waiting, like the sailors of the Empire, for the moment when all cannons would be face-on to their enemy.

'Fire!' came the cry from the Weaver ship, at the same time as it did from the captain of the junk; and at that moment, the entire port side of the enemy craft exploded. It heeled drastically, its cannons blasting into the water and passing beneath the keel of Kaiku's junk. The sailors slid howling over the gunwale and into the sea. And now its unarmoured deck was presented to the junk's artillery, which smashed it to ruin in a blitz of smoke and fire and sawdust.

It was all over so quickly that those aboard ship could barely believe they had escaped unscathed. The Tkiurathi rifles had not fired. They watched as the wrecked boat plunged into the water, sucking down those who had survived the initial assault, and like the other two boats they had seen in ruin it slid away from them and was masked once more by the murk.

Kaiku blinked, looked about the deck and met Tsata's gaze with her crimson eyes.

'You?' he asked.

'They should be have been more careful where they stored their ammunition,' she said.

And the ship sailed on, while the mist thinned around them and finally broke to a clear winter's day. The open sea was all around, sparkling under the gaze of Nuki's eye, and the ships of Lalyara were there, twelve of them, sailing at a swift clip towards the horizon.

TWENTY-FIVE

The Lord Protector Avun and the Weave-lord Kakre stood together on a balcony on the south face of the Imperial Keep. They were looking over the city to where the Jabaza and Kerryn met to form the Zan, in a place called the Rush. Once, on the hexagonal island in the centre, there had stood an enormous statue of Isisya, facing towards the Keep, but no more. In other times, Avun might have been glad of its loss, for he could not easily bear its accusing gaze. Today, though, he felt that it would not have troubled him. His spirits were high, and all was well.

Even Kakre seemed pleased with him. The sight of the Weavers' many mechanised barges gathering along the rivers of the city was an impressive one indeed, as was the horde of Aberrants that were being brought from their pens underground and herded on board by the black-robed Nexuses. And this represented only the tail of the undertaking: most had already departed eastward, upstream along the Kerryn and down the Rahn. From there, the troops would skirt the Xarana Fault and loop west of Lake Azlea, and then south into the enemy's territory, towards Saraku. The feya-kori would join them en route, six of them in total, including the two that had assaulted Lalyara several weeks ago. Those two were hardier now; they needed less time to recuperate in their pall-pits. The blight demons, it seemed, got stronger with age.

The prelude was done. The forces of the Empire, rocked by defeats at Juraka and Zila and Lalyara, did not know where the next strike would come from. Their armies would be spread in an attempt to cover the greatest amount of ground. Avun would cut through them like a sword and strike into their heart. By the time they could get their troops to Saraku it would be too late: the Weavers would hold the line of the River Ju, cutting off the marshland cities of Yotta and Fos to be despatched by their forces in Juraka. And after a short recuperation during which they could easily hold a city like Saraku, they would strike west, and nothing the Empire had could stand against them. At best, they could scatter into guerrilla armies, dogging the Weavers' efforts; but the Weavers would have the harvest, and the armies would be starved out and hunted down until nothing remained of them.

It would be over then. The desert lands could not stand alone. Their fall would swiftly follow.

Even the Weave-lord seemed happy today; or at least as happy as it was possible for such a creature to be. He was satisfied at Avun's progress now that action he deemed worthy was being taken. He had always been impatient with Avun's tactics, and had wanted to go in for the kill as soon as the feya-kori were first brought under their control. Avun allowed himself a wry smile. Idiots. If not for him, they would have been in a much worse situation by now.

Thoughts of that made him consider his encounter with Kakre, when he had convinced the Weave-lord of his worth. Kakre appeared to have forgotten about it, or was pretending to. It didn't matter. Kakre had been outmanoeuvred. Removing Avun would cause him far too much trouble, and it was trouble he could ill afford with time growing so short.

But more pleasing even than this to Avun was the behaviour of his wife. Since that day of her frankly miraculous recovery from sickness, she had seemed a different person. In public she was as quiet and meek as ever, but when they were alone she was no longer so demure. There was passion in her now, and after years of showing no interest whatsoever in him sexually she was suddenly, while not exactly wild, at least far more voracious than she used to be. In its absence, Avun had convinced himself that he did not need bedplay. He had always possessed torpid sexual appetites: he was slow to rouse and indifferent to the lures of a woman. But he had found, after so long, that the pleasures his wife's body might provide were immensely attractive again. He was loth to admit it to himself, but he felt more of a man for it.

Tomorrow he would depart, along with Kakre, to join the Weavers' army as their general. But first he had something else to look forward to. Until recently, he had all but needed to command Muraki to join him for meals; now, to his delight, she had asked him to come to one. She had something to celebrate, and when she told him he felt like celebrating too.

At long last, she had finished her book.

The wind whipped through the Tchamil Mountains, chasing itself among the barren peaks and valleys that formed the spine of Saramyr. The men of the desert had kept to the lower altitudes, for in winter there were snow and blizzards in the high passes; but still the ground was frosted and bitter, and they huddled in thick furs around their fires and listened anxiously to the dark. The land was cool and sharp as well-polished steel beneath the combined glow of Iridima and Aurus, and the sky was thick with pinpricks of starlight.

The desert army were seven thousand strong, all told, and they spread down the mountainside in a great clot of tents and lanterns. They had lost perhaps five hundred so far, all of them to Aberrant attacks. The cries of the beasts echoed across the peaks even now, some identifiable as ghauregs or latchjaws, others entirely unfamiliar. It was hard going to take an army through this kind of terrain, but the folk of Tchom Rin prided themselves on their endurance, and they travelled light and wore little armour. Rivalries between soldiers sworn to different families had dissipated out of the need for unity and cooperation in this hostile place, and they had made good progress. But the Aberrants' attacks were becoming more and more coordinated now, and by day gristle-crows wheeled overhead, cawing hoarsely.

The Weavers knew they were coming, and they were watching and waiting.

Reki walked slowly back through the camp towards his tent, a lean and thoughtful figure, the wind flicking his hair about his face. His boots crunched on the lifeless, stony soil. He was running over events in his mind as he had a hundred times before, examining them, turning them to consider from all angles.

The council with the nobles of the Empire and the Libera Dramach had been remarkably quick, all things considered. For the first time Reki had really appreciated what he had taken for granted all his life, that the Weavers, and latterly the Sisters, provided something so valuable that they simply could not ever go back to the way things had been. Men and women from Araka Jo, Saraku, and Izanzai had talked to each other face to phantom face via the power of the Sisters, though almost nine hundred miles separated them. A conference had been carried out, with terms and suggestions bandied back and forth, in less than a day. Without the Sisters, it would have been a labour of months, whether by an exchange of letters or by attempting to assemble them all in one place. He understood then, truly, why the Weavers had become so indispensible to his ancestors, and how they had come to the situation they had were in now.

When the desert folk's part in the plan had been laid out, Reki had agreed without much fuss. Unbeknownst to the Sisters, he had been intending something very similar anyway. It had become clear to him that they were fighting a losing battle in Tchom Rin. If they were content to merely defend against the Aberrants, then eventually the Weavers would come up with some way to overwhelm them, whether by new types of Aberrant, by demons, or by sheer weight of numbers. It was prudent to attack while they still had strength to do so. His scouts had traced the Aberrants from Izanzai, seeking a source to strike at. All those who had returned came back with the same news. Though they could not find the exact place, they knew the general area, and it was in the vicinity of Adderach. Reki had not been surprised.

And so, while he had been in the midst of plotting an assault on Adderach, the Red Order came to suggest he did exactly that. Yet he could not shrug an uncomfortable suspicion that the Sisters thought he and his men expendable, and that they were merely intended as a decoy.

Well, let them think what they would. He would show them how desert folk could fight. And they had Sisters too, gathered from the dozens scattered across Tchom Rin, to defend them against Weavers and to get them through the barrier of misdirection surrounding the mountain monastery.

If Reki could dispose of the threat of Adderach, then they would no longer be beleaguered on two fronts, and they could turn all their attention to Igarach in the south. If the Sisters' intelligence was accurate, then they needed only to hold the Weavers off till next winter; and with Adderach out of the picture, it could be done.

And then there was Cailin's assertion that maybe, just maybe, getting the Sisters to that witchstone might be enough to end this war. That was a prize worth trying for.

He picked his way between campfires, returning the greetings of the soldiers as he neared his tent. He was discomfited tonight, a subtle notion that something was amiss. Posting extra guards and sentries had not eased his fears. He tried to shake it off, to return his mind to matters at hand, but instead he found himself drifting, as he so often did, towards thoughts of Asara.

Trust is an overrated commodity. One of Asara's favourite sayings. And she should know. For he was beginning to suspect that trusting her had been something of a mistake.

He had not known peace since she left him all that time ago, heading to Araka Jo on some secret purpose of her own. At first, he had been tormented by not knowing, mocked by possibilities; and then, when that had become too much to bear and he had sent his spymaster Jikiel to find answers, he had been racked with guilt at betraying her. But now things were even worse. He had thought his love could withstand anything that Jikiel might discover about his wife's past, but when the spymaster returned it was with news that was entirely unexpected.

Asara *had* no past.

His initial reaction was to dismiss this as evidence of the spymaster's limits. After all, he had to fail sometimes. But Reki had had experience of Jikiel's abilities, and he could not convince himself of it in the end. The spymaster was far too good to come up blank like that. If he could not dig out the truth of any matter, then Reki was convinced that there was no truth to be had.

But of Asara, he had found nothing. Her family name, which she had said was Arreyia, yielded no answers. It was a common enough name, for it was very old and had spread widely. Saramyr names ranged from those derived from archaic Quraal, like Asara and Lucia, Adderach and Anais, to more modern ones which arose after Saramyrrhic had evolved, like Kaiku and Mishani and Reki. There were other Asaras, of course, but none matching her description, her talents and her circumstances. Jikiel had heard of a spy called Asara tu Amarecha who had worked for the Libera Dramach in recent years, but he discounted her eventually. She was not desert-born, and Reki's Asara certainly was, unless a person could fake their bone structure, their skin colour, the shape of their eyes.

Jikiel had probed the limits of his spy network as the puzzle became more intriguing. Whispers and hints were followed up and came to nothing. He sought information from those who had met her in the Imperial Keep during the time she had first seduced Reki, but they had no answers to give. He asked in places of learning, for she had been incredibly knowledgeable and well-travelled for one so young and it hinted at a childhood of study or adventure or both, but no clues were found. He worked on the assumption that she had changed her name, maybe even that she had disguised herself with a different manner, different hairstyles and clothes. He was adept at seeing through such basic deceptions. And still, nothing.

Eventually, he had exhausted all possibilities and was forced, shamefully, to admit defeat. In the end, he could report only this: that the woman who was to become Reki's wife had not appeared to exist prior to that day she turned up at the Imperial Keep.

Reki was still thinking about the implications of that when he walked past the guards outside his tent – not noticing the wry grin that one gave to the other – and found Asara waiting there.

The tent was tall and wide enough to stand up in, but inside it was bare and spartan except for a thick bed of blankets and a lamp placed on the groundsheet. The lamp threw light up and onto the curves of his wife's face and body, capturing her as she half-turned at his entrance. The surprise at her presence and the breathtaking beauty of her robbed him of speech for a moment.

'I promised I would be back, Reki,' she said. 'Even though it meant I had to track you through the mountains.'

He opened his mouth, but she stepped towards him and put a finger to his lips. The scent of her and the touch of her skin was intoxicating.

'There will be time for questions later,' she said.

'We have to talk,' he murmured, some remnant memory of his previous sour thoughts inspiring the need to protest, however feebly.

'Afterward,' she said. She kissed him, and he gave up any more attempt to resist. He had yearned for her every instant she had been gone, and now that she was here he could not restrain himself. Their kisses turned to caresses and took them onto the bed, where they sated their passions with one another long into the night and past the dawn.

When Avun arrived at the room where he and Muraki shared their meals, he barely recognised it. The table of black and red lacquer was surrounded by four standing lanterns, the flames burning inside metal globes with patterns cut into them to allow the light through. Exquisite drapes had been hung over the alcoves, hiding the statues there. A brazier of scented wood smoked gently in the far corner of the room, providing heat and a subtle fragrance of jasmine. No longer did the room seem cold and empty, but warm and intimate. The meal was already served, bowls and baskets steaming on the table, and Muraki knelt at her place, dappled by the light from the lanterns.

'This is wonderful,' he said, unexpectedly touched.

Muraki smiled, her eyes averted downward, her face half-hidden by her hair. Beyond the three tall window-arches at the back of the room, it was utterly dark: no stars or moons could penetrate the canopy now.

He settled himself, kneeling at the mat across the table from her. 'Wonderful,' he murmured again.

'I am glad you approve,' she said quietly.

'Will you eat?' he asked. It had become one of their rituals. At first, because she was always reluctant to dine with him, and later, as a wry joke between them at the way she had been. He began to take the lids from the baskets and serve her.

'It is done, then?' he asked. 'The book?'

'It is done,' she replied. 'As we speak it is being taken to the publisher.'

'You must be relieved,' he guessed. He really had no idea how she felt at any stage of her writing, for she had never discussed it with him.

'No,' she said. 'Saddened, perhaps.'

He paused in the act of spooning saltrice onto her plate, puzzled.

'I thought you were celebrating?'

'I am,' she said. 'But it is a bittersweet day. That was my last Nida-jan book.'

Avun was confounded by this. It was as if she had told him she was giving up breathing. 'Your last?'

Muraki nodded.

He passed the plate to her and started taking food for himself. 'But why?'

She was sliding on her finger-cutlery. 'His journey has run its course,' she said. 'It is time, I think, to begin anew.'

'Muraki, are you sure about this?'

She made a noise to the affirmative.

'Then what will you do? Will you create a new hero to write about?'

'I do not know,' she replied. 'Maybe I will stop writing altogether. Today, Nida-jan is ended, and all things are possible.'

Avun did not quite know how to gauge his wife's mood, and was careful in his words. Though he had always found Muraki's constant writing a source of irritation, he found himself unable to imagine her any other way, and now that it came to it he was not sure he *wanted* her to stop.

'Are you doing this for my sake?' he asked. 'I would not have you change yourself for me.' The hypocrisy of this passed him by entirely.

She met his eyes for a moment with something like amusement. 'It is not for you I do this, Avun,' she replied. 'Too long I have lived in the safety of my own world and ignored the one that surrounds me. Today I have closed my world away, and I am ready to face what is real.'

He set down his plate, hiding his wariness. He was unsure whether to be glad or worried about her decision. Writing had been such a big part of her life for so long that he was afraid she might not cope without it. And he would not be there to watch over her; there was no way he could delay the movement of the Aberrant forces now, even if he wanted to. After all the effort he had spent to make himself indispensible to the Weavers, he could not back out. Kakre would shred him.

'You must tell me,' he said, to cover his thoughts. 'How does it end?' He poured each of them a glass of amber wine.

'It ends well for him,' she said. 'He finds his son at last, in the Golden Realm where Omecha has taken him. There he wins him back after facing Omecha and beating him in a game of wits. They return to their home, and the son acknowledges Nida-jan as his father, for only a father's love could drive him to seek his son even beyond the realms of death. And so the curse laid upon him by the demon with a hundred eyes is lifted.'

'It is a good ending indeed,' Avun said. And yet privately, he wondered. For it was no secret to him that she had been mourning the loss of their daughter in her books, mirroring her grief in the actions of Nida-jan, and this sudden turn to happiness made him suspect that something had happened which he was unaware of.

'Come to the window, Avun,' she said, picking up her glass of wine and holding out her hand to him across the table. Surprised by her uncharacteristic impetuousness, he took up his own glass and rose with her. Together, they walked across the room to the window-arches that faced out over Axekami.

In the night, the miasma overhead could not be seen, and Axekami seemed peaceful. Lights were lit, tumbling down in profusion towards the Kerryn and the River District. Not as many as there had been in days gone by, but enough. It was almost possible to believe the city was beautiful again.

Muraki turned to him. 'While I was dreaming, you have become the most powerful man in Saramyr, my husband,' she said. She kissed him deeply, and there was a hunger in it that made him dizzy. He wanted to have her then and there, but he did not yet dare to do so, did not trust that he would not embarrass himself by overstepping the mark. Presently, she drew away from him, her eyes searching his, and she took a sip of wine, regarding him over the rim of her glass. He slid his arm around her tiny waist. His wife's words made him burn with pride. It was true: he had done all this, he had made this of himself. He sipped his own glass as he surveyed his conquest, the great capital of Axekami, and he was content.

It took him only seconds to realise that the wine was deadly poison, but by then it was far too late.

The first he knew of it was the awful tightening of his throat and chest, as if he was choking on a bone. His hand came free of Muraki and went to his collar; his other, absurdly, still held the glass out of instinctive reluctance to drop it. He could not draw breath. Gaping, he staggered backwards and tripped on his heel, falling to the floor. The glass shattered in his hand, cutting it badly. His chest was a blaze of pain as if he had swallowed the sun. His lungs would not respond to the urging of his brain, would not expand to fill with oxygen.

Wildly, in blind animal panic, he reached for his wife, but Muraki was standing by the window, her face shadowed by her hair, and she was not moving to help him. His eyes widened in horror and disbelief. That appalled gaze still rested on his wife when his body went slack and his life left him.

Muraki regarded him for a long time. She had expected tears to come, but there were none. She had expected, at least, to be consumed by remorse or guilt, but she felt none of that either. If she were writing this scene, she thought, she would not do so with such a dearth of emotion. Real life was infinitely stranger and unpredictable than the one she lived in her imagination.

She turned away from her husband and looked out over the city once again. She could smell the oily tang of the miasma, overpowering the jasmine from the brazier. She had never quite become accustomed to it. Her lips tingled where the poison wine had touched them, but she had not let it past into her mouth. Simple enough to procure poison from Ukida: she had only to order him, and he obeyed. He was loyal enough to keep her secret and not to ask what it was for.

She glanced at the corpse of Avun again, trying for some last time to stir something in her breast. The newly awakened passion for him had not been faked by her. She had wanted to enjoy what she could while she could, and she wanted to make him happy too. After all, she thought he deserved that much before she killed him.

She realised what would follow now. The Weavers would take their revenge, would scour her mind agonisingly until they knew all about her code, and about Ukida, and Mishani's visit. They would know their plans had been compromised, and would alter them.

That could not be allowed to happen. From the time she had decided to murder her husband, she knew she would have to die too. She had found that knowledge an immensely liberating sensation.

Thoughts of her daughter brought back words she had spoken during those precious minutes when they were together, a few short minutes in ten terrible years – ten years for which Avun had been responsible.

We are on two sides of a war now. Mother, and one side or the other must win eventually. Whichever of us is on the losing side will not survive, I think. We are both of us too involved.

She was right. She always had the gift of cutting to the point. So let it be Muraki on the losing side, then, for she could not bear the thought of her daughter suffering such a fate.

Avun had indeed been clever in arranging the Weavers' power base so that so much relied on him. He had carefully guarded his battle tactics, kept them close to his chest, and ensured that there was nobody else in a position to easily succeed him. His death would be a major blow to the Weavers, at the time when they could least afford it. And from what she knew of Kakre, she did not think he would turn back from his assault now, no matter what speculation might arise as to what happened in this room tonight. The

Aberrants would move according to plan, and their enemies would be waiting for them.

Would it be worth it, in the end? Only the gods could say. There were no certainties in the real world.

She gave a long sigh, and her eyes turned to the night, the impenetrable blackness with no moons and no stars. What a cold and dreary prison her husband had made for her. She much preferred her dreams.

She drained her glass, and soon she was dreaming once more.

TWENTY-SIX

Nuki's eye was sinking in the west, igniting cottony bands of cloud. The surface of the River Ko glittered in fitful red and yellow. It had been unseasonably hot today, but the folk of Saramyr were glad of it, for winter was drawing to an end and it was their first hint of a spring to come. Now the temperature dropped as Nuki retreated towards the far side of the world, afraid of the tumult that the moon-sisters would bring when they took the sky. For tonight the moons' orbits would cross at shallow angles, and they would drag screeching fingers across the darkness. There would be a moonstorm, and a particularly long and vicious one.

It would be a suitably apocalyptic backdrop, Yugi thought, to the battle that was to come. He stood holding the reins of his horse on a rise a little way south of the river, and looked to the north. Waiting for the Aberrants.

The lands to the north and south of the Ko were rolling downs, a gentle sway of hills that ran from the Forest of Xu twenty miles to their west to peter out on the shores of Lake Azlea, a similar distance to their east. In between was the Sakurika Bridge, a sturdy arch of wood and stone that spanned the river. It was a plain construction, not as grand as many in Saramyr, and little used. Its abutments, spandrels and parapets were painted in faded terracotta to blend with the honey-coloured varnish on the wood, but beyond that there was no decoration. It had been built during a campaign in the far past to facilitate troop movement along the west side of the Azlea, but no road had ever been laid to it. The thin strip of land sandwiched between Xu, Azlea and the Xarana Fault was considered too perilous back then to merit a tradeway. Still, it had been maintained all this time, for it was the only crossing-place for this river east of the forest, and wide enough for twenty men abreast.

And it was here that the forces of the Empire hoped to halt the advance of the Weavers.

Yugi felt sick. He wished he could smoke a little amaxa root to take the edge off his fear. Instead he surveyed the scene below him, the sea of armour and blades and rifles. Several artillery positions were dug in on the hilltops to either side of the bridge, densely packed with mortars and fire-cannons and even old trebuchets and ballistae that they had managed to acquire. The flat ground in between was thick with soldiers, representing almost all of the remaining high families and the Libera Dramach. Their banners hung limp in the failing breeze.

A barricade of spikes had been built along the centre point of the bridge, and behind it soldiers waited. Beneath their feet, well hidden inside the arch, were enough explosives to blow the bridge to matchwood.

'Gods, I can't stand this waiting,' Yugi murmured to those nearby: a few generals, a black-haired Sister that might have been a twin to Cailin in her make-up, Barak Zahn, Nomoru, Mishani and Lucia. Horses shifted and whinnyed restlessly; there was the creak of leather armour and subdued coughing.

'Are we certain that they are coming this way at all?' Mishani asked. It was a measure of how tense she was that she asked such a redundant question; she already knew the reports of the scouts.

'They are coming,' said the Sister, whose irises were red.

Yugi glanced down at Lucia. Her expression was bland. The enemy had to be on time. There were better places in which they could have met the Aberrants, places further south where they could mount ambushes and which were far more defensible than this. But they would not win without Lucia, and it was at her insistence that they chose to meet the threat here. This, their scholars promised, was the night of the moonstorm; and it was on this night that the Aberrants – whose steady and unwavering advance had been marked by scouts all along their route – would reach the river. This night, in this place, Lucia would draw the spirits to the defence of their land.

They could only pray that Lucia knew exactly what she was doing, for without the intervention she had promised their stand would not last for long. Thousands upon thousands of lives were staked on the word of a girl barely into adulthood. Yugi thought they could be forgiven a little nervousness at this point.

Mishani, not for the first time, was asking herself why she was here at all. For someone who prided herself on her self-control and level-headedness, she seemed to have been remarkably rash of late. First her visit to Muraki and now this.

But if not for my rashness, we would not have even this chance, she thought. *Oh, Mother.*

She took a steadying breath to keep down the tears. No, she would not cry again. The thought of that last meeting still burned her with grief, but she was glad, at least, that she had made amends to Muraki. If she died today, she would have done that much.

Had she known then that her mother and father had already been dead for weeks, her grief would have been keener still. But the Weavers had been careful to keep that matter secret.

In the end, Mishani thought, it came down to Lucia. Mishani and Kaiku had been her guardians throughout her childhood in the Fold, and they had acted as elder sisters to her. Though time and circumstances had made them distant, they still had that bond. But Kaiku was needed elsewhere, and

Mishani could not bear the notion of leaving Lucia to face this alone. She knew how easily manipulated Lucia was, and there was nobody here who truly cared for her except her father Zahn, but he would be down in the battle. Mishani could not contribute much to war, but she could stand alongside Lucia. She felt that it would be dishonourable to abandon her.

Once, she had almost killed the young Heir-Empress, when she brought her a nightdress which she thought was infected with bone fever. When it came to it she had backed out; but she still felt responsible for harbouring the intention, and she had come terrifyingly close to executing it. She owed Lucia this, at least. And if Lucia fell, there would soon be little left to live for anyway. As with her visit to her mother, this was something Mishani had to do, no matter what the risks. A moral need that would not be overmatched by sense or logic.

You are getting impulsive in your old age, Mishani, she told herself wryly.

There was a cry from somewhere to their left, echoed by another voice closer by. The lookouts with their spyglasses had seen something on the horizon. A few moments passed, during which Mishani felt her blood slowly chill, before the Sister spoke.

'Our enemy has arrived,' she said.

Zahn exchanged glances with Yugi and the generals, a grim understanding in their eyes. Zahn was overall commander of this force, by consent of the council of high families. The generals mounted up and began to disperse to their positions. Yugi looked at Lucia, who did not acknowledge him, then he swung on to his horse, and pulled Nomoru up behind. Zahn put his hand on his daughter's shoulder, and her gaze shifted to him.

'We will do a great thing this night,' he murmured. 'Be strong. I will return to you; I promise you that.'

She nodded, her face set.

'Keep her safe,' he said to Mishani, and then he launched himself up onto his horse. He sidled the mount over to Yugi's, and the two of them clasped arms. Nomoru turned her scarred face to Lucia and Mishani and regarded them with an impenetrable stare, then both Zahn and Yugi spurred their horses and she was carried away, down the hill and towards the front.

Lucia and Mishani were left together on the hill with the Sister and a group of bodyguards. They watched and waited.

Night was drawing in as the Aberrants came, pounding through the twilight in a filthy tide of teeth and claws. They swept across the downs like the shadow of an eclipse, at a speed just short of a headlong run. Even at such a pace, they were virtually tireless, and could travel all hours with very little rest. More than once the Weavers' ability to move armies so quickly had surprised the forces of the Empire.

There were no gristle-crows in the sky. Like Lucia's ravens, they were useless at night, for they could not see well without the sun. And so the Weavers had no warning of the army ranged across the south bank of the Ko until they were close enough for the front ranks to be able to see the artillery on the hills.

The guiding minds of the Weaver forces were safely protected amid the mass of expendable soldiers. Nexuses were scattered about, riding on Aberrant manxthwa. With them rode Weavers, to whom the Nexuses signed when they had information to pass on from their connection to the Aberrants. The Weavers then penetrated deep into their servants' minds, through conditioned channels that made it an easy process, and learned what the Nexuses knew. They conversed among themselves along the Weave and then gave their orders to the Nexuses, never knowing that they themselves were in turn enslaved by the will of the witchstones and of the moon-god Aricarat. Through such a chain of command were the Weavers' affairs conducted.

The passage of information throughout the Aberrant army from the moment that the forces of Empire were spotted took less than a minute. The reaction was immediate, and unexpected. The high families had predicted that the Aberrants would slow, to take stock of the situation. But they did not know that Avun was dead, and that Kakre was in command here. Kakre had a different way of doing things to Avun.

He sent his orders, and the Aberrants charged.

Thousands of animals bayed and roared as they were goaded into a berserk rage by their handlers. The colossal swell of noise washed over the downs and reached the soldiers of the Empire. They stood grimly along the riverbank, on the flanks of the surrounding hills or packed thick on the bridge. They would not dishonour themselves by showing fear, but they felt dread settle on their hearts as they saw the hills aswarm with an army that vastly outnumbered theirs. They thought of their families, of moments of joy and pleasure, of things left undone. Some of them felt regret at their mistakes and hoped that the gods would find them worthy when they came to the Golden Realm. Some of them regretted nothing, and waited coldly for the end. Some of them felt the fire in their veins and thirsted for combat. Some felt noble, proud to be part of this; some were angry at throwing away their lives when they could have run and seen another day, another month or year, and honour be hanged.

But none of them broke ranks, and none of them shed a tear, and none of them showed their weakness. Though some sweated and trembled, though some fought to keep down the contents of their stomachs, they held at the riverbank as the Aberrants raced towards them, each second bringing them closer and closer.

And closer.

The air was torn by the scream of a firework as it spat into the twilight, trailing dazzling white fire; then the artillery opened up.

The first salvo drew a billowing line of fire across the downs, and ripped the leading edge of the Aberrants apart. Broken bodies spewed into the air in clouds of dirt and flame, shrapnel tore away limbs and sliced through hide. Those that survived the concussion and the heat were knocked to the ground where they were crushed by the stampede. The entire front line collapsed and was driven into the earth by the predators behind, who ran on through the blazing slicks left by the fire-cannons. A second salvo followed the first, pitched shorter. Shellshot sprayed burning jelly, mortars maimed and blinded, and heavy trebuchets lobbed bags of explosives that clattered to the earth amid the horde and then erupted, sending flailing corpses in every direction. The Aberrants were a target that was impossible to miss, and each shell or bomb accounted for a dozen or more. Hundreds fell as a result of those initial salvos, but they were a drop in the ocean. And the tide kept on coming.

The artillery continued firing without cease as the Aberrants reached the Ko. No longer were they aiming at the leading edge of the horde; instead, they placed their strikes carelessly into the heaving mass, confident that it was impossible to miss. The deafening barrage faded into a background noise, a constant roar of slaughter; the ground became a bloody trench of body parts, the soil red and churned and scorched. But the soldiers of the Empire had a greater concern: the Aberrants were upon them now.

The creatures swarmed onto the Sakurika Bridge or ploughed into the river, not slowing for anything. The spiked barricade across the bridge's centre took care of the first few dozen Aberrants before it collapsed: they simply threw themselves onto it with nauseating force until it cracked beneath their weight. Their brethren swarmed over their impaled corpses.

The soldiers of the Empire were ranked across the bridge to meet them. Riflemen stood behind kneeling swordsmen, aiming over their shoulders. A volley of shots cut the first row of Aberrants down like wheat. Then the swords swung, and battle was joined.

The fury of close-quarters combat was terrible. The huge, shaggy ghauregs tore into the soldiers, flinging them off the bridge into the water, or else picking them up and biting off their heads. Skrendel wound along the parapets of the bridge to insinuate themselves in the ranks of the defenders, scratching and biting, blinding and strangling. Shrillings filled the air with their insidious ululations as they pounced and tore with their claws. Other creatures fought too, nightmare things of bony hide and jagged tooth, beasts that were too strange or uncommon to be recognised as a species.

The soldiers cut and sliced, but hand-to-hand the Aberrants had a great advantage. The shrillings' natural armour turned sword blades away; the ghauregs' tough skin and thick pelt made it hard to cut them deeply, and even then nothing short of a strike in a vital organ would take them down. Skrendel were too fast to hit easily, and the soldiers were crammed too tight on the bridge to make wild swings for fear of hitting each other. The Aberrants pressed forward as the soldiers fought and died. The bridge became greasy with gore and cluttered with bodies as the men of the Empire were pushed back.

And, in the river beneath, the Aberrants were swimming across.

*

'It is time, Lucia,' Mishani murmured.

Lucia ignored her. She could see what was going on below as well as Mishani could. From their vantage point on the crest of the hill, the battle seemed strangely removed and insignificant in the last of the light, the deaths too distant to be real. Nuki's eye had gone now, leaving only a soft blue glow in the sky through which the stars were visible. The three moons, all of them full, had risen from the same horizon and were converging slowly. There was something eerily malevolent in their steady movement, heavy with purpose.

Four guards stood around them, doing their best not to glance at Lucia or the Sister who stood by her. Mishani waited for a reaction to her comment, then turned her head to regard the young woman at her side.

'Lucia, it is time,' she repeated.

Lucia slowly met her gaze, a deep sorrow in her eyes. For a moment, Mishani was struck by an awful thought: that Lucia would confess it was all a sham, that there *were* no spirits coming to their aid. But what she said instead was almost as worrying.

'Whatever comes after, Mishani, think well of me,' she murmured. 'I made a choice that nobody should ever have to make.'

Mishani did not reply. She sensed that she did not need to. There was no time to discuss this, anyway, for the Aberrants were almost across the river now. The soldiers on the south bank were riddling them with rifle balls as they swam, but there were too many of them to stop.

Lucia bowed her head and closed her eyes.

The change in the atmosphere was swift and immediately noticable. At first, Mishani thought it was the onset of the moonstorm, somehow beginning before the great satellites had aligned. But though it was similar, it was not that. The air tautened, stretching across the senses and bringing with it a sense of dislocation, a faint notion that the eyes and ears had become detached from the mind. The wind began to pick up, at first in sporadic gusts and then rising to a fitful bluster, whipping back and forth. Lucia's cropped blonde locks, now grown a little wild, began to lash against her cheeks; Mishani's newly cut hair did the same, escaping the jewelled combs she had used to tame it. She had the impression of movement on the periphery of her vision, slender, shadowy figures darting between the guards that surrounded them. But they were phantoms, and when she tried to catch them with her eye they were not there.

The surface of the river became a chaos of ripples, coldly glinting frills chasing each other with the switching of the wind. The Aberrants swam through, oblivious, cutting across the slow current of the Ko.

Then there was a howl, rising above the battlefield, and the first of them disappeared under the water.

The river was suddenly alive with a white churning. The Aberrants began to bay and shriek and hoot as their companions were sucked down, and the white froth turned pink. Spectral shapes, sinuous like eels, arced and slid among the Aberrants. They curled and swept and plunged, encircling their victims in the knots of their bodies and dragging them under as they dived. The Aberrants thrashed and twisted, but it did them no good. The river spirits caught them all, and none survived to reach the other side.

Some of the Aberrants, their fear of the spirits overriding even the urging of the Nexuses, tried to brake themselves at the river bank; but the momentum behind them tumbled them over, tripping those that followed, and in a clutter they slumped into the water. Hundreds more fell in that way, to be drowned in the Ko, until the Nexuses managed to gain control of the horde and check their assault. Gradually, the headlong rush dissipated, and the Aberrant army was still. Their only way to cross now was the Sakurika Bridge, and only a finite amount could cram onto that at once. The artillery, relentless, continued to pound them without mercy; but the animals paid no attention to the carnage being wreaked upon them, and whenever a hole was blown in the horde more simply moved in to fill it.

Seeing their enemy halted and frustrated, the forces of the Empire raised a triumphant cheer, echoed by the guards who stood on the hilltop with Lucia and Mishani. They gazed at her with fear and wonder and a kind of adoration, and though she did not see it through her closed eyes she sensed their emotion.

'I'm sorry,' she whispered, so quiet that only Mishani heard it; and Mishani felt a chill clutch of trepidation take her.

The air crawled with invisible conflict as the Sisters and Weavers engaged. The scope of their combat was immense. Not only did they seek to kill each other, and in greater numbers than had ever matched before, but they sought to manipulate the battlefield as well. The Weavers probed tendrils towards Lucia, trying to find her even though she, by dint of her unusual abilities, was invisible to them. They reached towards men's minds, to persuade generals to make rash choices, soldiers to turn on their brethren, to shift their fire-cannons so that they fired into their own allies. The Weavers were trying to take down the artillery positions that were accounting for so many of their troops, for they had no ranged weaponry to fight back with, but the Sisters worked to foil them, and thus far they had been successful.

Still, there were too many options, too many possibilities. Sooner or later, something had to get through.

Yugi, Nomoru and Barak Zahn watched the battle on the bridge from horseback. They were down near the river bank, in the thick of the men but out of reach of the fighting. Here, a circle of soldiers and a Sister was gathered round a sapper who crouched with his lantern at the end of a fuse. The fuse was threaded through a long, thin pipe that was buried just beneath the turf. It emerged from the end of the pipe near the bridge, where it was connected to a package of hidden explosives. Detonating this one would detonate the others that had been placed around the structure, and bring the bridge down. In case anything went wrong, there was another sapper nearby who had a secondary fuse.

The Aberrants were cramming onto the bridge now, and though they were gaining ground the soldiers made them pay dearly for every inch. The boards of the bridge were slippery with fluids, and the combatants stumbled as they fought. Terrible wounds were sustained on either side as blades and claws chopped through flesh, sometimes severing cleanly, more often not. Men were opened to the bone from armpit to thigh, shrillings tore away faces from skulls, ghauregs were hamstrung and crippled. Up close, the savagery of man against animal was unparalleled.

'Pull them back,' Zahn said to the Sister. 'Prepare to blow the bridge.'

The Sister wordlessly passed on the order to another of her kind, nearer the front, who advised the general that she accompanied. The rising wail of a wind-alarm signalled the retreat, and at once the soldiers on the bridge began to back away, allowing more of the Aberrants to crowd in.

'Light it,' Zahn said to the sapper, who touched the flame to the fuse. It hissed into life and disappeared into the mouth of the tube, burning its way along the darkness within. Elsewhere, the secondary fuse was also being lit.

The soldiers had retreated to the south edge of the Sakurika now, and they pressed forward again, bolstered by riflemen who picked off the taller ghauregs with headshots.

The fuse sparkled its way through the tube, across the arch and up one of the spandrels of the bridge, accompanied by another which burned up a different route. Two tiny lights in the darkness, racing towards a single destination. With the bridge down and the river impassable, they had only the feya-kori to worry about, and the blight demons had yet to make an appearance.

The second fuse caught up with the first, and they reached the hidden package at the same time.

And went out, inches short of the end.

Yugi's vision was not sharp enough to see the fuses being extinguished, but it was not long before he realised that the bombs had not gone off. He saw the line of soldiers at the far end of the bridge bowing under the press of predators, and knew that it was about to collapse.

'What happened?' he cried. 'Where's our gods-damned explosion?'

'The Weavers,' said the Sister, her red eyes unfocused. 'Heart's blood. The Weavers got to the fuses before we could stop them. They slipped past us. A trick . . . a trick that we did not know they had.'

Yugi looked back at the bridge in horror, and finally the line broke and the Aberrants surged through. They spread like oil onto the south bank of the river, and there they began to kill.

TWENTY-SEVEN

'Destroy it!' Yugi cried. 'We need that bridge down!'

The Sister to whom he was addressing this barely heard him. She was already immersed in the effort to do just that. Though the fuses might have failed, the Sisters could detonate the explosives themselves easily enough; in fact, they could tear the bridge apart without the need for explosives at all. It had always been intended as another backup in a situation such as this.

But the Weavers had guessed how crucial the Sakurika was to the Empire's battle plan, and they had got there first. By spinning false images of themselves, they had duped the Sisters into thinking that all their opponents were accounted for, when in reality several of them were slipping unnoticed through the Weave to the bridge, where they found the explosives and choked their fuses. The Sisters had not expected such deftness and cooperation in their enemy, and it had cost them. Before they could react, the Weavers had stitched a defensive position around the bridge, abandoning their attempts to influence other parts of the battlefield in favour of consolidating there. The Sisters swarmed around them, probing at them, feinting and retreating, but they had meshed solid and they were impenetrable. The Sisters had met their match.

'We cannot,' said the Sister who stood near to Yugi. 'We cannot destroy it.'

Yugi swore, looking over the heads of the soldiers to where the Aberrants were carving bloody swathes into the ranks. Close in, the predators had the advantage of greater strength; the secret to victory lay in keeping them at a distance, where they could be hammered by mortars and fire-cannons. He glanced back at the hill where Lucia stood, but it was too dark to see her now.

What is she waiting for? he thought angrily. If those river spirits were the best she could do, then they were all doomed.

'The artillery,' Zahn said. 'They are making for the artillery.'

Yugi looked, and saw he was right. The Aberrants were cutting a path towards one of the hills where the artillery positions were steadily massacring Aberrants on the far side of the river. Their push was costing them dear, for it was exposing them to attacks from the flanks, but by sheer weight of numbers they were winning through.

A portion of the artillery had been turned toward the bridge now; through the Sisters, word had already spread about the failure of the explosives. But any shells that came near were plucked from the air by the Weavers and fell harmlessly into the river.

Yugi and Zahn looked at each other stonily. 'Defend the artillery,' Yugi said. 'I'll take back the bridge. We have to hold them on the north side.'

Zahn nodded. 'May Ocha and Shintu favour you,' he said, and then spurred his horse and rode away, accompanied by his bodyguard. Yugi could hear his rallying cry as he went, and other soldiers began to join him as he raced to intercept the enemy.

Yugi looked over his shoulder at Nomoru. 'Can you get a position on the riverbank to hit the explosives?'

'They're hidden under the bridge. And it's dark. Won't be easy,' Nomoru said. She slid down from the saddle behind him. 'I'll try.'

'Don't forget the Weavers. They can stop a rifle ball.'

'We will be ready,' said the Sister. 'They can intercept shells, but a rifle ball is smaller and faster. We could get it through.'

Nomoru shouldered her rifle, cast a disparaging glance at the painted woman, and then looked up at Yugi. Her eyes were flat.

His gaze flickered over the radial scars on the side of her face. 'I'll send up a signal rocket.' He patted his belt, from which hung a small and innocuous cylindrical tube. 'Don't hesitate.'

'I won't.'

They paused a moment longer. There was something left to be said, but neither would say it. Then Yugi spurred his horse towards the pennant of the Libera Dramach, which was raised near the mouth of the bridge.

As he forged through the troops, smelt the stink of sweat, of cured leather and blade oil and smoke and blood and death from upwind, he could not shed the feeling that he was dreaming all of this. The withdrawal from amaxa root – he had not had the opportunity to smoke any tonight – and the presence of the spirits charging the air suffused everything with a muffling haze. It seemed as if they were all complicit in some sort of game in which the stakes were trivial things instead of lives. He simply could not encompass the sheer number of people who would die here today, who had died already. This kind of slowly settling unreality had threatened him in the past, but he had never been a general in a battle of such scope before. War was too big for him, and his only defence was not to think about it at all.

He reached the pennant. Faces were upturned in the green wash of moonlight, looking to him. It seemed easier to do what he had to than to consider it any longer. He raised his sword and shouted:

'Libera Dramach! We're taking back the bridge!'

The roar of approval, full-throated and bestial, was loud enough to shock him. His senses sharpened, his blood began to pound, and the haze disappeared. Suddenly, he saw everything with an incredible clarity. The wind lashed against him, blowing the rag tied around his forehead like a streamer.

'Forward!'

The soldiers surged around him in an intoxicating wave, and he was borne along on its crest, unable to stop a fierce cry rising from his own lips. The ranks before them either parted or joined the charge. The Libera Dramach collided with the Aberrants in a brutal smash of bodies and blades.

Yugi was one of several mounted men, and they rode behind the leading edge with their rifles at their shoulders, using their height advantage to shoot the Aberrants at close range. He primed, fired, primed, fired, drawing the bolt on his weapon with fluid ease between each shot, controlling his mount with his knees. His shots smacked into their targets with shattering force, spewing ribbons of dark blood: a ghaureg went down with a hole in the side of its neck; a feyn took a neat headshot and went limp; he put three in the hump of a rampaging furie before he got something vital and killed it. He did not have time to think about anything but aiming and shooting until his rifle clicked dry and he was forced to break open the powder chamber and refill.

He was in the midst of doing so when there was a shove from the side, and his horse toppled into a group of men with a neigh of distress. Yugi's rifle fell from his hand as he fought for balance, but somehow his mount righted itself. Only long enough, however, for the ghaureg that had forced its way through the soldiers to grab the horse's head in both hands and break its neck with a sharp twist.

But it had chosen the wrong adversary of the two to attack first. Yugi's blade flew from its scabbard and he hacked downward with all his weight behind it. The ghaureg's arms were cut through at the elbows, and it flailed backward, roaring in pain, until someone drove a dagger into the glistening black nexus-worm in its neck.

Yugi did not see the demise of his opponent. He felt the tip of the horse as it went over, and tried to scramble free of the saddle. By good fortune, he managed to jump aside and tumble as the horse crashed down, and he fetched up against the legs of a soldier who dragged him to his feet before he could be trampled.

'Are you hurt?' came a gruff demand. He shook his head, and the man patted him roughly on the shoulder. 'Then come on! We've got a bridge to win back!'

Heartened and strangely touched by the soldier's bravado, he grinned and shoved his way forward, with the other man closely accompanying him. At the point where the armies met, the battle lines were like liquid, flowing uneasily as men or Aberrants fell and the victors surged into the gap. Down here, in amongst the press instead of above it on horseback, the reek of sweat and the claustrophobia was overwhelming; Yugi was too charged with adrenaline to care.

He saw a man killed in front of him, and there in his place was a chichaw, a nightmarish thing like a giant four-legged spider, its head thick with curling horns like a ram's and with a long, beak-like jaw full of tiny teeth. He stepped into the gap left by the fallen man, his sword already sweeping a cold arc in the moonlight, trailing spatters of its last victim's blood.

The Aberrant lunged at him, lashing its forelegs, which he belatedly noted were edged with chitinous blades along their length. He pulled his body aside and they glanced across the leather armour on his chest, cutting a deep groove but not getting through; and he turned his sword stroke so that it hacked one foreleg off. The chichaw recoiled automatically at the pain. He used that instant to gather a great lateral swing into the creature's flank, opening it along the side so that its internal organs crowded out in a great steaming spume. It collapsed, juddering, in the throes of shock and imminent death.

A flash of movement on his right among the chaos of swords and teeth. He turned in time to see a furie charging him over the bodies of the fallen, a wall of muscle and tusk; but the corpses shifted beneath its weight and it stumbled, and then a great overhand chop from the soldier at Yugi's side severed it nearly in half. It slid in a broken heap at Yugi's feet, the sword still stuck in its ribs. Yugi wrenched the weapon out and threw it back to his saviour, who offered him a quick salute of thanks and was then swallowed by the fray.

Yugi lost track of time after that. His past and future contracted to a single instant in which he was *still alive*, where the aching of his body was a distant and dull nothing and his muscles and mind were geared only towards his blade. He cut and slashed, not out of conscious desire to kill but because it would make them stop trying to kill him. He moved along lines drawn by years of practice, dodging and slashing and parrying without thought as to where the next strike would go, not daring to imagine how close he had inched by death since this battle had begun, for to do so would break his nerve and crush him. At some point, he became aware of wounds on his body, deep cuts that he had felt as tiny nicks, dribbling warm blood across his skin. He ignored them. He could do little else.

And then a gap appeared in the moon-drenched phantasmagoria of horrors that faced him, and he saw the end of the bridge, a mere dozen metres away.

The sight of it caused him to pause. How long had he been fighting? How far had they come? He became aware of the yells and screams of men all around him, but there was a predominant tone which sounded like defiance. Their assault had been bolstered by other troops, men eager to lend their blades to a winning cause, and the rally had multiplied and invigorated the soldiers. Now, as the bridge neared and the Aberrants on the south of the Ko were being cut off from their reinforcements, the other soldiers pressed in with new zeal to drive the creatures against the river bank and into the water. The spirits embarked on a fresh frenzy, drowning any living thing that came within their reach. Yugi could taste cold, wet dirt on his lips. The air was becoming tighter still now, seeming to pluck at them, to lift them upwards. The moonstorm would soon be upon them.

Yugi wanted that bridge. With a cry that was more like a shriek, he fought on, and his men fought with him.

*

Nomoru ran low through the dark forest of soldiers on the south bank, careful to stay behind the lines of riflemen that loosed shot after shot over the river. Far behind her, there was the churn of combat on one of the hills, where Zahn was making a stand against the Aberrants that had made for the artillery position. Now that Yugi was steadily advancing to plug the mouth of the Sakurika Bridge, the creatures were finding themselves becoming isolated and were steadily being whittled away on all sides. Nomoru could not see over the heads of the soldiers, but she heard the reports, spreading from the mouths of the Sisters, out through the troops.

Idiot, she thought. *He will get himself killed.*

She was thinking of Yugi. She had not imagined him as one for heroics – and indeed, she suspected that the stories being circulated were more than a little exaggerated for the purposes of morale – but it bothered her. As she slipped along the river bank, accompanied by the clip and stutter of rifle fire, she wondered how she would feel if he *did* die. Probably very little, she had to admit. Their affair so far had been pleasurable, but no more than that. She was a woman who had grown up amid the depravity and impermanence of the Poor Quarter of Axekami, and her heart was thickly calloused because of it. Death did not really affect her. She did not allow any feeling to dig in deeply. It was not a conscious decision, but it was her way and she had never felt it necessary to examine that or try to change it. She existed on a constant level, untroubled by spikes of wild happiness or terrible sorrow. She was a survivor, and survival was a business best enacted without the luxuries of emotion.

She brought her concentration back to the matter at hand. She had gone some way along the river bank now, heading away from the bridge. The explosives had been secreted carefully: that meant that they presented a very tricky target, concealed as they were in the corners of the stonework. Nomoru, with a sniper's instinct, had taken account of where they were and was making for the angle that would present the best shot.

Well, that was not strictly true: the easiest angle to fire from was right at the side of the bridge, but there was no way she was going to be that close to the Sakurika when it went up.

Judging that the time was right, she slipped through the riflemen. The bank dipped sharply towards the water, and she clambered carefully down it and settled herself into a crouch, so that she was below the level of the guns firing over her head. The River Ko, a mere foot or two away, was quiet now, though the ripples of its surface still flocked this way and that with the unpredictable wind. Nomoru gave it an uneasy glance. The river spirits were still down there. Nomoru had a suspicion that if she so much as touched the water they would take her too.

She put it out of her mind and allowed herself to relax. She ignored the threat of the river, the fusillade ripping over her head, the oppressive atmosphere of the oncoming moonstorm. She ignored the endless barrage of artillery bombardment, and the distant sound of swords clashing and the bellow of ghauregs and furies. She set her rifle against her shoulder.

Gods, it was dark. The greenish, steely light, bright as it was with the clear sky and the three moons out, was barely adequate. When the moonstorm began, she would hardly have a hope. She calculated where she thought the explosives were, sighting past the near spandrels and up into the corner of one of the further ones. There; it had to be there. She shifted her aim slightly, sighting on another spot. There too. She could not see them in the shadow, but unless they had moved somehow, that was where they were. She only had an angle on two of them; the rest were obscured by the architecture.

Most would have said it was an impossible shot. But Nomoru liked a challenge.

The conflict between the Weavers and the Sisters around the bridge was so intense that Yugi could physically feel the atmosphere crawl. He looked more like some golem of the earth than a man now: he was caked and gloved in blood and muck, his muscles fuelled only by animal fury. They had stopped aching now: he had gone beyond tiredness. His strikes were unsubtle and clumsier than before, but enacted with more viciousness than he had believed himself capable of. His ears rang with the cries of men and he felt their burning adulation. Some faint, rational corner of his mind knew that they were inspired by him, but it was not clear why that was. He knew only that he fought in the forefront of a great column of soldiers that had carved its way deep into the clot of Aberrants on the south bank, and that at some point, as he wormed his boot through the slither of corpses to find solid ground, his foot came down on wood instead of dirt and he was on the bridge.

The realisation triggered something hitherto forgotten. Nomoru. He reached for the signal rocket at his belt, but the instant he took his attention away from the battle he almost lost his hand to some whip-tailed creature and was saved only by the intervention of one of the men who fought alongside him.

'The bridge! The bridge!' someone was crying, and a great cheer went up. Then Yugi felt himself propelled from behind as the soldiers of the Empire surged forward.

'No! No! Hold here!' he managed to shout, but his voice was overwhelmed. A clot of Aberrants on the bridge collapsed under the force of the surge, pulling one another down as they fell. Yugi tried to resist, but it was too much. He could only ride the crest of the wave.

He beheaded a ghaureg with a two-handed swipe, then twisted to break a skrendel's jaw with the pommel of his blade. In the frenzy he lost what it was he was trying to remember: there was no time for anything but combat. Trapped in a seething, whirling world of chaos and madness, Yugi managed only swift episodes of sense in among the blur of constant movement, and at some point he realised that they had managed to make it a third of the way across the bridge, and that the Aberrants were being driven back by the soldiers of the Empire, who fought with a primal elation at their own heroism.

Where would it end? Would they push onward into the Aberrant horde, into certain death, driven by a false sense of invincibility? Yugi did not know, and he could not have resisted it even if that were the case. It had gone too far to stop now.

But there was another enemy here, one he had not accounted for. He only realised it when the man to his left suddenly keeled over, fitting and spewing blood from his mouth and nose. The man who tried to help him did the same.

Weavers.

He felt the wrench as his muscles clamped up on him. He had experienced that agony before, in the Fold when he was forced to watch powerlessly as his friend and leader, Zaelis, shot himself. Then it had unmanned him. Now it was worse. It was no mere paralysis, this; he felt himself juddering, in the preliminary throes of a seizure. Soon the contractions would intensify to a strength sufficient to break bones, to crush organs. He fell, cushioned by the rough hide of his dead enemies, his eyes rolling wildly.

And suddenly it was gone, the grip loosened. Stamping feet were all around him. Blood dripped from his lips. But he was not dead. Somehow, through some twist of battle in the invisible realm, the Weaver that had been about to kill him had been distracted, forced to divert its attention elsewhere. But he could hear the shrieks around him as other men died, saw someone collapse nearby, milky foam frothing from between clenched teeth.

He did not need to think. Anything, anything was better than the touch of a Weaver. He wrenched the signal rocket from his belt and tore off the cap of the cylinder. On its top was a strip of coarse paper, which could be struck against another strip on the bottom of the cylinder, lighting the fuse through friction. He struck it.

A rain of sparks spewed from the cylinder. Lying in an island of burning white light on a shallow heap of corpses, surrounded by the pounding feet of soldiers, he held the rocket out shakily.

The ignition powder caught, and it shot upwards into the night with a scream, crisping the flesh on his hand with the backwash of heat.

Nomoru had observed the troops of the Empire as they battled their way onto the bridge. When she saw the rocket, she saw also that it had come from near the front of those troops, and knew that it had come from Yugi.

It did not give her an instant's pause. She fired four times in rapid succession, priming in between each shot: two at her secondary target as a decoy, and two at the largest package of explosives, the one which Yugi had intended to detonate in the first place.

The Sisters were true to their word, and were ready at the signal; but even with the Sister's best defence, the Weavers took out the first two rifle balls, stunning them in mid-air before they reached their target.

Two, however, was not good enough.

The Sakurika Bridge exploded, annihilated in a terrific bloom of flame and smoke all along its length. It blasted great tracks of white spume along the river, and sent wheeling planks of wood and lumps of stone high into the night, to splash into the water or to fall amongst the armies on the banks. Those men and Aberrants who were on the bridge when it was destroyed were obliterated instantly, and to either side dozens fell with burns or other injuries, or were thrown down by the concussion. The violence of the eruption rolled over the downs and echoed away into the night.

The author of that destruction put down her rifle, and looked at the pitiful shreds of wood that were left, their ends ablaze. She considered saying something, a few short words to herself in memory of the man she had just killed. But it would be pointless, and so she kept silent. She slipped up the bank and ducked under the riflemen, and was lost amid the ranks of the soldiers.

Zahn had finished off the last of the nearby Aberrants when the river lit up in fire. He reined in his horse, panting and wet with sweat, and looked down the hillside. Behind him, the fire-cannons and mortars still boomed, and the trebuchets creaked, flinging missiles which tore ragged chunks out of the endless expanse of predators on the far shore. It was safe now; the bridge was down at last. The enemy was trapped on the north side of the Ko. They could only retreat out of range and try to find another way around – a journey of many hundred miles, for they faced the Forest of Xu to the west and Lake Azlea to the east – or wait to see how long the spirits of the river would hold against them.

Then he heard a cry from the men around him, and he saw that the Weavers had unleashed their greatest weapon at last.

They rose over the crests of the distant hill, shadows against the horizon, but their incandescent eyes could be seen even from miles away, and they shone in the dark. Slowly they lumbered closer, their silhouettes growing as they ascended the hill, towering to the height of great siege-towers.

Feya-kori. Six of them.

Mishani and Lucia stood together on another hilltop. A light rain began to fall, chill droplets brushing against their skin and soaking into their clothes, blooms of darker colour spreading across the fibres.

'Yugi is dead,' said Lucia, her eyes still closed and her head bowed. Mishani looked questioningly at the Sister, who nodded in confirmation. The news glanced off her. It was mere fact, meaning nothing. She would find time to grieve when she could, but Yugi had never been a great friend of hers.

'The feya-kori are on their way,' said Mishani, her words caught up and lost in the wind. She looked at the sky, where the moons were drifting together. Clouds were boiling out of the air, sucking inward to the point where they would meet. Mishani felt her senses twining tighter and tighter; the storm was only moments from breaking.

'I know,' said Lucia.

The rain gathered in intensity; the wind picked up, keening across the battlefield. The feya-kori's moans drifted through the air as they approached.

'Lucia . . .' Mishani murmured.

'Not yet,' she replied.

'They are getting close, Lucia.'

'Not *yet*.'

The downs were ripped with a terrible shriek, making Mishani shudder, and a jagged fork of purple lightning split the night. The sky exploded in a thunderous roar. Wind howled, jostling them, and the rain drove down hard enough to hurt. Lucia lifted her face up, tilting it to receive the full force of the downpour. Above them, the moons formed an uneven triangle, scratched with churning clouds.

Her eyes flickered open.

'Now.'

TWENTY-EIGHT

The men surrounding Lucia fell back from her with oaths of terror as she called, at last, the full force of the spirits to their aid. Even Mishani stumbled away, shocked at the thing she saw in Lucia's place. Nothing physical had changed, but her aspect had warped. No longer were her features pretty and naïve in appearance, but sly and evil and chilling. The air became flat, difficult to breathe, tasting of iron. Mishani looked around her and saw that it was not only Lucia who had changed: the soldiers' faces were narrow and hateful, the Sister's painted countenance was shrewish and full of spite. Subtle whispers, promising half-imagined horrors, hissed in Mishani's ears. Flitting figures massed thickly in the moon-shadows. The presence of the spirits twisted perception, and never had it been so strong as now.

Lucia was standing still, her arms loose, her face upturned to the barrage of the rain as if it were a balm, blinking rapidly against its fury. She was soaked to the skin. Mishani, small and light as she was, had to fight to keep steady in the wind. She shielded her eyes with her hand and looked on fearfully. Steam was wisping from Lucia's clothes now, thin trails of vapour that congealed and thickened until Mishani realised what she was seeing.

Something was rising out of her.

The Xhiang Xhi unfolded from Lucia's body like the wings of some mythical demon, spreading and looming, its impossibly long fingers giving it the appearance of some vaporous and skeletal bat. A thin chalk figure, a shadow cast in mist, it was attached to her lower back like a ghostly incubus, covering her with the parasol of its hands. Its face was a blur, its size defying the eye as it seemed to change with every new angle. The soldiers cringed, and some of them ran, unable to take the overbearing weight of its presence.

Mishani would have run, too, if not for Lucia. But she had sworn to herself that she would not desert the child she had once thought of as a sister, and so she stayed, caught between honour and dread.

The feya-kori unleashed a long, discordant drone across the downs, loud enough to rattle swords in their scabbards. They had sensed their adversary and were issuing a challenge.

The Xhiang Xhi raised its hands, splaying its spindly fingers wide; Lucia opened her mouth, and the answering screech that came from her blasted outward like the concussion of a bomb, making Mishani clamp her hands to her ears, staggering back under the force of it.

The armies stilled. The artillery fell silent. The night was darkening as a blanket of cloud boiled out from the triad of moons, its underside flashing with lightning. There was a rumbling in the earth, at first so low that it could not be heard, but growing ominously louder. The wind had roused to a gale strong enough to push men over, and the armies of the Empire and Aberrants alike were thrown into disorder. Mishani fell to her knees in the mud, bracing herself as best she could on the hilltop. Lucia's bodyguards slipped and slid and held onto each other for support. Only the Sister stood firm against it, the pressure of the wind diverting around her and leaving her untouched.

The Aberrants went scrambling aside as the feya-kori walked through them on all fours. Some of them, blown by the wind or trapped by the press, were crushed like beetles, or burned by the noisome filth that dripped from the demons. The feya-kori drove on through the tempest, not slowed by it in the least.

The rumbling had become huge now, and the earth trembled in small judders. The soldiers cried prayers to the gods and almost broke ranks to run, but their generals barked at them and their legendary discipline held them in place.

The sky shrieked and boomed. A crooked tine of lightning struck the flank of one of the feya-kori, blowing a hole there, spraying acidic muck in great gobbets over the Aberrants below. The demon groaned and crabstepped sideways; then it continued onward, toward the river. The ooze from its body was seeping inward to close the wound in its side.

Mishani looked on, huddled low against the storm and slimed in mud, as more lightning came flashing from the clouds in strikes as fast as the flicker of a snake's tongue. Each one was accompanied by a resonant explosion that battered the ears and made her cringe. The world was turning to madness: everywhere was noise, the crashing and keening of the sky, the ceaseless bellow of the earth, the shaking of the ground, the shoving of the wind and relentless lash of the rain. And all this made worse by the disorientating influence of the spirits and the moonstorm combined, leaving her scared and paranoid. If she had had anywhere to run to then, even her honour would not have kept her by Lucia's side; but there was nowhere to go.

The feya-kori were being hit again and again, rocked by the lightning. And now their advance faltered, for the blows hurt them, and though they forged on towards the river they stumbled and flinched under the barrage. Mishani, staring through the sodden mesh of her hair, could see faces of spirits in the lightning, leering sketches in jagged light burned onto the darkness, slow to fade. And not only that: the wind's howls had changed tone now, becoming more and more like voices, distorted mutters, cooing and shrieks of nonsense, barely definable but intimating some kind of language.

Gods, let it stop, let it stop!

But though the lightning could slow the feya-kori, their wounds closed again. And though the wind could batter and shove them, they were too massive and too solid to be toppled. They came onward, towards the river.

Far back in the ranks of the Aberrant army, hidden from sight, the Weave-lord Kakre worked, surrounded by his retinue of ghauregs. His mind was largely gone, the connections in his brain fused and muddled by the impossible task of overseeing six feya-kori. Yet while he was with the demons, as part of this gestalt of Weavers, his faculties still held together. He had been subsumed into the whole, borrowing from it heavily. When this all was over and he was released from the net they had woven, he would be left a gibbering lunatic.

His judgement had gone awry long ago. Reluctant to relinquish power, he had given himself the most important position among those Weavers that pooled their abilities to call and guide the initial pair of blight demons. He had done so again with this larger gestalt, and it had been far beyond him, far beyond the powers of any one Weaver; but they would not know that until afterward, when they disentangled themselves. For now, he was entirely occupied with the feya-kori, attempting to steer them to his will.

The strikes that hurt the demons hurt Kakre also, as they did the other Weavers of the gestalt, who were hidden around the battlefield. Kakre cared nothing for the pain, however, nor for the Aberrants his demons were trampling. Without Avun, the Weavers did not see the need to preserve their troops so carefully; after all, their numbers were overwhelming, and even the great army ranged against them could not have held them off if it were not for the spirits brought into play.

But the feya-kori knew what to do about that. Though Lucia could not be touched by the Weavers, the demons could sense the Xhiang Xhi like a beacon.

Yes, Kakre saw the girl's plan, oh indeed. The Xhiang Xhi *was* the Forest of Xu: it had become so much a part of that place that it could not possibly leave its home without a host to carry it. And as it was a beacon to the demons, it was also a beacon to the spirits; Lucia had had to bring it here so that the spirits would flock to it.

He wished his predecessor had killed her when he had the chance. But even the best efforts of the spirits thus far were not enough to destroy his demons. The feya-kori were made strong by the blight that spread through the land, even as it weakened their opponents. Perhaps they were too strong to be stopped by any force left in Saramyr. They had only to get to Lucia, and it would all be over, the Empire's last hope gone.

Behind his Mask, Kakre's ruined face twisted in an idiot grin.

The rumbling became unbearable, and the earth split.

The noise was colossal. The ground was shaking so violently now that the soldiers were falling over, grasping at each other for support. The artillery juddered out of position; mortars went toppling. On the north side of the Ko, a vast slice of land suddenly dropped away, plunging downward with a grinding roar and a billow of dust. Hundreds of Aberrants pitched squealing into its depths; an instant later a great fan of magma blasted out, high into the night, a pyroclastic fury of black smoke and flame.

Mishani, near-mad with terror, could not be sure if the fearsome cackling visage she saw in the fire was real or imaginary.

The smoke of the explosion spread across the battlefield, whipped and torn by the wind. As the magma splashed to the ground to scald and kill, Mishani thought she saw shapes moving in the smoke, swift darting things like monkeys. At first she imagined they must be skrendel, but they moved with a jerky flicker, never seeming to be quite where she thought they were. They passed among the Aberrants, springing upon them, bending to bite and springing away again. The Aberrant predators were in a panic: even the Nexuses could not control them now. And still the earth shook and smaller rifts spread across the downs, slumped trenches of broken grass and turf.

The smoke blew clear in one patch, and the purple stutter of lightning illuminated the uncovered scene for a moment. Nothing moved there. It was as if the Aberrants had all frozen in place. It was only when she saw one of them crumble that Mishani realised they had been turned to earth, sod effigies of themselves, by the bite of the nimble spirits.

The ground split again, this time beneath one of the feya-kori. With a wail, the demon toppled, and the chasm swallowed it with another fountain of magma.

The armies of the Weavers were being slaughtered. The wind had turned to knives and was cutting the predators and their handlers to pieces. The land was bucking and heaving, and within the smoke that belched from the chasms deadly spirits moved. Lightning played, killing dozens wherever it touched. Only the Weavers remained safe, their defences too strong to be easily tackled.

But through it all came the feya-kori. One of their number had fallen, but they had reached the River Ko now, which seethed as fleeing Aberrants were drowned by the spirits there.

She cannot hold them back! Mishani thought wildly. *All this, and she cannot hold them back!*

Lucia was motionless, unaffected by the rain or the wind or the shivering of the land. Her face was still uptilted, her eyes now closed, her arms hanging limp at her sides. It took Mishani a moment to notice that her feet were not touching the ground, but that she hovered an inch above it. Only the Xhiang Xhi moved, its fingers flexing as if it were a puppeteer, its wispy body writhing slowly above its host. The moons glared down upon them from behind the churning mess of tattered cloud, as lightning raked across the feya-kori again.

Then the demons halted, right on the bank of the river. Behind them, their army was being decimated. Many were scattering as their handlers died and they reverted to their animal instincts. The demons paid no attention. Their burning eyes were fixed on a single spot, something invisible which had arrested their progress.

Mishani squinted against the storm, and she *could* see something there. A strange glittering in the rain on the south bank of the Ko, a shimmer in the air as if the veils of droplets had turned to crystal. The soldiers were retreating from that spot as the phenomenon became more pronounced. It separated into three, the light tightening and hardening into form and shape.

Mishani knew what was happening before it was finished. She had heard this tale from Kaiku, long ago.

They were the mad spirits of the moonstorm, the offspring of the goddesses that ruled the night sky. The Children of the Moons had come.

They towered over the soldiers of the Empire. In Kaiku's story they had been twice her height, but now they had manifested themselves as giantesses, forty feet tall, the same as the demons they faced. They wore the form of women, clothed in decayed grandeur. Their robes were of exquisite finery that had fallen into ruin, and from their wrists and elbows hung ancient artifacts that swung gently as they moved. A cold glow exuded from them, like the brightness of their parents, casting a grim and unforgiving light, and their hair was like feathers. But it was their faces that were most terrible, for their features were smooth like partially melted masks of wax, and they blurred and shifted. Only their eyes were stable, holes of utter black through which might be caught a pulverising glimpse of eternity.

The discipline of the soldiers broke at last and they ran from the monstrous entities. But the spirits were not interested in them. Their abyssal eyes were turned upon the feya-kori, and from beneath their robes they drew thin blades which shone with a cruel luminescence.

Lightning flickered and the sky shrieked as the demons and the spirits faced each other across the river. Then, as one, they plunged in.

The clash was brutal and short. The feya-kori had greater numbers and strength, but they were ponderous in their movements, and the Children of the Moons flowed around them like liquid. The feya-kori swiped and swung, beleaguered by the insignificant attacks of the river spirits, but they could not hit the Children. When the counterstrikes came, the effects were devastating. Mishani saw one of the whirling spirits cut the forelegs away from a feya-kori, so that it toppled face-forward into the river. Another was sliced in half along its midriff and fell into two pieces, the water steaming and bubbling as it toppled. In moments, the five feya-kori had sunk, and the Children of the Moon stood alone.

But they were not alone for long. Scalding vapour rising from their back and flanks, the demons rose out of the Ko with defiant groans, their bodies whole again, rejoined where they had been sundered. The water was turning black with the poison of their presence. The Children, their reactions unreadable, stood motionless.

Then the feya-kori attacked: five of them lunging at the same enemy.

Though two of them were cut to ribbons and splashed once again into the befouled river, their target could not avoid the rest. The feya-kori slumped onto one of the Children and it was borne under with an earsplitting shriek. Its brethren were upon the remaining feya-kori instantly, chopping them apart with surgical precision; but when the spirit got back to its feet again, Mishani noted how its movements were jerky, its outline indistinct and its aura less bright. The feya-kori had wounded it.

And the demons were reforming and emerging anew, sloughing off the small spirits of the river that were making futile attempts to drag them under again.

The entities met and matched. The splashing of their combat was like dull explosions under the cries of the storm. Rain-wet blades flickered and darted through the vile muck of the feya-kori, and the demons fell to pieces at their touch; but the spirit that they had hurt was slower now, and one of them caught it with a swipe of one club-like stump, smashing it hard so that it staggered. It guttered like a candle and then stabilised, but its light was noticably dimmer than before. As if it were not quite *there* as much as the other two.

As this was going on, the remaining spirits had not been idle. The Aberrant army had all but disappeared beneath the maelstrom. The ground was scored with chasms, smoke rolled over everything, small tornados roamed and lightning stabbed from the clouds; yet no move was made by the Weavers to retreat. They knew they would not get far if they turned and ran. Their only hope now lay in getting to Lucia, and that meant going through the Children. So they bent all their will to the feya-kori, and the Sisters did their best to harass and distract the Weavers; but between them, there was still a stalemate, and neither had much influence here.

Now the Children of the Moons raised their swords together and screeched. The noise made Mishani shudder and cover her ears. She was sodden and frozen, huddled and filthy, insensible with fear. The Xhiang Xhi raised its own hands, the spindly digits of mist splaying wide, and from Lucia's mouth came an equally inhuman scream in reply.

The effect was immediate. Mishani could hear it even over the storm. The sussurus of the river, hitherto a background murmuring, increased to an angry hiss. She looked down from the hilltop and saw that the rain-speckled surface of the water, churned with spume, was flowing faster now, dragging the white foam and the dark pollution downstream. The noise intensified, underpinned by a low roar, until it had become a rushing torrent, breaking its banks. The river was in flood.

The armies of the Empire – who had settled at a wary distance from the Ko after the Children had appeared – scrambled to draw back from their positions, but they were too close-pressed to move quickly enough. Some of those at the fringes were caught up in the drastic rise of the river and swept away. Men fought to rescue their companions or fled for cover. The misfortune struck the Aberrants also, but there were none surviving so close to the bank on the north side, and the flood waters merely swept away the dead and those that had been turned to sculptures of earth.

In the river, the spirits and demons faced each other again. Both were noticably struggling against the flow, but they kept their feet. The Children screeched again, and then they struck, cutting through their enemies: five feya-kori went down in pieces.

But this time there was no quarter. The Children allowed them no time to reform. They chopped into the water where the demons had fallen, slicing through the black scum to the sludgy bodies beneath. They squealed in a frenzy, hacking with gleeful cries, their blades throwing polluted water and bits of burning muck in all directions. The river boiled around them, and the slim, ghostly eels of the river spirits thrashed and dodged in between.

Downstream, a small gobbet of filth bobbed to the surface and was carried away for a second before the river spirits enwrapped it and pulled it under. Then came more, chunks of varying sizes that gradually dissolved in the flow.

The Children of the Moons butchered the feya-kori over and over, and the river caught up the pieces and flung them away so that they could not reform again. For almost five minutes the appalling violence continued, until one by one the Children of the Moons stopped cutting, and the river ran clear.

They raised their swords again and gave a scream that could be heard all the way to Saraku, and in response the spirits that were attacking the Aberrant army renewed their assault with savage enthusiasm. The Weavers' defences crumbled as the feya-kori fell: they had invested so much in the demons that their loss tipped the balance. The Sisters took them apart rapaciously, and as they began to fall the spirits turned on the Weavers too, no longer afraid of their power. In moments, none were left alive.

The Weavers were dead, the Aberrant army scattered or destroyed. Gradually, the smoke dissipated and the extent of the carnage was laid bare to the eyes of the soldiers of the Empire. A cheer went up, swelling as it was joined by others, until the sound of it carried over the storm, over the restless tremors in the ground and the din of the moonstorm and the howl of the wind. The cheer gained shape, and became a chant:

Lucia! Lucia! Lucia!

They had stopped the Weavers, crippled their forces utterly. Even if the Weavers could muster another army now, the forces of the Empire would be able to hold them. For they had Lucia, the girl who commanded the spirits. At last, their saviour had revealed her power. With her, they could march into Axekami and take it back. With her, they could do anything.

But only Mishani was close enough to see that the droplets running down Lucia's face were not only rainwater. There were tears squeezing from beneath her lids.

Slowly, the Children of the Moons turned their dreadful black eyes upon the soldiers, and the chant faltered and died.

'Lucia!' Mishani cried. 'Lucia, what have you *done?*'

The first strike of lightning hit one of the artillery positions and annihilated it, destroying the hilltop and everyone on it in a tiara of flame. The second lashed down in the midst of the army, killing a dozen men instantly. The soldiers barely understood what was happening until the shaking of the earth suddenly intensified and it opened beneath them: a long, jagged split ripped the downs, and hundreds of men fell screaming. The wind turned to a localised hurricane, picking people up and flinging them into the river where they were drowned. The army broke down entirely. Soldiers fled, their weapons discarded, crushing each other in their desperate attempts to get away. Thousands upon thousands descended into complete disorder, every one interested only in preserving their own lives against the awful, unknowable forces that had suddenly turned against them.

The Children of the Moons stepped out onto the shore, surveyed the scene of abject panic all around, and began to kill.

The banks of the Ko ran with blood on both sides now. The Children swept here and there with their blades, scything through bodies. Men fell in uneven fractions. The river lapped hungrily outward, flooding ever more, sucking in those who could not escape the torrent. Blackened corpses still crackling with purple electricity lay in ragged circles where the lightning had hit. The smoke was rising again from the gash in the earth, and movement could be seen within it; when it passed, it left turf statues in its wake.

'*Lucia!*' Mishani shrieked from where she lay in the mud. '*Lucia! Stop them!*'

But Lucia could not hear her, and the Xhiang Xhi paid no attention. It waved its hands above its host's head like the conductor of an orchestra. The Sister that had accompanied her as a bodyguard was looking from the carnage below to Lucia and back, uncertainty in her eyes.

A soldier came crawling up the hillside, fighting against the wind and rain, his eyes fixed on Lucia in supplication.

'Save us!' he cried. 'Save your people!'

But Lucia did not answer.

'Why won't you help us?' he demanded.

The Xhiang Xhi reached down to him, encircling him in its huge, spindly hands, and crushed him to a pulp with a cracking of bones.

Mishani screamed as blood spattered her. The horror and shock were too much. Her mind was frozen, her body paralysed.

Then Lucia jerked violently, as if some invisible force had punched her in the gut. The Xhiang Xhi shrieked, a long, drawn-out wail. And Lucia dropped, falling from where she hovered just above the ground. She collapsed as she hit the earth, crumpling like a ball of paper. The Xhiang Xhi, still attached to her, began to darken and attenuate, reaching toward the west, lengthening like a shadow at the end of the day until it stretched across the whole battlefield and over the horizon, to where the Forest of Xu lay. Then perspective twisted, and it was gone.

The effect on the spirits was immediate: they began to settle and fade. The river went quiet, its flow diminishing and retreating. The smoke from the chasm no longer hung in the air but sank and dispersed. The wind died, dropping from a hurricane to a light breeze. The lightning stopped.

Silence ached. Only the Children of the Moons remained amid the death that surrounded them. Their swords had lowered, and they looked up at the moons above. The clouds were coming apart; the unreal sensation in the air was passing. Even the rain had lessened to a drizzle, and finally stopped altogether.

The moonstorm was over. A shimmer passed across the Children and they disappeared. The three moons drifted their steady way apart in a gradually clearing sky.

Mishani was curled up, trembling, still in shock. The sense that the danger had passed was a relief too precious to believe. She was alive, she was alive, beyond all hope it had seemed. She would have lay there for much longer, if not for one thing: the reason she was even here in the first place.

Lucia.

She crawled on her hands and knees to where Lucia lay. A frail thing, eighteen harvests, her clothing plastered to her body. And red, red blood, soaking her stomach, where she had been shot.

Mishani sobbed her name, gathering her up so that Lucia's head lay in her lap, and shook her. Lucia's eyes flickered open, and they were blue and distant. She tried to smile, and coughed instead. Blood ran over her lips and down her chin.

'I'm sorry, Mother,' she whispered. Mishani knew then that it was not her face Lucia was seeing, but Anais'. Already her gaze was becoming dim.

'Ssh,' she said. 'Ssh, do not speak.' She looked up at the Sister, who was standing over them and looking down. Her make-up had not even been smudged by the rain. 'Can you not help her?' she demanded, her voice shrill.

The Sister shook her head sadly. 'The power that kept her from the Weavers' attentions keeps her from ours as well. We cannot touch her. I cannot heal her.'

'Then what good are you?' Mishani shrieked. The Sister did not answer, and Mishani turned back to Lucia. 'What good are you?' she murmured again, helplessly.

'I didn't know,' Lucia was saying, her eyes roving. 'I didn't know they'd take so many. They took so *many*, Mother. They said they'd only take a few. A few lives to satisfy them. Because they hate us. Because that was their price.'

'Oh, child,' Mishani wept. 'Why? Why did you do it? Why did you agree?'

Lucia coughed again. Her chin and breast were soaked in crimson now. The night had gone still. There seemed nothing in the world but the three of them on the hilltop.

'I couldn't let them down . . .' she whispered.

Mishani began to weep anew at that. Gods, this poor girl, this appointed saviour who had spent every moment of ten years under the crushing expectation of the world. Could she have walked out of that forest a failure, after all the lives already given in her name? No. She had taken the Xhiang

Xhi's bargain: a sacrifice in return for the spirits' help. Mishani could only imagine how that had torn her apart.

And now she was here in Mishani's arms, a rifle ball in her. Her skin was grey, her hair in wet draggles. Her slowing heartbeat pulsed in the crook of her collarbone. She was seeing beyond, into somewhere Mishani could not follow.

'Help me, Mother,' she said, her voice trembling. 'I don't want to die. I don't want to die.'

But Mishani could not form a reply. Her throat was locked with grief, her body racked by it, and all she could do was cry as Lucia gave a long sigh, and her last breath was driven from her lungs.

It was some time before Mishani heard the footsteps of Barak Zahn, and she looked up. He slumped to his knees, his face a mask of disbelief. He did not try to take Lucia from her. To do so would be to admit that it was real, that this had really happened, that he had lost his child for the second and final time.

She wondered how historians might one day justify this loss. Would they count it worthy that the Weavers' army had been stopped, even at such a terrible cost? No, there was not even that to offer succour. To destroy the enemy was one thing, but the armies of the Empire were destroyed too. There was barely enough in reserve to defend their lands now. The same could be said of the Weavers, but the Weavers bred armies faster and stronger than humans did. The two forces had wiped each other out, levelled the score temporarily, but the reality was that the Weavers had won in the long term. Without this army, they needed less food. They could survive another two years, perhaps three, on what they had. And in that time they could launch a new offensive, one that nobody could stand up to. The Empire had bought itself a stay of execution, no more.

Everything now relied on one thing. Cailin's plan had to work. They had to destroy the witchstones. It was their last and only hope.

Those soldiers that had survived stood around the tableau on the hilltop: their fallen saviour, her head in Mishani's lap; the broken Barak on his knees; the impassive Sister. They felt the uncertainty that Mishani felt, and they dared not think of the future now.

Among them stood a thin woman with tangled hair and a sullen cast to her face. She watched the scene for a time, then turned away. Grief and death were not new to Nomoru: she had seen enough as a child to last her a lifetime. Her only concern was that nobody knew who it was that fired the shot which killed their beloved Lucia. And beneath that, there was the slightest twinge of embarrassment at her shoddy marksmanship. After all, she had been aiming for Lucia's head.

When dawn came, the battlefield was empty. Starfall drifted down in the aftermath of the moonstorm like tiny flakes of glass, glinting as it caught the sun. The armies of the Empire would search for their comrades and loved ones when Nuki's eye had risen high, but until then they had retreated, unable to bear staying in the abattoir that the banks of the River Ko had become. No carrion birds or flies troubled the corpses: the residue of the spirits was too strong here.

On the north side of the river, amid the uncountable thousands of those that had died, there stood a mound of earth the size and shape of a small, hunched man. Its visage, what there could be seen of it, was a gaping face, emaciated like that of a corpse.

The effigy lasted until mid-morning, when the sun warmed and dried it. It began to crack slowly; and then the Weave-lord Kakre crumbled, bit by bit, until he was nothing more than powdery dirt on the wind.

TWENTY-NINE

Kaiku stood on the foredeck of the junk and looked bleakly towards the grey peaks. She clutched her robe to her chest with one hand, cinching it tight against the chill sea breeze. She could have warmed herself up with a thought, but she wanted to suffer. It suited her mood.

The sky was overcast, and though it was spring there was no hint of it today. A dozen ships swayed at anchor before and behind her. They shed small rowing-boats periodically that ferried back and forth from the drab shingle beach to the south, a slender finger of the Newlands that extended along the line of the coast and stopped just east of the looming, slanted bulk of Mount Aon.

For days they had been skirting the northern edge of Saramyr and there had been nothing but sheer black rock, great mountain walls that plunged vertically into the sea and offered no purchase for a landing. Kaiku had gone to starboard every morning and watched the thin plume of dark smoke from the volcanic Mount Makara drift steadily away to her right. And now here they were at their destination, a bay of stony beaches and hard planes of slate which ran inland for a few short miles before the mountains rose up again. This was where they were to make landfall, where the seven hundred Tkiurathi would disembark and make their way southwest to Adderach.

Their voyage had been favoured by Assantua, it seemed. The moon-tides had gone their way and the winds had been good. And though they had been forced to take a somewhat indirect route – passing Fo on its western side to avoid the heavily trafficked Camaran Channel – and more than once they had been forced to detour while the Sisters cloaked them from the attention of distant ships, still they had arrived on the exact day they had intended to. Or so Cailin assured them, anyway. Kaiku had stopped counting long ago.

The journey had been a miserable affair even before Kaiku had learned of the Empire's pyrrhic victory and Lucia's death. After that, she remembered little, and the discomfort and boredom of their confinement seemed insignificant in comparison to her grief.

She was trapped on this ship. Even her cabin held no privacy, for she shared it with two other Sisters, and that she counted as a luxury compared to the holds of the junks, where the Tkiurathi slept in cramped confinement.

She took to wearing the make-up of the Order, because when she did so people tended to leave her alone. Often she was seen wandering the decks at night like some dark spectre, and the sailors became used to the sight after a time and ignored her. The other Sisters mistrusted her; though Cailin had told nobody of their argument at Araka Jo, Kaiku's disdain for their cause was subtly evident, and they sensed this. Cailin was on another ship, and had maintained an icy silence which suited Kaiku.

In her more bitter moments, she found a dark satisfaction in the knowledge that Lucia's death had robbed Cailin of her champion, that the Pre-Eminent must have been furious to learn how her carefully laid plans for the Sisterhood's future had been ruined. But that was small comfort: it was a setback at worst, and Kaiku knew Cailin would overcome it. If the Weavers fell, it would be the Sisters that claimed the victory, and the Sisters that would rise to take their place. Kaiku could scarcely bring herself to care. Why should she concern herself with a world so full of horror and sadness, a world that seemed to exist only to break her heart over and over? She cared only for her sorrow, and nursed it well.

Now she watched the sailors taking the Tkiurathi to shore. They were eager to get off the junks, having been tormented by conditions during the long journey. Though they had endured it without complaint, they hated to be penned in, and the overcrowded ships – much smaller than the massive vessels that had brought them across the sea from Okhamba – were claustrophobic in the extreme.

In less than a week, it would all be over. Seventy miles across the mountains lay the first monastery of the Weavers, and beneath it the first witchstone. Given that they were unsure of the terrain, they could not be certain of the exact timing of their arrival, but they kept in sporadic contact with the Sisters that accompanied the desert forces which approached from the south, and they coordinated in that way. Their activity in the Weave was heavily disguised: each communication was attended by several Sisters to ensure that no hint of their location could be divined. Their part of the operation relied on stealth.

If all went to plan, the Weavers' forces would be drawn out of Adderach to meet Reki's army in the south, whose progress had been well marked. They would not expect an attack from the north, from the sea. Kaiku doubted greatly if the Weavers would extrapolate a threat to Adderach from the daring breakout the Sisters had achieved at Lalyara: for all the Weavers knew, they were simply trying to save the Empire's fleet, and had sailed south to the safer ports of Suwana or Eilaza. Besides, the Weavers did not know that Muraki tu Koli had given away their plans; that much was evident by the way they fell into the ambush at the River Ko.

The prospect of having done with it all, one way or another, was comforting to Kaiku. She did not consider the shades of grey between success and failure: either the Weavers would be destroyed, or she would. She held on to the memories of her family, of Tane, of Lucia, and used it to fuel her hatred.

Death would not be so bad now, if it could take her away from the cruelty of this world.

But first there was something she had to do. When they reached the barrier of misdirection that the Weavers would certainly have erected around their monastery, she would have to wear the Mask again.

It lay still in her pack in her cabin, now at the bottom and buried in clothes. At night, it whispered to her, tempting her with promises of her father. It was infused in some way with his essence, an essence that it had robbed from him, as it was also infused with hers now. If she wore it, could she once again attain that peace of her childhood, the comfort of her father's presence, the unthinking security he offered? No, she would not allow herself the luxury. It was a narcotic, offering anything she wanted in return for taking everything she was. But each time she was forced to use it, it became harder to resist, and after so long in such close proximity she had almost caved in more than once, hoping for refuge in its warm folds. Only her sour and venomous abhorrence of the Weavers and their devices kept her from doing so.

But when they came to the barrier she would have to put it on. Though the Sisters were capable of getting through without much effort, there was no guarantee that the Weavers would not detect their intrusion, and the element of surprise would be lost then. The only sure way they had of passing unnoticed was the Mask.

This Mask, this Mask that had cost her family's lives, was still one of the most important weapons they had. There had been no others: those Masks that the Sisters had taken from dead adversaries were too old and powerful to dare investigate, and would kill or corrupt any Sister that wore them.

So it was down to Kaiku. She would have to lead seven hundred Tkiurathi and almost fifty Sisters through the barrier. It would take hours, and she would be wearing that awful Mask all that time.

Her eyes flickered over the mountain peaks, and she sighed. Let it all be over. Just let it be finished.

She sensed somebody by her side, and turned slightly to acknowledge Tsata. He had been wary around her ever since she had learned of Lucia's death, unsure whether she needed him to comfort her or if she wanted to be left alone. There had been little talk between them lately. He had busied himself with matters among his people in the hold.

'How are the Tkiurathi?' she asked. Her voice seemed foreign to her, older than before.

'Well enough,' he replied. 'They know how much is at stake since the battle at the River Ko. They will not falter. The journey through the mountains will restore their spirits after so long trapped in these ships.'

Kaiku brushed her hair away from her face. 'What will you do . . . afterward?' She looked at him. 'When this is all done?'

Tsata held her gaze for a long time before replying. 'That will depend on how things turn after we have reached Adderach,' he said. 'I will not say I have not thought on it, but there are too many factors.'

Kaiku nodded in understanding. It was no evasion; he was being honest. But honest though he was, he had picked up a habit of employing Saramyr ways while dealing with Saramyr, and the unspoken implication was clear. What it depended on was her.

And what did *she* want to do? She had no answer to that. The only person other than Tsata she had left was Mishani, but who could say in what direction their lives might take them? Tsata would probably return with his people, and Mishani would engage herself in something diplomatic which would keep her travelling. But for Kaiku, there was only a void, an emptiness that would be left by the fulfilment of her promise of revenge. In happier times she might have thought of it as boundless opportunity, but now she saw only a frightening loss of purpose.

She felt a surge of resentment. Why *should* he rely on her? Why should her decisions be so important to others? Why, if the world was so determined to wound her, was it so reluctant to let her divorce herself from it?

She realised that she was succumbing to self-pity again, and caught herself. No, she would not go that way. This man at her side loved her, and he was a man worthy of her love in return; it was her fault that she was reluctant to give it, and no one else's. There were things she wanted to say to him, things that nestled so deep in her that she did not know whether they would survive the journey out, the harsh process of speech. Promises, pledges, oaths. Words that were solid and real, to fix her back to the world of light and laughter that she had drifted away from. But everything seemed so frail and ephemeral to her now. She wanted to tell him these truths in case either of them should die in the coming conflict, so that he would not be left unknowing, but she realised also that if they did *not* die, she would have to live with the things that she had said, and she was not yet ready for that.

She could not think on it. It was a decision too great for her in the face of all that was to come. Afterward, let things fall as they may. For now, there was only revenge, and the promise of an ending. The world was glutted with death these days, but it could stand a little more.

'Are you ready?' Tsata asked at length. 'It will soon be my turn to go. I would like it if we went together.'

'I will get my pack from my cabin,' she said. *And my Mask*, she added silently, and heard its glee like a whisper behind a wall.

'I will wait for you, then,' he said after her, as she began to walk away.

She stopped and looked over her shoulder. '*Would* you wait for me?' she asked, and by her tone he knew she was talking about something entirely larger than a simple boat journey. 'How long would you wait?'

'Until all hope was gone,' Tsata replied, without a trace of embarrassment. 'Until it hurt me more to be with you than to be without.'

Kaiku felt something buck painfully in her chest at that. She found that she could not meet his eye, and that if she stayed any longer under the intensity of that gaze then she would begin to cry. She was so terribly fragile, and she hated herself for it.

'I will not be long,' she said, and left; but whether she meant it in answer to Tsata or in relation to fetching her pack, even she did not know.

It took them six days to reach the Weavers' barrier. Six days before Kaiku put the Mask on again, and for the first time in what seemed like forever, she was happy.

The hooves of Reki's manxthwa crunched steadily over the loose gravel on the floor of the pass. He was watching the gristle-crows circling overhead in the flat light of the dawn, his eyes tight with distrust. The air was dead and still.

He rode with his hand near the hilt of his nakata. His hair was tied back in a short queue to keep it out of his face in battle; it made his scar more obvious. The beige leather of his armour creaked as he moved, and his expression was grim with concentration.

Reki had been keeping in contact with the Tkiurathi force since landfall, and in that time the tension in his men had grown unbearable. The Aberrants had all but disappeared, except for the gristle-crows that shadowed them from high above, out of rifle range. In less than an hour, if the Sisters' estimations were correct, they would be coming up against the Weavers' barrier. The Tkiurathi had already successfully penetrated it during the night, and were lying in wait in the mountains just inside the perimeter. But there was no sign of any opposition. Even the skirmishes that had whittled at his army in those first weeks had ceased.

It was too easy. And this pass was too dangerous: a shallow-sided valley of shale and granite, bulwarked on either side by peaks. After so many days of struggling to find navigable trails through the hostile heights, he should have been glad that they at last had a few smooth miles to walk. His men had been taxed to their limits by the journey, and they needed a rest, but the pressures of time would not allow it. The longer the day wore on, the more chance that the Tkiurathi would be discovered by roaming gristle-crows within the perimeter of Adderach, and their deceit would be revealed.

So they had to come through this eerily silent pass.

All the scouts he had were scouring the surrounding land, but they reported nothing. He asked the Sisters that travelled with him, but they had no answer. Perhaps the Weavers were consolidating around Adderach. Perhaps even inside it. That would make things extremely problematic. It would be much harder to winkle the Weavers out of their lair if they had settled in to a defensive position, and it would give them time to destroy their own witchstone if it came to a last resort. That, as far as Reki understood, would be disastrous.

Asara rode alongside him, in the midst of the army of desert warriors that moved uneasily down the narrow route through the mountains. Her manxthwa murmured and snorted and shook its head as it plodded, apparently oblivious to the prevailing mood of foreboding.

She was trying to reconcile the man at her side with the boy she had first seduced, long ago, in her capacity as a spy for the Libera Dramach. It was no good. He was no great warrior – his skills lay in tactics, and he never fought in the frontline like some Baraks did – but he certainly looked like one now. Once he had been shy and uncertain of himself; now he was lordly and assured, and people responded to that and followed him.

Asara had watched that change, due in no small part to her. Having a lover and later a wife of such staggering beauty did wonders for his self-esteem. She had been unfailingly supportive and loyal, guiding him towards strength, and he had done whatever she suggested. When he was with her, he believed he could achieve anything, and believing made it so. Four years had passed swiftly for her. At her age, time was accelerating faster and faster. She had the body and face of a twenty-harvest goddess, but the soul of a woman of ninety.

However, things were not as they were. A cloud had gathered over their relationship and was darkening rapidly. He was asking about her past, and he would not let it lie. His love for her was poisoning him. His imagination fashioned dozens of different scenarios that he tested her with to see her reaction: desperate suggestions as to how she might have lived her childhood, as if she might give away some signal when he struck on the right one. It had become an obsession, a worm of doubt that had grown into something monstrous and gnawed him inside, feeding on the magnitude of his passion for her. Had she not won him so utterly, he might have managed to be content with ignorance; but she had long experience of men and their ways, and she knew that this would consume him until he was either satisfied or driven to some mad act. She had known men slay their partners in frustration when in the throes of such torment, or cast themselves from cliffs.

Even a lie would not be enough, now. Soon it would be time to leave.

Her whole life had been a sequence of transitory episodes, always forced to move on as her nature became apparent. Eventually people noticed that she did not become old, or that she healed from wounds uncommonly fast, or that people had a strange tendency to die in any place where she settled. The Sleeping Death had struck several times in the last few weeks, causing consternation among the men and fears of a plague. It was unwise, but Asara was hungry. Hungrier, in fact, than she had ever been. And she knew exactly why; had suddenly, unequivocably understood when she woke in the night less than a week past.

She was pregnant with Reki's child.

Even the Libera Dramach, where her Aberrancy was acceptable and known to some, she must leave behind now. Cailin would learn in the end that Kaiku had been persuaded into completing her part of the bargain struck with Asara long ago. Asara was beholden to Cailin no more. She had what she wanted. But Kaiku's misgivings at allowing her to become pregnant would be shared by Cailin. It was simply not politic to let Asara breed, to run the risk of allowing her to become the first of a race of beings that could change their outward shape at will.

Asara believed that Cailin would kill her if she ever knew. And kill her children too. So she would never return to Araka Jo, nor ever have any part of the Libera Dramach or the Sisters again.

Then why not go now? said the new voice in her mind, the voice that thought of her child first and only and always. *You have what you want from him. If you make yourself part of this battle, you could die; and what you carry is too precious to lose. You have a duty to survive now.*

But as much as she believed that, she could not leave. There was one thing left to do.

A cry from somewhere in the army brought her attention sharply back to her surroundings, and, seeing that everyone was looking up, she followed their gaze, and saw the Aberrants.

They were swarming down one side of the pass, a heaving mass of claws and fur and hide and teeth; and there, on the other side, more of them, coming from behind as well.

'How did we not see them?' Reki cried, unsheathing his sword. He turned to the Sister that rode nearby. 'How did you not know?'

Her expression was grim; she did not seem surprised or horrified, but resigned. 'They have learned to disguise themselves well,' she said.

Reki shot her a look of disgust and dismissed her with a snort. The sound of rifles was crackling along the flanks of the army as they arranged themselves defensively. The gods only knew what chance they would have against this. The Aberrants kept coming, thundering down the sides of the pass.

'Stay with me, Asara,' he said; then he muttered a quick prayer to Suran, and the first of the Aberrants reached them.

THIRTY

The pale light of Nuki's eye grew over Adderach, illuminating madness.

The oldest monastery of the Weavers was a testament to the insanity that saturated their kind. Though the other monasteries were similarly chaotic in their architecture, nothing came close to the nightmarish creation that they had raised on the spot where they had first found a witchstone, where Aricarat had ensnared them and turned them, unknowing, to his will.

It towered at the foot of Mount Aon, built primarily of stone the colour of sand, a bewildering agglutination of forms fused together in a pile that possessed a fractured logic all its own. Domes like bubbles poked out at odd angles from brickwork that varied wildly in size and shape. Walls slumped or curved, perhaps once intended to encircle something but never completed. Surreal statues, dream-images both fascinating and terrifying, were frozen in place, scattered randomly about the surroundings or growing out of the monastery itself. Walkways jabbed from the main body of the structure, half-completed. Spires tipped crazily, corkscrewing along their length.

The monastery sprawled in all directions. Half of the place was derelict, as were the majority of the outbuildings, which were themselves incredible demonstrations of caprice. Most of them looked ridiculous, but some showed hints of genius in their construction that the best sane minds in the Empire had never come close to matching.

Where the Weavers' ideas came from, even they did not know. But just as the Masks took pieces of their owners and passed them on, so did they possess pieces of their progenitor. The knowledge they contained – most of it far beyond the grasp of the Weavers' minds – would reveal itself in dreams and visions and moments of insight that the Weavers could not possibly have attained by themselves. Through the addle of benighted understanding, revelations were glimpsed like lanterns in the fog, some so incomprehensible that they sent their witnesses further into madness, and others lying just on the cusp of reason, that the Weavers might act on. Strange mathematics, unheard-of techniques of manufacture, combinations of reagents that would produce astounding results, patterns of logic: ideas, ideas, ideas.

The Weavers were inefficient conduits for their unseen master, but eventually the results leaked through. For every thousand misfires there was one moment of shocking clarity, and the Weavers built on these. Beneath the anarchy of Adderach there was cold, hard purpose.

The Tkiurathi attacked in the early morning, not long after they received the news that Reki's forces had been ambushed. They had crept inward from the perimeter as the dawn broke, their progress cloaked by the power of the Sisters. When the first of the gristle-crows began to appear, the Red Order deflected them so that they turned away and looked elsewhere. Once a Weaver surveyed their area, his attention crackling over them, but he was easily blinded by his skilful opponents. The Weavers were evidently not on any alert: after all, they had been steadily tracking the progress of Reki and his men for days now, and knew exactly where they were. They were confident of having their enemy safely within their grasp.

As Cailin had hoped, they did not expect an assault from the north.

When the moment came, the Tkiurathi broke cover at a run, howling battle-cries. Kaiku ran in the rearguard with some of the other Sisters. There were perhaps two hundred Aberrants, scattered across the rocky surrounds of Adderach as guards. As soon as they noticed the enemy, they raced to intercept.

Two hundred Aberrants could have done a lot of damage, even to such consummate warriors as the Tkiurathi, but they did not coordinate themselves, instead rushing at the army in clots and drabs. The Tkiurathi took them to pieces.

Kaiku felt a surge of fierce joy at the sight of Adderach, revealed there before her as the incline bottomed out and they rounded an outthrust root of the colossal Mount Aon, which rose into the insipid sky to her right. The proximity of their target and the battle ahead served to stir her from the maudlin reverie she had sunk into ever since she had removed the Mask the night before. Gods, even now she could remember the awful joy of it, and half her mind was telling her to take it from inside her dress and put it on, that she would seem so much more fearsome and formidable wearing it over her face. But she was already wearing one mask, that of the Red Order. She told herself that it was enough to serve her, and held onto that one to stave away the temptations of the other.

She caught sight of Tsata at the fringe of the horde, but then he was gone again. She had only a glimpse of him, his face fiercely intense as he swept toward a rampaging group of furies, and then the Weavers attacked.

The force of it was staggering. The Sisters had not expected such *rage*. Their enemies came through the Weave like demons, with a vigour beyond anything Kaiku had ever faced from them. They were angry at being duped, that much was evident; but more, they were angry that *women* were here, that they had penetrated the sanctuary of man this way and appeared, uninvited, so close to the heart of them. And under that anger they were desperately afraid, because they knew now that they had made a mistake and that their adversaries were close enough to reach their most precious treasure.

That first clash was a brutal one, and the Sisters almost buckled under the power of it, for they could not devote all their resources to the combat while they were still attending to the physical world in some degree. They were hampered by the necessity of running towards the monastery, and were fighting on the fly. But the Weavers' rage worked against them and made them clumsy, and after the shock of the initial impact the Sisters rallied and fought back, spinning traps and tricks into their path.

Kaiku was guarded by several Tkiurathi, as were the other Sisters, and she took her cues from their movements as to where to place her feet while she looked into the Weave. She was darting and shuttling, meshing with the efforts of her companions, as if she were one of a dozen needles working in perfect unison to knit fabric. She felt a blaze of satisfaction as the Weavers ran into their traps, or pulled up short to avoid them. Those that were too slow became ensnared and were pulled to pieces by the Sisters, or lost themselves in closed labyrinths, leaving their bodies in a drooling, vegetative state while their minds ceaselessly wandered.

Cailin had schooled the Sisters ruthlessly in the tactics they would employ, and Kaiku sensed several of the Order tracing away under cover of the battle to find Nexuses. With the Weavers distracted, the Sisters were free to hunt the masters of the Aberrants through the links that were strung between the nexus-worms embedded in both Nexus and predator. It was a discipline that they had learned from Kaiku. She had been able to do it intuitively the first time she tried, back in the Xarana Fault, but it had proved oddly difficult for most of the other Sisters. Now they had the art of it, and the Weavers were too busy to prevent them. They followed the links back to where the Nexuses were and burst their internal organs. The controlling minds behind the Aberrants faded, and those beasts that the Tkiurathi had not killed ran into the safety of the mountains.

At some point during the conflict, Kaiku noted a diffuse spray of threads heading away from them across the golden vista that she operated in. A call for help, directed south. Just as Cailin had planned.

The Sister to Kaiku's right stumbled, fell with a strangled cry. The Tkiurathi behind her caught her, bearing her up, but Kaiku knew it was useless. The Weavers had got to her. Her essence was destroyed now, and her body was an empty husk, which would soon wind down and stop without the spark of life to empower it.

There were many Weavers here, more than there were Sisters; but the Sisters were better, even with the new tricks that their opponents seemed to learn with every conflict. It would be a hard fight, but it was one they could win. At least until the other Weavers that had been occupied with Reki's forces joined in.

Time was against them. They had to find and penetrate the witchstone before then, or they would be overwhelmed.

Obsessed with the fight, Kaiku barely noticed the deafening tumult of the Tkiarathi, the thudding of feet and the giddy rush of the charge. The Aberrants had all but ceased to be a threat now, and it was only the Weavers that concerned her. But as she neared the monastery, its baroque and twisted spires reaching high above, she began to notice something else. The witchstone. She could feel it, all the way out here, throbbing through the earth. Its power dwarfed the other witchstones she had come across before, a venomous and malevolent strength like nothing she had ever encountered. If they could sense it all the way out here, what must it be like to stand before it? For the first time, doubts began to creep in.

I will ease your mind, promised the Mask that was hidden in her dress, close to her breast.

For an instant she faltered, stumbled a little, and in that moment a Weaver slid at her along the Weave like the thrust of a rapier. It was only by Cailin's intercession that the strike was turned aside: she wrapped the point of the attack in threads like swaddling a hot poker in towels, and thrust it away.

((Kaiku, concentrate!)) came the swift admonishment. Kaiku felt a surge of resentment at being scolded so, and used it to clear her mind of the Mask's whisperings. Hatred was her ally here, no matter whom it was directed at.

Then they were at one of Adderach's many walls, a spot between two wings that snaked away like angular tentacles on either side on them. It was curved and bowed inwards, constructed of uneven layers of brick and what looked like whole boulders suspended in a matrix of mortar. The Tkiurathi were bunching around it expectantly.

((With me)) came the order, and Kaiku and several other Sisters broke off portions of their consciousness from the front line of the battle in the Weave and sent them spinning in Cailin's wake. They sewed themselves along the length of the wall, and it detonated in a blast of sandy powder. It slumped inward on itself, leaving a wide hole, strewn with rubble.

The Tkiurathi headed for the breach and poured inside. Kaiku followed, pulling out of the Weave as she clambered over the shifting chunks of stone amid the flood of tattooed folk. Several Weavers had already fallen, and there were enough Sisters to do without her now.

The morning light brought unbearable brightness to the shadowy interior of the monastery, and it echoed with the sound of the Tkiurathi's feet and voices. Much of the room was covered in debris, but she could see that it was cavernous, and that its walls were built at drastically uneven angles, higher at one end than the other. A great semicircular opening fringed with what looked like human hair led out of the room. There were other doorways, but they were too small for anything bigger than a dog. The twisted perspective made her head hurt.

Then Tsata was at her side, scrambling up from behind and taking her arm. She welcomed the sight of him; together they ran through the debris and onward, where the Tkiurathi were spreading through the building. Small clashes began as they came across those Aberrants that were still trapped inside.

Adderach was just as demented within as without. Rooms narrowed to nothing; doors had been built but no doorways; corridors were like mazes.

Every room brought some new strangeness. They came across a chandelier of crystal hanging incongruously over what looked like a butcher's table, with fresh and bloody meat strewn everywhere. There was a sculpture twice the height of a man that was shockingly hideous and yet masterfully crafted, standing in a room that had been built with no doors. It was only revealed when one of the Sisters blasted a hole in the wall. One room was round and sloped down towards a circular pit, and from the blackness came hungry howls. There was little they came across that had any obvious purpose, and certainly there seemed to be nothing like dining rooms or other places of gathering. There was only the evidence of a speedy evacuation: food and rubbish everywhere, fires left burning while stew bubbled over, torches still blazing where they had been dropped. Kaiku had expected to find golneri everywhere, the diminutive servants of the Weavers, but while the presence of cooking equipment and their footprints in the dust suggested that they were around, there were none to be seen.

There were, however, dead Nexuses. Their elongated bodies, freakishly tall and thin and clad in black robes, were twisted in the throes of death. They lay in various contortions, blood weeping through the eyeholes of their blank white masks. Kaiku's stomach turned as she remembered what she had seen when they had looked beneath those masks. Tsata, who had shared her experience, gripped her shoulder reassuringly; she laid her hand on the back of his in acknowledgement.

These, then, were the Nexuses who had been coordinating the small defence force outside. And yet still it all seemed too easy, and there were too few of them.

She rushed from room to room with Tsata and several other Tkiurathi, often backtracking as they were foiled by the Weavers' architecture, sometimes blasting through the wall when it was possible to do so without bringing the upper levels down on them. She could sense other Sisters there, scouring the corridors above her, hunting their way up to the spires.

Presently, she came face-to-face with Cailin, who stalked into the room from another doorway. Semicircular discs of metal had been embedded in the walls and floor and ceiling of this chamber, their edges etched with markings that Kaiku could not identify. Cailin picked her way across to Kaiku, accompanied by the Tkiurathi that were guarding her.

'This is wrong, Cailin,' Kaiku said.

'Indeed,' she replied. 'Where are they all? Where is the resistance? They are not in the levels above; that much I am certain.'

Kaiku tapped her foot on stone. 'They are below. They have retreated and they are waiting for us to come to them.'

Cailin met her eyes, and it was clear that she had thought the same. The conflict in the Weave buzzed around them, tickling their senses. Kaiku was keeping sporadic checks on it, but the Sisters had matters in hand.

'Can you sense it?' Kaiku asked. 'The witchstone. Already it hampers my Weaving; I cannot see the layout of this cursed place, nor see a way down.'

'There are many ways down,' said Cailin. 'It does not foil me as it does you, but I think that will change as we get nearer.' And Kaiku saw the ways as Cailin broadcast a blaze of knowledge to all her brethren. The answering mesh of information came smoothly back: the Sisters all knew their place, whether it be continuing to fight off the the Weavers, checking the remainder of the upper levels, keeping in contact with the Sisters who fought with Reki or heading downward to whatever lay beneath Adderach.

Abruptly the battle in the Weave collapsed. The Weavers, as one, faded from the field, drawing back into themselves. The Sisters, bewildered, made to follow, but Cailin forbade them.

((Do not be drawn in. We will descend and face them there))

Adderach was eerily silent. There was no fighting, whether physical or in the Weave. The place was still, but for the pulsing of the witchstone beneath their feet.

'Come,' said Cailin, and she swept away. Kaiku followed, Tsata and the other Tkiurathi with her. They were somewhere near the centre of the edifice, Kaiku knew that much. Other Sisters were heading for other routes down. The Tkiurathi were draining into them too, leaving Adderach and its surrounds empty. They did not have a large enough force to retain a guard on the surface, in case an enemy army should arrive. If they did not succeed below, then their only chance at survival was to get out and away before the Weavers answered the distress call sent a short while ago.

Otherwise, they would be trapped down there.

Asara fired, primed, fired again. It took two more shots to get through the latchjaw's thick skull, but eventually she hit the brain. It slumped to the ground, its great porcupine-like quills shivering as it settled.

Grimed with sweat and dust, she took quick stock of her surroundings and located Reki. He was in the midst of a crowd of men, his nakata drawn but unbloodied; he was well protected. They struggled with another pair of latchjaws, squat monstrosities with fanged snouts, covered in deadly spines. They had stubby feet that protruded before them, their three digits stumpy and clawed; they had no back feet at all, only a short tail which they dragged behind them. Though they were cumbersome, they were fast enough in a lunge and their spiky armour meant that they were incredibly dangerous at close quarters.

She looked around. The floor of the pass was thick with fighting, but the desert warriors' core still held strong, due in no small part to the fact that most of the Aberrants had already left. At first the overwhelming tide of predators had taken a great toll on them, but Reki's generals had wisely kept up the defensive until their reprieve came. At some unseen signal, which Asara guessed had come from the Weavers at Adderach, the larger proportion of their attackers had broken away and headed northward up the pass. But they had left enough to keep the desert warriors busy for quite some while, and the battle continued on. Their situation was not quite so desperate now, but it was far from comfortable.

Reki was casting about for a sight of his wife, and relief showed on his face when their eyes met. She had become separated in the melee; now she slung her rifle across her back, drew a dagger and began to make her way to him, shying away from the swell of conflict as it loomed close to her.

The latchjaws had succumbed at last to their wounds, after taking down three of Reki's men, and his Blood Tanatsua bodyguards were regrouping around their Barak. They parted to allow Asara through. Reki regarded her for a moment, then unexpectedly he embraced her, driving the breath from her. He recoiled with a grunt, looking down at his hand.

Asara took it, concern on her face. There was a deep scratch along his palm, where the tip of the dagger she held had caught him. Blood welled up from within. 'Careful, my Barak,' she muttered. 'You will hurt yourself.' She turned the hand over, then looked up at him with a smile. 'I pray that is the worst of the wounds you sustain today.'

'These men will see to that,' he grinned. 'I even find myself eager to join in at times, but they will not hear of it.'

Asara brought out a bandage from a pocket in her travel clothes and expertly bound his hand. He flexed it; there was still perfect freedom of movement.

'Where did you learn to do that?'

'Don't,' Asara warned, her eyes hardening a little, and the moment of tenderness between them was gone.

Reki opened his mouth to speak, then closed it again and looked away. Now was not the time. He would have answers from her, whatever it took; but that would come later.

A shout of alarm made him snap his head round in time to see five ghauregs powering their way through a group of soldiers, heading for him and his men.

'Get back!' he cried, pushing Asara behind him. His bodyguards arranged themselves to tackle the menace. One of the creatures was taken down by rifles before it reached them; the other four crashed bellowing into their midst.

Reki's bodyguards were the best warriors Blood Tanatsua had to offer, but even they could not easily kill a ghaureg. Reki stumbled and fell as his men were driven back into him. He scrambled to his feet, looking around for Asara but unable to see her in the press. Blades sang: one of the ghauregs lost the fingers of its hand, another one had its leg cut off at the knee and fell. Someone split its face with their sword. Suddenly Reki's bravado seemed ridiculous: he was no fighter, and had no wish to be anywhere near combat if he could help it. But he was no coward either, and he would not run.

The battle had suddenly grown around him. Everything pressed in closer. He cast about for the enemy, but he could not see over the jostle of his bodyguards. A man screamed somewhere. There was a volley of rifle shots. A gap opened in the crush, and he saw a ghaureg on its knees, being hacked to pieces by his soldiers.

Then the army flexed and flowed away from him, and there was space again. The battle was no longer so near. His bodyguards moved to surround him. The ghauregs were dead, and shortly afterward a runner told him that the Sisters had begun to overcome the nearby Weavers and were killing the Nexuses that plagued them. The battle was turning.

Reki listened with half an ear: he was searching, becoming increasingly frantic.

'Where is your Barakess?' he demanded of the people around him. 'Where is Asara?'

But they could not answer him, and he himself had not seen her since the ghauregs had attacked.

In the end, he did not find her. Not even after the battle was over, and the remainder of the army – almost half its size now – forged on to Adderach in the hope of saving their allies there. Grief-stricken, he stayed with a small retinue and walked the corpse-strewn pass, praying to Suran that she might still somehow be alive.

Perhaps he would have found her, if he had been given time. He would have hunted for her over every inch of Saramyr if there was but the faintest shred of hope. Maybe, when he found her, he would have found her with the child that was his.

But Asara knew that. It was the reason she had disappeared into the mountains, and it was the reason she had smeared her dagger in poison. She had taken the unguent from the master poisoner who had collaborated with the assassin Keroki in an attempt to kill her husband months ago. It would be almost two hours before it would be felt, and by the time it struck it would be too late to remove it and too sudden for even a Sister of the Red Order to do anything but watch.

Barak Reki tu Tanatsua spent the last of his life looking desperately for the woman he loved, not realising that she had already murdered him, as she had murdered his sister long ago.

THIRTY-ONE

Cailin, Kaiku and the Tkiurathi emerged from the end of a sloping shaft, and into the sub-levels of Adderach.

Kaiku looked down the corridor that lay before them. It had once been a mine tunnel – that much was evident by the glimpses of rough stone that could occasionally be found – but its surface was almost entirely covered in metal. The walls were thick with black pipes that dripped a noxious liquid; the floor was of iron or some alloy of that. Gas-torches burned with smoky flames, connected by cables that ran along the ceiling.

The Tkiurathi were eager to be on with their task, distrusting their surroundings. They took point, with Cailin and Kaiku just behind and Tsata with them. Kaiku caught his nervousness and laid a hand on his forearm when nobody was looking.

'*Hthre*,' she murmured to him, offering the Tkiurathi pledge of mutual support.

Surprised, he grinned at her. '*Hthre*,' he replied. It did not matter that she had got it wrong, that *hthre* was supposed to be the response and not the offer. The sentiment was what counted, and he found it heartened him immensely in this dark and horrible place.

They hurried down the corridors, following Cailin's directions. Kaiku suspected that the Pre-Eminent did not know exactly where she was going: the witchstone's influence was overwhelming and made it hard to navigate. But that was a double-edged sword, for it also gave them a very definite target. They merely had to head for the epicentre of that influence, and there would be the witchstone.

But they saw no sign of their enemy at all. There were small rooms, like cells, some of them full of noisy devices and others standing empty and apparently without purpose. They looked into them as they passed by, but did not stop. They had other priorities.

They met up with another group of Tkiurathi and a half-dozen Sisters at a junction, swelling their numbers. Keeping in contact was harder now: it was like trying to shout over a hurricane. The brooding energy beneath them was confusing the Weave, sending it into disarray. Kaiku hoped it would hamper the Weavers as much as it would the Sisters, but somehow she doubted it.

The Sisters and the Tkiurathi were descending from above, spreading out through the tunnels of the old mine, an army of ants invading an enemy nest. But still the enemy would not meet them.

Cailin's force was the first to come out of the corridors. The claustrophobic tunnels opened into a massive room, bigger than any great hall ever built in Saramyr. It was circular in shape and flat-roofed, and as the invaders poured in from the tunnel they gradually faltered and stood there, aghast, at the sight.

It was stultifyingly hot and oppressive. The air was tinged with a coppery taste and thick with steam and smoke. There were two upper levels to the room: wide, ringed platforms that ran around the edge, walkways of metal. At ground level, furnaces roared from within their casings, glowing red through the vents at their sides and spewing strange gases. Contraptions clattered and jerked, chattering through cycles of activity incomprehensible to the observers.

Placed in concentric rows around the room were elaborate metal cradles. Hanging amid the cradles' frames were veiny, transparent sacs of flesh that looked like the stomach of some huge animal. Within, there were dark shapes suspended in liquid, lit by a greenish inner glow, visible only as smears from a distance.

Kaiku walked up to one, dazed by the scale of what they had discovered, and knelt down to look inside it.

It was a child, an infant, perhaps three harvests old but out of proportion, its bones too long. Its tiny chest sucked in and out as it breathed the liquid. It was on its side, facing her, and on top of its bald head there was the glistening diamond shape of a nexus-worm female embedded in its flesh. Kaiku could see a face tracked with ridges where the tendrils ran just beneath the skin, reaching to its eyes and mouth and nose, around which thin purple capillaries showed through. Its eyes were open, but they did not follow Kaiku as she moved. They were purest black.

A young Nexus. They grew them here, in these wombs.

Kaiku stared at the thing in the tank, numb. Cailin came up next to her.

'Is this what knowledge their god gives them?' Kaiku said. 'They blaspheme against Enyu herself.'

'That is not all,' Cailin said, motioning across the room.

Kaiku got to her feet and went to where a trio of larger cradles stood. The Tkiurathi were gathered around them, talking in hushed tones. She caught a word she knew: *maghkriin.* It was the name they gave to the beings created by the Fleshcrafters in Okhamba, who shaped babies in the bellies of their captured enemies to make them monstrous killers.

As she neared the cradles, she understood.

It was difficult to tell what the things that hung in the sacs had originally been, nor what they might become. But they moved fitfully, here twitching a leg, there curling a claw. They were baby Aberrants, three of the same species but each one different from the other. One was growing little fins along its arms, another was developing outsize teeth, while the last was a true horror with two three-quarter heads fused together in the centre, its animal features colliding and merging. The sacs glowed from within with the same nauseating light which Kaiku recognised as that given off by witchstone.

She had seen what happened to the Edgefathers who were in contact with the witchstone for too long. She knew how the Weavers changed through even the tiny dose of dust in their Masks. The Weavers were using witchstone to mutate these creatures, who were probably themselves the offspring of mutants. Like the Fleshcrafters, they were shaping their troops. Designing Aberrants through forced mutation and selective breeding. Was this where the latchjaws had come from? The nexus-worms? The *golneri*?

To Kaiku, the noise of the room faded until she could hear only the sound of her own breathing. The hate in her was choking all else. She wanted to lash out, to ruin this place, to kill every one of the Weavers and eradicate their practices from a world she had once loved. She thought suddenly of Tane, the priest of Enyu who had died to save Lucia, a man who had dedicated himself to understanding nature. How this would have destroyed him. All this time, these two and a half centuries, the Weavers had been learning the dark art of subverting Enyu's plans, using these poisonous devices to imitate her processes and turn them to their advantage.

She felt a hand on her shoulder.

'We must go,' Tsata said. Behind him the Tkiurathi were beginning to move again. They crossed the room and out through the far doorway, the Sisters following behind. Kaiku paused beneath the coiled-iron frame, her shoulders tight.

'Cailin,' she said, and the Pre-Eminent, who had been just ahead of her, stopped. She saw the look in Kaiku's eyes, and nodded.

When the last of the Tkiurathi had left the room, the two of them remained in the doorway, like estranged twins, their appearance uniting them in ways that they did not feel. The only thing between them now was a common goal.

Kaiku waved a dismissive hand, and the sacs detonated from within, spewing a green flood. Those that lined the upper levels burst at the same time, slopping forth their embryonic cargo like rough abortions. A great deluge of the amniotic liquid came splashing over the edge of the walkways and washed around the boots of the Sisters.

'I wish you would change your mind, Kaiku,' Cailin said at length. 'Stay with us. We have need of your strength. And there is so much more you could learn from me.'

But Kaiku turned away and stalked down the corridor after the departing Tkiurathi, and Cailin, after appraising the destruction for a few moments more, followed her.

The first attack on the intruders occurred not long afterward.

It was Cailin who sensed it. She was somehow able to filter through the baffling effect that the witchstone produced, at least to a better extent than

Kaiku could. Kaiku's *kana* was limited to her line of sight now; the very walls seemed infused with the stuff of the witchstone, and it was extraordinarily hard to try and Weave through it. She had only been given hints of how much greater Cailin's mastery of her *kana* was than her own, for Cailin kept her secrets close; but she was becoming more and more assured that the Pre-Eminent and some of the most proficient Sisters operated in an entirely different league.

What Cailin sensed she rebroadcast with greater clarity for those nearby, and that was how Kaiku learned of it. Garbled empathic impressions of surprise, pain, and combat. Then silence, and the soft ache of death.

Cailin said nothing, but she continued on and the others went with her.

It happened again later, as they hunted through another empty series of rooms. This time it was a bigger group of Sisters and Tkiurathi, and there was a clearer picture. Aberrants, swamping into the corridor, bolstered by Weavers. They were systematically assaulting the Sisters, group by group, taking advantage of the fact that they had to split up to search the complex. This was what they had lured them down here for. They knew their best chance for survival lay in picking the Sisters apart.

But that was not a usual Weaver tactic, Kaiku thought. If they had the strength of numbers, they would have attacked outright. They were delaying until their reinforcements could arrive. They were on the defensive.

As Cailin had hoped, they had been drawn off by Reki's men, and had not left enough of their forces behind to protect themselves from something like this.

As it turned out, the second group of Sisters were not taken down so easily. The Tkiurathi put up a vicious fight, and it was still ongoing by the time Cailin and Kaiku were ambushed.

The Aberrants boiled out of a side-corridor, filling the junction with their bodies and ploughing towards the Tkiurathi, howling. They almost caught the front line by surprise: they had been virtually soundless in their approach, and the Weavers had cloaked themselves from the Sisters well enough that, in this difficult environment, not even Cailin had detected them. But the soft warbling of the shrillings had given them away at the last moment. The Tkiurathi met the charge with their gutting-hooks sweeping.

The two groups crashed together. The corridors were wide enough for seven or eight to fight at a time, but the Aberrants in their frenzy clambered over the top of the combatants to reach those behind. Most found themselves eviscerated as they did so, their exposed underbellies ripped open and their steaming innards spilling out. The front line of the Tkiurathi collapsed under the weight of the creatures and were either dragged free or savaged. But the Okhambans were taking down the Aberrants faster than they themselves were dying. Their twin-bladed weapons, one in each hand, hacked and plunged and parried. The warriors, men and women both, were possessed of an uncanny harmony of movement that kept their blows from interfering with their neighbour's even when they were packed tight like this.

The Weavers had made one bad mistake. The Tkiurathi were born for close combat. Their weapons were adapted to its purpose and their fighting technique tailored to those conditions. Life in the jungle had meant that they had evolved short, fast, controlled movements so that they would not tangle their blades in vines or trees, and they had reactions honed by generations of living in one of the most hostile places in the Near World. Here in the confines of the tunnels they outclassed the Aberrants, who were used to the open spaces of the mountains.

The Tkiurathi were as animals themselves when they fought, primal and ferocious, and they dodged and slashed and killed until they were drenched in the blood of their enemies.

Kaiku and the Sisters dealt with the Weavers. There were only four of them, and the Sisters in Kaiku's group outnumbered them two to one. It was no contest. The Sisters attacked in a whirling chaos of threads and the Weavers' defences could not stand it. They held out briefly and then collapsed. The Sisters ripped into the fibres of their enemy's bodies, and the force released by the sundering turned the Weavers to pillars of fire.

With the Weavers gone, they broke the necks of the three Nexuses who were controlling the Aberrants, and the predators collapsed in disarray, some of them fleeing or attacking each other. The Tkiurathi made short work of the rest.

Kaiku caught sight of Tsata nearby. He was breathing hard, flecked in blood, his eyes sharp with an intensity that she only saw when he fought. A quiet and introspective man in the main, his flipside was this feral killer. She wondered briefly what that meant for the future, how deeply that ferocity was suppressed and whether it might one day be turned on her, if she should stay with him. Was he capable of that? How could she tell? How well, in the end, did she know him?

Tsata sensed her gaze upon him and turned to meet it. She felt a shock of guilt, as if he had realised what she was thinking. Then, expressionless, he turned away, and the group began to move on, deeper into the maze of corridors.

The Weavers attacked them three more times over the next hour. Other groups of Sisters who were searching elsewhere in the complex were similarly assaulted by forces of varying size. Some were overwhelmed and slain; some managed to kill their attackers. Cailin's group, with eight Sisters among them, had the strength to outmatch the Weavers; but some were not so lucky.

Kaiku could sense Cailin's mood growing graver. The Weavers' plan, costly though it was, was working. The invaders' numbers were dwindling slowly, and still there had been no sign of a way down to the witchstone beneath them. They could be running around these colossal sub-levels for hours yet, being gradually whittled away; but long before that, the Weavers' reinforcements would arrive, and flood down through the mine. Nobody thought of giving up and going back to the surface. They were just too close. But the enemy army could not be far from Adderach now.

Reports of other places like the chamber that Kaiku had destroyed came through to them. One group found a huge complex of grim workshops, forges and lathes and whittling benches where the Masks of the Weavers were crafted; but there were no Edgefathers to be seen, for they had all been taken elsewhere, presumably to the same place that the absent golneri had gone. There was also a bigger forge nearby, something entirely different to that of a blacksmith or an artisan: a monstrous, sweltering place with huge vats of molten metal and great moulds, where they found newly-made pipes and cogs and other components of the Weavers' devices. Another found a room full of roaring machines that pumped up and down, and in its centre a pool of bubbling mud that belched foul-smelling gas. Unusually, there was a marked lack of evidence of the Weavers' insanity in these sub-levels: there were no corpse-pits, no wild scrawls or strange sculptures. Here there was only the chill efficiency of machinery, designed by the Weavers and built by the golneri. Aricarat kept a tighter rein on his subjects down here.

Whether by Shintu's will or Cailin's guidance, it was Kaiku's group who found the way down. And they found it held against them.

They were directly above the witchstone at this point: Kaiku could feel it through the great weight of rock beneath their feet. They had reached what appeared to be a wall of metal at the end of the corridor, but which turned out on closer inspection to be a door of some kind. Cailin rested her hand against it and closed her eyes; a moment later there was a loud crunch, and Cailin stepped back as the wall began to part in the centre, sliding into recesses on either side.

The chamber it revealed was dimly lit by a scattering of gas-torches, but it was too large for them to do anything more than offer faint contrast to the shadows which cloaked the far end. It was circular, like the incubation room they had passed through, and its walls were metal and lined with cables and heavy pipes that leaked steam at regular intervals with a soft sigh, as if the mines themselves were breathing. In the centre of the room was a tower of machinery, bristling with cogs and chains. In the tower was a featureless metal doorway.

They stepped into the chamber, spreading out around the entrance, and regarded the strange edifice before them.

'There it is,' said Cailin. 'That is how we get to the witchstone.'

Tsata took a step forward, but Kaiku held out her hand to block him.

'It is too easy,' she said.

Something massive shifted in the shadows at the back of the chamber, moving from behind the obscuring bulk of the tower. There were smaller figures, also, strangely indistinct even to Kaiku's *kana*-adapted eyes.

'Trickery!' Cailin hissed, and swept a hand out. The shadows flexed and a veil dropped from their sight.

Kaiku paled. Twenty Weavers, a dozen Nexuses, and at least fifty Aberrants were emerging from the gloom, sidelit in the faint yellow glow. And behind them came something worse still.

Kaiku had seen giant Aberrants before; she had almost been killed by one on the way across Fo many years ago, and since then there had been reports of them from time to time in the mountains. But this was something altogether more terrible than any she had heard of. It must have been twenty feet high at the shoulder, its skin black and leathery and thick with sinew. It walked on all fours, its feet flat and its bulk enormous to support its weight. Its head was all jaw and teeth, crooked fangs far too big for its mouth, and its twisted muzzle was deeply scarred and torn because of it. It drooled a frothy milk of spittle and blood which drizzled onto the metal floor. Asymmetrical features were warped out of true: a tiny eye was lower on one side of its face than the other, almost upon the ridge of its cheek. A fringe of spikes that were somewhere between fangs, tusks and horns stuck out at random angles, sprouting from the edge of its mouth, its forehead, and its lower jaw. Its back was ridged in the same spikes, as was its tail – which was flaccid and appeared broken – but they were set to no pattern. Rather, they gave the impression of rampant growth, as if its skeleton had thrust protrusions through its flesh wherever it could. At its neck, visible only as a wet patch against its skin, Kaiku could see a nexus-worm.

It was a freak, a beast spawned from generations of creatures breeding in the mines beneath Adderach, where the mutating influence of the witchstone had created horrors beyond imagining. Though much of the mine was sealed for the Weavers' own safety, and it was suicide even for them to set foot in its depths, they had managed to secure this one and tamed it as the guardian of this place. It lived in the chamber just beyond this, through a dark doorway and down a long corridor to a room full of bones and the stench of musk and dung.

The Weavers shuffled to a halt at the edge of the light. The predators stopped also, shifting restlessly. Behind them, the giant Aberrant growled, a rumbling from deep within its chest.

For a long moment, the two forces faced each other across the chamber. Then, possessed by some feeling that she could not name, a mixture of resignation and anger and deep, deep hatred, Kaiku stepped forward. Her hair hung over one painted eye, and with the other she stared coolly at the Weavers ranged before them.

'You are in our way,' she said.

It was like the spark to a powder keg. Both sides erupted in a roar, and the Aberrants and Tkiurathi charged each other.

Kaiku plunged into the Weave, and the scene slowed around her. The golden knitwork figures of the Tkiurathi and the Aberrants became transparent: she saw the clench and tug of their muscles, saw the air sucked into their lungs through gritted teeth, the minute disturbance of soundwaves as their shoes and claws hit the floor. The Weavers came fast, but she realised their tactics immediately. They had divided: half were guarding the Nexuses and the giant beast while the rest attacked. Cailin and the Sisters were with her in the Weave, their own tactics already assigned and agreed in a communication faster than thought. And then Kaiku was spiralling towards her nearest adversaries, drawing two of them in together, and as they hit they burst into a ball of threads and sucked back inward onto each other, a tight knot of conflict that would only untangle when either Kaiku or the Weavers were dead.

Tsata jumped the swipe of a shrilling's sickle claw and struck down with his *kntha*, half-severing its foreleg. His leap landed him some way past the beast, and he left it for his kinfolk behind him while he tackled a ghaureg. In these moments of combat, he felt a stillness unlike any other, a perfection of focus that no other activity could bring him. In the sweep and slice of his gutting-hooks, in the dance of his body as he avoided the blows of his enemies by inches, he found that the chaff of existence sloughed from him like falling leaves from the trees. He was as his Okhamban ancestors had been, and their ancestors, all the way back to a time before civilisation had touched mankind. He was a hunter, a predator, streamlined to that one purpose. There was no fear of death. Death was simply impossible.

The ghaureg reached for him; he ducked under its elbow and buried his gutting-hook to the hilt in its armpit, angling in toward its heart. The creature's reflex was to swipe its arm back at him, but he had expected it and dropped beneath the swing; then he braced his foot against its ribs and in one quick motion he pulled the blade free. Blood sprayed from the wound, and the creature went down.

Rifles cracked behind him, and he saw an Aberrant he could not identify fall with its skull in ruins. The Tkiurathi, out of the cramped corridors, now had space to employ their ranged weapons without killing their own folk. Some of them took down Aberrants from a distance, but others fired at the Nexuses that hid in the shadows, and the Weavers were kept busy protecting their allies.

Kaiku saw none of this: her world had diminished to the frantic scurry inside the Weave-knot, the battlefield between her and the two Weavers. They struck at her hungrily, heartened by their numerical superiority; Kaiku barely fended them off. She spun herself a tight ball of defence in the centre of the knot, sheltering from the Weavers' attacks. They were harrying her instantly, picking at stray threads, trying to unravel her. She kept curled like a hedgehog, building a construct within the confines of her defences. The Weavers, puzzled by this sudden cessation of aggression, were determined to get at her. They wound themselves together and, as one, drilled inward. Even Kaiku could not withstand an attack like that in concert, and her ball came apart, its threads scattering.

Inside was a labyrinth, an insoluble jumble of threads with no beginning and no end, and the Weavers fell right into it and were lost.

Kaiku stayed there just long enough to be sure that they would never get out, and then threw herself back into the fight. One of the Sisters had fallen, but four Weavers had also been taken out of the action. Kaiku let her hate and anger spur her to new vigour. This was a battle they could not afford to lose. Much more than their own lives depended on it.

The giant Aberrant, meanwhile, was making its presence known. It roared and snapped and stamped among the combatants. The metal floor trembled with the impact. Tkiurathi swarmed around it, trying to take it down, but it was too big. Its jaws dripped with blood as evidence of the dozen lives it had already accounted for. The Sisters tried to get to it, to stop its heart or blind it, but the Weavers had made it the focus of their keenest protective measures and there were not enough Sisters to get through.

Tsata was among those who were attacking the monster. His efforts were futile. He ducked in and tried to hamstring its foreleg with his blade, but his hardest swipe made little more than a shallow cut against the creature's hide. Another Tkiurathi to his left made an attempt to get to the nexus-worm which kept the creature under control. The Aberrant swept its head to the side and gored him, then flung him shrieking into the air and caught him in its mouth with a crunch of bones.

Tsata saw the furie charging him out of the corner of his eye, and he moved just in time. The boar-like Aberrant skidded past him, and was taken in the side of the head by another Tkiurathi blade. The force of its momentum tore the weapon from its killer's hand, and it crashed into a heap, bleeding from the eyes.

Tsata looked up at the man who had slain it. It was Heth, his hair wet with sweat, his tattooed face gleaming. He gave Tsata a grave stare and then tipped his head at the roaring monstrosity that was tearing through their people.

'I'll be the lure,' he said in Okhamban. 'You kill that thing.'

Tsata tilted his chin at his friend, knowing that Heth would probably pay for it with his life. Neither of them had the slightest hesitation. It was a matter of *pash.*

Kaiku sensed the wave of alarm across the Weave through the muting effect of the witchstone, and knew what it meant even before Cailin amplified and clarified it. It had come from one of the Sisters in another part of the complex, and its message was simple.

The enemy army had arrived, and were already pouring down through Adderach.

Kaiku felt terror clutch at her. Not at the prospect of dying: death was something she was not afraid of at this point, and part of her would welcome it. It was the thought that she might fail here, when she was so close to fulfilling her oath to Ocha, to avenging her family. She redoubled the intensity of her assaults, but it was hopeless. The Weavers had dug in; they knew what the Sisters knew. They had only to hold out for a few minutes and the reinforcements would be here.

It will not end like this, she told herself, but it was an empty thought. There was nothing she could do about it.

((Sisters)) said Cailin. *((Time has run out))*

And with that came an empathic blaze of instructions. Kaiku did not question them; she had no other inspiration. The Sisters moved as one, breaking off their attacks and whirling into a frenzy, setting false resonances and weaving a screen of confusion. With the portion of her mind that attended the physical battle which raged across the chamber, Kaiku saw Cailin drawing a slender blade from inside her robe. She had a fraction of an instant to wonder what it was she hoped to do with that, when Cailin disappeared.

She had never witnessed anything like it. Even the display Cailin had shown her at Araka Jo, when she had made herself simply *not there*, was nothing compared to this. For as she disappeared, she dissassembled herself in the Weave, her very being coming apart into its component fibres and racing away in a diffuse burst before knotting together again elsewhere. Again, and again and again, she darted back and forth through the Weave, and finally returned to her original position and reappeared.

In the space of a heartbeat she had appeared behind several of the Weavers in rapid succession, so quick that it seemed almost simultaneous, each time stabbing with her blade. Then she was back where she had begun, the whole process enacted fast enough so that it might have been a trick of the brain. But on the far side of the room, in the gloomy shadows, eight Weavers collapsed, pierced through the nape of the neck.

Kaiku was dumbstruck. She had never imagined Cailin capable of such a thing; no wonder the Weavers were caught by surprise. Just for an instant, she had glimpsed the unplumbed depths of her own abilities, what she might be able to do if she took up Cailin's offer and returned to the fold.

But there was no time for such musings now. The Weavers were rocked by their loss, and the Sisters, scenting victory, threw themselves into the offensive.

The giant Aberrant swung its head around at Heth's cry. Even from a being so small to a creature so massive, it recognised a challenge. Its mismatched eyes squinted down at the blurred figure at its feet. This little thing was becoming a torment: already the Aberrant had tried to catch Heth twice, and he kept dodging out of the way. Frustrated, it lunged for him.

Heth moved as the great jaws gaped, and when they snapped shut he was not between them. As the head came down, Tsata darted in from the side, driving his gutting-hook in towards the creature's neck, where the nexus-worm glistened. His blade hit one of the Aberrant's many facial spikes, glanced away, and Tsata was forced to jump backwards to avoid being gored as it raised its head again.

Heth was already running to a new position, and Tsata went with him, keeping himself clear of the other Aberrants that were engaged in battling his brethren. He spared an instant to glance back at Kaiku, but she was anonymous among the other Sisters, and he had no idea how their endeavours were going. He had only this purpose: to bring down the beast. And every time he failed, Heth was forced to make himself the bait once more. But the creature was too well-armoured, making what was already a hard target near to impossible.

His knuckles whitened on the hilt of his *kntha.* He would not fail next time.

The giant Aberrant was following Heth now, ignoring the other Tkiurathi that hacked pointlessly at its legs and tail. Heth glanced over at Tsata, to be sure he was near enough; but in the instant that Heth took his attention away, it struck.

Heth only dodged at all because of the alarm on Tsata's face, but he was a fraction too slow. Though the beast missed most of him, its jaws snapped shut on his trailing arm with a terrible cracking noise. Heth screamed; blood squirted through the monster's teeth. It shook him violently, pulling him over and tearing the rest of his arm off.

Then Tsata was there. The beast's head had sunk low to the ground, and Tsata threw himself at his target. He felt a blaze of pain in his ribs: the thing had turned slightly, and he caught one of the spikes in his side. But he took his gutting-hook and rammed it into the soft, slimy flesh of the nexus-worm, then twisted hard. The beast roared, flexing spasmodically; Tsata was lifted up and flung away. He sailed through the air for a few awful instants and landed in a heap on the hard metal floor with a loud snap.

But the beast buckled. Its legs gave way as the nexus-worm died, and it staggered sideways and collapsed with a thunderous boom, crushing Aberrants and Tkiurathi alike underneath its massive bulk. The death of the worm, so closely tied in with its brain and nervous system, triggered a stroke and a heart attack simultaneously, and after a few violent spasms it gave a bubbling sigh and was still.

The Weavers fell to pieces all at once. The remainder of them had consolidated their efforts as best they could into one defensive force, but eventually it could bear the strain of the Sisters' furious assault no longer. The six Sisters that were left shredded the remaining eight Weavers, blowing them apart from within in a flaming rain of flesh and bone.

After that, it was a slaughter. The Sisters went for the Nexuses next. The black-robed beings went up like torches, silently burning. They showed no indication of pain, nor made a sound, but collapsed into blazing heaps. The Aberrants lost their minds as they lost their masters; some fled, some kept fighting, but the Tkiurathi were still thirty strong and the Aberrants half that now. The remaining beasts were destroyed by the Sisters or by the Tkiurathi, and then there was silence. As if waking from a dream, Kaiku realised that the fighting had stopped.

But a new sound was growing. The roar of an approaching horde, coming from the doorway through which they had entered. The Weavers' reinforcements were here.

'Seal that door!' Cailin cried, and the Sisters responded immediately. The mechanism that drove the metal barrier jerked into life, and the two halves began to slide from their recesses and grind shut. The sounds of the enemy got louder, louder, until Kaiku thought they must surely be upon them; and then there was a reverberant clang, and the door was closed.

Kaiku turned away, looking for Tsata, and found him kneeling, one arm cradled in the other. She hurried over to him, slowing as she neared. His trousers were black with blood which had soaked into them from the great slick all around him. Heth lay in the midst of that, his yellow skin gone white, his tattooes pallid. His arm had been ripped away, leaving only a wet mess at the shoulder through which a knob of bone showed. He was clearly dead.

'Tsata . . .' she murmured, then realised she did not know what to say. He did not look up. She noticed that his left forearm kinked at an angle, and he was holding it to his chest. 'Let me see to that . . .' she began, but then Cailin swept up to her.

'Kaiku. Come with me now,' she said. She looked down at Tsata. 'The Weavers will not be long getting through that door. We need what time you can give us.'

'You will have every moment our lives can buy,' he said quietly, and still he did not raise his head.

Cailin cast one last glance at Kaiku and then made for the doorway in the tower, where the other Sisters were heading. Kaiku waited there for a short time, trying to think of something to say, something suitable for this parting. But there were no words that could express her sorrow, nothing adequate to ease his hurt. In the end, she turned and walked away without a word. She was last through the doorway, and as soon as she was in Cailin used her *kana* to decipher and activate the mechanism. The door slid shut with a squeal of metal. Kaiku's gaze lingered on Tsata until he disappeared from view.

The elevator began to descend with a lurch, and they went down, down towards the witchstone.

THIRTY-TWO

None of the Sisters spoke as the machinery whirred and squeaked. They could sense that they were sinking by the feeling in their stomachs, but they were encased in the circular metal room of the elevator, and there was nothing to look at but each other. With every passing second, the power exuded by the witchstone was growing, becoming fiercer and more intense. Cailin had not brought the Tkiurathi with them because she believed they would not be able to survive such proximity to the thing; Kaiku wondered now if any of them would. This witchstone was older by far than the one she had destroyed in the mine long ago, older even than the stone that had been shattered at Utraxxa. It was the heart of a god, and merely to look on it might be enough to kill them.

After what seemed like an age, the elevator shuddered and stopped. There was a pregnant silence. Then the doors opened.

The force of the witchstone's presence made the Sisters cry out and recoil, their arms instinctively raised before their eyes as if by blocking the brightness they could mute its strength. The thick metal of the elevator had been shielding them until now; robbed of that barrier, they were blasted by it like a hurricane.

Kaiku fell backwards to the cold, hard floor, breaking her fall with her arm. The Weave was a maelstrom, its churning so violent that it physically pushed her over. She clung to control, trying to ride the chaos before she was swept away by it entirely. The very touch of the witchstone was foul, tainting the golden threads black, a sucking morass of malevolent darkness. The rage of Aricarat was palpable, a hatred pure enough to drive them insane.

But somehow Kaiku held on, long enough to sew a skin around herself, a protective cocoon that screened out the worst of the barrage. She found her level and allowed herself to flow with the maelstrom like a boat on stormy waters. Then she set about rescuing those of the Sisters that had not managed to do so yet. Finally, they were stable enough to stand again; but Kaiku's *kana* was already being taxed, and she knew she could not hold out like this for long.

They staggered out of the elevator and into the chamber of the witchstone.

It was gargantuan, towering almost a hundred feet high and half that in width, filling the cavern. There was no discernible overall shape to it; it was simply a mass, a crooked lump of rock that sprouted roots and protuberances all over its surface, and from those extrusions other extrusions came. It was growth gone mad, multiplying over and over in ridiculous plethora until there was barely any space at all between its branches. Like the other witchstones, it thrust into the wall of the surrounding cavern, melding with it; but unlike the others, its branches were so dense that it was almost impossible to tell where the witchstone ended and the cavern began. It had assimilated itself into its surroundings almost totally.

The nauseating luminescence of the witchstone blanched the faces of the Sisters as they came cringing into its presence, casting stark shadows across the broken floor. Several great roots reared over them, dwarfing them by comparison.

But Cailin straightened herself, her expression made hideous by the unnatural light, and her voice rang out across the chamber.

'Sisters! Cleanse our land of this abomination!'

Kaiku steeled herself and unleashed her *kana* at it. The vast, pulsing black tangle filled her world and engulfed her. The touch of it was like acid, but through the burning she fought to untangle the threads of the witchstone, to find purchase to get inside it. Its radiance was so terrible that even the Weavers had not been able to come near to plant explosives, like they must have done at Utraxxa. The Sisters had only to bore inward and they would be inside the web of the witchstones, able to spread to every stone in Saramyr. But each moment they wasted was a moment closer to that when the Weavers would break through the lingering defences that the Sisters had left on the door to the chamber above. Then the Tkiurathi would be killed – *Tsata* would be killed – and the Sisters would be next. The Weavers would send an elevator full of Aberrants down, and it would be the end.

She gritted her teeth, scratched and picked at the witchstone ferociously, but it did no good. Frustration grew in her. She could find nowhere amid the awful mass that would permit her entry to the thing: its exterior defences were too dense. No Sister had ever Weaved into a witchstone before, and now they found that they had underestimated the difficulty greatly.

Cailin sent an instruction to them all, and they battled their way through the whirling disorder and sewed themselves together. In one slender needle of intent, they thrust at the witchstone, driving into it; but incredibly, it held. They managed to make fractional headway before the point of the needle was blunted and expelled. They struck again, to no avail.

The Sisters began to try anything and everything they could. They attempted to make themselves diffuse, to seep into it like gas through the pores of a membrane; they tried attacking it from many angles at once; they worked at unpeeling it like an onion. Nothing worked. It remained invincible, and their best efforts did not even scratch it.

Kaiku was exhausted. The sheer mental strain of being in its presence was becoming too much, and Weaving on top of that was draining her utterly. What was more, her *kana* was being diverted to repair the damage that was being done to her physical body. She could feel the witchstone's insidious rays changing her, making minuscule alterations, causing tiny cancers and encouraging unusual and unnatural processes into life. Her *kana* was automatically fixing this corruption as it occurred. If not for that, it would not have been long before she became like the elder Edgefathers were: repulsive freaks, warped beyond recognition.

She dropped out of the Weave, and realised that she was on her knees on the rough floor of the cavern. Her legs had been unable to support her any longer. She was gasping for breath, her body aching.

Spirits, no. Not when we are so close. We cannot fail here. Ocha, emperor of the gods, help us now if you can. Help me fulfil my oath. Show me how to end this evil.

And the answer came to her. A possibility so awful that she at first dismissed it out of hand, but then, despairingly, she realised that it was the only chance they had left. She could sense the Sisters fruitlessly battering at the witchstone, and knew that even Cailin's skill could not help them now.

She thought of all that would be lost if the Sisters fell here. Of all the beauty she remembered from her childhood: the rinji birds on the Kerryn, the sun through the leaves of the Forest of Yuna, the dazzling waters of Mataxa Bay. All that would pass into a memory, and eventually even memories would fade. The skies would die. And after the Near World was gone, after their planet had been enshrouded as the Xhiang Xhi had predicted, then Aricarat would spread outward, into whatever was beyond.

It was too much, too much responsibility to comprehend. So she thought only of Tsata. She would save *his* life, if she could. Even if it meant trading her own. For *pash.*

She drew the leering red and black Mask from her dress and slipped it over her head.

'Kaiku!' Cailin shrieked, seeing what she was doing. 'Kaiku, *no!*'

With the Mask on her face, she Weaved.

The world shattered, and there was nothing but delirium and pain. Sense unravelled, connections of logic becoming estranged. There was no Kaiku, no *self* at all; she was a part of everything, subsumed, a curl of wind in a cyclone of derangement.

But she felt a gentle and insistent tugging, drawing her. For no reason she could fathom, it was a comfort, and she went to it. The disassembled parts of her consciousness gradually came together, reaching tendrils of sanity to each other, cohering into a structure around the warm, blessed clot of emotion that attracted them.

Father.

It was him. Or rather, it was the part of him that the Mask had robbed all that time ago, an imprint of his thoughts and mind that Kaiku had subconsciously recognised and gravitated towards. She wished somehow that she could gather it up, treasure it; but it was only a faint recollection, a sensation of trust and safety that she had lost long ago.

That the Weavers had taken from her.

She struggled to gain control of the madness around her. Anger rose within, anger at how this sanctuary had been stolen by her enemies, how her father had been so *broken* that he had poisoned his own family rather than let them fall into the hands of the Weavers. *They* had done that to him. *Them!*

With one colossal effort of will, she dragged herself into focus, until she was Kaiku again.

She was in the Mask, in the fibres that formed the wood and lacquer of the thing. And she was in the witchstone dust, tiny particles of the enormous entity that they had come to destroy. They were part of her surroundings, bending the Weave unnaturally, befouling and violating her. She saw the dementia they engendered, the way they fractured the Weave in such a way that even she found it hard to understand. No wonder that it drove the Weavers mad in the end. No wonder the Sisters had never dared to attempt this. It was only because the Mask was exceptionally young and therefore weak, and because she had worn it before and was used to it, that she had not entirely shed her mind upon entering; that, and the fact that her father had been here before her.

She let herself sink into the dark threads of the witchstone dust. These were mindless things, possessing none of the fearsome hatred of Aricarat, and yet they did live. In those little particles were a multitude of infinitesimally small organisms, so incredibly minute that Kaiku could only sense them and not identify them at all. But they possessed a portion of their parent, ingrained memory and power held in suspension. Each one possessed a tiny glimmer of energy, the force that twisted plant and flesh into new configurations. They were like tiny synapses: individually they were nothing at all, but in a group they made connections, and the connections made them greater than the sum of their parts.

And as Kaiku touched them, a flash of understanding bloomed in her mind. How one of these organisms could link with another, how the links increased in number exponentially as the number of organisms increased until they were sufficiently complex to become aware, like the processes of the human brain. How the organisms, multiplying endlessly, became legion, their intelligence and their ability growing as the gestalt entity grew until it was beyond human comprehension. And how the more them that gathered, the greater the energy they exuded, and the more they warped anyone or anything that came near.

Once these things had dominated a *moon*, until the spear of Jurani destroyed it. The god had been smashed, and the pieces had rained down on Saramyr. But the organisms in the rock had survived: senseless, stupid, like newborns once again, but *alive.* And some pieces, like this one beneath Adderach, had been large enough to exert their influence over the weak minds of humans when they were at last uncovered. They discovered blood, which had been absent on the moon; they converted its organic energy to strength, building pathways, altering the rock that sheltered them to better distribute the life-giving matrix, full of the nutrients they needed for growth. They took the designs from the beings that had discovered them. They built hearts and veins and used them.

I know you now, she thought darkly. And with that, she attacked the witchstone.

She burst from the Mask, tearing through the Weave towards the seething snarl of her enemy. She was aware of the shock of the Sisters as she raced past them, and then she hit the skin of the witchstone's defences.

But this time it was different. She had found the tiny threads that connected the Mask to its parent, just as the greater links joined witchstone to witchstone across the land. And she rode those threads, piggybacking them inward, and permeated the rock at last.

The witchstone's alarm was a blare that stunned her. It knew she was here, knew she was inside it. She sensed the billions upon billions of organisms that surrounded her, the crushing foulness of their presence. There, at the core, she found a junction, a nexus of tendrils, each snaking away to another, distant witchstone, assimilating them as part of the matrix, making them nodes in the unfathomable mind that the people of Saramyr called Aricarat.

But then the world around Kaiku began to wrench apart. The threads of the Weave twisted and snapped. And Kaiku realised in terror what was happening, and what had happened to the witchstone at Utraxxa. It had not been destroyed by the Weavers at all. It had realised that it was compromised, and had destroyed *itself.*

No! No! It was not enough that this witchstone should crumble into ruin. It was not enough that they won here today. It had to end now.

And as the witchstone began to tear itself apart around her, Kaiku sewed herself into it and she held it together.

It almost pulled her mind to pieces. The agony was appalling. She was being ripped asunder from every direction at once, and only her will kept her from being shredded into raving lunacy. But she would not let go. She would not let the witchstone come apart. And though the pain was more than she could bear, and the power that burst from her scorched her insides, the witchstone did not shatter. Though it shook and pulsed and deep cracks appeared along its length, though chunks of it rained down upon the Sisters so that they were forced to deflect them, it did not split.

Kaiku, both Sister and Weaver, bound it together. And with the last fraction of her energy, she punched a hole out through its defences from within, a conduit for the Sisters outside. They flooded in eagerly, passing through her and into the nexus at the core of the witchstone; and from there they spread outward, flashing along the links between the other witchstones across Saramyr. Possessing them. Infecting them.

Destroying them.

The first blast of a witchstone's death rolled across the Weave, buffeting Kaiku like a tsunami. But still she held, still she refused to let the witchstone go. She would not release it until she was sure that every one of them was gone. The suffering was unearthly, more than she could take, and had she a voice she would have screamed; but she held on, beyond endurance, possessed of a power greater than she had ever known. The Mask was turned against its master, and she had dominated it and taken its strength for her own. The world around her was frantically trying to twist itself apart even now, wrenching her so that she felt she would burst.

But still she held. Holding on was all she had left now. She knew nothing else.

Another shockwave rolled over her, and another. Aricarat was convulsing, his death throes ripping across the Weave, anguished and terrible and desperate. A vicious, bitter satisfaction sparked in her breast.

Die, she thought savagely. *Die for what you did to me.*

The Weave knotted before her, shrinking to a point of infinite density. A moment before it sprang back Kaiku realised what was about to happen and braced herself for the arrival of the Weave-whale.

It smashed into existence, its sheer mind-bending immensity crushing her. She hung in the Weave, the centre of a web of millions of straining tendrils all trying to break away from her, stretched as if on a rack; and now she was pierced also by the dread regard of one of the monstrous beings who haunted the Weave. She had gone beyond pain: her mind trembled on the edge of snapping, unable to exist in such conditions. The indescribable torment of continuance was all that had ever been, all there ever would be, a timeless hell with nothing beyond it, and all there was left of her was that slender thread of will that told her to endure, and which would not break.

The witchstones were dying. One by one they shattered, pulverised from within by the Sisters.

More singularities sucked and bloomed. More Weave-whales arrived. Kaiku did not even realise. She had gone beyond sense, beyond sight. She was only a force of purpose now, driven far beyond the limits of her body and mind.

The Sisters were returning. She felt them flow through her, and a tiny sliver of comprehension penetrated. The witchstones were all gone, all but the one that she held together that was still desperately trying to pull itself to pieces. It would not bear an invader, though all hope of saving the rest of the network had long passed. It would rather have non-existence.

It is done, Kaiku thought, and she let go.

Tsata and the remaining Tkiurathi waited in the chamber above, hardly daring to breathe. They feared some kind of trick. The great metal barriers were gradually sliding aside, their mechanism activated at last by the Weavers without; but the scene they revealed was far from the ravening horde that the Tkiurathi had expected.

There were perhaps thirty Weavers there, and all of them were dead. Behind them, several dozen Aberrants fought among themselves, some of them fleeing away up the corridor, others attacking members of different predator species. A dozen Nexuses stood still, their shoulders slack, and even behind their blank white masks it was evident that something had been extinguished inside them. Tsata watched in disbelief as one of them was knocked down and savaged by a shrilling. The Nexus did not react as the beast tore him apart.

'Fire!' one of the Tkiurathi cried, and a hail of bullets ripped into the Aberrants and Nexuses alike. Those Aberrants that were not killed ran howling; the Nexuses keeled over silently and lay still.

Tsata, his broken arm held to his chest, his teeth gritted against the pain, merely stared. Then a cheer rose from the Tkiurathi, a full-throated bellow of victory. They had realised what had happened before Tsata had. The witchstones were destroyed.

All across the land, the effects were the same. The Weavers died, simply falling over like puppets whose strings had been cut. The Nexuses, bereft of instruction, went still and did not move again. Their minds were void, utterly empty, and most stood where they were until they starved to death, unless they were first eaten by the predators that they had controlled or killed by vengeful townsfolk. It took the people of Saramyr a long time to understand what had happened at that instant when a god had been slain, but when they did they rejoiced, whole cities erupting in scenes such as none in living memory could recall; for their world was theirs again.

But for Tsata, there was only one thing that concerned him. The great mechanism that had taken the Sisters away was grinding and clanking again, bringing them back. Bringing Kaiku back to him. He walked over to the doorway to the metal edifice in the centre of the chamber. His brethren gathered around him, their gazes expectant. Finally, the elevator settled with a racket of machinery, and the door slid open.

Five Sisters were there, but they were crouching around a sixth, who lay in the arms of Cailin. Cast aside on the floor of the elevator was a Mask that had split in half. Kaiku's Mask.

Cailin looked up at him, and in her red eyes he saw all that he had to know. Numbness clouded him, killing even the pain of his arm. He took a few steps forward and sank to his knees before the fallen Sister. He had not recognised her at first, but he recognised her now.

Her hair had turned from tawny brown to bright white, and her irises were rich crimson, but it was unmistakably her. Her, and yet not her. She still breathed, but her features were vacant. The life that had animated them had gone. She was not there.

'She gave too much, in the end,' Cailin said quietly, and there was real grief in her voice. 'Nobody could master a Weaver's Mask like that and hope to come out unscathed.'

'Where is she?' Tsata whispered, his eyes filling with hot tears. 'Where has she gone?'

'She is lost to the Weave, Tsata. She has lost her mind to the Weave.'

THIRTY-THREE

The year that followed was a turbulent one.

The restoration of the Empire was not to be achieved in a day; nor would the famine that gripped most of the land disappear overnight. Saramyr was like a wounded animal which had licked its injuries clean of infection: it was healing itself, but it was still weak, and the process was slow and painful.

Against all expectations, there was little civil conflict in the wake of the Weavers' demise. It had been predicted that riots would occur as the redistribution of limited foodstuffs left some areas hungrier than others, that lack of medical supplies and malnutrition would encourage plague, and this would spark further unrest. It was expected that opportunist leaders, demagogues and bandits would rise up to fill the power vacuum before the Empire could regain what it once had lost. But Saramyr was exhausted. It was tired of war and suffering, and there was little enthusiasm for it any more. Even through their strife, the people were prepared to be patient. They had been given a taste of what an alternative to the Empire might be like, and in the light of that they would endure anything to get back the days that already seemed like a fond dream.

Though the high families' armies had been decimated and they barely had enough strength to defend their borders against the roaming Aberrants that were now a feature of the Saramyr wilds, they returned to their lands and were rapturously welcomed. With them went the Sisters. There were few of them left, dangerously few, for despite Cailin's best efforts they had been brought perilously close to extinction in the war with the Weavers. But those few knitted the continent together. And if there were murmurings of dissent at the idea of replacing the Weavers with women like these, they were drowned out by the acclaim. The Sisters, after all, had saved their country where even the high families and the legendary Lucia had failed. Cailin made very certain that everyone knew that.

The accession of Emperor Zahn tu Ikati was due in no small part to the support of the Sisters. Cailin could have thrown her weight behind a more tractable candidate, but she knew that Zahn was the strongest, and she wanted to be sure of being on the winning side. His old treaties with the minor families had held firm even through the war, and the generals knew him as a warrior and a tactician. Though his detractors pointed out that the death of his daughter would leave him a broken man – as it had in the past when he had believed her dead – Zahn's reaction surprised everyone. Though he grieved, he accepted that there was no question this time that Lucia had died and no possibility of her coming back. He became grim and cold, but he did not retreat into himself. Though there was no spark of compassion in him any more, and he was stern sometimes to the point of cruelty, he was in perfect possession of his faculties. The nobles believed a firm leader was what they needed to restore their country. There was the usual squabbling, but Zahn took the throne at the last.

As to Cailin, she lived in the Imperial Keep and nursed her plans. The reconstruction of Axekami went on around her: the destruction of the pall-pits, the rebuilding of the great temples, the dismantling of the Blackguard. But she had little interest in that. She was thinking, as always, of her Sisterhood.

The retreat of the blight across the land meant fewer Aberrants, and soon there would be no more born with the power to manipulate *kana*. The time would come when she would allow the Sisters to breed, under closely controlled conditions and with carefully chosen stock. Without the Weavers, they had no competition in the field of the Weave any more, and she could count them relatively safe. But one day, that might change, and she must be ready for it. The Sisterhood would grow and diversify, and their powers would grow also. They would sink into the fabric of society and become inextricable, even more so than the Weavers had. Who knew what might be possible in a century, in ten centuries? Would they be as gods? Or would they wane and fade into history? Perhaps she would not live to see it; perhaps her *kana* would dry up and she would age and die. Perhaps she would be here until the apocalypse predicted by the Xhiang Xhi would come to pass, engulfing the planet in fire. Or perhaps, even, she would be elsewhere by then.

She thought of the Weave-whales, and what they had left when they departed, and she knew they would not be safe for ever.

And so, more and more, her mind strayed to the empty Weaver monasteries, that had been sealed by the Sisters and surrounded by defences. More and more she wondered about what was inside them, what secrets they might hold that she could use to protect herself and her kind.

More and more, she wondered about the machines.

Two hundred Tkiurathi were left alive of the thousand that sailed to Saramyr in the winter of the war. Seventy of them went back to Okhamba, to spread the word of what had happened. The rest stayed.

For their part in the destruction of Adderach, the Emperor Zahn gave them a gift of land. At Mishani's request, they were mandated a small stretch of the western coast, northeast of Hanzean and just south of Blood Koli's ancestral territories around Mataxa Bay. The minor noble who had owned it had been one of the many casualties of the war, his property annexed by the

Weavers. The Tkiurathi built a small settlement there, of *repka* and precarious dwellings raised on stilts and poles, with aerial walkways and rope bridges built between the trees. And there they went on with their way of life, puzzling the local Saramyr with their strange and foreign customs and philosophies.

Mishani was never quite clear why the majority of the Tkiurathi had decided to stay. She suspected, from what she had learned of them, that it was simply a matter of whim, that there was no deeper meaning behind it other than that they wanted to. But for Tsata, it was different. He stayed for a reason.

Mishani had returned to Mataxa Bay after the high families were restored. She was, after all, still the heir to Blood Koli, and with her mother and father dead she was entitled to inhabit her childhood home again. Blood Koli were much diminished, having had most of their power taken away after the restoration of the Empire began. Much of their army had formed the Blackguard and were executed for their crimes. But Blood Koli still held powerful concessions, not least with Blood Mumaka, who had begun to trade with Saramyr from Okhamba again, transporting much-needed supplies from the Colonial Merchant Consortium to ease the famine. Mishani had once considered freeing Blood Mumaka of their obligations to her family in gratitude for what their scion Chien had done for her in the past, but she decided against it now. Blood Mumaka had weathered the conflict overseas; though they were mighty they had not acted with honour. And Mishani, as the head of a high family, needed all the advantage she could get.

Though there was grief and pain at the news of her parents' death, it passed. But there was another source of sorrow that did not heal with time. For Mishani had taken it upon herself to care for Kaiku, and every day the sight of her friend wandering listlessly through the grounds of her house pried open the wound in her heart.

Tsata visited Kaiku every day, travelling from the Tkiurathi settlement. He walked with her when the weather was fine, and talked with her often, though she never replied. She drifted like a ghost at his side, uncomprehending. Mishani watched them from the house sometimes, two distant figures on the cliff edge. His broken arm had healed clean and he was physically none the worse for his experiences in Adderach. But like Mishani, his wounds were of a different kind.

She wished sometimes that Kaiku had died on that day when she destroyed the witchstone. Anything would have been better than this torment. Kaiku was aware of her surroundings, and capable of learning ritual and reaction to certain situations, but inside her mind she was a wiped slate.

Mishani let her roam the house and along the cliffs above the bay on her own. Kaiku had demonstrated that she had enough sensibility to avoid harming herself. She made toilet of her own accord, she ate when she was presented with food, she went to bed and slept when she was tired. But she did not speak, nor did she appear interested in anything, and there was no indication that there was any intelligence left in her beyond the rudimentary logic of an animal. When she was awake, she shuffled around without purpose, or sat and stared at nothing. Her presence was disconcerting, but Mishani tolerated it; and though Mishani was ever busy, she always made time to talk to Kaiku, or read to her. But it had been a long time since she had any hope of bringing her friend back from wherever she had gone. Though Kaiku's *kana* still ministered to her, keeping her healthy and strong and fit, it was attending to an empty house waiting for a mistress that would not come home.

Her hair grew white from the day when she had lost her mind, and her eyes never changed back from their deep crimson hue. The Sisters and Cailin herself did what they could, but that amounted to nothing in the end. Once she had become untethered from her body they had no way to find her in the vastness of the Weave: it was like searching for one fish in all of the oceans.

'She has to make her own way back,' Cailin said to Mishani. But no one had ever done so, and privately she considered it impossible.

Tsata travelled from time to time, seeking medicines and physicians. The other Tkiurathi would take turns visiting Kaiku in his place. He sought out remedies both Saramyr and Okhamban, and even managed to arrange for a Muhd-taal from far Yttryx to visit and try his exotic techniques. But his chants and potions and crystals did nothing, and Kaiku remained a shell with no inhabitant. Tsata would only try again. After a year, Mishani wanted to suggest that he not exhaust himself over and over in a futile task when there was a life for him to lead. But she felt unworthy even thinking that, and she knew he would not listen anyway. Whether it was some memory of love that he bore, or loyalty to a companion as dictated by his beliefs, he would not give up.

But the spring of the second year since the witchstones' destruction turned to summer, and still Kaiku was not there.

She slept in a bedchamber near the back of the Koli family house, which faced east over the cliffs to the bay. The sunlight drenched her room in the early morning as it shone low across the land, glowing through the wispy veil that hung across her window, and the sultry heat of midsummer began to ascend. The walls were cool stone and the floor was coral marble. She lay on a simple sleeping mat in the centre of the room, and dreamed of nothing.

Mishani and her visitor stood in the doorway, looking in on her.

'This is Kaiku,' Mishani said.

The woman nodded. She was tall and long-boned, with the narrow, sharp features of the Newlands, coolly elegant and beautiful. Her summer robe was light blue and white, and her skin was pale. Her hair was worn in looped braids, a fashion from the north-east that had never caught on in the west.

'Please, leave us alone,' the woman replied.

Mishani agreed without really knowing why. Certainly, this stranger's appearance at such an early hour was unusual, as was her tale: she was a healer, who had heard of Kaiku's plight and come to help her. She had arrived on a manxthwa-drawn cart, with her two children in the back, a twin son and daughter aged six harvests by the look of them. They were playing with the servants' children in the great tiered garden that ran down to the cliff edge, watched over by retainers.

Mishani felt that she should be suspicious, but could not think of any reason why someone should want to harm Kaiku. And though she did not admit it to herself, she almost hoped someone would. To end this half-life, to release her to Omecha's care, would be a mercy.

When Mishani had left, the healer crossed the room and knelt by Kaiku's side. The sleeping woman's cheek was limned in gold in the morning sun, the fine hairs of her skin incandescent. Her face was unlined, her expression peaceful, her mouth slightly open. For a long while, the healer watched her.

'They say you are lost, Kaiku,' she said quietly. 'That your mind wanders far from your body and cannot trace its way home.' She laid the palm of her hand lightly against the side of Kaiku's jaw, caressing her. 'I have carried a piece of you for many years, and you a piece of me. Perhaps this will help you.'

She bent down and put her lips to Kaiku's, and exhaled. And after a moment the breath became more than breath, a glittering passage of some ephemeral energy crossing between the women, gushing from one mouth to another. It went on for some minutes, longer than lungs could sustain, until finally Asara broke away, drawing her lips softly across Kaiku's as she did so.

Still Kaiku slept. From beyond the window came the high laughter of children.

'Do you hear them, Kaiku?' Asara said. 'My kind grow fast, it seems. Too soon they will be adults, and I will be a grandmother. I think it appropriate. I am not too far from my first century.' She smiled sadly, looking down at the woman she had once known. Maybe she had once loved her. She could not say.

She got to her feet. 'I have you to thank for them, Kaiku,' she murmured. 'You gave them life.'

Mishani offered her a meal, and they spoke of matters in the distant steppes of the Newlands. She left in the afternoon, taking her children with her.

Kaiku collapsed later that day.

It happened towards sunset, as she was walking with Tsata. They were meandering along a path on the cliff edge, and the temperature had diminished to pleasant warmth, leavened by a breeze off the sea. Since Kaiku never replied to him and conversation was impossible, Tsata had developed a tendency towards storytelling, recounting to her the events of the settlement and the tales of the people who lived there. He had become well practised in making even the most mundane of incidents entertaining, though really it was only himself he was keeping amused.

He was in the middle of such an anecdote when, without warning, she went limp and sighed to the ground. He was so surprised that he was not fast enough to catch her. He squatted down and raised up her shoulders, patting her cheek with his palm and shaking her. She did not respond; her head lolled. He looked around, but there was no one nearby, and the squat shape of Blood Koli's house was far away. He would have to carry her, then.

He scooped her up easily. Her head hung, her white hair – somewhat longer since the day it had turned that colour – spilling down. He tipped her weight, jogging her head so that it lay against his shoulder.

She put her arms around him like a child clinging to its parent and held on tight.

It took him an instant to realise what she had done, what the pressure of her grip could mean. He did not dare to run with her, for to do so would be to break this moment, to shatter the possibility of it.

'Kaiku?' he said, his tongue thick.

She clutched him harder, pressing her head into his shoulder.

'*Kaiku?*'

Her body began to shake, and she was making a small sound in her throat. Tsata's heart jumped painfully in his chest.

She was sobbing, and Tsata was soon crying too, but his tears were of joy.

Kaiku's recovery was phenomenally quick. Though for the first few days she was skittish, prone to taking fright at loud noises and sudden movements, it was as if she had merely awoken from a deep sleep. Her mind was fogged, but it cleared rapidly; and though Mishani and Tsata and the entire Tkiurathi settlement celebrated, they managed to restrain themselves from taxing her too much with their visits.

In less than a week, it was like nothing had ever happened. The bad memories of Kaiku's fugue seemed like some disconnected reality that they had observed but not participated in, and the only reminder of it was Kaiku's hair of pure white and her eyes of deep red, which did not revert to normal even after everything else had.

She could not explain what had befallen her during the time she was away. She remembered only that she had been lost and searching, thinking that she was dead but unable to find Yoru and the gate to the Fields of Omecha. She had no conception of time, only an endless instant of uncertainty, caught in between one state and another. Then she had sensed something that she recognised, some*one* she recognised, a blaze in the Weave that had drawn her like a moth to a flame. And there she found herself at last.

Mishani told her of the healer from the Newlands, but Kaiku could shed no further light on the matter. They could only count her a blessing from the gods. The servants already believed that Kaiku had been visited by Enyu herself, the goddess of nature come to reward the one who had saved her from the Weavers. Others took her icy beauty as a sign that she was in fact an aspect of Iridima, the moon-goddess, who was grateful to Kaiku for slaying her brother Aricarat.

Kaiku did not know. But deep down, where reason and logic held no sway, she had her suspicions.

One evening she sought out Tsata, and found him in the spot where she had woken up, standing a little way off the path at the edge of the precipice. He was gazing out to sea.

A dull heat was thickening the air. The waters of Mataxa Bay were reddening, and the shadow of the cliff was reaching out to the great limestone islands in the mouth of the bay, their bases narrower than their broad tops, which were shaggy with vegetation. Hookbeaks cawed to each other as they hung on the breeze, watching the tiny junks and fishing boats below.

'Do you miss home?' she asked as she joined him.

'Sometimes,' he replied. 'Today I do.' He looked across at her. 'You should come to the settlement with me tomorrow. Many of my kinfolk have not seen you since your recovery, and they are eager.'

She smiled. 'I would be honoured,' she said.

They stood together a short while, observing the distant birds, sharing silent company.

'Mishani has been telling me a great many things,' she said at length. 'How matters have gone in the land while I was absent.'

'And that troubles you,' Tsata said.

She made an affirmative noise, brushed back her hair from her face. 'What did we do, Tsata? What did we achieve in all this?'

'We stopped the Weavers,' he said, but it was unconvincing, for she knew he felt the same as her.

'But we changed nothing. We *learned* nothing. We have merely set the calendar back a little. The Weavers are still here, only wearing a more pleasing form. Like them, the Sisters will one day decide that they no longer need the nobles as much as the nobles need them. The Empire survives, but . . .' She trailed away. 'After so much, the only winner is Cailin. I cannot help feeling that we followed paths of her making.'

'Perhaps,' Tsata said. 'And perhaps we are not right to despair. At least the Aberrants no longer have to hide. All fortune is relative, and the future is brighter than it was. You could consider that an ending.'

Kaiku shook her head. 'No, Tsata. That is what I came to tell you. This is anything but an ending.'

Tsata turned away from the vista, his full attention on her now. Though he had become used to her new appearance, he was still sometimes taken aback by the otherworldly quality it lent her. Those eyes, that hair, were the marks of a place she had been that nobody but her could ever know.

'I Weaved today,' she said. 'For the first time since I returned, I Weaved. And I know now something which the Sisters have not told us, which they have not told anyone. The Weave-whales have gone.'

Tsata's eyes showed his puzzlement. Kaiku had told him of the Weave-whales, but he did not understand the relevance.

'They have been there, in the Weave, since any of us can remember. They were always distant, unreachable, until *we* drew them. You and I, Tsata, when we destroyed the first of the witchstones in the Xarana Fault. But now they are not here.'

'What does it mean?'

'I do not know,' Kaiku said. 'But they left something behind them. Something in the Weave. A construct, a pattern, a . . .' She stalled. 'I cannot describe it. It is incomprehensible. But it is *active*.'

'Active?'

'Imagine a leaf that nods into the surface of a still pool, its tip touching the water. That pool is like the Weave, and this thing is sending ripples. The ripples spread, further and wider, far past where we dare go.'

Tsata frowned. He found always found it hard to follow Kaiku when she talked of the Weave, even when she simplified it with analogies.

'Then what is it?' he asked, feeling ignorant.

'It is a *beacon*, Tsata,' she said, animated. Then she calmed, and looked down to the bay. 'Perhaps it is a message also, though if that is true then I am sure we cannot understand it. But ripples in the pond draw the attention of the fish who swim there.'

'Kaiku, I still do not know what you are saying.'

'I am saying that this war will not be remembered as a fight for the Empire,' she said. 'It will be remembered as the time we came of age. Our conflict has attracted the notice of entities greater than we can imagine. The Xhiang Xhi told Lucia how Aricarat's influence changed us. We learned to meddle with forces beyond our understanding long before our due time. We tore the veil of ascendancy when we were but infants.' She met Tsata's gaze. 'And now our presence is being made known.'

'Made known to whom?'

'To those who dwell in places impenetrable to us. It may be a day, a year, a thousand years or longer; but sooner or later, something will come looking.' She dropped her eyes. 'What that may mean, whether that will be blessing or catastrophe, I cannot say.'

Tsata had no response to that. He did not believe in gods, but he knew enough to respect the world beyond the senses, and her words evoked a subtle dread in him that he could not define.

She laughed suddenly. 'But listen to me. I should be anything but maudlin. Forgive my foolishness. The future *is* brighter, at least for a time. I will enjoy that for now. Cailin can wait, the Sisters can wait, the Empire can wait. Maybe I will leave it all behind, and maybe I will rail against it; but not today.'

He caught her grin and was infected by it.

'I have something to ask,' she said. 'There is one more thing for me to do. I must travel east, to the Forest of Yuna, to a temple of Enyu that sits on the north bank of the Kerryn. Nearby there is a sacred glade, where once I made a promise to Ocha and to my family. I must return there, and offer thanks, and let my family know that they may rest now.' She touched his upper arm lightly, her eyes alive again. 'Come with me.'

'I will,' he said, without hesitation. Then, his expression faltered, and Kaiku became concerned.

'What is it?'

He steeled himself, and asked the question he had been putting off for some days now.

'After you have made your peace, Kaiku, what then?' he said. 'The war is over. The world goes on, and we go on with it. Where will *you* go?'

Her smile returned, and her fingers slid down his arm until her hand lay in his.

'I will go with you,' she said.

ACKNOWLEDGEMENTS

The Braided Path trilogy owes its existence to the following people:

Carolyn Whitaker for persuading me to rewrite the entire first book from scratch.

Simon Spanton for taking a chance on an unknown kid and sage advice throughout.

Nicola, Ilona, Steve, Tom, Gillian, Sara and everyone else at Gollancz who either contributed their efforts or made me feel welcome there.

And lastly my parents, for unconditional and unwavering support ever since they bought me my first typewriter at sixteen. The Braided Path trilogy is dedicated to them, with love.